SHANTARAM

SHANTARAM

Gregory David Roberts

St. Martin's Press ✖ New York

www.stmartins.com

Library of Congress Cataloging-in-Publication Data

Roberts, Gregory David.
    Shantaram : a novel / Gregory David Roberts.—1st U.S. ed.
        p. cm.
    ISBN 0-312-33052-9
    EAN 978-0312-33052-1
    1. Australians—Foreign countries—Fiction. 2. Fugitives from justice—Fiction.
  3. Australians—India—Fiction. 4. Bombay (India)—Fiction. 5. Criminals—Fiction.
  6. Clinics—Fiction. I. Title.

PR9619.4.R625S53 2004
823'.92—dc22   2004050316

First published in Australia and New Zealand by Scribe Publications

10 9 8 7 6 5 4 3

CONTENTS

For my mother

PART ONE

CHAPTER ONE

It took me a long time and most of the world to learn what I know about love and fate and the choices we make, but the heart of it came to me in an instant, while I was chained to a wall and being tortured. I realised, somehow, through the screaming in my mind, that even in that shackled, bloody helplessness, I was still free: free to hate the men who were torturing me, or to forgive them. It doesn't sound like much, I know. But in the flinch and bite of the chain, when it's all you've got, that freedom is a universe of possibility. And the choice you make, between hating and forgiving, can become the story of your life.

In my case, it's a long story, and a crowded one. I was a revolutionary who lost his ideals in heroin, a philosopher who lost his integrity in crime, and a poet who lost his soul in a maximum-security prison. When I escaped from that prison, over the front wall, between two gun-towers, I became my country's most wanted man. Luck ran with me and flew with me across the world to India, where I joined the Bombay mafia. I worked as a gunrunner, a smuggler, and a counterfeiter. I was chained on three continents, beaten, stabbed, and starved. I went to war. I ran into the enemy guns. And I survived, while other men around me died. They were better men than I am, most of them: better men whose lives were crunched up in mistakes, and thrown away by the wrong second of someone else's hate, or love, or indifference. And I buried them, too many of those men, and grieved their stories and their lives into my own.

But my story doesn't begin with them, or with the mafia: it goes back to that first day in Bombay. Fate put me in the game there. Luck dealt the cards that led me to Karla Saaranen. And I started to play it out, that hand, from the first moment I looked into her green eyes. So it begins, this story, like everything else—with a woman, and a city, and a little bit of luck.

The first thing I noticed about Bombay, on that first day, was the smell of the different air. I could smell it before I saw or heard anything of India, even as I walked along the umbilical corridor that connected the plane to the airport. I was excited and delighted by it, in that first Bombay minute, escaped from prison and new to the wide world, but I didn't and couldn't recognise it. I know now that it's the sweet, sweating smell of hope, which is the opposite of hate; and it's the sour, stifled smell of greed, which is the opposite of love. It's the smell of gods, demons, empires, and civilisations in resurrection and decay. It's the blue skin-smell of the sea, no matter where you are in the Island City, and the blood-metal smell of machines. It smells of the stir and sleep and waste of sixty million animals, more than half of them humans and rats. It smells of heartbreak, and the struggle to live, and of the crucial failures and loves that produce our courage. It smells of ten thousand restaurants, five thousand temples, shrines, churches, and mosques, and of a hundred bazaars devoted exclusively to perfumes, spices, incense, and freshly cut flowers. Karla once called it the worst good smell in the world, and she was right, of course, in that way she had of being right about things. But whenever I return to Bombay, now, it's my *first* sense of the city—that smell, above all things—that welcomes me and tells me I've come home.

The next thing I noticed was the heat. I stood in airport queues, not five minutes from the conditioned air of the plane, and my clothes clung to sudden sweat. My heart thumped under the command of the new climate. Each breath was an angry little victory. I came to know that it never stops, the jungle sweat, because the heat that makes it, night and day, is a wet heat. The choking humidity makes amphibians of us all, in Bombay, breathing water in air; you learn to live with it, and you learn to like it, or you leave.

Then there were the people. Assamese, Jats, and Punjabis; people from Rajasthan, Bengal, and Tamil Nadu; from Pushkar, Cochin, and Konarak; warrior caste, Brahmin, and untouchable; Hindu, Muslim, Christian, Buddhist, Parsee, Jain, Animist; fair skin and dark, green eyes and golden brown and black; every different face and form of that extravagant variety, that incomparable beauty, India.

All the Bombay millions, and then one more. The two best friends of the smuggler are the *mule* and the *camel*. Mules carry contraband across a border control for a smuggler. Camels are unsuspecting tourists who help the smuggler to get across the border. To camouflage themselves, when using false passports and identification papers, smugglers insinuate themselves into the company of fellow travellers—camels, who'll carry them safely and unobtrusively through airport or border controls without realising it.

I didn't know all that then. I learned the smuggling arts much later, years later. On that first trip to India I was just working on instinct, and the only commodity I was smuggling was my *self*, my fragile and hunted freedom. I was using a false New Zealand passport, with my photograph substituted in it for the original. I'd done the work myself, and it wasn't a perfect job. I was sure it would pass a routine examination, but I knew that if suspicions were aroused, and someone checked with the New Zealand High Commission, it would be exposed as a forgery fairly quickly. On the journey to India from Auckland, I'd roamed the plane in search of the right group of New Zealanders. I found a small party of students who were making their second trip to the sub-continent. Urging them to share their experience and travellers' tips with me, I fostered a slender acquaintance with them that brought us to the airport controls together. The various Indian officials assumed that I was travelling with that relaxed and guileless group, and gave me no more than a cursory check.

I pushed through alone to the slap and sting of sunlight outside the airport, intoxicated with the exhilaration of escape: another wall scaled, another border crossed, another day and night to run and hide. I'd escaped from prison almost two years before, but the fact of the fugitive life is that you have to keep on escaping, every day and every night. And while not completely free, never completely free, there was hope and fearful excitement in the new: a new passport, a new country, and new lines of excited dread on my young face, under the grey eyes. I stood there on the trample street, beneath the baked blue bowl of Bombay sky, and my heart was as clean and hungry for promises as a monsoon morning in the gardens of Malabar.

'Sir! Sir!' a voice called from behind me.

A hand grabbed at my arm. I stopped. I tensed every fighting muscle, and bit down on the fear. *Don't run. Don't panic.* I turned.

A small man stood before me, dressed in a grimy brown uniform, and carrying my guitar. More than small, he was a tiny man, a dwarf, with a large head, and the startled innocence of Down syndrome in his features. He thrust the guitar at me.

'Your music, sir. You are losing your music, isn't it?'

It *was* my guitar. I realised at once that I must've forgotten it near the baggage carousel. I couldn't guess how the little man had known that it belonged to me. When I smiled my relief and surprise, the man grinned back at me with that perfect sincerity we fear and call simple-minded. He passed the guitar to me, and I noticed that his hands were webbed like the feet of a wading bird. I pulled a few notes from my pocket and offered them to him, but he backed away awkwardly on his thick legs.

'Not money. We are here to help it, sir. Welcome in India,' he said, and trotted away into the forest of bodies on the path.

I bought a ticket to the city with the Veterans' Bus Service, manned by ex-servicemen from the Indian army. I watched as my backpack and travel bag were lifted to the top of a bus, and dumped onto a pile of luggage with precise and nonchalant violence, and decided to keep the guitar in my hands. I took a place on the bench seat at the back of the bus, and was joined there by two long-haired travellers. The bus filled quickly with a mix of Indians and foreigners, most of them young, and travelling as inexpensively as possible.

When the bus was close to full, the driver turned in his seat, scowled at us menacingly, spat a jet of vivid red betel juice through the open doorway, and announced our imminent departure.

'*Thik hain, challo!*'

The engine roared, gears meshed with a growl and thunk, and we sped off at alarming speed through crowds of porters and pedestrians who limped, sprang, or side-stepped out of the way with only millimetres to spare. Our conductor, riding on the bottom step of the bus, cursed them with artful animosity.

The journey from the airport to the city began on a wide, modern motorway, lined with shrubs and trees. It was much like the neat, pragmatic landscape that surrounded the international airport in my home city, Melbourne. The familiarity lulled me into a complacency that was so profoundly shattered, at the first narrowing of the road, that the contrast and its effect seemed calculated. For the first sight of the slums, as the many lanes of the motorway became one, and the trees disappeared, clutched at my heart with talons of shame.

Like brown and black dunes, the acres of slums rolled away from the roadside, and met the horizon with dirty heat-haze mirages. The miserable shelters were patched together from rags, scraps of plastic and paper, reed mats, and bamboo sticks. They slumped together, attached one to another, and with narrow lanes winding between them. Nothing in the enormous sprawl of it rose much above the height of a man.

It seemed impossible that a modern airport, full of prosperous and purposeful travellers, was only kilometres away from those crushed and cindered dreams. My first impression was that some catastrophe had taken place, and that the slums were refugee camps for the shambling survivors. I learned, months later, that they *were* survivors, of course, those slum-dwellers: the catastrophes that had driven them to the slums from their villages were poverty, famine, and bloodshed. And five thousand new survivors arrived in the city every week, week after week, year after year.

As the kilometres wound past, as the hundreds of people in those slums became thousands, and tens of thousands, my spirit writhed. I felt defiled by my own health and the money in my pockets. If you feel it at all, it's a lacerating guilt, that first confrontation with the wretched of the earth. I'd robbed banks, and dealt drugs, and I'd been beaten by prison warders until my bones broke. I'd been stabbed, and I'd stabbed men in return. I'd escaped from a hard prison full of hard men, the hard way— over the front wall. Still, that first encounter with the ragged misery of the slum, heartbreak all the way to the horizon, cut into my eyes. For a time, I ran onto the knives.

Then the smoulders of shame and guilt flamed into anger, became fist-tightening rage at the unfairness of it: *What kind of a government,* I thought, *what kind of a system allows suffering like this?*

But the slums went on, kilometre after kilometre, relieved only by the awful contrast of the thriving businesses and crumbling, moss-covered apartment buildings of the comparatively affluent. The slums went on, and their sheer ubiquity wore down my foreigner's pieties. A kind of wonder possessed me. I began to look beyond the immensity of the slum societies, and to see the people who lived within them. A woman stooped to brush forward the black satin psalm of her hair. Another bathed her children with water from a copper dish. A man led three goats with red ribbons tied to the collars at their throats. Another man shaved himself at a cracked mirror. Children played everywhere. Men carried water in buckets. Men made repairs to one of the huts. And everywhere that I looked, people smiled and laughed.

The bus stopped in a stutter of traffic, and a man emerged from one of the huts near my window. He was a foreigner, as pale-skinned as any of the new arrivals on the bus, and dressed only in a wrap-around sheet of hibiscus-patterned cotton. He stretched, yawned, and scratched unselfconsciously at his naked belly. There was a definitive, bovine placidity in his face and posture. I found myself envying that contentment, and the smiles of greeting he drew from a group of people who walked past him to the road.

The bus jerked into motion once more, and I lost sight of the man. But that image of him changed everything in my attitude to the slums. Seeing him there, a man as alien to the place as I was, let me picture myself in that world. What had seemed unimaginably strange and remote from my experience suddenly became possible, and comprehensible, and, finally, fascinating.

I looked at the people, then, and I saw how *busy* they were — how much industry and energy described their lives. Occasional sudden glimpses inside the huts revealed the astonishing cleanliness of that poverty: the spotless floors, and glistening metal pots in neat, tapering towers. And then, last, what should've been first, I saw how beautiful they were: the women wrapped in crimson, blue, and gold; the women walking barefoot through the tangled shabbiness of the slum with patient, ethereal grace; the white-toothed, almond-eyed handsomeness of the men; and the affectionate camaraderie of the fine-limbed children, older ones playing with younger ones, many of them supporting baby brothers and sisters on their slender hips. And half an hour after the bus ride began, I smiled for the first time.

'It ain't pretty,' the young man beside me said, looking at the scene beyond the window. He was Canadian, the maple leaf patch on his jacket declared: tall and heavy-set, with pale eyes, and shoulder-length brown hair. His companion looked like a shorter, more compact version of himself; they even wore identical stonewashed jeans, sandals, and soft, calico jackets.

'Come again?'

'This your first time?' he asked in reply. I nodded. 'I thought so. Don't worry. From here on, it gets a little better. Not so many slums and all. But it ain't good anywheres in Bombay. This here is the crummiest city in India, y'can take my word.'

'You got that right,' the shorter man agreed.

'But from here on in, you got a couple nice temples and some big British buildings that are okay—stone lions and brass street lights and like that. But this ain't India. The real India is up near the Himalayas, at Manali, or at the holy city of Varanasi, or down the coast, at Kerala. You gotta get outta the city to find the real India.'

'Where are you guys headed?'

'We're going to stay at an ashram,' his friend announced. 'It's run by the Rajneeshis, at Poona. It's the best ashram in the country.'

Two pairs of clear, pale-blue eyes stared at me with the vague, almost accusatory censure of those who've convinced themselves that they've found the one true path.

'You checkin' in?'

'Sorry?'

'You checkin' into a room, or you passin' on through Bombay today?'

'I don't know,' I replied, turning to look through the window once more. It was true: I didn't know whether I wanted to stay in Bombay for a while or continue on to … somewhere else. I didn't know, and it didn't matter to me. Just at that moment, I was what Karla once called the most dangerous and fascinating animal in the world: a brave, hard man, without a plan. 'I haven't really got any plans. But I think I'll stay in Bombay for a while.'

'Well, we're stayin' overnight, and catchin' the train tomorrow. If you want, we can share a room. It's a lot cheaper with three.'

I met the stare in his guileless, blue eyes. *Maybe it would be better to share a room at first*, I thought. Their genuine documents and their easy smiles would smother my false passport. Maybe it would be safer.

'And it's a lot safer,' he added.

'Yeah, right,' his friend agreed.

'Safer?' I asked, assuming a nonchalance I didn't feel.

The bus was moving more slowly, along narrow channels of three-and four-storey buildings. Traffic churned through the streets with wondrous and mysterious efficiency—a ballistic dance of buses, trucks, bicycles, cars, ox-carts, scooters, and people. The open windows of our battered bus gave us the aromas of spices, perfumes, diesel smoke, and the manure of oxen, in a steamy but not unpleasant mix, and voices rose up everywhere above ripples of unfamiliar music. Every corner carried gigantic posters, advertising Indian films. The supernatural colours of the posters streamed behind the tanned face of the tall Canadian.

'Oh, sure, it's a lot safer. This is Gotham City, man. The street kids here have more ways to take your money than hell's casino.'

'It's a *city* thing, man,' the short one explained. 'All cities are the same. It's not just here. It's the same in New York, or Rio, or Paris. They're all dirty and they're all crazy. A *city* thing, you know what I'm sayin'? You get to the rest of India, and you'll love it. This is a great country, but the cities are truly fucked, I gotta say.'

'And the goddamn hotels are in on it,' the tall one added. 'You can get ripped off just sittin' in your hotel room and smokin' a little weed. They do deals with the cops to bust you and take all your money. Safest thing is to stick together and travel in groups, take my word.'

'And get outta the cities as fast as you can,' the short one said. 'Holy shit! D'you see that?'

The bus had turned into the curve of a wide boulevard that was edged by huge stones, tumble-rolled into the turquoise sea. A small colony of black, ragged slum huts was strewn upon those rocks like the wreckage of some dark and primitive ship. The huts were burning.

'God-*damn*! Check *that* out! That guy's *cookin'*, man!' the tall Canadian shouted, pointing to a man who ran towards the sea with his clothes and hair on fire. The man slipped, and smashed heavily between the large stones. A woman and a child reached him and smothered the flames with their hands and their own clothes. Other people were trying to contain the fires in their huts, or simply stood, and watched, as their flimsy homes blazed. 'D'you see that? That guy's gone, I tell ya.'

'Damn right!' the short one gasped.

The bus driver slowed with other traffic to look at the fire, but then revved the engine and drove on. None of the cars on the busy road stopped. I turned to look through the rear window of the bus until the charred humps of the huts became minute specks, and the brown smoke of the fires was just a whisper of ruin.

At the end of the long, seaside boulevard, we made a left turn into a wide street of modern buildings. There were grand hotels, with liveried doormen standing beneath coloured awnings. Near them were exclusive restaurants, garlanded with courtyard gardens. Sunlight flashed on the polished glass and brass facades of airline offices and other businesses. Street stalls sheltered from the morning sunlight beneath broad umbrellas. The Indian men walking there were dressed in hard shoes and western business suits, and the women wore expensive silk. They looked purposeful and sober, their expressions grave as they bustled to and from the large office buildings.

The contrast between the familiar and the exceptional was everywhere around me. A bullock cart was drawn up beside a modern sports car at a traffic signal. A man squatted to relieve himself behind the discreet shelter of a satellite dish. An electric forklift truck was being used to unload goods from an ancient wooden cart with wooden wheels. The impression was of a plodding, indefatigable, and distant past that had crashed intact, through barriers of time, into its own future. I liked it.

'We're almost there,' my companion declared. 'City centre's just a few blocks. It's not really what you'd call the downtown area. It's just the tourist beat where most of the cheap hotels are. The last stop. It's called Colaba.'

The two young men took their passports and travellers' cheques from their pockets and pushed them down the fronts of their trousers. The shorter man even removed his watch, and it, too, joined the currency, passport, and other valuables in the marsupial pouch of his underpants. He caught my eye, and smiled.

'Hey,' he grinned. 'Can't be too careful!'

I stood and bumped my way to the front. When the bus stopped I was the first to take the steps, but a crowd of people on the footpath prevented me from moving down to the street. They were touts—street operatives for the various hoteliers, drug dealers, and other businessmen of the city—and they shouted at us in broken English with offers of cheap hotel rooms and bargains to be had. First among them in the doorway was a small man with a large, almost perfectly round head. He was dressed in a denim shirt and blue cotton trousers. He shouted for silence from his companions, and then turned to me with the widest and most radiant smile I'd ever seen.

'Good mornings, great sirs!' he greeted us. 'Welcome in Bombay! You are wanting it cheap and excellent hotels, isn't it?'

He stared straight into my eyes, that enormous smile not wavering. There was something in the disk of his smile—a kind of mischievous exuberance, more honest and more excited than mere happiness—that pierced me to the heart. It was the work of a second, the eye contact between us. It was just long enough for me to decide to trust him—the little man with the big smile. I didn't know it then, but it was one of the best decisions of my life.

A number of the passengers, filing off the bus, began beating and swatting at the swarm of touts. The two young Canadians made their way through the crowd unmolested, smiling broadly and equally at the bustling touts and the agitated tourists. Watching them dodge and weave through the crowd, I noticed for the first time how fit and healthy and handsome they were. I decided there and then to accept their offer to share the cost of a room. In their company, the crime of my escape from prison, the crime of my existence in the world, was invisible and inconceivable.

The little guide grabbed my sleeve to lead me away from the fractious group, and toward the back of the bus. The conductor climbed to the roof with simian agility, and flung my backpack and travel bag into my arms. Other bags began tumbling to the pavement in an ominous cadenza of creaks and crashes. As the passengers ran to stop the hard rain of their valuables, the guide led me away again, to a quiet spot a few metres from the bus.

'My name is Prabaker,' he stated, in his musically accented English. 'What is your good name?'

'My good name is Lindsay,' I lied, using the name from my false passport.

'I am Bombay guide. Very excellent first number Bombay guide, I am. All Bombay I know it very well. You want to see everything. I know exactly where is it you will find the most of everything. I can show you even *more* than everything.'

The two young travellers joined us, pursued by a persistent band of ragged touts and guides. Prabaker shouted at his unruly colleagues, and they retreated a few paces, staring hungrily at our collection of bags and packs.

'What I want to see right now,' I said, 'is a clean, cheap hotel room.'

'Certainly, sir!' Prabaker beamed. 'I can take you to a cheap hotel, and a *very* cheap hotel, and a *too much* cheap hotel, and even such a cheap hotel that *nobody* in a right minds is *ever* staying there also.'

'Okay, lead on, Prabaker. Let's take a look.'

'Hey, wait a minute,' the taller of the two young men interjected. 'Are you gonna pay this guy? I mean, I know the way to the hotels. No offence to you, buddy—I'm sure you're a good guide and all—but we don't need you.'

I looked at Prabaker. His large, dark brown eyes were studying my face with open amusement. I've never known a man who had less hostility in him than Prabaker Kharre: he was incapable of raising his voice or his hand in anger, and I sensed something of that even then, in the first minutes with him.

'Do I *need* you, Prabaker?' I asked him, my expression mock-serious.

'Oh, yes!' he cried in reply. 'You are so very needing me, I am almost *crying* with your situation! Only God knows what terrible things are happening to you without my good self to guide your body in Bombay!'

'I'll pay him,' I told my companions. They shrugged, and lifted their packs. 'Okay. Let's go, Prabaker.'

I began to lift my pack, but Prabaker grabbed at it swiftly.

'I am carrying it your luggages,' he insisted politely.

'No, that's okay. I'm fine.'

The huge smile faded to a pleading frown.

'Please, sir. It is my job. It is my duty. I am strong in my backs. No problem. You will see.'

All my instincts revolted at the idea.

'No, really ...'

'Please, Mr. Lindsay, this is my honour. See the people.'

Prabaker gestured with his upturned palm to those touts and guides who'd managed to secure customers from among the tourists. Each one of them seized a bag, suitcase, or backpack and trudged off, leading his party into the flak-traffic with brisk determination.

'Yeah, well, all right ...' I muttered, deferring to his judgment. It was just the first of countless capitulations that would, in time, come to define our relationship. The smile stretched his round face once more, and he grappled with the backpack, working the straps onto his shoulders with my help. The pack was heavy, forcing him to thrust his neck out, lean over, and launch himself forward into a trundling gait. My longer steps brought me up level with him, and I looked into his straining face. I felt like the white bwana, reducing him to my beast of burden, and I hated it.

But he laughed, that small Indian man. He chattered about Bombay and the sights to be seen, pointing out landmarks as we walked. He spoke with deferential amiability to the two Canadians. He smiled, and called out greetings to acquaintances as he passed them. And he was strong, much stronger than he looked: he never paused or faltered in his step throughout the fifteen-minute journey to the hotel.

Four steep flights in a dark and mossy well of stairs, at the rear of a large, sea-front building, brought us to the foyer of the India Guest House. Every floor on the way up had carried a different shield—Apsara Hotel, Star of Asia Guest House, Seashore Hotel—indicating that the one building was actually four separate hotels, each one of them occupying a single floor, and having its own staff, services, and style.

The two young travellers, Prabaker, and I tumbled into the small foyer with our bags and packs. A tall, muscular Indian, wearing a dazzlingly white shirt and a black tie, sat behind a steel desk beside the hallway that led to the guest rooms.

'Welcome,' he said, a small, wary smile dimpling his cheeks. 'Welcome, young gentlemen.'

'What a dump,' my tall companion muttered, looking around him at the flaking paint and laminated wooden partitions.

'This is Mr. Anand,' Prabaker interjected quickly. 'Best manager of the best hotel in Colaba.'

'Shut up, Prabaker!' Mr. Anand growled.

Prabaker smiled the wider.

'See, what a great manager is this Mr. Anand?' he whispered, grinning at me. He then turned his smile to the great manager. 'I am bringing three excellent tourists for you, Mr. Anand. Very best customers for the very best hotel, isn't it?'

'I told you to shut up!' Anand snapped.

'How much?' the short Canadian asked.

'Please?' Anand muttered, still glowering at Prabaker.

'Three people, one room, one night, how much?'

'One hundred twenty rupees.'

'*What!*' the shorter one exploded. 'Are you kidding me?'

'That's too much,' his friend added. 'C'mon, we're outta here.'

'No problem,' Anand snapped. 'You can go to somewhere else.'

They began to gather their bags, but Prabaker stopped them with an anguished cry.

'No! No! This is the very most beautiful of hotels. Please, just see it the room! Please, Mr. Lindsay, just see it the lovely room! Just see it the lovely room!'

There was a momentary pause. The two young men hesitated in the doorway. Anand studied his hotel register, suddenly fascinated by the hand-written entries. Prabaker clutched at my sleeve. I felt some sympathy for the street guide, and I admired Anand's style. He wasn't going to plead with us, or persuade us to take the room. If we wanted it, we took it on his terms. When he looked up from the register, he met my eyes with a frank and honest stare, one confident man to another. I began to like him.

'I'd like to see it, the lovely room,' I said.

'Yes!' Prabaker laughed.

'Okay, here we go!' the Canadians sighed, smiling.

'End of the passage,' Anand smiled in return, reaching behind him to take the room key from a rack of hooks. He tossed the key and its heavy brass nameplate across the desk to me. 'Last room on the right, my friend.'

It was a large room, with three single beds covered by sheets, one window to the seaward side, and a row of windows that looked down upon a busy street. Each of the walls was painted in a different shade of headache-green. The ceiling was laced with cracks. Papery scrolls of paint dangled from the corners. The cement floor sloped downwards, with mysterious lumps and irregular undulations, toward the street windows. Three small plywood side-tables and a battered wooden dressing table with a cracked mirror were the only other pieces of furniture. Previous occupants had left evidence of their tenure: a candle melted into the neck of a Bailey's Irish Cream bottle; a calendar print of a Neapolitan street scene taped to one wall; and two forlorn, shrivelled balloons hanging from the ceiling fan. It was the kind of room that moved people to write their names and other messages on the walls, just as men do in prison cells.

'I'll take it,' I decided.

'Yes!' Prabaker cried, scurrying away at once toward the foyer.

My companions from the bus looked at one another and laughed.

'I can't be bothered arguin' with this dude. He's crazy.'

'I hear ya,' the shorter one chuckled. He bent low and sniffed at the sheets before sitting down gingerly on one of the beds.

Prabaker returned with Anand, who carried the heavy hotel register. We entered our details into the book, one at a time, while Anand checked our passports. I paid for a week in advance. Anand gave the others their passports, but lingered with mine, tapping it against his cheek thoughtfully.

'New Zealand?' he murmured.

'So?' I frowned, wondering if he'd seen or sensed something. I was Australia's most wanted man, escaped from a jail term of twenty years for armed robberies, and a hot new name on the Interpol fugitive list. *What does he want? What does he know?*

'Hmmm. Okay, New Zealand, New Zealand, you must be wanting something for smoke, some lot of beer, some bottles whisky, change money, business girls, good parties. You want to buy something, you tell me, na?'

He snapped the passport back into my hand and left the room, glaring malevolently at Prabaker. The guide cringed away from him in the doorway, cowering and smiling happily at the same time.

'A great man. A great manager,' Prabaker gushed, when Anand was gone.

'You get a lot of New Zealanders here, Prabaker?'

'Not so many, Mr. Lindsay. Oh, but very fine fellows they are. Laughing, smoking, drinking, having sexes with women, all in the night, and then more laughing, smoking, and drinking.'

'U-huh. I don't suppose you'd happen to know where I could get some hashish, Prabaker?'

'Noooo problem! I can get it one tola, one kilo, ten kilos, even I know where it is a full warehouse ...'

'I don't need a warehouse full of hash. I just want enough for a smoke.'

'Just it happens I have it one tola, ten grams, the best Afghan charras, in my pocket. You want to buy?'

'How much?'

'Two hundred rupees,' he suggested, hopefully.

I guessed that it was less than half that price. But two hundred rupees —about twelve dollars American, in those years—was one-tenth of the price in Australia. I tossed a packet of tobacco and cigarette papers to him. 'Okay. Roll up a joint and we'll try it out. If I like it, I'll buy it.'

My two roommates were stretched out on their parallel beds. They looked at one another and exchanged similar expressions, raising their foreheads in sedimentary wrinkles and pursing their lips as Prabaker pulled the piece of hashish from his pocket. They stared with fascination and dread while the little guide knelt to make the joint on the dusty surface of the dressing table.

'Are you sure this is a good idea, man?'

'Yeah, they could be settin' us up for a drug bust or somethin'!'

'I think I feel okay about Prabaker. I don't think we'll get busted,' I replied, unrolling my travel blanket and spreading it out on the bed beneath the long windows. There was a ledge on the window sill, and I began to place my keepsakes, trinkets, and lucky charms there—a black stone given to me by a child in New Zealand, a petrified snail shell one friend had found, and a bracelet of hawk's claws made by another. I was on the run. I had no home and no country. My bags were filled with things that friends had given me: a huge first-aid kit that they'd pooled their money to buy for me, drawings, poems, shells, feathers. Even the clothes I wore and the boots on my feet were gifts that friends had given me. Every object was significant; in my hunted exile, the windowsill had become my home, and the talismans were my nation.

'By all means, guys, if you don't feel safe, take a walk or wait outside for a while. I'll come and get you, after I have a smoke. It's just that I promised some friends of mine that if I ever got to India, the first thing I'd do is smoke some hash, and think of them. I mean to keep that promise. Besides, the manager seemed pretty cool about it to me. Is there any problem with smoking a joint here, Prabaker?'

'Smoking, drinking, dancing, music, sexy business, no problem here,' Prabaker assured us, grinning happily and looking up momentarily from his task. 'Everything is allow no problem here. Except the fighting. Fighting is not good manners at India Guest House.'

'You see? No problem.'

'And dying,' Prabaker added, with a thoughtful wag of his round head. 'Mr. Anand is not liking it, if the people are dying here.'

'Say what? What is he talking about dying?'

'Is he fuckin' serious? Who the fuck is *dyin'* here? *Jesus!*'

'No problem dying, baba,' Prabaker soothed, offering the distraught Canadians his neatly rolled joint. The taller man took it, and puffed it alight. 'Not many people are dying here in India Guest House, and mostly only junkies, you know, with the skinny faces. For you no problem, with your so beautiful big fat bodies.'

His smile was disarmingly charming as he brought the joint to me. When I returned it to him, he puffed at it with obvious pleasure, and passed it to the Canadians once more.

'Is good charras, yes?'

'It's real good,' the taller man said. His smile was warm and generous —the big, open-hearted smile that the long years since then have taught me to associate with Canada and Canadians.

'I'll take it,' I said. Prabaker passed it to me, and I broke the ten-gram lump into two pieces, throwing one half to one of my roommates. 'Here. Something for the train ride to Poona tomorrow.'

'Thanks, man,' he answered, showing the piece to his friend. 'Say, you're all right. Crazy, but all right.'

I pulled a bottle of whisky from my pack and cracked the seal. It was another ritual, another promise to a friend in New Zealand, a girl who'd asked me to have a drink and think of her if I managed to smuggle myself safely into India with my false passport. The little rituals—the smoke and the drink of whisky—were important to me. I was sure that I'd lost those friends, just as I'd lost my family, and every friend I'd ever known, when I'd escaped from prison. I was sure, somehow, that I would never see them again. I was alone in the world, with no hope of return, and my whole life was held in memories, talismans, and pledges of love.

I was about to take a sip from the bottle, but an impulse made me offer it to Prabaker first.

'Thank you too much, Mr. Lindsay,' he gushed, his eyes wide with delight. He tipped his head backward and poured a measure of whisky into his mouth, without touching the bottle to his lips. 'Is very best, first number, Johnnie Walker. Oh, yes.'

'Have some more, if you like.'

'Just a teeny pieces, thank you so.' He drank again, glugging the liquor down in throat-bulging gulps. He paused, licking his lips, then tipped the bottle back a third time. 'Sorry, aaah, very sorry. Is so good this whisky, it is making a bad manners on me.'

'Listen, if you like it that much, you can keep the bottle. I've got another one. I bought them duty free on the plane.'

'Oh, thank you ...' he answered, but his smile crumpled into a stricken expression.

'What's the matter? Don't you want it?'

'Yes, yes, Mr. Lindsay, very yes. But if I knew this was *my* whisky and not *yours*, I would not have been so generous with my good self in the drinking it up.'

The young Canadians laughed.

'I tell you what, Prabaker. I'll give you the full bottle, to keep, and we'll all share the open one. How's that? And here's the two hundred rupees for the smoke.'

The smile shone anew, and he swapped the open bottle for the full one, cradling it in his folded arms tenderly.

'But Mr. Lindsay, you are making a mistake. I say that this very best charras is *one* hundred rupees, not two.'

'U-huh.'

'Oh, yes. *One* hundred rupees only,' he declared, passing one of the notes back to me dismissively.

'Okay. Listen, I'm hungry, Prabaker. I didn't eat on the plane. Do you think you could show me to a good, clean restaurant?'

'Very certainly, Mr. Lindsay sir! I know such excellent restaurants, with such a wonder of foods, you will be making yourself sick to your stomach with happiness.'

'You talked me into it,' I said, standing and gathering up my passport and money. 'You guys coming?'

'What, out *there?* You gotta be kidding.'

'Yeah, maybe later. Like, *much* later. But we'll watch your stuff here, and wait for you to come back.'

'Okay, suit yourselves. I'll be back in a couple of hours.'

Prabaker bowed and fawned, and politely took his leave. I joined him, but just as I was about to close the door, the tall young man spoke.

'Listen ... take it easy on the street, huh? I mean, you don't know what it's like here. You can't trust no-one. This ain't the village. The Indians in the city are ... well, just be careful, is all. Okay?'

At the reception desk, Anand put my passport, travel cheques, and the bulk of my cash in his safe, giving me a detailed receipt, and I stepped down to the street with the words of the young Canadian's warning wheeling and turning in my mind like gulls above a spawning tide.

Prabaker had taken us to the hotel along a wide, tree-lined, and relatively empty avenue that followed a curve of the bay from the tall, stone arch of the Gateway of India Monument. The street at the front of the building was crammed with people and vehicles, however, and the sound of voices, car horns, and commerce was like a storm of rain on wood and metal roofs.

Hundreds of people walked there, or stood in talking groups. Shops, restaurants, and hotels filled the street side by side along its entire length. Every shop or restaurant featured a smaller sub-shop attached to the front of it. Two or three attendants, seated on folding stools, manned each of those small encroachments on the footpath. There were Africans, Arabs, Europeans, and Indians. Languages and music changed with every step, and every restaurant spilled a different scent into the boiling air.

Men with bullock wagons and handcarts wound their way through heavy traffic to deliver watermelons and sacks of rice, soft drinks and racks of clothes, cigarettes and blocks of ice. Money was everywhere: it was a centre for the black-market trade in currencies, Prabaker told me, and thick blocks of bank notes were being counted and changing hands openly. There were beggars and jugglers and acrobats, snake charmers and musicians and astrologers, palmists and pimps and pushers. And the street was filthy. Trash tumbled from the windows above without warning, and garbage was heaped in piles on the pavement or the roadway, where fat, fearless rats slithered to feast.

Most prominent on the street, to my eyes, were the many crippled and diseased beggars. Every kind of illness, disability, and hardship paraded there, stood at the doorways of restaurants and shops, or approached people on the street with professionally plaintive cries. Like the first sight of the slums from the windows of the bus, that glimpse of the suffering street brought a hot shame to my healthy face. But as Prabaker led me on through the roistering crowd, he drew my attention to other images of those beggars that softened the awful caricature presented by the performance of their piteousness. One group of beggars sat in a doorway, playing cards, some blind men and their friends enjoyed a meal of fish and rice, and laughing children took turns to ride with a legless man on his little trolley.

Prabaker was stealing sideways glances at my face as we walked.

'How are you liking our Bombay?'

'I love it,' I answered, and it was true. To my eyes, the city was beautiful. It was wild and exciting. Buildings that were British Raj-romantic stood side to side with modern, mirrored business towers. The haphazard slouch of neglected tenements crumbled into lavish displays of market vegetables and silks. I heard music from every shop and passing taxi. The colours were vibrant. The fragrances were dizzyingly delicious. And there were more smiles in the eyes on those crowded streets than in any other place I'd ever known.

Above all else, Bombay was free—exhilaratingly free. I saw that liberated, unconstrained spirit wherever I looked, and I found myself responding to it with the whole of my heart. Even the flare of shame I'd felt when I first saw the slums and the street beggars dissolved in the understanding that they were free, those men and women. No-one drove the beggars from the streets. No-one banished the slum-dwellers. Painful as their lives were, they were free to live them in the same gardens and avenues as the rich and powerful. They were free. The city was free. I loved it.

Yet I *was* a little unnerved by the density of purposes, the carnival of needs and greeds, the sheer intensity of the pleading and the scheming on the street. I spoke none of the languages I heard. I knew nothing of the cultures there, clothed in robes and saris and turbans. It was as if I'd found myself in a performance of some extravagant, complex drama, and I didn't have a script. But I smiled, and smiling was easy, no matter how strange and disorienting the street seemed to be. I was a fugitive. I was a wanted man, a hunted man, with a price on my head. And I was still one step ahead of them. I was free. Every day, when you're on the run, is the whole of your life. Every free minute is a short story with a happy ending.

And I was glad of Prabaker's company. I noticed that he was well known on the street, that he was greeted frequently and with considerable warmth by a wide range of people.

'You must be hungry, Mr. Lindsay,' Prabaker observed. 'You are a happy fellow, don't mind I'm saying it, and happy always has it the good appetites.'

'Well, I'm hungry enough, all right. Where is this place we're going to, anyway? If I'd known it would take this long to get to the restaurant, I would've brought a cut lunch with me.'

'Just a little bit not much too very far,' he replied cheerfully.

'Okay ...'

'Oh, yes! I will take you to the best restaurant, and with the finest Maharashtra foods. You will enjoy, no problem. All the Bombay guides like me eat their foods there. This place is so good, they only have to pay the police half of usual baksheesh money. *So* good they are.'

'Okay ...'

'Oh, yes! But first, let me get it Indian cigarette for you, and for me also. Here, we stop now.'

He led me to a street stall that was no more than a folding card table, with a dozen brands of cigarettes arranged in a cardboard box. On the table there was a large brass tray, carrying several small silver dishes. The dishes contained shredded coconut, spices, and an assortment of unidentifiable pastes. A bucket beside the card table was filled with spear-shaped leaves, floating in water. The cigarette seller was drying the leaves, smearing them with various pastes, filling them with ground dates, coconut, betel, and spices, and rolling them into small packages. The many customers crowded around his stall purchased the leaves as fast as his dexterous hands could fill them.

Prabaker pressed close to the man, waiting for a chance to make his order. Craning my neck to watch him through the thicket of customers, I moved closer toward the edge of the footpath. As I took a step down onto the road, I heard an urgent shout.

'*Look out!*'

Two hands grasped my arm at the elbow and jerked me back, just as a huge, fast-moving, double-decker bus swept past. The bus would've killed me if those hands hadn't halted me in my stride, and I swung round to face my saviour. She was the most beautiful woman I'd ever seen. She was slender, with black, shoulder-length hair, and pale skin. Although she wasn't tall, her square shoulders and straight-backed posture, with both feet planted firmly apart, gave her a quietly determined physical presence. She was wearing silk pants, bound tightly at the ankles, black low-heeled shoes, a loose cotton shirt, and a large, long silk shawl. She wore the shawl backwards, with the double-mane of the liquid fabric twirling and fluttering at her back. All her clothes were in different shades of green.

The clue to everything a man should love and fear in her was there, right from the start, in the ironic smile that primed and swelled the archery of her full lips. There was pride in that smile, and confidence in the set of her fine nose. Without understanding why, I knew beyond question that a lot of people would mistake her pride for arrogance, and confuse her confidence with impassivity. I didn't make that mistake. My eyes were lost, swimming, floating free in the shimmering lagoon of her steady, even stare. Her eyes were large and spectacularly green. It was the green that trees are, in vivid dreams. It was the green that the sea would be, if the sea were perfect.

Her hand was still resting in the curve of my arm, near the elbow. The touch was exactly what the touch of a lover's hand should be: familiar, yet exciting as a whispered promise. I felt an almost irresistible urge to take her hand and place it flat against my chest, near my heart. Maybe I should've done it. I know now that she would've laughed, if I'd done it, and she would've liked me for it. But strangers that we were then, we stood for five long seconds and held the stare, while all the parallel worlds, all the parallel lives that might've been, and never would be, whirled around us. Then she spoke.

'That was close. You're lucky.'

'Yes,' I smiled. 'I am.'

Her hand slowly left my arm. It was an easy, relaxed gesture, but I felt the detachment from her as sharply as if I'd been roughly woken from a deep and happy dream. I leaned toward her, looking behind her to the left and then to the right.

'What is it?' she asked.

'I'm looking for your wings. You *are* my guardian angel, aren't you?'

'I'm afraid not,' she replied, her cheeks dimpling with a wry smile. 'There's too much of the devil in me for that.'

'Just how much devil,' I grinned, 'are we talking about here?'

Some people were standing in a group, on the far side of the stall. One of them—a handsome, athletic man in his mid-twenties—stepped to the road and called to her. 'Karla! Come on, *yaar!*'

She turned and waved to him, then held out her hand to shake mine with a grip that was firm, but emotionally indeterminable. Her smile was just as ambiguous. She might've liked me, or she might've just been happy to say goodbye.

'You still haven't answered my question,' I said, as her hand slipped from mine.

'How much devil have I got in me?' she answered me, the half-smile teasing her lips. 'That's a very personal question. Come to think of it, that might just be the most personal question anyone ever asked me. But, hey, if you come to Leopold's, some time, you could find out.'

Her friends had moved to our side of the little stand, and she left me to join them. They were all Indians, all young, and dressed in the clean, fashionably western clothes of the middle class. They laughed often and leaned against one another familiarly, but no-one touched Karla. She seemed to project an aura that was attractive and inviolable at the same time. I moved closer, pretending to be intrigued by the cigarette seller's work with his leaves and pastes. I listened as she spoke to them, but I couldn't understand the language. Her voice, in that language and in that conversation, was surprisingly deep and sonorous; the hairs on my arms tingled in response to the sound of it. And I suppose that, too, should've been a warning. *The voice*, Afghan matchmakers say, *is more than half of love*. But I didn't know that then, and my heart rushed in, where even matchmakers might've feared to tread.

'See, Mr. Lindsay, I bought it just two cigarettes for us,' Prabaker said, rejoining me and offering one of the cigarettes with a flourish. 'This is India, country of the poor fellows. No need for buying whole packet of cigarettes here. Just one cigarette, you can buy only. And no need for buying it any matches.'

He leaned forward and took up a length of smouldering hemp rope that was hanging from a hook on the telegraph pole, next to the cigarette stall. Prabaker blew the ash from the end of it, exposing a little orange ember of fire, which he used to puff his cigarette alight.

'What is he making? What are they chewing in those leaves?'

'Is called *paan*. A most very excellent taste and chewing it is. Everyone in Bombay is chewing and spitting, chewing and more spitting, no problem, day and night also. Very good for health it is, plenty of chewing and full spitting. You want to try it? I will get it for you some.'

I nodded and let him make the order, not so much for the new experience of the paan as for the excuse it offered to stand there longer, and look at Karla. She was so relaxed and at home, so much a part of the street and its inscrutable lore. What I found bewildering, all around me, seemed to be mundane for her. I was reminded of the foreigner in the slum—the man I'd seen from the window of the bus. Like him, she seemed calm and content in Bombay. She seemed to belong. I envied her the warmth and acceptance she drew from those around her.

But more than that, my eyes were drawn to her perfect loveliness. I looked at her, a stranger, and every other breath strained to force its way from my chest. A clamp like a tightening fist seized my heart. A voice in my blood said *yes, yes, yes* ... The ancient Sanskrit legends speak of a destined love, a karmic connection between souls that are fated to meet and collide and enrapture one another. The legends say that the loved one is instantly recognised because she's loved in every gesture, every expression of thought, every movement, every sound, and every mood that prays in her eyes. The legends say that we know her by her wings—the wings that only we can see—and because wanting her kills every other desire of love.

The same legends also carry warnings that such fated love may, sometimes, be the possession and the obsession of one, and only one, of the two souls twinned by destiny. But wisdom, in one sense, is the opposite of love. Love survives in us precisely because it isn't wise.

'Ah, you look that girl,' Prabaker observed, returning with the paan and following the direction of my gaze. 'You think she is beautiful, *na*? Her name is Karla.'

'You *know* her?'

'Oh, yes! Karla is everybody knows,' he replied, in a stage whisper so loud that I feared she might hear. 'You want to meet her?'

'Meet her?'

'If you want it, I will speak to her. You want her to be your friend?'

'What?'

'Oh, yes! Karla is my friend, and she will be your friend also, I think so. Maybe you will make a lot of money for your very good self, in business with Karla. Maybe you will become such good and closely friends that you will have it a lot of sexes together, and make a full enjoyment of your bodies. I am sure you will have a friendly pleasure.'

He was actually rubbing his hands together. The red juices of the paan stained the teeth and lips of his smile. I had to grasp at his arm to stop him from approaching her, there, in the group of her friends.

'No! Stop! For Christ's sake, keep your voice down, Prabaker. If I want to speak to her, I'll do it myself.'

'Oh, I am understand,' he said, looking abashed. 'It is what foreigners are calling *foreplay*, isn't it?'

'No! Foreplay is ... never mind what foreplay is!'

'Oh, good! I never mind about the foreplays, Mr. Lindsay. I am an Indian fellow, and we Indian fellows, we don't worry about the foreplay-ings. We go straight to the bumping and jumping. Oh yes!'

He was holding an imaginary woman in his hands and thrusting his narrow hips at her, smiling that red-juiced smile all the while.

'Will you stop that!' I snapped, looking up to see if Karla and her friends were watching him.

'Okay, Mr. Lindsay,' he sighed, slowing his rhythmic thrusts until they stopped altogether. 'But, I can still make a good offer of your friendship to the Miss Karla, if you like?'

'No! I mean—no, thank you. I don't want to proposition her. I ... Oh God, what's the use. Just tell me ... the man who's talking now—what language is he speaking?'

'He is speaking Hindi language, Mr. Lindsay. You wait one minute, I will tell you what is it he is saying.'

He moved to the far side of the stall and joined her group quite unself-consciously, leaning in to listen. No-one paid any attention to him. He nodded, laughed with the others, and returned after a few minutes.

'He is telling it one very funny story, about an inspector of Bombay Police, a very great powerful fellow in this area. That inspector did lock up a very clever fellow in his jail, but the clever fellow, he did convince the inspector to let him out again, because he told the inspector he had some gold and jewels. Not only that, but when he was free, the clever fellow sold the inspector some of the gold and some jewels. But they were not really gold and not really jewels. They were the imitations, and very cheaply not the really things. And the worst mischief, the clever fellow lived in the inspector's house for one week before he sold the not-really jewels. And there is a big rumour that the clever fellow had sexy business with that inspector's wife. Now the inspector is crazy, and so much angry, that everybody is running when they see him.'

'How do you know her? Does she live here?'

'Know who, Mr. Lindsay—that inspector's wife?'

'No, of course not! I mean the girl—Karla.'

'You know,' he mused, frowning hard for the first time, 'there are a lots of girls in this Bombay. We are only five minutes from your hotel. In this five minutes, we have seen it hundreds of girls. In five minutes more, there is more hundreds of girls. Every five minutes, more hundreds of girls. And after a little of walking, we will see hundreds, and hundreds, and hundreds, and hundreds —'

'Oh, hundreds of girls, great!' I interrupted sarcastically, my voice much louder than I'd intended it to be. I glanced around. Several people were staring at me with undisguised contempt. I continued, in a hushed tone. 'I don't want to know about hundreds of girls, Prabaker. I'm just ... curious ... about ... about *that* girl, okay?'

'Okay, Mr. Lindsay, I will be telling you everything. Karla—she is a famous businessman in Bombay. Very long she is here. I think five years maybe. She has one small house, not far. Everybody knows the Karla.'

'Where is she from?'

'I think, German, or something like that.'

'But she sounded American.'

'Yes, is *sounding*, but she is from German, or like to the German. And now, anyway, is almost very Indian. You want to eat your foods now?'

'Yeah, just a minute.'

The group of young friends called out their goodbyes to others near the paan stand, and walked off into the mill and swirl of the crowd. Karla joined them, walking away with her head held high in that curiously straight-backed, almost defiant posture. I watched her until she was swallowed by the people-tide of the crowds, but she never looked back.

'Do you know a place called Leopold's?' I asked Prabaker as he joined me, and we started to walk once more.

'Oh, yes! Wonderful and lovely place it is, Leopold's Beer Bar. Full of the most wonderful, lovely peoples, the very, very fine and lovely people. All kind of foreigners you can find there, all making good business. Sexy business, and drugs business, and money business, and black-market business, and naughty pictures, and smuggler business, and passport business, and —'

'Okay, Prabaker, I get it.'

'You want to go there?'

'No. Maybe later.' I stopped walking, and Prabaker stopped beside me. 'Listen, what do your friends call you? I mean, what's your name for short, instead of Prabaker?'

'Oh, yes, short name I am having also. My short name is Prabu.'

'Prabu … I like it.'

'It's meaning *the Son of Light*, or like to that. Is good name, yes?'

'Is good name, yes.'

'And your good name, Mr. Lindsay, it is really not so good, if you don't mind I'm telling your face. I don't like it this long and kind of a squeaky name, for Indian people speaking.'

'Oh, you don't?'

'Sorry to say it, no. I don't. Not at all. Not a bit. Not even a teensy or a weensy —'

'Well,' I smiled, 'I'm afraid there's not a lot I can do about it.'

'I'm thinking that a short name—*Lin*—is much better,' he suggested. 'If you're not having objections, I will call you Lin.'

It was as good a name as any, and no more or less false than the dozen others I'd assumed since the escape. In fact, in recent months I'd found myself reacting with a quirky fatalism to the new names I was forced to adopt, in one place or another, and to the new names that others gave me. *Lin*. It was a diminutive I never could've invented for myself. But it sounded right, which is to say that I heard the voodoo echo of something ordained, fated: a name that instantly belonged to me, as surely as the lost, secret name with which I was born, and under which I'd been sentenced to twenty years in prison.

I peered down into Prabaker's round face and his large, dark, mischievous eyes, and I nodded, smiled, and accepted the name. I couldn't know, then, that the little Bombay street guide had given me a name thousands of people, from Colaba to Kandahar, from Kinshasa to Berlin, would come to know me by. Fate needs accomplices, and the stones in destiny's walls are mortared with small and heedless complicities such as those. I look back, now, and I know that the naming moment, which seemed so insignificant then, which seemed to demand no more than an arbitrary and superstitious *yes* or *no*, was in fact a pivotal moment in my life. The role I played under that name, and the character I became—*Linbaba*— was more real, and true to my nature, than anyone or anything that I ever was before it.

'Yes, okay, Lin will do.'

'Very good! I am *too* happy that you like it, this name. And like my name is meaning *Son of Light* in Hindi language, your name, *Lin*, has it also a very fine and so lucky meaning.'

'Yeah? What does *Lin* mean in Hindi?'

'It's meaning *Penis!*' he explained, with a delight that he expected me to share.

'Oh, great. That's just … great.'

'Yes very great, very lucky. It is not exactly meaning this, but it is sounding like *ling*, or *lingam*, and that is meaning *penis.*'

'Come off it, man,' I protested, beginning to walk once more. 'How can I go around calling myself Mr. *Penis*? Are you kidding me? I can see it now — *Oh, hello, pleased to meet you, my name is Penis.* No way. Forget it. I think we'll stick to Lindsay.'

'No! No! Lin, really I'm telling you, this is a fine name, a very power name, a very lucky, a *too* lucky name! The people will love this name, when they hear it. Come, I will show you. I want to leave it this bottle of whisky you gave to me, leave it with my friend, Mr. Sanjay. Here, just here in this shop. Just you *see* how he likes it your name.'

A few more paces along the busy street brought us to a small shop with a hand-painted sign over the open door:

RADIO SICK
Electric Repair Enterprises
Electrical Sales and Repairs, Sanjay Deshpande Proprietor

Sanjay Deshpande was a heavy-set man in his fifties with a halo of grey-white hair, and white, bushy eyebrows. He sat behind a solid wooden counter, surrounded by bomb-blast radios, eviscerated cassette players, and boxes of parts. Prabaker greeted him, chattering in rapid Hindi, and passed the bottle of whisky over the counter. Mr. Deshpande slapped a meaty hand on it, without looking at it, and slid it out of sight on his side of the counter. He took a sheaf of rupee notes from his shirt pocket, peeled off a number, and passed them across with his palm turned downward. Prabaker took the money and slipped it into his pocket with a movement as swift and fluid as the tentacle-grab of a squid. He finished talking, at last, and beckoned me forward.

'This is my very good friend,' he informed Mr. Deshpande, patting me on the arm. 'He is from New Zealand.'

Mr. Deshpande grunted.

'He is just today coming in Bombay. India Guest House, he is staying.'

Mr. Deshpande grunted again. He studied me with a vaguely hostile curiosity.

'His name is Lin. Mr. Linbaba,' Prabaker said.

'What's his name?' Mr. Deshpande asked.

'Lin,' Prabaker grinned. 'His name is Linbaba.'

Mr. Deshpande raised his impressive eyebrows in a surprised smile.

'Linbaba?'

'Oh, yes!' Prabaker enthused. 'Lin. Lin. Very fine fellow, he is also.'

Mr. Deshpande extended his hand, and I shook it. We greeted one another, and then Prabaker began to tug at my sleeve, pulling me towards the doorway.

'Linbaba!' Mr. Deshpande called out, as we were about to step into the street. 'Welcome in Bombay. You have any Walkman or camera or any ghetto-blasting machine for selling, you come to me, Sanjay Deshpande, at Radio Sick. I am giving best prices.'

I nodded, and we left the shop. Prabaker dragged me a few paces further along the street, and then stopped.

'You see, Mr. Lin? You see how he likes it your name?'

'I guess so,' I muttered, bewildered as much by his enthusiasm as by the brief exchange with Mr. Deshpande. When I got to know him well enough, when I began to cherish his friendship, I discovered that Prabaker believed with the whole of his heart that his smile made a difference, in people's hearts and in the world. He was right, of course, but it took me a long time to understand that truth, and to accept it.

'What's the *baba* part, at the end of the name? Lin, I can understand. But what's the Lin*baba* bit all about?'

'Baba is just a respecting name,' Prabaker grinned. 'If we put *baba* up on the back of your name, or on the name of anybody special, it is like meaning the respect we give it to a teacher, or a holy persons, or a very old, old, old—'

'I get it, I get it, but it doesn't make me any more comfortable with it, Prabu, I gotta tell ya. This whole *penis* thing ... I don't know.'

'But you did see, Mr. Sanjay Deshpande! You did see how he liked it your name! Look, see how the people love this name. You see now, you look, I will tell it to everybody! Linbaba! Linbaba! Linbaba!'

He was speaking in a shout, addressing strangers as they passed us on the street.

'All right, Prabu, all right. I take your word for it. Calm down.' It was my turn to tug at *his* sleeve, and move him along the street. 'I thought you wanted to *drink* the whisky?'

'Ah, yes,' he sighed, 'was wanting it, and was already drinking it in my mind also. But now, Linbaba, with this money from selling your good present to Mr. Sanjay, I can buy two bottles of very bad and nicely cheap Indian whisky, to enjoy, and plenty of money left for one nice new shirt, red colour, one tola of good charras, tickets for enjoying air condition Hindi picture, and two days of foods. But wait, Linbaba, you are not eating it your paan. You must put it now in the side of your mouth and chew it, before it is getting stale and not good for taste.'

'Okay, how do I do it? Like this?'

I put the leaf-wrapped parcel, almost the size of a matchbox, into the side of my mouth between the cheek and the teeth, as I'd seen the others do. Within seconds, a suffusion of aromatic sweetnesses possessed my mouth. The taste was sharp and luscious—honeyed and subtly piquant at the same time. The leaf wrapping began to dissolve, and the solid, crunchy nibbles of shaved betel nut, date, and coconut swirled in the sweet juices.

'You must spit it out some paan now,' Prabaker said, staring at my grinding jaws with earnest concentration. 'You make like this, see? Spit him out like this.'

He spat out a squirt of red juice that landed on the road, a metre away, and formed a palm-sized blotch. It was a precise, expert procedure. Not a speck of the juice remained on his lips. With his enthusiastic encouragement, I tried to imitate him, but the mouthful of crimson liquid bubbled out of my mouth, left a trail of slobber on my chin and the front of my shirt, and landed with an audible splat on my right boot.

'No problem this shirt,' Prabaker frowned, pulling a handkerchief from his pocket, and smearing the blood-red fluid deeper into my shirtfront with vigorously ineffective rubbing. 'No problem your boots also. I will wipe him just like this, see? I must ask it now, do you like the swimming?'

'Swimming?' I asked, swallowing the little paan mixture that was still in my mouth.

'Oh, yes. Swimming. I will take you to Chowpatty beach, so nice beach it is, and there you can practise chewing and spitting and chewing and more spitting the paan, but without so many of all your clothes only, for a good saving on your laundry.'

'Listen, about that—going around the city—you work as a guide, right?'

'Oh, yes. Very best Bombay guide, and guiding all India also.'

'How much do you charge per day?'

He glanced at me, his cheeks appled in the impish grin I was learning to recognise as the clever under-side of his broad and gentle smile.

'I charge hundred rupees all day,' he said.

'Okay ...'

'And tourists buy it the lunch.'

'Sure.'

'And taxi also, tourists pay.'

'Of course.'

'And Bombay bus tickets, all they pay.'

'Yeah.'

'And chai, if we drink it on a hot afternoon, for refreshing our good selves.'

'U-huh —'

'And sexy girls, if we go there, on a cool night, if we are feeling a big needy swelling in our —'

'Yeah, okay, okay. Listen, I'll pay you for the whole week. I want you to show me Bombay, teach me a bit about the city. If it works out okay, there'll be a bonus for you at the end of the week. How does that sound?'

The smile sparked his eyes, but his voice was surprisingly sombre as he replied.

'This is your good decision, Linbaba. Your *very* good decision.'

'Well,' I laughed, 'we'll see. And I want you to teach me some Hindi words, okay?'

'Oh, yes! I can teach everything! *Ha* means *yes*, and *nahin* means *no*, and *pani* means *water*, and *khanna* means *foods*, and —'

'Okay, okay, we don't have to learn it all at once. Is this the restaurant? Good, I'm starved.'

I was about to enter the dark and unprepossessing restaurant when he stopped me, his expression suddenly grave. He frowned, and swallowed hard, as if he was unsure how to begin.

'Before we are eating this good foods,' he said, at last, 'before we ... before we make any business also, something there is, I must tell it to you.'

'O-*kay* ...'

His manner was so dejected that I felt a twinge of apprehension.

'Well, now I am telling ... that tola charras, the one I was selling to you in hotel ...'

'Yes?'

'Well ... that was the *business* price. The *really* price—the friendship price—is only fifty rupees for one tola Afghani charras.' He lifted his arms, and then let them slap down at his thighs. 'I charged it fifty rupees too much.'

'I see,' I answered quietly. The matter was so trivial, from my point of view, that I was tempted to laugh out loud. It was obviously important to him, however, and I suspected that he wasn't often moved to make such admissions. In fact, as he told me much later, Prabaker had just then decided to like me, and for him that meant he was bound to a scrupulous and literal honesty in everything he said or did. It was at once his most endearing and most irritating quality, that he always told me the whole of the truth.

'So ... what do you want to do about it?'

'My suggestion,' he said seriously, 'we smoke it that *business* price charras very fast, until finish that one, then I will buy *new* one for us. After from now, it will be everything *friendship* prices, for you and for me also. This is a no problem policy, isn't it?'

I laughed, and he laughed with me. I threw my arm around his shoulder and led him into the steamy, ambrosial activity of the busy restaurant.

'Lin, I think I am your very good friend,' Prabaker decided, grinning happily. 'We are the lucky fellows, isn't it?'

'Maybe it is,' I replied. 'Maybe it is.'

Hours later, I lay back in a comfortable darkness, under the sound-strobe of a ceaselessly revolving ceiling fan. I was tired, but I couldn't sleep. Beneath my windows the street that had writhed and toiled in daylight was silent, subdued by a night-sultriness, moist with stars.

Astounding and puzzling images from the city tumbled and turned in my mind like leaves on a wave of wind, and my blood so thrilled with hope and possibility that I couldn't suppress a smile, lying there in the dark. No-one, in the world I'd left behind me, knew where I was. No-one, in the new world of Bombay, knew who I was. In that moment, in those shadows, I was almost safe.

I thought of Prabaker, and his promise to return early in the morning to begin my tours of the city. *Will he come?* I wondered. *Or will I see him somewhere later in the day, walking with another newly arrived tourist?* I decided, with the faint, impersonal callousness of the lonely, that if he were as good as his word, and turned up in the morning, I would begin to like him.

I thought of the woman, Karla, again and again, surprised that her composed, unsmiling face intruded so often. *If you go to Leopold's, some time, maybe you'll find out.* That was the last thing she'd said to me. I didn't know if it was an invitation, a challenge, or a warning. Whatever it was, I meant to take her up on it. I meant to go there, and look for her. But not yet. Not until I'd learned a little more about the city she seemed to know so well. *I'll give it a week*, I thought. *A week in the city ...*

And beyond those reflections, as always, in fixed orbits around the cold sphere of my solitude, were thoughts of my family and my friends. Endless. Unreachable. Every night was twisted around the unquenchable longing of what my freedom had cost me, and all that was lost. Every night was pierced by the spike of shame for what my freedom continued to cost them, the loved ones I was sure I would never see again.

'We could'a beat him down, you know,' the tall Canadian said from his dark corner on the far side of the room, his sudden voice in the whirring silence sounding like stones thrown on a metal roof. 'We could'a beat that manager down on the price of this room. It's costin' us six bucks for the day. We could'a beat him down to four. It's not a lotta money, but it's the way they do things here. You gotta beat these guys down, and barter for everything. We're leavin' tomorrow for Delhi, but you're stayin' here. We talked about it before, when you were out, and we're kinda worried about you. You gotta beat 'em down, man. If you don't learn that, if you don't start thinkin' like that, they're gonna fuck you over, these people. The Indians in the cities are real mercenary, man. It's a great country, don't get me wrong. That's why we come back here. But they're different than us. They're ... hell, they just expect it, that's all. You gotta beat 'em down.'

He was right about the price of the room, of course. We could've saved a dollar or two per day. And haggling *is* the economical thing to do. Most of the time, it's the shrewd and amiable way to conduct your business in India.

But he was wrong, too. The manager, Anand, and I became good friends, in the years that followed. The fact that I trusted him on sight and didn't haggle, on that first day, that I didn't try to make a buck out of him, that I worked on an instinct that respected him and was prepared to like him, endeared me to him. He told me so, more than once. He knew, as we did, that six of our dollars wasn't an extravagant price for three foreign men to pay. The owners of the hotel received four dollars per day per room. That was their base line. The dollar or two above that minimum was all Anand and his staff of three room boys shared as their daily wage. The little victories haggled from him by foreign tourists cost Anand his daily bread, and cost them the chance to know him as a friend.

The simple and astonishing truth about India and Indian people is that when you go there, and deal with them, your heart always guides you more wisely than your head. There's nowhere else in the world where that's quite so true.

I didn't know that then, as I closed my eyes in the dark and breathing silence on that first night in Bombay. I was running on instinct, and pushing my luck. I didn't know that I'd already given my heart to the woman, and the city. And knowing none of it, I fell, before the smile faded from my lips, into a dreamless, gentle sleep.

CHAPTER TWO

S HE WALKED INTO LEOPOLD'S at the usual time, and when she stopped at a table near me to talk with friends, I tried once more to find the words for the foliant blaze of her green eyes. I thought of leaves and opals and the warm shallows of island seas. But the living emerald in Karla's eyes, made luminous by the sunflowers of gold light that surrounded the pupils, was softer, far softer. I did eventually find that colour, the green in nature that was a perfect match for the green in her lovely eyes, but it wasn't until long months after that night in Leopold's. And strangely, inexplicably, I didn't tell her about it. I wish now with all my heart that I did. The past reflects eternally between two mirrors—the bright mirror of words and deeds, and the dark one, full of things we didn't do or say. I wish now that from the beginning, even then in the first weeks that I knew her, even on that night, the words had come to tell her ... to tell her that I liked her.

And I did—I liked everything about her. I liked the Helvetian music of her Swiss-American English, and the way she pushed her hair back slowly with a thumb and forefinger when she was irritated by something. I liked the hard-edged cleverness of her conversation, and the easy, gentle way she touched the people she liked when she walked past them or sat beside them. I liked the way she held my eyes until the precise moment when it stopped being comfortable, and then smiled, softening the assail, but never looked away.

She looked the world in the eye and stared it down, and I liked that about her because I didn't love the world then. The world wanted to kill me or catch me. The world wanted to put me back in the same cage I'd escaped from, where the good guys, the guys in prison-guard uniforms who got paid to do the right thing, had chained me to a wall and kicked me until they broke my bones. And maybe the world was right to want that. Maybe it was no worse than I deserved. But repression, they say, breeds resistance in some men, and I was resisting the world with every minute of my life.

The world and I are not on speaking terms, Karla said to me once in those early months. *The world keeps trying to win me back,* she said, *but it doesn't work. I guess I'm just not the forgiving type.* And I saw that in her, too, right from the start. I knew from the first minute how much like me she was. I knew the determination in her that was almost brutal, and the courage that was almost cruel, and the lonely, angry longing to be loved. I knew all that, but I didn't say a word. I didn't tell her how much I liked her. I was numb, in those first years after the escape: shell-shocked by the disasters that warred in my life. My heart moved through deep and silent water. No-one, and nothing, could really hurt me. No-one, and nothing, could make me very happy. I was tough, which is probably the saddest thing you can say about a man.

'You're becoming a regular here,' she teased, ruffling my hair with one hand as she sat down at my table.

I loved it when she did that: it meant that she'd read me accurately, that she was sure I wouldn't take offence. I was thirty then—ugly, taller than average, with wide shoulders, a deep chest, and thick arms. People didn't often ruffle my hair.

'Yeah. I guess I am.'

'So, you went around on tour with Prabaker again? How was it today?'

'He took me to the island, Elephanta, to see the caves.'

'A beautiful place,' she remarked quietly, looking at me, but dreaming of something else. 'If you get the chance, you should visit the Ajanta and Ellora caves, in the north of the state. I spent the night there, once, at Ajanta, in one of the caves. My boss took me there.'

'Your boss?'

'Yes, my boss.'

'Is he European, your boss, or Indian?'

'Neither one, actually.'

'Tell me about him.'

'Why?' she asked with a direct, frowning stare.

I was simply making conversation, trying to keep her near me, talking to me, and the sudden wariness that bristled in the single word of her question surprised me.

'It's no big deal,' I replied, smiling. 'I'm just curious about how people get work here, how they make a living, that's all.'

'Well, I met him five years ago, on a long-distance flight,' she said, looking down at her hands and seeming to relax once more. 'We both got on the plane at Zurich. I was on my way to Singapore, but by the time we got to Bombay he'd convinced me to get off the plane and work for him. The trip to the caves was ... something special. He arranged it, somehow, with the authorities, and I went up there with him, and spent the night in a big cave, full of stone sculptures of the Buddha, and a thousand chattering bats. I was safe. He had a bodyguard posted outside. But it was incredible. A fantastic experience. And it really helped me to ... to put things in focus. Sometimes you break your heart in the right way, if you know what I mean.'

I wasn't sure what she meant; but when she paused, expecting a reply, I nodded as if I did understand.

'You learn something or you *feel* something completely new, when you break your heart that way,' she said. 'Something that only *you* can know or feel in that way. And I knew, after that night, I would never have that feeling anywhere but India. I knew—I can't explain it, I just *knew* somehow—that I was home, and warm, and safe. And, well, I'm still here ...'

'What kind of business is he in?'

'What?'

'Your boss—what does he do?'

'Imports,' she said. 'And exports.'

She lapsed into silence, turning her head to scan the other tables.

'Do you miss your home?'

'My home?'

'Yeah, I mean your *other* home. Don't you ever get homesick for Switzerland?'

'In a way, yes I do. I come from Basel—have you ever been there?'

'No, I've never been to Europe.'

'Well, you must go, and when you go there you must visit Basel. It's really a very European city, you know? It's divided by the river Rhine into Great Basel and Small Basel, and the two halves of the city have really different styles and attitudes, so it's like living in two cities at the same time. That used to suit me once. And it's right on the meeting place of three countries, so you can just walk across the border into Germany and France. You can have breakfast in France, you know, with coffee and baguettes, and lunch in Switzerland, and dinner in Germany, without leaving the city by more than a few kilometres. I miss Basel, more than I miss Switzerland.'

She stopped, catching her breath, and looked up at me through soft, unpainted lashes.

'Sorry, I'm giving you a geography lesson here.'

'No, no, please go on. It's interesting.'

'You know,' she said slowly, 'I like you, Lin.'

She stared that green fire into me. I felt myself reddening slightly, not from embarrassment, but from shame, that she'd said so easily the very words, *I like you*, that I wouldn't let myself say to her.

'You do?' I asked, trying to make the question sound more casual than it was. I watched her lips close in a thin smile.

'Yes. You're a good listener. That's dangerous, because it's so hard to resist. Being listened to — really listened to — is the second-best thing in the world.'

'What's the first best thing?'

'Everybody knows that. The best thing in the world is power.'

'Oh, is it?' I asked, laughing. 'What about sex?'

'No. Apart from the biology, sex is all about power. That's why it's such a rush.'

I laughed again.

'And what about love? A lot of people say that love is the best thing in the world, not power.'

'They're wrong,' she said with terse finality. 'Love is the opposite of power. That's why we fear it so much.'

'Karla, dear one, the things you say!' Didier Levy said, joining us and taking a seat beside Karla. 'I must make the conclusion that you have wicked intentions for our Lin.'

'You didn't hear a word we said,' she chided.

'I don't have to *hear* you. I can see by the look on his face. You've been talking your riddles to him, and turning his head around. You forget, Karla, that I know you too well. Here, Lin, we'll cure you at once!'

He shouted to one of the red-jacketed waiters, calling the man by the number '4' emblazoned on the breast pocket on his uniform. 'Hey! *Char number*! *Do battlee beer*! What will you have, Karla? Coffee? Oh, *char number*! *Ek coffee aur. Jaldi karo*!'

Didier Levy was only thirty-five years old, but those years were stitched to him in lumpy wads of flesh and deep lines that gave him the plump and careworn look of a much older man. In defiance of the humid climate, he always wore baggy canvas trousers, a denim shirt, and a rumpled, grey woollen sports coat. His thick, curly black hair never seemed to be shorter or longer than the line of his collar, just as the stubble on his tired face never seemed to be less than three days from its last shave. He spoke a lavishly accented English, using the language to provoke and criticise friend and stranger alike with an indolent malignity. There were people who resented his rudeness and rebukes, but they tolerated them because he was frequently useful and occasionally indispensable. He knew where everything—from a pistol, to a precious gem, to a kilo of the finest Thai-white heroin—might be bought or sold in the city. And, as he sometimes boasted, there was very little he wouldn't do for the right amount of money, provided there was no significant risk to his comfort and personal safety.

'We were talking of the different ideas people have about the best thing in the world,' Karla said, 'But I don't have to ask what you think.'

'You would say that *I* think money is the best thing in the world,' he suggested lazily, 'and we'd both be right. Every sane and rational person one day realises that money is almost everything. The great principles and the noble virtues are all very well, in the long run of history, but from one day to the next, it's money that keeps us going—and the lack of it that drives us under the great wheel. And what about you, Lin? What did you say?'

'He didn't say anything yet, and now that you're here, he won't get a chance.'

'Now be fair, Karla. Tell us, Lin. I would like to know.'

'Well, if you press me, I'd have to say freedom.'

'The freedom to do what?' he asked, putting a little laugh in the last word.

'I don't know. Maybe just the freedom to say no. If you've got that much freedom, you really don't need any more.'

The beer and coffee arrived. The waiter slammed the drinks onto the table with reckless discourtesy. The service in the shops, hotels, and restaurants of Bombay, in those days, moved from a politeness that was charming or fawning to a rudeness that was either abrupt or hostile. The churlishness of Leopold's waiters was legendary. *It's my favourite place in the whole world*, Karla once said, *to be treated like dirt*.

'A toast!' Didier declared, raising his glass to touch mine. 'To the freedom ... to drink! *Salut!*'

He drank half the long glass, let out a loud, wide-mouthed sigh of pleasure, and then drank the rest. He was pouring himself a second glass when two others, a man and a woman, joined our group, sitting between Karla and me. The dark, brooding, undernourished young man was Modena, a dour and taciturn Spaniard who did black-market business with French, Italian, and African tourists. His companion, a slim and pretty German prostitute named Ulla, had for some time allowed him to call himself her lover.

'Ah, Modena, you are just in time to buy the next round,' Didier shouted, reaching past Karla to slap him on the shoulder. 'I will have a whisky and soda, if you please.'

The shorter man flinched under the blow and scowled unhappily, but he called the waiter to his side, and ordered drinks. Ulla was speaking with Karla in a mixture of German and English that, by accident or intent, obscured the most interesting parts of her conversation.

'How could I know it, *na*? How was it possible for me to know that he was a *Spinner*? *Total verruckt*, I tell you. At the start, he looked totally straight to me. Or, maybe, do you think that was a sign? Maybe he was a little bit *too* straight looking. *Na ja*, ten minutes in the room and *er wollte auf der Klamotten kommen*. On my best dress! I had to fight with him to save my clothes, *der Sprintficker! Spritzen wollte er*, all over my clothes! *Gibt's ja nicht*. And later, when I went to the bathroom for a little sniff of cokes, I came back to see *daß er seinen Schwanz ganz tief in einer meiner Schuhe hat*! Can you believe it! In my shoe! *Nicht zu fassen*.'

'Let's face it,' Karla said gently, 'The crazy ones always know how to find you, Ulla.'

'*Ja, leider*. What can I say? Crazy people love me.'

'Don't listen to her, Ulla my love,' Didier consoled her. 'Craziness is the basis of many a fine relationship. In fact, craziness is the basis of *every* fine relationship!'

'Didier,' Ulla sighed, mouthing his name with a smile of exquisite sweetness, 'have I told you to get fucked yet?'

'No!' he laughed, 'But I forgive you for the lapse. Between us, my darling, such things are always implied, and understood.'

The whisky arrived, in four small flasks, and the waiter prised the tops off two soda bottles with a brass bottle opener that hung from a chain at his belt. He let the tops bounce on the table and fall to the floor, then swished a grimy rag over the wet surface of the table, forcing us to duck and weave as the moisture spilled in all directions.

Two men approached our table from different parts of the restaurant, one to speak to Didier and the other with Modena. Ulla used the moment to lean close to me. Under the table she pressed something into my hand —it felt like a small roll of bank notes—and her eyes pleaded with me not to draw attention to it. As she talked to me, I slipped the notes into my pocket without looking at them.

'So have you decided how long you're going to stay?' she asked.

'I don't really know. I'm in no hurry.'

'Don't you have someone waiting for you somewhere, or someone you should go to?' she asked, smiling with adroit but passionless coquetry. Seduction was a habit with her. She turned that same smile on her customers, her friends, the waiters, even on Didier, whom she openly disliked—on everyone, in fact, including her lover, Modena. In the months and years that followed, I heard a lot of people criticise Ulla, some of them cruelly, for her flirtations. I didn't agree with them. It seemed to me, as I got to know her well, that she flirted with the world because flirting was the only real kindness she ever knew or shared: it was her way of being nice, and of making sure that people—men—were nice to her. She believed that there wasn't enough niceness in the world, and she said so, in exactly those words, more than once. It wasn't deep feeling, and it wasn't deep thinking, but it was right, as far as it went, and there was no real harm in it. And what the hell, she was a beautiful girl, and it was a very good smile.

'No,' I lied. 'There's no-one waiting, and no-one I should go to.'

'And don't you have any, *wie soll ich das sagen*, any program? Any plan?'

'Not really. I'm working on a book.'

During the time since the escape, I'd learned that telling people a small part of the truth—that I was a writer—provided me with a useful and flexible cover story. It was vague enough to explain extended stays or sudden departures, and the word *research* was comprehensive enough to account for inquiries about certain subjects, such as transport and travel and the availability of false documents, that I was sometimes forced to make. Moreover, the cover story guaranteed me a measure of privacy: the simple threat to tell people, at length, of my work in progress usually discouraged all but the most persistently curious.

And I *was* a writer. In Australia I'd written since my early twenties. I'd just begun to establish myself through my first published work when my marriage collapsed, I lost the custody of my daughter, and I lost my life in drugs, crime, imprisonment, and escape. But even as a fugitive, writing was still a daily custom and part of my instinctual routine. Even there, in Leopold's, my pockets were full of notes, scribbled onto napkins, receipts, and scraps of paper. I never stopped writing. It was what I did, no matter where I was or how my circumstances changed. One of the reasons I remember those early Bombay months so well is that, whenever I was alone, I wrote about those new friends and the conversations we shared. And writing was one of the things that saved me: the discipline and abstraction of putting my life into words, every day, helped me to cope with shame and its first cousin, despair.

'Well, *Scheisse*, I don't see what's to write about in Bombay. It's no good place, *ja*. My friend Lisa says this is the place they were thinking about, when they invented the word *pits*. And I think it is a good place for calling a *pits*. Better you should go somewhere else to write about, like Rajasthan maybe. I did hear that it's not a pits there, in Rajasthan.'

'She's right, Lin,' Karla added. 'This is not India. There are people here from every part of India, but Bombay isn't India. Bombay is an *own-world*, a world in itself. The real India is out there.'

'Out there?'

'Out there, where the light stops.'

'I'm sure you're right,' I answered, smiling in appreciation of the phrase. 'But I like it here, so far. I like big cities, and this is the third-biggest city in the world.'

'You're beginning to sound like your tour guide,' Karla joked. 'I think, maybe, Prabaker has been teaching you too well.'

'I guess he has. He's been filling my head with facts and figures every day for two weeks—quite amazing really, for a guy who left school when he was seven, and taught himself to read and write here on the streets.'

'What facts and figures?' Ulla asked.

'Well, for instance, the official population of Bombay is eleven million, but Prabu says the guys who run the illegal numbers racket have a better idea of the real population, and they put it at anything from thirteen to fifteen million. And there are two hundred dialects and languages spoken in the city every day. Two *hundred*, for God's sake! It's like being in the centre of the world.'

As if in response to that talk of languages, Ulla spoke to Karla quickly and intently in German. At a sign from Modena she stood, and gathered her purse and cigarettes. The quiet Spaniard left the table without a word, and walked toward the open archway that led to the street.

'I have a job,' Ulla announced, pouting winsomely. 'See you tomorrow, Karla. About eleven o'clock, *ja*? Maybe we'll have dinner together tomorrow night, Lin, if you're here? I would like that. Bye! *Tschus!*'

She walked out after Modena, followed by leers and admiring stares from many of the men in the bar. Didier chose that moment to visit several acquaintances at another table. Karla and I were alone.

'She won't, you know.'

'Won't what?'

'She won't have dinner with you tomorrow night. It's just her way.'

'I know,' I grinned.

'You like her, don't you?'

'Yeah, I do. What—does that strike you as funny?'

'In a way, yes. She likes you, too.'

She paused, and I thought she was about to explain her remark, but when she spoke again it was to change the subject.

'She gave you some money. American dollars. She told me about it, in German, so Modena wouldn't understand. You're supposed to give it to me, and she'll collect it from my place at eleven tomorrow.'

'Okay. Do you want it now?'

'No, don't give it to me here. I have to go now. I have an appointment. I'll be back in about an hour. Can you wait till then? Or come back, and meet me then? You can walk me home, if you like.'

'Sure, I'll be here.'

She stood to leave, and I stood also, drawing back her chair. She gave me a little smile, with one eyebrow raised in irony or mockery or both.

'I wasn't joking before. You really should leave Bombay.'

I watched her walk out to the street, and step into the back of a private taxi that had obviously been waiting for her. As the cream-coloured car eased into the slow stream of night traffic, a man's hand emerged from the passenger window, thick fingers clutching a string of green prayer beads, and warning away pedestrians with a wave.

Alone again, I sat down, set my chair against the wall, and let the activity of Leopold's and its clamorous patrons close over me. Leopold's was the largest bar and restaurant in Colaba, and one of the largest in the city. The rectangular ground-floor room occupied a frontage equal to any four other restaurants, and was served by two metal doors that rolled up into wooden arches to give an expansive view of the Causeway, Colaba's busiest and most colourful street. There was a smaller, more discreet, air-conditioned bar on the first floor, supported by sturdy columns that divided the ground floor into roughly equal sections, and around which many of the tables were grouped. Mirrors on those pillars, and on much of the free wall space, provided the patrons with one of the bar's major attractions: the chance to inspect, admire, and ogle others in a circumspect if not entirely anonymous fashion. For many, the duplication of their own images in two or more mirrors at the same time was not least among the pleasures of the pastime. Leopold's was a place for people to see, to be seen, and to see themselves in the act of *being* seen.

There were some thirty tables, all of them topped with pearl-smoked Indian marble. Each table had four or more cedar chairs—*sixty-minute chairs*, Karla used to call them, because they were just uncomfortable enough to discourage customers from staying for more than an hour. A swarm of broad fans buzzed in the high ceiling, stirring the white-glass pendulum lights to a slow, majestic sway. Mahogany trim lined the painted walls, surrounded the windows and doors, and framed the many mirrors. Rich fruits used in desserts and juices—paw paw, papaya, custard apples, mosambi, grapes, watermelon, banana, santra, and, in the season, four varieties of mango—were displayed across the whole surface of one wall in gorgeous abundance. A vast, solid-teak manager's counter presided, like the bridge of a sailing ship, over the busy deck of the restaurant. Behind that, along a narrow corridor, one corner of the frantic kitchen was occasionally visible beyond the scurry of waiters and the sweating clouds of steam.

A faded but still sumptuous elegance struck and held the eyes of all who walked through those wide arches into Leopold's little world of light, colour, and richly panelled wood. Its chief splendour was truly admired by none but its humblest workers, however, for it was only when the bar was closed, and the cleaners removed all the furniture each morning, that the beauty of the floor was exposed. Its intricate tile-work replicated the pattern used in a north Indian palace, with hexagons in black, cream, and brown radiating from a central sunburst. And thus a paving designed for princes, all but invisible to the tourists with their eyes on their own reflections in the dazzling mirrors, revealed its luxurious perfections only in secret to the naked feet of cleaners, the city's poorest and meekest working men.

For one cool, precious hour each morning after it opened, and the floors had been cleaned, Leopold's was an oasis of quiet in the struggling city. From then, until it closed at midnight, it was constantly crowded with visitors from a hundred countries, and the many locals, both foreign and Indian, who came there from every part of the city to conduct their business. The business ranged from traffic in drugs, currencies, passports, gold, and sex, to the intangible but no less lucrative trade in influence — the unofficial system of bribes and favours by which many appointments, promotions, and contracts were facilitated in India.

Leopold's was an unofficial free zone, scrupulously ignored by the otherwise efficient officers of the Colaba police station, directly across the busy street. Yet a peculiar dialectic applied to the relationships between upstairs and down, inside and outside the restaurant, and governed all of the business transacted there. Indian prostitutes, garlanded with ropes of jasmine flowers and plumply wrapped in bejewelled saris, were prohibited downstairs, and only accompanied customers to the upstairs bar. European prostitutes were only permitted to sit downstairs, attracting the interest of men who sat at other tables, or simply paused on the street outside. Deals for drugs and other contraband were openly transacted at the tables, but the goods could only be exchanged outside the bar. It was common enough to see buyer and seller reach agreement on price, walk outside to hand over money and goods, then walk back inside to resume their places at a table. Even the bureaucrats and influence peddlers were bound by those unwritten rules: agreements reached in the dark booths of the upstairs bar could only be sealed, with handshakes and cash, on the pavement outside, so that no man could say he'd paid or received bribes within the walls of Leopold's.

While the fine lines that divided and connected the legal and illegal were nowhere more elegantly drawn, they weren't unique to the diverse society of Leopold's. The traders in the street stalls outside sold counterfeits of Lacoste, Cardin, and Cartier with a certain impudent panache, the taxi drivers parked along the street accepted tips to tilt their mirrors away from the unlawful or forbidden acts that took place on the seats behind them, and a number of the cops who attended to their duties with diligence, at the station across the road, had paid hefty bribes for the privilege of that lucrative posting in the city centre.

Sitting at Leopold's, night after night, and listening to the conversations at the tables around me, I heard many foreigners and not a few Indians complain about the corruption that adhered to every aspect of public and commercial life in Bombay. My few weeks in the city had already shown me that those complaints were often fair, and often true. But there's no nation uncorrupted. There's no system that's immune to the misuse of money. Privileged and powerful elites grease the wheels of their progress with kickbacks and campaign contributions in the noblest assemblies. And the rich, all over the world, live longer and healthier lives than the poor. *There is a difference between the dishonest bribe and the honest bribe,* Didier Levy once said to me. *The dishonest bribe is the same in every country, but the honest bribe is India's alone.* I smiled when he said that, because I knew what he meant. India was open. India was honest. And I liked that from the first day. My instinct wasn't to criticise. My instinct, in the city I was learning to love, was to observe, and become involved, and enjoy. I couldn't know then that, in the months and years to come, my freedom and even my life would depend on the Indian willingness to tilt the mirror.

'What, *alone?*' Didier gasped, returning to the table. '*C'est trop!* Don't you know, my dear friend, it is faintly disgusting to be alone here? And, I must tell you that being disgusting is a privilege I reserve, exclusively, for myself. Come, we will drink.'

He flopped into a chair beside me, calling his waiter to order more drinks. I'd spoken to him at Leopold's almost every night for weeks, but we'd never been alone. It surprised me that he'd decided to join me before Ulla, Karla, or another of his friends returned. In a small way, it was a kind of acceptance, and I felt grateful for it.

He drummed his fingers on the table until the whisky arrived, drank half his glass in a greedy gulp and then relaxed at last, turning to me with a narrow-eyed smile.

'You are heavy in thoughts.'

'I was thinking about Leopold's—looking around, and taking it all in.'

'A terrible place,' he sighed, shaking his head of thick curls. 'I hate myself for enjoying it so much here.'

Two men, wearing loose trousers gathered tightly at the ankles and dark green vests over their long-sleeved, thigh-length shirts, approached us, and drew Didier's keen attention. They nodded to him, provoking a broad smile and a wave, and then joined a group of friends at a table not far from our own.

'Dangerous men,' Didier muttered, the smile still creasing his face as he stared at their backs. 'Afghans. Rafiq, the small one, he used to run the black market in books.'

'Books?'

'Passports. He was the boss. A very big fellow, previously. Now he runs brown sugar through Pakistan. He makes a lot more money from the brown sugar, but he is very bitter about this losing of the book business. Men were killed in that struggle—most of them *his* men.'

It wasn't possible that they could've heard the remark, but just then the two Afghans turned in their seats and stared at us with dark, serious expressions, as if responding to his words. One of their companions at the table leaned close, and spoke to them. He pointed at Didier, then at me, and they shifted their gaze to look directly into my eyes.

'Killed ...' Didier repeated softly, smiling even more broadly until the two men turned their backs to us once more. 'I would refuse to do business with them, if only they did not do such good business.'

He was speaking out of the corner of his mouth, like a prisoner under the eyes of the warders. It struck me as funny. In Australian prisons, that whispering technique is known as *side-valving*. The expression spoke itself clearly in my mind and, together with Didier's mannerism, the words put me back in a prison cell. I could smell the cheap disinfectant, hear the metal hiss of the keys, and feel the sweating stone under my fingertips. Flashbacks are common to ex-prisoners, cops, soldiers, ambulance drivers, fire fighters, and others who see and experience trauma. Sometimes the flashback is so sudden, and so inappropriate to the surrounding circumstance, that the only sane reaction is foolish, uncontrollable laughter.

'You think I'm joking?' Didier puffed indignantly.

'No, no, not at all.'

'This is the truth, I assure you. There was a small war over this business. See, here, even now as we speak, the victors arrive. That is Bairam, and his men. He is Iranian. He is an enforcer, and one of those who works for Abdul Ghani, who, in his turn, works for one of the great crime lords of the city, Abdel Khader Khan. They won this little war, and now it is they who control the business in passport books.'

He gestured with a slight nod of his head to point out a group of young men, dressed in stylish western jeans and jackets, who'd just entered through one of the arches. They walked to the manager's desk and greeted the owners of Leopold's warmly before taking a table on the far side of the room. The leader of their group was a tall, heavy-set man in his early thirties. He lifted his plump, jovial face above the heads of his friends and swept the room from right to left, acknowledging deferential nods and friendly smiles from a number of acquaintances at other tables. As his eyes found us, Didier waved a greeting.

'Blood,' he said softly, through his bright smile. 'For a time yet, these passports will be stamped in blood. For me it is nothing. In matters of food I am French, in matters of love I am Italian, and in matters of business I am Swiss. Very Swiss. Strictly neutral. But there will be more blood on these books, of that I am sure.'

He turned to me and blinked once, twice, as if severing the thread of daydream with his thick lashes.

'I must be drunk,' he said with pleasurable surprise. 'Let's have another drink.'

'You go ahead. I'll sit on this one. How much do these passports cost?'

'Anything from one hundred to one thousand—dollars, of course. Do you want to buy one?'

'No ...'

'Ah. This is a Bombay gold dealer's *no*. It is a *no* that means *maybe*, and the more passionate the *no*, the more definite the *maybe*. When you want one, come to me. I will arrange it for you—for a small commission, of course.'

'You make a lot of ... *commissions* here?'

'Mmm, it goes. I cannot complain,' he grinned, his blue eyes gleaming through lenses of pink, alcoholic wetness. 'I make ends meet, as they say, and when they meet I get a payment from both of the ends. Just now, tonight, I made the arrangements for a sale—two kilos of Manali hashish. You see those Italian tourists, over there, by the fruits, the fellow with the long, blonde hair, and the girl in red? They wanted to buy. Someone—you see him, out there on the street, the one with a dirty shirt and no shoes, waiting for his commission—he put them to me, and then I in my turn put them to Ajay. He makes hashish business, and he is an excellent criminal. See now, he sits with them, and all are smiling. The deal is done. My work for this night is finished. I am a free man!'

He thumped the table for another drink, but when the small bottle arrived he grasped it for a while with both hands, staring at it with a brooding, pensive expression.

'How long will you stay in Bombay?' he asked, without looking at me.

'I don't know. It's funny, everyone seems to ask me that in the last few days.'

'You have already stayed longer than the usual. Most people cannot depart the city too quickly.'

'There's a guide, Prabaker's his name, do you know him?'

'Prabaker Kharre? The big smile?'

'That's him. He's been showing me around for weeks now. I've seen all the temples and museums and art galleries, and a lot of the bazaars. From tomorrow morning he's promised to show me something of the other side of the city—the *really* city, he called it. He made it sound interesting. I'll stick around for that, and make my mind up then where I want to go next. I'm in no hurry.'

'It's a very sad thing, to be in no hurry, and I would not be so free in admitting it, if I were you,' he said, still staring at the bottle. When he wasn't smiling his face looked flabby, slack, and pallid grey. He was unwell, but it was the kind of unwell you have to work at. 'We have a saying in Marseilles: a man in no hurry gets nowhere fast. I have been in no hurry for eight years.'

Suddenly his mood changed. He poured a splash from the bottle, looked at me with a smile, and raised his glass.

'So, let's drink! To Bombay, a fine place to be in no hurry! And to civilised policemen, who will accept a bribe, in the interests of the order, if not of the law. To *baksheesh*!'

'I'll drink to that,' I said, clattering my glass against his in the toast. 'So, tell me, Didier, what keeps *you* here in Bombay?'

'I am French,' he replied, admiring the dew on his half-raised glass, 'I am gay, I am Jewish, and I am a criminal, more or less in that order. Bombay is the only city I have ever found that allows me to be all four of those things, at the same time.'

We laughed, and drank, and he turned his gaze on the wide room, his hungry eyes finally coming to rest on a group of Indian men who sat near one of the entrances. He studied them for a while, sipping slowly at his drink.

'Well, if you decide to stay, you have picked a good time for it. This is a time of changes. Great changes. You see those men, eating foods with such strong appetite? They are Sainiks, workers for the Shiv Sena. *Hatchet men*, I think, is the charming English political phrase. Your guide, has he told you of the Sena?'

'No, I don't think so.'

'A conscious lapse, I would say. The Shiv Sena Party is the face of the future in Bombay. Perhaps their mode and their *politique* is the future everywhere.'

'What kind of politics?'

'Oh, regional, language-based, ethnic, us-against-them,' he replied, sneering cynically as he ticked each characteristic off on the fingers of his left hand. They were very white, soft hands. His long fingernails were black with dirt under the edges. 'The politics of fear. I hate politics, and politicians even more. They make a religion of being greedy. It's unforgivable. A man's relationship to his greed is a deeply personal thing, don't you think? The Shiv Sena controls the police, because they are a Maharashtrian party, and most of the lower ranks of the police are Maharashtrians. They control a lot of the slums, too, and many of the unions, and some of the press. They have everything, in fact, except the money. Oh, they have the support of the sugar barons, and some of the merchants, but the real money—the industrial money and the black money—that is in the hands of the Parsees and the Hindus from other cities in India and, most hated of all, the Muslims. And here is the struggle, the *guerre économique*, the truth behind their talk of race and language and region. They are changing the city, a little less and a little more every day. Even the name has been changed, from Bombay to Mumbai. They haven't managed to change the maps, yet, but they will do it. And they will do almost anything, join with almost anyone, in their quest. There are opportunities. Fortunes. Just in the last few months some Sainiks—oh, not the public ones, not the highly placed ones—made a deal with Rafiq and his Afghans and the police. In exchange for certain cash and concessions, the police closed down all but a few of the opium dens in the city. Dozens of the finest smoking parlours, places that have served the community for generations, were closed in a single week. Closed forever! Normally, I do not interest myself in the pigsty of politics, or in the slaughterhouse of big business, for that matter. The only force more ruthless and cynical than the business of big politics is the politics of big business. But this is big politics and big business together, in the destruction of the opium smoking, and I am incensed! I ask you, what is Bombay without its *chandu*—its opium—and its opium dens? What is the world coming to? It's a disgrace!'

I watched the men he'd described, as they concentrated with energetic single-mindedness on their meal. The table was heaped with platters of rice, chicken, and vegetable dishes. None of the five men spoke, nor did they so much as look at one another as they ate, bending low to their plates and scooping the food into their mouths rapidly.

'That's a pretty good line,' I commented, grinning widely. 'The one about the business of big politics, and the politics of big business. I like it.'

'Ah, my dear friend, I cannot claim it as my own. It was Karla who said it to me the first time, and I have used it ever since. I am guilty of many crimes—of *most* crimes, to say the truth—but I have never claimed a cleverness that was not my own.'

'Admirable,' I laughed.

'Well,' he puffed, 'a man has to draw the line somewhere. Civilisation, after all, is defined by what we forbid, more than what we permit.'

He paused, drumming the fingers of his right hand on the cold marble tabletop. After a few moments, he glanced around at me.

'That is one of mine,' he said, apparently peeved that I hadn't drawn attention to the phrase. When I didn't react, he spoke again. 'About the civilisation ... it was one of mine.'

'And damn clever,' I responded quickly.

'Nothing at all,' he said modestly, then he caught my eye, and we both laughed out loud.

'What was in it for Rafiq, if you don't mind my asking. That stuff about closing all the opium dens. Why did he go along with it?'

'Go along with it?' Didier frowned, 'Why, it was his idea. There is more money to be made from *garad*—brown sugar heroin—than there is from opium. And now everyone, all the poor who were chandu smokers, they have become garad smokers. Rafiq controls the garad, the brown sugar. Not all of it, of course. No one man controls all the thousands of kilos of brown sugar that come from Afghanistan, through Pakistan, into India. But a lot of it is his, a lot of the Bombay brown heroin. This is big money, my friend, big money.'

'Why did the politicians go along with it?'

'Ah, it is not only brown sugar and hashish that comes from Afghanistan into India,' he confided, lowering his voice and speaking from the corner of his mouth once more. 'There are guns, heavy weapons, explosives. The Sikhs are using these weapons now, in Punjab, and the Muslim separatists in Kashmir. There are weapons, you see. And there is power, the power to speak for many of the poor Muslims who are the enemies of the Shiv Sena. If you control one trade, the drugs, you can influence the other, the guns. And the Sena Party is desperate to control the flow of guns into their state, their Maharashtra. Money and power. Look there, at the table next to Rafiq and his men. You see the three Africans, two men and a woman?'

'Yes. I noticed her before. She's very beautiful.'

Her young face, with its prominent cheekbones, softly flared nose, and very full lips, looked as if it had been carved in volcanic stone by the rush of a river. Her hair was braided into a multitude of long, fine, beaded plaits. She laughed, sharing a joke with her friends, and her teeth gleamed large and perfectly white.

'Beautiful? I think not. Among the Africans, the men are beautiful, in my opinion, whereas the women are merely very attractive. For Europeans, the opposite is true. Karla is beautiful, and I never knew a European man who is beautiful in that way. But that is another matter. I mean only to say that they are customers of Rafiq, Nigerians, and that their business between Bombay and Lagos is one of the concessions—a *spin-off* is the term, I think—of this deal with the Sainiks. The Sena has a man at Bombay Customs. So much money is moving from hand to hand. Rafiq's little scheme is a tangle of countries, Afghanistan and India, Pakistan and Nigeria, and of powers—police and customs and politicians. All of it is a part of the struggle for control here in our cursed and beloved

Bombay. And all of it, all this intrigue, grows from the closing down of my dear old opium dens. A tragedy.'

'This Rafiq,' I muttered, perhaps sounding more flippant than I'd intended, 'is quite a guy.'

'He is Afghan, and his country is at war, my friend. That gives him an *edge*, as the Americans say. And he works for the Walidlalla mafia council —one of the most powerful. His closest associate is Chuha, one of the most dangerous men in Bombay. But the real power here, in this part of the city, is the great don, lord Abdel Khader Khan. He is a poet, a philosopher, and a lord of crime. They call him Khader*bhai*. Khader-*Elder Brother*. There are others, with more money and more guns than Khaderbhai— he is a man of rigid principles, you see, and there are many lucrative things that he will not do. But those same principles give him—I am not sure how to say it in English—the *immoral* high ground, perhaps, and there is no-one, in this part of Bombay, who has more real power than he does. Many people believe that he is a saint, with supernatural capabilities. I know him, and I can tell you that Khaderbhai is the most fascinating man I ever met. If you will allow me the small immodesty, this makes him a truly remarkable individual, for I have met a great many interesting men in my life.'

He left the words to swirl for a moment in the eye contact between us.

'Come, you are not drinking! I hate it when people take so long to drink a single glass. It is like putting on a condom to masturbate.'

'No really,' I laughed. 'I, er, I'm waiting for Karla to come back. She's due any minute now.'

'Ah, Karla ...' He said her name with a long, purring roll. 'And just what are your intentions with our inscrutable Karla?'

'Come again?'

'Perhaps it is more useful to wonder what intentions she has for *you*, no?'

He poured the last of the one-litre bottle into his glass and topped it up with the last of the soda. He'd been drinking steadily for more than an hour. His eyes were as veined and bloodshot as the back of a boxer's fist, but the gaze that stared from them was unwavering, and his hands were precise in their movements.

'I saw her on the street, just hours after I landed in Bombay,' I found myself saying. 'There was something about her that ... I think she's one of the reasons why I've stayed here this long. Her and Prabaker. I like them—I liked them both on sight. I'm a people person, if you know what I mean. If the people in it were interesting, I'd prefer a tin shed to the Taj Mahal—not that I've seen the Taj Mahal yet.'

'It leaks,' Didier sniffed, dismissing the architectural wonder with two words. 'But did you say *interesting*? Karla is *interesting*?'

He laughed out loud again. It was a peculiarly high-pitched laugh, harsh and almost hysterical. He slapped me hard on the back, spilling a little of his drink.

'Ha! You know, Lin, I *approve* of you, even if a commendation from me is a very fragile endorsement.'

He drained his glass, thumped it on the table, and wiped his closely trimmed moustache with the back of his hand. When he saw my puzzled expression, he leaned close until our faces were only a few centimetres apart.

'Let me explain something to you. Look around here. How many people do you count?'

'Well, maybe, sixty, eighty.'

'Eighty people. Greeks, Germans, Italians, French, Americans. Tourists from everywhere. Eating, drinking, talking, laughing. And from Bombay —Indians and Iranians and Afghans and Arabs and Africans. But how many of these people have real power, real destiny, real *dynamique* for their place, and their time, and the lives of thousands of people? I will tell you—four. Four people in this room with power, and the rest are like the rest of the people everywhere: powerless, sleepers in the dream, *anonyme*. When Karla comes back, there will be five people in this room with power. That is Karla, the one you call *interesting*. I see by your expression, my young friend, you do not understand what I am saying. Let me put it this way: Karla is reasonably good at being a friend, but she is stupendously good at being an enemy. When you judge the power that is in a person, you must judge their capacities as both friend and as enemy. And there is no-one in this city that makes a worse or more dangerous enemy than Karla.'

He stared into my eyes, looking for something, moving from one eye to the other and back again.

'You know the kind of power I'm talking about, don't you? *Real* power. The power to make men shine like the stars, or crush them to dust. The power of secrets. Terrible, terrible secrets. The power to live without remorse or regret. Is there something in your life, Lin, that you regret? Is there anything you have done, that you regret it?'

'Yes, I guess I —'

'Of *course* you do! And so do I, regret … things I have done … and not done. But not Karla. And that is why she is like the others, the few others in this room, who have real power. She has a heart like theirs, and you and I do not. Ah, forgive me, I am almost drunk, and I see that my Italians are leaving. Ajay will not wait for much longer. I must go, now, and collect my little commission, before I can allow myself to be completely drunk.'

He sat back in his chair, and then pushed himself to his feet by leaning heavily on the table with both of his soft, white hands. Without another word or look he left, and I watched him walk toward the kitchen, threading his way through the tables with the rolling, spongy step of the practised drinker. His sports coat was creased and wrinkled at the back, where he'd been leaning against the chair, and the seat of his trousers hung in baggy folds. Before I knew him well enough, before I realised how much it meant that he'd lived by crime and passion for eight years in Bombay without making a single enemy and without borrowing a single dollar, I tended to dismiss Didier as little more than an amusing but hopeless drunkard. It was an easy mistake to make, and one that he himself encouraged.

The first rule of black business everywhere is: *never let anyone know what you're thinking.* Didier's corollary to the rule was: *always know what the other thinks of you.* The shabby clothes, the matted, curly hair, pressed flat in places where it had rested on the pillow the night before, even his fondness for alcohol, exaggerated into what seemed to be a debilitating addiction—they were all expressions of an image he cultivated, and were as carefully nuanced as a professional actor's. He made people think that he was harmless and helpless, because that was the precise opposite of the truth.

I had little time to think about Didier and the puzzling remarks he'd made, however, because Karla soon returned, and we left the restaurant almost at once. We took the long way to her small house, walking beside the sea wall that runs from the Gateway of India to the Radio Club Hotel. The long, wide street was empty. On our right, behind a row of plane trees, were hotels and apartment buildings. A few lights, here and there, showed windowgraphs of the lives being lived in those rooms: a sculpture displayed on one wall, a shelf of books on another, a poster of some Indian deity, framed in wood, surrounded by flowers and smoky streamers of incense and, just visible in the corner of a street-level window, two slender hands pressed together in prayer.

On our left was a vast segment of the world's largest harbour, the dark water starred by the moorage lights of a hundred ships at anchor. Beyond them, the horizon quivered with fires flung from the towers of offshore refineries. There was no moon. It was nearly midnight, but the air was still as warm as it had been in the early afternoon. High tide on the Arabian Sea brought occasional sprays over the waist-high stone wall: mists that swirled, on the Simoom, all the way from the coast of Africa.

We walked slowly. I looked up often at the sky, so heavy with stars that the black net of night was bulging, overflowing with its glittering haul. Imprisonment meant years without a sunrise, a sunset, or a night sky, locked in a cell for sixteen hours each day, from early afternoon to late morning. Imprisonment meant that they took away the sun and the moon and the stars. Prison wasn't hell, but there was no heaven in it, either. In its own way, that was just as bad.

'You can take this good-listener business a little too far, you know.'

'What? Oh, sorry. I was thinking.' I apologised, and shook myself into the moment. 'Hey, before I forget, here's that money Ulla gave me.'

She accepted the roll of notes from me and shoved it into her handbag without looking at it.

'It's strange, you know. Ulla went with Modena to break away from someone else who was controlling her like a slave. Now she's Modena's slave, in a way. But she loves him, and that makes her ashamed that she has to lie to him, to keep a little money for herself.'

'Some people need the master-slave thing.'

'Not just *some* people,' she responded, with sudden and disconcerting bitterness. 'When you were talking to Didier about freedom, when he asked you *the freedom to do what?*—you said, the freedom to say *no*. It's funny, but I was thinking it's more important to have the freedom to say *yes*.'

'Speaking of Didier,' I said lightly, trying to change the subject and lift her spirits, 'I had a long talk with him tonight, while I was waiting for you.'

'I think *Didier* would've done most of the talking,' she guessed.

'Well, yes, he did, but it was interesting. I enjoyed it. It's the first time we've ever talked like that.'

'What did he tell you?'

'*Tell* me?' The phrase struck me as peculiar; it carried the hint that there were things he shouldn't tell. 'He was giving me some background on some of the people at Leopold's. The Afghans, and the Iranians, and the Shiv Sainiks—or whatever they're called—and the local mafia dons.'

She gave a wry little smile.

'I wouldn't take too much notice of what Didier says. He can be very superficial, especially when he's being serious. He's the kind of guy who gets right down to the skin of things, if you know what I mean. I told him once he's so shallow that the best he can manage is a *single entendre*. The funny thing is, he liked it. I'll say this for Didier, you can't insult him.'

'I thought you two were friends,' I remarked, deciding not to repeat what Didier had said about her.

'Friends … well, sometimes, I'm not really sure what friendship is. We've known each other for years. We used to live together once—did he tell you?'

'No, he didn't.'

'Yeah. For a year, when I first came to Bombay. We shared a crazy, fractured little apartment in the Fort area. The building was crumbling around us. Every morning we used to wake with plaster on our faces from the pregnant ceiling, and there were always new chunks of stone and wood and other stuff in the hallway. The whole building collapsed in the monsoon a couple of years ago, and a few people were killed. I walk that way sometimes, and look up at the hole in the sky where my bedroom used to be. I suppose you could say that we're close, Didier and I. But *friends*? Friendship is something that gets harder to understand, every damn year of my life. Friendship is like a kind of algebra test that nobody passes. In my worst moods, I think the best you can say is that a friend is anyone you don't despise.'

Her tone was serious, but I allowed myself a gentle laugh.

'That's a bit strong, I think.'

She looked at me, frowning hard, but then she, too, laughed.

'Maybe it is. I'm tired. I haven't had enough sleep for the last few nights. I don't mean to be hard on Didier. It's just that he can be very annoying sometimes, you know? Did he say anything about me?'

'He ... he said that he thinks you're beautiful.'

'He said that?'

'Yes. He was talking about beauty in white people and black people, and he said *Karla is beautiful.*'

She raised her eyebrows, in mild and pleased surprise.

'Well, I'll take that as a significant compliment, even if he is an outrageous liar.'

'I like Didier.'

'Why?' she asked quickly.

'Oh, I don't know. It's his professionalism, I think. I like people who are expert at what they do. And there's a sadness in him that ... kind of makes sense to me. He reminds me of a few guys I know. Friends.'

'At least he makes no secret of his decadence,' she declared, and I was suddenly reminded of something Didier had told me about Karla, and the power of secrets. 'Perhaps that's what we really have in common, Didier and I—we both hate hypocrites. Hypocrisy is just another kind of cruelty. And Didier's not cruel. He's wild, but he's not cruel. He's been quiet, in the last while, but there were times when his passionate affairs were the scandal of the city, or at least of the foreigners who live here. A jealous lover, a young Moroccan boy, chased him down the Causeway with a sword one night. They were both stark naked—quite a shocking event in Bombay, and in the case of Didier, something of a spectacle, I can report. He ran into the Colaba police station, and they rescued him. They are very conservative about such things in India, but Didier has one rule—he never has any sex-involvement with Indians—and I think they respect that. A lot of foreigners come here just for the sex with very young Indian boys. Didier despises them, and he restricts himself to affairs with foreigners. I wouldn't be surprised if that's why he told you so much of other people's business tonight. He was trying to seduce you, perhaps, by impressing you with his knowledge of dark business and dark people. Oh, hello! *Katzeli!* Hey, where did *you* come from?'

We'd come upon a cat that was squatting on the sea wall to eat from a parcel someone had discarded there. The thin, grey animal hunkered down and scowled, growling and whining at the same time, but it allowed Karla to stroke its back as it lowered its head to the food once more. It was a wizened and scabrous specimen with one ear chewed to the shape of a rosebud, and bare patches on its sides and back where unhealed sores were exposed. I found it amazing that such a feral, emaciated creature should permit itself to be petted by a stranger, and that Karla would want to do such a thing. Even more astounding, it seemed to me then, was that the cat had such a keen appetite for vegetables and rice, cooked in a sauce of whole, very hot chillies.

'Oh, look at him,' she cooed. 'Isn't he beautiful?'

'Well ...'

'Don't you admire his courage, his determination to survive?'

'I'm afraid I don't like cats very much. I don't mind dogs, but cats ...'

'But you *must* love cats! In a perfect world, all the people would be like cats are, at two o'clock in the afternoon.'

I laughed.

'Did anyone ever tell you you've got a very peculiar way of putting things?'

'What do you mean?' she asked, turning to me quickly.

Even in the streetlight I could see that her face was flushed, almost angry. I didn't know then that the English language was a gentle obsession with her: that she studied and wrote and worked hard to compose those clever fragments of her conversation.

'Just that you have a unique way of expressing yourself. Don't get me wrong, I like it. I like it very much. It's like ... well ... take yesterday, for instance, when we were all talking about truth. Capital T Truth. Absolute truth. Ultimate truth. And *is there* any truth, is *anything* true? Everybody had something to say about it—Didier, Ulla, Maurizio, even Modena. Then you said, *The truth is a bully we all pretend to like.* I was knocked out by it. Did you read that in a book, or hear it in a play, or a movie?'

'No. I made it up myself.'

'Well, that's what I mean. I don't think I could repeat anything that the others said, and be sure of getting it exactly right. But that line of yours —I'll never forget it.'

'Do you agree with it?'

'What—that the truth is a bully we all pretend to like?'

'Yes.'

'No, I don't, not at all. But I love the idea, and the way you put it.'

Her half-smile held my stare. We were silent for a few moments, and just as she began to look away I spoke again to hold her attention.

'Why do you like Biarritz?'

'What?'

'The other day, the day before yesterday, you said that Biarritz is one of your favourite places. I've never been there, so I don't know, one way or the other. But I'd like to know why *you* like it so much.'

She smiled, wrinkling her nose in a quizzical expression that might've been scornful or pleased.

'You remember that? Then, I guess I better tell you. Biarritz ... how to explain it ... I think it's the ocean. The Atlantic. I love Biarritz in the wintertime, when the tourists are gone, and the sea is so frightening that it turns people to stone. You see them standing on the deserted beaches, and staring at the sea—statues, scattered along the beach between the cliffs, frozen stiff by the terror they feel when they look at the ocean. It's not like other oceans—not like the warm Pacific or the Indian. The Atlantic there, in winter, is really unforgiving, and ruthlessly cruel. You can feel it calling to you. You know it wants to drag you out and pull you under. It's so beautiful, I just burst into tears the first time I really looked at it. And I wanted to go to it. I wanted to let myself go out and under the big, angry waves. It's the scariest thing. But the people in Biarritz, they're the most tolerant and easy-going people in Europe, I think. Nothing freaks them out. Nothing is too over-the-top. It's kind of weird—in most holiday places, the people are angry and the sea is calm. In Biarritz, it's the other way around.'

'Do you think you'll go back there one day—to stay, I mean?'

'No,' she said quickly. 'If I ever leave here, for good, it'll mean going back to the States. I grew up there, after my parents died. And I'd like to go back, some day. I think I love it there, most of all. There's something so confident and open-hearted and ... and *brave* about America, and the American people. I don't feel American—at least, I don't think I do—but I'm *comfortable* with them, if you know what I mean, more than I am with any other people, anywhere.'

'Tell me about the others,' I asked, wanting to keep her talking.

'The others?' she asked, frowning suddenly.

'The crew at Leopold's. Didier and the others. Tell me about Letitia, to start with. How do you know her?'

She relaxed, and let her eyes roam the shadows on the far side of the street. Still thinking, still considering, she lifted her gaze to the night sky.

The blue-white light from a street lamp melted to liquid on her lips and in the spheres of her large eyes.

'Lettie lived in Goa for a while,' she began, affection playing in her voice. 'She came to India for the usual mix—parties and spiritual highs. She found the parties, and she enjoyed them, I think. Lettie loves a party. But she never had much luck with the spiritual side of things. She went back to London—twice in the same year—but then she came back to India for one last try at the soul thing. She's on a soul mission. She talks tough, but she's a very spiritual girl. I think she's the most spiritual of all of us, really.'

'How does she live? I don't mean to pry—it's what I was saying before, I just want to learn how people make a living here. How foreigners get by, I mean.'

'She's an expert with gems—gemstones and jewels. She works on a commission basis for some of the foreign buyers. It was Didier who got her the job. He has contacts everywhere in Bombay.'

'Didier?' I smiled, genuinely surprised. 'I thought that they hated each other—well, not *hate* exactly. I thought they couldn't stand each other.'

'Oh, they annoy one another, sure. But there's a real friendship there. If anything bad happened to one of them, the other would be devastated.'

'How about Maurizio?' I asked, trying to keep my tone even. The tall Italian was too handsome, too confident, and I envied him for what I saw as his deeper knowledge of Karla, and his friendship with her. 'What's his story?'

'His story? I don't know what his *story* is,' she replied, frowning again. 'His parents died, leaving him a lot of money. He spent it, and I think he developed something of a talent for spending money.'

'Other people's money?' I asked. I might've seemed too eager for that to be true, because she answered me with a question.

'Do you know the story of the scorpion and the frog? You know, the frog agrees to carry the scorpion across the river, because the scorpion promises not to sting him?'

'Yeah. And then the scorpion stings the frog, half way across the river. The drowning frog asks him why he did it, when they'll both drown, and the scorpion says that he's a scorpion, and it's his nature to sting.'

'Yes,' she sighed, nodding slowly until the frown left her brow. 'That's Maurizio. And if you *know* that, he's not a problem, because you just don't offer to carry him across the river. Do you know what I mean?'

I'd been in prison. I knew exactly what she meant. I nodded, and asked her about Ulla and Modena.

'I like Ulla,' she answered quickly, turning that half-smile on me again. 'She's crazy and unreliable, but I have a feeling for her. She was a rich girl, in Germany, and she played with heroin until she got a habit. Her family cut her off, so she came to India—she was with a bad guy, a German guy, a junkie like her, who put her to work in a very tough place. A horrible place. She loved the guy. She did it for him. She would've done anything for him. Some women are like that. Some loves are like that. *Most* loves are like that, from what I can see. Your heart starts to feel like an over-crowded lifeboat. You throw your pride out to keep it afloat, and your self-respect and your independence. After a while you start throwing people out—your friends, everyone you used to know. And it's still not enough. The lifeboat is still sinking, and you know it's going to take you down with it. I've seen that happen to a lot of girls here. I think that's why I'm sick of love.'

I couldn't tell if she was talking about herself, or pointing the words at me. Either way, they were sharp, and I didn't want to hear them.

'And how about Kavita? Where does she fit in?'

'Kavita's great! She's a freelancer—you know that—a freelance writer. She wants to be a journalist, and I think she'll get there. I *hope* she gets there. She's bright and honest and gutsy. She's beautiful, too. Don't you think she's a gorgeous girl?'

'Sure,' I agreed, recalling the honey-coloured eyes, the full and shapely lips, and the long, expressive fingers. 'She's a pretty girl. But they're *all* good-looking people, I think. Even Didier, in his crumpled-up way, has got a touch of the Lord Byron about him. Lettie's a lovely girl. Her eyes are always laughing—they're a real *ice*-blue, her eyes, aren't they? Ulla looks like a doll, with those big eyes and big lips on such a round face. But it's a pretty doll's face. Maurizio's handsome, like a magazine model, and Modena's handsome in a different way, like a bullfighter or something. And you're ... you're the most beautiful woman I've ever seen with my own eyes.'

There, I'd said it. And even in the shock of speaking the thought out loud, I wondered if she'd understood, if she'd pierced my words about their beauty, and hers, to find the misery that inspired them: the misery that an ugly man feels in every conscious minute of love.

She laughed—a good, deep, wide-mouthed laugh—and seized my arm impulsively, pulling me along the footpath. Just then, as if drawn from the shadows by her laughter, there was a clattering rattle of noise as a beggar, riding on a small wooden platform with metal ball-bearing wheels, rolled off the footpath on the opposite side of the street. He pushed himself forward with his hands until he reached the centre of the deserted road, wheeling to a stop with a dramatic pirouette. His piteously thin mantis-legs were folded and tucked beneath him on the platform, which was a piece of wood no bigger than a folded newspaper. He wore a boy's school uniform of khaki shorts and a powder-blue shirt. Although he was a man in his twenties, the clothes were too big for him.

Karla called out, greeting him by name, and we stopped opposite him. They spoke for some time in Hindi. I stared across the ten metres that separated us, fascinated by the man's hands. They were huge hands, as wide across the back, from knuckle to knuckle, as his face. In the street-light I could see that they were thickly padded on the fingers and palms like the paws of a bear.

'Good night!' he called out in English, after a minute. He lifted one hand, first to his forehead and then to his heart, in a delicate gesture of consummate gallantry. With another swift, show-off's pirouette, he pro-pelled himself forward along the road, gaining speed as he rolled down the gentle slope to the Gateway Monument.

We watched him out of sight, and then Karla pulled at my arm, lead-ing me along the path once more. I allowed myself to be led. I allowed myself to be drawn by the soft pleading of the waves, and the roulade of her voice; by the black sky, and the darker night of her hair; by the sea-tree-stone smell of the sleeping street, and the perfume sublime on her warm skin. I allowed myself to be drawn into her life, and the life of the city. I walked her home. I said good night. And I was singing quietly to myself as I went back along the silent brood of streets to my hotel.

CHAPTER THREE

'What you're saying is that we're finally going to get down to the real deal.'

'*Real* will be full, baba,' Prabaker assured me, 'and *deal* will be plenty also. Now you will see it the really city. Usually, I am never taking the tourists to these places. They are not liking it, and I am not liking their not liking. Or maybe sometimes they are liking it too much, in these places, and I am liking that even less, isn't it? You must have it a good heads, to like these things, and you must be having a good hearts, to not like them too much. Like you, Linbaba. You are my good friend. I knew it very well, on that first day, when we were drinking the whisky, in your room. Now my Bombay, with your good heads and your good hearts, you will see it all.'

We were riding in a taxi along Mahatma Gandhi Road past Flora Fountain and towards Victoria Station. It was an hour before noon, and the swash of traffic that coursed through that stone canyon was swollen by large numbers of runners pushing tiffin carts. The runners collected lunches from homes and apartments, and placed them in tin cylinders called *jalpaans*, or tiffins. They pushed huge trays of the tiffins on long wooden carts, six men and more to a cart. Through the heavy metal-traffic of buses, trucks, scooters, and cars, they made deliveries at offices and businesses all over the city. None but the men and women who operated the service knew exactly how it was done: how barely literate men evolved the bafflingly complex system of symbols, colours, and key numbers to mark and identify the cylinders; how, day after day, hundreds of thousands of those identical containers swept through the city on their wooden axles, oiled with sweat, and reached the right man or woman, among millions, every time; and how all that was achieved at a cost measured in cents rather than dollars. Magic, the trick that connects the ordinary to the impossible, was the invisible river that ran through every street and beating heart in Bombay in those years, and nothing, from the postal service to the pleading of beggars, worked without a measure of it.

'What number that bus, Linbaba? Quickly, tell it.'

'Just a second.' I hesitated, peering out of the half-open window of the taxi and trying to read the curlicue numbers on the front of a red, double-decker bus that had stopped opposite us momentarily. 'It's, ah, it's a one-zero-four, isn't it?'

'Very, very fine! You have learn your Hindi numbers so nicely. Now no problem for you, reading numbers for bus, and train, and menu card, and drugs purchase, and other good things. Now tell me, what is *alu palak*?'

'*Alu palak* is potato and spinach.'

'Good. And nice eating also, you have not mention. I love to eat it, *alu palak*. What is *phul gobhi* and *bhindi*?'

'That's … oh yeah, cauliflower and … and okra.'

'Correct. And also good eating, again you are not mention. What is *baingan masala*?'

'That's, ah, spiced eggplant.'

'Again right! What is it, you're not enjoying eating baingan?'

'Yes, yes, all right! Baingan is good eating, too!'

'I don't like it baingan so much,' he sneered, wrinkling up his short nose. 'Tell me, what am I calling *chehra*, *munh*, and *dil*?'

'Okay … don't tell me … face, mouth, and heart. Is that right?'

'Very right, no problem. I have been watching it, how nicely you eat up your foods with the hand, like a good Indian style. And how you learn to ask for the things—how much this, how much that, give me two cups of tea, I want more hashish—speaking only Hindi to the people. I have seen this all. You are my best student, Linbaba. And I am your best teacher also, isn't it?'

'It is, Prabu,' I laughed. 'Hey! Watch out!'

My shout alerted the taxi driver, who swerved just in time to avoid an ox-cart that was attempting to make a turn in front of us. The taxi driver —a burly, dark-skinned man with a bristling moustache—seemed to be outraged at my impertinence in saving our lives. When we first took the taxi he'd adjusted his mirror until he saw nothing in it but my face. After the near miss he glared at me, snarling a growl of insults in Hindi. He drove the cab like a getaway car, slewing left and right to overtake slower vehicles. There was an angry, bullying pugnacity in his attitude to everyone else on the road. He rushed to within centimetres of every slower car in his path, sounding his horn, then all but nudging it out of the way. If the slower car moved a little to the left, in order to let him pass, our driver drew beside it, pacing it for a time and shouting insults. When he spied another slow vehicle ahead, he sped forward to repeat the procedure. From time to time he opened his door and leaned out over the road to spit paan juice, taking his eyes off the traffic ahead for long seconds as we hurtled along in the rattling cab.

'This guy's a nut-case!' I muttered to Prabaker.

'Driving is not so good,' Prabaker replied, bracing himself with both arms against the back of the driver's seat. 'But I have to say, the spitting and insulting is a first-class job.'

'For Christ's sake, tell him to stop!' I shouted as the cab accelerated into a squall of traffic, lurching in the swerve left and right. 'He's going to kill us!'

'*Band karo!*' Prabaker shouted. *Stop!*

He added a pithy curse, for good measure, but the driver only became more enraged. With the car hurtling along at top speed, he turned his head to snarl at us. His mouth was wide open, and his teeth were bared. His eyes were huge, their blackness streaked with rage.

'*Arrey!*' Prabaker shrieked, pointing past the driver.

It was too late. The man turned quickly. His arms stiffened at the wheel, and he hit the brakes hard. There was a skating, sliding second ... two seconds ... three seconds. I heard a guttural gasp of air from deep in his throat. It was a sucking sound, like the lifting of a flat stone from the moist clay on the edge of a riverbed. Then there was the whump and crash as we slammed into a car that had stopped in front of us to make a turn. We were thrown forward into the back of his seat, and heard two thumping explosions as two other cars rammed into us.

Shattered glass and chrome fragments rattled on the road like thin metallic applause in the sudden silence that followed the impacts. My head had hit the door in the tumble spill of the accident. I felt blood flowing from a cut above my eye, but I was otherwise unhurt. As I wriggled myself up from the floor, and onto the back seat once more, I felt Prabaker's hands on me.

'Nothing broken you are, Lin? You are okay?'

'I'm okay, I'm okay.'

'You are sure? Everything not broken?'

'Jesus, Prabu, I don't care how good this guy's spitting is,' I said, laughing nervously, and ragged with relief, 'he doesn't get a tip. Are you all right?'

'We must get out, Lin!' he answered, his voice rising to a hysterical whine. 'Out! Out of here! Now!'

The door on his side was jammed shut, and he began to push at it with his shoulder. He couldn't budge it. He reached across me to try the door on my side, but saw at once that another car was jammed against it, pinning it shut. Our eyes met, and there was such fear in him, such terror in the white-rimmed bulge of his eyes, that I felt the coldness of it deep in my chest. He turned at once, and threw himself again at the door on his side.

My mind was muddy water, and one idea splashed up from it, clear and exclusive: FIRE. *Is that what he's afraid of?* Once I'd asked myself the question I couldn't stop thinking it. I looked at the terror that pulled at Prabaker's gasping mouth, and I was sure the taxi was going to catch fire. I knew we were trapped there. The rear windows, in all the Bombay taxis I'd seen, didn't open beyond a few centimetres. The doors were jammed, and the windows wouldn't open, and the taxi was going to explode in fire, and we were trapped. *Burned alive … Is that why he's so scared?*

I looked to the driver. He was slumped, awkwardly, between the steering wheel and the door. His body was still, but I heard him moaning. Beneath the thin shirt, the abacus ridge of his spine rose and fell with each slow and shallow breath.

Faces appeared at the windows of the cab, and I heard excited voices. Prabaker looked out at them, turning this way and that, his face cramped in an expression of terrible anguish. Suddenly, he clambered over the seat into the front of the car and wrestled the passenger door open. Turning swiftly and grabbing at my arms with surprising strength, he tried to drag me by main force over the seat that divided us.

'This way, Lin! Get out, now! Hurry! Hurry!'

I climbed up and over the seat. Prabaker got out of the car, pushing his way into a crowd of onlookers. I reached out to the driver, trying to prise him from the obstructing rim of the steering wheel, but Prabaker's hands were on me again, brutally rough. The fingernails of one hand tore into the skin of my back, and the other wrenched at the collar of my shirt.

'Don't touch him, Lin!' he almost screamed. 'Don't touch him! Leave him and get out. Get out now!'

He dragged me from the car and through the hedge of bodies pressing in on the accident. On a footpath nearby, we sat beneath a fringe of hawthorn leaves that overhung a fence of wrought-iron spears, and inspected one another for injuries. The cut on my forehead, above my right eye, wasn't as serious as I'd thought. The bleeding had already stopped, and it began to weep a clear, plasmic fluid. I was sore in a few places, but it was no cause for concern. Prabaker cradled his arm—the same arm that had pulled me from the car with such irresistible power—and it was obvious that he was in pain. A large swelling had already formed near the elbow. I knew it would leave a nasty bruise, but nothing seemed to be broken.

'Looks like you were wrong, Prabu,' I chided, smiling as I lit a cigarette for him.

'Wrong, baba?'

'Getting us out of the car in such a panic and all. You really had me going. I thought the damn thing was going to catch fire, but it looks okay.'

'Oh,' he replied softly, staring straight ahead. 'You think I was frightening for fire? Not fire in the car, Lin, but fire in the *people*. Look, now. See the public, how they are.'

We stood, stretching the ache from shoulders and whip-lashed necks, and looked toward the wreckage some ten metres away. About thirty people had gathered around the four crashed vehicles. A few of them were helping drivers and passengers from the damaged cars. The rest huddled together in groups, gesturing wildly and shouting. More people streamed toward the site from every direction. Drivers of other cars that had been blocked from travelling further, left their vehicles and joined the crowd. The thirty people became fifty, eighty, then a hundred as we watched.

One man was the centre of attention. It was his car that had been trying to turn right, his car we'd smashed into with the brakes on full lock. He stood beside the taxi, bellowing with rage. He was a round-shouldered man, in his middle forties, wearing a grey, cotton safari suit that had been tailored to accommodate the extravagant boast of his large paunch. His thinning hair was awry. The breast pocket of his suit had been torn, there was a rip in his trousers, and he'd lost one sandal. That dishevelment combined with his theatrical gestures and persistent shouting to present a spectacle that seemed to be more enthralling, for the crowd of onlookers, than the wreckage of the cars. His hand had been cut from the palm to the wrist. As the staring crowd grew more silent, subdued by the drama, he smeared blood from the wound on his face and beat the redness into the grey of his suit, shouting all the while.

Just then, some men carried a woman into the little clear space around the man, and placed her on a piece of cloth that was stretched out on the ground for her. They shouted instructions to the crowd, and in moments a wooden cart appeared, pushed by bare-chested men wearing only singlets and short lungis. The woman was lifted onto the cart, her red sari gathered up in folds and wrapped about her legs. She may have been the man's wife—I couldn't be sure—but his rage suddenly grew hysterical. He seized her roughly by the shoulders and shook her. He pulled at her hair. He appealed to the crowd with enormous, histrionic gestures, flinging his arms wide and then striking his own blood-streaked face. They were the gestures of pantomime, the exaggerated simulations of silent films, and I couldn't help thinking they were absurd and funny. But the injuries people had sustained were real, as were the rumbling threats that surged through the ever-increasing crowd.

As the semi-conscious woman was trundled away on the humble cart, the man hurled himself at the door of the taxi, wrenching it open. The crowd reacted as one. They dragged the dazed and injured taxi driver from his cab in an instant and flung him on the bonnet of the car. He raised his arms in feeble pleading, but a dozen, twenty, fifty hands punched and tore at him. Blows drummed on his face, chest, stomach, and groin. Fingernails scratched and ripped, tearing his mouth open on one side almost to the ear, and shredding his shirt to rags.

It happened in seconds. I told myself, as I watched the beating, that it was all too fast, that I was dazed, and there was no time to react. What we call cowardice is often just another name for being taken by surprise, and courage is seldom any better than simply being well prepared. And I might've done more, I might've done something, anything, if it had happened in Australia. *It's not your country*, I told myself, as I watched the beating. *It's not your culture …*

But there was another thought, dark and secret then, and all too clear to me now: the man was an idiot, an insulting and belligerent idiot, whose reckless stupidity had risked Prabaker's life and mine. A splinter of spite had pierced my heart when the crowd turned on him, and at least some small particle of their revenge—a blow or a shout or a shove—was my own. Helpless, craven, ashamed, I did nothing.

'We've got to do something …' I said lamely.

'Enough people are doing, baba,' Prabaker replied.

'No, I mean, we've got to … can't we help him, somehow?'

'For this fellow is no helping,' he sighed. 'Now you see it, Lin. Accidents is very bad business in Bombay. Better you get out of that car, or taxi, or what is it you are in, very, very quickly. The public are not having patience for such business. See now, it is too late for that fellow.'

The beating was swift, but savage. Blood streamed from many cuts on the man's face and naked torso. At a signal, perceived, somehow, through the howl and shriek of the crowd, the man was lifted up and carried off at head height. His legs were pressed together and stretched out, held rigid by a dozen hands. His arms were splayed out at right angles to his body and held fast. His head lolled and fell back, the soft, wet flap of skin hanging from cheek to jaw. His eyes were open, conscious, staring backward and upside down: black eyes, scudded with fear and imbecile hope. Traffic on the far side of the road parted to let the people pass, and the man slowly disappeared, crucified on the hands and shoulders of the crowd.

'Come on, Lin. Let's go. You are okay?'

'I'm all right,' I mumbled, forcing myself to shuffle into step beside him. My self-assurance had melted through muscle and bone to settle in my knees. Each step was leaden and willed. It wasn't the violence that had shaken me. I'd seen worse, and with far less provocation, in prison. It was, instead, the too-sudden collapse of my stilted complacencies. The weeks of the city I'd thought I was beginning to know—the Bombay of temples, bazaars, restaurants, and new friends—had cindered in the fires of that public rage.

'What … what are they going to do with him?'

'They will take him to police, I think so. Behind Crawford Market is one police station, for this area. Maybe he will have the luck—maybe alive, he will reach there. Maybe not. He has a very quickly Karma, this fellow.'

'You've seen this before?'

'Oh, many times, Linbaba. Sometimes, I drive it my cousin Shantu's taxi. I have seen so many angry publics. That is why I was getting so afraid for you, and for my good self also.'

'Why does it happen like that? Why did they get so crazy about it?'

'That is nobody knows, Lin,' Prabaker shrugged, quickening his pace a little.

'Wait a minute,' I paused, slowing him with a hand to his shoulder. 'Where are we going?'

'Still going for the tour, isn't it?'

'I thought ... maybe ... you want to call it off, for today.'

'Calling off *why*? We have it a real and full deal to see, Linbaba. So, let's go, *na*?'

'But what about your arm? Don't you want to get it seen to?'

'No problem this arms, Lin. For last of the touring, we will have some whisky drinks in a terrible place I know. That will be a good medicine. So come on, let's go now, baba.'

'Well, okay, if you say so. But we were going the other way, weren't we?'

'*Still* going the other way, baba,' Prabaker replied with some urgency. 'But first going *this* way only! Over there is a telephone, at the station. I must call my cousin, working now at Sunshine restaurant, as the dishes-washing boy. He is wanting a taxi-driving job, for his brother, Suresh, and I must give it the number and boss-name of the driver, now gone with the people. That fellow's boss will be needing a new driver now, and we must hurry for such a good chance, isn't it?'

Prabaker made that call. Seconds later, he continued his tour of the dark side of the city without a heartbeat of hesitation, in another taxi, as if nothing had happened. Nor did he ever raise the matter with me again. When I occasionally spoke of it, he responded with a shrug, or some bland comment about our *good luck* in avoiding serious injury. For him, the incident was like a brawl in a nightclub, or a clash of rival supporters at a football match — commonplace and unremarkable, unless you happen to be in the centre of it.

But for me that sudden, savage, bewildering riot, the sight of that taxi-driver floating away on a rippling wave of hands, shoulders, and heads was a turning point. A new understanding emerged from it. I suddenly realised that if I wanted to stay there, in Bombay, the city I'd already fallen in love with, I had to change. I had to get involved. The city wouldn't let me be a watcher, aloof and apart. If I wanted to stay, I had to expect that she would drag me into the river of her rapture, and her rage. Sooner or later, I knew, I would have to step off the pavement and into the bloody crowd, and put my body on the line.

And with the seed of that resolve, born in that convulsion and portent, Prabaker's dark circuit of the city began. When we resumed our tour, he took me to a slave market not far from Dongri, an inner suburb famous for its mosques, bazaars, and restaurants specialising in Mughlai dishes. The main road became streets and the streets became lanes and, when those proved too narrow for the taxi to negotiate, we left the vehicle and walked together in the sinuous busyness of the crowds. The further we travelled into the Catiline lanes, the more we lost of the day, the year, the very age in which we lived. As automobiles and then scooters disappeared, the air became clearer, sharper, with the scents of spices and perfumes undulled by the diesel and petrol fumes prevalent elsewhere. Traffic noise faded, ceased, and was replaced by street sound—a class of children reciting verses from the Koran in a little courtyard; the whirr and scrape of stone on stone, as women ground spices in doorways; and the whining optimism of cries from knife sharpeners, mattress-fluffers, stove repairers, and other hawkers. They were people sounds, everywhere, played with voice and hand.

At one turn in the puzzle alleyways we passed a long metal rack where bicycles were parked. From then on, even those simple machines vanished. Goods were transported by bearers with enormous bundles on their heads. One burden usually carried by all, the thudding pressure of the Bombay sun, was lifted from us: the lanes were dark, cool, shadowless. Although only three and at most four storeys tall, the buildings leaned in upon the winding pathways, and the sky was reduced to a thin brush stroke of pale blue.

The buildings themselves were ancient and dilapidated. Stone facades, which had once been splendid and impressive, were crumbling, grimed, and patched with haphazard necessity. Here and there, small balconies jutted out to meet one another overhead, so close that neighbours could reach across and pass things with an out-stretched hand. Glimpses inside the houses showed unpainted walls and sagging staircases. Many ground-floor windows were held open to reveal makeshift shops for the sale of sweets, cigarettes, groceries, vegetables, and utensils. It was clear that the plumbing was rudimentary, where it was connected at all. We passed several places where women gathered with metal or clay pots to collect water from a single, outside tap. And skeined over all the buildings like metal cobwebs were complicated traceries of electrical conduits and wires, as if even that symbol and source of the modern age and its power was no more than a fragile, temporary net that might be swept away by a rough gesture.

Just as the contracted lanes seemed, with every twist and turn, to belong to another age, so too did the appearance of the people change as we moved deeper into the maze. I saw less and less of the western-style cotton shirts and trousers, so common everywhere else in the city, until finally those fashions disappeared from all but the youngest children. Instead, the men wore traditional garments of colourful diversity. There were long silk shirts that descended to the knee and were fastened with pearl buttons, from neck to waist; kaftan robes in plain colours or stripes; hooded cloaks that resembled the garb of monks; and an endless variety of skull caps, in white or beaded colours, and turbans in yellow, red, and electric blue. The women were more conspicuously bejewelled, despite the indigence of the quarter, and what those jewels lacked in money's worth was found in the extravagance of their design. No less prominent were caste mark tattoos on some foreheads, cheeks, hands, and wrists. And every bare feminine foot was graced by anklets of silver bells and coiled brass toe-rings.

It was as if all of those hundreds of people were costumed for home, for themselves, not for the public promenades. It was as if they were safe, there, to clothe themselves in tradition and display. And the streets were clean. The buildings were cracked and smeared, the constricted passage-ways were crowded with goats, chickens, dogs, and people, and each thin face showed the shade and hollows of penury, but the streets and the people were stainlessly, scrupulously clean.

We turned then into more ancient alleyways, so narrow that two persons passed one another only with difficulty. People stepped into door-ways, waiting for us to walk past before they moved on. The passages had been covered with false ceilings and stretched awnings, and in the darkness it wasn't possible to see more than a few metres in front or behind. I kept my eyes on Prabaker, fearful that I wouldn't find my way out alone. The little guide turned often, drawing my attention to a loose stone in the path ahead, or a step, or some obstruction overhead. Concentrating on those perils, I lost my orientation. My mental map of the city turned, blurred, faded, and I couldn't guess at the direction of the sea, or the major land-marks—Flora Fountain, V.T. station, Crawford Market—we'd passed on our way to the quarter. I felt myself to be so deep in the flow and reflux of those narrow lanes, so smothered by the intimacy of open doors and per-fumed bodies, that it seemed I was walking inside the buildings, inside the very homes, rather than between them.

We came upon a stall where a man in a sweat-stained cotton vest stirred battered foods frying in a dish of bubbling oil. The blue flames of his kerosene stove, eerie and claustral, provided the only light. Emotion haunted his face. It was anguish, some kind of anguish, and the dull, stoic anger that hangs in the eyes of repetitive, ill-paid work. Prabaker moved past him and into the darkness beyond. As I approached the man he turned to face me, and his eyes met mine. For a moment, the full-force of his blue-lit anger was directed at me.

Long years after that day, the Afghan guerrillas I came to know as friends, on a mountain near the siege of Kandahar, talked for hours about Indian films and their favourite Bollywood movie stars. *Indian actors are the greatest in the world*, one of them said once, *because Indian people know how to shout with their eyes*. That back-street fried-foods cook stared at me, with shouting eyes, and stopped me as surely as if he'd pushed a hand into my chest. I couldn't move. In my own eyes, there were words—*I'm sorry, I'm sorry that you have to do this work, I'm sorry that your world, your life, is so hot and dark and unremembered, I'm sorry that I'm intruding* ...

Still staring at me, he grasped the handles of his dish. For one, two, thudding heartbeats, I was gripped by the ridiculous, terrifying thought that he was going to throw the boiling oil in my face. Fear jerked at my feet and I moved, easing my way past him with my hands flat against the damp surface of the stone wall. Two steps beyond him, my foot struck a crack in the path and I stumbled, and fell, dragging another man down with me. He was an elderly man, thin and frail. I could feel the wicker-basket of his bones through his coarse tunic. We fell heavily, landing near the open entrance to a house, and the old man struck his head. I scrambled to my feet, slipping and sliding on a pile of shifting stones. I tried to help the man to stand, but there was an elderly woman who squatted on her haunches there, in the open doorway, and she slapped at my hands, warning me away. I apologised in English, struggling to find the words for *I'm sorry* in Hindi—*What are they? Prabaker taught me the words* ... *Mujhako afsos hain ... that's it*—I said it three, four times. In that dark, quiet corridor between the buildings, the words echoed like a drunkard's prayer in an empty church.

The old man moaned quietly, slouching in the doorway. The woman wiped his face with a corner of her headscarf, and held the cloth out for me to see the bright stain of blood. She said nothing, but her wrinkled face was creased with a frown of contempt. With that simple gesture, holding out the bloodstained cloth, she seemed to be saying *Look, you stupid oaf, you great clumsy barbarian, look what you've done here ...*

I felt choked by the heat, smothered by the darkness and the strangeness of the place. The walls seemed to press upon my hands, as if only my arms prevented them from closing in on me altogether. I backed away from the elderly couple, stumbling at first, and then plunging headlong into the shadow-land of the tunnel street. A hand reached out to grab at my shoulder. It was a gentle touch, but I almost shouted out loud.

'This way, baba,' Prabaker said, laughing quietly. 'Where are you taking yourself? *This* way only. Along this passage now, and you must be keeping your two feets to the outside because too much dirty it is, in the middle of the passages, okay?'

He was standing in the entrance to a narrow gap formed between the blank walls of two buildings. Feeble light gleamed in the teeth and eyes of his smile, but beyond him was only blackness. He turned his back to me, spread his feet out until they touched the walls, braced himself with his hands, and then shuffled off, sliding his feet along the walls in small, dragging steps. He expected me to follow. I hesitated, but when the awkward star of his shuffling form melted in the darkness and vanished, I too put my feet out against the walls and shambled after him.

I could hear Prabaker ahead of me, but it was so dark that I couldn't see him. One foot strayed from the edge of the wall, and my boot squelched into a muddy slime that rested in the centre of the path. A foul smell rose up from that viscous ooze, and I kept my feet hard against the walls, sliding them along in short steps. Something squat and heavy slithered past me, rasping its thick body against my boot. Seconds later, another and then a third creature waddled past me in the darkness, rolling heavy flesh over the toes of my boots.

'Prabu!' I bellowed, not knowing how far ahead of me he was. 'There are things in here with us!'

'Things, baba?'

'On the ground! Something's crawling on my feet! Something heavy!'

'Only rats are crawling here, Lin. There are no *things*.'

'Rats? Are you kidding? These things are as big as bull terriers. Jesus, this is some tour, my friend!'

'No problem big rats, Lin,' Prabaker answered quietly from the darkness in front of me. 'Big rats are friendly fellows, not making mischief for the people. If you don't attack them. Only one thing is making them bite and scratch and such things.'

'What's that, for God's sake?'

'Shouting, baba,' he replied softly. 'They don't like the loud voices.'

'Oh, great! Now you tell me,' I croaked. 'Is it much further? This is starting to give me the creeps and—'

He'd stopped, and I bumped into him, pressing him against the panelled surface of a wooden door.

'We are here,' he whispered, reaching out to knock with a complex series of taps and pauses. There was a scrape and clunk as a heavy bolt slid free, and then the door swung open, dazzling us with sudden bright light. Prabaker grasped my sleeve and dragged me with him. 'Quickly, Lin. No big rats allowed inside!'

We stepped inside a small chamber, hemmed in by blank walls and lit from high above by a raw silk rectangle of sky. I could hear voices from deeper within the cul-de-sac. A huge man slammed the gate shut. He put his back to it and faced us with a scowl, teeth bared. Prabaker began to talk at once, placating him with soft words and fawning gestures. The man shook his head repeatedly, interjecting regularly to say *no, no, no*.

He towered over me. I was standing so close to him that I could feel the breath from his wide nostrils, the sound of it like wind whistling through caves on a rocky shore. His hair was very short, exposing ears as large and nubbled as a boxer's practice mitts. His square face seemed to be animated by more strong muscle tissue than the average man has in his back. His chest, as wide as I was from shoulder to shoulder, rose and fell with each breath, and rested upon an immense belly. The fine dagger-line of his moustache accentuated his scowl, and he looked at me with such undiluted loathing that a little prayer unfurled itself in my mind. *Please God, don't make me fight this man.*

He raised the palms of his hands to stop Prabaker's wheedling cajolery. They were huge hands, gnarled and calloused enough to scrape the bar-nacles off the side of a dry-docked oil tanker.

'He says we are not allowed inside,' Prabaker explained.

'Well,' I replied, reaching past the man and attempting with unforced enthusiasm to open the door, 'you can't say we didn't try.'

'No, no, Lin!' Prabaker stopped me. 'We must argue with him about this matter.'

The big man folded his arms, stretching the seams of his khaki shirt with little ripples of sound.

'I don't think that's such a good idea,' I mumbled, under a tight smile.

'Certainly it is!' Prabaker insisted. 'Tourists are not allowed here, or to any of the other people-markets, but I have told him that you are not one of these tourist fellows. I have told him that you have learned the Marathi language. He does not believe me. That is our problem only. He doesn't believe any foreigner will speak Marathi. You must for that reason speak it a little Marathi for him. You will see. He will allow us inside.'

'I only know about twenty words of Marathi, Prabu.'

'No problem twenty words, baba. Just make a begin. You will see. Tell him your name.'

'My name?'

'Yes, like I taught it to you. Not in Hindi, but in Marathi. Okay, just begin ...'

'Ah, ah, *maza nao Lin ahey*,' I muttered, uncertainly. *My name is Lin.*

'*Baapree!*' the big man gasped, his eyes wide with genuine surprise. *Good Lord!*

Encouraged, I tried a few more of the phrases Prabaker had taught me during the last few weeks.

'*Maza Desh New Zealand ahey. Ata me Colabala rahella ahey.*' *My country is New Zealand. I am living in Colaba now.*

'*Kai garam mad'chud!*' he roared, smiling for the first time. The phrase literally means, *What a hot motherfucker!* It's so frequently and inventively applied in conversation, however, that it can be loosely translated as *Son of a gun!*

The giant grasped my shoulder, squeezing it with amiable severity.

I ran through the range of my Marathi phrases, beginning with the first words I'd asked Prabaker to teach me — *I love your country very much* — and concluding with a request I was often forced to make in restaurants, but which must've seemed spectacularly inappropriate in the little alcove: *Please turn off the fan, while I am eating my soup* ...

'Enough now, baba,' Prabaker gurgled through his wide grin. When I fell silent, the big man spoke swiftly and exuberantly. Prabaker translated for him, nodding and gesturing expressively with his hands. 'He says he is Bombay policeman, and his name is Vinod.'

'He's a cop?'

'Oh yes, Lin. A police-cop, he is.'

'Do the cops run this place?'

'Oh, no. This is part-time work only. He says he is so very, very happy to meet you ...

'He says you are the first gora he ever met who can speak Marathi ...

'He says some foreigners speak Hindi, but nobody foreigner can speak Marathi ...

'He says Marathi is his language. His native place is Pune ...

'He says they speak it a very pure Marathi in Pune, and you must go there to hear it ...

'He says he is too happy! You are like a son to him ...

'He says you must come to his house, and eat foods and meet his family ...

'He says that will be one hundred rupees.'

'What was that?'

'Baksheesh, Lin. To go inside. One hundred rupees, it is. Pay him now.'

'Oh, sure.' I fumbled a few notes from my pocket, peeled off one hundred rupees, and handed it over. There's a special sleight of hand that's peculiar to policemen: the conjuring trick that palms and conceals banknotes with a skill that experienced shell-game swindlers envy. The big man collected the money with a two-handed handshake, smeared a palm across his chest as if brushing away crumbs after eating a sandwich, and then scratched at his nose with practised innocence. The money had vanished. He pointed along the narrow corridor. We were free to enter.

Two sharp turns and a dozen paces beyond the gate and its shaft of bright light, we came upon a kind of courtyard. Several men sat on rough wooden benches, or stood in talking groups of two or three. Some were Arabs, dressed in loose, cotton robes and kaffiyehs. An Indian boy moved among them, serving black tea in long glasses. Some of the men looked at Prabaker and me with frowning curiosity. When Prabaker smiled widely and waved a greeting they turned away, concentrating their attention once more on their conversation. Occasionally, one or another of them looked up to inspect a group of children who sat together on a long wooden bench beneath a ragged canvas awning.

It was darker there, after the bright light of the entrance chamber. A patchwork of canvas scraps provided an uneven cover that screened out most of the sky. Blank brown and magenta walls rose up all around us. The few windows I could see, through tears in the canvas coverings, were boarded over. Not a real courtyard, the roughly square space seemed unplanned, a kind of mistake, an almost forgotten architectural accident formed by building and rebuilding on the ruins of other structures within the congested block. The ground was paved with haphazard collections of tiles that had once been the floors of kitchens and bathrooms. Two naked bulbs, strange fruit on the withered vines of bare wires, provided the poor light.

We moved to a quiet corner, accepted tea when it was offered, and sipped it in silence for a while. Then, speaking quietly and slowly, Prabaker told me about the place he called the people-market. The children sitting beneath the tattered canopy were slaves. They'd come from the cyclone in West Bengal, the drought in Orissa, the cholera epidemic in Haryana, the secessionist fighting in Punjab. Sourced in calamity, recruited and purchased by scouts, the children had journeyed to Bombay by train, often alone, through all the many hundreds of kilometres.

The men gathered in the courtyard were purchasers or agents. Although they seemed to express no great interest, talking amongst themselves and for the most part ignoring the children on the wooden bench, Prabaker assured me that a restrained haggling was taking place, and that bargains were being struck, even as we watched.

The children were thin, vulnerable, and small. Two of them sat with their four hands bunched together in a beehive-ball. One child embraced another within the huddle of a protective arm. All of them stared out at the well-fed, well-clothed purchasers and agents, following every change of expression or emphatic gesture of their bejewelled hands. And the eyes of those children were like the black gleam at the bottom of a sweetwater well.

What does it take to harden a man's heart? How could I see that place, look at those children, and not put a stop to it? Why didn't I contact the authorities? Why didn't I get a gun, and put a stop to it myself? The answer to that, like the answers to all the big questions, came in many parts. I was a wanted man, a hunted criminal, living on the run. Contacting police or government authorities wasn't an option for me. I was a stranger in that strange land: it wasn't my country, and it wasn't my culture. I had to know more. I had to know the language that was spoken, at the very least, before I could presume to interfere. And I'd learned, the hard way, that sometimes, even with the purest intentions, we make things worse when we do our best to make things better. If I came back with a gun and stopped the slave market there, in that crooked concrete maze, it would start up again somewhere else. Stranger that I was, I knew that much. And maybe the new slave market, in a different place, would be worse. I was helpless to stop it, and I knew it.

What I didn't know then, and what troubled me for a long time after that Day of the Slaves, was how I could be there, and look at the children, and not be crushed by it. I realised, much later, that a part of the answer lay in the Australian prison, and the men I'd met there. Some of those men, too many of them, were serving their fourth or fifth prison sentences. Many of them had begun their imprisonment in reform schools —Boys' Homes, they were called, and Youth Training Centres—when they were no older than those Indian slave children. Some of them had been beaten, starved, and locked in solitary confinement. Some of them, too many of them, had been sexually abused. Ask any man with a long-enough experience of prisons, and he'll tell you that all it takes to harden a man's heart is a system of justice.

And strange and shameful as it is to admit it, I was glad that something, someone, some experience had flinted my heart. That hard stone within my chest was all that protected me from those first sounds and images of Prabaker's dark tour of the city.

Hands clapped in brittle echoes, and a little girl stood up from the bench to sing and dance. It was a love song from a popular Hindi movie. I heard it many times, hundreds of times, during the following years, and it always reminded me of that child, ten years old, and her surprisingly strong, high, thin voice. She swayed her hips, pushing up her non-existent breasts in a child's imitation of a temptress burlesque, and new interest quirked the heads of the purchasers and agents.

Prabaker played the Virgil. His soft voice was ceaseless, explaining all that we saw, and all that he knew. He told me that the children would've died, if they hadn't found their way to the people-market. Professional recruiters, known as talent scouts, roamed from one catastrophe to another, from drought to earthquake to flood. Starving parents, who'd already watched one or more of their children sicken, and die, blessed the scouts, kneeling to touch their feet. They begged them to buy a son or a daughter, so that at least that one child would live.

The boys on sale there were destined to work as camel jockeys in Saudi Arabia, Kuwait, and other Gulf States. Some would be maimed in the camel races that provided afternoon entertainment for the rich sheiks, Prabaker said. Some would die. The survivors, grown too tall to ride in the races, were often abandoned to fend for themselves. The girls would work in households throughout the Middle East. Some of them would be used for sex.

But they were alive, Prabaker said, those boys and girls. They were the lucky ones. For every child who passed through the people-market there were a hundred others, or more, who'd starved in unutterable agonies, and were dead.

The starving, the dead, the slaves. And through it all, the purr and rustle of Prabaker's voice. There's a truth that's deeper than experience. It's beyond what we see, or even what we feel. It's an order of truth that separates the profound from the merely clever, and the reality from the perception. We're helpless, usually, in the face of it; and the cost of knowing it, like the cost of knowing love, is sometimes greater than any heart would willingly pay. It doesn't always help us to love the world, but it does prevent us from hating the world. And the only way to know that truth is to share it, from heart to heart, just as Prabaker told it to me, just as I'm telling it to you now.

CHAPTER FOUR

'Do you know the Borsalino hat test?'

'The what?'

'The Borsalino hat test. It is the test that reveals whether a hat is a genuine Borsalino, or an inferior imitator. You know about the Borsalino, *non*?'

'No, I can't say I do.'

'Aaaaah,' Didier smiled. The smile was composed of one part surprise, one part mischief, and one part contempt. Somehow, those elements combined in an effect that was disarmingly charming. He leaned slightly forward and inclined his head to one side, his black curly hair shaking as if to emphasise the points in his explanation. 'The Borsalino is a garment of the first and finest quality. It is believed by many, and myself included, to be the most outstanding gentleman's head covering ever made.'

His hands shaped an imaginary hat on his head.

'It is wide-brimmed, in black or white, and made from the furs of the *lapin*.'

'So, it's just a hat,' I added, in what I thought to be an agreeable tone. 'We're talking about a rabbit-fur hat.'

Didier was outraged.

'Just a hat? Oh, no, my friend! The Borsalino is more than just a hat. The Borsalino is a work of art! It is brushed ten thousand times, by hand, before it is sold. It was the style expression of first choice by discerning French and Italian gangsters in Milan and Marseilles for many decades. The very name of Borsalino became a *synonyme* for gangsters. The wild young men of the underworld of Milano and Marseilles were called *Borsalinos*. Those were the days when gangsters had some style. They understood that if you were to live as an outlaw and steal and shoot people for a living, you had a responsibility to dress with some elegance. Isn't it so?'

'It's the least they could do,' I agreed, smiling.

'But of course! Now, sadly, there is all attitude and no style. It is the mark of the age in which we live that the style becomes the attitude, instead of the attitude becoming the style.'

He paused, permitting me a moment to acknowledge the turn of phrase.

'And so,' he continued, 'the test of a real Borsalino hat is to roll it into a cylinder, roll it up into a very tight tube, and pass it through a wedding ring. If it emerges from this test without permanent creases, and if it springs back to its original shape, and if it is not damaged in the experience, it is a genuine Borsalino.'

'And you're saying ...'

'Just so!' Didier shouted, slamming a fist down on the table.

We were sitting in Leopold's, near the square arch of the Causeway doors, at eight o'clock. Some foreigners at the next table turned their heads at the noisy outburst, but the staff and the regulars ignored the Frenchman. Didier had been eating and drinking and expostulating at Leopold's for nine years. They all knew there was a line you could cross with him, a limit to his tolerance, and he was a dangerous man if you crossed it. They also knew that the line wasn't drawn in the soft sand of his own life or beliefs or feelings. Didier's line was drawn through the hearts of the people he loved. If you hurt them, in any way, you roused him to a cold and deadly rage. But nothing anyone said or did to him, short of actual bodily harm, ever really offended or angered him.

'*Comme ça*! That is my point! Your little friend, Prabaker, has put you through the hat test. He rolled you into a tube, and dragged you through the wedding ring, to see if you are a real Borsalino or not. That was his purpose in taking you on the tour of the bad sights and sounds of the city. It was a Borsalino test.'

I sipped my coffee in silence, knowing that he was right—Prabaker's dark tour *had* been a kind of test—but not willing to give Didier the trophy of conceding the point.

The evening crowd of tourists from Germany, Switzerland, France, England, Norway, America, Japan, and a dozen other countries thinned out, giving way to the night crowd of Indians and expatriates who called Bombay home. The locals reclaimed places like Leopold's, the Mocambo, Café Mondegar, and the Light of Asia every night, when the tourists sought the safety of their hotels.

'If it was a test,' I did at last concede, 'he must've given me a pass. He invited me to go with him to visit his family, in his village in the north of the state.'

Didier raised his eyebrows in theatrical surprise.

'For how long?'

'I don't know. A couple of months, I think. Maybe more.'

'Ah, then it is so,' he concluded. 'Your little friend is beginning to love you.'

'I think that's putting it a bit strong,' I objected, frowning.

'No, no, you do not understand. You must be careful, here, with the real affection of those you meet. This is not like any other place. This is India. Everyone who comes here falls in love—most of us fall in love many times over. And the Indians, they love most of all. Your little friend may be beginning to love you. There is nothing strange in this. I say it from a long experience of this country, and especially of this city. It happens often, and easily, for the Indians. That is how they manage to live together, a billion of them, in reasonable peace. They are not perfect, of course. They know how to fight and lie and cheat each other, and all the things that all of us do. But more than any other people in the world, the Indians know how to love one another.'

He paused to light a cigarette, and then waved it like a little flagpole until the waiter noticed him and nodded to his request for another glass of vodka.

'India is about six times the size of France,' he went on, as the glass of alcohol and a bowl of curried snacks arrived at our table. 'But it has almost twenty times the population. Twenty times! Believe me, if there were a billion Frenchmen living in such a crowded space, there would be rivers of blood. Rivers of blood! And, as everyone knows, we French are the most civilised people in Europe. Indeed, in the whole *world*. No, no, without love, India would be impossible.'

Letitia joined us at our table, sitting to my left.

'What are you on about now, Didier, you bastard?' she asked companionably, her South London accent giving the first syllable of the last word an explosive ring.

'He was just telling me that the French are the most civilised people in the world.'

'As all the world knows,' he added.

'When you produce a Shakespeare, out of your *villes* and vineyards, mate, I might just agree with you,' Lettie murmured through a smile that seemed to be warm and condescending in equal parts.

'My dear, please do not think that I disrespect your Shakespeare,' Didier countered, laughing happily. 'I *love* the English language, because so *much* of it is French.'

'*Touché*,' I grinned, 'as we say in English.'

Ulla and Modena arrived at that moment, and sat down. Ulla was dressed for work in a small, tight, black, halter-neck dress, fishnet stockings, and stiletto-heel shoes. She wore eye-dazzling fake diamonds at her throat and ears. The contrast between her clothing and Lettie's was stark. Lettie wore a fine, bone-coloured brocade jacket over loose, dark-brown satin culottes, and boots. Yet the faces of the two women produced the strongest and most unexpected contrast. Lettie's gaze was seductive, direct, self-assured, and sparkling with ironies and secrets, while Ulla's wide blue eyes, for all the make-up and clothing of her professional sexuality, showed nothing but innocence—honest, vacuous innocence.

'You are forbidden to speak to me, Didier,' Ulla said at once, pouting inconsolably. 'I have had a very disagreeable time with Federico—three hours—and it is all your fault.'

'*Bah!*' Didier spat out. 'Federico!'

'Oh,' Lettie joined in, making three long sounds out of one. 'Something's happened to the beautiful young Federico, has it? Come on, Ulla me darlin', let's have all the gossip.'

'*Na ja*, Federico has got a religion, and he is driving me crazy about it, and it is all Didier's fault.'

'Yes!' Didier added, clearly disgusted. 'Federico has found religion. It is a tragedy. He no longer drinks or smokes or takes drugs. And of *course* he will not have sex with anyone—not even with himself! It is an appalling waste of talent. The man was a genius of the corruptions, my finest student, my *masterwork*. It is maddening. He is now a *good* man, in the very *worst* sense of the word.'

'Well, you win a few, you lose a few,' Lettie sighed with mock sympathy. 'You mustn't let it get you down, Didier. There'll be other fish for you to fry and gobble up.'

'Your sympathy should be for *me*,' Ulla chided. 'Federico came from

Didier in such a bad mood yesterday, he was at my door today in tears. *Scheisse! Wirklich!* For three hours he cried and he raved at me about being born again. In the end I felt so sorry for him. It was only with a great suffering that I let Modena throw him and his bible books onto the street. It's all your fault, Didier, and I will take the longest time to forgive you for it.'

'Fanatics,' Didier mused, ignoring the rebuke, 'always seem to have the same scrubbed and staring look about them. They have the look of people who do not masturbate, but who think about it almost all the time.'

'I really do love you, you know, Didier,' Lettie stuttered, through her bubbling laughter. 'Even if you are a despicable toad of a man.'

'No, you love him *because* he is a despicable toe of a man,' Ulla declared.

'That's *toad*, love, not *toe*,' Lettie corrected patiently, still laughing. 'He's a toad of a man, not a toe of a man. A despicable toe wouldn't make any sense at all, now would it? We wouldn't love him or hate him just for being a *toe* of a man, would we, darlin'—even if we knew what it meant?'

'I'm not so good with the English jokes, you know that, Lettie,' Ulla persisted. 'But I think he *is* a big, ugly, hairy toe of a man.'

'I assure you,' Didier protested, 'that my toes—and my feet, for that matter—are exceptionally beautiful.'

Karla, Maurizio, and an Indian man in his early thirties walked in from the busy night street. Maurizio and Modena joined a second table to ours, and then the eight of us ordered drinks and food.

'Lin, Lettie, this is my friend, Vikram Patel,' Karla announced, when there was a moment of relative quiet. 'He came back a couple of weeks ago, after a long holiday in Denmark, and I think you're the only two who haven't met him.'

Lettie and I introduced ourselves to the newcomer, but my real attention was on Maurizio and Karla. He sat beside her, opposite me, and rested his hand on the back of her chair. He leaned in close to her, and their heads almost touched when they spoke.

There's a dark feeling—less than hatred, but more than loathing—that ugly men feel for handsome men. It's unreasonable and unjustified, of course, but it's always there, hiding in the long shadow thrown by envy. It creeps out, into the light of your eyes, when you're falling in love with a beautiful woman. I looked at Maurizio, and a little of that dark feeling began in my heart. His straight, white teeth, smooth complexion, and thick, dark hair turned me against him more swiftly and surely than flaws in his character might've done.

And Karla *was* beautiful: her hair, in a French roll, was shining like water running over black river stones, and her green eyes were radiant with purpose and pleasure. She wore a long-sleeved Indian salwar top that reached to below her knees, where it met loose trousers in the same olive silk fabric.

'I had a great time, *yaar*,' the newcomer, Vikram, was saying when my thoughts returned to the moment. 'Denmark is very hip, very cool. The people are very sophisticated. They're so fucking controlled, I couldn't believe it. I went to a sauna, in Copenhagen. It was a fucking huge place, *yaar*, with a mixed set-up—with men and women, together, walking around stark naked. Absolutely, totally naked. And nobody reacted at all. Not even a flickering eye, *yaar*. Indian guys couldn't handle that. They'd be *boiling*, I tell you.'

'Were *you* boiling, Vikram dear?' Lettie asked, sweetly.

'Are you fucking kidding? I was the only guy in the place wearing a towel, and the only guy with a hard-on.'

'I don't understand,' Ulla said, when we stopped laughing. It was a flat statement—neither a complaint, nor a plea for further explanation.

'Hey, I went there every day for three weeks, *yaar*,' Vikram continued. 'I thought that if I just spent enough time there, I'd get used to it, like all the super-cool Danes.'

'Get used to what?' Ulla asked.

Vikram frowned at her, bewildered, and then turned to Lettie.

'It was no good. It was useless. After three weeks, I still had to wear the towel. No matter how often I went there, when I saw those bouncy bits going up and down, and side-to-side, I stiffened up. What can I say? I'm too Indian for a place like that.'

'It is the same for Indian women,' Maurizio observed. 'Even when they are making love, it is not possible to be naked.'

'Well, that's not always true,' Vikram went on, 'And anyway, it's the guys who are the problem here. Indian women are ready to change. Young Indian chicks from middle-class families are wild about change, *yaar*. They're educated, and they're ready for short hair, short dresses, and short love affairs. They're ready for it, but the guys are holding them back. The average Indian guy has a sexual maturity of about fourteen.'

'Tell me about it,' Lettie muttered.

Kavita Singh had approached our table moments before, and stood behind Vikram while he made his observations about Indian women. With short, styled hair, and wearing jeans and a white sweatshirt bearing the emblem of New York University, she was the living woman, the physical representation of what Vikram had been saying. She was the real thing.

'You're such a *chudd*, Vikkie,' she said, taking a place opposite him and on my right side. 'You say all this, but you're just as bad as all the rest. Look at how you treat your own sister, *yaar*, if she dares to wear jeans and a tight sweater.'

'Hey, I *bought* her that tight sweater, in London, last year!' Vikram protested.

'But you still gave her buckets of grief when she wore it to the jazz *yatra*, na?'

'Well, how was I to know that she would want to wear it *outside* the apartment?' he countered lamely, provoking laughter and derision from the whole group. None laughed harder than Vikram himself.

Vikram Patel was of average height and build, but average stopped just there, with those characteristics. His thick, curly, black hair framed a handsome, intelligent face. The bright and animated light brown eyes stared out confidently above a long, hawk-like nose and a sharp, immaculately trimmed Zapata moustache. His clothes were black—cowboy boots, jeans, shirt, and leather vest—and he wore a flat, black Spanish flamenco hat on his back, hanging from a leather thong at his throat. His bolo tie, dollar-coin belt, and hatband were all in silver. He looked like a hero in a spaghetti western movie, and that was, in fact, the inspiration for his style. Vikram had an obsession with Sergio Leone's films, *Once Upon A Time In The West*, and *The Good, The Bad and The Ugly*. Later, when I knew him better, when I watched him win the heart of the woman he loved, and when we stood together to face and fight enemies who wanted to kill me, I learned that he *was* a hero, and that he would've held his own with any of the gunslingers he adored.

Sitting opposite him on that first meeting, I was struck by the ease with which he assumed his black cowboy dream, and the stylish assurance that carried it off. *Vikram is the kind of man who wears his sleeve on his heart*, Karla once said. It was an affectionate joke, and one that we all understood, but there was a brittle filament of scorn in it, as well. I didn't laugh with the others when she said it. People like Vikram, people who can wear an obsession with panache, always win me over because their honesty speaks directly to my heart.

'No, it's true!' he persisted. 'In Copenhagen there was this club. It's what they call a telephone club. There's all these tables, *yaar*, and every table has a number that's lit up in red lights. If you see someone interesting, someone really hot, sitting at table twelve, you just dial up number twelve, and speak to them. Fucking *deadly* system, man. Half the time you don't know who's calling you, or they don't know who you are. Sometimes you talk for an hour, trying to guess who's talking to you, because everybody is talking at the same time. And then you tell each other what table you're at. I had a real nice party there, I can tell you. But if they tried to do it here, it wouldn't last five minutes, because the guys couldn't handle it. So many Indian guys are *chutias*, *yaar*. They'd be swearing, and saying all sorts of indecent shit, the childish motherfuckers. That's all I'm saying. In Copenhagen, the people were a lot cooler, and we've still got a damn long way to go, here, before India catches up to them on the cool scale.'

'I think that things are getting better,' Ulla volunteered. 'I get the feeling the future of India is a good future. I am sure things will be good, you know, like better than now, and there will be a lot of better living, for a lot of the people.'

We all turned to stare at her. The table was silent. We were stunned to hear such sentiments expressed by a young woman who made her living as the sexual plaything of those Indians who were rich enough to exploit her. She was used and abused, and I, for one, would've expected her to be more cynical. Optimism is the first cousin of love, and it's exactly like love in three ways: it's pushy, it has no real sense of humour, and it turns up where you least expect it.

'Really, my dear foolish Ulla, nothing changes at all,' Didier said, curling his lip in disgust. 'If you want to curdle the milk of your human kindness, or turn your compassion into contempt, get a job as a waitress or a cleaner. The two fastest ways to develop a healthy loathing for the human race and its destiny is to serve it food, or clean up after it, on the minimum wage. I have done both jobs, in those terrible days when I was forced to work for a living. It was horrible. I shudder now in thinking about it. That's where I learned that nothing ever really changes. And to speak the truth, I am glad of it. In a better world, or a worse one, I would make no money at all.'

'Bullshit,' Lettie declared. 'Things can get better, and things can get a lot worse. Ask the people in the slum. They're experts in how much worse things can get. Isn't that right, Karla?'

We all turned our attention to Karla. She toyed with her cup for an instant, turning it slowly in the saucer with her long index finger.

'I think that we all, each one of us, we all have to *earn* our future,' she said slowly. 'I think the future is like anything else that's important. It has to be earned. If we don't *earn* it, we don't have a future at all. And if we don't earn it, if we don't deserve it, we have to live in the present, more or less forever. Or worse, we have to live in the past. I think that's probably what love is—a way of earning the future.'

'Well, I agree with Didier,' Maurizio stated, finishing his meal with a glass of iced water. 'I like things just as they are, and I am content if they do not change.'

'How about you?' Karla asked, turning to face me.

'What about me?' I smiled.

'If you could be happy, really happy, for just a while, but you knew from the start that it would end in sadness, and bring pain afterwards, would you choose to have that happiness or would you avoid it?'

The attention and the question unsettled me, and I felt momentarily uncomfortable in the expectant silence that awaited my reply. I had the feeling that she'd asked the question before, and that it was a kind of test. Maybe she'd already asked the others at the table. Maybe they'd given their answers, and were waiting to hear mine. I wasn't sure what she wanted me to say, but the fact was that my life had already answered the question. I'd made my choice when I escaped from prison.

'I'd choose the happiness,' I replied, and was rewarded with a half-smile of recognition or amusement—perhaps it was both—from Karla.

'I wouldn't do it,' Ulla said, frowning. 'I hate sadness. I can't bear it. I would rather have nothing at all than even a little sadness. I think that's why I love to sleep so much, *na?* It's impossible to be really sad when you're asleep. You can be happy and afraid and angry in your dreams, but you have to be wide awake to be sad, don't you think?'

'I'm with you, Ulla,' Vikram agreed. 'There's too much fucking sadness in the world, *yaar*. That's why everybody is getting so stoned all the time. I know that's why *I'm* getting so stoned all the time.'

'Mmmmm—no, I agree with *you*, Lin,' Kavita put in, although I couldn't be sure how much was agreement with me, and how much merely the reflex of opposing Vikram. 'If you have a chance at real happiness, whatever the cost, you have to take it.'

Didier grew restless, irritated with the turn the conversation had taken. 'You are being much too serious, all of you.'

'*I'm* not!' Vikram objected, stung by the suggestion.

Didier fixed him with one raised eyebrow.

'I mean that you are making things to be more difficult than they are, or need to be. The facts of life are very simple. In the beginning we feared everything—animals, the weather, the trees, the night sky—everything except each other. Now we fear each other, and almost nothing else. No-one knows why anyone does anything. No-one tells the truth. No-one is happy. No-one is safe. In the face of all that is so wrong with the world, the very worst thing you can do is survive. And yet you *must* survive. It is this dilemma that makes us believe and cling to the lie that we have a soul, and that there is a God who cares about its fate. And now you have it.'

He sat back in his chair, and twirled the points of his D'Artagnan moustache with both hands.

'I'm not sure what he just said,' Vikram muttered, after a pause, 'but somehow I agree with him, and feel insulted, at the same time.'

Maurizio rose from his seat to leave. He placed a hand on Karla's shoulder, and turned to the rest of us with a brilliant smile of affability and charm. I had to admire that smile, even as I was working myself up to hate him for it.

'Don't be confused, Vikram,' he said pleasantly. 'Didier only has one subject—himself.'

'And his curse,' Karla added quickly, 'is that it is a fascinating subject.'

'*Merci*, Karla, darling,' Didier murmured, presenting her with a little bow.

'*Allora*, Modena, let's go. We may see you all later, at the President, *si*? *Ciao*.'

He kissed Karla on the cheek, put on his Ray-Ban sunglasses, and stalked out into the crowded night with Modena at his side. The Spaniard hadn't spoken once all evening, or even smiled. As their shapes were lost in the shifting, shuffling figures on the street, however, I saw that he spoke to Maurizio passionately, waving his clenched fist. I watched them until they were gone, and was startled and a little ashamed to hear Lettie speak aloud the smallest, meanest corner of my thoughts.

'He's not as cool as he looks,' she snarled.

'No man is as cool as he looks,' Karla said, smiling and reaching out to cover Lettie's hand with her own.

'You don't like Maurizio any more?' Ulla asked.

'I hate him. No, I don't hate him. But I despise him. It makes me sick to look at him.'

'My dear Letitia —' Didier began, but Karla cut him off.

'Not now, Didier. Give it a rest.'

'I don't know how I could've been so stupid,' Lettie growled, clenching her teeth.

'Na ja ...' Ulla said slowly. 'I don't want to say I told you so, but ...'

'Oh, why not?' Kavita asked. 'I love to say I told you so. I tell Vikram I told you so at least once a week. I'd rather say I told you so than eat chocolate.'

'I like the guy,' Vikram put in. 'Did you all know he's a fantastic horseman? He can ride like Clint Eastwood, yaar. I saw him at Chowpatty last week, riding on the beach with this gorgeous, blonde, Swedish chick. He rode just like Clint, in High Plains Drifter, I'm telling you. Fucking deadly.'

'Oh, well, he rides a horse,' Lettie said. 'How could I have been so wrong about him? I take it all back then.'

'He's got a cool hi-fi in his apartment, too,' Vikram added, apparently oblivious to Lettie's mood. 'And some damn fine original Italian movie scores.'

'That's it! I'm off!' Lettie declared, standing and grabbing her handbag and the book she'd brought with her. Her red hair, falling in gentle curls that framed her face, trembled with her irritation. Her pale skin stretched so flawlessly over the soft curves of her heart-shaped face that for a moment, in the bright white light, she was a furious, marble Madonna, and I recalled what Karla had said of her: I think Lettie's the most spiritual of all of us ...

Vikram jumped to his feet with her.

'I'll walk you to your hotel. I'm going your way.'

'Is that right?' Lettie asked, rounding on him so swiftly that he flinched. 'Which way would that be then?'

'I ... I ... I'm going, kind of, everywhere, *yaar*. I'm taking a very long walk, like. So ... so ... wherever you're going, I'll be going *your* way.'

'Oh, all right, if you must,' she murmured, her teeth clenched and her eyes flashing blue sparks. 'Karla me love, see you at the Taj, tomorrow, for coffee. I promise not to be late this time.'

'I'll be there,' Karla agreed.

'Well, bye all!' Lettie said, waving.

'Yeah, me too!' Vikram added, rushing after her.

'You know, the thing I like most about Letitia,' Didier mused, 'is that no little bit of her is French. Our culture, the French culture, is so pervasive and influential that almost everyone, in the whole world, is at least a little bit French. This is especially so for women. Almost every woman in the world is French, in some way. But Letitia, she is the most un-French woman I have ever known.'

'You're full of it, Didier,' Kavita remarked. 'Tonight more than most nights. What is it — did you fall in love, or out of love?'

He sighed, and stared at his hands, folded one on top the other.

'A little of both, I think. I am feeling very blue. Federico — you know him — has found religion. It is a terrible business, and it has wounded me, I confess. In truth, his saintliness has broken my heart. But enough of that. Imtiaz Dharker has a new exhibition at the Jehangir. Her work is always sensuous, and a little bit wild, and it brings me to myself again. Kavita, would you like to see it with me?'

'Sure,' Kavita smiled. 'I'd be happy to.'

'I'll walk to the Regal Junction with you,' Ulla sighed. 'I have to meet Modena.'

They rose and said goodbye, and walked through the Causeway arch, but then Didier returned and stood beside me at the table. Resting a hand on my shoulder as if to steady himself, he smiled down at me with an expression of surprisingly tender affection.

'*Go* with him, Lin,' he said. 'Go with Prabaker, to the village. Every city in the world has a village in its heart. You will never understand the city, unless you first understand the village. Go there. When you return, I will see what India has made of you. *Bonne chance!*'

He hurried off, leaving me alone with Karla. When Didier and the others were at the table, the restaurant had been noisy. Suddenly, all was quiet, or it seemed to be, and I had the impression that every word I spoke would be echoed, from table to table, in the large room.

'Are you leaving us?' Karla asked, mercifully speaking first.

'Well, Prabaker invited me to go with him on a trip to his parents' village. His *native place*, he calls it.'

'And you're going?'

'Yes, yes, I think I will. It's something of an honour to be asked, I take it. He told me he goes back to his village, to visit his parents, once every six months or so. He's done that for the last nine years, since he's been working the tourist beat in Bombay. But I'm the first foreigner he ever invited to go there with him.'

She winked at me, the start of a smile tugging at the corners of her mouth.

'You may not be the first one he asked. You may be the first one of his tourists crazy enough to actually say *yes*, but it amounts to the same thing.'

'Do you think I'm crazy to accept the invitation?'

'Not at all! Or at least, crazy in the right way, like the rest of us. Where is the village?'

'I don't know, exactly. It's in the north of the state. He told me it takes a train and two bus rides to get there.'

'Didier's right. You have to go. If you want to stay here, in Bombay, as you say, then you should spend some time in the village. The village is the key.'

A passing waiter took our last order, and moments later brought a banana lassi for Karla and a chai for me.

'How long did it take you to feel comfortable here, Karla? I mean, you always seem so relaxed and at home. It's like you've always been here.'

'Oh, I don't know. It's the right place for *me*, if you understand what I mean, and I knew that on the first day, in the first hour that I came here. So, in a sense, I was comfortable from the beginning.'

'It's funny you say that. I felt a bit like that myself. Within an hour of landing at the airport, I had this incredibly strong feeling that this was the right place for me.'

'And I suppose that the real breakthrough came with the language.

When I started to dream in Hindi, I knew that I was at home here. Everything has fallen into place since then.'

'Is that it now? Are you going to stay here forever?'

'There's no such thing as forever,' she answered in her slow, deliberate way. 'I don't know why we use the word.'

'You know what I mean.'

'Yeah. Yeah. Well, I'll stay until I get what I want. And then, maybe, I'll go somewhere else.'

'What do you want, Karla?'

She frowned in concentration, and shifted her gaze to stare directly into my eyes. It was an expression I came to know well, and it seemed to say, *If you have to ask the question, you have no right to the answer.*

'I want everything,' she replied with a faint, wry smile. 'You know, I said that once, to a friend of mine, and he told me that the real trick in life is to want nothing, and to succeed in getting it.'

Later, after we'd negotiated the crowds on the Causeway and the Strand, and walked the leafy arches of the empty streets behind the night-silent Colaba Market, we stopped at a bench beneath a towering elm near her apartment.

'It's really a paradigm shift,' I said, trying to explain a point I'd been making as we'd walked. 'A completely different way of looking at things, and thinking about things.'

'You're right. That's exactly what it is.'

'Prabaker took me to a kind of hospice, an old apartment building, near the St George Hospital. It was full of sick and dying people who'd been given a piece of floor-space to lie down and die on. And the owner of the place, who has this reputation as a kind of saint, was walking around, tagging the people, with signs that told how many useful organs they had. It was a huge organ-bank, full of living people who pay for the privilege of a quiet, clean place to die, off the street, by providing organs whenever this guy needs them. And the people were pathetically grateful to the guy for it. They revered him. They looked at him as if they loved him.'

'He put you through it in the last two weeks, your friend, Prabaker, didn't he?'

'Well, there was much worse than that. But the real problem is that you can't *do* anything. You see kids who ... well, they're in a lot of trouble, and you see people in the slums—he took me to the slum, where he lives, and the stink of the open latrine, and the hopeless mess of the place, and the people staring at you from the doorways of their hovels and ... and you can't change anything. You can't do anything about it. You have to accept that things could be worse, and they'll never be much better, and you're completely helpless in the face of it.'

'It's good to know what's wrong with the world,' Karla said, after a while. 'But it's just as important to know that sometimes, no matter how wrong it is, you can't change it. A lot of the bad stuff in the world wasn't really that bad until someone tried to change it.'

'I'm not sure I want to believe that. I know you're right. I know we make things worse, sometimes, the more we try to make them better. But I want to believe that if we do it right, everything and everyone can change for the better.'

'You know, I actually ran into Prabaker today. He told me to ask you about the water, whatever that means.'

'Oh, yeah,' I laughed. 'Just yesterday, I went down from my hotel to meet Prabaker on the street. But on the stairwell, there were these Indian guys, one after the other, carrying big pots of water on their heads, and climbing the stairs. I had to stand against the wall to let them pass. When I made it to the bottom, I saw this big wooden barrel with iron-rimmed wheels attached to it. It was a kind of water wagon. Another guy was using a bucket, and he was dipping it into the barrel and filling the big carry-pots with water.

'I watched this for ages, and the men made a lot of trips, up and down the stairs. When Prabaker came along, I asked him what they were doing. He told me that that was the water for my shower. That the shower came from a tank on the roof, and that these men filled the tank with their pots.'

'Of course.'

'Yeah, *you* know that, and I know that *now*, but yesterday was the first I heard of it. In this heat, I've been in the habit of taking three showers a day. I never realised that men had to climb six flights of stairs, to fill a damn tank, so that I could take those showers. I felt horrible about it, you know? I told Prabaker I'd never take another shower in that hotel again. Not ever.'

'What did he say?'

'He said, *No, no you don't understand.* He called it a *people-job*. It's only because of tourists like me, he explained, that those men have a job. And he told me that each man is supporting a family of his own from his wages. *You should have three showers, four showers, even five showers every day*, he told me.'

She nodded in agreement.

'Then he told me to watch the men while they got themselves ready to run through the city again, pushing their water wagon. And I think I knew what he meant, what he wanted me to see. They were strong, those guys. They were strong and proud and healthy. They weren't begging or stealing. They were working hard to earn their way, and they were proud of it. When they ran off into the traffic, with their strong muscles, and getting a few sly looks from some of the young Indian girls, I saw that their heads were up and their eyes straight ahead.'

'And you still take a shower in the hotel?'

'Three a day,' I laughed. 'Tell me, why was Lettie so upset with Maurizio?'

She looked at me, staring hard into my eyes for the second time that evening.

'Lettie has a pretty good contact at the Foreigner Registration Branch. He's a senior police official who has an obsession with sapphire gems, and Lettie supplies them to him at the wholesale rate, or a little below. Sometimes, in exchange for this ... favour ... she can arrange to have a visa renewed, almost indefinitely. Maurizio wanted to extend his visa for another year. He allowed Lettie to think he was in love with her—well, you can say he seduced her—and when he got what he wanted, he dumped her.'

'Lettie's your friend ...'

'I warned her. Maurizio is not a man to love. You can do everything else with him, but not love him. She didn't listen to me.'

'You still like Maurizio? Even after he did that to your friend?'

'Maurizio did exactly what I knew he would do. In his own mind, he made a trade of his affection for the visa, and it was a fair trade. He would never try anything like that with me.'

'Is he afraid of you?' I asked, smiling.

'Yes. I think he is, a little bit. That's one of the reasons I like him. I could never respect a man who didn't have the good sense to be at least a little bit afraid of me.'

She stood up, and I rose with her. Under the street lamp her green eyes were jewels of desire, wet with light. Her lips widened in a half-smile that was mine — a moment that was mine alone — and the beggar, my heart, began to hope and plead.

'Tomorrow,' she said, 'when you go to Prabaker's village, try to relax completely, and go with the experience. Just ... let yourself go. Sometimes, in India, you have to surrender before you win.'

'You've always got some wise advice, haven't you?' I said, laughing gently.

'That's not wise, Lin. I think wisdom is very over-rated. Wisdom is just cleverness, with all the guts kicked out of it. I'd rather be clever than wise, any day. Most of the wise people I know give me a headache, but I never met a clever man or woman I didn't like. If I *was* giving wise advice — which I'm not — I'd say don't get drunk, don't spend all your money, and don't fall in love with a pretty village girl. *That* would be wise. That's the difference between clever and wise. I prefer to be clever, and that's why I told you to surrender, when you get to the village, no matter what you find when you get there. Okay. I'm going. Come and see me when you get back. I look forward to it. I really do.'

She kissed my cheek, and turned away. I couldn't obey the impulse to hold her in my arms and kiss her lips. I watched her walk, her dark silhouette a part of the night itself. Then she moved into the warm, yellow light near the door of her apartment, and it was as if my watching eyes had made her shadow come to life, as if my heart alone had painted her from darkness with the light and colours of love. She turned once to see that I was watching her, before she softly closed and locked the door.

That last hour with her was a Borsalino test, I was sure, and all the walking way back to the hotel I asked myself if I'd passed it, or if I'd failed. I still think about it, all these years later. I still don't know.

CHAPTER FIVE

The long, flat interstate platforms at Victoria Terminus train station stretched out to vanishing points beneath a metal heaven of rolling vaulted ceilings. The cherubs of that architectural sky were pigeons, so far overhead in their flutter from roost to roost that they were only faintly discernible; distant, celestial beings of flight, and white light. The great station—those who used it every day knew it as V.T.—was justly famous for the splendour of its intricately detailed facades, towers, and exterior ornaments. But its most sublime beauty, it seemed to me, was found in its cathedral interiors. There, the limitations of function met the ambitions of art, as the timetable and the timeless commanded equal respect.

For a long hour I sat on and amid our pile of luggage at the street end of the northbound interstate platform. It was six o'clock in the evening, and the station was filled with people, luggage, bundles of goods, and an agricultural assortment of live and recently deceased animals.

Prabaker ran into the crowds milling between two stationary trains. It was the fifth time I'd watched him leave. And then, a few minutes later, for the fifth time, I watched him run back.

'For God's sake, sit down, Prabu.'

'Can't be sitting, Lin.'

'Well, let's get on the train, then.'

'Can't be getting on also, Lin. It is not now the time for the getting on the train.'

'So ... when *will* it be the time for the getting on the train?'

'I think ... a little bit almost quite very soon, and not long. Listen! Listen!'

There was an announcement. It might've been in English. It was the kind of sound an angry drunk makes, amplified through the unique distortions of many ancient, cone-shaped speakers. As he listened to it,

Prabaker's face moved from apprehension to anguish.

'Now! Now, Lin! Quickly! We must hurry! You must hurry!'

'Hang on, hang on. You've had me sitting here like a brass Buddha, for an hour. Now, all of a sudden, there's a big rush, and I have to hurry?'

'Yes, baba. No time for making Buddha — beg of pardons to the Holy One. You must make a big rush. He's coming! You must be ready. He's coming!'

'Who's coming?'

Prabaker turned to look along the platform. The announcement, whatever it was, had galvanised the crowds of people, and they rushed at two stationary trains, hurling themselves and their bundles into the doors and windows. From the broiling tangle of bodies, one man emerged and walked towards us. He was a huge man, one of the biggest men I'd ever seen. He was two metres tall, well muscled, and had a long, thick beard that settled on his burly chest. He wore the Bombay train porter's uniform of cap, shirt, and shorts, in rough red-and-khaki linen.

'Him!' Prabaker said, staring at the giant with admiration and dread. 'You go with this man now, Lin.'

Having long experience with foreigners, the porter took control of the situation. He reached out with both hands. I thought that he wanted to shake hands, so I extended my own in return. He brushed it aside with a look that left me in no doubt as to how repulsive he'd found the gesture. Then, putting his hands under my armpits, he lifted me up and dropped me out of the way to one side of the luggage.

It's a disconcerting, albeit exhilarating, experience, when you weigh 90 kilos yourself, to be lifted up so effortlessly by another man. I determined, there and then, to co-operate with the porter in so far as it was decently possible.

While the big man lifted my heavy back-pack onto his head and gathered up the rest of the bags, Prabaker put me at his back, and seized a handful of the man's red linen shirt.

'Here, Lin, take it a hold on this shirts,' he instructed me. 'Hold it, and never let it go, this shirts. Tell me your deep and special promise. You will never let it go this shirts.'

His expression was so unusually grave and earnest that I nodded in agreement, and took hold of the porter's shirt.

'No, say it also, Lin! Say the words — I will never let it go this shirts.

Quickly!'

'Oh, for God's sake. All right—*I will never let it go this shirts*. Are you satisfied?'

'Goodbye, Lin,' Prabaker shouted, running off into the mill and tumble of the crowd.

'What? *What*! Where are you going? Prabu! *Prabu*!'

'Okay! We go now!' the porter rumbled and roared in a voice that he'd found in a bear's cave, and cured in the barrel of a rusted cannon.

He walked off into the crowd, dragging me behind him and kicking outwards by raising his thick knees high with every step. Men scattered before him. When they didn't scatter, they were knocked aside.

Bellowing threats, insults, and curses, he thumped a path through the choking throng. Men fell and were pushed aside with every lift and thrust of his powerful legs. In the centre of the crowd, the din was so loud that I could feel it drumming on my skin. People shouted and screamed as if they were the victims of a terrible disaster. Garbled, indecipherable announcements blared from the loudspeakers over our heads. Sirens, bells, and whistles wailed constantly.

We reached a carriage that was, like all the others, filled to its capacity with a solid wall of bodies in the doorway. It was a seemingly impenetrable human barrier of legs and backs and heads. Astonished, and not a little ashamed, I clung to the porter as he hammered his way into the carriage with his indefatigable and irresistible knees.

His relentless forward progress stopped, at one point, in the centre of the carriage. I assumed that the density of the crowd had halted even that juggernaut of a man. I clung to the shirt, determined not to lose my grip on him when he started to move again. In all the furious noise of the cloying press of bodies, I became aware of one word, repeated in an insistent and tormented mantra: *Sarr ... Sarr ... Sarr ... Sarr ... Sarr ...*

I realised, at last, that the voice was my own porter's. The word he was repeating with such distress was unrecognisable to me because I wasn't used to being addressed by it: *Sir*.

'Sir! Sir! Sir! Sir!' he shouted.

I let go of his shirt and looked around to find Prabaker stretched to his full length along an entire bench seat. He'd fought his way ahead of us into the carriage to reserve a seat, and he was guarding it with his body. His feet were wrapped around the aisle armrest. His hands clasped the armrest at the window end. Half a dozen men had crammed themselves into that part of the carriage, and each tried with unstinting vigour and violence to remove him from the seat. They pulled his hair, punched his body, kicked him, and slapped at his face. He was helpless under the onslaught; but, when his eyes met mine, a triumphant smile shone through his grimaces of pain.

Incensed, I shoved the men out of the way, grabbing them by shirt collars, and hurling them aside with the strength that swarms into the arms of righteous anger. Prabaker swung his feet to the floor, and I sat down beside him. A brawl started at once for the remaining space on the seat. The porter dumped the luggage at our feet. His face and hair and shirt were wet with sweat. He gave Prabaker a nod, communicating his respect. It was fully equal, his glaring eyes left no doubt, to the derision he felt for me. Then he shoved his way through the crowd, roaring insults all the way to the door.

'How much did you pay that guy?'

'Forty rupees, Lin.'

Forty rupees. The man had battled his way into the carriage, with all of our luggage, for two American dollars.

'Forty rupees!'

'Yes, Lin,' Prabaker sighed. 'It is very expensive. But such good knees are very expensive. He has famous knees, that fellow. A lot of guides were making competition for his two knees. But I convinced him to help us, because I told him you were — I'm not sure how to say it in English — I told him you were not completely right on your head.'

'Mentally retarded. You told him I was mentally retarded?'

'No, no,' he frowned, considering the options. 'I think that *stupid* is more of the correctly word.'

'Let me get this straight — you told him I was stupid, and that's why he agreed to help us.'

'Yes,' he grinned. 'But not just a little of stupid. I told him you were very, very, very, very, very —'

'All right. I get it.'

'So the price was twenty rupees for each knees. And now we have it this good seat.'

'Are you all right?' I asked, angry that he'd allowed himself to be hurt for my sake.

'Yes, baba. A few bruises I will have on all my bodies, but nothing is broken.'

'Well, what the hell did you think you were doing? I gave you money for the tickets. We could've sat down in first or second class, like civilised people. What are we doing back here?'

He looked at me, reproach and disappointment brimming in his large, soft-brown eyes. He pulled a small bundle of notes from his pockets, and handed it to me.

'This is the change from the tickets money. Anybody can buy first-class tickets, Lin. If you want to buy tickets in first class, you can be doing that all on yourself only. You don't need it a Bombay guide, to buy tickets in comfortable, empty carriages. But you need a very excellent Bombay guide, like me, like Prabaker Kishan Kharre, to get into this carriage at V.T. Station, and get a good seats, isn't it? This is my job.'

'Of course it is,' I softened, still angry with him because I still felt guilty. 'But please, for the rest of this trip, don't get yourself beaten up, just so that I can have a goddamn seat, okay?'

He reflected for a moment with a frown of concentration, and then brightened again, his familiar smile refulgent in the dimly lit carriage.

'If it is absolutely *must* be a beating,' he said, firmly and amiably negotiating the terms of his employment, 'I will shout even more loudly, and you can rescue my bruises in the nicks of time. Are we a deal?'

'We are,' I sighed, and the train suddenly lurched forward and began to grind its way out of the terminus.

In the instant that the train started on its journey, the gouging, biting, and brawling ceased completely and were replaced by a studied and genteel courtesy that persisted throughout the entire journey.

A man opposite me shifted his feet, accidentally brushing his foot against mine. It was a gentle touch, barely noticeable, but the man immediately reached out to touch my knee and then his own chest with the fingertips of his right hand, in the Indian gesture of apology for an unintended offence. In the carriage and the corridor beyond, the other passengers were similarly respectful, sharing, and solicitous with one another.

At first, on that first journey out of the city into India, I found such sudden politeness infuriating after the violent scramble to board the train. It seemed hypocritical for them to show such deferential concern over a nudge with a foot when, minutes before, they'd all but pushed one another out of the windows.

Now, long years and many journeys after that first ride on a crowded rural train, I know that the scrambled fighting and courteous deference were both expressions of the one philosophy: the doctrine of necessity. The amount of force and violence necessary to board the train, for example, was no less and no more than the amount of politeness and consideration necessary to ensure that the cramped journey was as pleasant as possible afterwards. *What is necessary?* That was the unspoken but implied and unavoidable question everywhere in India. When I understood that, a great many of the characteristically perplexing aspects of public life became comprehensible: from the acceptance of sprawling slums by city authorities, to the freedom that cows had to roam at random in the midst of traffic; from the toleration of beggars on the streets, to the concatenate complexity of the bureaucracies; and from the gorgeous, unashamed escapism of Bollywood movies, to the accommodation of hundreds of thousands of refugees from Tibet, Iran, Afghanistan, Africa, and Bangladesh, in a country that was already too crowded with sorrows and needs of its own.

The real hypocrisy, I came to realise, was in the eyes and minds and criticisms of those who came from lands of plenty, where no-one had to fight for a seat on a train. Even on that first train ride, I knew in my heart that Didier had been right when he'd compared India and its billion souls to France. I had an intuition, echoing his thought, that if there were a billion Frenchmen or Australians or Americans living in such a small space, the fighting to board the train would be much more, and the courtesy afterwards much less.

And in truth, the politeness and consideration shown by the peasant farmers, travelling salesmen, itinerant workers, and returning sons and fathers and husbands did make for an agreeable journey, despite the cramped conditions and relentlessly increasing heat. Every available centimetre of seating space was occupied, even to the sturdy metal luggage racks over our heads. The men in the corridor took turns to sit or squat on a section of floor that had been set aside and cleaned for the purpose. Every man felt the press of at least two other bodies against his own. Yet there wasn't a single display of grouchiness or bad temper.

However, when I surrendered my seat, for four hours of the journey, to an elderly man with a shock of white hair and spectacles as thick as the lenses on an army scout's binoculars, Prabaker was provoked to an indignant exasperation.

'So hard I fought with nice peoples for your seat, Lin. Now you give it up, like a spit of paan juices, and stand up in the passage, and on your legs, also.'

'Come on, Prabu. He's an old guy. I can't let him stand while I sit.'

'That is easy—only you don't *look* at that old fellow, Lin. If he is standing, don't *look* at him standing. That is his business only, that standing, and nothing for your seat.'

'It's the way I am,' I insisted, laughing self-consciously in the conversation he was directing across the whole carriage of interested fellow passengers.

'Such scratches and bruises I have it on my bodies, Lin,' he whined, talking to me, but appealing to the curious gallery. He lifted his shirt and singlet to display what was indeed a rough scratch and gathering bruise. 'For this old fellow to put the left-side buttocks on the seat, I have these many scratches and bruises. For his right-side buttocks, I have more bruises, on my other side also. For him to put his two-sides buttocks on the seat, I am all bruising and scratching on my bodies. This is a very shame, Lin. That is all I'm telling you. It is a very shame.'

He'd drifted between English and Hindi until all of us knew the substance of his complaint. Every one of my fellow passengers looked at me with frowns or head-shakes of disapproval. The fiercest glance of reproof, of course, came from the elderly man for whom I'd surrendered my seat. He glared at me malevolently during the entire four hours. When at last he rose to leave, and I resumed my seat, he muttered such a vile curse that the other passengers sputtered into guffaws of laughter, and a couple of them commiserated with me by patting my shoulder and back.

Through the sleepy night, and into the rose-petal dawn, the train rattled on. I watched and listened, literally rubbing shoulders with the people of the interior towns and villages. And I learned more, during those fourteen constricted and largely silent hours in the crowded economy-class section, communicating without language, than I could've learned in a month of travelling first class.

No discovery pleased me more, on that first excursion from the city, than the full translation of the famous Indian head-wiggle. The weeks I'd spent in Bombay with Prabaker had taught me that the shaking or wiggling of the head from side to side—that most characteristic of Indian expressive gestures—was the equivalent of a forward nod of the head, meaning *Yes*. I'd also discerned the subtler senses of *I agree with you*, and *Yes, I would like that*. What I learned, on the train, was that a universal message attached to the gesture, when it was used as a greeting, which made it uniquely useful.

Most of those who entered the open carriage greeted the other seated or standing men with a little wiggle of the head. The gesture always drew a reciprocal wag of the head from at least one, and sometimes several of the passengers. I watched it happen at station after station, knowing that the newcomers couldn't be indicating *Yes*, or *I agree with you* with the head-wiggle because nothing had been said, and there was no exchange other than the gesture itself. Gradually, I realised that the wiggle of the head was a signal to others that carried an amiable and disarming message: *I'm a peaceful man. I don't mean any harm.*

Moved by admiration and no small envy for the marvellous gesture, I resolved to try it myself. The train stopped at a small rural station. A stranger joined our group in the carriage. When our eyes met for the first time, I gave the little wiggle of my head, and a smile. The result was astounding. The man beamed a smile at me so huge that it was half the brilliance of Prabaker's own, and set to such energetic head waggling in return that I was, at first, a little alarmed. By journey's end, however, I'd had enough practice to perform the movement as casually as others in the carriage did, and to convey the gentle message of the gesture. It was the first truly Indian expression my body learned, and it was the beginning of a transformation that has ruled my life, in all the long years since that journey of crowded hearts.

We left the railway at Jalgaon, a regional centre that boasted wide streets of commerce and bustle. It was nine o'clock, and the morning rush was in rumble, roll, rattle, and swing. Raw materials—iron, glass, wood, textiles, and plastic—were being unloaded from the train as we left the station. A range of products, from pottery to clothing to hand-woven tatami mats, was arriving at the station for dispatch to the cities.

The aroma of fresh, highly spiced food stirred my appetite, but Prabaker urged me on to the bus terminal. In fact, the terminal was simply a vast open patch of rough ground that served as a staging area for dozens of long-distance coaches. We drifted from bus to bus for half an hour, carrying our bulky luggage. I couldn't read the Hindi and Marathi texts on the front and side of each bus. Prabaker could read the signs, but still he felt it necessary to ask every driver about his destination.

'Doesn't it tell you where every bus is going, on the front of the bus?' I demanded, irritated by the delay.

'Yes, Lin. See, this one says Aurangabad, and that one says Ajanta, and that one says Chalisgao, and that one says —'

'Yeah, yeah. So ... why do we have to ask every driver where he's going?'

'Oh!' he exclaimed, genuinely surprised by the question. 'Because not every sign is a truly sign.'

'What do you mean, *not a truly sign?*'

He stopped, putting down his share of the luggage, and offered me a smile of indulgent patience.

'Well, Lin, you see, some of those driving fellows are going to places that is *nobody* wants to go to. Little places, they are, with a few people only. So, they put a sign for a more popular place.'

'You're telling me that they put a sign up saying they're going to a big town, where lots of people want to go, but they're really going somewhere else, where nobody wants to go?'

'That's right, Lin,' he beamed.

'Why?'

'You see, because those people who come to them, to go to the popular place, well, maybe the driver can convince them to go to the not-popular place. It's for business, Lin. It's a business thing.'

'That's crazy,' I said, exasperated.

'You must have it a bit of sympathies for these fellows, Lin. If they put the truly sign on their bus, no-one will talk to them, in the whole day, and they will be very lonely.'

'Oh, well, *now* I understand,' I muttered, sarcastically. 'We wouldn't want them to feel lonely.'

'I know, Lin,' Prabaker smiled. 'You have a very good hearts in your bodies.'

When at last we did board a bus, it seemed that ours was one of the popular destinations. The driver and his assistant interrogated the passengers, to determine precisely where each man or woman intended to set down, before allowing them to enter the bus. Those travelling the furthest were then directed to fill the rear seats. The rapidly accumulating piles of luggage, children, and livestock filled the aisle to shoulder height, and eventually three passengers crowded into every seat designed for two.

Because I had an aisle seat, I was required to take my turn at passing various items, from bundles to babies, backwards over the loaded aisle. The young farmer who passed the first item to me hesitated for a moment, staring into my grey eyes. When I wiggled my head from side to side, and smiled, he grinned in return and handed the bundle to me. By the time the bus rolled out of the busy terminal, I was accepting smiles and head-wiggles from every man in sight, and waggling and wiggling at them in return.

The sign behind the driver's head, in large red letters in Marathi and English, said that the bus was strictly licensed to seat forty-eight passengers. No-one seemed concerned that we were seventy passengers, and two or three tons of cargo. The old Bedford bus swayed on its exhausted springs like a tugboat in a storm tide. Creaks and groans and squeaks issued from the top, sides, and floor of the bus, and the brakes squealed alarmingly with every application. Nevertheless, when the bus left the city limits, the driver managed to crank it up to eighty or ninety kilometres per hour. Given the narrow road, the precipitous fall on the low side, the frequent columns of people and animals that lined the high side, the titanic mass of our swaying ark of a bus, and the vertiginous hostility with which the driver negotiated every curve, the speed was sufficient to relieve me of the need to sleep or relax on the ride.

During the following three hours of that perilous acceleration, we rose to the peak of a ridge of mountains marking the edge of a vast plateau, known as the Deccan, and descended once more to fertile plains within the rim of the plateau. With prayers of gratitude, and a new appreciation for the fragile gift of life, we left that first bus at a small, dusty, deserted stop that was marked only by a tattered flag flapping from the branch of a slender tree. Within an hour a second bus stopped.

'Gora kaun hain?' the driver asked, when we climbed aboard the step. *Who's the white guy?*

'Maza mitra ahey,' Prabaker answered with contrived nonchalance, trying in vain to disguise his pride. *He's my friend.*

The exchange was in Marathi, the language of Maharashtra State, which has Bombay as its capital. I didn't understand much of it then, but the same questions and answers were repeated so often during those village months that I learned most of the phrases, with some variations, by heart.

'What's he doing here?'

'He's visiting my family.'

'Where's he from?'

'New Zealand,' Prabaker replied.

'New Zealand?'

'Yes. New Zealand. In Europe.'

'Plenty of money in New Zealand?'

'Yes, yes. Plenty. They're all rich, white people there.'

'Does he speak Marathi?'

'No.'

'Hindi?'

'No. Only English.'

'Only English?'

'Yes.'

'Why?'

'They don't speak Hindi in his country.'

'They don't speak Hindi there?'

'No.'

'No Marathi? No Hindi?'

'No. Only English.'

'Holy Father! The poor fool.'

'Yes.'

'How old is he?'

'Thirty.'

'He looks older.'

'They all do. All the Europeans look older and angrier than they really are. It's a white thing.'

'Is he married?'

'No.'

'Not married? Thirty, and not married? What's wrong with him?'

'He's European. A lot of them get married only when they're old.'

'That's crazy.'

'Yes.'

'What job does he do?'

'He's a teacher.'

'A teacher is good.'

'Yes.'

'Does he have a mother and a father?'

'Yes.'

'Where are they?'

'In his native place. New Zealand.'

'Why isn't he with them?'

'He's travelling. He's looking at the whole world.'

'Why?'

'Europeans do that. They work for a while, and then they travel around, lonely, for a while, with no family, until they get old, and then they get married, and become very serious.'

'That's crazy.'

'Yes.'

'He must be lonely, without his mummy and his daddy, and with no wife and children.'

'Yes. But the Europeans don't mind. They get a lot of practice being lonely.'

'He has a big strong body.'

'Yes.'

'A very strong body.'

'Yes.'

'Make sure you feed him properly, and give him plenty of milk.'

'Yes.'

'Buffalo milk.'

'Yes, yes.'

'And make sure he doesn't learn any bad words. Don't teach him any swearing. There are plenty of arseholes and bastards around who will teach him the wrong sisterfucking words. Keep him away from mother-fuckers like that.'

'I will.'

'And don't let anyone take advantage of him. He doesn't look too bright. Keep an eye on him.'

'He's brighter than he looks, but yes, I will look after him.'

It troubled none of the other passengers on the bus that the conversation of several minutes had taken place before we could board the bus and move off. The driver and Prabaker had made sure to speak at a volume adequate to the task of including everyone in the bus. Indeed, once we were under way, the driver sought to include even those *outside* the bus in the novelty of the experience. Whenever he spied men and women strolling on the road, he sounded the horn to draw their attention, gesticulated with his thumb to indicate the foreigner in the rear of the bus, and slowed to a crawl, so that each pedestrian could examine me with satisfactory thoroughness.

With such democratic rationing of the astounding new attraction, the journey of one hour took closer to two, and we arrived at the dusty road to Sunder village in the late afternoon. The bus groaned and heaved away, leaving us in a silence so profound that the breeze against my ears was like a child's sleepy whisper. We'd passed countless fields of maize and banana groves in the last hour of the bus ride, and then on foot we trudged along the dirt road between endless rows of millet plants. Almost fully grown, the plants were well over head-height, and in a few minutes of the walk we were deep within a thick-walled labyrinth. The wide sky shrank to a small arc of blue, and the way ahead or behind us dissolved into curves of green and gold, like curtains drawn across the living stage of the world.

I'd been preoccupied for some time, nagged by something that it seemed I should've known or realised. The thought, half submerged, troubled me for the best part of an hour before it swam into the field of vision of my mind's eye. No telegraph poles. No power poles. For most of that hour I'd seen no sign of electric power—not even distant power lines.

'Is there electricity in your village?'

'Oh, no,' Prabaker grinned.

'No electricity?'

'No. None.'

There was silence, for a time, as I slowly turned off all the appliances I'd come to regard as essential. No electric light. No electric kettle. No television. No hi-fi. No radio. No music. I didn't even have a Walkman with me. How would I live without music?

'What am I going to do without music?' I asked, aware of how pathetic I sounded, but unable to suppress the whine of disappointment in my voice.

'There will be music full, baba,' he answered cheerfully. 'I will sing. Everybody will sing. We will sing and sing and sing.'

'Oh. Well. *Now* I feel all right.'

'And you will sing, too, Lin.'

'Don't count on it, Prabu.'

'In the village, everybody sings,' he said with sudden seriousness.

'U-huh.'

'Yes. Everybody.'

'Let's cross that bridge and chorus when we come to it. How much further is it to the village?'

'Oh, just a little bit almost not too very far. And you know, now we have water in our village also.'

'What do you mean, *now* you have water?'

'What I mean is, there is one tap in the village now.'

'One tap. For the whole village.'

'Yes. And the water is coming out of it for one whole hour, at two o'clock in every afternoon.'

'One whole hour per day …'

'Oh, yes. Well, on most days. Some days it is only coming for half an hour. Some days it is not coming out at all. Then we go back and scrape the green stuff off the top of the water in the well, and we are no problem for water. Ah! Look! Here is my father!'

Ahead of us, on the rambling and weedy path, was an ox-cart. The ox, a huge curve-horned beast, the colour of café latte, was shackled to a tall, basket-shaped cart mounted on two wooden, steel-rimmed wheels. The wheels were narrow but high, reaching to my shoulder. Smoking a beedie cigarette and sitting on the ox-bow yoke, his legs dangling free, was Prabaker's father.

Kishan Mango Kharre was a tiny man, shorter even than Prabaker, with very close-cropped grey hair, a short, grey moustache, and a prominent paunch on his otherwise slender frame. He wore the white cap, cotton kurtah shirt, and dhoti of the farmer caste. The dhoti is technically described as a loincloth, but the term robs the garment of its serene and graceful elegance. It can be gathered up to become work shorts for labour in the fields, or loosened to become pantaloon-style trousers with the ankles free. The dhoti itself is always moving, and it follows the human contour in every act from running to sitting still. It captures every breeze at noon, and keeps out the dawn chill. It's modest and practical, yet flattering and attractive at the same time. Gandhi gave the dhoti prominence on his trips to Europe, in the struggle for Indian independence from England. With all due respect to the Mahatma, however, it's not until you live and work with India's farmers that you fully appreciate the gentle and ennobling beauty of that simple wrap of fabric.

Prabaker dropped his bags and ran forward. His father sprang from his seat on the yoke, and they embraced shyly. The older man's smile was the only smile I've ever seen that rivalled Prabaker's own. It was a vast smile, using the whole of the face, as if he'd been frozen in the middle of a belly laugh. When Prabaker turned to face me, beside his father, subjecting me to a double dose of the gigantic smile—the original, and its slightly grander genetic copy—the effect was so overwhelming that I found myself grinning helplessly in return.

'Lin, this is my father, Kishan Mango Kharre. And father, this is Mr. Lin. I am happy, too much happy, that you are meeting each other's good selves.'

We shook hands, and stared into one another's eyes. Prabaker and his father had the same almost perfectly round face and the same upturned, button nose. However, where Prabaker's face was completely open, guileless, and unlined, his father's face was deeply wrinkled; and when he wasn't smiling, there was a weary shadow that closed over his eyes. It was as if he'd sealed shut some doors in himself, and stood guard over them, with his eyes alone. There was pride in his face, but he was sad, and tired, and worried. It took me a long time to realise that all farmers, everywhere, are just as tired, worried, proud, and sad: that the soil you turn and the seed you sow are all you really have, when you live and work the Earth. And sometimes, much too often, there's nothing more than that— the silent, secret, heartbreaking joy God puts into things that bloom and grow—to help you face the fear of hunger and the dread of evil.

'My father is a very success man,' Prabaker beamed, proudly, his arm around the older man's shoulders. I spoke very little Marathi, and Kishan spoke no English, so Prabaker repeated everything in both languages. Hearing the phrase in his own language, Kishan lifted his shirt with a graceful, artless flourish, and patted at his hairy pot-belly. His eyes glittered as he spoke to me, waggling his head all the while in what seemed to be an unnervingly seductive leer.

'What did he say?'

'He wants you to pat his tummies,' Prabaker explained, grinning.

Kishan grinned as widely.

'I don't think so.'

'Oh, yes, Lin. He wants you to pat his tummies.'

'No.'

'He *really* wants you to give it a pat,' he persisted.

'Tell him I'm flattered, and I think it's a fine tummies. But tell him I think I'll pass, Prabu.'

'Just give it a little pat, Lin.'

'No,' I said, more firmly.

Kishan's grin widened, and he raised his eyebrows several times, in encouragement. He still held the shirt up to his chest, exposing the round, hairy paunch.

'Go on, Lin. A few pats only. It won't bite you, my father's tummies.'

Sometimes you have to surrender, Karla said, *before you win*. And she was right. Surrender is at the heart of the Indian experience. I gave in. Glancing around me, on the deserted track, I reached out and patted the warm and fuzzy belly.

Just then, of course, the tall green stalks of millet beside us on the path separated to reveal four dark brown faces. They were young men. They stared at us, their eyes wide with the kind of amazement that's afraid, appalled, and delighted at the same time.

Slowly, and with as much dignity as I could muster, I withdrew my hand from Kishan's stomach. He looked at me, and then at the others, with one eyebrow raised and the corners of his mouth drawn down into the smug smile of a police prosecutor, resting his case.

'I don't want to intrude on your dad's moment here, Prabu, but don't you think we should be getting along?'

'*Challo!*' Kishan announced, making a guess at the meaning of my words. *Let's go!*

As we loaded our gear and climbed into the back of the cart, Kishan took his seat on the yoke attached to the ox-bow, raised a long bamboo stick that had a nail driven into the end of it, and moved us off with a tremendous blow to the animal's haunches.

Responding to the violent blow, the ox gave a lurch forward, and then set off with ponderous, thudding slowness. Our steady but very sluggish progress caused me to wonder at the choice of that beast, above others, to perform the task. It seemed to me that the Indian ox, known as the *baille*, was surely the slowest harness animal in the world. If I'd climbed down from the cart, and walked at a moderate pace, I would've doubled its speed. In fact, the people who'd stared at us through the millet plants were rushing ahead through the dense crops at the sides of the path to announce our arrival.

Every twenty to fifty metres or so, new faces appeared between the parted stalks of maize, corn, and millet. The expression on those faces was always the same—frank, stupefying, goggle-eyed amazement. If Prabaker and his father had captured a wild bear, and trained it to speak, the people couldn't have reacted with more gape-mouthed astonishment.

'The people are too happy,' Prabaker laughed. 'You are the first person from foreign to visit my village in twenty-one years. The last foreign fellow coming here was from Belgian. That was twenty-one years ago. All the people who are less than twenty-one years old have never seen a foreigner with their own eyes. That last fellow, that one from Belgian, he was a good man. But you are a very, very good man, Lin. The people will love you too much. You will be so happy here, you will be outside yourself. You will see.'

The people who stared at me from the groves and bushes at the side of the road seemed more anguished and threatened than happy. In the hope of dispelling that trepidation, I began to practise my Indian head-wiggle. The reaction was immediate. The people smiled, laughed, wiggled their heads in return, and ran ahead, shouting to their neighbours about the entertaining spectacle that was plodding along the track towards them.

To ensure the unflagging progress of the ox, Kishan beat the animal fiercely and often. The stick rose and fell with a resounding smack at regular intervals of minutes. The rhythm of those heavy blows was punctuated by sharp jabs at the animal's flanks with the nail attached to the end of the stick. Each thrust penetrated the thick hide, and raised a little tuft of cream brown fur.

The ox didn't react to those assaults, other than to continue its lumbering, drag-footed advance along the path. Nevertheless, I suffered for the beast. Each blow and jab accumulated within my sympathy until it was more than I could bear.

'Prabu, do me a favour, please ask your father to stop hitting the animal.'

'Stop ... stop *hitting*?'

'Yeah. Ask him to stop hitting the ox, please.'

'No, it is not possible, Lin,' he replied, laughing.

The stick slammed into the broad back of the ox, and was followed by two quick jabs of the nail.

'I mean it, Prabu. Please ask him to stop.'

'But, Lin ...'

I flinched, as the stick came down again, and my expression pleaded with him to intervene.

Reluctantly, Prabaker passed on my request to his father. Kishan listened intently, and then laughed helplessly in a fit of giggles. After a time, he perceived his son's distress, however, and the laughter subsided, and finally died, in a flurry of questions. Prabaker did his best to answer them, but at last he turned his increasingly forlorn expression to me once more.

'My father, Lin, he wants to know why you want him to stop using the stick.'

'I don't want him to hurt the ox.'

This time Prabaker laughed, and when he was able to translate my words for his father, they both laughed. They talked for a while, still laughing, and then Prabaker addressed me again.

'My father is asking, is it true that in your country people are eating cows?'

'Well, yes, it's true. But ...'

'How many of the cows do you eat there?'

'We ... well ... we export them from my country. We don't eat them all ourselves.'

'How many?'

'Oh, hundreds of thousands of them. Maybe millions, if you count the sheep. But we use humane methods, and we don't believe in unnecessarily hurting them.'

'My father is saying, he thinks it is very hard to *eat* one of these big animals, without *hurting* it.'

He then sought to explain my nature to his father by recounting for him the story of how I'd given up my seat, on the train journey, to allow an elderly man to sit, how I shared my fruit and other food with my fellow passengers, and how I often gave to beggars on the streets of Bombay.

Kishan pulled the cart to a sudden stop, and jumped down from the wooden yoke. He fired a stream of commands at Prabaker, who finally turned to me to translate.

'My father wants to know if we have it any presents with us, from Bombay, for him and the family. I told him we did. Now he wants us to give it those presents to him here, and in this place, before we go any more along the road.'

'He wants us to go through our bags, here, on this track?'

'Yes. He is afraid that when we get to Sunder village, you will have a good hearts, and give it away all those presents to other people, and he will not get his presents. He wants it all his presents now.'

So we did. Under the indigo banner of early-evening sky, on the scratch of track between fields of undulant maize and millet, we spread out the colours of India, the yellows and reds and peacock blues of shirts and lungi wraps and saris. Then we repacked them, with fragrant soaps and sewing needles, incense and safety pins, perfume and shampoo and massage oils, so that one full bag contained only those things we'd brought for Prabaker's family. With that bag safely tucked behind him on the rails of the ox-cart harness, Kishan Mango Kharre launched us on the last leg of our journey by striking the dumbly patient ox more often, and with a good deal more vigour, than he'd done before I tried to intercede on its behalf.

And then, at last, it was the voices of women and children, raised in laughter and cries of excitement, that welcomed us. The sounds reached us moments before we turned the last sharp curve and entered the village of Sunder along a single, wide street of swept, pressed, golden river sand. On either side were the houses, distributed so that no house faced into another across the street. The houses were round, made of pale brown mud, with round windows and curved doors. The roofs were made with little domes of thatched grasses.

Word had spread that the foreigner was arriving. The two hundred souls of Sunder village had been joined by hundreds more from neighbouring villages. Kishan drove us into the throng, stopping outside his own home. He was grinning so widely that everyone who looked at him was moved to laugh in return.

We climbed down from the cart, and stood with our luggage at our feet in the centre of six hundred stares and whispers. A breath-filled silence settled on the crowd, packed so tightly that each one pressed upon his neighbour. They were so close to me that I could feel the breath upon my face. Six hundred pairs of eyes fixed me with the intensity of their fascination. No-one spoke. Prabaker was at my side, and although he smiled and enjoyed the celebrity that the moment gave him, he too was awed by the press of attention and the surrounding wall of wonderment and expectation.

'I suppose you're wondering why I've called you all here,' I said, in just the serious tone of voice that would've been funny if there'd been a single person in the crowd who understood the joke. No-one did, of course, and the silence thickened, as even the faint murmurs died away.

What do you say to a huge crowd of strangers who are waiting for you to say something, and who don't speak your language?

My backpack was at my feet. In the top flap pocket there was a souvenir that a friend had given me. It was a jester's cap, in black and white, complete with bells on the ends of its three cloth horns. The friend, an actor in New Zealand, had made the jester's cap as part of a costume. At the airport, with minutes to go before my flight to India, he'd given me the cap as a good luck charm, a remembrance of him, and I'd stuffed it into the top of my backpack.

There's a kind of luck that's not much more than being in the right place at the right time, a kind of inspiration that's not much more than doing the right thing in the right way, and both only really happen to you when you empty your heart of ambition, purpose, and plan; when you give yourself, completely, to the golden, fate-filled moment.

I took the jester's cap out of the pack and put it on, pulling it tight under my chin, and straightening the cloth horns with my fingers. Everyone at the front of the crowd drew back with a little inrushing gasp of alarm. Then I smiled, and wiggled my head, ringing the bells.

'Hello, folks!' I said. 'It's show time!'

The effect was electrifying. Everyone laughed. The entire group of women, children, and men erupted as one, laughing and joking and crying out. One person reached out to touch me on the shoulder. The children at the front reached for my hands. Then everyone within grasping distance patted, stroked, and grabbed me. I caught Prabaker's eye. The look of joy and pride I found there was a kind of prayer.

He permitted the gentle assault for some minutes, and then asserted his authority over the new attraction by clearing the crowd away. He succeeded, at last, in opening the way to his father's house and, as we entered the dark circle of Kishan's home, the chattering, laughing crowd began to disperse.

'You must have a bath, Lin. After such a long travel you must be smelling unhappy. Come this way. My sisters have already heated the water on the fire. The pots are ready for your bath. Come.'

We passed through a low arch, and he led me to an area beside the house that was enclosed on three sides by hanging tatami mats. Flat river stones formed a shower base, and three large clay pots of warm water were arranged near them. A channel had been dug and smoothed out, allowing water to run off behind the house. Prabaker told me that a small brass jug was to be used to tip water over my body, and gave me the soap dish.

I'd been unlacing my boots while he spoke, and I cast them aside, threw off my shirt, and pulled off my jeans.

'Lin!' Prabaker screamed in panic, leaping, in a single bound, across the two metres that separated us. He tried to cover my body with his hands, but then looked around in anguish to see that the towel was on my backpack, a further two metres away. He jumped for the towel, snatched it up, and jumped back, giving a little shout of panic—*Yaaah!*—each time. He wrapped the towel around me, and looked around in terror.

'Have you gone crazy, Lin? What are you doing?'

'I'm trying to ... take a shower ...'

'But like that? Like *that?*'

'What's the matter with you, Prabu? You told me to take a shower. You brought me here to have a shower. So, I'm trying to take a shower, but you're jumping around like a rabbit. What's your problem?'

'You were *naked*, Lin! Naked, without any *clothes* also!'

'That's how I take a shower,' I said, exasperated by his mysterious terror. He was darting about, peering through the tatami matting at various places. 'That's how everyone takes a shower, isn't it?'

'No! No! No, Lin!' he corrected, returning to face me. A desperate expression contorted his normally happy features.

'You don't take your clothes off?'

'No, Lin! This is India. Nobody can take his clothes off, not even to wash his bodies. This is India. Nobody is ever naked in India. And especially, nobody is naked without clothes.'

'So ... how *do* you take a shower?'

'We wear it the underpants, for having a bath in India.'

'Well, that's fine,' I said, dropping the towel to reveal my black jockey shorts. 'I'm wearing underpants.'

'*Yaaah!*' Prabaker screamed, diving for the towel and covering me again.

'Those teeny pieces, Lin? Those are not the underpants. Those are the under-underpants only. You must have it the over-underpants.'

'The ... *over*-underpants?'

'Yes. Certainly. Like these, my ones, that I am wearing.'

He unbuttoned his own trousers enough to show me that he wore a pair of green shorts under his clothes.

'In India, the men are wearing this over-underpants, under their clothes, at all times, and in all the situations. Even if they are wearing *under*-underpants, *still* they are wearing *over*-underpants, over their unders. You see?'

'No.'

'Well, just you wait here. I will get you some over-underpants for your bath. But don't remove your towel. Please! Promise! If the people see you without the towel, in such teeny pieces, they will be like a wild people. Wait here!'

He darted off, and after a few minutes returned with two pairs of red football shorts.

'Here, Lin,' he puffed. 'You are such a big fellow, I hope we can get a good fits. These are from Fat Satish. He is so fat, I think they might fit you. I told him a story, and then he gave it this two pairs for you. I told him that on the journey you had loose motions, and you made such a mess in your over-underpants that we had to throw them away.'

'You told him,' I asked, 'that I shit my pants?'

'Oh, yes, Lin. I certainly couldn't tell him that you have no over-under-pants!'

'Well, of *course* not.'

'I mean, what would he be thinking about you?'

'Thank you, Prabu,' I muttered, through clenched teeth. If my tone had been any drier I wouldn't have needed a towel.

'That is my pleasure, Lin. I am your very good friend. So please, promise me that you will not be naked in India. Especially not without your clothes.'

'I promise.'

'I am so glad you make this promise, Lin. You are my very good friend, too, isn't it? Now I will take a bath also, like we are two brothers, and I will show you the Indian style.'

So, we both took a shower, in the bathing area of his father's house. Watching him, and following his lead, I wet my body in a first rinse with two jugs of water from one of the large pots, and worked the soap beneath my shorts without ever taking them off. After the final rinse, and a quick dry off with the towel, he taught me how to tie a lungi around the wet shorts. The lungi was a sarong-like rectangle of cotton, worn from waist to ankle. He gathered two long ends or corners of the lungi at the front, and then passed them around my waist, and rolled them under the top edge, in the small of my back. Within the encircling lungi, I removed and discarded my wet shorts and slipped on a dry pair of shorts underneath. With that technique, Prabaker assured me, I could take a shower in the open, and not offend his neighbours.

After the shower, and a delicious meal of dhal, rice, and homemade flatbreads, Prabaker and I watched as his parents and his two sisters opened their presents. We drank tea then, and for two hours we answered questions about me, and my home and family. I tried to answer truthfully—without the crucial truth that in my hunted exile, I didn't think I would ever see my home or family again. At last, Prabaker announced that he was too tired to translate any more, and that I should be permitted to rest.

A bed made from the wood of coconut trees and with a stretched mattress, formed from a web of coconut-fibre rope, was set up for me in the open, outside Kishan's house. It was Kishan's own bed. Prabaker told me that it might take two days to have a new one made to his father's satisfaction. Until then Kishan would sleep beside his son on the floor of the house, while I used his bed. I tried to resist, but my protests drowned in the sea of their gentle, relentless insistence. So I lay down on the poor farmer's bed, and my first night in that first Indian village ended, as it had begun, with surrender.

Prabaker told me that his family and his neighbours were concerned that I would be lonely, that I must be lonely, in a strange place, without my own family. They decided to sit with me on that first night, mounting a vigil in the dark until they were sure that I was peacefully deep in sleep. After all, the little guide remarked, people in my country, in my village, would do the same for him, if he went there and missed his family, wouldn't they?

They sat on the ground around my low bed, Prabaker and his parents and his neighbours, keeping me company in the warm, dark, cinnamon-scented night, and forming a ring of protection around me. I thought that it would be impossible to sleep within a circle of spectators, but in minutes I began to float and drift on the murmuring tide of their voices; soft and rhythmic waves that swirled beneath a fathomless night of bright, whispering stars.

At one point, Prabaker's father reached out from his place at my left side to rest his hand on my shoulder. It was a simple gesture of kindness and comfort, but its effect on me was profound. A moment before, I'd been drifting toward sleep. Suddenly I was hard awake. I plunged into memories and thoughts of my daughter, my parents, my brother; of the crimes I'd committed, and the loves I'd betrayed and lost forever.

It may seem strange, and it may in fact be impossible for anyone else to understand, but until that very moment I'd had no real comprehension of the wrong I'd done, and the life I'd lost. While I'd committed the armed robberies, I was on drugs, addicted to heroin. An opiate fog had settled over everything that I thought and did and even remembered about that time. Afterwards, during the trial and the three years in prison, I was sober and clear-headed, and I should've known then what the crimes and punishments meant, for myself and my family and the people I'd robbed at the point of a gun. But I didn't know or feel anything of it then. I was too busy being punished, and feeling punished, to put my heart around it. Even with the escape from prison, and the flight, running and hiding as a wanted man, a hunted man with a price on my head—even then, there was no final, clear, encompassing grasp of the acts and the consequences that made up the new, bitter story of my life.

It was only there, in the village in India, on that first night, adrift on the raft of murmuring voices, and my eyes filled with stars; only then, when another man's father reached out to comfort me, and placed a poor farmer's rough and calloused hand on my shoulder; only there and then did I see and feel the torment of what I'd done, and what I'd become— the pain and the fear and the waste; the stupid, unforgivable waste of it all. My heart broke on its shame and sorrow. I suddenly knew how much crying there was in me, and how little love. I knew, at last, how lonely I was.

But I couldn't respond. My culture had taught me all the wrong things well. So I lay completely still, and gave no reaction at all. But the soul has no culture. The soul has no nations. The soul has no colour or accent or way of life. The soul is forever. The soul is one. And when the heart has its moment of truth and sorrow, the soul can't be stilled.

I clenched my teeth against the stars. I closed my eyes. I surrendered to sleep. One of the reasons why we crave love, and seek it so desperately, is that love is the only cure for loneliness, and shame, and sorrow. But some feelings sink so deep into the heart that only loneliness can help you find them again. Some truths about yourself are so painful that only shame can help you live with them. And some things are just so sad that only your soul can do the crying for you.

CHAPTER SIX

P~RABAKER'S FATHER~ introduced me to Sunder village, but it was his mother who made me feel at home there. Her life enfolded mine within its triumph and sorrow, just as easily as her red shawl sometimes enswathed a crying child that passed the doorway of her house. Her story, told to me by many voices, month after month, became all the stories, even my own. And her love—her willingness to know the truth of my heart and to love me—changed the course of my life.

When I first met her, Rukhmabai Kharre was forty years old, and at the peak of her personal power and public prestige. She was a full head and shoulder taller than her husband, and that difference in height, combined with her ample, curvaceous figure, gave the false impression that she was something of an Amazon, whenever the couple stood together. Her black hair, gleaming with coconut oil, had never been cut, and the majestic rope of it reached to her knees. Her skin was tan brown. Her eyes were the colour of amber, set in rose gold. The whites of her eyes were pink, always, giving the impression that she'd just cried or was just about to cry. A wide gap between her front teeth gave an impish mischief to her smile, while the superb hook of her beaked nose endowed her serious expressions with an imposing authority. Her forehead was high and wide—it was Prabaker's forehead, exactly—and the high curves of her cheekbones were the mountains from which her amber eyes studied the world. She had a ready wit, and a deep sympathy for the distress of others. She stood aloof from disputes between her neighbours until she was asked to give her opinion, and then hers was usually the last word. She was a woman to admire and to desire, but the message in her eye and her bearing was unmistakable: offend or disesteem her at your peril.

The force of her personality maintained a status in the village that was derived from Kishan's ownership of land and her stewardship of their small personal fortune. Her marriage to Kishan had been arranged. As a shy sixteen-year-old, she'd peeped from behind a curtain to inspect her betrothed, seeing him then for the first and only time before the marriage. When I learned to speak her language well enough, she told me with disarming candour how disappointed she'd been when she'd scrutinised Kishan for the first time. He was short. His skin, tanned by farmer's toil until it matched the dark brown earth itself, was darker than hers, and that had worried her. His hands were rough and his speech was coarse. His clothes were clean but drab. And he was illiterate. Her father was head of a village council, a *panchayat*, and Rukhmabai could read and write, in Hindi and Marathi. As she looked at Kishan that first time, her heart beating its secrets so furiously that she feared he would hear it, she felt sure she couldn't love him, and that she was marrying beneath her status.

At the very moment of that distressing realisation, Kishan turned his head to stare directly at the hiding place, where she crouched behind the curtain. She was certain that he couldn't see her, yet he stared as if he was looking into her eyes. Then he smiled. It was the biggest smile she'd ever seen. It was radiant, and suffused with an irrepressible good humour. She looked into that prodigious smile, and a strange feeling took hold of her. She smiled back at him, despite herself, and felt a rush of well-being, an indefinable but overwhelmingly sanguine cheerfulness. *Things will turn out right*, the voice of her heart said to her. *Everything will be all right*. She knew, just as I'd known when I saw Prabaker for the first time, that no man who smiled with so much of his heart would knowingly hurt or harm another.

When he looked away again, it was as if the room had darkened, and she understood that she'd begun to love him for the reassuring incandescence of his smile alone. She offered no protest when her father announced the marriage arrangement, and within two months of that first glimpse of Kishan's magic smile she was wed, and pregnant with her first son, Prabaker.

Kishan's father settled two fertile fields on his eldest son at the time of the marriage, and Rukhmabai's father added a third to the young couple's endowment. From the earliest days of their union, the young bride assumed control of their small wealth. Using her reading and writing skills, she kept meticulous records of their profits and losses in simple school exercise books, which she tied into bundles and stored in a zinc trunk.

Judicious investments in the enterprises of her neighbours and a careful husbanding of their resources ensured that their losses were few. With the birth of their third child, when she was twenty-five years old, Rukhmabai had driven their modest fortune to become the largest in the village. They owned five fields. They planted cash crops. They kept three milking buffalo and three oxen, as well as two milking goats and a dozen laying hens. There was money in the bank sufficient to provide substantial dowries for her two daughters. The girls would marry well, she resolved, and give higher status to her grandchildren.

When he was nine years old, Prabaker was sent to Bombay, where he was apprenticed to an uncle who drove a taxi, and lived in a large inner-city slum. Rukhmabai began to expand her morning prayers, with the hopes and plans she made for the future of her family. Then she suffered a miscarriage. In less than a year, she miscarried twice more. Doctors concluded that her uterus had been scarred after the birth of her third child. They recommended, and carried out, a total hysterectomy. She was twenty-six years old.

Rukhmabai's heart wandered through the empty rooms of her life: the rooms reserved for the three babies lost in miscarriages, and all the other lives that might've been. For two years she was inconsolable. Even Kishan's wonderful smile, summoned through his own tears, failed to rouse her. Forlorn and broken-hearted, she languished in misery and the minimal routine of caring for her daughters. The laughter went out of her, and sadness settled on the neglected fields.

Rukhmabai's soul was dying, and she might've fallen into that sorrow forever, but a cataclysmic event that threatened the whole village roused her from her grieving. A band of dacoits, or armed bandits, settled in the area and began to demand tributes. A man in a neighbouring village was hacked with a machete. A woman in the same village was raped by the dacoits. Then they shot and killed a resister in Kishan's village.

Rukhmabai had known the dead man very well. He'd been one of Kishan's cousins, and had married a girl from Rukhmabai's own village. Every man, woman, and child in Sunder attended the funeral. At its end, Rukhmabai addressed the assembled villagers. Her hair was awry, and her amber eyes blazed with rage and determination. She harangued those who wanted to appease the dacoits, exhorting them to resist and fight and kill, if necessary, in defence of their lives and their land. Astonished as much by her sudden animation, after two years of grief's torpor, as by her martial speech, the villagers were inspirited. There and then, they devised a plan of action and resistance.

Word reached the dacoits that the people of Sunder village were determined to fight. Threats, skirmishes, and exploratory raids finally led the boiling conflict to the point where a battle was inevitable. The dacoits delivered a menacing warning that on a given day the villagers must surrender a considerable tribute, or suffer terrible consequences.

The people armed themselves with sickles, axes, staves, and knives. The women and children were evacuated to a neighbouring village. Fear and regret swept through the ranks of the men who remained. Several men argued that their struggle was foolhardy, and that tribute was less painful than death. The brothers of the murdered man stalked among them, giving encouragement and consolation while they castigated the backsliders for their cowardice.

The alarm went up that men were approaching on the city road. The villagers concealed themselves behind hastily erected barricades between their mud houses. Exhilarated and afraid, they were at the point of striking when they realised that the men were allies. Hearing of the war with the dacoits a week before, Prabaker had gathered a group of six friends and cousins from the city slum, where he lived, and he'd set out to join his family. He was just fifteen at the time, and the eldest of his friends was only eighteen, but they were street fighters from one of Bombay's toughest quarters. One of them, Raju, a tall boy with the handsome face and bouffant hairstyle of a Bombay movie star, had a gun. He showed the pistol to the villagers, and gave heart to them all.

The dacoits, arrogant and over-confident, swaggered into the village half an hour before sunset. The first blood-curdling threat was still on their leader's lips when Raju stepped from his concealment and walked toward the bandits, firing once for every third step. Axes, sickles, knives, staves, and rocks poured from the barricade walls, hurled to deadly effect by the desperate farmers. Raju never broke his stride, and with his last bullet he struck the leader of the dacoits in the chest at close range. The man was dead, the villagers said, before he hit the ground.

The rest of the wounded dacoits scattered, and were never seen again.

The body of the fallen leader was carried to Jamner District police post. All the villagers told the same story: they'd resisted the dacoits, and in the confusion of battle the bandits had shot one of their own men. Raju's name was never mentioned. After feasting for two days, the young men returned with Prabaker to the city. Wild, brave Raju died in a bar room fight a year later. Two of the other boys died in similarly violent circumstances. Another was serving a long sentence in prison for a crime of passion, involving the love of an actress and the enmity of a rival.

The villagers told me about the great battle many times as I learned to speak the Marathi language. They took me to the historic sites where the concealments and confrontations had occurred. They walked me through re-enactments of the event, the younger men often competing for the honour of playing Raju's part. No less important, in the telling of the tale, were the stories of the young men who'd fought beside them. The fate of each one—learned from Prabaker on his visits to the village—was recalled and told to me as part of the great saga. And through all of the stories and discussions, there was a special affection and pride for Rukhmabai Kharre. They loved and admired her for the galvanising role she'd played with her funeral speech—the first and last time she'd ever assumed a public position in the village. They acknowledged her courage, and they respected her strength of will. Above all, they celebrated her return to them, through the struggle with the dacoits, from grief and despair to the strong, shrewd, laughing woman she'd always been. In that poor and simple village, no-one doubted or forgot that its treasures were its people.

And it was all there, in her lovely face. The lines, high on her cheeks, were the dams she used to keep the tears in her eyes. Unspoken, unanswerable questions parted her full, red lips, whenever she was alone, or absorbed in her work. Determination stiffened the defiant thrust of her cleft chin. And her forehead was always slightly creased in the centre, between the brows, as if she was grasping, in those soft folds of skin, the monstrous and pitiable understanding that no happiness exists without its woe, no wealth without its cost, and no life without its full measure, sooner or later, of sorrowing and death.

My relationship with Rukhmabai was established on the first morning. I'd slept well on the rope bed outside Kishan's house—so well, in fact, that I was still snoring loudly when Rukhmabai drove her milking buffalo into the space, just after dawn. One of the creatures, drawn to the buzzing sound, decided to investigate. A wet, suffocating sensation woke me with a start of alarm. I opened my eyes to see the huge, pink tongue of a gigantic black water buffalo descending once again to smother my face. Shouting in fear and surprise, I fell off the bed and backed away on my hands and heels.

Rukhmabai led the laughter at my expense, but it was good laughter—honest, and kind, and with no knives in it. When she reached down to help me up, I took her hand and laughed with her.

'*Gaee!*' she said, pointing to the buffalo, and establishing the ground rule that if we were to be communicating with words, *I* would be the one learning a foreign language. *Water buffalo!*

She took a glass, and squatted by the udder of the immense, black, bow-horned beast to squeeze milk. I watched the milk squirt directly into the glass. She filled the glass with expert strokes, and then brought it to me, wiping the lip with the corner of her red cotton shawl.

I'm a city boy. I was born and raised in a fairly large city of three million people. One of the reasons I could remain for years on the run was that I love big cities, and feel completely confident and comfortable in them. The full range of a city boy's suspicion and dread of the country rose up in me when I held that glass of freshly squeezed milk. It was warm to the touch. It smelled of the cow. There seemed to be things floating in the glass. I hesitated. I had the sense that Louis Pasteur was standing just behind me, looking over my shoulder at the glass. I could hear him. *Er, I would boil that milk first, Monsieur, if I were you …*

I swallowed prejudice, fear, and the milk all at once, gulping it down as quickly as possible. The taste was not as bad as I'd expected it to be—creamy and rich, and with a hint of dried grasses within the bovine aftertaste. Rukhmabai snatched the glass from my hand and squatted down to fill it again, but my urgent, pleading protest convinced her that I was well satisfied with a single glass.

When we'd made our toilet, washed our faces, and cleaned our teeth, Rukhmabai stood over Prabaker and me while we ate a solid breakfast of roti and chai. The roti, or unleavened flatbreads, were made fresh for each breakfast, and cooked in a lightly oiled wok on an open fire. The hot, pancake-like bread was filled with a dab of ghee, or purified butter, and a large spoonful of sugar. It was then rolled into a tube, so thick that the hand only just curled around it, and eaten with a mug of hot, sweet, milky tea.

Rukhmabai watched every bite and chew, prodding us with a finger or slapping us on the head or shoulder if either of us showed the slightest inclination to pause for breath during the breakfast. Trapped, our jaws grinding away at the admittedly delicious food, we both cast surreptitious glances at the young women cooking at the wok, hoping that each roti, after the third or fourth we'd eaten, would be our last.

And so, for all the many weeks, every day in the village began with a glass of buffalo milk, then with a wash and, at last, with a long chai-roti breakfast. On most mornings, I joined the men in the fields tending to the crops of maize, corn, wheat, pulses, and cotton. The working day was divided into two brackets of about three hours, with a lunch break and siesta between. Children and young women brought the lunches to us in a multitude of stainless steel dishes. The meal usually consisted of the ubiquitous roti, spicy lentil dhal, mango chutney, and raw onions, served with lime juice. After eating the meal as a group, the men moved off to find quiet, shady spots to doze in for an hour or so. When work resumed, the fed and rested workers applied themselves with great energy and enthusiasm until the senior man in the group called a halt. Assembling on one of the main pathways, the farmers then walked back past fields they'd sown and tended themselves, often laughing and joking all the way to the village.

There was little work for the men to do in the village itself. Cooking, cleaning, washing, and even routine house-maintenance were all done by the women—mostly younger women, supervised in their tasks by older women. On average, the village women worked a four-hour day. They spent much of their free time playing with the young children. The village men worked six hours per day for an average four-day week. Special efforts were required for plantings and harvests, but in general the Maharashtrian villagers worked fewer hours than working men and women in cities.

It wasn't paradise. Some of the men exhausted themselves, after their work in the collective fields, trying to wring profits from a cash crop of cotton on a private patch of rocky ground. Rains came early or late. Fields flooded, or succumbed to the predations of insects and crop diseases. Women, with no outlet for their special creativities, endured the long, quiet ruin of their talents. Others watched the slow waste of bright children who could've been more and done more in some other, busier place, but never would know more than the village, the fields, and the river. Sometimes, rarely, a man or woman was so wretchedly miserable that the night for all of us, listening in the village dark, was ragged with sobbing.

But, just as Prabaker had said, the people did sing almost every day. If an abundance of good food, laughter, singing, and an amiable disposition can be taken as indicators of well-being and happiness, then the villagers eclipsed their western counterparts in those qualities of life. In my six months there, I never heard a cruel voice or saw a hand raised in anger. Moreover, the men and women in Prabaker's village were robustly healthy. The grandparents were plump, but not fat, the parents were bright-eyed and fit, and the children were straight-limbed, clever, and vivacious.

And there was a sense of certainty, in the village, that no city I've ever known provides: the certainty that emerges when the soil, and the generations who work it, become interchangeable; when the identities of the human beings and the nature of the place are one and the same. Cities are centres of constant and irreversible change. The definitive sound of a city is the rattlesnake chatter of a jackhammer—the warning sound you hear as the business reptile strikes. But change in the village is perennial. What changes in nature is restored with one wheel of the seasons. What comes from the earth always returns. What flourishes, dies away to bloom again.

And when I'd been in the village some three months, Rukhmabai and the people of Sunder gave me a fragment of that certainty: a part of them and their lives that changed my life forever. On the day the monsoon began, I was swimming in the river with a dozen other young men and about twenty children. The dark clouds, which had painted their sombre moods on the sky for weeks, gathered from horizon to horizon, and seemed to press upon the tops of the tallest trees. The air, after eight dry months, was so lavishly perfumed with rain that we were almost drunk with excitement.

'Paous alla! S'alla ghurree!' the children cried repeatedly, grasping my hands. They pointed to the clouds and dragged me toward the village. *The rain is coming! Let's go home!*

The first drops of rain fell as we ran. In seconds, the drops were a heavy fall. In minutes, the fall was a cascade. Within an hour, the monsoon was a ceaseless torrent, so thick that it was difficult to breathe in the open without cupping my hands to my mouth to make a little cave of air.

At first, the villagers danced in the rain and played pranks on one another. Some took soap, and washed in the heaven-sent shower. Some went to the local temple, where they knelt in the rain to pray. Others busied themselves with repairs to the roofs of their houses and the drainage trenches dug around every mud-brick wall.

Eventually, everyone stopped to simply stare at the drifting, flapping, curling sheets of rain. Every doorway of every house was crowded with faces, and each flash of lightning showed the frozen tableaux of wonder.

That downpour of several hours was followed by a lull just as long. The sun shone intermittently, and rainwater steamed from the warming earth. The first ten days of the season proceeded in the same way, with violent storms and tranquil lulls, as if the monsoon was probing the village for its weaknesses before mounting a final assault.

Then, when the great rain came, it was a lake of water in the air, and it rained almost without pause for seven days and nights. On the seventh day, I was at the river's edge, washing my few clothes as the drenching torrents fell. At one point I reached for my soap, and realised that the rock I'd placed it on was submerged. The water, which had merely caressed my bare feet, rose from my ankles to my knees in seconds. As I looked upstream at the tumbling crash of the river, the water reached to my thighs, and was still rising.

Awed and uneasy, I waded from the water with my wet clothes, and began the walk to the village. On the way I stopped twice to watch the progress of the river. The steep banks were quickly swamped, and then the wide sloping plain began to subside beneath the all-immersing flood. The advance was so rapid that the inevasible creep of the swollen, land-consuming river moved toward the village at a slow walking pace. Alarmed, I ran to warn the villagers.

'The river! The river is coming!' I shouted, in broken Marathi.

Sensing my distress but not really understanding me, the villagers gathered around and then called Prabaker, plying him with questions.

'What is your matter, Lin? The people are very upset for you.'

'The river! It's coming up fast. It'll wipe the village out!'

Prabaker smiled.

'Oh, no, Lin. That will not be happening.'

'I'm telling you! I've seen it. I'm not joking, Prabu. The fucking river's in flood!'

Prabaker translated my words for the others. Everyone laughed.

'Are you all crazy?' I shouted, in exasperation. 'It's not funny!'

They laughed all the harder and crowded around me, reaching out to calm my fear by patting and stroking me, their laughing voices full of soothing words and sighs. Then, with Prabaker leading the way, the crowd of villagers goaded, dragged, and pushed me toward the river.

The river, only a few hundred metres away, was a deluge: a vast muddy concrescence that tore through the valley in heaving waves and boiling eddies. The rain redoubled its intensity as we stood there, our clothes as drenched as the yielding soil. And still the tumid river grew, consuming new land with every thumping heartbeat.

'You see those sticks, Lin,' Prabaker said, in his most irritating attempt at a soothing tone. 'Those sticks are the flood-game sticks. Do you remember, when the people put them in the ground? Satish and Pandey, Narayan and Bharat ... do you remember?'

I did remember. Days before, there'd been a lottery of some kind. One hundred and twelve numbers—one for every man in the village—were written on small pieces of paper, and mixed together in an empty clay water-pot, called a *matka*. The men lined up to draw their numbers, and then a second set of the same numbers was mixed in the pot. A little girl was given the honour of drawing the six winning numbers from the pot. The whole village watched the ceremony, and applauded the winners happily.

The six men whose numbers had been drawn had won the chance to hammer a wooden stake, a little over a metre long, into the earth. As well, the three oldest men in the village were accorded the right to a wooden stake without the numbered lottery. They duly chose places for their stakes, and younger men obliged by hammering the wooden pegs into the ground. When all nine stakes were positioned, little flags with the names of the men were tied to each one, and the people drifted back to their homes.

I'd watched the affair from a shady spot beneath the branched dome of a tree. At the time, I was working on my own small reference dictionary of the

Marathi language, based on phonetic spellings of the words I heard every day in the village. I gave the ceremony little attention, and I never bothered to ask its purpose.

As we stood in the numbing, drumming rain and watched the prowling advance of the river, Prabaker explained that the wooden stakes were part of a flood-game that was played every year. The oldest men in the village, and six lottery winners, were given the chance to predict the point to which the river would rise. Each wooden stick, with its flag of yellow silk, represented a best guess.

'You see, this one little flag?' Prabaker asked, pointing to the stake that was furthest from where we stood. 'This one is almost gone. The river will reach to him, and cover him, tomorrow or tonight.'

He translated what he'd told me for the crowd, and they pushed Satish, a heavy-set cowherd, to the front of the group. The almost submerged stick was his, and he accepted, with shy laughter and downcast eyes, the good-natured jeers of his friends and the sneers of the older men.

'And this one here,' Prabaker went on, pointing to the stake nearest to our position. 'This one is the river will never be touching. The river never comes more far than this place. Old Deepakbhai has picked for himself this place, for the putting of his stick. He thinks this year will be a very heavy monsoon.'

The villagers had lost interest, and were already drifting or jogging back to the village. Prabaker and I stood alone.

'But ... how do you know that the river won't rise past this point?'

'We are here a long time, Lin. Sunder village has been in this place for two thousands of years. The next village, Natinkerra, has been there for much longer, about three thousands of years. In some other places—not near to here—the people do have a bad experiences, with the floods, in monsoon time. But not here. Not in Sunder. Our river has never come to this far. This year, also, I don't think it will come to this far, even so old Deepakbhai says it will. Everybody knows where the river will stop, Lin.'

He raised his eyes to squint at the unburdening clouds.

'But usually, we are waiting until the rain it stops, before we come out of the house to look at the flood-game sticks. If you don't mind, Lin, I'm swimming in my clothes, and I will have to squeeze the water out of my bones before I go in my house.'

I stared straight ahead. He glanced up at the black tumble of cloud once more, and asked a question.

'In your country, Lin, don't you know where the river stops?'

I didn't answer him. Eventually, he reached up to pat me on the back a few times, and then walked off. Alone, I stared at the rain-soaked world for a while, and at last I lifted my face to the drowning sky.

I was thinking about another kind of river, one that runs through every one of us, no matter where we come from, all over the world. It's the river of the heart, and the heart's desire. It's the pure, essential truth of what each one of us is, and can achieve. All my life I'd been a fighter. I was always ready, too ready, to fight for what I loved, and against what I deplored. In the end, I became the expression of that fight, and my real nature was concealed behind a mask of menace and hostility. The message of my face and my body's movement was, like that of a lot of other hard men, *Don't fuck with me*. In the end, I became so good at expressing the sentiment that the whole of my life became the message.

It didn't work in the village. No-one could read my body language. They knew no other foreigners, and had no point of reference. If I was grim or even stern, they laughed, and patted my back encouragingly. They took me as a peaceful man, no matter what expression I wore. I was a joker, someone who worked hard, played the fool for the children, sang with them, danced with them, and laughed with an open heart.

And I think I did laugh like that then. I was given a chance to reinvent myself, to follow that river within, and become the man I'd always wanted to be. On the very day that I learned about the wooden stakes of the flood-game, not three hours before I stood alone in the rain, Prabaker's mother had told me that she'd called a meeting of the women in the village: she'd decided to give me a new name, a Maharashtrian name, like her own. Because I was in Prabaker's house, it was decided that I should take the family name of Kharre. Because Kishan was Prabaker's father, and my adoptive father, tradition decreed that I should take his first name for my middle name. And because they judged my nature to be blessed with peaceful happiness, Rukhmabai concluded, the women had agreed with her choice for my first name. It was *Shantaram*, which means *man of peace*, or *man of God's peace*.

They nailed their stakes into the earth of my life, those farmers. They knew the place in me where the river stopped, and they marked it with a new name. Shantaram Kishan Kharre. I don't know if they found that name in the heart of the man they believed me to be, or if they planted it there, like a wishing tree, to bloom and grow. Whatever the case, whether they discovered that peace or created it, the truth is that the man I am was born in those moments, as I stood near the flood sticks with my face lifted to the chrismal rain. Shantaram. The better man that, slowly, and much too late, I began to be.

CHAPTER SEVEN

'SHE IS A BEAUTIFUL PROSTITUTES,' Prabaker pleaded. 'So fat she is, and in the most serious and the important places. A big handfuls you can grab, anywhere you like. You will be so exciting, you will make yourself sick!'

'It's a tempting offer, Prabu,' I responded, trying not to laugh, 'but I'm really not interested. We only left the village yesterday, and I guess my mind is still there. I'm just ... not in the mood.'

'Mood is no problem, baba. Only first you get bumping and jumping, then your bad moods will so quickly change, *futt-a-futt*!'

'Maybe you're right, but I think I'll pass, all the same.'

'But she is so experience!' he whined. 'Those fellows told me she has made sexy business *too* many times, and with too many hundred of customers, in *this* hotel only. I saw her. I looked on the inside of her eyes, and I know that she is a very big expert in the sexy business.'

'I don't want a prostitute, Prabu. No matter how expert she is.'

'But if you only *see* her. You will be crazy for her.'

'Sorry, Prabu.'

'But I told them ... that you will come and look at her. Only *look*. There is no harming for a look, Linbaba.'

'No.'

'But ... but I can't get back my cash deposits if you don't come and do some looking at her.'

'You paid a cash deposit?'

'Yes, Lin.'

'You paid a deposit, for me to have sex with a woman in this hotel?'

'Yes, Lin,' he sighed, raising his arms, and letting them fall to his sides in a helpless gesture. 'Six months in the village, you were. Six months with no sexy business. I was thinking you must be feeling a big amount of your needs. Now, no cash deposits returned for me, if you don't take one very small peeking at her.'

'Okay,' I sighed, copying his helpless gesture. 'Let's go take a look, just to get you off the hook.'

I pulled the door of our hotel room shut, and locked it. We set off along the wide corridor together. The Apsara Hotel in Aurangabad, north of Bombay, was more than a hundred years old, and built to serve a different, more splendid age. Its high, wide rooms were graced with open balconies facing the busy street, and they featured fine detail in their cornices and ceiling rosettes. The furniture was shoddy and thrown together in haphazard combinations, however, and the carpet in the corridors had worn through to shaggy holes in many places. The paint was peeling, the walls were bruised with dirt, and the rooms were cheap. Just the place, Prabaker had assured me, for us to spend a happy night on our way back to Bombay.

We stopped outside a door on the far side of our floor of the building. Prabaker was trembling with excitement. His eyes were alarmingly wide.

I knocked. Almost at once, the door opened. A woman, aged something over fifty, stood in the doorway. She was wearing a red and yellow sari, and she glared at us malevolently. Behind her in the room were several men. They were dressed in dhotis and white caps like the farmers in Prabaker's village, and they sat on the floor to eat a hearty meal of dhal, rice, and roti.

The woman stepped into the corridor, and pulled the door shut behind her. She fixed her gaze on Prabaker. He was a full head and shoulder shorter than she was, and he returned her baleful stare with the fixity of a school bully's minor henchman.

'You see, Lin?' he muttered, never taking his eyes off her. 'You see what I told you?'

What I saw was a plain, wide face with a bulbous nose, and lips so thin and curled with contempt that her mouth resembled a clam that someone had poked with a stick. The make-up on her face and neck was geisha thick, and gave her scowling expression a villainous intensity.

Prabaker spoke to the woman in Marathi.

'Show him!'

She responded by lifting aside the covering shawl of her sari to reveal a pudgy roll of stomach. She pinched a good pound or two of the flesh between her stubby fingers, and squeezed it, looking at me with one eyebrow raised to invite praise.

Prabaker let out a soft moan, and his eyes widened.

The woman then scowled dramatically left and right along the corridor before raising her blouse a few centimetres to reveal a long, thin, pendulous breast. She seized the breast and flapped it at me a few times, winking her eyebrow with a bafflingly inscrutable expression. My best guess, stabbing wildly in the dark, was that it might've been a menacing, derisive sneer.

Prabaker's eyes widened even more, and he began to breathe noisily through his open mouth.

The woman covered her breast, and then whipped her long plait of black hair over her shoulder with a jerk of her head. She took the plait in both hands and began to squeeze downward toward the tapering end with her fingers, as if it was a half-empty tube of toothpaste. A thick dribble of coconut oil gathered before her fingers, and dripped from the end of the plait onto the threadbare carpet.

'You know, Lin,' Prabaker mumbled, gaping hungrily and almost fearfully at the drips of oil. His right foot actually began to stamp, softly, on the carpet. 'If you don't want to have a sexy business with this woman ... if ... if you really don't want ... well ... I could use that cash deposits my own good self ...'

'I'll see you back at the room, Prabu,' I replied, smiling politely at the woman. I offered her a little bow, and took her scornful snarl with me back to our room.

I thought to use the time to update my Marathi dictionary. There were already some six hundred words from everyday usage in the list. I'd made the notes on scraps of paper, as people in the village had given me words and phrases, before transferring them to a sturdy journal for future reference. The last and latest of those notes were spread out on a little writing table, and I'd just begun to enter them in my journal when the door sprung open and Prabaker swaggered into the room. He walked past me without speaking, and fell onto his back on his bed. About nine minutes had passed since I'd left him at the prostitute's door.

'Oh, Lin!' he moaned happily, grinning up at the ceiling. 'I knew it. I knew she was a full-of-experience woman.'

I stared at him in bewilderment.

'Ah, yes!' he gushed, sitting up and letting his short legs swing from the bed. 'She gave me a big money's worth. And I gave it to her a very, very good sex also. And now! Let's go out! We will be having some foods, and some drinks, and a party!'

'If you're sure you've got the strength,' I muttered.

'Oh, no need for strength in this place, baba. This place I'm taking you is such a fine place that very often you can even sit down while you are drinking.'

As good as his word, Prabaker directed us to a hovel, about an hour's walk past the last bus stop on the outskirts of the town. With a round of drinks for the house, we insinuated ourselves into the crush of dusty, determined drinkers who occupied the bar's one narrow stone bench. The place was what Australians call a *sly grog shop*: an unlicensed bar, where men buy over-proof alcohol at under-the-counter prices.

The men we joined in the bar were workers, farmers, and a routine assortment of lawbreakers. They all wore sullen, persecuted expressions. They said little, or nothing at all. Fierce grimaces disfigured them as they drank the foul-tasting, homemade alcohol, and they followed each glass with a miscellany of grunts, groans, and gagging sounds. When we joined them, Prabaker and I consumed the drinks at a gulp, pinching our noses with one hand and hurling the noxious, chemurgic liquid down our open throats. By means of a fierce determination, we summoned the will to keep the poison in our bellies. And when sufficiently recovered we launched ourselves, with no little reluctance, into the next venomous round.

It was a grim and pleasureless business. The strain showed on every face. Some found the going too hard and slunk away, defeated. Some faltered, but were pressed on by the anguished encouragements of fellow sufferers. Prabaker lingered long over his fifth glass of the volatile fluid. I thought he was about to admit defeat, but at last he gasped and spluttered his way through to empty the glass. Then one man threw his glass aside, stood up, and moved to the centre of the shabby little room. He began to sing in a roaring, off-key voice, and because every man of us cheered our passionate and peremptory approval, we all knew that we were drunk.

One by one, we sang a song in turn. A weeping rendition of the Indian national anthem was followed by religious devotionals. Hindi love songs jingled beside heart-breaking gazals. The two burly waiters recognised the new stage of inebriation, and abandoned their drinks trays and glasses for a while. They took up their positions, sitting on stools on either side of the entrance door. They smiled broadly, nodded, wagged their heads, and cradled long, thick, wooden clubs in the tender embrace of their meaty arms. We all clapped and cheered, with every song. When it was my turn, I sang—I don't know why—the old Kinks' song, 'You Really Got Me':

> Girl, you really got me goin'
> You got me so I can't sleep at night …

I was drunk enough to coach Prabaker, and he was drunk enough to learn the chorus.

> Oh, yes, by God, you are a girl!
> And you really, really got me, isn't it going?

We were still singing on the dark, deserted stretch of road, leading back to town. We were still singing when the white Ambassador car cruised past us slowly, and turned. And we were still singing when the car cruised past us again, and then turned one more time to block our path on the shoulder of the road. Four men got out of the car, and one stayed behind the wheel. The tallest of the men grabbed at my shirt and barked a command at me in Marathi.

'What is this?' I slurred back at him, in Marathi.

Another man stepped in from the side and hit me with a short right hand that snapped my head back sharply. Two more quick punches crunched into my mouth and nose. I stumbled back, and felt one leg go out from under me. Falling, I saw Prabaker hurl himself at the four men with his arms wide, trying to hold them back from me. I roused myself, and rallied enough to make a charge. My left hook and overhand right elbow, the best hard punches in any street fight, were lucky, and both made tough contact. Beside me, Prabaker went down once, leapt to his feet, and collected a wild haymaker that sent him dazed and sprawling. I tried to stand near him and protect him with my legs, but I tripped and fell clumsily. Kicks and punches rained, and I covered up, hearing a quiet voice in my head that said, *I know this … I know this …*

The men held me down while one of them went through my pockets with practised thoroughness. Drunk and damaged, I was only dimly aware of the dark shapes looming over me. Then I heard another voice,

Prabaker's voice, and I understood some of the words in his pleading, and his defiant abuse of them. He castigated the men for shaming their own country and their own people by beating and robbing a foreigner, a visitor to their country who'd done them no harm. It was a wild speech that called them cowards and invoked Mahatma Gandhi, Buddha, the god Krishna, Mother Theresa, and the Bollywood film star Amitabh Bachchan in the same sentence. It had an effect. The leader of the group came to squat near me. I tried through my drunken haze to stand and fight again, but the others pushed me down and held me on the ground. *I know this ... I know this ...*

The man leaned over to look into my eyes. His face was hard, impassive, and very much like my own. He opened my torn shirt and shoved something inside. It was my passport and my watch.

They stood, gave Prabaker a last scowl of incomprehensible hatred, and then climbed into the car. Doors slammed as the car sped away, scattering us with dust and small stones.

Prabaker's wretchedness, when he was sure that I wasn't badly hurt, and he found time to wail and whine, was inconsolable. He blamed himself, loudly and often, for leading us to the remote bar and for allowing us to drink too much. He said with perfect honesty that he would happily take my bruises on his body, if it were possible. His pride in himself, as Bombay's best street guide, was a tattered banner. And his passionate, unqualified love for his country, *Bharat Mataji*, *Mother India*, suffered blows more grievous than any the body might endure.

'There's only one good thing for doing, Lin,' he concluded, as I washed my face at a hand-basin in the huge white-tiled bathroom of our hotel. 'When we get back to Bombay, you must be sending a telegram to your family and your friends for more monies, and you must go to your New Zealand embassy for making a complain of emergencies.'

I dried my face, and leaned on the basin to look into the mirror. The injuries weren't bad. A black eye was forming. My nose was swollen, but not broken. Both lips were cut and thickened, and there were some sweeping grazes on my cheeks and jaw, where kicks had scraped away the skin. It could've been a lot worse, and I knew it. I'd grown up in a tough neighbourhood, where working-class gangs preyed on one another and were merciless to loners, like me, who refused to join any of them. And then there was the prison. No beatings I'd ever suffered were as savage as those inflicted by the uniformed men who were paid to keep the peace, the prison guards. That was what the voice, my own voice, had recalled ... *I know this* ... That was the memory: being held down by three or four officers in the punishment unit while two or three others worked me over with fists, batons, and boots. It's always worse getting a beating from them, of course, because they're supposed to be the good guys. You understand and accept it when the bad guys work you over. But when the good guys use handcuffs to chain you to a wall, and then take turns to stomp and kick you, it's the whole system, it's the whole world, that's breaking your bones. And then there was the screaming. The other men, the other prisoners, screaming. Every night.

I looked into my own eyes in the mirror, and thought about Prabaker's suggestion. It was impossible to contact the New Zealand embassy — or any embassy. I couldn't contact family or friends because the police would be watching them, and waiting for a connection to be made. There was no-one. No help. No money. The thieves had taken every cent I had in the world. The irony of it wasn't lost on me: the escaped armed robber, robbed of everything he owned. What was it Karla had said, before I'd left for the village? *Don't drink any alcohol on the trip ...*

'There's no money in New Zealand, Prabu,' I told him as we walked back to our hotel room. 'There's no family who can help, no friends, and no help at the embassy.'

'No money?'

'None.'

'And you can't get any more? Not from any place?'

'No,' I answered, packing my few belongings into my backpack.

'This is a very serious trouble, Lin, if you don't mind I'm telling your bruise and scratchy face.'

'I know. Do you think we can sell my watch to the hotel manager?'

'Yes, Lin, I think so sure. It is a very nice watches. But I don't think so he will give us a big fair price. In such matters, the Indian businessman is putting his religion in his back pocket only, and he is driving very hard bargains on you.'

'Never mind,' I replied, clipping shut the catches on my backpack. 'So long as it's enough to pay the bill, and catch that night train you were talking about, back to Bombay. Come on, pack your things, and let's go.'

'It is a very, very, very serious trouble,' he said as we closed the door to the room for the last time, and walked down the corridor. 'No money is no funny in India, Lin, I'm telling you.'

The frown that compressed his lips and consumed his features remained with us all the way back to Bombay. The sale of my watch covered the hotel bill in Aurangabad, with enough left for two or three days at the India Guest House in Bombay. With my gear stowed in my favourite room, I walked Prabaker back to the small entrance foyer of the hotel, trying in vain to revive the little miracle of his wondrous smile.

'You will leave all those unhappy things in my caring,' he said, earnest and solemn. 'You will see, Lin. I will make a happy result on you.'

I watched him walk down the stairs, and then heard the manager, Anand, address me in friendly Marathi.

I turned with a smile, and we began to talk in Marathi. Six months in the village had given me the simple, everyday conversational phrases, questions, and sentences. It was a modest achievement, but Anand was obviously very pleased and surprised. After a few minutes of conversation, he called all the co-managers and room boys to hear me speak in their language. They all reacted with similarly delighted astonishment. They'd known foreigners who spoke a little Hindi, or even spoke it well, but none of them had ever met a foreigner who could converse with them in their own beloved Marathi language.

They asked me about the village of Sunder—they'd never heard of it —and we talked about the daily life that they all knew well from their own villages, and tended to idyllise in recollection. When the conversation ended, I returned to my room, and had barely shut the door when a tentative knock sounded at it.

'Excuse me, please. I am sorry to disturb.' The voice belonged to a tall, thin foreigner—German, or Swiss, perhaps—with a wispy beard attached to the point of his long face, and fair hair pulled back into a thick plait. 'I heard you speaking to the manager, and the room boys, before, and ... well, it is sure that you have been here in India very long ... and ... na ja, we just arrived today, my girlfriend and me, and we want to buy some hashish. Do you ... do you maybe know where we can get for ourselves some hashish, without somebody cheating us, and without trouble from the police?'

I did know, of course. Before the night was out, I also helped them to change money on the black market without being cheated. The bearded

German and his girlfriend were happy with the deal and they paid me a commission. The black marketeers, who were Prabaker's friends and contacts on the street, were happy that I'd brought new customers to them, and they paid me commissions as well. I knew there would be other foreigners, on every street in Colaba, who wanted to score. That casual conversation in Marathi with Anand and the room boys of the hotel, overheard by the German couple, had given me a way to survive in the city.

A more pressing problem, however, was my tourist visa. When Anand had signed me in to the hotel, he'd warned me that my visa had expired. Every hotel in Bombay had to supply a register of foreign guests, with a valid visa entry for each foreign name and passport number. The register was known as the C-Form, and the police were vigilant in its supervision. Overstaying on a visa was a serious offence in India. Prison terms of up to two years were sometimes imposed, and the police levied heavy fines on hotel operators who permitted C-Form irregularities.

Anand had explained all that to me, gravely, before he fudged the figures in his register and signed me in. He liked me. He was Maharashtrian, and I was the first foreigner he'd ever met who spoke the Marathi language with him. He was happy to break the rules for me, once, but he warned me to visit the Foreigner Registration Branch, at police headquarters, immediately, to see about an extension on my visa.

I sat in my room, and weighed the options. There weren't many. I had very little money. True, I'd inadvertently discovered a way to earn money as a middleman, a go-between, helping wary foreigners to deal with black marketeers. However, I wasn't sure if it would provide me with enough money to live in hotels and eat in restaurants. It certainly wouldn't pay for a plane ticket out of India. Moreover, I was already an overstayer on my visa, and technically guilty of a criminal offence. Anand assured me that the cops would see the lapsed visa as a mere oversight, and extend it without enquiry, but I couldn't risk my freedom on that chance. I couldn't visit the Foreigner Registration Branch. So, I couldn't alter my visa status, and I couldn't stay at a hotel in Bombay without a valid visa. I was caught between the rock of regulations and the hard place of the fugitive life.

I lay back on the bed, in the dark, listening to the sounds of the street that rose to my open window: the paanwalla, calling customers to the delights of his aromatic morsels; the watermelon man, piercing the warm, humid night with his plangent cry; a street acrobat, shouting through his sweaty exertions for a crowd of tourists; and music, always music. Did ever a people love music, I wondered, more than the Indians?

Thoughts of the village, thoughts I'd avoided and resisted until that music began, danced into my mind. On the day that Prabaker and I had left the village, the people had invited me to live with them. They'd offered me a house and a job. In the last three months of my stay I'd been helping the teacher at the local school with special lessons in spoken English. I gave him clear pronunciations of English words, helping him to correct the heavily accented versions of the language that he'd been teaching to the children. The teacher and the village council had urged me to stay. There was a place for me—a place and a purpose.

But it wasn't possible for me to return to Sunder village. Not then. A man can make his way in the city with his heart and his soul crushed within a clenched fist; but to live in a village, he has to unfurl his heart and his soul in his eyes. I carried crime and punishment with me in every hour of my life. The same fate that helped me to escape from prison had clamped its claws on my future. Sooner or later, if they looked hard enough and long enough, the people would see those claws in my eyes. Sooner or later, there would be a reckoning. I'd passed myself off as a free man, a peaceful man, and for a little while I'd known real happiness in the village, but my soul wasn't clean. What would I do to prevent my recapture? What wouldn't I do? Would I kill to save myself from prison?

I knew the answers to those questions, and I knew that my presence in Sunder defiled the village. I knew that every smile I took from them was swindled. Life on the run puts a lie in the echo of every laugh, and at least a little larceny in every act of love.

There was a knock at the door. I called out that it was open. Anand stepped into my room and announced with distaste that Prabaker had come to see me, with two of his friends. I clapped Anand on the back, smiling at his concern for me, and we walked to the hotel foyer.

'Oh, Lin!' Prabaker beamed, when our eyes met. 'I have the very good news for you! This is my friend, Johnny Cigar. He is a very important friend in the *zhopadpatti*, the slum where we live. And this is Raju. He helps Mr. Qasim Ali Hussein, who is the head man in the slum.'

I shook hands with the two men. Johnny Cigar was almost exactly my height and build, which made him taller and heavier than the Indian average. I judged him to be about thirty years old. His long face was candid and alert. The sand-coloured eyes fixed me with a steady, confident gaze. His thin moustache was trimmed to a precise line over an expressive mouth and determined jaw. The other man, Raju, was only a little taller than Prabaker, and of an even slighter build. His gentle face was stamped with a sadness that invited sympathy. It was the kind of sadness that's a companion, all too often, to scrupulous and uncompromising honesty. Thick brows hooded his intelligent, dark eyes. They stared at me, those knowing, mindful eyes, from a tired, sagging face that seemed much older than the thirty-five years I guessed him to be. I liked both men on sight.

We talked for a while, the new men asking me questions about Prabaker's village and my impressions of life there. They asked me about the city, as well, wanting to know my favourite places in Bombay, and the things that I liked to do most. When the conversation seemed likely to continue, I invited them to join me at one of the nearby restaurants for chai.

'No, no, Lin,' Prabaker declined, waggling his head. 'We must be leaving now. Only I wanted you to meet the Johnny and the Raju, and them to be meeting your good self, also. I think that Johnny Cigar has some things to tell you now, isn't it?'

He looked at Johnny, his eyes and his mouth wide open, and his hands raised in expectation. Johnny glowered at him, but the frown quickly softened into a broad smile, and he turned his attention to me.

'We made a decision for you,' Johnny Cigar declared. 'You will live with us. You are Prabaker's good friend. There is a place for you.'

'Yes, Lin!' Prabaker added quickly. 'One family is leaving tomorrow. And then, the day after tomorrow, that house will be yours.'

'But ... but ...' I stammered, flattered by the generous gesture, and yet horrified at the thought of life in the slum. I remembered my one visit to Prabaker's slum only too well. The smell of the open latrines, the heartbreaking poverty, the cramp and mill of people, thousands upon thousands of people—it was a kind of hell, in my memory, a new metaphor that stood for the worst, or almost the worst, that could happen.

'No problem, Lin,' Prabaker laughed. 'You will be too happy with us, you will see. And you know, you're looking like a different fellow now, it is true, but after a few months with us you will look exactly the same as everyone else there. People will think you are already living in the slum for years and years and years. You will see.'

'It is a place for you,' Raju said, reaching out slowly to touch my arm. 'A safe place, until you can save your money. *Our* hotel is *free*.'

The others laughed at that, and I joined them, inspired by their optimism and enthusiasm. The slum was filthy and crowded beyond imagining, but it was free, and there were no C-Forms for the residents. It would give me time to think, I knew, and time to plan.

'I ... well ... thanks, Prabu. Thanks, Johnny. Thanks, Raju. I accept your offer. I'm very grateful. Thank you.'

'No problem,' Johnny Cigar replied, shaking my hand, and meeting my eye with a determined, penetrating stare.

I didn't know then that Johnny and Raju had been sent by the head man of the slum, Qasim Ali Hussein, to look me over. In my ignorance and self-centeredness, I'd recoiled at the thought of the terrible conditions of the slum, and accepted their offer reluctantly. I didn't know that the huts were in much demand, and that there was a long list of families waiting for a place. I couldn't know, then, that offering a place to me meant that a family in need had missed out on a home. As the last step in making that decision, Qasim Ali Hussein had sent Raju and Johnny to my hotel. Raju's task was to determine whether I could live with them. Johnny's task was to make sure that *they* could live with *me*. All I knew, on the first night of our meeting, was that Johnny's handshake was honest enough to build a friendship on, and Raju's sad smile had more acceptance and trust in it than I deserved.

'Okay, Lin,' Prabaker grinned. 'Day after tomorrow, we come to pick up your many things, and your good self also, in the late of afternoon.'

'Thanks, Prabu. Okay. But wait! Day after tomorrow—won't that ... won't that mess up our appointment?'

'Appointment? What for an appointment, Linbaba?'

'The ... the ... Standing Babas,' I replied lamely.

The Standing Babas, a legendary cloister of mad, inspired monks, ran a hashish den in suburban Byculla. Prabaker had taken me there as part of his dark tour of the city, months before. On the way back to Bombay from the village, I'd made him promise to take me there again, with Karla. I knew she'd never been to the den, and I knew she was fascinated by the stories she'd heard of it. Raising the matter then, in the face of their hospitable offer, was ungrateful, but I didn't want to miss the chance to impress her with the visit.

'Oh yes, Lin, no problem. We can still make a visit to those Standing Babas, with the Miss Karla, and after that we will collect up all your things. I will see you here, day after tomorrow at three o'clock afternoon. I am so happy you are going to be a slum-living fellow with us, Lin! So happy!'

He walked out of the foyer and descended the stairwell. I watched him join the lights and traffic stirring on the noisy street, three floors below. Worries waned and receded. I had a way to make a little money. I had a safe place to stay. And then, as if that safety allowed them to, my thoughts wound and spiralled along the streets and alleys to Karla. I found myself thinking of her apartment, of her ground-floor windows, those tall French doors that looked out on the cobbled lane, not five minutes away from my hotel. But the doors I pictured in my mind stayed shut. And as I tried, and failed, to form an image of her face, her eyes, I suddenly realised that if I became a slum-dweller, if I lived in those squalid, squirming acres, I might lose her; I probably would lose her. I knew that if I fell that far, as I saw it then, my shame would keep me from her as completely and mercilessly as a prison wall.

In my room, I lay down to sleep. The move to the slum would give me time: it was a hard solution to the visa problem, but a practical one. I felt relieved and optimistic about it, and I was very tired. I should've slept well. But my dreams that night were violent and troubled. Didier once told me, in a rambling, midnight dissertation, that a dream is the place where a wish and a fear meet. *When the wish and the fear are exactly the same*, he said, *we call the dream a nightmare*.

CHAPTER EIGHT

THE STANDING BABAS were men who'd taken a vow never to sit down, or lie down, ever again, for the rest of their lives. They stood, day and night, forever. They ate their meals standing up, and made their toilet standing up. They prayed and worked and sang standing up. They even slept while they were standing, suspended in harnesses that kept the weight of their bodies on their legs, but prevented them from falling when they were unconscious.

For the first five to ten years of that constant standing, their legs began to swell. Blood moved sluggishly in exhausted veins, and muscles thickened. Their legs became huge, bloated out of recognisable shape, and covered with purple varicose boils. Their toes squeezed out from thick, fleshy feet, like the toes of elephants. During the following years, their legs gradually became thinner, and thinner. Eventually, only bones remained, with a paint-thin veneer of skin and the termite trails of withered veins.

The pain was unending and terrible. Spikes and spears of agony stabbed up through their feet with every downward pressure. Tormented, tortured, the Standing Babas were never still. They shifted constantly from foot to foot in a gentle, swaying dance that was as mesmerising, for everyone who saw it, as the sound-weaving hands of a flute player for his cobras.

Some of the Babas had made the vow when they were sixteen or seventeen years old. They were compelled by something like the vocation that calls others, in other cultures, to become priests, rabbis, or imams. A larger number of much older men had renounced the world as a preparation for death and the next level of incarnation. Not a few of the Standing Babas were businessmen who'd given themselves to ruthless pursuits of pleasure, power, and profit during their working lives. There were holy men who'd journeyed through many other devotions, mastering their punishing sacrifices before undertaking the ultimate vow of the Standing Baba. And there were criminals—thieves, murderers, major mafia figures, and even former warlords—who sought expiation, or propitiation, in the endless agonies of the vow.

The den was really a corridor between two brick buildings at the rear of their temple. Hidden from view forever, within the temple compound, were the secret gardens, cloisters, and dormitories that only those who made and kept the vow ever saw. An iron roof covered the den. The floor was paved with flat stones. The Standing Babas entered through a door at the rear of the corridor. Everyone else entered and left through an iron gate at the street end.

The customers, men from every part of the country and every level of society, stood along the walls of the corridor. They stood, of course: no-one ever sat in the presence of the Standing Babas. There was a tap fixed over an open drain near the entrance gate, where men drank water or leaned over to spit. The Babas moved from man to man and group to group, preparing hashish in funnel-shaped clay chillums for the customers, and smoking with them.

The faces of the Babas were radiant with their excruciation. Sooner or later, in the torment of endlessly ascending pain, every man of them assumed a luminous, transcendent beatitude. Light, made from the agonies they suffered, streamed from their eyes, and I've never known a human source more brilliant than their tortured smiles.

The Babas were also comprehensively, celestially, and magnificently stoned. They smoked nothing but Kashmiri—the best hashish in the world—grown and produced at the foothills of the Himalayas in Kashmir. And they smoked it all day, and all night, all their lives.

I stood with Karla and Prabaker at the back wall of the narrow den. Behind us was the sealed door through which the Standing Babas had entered. In front of us were two lines of men standing along the walls all the way to the iron gate at the street end of the passage. Some of the men were dressed in suits. Some wore designer jeans. Workmen, wearing faded lungis, stood beside men in traditional dress from various regions of India. They were young and old, rich and poor. Their eyes were often drawn to Karla and me, pale-skinned foreigners, standing with our backs against the wall. It was clear that some of them were shocked to see a woman in the den. Despite their open curiosity, no-one approached us or acknowledged us directly, and for the most part they gave their attention to the Standing Babas and the hashish. Conversations, buzzing softly, blended with music and devotional chanting, coming from somewhere inside the compound.

'So, what do you think?'

'It's incredible!' she replied, her eyes gleaming in the soft light of the shaded lamps. She was exhilarated, and perhaps a little unnerved. Smoking the charras had relaxed the muscles of her face and shoulders, but there were tigers moving quickly in the eyes of her soft smile. 'It's amazing. It's horrible and holy at the same time. I can't make up my mind which is the holy part, and which is the horrible part. Horrible— that's not the right word, but it's something like that.'

'I know what you mean,' I agreed, thrilled that I'd succeeded in impressing her. She'd been in the city for five years, and she'd heard about the Babas many times, but that visit with me was her first. My tone implied that I knew the place well, but I couldn't fairly claim credit for the experience. Without Prabaker, who'd knocked on the gate for us and gained access with his golden smile, we wouldn't have been permitted to enter.

One of the Standing Babas approached us slowly with an acolyte who held a silver tray containing chillums, charras, and the paraphernalia of smoking. Other monks rocked and swayed along the length of the corridor, smoking and chanting prayers. The Baba standing before us was tall and lean, but his legs were so thickly swollen that dreadful ropes of distended veins throbbed on their surfaces. His face was thin. The bones of his skull, near the temples, were sharply defined. His cheekbones, majestic, presided over deep valleys that ran to a hard and hungry jaw. His eyes were huge, within the caverns ridged by his brows, and there was such madness and longing and love in them that he was at once fearsome and immensely pitiable.

He prepared the chillum, rocking from side to side and smiling absently. He never looked at us, but still it seemed to be the smile of a very close friend: indulgent, knowing, forgiving. He was standing and swaying so close to me that I could see each wiry strand in the forest of his brows. I heard the little gasps of his breathing. The rapid outward rushes of air sounded like wavelets on a steep shore. He finished preparing the chillum, and looked up at me. For a moment I was lost in the vision that swarmed and screeched in his eyes. For a tiny moment in the infinitude of his suffering I almost felt it, what the human will can drive the human body to endure and achieve. I almost understood it, that smile of his, driven insane by the will that forced it to shine. I was sure that he was communicating it to me—that he wanted me to know. And I tried to tell him, with my eyes alone, that I could almost sense it, almost feel it. Then he held the chillum to his mouth, in the funnel of his hand, puffed it alight, and offered it to me. That terrible intimacy with his unending pain shrivelled, the vision shimmered, and the moment drifted away with the fading white shadows of the smoke. He turned, and tottered slowly back toward the street gate, muttering prayers in a soft drone.

A scream pierced the air. Everyone turned to the street-entrance gate. A man dressed in the red turban, vest, and silk trousers of a northern tribesman stood there, near the iron gate, shrieking at the very top of a strong voice. Before we could discern his message or react in any way, the man drew a long, thick-bladed sword from his belted sash and raised it over his head. Still screaming, he began to stalk along the corridor. He was staring directly at me as he walked, with a stomping, marching tread. I couldn't understand the words he was screeching, but I knew what he had in mind. He wanted to attack me. He wanted to kill me.

The men standing at the sides flattened their backs against the walls instinctively. The Standing Babas rocked themselves out of the madman's path. The door behind us was locked shut. There was no escape. We were unarmed. The man walked on towards us, waving the sword in circles over his head with both hands. There was nowhere to go, and nothing to do, but to fight him. I took one step back with the right foot, and raised my fists. It was a karate stance. Seven years of martial arts' training pulsed and flickered in my arms and legs. I felt good about it. Like every other tough, angry man I knew, I avoided fighting until it came to me, and then I enjoyed it.

At the last possible moment, a man stepped out from the wall at the side, tripped the goose-stepping tribesman, and sent him crashing to the stone floor. The sword fell from his hand and clattered to a stop at Karla's feet. I snatched it up, and watched as the man who'd tripped our assailant held him in a firm but merciful submission hold. He gripped the fallen man's arm in a hammerlock, behind his back. At the same time he twisted the collar of the man's shirt to choke off a little air. The anger or madness that had possessed the swordsman subsided, and he surrendered passively. Men who knew him stepped forward and escorted him out to the alley, beyond the iron gate. Seconds later, one of the men returned and approached me. Looking into my eyes, he held out his hands, palms upward, for the sword. I hesitated, but then handed it over. The man gave us a polite and apologetic bow, and left the den.

In the bubble and chatter that followed his departure, I checked on Karla. Her eyes were wide and she pursed her lips in a wondering smile, but she wasn't distressed. Reassured, I went to thank the man who'd stepped in to help us. He was tall, taller than I am by a few centimetres, and had a strong, athletic build. His thick, black hair was unusually long for Bombay in those years, and he wore it in a high ponytail. His silk shirt and loose trousers were black, and he wore black leather sandals.

'Abdullah,' he replied, when I'd told him my name, 'Abdullah Taheri.'

'I owe you one, Abdullah,' I said, giving him a smile that was as cautious as it was grateful. He'd moved with such lethal grace that he made the trick of disarming the swordsman seem effortless. But it wasn't as easy as it looked. I knew how much skill and courage it had taken, and how big a role instinct had played in his timing. The man was a natural; a born fighter. 'That was damn close.'

'No problem,' he smiled. 'He was drunk, I think, that fellow, or not right in his head.'

'Whatever his problem was, I still owe you one,' I insisted.

'No, really,' he laughed.

It was an easy laugh, revealing white teeth. The sound of it came from deep within his chest: a laugh from the heart. His eyes were the colour of sand, in the palm of your hand, a few minutes before the sun sinks below the sea.

'All the same, I want to thank you.'

'Okay,' he conceded, clapping a hand to my shoulder.

I returned to Karla and Prabaker. When we turned to leave the den, Abdullah was already gone. The alley outside was deserted, and within a few minutes we caught a taxi back to Colaba. Karla was silent during the ride, and I too said nothing, miserable that my attempt to impress her had ended in such confusion and near disaster. Only Prabaker felt free to speak.

'What a lucky escapes!' he said, from the front seat, grinning at us in turn as we sat together but apart in the back of the taxi. 'I thought a sure thing that fellow would chop us up in teeny pieces. Some of the people should not be smoking the charras, isn't it? Some of the people get very angry when they relax their brains.'

At Leopold's I got out of the taxi and stood with Karla while Prabaker waited. A late-afternoon crowd surged around the island of our silent stare.

'You're not coming in?'

'No,' I answered, wishing that the moment was more like the strong, confident scene I'd imagined through most of that day. 'I'm going to collect my stuff from the India Guest House, and move to the slum. In fact, I won't be coming to Leopold's for a while, or anywhere else for that matter. I'm going to ... you know ... get on my feet ... or ... I don't know ... find my feet ... or ... I'm going to ... what was I saying?'

'Something about your feet.'

'Yeah,' I laughed. 'Well, you gotta start somewhere.'

'This is kind of goodbye, isn't it?'

'Not really,' I muttered. 'Well, yes. Yes, it is.'

'And you only just got back from the village.'

'Yeah,' I laughed again. 'From the village, to the slum. It's quite a jump.'

'Just make sure you land on your —'

'—feet. Okay. I got it.'

'Listen, if it's a question of money, I could —'

'No,' I said quickly. 'No. I want to do this. It's not just money. I ...'

For three seconds I balanced on the edge of telling her about my visa problems. Her friend, Lettie, knew someone at the Foreigner Registration Branch. She'd helped Maurizio, I knew, and there was a chance that she could help me. But then I drew back from the edge, and covered the truth with a smile. Telling Karla about the visa would lead to other questions that I couldn't answer. I was in love with her, but I wasn't sure that I could trust her. It's a fact of life on the run that you often love more people than you trust. For people in the safe world, of course, exactly the opposite is true.

'I ... think this will be quite an adventure. I'm ... actually looking forward to it.'

'Okay,' she said, nodding her head slowly in acceptance. 'Okay. But you know where I live. Come by and see me, when you get the chance.'

'Sure,' I answered, and we both smiled, and we both knew that I wouldn't visit her. 'Sure. And you know where I am, with Prabaker. You do the same.'

She reached out to take my hand in hers, and then leaned over to kiss me on the cheek. She turned to leave, but I held her hand.

'Don't you have any advice for me?' I asked, trying to find another laugh.

'No,' she said impassively. 'I'd only give you advice if I didn't care what happens to you.'

It was something. It wasn't much, but it was something to hold on to and shape my love around, and keep me wishing. She walked away. I watched her step into the brittle brightness and banter of Leopold's, and I knew that a door to her world had closed, for a time. For as long as I lived in the slum, I would be exiled from that little kingdom of light. Living in the slum would consume me, and conceal me, as effectively as if the mad swordsman had struck me with his blade.

I slammed the door of the taxi and looked at Prabaker, whose wide and beaming smile across the seat in front of me became the world.

'Thik hain. Challo!' I said. Okay. Let's go!

We pulled up, forty minutes later, outside the slum in Cuffe Parade, beside the World Trade Centre. The contrast between the adjacent and roughly equal plots of land was stark. To the right, looking from the road, the World Trade Centre was a huge, modern, air-conditioned building. It was filled to three levels with shops, and displays of jewels, silks, carpets, and intricate craftworks. To the left was the slum, a sprawling ten acres of wretched poverty with seven thousand tiny huts, housing twenty-five thousand of the city's poorest people. To the right there were neon lights and floodlit fountains. To the left there was no electricity, no running water, no toilets, and no certainty that the whole shamble and bustle of it wouldn't be swept away, from one day to the next, by the same authorities that reluctantly tolerated it.

I turned my eyes from the glamorous limousines, drawn up outside the Trade Centre, and began the long walk into the slum. There was an open latrine near the entrance, concealed by tall weeds, and screens made from reed mats. The smell was appalling and almost overpowering. It was like a physical element permeating the air, and it seemed that I could feel it settle on my skin in a thickening, slimy ooze. Gagging and swallowing back the impulse to vomit, I glanced at Prabaker. His smile had dimmed, and for the first time I saw something like cynicism in it.

'See, Lin,' he said with that uncharacteristically hard little smile drawing down the corners of his mouth, 'See how the people live.'

Once past the latrines and within the first lane of huts, however, there were fitful gusts of wind from a wide arc of seacoast that formed the furthermost edge of the slum. The air was hot and steamy, but the breeze dispersed the noisome stink from the latrine. Smells of spices, cooking, and incense predominated. Seen up close, the huts were pitiful structures made from scraps of plastic and cardboard, thin bamboo poles, and flat reed mats for walls. They were erected over bare earth. Patches of concrete and stonework showed in some places where the old floors and foundations of the original buildings, cleared from the site years before, remained intact.

As I walked along the narrow rag-and-plastic lanes of the slum, word spread that the foreigner was on his way. A large crowd of children gathered and pooled around Prabaker and me, close to us but never touching. Their eyes were wide with surprise and excitement. They burst into fierce gusts of nervous laughter, shouted to one another, and leapt into jerky, spontaneous dances as we approached.

People came out of their huts to stand in every doorway. Dozens, and eventually hundreds, of people crowded into the side-lanes and the occasional gaps between the houses. They were all staring at me with such gravity, such a fixity of frowning intensity, that I felt sure they must bear me enormous ill-will. I was wrong, of course. I couldn't know then, on my first day, that the people were simply staring at my fear. They were trying to understand what demons haunted my mind, causing me to dread so terribly the place they knew to be a sanctuary from fates far worse than slum life.

And the fact was that for all my fear of its swarm and squalor, I did know a fate far worse than slum life. It was a fate so bad that I'd climbed a prison wall and given up everything that I knew, everything I was, everything I loved, to escape it.

'This is now your house, Lin,' Prabaker proudly announced over the giggling and chatter of the children when we reached the hut. 'Go inside. See all for yourself.'

The hut was identical to the others around it. The roof was a sheet of black plastic. The frame was made from thin bamboo poles bound together with coconut-fibre twine. The walls were made from hand-woven reed matting. The floor was bare earth, pressed flat and smooth by the feet of the hut's previous tenants. The door was a thin piece of ply-wood dangling on rope hinges. The plastic ceiling was so low that I had to stoop, and the whole room was about four paces long by two paces wide. It was almost exactly the same size as a prison cell.

I put my guitar in one corner, and then dragged the first-aid kit from the pack, setting it up in another corner. I had a couple of wire coat-hangers, and I was hanging my few clothes in the upper corners of the hut when Prabaker called me from outside.

I stepped out to find Johnny Cigar, Raju, Prabaker, and several other men standing together in the lane. I greeted those I knew, and was introduced to the others.

'This is Anand, your neighbour on the one side—on left side,' Prabaker said, bringing me to shake hands with a tall, handsome, young Sikh who wore his long hair in a tight yellow scarf.

'Hello,' I said, smiling in response to the warmth of his strong hand-shake. 'I know another Anand—the manager of the India Guest House.'

'Is he a good man?' Anand asked through a puzzled frown.

'He's a nice guy. I like him.'

'Good,' Anand replied, giving me a boyish smile that undermined the serious tone in his deep voice. 'Then we are half the way to being friends, na?'

'Anand, he shares his house with another of bachelors, with name Rafiq,' Prabaker continued.

Rafiq was about thirty years old. A straggly beard dangled from his pointed chin. His very prominent front teeth gaped from an impover-ished grin. His eyes narrowed unfortunately in the expression, and gave him a sly, almost malevolent appearance.

'On the other side is our very good neighbour, Jeetendra. His wife has the name Radha.'

Jeetendra was short and plump. He smiled happily and shook my hand, rubbing vigorously at his prominent paunch all the while. His wife, Radha, acknowledged my smile and nod of greeting by drawing her red cotton shawl over her head and holding it across her face with her teeth.

'Do you know,' Anand said in a gentle, conversational tone that caught me by surprise, 'it is a *fire*, I believe.'

He was standing on his stretched toes, and shading his eyes from the afternoon sun with his hand as he looked away across the black dunes of the huts. Everyone followed his gaze. There was a humid, ominous silence. Then, several hundred metres away, a gorgeous plume of orange flames erupted skyward. An explosion followed, sounding like a shotgun blast into a metal shed. Every man ran at top pace in the direction of the yellow spears of flame that rose in the distance.

I stood still, fascinated, bewildered, staring at the flames and spirals of smoke. As I watched, the jets of fire expanded to become a sheet and then a wall of searing flames. The red, yellow, and orange wall began to advance with the breeze from the sea, engulfing new huts every few seconds. It was heading directly toward me, at a slow walking pace, incinerating everything that stood in its path.

Explosions thundered in the blaze — one, two, another. I realised, at last, that they were kerosene stoves. Every one of the seven thousand huts had a stove. Those that were pumped up and under pressure were exploding when the flames reached them. The last monsoon rain had fallen weeks before. The slum was a huge pile of tinder-dry kindling, and a strengthening sea breeze fanned the flames through a whole acre of fuel and human lives.

Stunned, afraid, but not in panic, I watched the inexorable advance of the inferno, and decided that the cause was lost. I rushed into the hut, seized my pack and belongings, and scrambled for the door. At the threshold I dropped the pack, and stooped to retrieve the clothes and other items that had spilled to the ground. In the act, I looked up to see some twenty or more women and children, standing in a group and watching me. For an instant of perfect, wordless communication, I knew exactly what they were thinking. We stared across the open ground, and I heard their speaking minds.

Look at the big, strong foreigner, saving himself, and running away from the fire, while our men run towards it ...

Ashamed, I stuffed my belongings into the pack, and placed it at the feet of the woman, Radha, who'd been introduced as my neighbour. Then I turned and ran toward the fire.

Slums are planless, organic dispersements. There's purpose in the narrow, twisting lanes, but no order. Within three or four turns, I was lost. I ran in a line of men who were moving toward the smoke and flames. Beside us, running, staggering, and bumping along the lane in the opposite direction, was a constant file of other people moving away from the fire. They were helping the elderly and herding the children. Some carried possessions—clothes, cooking pots, stoves, and cardboard boxes of documents. Many of them were injured, showing cuts, bloody wounds, and serious burns. The smell of burning plastic, fuel, clothes, hair, and flesh was acrid and unnerving.

I turned a blind corner, and another, and another, until I was near enough to hear the roaring flames above the shouts and screams. Then a dazzlingly brilliant fireball burst through the gap between two huts. It was screaming. It was a woman, engulfed in flames. She ran straight at me, and we collided.

My first impulse was to spring away as I felt my hair, eyebrows, and eyelashes burn off in the contact with her. She stumbled, and fell over backwards, still screaming and thrashing. I ripped the shirt from my back. Using it to protect my hands and face, I threw myself on her, smothering the flames with my skin and clothes. Others rushed forward and tended to her. I ran on toward the fire again. She was still alive when I left her, but a voice in my mind was declaring her dead. *She's dead ... she's gone ... she won't make it ...*

The maw of the fire, when I did reach it, was terrifying. The flames roared to two or three times the height of the tallest hut, and ranged across a semi-circular front, arched away from us, that was fifty or more huts wide. Wilful gusts of wind drove the arc forward in probing feints, flaring up suddenly on one side, and then blazing toward us from a different direction. Behind it was the inferno, a cauldron of burning huts, explosions, and poisonous smoke.

A man stood in the centre of the large arc of open space before the wall of flames, directing those who were fighting the fire as if he was a general ordering troops into battle. He was tall and lean, with silver-grey hair, and a short, pointed, silver-grey beard. He was dressed in a white shirt, white trousers, and sandals. There was a green scarf tied at his neck, and he held a short, brass-tipped wooden stick in his hand. His name was Qasim Ali Hussein, and that was my first glimpse of the head man in the slum.

Qasim Ali's double tactic was to send beaters against the fire to slow it down while other teams demolished the huts that stood in the fire's path, and dragged away their contents to deprive the fire of fuel. That involved a staggered retreat, ceding land to the flames all the while, and then launching counter-attacks wherever the fire seemed to weaken. Slowly turning his head and sweeping his gaze back and forth across the front of the fire, Qasim pointed with the brass-tipped stick, and shouted commands.

The head man turned his gaze in my direction. A sliver of surprise gleamed in the polished bronze of his eyes. His scrutiny took in the blackened shirt in my hand. Without a word, he lifted his stick to point toward the flames. It was a relief and an honour to obey him. I trotted forward and joined a team of beaters. I was very glad to find Johnny Cigar in the same team.

'Okay?' he shouted. It was both encouragement and enquiry.

'Okay!' I shouted back. 'We need more water!'

'There is no more water!' he called back, gasping as the smoke eddied around us. 'The tank is empty. Trucks will fill it up tomorrow. The water that people are using here is their ration.'

I discovered later that every household, my own included, was rationed to two or three buckets of water per day for all cooking, drinking, and washing needs. The slum-dwellers were trying to put the fire out with their drinking water. Every bucket thrown, and there were many, forced one more household to spend a thirsty night, waiting for the morning delivery of water in city council trucks.

'I hate these fucking fires!' Johnny cursed, slamming downward with a wet sack to emphasise his words. 'Come on, you *fuck*! You want to *kill* me? Come on! We will *beat* you! We will *beat* you!'

A sudden quirk of the fire sent a burst of orange flame toward us. The man beside me fell backward, screaming and clutching at his burned face. Qasim Ali directed a rescue team to help him away. I seized his discarded sack and fell into line beside Johnny, slamming at the flames with one hand and shielding my face with the other.

We glanced over our shoulders, often, to receive directions from Qasim Ali Hussein. We couldn't hope to put the fire out with our wet rags. Our role was to gain time for the demolition teams scrambling to remove endangered huts. It was heartbreaking work. They were saving the slum by destroying their own houses. And to gain time for those wrecking teams, Qasim sent us left and right in desperate chess moves, starving the fire, and slowly winning ground.

When one squalling downdraft of wind swept black and brown smoke into our clearing, we lost sight of Qasim Ali Hussein completely. I wasn't the only man who thought to pull back in retreat. Then, through the smoke and dust, we saw his green scarf, held aloft and fluttering in the breeze. He stood his ground, and I glimpsed his calm face, summing up the status of the struggle and calculating his next move. The green scarf rippled above his head like a banner. The wind changed again, and we hurled ourselves to the task once more, inspired with new courage. The heart of the man with the green scarf was in me, and in all of us.

In the end, when we'd made our last sweep through the scorched lanes and charred lumps of houses, looking for survivors and counting the dead, we stood together in a mournful assembly to hear the tally. It was known that twelve persons were dead, six of them elderly men and women, and four of them children. More than one hundred were injured, with burns and cuts. Many of them were serious wounds. About six hundred houses were lost—one-tenth of the slum.

Johnny Cigar was translating the figures for me. I was listening to him with my head close to his, but watching Qasim Ali's face as he read from his hastily prepared list of the dead and injured. When I turned to look at Johnny, I found that he was crying. Prabaker pushed through the crowd to join us, just as Johnny told me that Raju was one of those who'd died in the fire. Raju, with the sad, honest, friendly face; the man who'd invited me to live in the slum. Dead.

'Damn lucky!' Prabaker summed up cheerfully, when Qasim Ali had called the tally. His round face was so blackened with soot that his eyes and teeth seemed almost supernaturally bright. 'Last year, in the last big fire, a full one-third of the zhopadpatti was burning up. One house from every three houses! More than two thousand houses gone! *Kalaass!* More than forty people dying also. *Forty.* It's too many, Lin, let me tell you. This year is a very lucky fire. And our houses are safe also! Bhagwan have blessings on our brother, Raju.'

Shouts from the edge of the sombre crowd drew our attention, and we turned to see one of the search teams pushing their way through to Qasim Ali. A woman from the team was carrying a baby they'd rescued from the smouldering rubble. Prabaker translated the excited shout and chatter for me. Three adjoining huts had collapsed in the blaze, falling on a family. In one of those inexplicable quirks of the fire's action, the parents of the child had suffocated and died, but the child, a baby girl, had survived. Her face and body were untouched, but her legs were severely burned. Something had fallen across them at mid-thigh, and they were black, split, and cracked. She was screaming in pain and terror.

'Tell them to come with us!' I shouted to Prabaker. 'Lead me back to my hut, and tell them to follow us. I've got medicine and bandages!'

Prabaker had seen the large and impressive first-aid kit many times. He knew it included bandages, salves, and creams, disinfectant solutions, swabs, probes, and an array of surgical instruments. Grasping my meaning at once, he shouted a message to Qasim Ali and the others. I heard the words *medicine* and *doctor* repeated several times. Then he grasped my sleeve and dragged me with him, jogging back to the hut.

With the kit open on the ground in front of my hut, I applied local anaesthetic cream to the baby's legs in a thick smear. It began to work almost at once. The baby settled down to a quiet whimper, and cuddled within her rescuer's arms.

'Doctor ... doctor ... doctor ...' people said, all around me.

Qasim Ali called for lamps to be brought as the sun set on the Arabian Sea, and the long Bombay evening finally succumbed to warm, star-filled night. By the yellow flickering lamplight we tended to the wounded slum-dwellers, using my first-aid kit as the basis of our little open-air clinic. Johnny Cigar and Prabaker worked with me as translators and nurses. The most common injuries were burns, cuts, and deep gashes, but a great many people were also affected by smoke inhalation.

Qasim Ali Hussein watched us for a short while, and then left to supervise the erection of emergency shelters, the rationing of remaining water supplies, the preparation of food, and the dozen other tasks that would fill the night to morning and beyond. A cup of tea appeared beside me. My neighbour Radha had made it and brought it to me. It was the first thing I ate or drank in the slum, and it was the best chai I ever tasted in my life. An hour later, she forced her husband and two other young men to drag me from the injured people to eat a meal of roti bread, rice, and bhajee. The curried vegetables were deliciously spiced, and I cleaned the plate with the last bite of roti.

And again, hours later, after midnight, it was Radha's husband, Jeetendra, who pulled at my arm and drew me into my hut, where a hand-crocheted blanket had been spread out on the bare earth. Unresisting, I collapsed on the blanket for my first night of sleep in the slum.

Seven hours later—hours that passed as if they were minutes—I woke to see Prabaker's face hovering in the air. I blinked, and squinted, and realised that he was squatting on his haunches, with his elbows on his knees, and his face cupped in his hands. Johnny Cigar was squatting beside him, on his left, and Jeetendra was on his right.

'Good morning, Linbaba!' he said, cheerfully, when my eyes settled on his. 'Your snorings is a fabulous thing. So loud! Like having a bullock in this hut, Johnny said so.'

Johnny nodded his agreement, and Jeetendra wagged his head from side to side.

'Old Sarabai is having a first-class cure for snorings,' Prabaker informed me. 'She can take one very sharp pieces of bamboo, about same as long as my finger, and push it up inside of your nose. After that, no more snoring. *Bas! Kalaass!*'

I sat up on the blanket, and stretched the stiffness from my back and shoulders. My face and eyes were still gritty from the fire, and I could feel that the smoke had stiffened in my hair. Lances of morning light stabbed through holes in the walls of the hut.

'What are you doing, Prabu?' I asked irritably. 'How long have you been watching me sleeping?'

'No so very long, Lin. Only for the half hours or so.'

'It's not polite, you know,' I grumbled. 'It's not nice to watch people when they're sleeping.'

'I'm sorry, Lin,' he said quietly. 'In this India we can see everybody sleeping, at some times. And we say that the face, when it is in sleeping, is the friend of the world.'

'Your face is so kind when you are sleeping, Lin,' Johnny Cigar added. 'I was very surprised.'

'I can't begin to tell you what this means to me, guys. Can I expect to find you in the hut, *every* morning, when I wake up?'

'Well, if you really, really want, Lin,' Prabaker offered, jumping to his feet. 'But this morning we only came to tell you that your patients are ready.'

'My … *patients*?'

'Yes. Come and see.'

They stood, and opened the door of the hut. Sunlight splintered into my burning eyes. I blinked, and stepped through, following the men into the brilliant, bayside morning to see a line of people squatting on the ground outside my hut. There were thirty or more of them forming a queue along the length of the lane to the first turn.

'Doctor … doctor …' people murmured and whispered when I emerged from the hut.

'Come on!' Prabaker urged, tugging at my arm.

'Come on where?'

'First to toilet,' he replied, happily. 'You must make a motions, isn't it? I will show you how we make a motions, into the sea, on the long cement jetty. That is where the young men and boys make their motions, every morning, into the oceans—motions into the oceans, isn't it? You just be squatting down, with your buttocks pointing on the oceans. Then you wash your good self with a shower, and you have it a happy breakfast. Then you can easily fix up all your patients. No problem.'

We walked along the length of the queue. They were young and old, men and women. Their faces were cut, bruised, and swollen. Their hands were blackened, blistered, and bloody. There were arms in slings, and legs in splints. And at the first turn, I saw to my horror that the queue extended into the next lane, and was longer, much longer.

'We've got to … do something …' I mumbled. 'They're all … waiting.'

'No problem, waiting, Lin,' Prabaker replied, airily. 'The people are waiting more than one hour already. If you are not with us, they would still be waiting, but waiting for nothing only. Waiting for nothing, that is what kills the heart of a man, isn't it? Now the people are waiting for *something*. Waiting for *you*, they are. And you are a *really* something, Lin-Shantaram, if you don't mind I'm saying it to your smoky face and sticking-up hairs. But first, you must make it motions, and then washing, and then breakfast. And we have to get going—some young fellows are waiting down there on the jetty, and wanting to see you make your motions.'

'They what?'

'Oh yes! They are a fascinating for you. You are like a movie hero for them. They are dying to see how you will make your motions. And then, after all these things, you will return, and fix the patients, like a really hero, isn't it so?'

And in that way was my role in the slum created. *If fate doesn't make you laugh*, Karla said, in one of my first conversations with her, *then you just don't get the joke*. As a teenager I'd trained in first-aid treatment. The formal course of study had covered cuts, burns, sprains, breaks, and a wide range of diagnostic and emergency procedures. Later, I'd earned my nickname, *Doc*, by using my training in CPR to pull junkies out of overdoses, and save their lives. There were hundreds of people who only knew me as *Doc*. Many months before that morning in the slum, my friends in New Zealand had given me the first-aid kit as a going-away present. I was sure those threads—the training, the nickname, the first-aid kit, the work as unofficial doctor in the slum—were all connected in some way that was more than accident or coincidence.

And it had to be me. Another man, with my first-aid training or better trained, wouldn't have been forced by crime and a prison-break to live in the slum. Another criminal, ready to live there with the poor, wouldn't have had my training. I couldn't make sense of the connection on that first morning. I didn't get the joke, and fate didn't make me laugh. But I knew there was something—some meaning, some purpose, leading me to that place, and that job, at exactly that time. And the force of it was strong enough to bind me to the work, when every intuition tried to warn me away.

So, I worked into the day. One by one, the people gave me their names and their smiles and, one by one, I did my best to treat their wounds. At some point during the morning, someone put a new kerosene stove in my hut. Someone else provided a metal box for rat-proof storage of food. A stool found its way into my hut, and a water pot—the ubiquitous matka—and a set of saucepans, and a few pieces of cutlery.

As evening throbbed in a scarlet arch of sky, we sat in a group, near my hut, to eat and talk. Sadness lingered in the busy lanes, and memories of those who'd died receded and returned like waves moving on the great ocean of the heart. Yet carried on that sadness, a part of sorrowing itself, was the determination of those who'd endured. The scorched earth had been cleared and cleaned, and many of the huts were already rebuilt. Hopes rose with every humble home that was restored.

I looked at Prabaker, laughing and joking as he ate, and I thought of our visit with Karla to the Standing Babas. One moment from that evening, one heartbeat's length of time as the crazed man had charged at us with a sword, was stretched in my memory. At the precise instant when I took that step backwards and raised my hands in a boxing stance to fight, Prabaker took a step to the side, and stood in front of Karla. He wasn't in love with her, and he wasn't a fighter. Yet his first instinct was to step sideways and protect Karla by shielding her with his body, while my first thought was to step back and fight.

If the mad swordsman hadn't been tripped, if he'd reached us, I would've been the one to fight him. And, probably, I would've saved us: I'd fought men with fists, knives, and clubs before, and I'd won. But even then, even if it had gone that far, Prabaker would've been the real hero, for the bravery of that little, instinctive, sideways step.

I'd grown to like Prabaker. I'd learned to admire his unshakeable optimism. I'd come to depend on the comforting warmth his great smile provided. And I'd enjoyed his company, day and night, through the months in the city and the village. But in that minute, on my second night in the slum, as I watched him laughing with Jeetendra, Johnny Cigar, and his other friends, I began to love him.

The food was good, and there was enough for all. Music played on a radio somewhere. It was the fine, almost unbearably sweet soprano and happy, boasting tenor of a duet from an Indian movie. The people talked, nourishing one another with their smiles and conversation. And some time during the course of that love-song, somewhere in the landscape of the slum-dwellers' reassurances, somehow through the fact of our survival, their world enfolded my life within its dreams, as gently and completely as a swollen tide closes over a stone that stands upon its shore.

PART TWO

PART TWO

CHAPTER NINE

I ESCAPED FROM PRISON in broad daylight, as they say, at one o'clock in the afternoon, over the front wall and between two gun-towers. The plan was intricate and meticulously executed, up to a point, but the escape really succeeded because it was daring and desperate. The bottom line for us, once we started, was that the plan had to succeed. If it failed, the guards in the punishment unit were quite capable of kicking us to death.

There were two of us. My friend was a wild, big-hearted twenty-five year old serving a life sentence for murder. We tried to convince other men to escape with us. We asked eight of the toughest men we knew, all of them serving ten straight years or more for crimes of violence. One by one, they found an excuse not to join in the attempt. I didn't blame them. My friend and I were young first-offenders with no criminal history. We were serving big years, but we had no reputation in the prison system. And the escape we'd planned was the kind that people call heroic if it succeeds, and insane if it fails. In the end, we were alone.

We took advantage of extensive renovations that were being carried out on the internal security-force building—a two-storey office and inter-rogation block near the main entrance gate at the front wall. We were working as maintenance gardeners. The guards who pulled shifts in the area saw us every day. When we went to work there, on the day of the escape, they watched us for a while, as usual, and then looked away. The security-force building was empty. The renovation workers were at lunch. In the few long seconds of the little eclipse created by the guards' bore-dom and their familiarity with us, we were invisible, and we made our move.

Cutting our way through the chain-link fence that closed off the reno-vation site, we broke open a door to the deserted building and made our way upstairs. The interior was hollowed out by the renovation.

Unplastered walls showed the skeleton structure of uprights and load-bearing beams. The bare, wooden steps on the stairway were white with dust, and littered with fragments of brick and plaster. There was a manhole in the ceiling on the top floor. Standing on my friend's strong shoulders, I punched out the wooden trapdoor in the manhole and climbed through. I had an extension cord with me, wrapped around my body under my coveralls. I uncoiled it and pulled it free, fixed one end to a roof beam, and passed the other down to my friend. He used it to climb up into the roof-space with me.

The roof stretched out in zigzag waves. We scrambled toward the narrowing pinch of space where the roof met the front wall of the prison. I chose a spot on one of the troughs to cut our way through, hoping that the peaks on either side would conceal the hole from the gun-towers. It was dark everywhere in the roof-space, but in that narrow wedge near the wall it was blacker than a guard's baton.

With a cigarette lighter for a lantern, we worked to cut our way through the double-thickness of hardwood that separated us from the tin on the outside of the roof. A long screwdriver, a chisel, and a pair of tin snips were our only tools. After fifteen minutes of hacking, scraping, and stabbing at the wood, we'd cleared a little space about the size of a man's eye. Waving the flame of the hot cigarette lighter back and forth, we could see the glint of the metal roof beyond the small hole. But the wood was too hard and too thick. With the tools we had, it would take us hours to make a man-sized hole.

We didn't have hours. We had thirty minutes, we guessed, or maybe a little more, before the guards did a routine check of the area. In that time we had to get through the wood, cut a hole in the tin, climb out on the roof, use our power extension cord as a rope, and climb down to freedom. The clock was ticking on us. We were trapped in the roof of the security building. And any minute, we knew, the guards might notice the cut fence, see the broken door, and find the smashed manhole. Any minute they could come up through the manhole into that black, sweating cave, and find us.

'We've gotta go back,' my friend whispered. 'We'll never get through the wood. We've gotta go back, and pretend it never happened.'

'We can't go back,' I said flatly, although the thought had screamed through my mind as well. 'They'll find all the broken stuff, the fence we cut, and they'll know it was us. We're the only ones allowed in the area. If we go back, we're in the Slot for a year.'

The Slot was prison slang for the punishment unit. In those years, that unit, in that prison, was one of the most inhumane in the country. It was a place of random, brutal beatings. A failed attempt to escape through the roof of the security-force building—*their* building, the head office for the punishment unit guards—would ensure that the beatings were less random and more brutal.

'Well what the *fuck* are we gonna do?' my friend demanded, shouting with everything but his voice. Sweat dripped from his face, and his hands were so wet with fear that he couldn't hold the cigarette lighter.

'I think there's two possibilities,' I declared.

'What are they?'

'First, we could use that ladder—the one that's chained to the wall downstairs. We could go down again, break the chain off the ladder, tie the extension cord to the top of it, slam it up against the wall, climb up, and throw down the cord on the other side. Then we can slide down to the street.'

'That's it?'

'That's the first plan.'

'But ... they'll see us,' my friend protested.

'Yeah.'

'And they'll start shooting at us.'

'Yeah.'

'They'll shoot us.'

'You said that.'

'Well, fuck *me*,' he hissed. 'I think it *bears* repeating. It's a fuckin' salient point, don't you think?'

'I figure that one of us will get through, maybe, and one of us will get shot. It's fifty-fifty.'

We considered the odds in silence for a while.

'I hate that plan,' my friend shuddered.

'So do I.'

'What's the second plan?'

'Did you notice that buzz saw, on the ground floor, as we came up here?'

'Yeah ...'

'If we bring it up here, we could use the buzz saw to cut through the wood. Then we can use the tin snips to cut through the tin. After that, it's back to the original plan.'

'But they'll hear the thing,' my friend whispered fiercely. 'I can hear them talking on the fuckin' telephone. We're that close. If we drag the saw up here, and fire it up, it'll sound like a fuckin' helicopter.'

'I know. But I think they'll just figure it's the workers, doing more work.'

'But the workers aren't here.'

'No, but the shift at the gate is changing. There's new guards coming on duty. It's a big chance to take, but I think if we do it they'll just hear the noise, as usual, and think it's the workers. They've been listening to drills and hammers and buzz saws for weeks. And there's no way they could imagine that it's *us* doing it. They'd never figure that crims would be crazy enough to use a power saw, right next to the main gate. I think it's our best shot.'

'I hate to be Mister-fuckin'-Negative here,' he objected, 'but there's no electricity in this building. They shut it off for the renovating. The only power point is outside. The extension cord is long enough to reach down there, I think, but the power is *outside* the building.'

'I know, I know. One of us will have to go down, creep out the door we busted open, and plug the extension cord into the outside power outlet. It's the only way.'

'Who goes down there?'

'I'll do it,' I said. I tried to sound confident and strong, but there are some lies that the body just won't believe, and the words came out as a squeak.

I scrambled over to the manhole. My legs were stiff with dread and tension-cramp. I slid down the extension cord and crept down the stairway to the ground floor, playing the cord out all the way. It reached to the door, with plenty to spare. The buzz saw was resting near the door. I tied the extension cord around the handle of the saw, and ran back up the stairs. My friend pulled the saw up into the manhole and then passed the cord back to me. Once more I crept down to the door. With my body pressed flat against a wall, I breathed hard, and tried to find the courage to open the door. At last, with a heart-wrenching rush of adrenaline, I pushed the door aside and stepped out into the open to plug the cord into the socket.

The guards, armed with pistols, were talking among themselves, not twenty metres from the door. If one of them had been facing my way, it would've been over. I glanced up to see that they were looking in every direction but mine. They were talking and walking about in the gate area, and laughing at a joke someone had just cracked. No-one saw me. I slipped back inside the building, crawled like a wolf on all fours up the stairs, and dragged myself up the cord to the manhole.

In the dark corner near the trough in the zigzag roof space, my friend lit the cigarette lighter. I saw that he'd connected the power saw to the cord. He was ready to make the cut. I took the lighter, and held it for him. Without a second of hesitation, he hoisted the heavy saw and clicked it to life. The machine screamed like the whine of a jet engine on a runway. My friend looked at me, and a huge grin tore his mouth open. His teeth were clenched in the smile, and his eyes were glittering with the reflected fire. Then he drove the saw into the thick wood. With four swift, ear-splitting cuts, he made a perfect hole that revealed a square of gleaming tin.

We waited in the silence that followed, our ears ringing with diminishing echoes, and our hearts thumping at our chests. After a moment we heard a telephone ring close by, at the main gate, and we thought we were finished. Then someone answered the phone. It was one of the gate guards. We heard him laugh and talk on in a relaxed, conversational tone. It was okay. We were safe. They'd heard the power saw, of course; but, just as I'd hoped, they'd dismissed it as noise made by the workmen.

Heartened, I punched a hole in the tin with the screwdriver. Sunlight from the free sky above shot in on us. I widened the hole, and then used the tin snips to cut a panel of tin around three sides. Pushing with two sets of hands, we shoved the flap of tin outwards, and I poked my head through the hole. I saw that we had indeed cut our way into one of the troughs of the roof. The deepest part of that V-shaped trench was a blind spot. If we lay down in that narrow defile we couldn't see the tower guards, and they couldn't see us.

We had one job left to do. The power cord was still plugged into the outlet, downstairs and outside the building. We needed the cord. It was our rope. We needed it to climb down the outside of the prison wall to the street. One of us had to go down the stairs, push out through the door in full view of the guards in the adjacent gate area, unplug the power cord, and then climb back up into the roof again. I looked at my friend, his sweating face clear in the bright light bathing us from the hole we'd cut in the roof, and I knew it had to be me.

Downstairs, with my back against the inside wall, next to the door, I paused again, and tried to will the strength into my arms and legs for the move out into the open. I was breathing so hard that I felt dizzy and nauseous. My heart, like a trapped bird, hurled itself against the cage of my chest. After a few long moments, I knew I couldn't do it. Everything, from judicious caution to superstitious terror, screamed at me not to go out there again. And I couldn't.

I had to cut the cord. There was no other way. I took the chisel from the side-pocket of my coveralls. It was very sharp, even after the work we'd done with it in trying to penetrate the wooden barrier in the roof. I placed it against the trailing power cord, where it entered under the door. I raised my hand to strike. The thought occurred to me that if I blew out the power by cutting through the cord it could sound an alarm, and perhaps send a guard into the building to investigate. It didn't matter. I didn't have any choice. I knew I couldn't go out into the open again. I slammed my hand down hard onto the chisel. It cut through the cord, and embedded itself in the wooden floor. I swept the snipped ends of the cord away from the metal chisel, and waited for the sound of an alarm or the tumble of voices to approach from the gate area. There was nothing. Nothing. I was safe.

I grabbed the loose end of the power cord, and rushed back upstairs and into the roof space. At the new manhole we'd cut in the roof, we secured the cord to a heavy, wooden bearer beam. Then my friend started out through the hole. When he was halfway onto the tin roof, he got stuck. For a few moments, he couldn't move upward and he couldn't move back. He began to thrash wildly, straining with all his strength, but it was hopeless. He was stuck fast.

It was dark again in the roof space, with his body blocking the hole we'd made. I scrabbled around with my hands in the dust, between the roof joists, and found the cigarette lighter. When I struck it, I saw at once what had trapped him. It was his tobacco pouch—a thick, leather wallet that he'd made for himself in one of the hobby groups. Telling him to hold still, I used the chisel to tear a flap in the pocket at the back of his coveralls. When I ripped the pocket away, the tobacco pouch fell free into my hands, and my friend went up through the hole and onto the roof.

I followed him up to the tin roof. Wriggling like worms in the gutter of the trough, we moved forward to the castellated front wall of the prison. We knelt to look over the wall. We were visible then, for a few seconds, but the tower guards weren't looking our way. That part of the prison was a psychological blind spot. The tower guards ignored it because they didn't believe that anyone would be crazy enough to attempt a daylight escape over the front wall.

Risking a quick, frantic glimpse at the street below, we saw that there was a queue of vehicles outside the prison. They were deliverymen, waiting to enter through the main gate. Because each vehicle was searched throughout, and checked with mirrors beneath, the queue made slow progress. My friend and I hunkered down in the trough to consider our options.

'That's a mess down there.'

'I say we go now,' he said.

'We have to wait,' I countered.

'Fuck it, just throw the cord over and let's go.'

'No,' I whispered. 'There's too many people down there.'

'So what?'

'One of them'll play hero, for sure.'

'Fuck him. Let him play hero. We'll just go over the top of him.'

'There's too many of them.'

'Fuck them all. We'll go straight through 'em. They won't know what hit 'em. It's us or them, mate.'

'No,' I said finally. 'We have to wait. We have to go over when there's no-one down there. We have to wait.'

And we did wait, for a twenty-minute eternity, and I wriggled forward again and again to look over the wall, risking exposure every time. Then, at last, I looked down to the street and saw that it was completely empty in both directions. I gave my friend the signal. He scrambled forward over the wall, and down out of sight. I crept forward to look, expecting to see him climbing down the cord, but he was already on the street. I saw him disappear into a narrow lane, across the street from the prison. And I was still inside, on the roof.

I clambered over the bluestone parapet, and took hold of the cord. Standing with my legs against the wall, and the cord in both hands, my back to the street, I looked at the gun-tower on my left. The guard was talking into a telephone and gesturing with his free hand. He had an automatic rifle slung over his shoulder. I looked to the other tower. The guard there, also armed with a rifle, was calling down to another guard inside the prison in the gate area. He was smiling and relaxed. I was invisible. I was standing on the front wall of the toughest maximum-security prison in the state, and I was invisible.

I pushed off with my legs and started the descent, but my hands slipped —the fear, the sweat—and I lost the cord. I fell. It was a very high wall. I knew it was a killing fall to the ground below. In an agony of terror and desperation, I grabbed at the cord and seized it. My hands were the brakes that slowed my fall. I felt the skin tear away from my palms and fingers. I felt it singe and burn. And slower, but still hard enough to hurt, I slammed into the ground, stood, and staggered across the road. I was free.

I looked back at the prison once. The cord was still dangling over the wall. The guards were still talking in their towers. A car drifted past on the street, the driver drumming his fingers on the steering wheel in time to a song. I turned my back. I walked on through the lane into a hunted life that cost me everything I'd ever loved.

When I committed the armed robberies, I put fear into people. From that time—even as I did the crimes—and on through prison and life on the run, fate put fear into me. The nights were steeped in it, and sometimes I felt as if the blood and the breath in my body were clotted with fright. The fear I'd put into others became ten terrors, fifty, a thousand, filling the loneliest hours of every night with dread.

By day, in those early Bombay months, when the world worked and worried around me, I wedged my life into a busy thickness of duties, needs, and small pleasures. But at night, when the sleeping slum dreamed, the horror crept across my skin. My heart backed away into a black cave of memory. And I walked most nights, while the city slept. I walked, and I forced myself not to look over my shoulder at the gun-towers and the dangling power cord on the high wall that wasn't there.

The nights, at least, were quiet. At midnight, every night in those years, the cops imposed a curfew on Bombay. Half an hour before twelve, police jeeps gathered in the main streets of the central city, and began the enforced closure of restaurants, bars, stores, and even the tiny pavement shops that sold cigarettes and paan. The beggars, junkies, and hookers who weren't already at home or hiding were chased from the footpaths.

Steel shutters came down over the shop windows. White calico cloths were thrown over the tables in all the markets and bazaars. Quiet and emptiness descended. In the whirl and crush of people and purposes in Bombay's daylight scramble, it was impossible to imagine those deserted silences. But each and every night was the same: soundless, beautiful, and threatening. Bombay became a haunted house.

For two to three hours after midnight, in an operation known as the *round-up*, squads of plain-clothes cops patrolled the vacant streets in search of criminals, junkies, suspects, and homeless, unemployed men. More than half the people in the city *were* homeless, of course, and many of them lived, ate, and slept on the streets. The sleepers were everywhere, stretched out on the footpaths with only a thin blanket and a cotton sheet to keep out the damp of night. Single people, families, and whole communities who'd escaped some drought, flood, or famine slept on the stone paths and in doorways, huddled together in bundled necessity.

It was technically illegal to sleep on the streets in Bombay. The cops enforced that regulation, but they were as pragmatic about it as they were about enforcing the laws against prostitution on the Street of Ten Thousand Whores. A certain discrimination was required, and in fact the list of those they *wouldn't* arrest for the crime of homelessness was quite long. Sadhus and all other religious devotees, for example, were exempted. Elderly people, amputees, the sick, or the injured didn't find much sympathy, and were sometimes forced to move on to another street, but they weren't arrested. Lunatics, eccentrics, and itinerant entertainers such as musicians, acrobats, jugglers, actors, and snake charmers were occasionally roughed up, but they were invariably excluded from the round-up. Families, particularly those with young children, usually received no more than a stern warning not to remain longer than a few nights in a given area. Any man who could prove he had a job, however menial, by displaying the business card or written address of his employer, was spared. Single men who were clean and respectful and could demonstrate some level of education could usually talk their way out of an arrest, even if they weren't employed anywhere. And, of course, anyone who could pay baksheesh was safe.

That left the very poor, homeless, unemployed, uneducated, single young men as the high-risk group in the midnight round-up. With no money to pay their way out of the police net, and not enough education to talk their way out, scores of those young men were arrested throughout the city, every night. Some of them were arrested because they fitted descriptions of wanted men. Some were found to have drugs or stolen goods in their possession. Some were well known, and the cops arrested them routinely, on suspicion. Many, however, were simply dirty and poor and stricken with a sullen helplessness.

The city didn't have the funds to provide thousands of pairs of metal handcuffs; and even if the money were found, the cops probably wouldn't have burdened themselves with heavy chains. Instead, they carried lengths of rough twine made from hemp and coconut fibres, and used it to tie the arrested men one to the other by the right hand. The thin rope was enough to hold the men because the victims of nightly round-ups were mostly too weak, under-nourished, and spiritually defeated to run. They submitted meekly, silently. When between a dozen and twenty men had been arrested and tied into the human chain, the six or eight cops in the round-up squad marched them back to holding cells.

For their part, the cops were fairer than I'd expected them to be, and undeniably brave. They were armed only with the thin bamboo cane known as the lathi. They carried no clubs, gas, or guns. They had no walkie-talkies, so they couldn't call for back-up if they ran into trouble on the patrols. There were no vehicles to spare for the round-up, so the squads walked the many kilometres of their beat. And although they struck out often with the lathi, savage or even serious beatings were rare —much less frequent than police beatings in the modern, western city where I'd grown up.

Nevertheless, the round-up did mean days, weeks, or even months of confinement for the young men in prisons that were as bad as any in Asia, and the caravans of roped, arrested men that shambled throughout the city, after midnight, were more melancholy and forlorn than most funeral processions.

In my late-night walks around the city, I was invariably alone when the round-up was done. My rich friends feared the poor. My poor friends feared the cops. Most foreigners feared everybody, and kept to their hotels. The streets were mine as I searched their cool silences.

On one of those night walks, about three months after the fire, I found myself on the sea wall at Marine Drive. The broad footpath beside the sea wall was bare and clean. A six-lane road separated the seaside path from a horizon-wide, incurving crescent of affluence: fine homes, expensive apartments, consular offices, first-class restaurants, and hotels that looked out over the black and heaving sea.

There were very few cars on the Drive, that night, only one every fifteen or twenty minutes, travelling slowly. Few lights shone in any of the rooms across the street behind me. A cool wind carried the clean, salt air in irascible gusts. It was quiet. The sea was louder than the city.

Some of my friends from the slum worried about me walking alone on the streets at night. *Don't walk at night*, they said. *The night is no safety in Bombay.* But it wasn't the city that I feared. I felt safe on the streets. Strange and troubled as my life was, the city enfolded it within the millions of others as if ... as if it belonged there, no less than any other.

And the work I was doing enhanced that sense of belonging. I gave myself assiduously to the role of slum doctor. I found books on diagnostic medicine, and studied them by lamplight in my hut. I accumulated a modest cache of medicines, salves, and bandages, buying them from local chemists with money I earned in black-market deals with tourists. And I stayed on there, in those squalid acres, even after I'd made enough money to leave. I stayed on in the cramped little hut when I could've moved to a comfortable apartment. I allowed my life to be swept up in the broiling, dancing struggle of their twenty-five thousand lives. I bound myself to Prabaker and Johnny Cigar and Qasim Ali Hussein. And although I tried not to think of Karla, my love put claws in the sky. I kissed the wind. I spoke her name, when I was alone.

On the sea wall, I felt the cool breeze wash across the skin of my face and chest like water poured from a clay matka. There was no sound but my own breath in the wind and the crash of deep water on the rocks, three metres below the wall. The waves, reaching up in splash and spindrift, pulled at me. *Let go. Let go. Get it over with. Just fall down and die. So easy.* It wasn't the loudest voice in my mind, but it came from one of the deepest sources—the shame that smothered my self-esteem. The shamed know that voice: *You let everyone down. You don't deserve to live. The world would be better off without you ...* And for all that I tried to belong, to heal myself with the work in the clinic, to save myself with the fool notion of being in love with Karla, the truth was that I was alone in that shame, and lost.

The sea surged and shoved at the rocks below. One push, and it would all be over. I could feel the fall, the crash as my body struck the rocks; the cold slipperiness of drowning death. *So easy.*

A hand touched my shoulder. The grip was soft and gentle, but firm enough to hold me there. I turned quickly in shocked surprise. There was a tall, young man standing behind me. His hand remained on my shoulder as if to brace me there; as if he'd read my thoughts a few moments before.

'Your name is Mr. Lin, I believe,' he said quietly. 'I don't know if you can remember me — my name is Abdullah. We met at the den of the Standing Babas.'

'Yes, yes,' I stammered. 'You helped us, helped me. I remember you well. You left — you disappeared — before I got to thank you properly.'

He smiled easily, and took away his hand to run it through his thick, black hair.

'No need for thanks. You would be doing the same for me, in your country, isn't it? Come, there is someone who wants to meet you.'

He gestured to a car that was parked at the kerb ten metres away. It had drawn up behind me, and the motor was still running, but somehow I'd failed to hear it. It was an Ambassador, India's modest version of a luxury car. There were two men inside — a driver, and one passenger in the back.

Abdullah opened the rear door and I stooped to look inside. A man in his middle to late sixties sat there, his face half illuminated by the street-lights. It was a lean, strong, intelligent face with a long, thin nose and high cheekbones. I was struck and held at once by the eyes, an amber brilliance of amusement and compassion and something else — ruthlessness, perhaps, or love. His hair and beard were close-cropped and white-grey.

'You are Mr. Lin?' he said. His voice was deep, resonant, and supremely confident. 'I am pleased to meet you. Yes, very pleased. I have heard something good about you. It is always a delight to hear good things — and even more pleasurable, when it concerns foreigners, here in our Bombay. Perhaps you have heard of me also. My name is Abdel Khader Khan.'

Sure, I'd heard of him. Everyone in Bombay had heard of him. His name appeared in the newspapers every other week. People spoke about him in the bazaars and nightclubs and slums. He was admired and feared by the rich. He was respected and mythologised by the poor. His discourses on theology and ethics, held in the courtyard of the Nabila Mosque in Dongri, were famous throughout the city, and drew many scholars and students from every faith. No less famous were his friendships with artists, businessmen, and politicians. He was also one of the lords of Bombay's mafia—one of the founders of the council system that had divided Bombay into fiefdoms ruled by separate councils of mafia dons. The system was a good one, people said, and popular, because it had brought order and relative peace to the city's underworld after a decade of bloody power struggles. He was a powerful, dangerous, brilliant man.

'Yes, sir,' I answered, shocked that I'd inadvertently used the word *sir*. I loathed the word. In the punishment unit we were beaten whenever we failed to address the guards as *sir*. 'I know your name, of course. The people call you Khaderbhai.'

The word *bhai*, at the end of his name, meant *elder brother*. It was a term of respectful endearment. He smiled and nodded his head slowly when I said it: Khaderbhai.

The driver adjusted his mirror and fixed me in it, staring expressionlessly. There were fresh jasmine flowers hanging in garlands from the mirror, and the perfume was intoxicating, almost dizzying after the fresh wind from the sea. As I leaned into the doorway of the car, I became acutely conscious of myself and my situation: my stooping posture; the wrinkles in my frown as I lifted my face to see his eyes; the rim of guttering at the edge of the car's roof under my fingertips; and a sticker, pasted to the dashboard, that read GOD BLESS I AM DRIVING THIS CAR. There was no-one else on the street. No cars passed. It was silent, but for the idling engine of the car and the muffled churning of the shuffling waves.

'You are the doctor in the Colaba hutments, Mr. Lin. I heard of it at once, when you went to live there. It is unusual, a foreigner, living in the hutments. This belongs to me, you understand. The land where those huts stand—it belongs to me. You have pleased me by working there.'

I was stunned into silence. The slum where I lived, known as the *zhopadpatti*, or the hutments, half a square kilometre, with twenty-five thousand men, women, and children, belonged to him? I'd lived there for months, and I'd heard Khaderbhai's name mentioned many times, but no-one had ever said that he owned the place. *It can't be*, I heard myself thinking. *How can any one man own such a place, and all its lives?*

'I, er, I'm not a doctor, Khaderbhai,' I managed to tell him.

'Perhaps that is why you are having such success in treating the sick, Mr. Lin. Doctors will not go into the hutments willingly. We can compel men not to be bad, but we cannot compel them to be good, don't you find? My young friend, Abdullah, recognised you just now, as we passed you, sitting on the wall. I turned the car to come back here for you. Come—sit inside the car with me. I will take you somewhere.'

I hesitated.

'Please, don't trouble yourself. I …'

'No trouble, Mr. Lin. Come and sit. Our driver is my very good friend, Nazeer.'

I stepped into the car. Abdullah closed the door behind me, and then sat in the front next to the driver, who adjusted the mirror to find and fix me in it again. The car didn't move off.

'*Chillum bono*,' Khaderbhai said to Abdullah. *Make a chillum.*

Abdullah produced one of the funnel-shaped pipes from his jacket pocket, placed it on the seat beside him, and set about mulling together a mix of hashish and tobacco. He pressed a ball, known as a *goli*, of hashish onto the end of a matchstick, and burned it with another match. The smell of the charras coiled into the perfume of the jasmine flowers. The engine of the car was still idling slowly and quietly. No-one spoke.

In three minutes the chillum was prepared, and offered to Khaderbhai for the first *dumm*, or puff. He smoked, and passed the pipe to me. Abdullah and the driver smoked then, passing the chillum for one more round. Abdullah cleaned the pipe quickly and efficiently, and returned it to his pocket.

'*Challo*,' Khader said. *Let's go.*

The car moved away from the kerb slowly. Streetlights began to stream into the sloping windshield. The driver snapped a cassette into the dashboard player. The soul-wrenching strains of a romantic gazal slammed out at maximum volume from speakers behind our heads. I was so stoned that I could feel my brain trembling within my skull, but when I looked at the other three men they appeared to be perfectly controlled and composed.

The ride was eerily similar to a hundred stoned drives with friends in

Australia and New Zealand when we'd smoked hash or grass, put loud music on the dashboard player, and cruised together in a car. Within my own culture, however, it was mainly the young who smoked and cruised with the music on max. There, I was in the company of a very powerful and influential senior man who was much older than Abdullah, the driver, and me. And while the songs followed regular rhythms, they were in a language that I couldn't understand. The experience was familiar and disturbing at the same time—something like returning, as an adult, to the schoolyard of childhood—and despite the soporific slump of the drug, I couldn't entirely relax.

I had no idea where we were going. I had no idea how or when we would return. We were travelling toward Tardeo, which was the opposite direction to my home in the Colaba slum. As the minutes passed, I reflected on that particularly Indian custom of amiable abduction. For months, in the slum, I'd succumbed to the vague and mysterious invitations of friends to accompany them to unspecified places, for unknown purposes. *You come,* people said with smiling urgency, never feeling the need to tell me where we were going, or why. *You come now!* I'd resisted it a few times, at first, but I soon learned that those obscure, unplanned journeys were invariably worthwhile, frequently interesting and enjoyable, and quite often important. Little by little, I learned to relax, and submit, and trust my instincts, just as I was doing with Khaderbhai. I never regretted it, and I was never once hurt or disappointed by the friends who abducted me.

As the car crested the long, slow hill, leading down to the Haji Ali Mosque, Abdullah turned off the cassette and asked Khaderbhai if he wanted to make his regular stop at the restaurant there. Khader stared at me reflectively for a moment, and then smiled and nodded to the driver. He tapped me on the hand twice with the knuckles of his left hand, and touched his thumb to his lips. *Be silent now,* the gesture said. *Look, but don't speak.*

We pulled into a parking bay, beside and a little apart from a row of twenty other cars outside the Haji Ali Restaurant. Although most of Bombay slept after midnight, or at least pretended to sleep, there were centres of sound and colour and activity in the city. The trick lay in knowing where to find them. The restaurant near the Haji Ali shrine was one of those places. Hundreds of people gathered there every night to eat, and meet, and buy drinks or cigarettes or sweets. They came in taxis and private cars and on motorcycles, hour after hour, until dawn. The restaurant itself was small and always full. Most of the patrons preferred to stand on the footpath, and sit in or on their cars, to eat. Music blasted from many of the cars. People shouted in Urdu, Hindi, Marathi, and English. Waiters scurried from the counter to the cars and back, carrying drinks, parcels, and trays with stylish skill.

The restaurant broke the business curfew, and should've been closed down by the officers of the Haji Ali police post, which was only twenty metres away. But Indian pragmatism recognised that civilised people in large, modern cities needed places to gather and hunt. The owners of certain oases of noise and fun were permitted to bribe various officials and cops in order to stay open, virtually all night. That wasn't, however, the same thing as having a licence. Such restaurants and bars were operating illegally, and sometimes the appearance of compliance had to be displayed. Regular phone calls alerted the police post at Haji Ali when a commissioner or a minister or some other VIP intended to drive past. With a co-operative bustle, the lights were turned out, the cars dispersed, and the restaurant was forced to a temporary close. Far from discouraging people, that small inconvenience added a touch of glamour and adventure to the commonplace act of buying snacks. Everyone knew that the restaurant at Haji Ali, like every other illegal nightspot in town that faked a close, would reopen in less than half an hour. Everyone knew about the bribes that were paid and taken. Everyone knew about the warning phone calls. Everyone profited, and everyone was well pleased. *The worst thing about corruption as a system of governance*, Didier once said, *is that it works so well.*

The headwaiter, a young Maharashtrian, hurried up to the car and nodded energetically as our driver ordered for us. Abdullah got out of the car, and walked to the long, crowded take-away counter. I watched him. He walked with an athlete's touchy grace. He was taller than most of the other young men around him, and there was a striking, heads-up confidence in his bearing. His black hair was long at the back, reaching almost to his shoulders. He wore simple, inexpensive clothes—soft black shoes, black trousers, and a white silk shirt—but they suited him well, and he carried them with a certain martial elegance. His body was well muscled, and he looked to be about twenty-eight years old. He turned toward the car, and I caught sight of his face. It was a handsome face, calm and composed. I knew the source of that composure. I'd seen the swift and lethal way he'd moved to disarm the swordsman at the den of the Standing Babas.

A few customers and all of the counter staff recognised Abdullah, and talked, smiled, or joked as he ordered cigarettes and paan. Their gestures were exaggerated. Their laughter was louder than it had been moments before. They crowded against one another, and reached out to touch him often. It seemed that they were almost desperate to be liked by him, even just to be noticed by him. But there was hesitancy as well—a kind of reluctance—as if, despite everything in their talk and smiles, they didn't really like or trust him. It was also very clear that they were afraid of him.

The waiter returned, and passed our food and drinks to the driver. He lingered at the open window beside Khaderbhai, his eyes pleading to speak.

'Your father, Ramesh, he is well?' Khader asked him.

'Yes, bhai, he is well. But … but … I have a problem,' the young waiter answered, in Hindi. He tugged nervously at the edge of his moustache.

Khaderbhai frowned, and stared hard into the worried face.

'What kind of problem are you having, Ramesh?'

'It's … it's my landlord, bhai. There is … there will be an eviction. I, we, my family, we are paying double rent already. But the landlord … the landlord is greedy, and he wants to evict us.'

Khader nodded thoughtfully. Drawing encouragement from his silence, Ramesh plunged on in rapid Hindi.

'It's not just my family, bhai. All the families in the building are to be evicted. We have tried everything, made very good offers, but the landlord will not listen to us. He has *goondas*, and those gangsters have made threats, and even done some beatings. My own father was beaten. I am ashamed that I have not killed that landlord, bhai, but I know that this would only bring more trouble on my family and the other families in the building. I told my very honoured father that we should tell you, and that you would protect us. But my father is too proud. You know him. And he loves you, bhai. He will not disturb your peace to ask for help. He will be very angry if he knows that I spoke of our trouble in this way. But when I saw you tonight, my lord Khaderbhai, I thought that … that the Bhagwan had brought you here to me. I … I am very sorry to disturb you …'

He fell silent, swallowing hard. His fingers were white in their grip on his metal tray.

'We will see what can be done about your problems, Ramu,' Khaderbhai said slowly. The affectionate diminutive of the name Ramesh, *Ramu*, provoked a wide, child's smile on the young face. 'You will come and see me tomorrow, at two o'clock sharp. We will talk further. We will help you, *Inshallah*. Oh, and Ramu—there will be no need to speak to your father about this, until the problem, *Inshallah*, has been solved.'

Ramesh looked as though he wanted to seize Khader's hand and kiss it, but he simply bowed and backed away, muttering his thanks. Abdullah and the driver had ordered plates of fruit salad and coconut yoghurt, and they ate with noisy appreciation when the four of us were alone. Khaderbhai and I had ordered only mango-flavoured lassi. As we sipped the iced drinks, another visitor came to the window of the car. It was the chief officer of the Haji Ali police post.

'A great honour to see you again, Khaderji,' he said, his face writhing into a grimace that was either a reaction to stomach cramp, or an oily smile. He spoke Hindi with the strong accent of some dialect, and I found it difficult to understand. He asked after Khaderbhai's family, and then made some reference to business interests.

Abdullah put his empty plate down on the front seat, and drew a packet, wrapped in newspapers, from under the seat. He passed it across to Khader, who opened a corner of the packet to reveal a thick bundle of hundred-rupee notes, and then passed it casually through the window to the cop. It was done so openly, and even ostentatiously, that I felt sure it was important to Khader that everyone within a hundred metres would see the bribe made and taken.

The cop scrunched the parcel into the front of his shirt, and leaned aside to spit twice noisily, for luck. He came close to the window once more, and began to speak in a quick, urgent murmur. I caught the words *body* and *bargain*, and something about the *Thief Bazaar*, but I couldn't make sense of it. Khader silenced him with a raised hand. Abdullah looked from Khader to me, and then broke into a boyish grin.

'Come with me, Mr. Lin,' he said quietly. 'We will see the mosque, isn't it?'

As we got out of the car I heard the cop say loudly, *The gora speaks Hindi? Bhagwan save us from foreigners!*

We walked to a deserted spot on the sea wall. The mosque, at Haji Ali, was built upon a small, flat island that was connected to the mainland by a stone path, three hundred and thirty-three steps long. From dawn to dusk, the tide permitting, that broad pathway was thronged with pilgrims and tourists. At high tide, the path was completely submerged, and deep waters isolated the island. Seen from the retaining wall on the road beside the sea, the mosque at night seemed like a great moored ship. Brass lanterns, throwing green and yellow light, swung from brackets on the marble walls. In the moonlight, the teardrop arches and rounded contours glowed white and became the sails of that mystic ship, and the minarets were so many towering spars.

On that night, the swollen, flattened, yellow moon—known in the slum as a *grieving moon*—hovered hypnotic-full, above the mosque. There was a breeze from the sea, but the air was warm and humid. Swarms of bats flying overhead, along the lines of electrical wires, thousands of them, were like musical notes on a strip of sheet music. A very small girl, awake past her bedtime and still selling ribbons of jasmine flowers, came up to us and gave Abdullah a garland. He reached into his pocket to give her some money, but she refused, laughing, and walked away singing the chorus of a song from a popular Hindi movie.

'There is no act of faith more beautiful than the generosity of the very poor,' Abdullah said, in his quiet tone. I had the impression that he never raised his voice above that softness.

'You speak English very well,' I commented, genuinely impressed by the sophisticated thought and the way he'd expressed it.

'No, I don't speak well. I knew a woman, and she taught me those words,' he replied. I waited for more, and he hesitated, looking out over the sea, but when he spoke again it was to change the subject. 'Tell me, Mr. Lin, that time at the den of the Standing Babas, when that man was coming for you with a sword—what would you have done if I was not there?'

'I would've fought him.'

'I think ...' He turned to stare into my eyes, and I felt my scalp tightening with an unaccountable dread. 'I think you would have died. You would have been murdered, and you would now be dead.'

'No. He had a sword, but he was old, and he was crazy. I would've beaten him.'

'Yes,' he said, not smiling. 'Yes, I think you are right—you would have beaten him. But the others, the girl and your Indian friend, one of them would have been hurt, or even killed, if you had survived. When the sword came down, if it did not strike you, it would have hit one of them, I think it is so. One of you would have died. You or your friends—one of you would be dead.'

It was my turn to be silent. The sense of dread I'd felt a moment before was suddenly a full-blown alarm. My heart was thumping a loudness of blood. He was talking about having saved my life, and yet I sensed a threat in his words. I didn't like it. Anger began to rise in me. I tensed, ready to fight him, and stared hard into his eyes.

He smiled, and put a hand on my shoulder, just as he'd done less than an hour before at another sea wall, on Marine Drive. As quickly as the tingling, intuitive sense of alarm arose, it also passed; as powerful as it had been, it was suppressed and gone. It was months before I thought of it again.

I turned to see the cop saluting and moving away from Khader's car.

'Khaderbhai was very conspicuous about giving that cop a bribe.'

Abdullah laughed, and I remembered the first time I'd heard him laugh out loud, in the den of the Standing Babas. It was a good laugh, guileless and completely unselfconscious, and I suddenly liked him because of it.

'We have a saying in Persian—*Sometimes the lion must roar, just to remind the horse of his fear*. This policeman has been making problems here at Haji Ali. The people do not respect him. For that, he is unhappy. His unhappiness is causing him to make problems. The more problems he makes, the less respect he gets from the people. Now they see such big baksheesh, more than a policeman like him is getting, and they will respect him a little. They will be impressed that the great Khaderbhai pays him so well. With this little respect, he will make less problems for all of us. But still, the message is very clear. He is a horse, but Khader is a lion. And the lion, it has roared.'

'Are you Khaderbhai's bodyguard?'

'No, no!' he laughed again. 'Lord Abdel Khader needs no protection. But ...' He paused, and we both looked at the grey-haired man in the back of the modest limousine. 'But I would die for him, if that is what you mean. That, and a lot more would I do for him.'

'There's not a lot more you can do for someone than die for them,' I replied, grinning at his earnestness as much as the strangeness of his idea.

'Oh yes,' he said, putting an arm around my shoulder and leading us back towards the car. 'There is a lot more.'

'You are making a friendship with our Abdullah, Mr. Lin?' Khaderbhai said as we climbed back into the car. 'This is a good thing. You should be close friends. You look like brothers.'

Abdullah and I looked at one another, and laughed gently at the words. My hair was blond, and his was ink black. My eyes were grey, and his were brown. He was Persian, and I was Australian. At first glance, we couldn't be more dissimilar. But Khaderbhai stared from one to the other of us with such a puzzled frown, and was so genuinely bewildered by our amusement, that we swallowed our laughter in smiles. And as the car headed out along the Bandra road, I thought about what Khader had said. I found myself thinking that, for all the differences between us, there just might be some perceptive truth in the older man's observation.

The car drove on for almost an hour. It slowed, at last, on the outskirts of Bandra, in a street of shops and warehouses, and then bumped into the entrance to a narrow lane. The street was dark and deserted, as was the lane. When the car doors opened, I could hear music and singing.

'Come, Mr. Lin. We go,' Khaderbhai said, feeling no compulsion to tell me where we were going or why.

The driver, Nazeer, remained with the car, leaning against the bonnet and finally allowing himself the luxury of unwrapping the paan that Abdullah had bought for him at Haji Ali. As I passed him to walk down the lane, I realised that Nazeer hadn't spoken a single word, and I wondered at the long silences so many Indian people practised in that crowded, noisy city.

We passed through a wide stone arch, along a corridor and, after climbing two flights of stairs, we entered a vast room filled with people, smoke, and clamorous music. It was a rectangular room, hung with green silks and carpets. At the far end there was a small, raised stage where four musicians sat on silk cushions. Around the walls there were low tables surrounded by comfortable cushions. Pale green, bell-shaped lanterns, suspended from the wooden ceiling, cast trembling hoops of yellow-gold light. Waiters moved from group to group, serving black tea in long glasses. At some of the tables there were hookah pipes, pearling the air with blue smoke, and the perfume of charras.

Several men rose immediately to greet Khaderbhai. Abdullah was also well known there. A number of people acknowledged him with a nod, wave, or spoken greeting. I noticed that the men in that room, unlike those at Haji Ali, embraced him warmly, and lingered as they held his hand between their own. I recognised one man in the crowd. It was Shafiq *Gussa*, or Shafiq *The Angry*, the controller of prostitution in the navy barracks area near the slum where I lived. I knew a few other faces —a well-known poet, a famous Sufi holy man, and a minor movie star— from photographs in newspapers.

One of the men near Khaderbhai was the manager of the private club. He was a short man, plumply buttoned into a long Kashmiri vest. The white lace cap of a *hajji*, one who'd made the pilgrimage to Mecca, covered his bald head. His forehead was discoloured by the dark, circular bruise some Muslims acquire through touching their foreheads to a stone in their devotions. He shouted instructions, and at once waiters brought a new table and several cushions, setting them up in a corner of the room with a clear view to the stage.

We sat cross-legged, with Khader in the centre, Abdullah at his right hand, and me at his left. A boy, wearing a hajji cap and Afghan pants and vest, brought us a bowl of popped rice, sharply spiced with chilli powders, and a platter of mixed nuts with dried fruits. The chai waiter poured hot, black tea from a narrow-spouted kettle through a metre of air without spilling a drop. He placed the tea before each of us and then offered sugar cubes. I was about to drink the tea without sugar, but Abdullah stopped me.

'Come, Mr. Lin,' he smiled, 'We are drinking Persian tea, in the real Iranian style, isn't it?'

He took a sugar cube and placed it in his mouth, holding it firmly between his front teeth. He lifted the glass then, and sipped the tea through the cube. I followed suit, imitating the steps. The sugar cube slowly crumbled and melted away and, although the taste was sweeter than I preferred, I enjoyed what was for me the strangeness of a new custom.

Khaderbhai also took a sugar cube and sipped his tea through it, endowing the little custom with a peculiar dignity and solemnity, as in fact he did with every expression and even the most casual gesture. He was the most imperial human being I'd ever met. Looking at him, then, as he inclined his head to listen to Abdullah's light-hearted conversation, the thought came to me that in any life, and in any world, he would command men, and inspire their obedience.

Three singers joined the musicians, and sat a little in front of them. A gradual silence settled in the room, and then all of a sudden the three men began to sing in powerful, thrilling voices. It was a luscious sound — a layered and gorgeous music of passionate intensity. The men weren't just singing, they were crying and wailing in song. Real tears ran from their closed eyes and dripped onto their chests. I was elated, listening to it; and yet, somehow, I felt ashamed. It was as if the singers had taken me into their deepest and most intimate love and sorrow.

They sang three songs then quietly left the stage, disappearing through a curtain into another room. No-one had spoken or moved during the performance, but then everyone spoke at once as we forced ourselves to break the spell that had enveloped us. Abdullah stood up and crossed the room to talk with a group of Afghans at another table.

'How do you like the singing, Mr. Lin?' Khaderbhai asked me.

'I like it very much. It's incredible, amazing. I've never heard anything like it. There was so much sadness in it, but so much power as well. What language was it? Urdu?'

'Yes. Do you understand Urdu?'

'No, I'm afraid I don't. I only speak a little Marathi and Hindi. I recognised it as Urdu because some of the people speak it around me, where I live.'

'Urdu is the language of gazals, and these are the best gazal singers in all Bombay,' he replied.

'Are they singing love songs?'

He smiled, and leaned across to rest his hand on my forearm. Throughout the city, people touched one another often during their conversations, emphasising the points they made with a gentle squeeze of pressure. I knew the gesture well from daily contact with my friends in the slum, and I'd come to like it.

'They are love songs, yes, but the best and most true of all love songs. They are love songs to God. These men are singing about loving God.'

I nodded, saying nothing, but my silence prompted him to speak again.

'You are a Christian fellow?' he asked.

'No. I don't believe in God.'

'There is no believing in God,' he declared, smiling again. 'We either *know* God, or we do not.'

'Well,' I laughed, 'I certainly don't *know* God, and frankly I'm inclined to think that God is impossible to believe in, at least most of the notions of God that I've come across.'

'Oh, of course, naturally, God is impossible. That is the first proof that He exists.'

He was staring at me intently, his hand still resting warm on my arm. *Be careful,* I thought. *You're getting into a philosophical discussion with a man who's famous for them. He's testing you. It's a test, and the water's deep.*

'Let me get this straight—you're saying that because something is impossible, it exists?' I asked, pushing a canoe of thought out into the uncharted water of his ideas.

'That is correct.'

'Well, wouldn't that mean that all the *possible* things *don't* exist?'

'Precisely!' he said, smiling more widely. 'I am delighted that you understand.'

'I can *say* those words,' I answered, laughing to match his smile, 'but that doesn't mean I *understand* them.'

'I will explain. Nothing exists as we see it. Nothing we see is really there, as we think we are seeing it. Our eyes are liars. Everything that seems real, is merely part of the illusion. Nothing exists, as we think it does. Not you. Not me. Not this room. Nothing.'

'I still don't get it. I don't see how *possible* things *don't* exist.'

'Let me put it another way. The agents of creation, the energy that actually animates the matter and the life that we think we see around us, cannot be measured or weighed or even put into time, as we know it. In one form, that energy is photons of light. The smallest object is a universe of open space to them, and the entire universe is but a speck of dust. What we call the world is just an idea—and not a very good one, yet. From the point of view of the light, the photon of light that animates it, the universe that *we* know is not real. Nothing is. Do you understand now?'

'Not really. It seems to me that if everything we think we know is wrong, or is an illusion, then none of us can know what to do, or how to live, or how to stay sane.'

'We lie,' he said with a flash of real humour in the gold-flecked amber of his eyes. 'The sane man is simply a better liar than the insane man. You and Abdullah are brothers. I know this. Your eyes lie, and tell you that this is not so. And you believe the lie, because it is easier.'

'And that's how we stay sane?'

'Yes. Let me tell you that I can see you as my son. I was not married, and I have no son, but there was a moment of time, yes, when it was possible for me to be married, and to have a son. And that moment of time was—how old are you?'

'I'm thirty.'

'Exactly! I knew it. That moment of time, when I could have been a father, was exactly thirty years ago. But if I tell you that I see it clearly, that you are my son, and I am your father, you will think that it is impossible. You will resist it. You will not see the truth, that I see now, and that I saw in the first moments when we met, a few hours ago. You will prefer to make a convenient lie, and to believe it—the lie that we are strangers, and that there is no connection between us. But fate—you know fate? *Kismet* is the word, in the Urdu language—fate has every power over us, but two. Fate cannot control our free will, and fate cannot lie. Men lie, to themselves more than to others, and to others more often than they tell the truth. But fate does not lie. Do you see?'

I did see. My heart knew what he was saying, even as my rebellious mind rejected the words and the man who spoke them. Somehow, he'd found that sorrow in me. The hole in my life that a father should've filled was a prairie of longing. In the loneliest hours of those hunted years, I wandered there, as hungry for a father's love as a cellblock full of sentenced men in the last hour of New Year's Eve.

'No,' I lied. 'I'm sorry, but I just don't agree. I don't think you can make things true, just by believing them.'

'I have not said that,' he replied, patiently. 'What I am saying is that reality—as you see it, and as most people see it—is nothing more than an illusion. There is another reality, beyond what we see with our eyes. You have to *feel* your way into that reality with your heart. There is no other way.'

'It's just ... pretty confusing, your way of looking at things. Chaotic, in fact. Don't you find it chaotic, yourself?'

He smiled again.

'It is strange, at first, to think in the right way. But there are a few things we can know, a few things to be sure of, and it is relatively easy. Let me show you. To know the truth, all you have to do is close your eyes.'

'It's that easy?' I laughed.

'Yes. All you have to do is close your eyes. We can know God, for example, and we can know sadness. We can know dreams, and we can know love. But none of these are real, in our usual sense of things that exist in the world and seem real. We cannot weigh them, or measure their length, or find their basic parts in an atom smasher. Which is why they are possible.'

My canoe of thought was taking water, and I decided to bail out, fast.

'I've never heard of this place before. Are there many places like this?'

'Perhaps five,' he replied, accepting the change of topic with tolerant equanimity. 'Is that many, do you think?'

'I guess it's enough. There aren't any women. Are women not allowed to come here?'

'Not forbidden,' he frowned, casting about for the right words. 'Women are permitted here, but they do not want to come. There are other places where women gather, to do their own things and to hear music and singers, and no man would want to disturb them there, either.'

A very elderly man approached us and sat at Khaderbhai's feet. He wore the simple cotton shirt and thin baggy pants known as a kurta-pyjama. His face was deeply lined, and his white hair was cropped into a short, punk cut. He was thin and stooped and obviously poor. With a curt but respectful nod to Khader, he began to mull tobacco and hashish in his gnarled hands. In a few minutes he passed a huge chillum to Khader, and waited with matches ready to light it.

'This man is Omar,' Khaderbhai said, pausing with the chillum almost to his lips. 'He is the best maker of the chillum in all Bombay.'

Omar lit the chillum for Khaderbhai, breaking into a toothless grin and basking in the praise. He passed it to me, studied my technique and lung-power with a critical eye, and grunted a sort of approval. After Khader and I had smoked twice, Omar took the chillum and finished it with gigantic puffs that swelled his thin chest to bursting. When he was finished, he tapped out a small residue of white ash. He'd sucked the chillum dry, and proudly accepted a nod of acknowledgement from Khaderbhai. Despite his great age, he rose easily from the seated position without touching his hands to the floor. He hobbled away as the singers returned to the stage.

Abdullah rejoined us, bringing a cut-glass bowl filled with slices of mango, papaya, and watermelon. The scents of the fruits surrounded us as their tastes dissolved in our mouths. The singers began their next performance, singing just one song that continued for almost half an hour. It was a lush, tripartite harmony built upon a simple melody and improvised cadenzas. The musicians accompanying the singers on the harmonium and the tablas were animated, but the singers themselves were expressionless, motionless, with their eyes closed and their hands limp.

As before, the silent crowd in the club broke out in rowdy chatter when the singers left the small stage. Abdullah leaned across to speak to me.

'While we were driving here in the car, I was thinking about being brothers, Mr. Lin. I was thinking about what Khaderbhai said.'

'That's funny, so was I.'

'My two brothers—we were three brothers in my family in Iran, and now my two brothers, they are dead. They were killed in the war against Iraq. I have a sister, in Iran, but I have no brother. I am just one brother now. One brother is a sadness, isn't it?'

I couldn't answer him directly. My own brother was lost to me. My whole family was lost, and I was sure I would never see them again.

'I was thinking that perhaps Khaderbhai saw something true. Perhaps we really are looking like brothers.'

'Maybe we are.'

He smiled.

'I have decided to like you, Mr. Lin.'

He said it with such solemnity, despite the smile, that I had to laugh.

'Well, I guess in that case you'd better stop calling me *Mr. Lin*. It gives me the heebie-jeebies, anyway.'

'Jeebies?' he asked, earnestly. 'It is an Arabic word?'

'Don't worry about it. Just call me Lin.'

'Okay. I will call you *Lin*. I will call you *Lin brother*. And you will call me Abdullah, isn't it so?'

'I guess it is.'

'Then we will remember this night, at the concert of the blind singers, because it is the night we begin brothering for each other.'

'Did you say, the *blind* singers?'

'Yes. You don't know them? These are the Blind Singers of Nagpur.

They are famous in Bombay.'

'Are they from an institution?'

'Institution?'

'Yeah, a school for the blind, maybe. Something like that.'

'No, Lin brother. At one time they could see, just as we are seeing. But in a small village, near Nagpur, there was a blinding, and these men became blind.'

The noise around me was dizzying, and the once pleasant smell of the fruits and the charras was beginning to cloy and stifle.

'What do you mean, there was a *blinding*?'

'Well, there were rebels and bandits, hiding in the mountains, near that village,' he explained in his slow, deliberate way. 'The villagers had to give them food, and other help. They had no choice. But when the police and soldiers came to the village, they made twenty people blind, as a lesson, as a warning to other people, in other villages. This happens sometimes. The singers were not from that village. They were visiting there, to sing at a festival. It was just bad luck. They were made blind, with the rest. All of them, those men and women, twenty people, were tied on the ground, and their eyes were put out, with sharp pieces of bamboo. Now they sing here, everywhere, and are very famous. And rich also ...'

He talked on. I listened, but I couldn't respond or react. Khaderbhai sat next to me, conversing with a young, turbaned Afghan. The young man bent low to kiss Khader's hand, and the butt of a gun appeared within the folds of his robe. Omar returned and began to prepare another chillum. He grinned up at me with his stained gums, and nodded.

'Yes, yes,' he lisped, staring into my eyes. 'Yes, yes, yes.'

The singers came back to sing again, and smoke spiralled up into the slash of slowly revolving fans, and that green silk room of music and conspiracies became a beginning for me. I know now that there *are* beginnings, turning points, many of them, in every life; questions of luck and will and fate. The naming day, the day of the flood sticks in Prabaker's village, when the women gave me the name Shantaram, was a beginning. I know that now. And I know that everything else I'd been and done in India up to that night and the concert of the blind singers, perhaps even the whole of my life, was a preparation for that beginning with Abdel Khader Khan. Abdullah became my brother. Khaderbhai became my father. By the time I realised that fully, and knew the reasons for it, my new life as brother and son had taken me to war, and involved me in murder, and everything had changed forever.

Khaderbhai leaned across after the singing stopped. His lips were moving, and I knew he was speaking to me, but for a moment I couldn't hear him.

'I'm sorry, I couldn't hear you.'

'I said that the truth is found more often in music,' he repeated, 'than it is in books of philosophy.'

'What *is* the truth?' I asked him. I didn't really want to know. I was trying to hold up my end of the conversation. I was trying to be clever.

'The truth is that there are no good men, or bad men,' he said. 'It is the deeds that have goodness or badness in them. There are good deeds, and bad deeds. Men are just men—it is what they do, or refuse to do, that links them to good and evil. The truth is that an instant of real love, in the heart of anyone—the noblest man alive or the most wicked—has the whole purpose and process and meaning of life within the lotus-folds of its passion. The truth is that we are all, every one of us, every atom, every galaxy, and every particle of matter in the universe, moving toward God.'

Those words of his are mine forever now. I can hear them. The blind singers are forever. I can see them. The night, and the men that were the beginning, father and brother, are forever. I can remember them. It's easy. All I have to do is close my eyes.

CHAPTER TEN

Abdullah took his brothering seriously. A week after the Night of the Blind Singers, he arrived at my hut in the Cuffe Parade slum carrying a satchel filled with medicines, salves, and bandages. He also brought a small metal case containing a few surgical instruments. We went through the bag together. He asked me about the medicines, wanting to know how useful they were and what quantities I might need in the future. When he'd satisfied himself, he dusted off the wooden stool and sat down. He was silent for a few minutes, watching me pack the supplies he'd brought into a rack of bamboo shelves. The crowded slum chattered, brawled, sang, and laughed around us.

'Well, Lin, where are they?' he finally asked.

'Where's who?'

'The patients. Where are they? I want to see my brother healing them. There can't be healing, without sick people, isn't it?'

'I, er, I don't have any patients just now.'

'Oh,' he sighed. He frowned, drumming his fingers on his knees. 'Well, do you think I should go and get you some?'

He half rose from his seat, and I had a vision of him dragging sick and injured people to my hut by force.

'No, no, take it easy. I don't see people every day. But if I *do* see people, if I'm *here*, they usually start coming around two o'clock. They don't come this early in the morning. Nearly everyone works until at least noon. I'm usually working myself. I have to earn money too, you know.'

'But not this morning?'

'No, not today. I made some money last week. Enough to last me for a while.'

'How did you make this money?'

He stared at me ingenuously, unaware that the question might embarrass me or be taken as rude.

'It's not polite to ask foreigners how they make their money, Abdullah,' I informed him, laughing.

'Oh, I see,' he said, smiling. 'You made it by the illegal means.'

'Well, that's not exactly the point. But yes, now that you mention it. There was this French girl who wanted to buy half a kilo of charras. I found it for her. And I helped a German guy get a fair price for his Canon camera. They were both commission jobs.'

'How much did you make with this business?' he asked, his eyes not wavering. They were a very pale brown, those eyes, almost a golden colour. They were the colour of sand dunes in the Thar Desert, on the last day before it rains.

'I made about a thousand rupees.'

'Each business, one thousand?'

'No, both jobs together made a thousand.'

'This is very little money, Lin brother,' he said, his nose wrinkling and his mouth puckering with contempt. 'This is tiny, tiny, very small money.'

'Well, it might be tiny to you,' I mumbled defensively, 'but it's enough to keep me going for a couple of weeks or so.'

'And now you are free, isn't it?'

'Free?'

'You have no patients?'

'No.'

'And you have no little commission business to do?'

'No.'

'Good. Then we go together, now.'

'Oh, yeah? Where are we going?'

'Come, I will tell you when we get there.'

We stepped out of the hut and were greeted by Johnny Cigar, who'd obviously been eavesdropping. He smiled at me, and scowled at Abdullah, then smiled at me again with traces of the scowl in the shadows of his smile.

'Hi, Johnny. I'm going out for a while. Make sure the kids don't get into the medicines, okay? I put some new stuff into the shelves today, and some of it's dangerous.'

Johnny thrust his jaw out to defend his wounded pride.

'Nobody will touch anything in your hut, Linbaba! What are you saying? You could put millions of rupees in there, and nobody would touch anything. Gold also you could put in there. The Bank of India is not as safe as this, Linbaba's hut.'

'I only meant that ...'

'And diamonds, also, you can leave in there. And emeralds. And pearls.'

'I get the picture, Johnny.'

'No need to worry about all that,' Abdullah interjected. 'He makes such tiny money that nobody would have the interest to be taking it. Do you know how much money he made last week?'

Johnny Cigar seemed suspicious of Abdullah. The hostile scowl pinched his face a little tighter, but he was intrigued by the question, and his curiosity got the better of him.

'How much?'

'I don't think we need to go into this right now, guys,' I grumbled, struggling to head off what I knew could become a one-hour discussion of my tiny money.

'One thousand rupees,' Abdullah said, spitting for emphasis.

I seized him by the arm and gave him a shove along the path between the huts.

'Okay, Abdullah. We were going somewhere, weren't we? Let's get on with it, brother.'

We took a few steps, but Johnny Cigar came after us and tugged at my shirtsleeve, pulling me a pace or two behind Abdullah.

'For God's sake, Johnny! I don't want to talk about how much money I made, right now. I promise, you can nag me about it later but ...'

'No, Linbaba, not about that,' he rasped, in a scratchy whisper. 'That man, that Abdullah—you shouldn't trust him! Don't do any business with him!'

'What is this? What's the matter, Johnny?'

'Just don't!' he said, and might've said more, but Abdullah turned and called to me, and Johnny sulked off, vanishing in a twist of lane.

'What is the problem?' Abdullah asked as I drew level with him, and we set off between the snaking lines of huts.

'Oh, no problem,' I muttered, knowing that there was. 'No problem at all.'

Abdullah's motorcycle was parked on the roadway, outside the slum, where several kids were watching over it. The tallest of them snapped up the ten-rupee tip Abdullah gave them, and then led his ragged urchin band away at a whooping run. Abdullah kicked the engine over, and I climbed up onto the pillion seat behind him. Wearing no helmets, and only thin shirts, we swung out into the friendly chaos of traffic, heading parallel to the sea towards Nariman Point.

If you know bikes at all, you can tell a lot about a man by how he rides. Abdullah rode from reflex rather than concentration. His control of the bike in motion was as natural as his control of his legs in walking. He read the traffic with a mix of skill and intuition. Several times, he slowed before there was an obvious need, and avoided the hard braking that other, less instinctive riders were forced to make. Sometimes he accelerated into an invisible gap that opened magically for us, just when a collision seemed imminent. Although unnerving at first, the technique did soon inspire a kind of grudging confidence in me, and I relaxed in the ride.

At Chowpatty Beach, we turned away from the sea, and the cool breeze from the bay was stilled and then choked off by streets of tall terraces. We joined shoals of traffic in a steamy drift towards Nana Chowk. The architecture there was from the middle period of Bombay's development as a great port city. Some of the buildings, constructed in the sturdy geometries of the British Raj, were two hundred years old. The detailed intricacies of balconies, window surrounds, and stepped facades reflected a luxurious elegance that the modern city, for all its chrome and glamour, rarely afforded itself.

The section from Nana Chowk to Tardeo was known as a Parsee area. It had surprised me, at first, that a city so polymorphous as Bombay, with its unceasing variety of peoples, languages, and pursuits, tended to such narrow concentrations. The jewellers had their own bazaar, as did the mechanics, plumbers, carpenters, and other trades. The Muslims had their own quarter, as did the Christians, Buddhists, Sikhs, Parsees, and Jains. If you wanted to buy or sell gold, you visited the Zhaveri bazaar, where hundreds of goldsmiths competed for your custom. If you wanted to visit a mosque, you found several of them within walking distance of one another.

But after a while I realised that the demarcations, like so many other long and short lines of division in the complex, culturally polyglot city, were not as rigid as they'd seemed. The Muslim quarter had its Hindu temples, the Zhaveri bazaar had its vegetable sellers among the glittering jewels, and almost every tower of luxury apartments had its adjacent slum.

Abdullah parked the bike outside the Bhatia Hospital, one of several modern hospitals and clinics which were endowed by charitable Parsee trusts. The large building housed expensive wards for the rich, and free treatment centres for the poor. We climbed the steps and entered a spotlessly clean marble foyer pleasantly cooled by large fans. Abdullah spoke to the receptionist and then led me down a corridor to the busy casualty and admissions section. After more questions to a porter and a nurse, he finally located the man he sought—a short and very thin doctor who sat at a cluttered desk.

'Doctor Hamid?' Abdullah asked.

The doctor was writing, and didn't look up.

'Yes, yes,' he answered testily.

'I have come from Sheik Abdel Khader. My name is Abdullah.'

The pen stopped at once, and Doctor Hamid slowly lifted his head. He stared at us with a look of apprehensive curiosity. It was a look you see sometimes on the faces of bystanders witnessing a fight.

'He telephoned to you yesterday, and told you to expect me?' Abdullah prompted quietly.

'Yes, yes of course,' Hamid said, regaining his composure in an easy smile. He stood up to shake hands across the desk.

'This is Mr. Lin,' Abdullah introduced me, as the doctor and I shook hands. It was a very dry and fragile hand. 'He is the doctor in the Colaba hutments.'

'No, no,' I protested. 'I'm not a doctor. I've just been sort of co-opted into helping out there. And I'm ... I'm not trained for it, and ... not really very good at it.'

'Khaderbhai tells me that when you spoke to him, you complained about the referrals you're making to the St. George and other hospitals,' Hamid said, getting down to business, and ignoring my protest with the air of a man who was too busy to indulge another's modesty. His eyes were dark brown, almost black, and glistening behind the polished lenses of his gold-framed glasses.

'Well, yes,' I replied, surprised that Khaderbhai had remembered my conversation with him, and that he'd found it important enough to tell the doctor. 'The problem is that I'm flying blind, if you know what I mean. I don't know enough to cope with all the problems people come to me with. When I come across illnesses that I can't identify, or what I think are probably illnesses, I send them to the diagnostic clinic at St. George Hospital. I don't know what else to do with them. But a lot of the time they come back to me without having seen anyone — no doctors, no nurses, no-one.'

'These people are not feigning illness, you think?'

'No. I'm sure.' I was a little offended for myself, and even more indignant for the slum-dwellers. 'They've got nothing to gain by pretending to be sick. And they're proud people. They don't ask for help lightly.'

'Of course,' he murmured, removing his glasses to rub at the deep ridges they'd imposed on his nose. 'And have you been to the St. George yourself? Have you seen anyone there to ask them about this?'

'Yes. I went there twice. They told me they're swamped with patients, and they do the best they can. They suggested that if I could get referrals from licensed medical practitioners, then the slum-dwellers could jump the queue, so to speak. I'm not complaining about them, at the St. George. They've got their own problems. They're under-staffed and over-crowded. In my little clinic, I look at about fifty patients a day. They get six hundred patients every day. Sometimes as many as a thousand. I'm sure you know how it is. I think they're doing the best they can, and they're pushed to the limit just trying to treat the emergency cases. The real problem is that my people can't afford to see a real doctor, to get the referral that would help them jump the queue at the hospital. They're too poor. That's why they come to *me*.'

Doctor Hamid raised his eyebrows, and offered me that easy smile.

'You said *my people*. Are you becoming such an Indian, Mr. Lin?'

I laughed, and answered him in Hindi for the first time, using a line from the theme song to a popular movie that was showing, then, in many cinemas.

'In this life, we do what we can to improve ourselves.'

Hamid also laughed, clapping his hands together once in pleased surprise.

'Well, Mr. Lin, I think I may be able to help you. I am on duty here two days a week, but the rest of the time I can be found at my surgery, in Fourth Pasta Lane.'

'I know Fourth Pasta Lane. That's very close to us.'

'Precisely, and, after speaking to Khaderbhai, I have agreed that you should begin referring your patients to me, when you need it, and I will arrange treatment at St. George Hospital when I think it is required. We can begin from tomorrow, if you wish.'

'Yes, I do,' I said quickly. 'I mean, it's great, thank you, thank you very much. I don't know how we're going to go about paying you but ...'

'No need for thanks, and no need to worry about payment,' he replied, glancing at Abdullah. 'My services will be free for *your people*. Perhaps you would like to join me for tea? I take a break here soon. There is a restaurant across the road from the hospital. If you can wait for me there, I will come across and join you. We have, I think, much to discuss.'

Abdullah and I left him, and waited for twenty minutes in the restaurant, watching through a large window as poor patients hobbled to the entrance of the hospital, and rich patients were delivered in taxis and private cars. Doctor Hamid joined us, and outlined the procedures I was to follow in referring the slum-dwellers to his practice in Fourth Pasta Lane.

Good doctors have at least three things in common: they know how to observe, they know how to listen, and they're very tired. Hamid was a good doctor, and when, after an hour of discussion, I looked into his prematurely lined face, the eyes burned and reddened by lack of sleep, I felt shamed by his honest exhaustion. He could accumulate wealth, I knew, and surround himself with luxury, in private practice in Germany or Canada or America, yet he chose to be there, with his own people, for a fraction of the reward. He was one of thousands of health professionals working in the city, with careers as distinguished in what they denied themselves as in what they achieved every working day. And what they achieved was no less than the survival of the city.

When Abdullah took us into the plaited traffic once more, his bike weaving a haphazard progress through the threads of buses, cars, trucks, bicycles, bullock wagons, and pedestrians, he called over his shoulder to tell me that Doctor Hamid had once lived in a slum himself. He said that Khaderbhai had taken especially gifted slum children from several slums throughout the city, and paid for their enrolment in private colleges. Through secondary and then tertiary studies, the children were provided for and encouraged. They graduated to become physicians, surgeons, nurses, teachers, lawyers, and engineers. Hamid was one of those gifted children who'd been selected more than twenty years before. In response to the needs of my small clinic, Khaderbhai was calling in some dues.

'Khaderbhai is a man who *makes* the future,' Abdullah concluded, as we stopped for a traffic signal. 'Most of us—me and you, my brother—we wait for the future to come to us. But Abdel Khader Khan dreams the future, and then he plans it, and then he makes it happen. That is the difference between him and the rest of us.'

'What about *you*, Abdullah?' I asked him in a shout as we roared off with the traffic once more. 'Did Khaderbhai plan *you*?'

He laughed out loud, his chest heaving with the pleasure and the force of the laugh.

'I think he did!' he replied.

'Hey! This isn't the way back to the slum. Where are we going now?'

'We are going to visit the place where you will be getting your medicines.'

'My what?'

'Khaderbhai has arranged for you to get medicines, every week. The things I brought you today—those are the first. We are going to the medicine black market.'

'A black market for medicine? Where is it?'

'In the slum of the lepers,' Abdullah answered, matter-of-factly. Then he laughed again as he pushed the bike to greater speed through a gap in the traffic that opened for him, even as he reached it. 'Just leave it to me, Lin brother. Now *you* are part of the plan, isn't it so?'

Those words—*now you are part of the plan*—should've woken some fear in me. I should've sensed ... something ... even then, right at the start. But I wasn't afraid. I was almost happy. The words seemed exciting. They rushed my blood. When my fugitive life began, I was exiled *from* my family, homeland, and culture. I thought that was the whole of it. Years into the banishment, I realised that I was exiled *to* something, as well. What I escaped to was the lonely, reckless freedom of the outcast. Like outcasts everywhere, I courted danger because danger was one of the few things strong enough to help me forget what I'd lost. And staring into the warmth of the afternoon wind, riding with Abdullah into the web of streets, I fell as fearlessly into my fate, that afternoon, as a man falls into love with a shy woman's best smile.

The journey to the lepers' camp took us to the outskirts of the city.

There were several treatment colonies for Bombay's lepers, but the men and women we went to see refused to live in them. Funded by state and private contributions, the colonies provided medical attention, caring support, and clean environments. The rules and regulations that governed them were strict, however, and not all the lepers could bring themselves to conform. As a result, some chose to leave, and some were forced out. At any one time, a few dozen men, women, and children lived outside the colonies, in the wider community of the city.

The elastic tolerance of slum-dwellers—who accommodated every caste and race and condition of person within their sprawl of huts— rarely extended to lepers. Local councils and street committees didn't endure their presence for long. Feared and shunned, the lepers formed themselves into mobile slums that settled, within an hour, in any open space they could find, and made a traceless departure in even less time. Sometimes they established themselves for several weeks beside a rubbish dump, fending off the permanent rag-pickers, who resisted their incursion. At other times they set up their camp on a swampy patch of vacant land or some outfall for industrial waste. When I first visited them with Abdullah, that day, I found that they'd built their ragged shelters on the rusty stones of a railway siding near the suburb of Khar.

We were forced to park Abdullah's bike, and enter the railway land as the lepers did, through gaps in fences and across ditches. The rusty plateau was a staging area for most trains on the urban route and many of the goods wagons carrying produce and manufactured articles out of the city. Beyond the sub-station itself were office outbuildings, storage warehouses, and maintenance sheds. Further on was a vast shunting area—an open space marked by dozens of railway lines and their confluences. At the outer edges, high wire fences enclosed the space.

Outside was the commerce and cosiness of suburban Khar: traffic and gardens, balconies and bazaars. Within was the aridity of function and systems. There were no plants, no animals, and no people. Even the rolling stock were ghost trains, trundling from shunting stop to shunting stop without staff or passengers. Then there was the lepers' slum.

They'd seized a diamond of clear space between the tracks for themselves, and patched their shelters together in it. None of the huts was taller than my chest. From a distance, they looked like the pup tents of an army bivouac wreathed in the smoke of cooking fires. As we neared them, however, we saw that their appalling raggedness made the slum huts where I lived seem like solid, comfortable structures. They were made from scraps of cardboard and plastic held aloft with crooked branches, and braced with thin string. I could've knocked the whole camp to rubble with an open hand, and it would've taken me less than a minute, yet thirty men, women, and children made their lives there.

We entered the slum unchallenged, and made our way to one of the huts near the center. People stopped and stared at us, but no-one spoke. It was hard not to look at them, and then hard not to stare when I did look. Some of the people had no noses, most of them had no fingers, the feet of many were bound in bloody bandages, and some were so advanced into the deteriorations that their lips and ears were missing.

I don't know why—the price, perhaps, that women pay for their loveliness—but the disfigurements seemed more ghastly for the women than they were for the men. Many of the men had a defiant and even a jaunty air about them—a kind of pugnacious ugliness that was fascinating in itself. But shyness just looked cowed in the women, and hunger looked predatory. The disease was indiscernible in the many children I saw. They looked fit, if uniformly thin, and quite well. And they worked hard, all of those children. Their small fingers did the grasping for the whole of their tribe.

They'd seen us coming, and must've passed the word because, as we approached the hut, a man crawled out and stood to greet us. Two children came at once and supported him. He was tiny, reaching to just above my waist, and severely stricken with the disease. His lips and the lower part of his face were eaten away to a hard, knobby ridge of dark flesh that extended downwards from the cheeks to the hinges of his jaw. The jaw itself was exposed, as were the teeth and gums, and the gaping holes where his nose had been.

'Abdullah, my son,' he said, in Hindi. 'How are you? Have you eaten?'

'I am well, Ranjitbhai.' Abdullah replied in respectful tones. 'I have brought the gora to meet you. We have just now eaten, but we will drink tea, thank you.'

Children brought stools to us, and we sat there in the open space in front of Ranjit's hut. A small crowd gathered and sat on the ground, or stood around us.

'This is Ranjitbhai,' Abdullah told me, in Hindi, speaking loudly enough for all to hear. 'He is the boss here, the senior fellow, in the slum of the lepers. He is the king here, in this club for *kala topis*.'

Kala topi means *black hat* in Hindi, and it's a phrase used, sometimes, to describe a thief, referring to the black-banded hats that convicted thieves were forced to wear in Bombay's Arthur Road Prison. I wasn't sure exactly what Abdullah had meant by the remark, but Ranjit and the other lepers took it well enough, smiling and repeating the phrase several times.

'Greetings, Ranjitbhai,' I said, in Hindi. 'My name is Lin.'

'*Aap doctor hain?*' he asked. *You are a doctor?*

'No!' I almost shouted in panic, disconcerted by the disease and my ignorance of it, and afraid he would ask me to help them. I turned to Abdullah, and switched to English. 'Tell him I'm not a doctor, Abdullah. Tell him I just do a little first aid, and treat rat bites and scratches caused by the barbed wire, and things like that. Explain to him. Tell him that I haven't had any real training, and I don't know the first thing about leprosy.'

Abdullah nodded, and then faced Ranjitbhai.

'Yes,' he said. 'He is a doctor.'

'Thank you very much, Abdullah,' I gnashed out through clenched teeth.

Children brought full glasses of water for us, and tea in chipped cups. Abdullah drank his water in quick gulps. Ranjit tilted his head back, and one of the children tipped the water in a gurgle down his throat. I hesitated, fearful of the grotesque sickness around me. One of the slum words in Hindi for *lepers* can be translated as *the undead*, and I felt that I was holding the nightmares of the undead in my hands. All the world of suffering disease was concentrated in that glass of water, it seemed to me.

But Abdullah had drunk his glass. I was sure he'd calculated the risks, and decided it was safe. And every day of my life was a risk. Every hour had its hazards, after the big gamble of escape from prison. The voluptuous recklessness of a fugitive moved my arm to my mouth, and I drank the water down. Forty pairs of eyes watched me drink.

Ranjit's own eyes were honey-coloured, and clouded by what I judged to be incipient cataracts. He examined me closely, those eyes roving from my feet to my hair and back, several times, with unshy curiosity.

'Khaderbhai has told me that you need medicines,' he said slowly, in English.

His teeth clicked together as he spoke, and with no lips to help him form the words, his speech was difficult to understand. The letters B, F, P, and V were impossible, for example, with M and W coming out as other sounds altogether. The mouth forms more than just words, of course: it forms attitudes and moods and nuances of meaning, and those expressive hints were also missing. And he had no fingers, so even that aid to communication was denied him. Instead, there was a child, perhaps his son, who stood at his shoulder and repeated his words in a quiet but steady voice, one beat behind the rhythm of his speech, just as a translator might.

'We are always happy to help lord Abdel Khader,' the two voices said. 'I have the honour to serve him. We can give you much medicine, every week, no problem. First-class stuff, as you see.'

He shouted a name, then, and a tall boy in his early teens pushed through the crowd to lay a canvas bundle at my feet. He knelt to roll out the canvas, and revealed a collection of ampoules and plastic bottles. There was morphine hydrochloride, penicillin, and antibiotics for staph and strep infections. The containers were labelled and new.

'Where do they get this stuff?' I asked Abdullah as I examined the medicines.

'They steal it,' he answered me, in Hindi.

'Steal it? How do they steal it?'

'*Bahut hoshiyaar*,' he replied. *Very cleverly*.

'*Yes, yes*.'

A chorus of voices surrounded us. There was no humour in that concord. They accepted Abdullah's praise solemnly, as if he was admiring some work of art they'd collectively produced. *Good thieves*, *clever thieves*, I heard people mutter around me.

'What do they do with it?'

'They sell it on the black market,' he told me, still speaking in Hindi, so that all those present could follow our conversation. 'They survive nicely from this, and other very good stealing.'

'I don't get it. Why would anyone buy medicine from them? You can buy this stuff from just about any chemist.'

'You want to know everything, brother Lin, isn't it? Well then, we must have another cup of tea, because this is a two-cups-of-tea story.'

The crowd laughed at that, and pressed a little closer, picking out places to sit near us for the story. A large, empty, unattended goods wagon rumbled past slowly on an adjacent track, perilously close to the huts. No-one gave it more than a cursory glance. A railway worker, dressed in khaki shirt and shorts, strolled between the lines, inspecting the rails. He looked up at the lepers' camp from time to time, but his mild curiosity faded as he passed us, and he never looked back. Our tea arrived, and we sipped it as Abdullah began his story. Several of the children were sitting against our legs, their arms wrapped around one another companionably. One little girl slipped her arm around my right leg, and hugged me with artless affection.

Abdullah spoke in very simple Hindi, repeating some passages in English, when he perceived that I hadn't understood. He began by talking of the British Raj, the time when Europeans controlled all of India from the Khyber Pass to the Bay of Bengal. The *firengi*, the foreigners, he said, gave lepers the lowest priority on their scale of privileges and entitlements. As the last in line, lepers often missed out on the limited supply of medicines, bandages, and medical treatment. When famine or flood struck, even the traditional medicines and herbal remedies were in short supply. The lepers became skilled at stealing what they couldn't obtain by other means—so skilled, in fact, that they accumulated surpluses, and began to sell medicines in their own black market.

In India's vastness, Abdullah went on, there were always conflicts— brigandage, rebellions, wars. Men fought, and blood was spilled. But many more men died through the festering of wounds and the ravages of disease than were killed in battles. One of the best sources of intelligence available to police forces and governments lay in the control of medicines, bandages, and expertise. All sales from chemists, hospital pharmacies, and pharmaceutical wholesalers were registered. Any purchase or string of purchases significantly greater than the established norm attracted attention that sometimes led to captures or killings. A telltale trail of medicines, particularly of antibiotics, had led to the downfall of many dacoits and revolutionaries. In their black market, however, the lepers asked no questions, and sold to anyone who could pay. Their networks and secret markets existed in every great city in India. Their customers were terrorists, infiltrators, separatists, or just more than usually ambitious outlaws.

'These people are dying,' Abdullah concluded, with the colourful turn of phrase that I was learning to expect from him, 'and they steal life for themselves, and then they sell life to others who are dying.'

When Abdullah finished speaking, there was a dense and ponderous silence. Everyone looked at me. They seemed to want some response, some reaction, to the story of their sadness and skill, their cruel isolation and violent indispensability. Whistling hisses of breath came through the clenched teeth of lipless mouths. Patient, serious eyes fixed me with expectant concentration.

'Can I ... can I have another glass of water, please?' I asked, in Hindi, and it must've been the right thing to say because the whole crowd started laughing. Several children rushed off to fetch the water, and a number of hands patted me on the back and shoulder.

Ranjitbhai explained, then, how Sunil, the boy who'd showed us the canvas bundle of medicines, would make deliveries to my hut in the slum as and when I required them. Before we could leave, he asked that I remain seated for a while longer. Then he directed every man, woman, and child in his group to come forward and touch my feet. It was mortifying, a torment, and I entreated him not to do it. He insisted. A stern, almost severe expression burned in his eyes, while the lepers hobbled forward, one by one, and tapped their leathery stumps or the blackened, curled claws of their fingernails to my feet.

An hour later, Abdullah parked his bike near the World Trade Centre. We stood together for a moment, and then he reached out impulsively and enclosed me in a warm, bearish hug. I laughed as we came apart, and he frowned at me, clearly puzzled.

'Is it funny?' he asked.

'No,' I reassured him. 'I just wasn't expecting a bear hug, that's all.'

'Bare? Do you mean it is naked?'

'No, no, we call that a *bear hug*,' I explained, gesturing with my hands, as if they were claws. 'Bears, you know, the furry animals that eat honey and sleep in caves. When you hold someone like that, we say you're giving them a bear hug.'

'Caves? Sleeping in caves?'

'It's okay. Don't worry about it. I liked it. It was ... good friendship. It was what friends do, in my country, giving a bear hug like that.'

'My brother,' he said, with an easy smile, 'I will see you tomorrow, with Sunil, from the lepers, with new medicine.'

He rode off, and I walked alone into the slum. I looked around me, and that place I'd once regarded as grievously forlorn seemed sturdy, vital, a miniature city of boundless hope and possibility. The people, as I passed them, were robust and invigorated. I sat down in my hut, with the thin plywood door closed, and I cried.

Suffering, Khaderbhai once told me, *is the way we test our love, especially our love for God.* I didn't *know* God, as he'd put it, but even as a disbeliever I failed the test that day. I couldn't love God—anyone's God—and I couldn't forgive God. The tears stopped after a few minutes, but it was the first time I'd cried for too long, and I was still deep in the mud of it when Prabaker came into my hut and squatted down beside me.

'He is a danger man, Lin,' he said without preamble.

'What?'

'This Abdullah fellow, who came here today. He is a very danger man. You are better not for any knowing of him. And *doings* with him are even worsely dangerous, also.'

'What are you talking about?'

'He is ...' Prabaker paused, and the struggle was explicit in his gentle, open face. 'He is a killing man, Lin. A murdering fellow. He is killing the people for money. He is a goonda—a gangster fellow—for Khaderbhai. Everybody knows this. Everybody, except of you.'

I knew it was true without asking any more, without a shred of proof beyond Prabaker's word. *It's true,* I said in my mind. In saying it, I realised that I'd always known, or suspected it. It was in the way other people treated him, the whispers he inspired, and the fear I'd seen in so many of the eyes that looked into his. It was in the ways that Abdullah was like the best and most dangerous men I'd known in prison. That, or something like that, had to be true.

I tried to think clearly about what he was, and what he did, and what my relationship to him should or shouldn't be. Khaderbhai was right, of course. Abdullah and I were very much alike. We were men of violence, when violence was required, and we weren't afraid to break the law. We were both outlaws. We were both alone in the world. And Abdullah, like me, was ready to die for any reason that seemed good enough on the day. But I'd never killed anyone. In that, we were different men.

Still, I liked him. I thought of that afternoon at the lepers' slum, and I recalled how self-assured I'd been there with Abdullah. I knew that a part of whatever equanimity I'd managed to display, perhaps most of it, had really been his. With him I'd been strong and able to cope. He was the first man I'd met, since the escape from prison, who'd had that effect on me. He was the kind of man that tough criminals call a *hundred-percenter*: the kind of man who'll put his life on the line if he calls you his friend; the kind who'll put his shoulder beside yours, without question or complaint, and stand with you against any odds.

Because men like that are so often the heroes in films and books, we forget how rare they are in the real world. But I knew. It was one of the things that prison taught me. Prison pulls the masks away from men. You can't hide what you are, in prison. You can't pretend to be tough. You are, or you're not, and everyone knows it. And when the knives came out against me, as they did more than once, and it was kill or be killed, I learned that only one man in hundreds will stand with you, to the end, in friendship's name.

Prison also taught me how to recognise those rare men when I met them. I knew that Abdullah was such a man. In my hunted exile, biting back the fear, ready to fight and die every haunted day, the strength and wildness and will that I found in him were more, and better, than all the truth and goodness in the world. And sitting there in my hut, striped with hot white light and cooling shadows, I pledged myself to him as brother and friend, no matter what he'd done, and no matter what he was.

I looked up into Prabaker's worried face, and smiled. He smiled back at me, reflexively, and in an instant of unusual clarity I saw that, for him, *I* was the one who inspired something of that confidence: as Abdullah was to me, so was I to Prabaker. Friendship is also a kind of medicine, and the markets for it, too, are sometimes black.

'Don't worry,' I said, reaching out to put a hand on his shoulder. 'It'll be all right. It'll be fine. Nothing's going to happen to me.'

CHAPTER ELEVEN

The long days, working in the slum and grinding commissions from the hard, jewelled eyes of tourists, unfolded one upon another through the tumble of crowded hours like lotus petals in a summer dawn. There was always a little money, and sometimes a lot of it. On one afternoon, a few weeks after that first visit to the lepers, I fell in with a party of Italian tourists who planned to sell drugs to other tourists at some of the bigger dance parties in Goa. With my help, they bought four kilos of charras and two thousand Mandrax tablets. I liked doing illegal business with Italians. They were single-minded and systematic in the pursuit of their pleasures, and stylish in the practice of their business. They were also generous, for the most part, believing in a fair minute's pay for a fair minute's work. The commission on that deal gave me enough money to retire for a few weeks. The slum absorbed my days, and most of my nights.

It was late April then, only a little more than a month before the monsoon. The slum-dwellers were busy making preparations for the coming of the rain. There was a quiet urgency in the work. We all knew what troubles the darkening sky would bring. Yet there was happiness in every lane, and excitement in the easy smiles of the young ones because, after the hot, dry months, all of us were hungry for clouds.

Qasim Ali Hussein appointed Prabaker and Johnny Cigar as the leaders of two teams who were responsible for helping widows, orphans, disabled people, and abandoned wives to repair their huts. Prabaker won the assistance of a few willing lads to gather bamboo poles and small lengths of timber from the piles of scrap at the construction site beside our slum. Johnny Cigar chose to organise several street kids into a marauding band of pirates who plundered the neighbourhood for pieces of tin, canvas, and plastic. All manner of things that might be used as weatherproofing materials began to vanish from the vicinity of the slum. One notable expedition by the tiny pilferers produced a huge tarpaulin that, from its shape, had clearly been the camouflage cover for a battle tank. That piece of military software was cut into nine pieces, and used to protect as many huts.

I joined a team of young men who'd been given the task of clearing the drains and gullies of snarls and snags. Months of neglect had filled those places with an accumulation of cans and plastic bottles and jars— everything that rats wouldn't eat and that scavengers hadn't found. It was dirty work, and I was glad to do it. It took me to every corner of the slum, and introduced me to hundreds of people I might otherwise never have known. And there was a certain kudos in the job: humble and important tasks were as esteemed in the slum as they were reviled in the wider community. All the teams who worked to defend the huts from the coming rain were rewarded with love. We only had to lift our heads from the filthy drains to find ourselves in a luxuriant garden of smiles.

As head man in the slum, Qasim Ali Hussein was involved in every plan and decision in those preparations. His authority was clear and unquestioned, but it was a subtle, unobtrusive leadership. An incident that occurred in those weeks before the rain brought me into the ambit of his wisdom, and revealed to me why it was so widely revered.

A group of us had gathered in Qasim Ali's hut, one afternoon, to hear his eldest son tell stories of his adventures in Kuwait. Iqbal, a tall, muscular twenty-four-year old with an honest stare and a shy smile, had recently returned after six months of work as a contract labourer in Kuwait. Many of the young men were eager to gain from his experience. What were the best jobs? Who were the best masters? Who were the worst ones? How did you make extra money between the flourishing black markets of the Gulf States and those of Bombay? Iqbal held impromptu classes every afternoon for a week in the main room of his father's hut, and the crowd spilled out into the forecourt to share in his precious knowledge. On that day, however, his discourses were interrupted abruptly by shouts and screaming.

We rushed out of the hut and ran towards the sound. Not far away, we discovered a noisy mob of men, women, and children. We pushed our way to the centre, where two young men were wrestling and punching at one another. Their names were Faroukh and Raghuram. They were from the team that was helping Prabaker to gather poles and lengths of wood. Iqbal and Johnny Cigar separated the combatants, and Qasim Ali stepped between them, his presence quieting the raucous crowd at once.

'What is happening here?' he asked, his voice unusually stern. 'Why are you fighting?'

'The Prophet, may Allah grant him peace!' Faroukh shouted. 'He insulted the Prophet!'

'And *he* insulted the Lord Ram!' Raghuram countered.

The crowd supported one or the other with shrieks and condemnations. Qasim Ali gave them half a minute of noise, and then raised his hands for silence.

'Faroukh, Raghuram, you two are friends, good friends,' he said. 'You know that fighting is no way to settle your differences. And you both know that fighting between friends and neighbours is the worst fighting of all.'

'But the *Prophet*, peace be upon him! Raghu insulted the Prophet. I *had* to fight with him,' Faroukh whined. He was still angry, but Qasim Ali's hard stare was causing him to wilt, and he couldn't meet the older man's eye.

'And what of insulting the Lord Ram?' Raghuram protested. 'Isn't that also a reason to —'

'There is no excuse!' Qasim Ali thundered, silencing every voice. 'There is no reason that is good enough to make us fight with each other. We are all poor men here. There are enemies enough for all of us outside this place. We live together, or we die. You two young fools have hurt our people, your own people. You have hurt all of our people, of every faith, and you have shamed me terribly.'

The crowd had grown to more than a hundred people. Qasim's words caused a stir of rumbling comments that rippled through them, as heads touched together. Those closest to him, at the centre, repeated what he'd said, relaying the message to others at the edges of the group. Faroukh and Raghuram hung their heads wretchedly. Qasim Ali's charge that they'd shamed *him*, rather than themselves, was a telling blow.

'You must both be punished for this,' Qasim said, a little more gently, when the crowd was quieter. 'Your parents and I will choose a punishment for you tonight. Until then, you will work for the rest of the day at cleaning the area around the latrine.'

New murmurs buzzed through the crowd. Conflicts based on religion were potentially dangerous, and people were glad to see that Qasim took the matter seriously. Many of the voices around me spoke of the friendship between Faroukh and Raghuram, and I realised that what Qasim had said was true—the fighting between close friends of different faiths had hurt the community. Then Qasim Ali removed the long green scarf that he wore around his neck, and held it aloft for all to see.

'You will work in the latrine now. But first, Faroukh and Raghuram, I will bind you together with this, my scarf. It will remind you that you are friends and brothers, while cleaning the latrine will fill your noses with the stink of what you have done to each other today.'

He knelt then, and tied the two young men together at the ankle, Faroukh's right to Raghuram's left. When it was done, he stood and told them to go, pointing with outstretched arm in the direction of the latrine. The crowd parted for them, and the young men tried to walk, but they stumbled at first, and soon realised that they had to hold on tightly and walk in step if they were to make any progress at all. They clasped their arms around one another, and hobbled away on three legs.

The crowd watched them walk, and began to chatter in praise of Qasim Ali's wisdom. Suddenly there was laughter where a minute before there'd been tension and fear. People turned to speak to him, but discovered that Qasim was already walking back to his hut. I was close enough to him to see that he was smiling.

I was lucky, and shared that smile often in those months. Qasim visited my hut two and sometimes three times a week, checking on my progress with the increasing number of patients who came to me after Doctor Hamid began to accept my referrals. Occasionally, the head man brought someone with him—a child who'd been bitten by rats, or a young man who'd been injured at the construction site beside the slum. After a while, I realised that they were people he'd chosen to bring to me, personally, because for one reason or another they were reluctant to come alone. Some were simply shy. Some had resentments against foreigners, and refused to trust them. Others were unwilling to try any form of medicine other than traditional, village remedies.

I had some trouble with the village remedies. In the main I approved of them, and even adopted them wherever it was possible, preferring some of the ayurvedic medicines to their western pharmaceutical equivalents.

Some treatments, however, seemed to be based on obscure superstitions rather than therapeutic traditions, and they were as contrary to common sense as they were to any notions of medical science. The practice of applying a coloured tourniquet of herbs to the upper arm as a cure for syphilis, for example, struck me as particularly counter-productive. Arthritis and rheumatism were sometimes treated by taking cherry-red coals from the fire with metal tongs, and holding them against the knees and elbows of the sufferer. Qasim Ali told me, privately, that he didn't approve of the more extreme remedies, but he didn't prohibit them. Instead, he visited me regularly; and because the people loved him, they followed his example and came to me in greater numbers.

Qasim Ali's nut-brown skin, stretched over his lean and sinewy body, was as smooth and taut as a boxer's glove. His thick, silver-grey hair was short, and he sported a goatee beard one shade lighter than his hair. He most often wore a cotton kurtah and plain, white, western-style trousers. Although they were simple, inexpensive clothes, they were always freshly washed and ironed, and he changed them twice every day. Another man, a less revered man with similar habits of dress, would've been considered something of a dandy. But Qasim Ali raised smiles of love and admiration wherever he went in the slum. His immaculately clean, white clothes seemed to all of us a symbol of his spirituality and moral integrity — qualities we depended on, in that little world of struggle and hope, no less urgently than we depended on the water from the communal well.

His fifty-five years sat lightly on his taller-than-average frame. More than once, I watched him and his young son run from the water tanks to their hut with heavy containers of water hoisted onto their shoulders, and they were neck-and-neck all the way. When he sat down on the reed mats, in the main room of his hut, he did so without touching his hands to the ground. He crossed his feet over and then lowered himself to a sitting position by bending his knees. He was a handsome man, and a great part of his beauty derived from the healthy vitality and natural grace that supported his inspirational and commanding wisdom.

With his short, silver-grey hair, lean figure, and deeply resonant voice, Qasim reminded me often of Khaderbhai. I learned, some time later, that the two powerful men knew each other well, and were in fact close friends. But there were considerable differences between them, and perhaps none more significant than the authority of their leadership, and how they'd come by it. Qasim was given his power by a people who loved him. Khaderbhai had seized his power, and held it by strength of will and force of arms. And in the contrast of powers, it was the mafia lord's that dominated. The people of the slum chose Qasim Ali as their leader and head man, but it was Khaderbhai who'd approved the choice, and who'd allowed it to happen.

Qasim was called upon to exercise his power frequently because his was the only real day-to-day authority in the slum. He resolved those disputes that had escalated into conflicts. He mediated claims and counterclaims concerning property and rights of access. And many people simply sought his advice about everything from employment to marriages.

Qasim had three wives. His first wife, Fatimah, was two years younger than he was. His second wife, Shaila, was younger by ten years. His third wife, Najimah, was only twenty-eight years old. His first marriage had been for love. The two subsequent marriages were to poor widows who might not otherwise have found new husbands. The wives bore him ten children between them—four sons and six daughters—and there were five other children who'd come to him with the widowed wives. To give the women financial independence, he bought four foot-treadle sewing machines for them. His first wife, Fatimah, set the machines up under a canvas canopy, outside the hut, and hired one, two, three, and eventually four male tailors to work at making shirts and trousers.

The modest enterprise provided living wages for the tailors and their families, and a measure of profit, which was divided equally among the three wives. Qasim took no part in the running of the business, and he paid all the household expenses, so the money made by his wives was their own to spend or save as they wished. In time, the tailors bought slum huts around Qasim's own, and their wives and children lived side by side with Qasim's, making up a huge, extended family of thirty-four persons who looked upon the head man as father and friend. It was a relaxed and contented household. There was no bickering or bad temper. The children played happily and did their chores willingly. And several times a week, he opened his large main room to the public as a *majlis*, or forum, where the slum-dwellers could air their grievances or make requests.

Not all the disputes or problems in the slum were brought to Qasim Ali's house for a timely resolution, of course, and sometimes Qasim was forced to take on the roles of policeman and magistrate in that unofficial and self-regulating system. I was drinking tea in the foreground of his house one morning, some weeks after Abdullah took me to the lepers, when Jeetendra rushed up to us with the news that a man was beating his wife, and it was feared that he might kill her. Qasim Ali, Jeetendra, Anand, Prabaker, and I walked quickly through the narrow lanes to a strip of huts that formed the perimeter of the slum at the line of mangrove swamp. A large crowd had gathered outside one of the huts and, as we neared it, we could hear a pitiable screaming and the smack of blows from within.

Qasim Ali saw Johnny Cigar standing close to the hut, and pushed his way through the silent crowd to join him.

'What's happening?' he demanded.

'Joseph is drunk,' Johnny replied sourly, spitting noisily in the direction of the hut. 'The *bahinchudh* has been bashing his wife all morning.'

'All morning? How long has this been going on?'

'Three hours, maybe longer. I just got here myself. The others told me about it. That's why I sent for you, Qasimbhai.'

Qasim Ali drew his brows together in a fierce frown, and stared angrily into Johnny's eyes.

'This is not the first time that Joseph has beaten his wife. Why didn't you stop it?'

'I ...' Johnny began, but he couldn't hold the stare, and he looked down at the stony ground at their feet. There was a kind of rage in him, and he looked close to tears. 'I'm not *afraid* of him! I'm not afraid of *any* man here! You know that! But, they are ... they are ... she is his wife ...'

The slum-dwellers lived in a dense, crowded proximity. The most intimate sounds and movements of their lives entwined, constantly, each with every other. And like people everywhere, they were reluctant to interfere in what we usually call domestic disputes, even when those so-called disputes became violent. Qasim Ali reached out and put a compassionate hand on Johnny's shoulder to calm him, and commanded that he stop Joseph's violence at once. Just then a new burst of shouting and blows came from the house, followed by a harrowing scream.

Several of us stepped forward, determined to put a stop to the beating. Suddenly, the flimsy door of the hut crashed open, and Joseph's wife fell through the doorway and fainted at our feet. She was naked. Her long hair was wildly knotted and matted with blood. She'd been cruelly beaten with some kind of stick, and blue-red welts crossed and slashed her back, buttocks, and legs.

The crowd flinched and recoiled in horror. They were as affected by her nakedness, I knew, as they were by the terrible wounds on her body. I was affected by it myself. In those years, nakedness was like a secret religion in India. No-one but the insane or the sacred was ever publicly naked. Friends in the slum told me with unaffected honesty that they'd been married for years and had never seen their own wives naked. We were all stricken with pity for Joseph's wife, and shame passed among us, burning our eyes.

A shout came from the hut then, and Joseph stumbled through the doorway. His cotton pants were stained with urine, and his T-shirt was torn and filthy. Wild, stupid drunkenness twisted his features. His hair was dishevelled, and blood stained his face. The bamboo stick he'd used to beat his wife was still in his hands. He squinted in the sunlight, and then his blurred gaze fell on his wife's body, lying face down between himself and the crowd. He cursed her, and took a step forward, raising the stick to strike her again.

The shock that had paralysed us escaped in a collective gasp, and we rushed forward to stop him. Surprisingly, little Prabaker was the first to reach Joseph, and he grappled with the much bigger man, pushing him backwards. The stick was wrenched from Joseph's hand, and he was held down on the ground. He thrashed and screamed, a string of violent curses spilling with the drool from his lips. A few women came forward, wailing as if in mourning. They covered Joseph's wife with a yellow silk sari, lifted her, and carried her away.

The crowd might've become a lynch mob, then, but Qasim Ali took charge of the scene immediately. He ordered the people to disperse, or stand back, and he told the men who were holding Joseph to keep him pinned on the ground. His next command astonished me. I thought he might call for the police, or have Joseph taken away. Instead, he asked what alcohol Joseph had been drinking, and demanded that two bottles of it be brought to him. He also called for charras and a chillum, and told Johnny Cigar to prepare a smoke. When the rough, home-brewed alcohol, known as daru, was produced, he instructed Prabaker and Jeetendra to force Joseph to drink.

They sat Joseph in a circle of strong, young men, and offered him one of the bottles. He glared at them suspiciously for a few moments, but then snatched the bottle and took a long, greedy swig. The young men around him patted him on the back, encouraging him to drink more. He gulped down more of the extremely powerful daru and then tried to push it away, saying that he'd had enough. The young men became forceful in their coaxing. They laughed and joked with him, holding the bottle to his lips and driving it between his teeth. Johnny Cigar lit the chillum, and passed it to Joseph. He smoked and drank and smoked again. Then, some twenty minutes after he'd first stumbled from the hut with the bloody stick in his hand, Joseph dipped his head and passed out cold on the rubble-strewn path.

The crowd watched him snore for a while, and then they gradually drifted away to their huts and their jobs. Qasim told the group of young men to stay in their circle around Joseph's body, and watch him closely. He left for about half an hour to perform the mid-morning prayer. When he returned, he ordered tea and water. Johnny Cigar, Anand, Rafiq, Prabaker, and Jeetendra were in the watchful circle. A strong, young fisherman named Veejay was also in the group, and a lean, fit cart-pusher known as *Andhkaara*, or *Darkness*, because of his luminously dark skin. They talked quietly while the sun rose to its zenith, and the sweltering humidity of the day clamped a moist grip on us all.

I would've left then, but Qasim Ali asked me to stay, so I sat down under the shade of a canvas veranda. Veejay's four-year-old daughter, Sunita, brought me a glass of water, without my asking for it. I sipped the lukewarm liquid gratefully.

'Tsangli mulgi, tsangli mulgi,' I thanked her, in Marathi. *Good girl, good girl.*

Sunita was delighted that she'd pleased me, and stared back at me with a furious little smiling-frown. She wore a scarlet dress with the words MY CHEEKY FACES printed in English across the front. I noticed that the dress was torn, and too tight for her, and I made a mental note to buy some clothes for her and a few of the other kids in the cheap clothing bazaar, known as Fashion Street. It was the same mental note I made every day, every time I talked to the clever, happy kids in the slum. She took the empty glass and skipped away, the metal bells of her ankle bracelets jingling their small music, and her tiny, bare feet tough against the stones.

When all the men had taken tea, Qasim Ali ordered them to wake

Joseph. They began to prod and poke him roughly, shouting at him to wake up. He stirred, and grumbled resentfully, waking very slowly. He opened his eyes and shook his groggy head, calling petulantly for water.

'*Pani nahin*,' Qasim said. *No water.*

They forced the second bottle on him, roughly insistent, but cajoling him with jokes and pats on the back. Another chillum was produced, and the young men smoked with him. He growled repeatedly for water. Every time, he found the strong alcohol thrust into his mouth instead. Before a third of the bottle was finished, he fainted again, collapsing to the side with his head lolling at an awkward angle. His face was bare to the climbing sun. No-one made any attempt to shade him.

Qasim Ali allowed him a mere five minutes to doze before ordering that he be woken. Joseph's grumbling was angry as he woke, and he began to snarl and curse. He tried to raise himself to his knees, and crawl back to his hut. Qasim Ali took the bloodied bamboo stick, and handed it to Johnny Cigar. He spoke one word of command. *Begin!*

Johnny raised the stick, and brought it down on Joseph's back with a resounding smack. Joseph howled, and tried to crawl away, but the circle of young men pushed him back to the centre of their group. Johnny struck him with the stick again. Joseph screamed angrily, but the young men slapped at him and shouted for silence. Johnny raised the stick, and Joseph cowered, trying to focus his bleary eyes.

'Do you know what you have done?' Johnny demanded harshly. He brought the stick down with a whack on Joseph's shoulder. 'Speak, you drunken dog! Do you know what a terrible thing you have done?'

'Stop hitting me!' Joseph snarled. 'Why are you doing this?'

'Do you know what you have done?' Johnny repeated. The stick struck again.

'Ow-ah!' Joseph shrieked. 'What? What have I done? I've done nothing!'

Veejay took the stick, and beat Joseph on the upper arm.

'You beat your wife, you drunken pig! You beat her, and maybe she will die!'

He passed the stick to Jeetendra, who used it to smack Joseph on the thigh.

'She's dying! You are a murderer! You murdered your own wife.'

Joseph tried to shield himself with his arms, casting his eyes about feverishly for some escape. Jeetendra lifted the stick again.

'You beat your wife all morning, and threw her naked from the hut. Take that, you drunkard! And that! Just as you beat her. How do you like it, you murderer?'

The slow creep of a foggy comprehension stiffened Joseph's face into a terrified anguish. Jeetendra passed the stick to Prabaker, and the next blow brought tears.

'Oh, no!' he sobbed. 'It's not true! I haven't done anything! Oh, what will happen to me? I didn't mean to kill her! God in heaven, what will happen to me? Give me water. I need water!'

'No water,' Qasim Ali said.

The stick came down again and again. It was in Andhkaara's hand.

'Worrying about yourself, dog? What about your poor wife? You didn't worry when you beat her. This is not the first time you took this stick to her, is it? Now it is finished. You killed her. You can never beat her again, not her or anyone. You will die in the jail.'

Johnny Cigar took the stick again.

'Such a big, strong fellow you are! So brave to beat your wife, who is half your size. Come on and beat *me*, hero! Come on, take this stick of yours, and beat a man with it, you cheap goonda.'

'Water ...' Joseph blubbered, collapsing to the ground in tears of self-pity.

'No water,' Qasim Ali said, and Joseph drifted into unconsciousness once more.

When they woke him the next time, Joseph had been in the sun for almost two hours, and his distress was great. He shouted for water, but they offered him only the daru bottle. I could see that he wanted to refuse it, but his thirst was becoming desperate. He accepted the bottle with trembling hands. Just as the first drops touched his parched tongue, the stick came down again. Daru spilled over his stubbled chin, and ran from his gaping mouth. He dropped the bottle. Johnny picked it up and poured the remaining alcohol over his head. Joseph shrieked and tried to scramble away on his hands and knees, but the circle of men wrestled him back to the centre. Jeetendra wielded the stick, smacking it onto his buttocks and legs. Joseph whined and wept and moaned.

Qasim Ali was sitting to one side, in the shaded doorway of a hut. He called Prabaker to him, and gave orders that a number of Joseph's friends and relatives should be sent for, as well as relatives of Maria, Joseph's wife. As the people arrived, they took the places of the young men in the circle, and Joseph's torment continued. For several hours, his friends and relatives and neighbours took turns to vilify and accuse him, beating him with the stick he'd used to assault his wife so savagely. The blows were sharp, and they hurt him, but they weren't severe enough to break the skin. It was a measured punishment that was painful, but never vicious.

I left the scene, and returned a few times during the afternoon. Many of the slum-dwellers who were passing that way stopped to watch. People joined the circle around Joseph, or left it, as they wished. Qasim Ali sat in the doorway of the hut, his back straight and his expression grave, never taking his eyes from the circle. He directed the punishment with a quiet word or a subtle gesture, keeping a relentless pressure on the man, but preventing any excesses.

Joseph passed out twice more before he finally broke down. When the end came, he was crushed. All the spite and defiance in him were defeated. He sobbed the name of his wife over and over again. *Maria, Maria, Maria ...*

Qasim Ali stood, and approached the circle. It was the moment he'd waited for, and he nodded to Veejay, who brought a dish of warm water, soap, and two towels from a nearby hut. The same men who'd been beating Joseph cradled him in their arms, then, and washed his face, neck, hands, and feet. They gave him water. They combed his hair. They soothed him with hugs and the first kind words he'd heard since the beginning of his chastisement. They told him that if he were genuinely sorry he would be forgiven, and given help. Many people were brought forward, myself included, and Joseph was made to touch our feet. They dressed him in a clean shirt, and propped him up, their arms and shoulders supporting him tenderly. Qasim Ali squatted close to him, and stared into his bloodshot eyes.

'Your wife, Maria, is not dead,' Qasim Ali said softly.

'Not ... not dead?' he mumbled.

'No, Joseph, she is not dead. She is very badly injured, but she is alive.'

'Thank God, thank God.'

'The women of your family, and Maria's family, have decided what is to be done,' Qasim said slowly, firmly. 'Are you sorry — do you know what you have done to your wife, and are you sorry for it?'

'Yes, Qasimbhai,' Joseph wept. 'I'm so sorry, so sorry.'

'The women have decided that you must not see Maria for two months. She is very ill. You almost killed her, and she must take two months to recover. In this time, you will work every day. You will work long hours and hard. You will save your money. You will not drink even one drop of daru or beer or anything but water. Do you understand? No chai or milk or anything but water. You must observe this fast, as part of your punishment.'

Joseph wagged his head feebly.

'Yes, yes. I will.'

'Maria may decide not to take you back. You must know this also. She may want to divorce you, even after the two months—and if she does, I will help her in this. But at the end of two months, if she wants to accept you again, you will use the money you have saved by this extra hard work, and you will take her on a holiday to the cool mountains. During retreat in that place, with your wife, you will face this ugliness in yourself, and you will try to overcome it. *Inshallah*, you will make a happy and virtuous future, for your wife and yourself. This is the decision. Go now. No more talking. Eat now, and sleep.'

Qasim stood, turned, and walked away. Joseph's friends helped him to his feet, and half-carried him to his hut. The hut had been cleaned, and all of Maria's clothes and personal articles had been removed. Joseph was given rice and dhal. He ate a little of it, and then lay back on his thin mattress. Two friends sat near him, and fanned his unconscious body with green paper fans. A cord was tied around one end of the bloody stick, and Johnny Cigar suspended it from a post outside Joseph's hut for all to see. It would remain there for the two months of Joseph's further punishment.

Someone turned a radio on in a hut not far away, and a Hindi love song wailed through the lanes and gullies of the busy slum. A child was crying somewhere. Chickens scratched and pecked at the place where Joseph's circle of torment had been. Somewhere else, a woman was laughing, children played, the bangle-seller sang out his enticement-call in Marathi. *A bangle is beauty, and beauty is a bangle!*

As the pulse and push of normal life returned to the slum, I walked back to my hut, through the winding lanes. Fishermen and fisherwomen were coming home from Sassoon Dock, bringing baskets of sea-smell with them. In one of those balancing contrasts of slum life, it was also the hour chosen by the incense-sellers to move through the lanes, burning their samples of sandalwood, jasmine, rose, and patchouli.

I thought about what I'd seen that day, what the people did for themselves in their tiny city of twenty-five thousand souls, without policemen, judges, courts, and prisons. I thought about something Qasim Ali had said, weeks before, when the two boys, Faroukh and Raghuram, had presented themselves for punishment, having spent a day tied together in work at the latrine. After they'd scrubbed themselves clean with a hot bucket-bath, and dressed in new lungis and clean, white singlets, the two boys stood before an assembly of their families, friends, and neighbours. Lamplights fluttered in the breeze, passing the golden gleam from eye to eye, as shadows chased one another across the reed-mat walls of the huts. Qasim Ali pronounced the punishment that had been decided upon by a council of Hindu and Muslim friends and neighbours. Their punishment, for fighting about religion, was that each had to learn one complete prayer from the religious observances of the other.

'In this way is justice done,' Qasim Ali said that night, his bark-coloured eyes softening on the two young men, 'because justice is a judgement that is both fair and forgiving. Justice is not done until everyone is satisfied, even those who offend us and must be punished by us. You can see, by what we have done with these two boys, that justice is not only the way we punish those who do wrong. It is also the way we try to save them.'

I knew those words by heart. I'd written them down in my work journal, not long after Qasim Ali had spoken them. And when I returned to my hut on that day of Maria's agonies, that day of Joseph's shame, I lit a lamp, and opened the black journal, and stared at the words on the page. Somewhere close to me, sisters and friends comforted Maria, and fanned her bruised and beaten body. In Joseph's hut, Prabaker and Johnny Cigar took the first shift to watch over their neighbour as he slept. It was hot, then, as evening's long shadows became the night. I breathed a stillness of air, dusty and fragrant with scents from cooking fires. And it was quiet, in those dark, thinking moments: quiet enough to hear sweat droplets from my sorrowed face fall upon the page, one after another, each wet circle weeping outward into the words *fair … forgiving … punish …* and *save …*

CHAPTER TWELVE

ONE WEEK became three weeks, and one month became five. From time to time, as I worked the streets of Colaba with my tourist clients, I ran into Didier, or Vikram, or some of the others from Leopold's. Sometimes I saw Karla, but I never spoke to her. I didn't want to meet her eyes while I was poor, and living in the slum. Poverty and pride are devoted blood brothers until one, always and inevitably, kills the other.

I didn't see Abdullah at all during that fifth month, but a succession of strange and occasionally bizarre messengers came to the slum with news of him. I was sitting alone at the table in my hut one morning, writing, when the ghetto dogs roused me from my work with a fury of barking more frenzied than anything I'd ever heard. There was rage and terror in it. I put down my pen, but didn't open my door or even move from my chair. The dogs were often vicious at night, but that was the first time I'd ever heard such ferocity in the daylight hours. The sound was fascinating and alarming. As I perceived that the pack was coming nearer and slowly nearer to my hut, my heart began to thump.

Shafts of golden morning stabbed through rents and gaps in the fragile reed walls of my hut. Those mote-filled rays stuttered and strobed as people rushed past in the lane outside. Shouts and screams joined the howling. I looked around me. The only weapon of any kind in my small house was a thick bamboo stick. I picked it up. The riot of barking and voices concentrated outside my hut, and seemed to be centred on my door.

I pulled open the thin piece of plywood I used as a door, and dropped the stick at once. There, half a metre away, was a huge, brown bear. The animal towered over me, filling the doorway with awesome, muscled fur. It stood easily on its hind legs, with its enormous paws raised to the height of my shoulders.

The presence of the beast provoked the ghetto dogs to madness. Not daring to come within reach, they turned on one another in their fierce rage. Ignoring them and the excited crowd of people, the bear stooped and leaned in toward the doorway to stare into my eyes. Its eyes were large, sentient, and topaz-coloured. It growled. Far from threatening, the bear's growl was a rumbling, tumbling, oddly soothing roll of sound, more eloquent than the prayer that muttered through my mind. My fear slipped away as I listened to it. Across that half-metre of air, I felt the reverberations of the feral noise throb against my chest. It leaned closer until its face and mine were centimetres apart. Froth dissolved to liquid, and dripped from its wet, black jaws. The bear meant me no harm. Somehow, I was sure of it. The eyes of the beast were speaking of something else. It was seconds only, but in that thudding stillness the communication of an animal sadness, undiluted by reason and complete in its passion, was so intense and pure, from eye to eye, that it seemed much longer, and I wanted it to go on.

The dogs slashed at one another, whining and howling an agony of hate and fear, wanting to rip at the bear, but more afraid than enraged. Children screamed, and people scrambled to avoid the thrashing dogs. The bear turned, ponderously slow, but then lashed out swiftly and swept a massive paw at the dogs. The dogs scattered, and a number of young men seized the opportunity to drive them further away with stones and sticks.

The bear swayed from side to side, scanning the crowd with those large, dolorous eyes. With a clear view of the animal, I noticed that it wore a leather collar studded with short spikes. Two chains were fastened to the collar, and they trailed away into the hands of two men. I hadn't seen them until then. They were bear-handlers, dressed in vests, turbans, and trousers, all of which were a startling electric blue colour. Even their chests and faces were painted blue, as were the metal chains and collar of the bear. The bear turned and stood to face me again. Impossibly, one of the men who held its chains spoke my name.

'Mr. Lin? You are Mr. Lin, I am thinking so?' he asked.

The bear tilted its head as if it, too, was asking the question.

'Yes!' a few voices in the crowd called out. 'Yes! This is Mr. Lin! This is Linbaba!'

I was still standing in the doorway of my hut, too surprised to speak or move. People were laughing and cheering. A few of the more courageous children crept almost close enough to touch the bear with darting fingers. Their mothers shrieked and laughed and gathered them back into their arms.

'We are your friends,' one of the blue-faced men said, in Hindi. His teeth were dazzling white, against the blue. 'We have come with a message for you.'

The second man took a crumpled, yellow envelope from the pocket of his vest and held it up for me to see.

'A message?' I managed to ask.

'Yes, an important message for you, sir,' the first man said. 'But first, you must do something. There is a promise for giving the message. A big promise. You will like it very much.'

They were speaking in Hindi, and I was unfamiliar with the word *vachan*, meaning promise. I stepped from the hut, edging around the bear. There were more people than I'd imagined, and they crowded together, just out of range of the bear's paws. Several people were repeating the Hindi word *vachan*. A babble of other voices, in several languages, added to the shouts and stone-throwing and barking dogs to produce the sound effects for a minor riot.

The dust on the stony paths rose up in puffs and swirls, and although we were in the centre of a modern city, that place of bamboo huts and gaping crowds might've been a village in a forgotten valley. The bear-handlers, when I saw them clearly, seemed fantastic beings. Their bare arms and chests were well muscled beneath the blue paint, and their trousers were decorated with silver bells and discs and tassels of red and yellow silk. Both men had long hair, worn in dreadlocks as thick as two fingers, and tipped with coils of silver wire.

I felt a hand on my arm, and almost jumped. It was Prabaker. His usual smile was preternaturally wide and his dark eyes were happy.

'We are so lucky to have you live with us, Lin. You are always bringing it so many adventures of a fully not-boring kind!'

'I didn't bring this, Prabu. What the hell are they saying? What do they want?'

'They have it a message for you, Lin. But there is a vachan, a promise, before they will give it the message. There is a ... you know ... a catches.'

'A catches?'

'Yes, sure. This is English word, yes? *Catches*. It means like a little revenge for being nice,' Prabaker grinned happily, seizing the opportunity to share one of his English definitions with me. It was his habit or fortuity, always, to find the most irritating moments to offer them.

'Yes, I know what a *catch* is, Prabu. What I don't know is, who are these guys? Who's this message from?'

Prabaker rattled away in rapid Hindi, delighted to be the focus of attention in the exchange. The bear-handlers answered him in some detail, speaking just as swiftly. I couldn't understand much of what was said, but those in the crowd who were close enough to hear broke out in an explosion of laughter. The bear dropped down on all fours and sniffed at my feet.

'What did they say?'

'Lin, they won't tell who is sending it the messages,' Prabaker said, suppressing his own laughter with some difficulty. 'This is a big secret, and they are not telling it. They have some instructions, to give this message to you, with nothing explanations, and with the one catches for you, like a promise.'

'What catch?'

'Well, you have to hug it the bear.'

'I have to what?'

'Hug it the bear. You have to give him a big cuddles, like this.'

He reached out and grabbed me in a tight hug, his head pressed against my chest. The crowd applauded wildly, the bear-handlers shrieked in a high-pitched keening, and even the bear was moved to stand and dance a thudding, stomp-footed jig. The bewilderment and obvious reluctance on my face drove the people to more and bigger laughter.

'No way,' I said, shaking my head.

'Oh, yes,' Prabaker laughed.

'Are you kidding? No way, man.'

'*Takleef nahin!*' one of the bear-handlers called out. *No problem!* 'It is safe. Kano is very friendly. Kano is the friendliest bear in all India. Kano loves the people.'

He moved closer to the bear, shouting commands in Hindi. When Kano the bear stood to his full height, the handler stepped in and embraced him. The bear closed its paws around him, and rocked backwards and forwards. After a few seconds, it released the man, and he turned to the tumultuous applause of the crowd with a beaming smile and a showman's bow.

'No way,' I said again.

'Oh, come on, Lin. Hug it the bear,' Prabaker pleaded, laughing harder.

'I'm not hugging it any bear, Prabu.'

'Come on, Lin. Don't you want to know what is it, the messages?'

'No.'

'It might be important.'

'I don't care.'

'You might *like* that hugging bear, Lin, isn't it?'

'No.'

'You might.'

'I won't.'

'Well, maybe, would you like *me* to give you another big hugs, for practice?'

'No. Thanks, all the same.'

'Then, just hug it the bear, Lin.'

'Sorry.'

'Oh, pleeeeeeese,' Prabaker wheedled.

'No.'

'Yes, Lin, please hug it the bear,' Prabaker encouraged, asking for support from the crowd. There were hundreds of people crammed into the lanes near my house. Children had found precarious vantage points on top of some of the sturdier huts.

'*Do it, do it, do it!*' they wailed and shouted.

Looking around me, from face to laughing face, I realised that I didn't have any choice. I took the two steps, reached out tremulously, and slowly pressed myself against the shaggy fur of Kano the bear. He was surprisingly soft under the fur—almost pudgy. The thick forelegs were all muscle, however, and they closed around me at shoulder height with a massive power, a non-human strength. I knew what it was to feel utterly helpless.

One fright-driven thought spun through my mind—Kano could snap my back as easily as I could snap a pencil. The bear's voice grumbled in his chest against my ear. A smell like wet moss filled my nostrils. Mixed with it was a smell like new leather shoes, and the smell of a child's woollen blanket. Beyond that, there was a piercing ammoniac smell, like bone being cut with a saw. The noise of the crowd faded. Kano was warm. Kano moved from side to side. The fur, in the grasp of my fingers, was soft, and attached to rolls of skin like that on the back of a dog's neck. I clung to the fur, and rocked with him. In its brawny grip, it seemed to me that I was floating, or perhaps falling, from some exalted place of inexpressible peace and promise.

Hands shook my shoulders, and I opened my eyes to see that I'd fallen to my knees. Kano the bear had released me from the hug, and was already at the end of the short lane, lumbering away with his slow, thumping tread in the company of his handlers and the retinue of people and maddened dogs.

'Linbaba, are you all right?'

'I'm fine, fine. Must have ... I got dizzy, or something.'

'Kano was giving you the pretty good squeezes, yes? Here, this is your message.'

I went back to my hut and sat at the small table made from packing crates. Inside the crumpled envelope was a typed note on matching yellow paper. It was typed in English, and I suspected that it had been typed by one of the professional letter-writers on the Street of the Writers. It was from Abdullah.

My Dear Brother,

Salaam aleikum. You told me that you are giving the bear hugs to the people. I think this is a custom in your country and even if I think it is very strange and even if I do not understand, I think you must be lonely for it here because in Bombay we have a shortage of bears. So I send you a bear for some hugging. Please enjoy. I hope he is like the hugging bears in your country. I am busy with business and I am healthy, thanks be to God. After my business I will return to Bombay soon, Inshallah. God bless you and your brother.

Abdullah Taheri

Prabaker was standing at my left shoulder, reading the note out aloud, slowly.

'Aha, this is the Abdullah, who I am not supposed to be telling you that he is doing all the bad things, but really he is, even at the same time that I am not telling you ... that he is.'

'It's rude to read other people's mail, Prabu.'

'Is rude, yes. Rude means that we like to do it, even when people tell us not to, yes?'

'Who are those bear guys?' I asked him. 'Where are they staying?'

'They are making money with the dancing bear. They are original from U.P., Uttar Pradesh, in the north of this, our Mother India, but travelling everywhere. Now they are staying at the zhopadpatti in Navy Nagar area. Do you want me to take you there?'

'No,' I muttered, reading the note over again. 'No, not now. Maybe later.'

Prabaker went to the open door of the hut and paused there, staring at me reflectively with his small, round head cocked to one side. I put the note in my pocket, and looked up at him. I thought he wanted to say something—there was a little struggle of concentration in his brow— but then he seemed to change his mind. He shrugged. He smiled.

'Some sick peoples are coming today?'

'A few. I think. Later.'

'Well, I will be seeing you at the lunch party, yes?'

'Sure.'

'Do you ... do you want me, for to do anything?'

'No. Thanks.'

'Do you want my neighbour, his wife, to wash it your shirt?'

'Wash my shirt?'

'Yes. It is smelling like bears. You are smelling like bears, Linbaba.'

'It's okay,' I laughed. 'I kinda like it.'

'Well, I'm going now. I'm going to drive my cousin Shantu's taxi.'

'Okay then.'

'All right. I'm going now.'

He walked out, and when I was alone again the sounds of the slum swarmed around me: hawkers selling, children playing, women laughing, and love songs blaring from radios running on maximum distortion. There were also animal sounds, hundreds of them. With only days to go before the big rain, many itinerants and entertainers, like the two bear-handlers, had sought shelter in slums throughout the city. Ours was host to three groups of snake charmers, a team of monkey men, and numerous breeders of parrots and singing birds. The men who usually tethered horses in open ground near the Navy barracks brought their mounts to our makeshift stables. Goats and sheep and pigs, chickens and bullocks and water buffalo, even a camel and an elephant—the acres of the slum had become a kind of sprawling ark, providing sanctuary from the coming floods.

The animals were welcome, and no-one questioned their right to shelter, but their presence did pose new problems. On the first night of their stay, the monkey men allowed one of their animals to escape while everyone was asleep. The mischievous creature scampered over the tops of several huts and lowered itself into the hut used by one group of snake charmers. The snake men housed their cobras in covered wicker baskets which were secured with a bamboo slip-catch and a stone placed on top of each cover. The monkey removed one of the stones, and opened a basket containing three cobras. From a safe vantage point at the top of the hut, the monkey shrieked the snake men awake, and they sounded the alarm.

'Saap alla! Saap alla! Saap!' Snakes are coming! Snakes!

There was pandemonium, then, as sleepy slum-dwellers rushed about with kerosene lanterns and flaming torches, striking at every shadow, and beating each other on the feet and shins with sticks and poles. A few of the flimsier huts were knocked over in the stampede. Qasim Ali finally restored order, and organised the snake men into two search parties that combed the slum systematically until they found the cobras and returned them to their basket.

Among their many other skills, the monkeys had also been trained to be excellent thieves. Like most of the slums throughout the city, ours was a stealing-free zone. With no locks on any of the doors, and no secret places for any of us to hide things, the monkeys were in a pilferer's paradise. Each day, the embarrassed monkey men were forced to set up a table outside their hut where all the items their monkeys had stolen could be displayed, and reclaimed by the rightful owners. The monkeys showed a marked preference for the glass bangles and brass anklets or bracelets worn by most of the little girls. Even after the monkey men bought them their own supply of the baubles, and festooned their hairy arms and legs with them, the monkeys still found the theft of such jewellery irresistible.

Qasim Ali decided at last to have noisy bells put on all the monkeys while they were within the slum. The creatures displayed an inventive resourcefulness in divesting themselves of the bells or in smothering them. I once saw two monkeys stalking along the deserted lane outside my hut, at dusk, their eyes huge with simian guilt and mischief. One of them had succeeded in removing the bells from around its neck. It walked on its hind legs, in tandem with the other ape, muffling the noise of the other's bells by holding on to them with both tiny hands. Despite their ingenuity, the bell music did make their usually noiseless capering more detectable, reducing their small felonies and the shame of their handlers.

Along with those itinerants, many of the people who lived on the streets near our slum were drawn to the relative security of our huts. Known as pavement dwellers, they were people who made homes for themselves on every available strip of unused land and any footpath wide enough to support their flimsy shelters, while still permitting pedestrian traffic. Their houses were the most primitive, and the conditions under which they lived the most harsh and brutalising, of all the millions of homeless people in Bombay. When the monsoon struck, their position was always dangerous and sometimes untenable, and many of them sought refuge in the slums.

They were from every part of India: Assamese and Tamils, Karnatakans and Gujaratis, people from Trivandrum, Bikaner, and Konarak. During the monsoon, five thousand of those extra souls squeezed themselves into the already over-crowded slum. With subtractions for the space taken up by animal pens, shops, storage areas, streets, lanes, and latrines, that allowed some two square metres for each man, woman, and child among us.

The greater-than-usual crowding caused some tensions and additional difficulties, but in the main the newcomers were treated tolerantly. I never heard anyone suggest that they shouldn't have been helped or made welcome. The only serious problems, in fact, came from outside the slum. Those five thousand extra people, and the many thousands who'd flocked to other slums as the monsoon approached, had been living on the streets. They'd all done their shopping, such as it was, in shops throughout the area. Their purchases were individually small—eggs, milk, tea, bread, cigarettes, vegetables, kerosene, children's clothes, and so on. Collectively, they accounted for large amounts of money and a considerable portion of the trade for local shops. When they moved to the slums, however, the newcomers tended to spend their money at the dozens of tiny shops within the slums. The small, illegal businesses supplied almost everything that could be bought in the legal shops of the well-established shopping districts. There were shops that supplied food, clothing, oils, pulses, kerosene, alcohol, hashish, and even electrical appliances. The slum was largely self-contained, and Johnny Cigar—a money and tax adviser to the slum businesses—estimated that the slum-dwellers spent twenty rupees within the slum for every one rupee they spent outside it.

Shopkeepers and small businessmen everywhere resented that attrition of their sales and the success of the thriving slum shops. When the threat of rain pulled even the pavement dwellers into the slums, their resentment turned to rage. They joined forces with local landlords, property developers, and others who feared and opposed the expansion of the slums. Pooling their resources, they recruited two gangs of thugs from areas outside Colaba, and paid them to attack the supply lines to slum shops. Those returning from the large markets with cartloads of vegetables or fish or dry goods for shops in the slum were harassed, had their goods spoiled, and were sometimes even assaulted.

I'd treated several children and young men who'd been attacked by those gangs. There'd been threats that acid would be thrown. Unable to appeal to the police for help—the cops had been paid to maintain a discreet myopia—the slum-dwellers banded together to defend themselves. Qasim Ali formed brigades of children who patrolled the perimeter of the slum as lookouts, and several platoons of strong, young men to escort those who visited the markets.

Clashes had already occurred between our young men and the hired thugs. We all knew that, when the monsoon came, there would be more and greater violence. Tensions ran high. Still, the war of the shopkeepers didn't dispirit the slum-dwellers. On the contrary, the shopkeepers within the slum experienced a surge of popularity. They became demi-heroes, and were moved to respond with special sales, reduced prices, and a carnival atmosphere. The ghetto was a living organism: to counter external threats, it responded with the antibodies of courage, solidarity, and that desperate, magnificent love we usually call the survival instinct. If the slum failed, there was nowhere and nothing else.

One of the young men who'd been injured in an attack on our supply lines was a laborer on the construction site beside the slum. His name was Naresh. He was nineteen years old. It was his voice, and a confident rapping on the open door of my hut, which scattered the brief, still solitude that I'd found when my friends and neighbours had followed Kano and his bear-handlers from the slum. Without waiting for me to reply, Naresh stepped into the hut and greeted me.

'Hello, Linbaba,' he greeted me, in English. 'You have been hugging it bears, everyone says.'

'Hello, Naresh. How's your arm? You want me to take a look at it?'

'If you have time, yes,' he answered, switching to Marathi, his native tongue. 'I took a break from work, and I have to return in fifteen or twenty minutes. I can come back another time if you are busy.'

'No, now is okay. Come and sit down, and we'll have a look.'

Naresh had been slashed on the upper arm with a barber's straight razor. The cut wasn't deep, and it should've healed quickly with no more than a wrap of bandage. The unclean humidity of his working conditions, however, accelerated the risk of infection. The bandage I'd placed on his arm just two days before was filthy and soaked with sweat. I removed it, and stored the soiled dressing in a plastic bag for disposal later in one of the communal fires.

The wound was beginning to knit well enough, but it was an angry red, with some flares of yellowish-white. Khaderbhai's lepers had supplied me with a ten-litre container of surgical disinfectant. I used it to wash my hands and then cleansed the wound, roughly scraping at it until there was no trace of the white infection. It must've been tender, but Naresh endured the pain expressionlessly. When it was dry, I squeezed antibiotic powder into the crease of the cut and applied a fresh gauze dressing and bandage.

'Prabaker tells me you had a narrow escape from the police the other night, Naresh,' I said as I worked, stumbling along in my broken Marathi.

'Prabaker has a disappointing habit of telling everybody the truth,' Naresh frowned.

'You're telling me,' I answered quickly, and we both laughed.

Like most of the Maharashtrians, Naresh was happy that I tried to learn his language, and like most of them he spoke slowly and very precisely, encouraging me to understand. There were no parallels between Marathi and English, it seemed to me: none of the similarities and familiar words that were shared by English and German, for example, or English and Italian. Yet Marathi was an easy language to learn because the people of Maharashtra were thrilled that I wanted to learn it, and they were very eager to teach.

'If you keep stealing with Aseef and his gang,' I said, more seriously, 'you're going to get caught.'

'I know that, but I hope not. I hope the Enlightened One is on my side. It's for my sister. I pray that no harm will come to me, you see, because I am not stealing for myself, but for my sister. She will be married soon, and there is not enough to pay the promised dowry. It is my responsibility. I am the oldest son.'

Naresh was brave, intelligent, hard working, and kind with the young children. His hut wasn't much bigger than my own, but he shared it with his parents, and six brothers and sisters. He slept outside on the rough ground to leave more space for the younger ones inside. I'd visited his hut several times, and I knew that everything he owned in the world was contained in one plastic shopping bag: a change of rough clothes, one pair of good trousers and a shirt for formal occasions and for visiting the temple, a book of Buddhist verses, several photographs, and a few toiletries. He owned nothing else. He gave every rupee that he earned from his job or made from petty thefts to his mother, asking her for small change in return as he required it. He didn't drink or smoke or gamble. As a poor man with no immediate prospects, he had no girlfriend and only a slender chance of winning one. The one entertainment he allowed himself was a trip to the cheapest cinema, with his workmates, once a week. Yet he was a cheerful, optimistic young man. Sometimes, when I came home through the slum late at night, I saw him curled up on the path, outside the family hut, his thin young face slackened in sleep's exhausted smile.

'And you, Naresh?' I asked, fastening the bandage with a safety pin. 'When will you get married?'

He stood, flexing his slender arm to loosen the tight bandage.

'After Poonam is married, there are two other sisters who must be married,' he explained, smiling and wagging his head from side to side. 'They must be first. In this, our Bombay, the poor man must look for husbands before he looks for a wife. Crazy, isn't it? *Amchi Mumbai, Mumbai amchi!*' *It's our Bombay, and Bombay is ours!*

He went out without thanking me, as was usual with the people I treated at my hut. I knew that he would invite me to dinner at his house one day soon, or bring me a gift of fruit or special incense. The people showed thanks, rather than saying it, and I'd come to accept that.

When Naresh emerged from my hut with a clean bandage, several people who saw him approached me for treatment. I attended to them one by one — rat bites, fever, infected rashes, ringworm — chatting with each, and catching up on the gossip that constantly swirled through the lanes and gullies like the ubiquitous dust-devils.

The last of those patients was an elderly woman accompanied by her niece. She complained of pains in her chest, on the left side, but the extremes of Indian modesty made examination a complex procedure. I asked the girl to summon others to help. Two of the niece's young friends joined her in my hut. The friends held a sheet of thick cloth up between the elderly woman and myself, completely obscuring her from my view. The girl was standing beside her aunt in a position where she could look over the blanket and see me sitting on the other side. Then, as I touched my own chest here and there, the young niece imitated me by touching her aunt's breast.

'Does it hurt here?' I asked, probing my own chest above the nipple.

Behind the screen, the niece probed at her aunt's breast, asking my question.

'No.'

'How about here?'

'No, not there.'

'What about here?'

'Yes. There it is hurting,' she answered.

'And here? Or here?'

'No, not there. A little bit here.'

With that pantomime, and through the invisible hands of her niece, I finally established that the elderly woman had two painful lumps in her breast. I also learned that she experienced some pain with deep breaths, and when lifting heavy objects. I wrote a note for Doctor Hamid, detailing my second-hand observations and my conclusions. I'd just finished explaining to the girl that she should take her aunt to Doctor Hamid's surgery at once, and give him my note, when a voice spoke behind me.

'You know, poverty looks good on you. If you ever got really down and out, you might be irresistible.'

I turned in surprise to see Karla leaning in the doorway with her arms folded. An ironic half-smile turned up the corners of her mouth. She was dressed in green—loose silk trousers and a long-sleeved top, with a shawl of darker green. Her black hair was free, and burnished with copper tints by the sun. The green of warm, shallow water in a dreamed lagoon blazed in her eyes. She was almost too beautiful: as beautiful as a blush of summer sunset on a sky-wide stream of cloud.

'How long have you been there?' I asked, laughing.

'Long enough to see this weird faith-healing system of yours in operation. Are you curing people by telepathy now?'

'Indian women are very obstinate when it comes to having their breasts handled by strangers,' I replied when the patient and her relatives had filed past Karla, and left the hut.

'Nobody's perfect, as Didier would say,' she drawled, with a smirk that fluttered just short of a smile. 'He misses you, by the way. He asked me to say hello to you. In fact, they all miss you. We haven't seen much of you at Leopold's, since you started this Red Cross routine.'

I was glad that Didier and the others hadn't forgotten me, but I didn't look her in the eye. When I was alone, I felt safe and satisfyingly busy in the slum. Whenever I saw friends from beyond those sprawling acres, a part of me shrivelled in shame. *Fear and guilt are the dark angels that haunt rich men*, Khader said to me once. I wasn't sure if that was true, or if he simply wanted it to be true, but I did know from experience that despair and humiliation haunt the poor.

'Come in, come in. This is a real surprise. Sit ... sit here, while I just ... clean up a bit.'

She came over and sat on the wooden stool as I gathered a plastic bag containing used swabs and bandages, and swept the last of the litter into it. I washed my hands with spirit once more, and packed the medicines into the little rack of shelves.

She looked around the small hut, examining everything with a critical eye. As my gaze followed hers, I saw my little house for the shabby, threadbare hovel that it really was. Because I lived alone in the hut, I'd come to think of it as luxuriously spacious, in contrast to the crowding that was everywhere around me. With her beside me, it seemed mean and cramped.

The bare earth floor was cracked, and formed in lumpy undulations.

Holes as big as my fist punctured every wall, exposing my life to the brawl and business of the bustling lane outside. Children peeped in through the holes at Karla and me, emphasising how unprivate my life there was. The reed matting of the roof sagged, and had even given way in a few places. My kitchen consisted of a single-burner kerosene stove, two cups, two metal plates, a knife, a fork, a spoon, and a few containers of spices. The whole of it fitted into a cardboard box, and was stored in one corner. I was in the habit of buying only enough for a single meal at a time, so there was no food. The water was stored in an earthenware matka. It was slum water. I couldn't offer it to her because I knew Karla couldn't drink it. My only furniture was a cupboard for medicines, a small table, a chair, and a wooden stool. I remembered how delighted I'd been when those sticks of furniture were given to me; how rare they were in the slum. With her eyes, I saw the cracks in the wood, the stains of mildew, the repairs made with wire and string.

I looked back to where she sat on the stool, lighting a cigarette and blowing the smoke out through the side of her mouth. A rush of irrational resentment seized me. I was almost angry that she'd made me see the unlovely truth of my house.

'It's ... it's not much. I ...'

'It's fine,' she said, reading my heart. 'I lived in a little hut like this in Goa for a year once. And I was happy. There isn't a day goes by when I don't feel like going back there. I sometimes think that the size of our happiness is inversely proportional to the size of our house.'

She raised her left eyebrow in a high arch as she said it, challenging me to respond and meet her on her level, and with that gesture it was all right between us. I wasn't resentful any more. I knew, I was certain somehow, that wanting my little house to be bigger or brighter or grander than it was had been in my mind, not hers. She wasn't judging. She was only looking, seeing everything, even what I felt.

My neighbour's twelve-year-old son, Satish, came into the hut, carrying his tiny, two-year-old cousin on his hip. He stood close to Karla, staring unselfconsciously. She stared back at him just as intently, and I was struck by how similar they were in that instant, the Indian boy and the European woman. Both had full-lipped, expressive mouths, and hair that was night-sky black; and although Karla's eyes were sea-green and the boy's were dark bronze, each pair wore the same grave expression full of interest and humour.

'Satish, *chai bono*,' I said to him. *Make some tea.*

He gave me a quick smile, and hurried out. Karla was the first *foreign miss* he'd ever seen in the slum, so far as I knew. He was excited to have the task of serving her. I knew he would talk about it to the other kids for weeks afterwards.

'So, tell me, how did you find me? How did you even get in here?' I asked her when we were alone.

'Get in?' she frowned. 'It's not illegal to visit you, is it?'

'No,' I laughed, 'but it's not common either. I don't get many visitors here.'

'Actually, it was easy. I just stepped off the street and asked people to take me to you.'

'And they brought you here?'

'Not exactly. They're very protective of you, you know. They took me to your friend, Prabaker, first, and he brought me to you.'

'Prabaker?'

'Yes, Lin, you want me?' Prabaker said, popping through the doorway from his eavesdropping post outside.

'I thought you were going to drive your taxi,' I muttered, adopting the stern expression that I knew amused him the most.

'My cousin Shantu's taxi,' he said, grinning. 'Was driving, yes, but now my other cousin, Prakash, he is driving, while I am taking it my two hours of lunch breaks. I was at Johnny Cigar, his house, when some people came there with Miss Karla. She wants to see you, and I came here. It is very good, yes?'

'It's good, Prabu,' I sighed.

Satish returned, carrying a tray with three cups of hot, sweet tea. He handed them to us, and tore open a small packet containing four *Parle Gluco* biscuits, which he presented to us with a solemn sense of ceremony. I expected him to eat the fourth biscuit himself, but he placed it on his palm instead, marked it off into even sections with his grubby thumb nail, and then broke it into two pieces. Measuring the fragments against one another, he picked the one that was minutely larger and handed it to Karla. The other went to his baby cousin, who sat in the doorway of the hut and nibbled at the biscuit happily.

I was sitting on the straight-backed chair, and Satish came over to squat on the floor beside my feet. He rested his shoulder against my knee. I was big enough to know that the rare show of affection was a breakthrough with Satish. At the same time I was small enough to hope that Karla had noticed it, and was impressed by it.

We finished the tea, and Satish gathered the empty cups, leaving the hut without a word. At the door, he gave Karla a long-lashed, lingering smile as he took his cousin's hand to lead her away.

'He's a nice kid,' she remarked.

'He is. My next-door neighbour's son. You really sparked something in him today. He's normally very shy. So, what brings you to my humble home, anyway?'

'Oh, I just happened to be in the area,' she said nonchalantly, looking at the gaps in my wall, where a dozen little faces stared in at us. The voices of other children could be heard, questioning Satish about her. *Who is she? Is she Linbaba's wife?*

'Passing by, huh? It couldn't be, maybe, that you *missed* me, just a little bit?'

'Hey, don't push your luck,' she mocked.

'I can't help it. It's a genetic thing. I come from a long line of luck-pushers. Don't take it personally.'

'I take everything personally—that's what being a *person* is all about. And I'll take you to lunch, if you're finished with your patients.'

'Well, I have a lunch date, actually —'

'Oh. Okay, then —'

'No, no. You're welcome to come, if you like. It's kind of an open invitation. We're having a celebration lunch today, right here. I'd be very happy if you'd ... be our guest. I think you'll like it. Tell her she'll like it, Prabu.'

'We will have it a very nice lunches!' Prabaker said. 'My good self, I have kept it a complete empty stomach for filling up to fat. *So* good is the food. You will enjoy so much, the people will think you are having a baby inside your dress.'

'Okay,' she said slowly, and then looked at me. 'He's a persuasive guy, your Prabaker.'

'You should meet his father,' I replied, shaking my head in a resigned shrug.

Prabaker's chest swelled with pride, and he wagged his head happily.

'So, where are we going?'

'It's at the Village in the Sky,' I told her.

'I don't think I've heard of it,' she said, frowning.

Prabaker and I laughed, and the vaguely suspicious furrows in her brow deepened.

'No, you won't have heard of it, but I think you'll like it. Listen, you go on ahead with Prabaker. I'll wash up, and change my shirt. I'll just be a couple of minutes, okay?'

'Fine,' she said.

Our eyes met, and held. For some reason, she lingered, watching me expectantly. I couldn't understand the expression, and I was still trying to read it when she stepped close to me and quickly kissed my lips. It was a friendly kiss, impulsive and generous and light-hearted, but I let myself believe that it was more. She walked out with Prabaker, and I spun around on one foot, whispering a shout of joy while I did an excited little dance. I looked up to see the children peering through the holes in the hut and giggling at me. I made a scary face at them, and they laughed harder, breaking into little whirling parodies of my dance. Two minutes later, I loped through the slum lanes after Prabaker and Karla, tucking my clean shirt into my pants as I ran, and shaking the water from my hair.

Our slum, like many others in Bombay, came into being to serve the needs of a construction site — two thirty-five-floor buildings, the World Trade Centre towers, being built on the shore of the Colaba Back Bay. The tradesmen, artisans, and labourers who built the towers were housed in hutments, tiny slum-dwellings, on land adjacent to the site. The companies that planned and constructed large buildings, in those years, were forced to provide such land for housing. Many of the tradesmen were itinerant workers who followed where their skills were needed, and whose real homes were hundreds of kilometres away in other states. Most of the workers who were native to Bombay simply had no homes, other than those they found with their jobs. In fact, many men accepted the risks of that hard and dangerous work for no other reason than to gain the security of one of those shelters.

The companies were happy enough to comply with the laws that made land and huts available because the arrangement was eminently suitable to them in other ways. The kinship fostered in workers' slums guaranteed a sense of unity, familial solidarity, and loyalty to the company, which served employers well. Travelling time to and from work was eliminated when men lived on the site. The wives, children, and other dependants of employed workers provided a ready source of additional labourers. They were hired from that pool and put to work, from day to day, at a moment's notice. And the entire work force of several thousand people were much more easily influenced, and to some extent even controlled, when they lived in a single community.

When the World Trade Centre towers were first planned, a large area was set aside and marked off into more than three hundred hut-sized plots. As workers signed on, they received one of the plots and a sum of money with which to buy bamboo poles, reed matting, hemp rope, and scrap timber. Each man then built his own house, assisted by family and friends. The sprawl of fragile huts spread outward like a shallow, tender root-system for the huge towers that were to come. Vast underground wells were sunk to provide water for the community. Rudimentary lanes and pathways were scraped flat. Finally, a tall, barbed wire fence was erected around the perimeter to keep out squatters. The legal slum was born.

Drawn by the regular wages that those workers had to spend, and no less by the plentiful supply of fresh water, squatters soon arrived and settled outside the fence-line. Entrepreneurs establishing chai shops and small grocery stores were the first, attaching their tiny shops to the fence. Workers from the legal compound stooped to crouch through gaps in the wire, and spend their money. Vegetable shops and tailor shops and little restaurants were next. Gambling dens and other dens for the sale of alcohol or charras soon followed. Each new business clung to the fence of the compound until at last there was no space left on the fence-line. The illegal slum then began to grow outward into the surrounding acres of open land leading to the sea. Homeless people joined in ever-larger numbers, picking out squares for their huts. New holes were stretched in the fence. Squatters used them to enter the legal slum to collect water, and workers used them to make purchases in the illegal slum, or visit new friends.

The squatters' slum grew rapidly, but with a haphazard, needs-driven planlessness that was a disorderly contrast to the neater lanes of the workers' slum. In time there were eight squatters for every person in the workers' compound, more than twenty-five thousand people in all, and the division between legal and illegal slums became blurred, camouflaged by the crowding.

Although the Bombay Municipal Corporation condemned the illegal slum, and construction company officers discouraged contact between workers and squatters, the people thought of themselves as one group; their days and dreams and drives were entangled in the ravel of ghetto life. To workers and squatters alike, the company fence was like all fences: arbitrary and irrelevant. Some of the workers who weren't permitted to bring more than immediate family into the legal slum invited their relatives to squat near them, beyond the wire. Friendships flourished among the children of both sides, and marriages of love or arrangement were common. Celebrations on one side of the wire were well attended by residents from both sides. And because fires, floods, and epidemics didn't recognise barbed-wire boundaries, emergencies in one part of the slum required the close co-operation of all.

Karla, Prabaker, and I bent low to step through an opening in a section of fence, and we passed into the legal slum. A covey of children trooped along beside us, dressed in freshly washed T-shirts and dresses. They all knew Prabaker and me well. I'd treated many of the young children, cleaning and bandaging cuts, abrasions, and rat bites. And more than a few of the workers, afraid that they might be stood down from work when they received minor injuries on the construction site, had visited my free clinic rather than the company's first-aid officer.

'You know everybody here,' Karla remarked as we were stopped for the fifth time by a group of neighbours. 'Are you running for mayor of this place, or what?'

'Hell, no. I can't stand politicians. A politician is someone who promises you a bridge, even when there's no river.'

'That's not bad,' she murmured. Her eyes were laughing.

'I wish I could say it was mine,' I grinned. 'An actor named Amitabh said it.'

'Amitabh Bachchan?' she asked. 'The Big B himself?'

'Yeah—do you like Bollywood movies?'

'Sure, why not?'

'I don't know,' I answered, shaking my head. 'I just didn't ... think you would.'

There was a pause, then, that became an awkward silence. She was first to speak.

'But you *do* know a lot of people here, and they like you a lot.'

I frowned, genuinely surprised by the suggestion. It never occurred to me that the people in the slum might *like* me. I knew that some men — Prabaker, Johnny Cigar, even Qasim Ali Hussein — regarded me as a friend. I knew that some others treated me with a respect that seemed honest and unfeigned. But I didn't consider the friendship or the respect as any part of being liked.

'This is a special day,' I said, smiling and trying to shift ground. 'The people have been trying for years to get their own primary school. They've got about eight hundred school-age kids, but the schools for miles around are full, and can't take them. The people got their own teachers organised, and found a good spot for a school, but the authorities still put up a hell of a fight.'

'Because it's a slum ...'

'Yeah. They're afraid that a school would give the place a kind of legitimacy. In theory, the slum doesn't exist, because it's not legal and not recognised.'

'We are the not-people,' Prabaker said happily, 'And these are the not-houses, where we are not-living.'

'And now we have a not-school to go with it,' I concluded for him. 'The municipality finally agreed to a kind of compromise. They allowed them to set up a temporary school near here, and there'll be another one organised soon. But they'll have to tear them down when the construction is finished.'

'When will that be?'

'Well, they've been building these towers for five years already, and there's probably about three more years' work in it, maybe more. No-one's really sure what'll happen when the buildings are finished. In theory, at least, the slum will be cleared.'

'Then all this will be gone?' Karla asked, turning to sweep the hutment city with her gaze.

'All will be gone,' Prabaker sighed.

'But today's a big day. The campaign for the school was a long one, and it got pretty violent sometimes. Now the people have won, and they'll have their school, so there'll be a big celebration tonight. Meanwhile, one of the men who works here has finally got a son, after having five daughters in a row, so he's having a special pre-celebration lunch, and everyone's invited.'

'The Village in the Sky!' Prabaker laughed.

'Just where is this place? Where are you taking me?'

'Right here,' I replied, pointing upwards. 'Right up there.'

We'd reached the perimeter of the legal slum, and the megalithic immensity of the twin skyscrapers loomed before us. Concreting had been completed to three-quarters of their height, but there were no windows, doors, or fittings on the unfinished buildings. With no flash or reflection or trim to relieve the grey massiveness of the structures, they swallowed light into themselves, extinguished it, and became silos for storing shadows. The hundreds of cave-like holes that would eventually be windows allowed a kind of cross-sectional view into the construction — an ant-farm picture of men and women and children, on every floor, walking to and fro, upward and down, about their tasks. At ground level, the noise was a percussive and exciting music of towering ambition: the nervous irritation of generators, the merciless metal-to-metal zing of hammers, and the whining insistence of drills and grinders.

Snaking lines of sari-clad women carrying dishes of gravel on their heads wove through all the workplaces, from man-made dunes of small stones to the yawning mouths of ceaselessly revolving cement-mixing machines. To my western eyes, those fluid, feminine figures in soft red, blue, green, and yellow silk were incongruous in the physical turmoil of the construction site. Yet I knew, from watching them through the months, that they were indispensable to the work. They carried the great bulk of stone and steel and cement on their slender backs, one round dish-full at a time. The uppermost floors hadn't been concreted, but the framework of upright, transom, and truss girders was already in place and even there, thirty-five storeys into the sky, women worked beside the men. They were simple people from simple villages, most of them, but their view of the great city was unparalleled, for they were building the tallest structures in Bombay.

'Tallest buildings in all India,' Prabaker said with a gesture of expansive, proprietal pride. He lived in the illegal slum, and had nothing whatsoever to do with the construction, but he boasted about the buildings as if they were his own design.

'Well, the tallest buildings in Bombay, anyway,' I corrected. 'You'll get a good view from up there. We're having lunch on the twenty-third floor.'

'Up ... *there?*' Karla said through an expression of exquisite dread.

'No problem, Miss Karla. We are not walking up it, this building. We are travelling first class, in that very fine lifts.'

Prabaker pointed to the freight elevator attached to the outside of the building in a yellow, steel framework. She watched as the platform jerked and rattled upwards on heavy cables with loads of men and equipment.

'Oh, swell,' Karla said. 'Now I feel great about it.'

'I feel great, too, Miss Karla!' Prabaker agreed, his smile huge as he tugged at her sleeve and pulled her toward the elevator. 'Come, we will catch the lifts on the next run. They are a beautiful buildings, yes?'

'I don't know. They look like monuments to something that died,' she muttered to me as we followed him. 'Something very unpopular ... like ... the human spirit, for example.'

The workmen who ran the freight elevator shouted safety instructions at us, gruff in their self-importance. We climbed onto the wobbling platform with several other men and women, and a wheelbarrow containing work tools and barrels of rivets. The driver blew two shrill blasts on his metal whistle and threw the lever that activated the powerful generators, controlling our ascent. The motor roared, the platform shuddered, throwing us at the panic-handles attached to the uprights, and the elevator groaned slowly upwards. There was no cage surrounding the platform, only a yellow pipe at waist height around the three open sides. In a few seconds, we were fifty, eighty, a hundred metres off the ground.

'How do you like it?' I shouted.

'I'm scared out of my brain!' she shouted back, her dark eyes shining. 'It's great!'

'Are you afraid of heights?'

'Only when I'm on them! I hope you got a reservation, at this god-damn restaurant of yours! What are we doing eating lunch here, anyway? Don't you think they should finish the building first?'

'They're working on the top floors now. This elevator is constantly in use. It's not usually available for the workers to use. It's reserved for wheelbarrows and building materials and stuff. It's a long climb, up thirty flights of steps every day, and it gets fairly tricky in places. A lot of the people who work these upper floors stay up here most of the time. They live up here. Eat, work, and sleep. They've got farm animals and kitchens and everything. Goats for milk, and chickens for eggs, everything they need is sent up to them. It's sort of like a base camp that mountaineers use when they climb Everest.'

'The Village in the Sky!' she shouted back.

'You got it.'

The elevator stopped at the twenty-third floor, and we stumbled out onto a concrete surface that sprouted clumps of steel rods and wires like metal weeds. It was a vast, cavernous space, divided by equidistant columns and canopied by a flat, concrete ceiling adorned with a creepery of cables. Every flat plane was an unrelieved grey, which gave a startling vividness to the human and animal figures grouped on the far side of the floor. An area around one of the pillars was fenced off with wicker and bamboo for use as an animal pen. Straw and hessian was strewn about to serve as bedding for the goats, chickens, cats, and dogs that foraged amid discarded food scraps and rubbish in the pen. Rolled blankets and mattresses, for the people who slept there, were heaped around another pillar. Yet another pillar had been designated as a play area for children, with a few games and toys and small mats scattered for their use.

As we approached the crowd of people, we saw that a great feast was being laid out on clean reed mats. Huge banana leaves served as plates. A team of women scooped out servings of saffron rice, alu palak, kheema, bhajee, and other foods. A battery of kerosene stoves stood nearby, and more food was cooking there. We washed our hands in a drum of water and joined the others, sitting on the floor between Johnny Cigar and Prabaker's friend Kishore. The food was much more piquantly spiced with chillies and curries than any available in restaurants in the city, and much more delicious. As was customary, the women had their own banquet, laid out some five metres away. Karla was the only female in our group of twenty men.

'How are you liking the party?' Johnny asked Karla as the first course of foods was being replaced by the second.

'It's great,' she replied. 'Damn nice food. Damn nice place to eat it.'

'Ah! Here is the new daddy!' Johnny called out. 'Come here, Dilip. Meet Miss Karla, a friend of Lin's who has come to eat with us.'

Dilip bowed low with his hands pressed together in greeting, and then moved away, smiling shyly, to supervise the preparation of tea at two large stoves. He worked as a rigger on the site. The site manager had given him the day off to organise the feast for his family and friends. His hut was on the legal side of the slum, but close to my own across the wire.

Beside the women's banquet area, just beyond Dilip's tea stoves, two men were attempting to clean something from the wall. A word that someone had painted there was still legible beneath their scrubbing. It was the word SAPNA, written in large English capitals.

'What *is* that?' I asked Johnny Cigar. 'I've seen it everywhere lately.'

'It's bad, Linbaba,' he spat out, crossing himself superstitiously. 'It's the name of a thief, a goonda. He's a bad fellow. He's been doing evil things all over the city. He's been breaking into houses, and stealing, and even killing.'

'Did you say *killing*?' Karla asked. The skin on her lips was tight, and her jaw was set in a hard, grim line.

'Yes!' Johnny insisted. 'First it was just words, in posters and such, and writing on the walls. Now, it has come to murder—cold blood murder. Two people were killed in their own houses just last night.'

'He is so crazy, this Sapna, he uses a *girl's* name,' Jeetendra sneered.

It was a good point. The word *sapna*, meaning *dream*, was feminine, and a fairly common girl's name.

'Not so crazy,' Prabaker disagreed, his eyes gleaming but his expression grave. 'He tells that he is the king of thieves. He talks about making it war, to help the poor people, and killing the rich peoples. This is crazy, yes, but it is the kind of a crazy that many people will agree with, inside the quiet of their own heads.'

'Who is he?' I asked.

'Nobody knows who he is, Lin,' Kishore said, his American-accented English, learned from tourists, flowing in a liquid drawl. 'A lot of people are talking about him, but nobody I spoke to has ever seen him. People say he's the son of a rich man. They say he's from Delhi, and that he got cut out of his inheritance. But some people also say he's a devil. Some people think that it's not a man at all, but a kind of organisation, like. There are posters stuck up around the place, posters telling the thieves and the poor buggers in the zhopadpattis to do crazy things. And like Johnny said, now two people *have* been murdered. The name Sapna is getting painted on walls and streets all over Bombay. The cops are asking a lot of questions. I think they're scared.'

'The rich peoples are scared, too,' Prabaker added. 'They were rich people, those unlucky fellows, killed in their homes. This Sapna fellow is writing his name in English letters, not the Hindi writing. This is an educated fellow. And who painted that name *here*, in this place? The peoples are always here, always work or sleep, but nobody has seen who painted his name. An educated ghost! Rich peoples are also scared. Not so crazy, this Sapna fellow.'

'*Madachudh! Pagal!*' Johnny spat again. *Motherfucker! Madman!* 'He's trouble, this Sapna, and the trouble will be ours, you know, because trouble is the only property that poor fellows like us are allowed to own.'

'I think we might change the subject, guys,' I interjected, looking at Karla. Her face was pale, and her eyes were wide with what seemed to be fright. 'Are you okay?'

'I'm fine,' she answered quickly. 'Maybe that elevator ride was scarier than I thought.'

'Sorry for problem, Miss Karla,' Prabaker apologised, his face pinched in a solicitous frown. 'From now, only happy talking. No more talking about killing and murders and blood all over the houses, and all that.'

'That should cover it, Prabu,' I muttered through clenched teeth, glaring at him.

Several young women came to clear the used banana leaves away, and lay out small dishes of sweet rabdi dessert for us. They stared at Karla with frank fascination.

'Her legs are too thin,' one of them said, in Hindi. 'You can see them, through the pants.'

'And her feet are too big,' said another.

'But her hair is very soft, and a good, black Indian colour,' said a third.

'Her eyes are the colour of stink-weed,' said the first with a contemptuous sniff.

'Be careful, sisters,' I laughed, speaking in Hindi. 'My friend speaks perfect Hindi, and she understands everything you're saying.'

The women reacted with shocked scepticism, chattering amongst themselves. One of them stooped to stare into Karla's face, and asked her loudly if she spoke Hindi.

'My legs may be too thin, and my feet may be too big,' Karla replied in fluent Hindi, 'but there's nothing wrong with my hearing.'

The women shrieked in delight and crowded around her, laughing happily. They pleaded with her to join them, sweeping her away to the women's banquet. I watched her for some time, surprised to see her smile and even laugh out loud in the company of the women and the young girls. She was the most beautiful woman I'd ever known. It was the beauty of a desert at dawn: a loveliness that filled my eyes, and crushed me into silent, unbreathing awe.

Looking at her there, in the Village in the Sky, watching her laugh, it shocked me to think that I'd deliberately avoided her for so many months. I was no less surprised by how tactile the girls were with her, how easily they reached out to stroke her hair or to take her hands in their own. I'd perceived her to be aloof and almost cold. In less than a minute, those women were more familiar with her than I'd dared to be in more than a year of friendship. I remembered the quick, impulsive kiss she'd given me, in my hut. I remembered the smell of cinnamon and jasmine in her hair, and the press of her lips, like sweet grapes swollen with the summer sun.

Tea arrived, and I took my glass to stand near one of the huge window openings that looked out over the slum. Far below, the tattered cloak of the ghetto spread outward from the construction site to the very edge of the sea. The narrow lanes, obscured by ragged overhangs, were only partially visible and seemed more like tunnels than streets. Smoke rose in drifts from cooking fires, and stuttered on a sluggish seaward breeze to disperse over a scattering of canoes that fished the muddy shore.

Inland from the slum there were a large number of tall apartment buildings, the expensive homes of the middle-rich. From my perch, I looked down at the fabulous gardens of palms and creepers on the tops of some, and the miniature slums that servants of the rich had built for themselves on the tops of others. Mould and mildew scarred every building, even the newest. I'd come to think of it as beautiful, that decline and decay, creeping across the face of the grandest designs: that stain of the end, spreading across every bright beginning in Bombay.

'You're right, it is a good view,' Karla said quietly as she joined me.

'I come up here at night, sometimes, when everyone's asleep,' I said, just as quietly. 'It's one of my favourite places to be alone.'

We were silent, for a while, watching the crows hover and dip over the slum.

'So, where's *your* favourite place to be alone?'

'I don't like to be alone,' she said flatly, and then turned in time to see my expression. 'What's the matter?'

'I guess I'm surprised. I just, well, I thought of you as someone who's good at being alone. I don't mean that in a bad way. I just think of you as … sort of aloof, sort of above it all.'

'Your aim is off,' she smiled. 'Below it all, would be more like it.'

'Wow, twice in one day.'

'What?'

'That's twice in one day that I've seen a big smile. You were smiling with the girls before, and I was thinking that it's the first time I've ever seen you really smile.'

'Well, of *course* I smile.'

'Don't get me wrong. I like it. Not-smiling can be very attractive. Gimme an honest frown over a false smile, any day. It looks right on you. You look, I don't know, sort of *satisfied* not smiling, or maybe *honest* is the right word. It looks right on you, somehow. Or I *thought* it did, until I saw you smiling today.'

'Of *course* I smile,' she repeated, her brow creasing in a frown, while her tightly pressed lips wrestled with the smile.

We were silent again, staring at each other instead of the view. Her eyes were reef-green, flecked with gold, and they shone with the luminous intensity that's usually a sign of suffering or intelligence, or both. A clean wind stirred her shoulder-length hair—very dark hair, the same black-brown as her eyebrows and long lashes. Her lips were a fine, unpainted pink, parted to reveal the tip of her tongue between even, white teeth. She leaned against the windowless frame with her arms folded. The tides of the breeze rippled through the loose silk of her blouse, revealing and concealing her figure.

'What were you and the girls laughing about?'

She raised one eyebrow in the familiar, sardonic half-smile.

'Are you making small talk with me?'

'Maybe I am,' I laughed. 'I think you're making me nervous. Sorry.'

'Don't worry about it. I take it as a compliment—to both of us. If you really want to know, it was mostly about you.'

'Me?'

'Yeah, they were talking about you hugging a bear.'

'Oh, that. Well, it *was* pretty funny, I guess.'

'One of the women was imitating the look you had on your face, just before you did it, and they cracked up over that. But the really funny thing to them was figuring out *why* you did it. Everyone took turns at guessing why. Radha—she said she's your neighbour, right?'

'Yeah, she's Satish's mother.'

'Well, Radha said you hugged the bear because you felt sorry for it. That got a big laugh.'

'I'll bet,' I mumbled dryly. 'What did *you* say?'

'I said you probably did it because you're a guy who's interested in everything, and wants to know everything.'

'It's funny you say that. A girlfriend of mine once told me, a long time ago, that she was attracted to me because I was interested in everything. She said she left me for the same reason.'

What I didn't tell Karla was that the girlfriend had described me as interested in everything, and committed to nothing. It still rankled. It still hurt. It was still true.

'Are you ... are you interested in helping *me* with something?' Karla asked. Her tone was suddenly serious, portentous.

So that's it, I thought. *That's why she came to see me. She wants something.* The spiteful cat of wounded pride arched behind my eyes. She didn't miss me—she wanted something from me. But she *had* come, she was asking *me*, not someone else, and there was salvage in that. Looking into those serious green eyes, I sensed that it was rare for her to ask anyone for help. I also had the feeling that a great deal, maybe too much, was balanced in it.

'Sure,' I said, careful not to hesitate for too long. 'What do you want me to do?'

She swallowed hard, pushing past an obvious reluctance, and spoke in a rush of words.

'There's this girl, a friend of mine. Her name's Lisa. She's got herself in a very bad situation. She started working at this place—a place for foreign call girls. Anyway, Lisa messed up. Now she owes money, a lot of it, and the Madame who runs the place where she works won't let her go. I want to get her out of there.'

'I don't have much, but I think ...'

'It's not the money. I've got the money. But the woman who runs the place has taken a liking to Lisa. Even if we pay, she won't let her go. I know what she's like. It's personal now. The money's just an excuse. What she really wants is to break Lisa, a little at a time, until there's nothing left. She hates her, because Lisa's beautiful and bright and she's got guts. She won't let her leave.'

'You want us to break her out of there?'

'Not exactly.'

'I know some people,' I said, thinking of Abdullah Taheri and his mafia friends. 'They're not afraid of a fight. We could ask them to help.'

'No, I've got friends here, too. They could get her out of there easy enough, but that wouldn't stop the heavies from finding her, and taking it out on her later. They don't mess around. They use acid. Lisa wouldn't be the first girl to get acid thrown in her face because she got on the wrong side of Madame Zhou. We can't risk it. Whatever we do, it has to be in a way that convinces her to leave Lisa alone, forever.'

I was uneasy about it. I sensed that there was more to it than Karla was telling me.

'Did you say Madame Zhou?'

'Yes—have you heard of her?'

'A bit,' I nodded. 'I don't know how much of it to believe. People say some pretty wild and dirty things about her.'

'The wild things ... I don't know ... but the dirty things are all true, take it from me.'

I didn't feel any better about it.

'Why doesn't she just run away, this friend of yours? Why doesn't she get on a plane, and get the hell back to—where did you say she came from?'

'She's American. Look, if I could make her go back to the States, there wouldn't be a problem. But she won't go back. She won't leave Bombay. She'll never leave Bombay. She's a junkie. That's a big part of it. But there's more than that—stuff from her past, stuff she can't face back there. So she won't go. I've tried to talk her into it, but it's no good. She ... she just won't. And I can't say that I blame her. I've got issues of my own —things in my past I'd rather not go back to. Things I *won't* go back to.'

'And you've got a plan—to get this girl out, I mean?'

'Yes. I want you to pretend that you're someone from the American embassy, some kind of consulate officer. I've already set it up. You won't have to do much. I'll do most of the talking. We'll tell them that Lisa's father is some big honcho in America with ties to the government, and that you've had orders to get her out of there and keep an eye on her. I'll have all that straight before you even walk in the door.'

'It sounds pretty fuzzy to me, Karla. You think that'll be enough?'

She took a bundle of beedies from her pocket and lit two of them with a cigarette lighter, holding the small cigarettes in one hand and playing the flame over them with the other. She passed one to me, and puffed deeply on her own before answering me.

'I think so. It's the best thing I've come up with. I talked it over with Lisa, and she says she thinks it'll work. If Madame Zhou gets her money, and if she believes you're from the embassy, and if she's convinced that she'll get into trouble with the embassy or the government if she hassles Lisa any more, I think she'll leave her alone. There's a lot of *ifs* in there, I know. A lot of it really depends on you.'

'It depends on her, too, this ... Madame. Do you think she'll believe it —believe *me*?'

'We'll have to play it exactly right. She's more cunning than clever, but she's not stupid.'

'Do *you* think I can do this?'

'How's your American accent?' she asked with a little embarrassed laugh.

'I was an actor once,' I muttered, 'in another life.'

'That's great!' she said, reaching out to touch my forearm. Her long, slender fingers felt cool against my warm skin.

'I don't know,' I frowned. 'It's a lot of responsibility if it doesn't go down right. If something happens to the girl, or to you ...'

'She's my friend. It's my idea. The responsibility's mine.'

'I'd feel better about it, you know, just fighting my way in there, and fighting my way out again. This embassy thing—there's so many ways it could go wrong.'

'I wouldn't ask you if I didn't think it was the right way to go, and if I wasn't sure you could do it, Lin.'

She fell silent, waiting. I let her wait, but I knew the answer already. She might've thought I was weighing it up, trying to make up my mind. In fact, I was only thinking about *why* I was going to do it. *Is it for her?* I asked myself. *Am I committed, or just interested? Why did I hug the bear?*

I smiled.

'When do we do this?'

She smiled back.

'In a couple of days. I've got to do a bit of stuff first, to set it all up.'

She threw the finished beedie away, and took a step towards me. I think she might've kissed me, but just then a frightened clamour of shouting and shrieks started up among the people, and they ran to join us at the windows. In the jam of bodies, Prabaker pushed his head through, under my arm and next to Karla.

'Municipality!' he shouted. 'B.M.C. is coming! Bombay Municipal Corporation. Look there!'

'What is it? What's happening?' Karla asked. Her voice was all but lost in the shouts and screams.

'It's the council. They're going to tear down some houses,' I called back, my lips close to her ear. 'They do this every month or so. They're trying to keep the slum under control, to stop it from spreading outside the edge, there, where it meets the street.'

We looked down near the main street to see four, five, six large, dark blue police trucks rolling into an open area that was a kind of no man's land, enclosed by the crescent of the slum. The heavy trucks were covered with canvas tarpaulins. We couldn't see inside them, but we knew they contained squads of cops, twenty or more men to each truck. An open tray-truck, loaded with council workers and their equipment, drove between the parked police vehicles and stopped near the huts. Several officers climbed down from the police trucks and deployed their men in two rows.

The council workers, themselves mostly slum-dwellers from other slums, leapt from their truck, and set about their task of demolition. Each man had a rope and grappling hook that he swung onto the roof of a hut until it caught fast. He then tugged on the rope, collapsing the fragile hut. The people had just enough time to gather the bare essentials—babies, money, papers. Everything else was tumbled and raked into the wreckage: kerosene stoves and cooking pots, bags and bedding, clothes and children's toys. People scattered in panic. The police stopped some of them, and then marched a few young men away to the waiting trucks.

The people at our windows grew silent as they watched. From our vantage point, we could see the destruction far below, but we couldn't hear even the loudest noise of it. Somehow, the soundlessness of that methodical, scouring obliteration struck at us all. I hadn't noticed the wind until then. It was a moaning wail in that eerie quiet. I knew that all through the thirty-five floors of the building, above and below us, other people stared mute witness, just as we did.

Although the houses of construction workers in the legal slum were safe, all work on the site stopped in sympathy. The workers understood that when the building was finished it would be their own homes that would lie in ruins. They knew that the ritual they'd all seen so many times before would be played out for the last time: the ghetto would be gutted and burned, and a car park for limousines would take its place.

I looked at the faces around me; faces struck with compassion and dread. In the eyes of some, I saw smoulders of shame for what the council's power had forced too many of us to think: *Thank God ... Thank God it's not me ...*

'Great luck, your house is safe, Linbaba! Yours and mine also!' Prabaker said as we watched the cops and council workers climb back onto their trucks and drive away. They'd scythed and smashed a swath, one hundred metres long and ten metres wide, at the north-eastern corner of the illegal slum. About sixty houses had been obliterated, the homes of at least two hundred people. The entire operation had taken less than twenty minutes.

'Where will they go?' Karla asked quietly.

'Most of it will be back again by this time tomorrow. Next month they'll come and knock them down again, or another bunch of huts just like them in another part of the slum. Then that'll be rebuilt. But it's still a big loss. All their things have been smashed up. They have to buy new bamboo and mats and stuff, to make new houses. And people got arrested—we might not see them again for months.'

'I don't know what scares me more,' she declared, 'the madness that smashes people down, or their ability to endure it.'

Most of the people had left the window, but Karla and I remained as close together as we'd been in the push and shove of the crowd. My arm was around her shoulder. On the ground, twenty floors below, people began to pick through the rubble of their homes. Canvas and plastic shelters were already being erected for the elderly, the babies, and the smallest children. She turned to face me, and I kissed her.

The taut bow of her lips dissolved on mine in concessions of flesh to flesh. There was such sad tenderness in it that, for a second or two, I floated free, and was adrift in its inexpressible kindnesses. I'd thought of Karla as street-wise and tough and almost cold, but that kiss was pure, undisguised vulnerability. The gentle loveliness of it shocked me, and I was the first to pull away.

'I'm sorry. I didn't ...' I faltered.

'It's okay,' she smiled, leaning away from me with her hands on my chest. 'But we might be making one of those pretty girls at the feast jealous.'

'Who?'

'Are you saying you don't have a girl here?'

'No. Of course not.' I frowned.

'I've got to stop listening to Didier,' she sighed. 'It was his idea. He thinks you must have a girlfriend here. He thinks that's the only reason you'd stay in the slum. He said that's the only reason *any* foreigner would stay in the slum.'

'I don't have a girlfriend, Karla, not here or anywhere. I'm in love with you.'

'No you're not!' she snapped, and it was like a slap.

'I can't help it. For a long time now I —'

'Stop it!' she interrupted me again. 'You're not! You're *not*! Oh, *God*, how I *hate* love!'

'You can't hate love, Karla,' I said, laughing gently, and trying to lighten her mood.

'Maybe not, but you sure as hell can be sick of it. It's such a huge arrogance, to love someone, and there's too much of it around. There's too much love in the world. Sometimes I think that's what heaven is—a place where everybody's happy because nobody loves anybody else, ever.'

The wind lashed her hair into her face, and she pushed it back with both hands, holding it there with her fingers fanned out across her forehead. She was staring down at her feet.

'What the fuck ever happened to good, old, meaningless sex, without any strings attached?' she rasped, her lips drawn tightly over her teeth.

It wasn't a question, but I answered it anyway.

'I'm not ruling that out—as a fall-back position, so to speak.'

'Look, I don't want to be in love,' she stated, in a softer tone. She raised her eyes to stare into mine. 'I don't want anyone to be in love with me. It hasn't been good to me, the romance thing.'

'I don't think it's kind to anyone, Karla.'

'My point, exactly.'

'But when it happens, you haven't got a choice. I don't think it's something any of us do by choice. And ... I don't want to put any pressure on you. I'm just in love with you, that's all. I've been in love with you for a while, and I finally had to say it. It doesn't mean you have to do anything about it—or me either, for that matter.'

'I'm still ... I don't know. I'm just ... *Jesus*! But I'm happy to *like* you. I like you a lot. I'll be head over heels in *like* with you, Lin, if that's enough.'

Her eyes were honest, and yet I knew there was a lot she wasn't telling me. Her eyes were brave, and yet she was afraid. When I relented, and smiled at her, she laughed. I laughed, too.

'Is it enough for now?'

'Sure,' I lied. 'Sure.'

But already, like the people in the ghetto, hundreds of feet below, I was picking through the smashed houses in my heart, and rebuilding on the ruin.

CHAPTER THIRTEEN

Despite the fact that only a handful of people could claim to have seen Madame Zhou with their own eyes, she was the main attraction, Karla assured me, for many of those who visited the Palace. Her clients were rich men: executive-level businessmen, politicians, and gangsters. The Palace offered them foreign girls—exclusively, for no Indian girls ever worked there—and elaborate facilities for the realisation of their wildest sexual fantasies. The strangest of those illicit pleasures, devised by Madame Zhou personally, were the subject of shocked, breathless whispers throughout the city, but influential contacts and substantial bribes meant that the Palace was immune from raids or even close scrutiny. And although there were other places in Bombay that provided equal indulgence and security, none of them were as popular as Madame Zhou's because none had the Madame herself. In the end, what kept men coming to the Palace wasn't the skill and loveliness of the women they *could* have there; it was the mystery of the woman they couldn't have—the invisible beauty of Madame Zhou.

People said she was Russian, but that detail, like all the others concerning her private life, seemed to be unverifiable. It was accepted, Karla said, simply because it was the most persistent rumour. One clear fact was that she'd arrived in New Delhi during the 1960s, a decade as wild for that city as it was for most western capitals. The new part of the city was celebrating its thirtieth year, then, and Old Delhi its three hundredth. Madame Zhou, most sources agreed, was twenty-nine. Legend had it that she'd been the mistress of a KGB officer who'd employed her unique beauty to suborn prominent Congress Party officials. The Congress Party governed India through those years with what seemed to be an unassailable lead in every national poll. Many of the party faithful—and even their enemies—believed that the Congress Party would continue to rule the Indian motherland for a hundred years. Power over Congress men, therefore, was power over the nation.

The gossip about her years in Delhi prowled from scandals and suicides to political murder. Karla said that she'd heard so many different versions of the stories, from such a wide variety of people, she began to think that the truth, whatever it might've been, wasn't really important to them. Madame Zhou had become a kind of portmanteau figure: people packed the details of their own obsessions into her life. One said she possessed a fortune in precious gems that she kept in a hessian sack, another talked with authority about her addiction to various drugs, and a third whispered of satanic rites and cannibalism.

'People say a lot of really weird stuff about her, and I think some of it's just crap, but the bottom line is, she's dangerous,' Karla said. 'Devious, and dangerous.'

'U-huh.'

'I'm not kidding. Don't underestimate her. When she moved from Delhi to Bombay, six years ago, there was a murder trial, and she was at the centre of it. Two very important guys ended up dead in her Delhi Palace, both of them with their throats cut. One of them happened to be a police inspector. The trial fell apart when one witness against her disappeared, and another was found hanging from the doorway of his house. She left Delhi to set up shop in Bombay, and within the first six months there was another murder, only a block away from the Palace, and a lot of people connected her with it. But she's got so much stuff on so many people — stuff that goes all the way to the top. They can't touch her. She can do pretty much what she likes, because she knows she'll get away with it. If you want to get out of this, now's your chance.'

We were in a Bumblebee, one of the ubiquitous black-and-yellow Fiat taxis, travelling south through the Steel Bazaar. Traffic was heavy. Hundreds of wooden handcarts, longer and taller and wider than a car when fully laden, trundled along between buses and trucks, pushed by barefoot porters, six men to each cart. The main streets of the Steel Bazaar were crammed with small and medium shops. They sold every kind of metal house-ware, from kerosene stoves to stainless steel sinks, and most of the cast-iron and sheet-metal products required by builders, shop-fitters, and decorators. The shops themselves were adorned with gleaming metal wares, strung in such brilliantly polished plenty and such artful array that they often attracted the camera lenses of tourists. Behind the glossy, commercial ramble of the streets, however, were the hidden lanes, where men who were paid in cents, rather than dollars, worked at black and gritty furnaces to produce those shining lures.

The windows of the cab were open, but no breeze stirred through them. It was hot and still in the sluggish churn of traffic. We'd stopped at Karla's apartment on the way, where I'd swapped my T-shirt, jeans, and boots for a pair of dress shoes, conservatively cut black trousers, a starched white shirt, and a tie.

'The only thing I'd like to get out of, at the moment, are these clothes,' I grumbled.

'What's wrong with them?' she asked, a mischievous gleam in her eye.

'They're itchy and horrible.'

'They'll be fine.'

'I hope we don't have an accident—I'd really hate to get killed in these clothes.'

'Actually, they look pretty good on you.'

'Oh, shit, make my day.'

'Hey, come on!' she chided, curling her lip in an affable smirk. Her accent, the accent I'd come to love and consider the most interesting in the world, gave every word a rounded resonance that thrilled me. The music of that accent was Italian, its shape was German, its humour and its attitude were American, and its colour was Indian. 'Being so fussy about dressing down, the way you do, is a kind of vanity, you know. It's fairly conceited, too.'

'I don't dress down. I just hate clothes.'

'No you don't, you *love* clothes.'

'What *is* this? I've got one pair of boots, one pair of jeans, one shirt, two T-shirts, and a couple of lungis. That's it—my whole wardrobe. If I'm not wearing it, it's hanging on a nail in my hut.'

'That's my point. You love clothes so much that you can't bear to wear anything but the few things that feel just right.'

I fidgeted with the prickly collar of the shirt.

'Well, Karla, these clothes are a long way from just right. How come you've got so many men's clothes at your place, anyway? You've got more men's clothes than I have.'

'The last two guys who lived with me left in kind of a hurry.'

'So much of a hurry that they left their clothes behind?'

'Yes.'

'Why?'

'One of them ... got very busy,' she said quietly.

'Busy doing what?'

'He was breaking a mess of laws, so he probably wouldn't want me to talk about it.'

'Did you kick him out?'

'No.'

She said it flatly, but with such a clear sense of regret that I let it go.

'And ... the other guy?'

'You don't want to know.'

I did want to know, but she turned her face away to stare out the window, and there was a finality in the gesture that warned and prohibited. I'd heard that Karla had once lived with someone named Ahmed, an Afghan. People didn't talk about it much, and I'd assumed that they'd broken up years before. In the year that I knew her, she'd lived alone in the apartment, and I hadn't realised until that moment how deeply that image of her had insinuated itself into my sense of who she was and how she lived. Despite her protest that she didn't like to be alone, I'd thought of her as one of those people who never lived with others: someone who let people visit or even stay overnight, but never more than that.

I looked at the back of her head, at the small part of her profile, at the barely perceptible bump of her breasts beneath the green shawl, and the long, thin fingers making prayer in her lap, and I couldn't imagine her living with someone. Breakfast and bare backs, bathroom noises and bad moods, domestic and demi-married: it was impossible to see her in that. Perversely, I found it easier to imagine Ahmed, the Afghan roommate I'd never met, than it was to imagine her as anything but alone and ... complete.

We sat in silence for five minutes, a silence calibrated by the slow metronome of the taxi's meter. An orange banner hanging from the dashboard of the car proclaimed that the driver, like many others in Bombay, was from Uttar Pradesh, a large and populous state in India's north-east. Our slow progress through the traffic jam gave him many chances to study us in the rear-vision mirror. He was intrigued. Karla had spoken to him in fluent Hindi, giving him precise, street-by-street directions to the Palace. We were foreigners who behaved like locals. He decided to test us.

'Sister-fucking traffic!' he muttered in street Hindi, as if to himself, but his eyes never left the mirror. 'The whole fucking city is constipated today.'

'A twenty-rupee tip might make a good laxative,' Karla fired back, in Hindi. 'What are you doing, renting this taxi by the hour? Get a move on, brother!'

'Yes, miss!' the driver replied in English, through delighted laughter. He applied himself with more energy to bullying his way through the traffic.

'So what *did* happen to him?' I asked her.

'To who?'

'To the other guy you lived with—the one who *didn't* break a mess of laws.'

'He died, if you must know,' she said, her teeth clenched.

'So ... how did he die?'

'They say he poisoned himself.'

'They *say?*'

'Yeah,' she sighed, looking away to let her eyes drift in the shuffle of people on the street.

We drove in silence for a few moments, and then I had to speak.

'Which ... which one of them owned this outfit I'm wearing? The law-breaking one, or the dead one?'

'The dead one.'

'O ... kay.'

'I bought it for him to get buried in.'

'Shit!'

'Shit ... *what?*' she demanded, turning to face me again, and frowning hard.

'Shit ... nothing ... but remind me to get the name of your dry cleaner.'

'We didn't need it. They buried him in ... in a different outfit of clothes. I bought the suit, but in the end we didn't use it.'

'I see ...'

'I told you that you didn't want to know.'

'No, no, it's okay,' I mumbled, and in fact I felt a cruel, secret relief that the former lover was dead, gone, no competition to me. I was too young, then, to know that dead lovers are the toughest rivals. 'Still, Karla, I don't mean to be picky, but you've got to admit it's just a tad creepy — we're off on a dangerous mission, and I'm sitting here in a dead guy's burial suit.'

'You're just being superstitious.'

'No I'm not.'

'Yes you are.'

'I'm not superstitious.'

'Yes you are.'

'No I'm not.'

'Of *course* you are!' she said, giving me her first real smile since we'd started in the taxi. 'Everyone in the whole world is superstitious.'

'I don't want to fight about it. It might be bad luck.'

'Don't worry,' she laughed. 'We'll be okay. Look, here are your business cards. Madame Zhou likes to collect them. She'll ask you for one. And she'll keep it, in case she needs a favour from you. But if it ever comes to that, she'll find that you're long gone from the embassy.'

The cards were made of pearl-white, textured, linen paper, and the words were embossed in liquid black italic. They declared that Gilbert Parker was a consular under-secretary at the embassy of the United States of America.

'Gilbert?' I grunted.

'So what?'

'So, this taxi crashes, and they gouge my body out of the wreckage, wearing *these* clothes, and they identify me as Gilbert. I'm not feeling any better about this, Karla, I have to say.'

'Well, you'll have to settle for Gilbert at the moment. There really is a Gilbert Parker at the embassy. His tour of duty in Bombay finishes today. That's why we picked him — he goes back to the States tonight. So everything will check out okay. I don't think she'll be checking up on you too much, anyway. Maybe a phone call, but she might not even do that. If she wants to get in touch with you, she'll do it through me. She had some trouble with the British embassy last year. It cost her plenty. And a German diplomat got into a real mess at the Palace a few months ago. She had to call in a lot of dues to cover that up. The embassies are the only people who can really hurt her, so she won't be pushing it. Just be polite and firm when you speak to her. And speak some Hindi. She'll expect it. And it'll smooth over any trouble with your accent. That's one of the reasons why I asked you to help me with this, you know? You've picked up a lot of Hindi, for someone who's only been here a year.'

'Fourteen months,' I corrected her, feeling slighted by her shorter estimate. 'Two months when I first got to Bombay, six months in Prabaker's village, and now nearly six months in the slum. Fourteen months.'

'Yes ... okay ... fourteen months.'

'I thought no-one got to meet this Madame Zhou,' I said, hoping to shift the puzzled, uncomfortable frown from her features. 'You said she kept herself hidden away, and never talked to anyone.'

'That's true, but it's a little more complicated than that,' Karla replied, softly. A meditation of memories clouded her eyes for a moment, but then she concentrated again with obvious effort. 'She lives on the top floor, and has everything she needs up there. She never goes out. She has two servants who bring food and clothes and stuff up to her. She can move around the building without being seen because there's a lot of hidden passageways and staircases. She can look in on most of the rooms through two-way mirrors or metal air vents. She likes to watch. Sometimes she talks to people through a screen. You can't see *her*, but she can see *you*.'

'So how does anyone know what she looks like?'

'Her photographer.'

'Her what?'

'She has photographs taken of herself. A new one, every month or so. She gives them out to favoured clients.'

'It's pretty weird,' I muttered, not really interested in Madame Zhou, but wanting Karla to go on talking. I watched her red-pink lips form each word—lips I'd kissed only days before—and her speaking mouth was a sublime performance of perfect flesh. She could've been reading from a month-old newspaper, and I would've been just as delighted to watch her face, her eyes, and her lips as she talked. 'Why does she do it?'

'Do what?' she asked, her eyes narrowing with the question.

'Why does she hide herself away like that?'

'I don't think anyone knows.' She took out two beedies, lit them, and gave me one. Her hands appeared to be trembling. 'It's like I was saying before—there's so much crazy talk about her. I've heard people say she was horribly disfigured in an accident, and she hides her face because of it. They say the photos are retouched to cover up the scars. I've heard people say she has leprosy or some other disease. One friend of mine says she doesn't exist at all. He says it's just a lie, a kind of conspiracy, to hide who really runs the place and what goes on there.'

'What do you think?'

'I ... I've spoken to her, through the screen. I think she's so incredibly, psychopathically vain that she, she sort of *hates* herself for getting older. I think she can't bear to be less than perfect. A lot of people say she was beautiful. Really, you'd be surprised. A *lot* of people say that. In her photos she hasn't aged past twenty-seven or thirty. There aren't any lines or wrinkles. There's no shadows under the eyes. Every black hair is in its place. I think she's so in love with her own beauty, she'll never let anyone see her as she really is. I think she's ... it's like she's mad with love for herself. I think that even if she lives to be ninety, those monthly photos will still show that same thirty-year-old blank.'

'How do you know so much about her?' I asked. 'How did you meet her?'

'I'm a facilitator. It was part of my job.'

'That doesn't tell me a lot.'

'How much do you need to know?'

It was a simple question, and there was a simple answer—*I love you, and I want to know everything*—but there was a hard edge to her voice and a cold light in her eyes, and I faltered.

'I'm not trying to pry, Karla. I didn't know it was such a touchy area. I've known you for more than a year and, okay, I haven't seen you every day, or even every month, but I've never asked you what you do, or how you make your living. I don't think that qualifies me as the nosey type.'

'I put people together,' she said, relaxing a little, 'and I make sure they're having the right amount of fun to seal a deal. I get paid to keep people in the deal-making mood, and give them what they want. Some of them—quite a few of them, as it happens—want to spend time at Madame Zhou's Palace. The real question is why people are so *crazy* about her. She's dangerous. I think she's completely insane. But people would do almost anything to meet her.'

'What do *you* think?'

She sighed, exasperated.

'I can't tell you. It's not just the sex thing. Sure, the prettiest foreign girls in Bombay work for her, and she trains them in some very weird specialties, but people would still come to her even if there weren't any gorgeous girls there. I don't get it. I've done what people want, and I've taken them to the Palace. A few of them even got to meet her in person, like I did, through the screen, but I've never been able to figure it out. They come out of the Palace like they've had an audience with Joan of Arc. They're high on it. But not me. She gives me the creeps, and she always has.'

'You don't like her much, do you?'

'It's worse than that. I hate her, Lin. I hate her, and I wish she was dead.'

It was my turn to withdraw. I wrapped the silence around myself like a scarf, and stared past her softly sculptured profile to the haphazard beauty of the street. In truth, Madame Zhou's mystery didn't matter to me. I had no interest in her, then, beyond the mission Karla had given me. I was in love with the beautiful Swiss woman sitting beside me in the cab, and she was mysterious enough. I wanted to know about *her*. I wanted to know how she came to live in Bombay, and what her connection was to the weirdness of Madame Zhou, and why she never talked about herself. But no matter how badly I wanted to know ... everything ... everything about her, I couldn't press it. I had no right to ask for more because I'd kept all of my secrets from her. I'd lied to her, saying that I came from New Zealand, and that I had no family. I hadn't even told her my real name. And because I was in love with her, I felt trapped by those fictions. She'd kissed me, and it was good; honest and good. But I didn't know if the truth in that kiss was the beginning for us or the end. My strongest hope was that the mission would bring us together. I hoped it would be enough to break through both our walls of secrets and lies.

I didn't underestimate the task she'd set for me. I knew it might go wrong, and I might have to fight to bring Lisa out of the Palace. I was ready. There was a knife in a leather scabbard tucked into the waistband of my trousers under my shirt. It had a long, heavy, sharp blade. I knew that with a good knife I could handle two men. I'd fought men in knife fights before, in prison. A knife, in the hand of a man who knows how to use it and isn't afraid to drive it into other human bodies, is still, despite its ancient origin, the most effective close-order weapon after the gun. Sitting there in the cab, silent and still, I prepared myself for the fight. A little movie, a preview of the bloodshed to come, played itself out in my mind. I would have to keep my left hand free, to lead or drag Lisa and Karla out of the Palace. My right hand would have to force a path through any resistance. I wasn't afraid. I knew that if the fighting started, when the fighting started, I would slash and punch and stab without thinking.

The cab had bluffed its way through the strangle of traffic, and we picked up speed on the wider streets near a steep overpass. A blessing of fresh wind cooled us, and hair that had been lank and wet with sweat was dry in seconds. Karla fidgeted, tossed her beedie cigarette out of the open window, and rifled through the contents of her patent-leather shoulder bag. She took out a cigarette packet. It contained thick, ready-made joints with tapered, twisted ends. She lit one.

'I need a kicker,' she said, inhaling deeply. The flower-leaf scent of hashish blossomed in the cab. She took a few puffs, and then offered the joint to me.

'Do you think it'll help?'

'Probably not.'

It was strong, Kashmiri hash. I felt the momentary loosening of stomach, neck, and shoulder muscles as the stone took hold. The driver sniffed loudly, theatrically, adjusting his mirror to see the back seat more clearly. I gave the joint back to Karla. She sucked at it a few more times, and then passed it to the driver.

'Charras pitta?' she asked. *You smoke charras?*

'Ha, munta!' he said, laughing and accepting it happily. *Say yes!* He smoked it halfway down, and passed it back. 'Achaa charras! First number. I have it Am'rikan music, disco, very first number United States Am'rikan music disco. You like you hear.'

He snapped a cassette into his dashboard player and threw the volume to maximum. Seconds later, the song We Are Family, by Sister Sledge, thumped out of the speakers behind our heads with numbing plangency. Karla whooped for joy. The driver switched the volume to zero, and asked if we liked it. Karla whooped again, and passed him the joint. He turned the music back to max. We smoked, and sang along, and drove past a thousand years of street, from barefoot peasant boys on bullock carts to businessmen buying computers.

Within sight of the Palace, the driver pulled over beside an open chai shop. He pointed to it, with a jerk of his thumb, and told Karla that he would wait for her there. I knew enough cab drivers, and had travelled enough in Bombay cabs, to know that the driver's offer to wait was a decent gesture of concern for her, and not just hunger for work or tips or something else. He liked her. I'd seen it before, that quirky and spontaneous infatuation. Karla was young and attractive, sure, but most of the driver's reaction was inspired by her fluency with his language, and the way she used it to deal with him. A German cab driver might be pleased that a foreigner had learned to speak German. He might even say that he was pleased. Or say nothing at all. The same might be true of a French cab driver, or an American, or an Australian. But an Indian will be so pleased that if he likes something else about you—your eyes, or your smile, or the way you react to a beggar at the window of his cab—he'll feel bonded to you, instantly. He'll be prepared to do things for you, go out of his way, put himself at risk, and even do dangerous or illegal things. If you've given him an address he doesn't like, such as the Palace, he'll be prepared to wait for you, just to be sure that you're safe. You could come out an hour later, and ignore him completely, and he would smile and drive away, happy to know that no harm had come to you. It happened to me many times in Bombay, but never in any other city. It's one of the five hundred things I love about Indians: if they like you, they do it quickly, and not by half. Karla paid his fare and the promised tip, and told him not to wait. We both knew that he would.

The Palace was a huge building, triple-fronted and three stories tall. The street windows were barred with wrought-iron curlicues beaten into the shape of acanthus leaves. It was older than many other buildings on the street, and restored, not renovated. Original detail had been carefully preserved. The heavy stone architraves over the door and windows had been chiselled into coronets of five-pointed stars. That meticulous craftsmanship, once common in the city, was all but a lost art. There was an alleyway on the right-hand side of the building, and the stonemasons had lavished their handiwork on the quoin—every second stone from the ground to below the eaves was faceted like a jewel. A glassed-in balcony ran the width of the third floor, the rooms within concealed by bamboo blinds. The walls of the building were grey, the door black. To my surprise, the door simply opened when Karla touched it, and we stepped inside.

We entered a long, cool corridor, darker than the sunlit street but softly illuminated by lily-shaped lamps of fluted glass. There was wallpaper — very unusual in humid Bombay — with the repetitive Compton pattern of William Morris in olive green and flesh pinks. A smell of incense and flowers permeated, and the eerie, padded silences of closed rooms surrounded us.

A man was standing in the hallway, facing us, with his hands loosely clasped in front of him. He was tall and thin. His fine, dark brown hair was pulled back severely and tied into a long plait that reached to his hips. He had no eyebrows, but very thick eyelashes, so thick that I thought they must be false. Some designs, in swirls and scrolls, were drawn on his pale face from his lips to his pointed chin. He was dressed in a black, silk kurta-pyjama and clear plastic sandals.

'Hello, Rajan,' Karla greeted him, icily.

'*Ram Ram*, Miss Karla,' he replied, using the Hindu greeting. His voice was a sneering hiss. 'Madame will see you immediately. You are to go straight up. I will bring cold drinks. You know the way.'

He stood to one side, and gestured towards the stairs at the end of the hall. The fingers of his outstretched hand were stained with henna stencils. They were the longest fingers I'd ever seen. As we walked past him, I saw that the scrolled designs on his lower lip and chin were actually tattoos.

'Rajan is creepy enough,' I muttered, as Karla and I climbed the stairs together.

'He's one of Madame Zhou's two personal servants. He's a eunuch, a castrato, and a lot creepier than he looks,' she whispered enigmatically.

We climbed the wide stairs to the second floor, our footsteps swallowed by thick carpet and heavy teakwood newels and handrails. There were framed photographs and paintings on the walls, all of them portraits. As I passed those images, I had the sense that there were other living, breathing people in the closed rooms, all around us. But there was no sound. Nothing.

'It's damn quiet,' I said as we stopped in front of one of the doors.

'It's siesta time. Every afternoon, from two to five. But it's quieter than usual because she's expecting you. Are you ready?'

'I guess. Yes.'

'Let's do it.'

She knocked twice, turned the knob and we entered. There was nothing in the small, square space but the carpet on the floor, lace curtains drawn across the window, and two large, flat cushions. Karla took my arm and steered me toward the cushions. The half-light of late afternoon glowed through the cream-coloured lace. The walls were bare and painted tan-brown, and there was a metal grille, about a metre square, set into one of them just above the skirting board. We knelt on the cushions in front of the grille as if we'd come to make our confession.

'I am not happy with you, Karla,' a voice said from behind the grille. Startled, I peered into the lattice of metal, but the room beyond it was black and I could see nothing. Sitting there, in the gloom, she was invisible. Madame Zhou. 'I do not like to be unhappy. You know that.'

'Happiness is a myth,' Karla snapped back angrily. 'It was invented to make us buy things.'

Madame Zhou laughed. It was a gurgling, bronchial laugh. It was the kind of laugh that hunted down funny things, and killed them stone dead.

'Ah, Karla, Karla, I miss you. But you neglect me. It really has been much too long since you visited me. I think you still blame me for what happened to Ahmed and Christina, even though you swear it is not so. How can I believe that you do not hold a grudge against me, when you neglect me so terribly? And now you want to take my favourite away from me.'

'It's her father who wants to take her, Madame,' Karla replied, a little more gently.

'Ah yes, the *father* ...'

She said the word as if it was a despicable insult. Her voice rasped the word across our skin. It had taken a lot of cigarettes, smoked in a particularly spiteful manner, to make that voice.

'Your drinks, Miss Karla,' Rajan said, and I almost jumped. He'd come in behind me without making the slightest sound. He bent low to place a tray on the floor between us, and for a moment I stared into the lambent blackness of his eyes. His face was impassive, but there was no mistaking the emotion in those eyes. It was cold, naked, incomprehensible hatred. I was mesmerised by it, bewildered, and strangely ashamed.

'This is your American,' Madame Zhou said, breaking the spell.

'Yes, Madame. His name is Parker, Gilbert Parker. He is attached to the embassy, but this is not an official visit, of course.'

'Of course. Give Rajan your card, Mr. Parker.'

It was a command. I took one of the cards from my pocket and handed it to Rajan. He held it at the edges, as if he was afraid of contamination, and backed out of the room, closing the door behind him.

'Karla did not tell me, when she telephoned, Mr. Parker—have you been in Bombay very long?' Madame Zhou asked me, switching to Hindi.

'Not so long, Madame.'

'You speak Hindi quite well. My compliments.'

'Hindi is a beautiful language,' I replied, using one of the stock phrases that Prabaker had taught me to recite. 'It is a language of music and poetry.'

'It is also a language of love and money,' she chuckled greedily. 'Are you in love, Mr. Parker?'

I'd thought hard about what she might ask me, but I hadn't anticipated that question. And just at that moment, there was probably no other subject that could've unsettled me more. I looked at Karla, but she was staring down at her hands, and she gave me no clue. I didn't know what Madame Zhou meant by the question. She hadn't asked me if I was married or single, engaged or involved.

'In love?' I mumbled, the words sounding like an incantation in Hindi.

'Yes, yes, romantic love. Your heart lost in the dream of a woman's face, your soul lost in the dream of her body. *Love*, Mr. Parker. Are you *in* it?'

'Yes. Yes, I am.'

I don't know why I said it. The impression that I was making an act of confession, there, on my knees before the metal grate, was even more pronounced.

'How very sad for you, my dear Mr. Parker. You are in love with Karla, of course. That's how she got you to do this little job of work for her.'

'I assure you —'

'No, Mr. Parker, I assure *you*. Oh, it may be true that my Lisa's father is pining for his daughter, and that he has the power to pull some strings. But it was Karla who talked you into this—of that, I'm quite sure. I know my dear Karla, and I know her ways. Don't think for a moment that she will ever love you in return, or keep any of her promises to you, or that anything but sorrow will come of the love you feel. She will never love you. I tell you this out of friendship, Mr. Parker. This is a little gift for you.'

'With respect,' I said, through clenched teeth, 'we're here to talk about Lisa Carter.'

'Of course. If I let my Lisa go with you, where will she live?'

'I ... I'm not sure.'

'You're not sure?'

'No, I ...'

'She will live at —' Karla began.

'Shut up, Karla!' Madame Zhou snapped. 'I asked Parker.'

'I don't know where she will live,' I answered, as firmly as I could. 'I think that's up to her.'

There was a lengthy pause. It was becoming an effort of concentration to listen and speak in Hindi. I felt lost, in over my head. It was going badly. She'd asked me three questions, and I'd stumbled badly on two of them. Karla was my guide in that strange world, but she seemed as confused and wrong-footed as I was. Madame Zhou had told her to shut up, and she'd swallowed it with a meekness I'd never seen or even imagined in her. I took a glass and drank some of the nimbu pani. The iced lime-juice was spiced with something hot to the taste like chilli powder. There was a shadowy movement and whisper in the darkness of the room behind the metal grate. I wondered if Rajan was in there with her. I couldn't make out the shape.

She spoke.

'You can take Lisa with you, Mr. Parker-in-love. But if she decides to come back here to me, I will not give her up. Do you understand me? She will stay here, if she comes back, and I will be unhappy if you trouble me about it again. You are, of course, free to enjoy our many delights, whenever you wish, as my guest. I would like to see you ... *relax*. Perhaps, when Karla is finished with you, you will remember my invitation? In the meantime, remember—Lisa is mine if she returns to me. That matter is finished between us, today, here and now.'

'Yes, yes, I understand. Thank you, Madame.'

The relief was enormous. I felt sapped with it. We'd won. It was done, and Karla's friend was free to come with us.

Madame Zhou began to speak again, very quickly, and in another language. I guessed it to be German. It sounded harsh and threatening and angry, but I couldn't speak German then, and the words might've been kinder than they sounded to me. Karla responded from time to time with *Ja* or *Natürlich nicht*, but little else. She was rocking from side to side, sitting back on her folded legs. Her hands were in her lap. Her eyes were closed. And as I watched her, she began to cry. The tears, when they came, slipped from her closed eyelids like so many beads on a prayer chain. Some women cry easily. The tears fall as gently as fragrant raindrops in a sun-shower, and leave the face clear and clean and almost radiant. Other women cry hard, and all the loveliness in them collapses in the agony of it. Karla was such a woman. There was terrible anguish written in the rivulets of those tears and the torment that creased her face.

From behind the grate, the smoky voice full of spitting sibilants and crunching words continued. Karla swayed and sobbed in utter silence. Her mouth opened, and then closed soundlessly. A pearl of sweat trickled from her temple across the folded wing of her cheek. More sweat stippled her upper lip, dissolving in the tears. Then there was nothing from behind the metal grate: no sound or movement or even the sense of a human presence. And with an effort of will that clenched her jaws to white and set her body trembling, Karla swept her hands over her face, and her crying ceased.

She was very still. She reached out with one hand to touch me. The hand rested on my thigh, and then pressed downward with regular, gentle pressures. It was the tender, reassuring gesture she might've used to calm a frightened animal. She was staring into my eyes, but I wasn't sure if she was asking me something or telling me something. She breathed deeply, quickly. Her green eyes were almost black in the shadowed room.

I didn't understand any of it. I couldn't understand the German chatter, and I had no idea what was going on between Karla and the voice behind the metal grille. I wanted to help her, but I didn't know why she'd cried, and I knew that we were probably being watched. I stood up, and then helped her to stand. For a moment, she rested her face against my chest. I put my hands on her shoulders, steadying her and easing her away from me. Then the door opened, and Rajan came into the room.

'She is ready,' Rajan hissed.

Karla brushed at the knees of her loose trousers, picked up her bag, and stepped past me toward the door.

'Come on,' she said. 'The interview's over.'

For a moment I looked at the marks, the curved indentations that her knees had made in the brocade cushion beside me on the floor. I felt tired and angry and confused. I turned to see Karla and Rajan staring at me impatiently in the doorway. As I followed them along the corridors of the Palace, I grew more sullen and resentful with every step.

Rajan led us to a room at the very end of a corridor. The door was open. The room was decorated with large movie posters—Lauren Bacall in a still from *To Have And Have Not*, Pier Angeli from *Somebody Up There Likes Me*, and Sean Young from *Blade Runner*. A young and very beautiful woman sat on the large bed in the centre of the room. Her blonde hair was long and thick, ending in spirals of lush curls. Her sky-blue eyes were large and set unusually wide apart. Her skin was flawless pink, her lips painted a deep red. A suitcase and a cosmetic case were snapped shut and resting on the floor at her golden-slippered feet.

'About fucking time. You're late. I'm going outta my mind here.' It was a deep voice. The accent was Californian.

'Gilbert had to change his clothes,' Karla replied, with something of her familiar composure. 'And the traffic, getting here—you don't want to know.'

'Gilbert?' Her nose wrinkled with distaste.

'It's a long story,' I said, not smiling. 'Are you ready to go?'

'I don't know,' she said, looking at Karla.

'You don't *know*?'

'Hey, fuck *you*, Jack!' she exploded, rounding on me with so much fury that I didn't see the fear behind it. 'What the hell business is it of yours, anyway?'

There's a special anger we reserve for people who won't let us do them a good turn. My teeth began to grind with it.

'Look, are you coming or not?'

'Did she say it's okay?' Lisa asked Karla. Both women looked to Rajan, and then to the mirror on the wall behind him. Their expressions told me that Madame Zhou was watching us, and listening, as we spoke.

'It's fine. She said you can go,' I told her, hoping she wouldn't comment on my imperfect American accent.

'Is this for real? No bullshit?'

'No bullshit,' Karla said.

The girl stood up quickly and grabbed at her bags.

'Well, what're we waiting for? Let's get the fuck outta here before she changes her goddamn mind.'

Rajan stopped me at the street door, and gave me a large, sealed envelope. He stared that perplexing malice into my eyes once more, and then closed the door. I caught up to Karla and pulled her round to face me.

'What was *that* all about?'

'What do you mean?' she asked, a little smile trying to light her eyes. 'It worked. We got her out.'

'I'm not talking about that. I'm talking about you and me, and that crazy game Madame Zhou was playing up there. You were crying your eyes out, Karla—what was it all about?'

She glanced at Lisa, who stood close by, impatient and shielding her eyes, even though the late-afternoon light wasn't bright. She looked at me again, her green eyes puzzled and tired.

'Do we have to talk about this now, in public?'

'No, we don't!' Lisa answered for me.

'I'm not talking to you,' I snarled, not looking at her. My eyes were fixed on Karla's face.

'You're not talking to me, either,' Karla said firmly. 'Not here. Not now. Let's just go.'

'What *is* this?' I demanded.

'You're over-reacting, Lin.'

'*I'm* over-reacting!' I said, almost shouting, and proving her right. I was angry that she'd told me so little of the truth, and prepared me so poorly for the interview. I was hurt that she didn't trust me enough to give me the whole story. 'That's funny, that's *really* funny.'

'Who *is* this fucking jerk?' Lisa snarled.

'Shut up, Lisa.' Karla said, just as Madame Zhou had said it to her, only minutes before. Lisa reacted just as Karla had, with meek, sullen silence.

'I don't want to talk about this now, Lin,' Karla said, turning to me with an expression of hard, reluctant disappointment. There are few things people can do with their eyes that hurt more, and I hated to see it. Passers-by stopped near us on the street, staring and eavesdropping openly.

'Look, I know there's a lot more going on here than getting Lisa out of the Palace. What *happened* up there? How did she … you know, how did she know about *us*? I'm supposed to be some guy from the embassy, and she starts talking about being in love with you. I don't get it. And who the hell are Ahmed and Christina? What happened to them? What was she talking about? One minute you're indestructible, and then the next minute you're breaking down, while Madame Nutcase is babbling away in German or whatever.'

'It was Swiss-German, actually,' she snapped, a flash of spite in the gleam of her clenched teeth.

'Swiss, Chinese, so what? I just want to know what's going on. I want to help you. I want to know ... well, where I stand.'

A few more people stopped to join the idlers. One group of three young men stood very close, leaning on one another's shoulders and gawking with aggressive curiosity. The taxi driver who'd brought us there was standing beside his cab, five metres away. He twirled his handkerchief to fan himself, watching us, smiling. He was much taller than I'd thought him to be; tall and thin and dressed in a tightly fitting white shirt and trousers. Karla glanced over her shoulder at him. He wiped at his moustache with the red handkerchief, and then tied it as a scarf around his neck. He smiled at her. His strong, white teeth were gleaming.

'Where you're *standing* is right *here*, on the street, outside the Palace,' Karla said. She was angry and sad and strong—stronger than I was at that moment. I almost hated her for it. 'Where I'm *sitting* is in that *cab*. Where I'm *going* is none of your damn business.'

She walked away.

'Where the hell did you get *that* guy?' I heard Lisa say, as they approached the cab.

The taxi driver greeted them, waggling his head happily. When they drove past me, there was music playing, *Freeway of Love*, and they were laughing. For one explosive moment of writhing fantasy I saw them all together, naked, the taxi driver and Lisa and Karla. It was improbable and ridiculous and I knew it, but the squirm was in my mind, and a white-hot thump of rage went pulsing along the thread of time and fate that connected me to Karla. Then I remembered that I'd left my boots and clothes at her apartment.

'Hey!' I called after the retreating cab. "My clothes! Karla!'

'Mr. Lin?'

There was a man standing beside me. His face was familiar, but I couldn't place it immediately.

'What?'

'Abdel Khader want you, Mr. Lin.'

The mention of Khader's name jolted my memory. It was Nazeer, Khaderbhai's driver. The white car was parked nearby.

'How ... how did you ... what are you doing here?'

'He say you come now. I am driving.' He gestured toward the car, and took two little steps to encourage me.

'I don't think so, Nazeer. It's been a long day. You can tell Khaderbhai that —'

'He say you come now,' Nazeer said grimly. He wasn't smiling, and I had the feeling that I would have to fight him if I wanted to avoid getting into the car. I was so angry and confused and tired, just then, that I actually considered it for a moment. *It might cost less energy, in the long run, to fight with him,* I thought, *than to go with him.* But Nazeer screwed his face into agonised concentration, and spoke with unaccustomed courtesy.

'Khaderbhai told it—*You come, please*—like that, Khaderbhai told it— *Please come see me, Mr. Lin.*'

The word *please* didn't sit well with him. It was clear that, in his view, lord Abdel Khader Khan gave orders that others quickly and gratefully obeyed. But he'd been told to request my company, rather than command it, and the English words he'd just spoken with such visible effort had been carefully memorised. I pictured him driving across the city and repeating the incantation of the foreign words to himself, as uncomfortable and unhappy with them as if they were fragments of prayer from another man's religion. Alien to him or not, the words had their effect on me, and he looked relieved when I smiled a surrender.

'Okay, Nazeer, okay,' I sighed. 'We'll go to see Khaderbhai.'

He began to open the back door of the car, but I insisted on sitting in the front. As soon as we pulled away from the kerb, he switched on the radio and turned the volume to high, perhaps to prevent conversation. The envelope that Rajan had given me was still in my hands, and I turned it over to examine both sides. It was hand-made paper, pink, and about the size of a magazine cover. There was nothing written on the outside. I tore the corner and opened it to find a black-and-white photograph. It was an interior shot of a room, half-lit, and filled with expensive ornaments from a variety of ages and cultures. In the midst of that self-conscious clutter, a woman sat on a throne-like chair. She was dressed in an evening gown of extravagant length that spilled to the floor and concealed her feet. One hand rested on an arm of the chair. The other was poised in a regal wave or an elegant gesture of dismissal. The hair was dark and elaborately coifed, falling in ringlets that framed her round and somewhat plump face. The almond-shaped eyes stared straight into the camera. They wore a faintly neurotic look of startled indignation. The lips of her tiny mouth were pinched in a determined pout that pulled at her weak chin.

A beautiful woman? I didn't think so. And a range of less than lovely impressions stared from that face—haughty, spiteful, frightened, spoiled, self-obsessed. The photograph said she was all of those things, and more. And worse. But there was something else on the photograph, something more repugnant and chilling than the unlovely face. It was the message she'd chosen to stamp in red, block letters, across the bottom. It said: MADAME ZHOU IS HAPPY NOW.

CHAPTER FOURTEEN

'Come in, come in, Mr. Lin. No, please, sit here. We have been expecting you.' Abdel Khader waved me to a place at his left hand. I kicked off my shoes at the doorway, where several other pairs of sandals and shoes had been discarded, and sat down on the plush, brocade cushion he'd indicated. It was a large room—nine of us, seated in a circle about a low marble table, occupied no more than a corner of it. The floor was surfaced with smooth, cream, pentagonal tiles. A square of Isfahan carpet covered the tiles in our part of the room. The walls and vaulted ceiling featured a mosaic of pale blue and white miniatures, presenting the effect of a sky with drifts of cloud. Two open arches connected the room to wide passageways. Three picture-seat windows overlooked a palm-filled courtyard. They were all framed with sculptured pillars and topped with minaret-shaped domes inscribed with Arabic lettering. The spill, splash, and stir of water in a cascade fountain came to us from beyond those windows, somewhere in the courtyard.

It was a room of diligently austere splendour. The only furniture was the low marble table and our nine cushions evenly arranged around the carpet. The only decoration was a framed black and gold-leaf depiction of the Kaaba at Mecca. The eight men who sat or reclined there seemed comfortable in that inornate simplicity, however, and certainly they were free to choose any style that they wanted, for there was the wealth and power of a small empire between them: an empire of crime.

'Are you feeling quite refreshed, Mr. Lin?' Khaderbhai asked.

When I'd arrived at the building beside the Nabila Mosque, in Dongri, Nazeer had shown me at once to a large, well-appointed bathroom, where I'd used the toilet and then washed my face and hands. Bombay, in those years, was the most voluptuously dirty city in the world. It wasn't only hot and cloyingly humid: in the eight rainless months of the year it was constantly aswirl with grimy dust clouds that settled on and smeared every exposed surface with a catholic variety of filths. If I wiped my face with a handkerchief after only half an hour's walk along any street, the cloth was streaked with black.

'Thank you, yes. I felt tired, when I arrived, but now I'm revived by a combination of politeness and plumbing.' I was speaking in Hindi, and it was a struggle to carry the humour, sense, and good intentions in the small phrase. We can't really know what a pleasure it is to run in our own language until we're forced to stumble in someone else's. It was a great relief when Khaderbhai spoke in English.

'Please speak English, Mr. Lin. I am very happy that you are learning our languages, but today we would like to practise yours. Each of us here can speak and read and write English, to some extent. In my own case, I have been educated in English, as well as in Hindi and Urdu. In fact, I often find myself thinking first in English, before other languages. My dear friend, Abdul, sitting near you, would call English his first language, I think. And all of us, no matter what our level of learning, are enthusiastic about the study of English. It is a critical thing for us. One of the reasons why I asked you to come here, this evening, was so that we might enjoy the speaking of English with you, a native of the language. This is our monthly discussion night, you see, and our little group talks about— but wait, let me first introduce you.'

He reached over to lay an affectionate hand on the bulky forearm of the heavy-set, elderly man who sat on his right. He was dressed in the green pantaloons and long tunic of Afghan traditional dress.

'This is Sobhan Mahmoud—let us use first names, after our introductions, Lin, for we are all friends here, yes?'

Sobhan wagged his grizzled, grey head at me in greeting, fixing me with a look of steely enquiry, perhaps to make sure that I understood the honour implied in the use of first names.

'The very ample and smiling gentleman next to him is my old friend from Peshawar, Abdul Ghani. Next to him is Khaled Ansari, originally from Palestine. Rajubhai, next to him, is from the holy city of Varanasi—have you seen it? No? Well, you must make the time to do so before too long.'

Rajubhai, a bald, thick-set man with a neat, grey moustache, smiled in response to Khaderbhai's introduction, and turned to me with his hands joined together in a silent greeting. His eyes, above the gentle steeple of his fingers, were hard and wary.

'Next to our dear Raju,' Khaderbhai continued, 'is Keki Dorabjee, who came to Bombay from Zanzibar, with other Indian Parsees, twenty years ago, when they were driven from the island by the nationalist movement.'

Dorabjee, a very tall, thin man in his middle fifties, turned his dark eyes on me. His expression seemed fixed in such distressing melancholy that I felt compelled to offer him a small, comforting smile in return.

'Next to our brother Keki is Farid. He is the youngest of our group, and the only one of us who is a native Maharashtrian, by virtue of being born in Bombay, although his family came here from Gujarat. Sitting next to you is Madjid, who was born in Teheran, but has lived here, in our city, for more than twenty years.'

A young servant entered with a tray of glasses and a silver pot of black tea. He served us, beginning with Khaderbhai and ending with me. He left the room, returned momentarily to place two bowls of ladoo and barfi sweets on the table, and then left us once more.

Immediately afterward, three men joined us in the room, making a place for themselves on another patch of carpet that was near, but a little apart from us. They were introduced to me—Andrew Ferreira, a Goan, and Salman Mustaan and Sanjay Kumar, both from Bombay—but from that moment they never spoke again. They were, it seemed, young gangsters on the next rung below council membership: invited to listen at the meetings, but not to speak. And they did listen, very attentively, while watching us closely. I turned, often, to find their eyes on me, staring out from the kind of grave appraisal I'd come to know too well in prison. They were deciding whether to trust me or not, and how hard it would be—as a purely professional speculation—to kill me, without a gun.

'Lin, we usually talk about some themes, at our discussion nights,' Abdul Ghani said in a clipped, BBC-accented English, 'but first we would like to ask you what you make of this.'

He reached across, pushing toward me a rolled poster that was lying on the table. I opened it out and read through the four paragraphs of large, bold typeface.

SAPNA

People of Bombay, listen to the voice of your King. Your dream is come to you and I am he, Sapna, King of Dreams, King of Blood. Your time is come, my children, and your chains of suffering will be lifted from you. I am come. I am the law. My first commandment is to open your eyes. I want you to see your hunger while they waste food. I want you to see your rags while they wear silk. See that you live in the gutter while they live in palaces of marble and gold. My second commandment is to kill them all. Do this with cruel violence.

Do this in memory of me, Sapna. I am the law.

There was more, a lot more, all of it in the same vein. It struck me as absurd at first, and I started to smile. The silence in the room and the stares of tense concentration they turned on me stifled the smile to a grimace. They took it very seriously, I realised. Stalling for time, because I didn't know what Ghani wanted from me, I read through the ranting, insane tract again. While I read the words, I remembered that someone had painted the name Sapna on the wall at the Village in the Sky, twenty-three floors off the ground. I remembered what Prabaker and Johnny Cigar had said about brutal murders done in Sapna's name. The continuing silence and expectant seriousness in the room filled me with a chill of menace. The hairs on my arms tingled with it, and a caterpillar of sweat inched down the groove of my spine.

'Well, Lin?'

'Sorry?'

'What do you make of it?'

The stillness was so complete that I could hear myself swallowing. They wanted me to give them something, and they expected it to be good.

'I don't know what to say. I mean, it's so ridiculous, so fatuous, it's hard to take it seriously.'

Madjid grunted, and cleared his throat loudly. He drew his thick black eyebrows down over a thick black scowl.

'If you call cutting a man from the groin to the throat, and then leaving his organs and his life's blood all around his house *serious*, then it is a serious matter.'

'Sapna did that?'

'His followers did it, Lin,' Abdul Ghani answered for him. 'That, and at least six more murders like it, in the last month. Some were even more hideous killings.'

'I've heard people talking about Sapna, but I thought it was just a story, like an urban legend. I haven't read anything about it in any of the newspapers, and I read them every day.'

'This matter is being handled in the most careful way,' Khaderbhai explained. 'The government and the police have asked for co-operation from the newspapers. They have been reported as unrelated things, as deaths that happened during simple, unconnected robberies. But we know that Sapna's followers have committed them, because the blood of the victims was used to write the word Sapna on the walls and the floors. And despite the terrible violence of the attacks, not much of any real value was stolen from the victims. For now, this Sapna does not officially exist. But it is only a matter of time before everyone knows of him, and of what has been done in his name.'

'And you ... you don't know who he is?'

'We are very interested in him, Lin,' Khaderbhai answered. 'What do you think about this poster? It has been seen in many markets and hutments, and it is written in English, as you see. Your language.'

I sensed a vague hint of accusation in those last two words. Although I had nothing whatsoever to do with Sapna and knew almost nothing about him, my face reddened with that special guilty blush of the completely innocent man.

'I don't know. I don't think I can help you with this.'

'Come now, Lin,' Abdul Ghani chided. 'There must be some impressions, some thoughts, that occur to you. There is no commitment here. Don't be shy. Just say the first things that come to your mind.'

'Well,' I began reluctantly, 'the first thing is, I think that this Sapna—or whoever wrote this poster—may be a Christian.'

'A Christian!' Khaled laughed. He was a young man, perhaps thirty-five, with short dark hair and soft green eyes. A thick scar swept in a smooth curve from his left ear to the corner of his mouth, stiffening that side of his face. His dark hair was streaked with premature white and grey. It was an intelligent, sensitive face, more scarred by its anger and hatreds than it was by the knife-wound on his cheek. 'They're supposed to *love* their enemies, not disembowel them!'

'Let him finish,' Khaderbhai smiled. 'Go on, Lin. What makes you think Sapna is a Christian fellow?'

'I didn't say Sapna is a Christian—just that whoever wrote this stuff is using Christian words and phrases. See, here, in the first part, where he says *I am come* ... and ... *Do this in memory of me*—those words can be found in the Bible. And here, in the third paragraph ... *I am the truth in their world of lies, I am the light in their darkness of greed, my way of blood is your freedom*—he's paraphrasing something ... *I am the Way and the Truth and the Light* ... and it's also in the Bible. Then in the last lines, he says ... *Blessed are the killers, for they shall steal lives in my name*—that's from the Sermon on the Mount. It's all been taken from the Bible, and there's probably more in here that I don't recognise. But it's all been changed around, it's as though this guy, whoever wrote this stuff, has taken bits of the Bible, and written it upside down.'

'Upside down? Explain please?' Madjid asked.

'I mean, it's against the *ideas* of the words in the Bible, but uses the same kind of *language*. He's written it to have exactly the opposite meaning and intention of the original. He's kind of turned the Bible on its head.'

I might've said more, but Abdul Ghani ended the discussion abruptly.

'Thank you, Lin. You've been a big help. But let's change the subject. I, for one, do sincerely dislike talking about such unpleasantness as this Sapna lunatic. I only brought it up because Khader asked me to—and Khader Khan's wish is my command. But we really should move on now. If we don't get started on our theme for tonight, we'll miss out altogether. So, let's have a smoke, and talk of other things. It's our custom for the guest to start, so will you be so kind?'

Farid rose and placed a huge, ornate hookah, with six snaking lines, on the floor between us next to the table. He passed the smoking tubes out, and squatted next to the hookah with several matches held ready to strike. The others closed off their smoking tubes with their thumbs and, as Farid played a flame over the tulip-shaped bowl, I puffed it alight. It was the mix of hashish and marijuana known as *ganga-jamuna*, named after the two holy rivers, Ganges and Jamner. It was so potent, and came with such force from the water-pipe, that almost at once my bloodshot eyes failed in focus and I experienced a mild, hallucinatory effect: the blurring at the edges of other people's faces, and a minuscule time-delay in their movements. The *Lewis Carrolls*, Karla called it. *I'm so stoned*, she used to say, *I'm getting the Lewis Carrolls*. So much smoke passed from the tube that I swallowed it and belched it out again. I closed off the pipe, and watched in slow motion as the others smoked, one after another. I'd just begun to master the sloppy grin that dumped itself on the plasticine muscles of my face when it was my turn to smoke again.

It was a serious business. There was no laughing or smiling. There was no conversation, and no man met another's eye. The men smoked with the same mirthless, earnest impassiveness I might've found on a long ride in an elevator full of strangers.

'Now, Mr. Lin,' Khaderbhai said, smiling graciously as Farid removed the hookah and set about cleaning the ash-filled bowl. 'It is also our custom for the guest to give us the theme for discussion. This is usually a religious theme, but it need not be so. What would you like to talk about?'

'I … I … I'm not sure what you mean?' I stammered, my brain soundlessly exploding in fractal repetitions of the pattern in the carpet beneath my feet.

'Give us a subject, Lin. Life and death, love and hate, loyalty and betrayal,' Abdul Ghani explained, waving a plump hand in effete little circles with each couplet. 'We are like a debating society here, you see. We meet every month, at least one time, and when our business and private matters are finished, we talk about philosophical subjects and the suchlike. It's our amusement. And now we have you, an Englishman, to give us a subject to discuss, in your language.'

'I'm not English, actually.'

'Not English? Then what are you?' Madjid demanded to know. Deep suspicions were planted in the furrows of his frown.

It was a good question. The false passport in my backpack in the slum said that I was a New Zealand citizen. The business card in my pocket said that I was an American named Gilbert Parker. People in the village at Sunder had re-named me Shantaram. In the slum they knew me as Linbaba. A lot of people in my own country knew me as a face on a wanted poster. *But is it my own country*, I asked myself. *Do I have a country?*

It wasn't until I'd asked myself the question that I realised I already had the answer. If I did have a country, a nation of the heart, it was India. I knew that I was as much a refugee, a displaced and stateless person, as the thousands of Afghans, Iranians, and others who'd come to Bombay across the burning bridge; those exiles who'd taken shovels of hope, and set about burying the past in the earth of their own lives.

'I'm an Australian,' I said, admitting it for the first time since I'd arrived in India, and obeying an instinct that warned me to tell Khaderbhai the truth. Strangely, I felt it to be more of a lie than any alias I'd ever used.

'How very interesting,' Abdul Ghani remarked, lifting one eyebrow in a sage nod to Khaderbhai. 'And what will you have as a subject, Lin?'

'Any subject?' I asked, stalling for time.

'Yes, your choice. Last week we discussed patriotism—the obligations of a man to God, and what he owes to the state. A most engaging theme. What will you have us discuss this week?'

'Well, there's a line in that poster of Sapna's ... *our suffering is our religion*—something like that. It made me think of something else. The cops came again, a few days ago, and smashed down a lot of houses in the zhopadpatti, and while we were watching it one of the women near me said ... *our duty is to work, and to suffer*—or as near to that as I can make out. She said it very calmly and simply, as if she accepted it, and was resigned to it, and understood it completely. But I don't understand it, and I don't think I ever will. So, maybe the question could be about that. Why do people suffer? Why do bad people suffer so little? And why do good people suffer so much? I mean, I'm not talking about me—all the suffering I've gone through, I brought most of it on myself. And God knows, I've caused a lot of it to other people. But I still don't understand it—especially not the suffering that the people in the slum go through. So ... suffering. We could talk about that ... do you think?'

I trailed off a little lamely into the silence that greeted my suggestion, but moments later I was rewarded with a warmly approving smile from Khaderbhai.

'It is a good theme, Lin. I knew that you would not disappoint us. Majidbhai, I will call on you to start us on this talk.'

Madjid cleared his throat and turned a gruff smile on his host. He scratched at his bushy eyebrows with thumb and forefinger, and then plunged into the discussion with the confident air of a man much used to expressing his opinions.

'Suffering, let me see. I think that suffering is a matter of choice. I think that we do not have to suffer anything in this life, if we are strong enough to deny it. The strong man can master his feelings so completely that it is almost impossible to make him suffer. When we do suffer things, like pain and so, it means that we have lost control. So I will say that suffering is a human weakness.'

'*Achaa-cha*,' Khaderbhai murmured, using the repetitive form of the Hindi word for *good*, which translates as *Yes, yes*, or *Fine, fine*. 'Your interesting idea makes me ask the question, where does strength come from?'

'Strength?' Madjid grunted. 'Everyone knows that it ... well ... what are you saying?'

'Nothing, my old friend. Only, is it not true that some of our strength comes from suffering? That suffering hardship makes us stronger? That those of us who have never known a real hardship, and true suffering, cannot have the same strength as others, who have suffered much? And if that is true, does that not mean that your argument is the same thing as saying that we have to be weak to suffer, and we have to suffer to be strong, so we have to be weak to be strong?'

'Yes,' Madjid conceded, smiling. 'Maybe a little bit is true, maybe a little bit of what you say. But I still think it is a matter of strength and weakness.'

'I don't accept everything that our brother Madjid said,' Abdul Ghani put in, 'but I do agree that there is an element of control that we have over suffering. I don't think you can deny that.'

'Where do we get this control, and how?' Khaderbhai asked.

'I would say that it is different for all of us, but that it happens when we grow up, when we mature and pass from the childishness of our youthful tears, and become adults. I think that it is a part of growing up, learning to control our suffering. I think that when we grow up, and learn that happiness is rare, and passes quickly, we become disillusioned and hurt. And how much we suffer is a mark of how much we have been hurt by this realisation. Suffering, you see, is a kind of anger. We rage against the unfairness, the injustice of our sad and sorry lot. And this boiling resentment, you see, this *anger*, is what we call suffering. It is also what leads us to the hero curse, I might add.'

'*Hero curse*! Enough of your hero curses! You bring *every* subject back to this,' Madjid growled, scowling to match the smug smile of his portly friend.

'Abdul has a pet theory, Lin,' said Khaled, the dour Palestinian. 'He believes that certain men are cursed with qualities, such as great courage, that make them commit desperate acts. He calls it the hero curse, the thing that compels them to lead other men to bloodshed and chaos. He might be right, I think, but he goes on about it so much he drives us all crazy.'

'Leaving that aside, Abdul,' Khaderbhai persisted, 'let me ask you one question about what you have said. Is there a difference, would you say, between suffering that we experience, and suffering that we cause for others?'

'Of course, yes. What are you getting at, Khader?'

'Just that if there are at least two kinds of suffering, quite different to each other, one that we feel, and one that we cause others to feel, they can hardly both be the anger that you spoke of. Isn't it so? Which one is which, would you say?'

'Why ... ha!' Abdul Ghani laughed. 'You've got me there, Khader, you old fox! You always know when I'm just making an argument for the sake of it, *na*? And just when I thought I was being bloody clever, too! But don't worry, I'll think it around, and come back at you again.'

He snatched a chunk of sweet barfi from the plate on the table, bit a piece of it, and munched happily. He gestured to the man on his right, thrusting the sweet in his pudgy fingers.

'And what about you, Khaled? What have you to say about Lin's topic?'

'I know that suffering is the truth,' Khaled said quietly. His teeth were clenched. 'I know that suffering is the sharp end of the whip, and *not* suffering is the blunt end—the end that the master holds in his hand.'

'Khaled, dear fellow,' Abdul Ghani complained. 'You are more than ten years my junior, and I think of you as dearly as I would of my own younger brother, but I must tell you that this is a most depressing thought, and you're disturbing the good pleasure we've gained from this excellent charras.'

'If you'd been born and raised in Palestine, you'd know that some people are born to suffer. And it never stops, for them. Not for a second. You'd know where real suffering comes from. It's the same place where love and freedom and pride are born. And it's the same place where those feelings and ideals die. That suffering never stops. We only pretend it does. We only tell ourselves it does, to make the kids stop whimpering in their sleep.'

He stared down at his strong hands, glowering at them as if at two despised and defeated enemies who were pleading for his mercy. A gloomy silence began to thicken in the air around us, and instinctively we looked to Khaderbhai. He sat cross-legged, stiff-backed, rocking slowly in his place and seeming to spool out a precise measure of respectful reflection. At last, he nodded to Farid, inviting him to speak.

'I think that our brother Khaled is right, in a way,' Farid began quietly, almost shyly. He turned his large, dark brown eyes on Khaderbhai. Encouraged by the older man's nod of interest, he continued. 'I think that happiness is a really thing, a truly thing, but it is what makes us crazy people. Happiness is a so strange and power thing that it makes us to be sick, like a germ sort of thing. And suffering is what cures us of it, the too much happiness. The—how do you say it, *bhari vazan?*'

'The *burden,*' Khaderbhai translated for him. Farid spoke a phrase rapidly in Hindi, and Khader gave it to us in such an elegantly poetic English that I realised, through the haze of the stone, how much better his English was than he'd led me to believe at our first meeting. *'The burden of happiness can only be relieved by the balm of suffering.'*

'Yes, yes, that is it what I want to say. Without the suffering, the happiness would squash us down.'

'This is a very interesting thought, Farid,' Khaderbhai said, and the young Maharashtrian glowed with pleasure in the praise.

I felt a tiny twitch of jealousy. The sense of well-being bestowed by Khaderbhai's benignant smile was as intoxicating as the heady mixture we'd smoked in the hookah pipe. The urge to be a son to Abdel Khader Khan, to earn the blessing of his praise, was overwhelming. The hollow space in my heart where a father's love might've been, should've been, wrapped itself around the contours of his form, and took the features of his face. The high cheekbones and closely cropped silver beard, the sensual lips and deep-set amber eyes, became the perfect father's face.

I look back on that time now—at my readiness to serve him as a son might serve a father, at my willingness to love him, in fact, and at how quickly and unquestioningly it happened in my life—and I wonder how much of it came from the great power that he wielded in the city, his city. I'd never felt so safe, anywhere in the world, as I did in his company. And I did hope that in the river of his life I might wash away the scent, and shake off the hounds. I've asked myself a thousand times, through the years, if I would've loved him so swiftly and so well if he'd been powerless and poor.

Sitting there, then, in that domed room, feeling the twinge of jealousy when he smiled at Farid and praised him, I knew that although Khaderbhai had spoken of adopting me as his son, on our first meeting, it was really I who'd adopted him. And while the discussion continued around me, I spoke the words, quite clearly, in the secret voice of prayer and incantation ... *Father, father, my father* ...

'You do not share our joy at the speaking of English, Sobhan Uncle,' Khaderbhai said, addressing the tough, grizzled older man on his right. 'So please, permit me to answer for you. You will say, I know, that the Koran tells us how our sin and wrong-doing is the cause of our suffering, isn't it so?'

Sobhan Mahmoud wagged his head in assent, his gleaming eyes nesting under a tufted ledge of grey eyebrows. He seemed amused by Khaderbhai's guess at his position on the theme.

'You will say that living by right principles, according to the teachings of the Holy Koran, will banish suffering from the life of a good Muslim, and lead him to the eternal bliss of heaven when life is at an end.'

'We all know what Sobhan Uncle thinks,' Abdul Ghani cut in, impatiently. 'None of us will disagree with your arguments, Uncle-*ji*, but you must permit me to say that you are inclined to be a little extreme, *na*? I well remember the time that you beat young Mahmoud with a rod of bamboo because he cried when his mother died. It is, of course, true that we should not question the will of Allah, but a touch of sympathy, in these matters, is only human, isn't it? But be that as it may, what I am interested in is *your* opinion, Khader. Please tell us, what do you think about suffering?'

No-one spoke or moved. There was a perceptible sharpening of focus and attention in the few silent moments as Khaderbhai gathered his thoughts. Each man had his own opinion and level of articulacy, yet I had the clear impression that Khaderbhai's contribution was usually the last word. I sensed that his response would set the tone, perhaps even becoming the answer those men would give, if the question about suffering were asked again. His expression was impassive, and his eyes were modestly cast down, but he was far too intelligent not to perceive the awe he inspired in others. I thought that he was far too human, as well, not to be flattered by it. When I came to know him better, I discovered that he was always avidly interested in what others thought of him, always acutely aware of his own charisma and its effect on those around him, and that every word he spoke, to everyone but God, was a performance. He was a man with the ambition to change the world forever. Nothing that he ever said or did— not even the quiet humility in his deep voice as he spoke to us then—was an accident, a chance, or anything but a calculated fragment of his plan.

'In the first place, I would like to make a general comment, and then I would like to follow it with a more detailed answer. Do you all allow me this? Good. Then, to the general comment—I think that suffering is the way we test our love. Every act of suffering, no matter how small or agonisingly great, is a test of love in some way. Most of the time, suffering is also a test of our love for God. This is my first statement. Does anyone wish to discuss this point, before I proceed?'

I looked from one face to another. Some men smiled in appreciation of his point, some nodded their agreement, and some others frowned in concentration. All of them seemed eager for Khaderbhai to continue.

'Very well, I will move on to my more detailed answer. The Holy Koran tells us that all things in the universe are related, one to another, and that even opposites are united in some way. I think that there are two points about suffering that we should remember, and they have to do with pleasure and pain. The first is this: that pain and suffering are connected, but they are not the same thing. Pain can exist without suffering, and it is also possible to suffer without feeling pain. Do you agree with this?'

He scanned the attentive, expectant faces, and found approval.

'The difference between them is this, I think: that what we learn from pain—for example, that fire burns and is dangerous—is always individual, for ourselves alone, but what we learn from suffering is what unites us as one human people. If we do not suffer with our pain, then we have not learned about anything but ourselves. Pain without suffering is like victory without struggle. We do not learn from it what makes us stronger or better or closer to God.'

The others wagged their heads at one another in agreement.

'And the other part, the pleasure part?' Abdul Ghani asked. A few of the men laughed gently, grinning at Ghani as he looked from one to the other. He laughed at them in return. 'What? *What?* Can't a man have a healthy, scientific interest in pleasure?'

'Ah,' Khader continued, 'I think that it's a little bit like what Mr. Lin tells us this Sapna fellow has done with the words from the Christian Bible. It is the reverse. Suffering is exactly like happiness, but backwards. One is the mirror image of the other, and has no real meaning or existence without the other.'

'I am sorry, I do not understand,' Farid said meekly, glancing at the others and blushing darkly. 'Please can you explain it?'

'It is like this,' Khaderbhai said gently. 'Take my hand, as an example. If I open my hand out like this, stretching the fingers and showing you the palm, or if I open my hand and put it on your shoulder, my fingers stretched out like this—that is happiness, or we may call it so for the sake of this moment. And if I curl my fingers, and close them tightly into a fist, just so, we may call that suffering. The two gestures are opposite in their meaning and power. Each one is completely different in appearance and in what it can do, but the hand that makes the gesture is the same. Suffering is happiness, backwards.'

Each man was then given another turn to speak, and the discussion itself moved backwards and forwards, reversing on itself as arguments were embellished or abandoned for two long hours. Hashish was smoked. Tea was served twice more, Abdul Ghani choosing to mix a small pellet of black opium in his, and drinking it down with a practised grimace.

Madjid modified his position by agreeing that suffering was not necessarily a sign of weakness, but insisting that we could toughen ourselves against it with a strong will; strength of will coming from strict self-discipline, a kind of self-imposed suffering. Farid added to his notion of suffering as an anti-toxin to the poison of happiness by recalling specific incidents from the lives of his friends. Old Sobhan whispered a few sentences in Urdu, and Khaderbhai translated the new point for us: there are some things we human beings will never understand, the things only God can understand, and that suffering may well be one of them. Keki Dorabji made the point that the universe, as those of the Parsee faith see it, is a process of struggle between opposites—light and darkness, hot and cold, suffering and pleasure—and that nothing can exist without the existence of its opposite. Rajubhai added that suffering is a condition of the unenlightened soul, locked within the wheel of Karma. Khaled Fattah said nothing more, despite the artful urgings of Abdul Ghani, who teased and cajoled him several times before finally giving up the attempt, visibly piqued by the stubborn refusal.

For his part, Abdul Ghani emerged as the most vocal and likeable of the group. Khaled was an intriguing man, but there was anger—too much anger, perhaps—brooding in him. Madjid had been a professional soldier in Iran. He seemed brave and direct, yet given to a simplistic view of the world and its people. Sobhan Mahmoud was undoubtedly pious, but there was a vaguely antiseptic scent of inflexibility about him. Young

Farid was openhearted, self-effacing and, I suspected, too easily led. Keki was dour and unresponsive, and Rajubhai seemed to be suspicious of me, almost to the point of rudeness. Of all of them, only Abdul Ghani displayed any sense of humour, and only he laughed aloud. He was as familiar with younger men as he was with those senior to him. He sprawled in his place, where others sat. He interrupted or interjected when he pleased, and he ate more, drank more, and smoked more than any man in the room. He was especially, irreverently, affectionate with Khaderbhai, and it was certain that they were close friends.

Khaderbhai asked questions, probed, made comments upon what was said, but never added another word to his own position. I was silent; drifting, tired, and grateful that no-one pressured me to speak.

When Khaderbhai finally adjourned the meeting, he walked with me to the door that opened into the street beside the Nabila Mosque, and stopped me there with a gentle hand on my forearm. He said he was glad I'd come, and that he hoped I'd enjoyed myself. Then he asked me to return on the following day because there was a favour I could do for him, if I was willing. Surprised and flattered, I agreed at once, promising to meet him at the same place on the following morning. I stepped out into the night, and almost put it out of my mind.

On the long walk home, my thoughts browsed among the ideas I'd heard presented by that scholarly group of criminals. I recalled other, similar discussions I'd shared with men in prison. Despite their general lack of formal education, or perhaps because of it, many men I'd known in prison had a fervent interest in the world of ideas. They didn't call it philosophy, or even know it as such, but the stuff of their conversations was often just that—abstract questions of moral and ethic, meaning and purpose.

It had been a long day, and an even longer night. With Madame Zhou's photograph in my hip pocket, my feet pinched by shoes that had been bought to bury Karla's dead lover, and my head clogged with definitions of suffering, I walked the emptying streets and remembered a cell in an Australian prison where the murderers and thieves I'd called my friends often gathered to argue, passionately, about truth and love and virtue. I wondered if they thought of me from time to time. *Am I a daydream for them now*, I asked myself, *a daydream of freedom and flight? How would they answer the question, what is suffering?*

I knew. Khaderbhai had dazzled us with the wisdom of his uncommon sense, and the cleverness of his talent for expressing it. His definition was sharp, and barbed enough—*suffering is happiness, backwards*—to hook a fish of memory. But the truth of what human suffering really means, in the dry, frightened mouth of life, wasn't in Khaderbhai's cleverness that night. It belonged to Khaled Ansari, the Palestinian. His was the definition that stayed with me. His simple, unbeautiful words were the clearest expression of what all prisoners, and everyone else who lives long enough, know well—that suffering, of every kind, is always a matter of what we've lost. When we're young, we think that suffering is something that's done to us. When we get older— when the steel door slams shut, in one way or another—we know that real suffering is measured by what's taken away from us.

Feeling small and alone and lonely, I walked by memory and touch through the dark, lightless lanes of the slum. As I turned into the last gully where my own empty hut waited, I saw lamplight. A man was standing not far from my door with a lantern in his hand. Beside him was a small child, a little girl, with knotted, teased hair. I drew near and saw that the man with the lantern was Joseph, the drunkard who'd beaten his wife, and that Prabaker was with him in the shadows.

'What's going on?' I whispered. 'It's late.'

'Hello, Linbaba. Nice clothes you're wearing for changes,' Prabaker smiled, his round face floating in the yellow light. 'I love it, your shoes— so clean and shining. Just in time you are. Joseph is doing it good things. He has paid money, to have it the good luck sign put on everybody his doors. Since not being a badly drinking fellow any more, he has been working full overtimes, and with some of his extra money he paid for this, to help us all with good luck.'

'The good luck sign?'

'Yes, look here at this child, look at her hand.' He lifted the little girl's wrists, and exposed the hands. In the feeble light, it wasn't clear what I was supposed to see. 'Look, here, only four fingers she has. See that! Four fingers only. Very good luck, this thing.'

I saw it. Two fingers on the child's hands were joined, imperceptibly, to make just one thick finger between the index and middle fingers. Her palms were blue. Joseph held a flat dish of blue paint. The child had been dipping her hands into it, and making handprints on the door of every hut in our lane to bring protection against the many afflictions attributed to the Evil Eye. Superstitious slum-dwellers apparently deemed her to be especially blessed because she was born with the rare difference of only four fingers on each hand. As I watched, the child reached over to press her small hands against my flimsy door. With a brief, serious nod, Joseph led the girl away to the next hut.

'I am helping that used-to-be-beating-his-wife-and-badly-drinking-fellow, that Joseph,' Prabaker said, in a stage whisper that could be heard twenty metres away. 'You are wanting any things, before I'm going?'

'No. Thanks. Good night, Prabu.'

'*Shuba ratri*, Lin,' he grinned. *Good night.* 'Have it sweet dreams for me, yes?'

He turned to leave, but I stopped him.

'Hey, Prabu.'

'Yes, Lin?'

'Tell me, what is suffering? What do you think? What does it mean, that people suffer?'

Prabaker glanced along the dark lane of ramshackle huts to the hovering glow-worm of Joseph's lamp. He looked back at me, only his eyes and his teeth visible, although we were standing quite close together.

'You're feeling okay, Lin?'

'I'm fine,' I laughed.

'Did you drink any daru tonight, like that badly-drinking-Joseph?'

'No, really, I'm fine. Come on, you're always defining everything for me. We were talking about suffering tonight, and I'm interested to know, what do you think about it?'

'Is easy—suffering is hungry, isn't it? Hungry, for anything, means suffering. Not hungry for something, means, not suffering. But everybody knows that.'

'Yes, I guess everybody does. Good night, Prabu.'

'Good night, Lin.'

He walked away, singing, and he knew that none of the people sleeping in the wretched huts around him would mind. He knew that if they woke they would listen for a moment, and then drift back to sleep with a smile because he was singing about love.

CHAPTER FIFTEEN

'Wake up, Lin! Hey, Linbaba, you must awake up now!'

One eye opened, and focused on a hovering, brown balloon that had Johnny Cigar's face painted on it. The eye closed again.

'Go away, Johnny.'

'Hello to you, too, Lin,' he chuckled, infuriatingly happy. 'You have to get up.'

'You're an evil man, Johnny. You're a cruel and evil man. Go away.'

'One fellow has an injury, Lin. We need your medicine box, and your good medical self also.'

'It's still dark, man.' I groaned. 'It's two o'clock in the morning. Tell him to come back in the daylight, when I'm alive.'

'Oh, certainly, I will tell him, and he will go, but I think you should know that he is bleeding very swiftly. Still, if you must have more sleep, I will beat him away from your door, this very instant, with three-four good shots from my slipper.'

I was leaning out over the deep pool of sleep but that word, *bleeding*, pulled me back from the edge. I sat up, wincing at the numbed stiffness of one hip. My bed, like most of the beds in the slum, was a blanket, folded twice and placed on the hard-packed earth. Kapok mattresses were available, but they were impractical. They took up too much space in the small huts, they quickly became infested with lice, fleas, and other vermin, and rats found them irresistible. After long months of sleeping on the ground, I was as used to it as a man gets, but there wasn't much flesh on my hips, and I woke up sore every morning.

Johnny was holding a lamp quite close to my face. I blinked, pushing it aside to see another man squatting in the doorway with his arm held out in front of him. There was a large cut or gash on the arm, and blood seeped from it, drip, drip, drop, into a bucket. Only half awake, as I was, I stared stupidly at the yellow plastic bucket. The man had brought his own bucket with him to stop the blood from staining the floor of my hut, and that seemed more disturbing, somehow, than the wound itself.

'Sorry for trouble, Mr. Lin,' the young man said.

'This is Ameer,' Johnny Cigar grunted, whacking the injured man on the back of the head with a resounding slap. 'Such a stupid fellow he is, Lin. *Now* he's sorry for trouble. I should take my slipper and beat your black, and beat some of your blue also.'

'God, what a mess. This is a bad cut, Johnny.' It was a long, deep slash from the shoulder almost to the tip of the elbow. A large, triangular flap of skin, shaped like the lapel of an overcoat, was beginning to curl away from the wound. 'He needs a doctor. This has to be stitched up. You should've taken him to the hospital.'

'Hospital *naya*!' Ameer whined. '*Nahin*, baba!'

Johnny slapped him on the ear.

'Shut up, you stupid! He won't go to a hospital or a doctor, Lin. He's a cheeky fellow, a goonda. He's afraid of police. Aren't you, hey, you stupid? Afraid of police, *na?*'

'Stop hitting him, Johnny. It's really not helping. How did this happen?'

'Fighting. His gang, with the other gang. They fight, with swords and choppers, these street gangsters, and this is the result.'

'The other fellows started it. They were doing the Eve-teasing!' Ameer complained. *Eve-teasing* was the name given to the charge of sexual harassment, under Indian law, and it covered a range of offences from insulting language to physical molestation. 'We warned them to stop it. Our ladies were not walking safely. For that reason only we did fight them.'

Johnny raised his broad hand, silencing Ameer's protest. He wanted to strike the young man again, but my frown gave him reluctant pause.

'You think this is a reason to fight with swords and choppers, you stupid? Your mummy will be very happy that you stop the Eve-teasing, and get yourself hacked up into teeny pieces, *na?* Very happy she'll be! And now you want Linbaba to sew you up, and make nice repairs to your arm. *Shameful*, you are!'

'Wait a minute, Johnny. I can't do this. It's too big, too messy ... it's too much.'

'You have the needles and cotton in your medical boxes, Lin.'

He was right. The kit contained suture needles and silk thread. But I'd never used them.

'I've never used them, Johnny. I can't do it. He needs a professional—a doctor or a nurse.'

'I told you, Lin. He won't go to a doctor. I tried to force him. Someone in the other gang was hurt even more seriously than this stupid boy. Maybe he will *die* also, this other fellow. It is a police matter now, and they are asking questions. Ameer won't go to any doctor or hospital.'

'If you give me, I will do myself,' Ameer said, swallowing hard.

His eyes were huge with fright and horror-struck resolve. I looked at him full in the face for the first time, and I saw how young he was: sixteen or seventeen years old. He was wearing Puma sneakers, jeans, and a basketball singlet with the number 23 printed on the front. The clothes were Indian copies of famous western brands, but they were considered fashionably hip by his peers in the slum, other young men with lean bellies and heads full of scrambled foreign dreams; young men who went without food to buy clothes that they imagined made them look like the cool foreigners in magazines and films.

I didn't know the kid. He was one of thousands I'd never seen, although I'd been there for almost six months, and no-one in the place lived more than five or six hundred metres from my hut. Some men, such as Johnny Cigar and Prabaker, appeared to know everyone in the slum. It seemed extraordinary to me that they should know intimate details from the lives of so many thousands of people. It was even more remarkable that they cared—that they encouraged and scolded and worried about all of them. I wondered how that young man was connected to Johnny Cigar. Ameer shivered in the swirling chill of night, pressing his lips into a wide, noiseless whine as he contemplated taking needle and thread to his own flesh. I wondered how it was that Johnny, standing above him, knew him well enough to be sure he would do it; to nod at me with the message, *Yes, if you give him the needle, he will do it himself.*

'Okay, okay, I'll do it,' I surrendered. 'It's going to hurt. I haven't got any anaesthetic.'

'Hurt!' Johnny boomed happily. 'Pain is no problem, Lin. Good you have pains, Ameer, you *chutia*. Pains in your *brains*, you should be having.'

I sat Ameer down on my bed, covering his shoulders with another blanket. Pulling the kerosene stove from my kitchen box, I pumped it up, primed it, and set a pot of water on it to boil. Johnny hurried off to ask someone to make hot, sweet tea. I washed my face and hands hurriedly, in the dark, at the open bathroom-space beside my hut. When the water boiled, I put a little into a dish, and threw two needles into the pot to sterilise them with further boiling. Using antiseptic and warm soapy water, I washed the wound and then dried it off with clean gauze. I bound the arm tightly with gauze, leaving it in place for ten minutes to press the wound together, in the hope that it would make the stitching easier.

Ameer drank two large mugs of sweet tea at my insistence, as a counter to the symptoms of shock that had begun to show. He was afraid, but he was calm. He trusted me. He couldn't know that I'd only done the procedure once before, and under ironically similar circumstances. A man had been stabbed during a prison fight. The problem between the two antagonists, whatever it was, had been resolved in the violent encounter, and the matter was finished so far as they were concerned. But if the stabbed man had reported to the prison infirmary for treatment, the authorities would've placed him in an isolation unit for prisoners on protection. For some men, child molesters and informers particularly, there was no alternative to being placed on protection because they wouldn't otherwise have survived. For others, men placed there against their will, the protection unit was a curse: the curse of suspicion, slanders, and the company of men they despised. The stabbed man had come to me. I'd stitched his wound closed with a leatherwork needle and embroidery thread. The wound healed, but it left an ugly, rippling scar. The memory of it never left me, and I wasn't confident about the attempt to stitch Ameer's arm. The sheepish, trusting smile that the young man offered me was no help. *People always hurt us with their trust,* Karla said to me once. *The surest way to hurt someone you like, is to put all your trust in him.*

I drank tea, smoked a cigarette, and then set to work. Johnny stood in the doorway, ineffectually scolding several curious neighbours and their children away from the door. The suture needle was curved and very fine. I supposed that it should've been used with some kind of pliers. I had none in my kit. One of the boys had borrowed them to fix a sewing machine. I had to push the needle into the skin, and pull it through with my fingers. It was awkward and slippery, and the first few cross-shaped stitches were messy. Ameer winced and grimaced inventively, but he didn't cry out. By the fifth and sixth stitches I'd developed a technique, and the ugliness of the work, if not the pain involved, had diminished.

Human skin is tougher and more resilient than it looks. It's also relatively simple to stitch, and the thread can be pulled quite tightly without tearing the tissue. But the needle, no matter how fine or sharp, is still a foreign object and, for those of us who aren't inured to such work through frequent repetition, there's a psychological penalty that must be paid each time we drive that alien thing into another being's flesh. I began to sweat heavily despite the cool night. It was a measure of the distress involved that Ameer became brighter as the work progressed, while I grew more tense and fatigued.

'You should've insisted that he go to a hospital!' I snapped at Johnny Cigar. 'This is ridiculous!'

'You're doing very excellent sewing, Lin,' he countered. 'You could make up a very fine shirt, with stitches like that.'

'It's not as good as it should be. He'll have a big scar. I don't know what the fuck I'm doing here.'

'Are you having trouble with toilet, Lin?'

'What?'

'Are you not going to toilet? Are you having it hard motions?'

'For Chrissakes, Johnny! What are you babbling about?'

'Your bad temper, Lin. This is not your usual behaviour. Maybe it is a problem with hard motions, I think so?'

'No,' I groaned.

'Ah, then it is *loose* motions you're having, I think.'

'He had it loose motions for three days last month,' one of my neighbours chipped in from the open doorway. 'My husband told me that Linbaba was going three-three-four times to toilet every day then, and again three-three-four times every night. The whole street was talking.'

'Oh yes, I remember,' another neighbour recalled. 'Such pain he had! What faces he pulled when he was at toilet, *yaar*. Like he was making a baby. And it was a very runny, loose motion. Like water, it was, and it came out so fast, like when they explode the cannons on Independence Day. *Da-dung*! Like that, it was! I recommended the drinking of chandu-chai that time, and his motions became harder, and a very good colour again.'

'A good idea,' Johnny muttered appreciatively. 'Go and get it some chandu-chai for Linbaba's loose motions.'

'No!' I moaned. 'I don't *have* loose motions. I don't have *hard* motions. I haven't had a chance to have *any* motions at *all* yet. I'm only half awake, for God's sake! Oh, what's the use? There, it's finished. You'll be okay, Ameer, I think. But you should have a tetanus injection.'

'No need, Linbaba. I had it injections before three months, after the last fighting.'

I cleaned the wound once more and dusted it with antibiotic powder. Covering the twenty-six stitches with a loose bandage, I warned him not to get it wet, and instructed him to come back within two days to have it checked. He tried to pay me, but I refused the money. No-one paid for the treatment I dispensed. Still, it wasn't principle that made me refuse. The truth was that I felt curiously, inexplicably angry—at Ameer, at Johnny, at myself—and I ordered him away curtly. He touched my feet, and backed out of the hut, collecting a parting slap on the head from Johnny Cigar.

I was about to clean up the mess in my hut when Prabaker rushed inside, grasped at my shirt, and tried to drag me out through the door.

'So good that you are not sleeping, Linbaba,' he gasped breathlessly. 'We can save the time of waking you up. You must come now with me! Hurry, please!'

'For God's sake, what is it now?' I grumbled. 'Let go of me, Prabu. I've got to clean up this mess.'

'No time for mess, baba. You come now, please. No problem!'

'*Yes* problem!' I contradicted him. 'I'm not going anywhere until you tell me what the hell is going on. That's it, Prabu. That's final. No problem.'

'You absolutely *must* come, Lin,' he insisted, dragging at my shirt. 'Your friend is in the jail. You must help!'

We abandoned the hut and rushed out through the narrow, shadow-clogged lanes of the sleeping slum. On the main street outside the President Hotel we caught a cab, and swept along the clean, silent streets past the Parsee Colony, Sassoon Dock, and the Colaba Market. The cab stopped outside the Colaba police station, directly across the road from Leopold's. The bar was closed, of course, with the wide metal shutters rolled down to the pavement. It seemed preternaturally quiet: the haunted stillness of a popular bar, closed for business.

Prabaker and I passed the gates of the police station and entered the compound. My heart was beating fast, but I looked outwardly calm. All the cops in the station spoke Marathi—it was a requirement of their employment. I knew that if they had no special reason to suspect or challenge me, my proficiency with the Marathi language would please them as much as it surprised them. It would make me popular with them, and that small celebrity would protect me. Still, it was a journey behind enemy lines, and in my mind I pushed the locked, heavy box of fear all the way to the back of the attic.

Prabaker spoke quietly to a *havaldar*, or *police constable*, at the foot of a long flight of metal stairs. The man nodded, and stepped to the side. Prabaker wagged his head, and I followed him up the steel steps to a landing, with a heavy door, on the first floor. A face appeared at the grille set into the door. Large brown eyes stared left and right, and then the door opened for us. We stepped into an antechamber that contained a desk, a small metal chair, and a bamboo cot. The guard who opened the door was the watchman on duty that night. He spoke briefly with Prabaker and then glared at me. He was a tall man with a prominent paunch and a large, expressively bristly moustache, tinged with grey. There was a metal gate made from hinged, concertina-style lattices behind him. Beyond the gate, the faces of a dozen prisoners watched us with intense interest. The guard turned his broad back on them, and held out his hand.

'He wants you to —' Prabaker began.

'I know,' I stopped him, fishing into the pocket of my jeans. 'He wants baksheesh. How much?'

'Fifty rupees,' Prabaker grinned, looking up with his biggest smile into the face of the tall officer.

I handed over a fifty-rupee note, and the watchman palmed it. He turned his back to me and approached the metal gate. We followed him. More men had gathered there, all wide awake and chattering, despite the late hour. The watchman stared at them, one by one, until all were silent. Then he called me forward. When I faced the bars of the steel gate, the crowd of men parted and two fantastic figures pushed their way to the front. They were the bear-handlers, the blue-skinned men who'd brought Kano the bear to my slum at Abdullah's request. They reached the gate and grasped at the bars, chattering at me so quickly and urgently that I only caught every fourth or fifth word.

'What's going on, Prabu?' I asked, completely mystified. When Prabaker told me that *my friend* was in jail, I'd assumed that he'd meant

Abdullah. I was expecting to find Abdullah behind the bars, and I moved left and right, trying to see beyond the bear-handlers and the other men crowding at the gate.

'These are your friends, isn't it?' Prabaker asked. 'Don't you remember, Lin? They came with Kano to have your bear hugs.'

'Yes, sure, I remember them. Did you bring me to see *them*?'

Prabaker blinked at me, and then turned quickly to check the expressions on the faces of the watchman and the bear-handlers.

'Yes, Lin,' he said quietly. 'These men were asking you to come. Do you ... do you want to leave?'

'No, no. I just ... never mind. What do they want? I can't make out what they're saying.'

Prabaker asked them to explain what they wanted, and the two blue-skinned men shouted their story, clutching at the lattices of the gate as if they were the boards of a raft on the open sea.

'They say, they tell it, that they are staying near to the Navy Nagar, and they found there some other fellows, who also are bear handling fellows, and having it one very sad and skinny bear,' Prabaker explained, urging the men to be calm and to speak more slowly. 'They say that these others were not treating their bear with respect. They were beating that bear with a whip, and that bear was crying, with pains all over him.'

The bear-handlers spoke in a rush of words that kept Prabaker silent, listening and nodding, with his mouth open to speak. Other prisoners approached the gate to listen. The corridor beyond the gate had long windows on one side covered by a metal grille. On the other side of the crowded prison corridor there were several rooms. Men streamed from those rooms, swelling the throng at the gate to a hundred or more prisoners, all of them listening with fascination to the bear-handler's story.

'So hard, those bad fellows were beating their poor bear,' Prabaker translated. 'And even when it cried, those fellows didn't stop beating it, that bear. And, you know, it was a *girl* bear!'

The men at the gate reacted with outraged, angry shouts and sympathetic cries.

'Our fellows here, they were very upset about the others, beating that other bear. So, they went up to those others, and they told them they must not be beating any bear. But they were very bad and angry, those fellows. There was a lot of shouting, and pushing, and bad language. One of those fellows, he called our fellows the sisterfuckers. Our fellows, they called the other ones the arse-holes. The bad ones, they called our fellows motherfucking bastards. Our fellows, they called them brotherfuckers. The other ones, they said a lot more about something-and-anything-fucking. Our fellows, they said back a lot about —'

'Get to the point, Prabu.'

'Yes, Lin,' he said, listening intently. There was a lengthy pause.

'Well?' I demanded.

'Still a lot of bad language, Lin,' he replied, shrugging helplessly. 'But some of it, I have to say, is very, very fine, if you want to hear it?'

'No!'

'Okay,' he said, at last, 'at the end, somebody called it the police to come. Then there was a big fight.'

He paused again, listening to the next instalment of the story. I turned to look at the watchman, and saw that he was as deeply engrossed in the unfolding saga as the prisoners were. He chewed paan as he listened, his thorn-bush of a moustache twitching up and down, and unconsciously emphasising his interest. A roar of approval for something in the story went up from the attentive prisoners, and the watchman was united with them in the appreciative shout.

'At first, the other fellows were winning that big fight. So much fighting there was, Lin, like in Mahabharata. Those bad fellows had a few friends, who all made a contribution of punches and kicking and slapping with slippers. Then, Kano the bear, he got upset. Just before the police arrived, Kano the bear got into that fight, to help his bear-handling fellows. He stopped that fight too fast. He was knocking those other fellows right, and left also. That Kano is a very good fighting bear. He beat those bad fellows, and all their friends, and gave them a solid pasting!'

'And then the blue guys got arrested,' I concluded for him.

'Sad to say it, yes. Arrested, they were, for the charge of Breaking the Peaces.'

'Okay. Let's talk.'

Prabaker, the watchman, and I took two steps away from the gate and stood at the bare metal desk. Over my shoulder, I could see that the men at the gate were straining to hear our conversation.

'What's the Hindi word for *bail*, Prabu? Find out if we can bail the guys out of jail.'

Prabaker asked, but the watchman shook his head, and told us that it was out of the question.

'Is it possible for me to pay the *fine?*' I asked in Marathi, using the commonly accepted euphemism for a police bribe.

The watchman smiled, and shook his head. A policeman was hurt in the scuffle, he explained, and the matter was out of his hands.

Shrugging my helplessness, I turned back to the gate and told the men that I couldn't bail or bribe them out of the jail. They rattled away at me in such a swift and garbled Hindi that I couldn't understand them.

'No, Lin!' Prabaker announced, beaming a smile at me. 'They don't worry for themselves. They worry for Kano! He is arrested also, that bear. They are very worried for their bear. *That* is what they want you to help them for!'

'The *bear* is arrested?' I asked the watchman, in Marathi.

'*Ji, ha!*' he replied, a flourish of pride rippling in his wild moustache. *Sir, yes!* 'The bear is in custody downstairs!'

I looked at Prabaker, and he shrugged.

'Maybe we should see it that bear?' he suggested.

'I think we *should* see it that bear!' I replied.

We took the steel steps down to the ground-floor level, and were directed to a row of cells directly beneath the rooms we'd seen upstairs. A ground-level watchman opened one of the rooms, and we leaned inside to see Kano the bear sitting in the middle of a dark and empty cell. It was a large room, with a keyhole toilet in the floor in one corner. The huge muzzled bear was chained at his neck and on his paws, and the chains passed through a metal grille at one of the windows. He sat with his broad back against a wall, and his lower legs splayed out in front of him. His expression—and I have no other way of describing the set of his features, other than as an expression—was disconsolate and profoundly distressed. He let out a long, heart-wrenching sigh, even as we watched him.

Prabaker was standing a little behind me. I turned to ask him a question, and found that he was crying, his face contorted with miserable sobbing. Before I could speak, he moved past me toward the bear, evading the outstretched hand of the watchman. He reached Kano, with his arms before him in a wide embrace, and pressed himself to the creature, resting his head against Kano's and stroking the shaggy fur with murmurs of tenderness. I exchanged glances with the ground-level watchman. The man raised his eyebrows, and wagged his head from side to side energetically. He was clearly impressed.

'I did that first, you know,' I found myself saying, in Marathi. 'A few weeks ago. I hugged that bear first.'

The watchman wrinkled his lips in a pitying and contemptuous sneer. 'Of course you did,' he mocked. 'Absolutely, you did.'

'Prabaker!' I called out. 'Can we get on with this?'

He pulled himself away from the bear and approached me, wiping tears from his eyes with the backs of his hands as he walked. His wretchedness was so complete that I was moved to put my arm around him to comfort him.

'I hope you are not minding, Lin,' he cautioned. 'I smell quite much like bears.'

'It's okay,' I answered him softly. 'It's okay. Let's see what we can do.'

Ten more minutes of discussion with the watchmen and the other guards resolved that it was impossible for us to bail out the handlers or their bear. There was nothing to be done. We returned to the metal gate and informed the bear-handlers that we were unable to help them. They broke into another animated dialogue with Prabaker.

'They know all that we cannot be helping,' Prabaker clarified for me, after a few minutes. 'What they want is to be in that lock-up cell with Kano. They are worried for Kano because he is lonely. Since a baby, he has never been sleeping alone, even one night. For that only, they are a big worried. They say that Kano, he will be frightened. He will have a bad sleep, and have too many bad dreams. He will be crying, for his loneliness. And he will be ashamed, to be in the jail, because he is normally a very fine citizen, that bear. They want only to go down to that lock-up cell with Kano, and keep him some good companies.'

One of the bear-handlers stared into my eyes when Prabaker finished his explanation. The man was distraught. His face was creased with worry. Anguish drew his lips back into something that resembled a snarl. He repeated one phrase again and again, hoping that with repetition and the force of his emotion he might make me understand. Suddenly, Prabaker burst into tears once more, sobbing like a child as he grasped the metal bars of the gate.

'What's he saying, Prabu?'

'He says *a man must love his bear*, Lin,' Prabaker translated for me. 'He says like that. *A man must love his bear.*'

Negotiations with the watchmen and the other guards were spirited once we presented them with a request that they could grant without bending the rules to their breaking point. Prabaker thrived in the theatrically energetic barter, protesting and pleading with equal vigour. At last he arrived at an agreed sum—two hundred rupees, about twelve American dollars—and the moustachioed watchman unlocked the gate for the bear-handlers while I handed over the bundle of notes. In a strange procession of people and purposes, we filed down the steel stairs, and the ground-floor watchman unlocked the cell that housed Kano. At the sound of their voices, the great bear rose from his seated position, and then fell forward on all fours, dragged downward by the chains. The bear swayed its head from side to side in a joyful dance, and pawed at the ground. When the bear-handlers rushed to greet him, Kano drove his snout into their armpits, and nuzzled in their long, dread-locked hair, snuffling and sniffing at their scent. For their part, the blue men smothered him in affectionate caresses, and sought to ease the stress of the heavy chains. We left them in the enclosure of that embrace. When the steel cell door slammed shut on Kano and his handlers the sound rattled through the empty parade ground, gouging echoes from the stone. I felt that sound as a shiver in my spine as Prabaker and I walked out of the police compound.

'It is a very fine thing that you have done tonight, Linbaba,' Prabaker gushed. 'A man must love his bear. That is what they said, those bear-handling fellows, and you have made it come true. It is a very, very, very fine thing that you have done.'

We woke a sleeping cab driver outside the police station, on Colaba Causeway. Prabaker joined me in the back seat, enjoying the chance to play tourist in one of the cabs he frequently drove. As the taxi pulled out from the kerb, I turned to see that he was staring at me. I looked away. A moment later, I turned my head and found that he was still staring. I frowned at him, and he wagged his head. He smiled his world-embracing smile for me, and placed his hand over his heart.

'What?' I asked irritably, although his smile was irresistible, and he knew it, and I was already smiling with him in my heart.

'A man ...' he began, intoning the words with sacramental solemnity.

'Not again, Prabu.'

'... must love his bear,' he concluded, patting at his chest and wagging his head frantically.

'Oh, God help me,' I moaned, turning again to look at the awkward stir and stretch of the waking street.

At the entrance to the slum, Prabaker and I separated as he made his way to Kumar's chai shop for an early breakfast. He was excited. Our adventure with Kano the bear had given him a fascinating new story—with himself cast in an important role—to share with Parvati, one of Kumar's two pretty daughters. He hadn't said anything to me about Parvati, but I'd seen him talking to her, and I guessed that he was falling in love. In Prabaker's way of courtship, a young man didn't bring flowers or chocolates to the woman he loved: he brought her stories from the wider world, where men grappled with demons of desire, and monstrous injustice. He brought her gossip and scandals and intimate secrets. He brought her the truth of his brave heart, and the mischievous, awe-struck wonder that was the wellspring of his laughter, and of that sky-wide smile. And as I watched him scurry toward the chai shop, I saw that already his head was wagging and his hands were waving as he rehearsed the story that he brought to her as the new day's gift.

I walked on into the grey pre-morning as the slum murmured itself awake. Smoke swirling from a hundred small fires roved the lanes. Figures wrapped in coloured shawls emerged, and vanished in the misty streams. The smells of rotis cooking on kerosene stoves, and chai boiling in fragrant pots joined the people-smells of coconut hair oil, sandalwood soap, and camphor-soaked clothing. Sleepy faces greeted me at every turn in the winding lanes, smiling and offering the blessings of the morning in six languages and as many different faiths. I entered my hut and looked with new fondness at the humble, comfortable shabbiness of it. It was good to be home.

I cleaned up the mess in my hut and then joined the morning procession of men who filed out onto the concrete pier that we used as a latrine. When I returned, I discovered that my neighbours had prepared two full buckets of hot water for my bath. I rarely bothered with the laborious and time-consuming procedure of heating several pots of water on the kerosene stove, preferring the lazier, if less luxurious, option of a cold-water bath. Knowing that, my neighbours sometimes provided it for me. It was no small service. Water, the most precious commodity in any slum, had to be carried from the communal well in the legal compound, some three hundred metres away beyond the barbed wire. Because the well was only open twice a day, there were hundreds of people in the shove and wrestle for water, and each bucket was dragged into the light with bluff and scratch and shout. Carried back and hoisted through the wire, the water had to be boiled in saucepans on small kerosene stoves, at some cost of the relatively expensive fuel. Yet when they did that for me, none of my neighbours ever took credit for it or expected thanks. The water I used might've been boiled and brought there by Ameer's family as a sign of appreciation for the treatment I'd given him. It might've come from my nearest neighbour, or it might've been provided by one of the half dozen people who stood around and watched me bathe. I would never know. It was one of the small, uncelebrated things people did for me every week.

In a sense, the ghetto existed on a foundation of those anonymous, unthankable deeds; insignificant and almost trivial in themselves, but collectively essential to the survival of the slum. We soothed our neighbours' children as if they were our own when they cried. We tightened a loose rope on someone else's hut when we noticed it sagging, and adjusted the lay of a plastic roof as we passed by. We helped one another, without being asked, as if we were all members of one huge tribe, or family, and the thousand huts were simply rooms in our mansion home.

At his invitation, I breakfasted with Qasim Ali Hussein. We drank sweet tea spiced with clove, and ate waffle-style rotis filled with ghee and sugar, and rolled into tubes. Ranjit's lepers had delivered a new batch of medicines and bandages on the previous day. Because I was away all afternoon, they'd left the bundles with Qasim Ali. We sorted through them together. Qasim Ali couldn't read or write English, and he insisted that I explain the contents and uses of the various capsules, tablets, and salves that I'd ordered. One of his sons, Ayub, sat with us, and wrote the name and description of each medicine in the Urdu script on tiny fragments of paper, and patiently attached a label to every container or tube of cream with adhesive tape. I didn't know it then, but Qasim Ali had chosen Ayub to be my assistant, to learn everything possible about medicines and their uses, so that he could replace me when the time came—as the head man was sure that it would—for me to leave the slum.

It was eleven o'clock when I finally found time to stop at Karla's small house near the Colaba Market. There was no answer to my knocking. Her neighbours told me she'd gone out an hour earlier. They had no idea when she would return. I was annoyed. I'd left my boots and jeans inside, and I was anxious to retrieve them, to get out of those loose but uncomfortable clothes, those clothes that were hers. I hadn't exaggerated when I'd told her that the jeans, T-shirt, and boots were my only clothes. In my hut there were only two lungis, which I wore for sleeping, bathing, or for when I washed my jeans. I could've bought new clothes—a T-shirt, jeans, and track shoes would've cost me no more than four or five American dollars in the clothing bazaar at Fashion Street—but I wanted my *own* clothes, the clothes I felt right in. I left a grumble of words for her in a note, and set off to keep my appointment with Khaderbhai.

The great house on Mohammed Ali Road seemed to be empty when I arrived. The six panels of the street door were folded back, and the spacious marble entrance hall was exposed. Thousands of people walked past every hour, but the house was well known and no-one on the street seemed to pay any attention to me as I entered, knocking on the green panels to announce my arrival. After a few moments, Nazeer came to greet me, his frown vaguely hostile. He directed me to swap my street shoes for a pair of house slippers, and then led me along a tall, narrow corridor in the opposite direction to that of the room I'd visited the night before. We passed a number of closed rooms as the corridor wound through two right turns, and eventually came out upon an inner courtyard.

The very large, oval space was open to the sky in the centre as if a great hole had been cut in the thick plasterwork of the ceiling. It was paved with heavy, square Maharashtrian stone, and surrounded by pillared arches that gave a cloister effect. There were many plants and flowering shrubs in the wide circle of the interior garden, and five tall, slender palms. The fountain that I'd heard from the meeting room, where we'd talked about suffering, was the centrepiece. It was a circle of marble about a metre in height and four metres in diameter with a single huge, uncut boulder in the centre. Water seemed to spout from the very core of the enormous stone. At its peak, the small fountain curved into a lily-shaped plume before splashing gently onto the smooth, rounded surfaces of the boulder and flowing with rhythmic, musical flourishes into the pond of the fountain. Khaderbhai was sitting in a cane emperor chair, to one side of the fountain. He was reading a book, which he closed and placed on a glass-topped table when I arrived.

'*Salaam aleikum*, Mr. Lin,' he smiled. *Peace be with you.*

'*Wa aleikum salaam. Aap kaise hain?*' *And with you be peace. How are you, sir?*

'I am well, thank you. Mad dogs and Englishmen may very well be out and about in the midday sun, but I prefer to sit here, in the shade of my humble garden.'

'Not so humble, Khaderbhai,' I remarked.

'Do you think it altogether too grand?'

'No, no. I didn't mean that,' I said hurriedly, because that's precisely what I'd been thinking. I couldn't help but recall that he owned the slum where I lived; the dusty, barren slum of twenty-five thousand people, where nothing green existed after eight rainless months, and the only water was rationed from wells that were padlocked shut, most of the time. 'This is the most beautiful place I've ever seen in Bombay. I couldn't have imagined this from the street outside.'

He stared at me, for a few moments as if measuring the exact width and depth of the lie, and then waved me to a small, backless stool that was the only other chair in the courtyard.

'Please sit down, Mr. Lin. Have you eaten?'

'Yes, thank you. I had a late breakfast.'

'Allow me to serve you tea, at least. Nazeer! *Idhar-ao!*' he shouted, his voice startling a pair of doves that had been pecking for crumbs at his feet. The birds flew up and flapped around Nazeer's chest as he entered. They seemed to be unafraid of him, even to recognise him, and they settled on the flagstones once more, following him like tame puppies.

'*Chai bono*, Nazeer,' Khaderbhai commanded. His tone with the driver was imperious, but not severe, and I guessed that it was the only tone Nazeer felt comfortable with and respected. The burly Afghan withdrew silently, the birds hop-running behind him into the very house.

'Khaderbhai, there's something I want to say before we ... talk about anything else,' I began quietly. My next words drew his head up swiftly, and I knew that I had his full attention. 'It's about Sapna.'

'Yes, go on,' he murmured.

'Well, I thought about it a lot last night, what we were talking about, and what you asked me to do at the meeting, to sort of help you and so on, and I've got a problem with it.'

He smiled, and raised one eyebrow quizzically, but he said nothing more, and I was forced to explain myself further.

'I know I'm not saying this very well, but I just don't feel right about it. No matter what this guy did, I don't want to be put in a position of being ... well, a kind of cop. I wouldn't feel right about working with them, even indirectly. In my country, the phrase *helping the police with their enquiries* is a euphemism for informing on someone. I'm sorry. I understand that this guy killed people. If you want to go after him, that's your business, and I'm happy to help you out in any way I can. But I don't want to be involved with the cops, or to help *them* do it. If you're working *outside* the law, on your own—if you want to go after him, and put him out of action personally, for whatever reason of your own—then I'll be glad to help. You can count me in, if you want to fight his gang, whoever they are.'

'Is there anything more?'

'No. That's ... that's ... pretty much it.'

'Very well, Mr. Lin,' he replied. His face was impassive as he studied me, but there was a puzzling laughter in his eyes. 'I may put your mind at rest, I think, in assuring you that while I do assist a large number of policemen financially, so to say, I do not ever work with them. I can tell you, however, that the matter of Sapna is a deeply personal one, and I would ask that if you should wish to confide anything at all about this terrible fellow, you will speak of it only to me. You will not speak to any of the gentlemen you met here, last night, about this Sapna or ... or to anyone else. Is that agreed?'

'Yes. Yes, that's agreed.'

'Was there anything else?'

'Well, no.'

'Excellent. Then, to business: I have very little time today, Mr. Lin, so I will come directly to the point of the matter. The favour that I mentioned yesterday—I want you to teach one small boy, named Tariq, the English language. Not everything, of course, but enough that his English will be considerably improved, and that he will have some little advantage when he begins his formal studies.'

'Well, I'll be happy to try,' I stammered, bewildered by the request, but not daunted by it. I felt competent to teach the fundamentals of the language that I wrote in every day of my life. 'I don't know how *good* I'll be at it. I think there must be a lot of people who'd be better than I would, but I'm happy to take a shot at it. Where do you want me to do it? Would I come here to teach him?'

He looked at me with benign, almost affectionate condescension.

'Why, he will stay with *you*, naturally. I want you to have him with you, constantly, for the next ten or twelve weeks. He will live with you, eat with you, sleep at your house, go where you go. I do not simply want that he learns the English *phrases*. I want that he learns the English *way*. *Your* way. I want that he learns this, with your constant company.'

'But ... but I'm not English,' I objected stupidly.

'This is no matter. You are English enough, don't you think? You are a foreigner, and you will teach him the ways of a foreigner. It is my desire.'

My mind was hot, my thoughts scattered and flapping like the birds that he'd startled with his voice. There had to be a way out. It was impossible.

'But I live at the zhopadpatti. You know that. It's very rough. My hut is really small, and there's nothing in it. He'll be uncomfortable. And it's ... it's dirty and crowded and ... where would he sleep and all that?'

'I am aware of your situation, Mr. Lin,' he replied, a little sharply. 'It is precisely this, your life in the zhopadpatti, that I want him to know. Tell me your honest opinion, do you think that there are lessons to be learned in the slum? Do you think he will benefit from spending some time with the city's poorest people?'

I did think that, of course. It seemed to me that *every* child, beginning with the sons and daughters of the rich, would benefit from the experience of slum life.

'Yes, I suppose I do. I do think it's important to see how people live there. But you have to understand, it's a huge responsibility for me. I'm not doing a spectacular job of looking after myself. I don't know how I could look after a kid.'

Nazeer arrived with the tea and a prepared chillum.

'Ah, here is our tea. We shall first smoke, yes?'

We first smoked. Nazeer squatted on his haunches to smoke with us. As Khaderbhai puffed on the clay funnel, Nazeer gave me a complex series of nods, frowns, and winks that seemed to say, *Look, see how the master smokes, see what a great lord he is, see how much he is, that you and I will never be, see how lucky we are to be here with him.*

Nazeer was a head shorter than I was, but I guessed that he was at least several kilos heavier. His neck was so thick that it seemed to draw his powerful shoulders up towards his ears. The bulky arms that stretched the seams of his loose shirt appeared to be only slightly more slender than his thighs. His broad, permanently scowling face was composed of three downward curves, something like the insignia of sergeant's stripes. The first of them consisted of his eyebrows, which began a little above and in the centre of his eyes, and descended with bristling unruliness along the slope of his frown to the level of the eyes themselves. The second curve began in the deep grooves at the wings of his nose, and divided his face all the way to the jaw. The third was drawn by the desperate, pugnacious unhappiness of his mouth, the upside-down horseshoe of bad luck that fate had nailed to the doorpost of his life.

A ridge of purplish scar tissue was prominent on the brown skin of his forehead. His dark eyes moved in their deep hollows like hunted things, constantly seeking concealment. His ears looked as though they'd been chewed by some beast that had blunted its teeth on them, and given up the task. His most striking feature was his nose, an instrument so huge and magnificently pendulous that is seemed designed for some purpose altogether more grand than merely inhaling air and fragrances. I thought him ugly, then, when I first knew him, not so much for the unbeautiful set of his features as for their joylessness. It seemed to me that I'd never seen a human face in which the smile had been so utterly defeated.

The chillum returned to me for the third time, but the smoke was hot and tasted foul. I announced that it was finished. Nazeer seized it from me roughly and puffed with furious determination, managing to extract a dirty brown cloud of smoke. He tapped the gitak stone out onto his palm to reveal a tiny residue of white ash. Making sure that I was watching, he blew the ash from his hand to the ground at my feet, cleared his throat menacingly, and then left us.

'Nazeer doesn't like me very much.'

Khaderbhai laughed. It was a sudden and very youthful laugh. I liked it, and I was moved to join him, though I didn't really understand why he was laughing.

'Do you like Nazeer?' he asked, still laughing.

'No, I guess I don't,' I answered, and we laughed all the harder.

'You do not want to teach Tariq English, because you do not want the responsibility,' he said, when the laughter had subsided.

'It's not just that ... well, yes, it *is* just that. It's ...' I looked into those golden eyes, pleading with them. 'I'm not very good with responsibility. And this ... this is a lot of responsibility. It's too much. I can't do it.'

He smiled, and reached out to rest his hand on my forearm.

'I understand. You are worried. It is natural. You are worried that something might happen to Tariq. You are worried that you will lose your freedom to go where you want, and to do what you want. This is only natural.'

'Yes,' I murmured, relieved. He did understand. He knew that I couldn't do what he asked. He was going to let me off the hook. Sitting there, on the low stool beside his chair, I had to look up at him, and I felt at some disadvantage. I also felt a sudden rush of affection for him, an affection that seemed to proceed from and depend upon the inequalities between us. It was vassal-love, one of the strongest and most mysterious human emotions.

'Very well. My decision is this, Lin—you will take Tariq with you, and have him remain with you for two days. If, after this forty-eight hours, you think it is impossible for the situation to continue, you will bring him back here, and I will ask no more of you. But I am sure that he will be no problem to you. My nephew is a fine boy.'

'Your ... *nephew?*'

'Yes, the fourth son of my youngest sister, Farishta. He is eleven years old. He has learned some English words, and he speaks Hindi, Pashto, Urdu, and Marathi fluently. He is not so tall for his age, but he is most sturdy in his health.'

'Your nephew—,' I began again, but he cut me off quickly.

'If you find that you *can* do this thing for me, you will see that my dear friend in the zhopadpatti, Qasim Ali Hussein—you know him, of course, as the head man—he will help you in every way. He will arrange for some families, including his own, to share your responsibility, and provide homes for the boy to sleep in, as well as your own. There will be many friends to help you look after Tariq. I want him to know the hardest life of the poorest people. But above all, I want him to have the experience of an English teacher. This last thing means a great deal to me. When I was a boy ...'

He paused, allowing his gaze to shift and settle on the fountain and the wet surface of the great, round boulder. His eyes gleamed, reflecting the liquid light on the stone. Then a grave expression passed across them like a cloud-shadow slinking over smooth hills, on a sunny day.

'So, forty-eight hours,' he sighed, bringing himself to the moment. 'After that, if you bring him back to me, I will not think the worse of you. Now it is time for you to meet the boy.'

Khaderbhai gestured toward the arches of the cloister, behind me, and I turned to see that the boy was already standing there. He *was* small for his age. Khaderbhai had said that he was eleven years old, but he seemed to be no more than eight. Dressed in clean, pressed kurta-pyjama and leather sandals, he clutched a tied calico bundle in his arms. He stared at me with such a forlorn and distrustful expression that I thought he might burst into tears. Khaderbhai called him forward, and the boy approached us, making a wide detour around me to the far side of his uncle's chair. The closer he came, the more miserable he seemed. Khaderbhai spoke to him sternly and swiftly in Urdu, pointing at me several times. When he finished, the boy walked to my stool and extended his hand to me.

'Hello very much,' he said, his eyes huge with reluctance and fear.

I shook hands with him, his small hand vanishing in mine. Nothing ever fits the palm so perfectly, or feels so right, or inspires so much protective instinct as the hand of a child.

'Hello to you, too, Tariq,' I said, smiling in spite of myself.

His eyes flickered a tiny, hopeful smile in response, but doubt quickly smothered it. He looked back to his uncle. It was a look of desperate unhappiness, drawing his closed mouth wide and pulling his small nose in so tightly that it showed white at the corners.

Khaderbhai returned the look, staring strength into the boy, then stood up and called for Nazeer once more in that half-shout.

'You will forgive me, Mr. Lin. There are a number of matters that require my urgent attentions. I will expect you in two days, if you are not happy, *na*? Nazeer will show you out.'

He turned without looking at the boy, and strode off into the shadowed arches. Tariq and I watched him leave, each of us feeling abandoned and betrayed. Nazeer walked with us to the door. As I changed into my street shoes, Nazeer knelt and pressed the boy to his chest with surprising and passionate tenderness. Tariq clung to him, grabbing his hair, and had to be prised from the embrace with some force. When we stood once more, Nazeer gave me a look of eloquent, lingering menace —*If anything happens to this boy, you will answer to me for it*—and turned away from us.

A minute later we were outside, on the street beside the Nabila Mosque, boy and man joined tightly at the hand but in nothing else except our bewilderment at the power of the personality that had pushed us together against our wills. Tariq had simply been obedient, but there was something craven in *my* helplessness to resist Khaderbhai. I'd capitulated too readily, and I knew it. Self-disgust quickly became self-righteousness. *How could he do this to a child,* I asked myself, *his own nephew, give him up so easily to a stranger? Didn't he see how reluctant the boy was? It's a callous disregard for the rights and well-being of a child. Only a man who thought of others as his playthings, would surrender a child to someone like ... like me.*

Furious at my feeble pliancy—*How did I let him force me to do this?*—and burning with spite and selfishness, I dragged Tariq along at a jogging trot as I marched through the swarming street. Just as we passed the main entrance to the mosque, the muezzin began to recite the call to prayer from the minarets above our heads.

Allah hu Akbar Allah hu Akbar
Allah hu Akbar Allah hu Akbar
Ash-hadu an-la Ila ha-illallah
Ash-hadu an-la Ila ha-illallah

God is great, God is great
I bear witness that there is no god but God ...

Tariq tugged at my wrists with both hands, pulling me to a stop. He pointed at the entrance to the mosque, and then to the tower above it, where loudspeakers amplified the voice of the muezzin. I shook my head, and told him we had no time. He planted his feet and tugged harder at my wrist. I told him in Hindi and Marathi that I wasn't a Muslim, and I didn't want to enter the mosque. He was adamant, straining to drag me toward the doorway until the veins stood out at his temples. At last he broke free from my grip and scampered up the steps of the mosque. Kicking his sandals aside, he darted inside before I could stop him.

Frustrated and wavering, I hesitated at the large, open archway of the mosque. I knew that it was permitted for non-believers to enter. People of any faith may enter any mosque and pray, or meditate, or simply admire and wonder. But I knew that the Muslims regarded themselves as a minority under siege in the predominantly Hindu city. Violent confrontations between religionists were common enough. Prabaker warned me, once, that clashes had occurred between militant Hindus and Muslims outside that very mosque.

I had no idea what to do. I was certain there were other exits, and if the boy decided to run off there would be little chance of finding him. A throbbing dread drummed in my heart at the thought that I might have to return to Khaderbhai and tell him I'd lost his nephew, not a hundred metres from where he'd entrusted the boy to me.

Just as I made up my mind to go inside and search the mosque, Tariq came into view, passing from right to left across the huge, ornately tiled vestibule. His hands, feet, and head were wet, and it seemed that he'd washed himself hurriedly. Leaning as far into the entrance as I dared, I saw the boy take up a position at the rear of a group of men, and begin his prayers.

I sat down on an empty push-cart, and smoked a cigarette. To my great relief, Tariq emerged after a few minutes, collected his sandals, and came over to join me. Standing very close to me, he looked up into my face and gave me a smile-frown; one of those splendidly contradictory expressions that only children seem to master, as if he were afraid and happy at the same time.

'Zuhr! Zuhr!' he said, indicating that it was the time of the noon prayer. His voice was remarkably firm for such a small child. 'I am thank you for God. Are *you* thank you for God, Linbaba?'

I knelt on one knee in front of him, and seized his arms. He winced, but I didn't relax the grip. My eyes were angry. I knew that my face looked hard and perhaps even cruel.

'Don't you ever do that again!' I snapped at him, in Hindi. 'Don't you *ever* run away from me again!'

He frowned at me, defiant and afraid. Then his young face hardened into the mask we use to fight back tears. I saw his eyes fill, and one tear escaped to roll down his flushed cheek. I stood, and took a step away from him. Glancing around me, I saw that a few men and women had stopped on the street to stare at us. Their expressions were grave, although not yet alarmed. I reached out to offer the boy an open palm. He put his hand in mine, reluctantly, and I struck out along the street toward the nearest taxi stand.

I turned once to look over my shoulder, and saw that the people were following us with their eyes. My heart was beating fast. A viscid mix of emotions boiled in me, but I knew that most of it was rage, and most of the anger was at myself. I stopped, and the boy stopped with me. I breathed deeply for a few moments, fighting for reasonable control. When I looked down at him, Tariq was staring at me intently with his head cocked to one side.

'I'm sorry I got angry with you, Tariq,' I said calmly, repeating the words in Hindi. 'I won't do it again. But *please*, please don't run away from me like that. It makes me very scared and worried.'

The boy grinned at me. It was the first real smile he gave me. I was startled to see that it was very similar to Prabaker's lunar disk of a smile.

'Oh, God help me,' I said, sighing all the way from the core of my bones. 'Not another one.'

'Yes, okay very much!' Tariq agreed, shaking my hand with gymnastic enthusiasm. 'God help you, and me, all day, please!'

CHAPTER SIXTEEN

'When will she be back?'

'How should I know? Not long, maybe. She said to wait.'

'I don't know. It's getting late. I gotta get this kid home to bed.'

'Whatever. It's all the same to me, Jack. She said to wait, that's all.'

I glanced at Tariq. He didn't look tired, but I knew he had to be getting sleepy. I decided that a rest was a good idea before the walk home. We kicked off our shoes and entered Karla's house, closing the street door behind us. I found some chilled water in the large, old-fashioned refrigerator. Tariq accepted a glass, and sat down on a pile of cushions to flip through a copy of India Today magazine.

Lisa was in Karla's bedroom, sitting on the bed with her knees drawn up. She was wearing a red silk pyjama jacket, and nothing else. A patch of her blonde pubic hair was visible, and I glimpsed reflexively over my shoulder to make sure that the boy couldn't see into the room. She cradled a bottle of Jack Daniels in her folded arms. Her long curly hair was tied up into a lopsided bun. She was staring at me with an expression of calculated appraisal, one eye almost closed. It reminded me of the look that marksmen concentrate on their targets in a firing range.

'So where'd ya get the kid?'

I sat on a straight-backed chair, straddling it, so that my forearms could rest on the back.

'I sort of inherited him. I'm doing someone a favour.'

'A favour?' she asked, as if the word was a euphemism for some kind of infection.

'Yeah. A friend of mine asked me to teach the kid a little English.'

'So, what's he doing here? Why isn't he at home?'

'I'm supposed to keep him with me. That's how he's supposed to learn.'

'You mean keep him with you all the time? Everywhere you go?'

'That's the deal. But I'm hoping to give him back after two days. I don't know how I got talked into it in the first place, really.'

She laughed out loud. It wasn't a pleasant sound. The state she was in gave it a forced and almost vicious edge. Still, the heart of it was rich and full, and I thought it might've been a nice laugh, once. She took a swig from the bottle, exposing one round breast with the movement.

'I don't like kids,' she said proudly, as if she was announcing that she'd just received some distinguished award. She took another long drink. The bottle was half full. I realised that she was early drunk, in that squall of coherence before slurred speech and clumsiness and collapse.

'Look, I just want to get my clothes,' I muttered, looking around the bedroom for them. 'I'll pick them up, and come back and see Karla another time.'

'I'll make you a deal, Gilbert.'

'The name's Lin,' I insisted, although that, too, was a false name.

'I'll make you a deal, Lin. I'll tell you where your clothes are, if you agree to put them on here, in front of me.'

We didn't like each other. We stared across the kind of bristling hostility that's sometimes as good as, or better than, mutual attraction.

'Assuming you can handle it,' I drawled, grinning in spite of myself, 'what's in it for me?'

She laughed again, and it was stronger, and more honest.

'You're all right, Lin. Get me some water, will ya? The more of this stuff I drink, the goddamn thirstier I get.'

On my way to the small kitchen, I checked on Tariq. The boy had fallen asleep. His head was tipped back onto the cushions, and his mouth was open. One hand was curled up under his chin, and the other still grasped weakly at the magazine. I removed it, and covered him with a light woollen shawl that was hanging from a set of hooks. He didn't stir, and seemed to be deep in sleep. In the kitchen I took a bottle of chilled water from the refrigerator, snatched up two tumblers, and returned to the bedroom.

'The kid's asleep,' I said, handing her a glass. 'I'll let him crash for a while. If he doesn't wake up by himself, I'll get him up later.'

'Sit here,' she commanded, patting at the bed beside her. I sat. She watched me over the rim of her glass as I drank first one, then a second full glass of the iced water.

'The water's good,' she said, after a while. 'Have you noticed that the water's good here? I mean, really good. You'd expect it to be fucking slime, I mean being Bombay and India and all. People are so scared of the water, but it's really much better than the chemical-tasting horse-piss that comes outta the faucet back home.'

'Where is home?'

'What the fuck difference does it make?' She watched me frown impatiently, and added quickly, 'Don't get mad, keep your goddamn shirt on. I'm not tryin' to be a smart-ass. I really mean it—what difference does it make? I'll never go back there, and you'll never go there in the first place.'

'I guess not.'

'God it's hot! I hate this time of the year. It's always worst just before the monsoon. It makes me crazy. Doesn't this weather make you crazy? This is my fourth monsoon. You start to count in monsoons after you've been here a while. Didier is a nine-monsoon guy. Can you believe that? Nine fucking monsoons in Bombay. How about you?'

'This is my second. I'm looking forward to it. I love the rain, even if it does turn the slum into a swamp.'

'Karla told me you live in one of the slums. I don't know how you can stand it—that stink, all those people living on top of each other. You'd never get me inside one of those places.'

'Like most things, and most people, it's not as bad as it looks from the outside.'

She let her head fall onto one shoulder, and looked at me. I couldn't read her expression. Her eyes glittered in a radiant, almost inviting smile, but her mouth was twisted in a disdainful sneer.

'You're a real funny guy, Lin. How did you really get hooked up with that kid?'

'I told you.'

'So what's he like?'

'I thought you didn't like kids.'

'I don't. They're so ... innocent. Except that they're not. They know exactly what they want, and they don't stop till they get it. It's disgusting. All the worst people I know are just like big, grown-up children. It's so creepy it makes me sick to my stomach.'

Children might've turned her stomach, but it seemed to be immune to the searing effects of the sour mash whisky. She tipped the bottle back and drank off a good quarter of it in long, slow swallows. *That's the one*, I thought. If she wasn't drunk before, she is now. She wiped her lips with the back of her hand and smiled, but the expression was lopsided, and the focus was spilling from the bowls of her china blue eyes. Falling and fading as she was, the mask of her many abrasive attitudes began to slip, and she suddenly looked very young and vulnerable. The set of her jaw — angry, fearing, and dislikeable — relaxed into an expression that was surprisingly gentle and compassionate. Her cheeks were round and pink. The tip of her nose was turned-up slightly, and formed in soft contours. She was a twenty-four-year-old woman with the face of a girl, unmarked by the hollows of compromise or the deeply drawn lines of hard decisions. From the few things that Karla had told me about her, and what I'd seen at Madame Zhou's, her life had in fact been harder than most, but none of that showed in her face.

She offered me the bottle and I accepted it, taking a sip. I held on to it for a few moments, and when she wasn't looking I placed it on the floor beside the bed, discreetly out of her reach. She lit a cigarette and messed at her hair, spilling the loosely tied bun until the long curls fell over one shoulder. With her hand poised there, on top of her head, the wide sleeve of her silk jacket slipped past her elbow, and exposed the pale stubble of a shaved armpit.

There was no sign of other drugs in the room, but her pupils were contracted to pinpoints, suggesting that she'd taken heroin or some other opiate. Whatever the combination, it was sending her swiftly over the edge. She was slumped uncomfortably against the bedstead, and she was breathing noisily through her mouth. A little trickle of whisky and saliva dribbled from the corner of her slack lower lip.

Still, she was beautiful. The thought struck me that she would always look beautiful, even when she was being ugly. Hers was a big, lovely, empty face: the face of a pom-pom girl at a football match, the face advertisers use to help them sell preposterous and irrelevant things.

'So go on, tell me. What's he like, that little kid?'

'Well, I think he's some kind of religious fanatic,' I confided, smiling, as I looked over my shoulder at the sleeping boy. 'He made me stop three times today, and this evening, so he could say his prayers. I don't know if it's doing his soul any good, but his stomach seems to be working fine. He can eat like they're giving prizes for it. He kept me in the restaurant for more than two hours tonight, eating everything from noodles and grilled fish to ice cream and jelly. That's why we're late. I would've been home ages ago, but I couldn't get him out of the restaurant. It's going to cost me an arm and a leg to keep him for the next couple of days. He eats more than I do.'

'Do you know how Hannibal died?' she asked.

'Come again?'

'Hannibal, that guy with the elephants. Don't you know your history? He crossed the Alps, with his elephants, to attack the Romans.'

'Yeah, I know who you're talking about,' I said testily, irritated by the conversational non sequitur.

'Well, how did he die?' she demanded. Her expressions were becoming exaggerated, the gross burlesque of the drunk.

'I don't know.'

'Ha!' she scoffed. 'You don't know everything.'

'No. I don't know everything.'

There was a lengthening silence. She stared at me blankly. It seemed that I could see the thoughts drifting downwards, through the blue of her eyes, like white flakes in the bubble of a snow-dome.

'So, are you going to tell me?' I probed after a while. 'How did he die?'

'Who die?' she asked, mystified.

'Hannibal. You were going to tell me how he died.'

'Oh, him. Well, he kinda led this army of thirty thousand guys over the Alps into Italy, and fought the Romans for like, sixteen years. Six-teen goddamn years! And he never got beaten, even one time. Then, after a lot of other shit, he went back to his own country, where he became a big honcho, what with being a big hero and all. But the Romans, those guys never forgot that he embarrassed the fuck outta them, so they used politics, and they got his own people to turn on him, and kick him out. Are you getting any of this?'

'Sure.'

'I mean really, am I wastin' my goddamn time here with this? I don't have to do this, you know. I can spend my time with a lot better people than you. I can be with anyone I like. Anyone!'

The forgotten cigarette was burning down to her fingers. I placed the ashtray under it and prised it loose, letting it fall from her hand into the bowl. She didn't seem to notice.

'Okay, so the Romans forced Hannibal's own people to kick him out,' I pressed, actually curious about the fate of the Carthaginian warrior.

'They exiled him,' she corrected grumpily.

'Exiled him. Then what happened? How did he die?'

Lisa stirred her head from the pillows suddenly, her movements groggy, and glared at me with what seemed to be real malevolence.

'What's so special about Karla, huh?' she demanded furiously. 'I'm more beautiful than she is! Take a good look—my tits are better than hers.'

She pulled the silk jacket open until she was quite naked, touching at her breasts clumsily. 'Well? Aren't they?'

'They're ... very nice,' I muttered.

'Nice? They're goddamn beautiful is what they are. They're perfect! You want to touch them, don't you? Here!'

She snatched at my wrist with surprising speed, and dragged my hand onto her thigh, near the hip. The flesh was warm and smooth and supple. Nothing in the world is so soft and pleasing to the touch as the skin of a woman's thigh. No flower, feather, or fabric can match that velvet whisper of flesh. No matter how unequal they may be in other ways, all women, old and young, fat and thin, beautiful and ugly, have that perfection. It's a great part of the reason why men hunger to possess women, and so often convince themselves that they do possess them: the thigh, that touch.

'Has Karla told you what I did at the Palace, huh? What I used to do there?' she said with puzzling hostility, moving my hand onto the hard little mound of blonde hair between her legs. 'Madame Zhou has us play games there. They're big on games at the Palace. Karla told you about those games, did she? Huh? Blind Man's Butt, did she tell you about that? The customers wear blindfolds and get a prize for guessing which one of us they push their cock into. No hands, ya see. That's the trick. Did she tell you any of this? Did she tell you about the Chair? That's a real popular number. One girl kneels down on her hands and knees, see, then another girl lies on top of her, back to back, and they tie them together. The customers go from one to another, kind of a multiple choice. Is this turnin' you on, Lin? Are you gettin' hot with this? It used to turn Karla's customers on, when she brought them to the Palace. Karla has a business head. Did you know that? I worked at the Palace, but it was just a job, and all I ever made out of it was money. She's the one who made it dirty. She's the one who made it a … a sick thing. Karla's the one who'll do anything to get what she wants. Damn right, a business head, and a heart to match …'

She was rubbing my hand against herself with both of her own hands, grinding against it with rolling motions of her hips. She drew up her knees, and her legs parted. My hand was drawn to the lips of her vagina, heavy and swollen and wet. She pushed two of my fingers inside the dark heat.

'You feel that?' she mumbled, her teeth clenched and exposed in a grim smile. 'That's muscle power, boy. That's what that is. That's training and practice, hours of it, months of it. Madame Zhou makes us squat, and squeeze down hard on a pencil, to build up a grip like a fist. I got so fuckin' good at it, I could write a letter with the goddamn thing. You feel how good that is? You'll never find anything as tight as this, not any-where. Karla isn't this good. I know she isn't. What's the matter with you? Don't you wanna fuck me? What are you, some kinda faggot? I …'

She was still squeezing down on my fingers, still grasping at my wrist, but the straining smile faded, and her face slowly turned away.

'I … I … I think I'm gonna throw up.'

I withdrew my fingers from her body, and my hand from her weaken-ing grip, and backed away from the bed towards the bathroom. Hurriedly soaking a towel in cold water and grabbing up a large dish from the bath-room, I returned to find her sprawled out awkwardly, her hands on her belly. I straightened her into a more comfortable position, covering her with a light cotton blanket. I draped the cool towel over her forehead. She stirred a little, but she didn't resist. Her frown gradually dissolved into the earnest mask of the unwell.

'He committed suicide,' she said softly, her eyes closed. 'That Hannibal. They were going to extradite him back to Rome, make him face charges at a trial, so he killed himself. How do ya like that? After all that fighting, all those elephants, all those big battles, he killed himself. It's true. Karla told me. Karla always tells the truth … even when she's lying… she said that to me once … I always tell the truth, even when I'm lying … Fuck, I love that girl. I love that girl. You know, she saved me from that place—and you did, too—and she's helping me to get clean … to dry out … gotta dry out, Lin … Gilbert … gotta get off the shit … I love that girl …'

She slept. I watched her for a while, waiting to see if she was sick, if she would wake, but she was wrapped in unworried sleep. I went to check on Tariq, and he too was sleeping soundly. I decided not to wake him. Being alone, in that stillness, was a piercing pleasure. Wealth and power, in a city where half the many millions were homeless, were measured by the privacy that only money could buy, and the solitude that only power could demand and enforce. The poor were almost never alone in Bombay, and I was poor.

There, in that breathing room, no sound reached me from the quieting street. I moved through the apartment freely, unwatched. And the silence was sweeter, it seemed, the peace more profound, for the presence of the two sleepers, woman and child. A balm of fantasy soothed me. There was a time, once, when I'd known such a life: when a woman and a sleeping child were my own, and I was their man.

I stopped at Karla's cluttered writing desk, and caught sight of myself in a wide mirror on the wall above it. The momentary fantasy of belonging, that little dream of home and family, hardened and cracked in my eyes. The truth was that my own marriage had crumbled to ruin, and I'd lost my child, my daughter. The truth was that Lisa and Tariq meant nothing to me, and I meant nothing to them. The truth was that I belonged nowhere and to no-one. Surrounded by people and hungry for solitude, I was always and everywhere alone. Worse than that, I was hollow, empty, gouged out and scraped bare by the escape and flight. I'd lost my family, the friends of my youth, my country and its culture—all the things that had defined me, and given me identity. Like all the fugitive kind, the more successful I was, the longer and further I ran, the less I kept of my self.

But there were people, a few who could reach me, a few new friends for the new self I was learning to become. There was Prabaker, that tiny, life-adoring man. There was Johnny Cigar, and Qasim Ali, and Jeetendra and his wife, Radha: heroes of chaos who propped up the collapsible city with bamboo sticks, and insisted on loving their neighbours, no matter how far they'd fallen; no matter how broken or unlovely they were. There was Khaderbhai, there was Abdullah, there was Didier, and there was Karla. And as I looked into my own hard eyes in the green-edged mirror, I thought about them all, and asked myself why those people made a difference. Why them? What is it about them? Such a disparate group—the richest and the most wretched, educated and illiterate, virtuous and criminal, old and young—it seemed that the only thing they had in common was a power to make me feel ... something.

On the desk in front of me was a thick, leather-bound book. I opened it and saw that it was Karla's journal, filled with entries in her own elegant handwriting. Knowing that I shouldn't, I turned through the pages and read her private thoughts. It wasn't a diary. There were no dates on any of the pages, and there were none of the day-to-day accounts of things done and people met. Instead, there were fragments. Some of them were culled from various novels and other texts, each one attributed to the respective author and annotated with her own comments and criticisms. There were many poems. Some had been copied out from selections and anthologies and even newspapers, with the source and the poet's name written beneath. Other poems were her own, written out several times with a word or a phrase changed and a line added. Certain words and their dictionary meanings were listed throughout the journal and marked with asterisks, forming a running vocabulary of unusual and obscure words. And there were random, stream-of-consciousness passages that described what she'd been thinking or feeling on a certain day. Other people were mentioned frequently, yet they were never identified except as he and she.

On one page there was a cryptic and disturbing reference to the name Sapna. It read:

THE QUESTION: What will Sapna do?
THE ANSWER: Sapna will kill us all.

My heart began to beat faster as I read the words through several times. I didn't doubt she was talking about the same man—the Sapna whose followers had committed the gruesome murders Abdul Ghani and Madjid had talked about, the Sapna who was hunted by the police and the underworld alike. And it seemed, from that strange couplet, that she knew something about him, perhaps even who he was. I wondered what it meant, and if she was in danger.

I examined the pages before and after the entry more carefully, but I found nothing more that might concern him, or Karla's connection to him. On the second-last page of the journal, however, there was one passage that clearly referred to me:

He wanted to tell me that he is in love with me. Why did I stop him? Am I so ashamed that it might be true? The view from that place was incredible, amazing. We were so high that we looked down on the kites that flew so high above the children's heads. He said that I don't smile. I'm glad he said that, and I wonder why.

Beneath that entry she'd written the words:

I don't know what frightens me more,
the power that crushes us
or our endless ability to endure it.

I remembered the remark very well. I remembered her saying it after the slum huts had been smashed and dragged away. Like so many of the things she said, it had the kind of cleverness that insinuated itself into my memory. I was surprised and perhaps a little shocked to see that she, too, had remembered the phrase, and that she'd copied it down there—even improving it, with more aphoristic roundness than the impromptu remark had possessed. *Is she planning to use those words again*, I asked myself, *with someone else?*

The last page carried a poem that she'd written—her most recent addition to the almost completed journal. Because it appeared on the page following her reference to me, and because I was so hungry for it, I read the poem and told myself that it was mine. I let myself believe that it was meant for me, or that at least some part of it was born in feelings that were mine. I knew it wasn't true, but love seldom concerns itself with what we know or with what's true.

To make sure none followed where you led
I used my hair to cover our tracks.
Sun set on the island of our bed
night rose
eating echoes
and we were beached there, in tangles of flicker,
candles whispering at our driftwood backs.

Your eyes above me
afraid of the promises I might keep
regretting the truth we did say
less than the lie we didn't,
I went in deep, I went in deep,
to fight the past for you.
Now we both know
sorrows are the seeds of loving.
Now we both know I will live and
I will die for this love.

Standing there, at the desk, I snatched up a pen and copied out the poem on a sheet of paper. With the stolen words folded secretly in my wallet, I closed the journal and replaced it exactly as I'd found it.

I walked to the bookshelf. I wanted to study the titles for clues to the woman who'd chosen them and read them. The small library of four shelves was surprisingly eclectic. There were texts on Greek history, on philosophy and cosmology, on poetry and drama. Stendhal's *The Charterhouse of Parma* in an Italian translation. A copy of *Madame Bovary* in the original French. Thomas Mann and Schiller in German. Djuna Barnes and Virginia Woolf in English. I took down a copy of *Maldoror*, by Isidore Ducasse. The pages were dog-eared, and heavily annotated in Karla's own hand. I took out another book, a German translation of Gogol's *Dead Souls*, and it too bore Karla's hand-written notes on many pages. She consumed her books, I saw. She devoured her books, and was unafraid to mark them, even to scar them, with her own comments and system of references.

A row of journals, similar to the one I'd discovered on the desk, occupied half of one shelf, some twenty books in all. I took one of them down and flipped through it. The fact that it, like the others, was written in English, struck me for the first time. She was born in Switzerland and she was fluent in German and French, I knew; but when she wrote out her most intimate thoughts and feelings she used English. I seized on that, telling myself that there were good and hopeful signs in it. English was my language. She spoke to herself, from her heart, in my language.

I moved around the apartment, studying the things she chose to surround herself with in her private living space. There was an oil painting of women carrying water from a river, with matkas balanced on their heads, and children following with smaller pots on their own heads. Prominently displayed on a dedicated shelf was a hand-carved, rosewood figure of the goddess Durga. It was surrounded by incense holders. I noticed an arrangement of everlastings and other dried flowers. They were my own favourites, and very unusual in a city where fresh flowers were plentiful and inexpensive. There was a collection of found objects— a huge frond from a date palm that she'd picked up somewhere and fixed to one wall; shells and river stones that filled a large and waterless fish tank; a discarded spinning wheel on which she'd draped a collection of small, brass temple-bells.

The most colourful articles in the apartment, her clothes, hung from an open rack in one corner of her room rather than in a wardrobe. The clothes were divided into two distinct groups, left and right of the rack. On the left were her networking clothes—smart suits with long, narrow skirts, and the silver sheath of a backless evening dress, among other glamorous dresses. On the right were her private clothes, the loose silk trousers, flowing scarves, and long-sleeved cotton blouses that she wore by choice.

Under the rack of clothes was a row of shoes, two dozen pairs. At the end of the row were my boots, newly polished and laced up to their tops. I knelt to pick them up. Her shoes looked so small, next to my own, that I took one of them up instead, and held it in my hands for a moment. It was Italian, from Milano, in dark green leather, and with a decorative buckle stitched to the side and looped around the low heel. It was an elegant, expensive shoe, but the heel was worn down slightly on one side, and the leather was scuffed in a few places. I saw that she, or someone, had tried to disguise the pale scratches by drawing over them with a felt-tipped pen that was almost, but not quite, the right shade of green.

I found my clothes in a plastic bag behind the boots. They'd been laundered and folded neatly. I took them, and changed into them in the bathroom. I held my head under the cold-water tap for a full minute. Dressed in my old jeans and comfortable boots, and with my short hair pushed back into its familiar, messy disorder, I felt refreshed, and my spirits revived.

I returned to the bedroom to check on Lisa. She was sleeping contentedly. A diffident smile flickered on her lips. I tucked the sheet into the sides of the bed to prevent her from falling, and adjusted the overhead fan to a minimum speed. The windows were barred, and the front door snapped to the lock position when it was shut from outside. I knew that I could leave her there, and she would be safe. As I stood beside the bed, watching the rise and fall of her chest in its sleeping rhythm, I thought about leaving a note for Karla. I decided against it because I wanted her to wonder about me—to ask herself what I'd been thinking and what I'd done there, in her house. To give myself an excuse to see her, I folded the clothes she'd given me, the dead lover's burial clothes that I'd just discarded, and put them in a plastic bag. I planned to wash them, and return with them in a few days.

I turned to wake Tariq for our journey home, but the boy was standing in the doorway, clutching his small shoulder bag. His sleepy face wore a look of hurt and accusation.

'You want leave me?' he asked.

'No,' I laughed, 'but you'd be a lot better off if I did. More comfortable, anyway. My place isn't as nice as this.'

He frowned, puzzled by the English words, and not at all reassured.

'Are you ready?'

'Yes, ready,' he mumbled, wagging his head from side to side.

Thinking of the latrine, and the lack of water at the slum, I told him to use the bathroom before we went, and directed him to wash his face and hands well. After he'd used the toilet, I gave him a glass of milk and a sweet cake that I found in Karla's kitchen. We stepped out into the deserted street, and pulled the door locked behind us. He looked back at the house and at all the buildings around it, searching for landmarks that would fix the place in his mental map. Then he fell into step, beside but a little apart from me.

We walked on the road because the footpaths were occupied in many places by sleeping pavement dwellers. The only traffic was the occasional taxi or police jeep. Every shop and business was closed, and only a few houses or apartments showed light at their windows. The moon was almost full, but obscured from time to time by dense, brooding drifts of cloud. They were harbingers of the monsoon: the clouds that gathered and thickened every night, and would swell, within the following days, until every part of the sky was clogged with them, and it would rain, everywhere and forever.

We made good time. Only half an hour after leaving Karla's apartment, we turned onto the wide track that skirted the eastern curve of the slum. Tariq had said nothing on the walk, and I, burdened by worry about how to cope with him and the responsibility for his welfare—burdened by the boy himself, it seemed to me then—kept a churlish silence. On our left, there was a large open area about the size of a soccer field that was set aside as a latrine zone, where women, young children, and elderly people went to relieve themselves. Nothing grew there, and the whole area was dusty and bare after eight months of continuous sunshine. On our right was the fringe of the construction site, marked here and there by low piles of timber, latticed steel, and other materials. Single bulbs, suspended from long extension wires, lit the mounds of supplies. There was no other light on the path, and the slum, still some five hundred metres away, showed only faint glimmers from a few kerosene lamps.

I told Tariq to follow my steps precisely, knowing that many people used the track as a latrine after dark because they were afraid of rats or snakes in the open field. By some mysterious, unspoken consensus, a narrow and erratic path was always left clean along the course of the track, so that latecomers might enter the slum without stepping in the filth that accumulated. I came home late at night so often that I'd learned how to negotiate the eccentric meander of that clean path without stumbling or tripping on the edges of the many large potholes that no-one ever seemed inclined to repair.

Tariq followed me closely, struggling dutifully to step exactly where I'd walked. The stench there at the edge of the slum was overpowering and sickening for a stranger, I knew. I'd grown accustomed to it, and had even come to think of it with a kind of affection, as the slum-dwellers did. That smell meant we were home, safe, protected by our collective wretchedness from the dangers that haunted poor people in the cleaner, grander city streets. Yet I never forgot the spasms of nausea I'd endured when I first entered the slum as a stranger. And I remembered the fear I'd felt, in that smear of air so foul it seemed to poison my lungs with every breath, and stain the very sweat on my skin.

I remembered, and I knew that Tariq was surely suffering and sickened and afraid. But I said nothing to comfort him, and I refused the impulse to take his hand. I didn't want the child with me, and I was furious with myself for being too weak to tell Khaderbhai as much. I wanted the boy to be sickened. I wanted him to be afraid. I wanted him so sickened and afraid and unhappy that he would plead with his uncle to take him from me.

The crackling tension of that cruel silence was shattered by a burst of ferocious barking. The howls of that one dog soon stirred violent barking from several, and then many others. I stopped suddenly, and Tariq bumped into me from behind. The dogs were in the open field, and not far away. I peered into the blackness, but I couldn't see them. I sensed that it was a large pack, and spread out over a wide area. I looked to the mass of huts, calculating the distance to the slum and the safety of its buildings. Just then, the baying howls reached a crescendo of violence, and they came trotting at us out of the night.

Twenty, thirty, forty maddened dogs formed the pack that advanced on us in a wide crescent, cutting off our retreat to the slum. The danger was extreme. Those dogs that were so cowed and obsequious in the daylight hours formed themselves into vicious, feral packs at night. Their aggression and ferocity was legendary in all the slums throughout the city, and inspired great fear. Attacks upon human beings were common. I treated dog bites and rat bites almost every day in the little clinic at my hut. A drunken man had been savaged by a pack of dogs on the edge of the slum, and was still recovering in hospital. A young child had been killed in that very spot, only a month before. His small body had been torn to pieces, and the fragments were strewn across such a wide area that it had taken the whole of a long day to locate and retrieve them all.

We were stranded on the dark path. The dogs closed to within a few metres, swarming around us and barking furiously. The noise was deafening and terrifying. The bravest of the hounds inched closer and closer. I knew they were only seconds from making the first snapping rush at us. The slum was too far away to reach safely. I thought I could make it alone, suffering a few bites, but I knew the dogs would cut Tariq down in the first hundred metres. Much closer, there was a pile of timbers and other construction materials. It would give us weapons, and a well-lit area for the fight. I told Tariq to prepare himself to run on my command. When I was sure he understood, I threw the plastic bag containing the clothes Karla had loaned me into the midst of the pack. They fell on it at once, snapping and snarling at one another in their frenzy to rip and tear at it.

'Now, Tariq! Now!' I shouted, shoving the boy in front of me and turning to cover his retreat. The dogs were so engrossed in the bundle that we were safe for a moment. I ran to the pile of scrap wood, and snatched up a length of stout bamboo just as the pack tired of the shredded bundle and advanced on us again.

Recognising the weapon, the enraged hounds hesitated a little further from us. They were many. *Too many*, I heard myself thinking. *There's too many of them.* It was the largest pack I'd ever seen. The wild howling goaded the most maddened of them to make a series of rushing feints from several directions. I raised the solid stick and told Tariq to climb onto my back. The boy did so at once, clambering up piggyback style, and wrapping his thin arms around my neck tightly. The pack crept closer. One black dog, larger than the rest, made a scrambling run with its jaws wide, and aimed at my legs. I brought the stick down with all my strength, missing the snout but smashing it into the animal's spine. It yelped in agony, and scuttled out of range. The battle began.

One after another, from left, right, and in front of us, they attacked. Each time, I lashed out with the stick to repulse them. It occurred to me that if I managed to cripple or even kill one of the dogs, the others might be frightened off, but none of the blows I landed was serious enough to discourage them for very long. In fact, they seemed to sense that the stick could hurt them but not kill them, and they grew bolder.

The whole pack crept inexorably closer. The individual attacks came more often. Ten minutes into the struggle, I was sweating heavily and beginning to tire. I knew it wouldn't be long before my reflexes slowed, and one of the dogs slipped through to bite my leg or arm. And with the first smell of blood, their ravening fury would become rabid, berserk, and fearless. I hoped that someone in the slum would hear the ear-splitting clamour and come to our rescue. But I'd been woken by that same barking from the outskirts of the slum a hundred times late at night. And a hundred times I'd turned over and gone back to sleep without thinking about it.

The large black dog that seemed to be the pack leader made a cunning double feint. As I turned, too quickly, to meet its rush, my foot struck a projecting timber and I fell. I'd often heard people say that at the moment of some accident or sudden danger they had the sensation that time was delayed or sluggish, and everything seemed to happen in slow motion.

That stumble sideways, as I fell to the ground, was my first experience of it. Between stumble and fall, there was a tunnel of lengthened time and narrowed perspectives. I saw the black dog hesitate in the rhythm of its instinctive retreats, and turn to face us once more. I saw its forepaws slip and slide beneath it with the energy of its scrambling turn, and then gouge out a purchase on the dusty track for the rush and spring. I saw the eyes of the beast, the almost human cruelty as it sensed my weakness and its nearness to the killing second. I saw the other dogs pause, almost as one, and then creep forward with little mincing steps. I had time to think how strange and inappropriate their stealth was, then, in the moments of my vulnerability. I had time to feel the rough stones scrape the skin back from my elbow as I struck the ground, and time to wonder at the ridiculous particle of worry, about the threat of infection, that strayed across the surface of the present and greater danger of the dogs, the dogs. They were everywhere.

And desperate, sickened with fear for him, I thought of Tariq, the poor child who'd been pressed into my care so reluctantly. I felt him slip from my neck, felt his fragile arms fall through my scrambling hands as I crashed into the slithering pile of timber. I watched him fall and scramble forward with feline agility to stand, one foot on either side of my extended legs. Then, his body rigid with the vehemence of his rage and courage, the little boy shrieked, seized a lump of wood, and crashed it down on the snout of the black dog. The beast was sorely wounded. Its yelping screams rose above the din of barks and howls and the shrieking of the boy.

'Allah hu Akbar! Allah hu Akbar!' Tariq shouted. He crouched, and swung at the empty air, his own face wild as any beast, and his posture as feral. In the last of those impossibly long seconds of my heightened sense, I had time to feel the hot sting of tears as I watched him crouch and swing and fight to defend us. I could see the knuckles of his spine thrust out against his shirt, and the bones of his thin, little knees outlined against his trousers. There was so much bravery in that small package. The emotion that burned my eyes was love, the pure, pride-filled love of father for son. I loved him with all my heart in that second. As I thrashed up to my feet, and time accelerated from its glue of fear and failure, some words repeated themselves in my mind, words from Karla's poem. I will die for this love, die for this love.

Tariq had wounded the pack leader, and it hung back behind the others, dispiriting them for a few moments. The howling grew louder, however, and there was another quality to it then, a throbbing moan of frustration. It was as if they were sickening for the kill, and tormented by their failure. I hoped that in their agony of disappointment they might turn on one another if they didn't bring us down soon. Then, without warning, they sprang at us again.

They came in groups of two and three. They attacked from two sides at once. The boy and I stood side-to-side and back-to-back, fighting them off with desperate jabs and slashes. The dogs were insane with the blood lust. We hit them hard, but they cowered only seconds before leaping at us again. Everywhere around us was fang and snarl, snap and howl. I leaned over Tariq to help him drive back a determined rush from three or four of the beasts, and one dog managed to sprint in behind me and bite down hard on my ankle. My leather boot protected me, and I drove the dog away, but I knew we were losing the war. We'd retreated hard up against the mound of timbers, and there was nowhere else to go. The whole pack was snarling and lunging at us from only two metres away. Then, from behind us, there was a sound of growling, and the crunching rattle of timbers slipping away under the weight of something that had jumped onto them. I thought that some of the dogs had somehow worked their way around onto the heap but, as I turned to meet the challenge, I saw the black-clad figure of Abdullah as he sprang, leaping over our heads into the midst of the thrashing jaws of the pack.

He whirled, striking out left and right. He jumped, drawing his knees up tight and landing with the supple tautness of a trained fighter. His movements were fluid, swift, and economical. It was the awful and beautiful frugality of snake and scorpion. Lethal. Exact. Perfect. He'd armed himself with a metal rod, about three centimetres in diameter and more than a metre in length. He swung it two-handed as if it was a sword. But it wasn't the superior weapon or even his uncanny agility that terrified the dogs and drove them back. What routed them in panicked flight, leaving two of their number skull-crack dead, was the fact that he'd taken the fight to them; that he'd attacked, where we'd defended; that he was sure of winning, where we'd merely struggled to survive.

It was over quickly. There was silence, where so much sound had screamed. Abdullah turned to look at us with the metal rod held above his shoulder like a samurai sword. The smile shining from his brave young face was like moonlight gleaming on the minaret of Haji Ali's white mosque.

Later, while we drank hot and very sweet Suleimani chai in my hut, Abdullah explained that he'd been waiting for me in the hut, and heard the dogs. He told us he came to investigate it because he'd sensed that something was dreadfully wrong. When we'd talked the adventure through several times, I prepared three places for us on the bare earth floor, and we stretched out to rest.

Abdullah and Tariq slipped effortlessly into a sleep that eluded me. I lay back, in a darkness that smelt of incense and beedie cigarettes and cheap kerosene, and I sifted the events of the last few days through a sieve of doubt and suspicion. So much more had happened during those days, it seemed, than in the months before them. Madame Zhou, Karla, Khaderbhai's council, Sapna—I felt myself to be at the mercy of personalities that were stronger, or at least more mysterious, than my own. I felt the irresistible draw and drift of a tide that was carrying me to someone else's destination, someone else's destiny. There was a plan or purpose. I sensed it. There were clues, I was sure, but I couldn't separate them from the busy collage of hours and faces and words. The cloud-mottled night seemed full of signs and portents, as if fate itself was warning me to go or daring me to stay.

Tariq woke with a start, and sat up, staring about him. My eyes were adjusted to the darkness. I saw the moment of fear on his pale face clearly, a fear that tightened into sorrow and resolve even as I watched. He looked to the peacefully sleeping form of Abdullah, and then to me. Without a sound, he stood and dragged his sleeping mat over until it met mine. Snuggling down under the cover of his thin blanket once more, he cuddled in beside me. I stretched out my arm, and he rested his head on it. The smell of the sun was in his hair.

As exhaustion finally claimed me, submerging my doubts and confusions, the shrewd clarity of near-sleep suddenly showed me what it was that those new friends—Khaderbhai, Karla, Abdullah, Prabaker, and all the others—had in common. They were all, we were all, strangers to the city. None of us was born there. All of us were refugees, survivors, pitched up on the shores of the island city. If there was a bond between us, it was the bond of exiles, the kinship of the lost, the lonely, and the dispossessed.

Realising that, understanding it, made me see the hard edges of the way I'd treated the boy, Tariq, himself a stranger in my raw and ragged fragment of the city. Ashamed of the cold selfishness that had stolen my pity, and pierced by the courage and loneliness of the little boy, I listened to his sleeping breath, and let him cling to the ache in my heart. Sometimes we love with nothing more than hope. Sometimes we cry with everything except tears. In the end that's all there is: love and its duty, sorrow and its truth. In the end that's all we have—to hold on tight until the dawn.

PART THREE

CHAPTER SEVENTEEN

'T HE WORLD IS RUN by one million evil men, ten million stupid men, and a hundred million cowards,' Abdul Ghani pronounced in his best Oxford English accent, licking the sweet honey cake from his short, thick fingers. 'The evil men are the power—the rich men, and the politicians, and the fanatics of religion—whose decisions rule the world, and set it on its course of greed and destruction.'

He paused, looking toward the whispering fountain in Abdel Khader Khan's rain-splashed courtyard as if he was receiving inspiration from the wetness and the shimmering stone. He reached out with his right hand and took another honey cake, popping it whole into his mouth. The little beseeching smile he gave me as he chewed and swallowed seemed to say, *I know I shouldn't, but I really can't help it.*

'There are only one million of them, the truly evil men, in the whole world. The very rich and the very powerful, whose decisions really count —they only number one million. The stupid men, who number ten million, are the soldiers and policemen who enforce the rule of the evil men. They are the standing armies of twelve key countries, and the police forces of those and twenty more. In total, there are only ten million of them with any real power or consequence. They are often brave, I'm sure, but they are stupid, too, because they give their lives for governments and causes that use their flesh and blood as mere chess pieces. Those governments always betray them or let them down or abandon them, in the long run. Nations neglect no men more shamefully than the heroes of their wars.'

The circular courtyard garden at the heart of Khaderbhai's house was open to the sky at its centre. Monsoon rain fell upon the fountain and surrounding tiles: rain so dense and constant that the sky was a river, and our part of the world was its waterfall. Despite the rain, the fountain was still running, sending its frail plumes of water upward against the cascade from above. We sat under cover of the surrounding veranda roof, dry and warm in the humid air as we watched the downpour and sipped sweet tea.

'And the hundred million cowards,' Abdul Ghani continued, pinching the handle of the teacup between his plump fingers, 'they are the bureaucrats and paper shufflers and pen-pushers who permit the rule of the evil men, and look the other way. They are the head of this department, and the secretary of that committee, and the president of the other association. They are managers, and officials, and mayors, and officers of the court. They always defend themselves by saying that they are just following orders, or just doing their job, and it's nothing personal, and if *they* don't do it, someone else surely will. They are the hundred million cowards who know what is going on, but say nothing, while they sign the paper that puts one man before a firing squad, or condemns one million men to the slower death of a famine.'

He fell silent, staring into the mandala of veins on the back of his hand. A few moments later, he shook himself from his reverie and looked at me, his eyes gleaming in a gentle, affectionate smile.

'So, that's it,' he concluded. 'The world is run by one million evil men, ten million stupid men, and a hundred million cowards. The rest of us, all six billion of us, do pretty much what we are told!'

He laughed, and slapped at his thigh. It was a good laugh, the kind of laugh that won't rest until it shares the joke, and I found myself laughing with him.

'Do you know what this means, my boy?' he asked, when his face was serious enough to frame the question.

'Tell me.'

'This formula—the one million, the ten million, the hundred million —this is the real truth of all politics. Marx was wrong. It is not a question of classes, you see, because all the classes are in the hands of this tiny few. This set of numbers is the cause of empire and rebellion. This is the formula that has generated our civilisations for the last ten thousand years. This built the pyramids. This launched your Crusades. This put the world at war, and this formula has the power to impose the peace.'

'They're not *my* Crusades,' I corrected him, 'but I get your point.'

'Do you love him?' he asked, changing the subject so swiftly that he took me by surprise. He did that so often, shifting the ground of his discourses from theme to theme, that it was one of the hallmarks of his conversation. His skill at performing the trick was such that even when I came to know him well, even when I came to expect those sudden deviations and deflections, he still managed to catch me off guard. 'Do you love Khaderbhai?'

'I ... what sort of question is that?' I demanded, still laughing.

'*He* has great affection for *you*, Lin. He speaks of you often.'

I frowned, and looked away from his penetrating gaze. It gave me a rush of intense pleasure to hear that Khaderbhai liked me and spoke of me. Still, I didn't want to admit, even to myself, how much his approval meant to me. The play of conflicting emotions—love and suspicion, admiration and resentment—confused me, as it usually did when I thought of Khader Khan, or spent time with him. The confusion emerged as irritation, in my eyes and in my voice.

'How long do you think we'll have to wait?' I asked, looking around at the closed doors that led to the private rooms of Khaderbhai's house. 'I have to meet with some German tourists this afternoon.'

Abdul ignored the question and leaned across the little table separating our two chairs.

'You must love him,' he said in an almost seductive whisper. 'Do you want to know why I love Abdel Khader with my life?'

We were sitting with our faces close enough for me to see the fine red veins in the whites of his eyes. The embroidery of those red fibres converged on the auburn iris of his eyes like so many fingers raised to support the golden, red-brown discs. Beneath the eyes were thick, heavy pouches, which gave his face its persistent expression of an inwardness filled with grieving and sorrow. Despite his many jokes and easy laughter, the pouches beneath his eyes were swollen, always, with a reservoir of unshed tears.

We'd been waiting half an hour for Khaderbhai to return. When I'd arrived with Tariq, Khader had greeted me warmly and then retired with the boy to pray, leaving me in the company of Abdul Ghani. The house was utterly silent, save for the splash of falling rain in the courtyard and the bubble of the fountain's over-burdened pump. A pair of doves huddled together on the far side of the courtyard.

Abdul and I stared at one another in the silence, but I didn't speak, I didn't answer his question. *Do you want to know why I love this man?* Of course I wanted to know. I was a writer. I wanted to know everything. But I wasn't so happy to play Ghani's question-and-answer game. I couldn't read him, and I couldn't guess where it was going.

'I love him, my boy, because he is a mooring post in this city. Thousands of people find safety by tying their lives to his. I love him because he has the task, where other men do not even have the *dream*, of changing the whole world. I worry that he puts too much time and effort and money into that cause, and I have disagreed with him many times about it, but I love him for his devotion to it. And most of all, I love him because he is the only man I ever met—he is the only man *you* will ever meet—who can answer the three big questions.'

'There are only *three* big questions?' I asked, unable to keep the sarcasm from my voice.

'Yes,' he answered equably. *'Where did we come from? Why are we here? Where are we going?* Those are the three big questions. And if you love him, Lin, my young friend, if you love him, he will tell *you* these secrets, as well. He will tell you the meaning of life. And when you hear him speak, when you listen to him, you will know that what he says is true. And no-one else you will ever meet will answer these three questions for you. I know. I have travelled the Earth many times over. I have asked all the great teachers. Before I met Abdel Khader Khan, and joined my life to his, as his brother, I spent a fortune—several fortunes—seeking out the famous seers and mystics and renowned scientists. None of them ever answered the three big questions. Then I met Khaderbhai. He answered the questions for me. And I have loved him, as my brother, my soul's brother, ever since that day. I have served him from that day until the little minute that we share. He will *tell* you. *The meaning of life!* He will solve the mystery for you.'

Ghani's voice was a new current in the wide, strong river that carried me: the river of the city and its fifteen million lives. His thick, brown hair was streaked with grey, and smudged completely white at the temples. His moustache, more grey than brown, rested on finely sculptured, almost feminine lips. A heavy gold chain gleamed at his neck in the afternoon light, and matched the gold that flashed in his eyes. And as we stared at one another in that yearning silence, tears began to fill the red-rimmed cups of his eyes.

I couldn't doubt the real depth of his feeling, but I couldn't fully understand it, either. Then a door opened behind us, and Ghani's round face dissolved into its usual mask of facetious affability. We both turned to see Khaderbhai enter with Tariq.

'Lin!' he said, with his hands resting on the boy's shoulders. 'Tariq has been telling us how much he learned with you in the last three months.'

Three months. At first I'd thought it impossible to endure the boy's company for three days. Yet three months had passed too swiftly; and when the time came to bring him home, I'd returned him to his uncle against the wishes of my heart. I knew that I would miss him. He was a good boy. He would be a fine man—the kind of man I once had tried, and failed, to be.

'He'd still be with us, if you hadn't sent for him,' I replied. There was a hint of reproach in my tone. It seemed to me a cruel arbitrariness that, without warning, had put the boy with me for months and had taken him away just as suddenly.

'Tariq completed his training at our Koranic school during the last two years, and now he has improved his English, with you. It is time for him to take his place at college, and I think he is very well prepared.'

Khaderbhai's tone was gentle and patient. The affectionate and slightly amused smile in his eyes held me as firmly as his strong hands held the shoulders of the solemn, unsmiling boy standing in front of him.

'You know, Lin,' he said softly, 'we have a saying, in the Pashto language, and the meaning of it is that you are not a man until you give your love, truly and freely, to a child. And you are not a good man until you earn the love, truly and freely, of a child in return.'

'Tariq's okay,' I said, standing to shake hands and take my leave. 'He's a good kid, and I'll miss him.'

I wasn't the only one who would miss him. He was a favourite with Qasim Ali Hussein. The head man had visited the boy often, and had taken him on his rounds of the slum. Jeetendra and Radha had spoiled him with their affection. Johnny Cigar and Prabaker had teased him good-naturedly, and they'd included him in their weekly cricket game. Even Abdullah had developed an emotional regard for the child. After the Night of the Wild Dogs, he'd visited Tariq twice every week to teach him the arts of fighting with sticks, scarves, and bare hands. I saw them often, during those months, their silhouettes carved on the horizon like figures from a shadow-play as they practised on the one small strip of sandy beach near the slum.

I shook hands with Tariq last, and looked into his earnest, truthful, black eyes. Memories from the last three months skipped across the fluid surface of the moment. I recalled his first fight with one of the slum boys. A much bigger boy had knocked him down, but Tariq drove him back with the power of his eyes alone, forcing shame into the boy with his stare. The other boy broke down and wept. Tariq embraced him in a solicitous hug, and their close friendship was sealed. I remembered Tariq's enthusiasm in the English classes that I'd set up for him, and how he soon became my assistant, helping the other children who joined in to learn. I saw him struggling against the first monsoon flood with us, digging a drainage channel out of the rocky earth with sticks and our bare hands. I remembered his face peeping around the flimsy door of my hut one afternoon when I was trying to write. *Yes! What is it, Tariq?* I'd asked him irritably. *Oh, I'm sorry*, he'd replied. *Do you want to be lonely?*

I left Abdel Khader Khan's house, and began the long walk back to the slum, alone and diminished by the absence of the boy. I was less important, somehow, or suddenly less *valuable* in the different world that closed in on me without him. I kept my appointment with the German tourists, at their hotel, quite near Khaderbhai's mosque. They were a young couple, on their first trip to the sub-continent. They wanted to save money by changing their Deutschmarks on the black market, and then buy some hashish for their journey around India. They were a decent, happy couple —innocent, generous-hearted, and motivated by a spiritual notion of India. I changed their money for them, on a commission, and arranged the purchase of the charras. They were very grateful, and tried to pay me more than we'd agreed. I refused the extra money—a deal is a deal, after all—and then accepted their invitation to smoke with them. The chillum I prepared was average strength for those of us who lived and worked on the streets of Bombay, but much stronger than they were accustomed to smoking. They were both stoned to sleep when I pulled the door of their hotel room closed, and walked on through dozy afternoon streets.

I made my way along Mohammed Ali Road to Mahatma Gandhi Road and the Colaba Causeway. I could've taken a bus, or one of the many prowling taxis, but I loved the walk. I loved those kilometres from Chor bazaar, past Crawford Market, V.T. Station, Flora Fountain, the Fort area,

Regal Circle, and on through Colaba to Sassoon Dock, the World Trade Centre, and the Back Bay. I walked them a thousand times in those years, and they were always new, always exciting, and always inspiring. As I rounded Regal Circle and paused momentarily to check the *Coming Attractions* posters outside Regal Cinema, I heard a voice calling my name.

'Linbaba! Hey! Oh, Lin!'

I turned to see Prabaker leaning from the passenger window of a black-and-yellow taxi. I walked over to shake his hand and greet the driver, Prabaker's cousin, Shantu.

'We're going back to home. Jump yourself inside, and we'll give you a lifts.'

'Thanks, Prabu,' I smiled. 'I'll keep walking. I've got a couple of stops to make on the way.'

'Okay, Lin!' Prabaker grinned. 'But you don't take too much time, like sometimes too much time you're taking, if you don't mind that I'm telling your face. Today is a special day, isn't it?'

I waved until his smile disappeared in the thicket of traffic, and then I jumped in fright as a car slammed to a screeching smash beside me. An Ambassador had tried to overtake a slower car and had crashed into a wooden hand-cart, forcing the heavy cart into the side of a taxi, only two metres away from me.

It was a bad accident. The hand-cart puller was seriously injured. I could see that the ropes attached to his neck and shoulders—the reins and harness—had trapped him in the yoke of the cart. His body, constrained by the ropes, had somersaulted, and he'd hit his head hard on the unyielding surface of the road. One arm was twisted backward at a sickeningly unnatural angle. A piece of shinbone on one leg protruded below the knee. And those ropes, the very ropes he used every day to drag his cart through the city, were tangled about his neck and chest, and dragging him toward choking death.

I rushed forward with others, pulling my knife from its scabbard in the belt at the back of my trousers. Working fast, but as carefully as possible, I cut through the ropes and freed the man from the wreckage of his cart. He was an older man, perhaps sixty years old, but he was fit and lean and healthy. His fast heartbeat was regular and strong: a powerful current with which to charge his recovery. His airways were clear, and he was breathing easily. When I opened his eyes gently with my fingers, his pupils reacted to the light. He was dazed and shocked, rather than unconscious.

With three other men, I lifted him from the road to the footpath. His left arm hung limply from its shoulder, and I eased it into a curve at the elbow. Onlookers donated their handkerchiefs when I called for them. Using four of the handkerchiefs, attached at the corners, I confined the arm to his chest in a makeshift sling. I was examining the break in his leg when a frenzy of screaming and shouts near the damaged cars forced me to my feet.

Ten or more men were trying to seize the driver of the Ambassador. He was a huge man, well over six feet, half again as heavy as I was, and twice as broad across the chest. He planted his thick legs against the floor of the vehicle, braced one arm against the roof, and gripped the steering wheel with the other. The furious crowd gave up after a minute of fruitless, desperate struggle, and turned their attention to the man in the back seat. He was a stocky man with strong shoulders, but he was much slighter and leaner. The mob dragged him from the back seat, and thrust him against the side of the car. He covered his face with his arms but the crowd began beating him with their fists and tearing at him with their fingers.

The two men were Africans. I guessed them to be Nigerians. Watching from the footpath, I remembered the shock and shame I'd felt when I'd seen mob rage like that for the first time, almost eighteen months before, on the first day of Prabaker's dark tour of the city. I remembered how helpless and cowardly I'd felt when the crowd had carried the man's broken body away. I'd told myself then that it wasn't my culture, it wasn't my city, it wasn't my fight. Eighteen months later, the Indian culture *was* mine, and that part of the city *was* my own. It was a black-market beat. My beat. I worked there every day. I even knew some of the people in the murderous crowd. I couldn't let it happen again without trying to help.

Shouting louder than the rest, I ran into the screaming crowd and began dragging men away from the tight press of bodies.

'Brothers! Brothers! Don't hit! Don't kill! Don't hit!' I shouted in Hindi.

It was a messy business. For the most part, they allowed me to drag them away from the mob. My arms were strong. The men felt the power that shoved them aside. But their killing rage soon hurled them back into the uproar, and I felt their fists and fingers pounding and gouging at me from everywhere at once. At last I succeeded in clearing a path to the passenger and then separating him from the leaders of the pack. With his back pressed defensively against the side of the car, the man raised his fists as if ready to fight on. His face was bloody. His shirt was torn and smeared with vivid, crimson blood. His eyes were wide and white with fear, and he breathed hard through clenched teeth. Yet there was determined courage in the set of his jaw and the scowl that bared his teeth. He was a fighter, and he would fight to the very end.

I took that in with a second's glance, and then turned my back to stand beside him and face the crowd. Holding my open hands in front of me, pleading and placating, I shouted for the violence to stop.

As I'd run forward and started the attempt to save the man I'd had a fantasy that the crowd would part and listen to my voice. Stones would fall from the limp hands of mortified men. The mob, swayed by my eloquent courage, would wander away from the scene with shamed and downcast eyes. Even now, in my recollections of that moment and that danger, I sometimes surrender to a wish that my voice and my eyes had changed their hearts that day, and that the circle of hate, humiliated and disgraced, had widened and dispersed. Instead, the crowd hesitated for only an instant and then pressed in upon us again in a brawling, hissing, screaming, boiling rage, and we were forced to fight for our lives.

Ironically, the very numbers of the crowd attacking us worked to our advantage. We were trapped in an awkward L-shape made by the tangle of vehicles. The crowd surrounded us, and there was no escape. But the crush of their numbers inhibited their movements. Fewer blows struck us than might've been the case had fewer men opposed us, and the thrashing crowd actually struck at themselves quite often in their fury.

And perhaps there really *was* some softening of their fury, some reluctance to *kill* us, despite their urgent desire to cause us pain. I know that reluctance. I've seen it many times, in many violent worlds. I can't fully explain it. It's as if there's a collective conscience within the group-mind of a mob, and the right appeal, at exactly the right moment, can turn murderous hate aside from its intended victim. It's as if the mob, in just that critical moment, *want* to be stopped, *want* to be prevented from the worst of their own violence. And in that one doubting moment, a single voice or fist raised against the gathering evil can be enough to avert it. I've seen it in prison, where men bent on the pack-rape of another prisoner can be stopped by one voice that stirs their shame. I've seen it in war, where one strong voice can weaken and wither the hate-filled cruelty that torments a captured prisoner. And perhaps I saw it on that day, as the Nigerian and I struggled with the mob. Perhaps the strangeness of the situation—a white man, a gora, pleading in Hindi for the lives of two black men—held them back from murder.

The car behind us suddenly roared to life. The heavy-set driver had managed to start the car. He gunned the engine, and began to gently reverse away from the wreckage. The passenger and I slowly shuffled and slithered along beside the car as it backed up into the crowd. We struck out, shoving men away from us and wrenching their hands from our clothes. When the driver reached backward over his seat and opened the rear passenger door, we both jumped into the car. The press of the crowd slammed the door. Twenty, fifty hands drummed, beat, slapped, and pounded on the outside of the car. The driver pulled away, heading at a crawl along the Causeway Road. A collection of missiles—tea glasses, food containers, dozens of shoes—rained on the car. Then we were free, speeding along the busy road and watching through the rear window to make sure we weren't followed.

'Hassaan Obikwa,' the passenger beside me said, offering his hand.

'Lin Ford,' I replied, shaking his hand and noticing for the first time how much gold he wore. There were rings on every finger. Some of them closed around blue-white, glittering diamonds. There was also a diamond-encrusted gold Rolex hanging loosely at his wrist.

'This is Raheem,' he said, nodding to the driver. The huge man in the front seat glanced over his shoulder to offer me a broad grin. He rolled his eyes in a survivor's happy prayer, and turned to face the road.

'I owe you my life,' Hassaan Obikwa said with a grim smile. 'We both do. They wanted to kill us, back there, that's for sure.'

'We were lucky,' I answered, looking into his round, healthy, handsome face and beginning to like him.

His eyes and his lips defined his face. The eyes were unusually wide-set and large, giving him a slightly reptilian stare, and the marvellous lips were so full and sumptuously shaped that they seemed to be designed for a much larger head. His teeth were white and even at the front, but all the teeth on either side were capped with gold. Rococo curves at the corners of his wide nose gave his nostrils a delicate flare, as if he was constantly inhaling a pleasantly intoxicating scent. A wide, gold earring, conspicuous beneath his short black hair and against the blue-black skin of his thick neck, pierced his left ear.

I glanced at his torn, bloody shirt, and at the cuts and bruises that were swelling on his face and every exposed centimetre of flesh. When I met his eyes again they were glittering with excited good humour. He wasn't too shaken by the violence of the mob, and neither was I. We were both men who'd seen worse, and had been through worse, and we recognised that in each other immediately. In fact, neither of us ever mentioned the incident directly after that day of our meeting. I looked into his glittering eyes, and I felt my smile stretching to match his.

'We were *damn* lucky!'

'Fuck yes! Yes, we were!' he agreed, laughing hard and slipping the Rolex watch from his wrist. He held it to his ear to make sure it was still ticking. Satisfied, he snapped the watch back on his wrist, and gave his full attention to me. 'But the debt is there, and the debt is still important, even if we were very lucky. A debt like this—it is the most important of all a man's obligations. You *must* allow me to repay you.'

'It'll take money,' I said. The driver glanced in the rear-vision mirror and exchanged a look with Hassaan.

'But ... this debt cannot be repaid with money,' Hassaan answered.

'I'm talking about the cart-puller—the one you hit with your car. And the taxi you damaged. If you give me some money, I'll see that it gets to them. It'll go a long way to calming things down at Regal Circle. That's in my beat—I have to work there, every day, and people are going to be pissed off for a while yet. Do that, and we'll call it square.'

Hassaan laughed, and slapped his hand on my knee. It was a good laugh—honest but wicked, and generous but shrewd.

'Please don't worry,' he said, still smiling broadly. 'This is not my area, it is true, but I am not without influence, even here. I will make sure that the injured man receives all the money he needs.'

'And the other one,' I added.

'The other one?'

'Yes, the other one.'

'The other ... *what?*' he asked, perplexed.

'The *taxi driver.*'

'Yes, yes, the taxi driver also.'

There was a little silence, humming with puzzles and questions. I glanced out the window of the cab, but I could still feel his enquiring eyes on me. I turned to face him again.

'I ... like ... taxi drivers,' I said.

'Yes ...'

'I ... I know a lot of taxi drivers.'

'Yes ...'

'And that cab being smashed up—it'll cause a lot of grief for the driver and his family.'

'Of course.'

'So, when will you do it?' I asked.

'Do what?'

'When will you put the money up, for the cart-puller and the cab driver?'

'Oh,' Hassaan Obikwa grinned, looking up again into the rear-vision mirror to exchange a look with Raheem. The big man shrugged, and grinned back into the mirror. 'Tomorrow. Is tomorrow okay?'

'Yeah,' I frowned, not sure what all the grinning was about. 'I just want to know, so that I can talk to them about it. It's not a question of the money. I can put the money up myself. I was planning to do it anyway. I've gotta mend some fences back there. Some of them are ... acquaintances of mine. So ... that's why it's important. If you're *not* going to do it, I need to know, so that I can take care of it myself. That's all.'

The whole thing seemed to be getting very complicated. I wished I'd never raised the matter with him. I began to feel angry at him, without really understanding why. Then he offered me his open palm in a hand-shake.

'I give you my word,' he said solemnly, and we shook hands.

We were silent again, and after a few moments I reached over to tap the driver on the shoulder.

'Just here is fine,' I said, perhaps a little more harshly than I'd intended. 'I'll get out here.'

The car pulled into the kerb, a few blocks from the slum. I opened the door to leave, but Hassaan gripped my wrist. It was a very strong grip. For a second, I calculated all the long way upward to the much greater strength I knew must be in Raheem's grip.

'Please, remember my name—Hassaan Obikwa. You can find me at the African ghetto, in Andheri. Everyone knows me there. Whatever I can do for you, please tell me. I want to clear my debt, Lin Ford. This is my telephone number. You can reach me, from here, at any time of the day or the night.'

I took the card—it bore only his name and number—and shook his hand. Nodding to Raheem, I left the car.

'Thank you, Lin,' Hassaan called out through the open window. '*Inshallah*, we'll meet again soon.'

The car drove off, and I turned toward the slum, staring at the gold-lettered business card for a full block before I put it in my pocket. A few minutes later, I passed the World Trade Centre and entered the compound of the slum, remembering, as I always did, the first time I entered those blest and tormented acres.

As I passed Kumar's chai shop, Prabaker came out to greet me. He was wearing a yellow silk shirt, black pants, and red-and-black patent leather high-heeled platform shoes. There was a crimson silk scarf tied at his throat.

'Oh, Lin!' he called out, hobbling across the broken ground on his platform shoes. He clung to me, as much for balance as in friendly greeting. 'There is someone, a fellow you know, he is waiting for you, in your house. But one minute please, what happened on your face? And your shirts? Have you been having it some fights, with some bad fellow? *Arrey!* Some fellow gave you a solid pasting. If you want me, I will go with you, and tell that fellow he is a bahinchudh.'

'It's nothing, Prabu. It's okay,' I muttered, striding toward the hut. 'Do you know who it is?'

'Who it ... is? You mean, who it is, who was hitting your face?'

'No, no, of course not! I mean, the man who's waiting in my hut. Do you know who it is?'

'Yes, Lin,' he said, stumbling along beside me and clutching my sleeve for support.

We walked on for a few more seconds in silence. People greeted us on every side, calling out invitations to share chai, food, or a smoke.

'Well?' I asked, after a while.

'Well? What well?'

'Well, who *is* it? Who's in my *hut*?'

'Oh!' he laughed. 'Sorry, Lin. I thought you want some surprises, so I didn't tell you.'

'It's hardly a surprise, Prabu, because you *told* me there was someone waiting for me in my hut.'

'No, no!' he insisted. 'You don't know it his *name* yet, so still you get the surprise. And that is a good things. If I don't tell you there is somebody, then you go to your hut, and you get the shocks. And that is a bad things. A shocks is like a surprise, when you are not ready.'

'Thank you, Prabu,' I replied, my sarcasm evaporating as it was uttered.

He needn't have concerned himself with sparing me the shock. The closer I came to my hut, the more often I was informed that a foreigner was waiting to see me. *Hello, Lin baba! There's a gora in your house, waiting for you!*

We arrived at my hut to find Didier sitting in the shade of the doorway on a stool, and fanning himself with a magazine.

'It's Didier,' Prabaker informed me, grinning happily.

'Yes. Thank you, Prabu,' I turned to Didier, who rose to shake hands. 'This is a surprise. It's good to see you.'

'And good to see you, my dear friend,' Didier replied, smiling despite the distressing heat. 'But, I must be honest, you look a little *worse for wear*, as Lettie would say.'

'It's nothing. A misunderstanding, that's all. Give me a minute to wash up.'

I stripped off my torn, bloody shirt, and poured a third of a bucket of clean water from the clay matka. Standing on the flattened pile of stones beside my hut, I washed my face, arms, and chest. Neighbours passed me as I washed, smiling when they caught my eye. There was an art to washing in that way, with no wasted drop of water and no excess of mess. I'd mastered that art, and it was one of the hundred little ways my life imitated theirs, and folded into the lotus of their loving, hoping struggle with fate.

'Would you like a chai?' I asked Didier as I slipped on a clean, white shirt in the doorway of my hut. 'We can go to Kumar's.'

'I just had one full cup,' Prabaker interjected before Didier could reply. 'But one more chai will be okay, for the friendship sake, I think so.'

He sat down with us in the rickety chai shop. Five huts had been cleared to make space for a single, large room. There was a counter made from an old bedroom dresser, a patchwork plastic roof, and benches for the customers made from planks resting precariously on piles of bricks. All the materials had been looted from the building site beside the slum. Kumar, the chai shop owner, fought a running guerrilla war with his customers, who tried to pilfer his bricks and planks for their own houses.

Kumar came to take our order himself. True to the general rule of slum life that the more money one made, the more poverty-stricken one had to look, Kumar's appearance was more dishevelled and ragged than the meanest of his customers. He dragged up a stained wooden crate for us to use as a table. Appraising it with a suspicious squint, he slapped at the crate with a filthy rag and then tucked the cloth into his singlet.

'Didier, you look terrible,' I observed, when Kumar left to prepare our tea. 'It must be love.'

He grinned back at me, shaking his head of dark curls and raising the palms of his hands.

'I am very fatigued, it is true,' he said, managing a shrug of elaborate self-pity. 'People do not understand the truly fantastic effort required in the corruption of a simple man. And the more simple the man, the more effort it requires. They do not realise what it takes out of me to put so much decadence into a man who is not born to it.'

'You might be making a rod for your own back,' I mocked.

'Each thing in its own time,' he replied, smiling thoughtfully. 'But *you*, my friend, you look very well. Only a little, how shall I say it, lonely for information. And to that end, Didier is here. I have all the latest news and gossip for you. You know the difference between news and gossip, don't you? News tells you *what* people did. Gossip tells you how much they *enjoyed* it.'

We both laughed, and Prabaker joined in, laughing so loudly that everyone in the chai shop turned to look at him.

'Well then,' Didier continued, 'where to start? Oh yes, Vikram's pursuit of Letitia proceeds with a certain bizarre inevitability. She began by loathing him —'

'I think *loathing* is bit strong,' I argued.

'Ah, yes, perhaps you're right. If she loathes *me*—and it is completely certain that she *does*, the dear and sweet English Rose—then her feeling for Vikram was indeed something less. Shall we say *detest*?'

'I think detest would cover it,' I agreed.

'*Et bien*, she began by detesting him but, through the persistence of his devoted romantic attentions, he has managed to arouse in her what I can only describe as an amiable revulsion.'

We laughed again, and Prabaker slapped at his thigh, hooting with such hilarity that every head turned toward him. Didier and I inspected him with quizzical looks of our own. He responded with an impish smile, but I noticed that his eyes darted away quickly to his left. Following the glance, I saw his new love, Parvati, preparing food in Kumar's kitchen. Her thick, black plait of hair was the rope by which a man might climb to heaven. Her petite figure—she was tiny, shorter even than Prabaker— was the perfect shape of his desire. Her eyes, when she turned in profile to look at us, were black fire.

Looking over Parvati's shoulder, however, was her mother, Nandita. She was a formidable woman, three times the combined width and weight of her petite daughters, Parvati and Sita, and she glowered at us, her expression managing to combine greed for our custom with contempt for our male sex. I smiled at her, and wagged my head. Her smile, in return, was remarkably similar to the fierce grimace that Maori warriors affect to intimidate their enemies.

'In his last episode,' Didier continued, 'the good Vikram hired a horse from the handlers on Chowpatty Beach, and rode it to Letitia's apartment on Marine Drive to serenade her outside her window.'

'Did it work?'

'Unfortunately, *non*. The horse left a package of *merde* on the front pathway—during an especially moving part of the song, no doubt—and the many other residents of the apartment building expressed their outrage by pelting the poor Vikram with rotting food. Letitia, it was noticed, threw more offensive missiles, and with a more deadly aim, than any of the neighbours.'

'*C'est l'amour*,' I sighed.

'Exactly—*merde* and bad food, *c'est l'amour*,' Didier agreed quickly. 'I do think that I must involve myself in this romance, if it is to succeed. The poor Vikram—he is a fool for love, and Lettie despises a fool above all else. But things are much more successful for Maurizio in the last time. He had some business venture with Modena, Ulla's paramour, and he is *in the chips*, as our dear Lettie would say. He is now a significant dealer, in Colaba.'

I forced my face to remain impassive while jealous thoughts of handsome Maurizio, flushed with success, spiked their way into my mind. The rain started again, and I glanced outside to see people running, hitching up their pants and their saris to avoid the many puddles.

'Just yesterday,' Didier went on, carefully tipping his tea from the cup into the saucer, and sipping it from the saucer as most of the slum-dwellers did, 'Modena arrived in a chauffeured car, at Leopold's, and Maurizio is wearing a ten-thousand-dollar Rolex watch. But ...'

'But?' I prompted, when he paused to drink.

'Well, there is terrible risk in their business. Maurizio is not always ... honourable ... in his business dealings. If he should upset the wrong people, there will be great violence.'

'And what about you?' I asked, changing the subject because I didn't want Didier to see the serpent of spite rising in me when he spoke of the trouble that might be finding its way to Maurizio. 'Aren't you flirting with danger yourself? Your new ... interest ... is one string short of the full marionette, or so I'm told. He's got a very bad temper, Lettie says, and a hair-trigger controlling it.'

'Oh, him?' he sniffed dismissively, turning down the corners of his expressive mouth. 'Not at all. He is not dangerous. Although he *is* annoying, and annoying is *worse* than dangerous, *n'est-ce pas*? It is easier to live with a dangerous man than an annoying one.'

Prabaker went to buy three beedie cigarettes from Kumar's shop counter, and lit them with the same match, holding them in one hand and burning the ends with the other. He passed one each to Didier and me, and sat down again, smoking contentedly.

'Ah, yes, there is another piece of news—Kavita has taken a new job at a newspaper, *The Noonday*. She is a features writer. It is a job with much prestige, I understand, and a fast track to a sub-editor's position. She won it in a field of many talented candidates, and she is very happy.'

'I like Kavita,' I felt moved to say.

'You know,' Didier offered, staring at the glowing end of his beedie and then looking up at me, genuinely surprised, 'so do I.'

We laughed again, and I deliberately included Prabaker in the joke. Parvati watched us from the corners of her smouldering eyes.

'Listen,' I asked, seizing the momentary pause in our conversation, 'does the name Hassaan Obikwa mean anything to you?'

Didier's mention of Maurizio's new, ten-thousand-dollar Rolex had reminded me of the Nigerian. I fished the gold-and-white business card from my shirt pocket, and handed it over.

'But, of course!' Didier replied. 'This is a famous Borsalino. They call him *The Body Snatcher*, in the African ghetto.'

'Well, that's a good start,' I muttered, a wry smile twisting my lips. Prabaker slapped at his thigh, and doubled over with near-hysterical laughter. I put a hand on his shoulder to calm him down.

'They say that when Hassaan Obikwa snatches a body away, not even the devil himself can find it. They are never again seen by living men. *Jamais!* How do you come to know him? How did you get his card?'

'I sort of, bumped into him, earlier today,' I answered, retrieving the card and slipping it into my pocket.

'Well, be careful, my dear friend,' Didier sniffed, clearly hurt that I hadn't provided the details of my encounter with Hassaan. 'This Obikwa is like a king, a black king, in his own kingdom. And you know the old saying—*a king is a bad enemy, a worse friend, and a fatal family relation.*'

Just then a group of young men approached us. They were labourers from the construction site, and most of them lived on the legal side of the slum. They'd all passed through my small clinic during the last year, most of them wanting me to patch up wounds they'd received in work accidents. It was payday at the site, and they were flushed with the excited optimism that a full pay packet puts into young, hard-working hearts. They shook hands with me, each in turn, and paused long enough to see the new round of chai and sweet cakes they'd bought for us delivered to our table. When they left, I was grinning as widely as they were.

'This social work seems to suit you,' Didier commented through an arch smile. 'You look so well and so fit—underneath the bruises and scratches, that is. I think you must be a very bad man, in your heart of hearts, Lin. Only a wicked man would derive such benefit from good works. A good man, on the other hand, would simply be worn out and bad tempered.'

'I'm sure you're right, Didier,' I said, still grinning. 'Karla said you're usually right, about the wrong you find in people.'

'Please, my friend!' he protested, 'You will turn my head!'

The sudden crash of many drums exploded, thumping music directly outside the chai shop. Flutes and trumpets joined the drums, and a wild, raucous music began. I knew the music and the musicians well. It was one of the jangling popular tunes that the slum musicians played whenever there was a festival or a celebration. We all went to the open front of the shop. Prabaker stood on a bench beside us to peer over the shoulders of the crowd.

'What is it? A parade?' Didier asked as we watched a large troupe slowly walk past the shop.

'It's Joseph!' Prabaker cried, pointing along the lane. 'Joseph and Maria! They're coming!'

Some distance away, we could see Joseph and his wife, surrounded by relatives and friends, and approaching us with ceremonially slow steps. In front of them was a pack of capering children, dancing out their unself-conscious and near-hysterical enthusiasm. Some of them adopted poses from their favourite movie dance scenes, and copied the steps of the stars. Others leapt about like acrobats, or invented jerky, exuberant dances of their own.

Listening to the band, watching the children, and thinking of Tariq—missing the boy already—I remembered an incident from the prison. In that other world-within-a-world, back then, I moved into a new prison cell and discovered a tiny mouse there. The creature entered through a cracked air vent, and crept into the cell every night. Patience and obsessional focus are the gems we mine in the tunnels of prison solitude. Using them, and tiny morsels of food, I bribed the little mouse, over several weeks, and eventually trained it to eat from the edge of my hand. When the prison guards moved me from that cell, in a routine rotation, I told the new tenant—a prisoner I thought I knew well—about the trained mouse. On the morning after the move, he invited me to see the mouse. He'd captured the trusting creature, and crucified it, face down, on a cross made from a broken ruler. He laughed as he told me how the mouse had struggled when he'd tied it by its neck to the cross with cotton thread. He marvelled at how long it had taken to drive thumbtacks into its wriggling paws.

Are we ever justified in what we do? That question ruined my sleep for a long time after I saw the tortured little mouse. When we act, even with the best of intentions, when we interfere with the world, we always risk a new disaster that mightn't be of our making, but that wouldn't occur without our action. *Some of the worst wrongs,* Karla once said, *were caused by people who tried to change things.*

I looked at the slum children dancing like a movie chorus and capering like temple monkeys. I was teaching some of those children to speak, read, and write English. Already, with just the little they'd learned in three months, a few of them were winning work from foreign tourists. Were those children, I wondered, the mice that fed from my hand? Would their trusting innocence be seized by a fate that wouldn't and couldn't have been theirs without me, without my intervention in their lives? What wounds and torments awaited Tariq simply because I'd befriended and taught him?

'Joseph beat his wife,' Prabaker explained as the couple drew near. 'Now the people are a big celebration.'

'If they parade like this when a man *beats* his wife, what parties they must throw when one is killed,' Didier commented, his eyebrows arched in surprise.

'He was drunk, and he beat her terribly,' I said, shouting above the din. 'And a punishment was imposed on him by her family and the whole community.'

'I gave to him a few good whacks with the stick my own self!' Prabaker added, his face aglow with happy excitement.

'Over the last few months, he worked hard, stayed sober, and did a lot of jobs in the community,' I continued. 'It was part of his punishment, and a way of earning the respect of his neighbours again. His wife forgave him a couple of months ago. They've been working and saving money together. They've got enough, now, and they're leaving today on a holiday.'

'Well, there are worse things for people to celebrate,' Didier decided, permitting himself a little shoulder and hip roll in time to the throbbing drums and snake-flutes. 'Oh, I almost forgot. There is a superstition, a famous superstition attached to that Hassaan Obikwa. You should know about it.'

'I'm not superstitious, Didier,' I called back over the thump and wail of the music.

'Don't be ridiculous!' he scoffed. 'Everyone in the whole world is superstitious.'

'That's one of Karla's lines,' I retorted.

He frowned, pursing his lips as he strained his memory to recall.

'It is?'

'Absolutely. It's a Karla line, Didier.'

'Incredible,' he muttered. 'I thought it was one of mine. Are you sure?'

'I'm sure.'

'Well, no matter. The superstition, about him, is that everyone who meets Hassaan Obikwa, and exchanges names with him in a greeting, will one day find himself a client of his—either a living client or a dead one. To avoid this fate, you don't tell him your name when you meet him the first time. No-one ever does. You didn't tell him your name, did you?'

A roar went up from the crowd surrounding us. Joseph and Maria were close. As they approached, I saw her radiant, hopeful, brave smile and his competing expressions of shame and determination. She was beautiful, with her thick hair trimmed short and styled to match the modern cut of her best dress. He'd lost weight, and looked fit, healthy, and handsome. He wore a blue shirt and new trousers. Husband and wife pressed against one another tightly, step for step, all four hands balled into a bouquet of clenched fingers. Family members followed them, holding a blue shawl to catch notes and coins thrown by the crowd.

Prabaker couldn't resist the call to dance. He leapt off the bench and joined the thick tangle of jerking, writhing bodies that preceded Joseph and Maria on the track. Stumbling and tottering on his platform shoes, he skipped to the centre of the dancers. His arms were outstretched for balance as if he was crossing a shallow river on a path of stones. His yellow shirt flashed as he whirled and lurched and laughed in the dance. Didier, too, was drawn into the avalanche of revelry that ploughed through the long lane to the street. I watched him glide and sway gracefully into the party, swept along in the rhythmic dance until only his hands were visible above his dark, curly hair.

Girls threw showers of flower petals plucked from chrysanthemums. They burst in brilliant white clusters, and settled on all of us in the converging crowd. Just before the couple passed me, Joseph turned to look into my eyes. His face was fixed between a smile and a frown. His eyes were burning, glistening beneath the tight brows of his frown, while his lips held a happy smile. He nodded twice before looking away.

He couldn't know it, of course; but with that simple nod of his head, Joseph had answered the question that had remained with me, as a dull ache of doubt, since the prison. Joseph was saved. That was the look simmering in his eyes as he nodded his head. It was the fever of salvation.

That look, that frowning smile, combined shame and exultation because both are essential—shame gives exultation its purpose, and exultation gives shame its reward. We'd saved him as much by joining in his exultation as we had by witnessing his shame. And all of it depended upon our action, our interference in his life, because no man is saved without love.

What characterises the human race more, Karla once asked me, *cruelty, or the capacity to feel shame for it?* I thought the question acutely clever then, when I first heard it, but I'm lonelier and wiser now, and I know it isn't cruelty or shame that characterises the human race. It's forgiveness that makes us what we are. Without forgiveness, our species would've annihilated itself in endless retributions. Without forgiveness, there would be no history. Without that hope, there would be no art, for every work of art is in some way an act of forgiveness. Without that dream, there would be no love, for every act of love is in some way a promise to forgive. We live on because we can love, and we love because we can forgive.

The drums staggered toward the distant street. Moving away from us, the dancers romped and rolled on the rhythm, their swaying heads like a field of wildflowers weaving back and forth on waves of wind. As the music dwindled to an echo in our minds, the day-to-day and minute-to-minute of slum life slowly reclaimed the lanes. We gave ourselves to our routines, our needs, and our harmless, hopeful scheming. And for a while, a little while, ours was a better world because the hearts and smiles that ruled it were almost as pure and clean as the flower petals fluttering from our hair, and clinging to our faces like still, white tears.

CHAPTER EIGHTEEN

T̲h̲e̲ ̲r̲o̲c̲k̲y̲ ̲c̲u̲s̲p̲ ̲o̲f̲ ̲c̲o̲a̲s̲t̲l̲i̲n̲e̲ bordering the slum began in mangrove swamp, at its left, and swept through deeper water around a long new-moon curve of white-crested wavelets to Nariman Point. The monsoon was at full strength, but just at that moment no rain fell from the grey-black ocean of the lightning-fractured sky. Wading birds swooped into the shallow swamp, and nestled among the slender, trembling reeds. Fishing boats plied their nets on the ragged waves of the bay. Children swam and played along the bouldered, pebble-strewn shoreline. On the golden crescent, across the small bay, apartment towers for the rich stood shoulder to shoulder to shoulder, all the way to the embassy district at the Point. In the large courtyards and recreation areas of those towers, the wealthy walked and took the air. Seen from the distant slum, the white shirts of the men and colourful saris of the women were like so many beads threaded by a meditating mind on the black strings of asphalt paths. The air, there, on that rocky fringe of the slum was clean and cool. The silences were large enough to swallow occasional sounds. The area was known as the Colaba Back Bay. There were few places in the city better suited to the spiritual and physical stocktaking that a wanted man worries himself with, when the omens are bad enough.

I sat alone, on a boulder that was larger and flatter than most, and I smoked a cigarette. I smoked in those days because, like everyone else in the world who smokes, I wanted to die at least as much as I wanted to live.

Sunlight suddenly pushed aside the sodden monsoon clouds, and for a few moments the windows of the apartment buildings across the bay were dazzling, brilliant mirrors of the golden sun. Then, horizon-wide, the rain clouds regrouped, and slowly sealed the splendent circle of sky, herding one against another until heaven matched the rolling sea with dark, watery waves of cloud.

I lit a new cigarette with the butt of the last, and thought about love, and thought about sex. Under pressure from Didier, who permitted his friends to keep any secrets but those of the flesh, I'd admitted that I hadn't made love to anyone since I'd arrived in India. *That is a very long time between the drinks, my friend*, he'd said, gasping in horror, *and I propose that it would be a good idea to get very drunk, if you have my meaning, and very soon.* And he was right, of course: the longer I went without it, the more important it seemed to become. I was surrounded, in the slum, by beautiful Indian girls and women who provoked small symphonies of inspiration. I never let my eyes or my thoughts wander too far in their direction —it would've compromised everything that I was, and did, as the slum doctor. But there *were* opportunities with foreign girls, tourists, in every other deal that I did with them, every other day. German, French, and Italian girls often invited me back to their hotel rooms for a smoke, once I'd helped them to buy hash or grass. I knew that something more than smoking was usually intended. And I was tempted. Sometimes I ached with it. But I couldn't get Karla out of my mind. And deep within me—I still don't know whether it's love, or fear, or good judgement that spawns such a feeling—I sensed with all of my intuition that if I didn't wait for her, it wouldn't happen.

I couldn't explain that love to Karla, or anyone else, including myself. I never believed in love at first sight until it happened to me. Then, when it did happen, it was as if every atom in my body had been changed, somehow: as if I'd become charged with light and heat. I was different, forever, just for the sight of her. And the love that opened in my heart seemed to drag the rest of my life behind it, from that moment onward. I heard her voice in every lovely sound the wind wrapped around me. I saw her face in brilliant mirrored flares of memory, every day. Sometimes, when I thought of her, the hunger to touch her and to kiss her and to breathe a cinnamon-scented minute of her black hair clawed at my chest and crushed the air in my lungs. Clouds, heavy with their burden of monsoon rain, massed above the city, above my head, and it seemed to me in those weeks that all grey heaven was my brooding love. The very mangroves trembled with my desire. And at night, too many nights, it was my restive sleep that rolled and turned the sea in lusted dreaming, until the sun each morning rose with love for her.

But she wasn't in love with me, she'd said, and she didn't want me to love her. Didier, trying to warn me, trying to help me or save me, perhaps, had said once that nothing grieves more deeply or pathetically than one half of a great love that isn't meant to be. And he was right, of course, up to a point. But I couldn't let it go, that hope of loving her, and I couldn't ignore the instinct that enjoined me to wait, and wait.

Then there was that other love, a father's love, and the son's love that I felt for Khaderbhai. Lord Abdel Khader Khan. His friend, Abdul Ghani, had called him a mooring post, with the lives of thousands tied to his life for safety. My own life seemed to be one of those harnessed to his. Yet I couldn't clearly see the means by which fate had bound me to him, nor was I completely free to leave. When Abdul had spoken of his search for wisdom, and the answers to his three big questions, he'd unwittingly described my own private search for something or someone to believe. I'd walked that same dusty, broken road toward a faith. But every time I'd heard the story of a belief, every time I'd seen some new guru, the result was the same: the story was unconvincing in some way, and the guru was flawed. Every faith required me to accept some compromise. Every teacher required me to close my eyes to some fault. And then there was Abdel Khader Khan, smiling at my suspicions with his honey-coloured eyes. *Is he the real thing*, I began to ask myself. *Is he the one?*

'It is very beautiful, isn't it?' Johnny Cigar asked, sitting beside me and staring out at the dark, impatient restlessness of the waves.

'Yeah,' I answered, passing him a cigarette.

'Our life, it probably began inside of the ocean,' Johnny said quietly. 'About four thousand million years before now. Probably near hot places, like volcanoes, under the sea.'

I turned to look at him.

'And for almost all of that long time, all the living things were water things, living inside the sea. Then, a few hundred million years ago, maybe a little more—just a little while, really, in the big history of the Earth—the living things began to be living on the land, as well.'

I was frowning and smiling at the same time, surprised and bewildered. I held my breath, afraid that any sound might interrupt his musing.

'But in a way you can say that after leaving the sea, after all those millions of years of living inside of the sea, we took the ocean with us. When a woman makes a baby, she gives it water, inside her body, to grow

373

in. That water inside her body is almost exactly the same as the water of the sea. It is salty, by just the same amount. She makes a little ocean, in her body. And not only this. Our blood and our sweating, they are both salty, almost exactly like the water from the sea is salty. We carry oceans inside of us, in our blood and our sweat. And we are crying the oceans, in our tears.'

He fell silent, and at last I spoke my amazement.

'Where the hell did you learn that?' I snapped, perhaps a little harshly.

'I read it in a book,' he replied, turning to me with shy concern in his brave, brown eyes. 'Why? Is it wrong? Have I said it wrongly? I have the book, in my house. Shall I get it for you?'

'No, no, it's right. It's ... perfectly right.'

It was my turn to lapse into silence. I was furious with myself. Despite my intimate knowledge of the slum-dwellers, and the debt I owed them —they'd taken me in, and given me all the support and friendship their hearts could hold—I still fell into the bigot's trap. Johnny shocked me with his knowledge because, somewhere in my deepest appraisal of the slum-dwellers, there was a prejudice that they had no right to such knowledge. In my secret heart I'd judged them as ignorant, even though I knew better, simply because they were poor.

'Lin! Lin!' my neighbour Jeetendra called out in a frightened shriek, and we turned to see him clambering over the rocks toward us. 'Lin! My wife! My Radha! She is very sick!'

'What is it? What's the matter?'

'She has bad loose motions. She is very hot with fever. And she is vomiting,' Jeetendra puffed. 'She's looking bad. She's looking very bad.'

'Let's go,' I grunted, jumping up and leaping from stone to stone until I reached the broken path leading back to the slum.

We found Radha lying on a thin blanket in her hut. Her body was twisted into a knot of pain. Her hair was wet, saturated with sweat, as was the pink sari she wore. The smell in the hut was terrible. Chandrika, Jeetendra's mother, was trying to keep her clean, but Radha's fever rendered her incoherent and incontinent. She vomited again violently as we watched, and that provoked a new dribble of diarrhoea.

'When did it start?'

'Two days ago,' Jeetendra answered, desperation drawing down the corners of his mouth in a grimace.

'Two *days* ago?'

'You were out some place, with tourists, very late. Then you were at Qasim Ali, his house, until late last night. Then you were also gone today, from very early. You were not here. At the first I thought it was just a loose motions. But she is very sick, Linbaba. I tried three times to get her in the hospital, but they will not take her.'

'She has to go back to hospital,' I said flatly. 'She's in trouble, Jeetu.'

'What to do? What to do, Linbaba?' he whined, tears filling his eyes and spilling on his cheeks. 'They will not take her. There are too many people at the hospital. Too many people. I waited for six hours today altogether—six hours! In the open, with all other sick peoples. In the end, she was begging me to come back to here, to her house. So ashamed, she was. So, I came back, just now. That's why I went searching for you, and called you only. I'm very worried, Linbaba.'

I told him to throw out the water in his matka, wash it out thoroughly, and get fresh water. I instructed Chandrika to boil fresh water until it bubbled for ten minutes and then to use that water, when it cooled, as drinking water for Radha. Jeetendra and Johnny came with me to my hut, where I collected glucose tablets and a paracetamol-codeine mixture. I hoped to reduce her pain and fever with them. Jeetendra was just leaving with the medicine when Prabaker rushed in. There was anguish in his eyes and in the hands that grasped me.

'Lin! Lin! Parvati is sick! Very sick! Please come too fast!'

The girl was writhing in the spasm of an agony that centred on her stomach. She clutched at her belly and curled up in a ball, only to fling her arms and legs outward in a back-arching convulsion. Her temperature was very high. She was slippery with sweat. The smells of diarrhoea and vomit were so strong in the deserted chai shop that the girl's parents and sister held cloths to their mouths and noses. Parvati's parents, Kumar and Nandita Patak, were trying to cope with the illness, but their expressions were equally helpless and defeated. It was a measure of their despondency and their fear that dread had banished modesty, and they allowed the girl to be examined in a flimsy undergarment that revealed her shoulders and most of one breast.

Terror filled the eyes of Parvati's sister, Sita. She hunched in a corner of the hut, her pretty face pinched and cramped by the horror she felt. It wasn't an ordinary sickness, and she knew it.

Johnny Cigar spoke to the girl in Hindi. His tone was harsh, almost brutal. He warned her that her sister's life was in her hands, and he admonished her for her cowardice. Moment by moment, his voice guided her out of the forest of her black fear. At last she looked up and into his eyes, as if seeing him for the first time. She shook herself, and then crawled across the floor to wipe her sister's mouth with a piece of wet towelling. With that call to arms from Johnny Cigar, and the simple, solicitous gesture from Sita, the battle began.

Cholera. By nightfall there were ten serious cases, and a dozen more possible. By dawn the next day there were sixty advanced cases, and as many as a hundred with some symptoms. By noon, on that day, the first of the victims died. It was Radha, my next-door neighbour.

The official from the Bombay Municipal Corporation's Department of Health was a tired, astute, condolent man in his early forties named Sandeep Jyoti. His compassionate eyes were almost the same shade of dark tan as his glistening, sweat-oily skin. His hair was unkempt, and he pushed it back frequently with the long fingers of his right hand. Around his neck there was a mask, which he lifted to his mouth whenever he entered a hut or encountered one of the victims of the illness. He stood together with Doctor Hamid, Qasim Ali Hussein, Prabaker, and me near my hut after making his first examination of the slum.

'We'll take these samples and have them analysed,' he said, nodding to an assistant who filed blood, sputum, and stool samples in a metal carry case. 'But I'm sure you're right, Hamid. There are twelve other cholera outbreaks, between here and Kandivli. They're small, mostly. But there's a bad one in Thane—more than a hundred new cases every day. All the local hospitals are overcrowded. But this is not bad, really, for the monsoon. We hope we can keep a cap on it at fifteen or twenty infection sites.'

I waited for one of the others to speak, but they simply nodded their heads gravely.

'We've got to get these people to hospital,' I said at last.

'Look,' he replied, glancing around him and drawing a deep breath, 'we can take some of the critical cases. I'll arrange it. But it's just not possible to take everyone. I'm not going to tell you any lies. It's the same in ten other hutments. I've been to them all, and the message is the same. You have to fight it out here, on your own. You have to get through it.'

'Are you out of your fucking mind?' I snarled at him, feeling the fear prowl in my gut. 'We already lost my neighbour Radha this morning. There's thirty thousand people here. It's ridiculous to say we have to fight it out ourselves. You're the *health* department, for God's sake!'

Sandeep Jyoti watched his assistant close and secure the sample cases. When he turned back to me, I saw that his bloodshot eyes were angry. He resented the indignant tone, especially coming from a foreigner, and was embarrassed that his department couldn't do more for the slum-dwellers. If it hadn't been so obvious to him that I lived and worked in the slum, and that the people liked me as much as they relied on me, he would've told me to go to hell. I watched all those thoughts shift across his tired, handsome face and then I saw the patient, resigned, almost affectionate smile that replaced them as he ran a hand through his untidy hair.

'Look, I really don't need a lecture from a foreigner, from a rich country, about how badly we look after our own people, or the value of a human life. I know you're upset, and Hamid tells me you do a good job here, but I deal with this situation every day, all over the state. There are a hundred million people in Maharashtra, and we value them all. We do our best.'

'Sure you do,' I sighed in return, reaching out to touch his arm. 'I'm sorry. I didn't mean to take it out on you. I'm just ... I'm way out of my depth here and ... I guess I'm scared.'

'Why do you stay here, when you can leave?'

It was an abrupt question, under the circumstances, and almost rude. I couldn't answer it.

'I don't know. I don't know. I love ... I love this city. Why do *you* stay?'

He studied my eyes for a moment longer, and then his frown softened again in a gentle smile.

'What help *can* you give us?' Doctor Hamid asked.

'Not much, I'm sorry to say.' He looked at the dread in my eyes, and heaved a sigh from the hill of exhaustion in his heart. 'I'll arrange for some trained volunteers to come and give you a hand. I wish I could do more. But I'm sure, you know, I'm sure that you all can handle it here — probably a lot better than you think, just at this moment. You've already made a good start. Where did you get the salts?'

'I brought them,' Hamid answered quickly, because the ORT salts had been supplied illegally by Khaderbhai's lepers.

'When I told him I thought we had cholera here, he brought the ORTs, and told me how to use them,' I added. 'But it's not easy. Some of these people are too sick to hold them down.'

ORT, or Oral Rehydration Therapy, had been devised by Jon Rohde, a scientist who worked with local and UNICEF doctors in Bangladesh during the late 1960s and early 1970s. The oral rehydration solution that he developed contained distilled water, sugar, common salt, and other minerals in carefully mixed proportions. Rohde knew that what kills people who are contaminated with the cholera bacterium is dehydration. The ugly fact is that they shit and vomit themselves to death. He discovered that a solution of water, salt, and sugar kept people alive long enough for the bacterium to pass through their systems. Ranjit's lepers, at Doctor Hamid's request, had given me boxes of the solution. I had no idea how much more of the stuff we could expect to receive, or how much we would need.

'We can get you a delivery of salts,' Sandeep Jyoti said. 'We'll get them to you as soon as possible. The city is stretched to its limits, but I'll make sure you get a team of volunteers here as soon as we can send them. I'll put a priority on it. Good luck.'

We watched in grim silence as he followed his assistant out of the slum. We were all afraid.

Qasim Ali Hussein took control. He declared his home to be a command centre. We called a meeting there, and some twenty men and women gathered to devise a plan. Cholera is largely a water-borne disease. The *vibrio cholerae* bacterium spreads from contaminated water and lodges itself in the small intestine, producing the fever, diarrhoea, and vomiting that cause dehydration and death. We determined to purify the slum's water, beginning with the holding tanks and then moving on to the pots and buckets in each of the seven thousand huts. Qasim Ali produced a bundle of rupee notes as thick as a man's knee, and gave it to Johnny Cigar, deputing him to buy the water-purification tablets and other medicines we would need.

Because so much rainwater had accumulated in puddles and rivulets throughout the slum, those too had provided breeding grounds for the bacteria. It was decided that a chain of shallow trenches would be established at strategic points in the lanes of the slum. They would be filled with disinfectant, and each person walking the lane would be required to pass through the ankle-deep antiseptic drench. Plastic bins for safe disposal of waste materials were to be placed at designated points, and antiseptic soap would be given to every household. Soup kitchens would be established in the chai shops and restaurants to provide safe, boiled food and sterilised cups and bowls. A team was also assigned to the task of removing the bodies of the dead and taking them on a trundle-cart to the hospital. My task was to supervise the use of the oral rehydration solution and to prepare batches of a homemade mixture as required.

They were all huge undertakings and onerous responsibilities, but no man or woman at the gathering hesitated in accepting them. It's a characteristic of human nature that the best qualities, called up quickly in a crisis, are very often the hardest to find in a prosperous calm. The contours of all our virtues are shaped by adversity. But there was another reason, far from virtue, for my own eagerness to accept the tasks—a reason found in shame. My neighbour Radha had been desperately ill for two days before she died, and I'd known nothing of it at the time. I was gripped by a feeling that my pride, my hubris, was responsible for the sickness in some way: that my clinic was founded in an arrogance—my arrogance—that had allowed the disease to breed in the smear of its conceits. I knew that nothing I'd done or neglected to do had caused the epidemic. And I knew that the disease would've attacked the slum, sooner or later, with or without my presence. But I couldn't shake off the feeling that, somehow, my complacency had made me complicit.

Just a week before, I'd celebrated with dancing and drinking because, when I'd opened my little clinic, no-one had come. Not one man, woman, or child in all the thousands had needed my help. The treatment queue that had begun with hundreds, nine months before, had finally dwindled to none. And I'd danced and drunk with Prabaker that day, as if I'd cured the whole slum of its ailments and illnesses. That celebration seemed vain and stupid as I hurried through the sodden lanes to the scores who were sick. And there was guilt in that shame as well. For the two days while my neighbour Radha lay dying, I'd been ingratiating myself with tourist customers in their five-star hotel. While she'd writhed and thrashed on a damp earth floor, I'd been calling down to room service to order more ice-cream and crepes.

I rushed back to the clinic. It was empty. Prabaker was looking after Parvati. Johnny Cigar had taken on the job of locating and removing the dead. Jeetendra, sitting on the ground outside our huts with his face in his hands, was sinking in the quicksand of his grief. I gave him the job of making several large purchases for me and checking on all the chemists in the area for ORTs. I was watching him shamble away down the lane toward the street, worrying about him, worrying about his young son, Satish, who was also ill, when I saw a woman in the distance walking toward me. Before I could actually *know* who it was, my heart was sure it was Karla.

She wore a salwar kameez—the most flattering garment in the world, after the sari—in two shades of sea green. The long tunic was a deeper green, and the pants beneath, tight at the ankle, were paler. There was also a long yellow scarf, worn backwards, Indian style, with the plumes of colour trailing out behind her. Her black hair was pulled back tightly and fastened at the nape of her neck. The hairstyle threw attention at her large green eyes—the green of lagoons, where shallow water laps at golden sand—and at her black eyebrows and perfect mouth. Her lips were like the soft ridges of dunes in the desert at sunset; like the crests of waves meeting in the frothy rush to shore; like the folded wings of courting birds. The movements of her body, as she walked toward me on the broken lane, were like storm-wind stirring in a stand of young willow trees.

'What are *you* doing here?'

'Those charm school lessons are paying off, I see,' she drawled, sounding very American. She arched one eyebrow, and pursed her lips in a sarcastic smile.

'It's not safe here,' I scowled.

'I know. Didier ran into one of your friends from here. He told me about it.'

'So, what are you doing here?'

'I came to help you.'

'Help me *what?*' I demanded, exasperated by my worry for her.

'Help you ... do whatever you *do* here. *Help other people.* Isn't that what you do?'

'You have to go. You can't stay. It's too dangerous. People are dropping down everywhere. I don't know how bad it'll get.'

'I'm not going,' she said calmly, staring her determination into me. The large, green eyes blazed, indomitable, and she was never more beautiful. 'I care about you, and I'm staying with you. What do you want me to do?'

'It's ridiculous!' I sighed, rubbing the frustration through my hair. 'It's bloody stupid.'

'Listen,' she said, surprising me with a wide smile, 'do you think you're the only one who needs to go on this salvation ride? Now, tell me, calmly —what do you want me to do?'

I did need help, not just with the physical work of nursing the people, but also with the doubt and fear and shame that throbbed in my throat and chest. One of the ironies of courage, and the reason why we prize it so highly, is that we find it easier to be brave for someone else than we do for ourselves alone. And I loved her. The truth was that while my words warned her away to safety, my fanatic heart connived with my eyes to make her stay.

'Well, there's plenty to do. But be careful! And the first sign that ... that you're not okay, you grab a taxi to my friend Hamid's. He's a doctor. Is that a deal?'

She reached out to place her long, slender hand in mine. The handshake was firm and confident.

'It's a deal,' she said. 'Where do we start?'

We started with a tour of the slum, visiting the sick and dispensing packets of the solution. There were, by then, more than a hundred people presenting symptoms of cholera, and half of them were serious cases. Allowing just a few minutes with each of the victims, it still took us twenty hours. Constantly on the move, we drank soup or sugary chai from sterile cups as our only food. By evening of the following day, we sat down to eat our first full meal. We were exhausted, but hunger drove us to chew through the hot rotis and vegetables. Then, somewhat refreshed, we set off on a second round of the most serious cases.

It was filthy work. The word *cholera* comes from the Greek word *kholera*, meaning *diarrhoea*. The diarrhoea of the cholera sickness has a singularly vile smell, and you never get used to it. Every time we entered a hut to visit the sick, we fought the urge to vomit. Sometimes, we did vomit. And when we vomited once, the impulse to retch and gag was stronger than ever.

Karla was kind and gentle, especially with the children, and she filled the families with confidence. She kept her sense of humour through the smell, and the endless stooping to lift and clean and give comfort in dark, humid hovels; through the sickness and the dying; and through the fear, when the epidemic seemed to be getting worse, that we, too, would sicken and die. Through forty hours without sleep, she smiled every time I turned my hungry eyes on her. I was in love with her, and even if she'd been lazy or a coward or miserly or bad-tempered I would've loved her still. But she was brave and compassionate and generous. She worked hard, and she was a good friend. And somehow, through those hours of fear and suffering and death, I found new ways and reasons to like the woman I already loved with all my heart.

At three after midnight on the second night, I insisted that she sleep, that we both sleep, before exhaustion crushed us. We began to walk back through the dark, deserted lanes. There was no moon, and the stars punctured the black dome of the sky with a dazzling intensity. In an unusually wide space, where three lanes converged, I stopped and raised a hand to silence Karla. There was a faint scratching sound, a whisper and scrape as of taffeta rustling, or cellophane being squeezed into a ball. In the blackness I couldn't tell where the sound began, but I knew it was close and getting closer. I reached around behind me to grab Karla, and held her pressed against my back, turning left and right as I tried to anticipate the sound. And then they came—the rats.

'Don't move!' I cautioned in a hoarse whisper, pulling her to my back as tightly as I could. 'Keep perfectly still! If you don't move, they'll think you're part of the furniture. If you move, they'll bite!'

The rats came in hundreds and then thousands: black waves of running, squealing beasts that poured from the lanes and swept against our legs like the swirling tide of a river. They were huge, bigger than cats, fat and slimy and rushing through the lanes in a horde that was two or three animals deep. They swept past us at ankle-height and then shin-high, knee-high, running on one another's backs and slapping and smacking into my legs with brutal force. Beyond us, they plunged on into the night toward the sewer pipes of the rich apartment towers, just as they did every night on their migration from nearby markets and through the slum. Thousands. The black waves of snapping rats seemed to go on for ten minutes, although it couldn't have been so long. At last, they were gone. The lanes were picked clean of rubbish and scraps, and silence clogged the air.

'What ... the fuck ... was that?' she asked, her mouth gaping open.

'The damn things come through here every night about this time.

Nobody minds, because they keep the place clean, and they don't worry you, if you're inside your hut, or asleep on the ground outside. But if you get in their way, and you panic, they just go right over the top of you, and pick you as clean as the lanes.'

'I gotta hand it to you, Lin,' she said, and her voice was steady, but fear was still wide in her eyes. 'You sure know how to show a girl a good time.'

Limp with weariness and relief that we weren't badly hurt, we clung to one another and staggered back to the clinic-hut. I spread one blanket down on the bare earth. We stretched out on it, propped up against a stack of other blankets. I held her in my arms. A sprinkling shower of rain rappled on the canvas awning overhead. Somewhere, a sleeper cried out harshly, and the tense, meaningless sound swooped from dream to dream until it disturbed answering howls from a pack of wild dogs roaming the edge of the slum. Too exhausted to sleep just yet, and tingling with sexual tension in the press of our tired bodies we lay awake and, piece by painful piece, Karla told me her story.

She was born in Switzerland, in Basel, and she was an only child. Her mother was Swiss-Italian, and her father was Swedish. They were artists. Her father was a painter, and her mother was a soprano coloratura. Karla Saaranen's memories of her early childhood years were the happiest of her life. The creative young couple was popular, and their house was a meeting place for poets, musicians, actors, and other artists in the cosmopolitan city. Karla grew up speaking four languages fluently, and spent many long hours learning her favourite arias with her mother. In her father's studio, she watched him magic the blank canvases with all the colours and shapes of his passion.

Then, one day, Ischa Saaranen failed to return from an exhibition of his paintings in Germany. At close to midnight, the local police told Anna and Karla that his car had left the road during a snowstorm. He was dead. Within a year, the misery that ruined Anna Saaranen's beauty, and killed her lovely voice, finally smothered her life as well. She took an overdose of sleeping tablets. Karla was alone.

Her mother's brother had settled in America, in San Francisco. The orphaned girl was only ten when she stood next to that stranger at her mother's grave and then travelled with him to join his family. Mario Pacelli was a big, generous-hearted bear of a man. He treated Karla with affectionate kindness and sincere respect. He welcomed her into his family as an equal in every way to his own children. He told her often that he loved her and that he hoped she would grow to love him, and to give him a part of the love for her dead parents that he knew she kept locked within her.

There was no time for that love to grow. Karla's uncle Mario died in a climbing accident, three years after she arrived in America. Mario's widow, Penelope, took control of her life. Aunt Penny was jealous of the girl's beauty and her combative, intimidating intelligence—qualities not discernible in her own three children. The more brightly Karla shined, in comparison to the other children, the more her aunt hated her. *There's no meanness too spiteful or too cruel,* Didier once said to me, *when we hate someone for all the wrong reasons.* Aunt Penny deprived Karla, punished her arbitrarily, chastised and belittled her constantly, and did everything but throw the girl into the street.

Forced to provide her own money for all her needs, Karla worked after school every night at a local restaurant, and as a baby-sitter on weekends. One of the fathers she worked for returned, alone and too early, on a hot summer night. He'd been to a party, and had been drinking. He was a man she'd liked, a handsome man she'd found herself fantasising about from time to time. When he crossed the room to stand near her on that sultry summer night, his attention flattered her, despite the stink of stale wine on his breath and the glazed stare in his eyes. He touched her shoulder, and she smiled. It was her last smile for a very long time.

No-one but Karla called it rape. He said that Karla had led him on, and Karla's aunt took his part. The fifteen-year-old orphan from Switzerland left her aunt's home, and never contacted her again. She moved to Los Angeles, where she found a job, shared an apartment with another girl, and began to make her own way. But after the rape, Karla lost the part of loving that grows in trust. Other kinds of love remained in her—friendship, compassion, sexuality—but the love that believes and trusts in the constancy of another human heart, romantic love, was lost.

She worked, saved money, and went to night school. It was her dream to gain a place at a university—any university, anywhere—and study English and German literature. But too much in her young life had been broken, and too many loved ones had died. She couldn't complete any course of study. She couldn't remain in any job. She drifted, and she began to teach herself by reading everything that gave her hope or strength.

'And then?'

'And then,' she said slowly, 'one day, I found myself on a plane, going to Singapore, and I met a businessman, an Indian businessman, and my life ... just ... changed, forever.'

She let out a sighing gasp of air. I couldn't tell if it was despairing or simply exhausted.

'I'm glad you told me.'

'Told you what?'

She was frowning, and her tone was sharp.

'About ... your life,' I answered.

She relaxed.

'Don't mention it,' she said, allowing herself a little smile.

'No, I mean it. I'm glad, and I'm grateful, that you trusted me enough to ... talk about yourself.'

'And *I* meant it, *too*,' she insisted, still smiling. 'Don't mention it—any of it—to anyone. Okay?'

'Okay.'

We were silent for a few moments. A baby was crying somewhere nearby, and I could hear its mother soothing it with a little spool of syllables that were tender and yet faintly annoyed at the same time.

'Why do you hang out at Leopold's?'

'What do you mean?' she asked sleepily.

'I don't know. I just wonder.'

She laughed with her mouth closed, breathing through her nose. Her head rested on my arm. In the darkness her face was a set of soft curves, and her eyes gleamed like black pearls.

'I mean, Didier and Modena and Ulla, even Lettie and Vikram, they all fit in there, somehow. But not you. You don't fit.'

'I think ... *they* fit in with *me*, even if I don't fit in with them,' she sighed.

'Tell me about Ahmed,' I asked. 'Ahmed and Christina.'

She was silent for so long, in response to the question, that I thought she must've fallen asleep. Then she spoke, quietly and steadily and evenly, as if she was giving testimony at a trial.

'Ahmed was a friend. He was my best friend, for a while, and kind of like the brother I never had. He came from Afghanistan, and was wounded in the war there. He came to Bombay to recover—in a way, we both did. His wounds were so bad that he never really did get his health back completely. Anyway, we kind of nursed each other, I guess, and we became very close friends. He was a science graduate, from Kabul University, and he spoke excellent English. We used to talk about books and philosophy and music and art and food. He was a wonderful, gentle guy.'

'And something happened to him,' I prompted.

'Yeah,' she replied, with a little laugh. 'He met Christina. That's what happened to him. She was working for Madame Zhou. She was an Italian girl—very dark and beautiful. I even introduced him to her, one night, when she came into Leopold's with Ulla. They were both working at the Palace.'

'Ulla worked at the Palace?'

'Ulla was one of the most popular girls Madame Zhou ever had. Then she left the Palace. Maurizio had a contact at the German Consulate. He wanted to oil the wheels on some deal that he was working on with the German, and he discovered that the German was crazy about Ulla. With some heavy persuasion from the consulate officer, and all his own savings, Maurizio managed to buy Ulla free from the Palace. Maurizio got Ulla to twist the consulate guy until he did ... whatever it was Maurizio wanted him to do. Then he dumped him. The guy lost it, I heard. He put a bullet in his head. By then, Maurizio had put Ulla to work, to pay the debt she owed him.'

'You know, I've been working up a healthy dislike for Maurizio.'

'It was a shitty deal, true enough. But at least she was free from Madame Zhou and the Palace. I have to give Maurizio his due there—he proved it could be done. Before that, nobody ever got away—not without getting acid thrown in her face. When Ulla broke away from Madame Zhou, Christina wanted to break out as well. Madame Zhou was forced to let Ulla go, but she was damned if she was going to part with Christina as well. Ahmed was crazy in love with her, and he went to the Palace, late one night, to have it out with Madame Zhou. I was supposed to go with him. I did business with Madame Zhou—I brought businessmen there for my boss, and they spent a lot of money—you know that. I thought she'd listen to me. But then I got called away. I had a job ... a job ... it was

... an important contact... I couldn't refuse. Ahmed went to the Palace alone. They found his body, and Christina's, the next day, in a car, a few blocks from the Palace. The cops ... said that they both took poison, like Romeo and Juliet.'

'You think she did it to them, Madame Zhou, and you blame yourself, is that it?'

'Something like that.'

'Is that what she was talking about, that day, through the metal grille, when we got Lisa Carter out of there? Is that why you were crying?'

'If you must know,' she said softly, her voice emptied of all its music and emotion, 'she was telling me what she did to them, before she had them killed. She was telling me how she played with them, before they died.'

I clamped my jaw shut, listening to the ruffle of air breathing in and out through my nose, until our two patterns of breath matched one another in rhythmic rise and fall.

'And what about you?' she asked, at last, her eyes closing more slowly and opening less often. 'We've got my story. When are you going to tell me your story?'

I let the raining silence close her eyes for the last time. She slept. I knew we didn't have her story. Not the whole of it. I knew the small daubs of colour she'd excluded from her summary were at least as important as the broad strokes she'd included. The devil, they say, is in the details, and I knew well the devils that lurked and skulked in the details of my own story. But she had given me a hoard of new treasures. I'd learned more about her in that exhausted, murmuring hour than in all the many months before it. Lovers find their way by such insights and confidences: they're the stars we use to navigate the ocean of desire. And the brightest of those stars are the heartbreaks and sorrows. The most precious gift you can bring to your lover is your suffering. So I took each sadness she confessed to me, and pinned it to the sky.

Somewhere out there in the night, Jeetendra wept for his wife. Prabaker mopped at Parvati's sweating face with his red scarf. Heaped up on the blankets, our bodies bound by weariness and her deep slumber, surrounded by sickness and hope, death and defiance, I touched the soft surrendered curl of Karla's sleeping fingers to my lips, and I pledged my heart to her forever.

CHAPTER NINETEEN

We LOST NINE PEOPLE in the cholera epidemic. Six of them were young children. Jeetendra's only son, Satish, survived, but two of the boy's closest friends died. Both of them had been enthusiastic students in my English class. The procession of children that ran with us behind the biers carrying those little bodies, garlanded with flowers, wailed their grief so piteously that many strangers on the busy streets paused in prayer, and felt the sudden burn and sting of tears. Parvati survived the sickness, and Prabaker nursed her for two weeks, sleeping outside her hut under a flap of plastic during the night. Sita took her sister Parvati's place at their father's chai shop; and, whenever Johnny Cigar entered or passed the shop, her eyes followed him as slowly and stealthily as a walking leopard's shadow.

Karla stayed for six days, the worst of it, and visited several times in the weeks that followed. When the infection rate dropped to zero, and the crisis had passed for the most serious cases, I took a three-bucket shower, changed into clean clothes, and headed for the tourist beat in search of business. I was almost broke. The rain had been heavy, and the flooding in many areas of the city was as hard on the touts, dealers, guides, acrobats, pimps, beggars, and black marketeers who made their living on the street as it was on the many businessmen whose shops were submerged.

Competition in Colaba for the tourist dollar was cordial, but creatively emphatic. Yemeni street vendors held up falcon-crested daggers and hand-embroidered passages from the Koran. Tall, handsome Somalis offered bracelets made from beaten silver coins. Artists from Orissa displayed images of the Taj Mahal painted on dried, pressed papaya leaves. Nigerians sold carved, ebony canes with stiletto blades concealed within their spiral shafts. Iranian refugees weighed polished turquoise stones by the ounce on brass scales hung from the branches of trees. Drum sellers from Uttar Pradesh, carrying six or seven drums each, burst into brief, impromptu concerts if a tourist showed the faintest interest. Exiles from Afghanistan sold huge, ornamental silver rings engraved with the Pashto script and encircling amethysts the size of pigeons' eggs.

Threading through that commercial tangle were those who made their living servicing the businesses and the street traders themselves—incense wavers, bringing silken drifts of temple incense on silver trays, stove cleaners, mattress fluffers, ear cleaners, foot massagers, rat catchers, food and chai carriers, florists, laundry-men, water carriers, gas-bottle men, and many others. Weaving their way between them and the traders and the tourists were the dancers, singers, acrobats, musicians, fortune-tellers, temple acolytes, fire-eaters, monkey men, snake men, bear-handlers, beggars, self-flagellators, and many more who lived from the crowded street, and returned to the slums at night.

Every one of them broke the law in some way, eventually, in the quest for a faster buck. But the swiftest to the source, the sharpest-eyed of all the street people, were those of us who broke the law professionally: the black marketeers. The street accepted me in that complex network of schemes and scammers for several reasons. First, I only worked the tourists who were too careful or too paranoid to deal with Indians; if I didn't take them, no-one did. Second, no matter what the tourists wanted, I always took them to the appropriate Indian businessman; I never did the deals myself. And, third, I wasn't greedy; my commissions always accorded with the standard set by decent, self-respecting crooks throughout the city. I made sure, as well, when my commissions were large enough, to put money back into the restaurants, hotels, and begging bowls of the area.

And there was something else, something far less tangible but even more important, perhaps, than commissions and turf-war sensitivities. The fact that a white foreigner—a man most of them took to be European—had settled so ably and comfortably in the mud, near the bottom of their world, was profoundly satisfying to the sensibility of the Indians on the street. In a curious mix of pride and shame, my presence legitimised their crimes. What they did, from day to day, couldn't be so bad if a gora joined them in doing it. And my fall raised them up because they were no worse, after all, than Linbaba, the educated foreigner who lived by crime and worked the street as they did.

Nor was I the only foreigner who lived from the black market. There were European and American drug dealers, pimps, counterfeiters, con men, gem traders, and smugglers. Among them were two men who shared the name George. One was Canadian and the other was English. They were inseparable friends who'd lived on the streets for years. No-one seemed to know their surnames. To make the distinction, they were known by their star signs: Scorpio George and Gemini George. The Zodiac Georges were junkies who'd sold their passports, as the last valuable things they'd owned, and then worked the heroin travellers— tourists who came to India to binge-hit heroin, for a week or two, before returning to the safety of their own countries. There were surprisingly large numbers of those tourists, and the Zodiac Georges survived from their dealings with them.

The cops watched me and the Georges and the other foreigners who worked the streets, and they knew exactly what we were doing. They reasoned, truly enough, that we caused no violent harm, and we were good for business in the black market that brought them bribes and other benefits. They took their cut from the drug and currency dealers. They left us alone. They left me alone.

On that first day after the cholera epidemic, I made about two hundred U.S. dollars in three hours. It wasn't a lot, but I decided it was enough. The rain had squalled through the morning, and by noon it seemed to have settled into the kind of sultry, dozing drizzle that sometimes lasts for days. I was sitting on a bar stool, and drinking a freshly squeezed cane juice under a striped awning near the President Hotel, not far from the slum, when Vikram ran in out of the rain.

'Hey, Lin! How you doin', man? Fuck this fuckin' rain, *yaar*.'

We shook hands, and I ordered him a cane juice. He tipped his flat, black Flamenco hat onto his back, where it hung from a cord at his throat. His black shirt featured white embroidered figures down the button-strip at the front. The white figures were waving lassoes over their heads. His belt was made from American silver dollar coins linked one to the other and fastened with a domed *concho* as a belt buckle. The black flamenco pants were embroidered with fine white scrolls down the outside of the leg, and ended in a line of three small silver buttons. His Cuban-heeled boots had crossover loops of leather that fastened with buckles at the outside.

'Not really riding weather, *na?*'

'Oh, shit!' he spat. 'You heard about Lettie and the horse? Jesus, man! That was fuckin' *weeks* ago, *yaar*. I haven't seen you in *too* fuckin' long.'

'How's it going with Lettie?'

'Not great.' He sighed as he said it, yet his smile was happy. 'But I think she's coming around, *yaar*. She's a very special kind of chick. She needs to get all the hating done, like, before she can kind of cruise into the loving part. But I'll get her, even if the whole world says I'm crazy.'

'I don't think you're crazy to go after her.'

'You don't?'

'No. She's a lovely girl. She's a great girl. You're a nice guy. And you're more alike than people think. You both have a sense of humour, and you love to laugh. She can't stand hypocrites, and neither can you. And you're interested in life, I think, in pretty much the same way. I think you're a good couple, or at least you *will* be. And I think you'll get her in the end, Vikram. I've seen the way she looks at you, even when she's putting shit on you. She likes you so much that she *has* to put you down. It's her way. Just stick with it, and you'll win her in the end.'

'Lin … *listen*, man. *That's* it! *Fuck* it! I *like* you. I mean, that's a fuckin' cool rave, *yaar*. I'm going to be your friend from now on. I'm your fuckin' *blood brother*, man. If you need anything, you call on me. Is it a deal?'

'Sure,' I smiled. 'It's a deal.'

He fell silent, staring out at the rain. His curly black hair had grown to his collar, at the back, and was trimmed at the front and sides. His moustache was fastidiously snipped and trimmed to little more than the thickness that a felt-tipped pen might've made. In profile, his face was imposing: the long forehead ended in a hawk-like nose and descended past a firm, solemn mouth to a prominent, confident jaw. When he turned to face me it was his eyes that dominated, however, and his eyes were young, curious, and shimmering with good humour.

'You know, Lin, I really *love* her,' he said softly. He let his eyes drift downward to the pavement and then he looked up again quickly. 'I really *love* that English chick.'

'You know, Vikram, I really *love* it,' I said, mimicking his tone of voice and the earnest expression on his face. 'I really *love* that cowboy shirt.'

'What, *this* old thing?' he cried, laughing with me. 'Fuck, man, you can have it!'

He jumped off the stool and began to unbutton his shirt.

'No! No! I was only joking!'

'What's that? You mean you *don't* like my shirt?'

'I didn't say that.'

'So, what's wrong with my fuckin' shirt?'

'There's nothing wrong with your fuckin' shirt. I just don't want it.'

'Too late, man!' he bellowed, pulling his shirt from his back and throwing it at me. 'Too fuckin' late!'

He wore a black singlet under the shirt, and the black hat was still hanging at his back. The cane juice crusher had a portable hi-fi at his stall. A new song from a hit Hindi movie started up.

'Hey, I *love* this song, *yaar!*' Vikram cried out. 'Turn it up, baba! *Arre, full karo!*'

The juice-wallah obligingly turned the volume up to the maximum, and Vikram began to dance and sing along with the words. Showing surprisingly elegant and graceful skill, he swung out from under the crowded awning and danced in the lightly falling rain. Within one minute of his twirling, swaying dance he'd lured other young men from the footpath, and there were six, seven, and then eight dancers laughing in the rain while the rest of us clapped, whooped, and hollered.

Turning his steps toward me once more, Vikram reached out to grasp my wrist with both of his hands, and then began to drag me into the dance. I protested and tried to fight him off, but many hands from the street assisted him, and I was pushed into the group of dancers. I surrendered to India, as I did every day, then, and as I still do, every day of my life, no matter where I am in the world. I danced, following Vikram's steps, and the street cheered us on.

The song finished after some minutes, and we turned to see Lettie standing under the awning and watching us with open amusement. Vikram ran to greet her, and I joined them, shaking off the rain.

'Don't tell me! I don't wanna know!' she said, smiling but silencing Vikram with the raised palm of her hand. 'Whatever you do, in the privacy of your own rain shower, is your own business. Hello, Lin. How are you, darlin'?'

'Fine, Lettie. Wet enough for you?'

'Your rain dance seems to be working a treat. Karla was supposed to join me and Vikram, right about now. We're going to the jazz concert at Mahim. But she's flooded in, at the Taj. She just called me, to let me know. The whole Gateway's flooded. Limousines and taxis are floatin' about like paper boats, and the guests can't get out. They're stranded at the hotel, and our Karla's stranded there, and all.'

Glancing around quickly, I saw that Prabaker's cousin Shantu was still sitting in his taxi, parked with several others outside the restaurants where I'd seen him earlier. I checked my watch. It was three-thirty. I knew that the local fishermen would all be back on shore with their catches. I turned to Vikram and Lettie once more.

'Sorry, guys, gotta go!' I pushed the shirt back into Vikram's hands. 'Thanks for the shirt, man. I'll grab it next time. Keep it for me!'

I jumped into Shantu's taxi, twirling the meter to the *on* position through the passenger window. Lettie and Vikram waved as we sped past them. I explained my plan to Shantu on the way to the kholi settlement, adjacent to our slum. His dark, lined face creased in a weathered smile and he shook his head in wonder, but he pushed the battered taxi a little faster through the short ride on the rain-drenched road.

At the fishermen's settlement, I enlisted the support of Vinod, who was a patient at my clinic and one of Prabaker's close friends. He selected one of his shorter punts, and we lifted the light, flat boat onto the roof of the taxi and sped back to the Taj Hotel area, near the Radio Club Hotel.

Shantu worked in his taxi sixteen hours a day for six days every week. He was determined that his son and two daughters would know lives that were better than his own. He saved money for their education and for the substantial dowries he would be required to provide if the girls were to marry well. He was permanently exhausted, and beset by all the torments, terrible and trivial, that poverty endures. Vinod supported his parents, his wife, and five children from the fish that he hauled from the sea with his thin, strong arms. On his own initiative, he'd formed a co-operative with twenty other poor fishermen. That pooling of resources had provided a measure of security, but his income seldom stretched to luxuries such as new sandals, or school books, or a third meal in any one day. Still, when they knew what I wanted to do, and why, neither Vinod nor Shantu would accept any money from me. I struggled to give it to them, even trying to force the money down the fronts of their shirts, but they refused to allow it. They were poor, tired, worried men, but they were Indian, and any Indian man will tell you that although love might not have been invented in India, it was certainly perfected there.

We put the long, flat punt down in the shallow water of the flooded road near the Radio Club, close to Anand's India Guest House. Shantu gave me the oilskin cape he used to keep himself dry with whenever the taxi broke down, and the weathered black chauffeur's cap that was his good-luck charm. He waved us off as Vinod and I struck out for the Taj Mahal Hotel. We poled our way along the road that was usually busy with taxis, trucks, motorcycles, and private cars. The water grew deeper with every stroke of the poles until, at Best Street corner, where the Taj Mahal Hotel complex began, it was already waist deep.

The Taj had experienced such floods in the surrounding streets many times. The hotel was built upon a tall platform of bluestone and granite blocks, with ten marble steps leading up to each wide entrance. The floodwaters were deep that year—they reached to the second step from the top—and cars were floating, drifting helplessly, and bumping together near the wall surrounding the great arch of the Gateway of India monument. We steered the boat directly to the steps of the main entrance. The foyer and doorways were crowded with people: rich businessmen, watching their limousines bubble and drift into the rain; women in expensive local and foreign designer dresses; actors and politicians; and fashionable sons and daughters.

Karla stepped forward as if she'd been expecting me. She accepted my hand, and stepped into the punt. I threw the cape around her shoulders as she sat in the centre of the boat, and handed her the cap. She slipped it on with a raffish tilt of the cap's peak, and we set off. Vinod sent us in a loop toward the Gateway Monument. As we entered its magnificent, vaulted chamber, he began to sing. The monument produced a spectacular acoustic. His love song echoed, and rang the bell in every heart that heard him.

Vinod brought us to the taxi stand at the Radio Club Hotel. I reached out to help Karla from the boat, but she jumped to the footpath beside me, and we held on to one another for a moment. Her eyes were a darker green beneath the peak of the cap. Her black hair glistened with raindrops. Her breath was sweet with cinnamon and caraway seed.

We pulled apart, and I opened the door of a taxi. She handed me the cap and the cape, and took a seat in the back of the cab. She hadn't spoken a single word since I'd arrived with the boat. Then she simply addressed the driver.

'Mahim,' she said. *'Challo!' Mahim area. Let's go!*

She looked at me once more as the taxi drew away from the kerb. There was a command or a demand in her eyes. I couldn't decide what it was. I watched the cab speed away. Vinod and Shantu watched it with me, and clapped their hands on my shoulders. We lifted Vinod's boat back onto the roof of the taxi. As I took my seat beside Shantu, reaching out with my left arm to hold the long boat on the roof, I glanced up to see a face in the crowd. It was Rajan, Madame Zhou's eunuch servant. He was staring at me. His face was a gargoyle mask of malevolence and hatred.

That face remained with me all the way back to the kholi settlement, but when we unloaded the boat, and Shantu agreed to join Vinod and me for dinner, I let the image of Rajan's malice melt into my memory. I ordered food from a local restaurant and it was delivered to us there, on the beach, steaming hot in metal containers. We spread the containers out on an old piece of canvas sail, and sat beneath a wide plastic awning to eat. Vinod's parents, wife, and five children took their places around the edge of the canvas sheet beside Shantu and me. Rain continued to fall, but the air was warm, and a faint breeze from the bay slowly stirred the humid evening. Our shelter on the sandy beach beside the many long boats looked out to the rolling sea. We ate chicken byriani, malai kofta, vegetable korma, rice, curried vegetables, deep fried pieces of pumpkin, potato, onion, and cauliflower, hot buttered naan bread, dhal, papadams, and green mango chutney. It was a feast, and the delight that spilled from the eyes of the children, while they ate their fill, put starlight in our smiles as we watched them.

When night fell, I rode back to Colaba's tourist beat in a cab. I wanted to take a room for a few hours at the India Guest House. I wasn't worried about the C-Form at the hotel. I knew that I wouldn't have to sign the register, and Anand wouldn't include me in his list of guests. The arrangement we'd agreed on months before—the same one that applied to most of the cheaper hotels in the city—allowed me to pay an hourly *rent*, directly to him, so that I could use the shower or conduct private business in one of the rooms from time to time. I wanted to shave. I wanted to spend a good half hour under a shower, using too much sham- poo and soap. I wanted to sit in a white-tiled bathroom where I could for- get the cholera, and scrape and scrub the last few weeks off my skin.

'Oh, Lin! So glad to see you!' Anand muttered through clenched teeth as I walked into the foyer. His eyes were glittering with tension, and his long, handsome face was grim. 'We have a problem here. Come quick!'

He led me to a room off the main corridor. A girl answered the door and spoke to us in Italian. She was distraught and dishevelled. Her hair was messed, and matted with lint and what looked like food. Her thin nightdress hung askew, revealing the hand-span of her ribs. She was a junkie, and she was stoned almost to sleep, but there was a numb, somnolent panic in her pleading.

On the bed there was a young man sprawled with one leg over the foot of the bed. He was naked to the waist, and his trousers were open at the front. One boot was discarded and the other was still on his left foot. He was about twenty-eight years old. He was dead.

No pulse. No heartbeat. No breathing. The overdose had thrown his body down the long black well, and his face was as blue as the sky at 5 p.m. on the darkest day of winter. I hauled his body up onto the bed, and put a roll of sheet behind his neck.

'Bad business, Lin,' Anand said tersely. He stood with his back to the closed door, preventing anyone from entering.

Ignoring him, I began cardio-pulmonary resuscitation on the young man. I knew the drill too well. I'd pulled junkies out of overdoses, dozens of them, when I was a junkie myself. I'd done it fifty, eighty times in my own country, pressing and breathing life into the living dead. I pressed at the young man's heart, willing it to beat, and breathed his lungs to their capacity for him. After ten minutes of the procedure he stuttered, deep in his chest, and coughed. I rested on my knees, watching to see if he was strong enough to breathe on his own. The breathing was slow, and then slower, and then it stopped in a hollow sigh. The sound was as flat and insentient as the air escaping from a fissure in layers of geyser stone. I began the CPR again. It was exhausting work, dragging his limp body back up the whole length of the well with my arms and my lungs.

The girl went under twice while I worked on her boyfriend. Anand slapped at her, and shook her awake. Three hours after I stepped into the hotel, Anand and I left the room. We were both soaked through with sweat, our shirts as wet as if we'd been standing in the rain that drummed and rattled beyond the windows. The couple was awake and sullen and angry with us, despite the girl's earlier plea for help, because we'd disturbed the pleasure of their stone. I closed the door on them, knowing that some time soon, someone else in that city, or some other, would close a door on them forever. Every time junkies go down the well they sink a little deeper, and it's just that little bit harder to drag them out again.

Anand owed me one. I showered and shaved, and accepted the gift of a freshly washed and ironed shirt. We sat in the foyer then, and shared a chai. Some men like you less the more they owe you. Some men only really begin to like you when they find themselves in your debt. Anand was comfortable with his obligation, and his handshake was the kind that good friends sometimes use in place of a whole conversation.

When I stepped down to the street, a taxi pulled in to the kerb beside me. Ulla was in the back seat.

'Lin! Please, can you get in for some time?'

Worry, and what might've been dread, pushed her voice almost to a whine. Her lovely, pale face was trapped in a fearful frown.

I climbed in beside her, and the taxi pulled out slowly from the kerb. The cab smelled of her perfume and the beedie cigarettes that she constantly smoked.

'*Seedha jao!*' she told the driver. *Go straight ahead!* 'I have a problem, Lin. I need some help.'

It was my night to be the white knight. I looked into her large blue eyes, and resisted the impulse to make a joke or a flirtatious remark. She was afraid. Whatever had scared her still possessed her eyes. She was looking at me, but she was still staring at the fear.

'Oh, I'm sorry,' she sobbed, breaking down suddenly, and then pulling herself together just as swiftly. 'I didn't even say any hello to you. How are you? I haven't seen you for a long time. Are you going good? You look very good.'

Her lilting German accent gave a fluttering music to her speech that pleased my ear. I smiled at her as the coloured lights streamed across her eyes.

'I'm fine. What's the problem?'

'I need someone to go with me, to be with me, at one o'clock after midnight. At Leopold's. I'll be there and ... and I need you to be there with me. Can you do it? Can you be there?'

'Leopold's is shut at midnight.'

'Yes,' she said, her voice breaking again on the edge of tears. 'But I'll be there, in a taxi, parked outside. I'm meeting someone, and I don't want to be alone. Can you be there with me?'

'Why me? What about Modena, or Maurizio?'

'I trust you, Lin. It won't take long—the meeting. And I'll pay you. I'm not asking you to help me for nothing. I'll pay you five hundred dollars, if you'll just be there with me. Will you do it?'

I heard a warning, deep within—we usually do, when something worse than we can imagine is stalking us, and set to pounce. Fate's way of beating us in a fair fight is to give us warnings that we hear, but never heed. Of course I would help her. Ulla was Karla's friend, and I was in love with Karla. I would help her, for Karla's sake, even if I didn't like her. And I *did* like Ulla: she was beautiful, and she was just naive enough, just sanguine enough to stop sympathy slipping into pity. I smiled again, and asked the driver to stop.

'Sure. Don't worry. I'll be there.'

She leaned across and gave me a kiss on the cheek. I got out of the cab. She put her hands on the window's edge, and leaned out. Misty rain settled on her long eyelashes, forcing her to blink.

'You'll be there? Promise?'

'One a.m.,' I said firmly. 'Leopold's. I'll be there.'

'You promise?'

'Yeah,' I laughed. 'I promise.'

The taxi pulled away, and she called out with a plaintive urgency that seemed harsh and almost hysterical in the stillness of the night.

'Don't let me down, Lin!'

I walked back toward the tourist beat, aimlessly, thinking about Ulla and the business, whatever it was, that her boyfriend, Modena, was involved in with Maurizio. Didier had told me they were successful, they were making money, but Ulla seemed afraid and unhappy. And there was something else that Didier had said—something about danger. I tried to remember the words he'd used. What were they? *Terrible risk ... great violence ...*

My mind was still shuffling through those thoughts when I realised that I was in Karla's street. I passed her ground-floor apartment. The wide French doors, leading directly from the street, were open. A desultory breeze riffled the gauze curtains, and I saw a soft yellow light, a candle, glowing within.

The rain grew heavier, but a restlessness I couldn't fight or understand kept me walking. Vinod's love song, the song that rang bells in the dome of the Gateway Monument, was running on a loop in my mind. My thoughts floated back to the boat sailing on the surreal lake that the monsoon had made of the street. The look in Karla's eyes—commanding, demanding—drove the restlessness to a kind of fury in my heart. I had to stop, sometimes, in the rain, to draw deep breaths. I was choking with love and desire. There was anger in me, and pain. My fists were clenched. The muscles of my arms and chest and back were tight and taut. I thought of the Italian couple, the junkies in Anand's hotel, and I thought of death and dying. The black and brooding sky finally ruptured and cracked. Lightning ripped into the Arabian Sea, and thunder followed with deafening applause.

I began to run. The trees were dark, their leaves wet through. They looked like small black clouds themselves, those trees, each one shedding its shower of rain. The streets were empty. I ran through puddles of fast-flowing water, reflecting the lightning-fractured sky. All the loneliness and all the love I knew collected and combined in me, until my heart was as swollen with love for her as the clouds above were swollen with their mass of rain. And I ran. I ran. And, somehow, I was back in that street, back at the doorway to her house. And then I stood there, clawed by lightning, my chest heaving with a passion that was still running in me while my body stood still.

She came to the open doors to look at the sky. She was wearing a thin, white, sleeveless nightgown. She saw me standing in the storm. Our eyes met, and held. She came through the doors, down two steps, and walked toward me. Thunder shook the street, and lightning filled her eyes. She came into my arms.

We kissed. Our lips made thoughts, somehow, without words: the kind of thoughts that feelings have. Our tongues writhed, and slithered in their caves of pleasure. Tongues proclaiming what we were. Human. Lovers. Lips slid across the kiss, and I submerged her in love, surrendering and submerging in love myself.

I lifted her in my arms and carried her into the house, into the room that was perfumed with her. We shed our clothes on the tiled floor, and she led me to her bed. We lay close, but not touching. In the storm-lit darkness, the beaded sweat and raindrops on her arm were like so many glittering stars, and her skin was like a span of night sky.

I pressed my lips against the sky, and licked the stars into my mouth. She took my body into hers, and every movement was an incantation. Our breathing was like the whole world chanting prayers. Sweat ran in rivulets to ravines of pleasure. Every movement was a satin skin cascade. Within the velvet cloaks of tenderness, our backs convulsed in quivering heat, pushing heat, pushing muscles to complete what minds begin and bodies always win. I was hers. She was mine. My body was her chariot, and she drove it into the sun. Her body was my river, and I became the sea. And the wailing moan that drove our lips together, at the end, was the world of hope and sorrow that ecstasy wrings from lovers as it floods their souls with bliss.

The still and softly breathing silence that suffused and submerged us, afterward, was emptied of need, and want, and hunger, and pain, and everything else except the pure, ineffable exquisiteness of love.

'Oh, *shit!*'

'What?'

'Oh, *Jesus!* Look at the *time!*'

'What? What is it?'

'I've gotta go,' I said, jumping out of the bed and reaching for my wet clothes. 'I've got to meet someone, at Leopold's, and I've got five minutes to get there.'

'*Now?* You're going *now?*'

'I have to.'

'Leopold's will be shut,' she frowned, sitting up in the bed and leaning against a little hill of pillows.

'I know,' I muttered, pulling on my boots and lacing them. My clothes and boots were soaking wet, but the night was still humid and warm. The storm was easing, and the breeze that had stirred the languid air was dying. I knelt beside the bed, and leaned across to kiss the soft skin of her thigh. 'I've gotta go. I gave my word.'

'Is it that important?'

A twitch of irritation creased my forehead with a frown. I was momentarily annoyed that she should press the point when I'd told her that I'd given my word: that should've been enough. But she was lovely in that moonless light, and she was right to be annoyed, while I wasn't.

'I'm sorry,' I answered softly, running my hand through her thick, black hair. How many times had I wanted to do that, to reach out and touch her, when we'd stood together?

'Go on,' she said quietly, watching me with a witch's concentration. 'Go.'

I ran to Arthur Bunder Road through the deserted market. White canvas covers on the market stalls gave them the appearance of shrouded cadavers in the cool-room of a morgue. My footsteps running made scattered echoes, as if ghosts were running with me. I crossed Arthur Bunder Road and entered Mereweather Road, running along that boulevard of trees and tall mansions, with no sight or sound of the million people who passed there during each busy day.

At the first crossroad I turned left to avoid the flooded streets, and I saw a cop riding a bicycle ahead. I ran on in the centre of the road, and a second bicycle cop pulled out of a dark driveway as I passed. When I was exactly half way into the side street, the first police jeep appeared at the end of the street. I heard the second jeep behind me and then the cyclists converged. The jeep pulled up beside me, and I stopped. Five men got out and surrounded me. There was silence for a few seconds. It was a silence of such delicious menace that the cops were almost drunk with it, and their eyes were lit with riot in the softly falling rain.

'What's happening?' I asked, in Marathi. 'What do you want?'

'Get in the jeep,' the commander grunted, in English.

'Listen, I speak Marathi, so can't we —' I began, but the commander cut me off with a harsh laugh.

'We know you speak Marathi, motherfucker,' he answered, in Marathi. The other cops laughed. 'We know everything. Now get in the fucking jeep, you sisterfucker, or we'll beat you with the lathis, and *then* put you in.'

I stepped into the back of the covered jeep, and they sat me on the floor. There were six men in the back of the jeep, and they all had their hands on me.

We drove the two short blocks to the Colaba police station, across the road from Leopold's. As we entered the police compound, I noticed that the street in front of Leopold's was deserted. Ulla wasn't there, where she'd said she would be. *Did she set me up?* I wondered, my heart thumping with dread. That made no sense, but still the thought became a worm that gnawed through all the walls I put up in my mind.

The night duty officer was a squat, overweight Maharashtrian who, like many of his colleagues in the police force, squeezed himself into a uniform that was at least two sizes too small for him. The thought occurred to me that the discomfort it must've caused might help to explain his evil disposition. There was certainly no humour in him or any of the ten cops who surrounded me, and I felt a perverse urge to laugh out loud as their scowling, heavy-breathing silence persisted. Then the duty officer addressed his men, and the laughter in me died.

'Take this motherfucker and beat him,' he said matter-of-factly. If he knew that I spoke Marathi, and could understand him, he gave no indication of it. He spoke to his men as if I wasn't there. 'Beat him hard. Give him a solid beating. Don't break any bones, if you can help it, but beat him hard, and then throw him into the jail with the others.'

I ran. I pushed through the circle of cops, cleared the landing outside the duty room in a single leap, and hit the gravel yard of the compound, running. It was a stupid mistake, and not the last I was to make in the next few months. *Mistakes are like bad loves,* Karla once said, *the more you learn from them, the more you wish they'd never happened.* My mistake that night took me to the front gate of the compound, where I collided with a round-up party, and collapsed in a tangle of tied and helpless men.

The cops dragged me back to the duty room, punching and kicking me all the way. They tied my hands behind my back with coarse, hemp rope, and removed my boots before tying my feet together. The short, fat duty officer produced a thick coil of rope, and ordered his men to bind me with it from ankles to shoulders. Puffing and panting with his rage, he watched as I was trussed in so many coils of rope that I resembled an Egyptian mummy. The cops then dragged me to an adjoining room, and hoisted me up to hang me at chest height from a hook, face down, with the hook jammed through several coils of rope at my back.

'Aeroplane ...' the duty officer growled, through clenched teeth.

The cops spun me around faster and faster. The hook held my bound hands in the bunched ropes, and my head hung down, level with my drooping feet. I whirled and spun until I lost my sense of up or down in the twirling room. Then the beatings began.

Five or six men hit my spinning body as hard and as often as they could, cracking their cane lathis against my skin. The stinging blows struck with piercing pain through the ropes, and on my face, arms, legs, and feet. I could sense that I was bleeding. The screaming rose up in me, but I clenched my jaws and gave the pain no sound of my own. I wouldn't let them have it. I wouldn't let them hear me scream. Silence is the tortured man's revenge. Hands reached out, stopping my body, holding it still, while the room continued to whirl. Then they spun me in the opposite direction, and the beating began again.

When their sport was done, they dragged me up the metal steps to the lock-up—the same metal steps I'd climbed with Prabaker when I'd tried to help Kano's bear-handlers. *Will someone come to help me?* I asked myself. No-one had seen my arrest on the deserted street, and no-one knew where I was. Ulla, if she came to Leopold's at all, if she wasn't actually *involved* in my arrest, wouldn't know that I'd been arrested. And Karla— what could Karla think, but that I'd abandoned her after we'd made love? She wouldn't find me. Prison systems are black holes for human bodies: no light escapes from them, and no news. With that mysterious arrest, I'd vanished into one of the city's darkest black holes. I'd disappeared from the city as completely as if I'd caught a plane to Africa.

And *why* was I arrested? The questions buzzed and swarmed in my whirling mind. Did they know who I really was? If they didn't know—if it was something else, if it had nothing to do with who I really was— there would still be questions, identification procedures, maybe even fingerprint checks. My prints were on file all over the world, through the Interpol agency. It was only a question of time before my real identity emerged. I had to get a message out to ... someone. Who could help me? Who was powerful enough to help me? Khaderbhai. Lord Abdel Khader Khan. With all of his contacts in the city, especially in the Colaba area, he would surely find out that I'd been arrested. In time, Khaderbhai would know. Until then, I had to sit tight, and try to get a message out to him.

Trussed up in the mummifying ropes, dragged up the hard metal stairs one bruising bump at a time, I forced my thoughts to settle on that mantra, and I repeated it to the thumping beat of my heart: *Get a message to Khaderbhai ... Get a message to Khaderbhai ...*

At the top landing of the stairs, they threw me into the long prison corridor. The duty officer ordered prisoners to remove the ropes from my body. He stood in the gateway of the lock-up, watching them with his fists on his hips. At one point, he kicked me two, three times to encourage them to work faster. When the last of the ropes was removed and passed through to the guards, he ordered them to lift me and stand me up, facing him at the open gate. I felt their hands numbly on my deadened skin, and I opened my eyes, through blood, to see his grimace of a smile.

He spoke to me in Marathi and then spat in my face. I tried to raise my arm to hit back at him, but the other prisoners held me fast. Their hands were gentle, but firm. They helped me into the archway of the first open cell-room, and eased me to the concrete floor. I looked up to see his face as he shut the gate. Loosely but accurately translated, he'd said to me, *You're fucked. Your life is over.*

I saw the steel bars of the gate swing shut, and felt the creeping coldness numb my heart. Metal slammed against metal. The keys jangled and turned in the lock. I looked into the eyes of the men around me, the dead eyes and the frenzied, the resentful eyes and the fearing. Somewhere, deep inside me, a drum began to beat. It might've been my heart. I felt my body, my whole body, tense and clench as if it was a fist. There was a taste, thick and bitter, at the back of my mouth. I struggled to swallow it down and then I knew, I remembered. It was the taste of hatred—my hatred, theirs, the guards', and the world's. Prisons are the temples where devils learn to prey. Every time we turn the key we twist the knife of fate, because every time we cage a man we close him in with hate.

CHAPTER TWENTY

THE FIRST FLOOR of the lock-up at Colaba police station had four big cell rooms beyond the flexi-steel gate. A corridor connected the four rooms. On one side the corridor gave access to the rooms. On the other side it looked out, through steel mesh, onto the quadrangle of the police compound. There were more cells below. It was in one of those ground-floor cells that Kano the bear had been detained. Transients, who spent only one or two nights in custody, were held on the ground floor. Anyone likely to stay for a week or longer in the Colaba lock-up climbed the steps or was dragged up them, as I was, and passed through the sliding steel gate into one of hell's antechambers.

There were no doors beyond the steel gate. Each of the four rooms was accessed through a blank arch that was slightly wider than the average house doorway. The rooms were roughly three metres square. The corridor was just wide enough for two men to pass each other with their shoulders touching, and it was about sixteen metres long. At the end of the corridor there was a urinal and a keyhole-shaped squatting-toilet, both without doors. A tap, providing water for washing and drinking, was fixed above the urinal.

The four rooms and corridor might've held forty men with an acceptable level of discomfort. When I woke up, on my first morning, I discovered that there were, in fact, two hundred and forty of us. The place was a hive, a termite's nest, a writhing mass of human beings, pressing against one another with every little movement of an arm or a leg. The toilet was ankle-deep in shit. The urinal overflowed. A stinking swamp oozed out of them into the far end of the corridor. The still, thickly humid monsoon air was clogged with moaning, murmurings, talking, complaining, shouting, and the screams, every few hours, of men going mad. I remained there for three weeks.

The first of the four rooms, where I'd slept the first night, held only fifteen men. It was furthest from the sickening smell of the toilet. It was clean. There was space to lie down. The men who lived in that room were all rich—rich enough to pay the cops to beat up anyone who tried to squeeze in without an invitation. The room was known as the Taj Mahal, and its residents were known as the *pandrah kumar*, the *fifteen princes*.

The second room held twenty-five men. I learned that they were all crooks: men who'd served hard time at least once before, and were prepared to fight, fast and dirty, to preserve a space for themselves. Their room was known as the *chor mahal*, the *abode of thieves*, and the men were known as the *black hats*, the *kala topis*—like Ranjit's lepers—because convicted thieves at the infamous Arthur Road Prison were forced to wear a black hat with their prison uniform.

The third room had forty men wedged into it, sitting shoulder to shoulder around the walls, and taking turns to stretch out in the little space left in the centre of the room. They weren't as hard as the men in the second room, but they were proud and willing. They claimed the small squares of space they sat in, and then struggled to hold them against incursions by newcomers. They were constantly under pressure: every day, at least one of them lost a fight and lost his place to a new, tougher man. Still, the optimal number for the third room was forty men and, since it rarely rose above that limit, it was known as the *chaaliss mahal*, or the *abode of the forty*.

The fourth room was known in the lock-up slang as the *dukh mahal*, or the *abode of suffering*, but many men preferred to use the name that the Colaba police had given the last cell in the row: the *detection room*. When a new man entered the corridor for the first time, through the steel gate, he sometimes tried his luck in the first room. Every one of the fifteen men in that room, and not a few lackeys in the corridor, would rise up, shoving and threatening him away, shouting: *Next room! Next room, bastard!* Driven along the corridor by the writhing, toiling press of bodies, the man might try to enter the second room. If no-one there knew him, whoever happened to be near the door would give him a clip, a smack in the mouth. *Next room, motherfucker!* If the man, badly rattled by then, tried to enter the third room as he was pushed further along the corridor, the two or three men who sat or stood in the doorway of that room would punch and kick at him. *Next room! Next room, sisterfucker!* When the new man found himself shoved all the way to the fourth room, the detection room, he would be greeted as an old and very welcome friend. *Come in, friend! Come in, brother!*

Those foolish enough to enter were beaten and stripped naked by the fifty or sixty men who crushed into that black and foetid room. Their clothes were distributed according to a waiting list determined by a precise and perpetually adjusted pecking order. Their body cavities were thoroughly searched for jewellery, drugs, or money. Any valuables went to the king of the detection room. During my weeks there, the king of the last room was a huge gorilla of a man with no neck, and a hairline that began little more than the thickness of a thumb above his single, thick eyebrow. The new men received filthy rags to wear—the rags that had been discarded by those who'd received their stolen clothes. They then had two options: to leave the room and fend for themselves with the hundred men who lived in the impossibly crowded corridor, or to join the detection-room gang and wait for opportunities to prey on other hapless new men in the chain of muggings. From what I saw in those three weeks, about one man in every five who was brutalised and dispossessed in that last room took the second option.

Even the corridor had its pecking order, its struggles over a foothold of space, and its claim-jumpers who challenged the strength or bravery of rivals. Places near the front gate and relatively far from the toilet were prized. Yet even at the foul end of the corridor, where shit and piss flowed onto the floor in a repulsive, reeking sludge, men fought each other for an inch of space that was slightly shallower in the muck.

A few of those men who were forced to the end of the corridor, forced to stand ankle-deep in shit all day and all night, finally fell down and died. One man died in the lock-up while I was there, and several others were carried out in a state so close to death that I'd found it impossible to rouse them to consciousness. Others summoned the raging madness required to fight their way, minute by minute, hour by hour, metre by metre, day by day, and man by man, along the concrete anaconda's intestine to a place where they could stand and go on living, until the beast disgorged them through the same steel jaws that had swallowed their lives whole.

We received one meal a day, at four in the afternoon. It was dhal and roti, mostly, or rice with a thin curry sauce. There was also chai and a slice of bread in the early morning. The prisoners tried to organise themselves into two orderly lines, approaching and leaving the gate where the cops gave out food. But the crush of bodies, and the desperate hunger, and the greed of a few caused chaos at every meal. Many men missed out. Some went hungry for a day or longer.

We all received a flat aluminium plate when we entered the lock-up. The plate was our only legal possession. There was no cutlery—we ate with our hands—and there were no cups: chai was ladled out onto the plates, and we sucked it off them with our mouths pressed into the thin pool of liquid. But the plates had other uses, first among which was in the manufacture of a makeshift stove. If two aluminium plates were bent into V shapes and used as stands, a third plate could rest on top of them. With a fuel source burning in the space between the bent, inverted plates and beneath the flat plate, a stove was created which could be used to re-heat tea or food. The ideal fuel source was a flat rubber sandal. When one of those rubber shoes was lit at one end, it burned evenly and slowly all the way to the other end. The smoke given off was acrid and thick with a greasy soot that settled on everything it touched. The detection room, where two such stoves burned for some time every night, was blackened across its filthy floor and walls, as were the faces of all the men who lived there.

The stoves were a source of income for the kingpins in the detection room: they used them to re-heat chai and saved food, at a price, for the rich men in room one. The guards allowed deliveries of food and drink— for those who could afford it—during the day, but nothing passed through the gate at night. The fifteen princes, unstinting in the pursuit of their comforts, had bribed the cops to provide a small saucepan, and several plastic bottles and containers, in which to store chai and food. In that way, when deliveries had ceased every night, the princes still enjoyed hot chai and snacks.

Because the aluminium plates could only be used as stoves for so long before they became brittle and collapsed, new plates were always in demand. Because food and chai and even the rubber sandals used as fuel could all be turned into money, they too were always required. The weakest men lost their sandals, their plates, and their food. Those with the heart to help them, by sharing the use of their plates, had to eat in scrambled gulps, and then hand on the plates to be used again. As many as four men often ate off one plate, in that way, during the six or seven minutes that the cops allowed for food to be distributed at the steel gate.

Every day I looked into the eyes of starving men. I saw them watching other men shove hot food too quickly into their mouths with their fingers while cops ladled out the last of the meals. I saw them, every day, watching and waiting and fearing that they might miss out. The truth that filled their eyes was something we only ever know about ourselves in cruel and desperate hunger. I took it into myself, that truth, and the part of my heart that broke to see it has never healed.

And every night in room one, the Taj Mahal, the fifteen princes ate a hot meal and drank hot, sweet tea, heated up on the makeshift stoves in the detection room, before stretching out to sleep.

Even the princes, of course, had to use the toilet. The procedure was as vile and dehumanising for them as it was for the poorest prisoner; and in that, if in nothing else, we were all nearly equal. The long journey through the jungle of limbs and bodies in the corridor ended in the stinking swamp. There, the rich men, like the rest of us, packed their nostrils with strips of cloth torn from a shirt or singlet, and clamped a lit beedie cigarette between their teeth to fight the smell. With pants hitched to their knees, and sandals held in their hand, they then waded barefoot into the sewage to squat over the keyhole toilet. The toilet was unblocked, and functioned well enough; but with more than two hundred men using it, once or twice a day, every day, it was soon fouled by those who missed the keyhole in the floor. Eventually, the piles of excrement slid down into the pools of urine that flowed from the shallow urinal. That was the filthy sludge through which we waded on our way to the toilet. Wading back to the urinal, the rich men then washed their hands and feet at the tap, without soap, and stepped on bundles of rags that were heaped like stepping-stones and formed a makeshift dam before the entrance to the detection room. For the price of a cigarette butt or a half-smoked beedie, men squatting in the muck would clean their feet once more with rags, and then they could begin the long struggle back along the corridor.

It was presumed that I had money, because I was a white foreigner, so the rich men in room one had invited me to join them when I'd woken in their room on my first morning. The idea appalled me. I'd been raised in a family of Fabian socialists, and I'd inherited their stubborn, impractical revulsion for social iniquity in all its forms. Imbued with their principles, and being a product, as a young man, of a revolutionary age, I'd become a revolutionary myself. Some of that commitment to *The Cause*, as my mother had called it, was still there in the core of my being. Moreover, I'd been living in a slum for many months with the city's poor. So I refused the offer—reluctantly, I must admit—to enjoy the comforts of the rich. Instead, I muscled my way into the second room with the hard men who'd all served time in prison. There was a brief scuffle at the doorway but, when it was clear that I was prepared to fight for a place in the abode of thieves, they shuffled themselves around, and made room for me. Still, there was some resentment. The black hats, like self-respecting crooks everywhere, were proud men. It wasn't long before they manufactured an opportunity to test me out.

On one of the long, squirming trips back from the toilet, three days after my arrest, a man in the crowd of prisoners tried to wrestle my plate away from me. I shouted a warning, in Hindi and Marathi, making the threat as anatomically impolite as my vocabulary would allow. It didn't stop him. The man was taller than I was, and bigger by some thirty kilos. His hands grasped the plate near my own, and we both pulled, but neither of us had the gross strength to wrest it away. All the men fell silent. Their breathing was a tidal swirl of sound and warm air around us. It was a face off. Make or break: I made my way in that world, right there and then, or I broke down, and let myself be forced into the foetid swamp at the end of the corridor.

Using the man's grip on the plate as leverage, I smashed my head onto the bridge of his nose, five, six, seven times, and then again on the point of his chin as he tried to pull away. Alarm surged through the crowd. A dozen pairs of hands shoved at us, crushing our bodies and faces together. Packed into the press of frightened men, unable to move my hands, and unwilling to release the plate, I bit into his face. My teeth pierced his cheek until I tasted his blood in my mouth. He dropped the plate and screamed. Thrashing wildly, he scrambled through the bodies in the corridor to the steel gate. I followed him, with my hand reaching out for his back. Grasping the bars, he shook the gate and screeched for help. I caught him just as the watchman turned his keys in the lock. I grabbed at him as he escaped through the gate. His T-shirt stretched behind him, and for a second he was stuck there, his legs running but his body quite still. Then the T-shirt gave way, and I was left with a chunk of it in my hand as the man staggered through the opening. He cowered behind the watchman, his back pressed against the wall. His face was opened at the cheek where my teeth had cut him, and blood streamed from his nose down his throat to his chest. The gate slammed shut. The cop stared, smiling inscrutably, as I used the T-shirt to wipe the blood from my hands and the plate. Satisfied, I threw the shirt at the gate. I turned and squeezed my way through the silent crowd, taking my place in the thieves' room once more.

'Nice move, brother,' the young man sitting beside me said in English.

'Not really,' I replied. 'I was trying for his ear.'

'Oooooh!' he winced, pursing his lips. 'But probably more of a nourishment in his ear, isn't it, than the fucking food they're giving us here, man. What is your case?'

'I don't know.'

'You don't *know*?'

'They picked me up at night and brought me here. They haven't told me what I'm charged with, or why I'm here.'

I didn't ask him what *he* was in for because the Australian prison protocol, followed by crooks of the old school—crooks who know there *is* a protocol, and who taught *me* about it, when I'd started my jail sentence with them—dictates that you don't ask a man about the crimes he might've committed until you like him enough to make him a friend, or dislike him enough to make him an enemy.

'They gave you a solid pasting, man.'

'The aeroplane, they called it.'

'Oooooh!' he winced again, hunching his shoulders. 'I hate that fucking aeroplane, brother! They tied me up in the ropes so tight, once, that it took three days for my arm to get the feeling back. And you know how your body swells the fuck up inside the ropes, when they've been beating you for a while, *na*? My name is Mahesh. What is your good name?'

'They call me Lin.'

'Lin?'

'Yeah.'

'Interesting name, man. Where did you learn to speak Marathi, like when you were calling that fellow a motherfucker, before you started eating on his face?'

'In a village.'

'Must be some sort of tough village, that one.'

I smiled for the first time since the police had picked me up. In prison, a man rations his smiles because predatory men see smiling as a weakness, weak men see it as an invitation, and prison guards see it as a provocation to some new torment.

'I learned the swearing here, in Bombay,' I explained. 'How long do people usually stay here?'

Mahesh sighed, and his broad, dark face folded inward in a resigned frown. His wide-spaced brown eyes were so deep-set that they seemed to be hiding or seeking shelter beneath the ridge of his scarred brow. His wide nose, broken more than once, dominated his face and gave him a tougher look than his small mouth and rounded chin might've managed on their own.

'That is *nobody* knows, brother,' he replied, the light dimming in his eyes. It was the sort of response Prabaker might've made, and I suddenly missed my little friend in a second of loneliness that speared my heart. 'I came here two days before you. There's a rumour we will be taking a truck to the Road, in two or three weeks.'

'The road?'

'Arthur Road jail, man.'

'I have to get a message out to someone.'

'You'll have to wait for that, Lin. The guards here, the cops, they've been telling all of us here not to help you. It's like somebody put a curse on you, my brother. I'm probably going to get some shit on my head just for *talking* to you only, but what the fuck, *yaar*.'

'I've *got* to get a message out,' I repeated, my lips bared from my teeth.

'Well, none of the guys leaving here will help you, Lin. They are afraid, like mice in a bag full of cobras. But you'll be able to get some messages out from Arthur Road. It's a fucking big jail, no problem. Twelve thousand men inside. Government says less than so many, but everybody of us, we know there is twelve thousands of men inside. But it's still a lot better than this. If you go to the Road, you'll be with me, in maybe three weeks. My case is stealing. Stealing from the constructions—copper wire, plastic pipes—three times in jail, already, for the same things. This time number four. What to say, brother? I am what they call a serial offensive, against the pilfering law. This time it is three years for me, if lucky, and five years, if not lucky. If you go to Arthur Road, you go with me.

Then we'll try to get your messages out of the jail. *Thik hain?* Until then, we smoke, and pray to the God, and bite any sisterfuckers who try to take our plates, *na?*'

And for three weeks we did just that. We smoked too much, and we troubled deaf heaven with our prayers, and we fought with some men, and sometimes we comforted other men who were losing the will to smoke and pray and fight. And one day they came to take our finger-prints, pressing the black, traitorous loops and whorls onto a page that promised to tell a truth, a vile truth, and nothing but that truth. And then Mahesh and I were crushed with other men into an ancient blue prison truck—eighty men in the black womb of the truck, where thirty would've been too many—and driven toward Arthur Road Prison at reckless speeds through the streets of the city that we all loved too much.

Inside the gates of the prison, guards dragged us off the tailgate of the truck and told us to squat on the ground, while other guards processed us and signed us into the prison, one by one. It took four hours, shuffling forward and squatting on our haunches, and they left me till last. The guards had been told that I understood Marathi. Their watch commander tested the assertion, when I was alone with them, by ordering me to stand. I stood up on painfully stiff legs, and he ordered me to squat again. When I squatted down, he ordered me to stand again. That might've gone on indefinitely, judging by the hilarity it provoked in the gallery of surrounding guards, but I refused to play. He continued to give the com-mands, but I ignored him. When he stopped, we stared at one another across the kind of silence I've only ever known in prisons or on the battle-field. It's a silence you can feel on your skin. It's a silence you can smell, and taste, and even hear, somehow, in a dark space at the back of your head. Slowly, the commander's sinful smile retreated into the snarl of hate that had spawned it. He spat on the ground at my feet.

'British built this jail, in the time of Raj,' he hissed at me, showing teeth. 'They did chain Indian men here, whip them here, hang them here, until dead. Now *we* run the jail, and you are a British prisoner.'

'Excuse me, sir,' I said, with the most formal politeness that the Marathi language offers, 'but I am not British. I am from New Zealand.'

'You are *British!*' he screamed, spraying my face with his saliva.

'I'm afraid not.'

'Yes! You are British! All *British!*' he replied, the snarl moving outward to a malignant smile once more. 'You are *British*, and *we* run the jail. You go through *that* way!'

He pointed toward an archway that led into the prison's interior. There was a hard right turn, just a little way into the arch, and I knew, the way all animals know, that harm waited for me there. To encourage me, the guards rammed their batons into my back. I stumbled into the arch, and took the right turn. Some twenty men were waiting for me, lined up on either side of the long corridor and armed with bamboo sticks.

I knew the gauntlet well—better than any man should. There'd been another tunnel of pain, in another country: the punishment unit in the prison I'd escaped from in Australia. Those guards had made us run their gauntlet down a long narrow corridor, leading to the tiny exercise yards. And as we ran they'd swung their batons and kicked us, all the way to the steel door at the end of the line.

I stood in the harsh electric light of that new tunnel, in Bombay's Arthur Road Prison, and I wanted to laugh. *Hey guys,* I wanted to say, *can't you be a little more original?* But I couldn't speak. Fear dries a man's mouth, and hate strangles him. That's why hate has no great literature: real fear and real hate have no words.

I walked slowly forward. The men were dressed in white shirts and shorts, with white caps on their heads, and wide black leather belts around their waists. The brass buckles on those belts carried numbers and a title. The title was *Convict Overseer*. They weren't prison guards, I soon discovered. In the Indian prison system, inherited from the days of the British Raj, the prison guards had very little to do with the day-to-day operation of the prison. Those everyday tasks of maintaining routines, order, and discipline were the preserve of convict overseers. Convicted murderers and other long-term serial offenders received sentences of fifteen years or more. During the first five of those years they were common prisoners. During the second five years they earned the privilege of a job in the kitchen, laundry, prison industries, or clean-up gangs. During the third and final five years they often accepted the hat, leather belt, and bamboo stick of a convict overseer. Then, the power of life and death was in their hands. Two lines of those convicted killers, who'd become guards themselves, awaited me in the tunnel. They raised their sticks and fixed their eyes on me, anticipating a charging run that might deprive them of the sporting chance to inflict some pain.

I didn't run. I wish I could say, now, that I walked that night and didn't run because of something noble and brave that I found inside myself, but I can't. I've thought about it often. I've recalled and relived that walk a thousand times, and each time I remember it, there's less certainty about the *why* of it. *Every virtuous act has some dark secret in its heart,* Khaderbhai once told me, *and every risk we take contains a mystery that can't be solved.*

I walked toward them slowly, and I began to think of the long concrete path that leads from the shore to the shrine at Haji Ali: the mosque that floats like a great moored ship on the moonlit sea. That view of the monument to the revered saint, and the journey between the waves to the floating pavilions, was one of my beloved images of the city. Its beauty, for me, was like the angel that a man sees in the sleeping face of the woman he loves. And it might've been just that, beauty alone, that saved me. I was walking into the worst of the city, one of her cruellest and most iniquitous defiles, but some instinct flooded my mind with a loveliness I'd found in her—that path, across the sea, to the white minarets of the saint's tomb.

The bamboo sticks whipped and cracked, ripping and slashing at my arms and legs and back. Some blows hit my head, my neck, and my face. Swung with maximum force, by strong arms against bare skin, the blows from the bamboo sticks were a cross between a hot metal burn and an electric shock. The sticks were split at the ends. They opened razor-thin cuts wherever they landed. Blood began to run from my face and the exposed skin on my arms.

I walked on as slowly and steadily as I could. I flinched often when the sticks smacked into my face or across my ear, but I never cringed or cowered or raised my hands. To keep my hands at my sides, I clutched at the legs of my jeans. And the attack, which had begun with frenzied violence, dwindled to fewer blows as I walked the gauntlet. It ceased altogether when I reached the last men in the lines. It was a kind of victory, seeing those men lower their sticks and their eyes as I passed them. *The only victory that really counts in prison,* an old-timer in the Australian jail once said to me, *is survival.* But survival means more than simply being alive. It's not just the body that must survive a jail term: the spirit and the will and the heart have to make it through as well. If any one of them is broken or destroyed, the man whose living body walks through the gate, at the end of his sentence, can't be said to have survived it. And it's for those small victories of the heart, and the spirit, and the will that we sometimes risk the body that cradles them.

The overseers and several guards brought me through the prison, in the darkening evening, to one of the many dormitory blocks. The large, high-ceilinged room was twenty-five paces long and ten paces wide. There were barred windows that gave views of open areas around the building, and there were two tall steel gates, one at either end of the room. In a bathroom near one entrance, there were three clean keyhole toilets. When the guards locked us in for the night, there were one hundred and eighty prisoners in that room, and twenty convict overseers.

One quarter of the room was reserved for the overseers. They had their own stack of clean blankets. They arranged them with free space all around, and in piles eight or ten thick to provide soft beds. The rest of us were squeezed into two lines in the remaining three-quarters of the room, with a no-man's land of about four paces between our part of the room and the area claimed by the overseers.

Each of us had one blanket, taken from a neatly folded stack at the crowded end of the room. The blankets were folded down their length, and placed side to side on the stone floor against the long walls. We lay down on the narrow blankets, with our shoulders rubbing against one another. Our heads touched the side walls, and our feet pointed in toward the centre of the room. The bright lights remained on all night. The overseers on night watch took turns to walk the length of the room between the rows of feet. They all carried whistles on chains around their necks, which they used to summon the guards in the event of any trouble they couldn't handle themselves. I soon learned that they were reluctant to use the whistle, and there was very little trouble that was beyond their power.

The overseers gave me five minutes to wash the drying blood off my face and neck and arms, and to use the immaculately clean squat toilet. When I returned to the main room they offered me the opportunity to sleep at their end of the room. They assumed, no doubt, that my white skin was connected to a supply of money. And they may have allowed themselves, in some small way, to be influenced by the fact that I'd walked their gauntlet without running. Whatever their reasons, I couldn't do it—they were the very men who'd beaten me only minutes before, the men who'd transformed themselves into prison guards—and I refused their offer. It was a huge mistake. As I walked to the far end of the room, took a blanket from the pile, and put it down next to Mahesh, they sneered and laughed. They were furious that I'd rejected the rare offer to join them, and they conspired, as cowards with power often will, to break my spirit.

In the night I woke from monstrous dreams with a piercing pain in my back. I sat up, scratching at my back to find an insect about the size of a small thumbtack attached to my skin. I wrenched it loose, and put it on the stone floor to examine it. The creature was dark grey, fat, swollen almost to round, with a multitude of legs. I squashed it with my hand. Blood spurted out. It was my own blood. The creature had feasted itself on me in my sleep. At once, a foul smell filled my nostrils. It was my first encounter with the parasite known as *kadmal*, the scourge of prisoners in the Arthur Road Prison. Nothing stopped them. They bit, and sucked blood, every night. The small, round wounds they made soon festered into poison-filled pustules. In any one night there were three to five bites; in a week, there were twenty; and, in a month, there were a hundred suppurating, infected sores on a man's body. And nothing stopped them.

I stared at the stupid mess that the squashed kadmal made, stunned to see how much blood the tiny creature had managed to drain from me. Suddenly there was a stabbing pain at my ear as the night watch overseer swung his bamboo lathi against my head. I started up in anger, but Mahesh stopped me. His hands locked onto my arm, and he dragged me down with all his weight.

The overseer glared at me until I lay down again. He resumed his pacing of the brightly lit room, and Mahesh mouthed a warning to me. Our faces were only a hand's width apart. All along the two lines of sleepers, men were jammed together, arms and legs intertwined in sleep. The terror that spiked in Mahesh's eyes, and the whimper that he clamped with a hand to his mouth, were the last things that I saw and heard on that first night.

'No matter what they do,' he whispered, 'for the sake of your life, don't do anything to them in return. This is not a living place, Lin. We are all dead men here. You can't do anything!'

I closed my eyes, and closed my heart, and willed myself to sleep.

CHAPTER TWENTY-ONE

THE OVERSEERS WOKE US a little after dawn, beating any man unfortunate enough to be asleep when they reached him. I was awake and ready, yet I too received a blow from a stick. I growled in anger and started up quickly, but Mahesh stopped me once again. We folded our blankets according to a precise pattern, and placed them in the pile at our end of the room. The guards opened the large steel gates from the outside, and we filed out of the room to assemble for the morning wash. The rectangular bathing area, something like an empty aboveground pool or a dry stone pond, had a huge cast-iron tank at one end. As we approached, a prisoner opened a valve at the base of the tank, allowing a small jet of water to escape from a pipe that protruded at about shin-height. He scampered up a steel ladder and sat on top of the tank to watch. Men rushed for the pipe, and held their flat aluminium plates under the thin stream of water that issued from it. The crush of men at the tank was ten deep and ten wide: a huge knot of muscle and bone, straining and struggling to reach the pipe.

I waited until the crowd thinned out, watching the men wash them-selves with the little water available. A few men, one in twenty, had pieces of soap, and attempted to lather themselves before returning to the pipe for more water. By the time I approached the pipe, the tank was almost empty. The trickle of water that I collected in my plate was wriggling with hundreds of maggot-like creatures. I thrust the plate away in disgust, and several men around me laughed.

'Water worms, brother!' Mahesh said, filling his plate with the squirm-ing, thrashing, semi-transparent creatures. He tipped the plate of wrig-gling things over his chest and back, and reached out to fill another plate. 'They live in the tanks. When the water gets low, the water worms come out of the tap so many, brother! But no problem. They can't hurt you.

They don't bite, like the kadmal. They just drop down and die in the cold air, you see? The other fellows fight to get water with not many worms inside. But if we wait, we get plenty of worms, but plenty of water also. This is better, yes? Come on. *Challo!* You better grab some, if you want a wash before tomorrow morning. This is it, brother. We can't be washing in the dormitory. That is a special for the overseers only. They let you wash there last night, because you had a lot of blood on you. But you'll never use that washing place again. We use the toilet inside, but we don't wash there. This is your only washing, brother.'

I held the plate under the ever-diminishing trickle of water and then tipped the seething mass of worms over my chest and back, as Mahesh had done. Like all the Indian men I knew, I wore a pair of shorts—the *over-underpants*, Prabaker had called them in the village—under my jeans. I discarded the jeans, and the next plate full of wriggling beasts went down the front of my shorts. By the time the overseers began hitting us with their sticks to herd us back into the dormitory, I was as clean as it was possible to be without soap, and using worm-infested water.

In the dormitory we squatted for an hour while we waited for the guards to make the morning head-count. After a time, the squatting caused us excruciating pain in our legs. Whenever anyone tried to stretch or straighten his legs, however, one of the patrolling overseers struck him a vicious blow. I didn't move in the line. I didn't want them to have the satisfaction of seeing me give in to the pain. But as I closed my eyes in sweating concentration, one of them struck me anyway, without cause or provocation. I began to stand, and once again I felt the restraining hands of Mahesh warning me to be still. When a second, third, and then a fourth blow ripped into my ear, over the space of fifteen minutes, I snapped.

'Come here, you *fuckin'* coward!' I shouted, standing and pointing at the last man who'd struck me. The overseer, a huge and obese man, known to friend and foe alike as Big Rahul, towered over most of the other men in the room. 'I'll take that *fuckin'* stick and jam it so far up your arse I'll be able to see it in your eyes!'

Silence imploded in the room, swallowing every sound. No-one moved. Big Rahul stared. His broad expression, a parody of amused condescension, was infuriating. Slowly, the convict overseers began to converge in support of him.

'Come here!' I shouted in Hindi. 'Come on, hero! Let's go! I'm ready!'

Suddenly Mahesh and five or six other prisoners rose up all around me and clung to my body, trying to force me down to a squatting position.

'*Please*, Lin!' Mahesh hissed. 'Please, brother, please! Sit down again. Please. I know what I'm telling you. Please. *Please!*'

There was a moment, while they pulled at my arms and shoulders, when Big Rahul and I made the kind of eye contact where each man knows everything about the violence in the other. His supercilious grin faded, and his eyes fluttered their signal of defeat. He knew it, and I knew it. He was afraid of me. I allowed the men to drag me down to a squatting position. He turned on his heel, and struck out reflexively at the nearest man crouching in the ranks. The tension in the room dissolved, and the head-count resumed.

Breakfast consisted of a single, large chapatti. We chewed them and sipped water during the five minutes allowed, and then the overseers marched us out of the room. We crossed several immaculately clean courtyards. In a broad avenue between fenced areas, the overseers forced us to squat in the morning sunlight while we waited to have our heads shaved. The barbers' wooden stools were in the shade of a tall tree. Every new prisoner had his hair clipped by one barber, and then a second barber shaved his head with a straight razor.

As we were waiting, we heard shouts coming from one of the fenced compounds near the barbers' courtyard. Mahesh nudged me, nodding his head for me to watch. Ten convict overseers dragged a man into the deserted compound beyond the wire fence. There were ropes attached to the man's wrists and waist. More ropes were attached to the buckles and rings of a thick leather collar fitted tightly around the man's neck. Teams of overseers were playing tug-of-war on the wrist ropes. The man was very tall and strong. His neck was as thick as the barrel of a cannon, and his powerful chest and back rippled with muscles. He was African. I recognised him. It was Hassaan Obikwa's driver, Raheem, the man I'd helped escape from the mob near Regal Circle.

We watched in a tight, fast-breathing silence. They manoeuvred Raheem to the centre of the compound, near a stone block about a metre high and a metre wide. He struggled and resisted them, but it was useless. More overseers joined in, with more ropes. Raheem's legs went out from under him. Three men pulled on each wrist-rope with all their strength.

His arms were drawn out so hard from his sides that I thought they might be torn from the sockets. His legs were splayed out at an excruciatingly unnatural angle. Other men, pulling on the ropes that passed through the leather collar, dragged his body toward the stone block. Using the ropes, the overseers stretched his left arm out, with the hand and forearm resting on the block. Raheem lay beside the block, his other arm stretched out by another team of overseers. One of the overseers then climbed onto the block and jumped off onto Raheem's arm, with both feet, snapping the arm backwards in a sickening crunch of gristle and bone.

He couldn't scream, because the collar at his throat was too tight, but his mouth opened and closed on the scream that we made for him in our minds. His legs began to twitch and spasm. A violent shiver passed through his whole body, ending in a rapid shaking of his head that would've been funny if it wasn't so frightening. The overseers dragged him around until his right arm was resting on the block. The same man climbed the stone, talking all the while to one of his friends, pulling tension on a rope. After a pause, he blew his nose with his fingers, scratched himself, and jumped onto the right arm, snapping it backwards. Raheem lost consciousness. The convict overseers looped their ropes around his ankles and then dragged his body out of the compound. His arms flopped and flapped behind his body, as limp and lifeless as long black socks filled with sand.

'You see?' Mahesh whispered.

'What was *that* all about?'

'He hit one of the overseers,' Mahesh answered in a terrified whisper. 'That's why I stopped you. That's what they can do.'

Another man leaned close to us, speaking quickly.

'And here, there is no guarantee of doctor,' he breathed. 'Maybe you see doctor, maybe no. Maybe that black fellow will live, maybe not live. No good luck to hit overseer, baba.'

Big Rahul walked toward us, resting the bamboo stick on his shoulder. He paused beside me, and brought the stick down with a lazy smack across my back. His laughter as he walked away down the line of waiting men was brutally loud, but it was also weak and false, and it didn't fool me. I'd heard that laugh before, in another prison across the world. I knew it well. Cruelty is a kind of cowardice. Cruel laughter is the way cowards cry when they're not alone, and causing pain is how they grieve.

Squatting in the queue, I noticed with a revulsive flinch that tiny insects, lice, were crawling in the hair of the man in front of me. I'd been feeling itchy since I'd woken. Until that moment, I'd put it down to the bites of the kadmal, the rough blanket I'd slept on, and the many cuts I'd sustained in walking the gauntlet. I looked at the next man's hair. It, too, was crawling with writhing, white lice. I knew what that itchiness was, on my body and in my hair. I turned to look at Mahesh. His hair was alive with lice. I ruffled my own hair onto the palm of my hand, and there they were—white and crab-like, and too many to count at a glance.

Body lice. The blankets they'd forced us to use as sleeping mats were infested with them. Suddenly, the itchiness I felt was a crawling horror, and I knew that the filthy pests were all over my body. When my head was shaved, and we made our way back to the dormitory, Mahesh explained about the body lice, known as *sheppesh*.

'Sheppesh are fuckin' horrible, brother. The little fucks are everywhere. That's why the overseers have their own blankets, and sleep at their own end of the room. No sheppesh there. Come on, watch me, Lin, and I will show you what it is you must be doing.'

He took off his T-shirt, and pulled it inside out. Holding the ribbed seam at the neck, he prised it apart and revealed the sheppesh crawling in the crease at the seam.

'They're fuckin' hard to see, brother, but you don't have any trouble *feeling* them, crawling on you, *yaar*? Don't worry. They're easy enough to kill. You just squeeze the little fucks between your thumbnails, like this.'

I watched him as he worked his way around the neck of his T-shirt, killing the body lice one by one. He moved on to the seams at the sleeves, then, and finally to the hem at the bottom of the shirt. There were scores of the lice, and he squashed each one expertly between his thumbnails.

'Now this shirt is clean,' he said, folding it carefully, away from his body, and placing it on the bare stone floor. 'No more sheppesh. Next you wrap a towel around yourself, like this, then take off your pants, and you kill all the sheppesh on your pants. When clean, put your pants with your shirt. Then your body—your arms underneath, your arse, your balls. And when your clothes they are clean, and your body it is clean, you get dressed again. And you'll be okay, not so many sheppesh, until the night. And then you'll get too many new sheppesh on you from the blanket. And no chance for sleeping without blanket, because the overseers will give you a solid pasting if you try. You can't avoid it. And then tomorrow, you start the whole business again. This is what we call sheppesh farming, and we are farmers every day at Arthur Road.'

I looked around the open, rain-drenched courtyard beside the long dormitory, and a hundred men were busy farming, picking the lice from their clothes and killing them methodically. Some men didn't care. They scratched and shivered like dogs, and allowed the lice to breed on them. For me, the itchy, crawling violation of the body lice was a frenzy on the surface of my skin. I ripped my shirt off and examined the seam at the collar. The shirt was alive with them, squirming, burrowing, and breeding. I began to kill them, one by one, seam by seam. It was the work of several hours, and I practised it with fanatical assiduity, every morning that I spent in Arthur Road Prison, but I never felt clean there. Even when I knew that I'd killed the lice, and rid myself of them temporarily, I still felt their wriggling, itching, crawling loathsomeness on my skin. And little by little, month by month, the horror of that creeping infestation pushed me to the edge.

For the whole of each day, between the early-morning head-count and the evening meal, we moved about within a large courtyard that was attached to our dormitory room. Some men played cards or other games. Some talked with friends, or tried to sleep on the stone paths. Not a few men, shuffling uncertainly on thin, tottering legs, talked a twitching madness to themselves, and stumbled into the walls until we turned them gently and set them on a new course.

Lunch, at Arthur Road, consisted of a watery soup ladled out onto our flat aluminium plates. The evening meal, served at four-thirty with the addition of a single chapatti, was a repetition of that soup of the day. It was made with the peelings and discarded ends of various vegetables — peelings from beetroot on one day, from carrots the next, from pumpkins on the third day, and so on. The eyes and bruises, cut from potatoes, were used, as were the hard ends of courgettes, the papery outer skins of onions, and the muddy scrapings from turnips. We never saw pieces of the vegetables — those went to the guards and the convict overseers. In our soup, the scraps of peelings or stalky ends floated in a colourless, watery liquid. The large vat that the overseers wheeled into our compound for every meal brought one hundred and fifty ladled servings from the kitchens. There were one hundred and *eighty* men in the room. To remedy the deficiency, the overseers poured two buckets of cold water into the vat. They did that at every meal, with a ritual head-count and a pantomime display of inspiration as they solved the problem by adding the buckets of water. It never failed to rouse them to raucous laughter.

At six o'clock, after the evening meal, the guards counted us once more, and locked us in the long dormitory room. For two hours, then, we were permitted to talk, and to smoke charras, purchased from the overseers. Inmates at Arthur Road Prison received five ration tickets, called coupons, per month. Men with access to money could also purchase coupons. Some men held rolls with several hundred coupons in them. They used them to buy tea—two coupons bought a cup of hot tea —bread, sugar, jam, hot food, soap, shaving accessories, cigarettes, and the services of men who washed clothes or did other odd jobs. They were also the black-market currency in the prison. For six coupons, a man could buy a tiny *goli*, or a *ball*, of charras. For fifty, he could buy a shot of penicillin. A few dealers also traded in heroin, for sixty coupons a fix, but the overseers were ruthless in their attempts to exterminate it. Heroin addiction was one of the few forces strong enough to overcome terror and challenge the torturers' authority. Most men, sane enough to fear the overseers' almost limitless power, satisfied themselves with the semi-legal charras, and the perfume of hashish often drifted through the room.

Every night the men gathered in groups to sing. Sitting in circles of twelve or more men, and tapping on their upturned aluminium plates as if they were tabla drums, the prisoners sang love songs from their favourite movies. They sang of heartbreak, and all the sorrows of loss. A particularly beloved song might start in one circle, be taken up by a second group for the next verses, and then move to a third group and a fourth before working its way back to the first. Around each circle of twelve or fifteen singers were twenty or thirty more men who provided the chorus of clapping hands and supporting voices. They cried openly as they sang, and they laughed together often. And with their music they helped one another to keep love alive in hearts that the city had forsaken, and forgotten.

At the end of the second week at Arthur Road, I met with two young men who were due for release within the hour. Mahesh assured me that they would carry a message for me. They were simple, illiterate village boys who'd visited Bombay and had found themselves caught in the round-up of unemployed youths. After three months in Arthur Road without any formal charge, they were finally being released. On a piece of paper I wrote the name and address of Abdel Khader Khan, and a short note informing him that I was in prison. I gave it to the men and promised to reward them when I was released. They joined their hands together in a blessing and then left me, their smiles bright and hopeful.

Later that day the overseers called our dormitory together with more than usual violence, and forced us to squat in close ranks. As we watched, the two young men who'd tried to help me were dragged into the room and dumped against a wall. They were only semi-conscious. They'd been beaten viciously. Blood wept from wounds on their faces. Their mouths were swollen and their eyes were blackened. A snakeskin pattern of lathi bruises covered their bare arms and legs.

'These dogs tried to take a message out of the jail for the gora,' Big Rahul the overseer roared at us in Hindi. 'Anyone who tries to help the gora, will get the same. Understand? Now these two dogs have six more months in jail, in *my* room! Six months! Help him, any of you, and you will get the same.'

The overseers left the room to share a cigarette, and we rushed forward to help the men. I washed their wounds, and dressed the worst of them with strips of cloth. Mahesh helped me, and when we finished the job he took me outside to smoke a beedie.

'It's not your fault, Lin,' he said, looking out at the yard, where men walked or sat or picked lice from their clothes.

'Of *course* it's my fault.'

'No, man,' he said compassionately. 'It's this place, this Arthur Road. That business, that happens every day. It's not your fault, brother, and it's not mine. But now, it is a real problem for you. Nobody will be helping you now—just like in the lock-up at Colaba. I don't know how long you will stay here. You see old Pandu, over there? He is in this room three years now, and still not any court action for him. Ajay is more than one year here. Santosh is two years in this room, for no charge, and he doesn't know when he will go to court. I ... I don't know how long you will be in this room. And, sorry, brother, nobody will help you now.'

The weeks passed, and Mahesh was right—no-one risked the anger of the overseers to help me. Men were released from the room every week, and I approached as many of them as I could, and as carefully as possible, but none would help. My situation was becoming desperate. After two months at the prison, I guessed that I'd lost about twelve kilos. I looked thin. My body was covered in the small, suppurating sores caused by the bites of the nocturnal kadmal. There were bruises caused by blows from overseers' canes on my arms, legs, back, face, and bald, shaved head. And all the time, every minute of every day and night, I worried that the report on my fingerprints would reveal who I really was. Almost every night the worry worked me into a sweating nightmare of the ten-year sentence I'd escaped from in Australia. That worry settled in my chest, squeezing my heart and often swelling to such a grotesque anguish that I felt myself choking, suffocating on it. Guilt is the hilt of the knife that we use on ourselves, and love is often the blade; but it's worry that keeps the knife sharp, and worry that gets most of us, in the end.

The frustration, dread, worry, and pain finally peaked when Big Rahul, the overseer who'd found in me a focus for the hatred and wretchedness *he'd* suffered in his twelve years at the prison, hit me one time too often. I was sitting near the entrance to the empty dormitory, and attempting to write down a short story that had emerged and developed in my mind over the last weeks. I'd been repeating the phrases of the story line by line and day after day as I'd created them. It was one of the meditations that kept me sane. When I managed, that morning, to scrounge a stub of pencil and a small sheaf of discarded sugar-ration wrappers, I felt ready at last to write down the lines of the first page. In a quiet moment, after farming for sheppesh, I began to write. With all the stealth that malice manufactures, even in the gross and clumsy, Rahul crept up behind me and brought his lathi down on my left upper arm with bone-rattling force. His punishment stick was split at the end, and the blow ripped the skin of my arm open along the length of the muscle, almost from the shoulder to the elbow. Blood erupted from the deep cut and spilled over the fingers that I clamped on the wound.

Springing to my feet in red-vision rage, I reached out quickly and snatched the stick from Rahul's startled hand. Advancing towards him, I forced him backwards several paces into the empty room. There was a barred window beside me. I threw the stick through the bars. Rahul's eyes bulged with fear and astonishment. It was the last thing he'd expected. He fumbled at his chest for his whistle. I kicked out in a twisting, flying front kick. He hadn't expected that, either. The ball of my foot struck him in the face between the nose and the mouth. He took several stumbling, backward steps. Rule number one of street fighting: stand your ground and never walk backwards, unless you're preparing a counter-strike. I followed him, pushing him on to the back foot and hitting him with a flurry of jabs and overhand rights. He put his head down, and covered up with his hands. Rule number two of street fighting: never put your head down. Aiming the punches for maximum damage, I punched him directly in the ear, on the temples, and at the throat. He was a bigger man than I was, and at least as strong, but he was no fighter. He buckled, and went to his knees, rolling over onto his side and pleading for mercy.

I looked up to see the other overseers running toward me from the yard outside. Backing up into a corner of the room, I took up a karate stance and waited for them. They ran at me. One of them was faster than the others. He rushed into striking range. I kicked out quickly. My foot struck him between the legs, with all the strength I had. I punched him three times before he hit the ground. His face was bloody. The blood smeared on the polished stone floor as he crawled away from me. The rest of them baulked. They stood in a semi-circle around me, startled and confused, with their sticks raised in the air.

'Come on!' I shouted, in Hindi. 'What can you do to me? Can you do worse than *this*?'

I punched my own face, hard, and punched it again, drawing blood from my lip. I swiped my right hand through the blood on my wounded arm and smeared it on my forehead. Lesson number three of street fighting: always get crazier than the other guy.

'Can you do worse than *this*?' I shouted, switching to Marathi. 'Do you think I'm afraid of *this*? Come on! I *want* this! I *want* you to get me out of this corner! You'll get me, you'll get me, but one of you, standing there, will lose an eye. One of *you*. I'll rip someone's eye out with my fingers, and *eat* it! So come on! Let's get on with it! And hurry up, because God knows, I'm *fuckin' hungry!*'

They hesitated, and then drew back in a huddle to discuss the situation. I watched them, every muscle in my body as tight and taut as a leopard leaping to the kill. After half a minute of harsh whispering, the overseers reached a decision. They drew back further, and some of their number ran out of the room. I thought they must be running for the guards, but they returned in seconds with ten prisoners from my room. They ordered the men to sit on the ground, facing me, and then they began to beat them. The sticks rose and fell swiftly. The men shrieked and yowled. The beating ceased, after a minute, and they sent the ten men away. In a few seconds, they replaced them with ten more.

'Come out of the corner, now!' one of the overseers commanded.

I looked at the men sitting on the ground, and then back at the overseer. I shook my head. The overseer gave the command, and the second group of ten men was beaten with the bamboo canes. Their cries rose up in piercing echoes, and wheeled about us in the stone room like a flock of frightened birds.

'Come out of the corner!' the overseer shouted.

'No.'

'*Aur dass!*' he screamed. *Bring ten more!*

The next group of ten frightened men was assembled, facing me. The overseers raised their sticks. Mahesh was in the third group. One of the two men who'd been beaten and given an extra six-month sentence for trying to help me was also in the huddle of ten. They looked at me. They were silent, but their eyes were pleading with me.

I put my hands down and took a step forward out of the corner. The overseers rushed at me, and seized me with six pairs of hands. They shoved and dragged me to one of the barred steel gates, and forced me down on my back, with the top of my head resting against the steel bars. They kept several pairs of handcuffs in a locker at their end of the room. Using two sets of those antique iron devices, they chained my outstretched arms to the bars at the wrists, level with my head. They used coconut fibre rope to tie my legs together at the ankles.

Big Rahul knelt beside me, and brought his face close to mine. The exertion of kneeling and bending and coping with his monstrous hatreds caused him to sweat and wheeze. His mouth was cut, and his nose was swollen. I knew that his head would ache for days from the punches I'd landed on his ear and his temple. He smiled. You can never tell just how much badness there is in a man until you see him smile. I suddenly remembered a comment Lettie had made about Maurizio. *If babies had wings,* she said, *he'd be the kind who'd pull them off.* I started to laugh. Helpless, with my arms stretched out and chained beside me, I laughed. Big Rahul frowned at me. His slack-lipped, cretinous puzzlement made me laugh the harder.

The beating began. Big Rahul exhausted himself in a furious assault that concentrated on my face and my genitals. When he could lift the stick no more, and was gasping for breath, the other overseers stepped in and continued the attack. They hammered at me with the bamboo lathis for twenty minutes or more. Then they took a break to smoke cigarettes. I was wearing shorts and a singlet, nothing else. The canes had cut into me, flaying my skin, slicing and tearing it open from the soles of my feet to the top of my head.

After they'd smoked, the beating resumed. Some time later, I heard from the conversation around me that another group of overseers, from another room, had arrived. The new men, with fresh arms, lashed at my body. Their fury was merciless. When they were done, a third group of overseers launched a savage attack. Then there was a fourth group. Then the first group, from my own room, cracked and whipped their sticks at me with murderous brutality. It was ten thirty in the morning when the floggings began. They continued until eight o'clock that night.

'Open your mouth.'

'What?'

'Open your mouth!' the voice demanded. I couldn't open my eyes, because my eyelids were fused together with dried blood. The voice was insistent but gentle, and coming from behind me, on the other side of the bars. 'You must take your medicine, sir! You must take your medicine!'

I felt the neck of a glass bottle press against my mouth and teeth. Water flowed down my face. My arms were still stretched out beside me, and chained to the bars. My lips parted, and water flowed into my mouth. I swallowed quickly, gulping and spluttering. Hands held my head, and I felt two tablets enter my mouth, pushed by someone's fingers. The water bottle returned, and I drank, coughing water back through my nose.

'Your mandrax tablets, sir,' the guard said. 'You will be sleeping now.'

Floating on my back, arms outstretched, my body was bruised and cut so extensively that no part of it escaped the pain. There was no way to measure or judge it because it was all pain, everywhere. My eyes were sealed shut. My mouth tasted blood and water. I drifted to sleep on a lake of sticky, numbing stone. The chorus of voices I heard was my own choir of screams and the shouts of pain I'd kept inside, and didn't give them, and wouldn't give them.

They woke me, at dawn, by throwing a bucket of water on me. A thousand shrieking cuts woke with me. They permitted Mahesh to wash my eyes with a damp towel. When I could open them to see, they unlocked the handcuffs, lifted me by my stiff arms, and led me out of the room. We marched through empty courtyards and immaculately swept footpaths lined with geometrically perfect beds of flowers. At last we stopped before one of the senior prison officials. He was a man in his fifties. His grey hair and moustache were closely trimmed around his fine, almost feminine features. He was dressed in pyjamas and a silk brocade dressing gown. In the middle of a deserted courtyard, he was sitting in an elaborately carved, high-backed chair, something like a bishop's chair. Guards stood beside and behind him.

'This is not exactly how I like my Sundays to commence, my dear fellow,' he said, covering a yawn with a ringed hand. 'Just what the devil do you think you're playing at?'

His English was the precise and rounded version of the language that was taught in good Indian schools. I knew, from those few sentences and the way he'd spoken them, that his education was a post-colonial parallel to my own. My mother, poor and worked into exhaustion every day of her life, had earned the money to send me to a school exactly such as his. Under other circumstances we might've discussed Shakespeare or Schiller or Bulfinch's *Mythology*. I knew that about him from those two sentences. What did he know about me?

'Not talking, eh? What is it? Have my men been beating you? Have the overseers done anything to you?'

I stared at him in silence. In the old school of Australian prisons you don't *lag*—or inform on—anyone. Not even the screws. Not even convict overseers. You never tell on anyone, ever, for any reason.

'Come now, have the overseers been beating you?'

The silence that followed his question was suddenly disturbed by the morning song of mynah birds. The sun was fully above the horizon, and golden light streamed through the misty air, scattering the dew. I felt the morning breeze on every one of the thousand cuts that stretched and cracked dried blood each time that I moved. With my mouth firmly shut, I breathed in the morning air of the city that I loved with all my heart.

'Are you beating him?' he asked one of the overseers, in Marathi.

'Absolutely, sir!' the man responded, clearly surprised. 'You *told* us to beat him.'

'I didn't tell you to kill him, you idiot! Look at him! He looks like his skin is gone.'

The official examined his gold wristwatch for a moment, and then sighed his exasperation loudly.

'Very well. This is your punishment. You will wear chains on your legs. You must learn not to hit the overseers. You must learn that lesson. And from now on, until further notice, you will have half your ration of food. Now take him away!'

I held my silence, and they led me back to the room. I knew the drill. I'd learned the hard way that it's wise to keep silent when prison authorities abuse their power: everything you do enrages them, and everything you say makes it worse. Despotism despises nothing so much as righteousness in its victims.

The chain-fitter was a cheerful, middle-aged man in the ninth year of a seventeen-year sentence for a double murder. He'd killed his wife and his best friend as they lay sleeping together, and then he'd turned himself in at the local police station.

'It was peaceful,' he told me in English as he collapsed a steel band around my ankle with a set of crunching pliers. 'They went in their sleeping. Well, you can say that *he* went in his sleeping. When the axe came on *her*, she was awake, a little bit awake, but not for very long.'

With the ankle-chains fitted, he lifted the length of chain that would hobble my step. At its centre there was a wider link in the form of a ring. He gave me a long strip of coarse cloth, and showed me how to thread the strip through the ring, and fasten the cloth around my waist. In that way, the ring in the centre of the leg chain hung from the thread, at a little below the knees, and kept the leg chain from dragging on the ground.

'They told me, you know, in two more years only, I am overseer,' he informed me, sharing a wink and a broad smile as he packed up his tools. 'Don't you be worry. When that will happen, in two years, I am looking after you. You are my very good English friend, isn't it? No problem.'

The chain restricted my stride to tiny steps. Walking at any faster pace required a shuffling, hip-swinging gait. There were two other men in my room with leg-irons, and by studying their movements I gradually learned the technique. Within a few days, I walked that rolling, shambling dance as unselfconsciously as they did. In fact, by studying them and imitating them, I gradually discovered that there was something more than necessity in their shuffling dance. They were trying to give some grace to their movements, put something beautiful in the sliding, weaving steps, to soften the indignity of the chain. Even in that, I discovered, human beings will find an art.

But it *was* a terrible humiliation. The worst things that people do to us always make *us* feel ashamed. The worst things that people do always strike at the part of us that wants to love the world. And a tiny part of the shame we feel, when we're violated, is shame at being human.

I learned to walk with the chains, but half rations took their toll, and I lost weight steadily: as much as fifteen kilos in a month, by my guess. I was living on a palm-sized piece of chapatti bread and one saucer of watery soup every day. My body was thin, and seemed to be weakening by the hour. Men tried to help me with smuggled food. They were beaten for it, but still they tried. I refused their offers of help, after a while, because the guilt I felt whenever they received a beating on my behalf was killing me just as surely as the malnutrition.

The many hundreds of small and large cuts that I'd sustained on the day and the night of the beating caused me agonising pain. Most of them were infected, and some were swollen with yellow poison. I tried to wash them with the worm-infested water, but it didn't make them clean. The bites from the kadmal were accumulating every night. There were hundreds of bites, and many of them, too, became infected, weeping sores. Body lice swarmed on me. I followed the routine slaughter of the filthy, wriggling, crawling pests, every day, but they were drawn to the cuts and wounds on my body. I woke with them feeding on me and breeding in the warm, damp sores.

The beatings, however, had stopped after my meeting with the prison official on that Sunday morning. Big Rahul still whacked me occasionally, and some of the other overseers struck me from time to time, but they were habitual gestures, and not delivered with full force.

Then one day, as I lay on my side, conserving energy and watching the birds peck for crumbs in the courtyard next to our dormitory, I was attacked by a powerful man who jumped on me and seized my throat in both of his hands.

'Mukul! Mukul, my young brother!' he growled at me in Hindi.

'Mukul! The young brother you bit on his face! My brother!'

He might've been the man's twin. He was tall and heavyset. I recognised the face, and in the instant that I heard the words I remembered the man who'd tried to take my aluminium plate in the Colaba lock-up. I'd lost too much weight. I was too weakened by the hunger and the fever. The press of his body was crushing me, and his hands were closing my throat to air. He was killing me.

Lesson number four of street fighting: always keep something in reserve. The last of my energy exploded in a thrust, with one arm. I drove the arm downward, between our bodies, and grabbed his balls, squeezing and twisting with all the strength I had. His eyes and mouth opened in a gurgling scream, and he tried to roll off me to his left. I rolled with him. He pressed his legs together and drew his knees up, but my right hand wouldn't surrender the crushing grip. I plunged the fingers of my other hand into the soft skin above his collarbone. Closing my fingers and thumb around the collarbone, I used it as a handle, for leverage, and began to hit him in the face with my forehead. I hit him six times, ten times. I felt his teeth open a cut in my forehead, felt his nose break, felt his strength oozing from him with his blood, felt the collar bone wrench and tear away in the socket. I kept hitting him with the head butt. We were both bloody, and he was weakening, but he wouldn't lie still. I kept hitting him.

I might've beaten him to death with the blunt instrument of my head, but the overseers dragged me off him and back to the gate. The chains clamped around my wrists again, but they changed their tactics, and chained me to the gate face down on the stone floor. Rough hands tore my thin shirt from my back. The bamboo sticks rose and fell with new fury. The overseers had arranged for the man to attack me—it was a set-up, and they admitted it during one of the breaks while they rested their arms. They'd wanted the man to beat me senseless, maybe even kill me. He had the perfect motive, after all. They'd allowed him into the room, and they'd sanctioned his revenge attack. But it didn't work. I beat their man. And they were outraged that their plans had gone awry. So the beatings went on for hours, with breaks for cigarettes and chai and snacks, and private showings of my bloodied body for selected guests from other parts of the prison.

At the end of it, they released me from the gate. I listened, my ears filled with blood, as they argued about what to do with me. The beating that had followed the fight, the beating they'd just inflicted on me, was so savage and bloody that the overseers were worried. They'd gone too far, and they knew it. They couldn't report any part of it to the prison officials. They decided to keep the matter quiet, and they ordered one of their flunkies to wash my flayed and razored body with soap. Understandably, the man complained about the odious task. A flurry of blows encouraged him, and he applied himself to the job with some thoroughness. I owe my life to him and, in a strange way, to the man who'd tried to kill me. Without the attack, and their furious torture after it, the overseers wouldn't have allowed a soap and warm-water wash—it was the first and last I ever knew in the prison. And the soapy wash saved my life, I'm sure, because the many wounds and lesions on my body had become so badly infected that my temperature was constantly fevered, and the poison was killing me. I was too weak to move. The man who washed me—I never even knew his name—gave my cuts and wounds and abscessed sores such soothing solace, with the soapy water and soft wash cloth, that tears of relief streamed down my cheeks, mixing with my blood on the stone floor.

The fever fell to a simmering shiver, but I still starved, and I got thinner every day. And every day, at their end of the room, the overseers feasted themselves on three good meals. A dozen men worked as their flunkies. They washed clothes and blankets, scrubbed the floors, prepared the dining area, cleaned the mess after each meal and, whenever the whim possessed one of the overseers, gave foot, back, or neck massages. They were rewarded with fewer beatings than the rest of us, a few beedie cigarettes, and scraps of food from every meal. Sitting around a clean sheet on the stone floor, the overseers dipped into the many dishes that went into their meals: rice, dhals, chutneys, fresh roti, fish, meat stews, chicken, and sweet desserts. As they ate noisily, they threw scraps of chicken, bread, or fruit outwards to the surrounding flunkies sitting on their haunches in simian obsequiousness, and waiting with bulging eyes and salivating mouths.

The smell of that food was a monstrous torment. No food ever smelled so good to me, and as I slowly starved, the smell of their food came to represent the whole of the world I'd lost. Big Rahul took relentless delight in offering me food at every meal. He would hold out a drumstick of chicken, waving it in the air and feigning a dummy throw, enticing me with his eyes and raised eyebrows, and inviting me to become one of his dogs. Occasionally, he threw a drumstick or a sweet cake toward me, and warned the waiting flunkies to leave it for me, for the gora, urging me to crawl for it. When I didn't react, and wouldn't react, he gave the signal for the flunkies, and then laughed that weak, vicious laugh as the men scrambled and fought for it.

I couldn't bring myself to crawl across the floor and accept that food, although I was weaker by the day, by the hour. Eventually my temperature soared again until my eyes burned with the fever day and night. I visited the toilet, limping, or crawling on my knees when the fever crippled me, but the visits grew less frequent. My urine was a dark, orange colour. Malnutrition robbed my body of energy, and even the simplest movement—rolling over from one side to another, or sitting up—demanded so much of the precious, limited resource that I considered long and hard before undertaking it. I lay motionless for most of every day and night. I still tried to remove the body lice, and I still tried to wash. But those simple tasks left me wretched and panting. My heartbeat was unnaturally high, even while lying down, and my breath came in short puffs, often accompanied by soft, involuntary moans. I was dying of hunger, and I was learning that it's one of the cruellest ways to kill a man. I knew that Big Rahul's scraps would save me, but I couldn't crawl across that room to the edge of his feast. Still, I couldn't look away either, and every meal he gluttonised found its witness in my dying eyes.

I drifted, often, in fevered visions to my family, and the friends I'd known and had lost forever in Australia. I also thought of Khaderbhai, Abdullah, Qasim Ali, Johnny Cigar, Raju, Vikram, Lettie, Ulla, Kavita, and Didier. I thought of Prabaker, and I wished that I could tell him how much I loved his honest, optimistic, brave, and generous heart. And sooner or later, my thoughts always found their way to Karla, every day, every night, every hour that I counted out with my burning eyes.

And it seemed, to my dreaming mind, that Karla saved me. I was thinking of her when strong arms lifted me, and the chains fell from my wounded ankles, and guards marched me to the prison official's office. I was thinking of her.

The guards knocked. At an answering call, they opened the door. They waited outside when I entered. In the small office, I saw three men—the prison official with the short grey hair, a plain-clothes cop, and Vikram Patel—sitting around a metal desk.

'Oh, *fuck*!' Vikram shouted. 'Oh, man, you look ... you look fuckin' *terrible*! Oh, fuck! Oh, *fuck*! What have you *done* to this guy?'

The official and the cop exchanged neutral glances, but didn't reply.

'Sit down,' the prison official commanded. I remained standing, on weakening legs. 'Sit down, *please*.'

I sat, and stared at Vikram with tongue-locked amazement. The flat, black hat hanging on his back by the cord at his throat, and his black vest, shirt, and scrolled flamenco pants seemed wildly exotic, and yet the most reassuringly familiar costume I could imagine. My eyes began to lose focus in the elaborate whirls and scrolls on his embroidered vest, and I pulled my stare back to his face. That face wrinkled and winced as he stared at me. I hadn't looked into a mirror for four months. Vikram's grimaces gave me a fairly good idea of how near to death he believed me to be. He held out the black shirt with the lasso figures that he'd taken off his back to give to me in the rain four months before.

'I brought ... I brought your shirt ...' he said falteringly.

'What ... what are you doing here?'

'A friend sent me,' he replied. 'A very good friend of yours. Oh, fuck, Lin. You look like dogs have been chewing on you. I don't want to freak you out or nothing, but you look like they dug you up, after they fuckin' killed you, man. Just stay cool. I'm here, man. I'm gonna get you the fuck outta this place.'

Taking that as his cue, the official coughed, and gestured toward the cop. The cop gave the lead back to him, and he addressed Vikram, a kind of smile pinching the soft skin around his eyes.

'Ten thousand,' he said. 'In American dollars, of course.'

'Ten fuckin' *thousand*?' Vikram exploded. 'Are you *crazy*? I can buy *fifty* guys out of this place with ten thousand. Fuck *that*, man.'

'Ten thousand,' the official repeated, with the calm and authority of a man who knows that he brought the only gun to a knife-fight. He rested his hands flat on the metal desk, and his fingers rolled through once in a little Mexican wave.

'No fuckin' way, man. *Arrey*, take a *look* at the guy. What are you *giving* me, *yaar*? You fuckin' destroyed the guy. You think he's *worth* ten thousand, in this condition?'

436

The cop took a folder from a slender vinyl briefcase, and slid it across the desk to Vikram. The folder contained a single sheet of paper. Reading it quickly, Vikram's lips pressed outward, and his eyes widened in an expression of impressed surprise.

'Is this you?' he asked me. 'Did you escape from jail in Australia?'

I stared at him evenly, my feverish eyes not wavering. I didn't reply.

'How many people know about this?' he asked the plain-clothes cop.

'Not so many,' the cop replied in English. 'But, enough to need ten thousand, for keeping this information a private matter.'

'Oh, shit,' Vikram sighed. 'There goes my bargaining. Fuck it. I'll have the money in half an hour. Clean him up, and get him ready.'

'There's something else,' I interrupted, and they all turned to look at me. 'There are two men. In my dormitory. They tried to help me, and the overseers or the guards gave them six months more. But they finished their time. I want them to walk out the gate with me.'

The cop gave an inquiring look at the prison official. He responded by waving his hand dismissively and wagging his head in agreement. The matter was a mere trifle. The men would be freed.

'And there's another guy,' I said flatly. 'His name's Mahesh Malhotra. He can't raise his bail. It's not much, a couple of thousand rupees. I want you to let Vikram pay his bail. I want him to walk out with me.'

The two men raised their palms, and exchanged identical expressions of bewilderment. The fate of such a poor and insignificant man never intruded upon their material ambitions or their spiritual disenchantments. They turned to Vikram. The prison official thrust out his jaw as if to say, *He's insane, but if that's what he wants …*

Vikram stood to leave, but I raised my hand, and he sat down again quickly.

'And there's another one,' I said.

The cop laughed out loud.

'*Aur ek?*' he spluttered, through the laugh. *One more?*

'He's an African. He's in the African compound. His name's Raheem. They broke both his arms. I don't know if he's alive or dead. If he's alive, I want him, too.'

The cop turned to the prison official, hunching his shoulders and raising the palm of his hand in a question.

'I know the case,' the prison official said, wagging his head. 'It is … a police case. The fellow carried on a shameless affair with the wife of a police inspector. The inspector quite rightly arranged to have him put in here. And once he was here, the brute made an assault on one of my overseers. It is quite impossible.'

There was a little silence, then, as the word *impossible* swirled in the room like smoke from a cheap cigar.

'Four thousand,' the cop said.

'Rupees?' Vikram asked.

'Dollars,' the cop laughed. 'American dollars. Four thousand extra. Two for us and our associates, and two for the inspector who's married to the slut.'

'Are there any more, Lin?' Vikram muttered, earnestly. 'I'm just asking, like, because we're workin' our way up to a group discount here, you know.'

I stared back at him. The fever was stinging my eyes, and the effort it took to sit upright in the chair was causing me to sweat and shiver. He reached out, leaning over so that his hands were resting on my bare knees. I had the thought that some of the body lice might creep from my legs onto his hands, but I couldn't brush that reassuring touch aside.

'It's gonna be cool, man. Don't worry. I'll be back soon. We'll get you the fuck outta here within the hour. I promise. I'll be back with two taxis, for us and your guys.'

'Bring three taxis,' I answered, my voice sounding as though it came from a new, dark, deep place that was opening up as I began to accept that I might be free.

'One taxi for you, and the other two for me and the guys,' I said. 'Because ... body lice.'

'Okay,' he flinched. 'Three taxis. You got it.'

Half an hour later, I rode with Raheem in the back of a black-and-yellow Fiat taxi through the tectonic spectacle and pedestrian pageant of the city. Raheem had obviously received some treatment—his arms were encased in plaster casts—but he was thin and sick, and horror clogged his eyes. I felt nauseous just looking into those eyes. He never said a word, except to tell us where he wanted to go. He was crying, softly and silently, when we dropped him off at a restaurant that Hassaan Obikwa owned in Dongri.

As we drove on, the driver kept staring at my gaunt, starved, beaten face in his rear-vision mirror. Finally, I asked him in rough, colloquial Hindi if he had any Indian movie songs in his cab. Stunned, he replied that he did. I nominated one of my favourites, and he found it, cranking it up to the max as we buzzed and beeped our way through the traffic. It was a song that the prisoners in the long room had passed from group to group. They sang it almost every night. I sang it as the taxi took me back into the smell and colour and sound of my city. The driver joined in, looking often into the mirror. None of us lie or guard our secrets when we sing, and India is a nation of singers whose first love is the kind of song we turn to when crying just isn't enough.

The song was still soaring in me as I shed my clothes into a plastic bag for disposal, and stood under the strong warm jet of water in Vikram's shower. I tipped a whole bottle of Dettol disinfectant over my head, and scrubbed it into my skin with a hard nailbrush. A thousand cuts and bites and gashes cried out, but my thoughts were of Karla. Vikram told me she'd left the city two days before. No-one seemed to know where she'd gone. *How will I find her? Where is she? Does she hate me now? Does she think I dumped her, after we made love? Could she think that about me? I have to stay in Bombay—she'll come back here, to the city. I have to stay and wait for her.*

I spent two hours in that bathroom, thinking, scrubbing, and clenching my teeth against the pain. My wounds were raw when I emerged to wrap a towel round my waist and stand in Vikram's bedroom.

'Oh, man,' he groaned, shaking his head and cringing in sympathy.

I looked into the full-length mirror on the front of his wardrobe. I'd used his bathroom scales to check my weight: I was forty-five kilos—half the ninety kilos I'd been when I was arrested four months before. My body was so thin that it resembled those of men who'd survived concentration camps. The bones of my skeleton were all visible, even to the skull beneath my face. Cuts and sores covered my body, and beneath them was the tortoise-shell pattern of deep bruises, everywhere.

'Khader heard about you from two of the guys who got out of your dormitory—some Afghan guys. They said they saw you with Khader, one night, when you went to see some blind singers, and they remembered you from there.'

I tried to picture the men, to remember them, but I couldn't. *Afghans,* Vikram had said. They must've been very good at keeping secrets because they'd never spoken to me in all those months in the locked room.

Whoever they were, I owed them.

'When they got out, they told Khader about you, and Khader sent for me.'

'Why you?'

'He didn't want anyone to know that *he* was the one getting you out. The price was steep enough, *yaar*. If they knew it was *him* paying the baksheesh, the price would've been a lot higher.'

'But how do you know him?' I asked, still staring with fascinated horror at my own torture and emaciation.

'Who?'

'Khaderbhai. How do you know him?'

'Everybody in Colaba knows him, man.'

'Sure, but how do *you* know him?'

'I did a job for him once.'

'What sort of a job?'

'It's kind of a long story.'

'I've got time, if you have.'

Vikram smiled and shook his head. He stood, and crossed the bedroom to pour two drinks at a small table that served as his private bar.

'One of Khaderbhai's goondas beat up a rich kid at a nightclub,' he began, handing me a drink. 'He did him over pretty bad. From what I hear, the kid had it coming. But his family pressed charges, with the cops. Khaderbhai knew my dad, and from him he found out that I knew the kid —we went to the same damn college, *yaar*. He got in touch with me, and asked me to find out how much they wanted to drop the case. Turns out they wanted plenty. But Khader paid it, and a little more. He could've got heavy with them, you know, and scared the shit out of them. He could've fuckin' *killed* them, *yaar*. The whole fuckin' family. But he didn't. His guy was in the wrong, *na*? So, he wanted to do the right thing. He paid the money, and everyone ended up happy. He's okay, that Khaderbhai. A real serious type, if you know what I mean, but he's okay. My dad respects him, and he likes him, and that's saying quite a lot, because my pop, he doesn't respect many members of the human race. You know, Khader told me he wants you to work for him.'

'Doing what?'

'Don't ask me,' he shrugged. He began to toss some clean, pressed clothes from his wardrobe onto the bed. One by one I accepted the shorts, trousers, shirt, and sandals, and began to dress. 'He just told me to bring you to see him when you feel well enough. I'd think about it if I was you, Lin. You need to feed yourself up. You need to make some fast bucks. And you need a friend like him, *yaar*. All that stuff about Australia —it's a fuckin' wild story, man. I swear, being on the run and all, it's *damn* heroic. At least with Khader on your side, you'll be safe here. With him behind you, nobody will ever do this shit to you again. You got a powerful friend there, Lin. Nobody fucks with Khader Khan in Bombay.'

'So why don't *you* work for him?' I asked, and I knew that the tone of my voice was harsh—harsher than I'd intended it to be—but everything I said sounded like that then, with memories of the beatings and the body lice still slicing and itching across my skin.

'I never got invited,' Vikram replied evenly. 'But even if I *did* get invited to join him, I don't think I'd take him up on it, *yaar*.'

'Why not?'

'I don't need him the way you do, Lin. All those mafia guys, they need each other, you know what I mean? They need Khaderbhai as much as he needs them. And I don't need him like that. But you do.'

'You sound very sure,' I said, turning to meet his eye.

'I *am* sure. Khaderbhai, he told me that he found out why you got picked up and put in jail. He said that someone powerful, someone with a lot of influence, had you put away, man.'

'Who was it?'

'He didn't say. He told me he doesn't know. Maybe he just didn't want to tell *me*. Whatever the case, Lin my brother, you're paddling in some fuckin' deep shit. The bad guys don't fuck around in Bombay—you know that much by now—and if you've got an enemy here, you're going to need all the protection you can get. You got two choices—get the fuck out of town, or get some firepower on your side, like the guys at the OK Corral, you know?'

'What would you do?'

He laughed, but my expression didn't change, and he let the laughter quickly fade. He lit two cigarettes and passed one to me.

'Me? I'd be fuckin' angry, *yaar*. I don't wear this cowboy stuff because I like cows—I wear it because I like the way those cowboy fuckers handled things in those days. Me, I'd want to find out who tried to fuck me over, and I'd want to get some damn revenge on him. Me, when I was ready, I'd accept Khader's offer, and go to work for him, and get my revenge. But hey, that's me, and I'm an Indian madachudh, *yaar*. And that's what an Indian madachudh would do.'

I looked in the mirror once more. The new clothes felt like salt on the raw wounds, but they covered the worst of it, and I looked less alarming, less confronting, less hideous. I smiled at the mirror. I was practising, trying to remember what it was like to be me. It almost worked. I almost had it. Then a new expression, not quite my own, swirled into the grey of my eyes. *Never again.* That pain wouldn't happen to me again. That hunger wouldn't threaten me. That fear wouldn't pierce my exiled heart. *Whatever it takes*, my eyes said to me. *Whatever it takes from now on.*

'I'm ready to see him,' I said. 'I'm ready right now.'

CHAPTER TWENTY-TWO

Working for Abdel Khader Khan was my first real instruction in organised crime—until then I'd been no more than a desperate man, doing stupid, cowardly things to feed a stupid, cowardly heroin habit, and then a desperate exile earning small commissions on random deals. Although they *were* crimes that I'd committed, and some of them were very serious, I was never really a criminal until I accepted Khaderbhai as my teacher. I'd been a man who committed crimes, up to then, rather than a criminal, and there's a difference between the two. The difference, as with most things in life, lay in the motive and the means. Being tortured in Arthur Road Prison had given me the motive to cross the line. Another man, a smarter man than I was, might've run away from Bombay as soon as he was freed from the prison. I didn't. I couldn't. I wanted to know who'd put me in there, and why. I wanted revenge. The safest and fastest way to that vengeance was to join Khaderbhai's branch of the mafia.

His instruction in the lawbreaker's arts—he sent me first to the Palestinian, Khaled Ansari, to learn the black-market money trade—gave me the means to become what I'd never tried or wanted to be: a professional criminal. And it felt good. It felt so good within the protective circle of that band of brothers. When I rode the train to Khaled's apartment every day, hanging out the door of a rattling carriage in the hot, dry wind with other young men, my heart swelled with the excitement of freedom's wild, reckless ride.

Khaled, my first teacher, was the kind of man who carried his past in the temple fires of his eyes, and fed the flames with pieces of his broken heart. I've known men like Khaled in prisons, on battlefields, and in the dens where smugglers, mercenaries, and other exiles meet. They all have certain characteristics in common. They're tough, because there's a kind of toughness that's found in the worst sorrow. They're honest, because the truth of what happened to them won't let them lie. They're angry, because they can't forget the past or forgive it. And they're lonely. Most of us pretend, with greater or lesser success, that the minute we live in is something we can share. But the past for every one of us is a desert island; and those like Khaled, who find themselves marooned there, are always alone.

Khaderbhai had told me some of Khaled's history when he'd briefed me for my first lessons. I'd learned that Khaled, at only thirty-four, was alone in the world. His parents, both renowned scholars, had been prominent in the Palestinian struggle for an independent nation-state. His father had died in prison, in Israel. His mother, his two sisters, his aunts and uncles, and his mother's parents had all been killed in the massacres at Shatila, in Lebanon. Khaled, who'd trained with Palestinian guerrilla units in Tunisia, Libya, and Syria, and had fought for nine years in dozens of operations across a score of conflict zones, broke down after the bloody deaths of his mother and all the others at the refugee camp. His Fattah Group commander, knowing the signs of that breakdown and the risks it posed, had released him from duty.

Although still devoted to the cause of Palestinian statehood in his words, he was in fact lost to any cause but the suffering he'd endured and the suffering he lived to inflict. He'd drifted to Bombay on the recommendation of a senior guerrilla fighter who knew Khaderbhai. The mafia don took him in. Impressed with his education, language skills, and obsessive dedication, the permanent members of Khaderbhai's council had rewarded the young Palestinian with successive promotions. Three years after Shatila, at the time that I met him, Khaled Ansari was in charge of Khaderbhai's black-market currency operation. The position carried with it a place on the council. And when I felt strong enough to put in a full day of study, not long after my release from Arthur Road Prison, the bitter, lonely, battle-scarred Palestinian began my instruction.

'People say that money is the root of all evil,' Khaled told me when we met in his apartment. His English was rich with accents of New York and Arabic and the Hindi that he spoke reasonably well. 'But it's not true. It's the other way round. Money isn't the root of all evil. *Evil* is the root of all *money*. There's no such thing as clean money. All the money in the world is dirty, in some way, because there's no clean way to make it. If you get paid in money, somebody, somewhere, is suffering for it. That's one of the reasons, I think, why just about everybody—even people who'd never break the law in any other way—is happy to add an extra buck or two to their money on the black market.'

'You make your living from it,' I said, curious to know how he would respond.

'So?'

'So, how do *you* feel about it?'

'I don't feel anything about it, one way or the other. Suffering is the truth. Not suffering is the lie. I told you that, once before. That's just the way the world is.'

'But surely some money has more suffering attached to it,' I persisted, 'and some money has less.'

'Money only comes in two kinds, Lin—*yours*, and *mine*.'

'Or, in this case, *Khader's* money.'

Khaled laughed. It was a short, sad laugh, and the only one that was left in him.

'We make money for Abdel Khader, true, but a part of everything we make is ours. And it's the little part of everything that belongs to *us* that keeps us in the game, *na*? Okay, let's get started. *Why* do black markets for money exist?'

'I'm not sure what you mean.'

'I'll ask it in a different way,' Khaled smiled. The thick scar that started at his throat, below the left ear, and cut a groove in his face all the way to the corner of his mouth, gave the smile a lopsided and unsettling twist. The scarred half of his face didn't smile at all, which meant that the other half seemed menacing, or pained, when he was trying hardest to be kind. 'How is it that we can buy one American dollar from a tourist for, say, eighteen rupees, when the banks are only offering fifteen or sixteen?'

'Because we can sell them for *more* than eighteen?' I offered.

'Good. Good. Now, how can we do that?'

'Because ... someone wants to buy them at that price, I guess.'

'Exactly. But who are we selling them to?'

'Look, the most I ever did was put tourists together with black-market guys, and take my cut. I don't really know what happens to the dollars after that. I never went that far into it.'

'Black markets for things exist,' he said slowly, as if confiding a personal secret rather than a commercial fact, 'because the white markets are too strict. In this case, in the case of currencies, the government and the Reserve Bank of India control the white markets, and they're too strict. It's all about greed, and control. These are the two elements that make for commercial crime. Any one of them, on its own, is not enough. Greed without control, or control without greed won't give you a black market. Men can be greedy for the profit made from, let's say, *pastries*, but if there isn't strict control on the baking of pastries, there won't be a black market for apple strudel. And the government has very strict controls on the disposal of sewage, but without greed for profit from sewage, there won't be a black market for shit. When greed meets control, you get a black market.'

'You've put a lot of thought into this,' I commented, laughing, but impressed and genuinely glad that he wanted to give me the ontology of currency crime, and not just the ways I could go about committing it.

'Not really,' he answered self-deprecatingly.

'No, I'm serious. When Khaderbhai sent me here, I thought you were going to give me a few tables of figures—you know, today's currency exchange rates and all that—and then send me on my way.'

'Oh, we'll get to the rates and stuff soon enough,' he smiled again, sounding very American in the light-hearted aside. I knew he'd studied in New York when he was much younger. Khaderbhai had told me that he'd been happy there, for a time. A little of that happiness seemed to have survived in the long, rounded vowels and other Americanisms of his speech. 'But first you need the theory, before you can make a profit from the practice.'

The Indian rupee, Khaled explained, was a restricted currency. It couldn't be taken out of India, and it couldn't legally be changed for dollars anywhere in the world but in India. With its vast population, India sent many thousands of businessmen, businesswomen, and travellers out of the country every day. Those people were permitted to take out only a limited amount of American currency with them. They could change a fixed amount of their rupees into American dollars, and the rest had to be converted in the form of travellers' cheques.

The regulation was enforced in various ways. When someone wanted to leave the country and change rupees into dollars to the legal limit, he or she had to present a passport and plane ticket at the bank. The bank teller confirmed the departure date on the ticket, and marked both the ticket and the passport to indicate that the holder had been granted the full limit of American dollars in exchange for rupees. The transaction couldn't be duplicated. There was no legal way for the traveller to buy more American dollars for that journey.

Almost everyone in India had at least *some* black money under the bed. From the few hundred rupees that a working man earned and didn't report to the Tax Office, all the way to the billions of rupees accumulated as profits from crime, the black economy was said to be almost half as large as the legal, white economy. Anyone who had thousands, or hundreds of thousands, of undeclared rupees—as many Indian business travellers did—couldn't buy legal travellers' cheques with them: the bank or the Tax Office always wanted to know where the money came from. So the only real alternative was to buy dollars from the black-market currency dealers. And every day, in Bombay, millions of rupees worth of black American dollars, English pounds, Deutschmarks, Swiss francs, and other currencies were bought and sold in a trade that was a dark mirror of the legal money exchanges.

'I buy a thousand American dollars, from a tourist, for *eighteen* thousand rupees, when the bank exchange rate is set at *fifteen*,' Khaled summarised. 'He's happy, because he's three thousand rupees better off than he would've been at the bank. Then I sell the dollars, to an Indian businessman, for *twenty-one* thousand rupees. He's happy, because he bought the dollars with black money that he couldn't declare. Then I put three thousand rupees in the kitty, and I buy another thousand dollars, from another tourist, for eighteen thousand. That's the simple equation at the heart of the currency racket.'

To find the tourists, and entice them to change their money, Khaderbhai's mafia council employed a small army of touts, guides, beggars, hotel managers, bellboys, restaurateurs, waiters, shopkeepers, airline officials, travel agents, nightclub owners, prostitutes, and cab drivers. Keeping tabs on them was one of Khaled's jobs. In the mornings he phoned all the businesses to establish exchange rates for all the important currencies. There were update calls every two hours throughout the day, advising of any fluctuations in the rates. A taxi was at his disposal around the clock, with two drivers operating in shifts. Every morning he visited the bagmen for each area, and handed over bundles of rupees for the street traders to use as their float. Touts and other street-level crooks dealt with the street traders, guiding tourists and businessmen to them. The traders changed money, and kept the foreign currencies in bundles to be collected. Bagmen did the rounds of traders throughout the day, supplying them with cash as they needed it. Collectors made several sweeps during each working day and night to pick up bundles of foreign currency.

Khaled supervised personal collections and exchanges at hotels, airline offices, travel agencies, and other businesses that required a greater degree of discretion. He made two major pick-ups from his collectors in the key areas; one at noon, and one in the late evening. Relevant cops in every area were paid to look away from anything that might offend their sensibilities. In return, Khaderbhai promised that any violence he deemed necessary, in the event that someone tried to rob his men or hold out on them, would be swift and sure, and would never involve the police or threaten their interests in any way. The responsibility for maintaining discipline and enforcing Khader's control fell to Abdullah Taheri. His team of Indian goondas and Iranian veterans of the war with Iraq ensured that irregularities were rare, and ruthlessly punished.

'You'll work with me, on the collections,' Khaled announced. 'You'll learn it all, in time, but I really want you to concentrate on the tricky ones—the five-star hotels, and the airline offices. The shirt and tie jobs. I'll go with you, especially at the start, but I think it'll be good if a gora, a well-dressed, white foreigner, does the hand-overs in those places. You'll be invisible. They won't look at you twice. And our contacts will be a lot less edgy, dealing with you. After that, I want you to get into the travel business. I can use a gora there, too.'

'The travel business?'

'Oh, you're gonna love it,' he said, meeting my eyes with that same sad smile. 'It'll make that stint you did in Arthur Road seem worth it, because it's first class all the way.'

The travel racket, he explained, was an especially lucrative part of the currency trade. It involved large numbers of people from the millions of Indians who worked in Saudi Arabia, Dubai, Abu Dhabi, Muscat, Bahrain, Kuwait, and elsewhere throughout the Arab Gulf. The Indian workers, employed on contracts for three, six, or twelve months as domestics, cleaners, and labourers, were usually paid in foreign currency.

Most of the workers tried to exchange their wages on the black market as soon as they got back to India, in order to gain a few extra rupees. Khader's mafia council offered the employers and the workers a short-cut. When they sold their foreign currencies in bulk to Khaderbhai, the Arab employers received a slightly more favourable rate, allowing them to pay their workers in rupees, at the black-market rate, in India. That left them with a surplus of rupees, and gave them a net profit from *paying* their workers.

For many Gulf State employers, the temptation to such currency crime was irresistible. They, too, had caches of undeclared, untaxed money under their opulent beds. Syndicates developed to organise the payment of Indian guest workers in rupees when they returned to India. The workers were happy because they got the black-market rate but didn't have to negotiate with hard-nosed black-market dealers personally. The bosses were happy because they made profits from the payment through their syndicates. The black marketeers were happy because a steady stream of dollars, Deutschmarks, riyals, and dirhams flowed into the river of demand created by Indian business travellers. Only the government missed out, and no-one in the thousands upon thousands of people involved in the trade shamed himself beyond endurance on that account.

'I ... this whole business was once something of a specialty with me ...,' Khaled said, when that long first lesson finally ended. His voice trailed off, and I couldn't be certain whether he was reminiscing or simply reluctant to talk further. I waited.

'When I was studying, in New York,' he went on at last, 'I was working on a thesis ... well, I *wrote* a thesis, on *un*-organised trade in the ancient world. It's an area that my mother was researching, before the '67 war. When I was a kid, she got me interested in the black markets of Assyria, Akkad, and Sumer, and how they related to trade routes, and taxes, and the empires that built up around them. When I started to write it myself, I called it *Black Babylon*.'

'It's a catchy title.'

He fired a glance at me to reassure himself that I wasn't mocking him.

'I mean it,' I said quickly, wanting to put him at ease because I was beginning to like him. 'I think it's a good topic for a thesis, and it's a very catchy title. I think you should go ahead and finish it.'

He smiled again.

'Well, Lin, life has a lot of surprises, and, as my uncle in New York used to say, most of them ain't happy ones for a working stiff. Now I'm working *for* a black market, instead of working *on* one. Now, it's *Black Bombay*.'

The bitterness in his voice was disconcerting. His jaw began to set in a grim and almost angry expression as he stared at his joined hands. I moved to steer the conversation away from the past.

'You know, I've been involved with a part of the black market that might interest you. Have you heard of the lepers' medicine market?'

'Sure,' he replied, interest glittering in his dark brown eyes. He ran a hand over his face and up across the short, military haircut, prematurely streaked with grey and white. The gesture wiped his gloomy recollections away, and he gave me his full attention. 'I heard that you met Ranjit —he's incredible, isn't he?'

We talked about Ranjitbhai, the king of his little group of lepers, and the black market they'd organised across the country. Their mysterious trade fascinated us equally. As a historian—or a man who'd once dreamed of becoming a historian, like his scholarly mother—Khaled was intrigued by the long evolution and secret conduct of the lepers' organisation. As a writer, I was provoked by the story of their suffering and their unique response to it. After twenty minutes of excited, actuating discussion, we agreed to visit Ranjit together to find out more about the history of the black market in medicines.

And with that pledge between exiles, between scholar and writer, Khaled and I established a simple but enduring bond of intellectual respect. We became friends in the rapid, unquestioning way of criminals, soldiers, and other survivors of disaster. I visited him every day in his sparsely furnished, Spartan apartment near Andheri station. The sessions lasted five or six hours. They roved freely from ancient history to reserve bank interest-rate policies, from anthropology to fixed and floating currencies, and I learned more about that very common but complex crime in one month, with Khaled Ansari, than most street traders in dollars and Deutschmarks learned in a year of dealing.

And when the lessons were complete, I went to work with Khaled every morning and every evening, seven days a week. The pay was good. The wages I earned came in such quantities that I was often paid in thick blocks of rupees, direct from the bank and still bearing their steel staples all the way through the notes. Compared to the slum-dwellers I'd known as neighbours, friends, and patients for almost two years, I was already a rich man.

To ensure that the cuts and wounds of prison healed as quickly as possible, I'd taken a room at the India Guest House, at Khaderbhai's expense. The clean, tiled shower and soft mattress did help me to heal, but there was more to the move than physical convalescence. The truth was that the months in Arthur Road Prison had damaged my spirit more than my body. And the lingering shame I felt over the deaths of my neighbour Radha in the cholera epidemic, and the two boys from my English class, gave me no peace. The prison torment, and my failures in the cholera epidemic: I might've survived either one of them on its own, and gone back to those loving, wretched acres when I was well enough. But both of them, together, were more than my frail self-respect could endure, and I couldn't live in the slum or even sleep the night there.

I visited Prabaker, Johnny, Qasim, and Jeetendra often, and I continued to help out at the clinic, attending to patients for two afternoons every week. But the strange mix of arrogance and insouciance that had permitted me to be the slum doctor was gone, and I didn't expect it to return. There's a little arrogance at the heart of every better self. That arrogance left me when I failed to save my neighbour's life—failed even to know that she was ill. And there's an innocence, essential and unblinking, in the heart of every determination to serve. That innocence faltered when I stumbled from the Indian prison: my smile, no less than my footsteps, hobbled by the memory of the leg-irons. Moving out of the slum had as much or more to do with the state of my soul as it did with the wounds on my body.

For their part, my friends from the slum accepted my decision without question or comment. They greeted me warmly whenever I visited, and involved me in the daily routines and celebrations of the slum—weddings, festivals, community meetings, or cricket games—as if I still lived and worked with them. And despite their shock and sorrow when they saw my emaciated frame, and the scars that the overseers had branded on my skin, they never once mentioned the prison. A part of that, I think, was sensitivity to the shame they knew I must've been feeling; the shame that they would've felt had they been imprisoned. Another part, in the hearts of Prabaker, and Johnny Cigar, and perhaps even Qasim Ali, might've been found in guilt—that they hadn't been able to help me because they hadn't thought to search for me. None of them had realised that I'd been arrested. They'd assumed that I'd simply tired of life in the slum, and that I'd returned to my comfortable life in my comfortable country, like every other tourist or traveller they'd ever known.

And that, too, found its way into my reluctance to return to the slum. It astonished me, and it hurt me, after all I'd done there, and for all that they'd included me in the ragged skein of their too-many lives, that they still expected me to leave them, without a word of farewell, whenever the whim possessed me.

So, when my health improved and I began to earn real money, I didn't move back to the slum. Instead, with Khaderbhai's help, I rented an apartment in Colaba at the landward end of Best Street, not far from Leopold's. It was my first apartment in India, and my first indulgence of space and privacy and domestic luxuries such as a hot shower and a functioning kitchen. I ate well, cooking high-protein and high-carbohydrate meals, and forcing myself to finish off a bucket of ice cream every day. I put on body weight. I slept for ten hours at a stretch, night after night, healing my lacerated body with sleep's ravelling repair. But I woke often, with my arms flailing, fighting, and the wet-metal smell of blood still fresh from the nightmare.

I trained in karate and weightlifting with Abdullah at his favourite gym in the fashionable suburb of Breach Candy. Two other young gangsters—Salman Mustaan and his friend Sanjay, whom I'd met at my first visit to Khader's council—often joined us. They were strong, healthy men in their late-twenties who liked to fight about as much as they liked sex, and they liked sex just fine. Sanjay, with his movie-star looks, was the joker. Salman was quieter and more serious. Although inseparable friends since childhood, they were as hard on one another in the ring as they were when they boxed Abdullah and me. We worked out five times each week, with two days off to allow our torn and swollen muscles to recover. And it was good. It helped. Pumping iron is Zen for violent men. Little by little, my body regained its strength, muscular shape, and fitness.

But no matter how fit I became, I knew that my mind wouldn't heal, couldn't heal, until I found out who'd arranged with the police to have me picked up and sent to Arthur Road Prison. I needed to know who did it. I needed to know the reason. Ulla was gone from the city—in hiding, some said, but no-one could guess from whom, or why. Karla was gone, and no-one could tell me where she was. Didier and several other friends were digging around for me, trying to find the truth, but they hadn't found anything that might tell me who'd set me up.

Someone had arranged with senior cops to have me arrested, without charge, and imprisoned at Arthur Road. The same person had arranged to have me beaten—severely and often—while I was in the prison. It was a punishment or an act of revenge. Khaderbhai had confirmed that much, but he couldn't or wouldn't say more, except to tell me that who-ever it was who'd set me up hadn't known that I was on the run. That information, about the escape from Australia, had emerged from the routine fingerprint check. The cops concerned had realised, at once, that there might be profit in keeping quiet about it, and they'd shelved my file until Vikram approached them on Khader's behalf.

'Those fuckin' cops *liked* you, man,' Vikram told me as we sat together in Leopold's one afternoon, a few months after I'd started work with Khaled as a currency collector.

'U-huh.'

'No, really, they did. That's why they let you go.'

'I never saw that cop before in my life, Vikram. He didn't know me at all.'

'You don't get it,' he replied patiently. He poured another glass of cold Kingfisher beer, and sipped it appreciatively. 'I talked to that guy, the cop, when I got you out of there. He told me the whole story. See, when the first guy in the fingerprint section found out who the fuck you really were—when your fingerprint check came back with the news that you were this wanted guy, from Australia—he freaked out on it. He freaked out on how much *money* he might get, you know, to keep the shit quiet. A chance like that doesn't come along every day, *na*? So, without saying any-thing to anyone else, he goes to a senior cop he knows, and shows him the file report on your prints. That cop freaks out, too. He goes to another cop—the one *we* saw at the jail—and shows him the file. That cop tells the others to keep quiet about it, and leave it to him to find out how much money there is in it.'

A waiter brought my cup of coffee, and chatted with me for a while in Marathi. Vikram waited until we were alone again before he spoke.

'They love it, you know, all these waiters and cab drivers and post office guys—and the cops, too—they love it, all these guys, that you speak

Marathi to them. Fuck, man, I'm *born* here, and you speak Marathi better than I do. I never learned to speak it properly. I never had to. That's why so many Marathis are so pissed off, man. Most of us don't give a shit about the Marathi language, or who all comes to live in Bombay, or wherever the fuck they come from, *yaar*. Anyway, where was I? Oh yeah, so the cop has this file on you, and he's keeping it quiet. But he wants to know more about this Australian fucker, who escaped from jail, before he does anything, *yaar*.'

Vikram stopped, and grinned at me until the grin became a playful laugh. He wore a black leather vest over his white silk shirt, despite the thirty-five-degree heat. In his heavy, black jeans and ornate black cowboy boots, he must've been very hot, but he seemed cool; almost as cool as he looked.

'It's fuckin' *great*, man!' he laughed. 'You busted out of a maximum-security jail! Fuckin' *deadly*! It's the greatest thing I ever heard, Lin. It's tearing my heart out that I can't tell anyone about it.'

'Do you remember what Karla said about secrets, when we were sitting here one night?'

'No, man. What was it?'

'It isn't a secret, unless keeping it hurts.'

'That's pretty fuckin' good,' Vikram mused, grinning 'So where was I? I'm losing it today, man. It's this *Lettie* thing. It's driving me insane, Lin. Oh yeah, the cop in charge, the cop with your file, he wants to do some checking on you. So, he sends two of his guys around, asking questions about you. All the street guys you used to work with, they gave you solid support, man. They said you never cheated anyone, never fucked anybody over, and you put a lot of money around with the poor street guys when you had it.'

'But the cops didn't tell anyone I was in Arthur Road?'

'No, man, they were checking up on you to find out if they wanted to fuck you over, and send you back to the Australian cops, or not— depending on how you checked out. And there's more to it. One of the moneychangers tells the cops, *Hey, if you wanna know about Lin, go ask in the zhopadpatti, because he lives there.* Well, the cops are now real intrigued, like—a gora, living in the slum. So they go there, and they take a look. They don't tell anybody in the slum what happened to you, but they start asking about you, and the people say stuff like, *You see that clinic? Lin built* it, and he's been working there for a long time, helping the people ... And they say stuff like, *Everybody here has been treated at Lin's clinic, free of charge, at one time or another, and he did a great job when the cholera came ...* And they told the cops about that little school you started, *You see that little school for English? Lin started it ...* And the cops get an earful of this *Lin,* this Linbaba, this foreign guy who does all this good shit, and they go back to their boss, telling him what they heard.'

'Oh, come on, Vikram! You *really* think that made a difference? It was about money, that's all, and I'm just glad you were there to pay it.'

Vikram's eyes widened in surprise, and then narrowed into a disapproving frown. He lifted the hat from his back and examined it, turning it in his hands and flicking specks of dust from the rim.

'You know, Lin, you've been here for a while now, and you've learned some language, and been to the village, and lived in the slum, and even been the fuck to jail and all, but you still don't get it, do you?'

'Maybe not,' I conceded. 'Probably not.'

'Damn right you don't, man. This is not England, or New Zealand, or Australia, or wherever the fuck else. This is India, man. This is *India.* This is the land of the heart. This is where the heart is *king,* man. The fuckin' *heart.* That's why you're free. That's why that cop gave you back your phoney passport. That's why you can walk around, and not get picked up, even though they *know* who you are. They could've fucked you, Lin. They could've taken your money, Khader's money, and let you go, and then get some *other* cops to bust you, and send you the fuck home. But they didn't do it, and they won't do it, because you got them in their heart, man, in their Indian fuckin' *heart.* They looked at all what you did here, and how the people in that slum love you, and they thought, *Well, he fucked up in Australia, but he's done some good shit here. If he pays up, we'll let the fucker go.* Because they're Indians, man. That's how we keep this crazy place together—with the *heart.* Two hundred fuckin' languages, and a billion people. India *is* the heart. It's the *heart* that keeps us together. There's no place with people like my people, Lin. There's no heart like the Indian heart.'

He was crying. Stunned, I watched him wipe the tears from his eyes, and I reached out to put a hand on his shoulder. He was right, of course. Even though I'd been tortured in an Indian prison, and almost killed there, I *had* been set free, and they *had* given me my old passport when I left the prison. *Is there any other country in the world*, I asked myself, *that would've let me go, as India did?* And even in India, if the cops had checked on me and discovered a different story—that I cheated Indians, say, or ran Indian prostitutes, or beat up defenceless people—they would've taken the money, and then sent me back to Australia anyway. It *was* the land where the heart is king. I knew that from Prabaker, from his mother, from Qasim Ali, from Joseph's redemption. I'd known it even in the prison, where men like Mahesh Malhotra had taken a beating in order to smuggle food to me when I was starving.

'What's this? A lover's quarrel, perhaps?' Didier asked, inviting himself to sit down.

'Oh, fuck you, Didier!' Vikram laughed, pulling himself together.

'Ah, well, it's a touching thought, Vikram. But, perhaps when you are feeling a little better. And how are you today, Lin?'

'I'm fine,' I smiled. Didier was one of three people who'd burst into tears when they saw me, flesh-withered and still ripped with cuts and wounds, soon after my release from Arthur Road Prison. The second was Prabaker, whose weeping was so violent that it took me a full hour to console him. The third person, unexpectedly, was lord Abdel Khader, whose eyes filled with tears when I thanked him: tears that flowed on my neck and shoulder when he hugged me.

'What'll you have?' I asked him.

'Oh, very kind,' he murmured, purring with pleasure. 'I believe that I will begin with a flask of whisky, and a fresh lime, and a cold soda. Yes. That will be a good *commencement*, no? It is very strange, and a very unhappy business, don't you think, this news about Indira Gandhi?'

'What news?' Vikram asked.

'They are saying on the news, just now, that Indira Gandhi is dead.'

'Is it true?' I asked.

'I fear that it is,' he sighed, suddenly and uncharacteristically solemn. 'The reports are not confirmed, but I think there is no doubt.'

'Was it the Sikhs? Was it because of Bluestar?'

'Yes, Lin. How did you know?'

'When she stormed the Golden Temple, to get Bhindranwale, I had a feeling it was going to catch up with her.'

'What happened? Did the KLF do it?' Vikram asked. 'Was it a bomb?'

'No,' Didier answered, gravely. 'They say it was her bodyguards—her

Sikh bodyguards.'

'Her own *bodyguard*, for fuck's sake!' Vikram gasped. His mouth gaped open, and his gaze drifted on the tide of his thoughts. 'Guys—I'll be back in a minute. Do you hear that? They're talking about the story, right now, on the radio, at the counter. I'll go and listen, and come back.'

He jogged to the crowded counter where fifteen or twenty men pressed together, arms around shoulders to listen, while an almost hysterical announcer gave details of the murder in Hindi. Vikram could've listened to the broadcast from his seat at our table—the volume was switched up to the maximum, and we heard every word. It was something else that drew him to that crowded counter: a sense of solidarity and kinship; a huddled need to *feel* the astounding news, through contact with his countrymen, even as he listened to it.

'Let's have that drink,' I suggested.

'Yes, Lin,' Didier answered, pouting with his lower lip, and offering a flourish of his hand to dismiss the distressing subject. The gesture failed. His head lolled forward, and he stared vacantly at the table in front of him. 'I can't believe it. It is simply not believable. *Indira Gandhi, dead* ... It is almost unthinkable. It is almost impossible to force myself to think of it, Lin. It is ... you know ... impossible.'

I ordered for Didier, and let my thoughts wander while we listened to the plaintive screech of the radio announcer. Selfishly, I wondered first what the assassination might mean for my security, and then what it might do to the exchange rates on the black money market. Some months before, Indira Gandhi had authorised an assault on the Sikh holy-of-holies, the Golden Temple, in Amritsar. Her goal was to drive out a large, well-armed company of Sikh militants who'd entered the temple and fortified themselves there under the leadership of a handsome, charismatic separatist named Bhindranwale. Using the temple complex as a base, the militants had launched punitive attacks against Hindus, and those they described as *recalcitrant* Sikhs, for many weeks. Indira Gandhi, on the eve of a fiercely contested general election, had been deeply concerned that she would appear weak and indecisive if she failed to act. In what many judged to be the worst of her admittedly limited options, Indira had sent the army into battle with the Sikh rebels.

The army operation to dislodge the militants from the Golden Temple was known as Operation Bluestar. Bhindranwale's militants, believing themselves to be freedom fighters and martyrs for the Sikh cause, met the army force with reckless and desperate resistance. More than six hundred lives were lost, and many hundreds of people were injured. In the end, the Golden Temple complex was cleared, and Indira emerged as anything but indecisive or weak. Her goal of reassuring the Hindu heartland of voters had been achieved, but the Sikh struggle for a separate homeland, called *Khalistan*, was rich in new martyrs. And across the world, Sikh hearts clenched around their determination to avenge the profane and bloody invasion of their holiest shrine.

The radio at the counter gave us no other details, but the message wailed from the speaker that she'd been murdered. Only a few months after Bluestar, Indira's own Sikh bodyguards had killed her. The woman who'd been reviled as a despot by some, adored as the mother of the country by many others, and so closely identified with the nation as to be indistinguishable from its past, and from its destiny, was gone. She was dead.

I had to think. I had to calculate the danger. Security forces across the country would be on special alert. There would be ramifications—riots, killings, looting, and burning, as revenge exacted on the Sikh communities for her murder. I knew it. Everyone in India knew it. On the radio, the announcer was talking about troop deployments in Delhi and in Punjab aimed at quelling anticipated disturbances. The tension would bring new dangers for me, a wanted man, working for the mafia, and living in the country with an expired visa. For a few moments, sitting there as Didier sipped his drink, as the men in the restaurant strained in silence to listen, and the early evening blushed our skin with rose-gold, my heart thumped with fear. *Run*, my thoughts whispered. *Run now, while you can. This is your last chance ...*

But even then, as I formed the clear thought to flee the city, I felt myself relaxing into a dense, fatalistic calm. I wouldn't leave Bombay. I couldn't leave Bombay. I knew that, as surely as I'd ever known anything in my life. There was the issue of Khaderbhai: my financial debt to him had been repaid from the wages I'd made in his service with Khaled, but there was a moral debt that was harder to repay. I owed him my life, and we both knew it. He'd hugged me when I came out of the prison and, crying at my pitiful state, he'd promised me that for so long as I remained in Bombay, I would be under his personal protection. Nothing like Arthur Road would ever happen to me again. He'd given me a gold medal featuring the Hindu *aum* symbol joined to a Muslim crescent and star, which I wore on a silver chain around my neck. Khaderbhai's name was inscribed on the back, in Urdu, Hindi, and English. In the event of trouble I was to show the medal, and ask that he be contacted at once. That security was imperfect, but it was better than anything I'd known since my exile had begun. His request for me to stay in his service, the unspoken debt that I owed him, and the safety that being Khader's man offered—all of those elements held me in the city.

And there was Karla. She'd disappeared from the city while I was in prison, and no-one knew where she'd gone. I had no idea where in all the wide world I might begin to look for her. But she loved Bombay. I knew that. It seemed reasonable to hope she might return. And I loved her. It grieved me—an emotion that was, in those months, even stronger than my love for her—that she must be thinking I'd abandoned her: that I got what I wanted, when we made love, and then dumped her. I couldn't move on without seeing her again, and explaining what had happened that night. So I stayed there, in the city, a minute's walk from the corner where we'd met, and I waited for her to return.

I glanced around the subdued, listening restaurant, and caught Vikram's eye. He smiled at me, and wagged his head. It was a heart-broken smile, and his eyes were inflamed with unshed tears. Still, he smiled to comfort me, to reassure me, to include me in his bewildered grieving. And with that smile I suddenly knew that there was something else holding me there. In the end I realised that it was the heart, the Indian heart that Vikram had talked about—*the land where heart is king*—that held me when so many intuitions told me I should leave. And the heart, for me, was the city. Bombay. The city had seduced me. I was in love with her. There was a part of me that she invented, and that only existed because I lived there, within her, as a *Mumbaiker*, a Bombayite.

'It's a fuckin' bad business, *yaar*,' Vikram muttered as he rejoined us. 'There's going to be a lot of blood spilled over this, *yaar*. On the radio, they're saying that Congress Party gangs are roaming in Delhi, going from house to house, and spoiling for a fight with the Sikhs.'

We were silent, all three of us, lost in our own speculations and worry. Then Didier spoke.

'I think I have a lead for you,' he said softly, wrenching us into the moment once more.

'About the jail?'

'*Oui.*'

'Go on.'

'It is not much. It does not add much to what you already know—that it was a person of some power, as your patron, Abdel Khader, has told you.'

'Whatever it is, Didier, it's more than I've got now.'

'As you wish. There is a ... man of my acquaintance ... who must visit the Colaba police station on a daily basis. We were talking, earlier today, and he mentioned the foreigner who was in the lock-up there some months ago. The name he used was the *Bite of the Tiger*. I cannot imagine how you came to win such a name for yourself, Lin, but I make a wild guess that it is not entirely flattering, the story, *non*? *Alors*, he told me that the *Bite of the Tiger*—you—was betrayed by a woman.'

'Did he give you a name?'

'No. I asked him, and he said that he did not know who she is. He did say that she is young, and very beautiful, but he may have invented those last details.'

'How reliable is this *man of your acquaintance*?'

Didier pursed his lips, and let out a puff of air.

'He can be relied upon to lie, and cheat, and steal. That is the extent of his reliability, I am afraid, but in these things he does show a marvellous predictability. However, in this case I think he has no reason to lie. I think you were the victim of a woman, Lin.'

'Well, that makes two of us, *yaar*. You and me both, brother,' Vikram put in. He finished his beer, and lit one of the long, thin, cheroots that he smoked as much for the complement they made to his costume as for the enjoyment of the smoke.

'You have been going out with Letitia for three months now,' Didier observed. His frown was irritated and profoundly unsympathetic. 'What is your problem?'

'You tell *me*! I'm going out with her all over the place, and I *still* can't get to first base. I'm not even in the ballpark. Fuck the ballpark, *yaar*— I'm not even in the fuckin' zip code. This chick is killin' me. This *love* is killin' me. She's playing hard to get. And brother, I'm hard but not *getting* any. I swear, I'm about to fuckin' *explode*!'

'You know, Vikram,' Didier said, his eyes shining once more with shrewdness and good humour, 'I have a strategy that just might work for you.'

'Didier, man, I'll try anything. The way things are, with this Indira thing and all, I gotta grab any chance while I can. Who knows where we'll all be tomorrow, *na*?'

'Yes, well, *attention*! This plan, it involves great daring, and careful planning, and a precise timing. If you are careless, it might cost you your life.'

'My ... my *life*?'

'Yes. Make no mistake. But if you succeed, I think you will win her heart forever. Are you, how do they say it, are you *game*, to try it?'

'I'm the *game-iest* motherfucker in the whole damn saloon, *yaar*. Let's hear it!'

'I might take this as my cue to leave, before you guys get too deep into this,' I interrupted, standing and shaking hands with both men. 'Thanks for the tip, Didier. I appreciate it. And a tip for you, Vikram—whatever you plan to try with Lettie, you can start by losing the phrase *hot-titty English chick*. Every time you call her that, she winces like you just strangled a baby rabbit.'

'You really think so?' he asked, frowning his puzzlement.

'Yes.'

'But it's one of my best lines, *yaar*. In Denmark —'

'You're not in Denmark any more, Toto.'

'Okay, Lin,' he conceded, laughing. 'Listen, when you find out what went down with the jail thing ... I mean, who the motherfucker was who put you in there, and all ... well, if you need a hand, count me in. Okay?'

'Sure,' I said, enjoying the good eye contact. 'Take it easy.'

I paid the bill and left, walking along the Causeway to Regal Cinema roundabout. It was early evening, one of the three best times of day in Bombay city. Early morning before the heat, and late night after the heat are special times of day, with special pleasures; but they're quiet times, with few people. Evening brings the people to their windows, balconies, and doorways. Evening fills the streets with strolling crowds. Evening is an indigo tent for the circus of the city, and families bring children to the entertainments that inspire every corner and crossroad. And evening is a chaperone for young lovers: the last hour of light before the night comes to steal the innocence from their slow promenades. There's no time, in the day or night, when there are more people on the streets of Bombay than there are in the evening, and no light loves the human face quite so much as the evening light in my Mumbai.

I walked through the evening crowds, loving the faces, loving the perfumes of skin and hair, loving the colours of clothes and the cadences of words that surrounded me. Yet I was alone, too much alone with my love of evening in the city. And all the while a black shark slowly circled in the sea of my thoughts: a black shark of doubt and anger and suspicion. *A woman betrayed me. A woman. A young and very beautiful woman ...*

The persistent blaring of a car horn drew my attention, and I saw Prabaker waving to me from his taxi. I got into the cab and asked him to drive me to my evening meeting with Khaled, near Chowpatty Beach. One of the first things I'd done with the first real money I'd made in Khaderbhai's service was pay for Prabaker's taxi licence. The cost of the licence had always been prohibitive for Prabaker, and it had eluded his sub-miniature talent for thrift. He drove occasional shifts in his cousin Shantu's taxi without the required licence, but ran considerable risks in doing it. With his own licence, he was free to approach any of the taxi lords who owned fleets of cabs and hired them out to licensed taxi drivers.

Prabaker was a hard worker and an honest man; but, more than that, he was the most likable man that most of those who knew him ever met. Even the hard-nosed taxi lords weren't immune to his sanguine charm. Within a month he had a semi-permanent lease on a taxi, which he cared for as if it was his own. On the dashboard he'd installed a plastic shrine to Lakshmi, the goddess of wealth. The gold, pink, and green plastic figure of the goddess blazed an alarmingly fierce expression through the bulbs in her red eyes whenever he hit the brakes of the car. From time to time he reached over, with a showman's flourish, to squeeze a rubber tube at the base of the figure. That action sprayed, through what appeared to be a valve in the navel of the goddess, a potent and disquietingly industrial mix of chemical perfumes onto the shirt and trousers of his passenger. Every squeeze of the spray was followed by a reflexive, polishing rub of his brass taxi driver's identification badge, which he wore with swaggering pride. Only one thing, in the whole city, rivalled the affection he felt for the black-and-yellow Fiat taxi.

'Parvati. Parvati. Parvati ...' he said, as we sped past Churchgate Station towards Marine Drive. He was drunk on the music of her name.

'I love her *too* much, Lin! Is love, yes, when a terrible feeling makes you happy? When you worry about a girl, more even than you worry about your taxi? That's a love, isn't it? A *great* love, isn't it? My *God*! Parvati. Parvati. Parvati ...'

'It's love, Prabu.'

'And Johnny has it too much love for Sita, my Parvati her sister. *Too* much love.'

'I'm happy for you. And for Johnny. He's a good man. You're both good men.'

'Oh, *yes*!' Prabaker agreed, slapping his hand on the horn a few times for emphasis. 'We are fine fellows! And tonight we are going out for a triple dates, with the sisters. It will be *too* much fun.'

'There's *another* sister?'

'Another?'

'Yeah—you said a triple date. Are there three sisters? I thought there were only two.'

'Yes, Lin, absolutely only two sisters.'

'Well, don't you mean a *double* date?'

'No, Lin. Parvati and Sita, they always bring their mummy, the wife of Kumar, Mrs. Patak. The girls, they are sitting on one side only, and Mrs. Nandita Patak, she is sitting in middle, and Johnny Cigar is with me, sitting on the other side. It is a triple date.'

'It sounds ... like ... a lotta fun.'

'Yes, fun! Of course fun! So much of fun! And when we offer it some foods and some drinks to Mrs. Patak, we can look at the girls, and they can look at us also. This is our system. This is how we smile at the girls and give them big winks with our eyes. We are having such good luck that Mrs. Patak, she has a happy appetites, and she will eat, without stopping, for three hours in a movie. So there is a very constant passing of foods, and plenty of looking at the girls. And Mrs. Patak—thanks to the God, it is impossible to fill up that woman in one movie only.'

'Hey, slow down ... that looks like a ... a riot.'

A mob of people, hundreds, thousands, streamed around a corner and onto wide Marine Drive, some three hundred metres in front of us. They advanced toward us across the whole width of the street.

'Not a riots, Linbaba,' Prabaker replied, slowing the cab to a stop. '*Riot nahin, morcha hain.*' It's not a riot, it's a demonstration.

It was clear that the people were passionately angry. The men and the women shook their fists in time with their furious chanting. Their anguished faces stiffened on necks and shoulders made rigid with their rage. They chanted about Indira Gandhi, and about revenge, and about the punishments they wanted to visit upon the Sikhs. I tensed as they neared us, but the human torrent parted for the cab, and then swept around and beyond us without so much as the scrape of a sleeve against the side of the car. Nevertheless, the eyes that looked in upon us were hate-stricken and cruel. I knew that if I were a Sikh, if I'd been wearing a Sikh turban or Sardarji scarf, the door would've been wrenched open.

As the crowd passed us and the road ahead became clear, I turned to see that Prabaker was wiping tears from his eyes. He fumbled in his pocket for a handkerchief, dragging a huge, red-checked sheet out at last, and dabbing at his eyes with it.

'It is a too much very sad situations, Linbaba,' he sniffed. 'That is the end of *She*. What is to become of our India now, without *She*? I am asking myself, and not having much of answers.'

She was one of the most common names for Indira: journalists, peasants, politicians, and black marketers all referred to her as *She*.

'Yeah. It's a mess, Prabu.'

He seemed so distraught that I sat with him in silence, for a while, staring out my window toward the darkening sea. When I turned to look at him once more, I saw that he was praying, with his head bowed forward and his hands pressed together at the base of the steering wheel. I watched his lips twitch and ripple in the whispered prayer, and then he opened his hands, turned his head, and smiled at me. His eyebrows rose and fell twice as he held the huge smile.

'So, Lin, how is about some sexy perfumes, on your good self?' he asked, reaching across to press the bulb beneath the plastic Lakshmi goddess on the dashboard of his cab.

'*No!*' I shrieked, trying to stop him.

Too late. He crushed the bulb, and a swirling belch of the noxious chemical mixture spurted from the belly of the goddess and settled on my trousers and my shirt.

'Now,' he grinned, starting the engine and pulling out onto Marine Drive again, 'we are ready for the life again! We are the lucky fellows, isn't it?'

'Sure it is,' I grumbled, gasping for a clean breath of air at the open window. A few minutes later we neared the car park, where I'd arranged to meet Khaled. 'You can let me out just here, Prabu. This is my stop, near that big tree.'

He parked beside a tall date palm, and I climbed out. We fought over payment for the cab ride. Prabaker refused the money, and I insisted that he take it. I suggested a compromise. He should take the money, and use it to buy some new perfume for his plastic goddess.

'Oh, *yes*, Linbaba!' he cried, accepting the money at last. 'What a good ideas you're having! I was just thinking that I have almost finished my perfumes bottle, and it is so much expensive that I didn't want to buy it another gallon any more. Now I can buy a big bottle, a new big bottle, and for weeks I can fill up my Lakshmi like new! Thank you, too much!'

'Don't mention it,' I answered him, laughing in spite of myself. 'Good luck on your triple date.'

He swung the car away from the kerb and out into the stream of traffic. I heard the car horn blaring a musical good-bye until he was out of sight.

Khaled Ansari was waiting for me in our chartered cab, fifty metres away. He sat in the back, with both doors opened for the breeze. I wasn't late, and he couldn't have been waiting more than fifteen or twenty minutes, but still there were ten cigarette butts on the ground beside the open door of the cab. Each one of them, I knew, was an enemy crushed under his heel, a violent wish, a brutal fantasy of the suffering he would one day inflict on those he hated.

And they were many, the ones he hated. Too many. The images of violence that filled his mind were so real, he'd told me, that sometimes he was nauseous with it. The anger was an ache in his bones. The hatred locked his jaws, and made him grind his teeth on the fury. The taste of it was bitter, always, all day and night, every waking minute, as bitter as the taste of the blackened knife he'd clamped between his teeth, as a Fattah guerrilla, when he'd crawled across broken ground toward his first kill.

'It's gonna kill you, Khaled, you know.'

'So I smoke too much. So what the fuck. Who wants to live forever?'

'I'm not talking about the cigarettes. I'm talking about what's inside you, making you chain-smoke them. I'm talking about what you're doing to yourself by hating the world. Someone told me once that if you make your heart into a weapon, you always end up using it on yourself.'

'You're a fine one to come on with a lecture, brother,' he said, and he laughed. The small laugh. The sad laugh. 'You're not exactly Father Fucking Christmas, Lin.'

'You know, Khader told me ... about Shatila.'

'What did he tell you?'

'That ... you lost your family there. It must've been incredibly hard for you.'

'What do you know about it?' he demanded.

It wasn't an offensive question, and it wasn't asked in an aggressive way, but there was too much hurt in it, too much of his pain for me to let it go.

'I know about Sabra and Shatila, Khaled. I've been into politics all my life. I was on the run, at the time, when it happened, but I followed the news every day, for months. It was ... it was a heartbreaking story.'

'I was in love with a Jewish girl once, you know?' Khaled asked. I didn't reply. 'She was ... she was a beautiful girl, and smart, and maybe, I don't know, maybe the nicest human being I'm ever gonna meet. That was in New York. We were students together. Her parents, they were reform Jews—they supported Israel, but they were against the occupation of the territories. I was with that girl, making love to her, on the night my father died in an Israeli prison.'

'You can't blame yourself for being in love, Khaled. And you can't blame yourself for what other people did to your father.'

'Oh, sure I can,' he said, offering me that small, sad smile. 'Anyway, I went back home, and I was just in time for the October War—the one the Israelis call the Yom Kippur War. We got smashed. I made it to Tunis, and got some training. I started fighting, and I kept on fighting, all the way to Beirut. When the Israelis invaded, we made a stand at Shatila. My whole family was there, and a lot of my neighbours from the old days. All of them, all of us, we were all refugees, with nowhere else to go.'

'Were you evacuated, with the other fighters?'

'Yeah. They couldn't beat us, so they worked out a truce. We left the camps—with our weapons, you know, to show that we weren't defeated. We marched, like soldiers, and there was a lot of firing in the air. Some people got killed just watching us. It was weird, like a parade or some kind of bizarre celebration, you know? And then, when we were gone, they broke all their promises, and they sent the Phalange into the camps, and they killed all the old men, and the women, and the children. And they all died. All my family. All the ones I left behind. I don't even know where their bodies are. They hid them, because they knew it was a war crime. And you think ... you think I should *let it go*, Lin?'

We were facing the sea, looking down on a section of Chowpatty Beach from a car park on the steep rise above Marine Drive. Beneath us the first wave of families, and couples, and young men out for the night tried their luck at throwing darts or shooting balloons pinned to a target. The ice cream and sherbet-drink vendors called out from their flamboyantly decorated bowers like birds of paradise singing for mates.

The hatred that had coiled around Khaled's heart was the only thing we ever argued about. I'd been raised among Jewish friends. Melbourne, the city where I grew up, had a large Jewish community, many of them Holocaust survivors and their children. My mother had been prominent in Fabian socialist circles, and she'd attracted left-leaning intellectuals from the Greek, Chinese, German, and Jewish communities. Many of my friends had attended a Jewish school, Mt. Scopus College. I grew up with those kids, reading the same books, enjoying the same movies and music, marching together in support of the same causes. Some of those friends were among the few who'd stood by me when my life imploded in agony and shame. It was a Jewish friend, in fact, who'd helped me to escape from Australia after I broke out of prison. I respected, admired, and loved all of those friends. And Khaled hated every Israeli, and every Jew in the world.

'It would be like me hating *all* Indians, just because *some* Indians tortured me in an Indian prison.' I said softly.

'It's not the same.'

'I'm not saying it's the same. I'm trying to ... look, when they had me chained to the wall there, at Arthur Road, and they went to work on me, it went on for hours. After a while, all I could smell and taste was my own blood. All I could hear was the lathis ripping into me.'

'I know, Lin —'

'No, let me finish. There was a minute, right in the middle of it, that was ... so weird ... it was like I was floating, outside myself, looking down at my own body, and at them, and watching everything that was going on. And ... I got this weird feeling ... this really strange kind of *understanding* ... of everything that was happening. I knew *who* they were, and *what* they were, and *why* they were doing it. I knew it all really clearly, and then I knew that I had two choices—to hate them or to forgive them. And ... I don't know why, or how, but it was absolutely clear to me that I had to forgive them. I had to, if I wanted to survive. I know it sounds crazy—'

'It doesn't sound crazy,' he said flatly, almost regretfully.

'It still seems crazy to me. I haven't really ... figured it out, yet. But that's exactly what happened. And I did forgive them. I really did. And I'm sure, somehow, that *that's* what got me through it. I don't mean that I stopped being angry—shit, if I'd gotten free and gotten a gun, I probably would've killed them all. Or maybe not. I don't know. But the point is, I *did* forgive them, right there and then, in the middle of it. And I'm sure that if I didn't do that—if I'd just hated them—I wouldn't have made it through till Khader got me out. I would've gone under. The hate would've killed me.'

'It's still not the same, Lin. I understand what you're saying, but the Israelis did more to me than that. And anyway, if I *was* in an Indian prison, and they did that to *me*, what they did to *you*, I *would* hate Indians forever. I'd hate them all.'

'But I don't hate them. I love them. I love this country. I love this city.'

'You can't say you don't want revenge, Lin.'

'I do want revenge. You're right. I wish I didn't. I wish I was better than that. But I only want it on one person—the one who set me up—not the whole nation that she comes from.'

'Well, we're different people,' he said flatly, staring out at the distant fires of the offshore oil refinery. 'You don't understand. You *can't* understand it.'

'I understand that hate kills you, Khaled, if you can't let it go.'

'No, Lin,' he answered, turning to look at me in the faint light of the cab. His eyes were gleaming, and there was a broken smile fixed to his scarred face. It was something like the expression Vikram wore when he talked about Lettie, or like Prabaker's face when he talked about Parvati. It was the kind of expression some men assume when they talk about their experience of God.

'My hate is what saved me,' he said quietly, but with an excited, feverish zeal. Softly rounded American vowels blended with breathy, aspirated

Arabic in a sound, a voice, that was somewhere between Omar Sharif and Nicholas Cage. In another time, another place, another life, Khaled Ansari would've read poetry aloud, in Arabic and English, moving all those who heard him to joy and tears. 'Hate is a very resilient thing, you know. Hate is a survivor. I had to hide my hate for a long time. People couldn't handle it. They got spooked by it. So I sent my hate outside myself. It's weird that I was a refugee for years—I still am—and my hate was a refugee, just like me. My hate was outside me. My family ... they were all killed ... raped and butchered ... and I killed men ... I shot them ... I cut their throats ... and my hate survived out there. My hate got stronger and harder. And then, I woke up one day, working for Khader, with money and power, and I could feel the hate creeping back into me. And it's here now, inside me, where it belongs. And I'm glad. I enjoy it. I need it, Lin. It's stronger than I am. It's braver than I am. My hate is my hero.'

He held that fanatic stare for a moment, and then turned to the driver, who was dozing in the front seat of the car.

'Challo, bhai!' he snapped. Let's go, brother!

A minute later, he broke the silence to ask me a question.

'You heard about Indira?'

'Yeah. On the radio, at Leopold's.'

'Khader's guys in Delhi got the details. The inside story. They phoned it through to us just before I came to meet you. It was pretty messy, the way she went.'

'Yeah?' I replied, still thinking about Khaled's song of hate. I didn't really care about the details of Indira's assassination, but I was happy that he'd changed the subject.

'At nine o'clock in the morning, this morning, she walked down to a security gate at her residence—the prime minister's residence. She folded her hands together in a greeting, you know, for the two Sikh bodyguards at the gate. She knew those guys. They were only there, on duty, because she insisted on it. After the Golden Temple, after Bluestar, they advised her not to have Sikhs in her security detail. But she insisted because she couldn't believe that her loyal Sikh bodyguards would turn against her. She just didn't get it—how much hatred she put in them, when she ordered the army to attack the Golden Temple. Anyway, she put her hands together in a greeting, and she smiled at them, and said the word

Namaste. One bodyguard, he pulled out his service revolver—it was a .38 —and fired three shots. He got her right in the guts, in the abdomen. She crumpled to the pathway. The second bodyguard turned his Sten gun on her. He emptied the whole magazine. Thirty rounds. It's an old gun, the Sten, but it packs a hell of a punch at close range. At least seven bullets got her in the abdomen, three bullets went into her chest, and one went through her heart.'

We rode in silence for a while. I was the first to speak.

'So, how do you think the money market will react?'

'I think it'll be good for business,' he replied dispassionately. 'So long as there's a clear line of succession—as there is here, with Rajiv—an assassination is always good for business.'

'But there'll be riots. They're already talking about gangs going after Sikhs. I saw a morcha, on my way up here.'

'Yeah, I saw it, too,' he said, turning to face me. His eyes were dark, almost black, and gleaming with the vehemence of his wilful induration. 'But even that'll be good for business. The more riots there are, and the more people get killed, the more demand there'll be for dollars. We'll put the rates up tomorrow morning.'

'The roads might be tangled up. If there's morchas or riots, it might not be so easy to get around.'

'I'll pick you up at your place, seven o'clock, and we'll go straight to Rajubhai's,' he said, referring to the mafia's black money counting room in the Fort area, and to Raju, the man who ran it. 'They won't stop me. My car will get through. What are you doing now?'

'Right now—after we finish the collections?'

'Yeah. Have you got some time?'

'Sure. What do you want me to do?'

'Drop me off, and keep the cab,' he said, resting back against the seat and letting his face and body sag in a sigh of exhaustion or dejection. 'Do the rounds of the guys. Tell them to make their way to Rajubhai's early tomorrow. Find as many as you can, and let them know. If it gets real bad, we'll need everyone.'

'Okay. I'll get on it. You should get some sleep, Khaled. You look tired.'

'I think I will,' he smiled. 'There won't be much sleep in the next couple days.'

He closed his eyes for a moment, and allowed his head to loll and roll with the movement of the car. Then he was suddenly awake, sitting upright, and sniffing the air around him.

'Say, what the fuck is that *smell*, man? Is that some kind of aftershave or what? I've been gassed with tear gas that smelled better than that!'

'Don't ask,' I replied, suppressing a grin through clenched teeth, and rubbing at Prabaker's perfume stain on the front of my shirt. Khaled laughed, and turned his eyes to the starless dark, where night met the sea.

Sooner or later, fate puts us together with all the people, one by one, who show us what we could, and shouldn't, let ourselves become. Sooner or later we meet the drunkard, the waster, the betrayer, the ruthless mind, and the hate-filled heart. But fate loads the dice, of course, because we usually find ourselves loving or pitying almost all of those people. And it's impossible to despise someone you honestly pity, and to shun someone you truly love. I sat beside Khaled in the darkness as the taxi took us to the business of crime. I sat beside him in the drift of coloured shadows, loving the honesty and toughness in him, and pitying the hatreds that weakened him and lied to him. And his face, reflected sometimes in the night that filled the window, was as drenched in destiny, and as radiant, as the faces found in paintings of doomed and haloed saints.

CHAPTER TWENTY-THREE

'Wherever you go in the world, in any society, it is always the same when it comes to questions of justice,' lord Abdel Khader Khan, my mafia boss and my surrogate father, told me when I'd been six months in his service. 'We concentrate our laws, investigations, prosecutions, and punishments on how much crime is in the sin, rather than how much sin is in the crime.'

We were sitting in the busy, steamy, wondrously aromatic Restaurant Saurabh, in the Sassoon Dock area. The Saurabh served what many regarded as Bombay's best masala dhosas, in a city where five thousand restaurants vied for the honour. Despite that distinction, or because of it, the Saurabh was small and relatively unknown. Its name didn't appear in any of the guidebooks for tourists or the epicure columns in the daily newspapers. It was a worker's restaurant, and it was full, from morning until evening, with working men and women who cherished it and kept its secret to themselves. Accordingly, the meals were cheap and the décor was a functional minimum. Nevertheless, the restaurant was spotlessly clean, and the spectacular, baroque sails of the crispy dhosas, swept to the tables by waiters who worked at a run, housed the most delicious mixes of spices that could be found in any dish, anywhere in the city.

'For me,' he went on as we ate, 'the opposite is true. For me, the most important thing is the amount of sin that is in the crime. You asked me, just now, why we do not make money from prostitution and drugs, as the other councils do, and I tell you it is because of the sin that is in those crimes. It is for *this* reason that I will not sell children, or women, or pornography, or drugs. It is for *this* reason that I will not permit those businesses in any of my areas. In all of these things, the sin in the crime is so great that a man must give up his soul for the profit he makes. And if a man gives his soul, if he becomes a soul-less man, it takes nothing less than a miracle for him to regain it.'

'Do you believe in miracles?'

'Certainly, I do. In our hearts, we all believe in miracles.'

'I'm afraid I don't,' I stated, smiling.

'I'm sure that you *do*,' he insisted. 'Wouldn't you say that your rescue from the prison at Arthur Road was a miracle, for example?'

'It *felt* like a miraculous thing at the time, I have to admit.'

'And when you escaped from the prison in your home country, Australia—was that not a miraculous thing?' he asked quietly.

It was the first time he'd ever mentioned the escape. I was sure that he knew, of course, and I was sure he must've thought about it many times. But by broaching the subject with me he was raising the real nature of the rescue from Arthur Road Prison. The fact was that he'd rescued me from two prisons—one in India and one in Australia—and I owed him a double debt.

'Yes,' I answered, slowly but steadily. 'It was something of a miracle, I guess.'

'If you do not object—that is, if you do not find it painful—I would like you to tell me about the escape from the prison in Australia. I might tell you that I find it to be fascinating, for my own very personal reasons, and I am deeply impressed by it.'

'I don't mind talking about it,' I replied, meeting his stare. 'What would you like to know?'

'*Why* did you escape?'

Khaderbhai was the only person who'd ever asked me that question. People in Australia and New Zealand had asked me about the escape. They'd wanted to know how I broke out of the prison, and how I stayed on the run. But only Khader asked me *why* I escaped.

'There was a punishment unit in the prison. The guards who ran it— not all of them, but enough of them—were crazy. They hated us. They were insane with hate for the prisoners. I don't know why. I can't explain it. That's just how it was down there then. And they tortured us, nearly every night. And I fought back. I had to fight them. It's my nature, I guess. It's just how I am. I'm not the kind of man who could take it from them, without fighting back. Which made it all worse, of course. I got ... well, they went to work on me, and it was ... pretty bad. I was only down there, in that punishment unit, for a little while. But I had a long sentence, and I knew that sooner or later they'd find a reason to put me down there again, or I'd be stupid enough to give them one—it wasn't hard, believe me. I thought that when they did get me there again, when they got their hands on me, they'd torture me again, and I'd fight them again, and they'd probably kill me. So ... I escaped.'

'How did you do it?'

'After that last beating, I let them think they'd broken my spirit. So they gave me the kind of job that only beaten men were allowed to do. They gave me a job near the front wall of the prison, pushing a wheelbarrow and making repairs. When the time was right, I escaped.'

He listened as I told him the story. We continued to eat while I talked. Khader never interrupted. He watched me throughout, and the smiling light in his eyes reflected the fire in mine. He seemed to enjoy the telling of the story as much as the tale itself.

'Who was the other man—the one with you, when you escaped?'

'The other guy was doing time for murder. He was a good man, with plenty of heart.'

'But you did not stay together?'

'No,' I answered, allowing my gaze to shift from Khader's for the first time. I looked at the doorway of the restaurant, and watched the rhythmic, unceasing flow of people on the street. How could I explain my reasons for leaving my friend after the escape, and going off on my own? I hardly understood it myself. I decided to give him the facts, and let him make of them what he would.

'At first, we went to stay with an outlaw bike club—a gang of men who rode motorcycles. The leader of the motorcycle gang had a young brother who was in the prison. He was a brave young kid, and about a year before I escaped he'd upset a very dangerous man by doing nothing more than being brave. I got involved, and I saved the kid from being killed. When the kid found out about it, he told his brother. The older brother, who was the president of the motorcycle gang, had let me know that he owed me one. When I escaped, I went to stay with the older brother and his gang, and I took my friend with me. They gave us guns, drugs, and money. They protected us and gave us shelter, for the first thirteen days and nights, while the cops tore the city up looking for us.'

I paused, mopping up the last of my food with a corner of pea-flour roti. Khaderbhai ate the last of the food on his own plate. We chewed vigorously, watching one another with thoughts and questions glittering in our eyes.

'On the thirteenth night after the escape, when I was still hiding with the motorcycle gang, I got this overwhelming urge to visit a man who used to be my teacher,' I continued at last. 'He was a lecturer in philosophy at a university in my city. He was a Jewish intellectual, a brilliant guy, and very highly respected in the city where I grew up. But brilliant and all as he was, I still don't know why I went to see him. I can't explain it—I don't really understand it, even now. I just *had* to speak to him. The feeling was so strong, I couldn't fight it. So I went across the city, risking my life to see him. He said that he'd *expected* to see me, and that he was waiting for me to come to him. He told me that I had to give up my guns, first of all. He tried to convince me that I wouldn't need them, and that they'd bring me grief if I didn't get rid of them. He told me that I had to give up the crime of armed robbery, and never commit it again. He said that I'd paid my dues for the crimes I'd committed, but that if I ever did that crime again I would be killed or captured straight away. *Whatever else you have to do to stay free,* he said, *don't ever do that crime again.* He told me to split from my friend, because he was sure to get caught, and if I was with him I'd be caught, too. And he told me to travel the world. *Tell people as much as they need to know,* he said. I remember that he was smiling when he said it, like there was nothing to it. *And ask people for help,* he said. *You'll be all right ... Don't worry ... It's a great adventure, your life, and it has only just begun ...*'

There was a pause as I lapsed into silence once more. A waiter approached the table to clear away our empty plates, but Khader waved him away. The mafia don stared at me, his golden eyes unwavering, but it was a sympathetic and encouraging stare.

'I left his office—the philosopher's office, at the university—and I knew that everything had changed with just that little conversation. I went back to the motorcycle gang and my friend. I gave him my guns, and I told him that I had to leave. I went off on my own. He was captured, six months later, after a gun battle with the cops. I'm still free, if that word means anything when you're a wanted man with nowhere to go. And that's it. Now you know the story.'

'I would like to meet this man,' Khaderbhai said slowly. 'This lecturer in philosophy. He gave you good advice. But tell me, I understand that Australia is a very different country, not like India—why do you not return there, and tell the authorities about the torture you endured in the prison? Would this not make you safe, and return you to your life and your family?'

'Where I come from, we don't inform on anyone,' I replied. 'Not even on torturers. And even if I did—even if I went back there and stood in the dock as a Crown witness, and gave evidence against the screws who torture prisoners—there'd be no guarantee it would stop. The system would look after them. No sane man trusts the British justice system. When was the last time you ever heard of a rich man throwing himself on the mercy of the court? It doesn't happen. The system would look after the torturers, and they'd get away with it, no matter what they did and no matter how much proof there was. And I'd go back in jail. And I'd be in their power again. And they'd make a pretty good mess of me. I think ... I think they'd kick me to death down there, in the punishment unit. Anyway, it's not an option. You don't lag people. You don't inform on people, not for any reason. It's a principle. It's probably the only one we've got left when we get locked up in a cage.'

'But you believe that these prison guards are still torturing other men in that prison, just as they tortured you?' he pressed.

'Yes, I do.'

'And you are in a position to do something about this, to try to alleviate their suffering?'

'I might be. I might not be. Like I said, I don't think the system would be in any hurry to bring them to justice, or to rush to our defence.'

'But there is a chance, just a chance, that they would listen to you, and put an end to the torture of the other men?'

'There's a chance. I don't think it's a big one.'

'But still there is a chance?' he insisted.

'Yes,' I said flatly.

'So it could be said that you are in a way responsible for the suffering of the other men?'

The question was offensive, but his tone was entirely gentle and compassionate. I stared into his eyes, and was sure that he meant no offence or harm. It was Khader who'd rescued me from the Indian prison, after all and, indirectly, from the Australian prison that we were discussing.

'You could say that,' I answered calmly. 'But that doesn't change the principle. You don't tell on people—not for any reason.'

'I am not trying to trap you, Lin, or trick you. But you will agree, I think, from this example, that it is possible to do the *wrong thing* for the *right reasons.*' He smiled again, for the first time since the story of the escape had begun. 'This will come back to us, at another time. I have raised it in this way because it is a very important point about how we *do* live our lives, and how we *should* live our lives. There is no need to talk of it now, but this question will come back to us in another discussion, I am sure, so I would like you to remember it.'

'And what about currencies?' I asked, seizing the opportunity to change the subject away from me, and toward the rules of his moral universe once more. 'Don't currencies come under your heading of sin-full crimes?'

'No. Not currencies,' he said firmly. The voice was deep, the words surging upwards from the diaphragm into the chest, and passing through the rumbling gemstone-tumbler of his throat. What emerged was a tone of voice that resonated with the hypnotic piety of a sermoner, reading from the Koran, even as he talked of his most profitable crimes.

'And gold smuggling?'

'No. Not gold. Not passports. Not influence.'

Influence was Khader's euphemism for the full range of interactions between his mafia group and the society in which it thrived. They began with bribery, in a schedule of venalities ranging from insider trading to the securing of profitable tenders. When bribes failed, Khader's influence extended to debt collection and protection rackets, aimed at businesses that operated in the areas he controlled. Not least in the spheres of his influence was intimidation, through force or blackmail, of political and bureaucratic recalcitrants.

'So, how do you determine how much sin is in any one crime? Who judges that?'

'Sin is a measure of evil,' he replied, leaning back to allow the waiter to clear away his plate and the crumbs on the table in front of him.

'Okay. How do you determine how much *evil* is in any one crime? Who judges the evil in it?'

'If you really want to know about good and evil, we'll have a walk, and talk further.'

He rose, and Nazeer, his constant companion, rose like his shadow and followed him to the sink, tap, and mirror housed in an alcove that was set into the back wall of the restaurant. They washed their hands and faces, hawking and spitting noisily into the sink, as did every other man in the restaurant at the conclusion of his meal. When my turn at washing, hawking, and spitting was complete, I found Khaderbhai talking with the owner of the Saurabh on the footpath outside the restaurant. When they separated, the owner embraced Khader and asked for his blessing. The man was a Hindu, and his forehead bore the mark of blessing he'd received at a temple only hours before. Yet when Khaderbhai held the man's hands in his own, and softly mumbled a Muslim blessing, the devout Hindu responded with delight and gratitude.

Khader and I strolled back towards Colaba. Stocky, ape-like Nazeer walked a metre or so behind us, scowling at the street. At Sassoon Dock we crossed the road and passed beneath the arch at the main entrance to the old dockyard. The smell of prawns, drying in the sun in pink mountains, made my stomach flip, but when we caught sight of the sea the stench was lost in the strong breeze. Nearer to the docks we threaded our way through crowds of men pushing handcarts, and women carrying baskets on their heads, all bearing crushed ice and a burden of fish. Factories that produced the ice and processed the fish added their industrious clangour to the wailing of auctioneers and salesmen. At the edge of the dock itself, there were twenty large, wooden fishing boats, built to the same designs used for vessels that had sailed the Arabian Sea, on the Maharashtrian coast of India, five hundred years before. Here and there between them were larger, more expensive metal boats. The contrast between those rusted, graceless hulks and the elegant wooden boats beside them spoke a history, a modern saga, a world story that moved from life at sea, as a romantic calling, to the profiteer's cold, efficient lusting for the bottom line.

We sat on a wooden bench in a quiet, shaded corner of the dock where fishermen sometimes rested to share a meal. Khader stared at the vessels, which were shifting and genuflecting at their moorings on the lapping tide.

His short hair and beard were almost white. The tight, unblemished skin of his lean face was tanned to the colour of sun-ripened wheat. I looked at the face—the long, fine nose and wide brow and upward curving lips—and wondered, not for the first time, and not for the last, if my love for him would cost me my life. Nazeer, ever watchful, stood near us and scanned the dock with a glowering expression that approved of nothing in the world but the man who sat beside me.

'The history of the universe is a history of motion,' Khader began, still looking at the boats nodding together like horses in harness. 'The universe, as we know it, in this one of its many lives, began in an expansion that was so big, and so fast that we can talk about it, but we cannot in any truth *understand* it, or even *imagine* it. The scientists call this great expansion the Big Bang, although there was no *explosion*, in the sense of a bomb, or something like that. And the first moments after that great expansion, from the first fractions of attoseconds, the universe was like a rich soup made out of simple bits of things. Those bits were so simple that they were not even atoms yet. As the universe expanded and cooled down, these very tiny bits of things came together to make particles. Then the particles came together to make the first of the atoms. Then the atoms came together to make molecules. Then the molecules came together to make the first of the stars. Those first stars went through their cycles, and exploded in a shower of new atoms. The new atoms came together to make more stars and planets. All the stuff we are made of came from those dying stars. We are made out of stars, you and I. Do you agree with me so far?'

'Sure,' I smiled. 'I don't know where you're going yet, but so far, so good.'

'Precisely!' he laughed. 'So far, so *good*. You can check the science of what I am saying to you—as a matter of fact, I *want* you to check everything that I say, and everything you ever learn from anyone else. But I am sure that the science is right, within the limit of what we know. I have been studying these matters with a young physicist for some time now, and my facts are essentially correct.'

'I'm happy to take your word for it,' I said, and I *was* happy, just to have his company and his undivided attention.

'Now, to continue, none of these things, none of these processes, none of these *coming together* actions are what one can describe as random events. The universe has a *nature*, for and of itself, something like *human nature*, if you like, and its *nature* is to combine, and to build, and to become more complex. It *always* does this. If the circumstances are right, bits of matter will always come together to make more complex arrangements.

And this fact about the way that our universe works, this moving towards order, and towards combinations of these ordered things, has a name. In the western science it is called *the tendency toward complexity*, and it is the way the universe works.'

Three fishermen dressed in lungis and singlets approached us shyly. One of them carried two wire baskets containing glasses of water and hot chai. Another grasped a plate bearing several sweet ladoo. The last man held a chillum and two golis of charras in his extended palms.

'Will you drink tea, sir?' one of the men asked politely in Hindi. 'Will you smoke with us?'

Khader smiled, and wagged his head. The men came forward quickly, handing glasses of chai to Khader, Nazeer, and me. They squatted on the ground in front of us and prepared their chillum. Khader received the honour of lighting the pipe, and I took the second dumm. The pipe went twice around the group and was tipped up clean by the last man, who exhaled the word *Kalaass ... Finished ...* with his stream of blue smoke.

Khader continued talking to me in English. I was sure that the men couldn't understand him, but they remained with us, and watched his face intently.

'To continue this point, the universe, as we know it, and from everything that we can learn about it, has been getting always more complex since it began. It does this because *that is its nature.* The *tendency toward complexity* has carried the universe from almost perfect simplicity to the kind of complexity that we see around us, everywhere we look. The universe is always doing this. It is always moving from the simple to the complex.'

'I think I know where you're going with this.'

Khader laughed. The fishermen laughed with him.

'The universe,' he continued, 'this universe that we know, began in almost absolute simplicity, and it has been getting more complex for about fifteen billion years. In another billion years it will be still more complex than it is now. In five billion, in ten billion—it is always getting more complex. It is moving toward ... *something*. It is moving toward some kind of ultimate complexity. We might not get there. An atom of hydrogen might not get there, or a leaf, or a man, or a planet might not get there, to that ultimate complexity. But we are all moving towards it— everything in the universe is moving towards it. And that final complexity, that thing we are all moving to, is what I choose to call God. If you don't like that word, God, call it the Ultimate Complexity. Whatever you call it, the whole universe is moving toward it.'

'Isn't the universe a lot more random than that?' I asked, sensing the drift of his argument, and seeking to head it off. 'What about giant asteroids and so on? We, I mean our planet, could get smashed to fragments by a giant asteroid. In fact, there's a statistical probability that major impacts *will* occur. And if our sun is dying—and one day it will—isn't that the *opposite* of complexity? How does that fit in with the movement to complexity, if all this complex planet is smashed to atoms, and our sun dies?'

'A good question,' Khaderbhai replied. A happy smile revealed the run of his slightly gapped, ivory-cream teeth. He was enjoying himself in the discussion, and I realised that I'd never seen him quite so animated or enthused. His hands roved the space between us, illustrating some points and emphasising others. 'Our planet may be smashed, it is true, and one day our beautiful sun will die. And we are, to the best of our knowledge, the most developed expression of the complexity in our bit of the universe. It would certainly be a major loss if we were to be annihilated. It would be a terrible waste of all that development. But the *process* would continue. We are, ourselves, expressions of that process. Our bodies are the children of all the suns and other stars that died, before us, making the atoms that *we* are made of. And if we were destroyed, by an asteroid, or by our own hand, well, somewhere else in the universe, our level of complexity, *this* level of complexity, with a consciousness capable of understanding the process, would be duplicated. I do not mean *people* exactly like us. I mean that thinking beings, that are as complex as we are, would develop, somewhere else in the universe. *We* would cease to exist, but the process would go on. Perhaps this is happening in millions of worlds, even as we speak. In fact, it is very likely that it *is* happening, all over the universe, because *that* is what the universe *does*.'

It was my turn to laugh.

'Okay, okay. And you want to say—let me guess—that everything that helps this along is good, right? And anything that goes in the other direction—your spin on it is that it's evil, *na?*'

Khaderbhai turned his full attention on me, with one eyebrow raised in amusement or disapproval, or both. It was an expression I'd seen on Karla's face more than once. He might've thought that my slightly mocking tone was rude. I didn't mean it to be. It was defensive, in fact, because I couldn't find a flaw in his logic, and I was profoundly impressed by his argument. Perhaps he was simply surprised. He told me once, much later, that one of the first things he liked about me was that I wasn't afraid of him; and my fearlessness often took him by surprise with its impudence and its folly. Whatever the cause for his little smile and arched eyebrow, it was some time before he continued.

'In essence, you are right. Anything that enhances, promotes, or accelerates this movement toward the Ultimate Complexity is *good*,' he said, pronouncing the words so slowly, and with such considered precision, that I was sure he'd spoken the phrases many times. 'Anything that inhibits, impedes, or prevents this movement toward the Ultimate Complexity is *evil*. The wonderful thing about *this* definition of good and evil is that it is both objective and universally acceptable.'

'Is anything really objective?' I asked, believing myself to be on surer ground at last.

'When we say that this definition of good and evil is objective, what we mean is that it is as objective as we can be at this time, and to the best of our knowledge about the universe. This definition is based on what we *know* about how the universe works. It is not based on the revealed wisdom of any one faith or political movement. It is common to the best principles of all of them, but it is based on what we *know* rather than what we *believe*. In that sense, it is objective. Of course, what we *know* about the universe, and our place in it, is constantly changing as we add more information and gain new insights. We are never *perfectly* objective about anything, that is true, but we can be less objective, or we can be more objective. And when we define good and evil on the basis of what we *know*—to the best of our knowledge at the present time—we are being as objective as possible within the imperfect limits of our understanding. Do you accept that point?'

'When you say that objective doesn't mean absolutely objective, then I accept it. But how can the different religions, not to mention the atheists and agnostics and the just plain confused, like me, ever find any definition *universally* acceptable? I don't mean to be insulting, but I think most believers have got too much of a vested interest in their own God-and-Heaven franchises, if you know what I mean, to ever agree on anything.'

'It is a fair point, and I am not offended,' Khader mused, glancing at the silent fishermen sitting at his feet. He exchanged a broad smile with them and then continued. 'When we say that this definition of good and evil is universally acceptable, what we mean is that any rational and reasonable person—any rational and reasonable Hindu or Muslim or Buddhist or Christian or Jew or any *atheist*, for that matter—can accept that this is a *reasonable* definition of good and evil, because it is based on what we know about how the universe works.'

'I think I understand what you're saying,' I offered when he fell silent. 'But I don't really follow you, when it comes to the ... *physics*, I guess, of the universe. Why should we accept *that* as the basis of our morality?'

'If I can give you an example, Lin, perhaps it will be clearer. I will use the analogy of the way we measure length, because it is very relevant to our time. You will agree, I think, that there is a need to define a common measure of length, yes?'

'You mean, in yards and metres, and like that?'

'Precisely. If we have no commonly agreed criterion for measuring length, we will never agree about how much land is yours, and how much is mine, or how to cut lengths of wood when we build a house. There would be chaos. We would fight over the land, and the houses would fall down. Throughout history, we have always tried to agree on a common way to measure length. Are you with me, once more, on this little journey of the mind?'

'I'm still with you,' I replied, laughing, and wondering where the mafia don's argument was taking me.

'Well, after the revolution in France, the scientists and government officials decided to put some sense into the system of measuring and weighing things. They introduced a decimal system based on a unit of length that they called the *metre*, from the Greek word *metron*, which has the meaning of a *measure*.'

'Okay ...'

'And the first way they decided to measure the length of a metre was to make it one ten-millionth of the distance between the equator and the North Pole. But their calculations were based on the idea that the Earth was a perfect sphere, and the Earth, as we now know, is *not* a perfect sphere. They had to abandon that way of measuring a metre, and they decided, instead, to call it the distance between two very fine lines on a bar of platinum-iridium alloy.'

'Platinum ...'

'Iridium. Yes. But platinum-iridium alloy bars decay and shrink, very slowly—even though they are very hard—and the unit of measure was constantly changing. In more recent times, scientists realised that the platinum-iridium bar they had been using as a measure would be a very different size in, say, a thousand years, than it is today.'

'And ... that was a problem?'

'Not for the building of houses and bridges,' Khaderbhai said, taking my point more seriously than I'd intended it to be.

'But not nearly accurate enough for the scientists,' I offered, more soberly.

'No. They wanted an unchanging criterion against which to measure all other things. And after a few other attempts, using different techniques, the international standard measure for a metre was fixed, only last year, as the distance that a photon of light travels in a vacuum during, roughly, one three-hundred-thousandth of a second. Now, of course, this begs the question of how it came to be that a *second* is agreed upon as a measure of *time*. It is an equally fascinating story—I can tell it to you, if you would like, before we continue with the point about the metre?'

'I'm ... happy to stay with the metre right now,' I demurred, laughing again in spite of myself.

'Very well. I think that you can see my point here—we avoid chaos, in building houses and dividing land and so forth, by having an agreed standard for the measure of a unit of length. We call it a metre and, after many attempts, we decide upon a way to establish the length of that basic unit. In the same way, we can only avoid chaos in the world of human affairs by having an agreed standard for the measure of a unit of morality.'

'I'm with you.'

'At the moment, most of our ways of defining the unit of morality are similar in their intentions, but they differ in their details. So the priests of one nation bless their soldiers as they march to war, and the imams of *another* country bless *their* soldiers as they march out to meet them. And everybody who is involved in the killing, says that he has God on his side. There is no objective and universally acceptable definition of good and evil. And until we have one, we will go on justifying our own actions, while condemning the actions of the others.'

'And you're putting the *physics* of the universe up as a kind of platinum-iridium bar?'

'Well, I do think that our definition is closer, in its precision, to the photon-second measure than it is to the platinum-iridium bar, but the point is essentially correct. I think that when we look for an objective way to measure good and evil, a way that all people can accept as reasonable, we can do no better than to study the way that the universe works, and its nature—the quality that defines the entire history of it—the fact that it is constantly moving towards greater complexity. We can do no better than to use the nature of the universe itself. And all the holy texts, from all the great religions, tell us to do this. The Holy Koran, for example, is often telling us, instructing us, to study the planets and the stars to find truth and meaning.'

'I still have to ask the question, why use *this* fact about the tendency toward complexity, and not some other fact? Isn't it still arbitrary? Isn't it still a matter of choice as to which *fact* you choose to use as the basis for your morality? I'm not trying to be obtuse here—I really think it still seems quite arbitrary.'

'I understand your doubt,' Khader smiled, raising his eyes to the sea-sky horizon for a moment. 'I, too, felt very sceptical when I first began along this road. But I am now convinced that there is no better way to think of good and evil, at this time. That is not to say that it will *always* be the best definition. With the measure of the metre, as well, there will be another, slightly better way to measure it, in the future. As a matter of fact, the current best definition uses the distance travelled by a photon of light in a *vacuum*, as if nothing happens in a vacuum. But we know that all sorts of things are happening in a vacuum. There are many, many reactions taking place in a vacuum, all of the time. I am sure that in the future an even better way to measure the metre will be found. But, at the moment, it is the best way that we have. And with morality, the fact of the tendency toward complexity—that the whole universe is doing this all the time, and always has—is the best way we have to be objective about good and evil. We use that fact, rather than any other, because it is the *largest* fact about the universe. It is the one fact that involves the whole universe, throughout the whole of its history. If you can give me a better way to be objective about good and evil, and to involve all the people of all the faiths, and all the non-believers, and the whole history of the whole universe, then I would be very, very happy to hear it.'

'Okay. Okay. So the universe is moving along toward God, or toward some Ultimate Complexity. Anything that helps it along is good. Anything that holds it back is evil. That still leaves me with the problem of who *judges* the evil. How do we *know*? How do we tell whether any one thing we do will get us there or hold us back?'

'A good question,' Khader said, standing and brushing the creases from his loose, linen trousers and his knee-length, white cotton shirt. 'In fact, it is the *right* question. And at the right *time*, I will give you a good answer.'

He turned away from me to face the three fishermen, who'd stood with him and were waiting attentively. For a moment, I teased myself with the conceit that I'd stumped him with my question. But that prideful hope dissolved as I watched him talk with the barefoot fishermen. There was such apodictic certitude in Khader's every pronouncement, such a decisive, incontrovertible assurance in the man, that it informed and composed even his stillnesses and silences. I knew that there *was* an answer to my question. I knew that he *would* give it to me when he judged the time to be right.

Standing near him, I eavesdropped on his conversation. He asked them if they had any complaints, if there was any bullying of the poor men on the dock. When they told him there was none, just at that time, he asked them about the available work, and if the jobs were fairly distributed among those with greatest need. Reassured on that point as well, he asked them about their families and their children. The last of their conversation was about the work on Sassoon Dock's fishing fleet. They told him about the mountainous, stormy waves, the fragile boats, the friends made at sea, and the friends lost at sea. He told them about the one and only time he'd sailed the deep water, during a violent storm, in one of the long, wooden fishing boats. He told them how he'd tied himself to the boat, and how fervently he'd prayed until they'd sighted land. They laughed, and then tried to touch his feet in a respectful goodbye, but he lifted them by the shoulders and shook hands with them, one by one. When he parted from them, they walked away with their backs straight and their heads high.

'How was your work with Khaled?' Khader asked me when we walked back through the dock.

'Very good. I like him. I liked working with him. I'd still be with him if you hadn't put me to work with Madjid.'

'And how is that? How is it, with our Madjid?'

I hesitated. Karla once said that men reveal what they *think* when they look away, and what they *feel* when they hesitate. *With women*, she said, *it's the other way around*.

'I'm learning what I need to know. He's a good teacher.'

'But ... you made a more personal connection with Khaled Ansari, isn't it so?'

It was true. Khaled was angry, and there was a part of his heart that was always hate-filled, but I liked him. Madjid was kind and patient and generous with me, yet I had no feeling for him at all beyond a vague, premonitory unease. After four months in the black-market currency business, Khaderbhai had decided that I should learn the gold-smuggling trade, and he'd sent me to Madjid Rhustem. In his house overlooking the sea, among the affluent elite at Juhu, I'd discovered the many ways in which gold was smuggled into India. Khaled's formula of *greed and control* applied to the trade in gold. Strictly enforced government controls on the import of gold crashed head-on with India's insatiable demand for the yellow metal.

Grey-haired Madjid controlled Khader's substantial gold imports, and had been running the business for almost ten years. With inexhaustible forbearance, he'd taught me everything that he thought I needed to know about gold and the smuggler's arts. His dark eyes had stared at me from beneath his bushy grey brows, hour after hour in the lessons. Although he commanded a large number of strong men, and could be ruthless with them when it was required, his rheumy eyes only ever showed me kindness. Still, I felt nothing for him but that bodeful uneasiness. When I left his house, after any lesson, a sense of relief flooded into me: a relief that washed the sound of his voice and the sight of his face from my mind, just as water might wash a stain from my hands.

'No. There's no connection. But he's a good teacher, as I say.'

'Linbaba,' Khader replied, his deep voice rumbling over the name that the slum-dwellers used, 'I like you.'

My face flushed with emotion. It was as if my own father had said the last three words to me. And my own father never did. The power that those simple words had—the power that Khader had over me—made me realise how neatly and completely he'd come to fill the father's role in my life. In my innermost, secret heart, a small boy that I used to be was wishing that Khader was my father—my real father.

'How's Tariq?' I asked him.

'Tariq is very well, *nushkur Allah*.' *Thanks be to God*.

'I miss him. He's a great kid,' I said. Missing him, I missed my own daughter. I missed my family. I missed my friends.

'He misses you, too,' Khader said slowly, and with what seemed to be regret. 'Tell me, Lin, what do you want? Why are you here? What do you really want here, in Bombay?'

We were approaching his parked car. Nazeer ran ahead on his short, thick legs to open the doors and start the engine. Khader and I stood close together, holding a stare.

'I want to be free,' I said.

'But you *are* free,' he replied.

'Not really.'

'Are you talking about Australia?'

'Yes. Not only that. But mostly that.'

'Don't worry,' he said. 'Nothing will ever harm you in Bombay. I give you my word. No harm will come to you, now, while you wear my name on the medal around your neck and while you work for me. You are safe here, *Inshallah*.'

He held both my hands in his and murmured a blessing, just as he'd done with the owner of the Saurabh. I walked him to his car, watching as he stooped to sit. Someone had daubed the name Sapna on a grubby wall nearby. The paint was reasonably fresh, no more than a week old. If Khader had noticed, he gave no indication of it. Nazeer slammed the door, and ran around to the other side of the car.

'Next week, I want you to start with my friend Ghani on passports,' Khader said. Nazeer revved the engine, awaiting the instruction to leave. 'I think you will find the passport business interesting.'

He was smiling at me as Nazeer drove away, but it was Nazeer's scowl, behind him, that lingered longest in my mind. The man hated me, it seemed, and sooner or later I would have to settle the matter with him. It was a measure of just how lost and lonely I was, in my exile, that I looked forward to fighting him. He was shorter than I was, but every bit as strong, and perhaps a little heavier. I knew it would be a good fight.

I filed that future violence away under pending and impending, hailed a cab, and made my way to the Fort area. The commercial district of printers, stationers, warehouses, and light manufacturers, known simply as the Fort, served the office districts that surrounded it. The buildings and narrow streets of the Fort were some of the oldest in the city. The atmosphere of another age, an age of starched and formal courtesies, remained in those law firms, publishing houses, and other cerebral enterprises that had been fortunate enough to boast a Fort address for several decades.

One of the newer businesses in the Fort was the travel agency owned through proxies by Khaderbhai, and managed by Madjid Rhustem. The agency handled the travel arrangements for thousands of men and women who worked on contracts in the Gulf States. On the legitimate side, the agency organised plane tickets, visas, work permits, and hostel accommodation in the Gulf. On the black-market side, Madjid's agents arranged for most of the returning workers to wear from one to three hundred grams of our gold, per person, in chains, bracelets, rings, and brooches. The gold arrived in the Gulf ports from many sources. Some of it was obtained in legal bulk purchases. Much of it was stolen. Junkies and pickpockets and housebreakers from all over Europe and Africa stole gold jewellery and then sold it to their drug dealers and fences. A percentage of that gold, stolen in Frankfurt or Johannesburg or London, found its way through black marketeers to the Gulf ports. Khader's men in Dubai, Abu Dhabi, Bahrain, and every other Gulf capital melted the gold into thick bracelets and chains and brooches. For a small fee, the contract workers wore the gold jewellery on their return to India, and our men collected it from them at the international airport in Bombay.

Each year, the travel agency in the Fort area handled travel arrangements for at least five thousand contract workers. The gold they carried in was re-worked, when necessary, at a small workshop near the agency and then sold throughout the Zhaveri bazaar, or jewellery market. The profit from that one part of the gold operation was greater than four million American dollars a year, tax free, and Khader's senior managers were all wealthy, well-respected men.

I checked in with the staff at the Transact Travel Agency. Madjid was out, but the three managers were busy. When I'd learned how the gold-smuggling operation worked, I suggested that Khader's agency should computerise its files, and maintain a database on the contract workers who'd successfully completed one mission for us. Khader had approved the suggestion, and the men were busy transferring hard-copy paper files onto the computers. I looked over their work, and was satisfied with their progress. We talked for a while, and when Madjid didn't return I went to look for him at the small gold workshop nearby.

Madjid looked up with a smile when I entered the factory, and then concentrated on the scales once more. Gold chains and bracelets, sorted into various grades, were weighed as individual pieces and weighed again in lots. The amounts were entered into a ledger and crossed-checked against a separate ledger kept for sales in the Zhaveri bazaar.

On that day, not two hours after Khaderbhai had talked to me of good and evil, I watched the heaps of gold chains and heavy home-made bracelets being weighed and catalogued, and I felt myself plunging into a dark mood that I couldn't shake off. I was glad that Khaderbhai had directed me to leave Madjid and to begin work with Abdul Ghani. The golden-yellow metal that excited so many millions, in India, made me uneasy. I'd enjoyed working with Khaled Ansari and his currencies. I knew that I would enjoy working with Abdul Ghani in the passport business: passports were, after all, the main game for a man on the run. But working with gold in such huge quantities was unsettling. Gold fires the eyes with a different kind and colour of greed. Money's almost always just a means to an end; but, for many men, gold is an end in itself, and their love for it is the kind of thing that can give love a bad name.

I left Madjid for the last time, telling him that Khaderbhai had other work for me. I didn't volunteer the information that I was set to begin work with Abdul Ghani in the passport business. Madjid and Ghani were both members of Khader's mafia council. I was sure they knew the substance of every decision affecting me before I knew it myself. We shook hands. He pulled me toward him in a clumsy, stiff-armed attempt at a hug. He smiled, and wished me luck. It was a false smile, but there wasn't any malice in it. Madjid Rhustem was simply the kind of man who thought that smiling was an act of will. I thanked him for his patience, but I didn't return the smile.

When I made my last round of the jewellers at the Zhaveri bazaar, there was a quivering, agitated restlessness in me. It was the random anger that attaches itself to a sense of futility: the wide-eyed, fist-clenching anxiety that flares up often in a wasted life. I should've been happy, or at least happier. I had Khader's assurance of safety. I was making good money. I worked every day with hoards of gold a metre high. I was about to learn everything I needed to know about the passport business. I could buy whatever I wanted. I was fit and healthy and free. I should've been happier.

Happiness is a myth, Karla once said. *It was invented to make us buy things.* And as her words rippled on the stream of my dark feelings, as I remembered her face and her voice, I thought that maybe she was right, after all. Then I recalled those moments, earlier that day, when Khaderbhai had spoken to me as if he was speaking to his son. And there'd been happiness in that; I couldn't deny it. But it wasn't enough: true, and profound, and somehow pure as that feeling had been, it wasn't strong enough to lift my spirits.

My training session with Abdullah that day was intense. He accepted my taciturn mood, and we worked through the strenuous exercise-routine in silence. After a shower, he offered to give me a ride to my apartment on his motorcycle. We cruised along August Kranti Marg on our way inland from the coast at Breach Candy. We had no helmets, and the breeze of hot dry air streaming through our hair and loose silk shirts was a river of wind. Abdullah's attention was suddenly taken by a group of men standing together outside a café. I guessed them to be Iranian, as he was. He wheeled the bike around, and pulled up about thirty metres from them.

'You stay here with the bike,' he said, killing the engine and kicking out the side stand. We both climbed off. He never took his eyes off the group. 'If there is any trouble, you take the bike, and leave.'

He strolled along the footpath toward the men, pulling his long black hair into a ponytail and removing his watch as he walked. I snatched the keys from the ignition of the bike, and set out after him. One of the men saw Abdullah and recognised him just as he approached. He gave a warning of some kind. The other men turned quickly. The fight started without a word. They swung wildly, flailing at him, and crashing into one another in their frenzy to land a punch on him. Abdullah stood his ground, covering his head with his fists held tightly to his temples. His elbows protected his body. When the fury of their initial attack abated, he struck out left and right, connecting with every punch. I ran up and joined him, dragging a man from his back. I tripped the man, forcing him against the straight edge of my leg until he fell. He tried to twist free of my grip, and dragged me down with him. I landed sideways to his body, with my knee on his chest, and punched him in the groin. He started to get up, and I swung round to hit him again, four or five times, on the cheek and the hinge of his jaw. He rolled over onto his side, and curled his knees into his chest.

I looked up to see Abdullah drive off one of his attackers with a text-book right cross that splattered the man's nose in a sudden explosion of blood. I jumped up to put my back against Abdullah's, and shaped up in a karate stance. The three men who remained standing backed off, unsure of themselves. When Abdullah made a charge at them, shouting at the top of his voice, they turned and ran. I looked at Abdullah. He shook his head. We let them go.

The Indian crowd that had gathered to watch the fight followed us with their eyes while we walked back to the bike. I knew that if we'd fought Indians—from any part of India, and any ethnic, religious, or class divide—the whole street would've joined in against us. Since the fight was between foreigners, the people were curious and even excited, but they had no desire to get involved. As we rode past them, heading for Colaba, they began to disperse.

For his part, Abdullah never told me what the fight was about, and I never asked him. The one time we did talk of it, years later, he told me that he began to love me on that day. He loved me, he said, not because I joined the fight, but because I never once asked him what it was about. He admired that, he said, more than anything else he ever knew about me.

In the Colaba Causeway near my home, I asked Abdullah to slow down. I'd noticed a girl who was walking on the road, like a local, to avoid the crowds on the footpath. She looked different, changed somehow, but I recognised the blonde hair, the long, shapely legs, and hip-roll walk instantly. It was Lisa Carter. I told Abdullah to pull up just in front of her.

'Hi, Lisa.'

'Ah,' she sighed, lifting her sunglasses to rest them on the top of her head. 'It's Gilbert. How's things at the embassy?'

'Oh, you know,' I laughed. 'A crisis here, a rescue there. You look great, Lisa.'

Her blonde hair was longer and thicker than when I'd last seen her.

Her face was fuller and healthier, but her figure was trim and more athletic. She was wearing a white halter-neck top, a white mini-skirt, and Roman sandals. Her legs and slender arms were tanned to a golden chestnut. She looked beautiful. She *was* beautiful.

'I stopped being a fuck-up, and took the cure,' she snarled, scowling through a bright, false smile. 'What can I tell ya? It's either one or the other, and you can't have it both ways. When you're sober and fit, it's the *world* that's fucked.'

'That's the spirit,' I replied, laughing until she laughed with me.

'Who's your friend?'

'Abdullah Taheri, this is Lisa Carter. Lisa, this is Abdullah.'

'Nice bike,' she purred.

'Would you like to ... ride it?' he asked, smiling with all of his white, strong teeth.

She looked at me, and I raised my hands in a gesture that said, *You're on your own, kid.* I got off the bike and joined her on the road.

'This is my stop,' I said. Lisa and Abdullah were still staring at one another. 'There's a free seat, if you want it.'

'Okay,' she smiled. 'Let's do it.'

She hitched up her skirt and climbed onto the back of the bike. The two or three men, out of several hundred on the street, who weren't already looking at her, joined in the chorus of stares. Abdullah shook hands with me, grinning like a schoolboy. He kicked the bike into gear, and roared off into the meandering traffic.

'Nice bike,' a voice behind me said. It was Gemini George.

'Not real safe, though, those Enfields,' answered another voice, with a strong Canadian accent. It was Scorpio George.

They lived on the street, sleeping in doorways and foraging for commissions among the tourists who wanted to buy hard drugs. And it showed. They were unshaven, unwashed, and unkempt in appearance. They were also intelligent, honest, and unconditionally loyal to one another.

'Hi, guys. How's it going?'

'Well, son, very well,' Gemini George answered, the song of Liverpool in his accent, 'We've got a client, you know, at about six o'clock tonight.'

'Touch wood,' Scorpio added, his dour frown already focusing on the troubles the evening might bring.

'Should do all right out of it,' Gemini said cheerily. 'Nice client. Nice little earner.'

'If it all goes okay, and nothing goes wrong,' Scorpio mused fretfully.

'Must be something in the water,' I muttered, watching the tiny white speck of Abdullah's shirt, or Lisa's skirt, disappear in the distance.

'How's that?' Gemini asked.

'Oh, nothing. Just, everyone seems to be falling in love lately.'

I was thinking of Prabaker, Vikram, and Johnny Cigar. And I knew the look I'd seen in Abdullah's eyes as he'd ridden off. He was a long way more than interested.

'Funny you should mention that—what do you make of sexual motivation, Lin?' Scorpio asked me.

'Come again?'

'In a manner of speakin',' Gemini innuendoed, winking indecently.

'C'mon, be serious for a minute,' Scorpio scolded. 'Sexual motivation, Lin—what do you make of it?'

'What, exactly, do you mean?'

'Well, we're having a debate, you know —'

'A *discussion*,' Gemini interrupted. 'Not a debate. I'm *discussin'* with you, not *debatin'* you.'

'We're having this *discussion*, about what it is that motivates people.'

'I give you fair warnin', Lin,' Gemini said, sighing mightily. 'We've been having this discussion for two weeks, and Scorpio still won't see reason.'

'As I said, we're having this discussion about what it is that motivates people,' Scorpio George pressed on, his Canadian accent and professorial manner combining in the documentary voice-over style that most irritated his English friend. 'Y'see, Freud said we're motivated by the drive for *sex*. Adler disagreed, and said that it was the drive for *power*. Then Victor Frankl, he said sex and power were important drives, but when you can't get either one—no sex and no power—there's still something else that drives us on and keeps us goin' —'

'Yes, yes, the drive for *meaning*,' Gemini added. 'Which is really just the same thing in different words. We have a drive for power because power gives us sex, and we have a drive for meaning because that helps us to understand sex. It all comes down to sex in the end, no matter what you call it. Those other ideas, they're just the *clothes*, like. And when you get the clothes off, it's all about sex, innit?'

'No, you're wrong,' Scorpio contradicted him. 'We're all driven by a desire to find meaning in life. We have to know what it's all about. If it was just sex or power we'd still be chimpanzees. It's *meaning* that makes us human beings.'

'It's sex that makes human beings, Scorpio,' Gemini put in, his wicked leer working even harder. 'But it's been so long, you've probably forgotten that.'

A taxi pulled up beside us. The passenger in the back seat waited in a band of shadow for a moment, and then slowly leaned closer to the window. It was Ulla.

'Lin,' she gasped, 'I need your help.'

She was wearing black-framed sunglasses, and there was a scarf tied around her head, covering her ash-blonde hair. Her face was pale and drawn and thin.

'This ... has a vaguely familiar ring to it, Ulla,' I replied, not moving toward the cab.

'Please. I mean it. Please, get in. I have something to tell you ... something you want to know.'

I didn't move.

'Please, Lin. I know where Karla is. I will tell you, if you help me.'

I turned and shook hands with the Georges. In the handshake with Scorpio, I passed over an American twenty-dollar bill. I'd taken it from my pocket when I first heard their voices, and I'd kept it ready to hand over when we parted. In their world, I knew, it was enough money—if their *nice little earner* client fell through—to make them rich men for the night.

I opened the door and got into the cab. The driver pulled away into the traffic, checking me out often in his rear vision mirror.

'I don't know why you're angry with me,' Ulla whined, removing her sunglasses and stealing glances at me. 'Please don't be angry, Lin. Please don't be angry.'

I wasn't angry. For the first time in too long, I wasn't angry. *Scorpio's right*, I thought: *it's meaning that makes us human*. There I was, with just the mention of a name, diving into the ocean of feeling again. I was looking for a woman, looking for Karla. I was involving myself in the world, and taking risks. I had a reason. I had a quest.

And then I knew, in the excited moment, what it was that had caused my desolate mood at Madjid's, and put so much anger in me that day. I knew with perfect understanding that the momentary dream—the little boy's wish that Khader really *was* my father—had plunged me into that restless, tide-rip of despair that fathers and sons too often let their love become. And seeing it, realising it, remembering it, I found the strength to lift the darkness from my heart. I looked at Ulla. I stared into the blue labyrinth of her eyes and I wondered, without anger or sorrow, if she'd played a part in betraying me, and having me put in prison.

She reached out to put a hand on my knee. The grip was strong, but her hand was shaking. I felt the scent-filled seconds expand around us. We were trapped, both of us, held fast, each in our different ways. And once again, we were about to set the web of our connection trembling.

'Relax. I'll help you if I can,' I said, calmly and firmly. 'Now, tell me about Karla.'

CHAPTER TWENTY-FOUR

At midnight's horizon the great milky wheel of stars rose wet and shivering from the waves, and the silver yellow light of a gibbous moon settled on the sea, glistening the tinsel-crested swell. It was a warm, still, and perfectly clear night. The deck of the Goa ferry was crowded, but I'd managed to stake out a clear space a little distance apart from a large group of young tourists. They were stoned, most of them, on grass, hash, and acid. Dance music thumped from the black, shouting mouths of a portable hi-fi. Sitting among their backpacks, they swayed and clapped in time, called out to one another over the music, and laughed, often. They were happy, on their way to Goa. The first-time tourists were moving toward a dream. The old hands were returning to the one place in the world where they felt truly free.

Sailing toward Karla, looking out at the stars, listening to the kids who'd bought spaces on the deck of the ferry, I understood their hopeful, innocent excitement, and in a small and distant way I even shared it. But my face was hard. My eyes were hard. And that hardness divided my feelings from theirs as cleanly and inviolably as the metre-wide space on the deck separated me from their tangled, high-spirited party. And as I sat there, on the swaying, gently plunging ferry, I thought about Ulla: I thought about the fear that had glittered in her sapphire-blue eyes when she'd talked to me in the back of the cab.

Ulla needed money that night, a thousand dollars, and I gave it to her. She needed me to accompany her to the hotel room where she'd left her clothes and personal belongings. We went there together and, despite her trembling fear, we collected her things and paid the bill without incident. She was in trouble, through some business deal involving Modena and Maurizio. The deal, like too many of Maurizio's quick scams, had soured. The men who'd lost their money weren't content, as others had been, to accept the loss and let the matter ride. They wanted their money, and they wanted someone to bleed, and not necessarily in that order.

She didn't tell me who they were. She didn't tell me why they considered her a target, or what they planned to do with her if they caught her. I didn't ask. I should've asked her, of course. It would've saved me a lot of trouble. In the long run, it might've saved a life or two. But I wasn't really interested in Ulla. I wanted to know about Karla.

'She's in Goa,' Ulla said, when we'd checked her out of her hotel.

'Where in Goa?'

'I don't know. One of the beaches.'

'There's a lot of beaches in Goa, Ulla.'

'I know, I know,' she whined, flinching at my irritated tone.

'You said you know where she is.'

'I do. She's in Goa. I *know* she's in Goa. She wrote to me, from Mapusa. I got her last letter only yesterday. She's somewhere near Mapusa.'

I relaxed a little. We loaded her belongings into the waiting cab, and I gave the driver directions to Abdullah's apartment in Breach Candy. I checked the streets around us carefully, and was fairly sure that we weren't being watched. When the cab moved off I sat back in silence for a while, watching the dark streets run in the window.

'Why did she leave?'

'I don't know.'

'She must've said something to you. She's a talkative girl.'

Ulla laughed.

'She didn't say to me anything about leaving. If you want to know what I think, I am in the opinion that she left because of you.'

My love for Karla cringed at the thought. My vanity preened itself in the flattery. I smothered the conflict in a harsher tone.

'There *must* be more to it. Was she afraid of something?'

Ulla laughed again.

'Karla's not afraid of anything.'

'Everyone's afraid of something.'

'What are *you* afraid of, Lin?'

I turned, slowly, to stare at her, searching in the faint light for some hint of spite, some hidden meaning or allusion in the question.

'What happened on the night you were supposed to meet me at Leopold's?' I asked her.

'I couldn't make it that night. I was prevented from coming there. Modena, him and Maurizio, they changed their plans at the last minute, and they stopped me.'

'I seem to recall that you wanted *me* there because you didn't *trust* them.'

'That's true. Well, I trust Modena, you know, kind of, but he is not strong against Maurizio. He can't stay in his own mind, when Maurizio tells him what to do.'

'That still doesn't explain it,' I grumbled.

'I know,' she sighed, clearly upset. 'I'm trying to explain it. Maurizio, he had a deal planned—well, actually, he had a rip-off planned—and I was the one in the middle. Maurizio was using me because the men he was planning to steal money from, they liked me, and they kind of trusted me, you know how it is.'

'Yeah, I know how it is.'

'Oh, please, Lin, it wasn't my fault that I wasn't there that night. They wanted me to meet the customers, alone. I was afraid of those men, because I knew what Maurizio was planning to do, and that's why I asked you to be with me, as my friend. Then, they changed their plans and we had the meeting all together, in another place, and I couldn't get away to let you know about it. I tried to find you the next day, to explain to you and make an apology, but ... you were gone. I looked everywhere, I promise you I did. I was very sorry that I didn't go there to meet you at Leopold's, like I promised you that night.'

'When did you find out that I was in jail?'

'After you got out. I saw Didier, and he told me that you looked terrible. That was the first thing that I ... just a moment ... do you ... do you think *I* had something to do with you going in the prison? Is *that* what you think?'

I held the stare for a few seconds before replying.

'*Did* you?'

'Oh, fuck! Oh, God!' she moaned, creasing her lovely face in miserable distress. She rocked her head from side to side swiftly, as if trying to prevent a thought or feeling from taking root. 'Stop the car! Driver! *Band karo! Abi, abi! Band karo!'* Now, now! Stop!

The cab driver pulled over to the pavement beside a row of shuttered shops. The street was deserted. He switched off the cab, and watched us in his rear-vision mirror.

Ulla tried to wrestle open the door. She was crying. In her agitation, she jammed the door handle, and the door wouldn't open.

'Take it easy,' I said, prizing her hands gently from the handle and holding them in my own. 'It's okay. Take it easy.'

'Nothing's okay,' she sobbed. 'I don't know how we got in this mess. Modena, he's not good at business. They messed everything up, him and Maurizio. They were cheating a lot of people, you know, and they just were always getting away with it. But not with these guys. They're different. I'm so scared. I don't know what to do. They're going to kill us. All of us. And you think *I* put the police on you? For what reason, Lin? Do you think I am such a person? Am I so bad that you can think such a thing about me? What do you think I am?'

I reached across to open the door. She stepped out, and leaned against the side of the car. I got out and joined her. She was trembling and sobbing. I held her in my arms until she cried it out.

'It's okay, Ulla. I don't think you had anything to do with it. I didn't ever think you did—not really—not even when you weren't there, at Leopold's that night. Asking you … it was just a way of closing a door on it. It's just something I had to ask. Do you understand?'

She looked up into my face. Streetlights arced in her large, blue eyes. Her mouth was slack with exhaustion and fear, but her eyes were drawn to a distant, ineradicable hope.

'You really love her, don't you?'

'Yes.'

'That's good,' she said dreamily, wistfully, looking away. 'Love is a good thing. And Karla—she needs love, very much. Modena loves me too, you know. He really and truly loves me …'

She drifted in that reverie for a few moments and then snapped her head back to stare at me. Her hands gripped my arms as I held her.

'You'll find her. Start at Mapusa, and you'll find her. She will stay in Goa for some little time yet. She told me so, in her letter. She is somewhere exactly on the beach. In her letter she told me she can see the ocean from her front door. Go there, Lin, and find her. Look for her, and find her. There is only love, you know, in the whole world. There is only love …'

And they remained with me, Ulla's tears, swarming with light, until they dissolved in the glittering, moonlit sea off the ferry. And her words, *there is only love*, passed like prayer-bead wishes on a thread of possibility as the music and laughter crashed around me.

When the light on that long night became the dawn, and the ferry docked at the Goan capital of Panjim, I was the first to board a bus to Mapusa. The fifteen-kilometre journey from Panjim to Mapusa, pronounced as *Muppsa*, wound through lush, leafy groves, past mansions built to the styles and tastes of four hundred years of Portuguese colonial rule. Mapusa was a transportation and communication centre for the northern region of Goa. I arrived on a Friday, market day, and the morning crowds were already busy with business and bargains. I made my way to the taxi and motorcycle stands. After a bout of bartering that invoked an august assembly of deities from at least three religions, and incorporated spirited, carnal references to the sisters of our respective friends and acquantainces, a dealer agreed to hire out an Enfield Bullet motorcycle for a reasonable rental. I paid a bond and a week's rent in advance, kick-started the bike, and set off through the market's maul toward the beaches.

The Enfield of India 350cc Bullet was a single-cylinder, four-stroke motorcycle, constructed to the plans of the original 1950s' model of the British Royal Enfield. Renowned for its idiosyncratic handling as much as for its reliability and durability, the Bullet was a bike that demanded a relationship with its rider. That relationship involved tolerance, patience, and understanding on the part of the rider. In exchange, the Bullet provided the kind of soaring, celestial, wind-weaving pleasure that birds must know, punctuated by not infrequent near-death experiences.

I spent the day cruising the beaches, from Calangute to Chapora. I checked every hotel and guesthouse, sprinkling the arid ground with a shower of small but tempting bribes. I found local moneychangers, drug dealers, tour guides, thieves, and gigolos at each of the beaches. Most of them had seen foreign girls who answered her description, but none could be sure that he'd seen Karla. I stopped for tea or juice or a snack at the main beach restaurants, asking waiters and managers. They were all helpful, or tried to be helpful, because I spoke to them in Marathi and Hindi. None of them had seen her, however, and when the few leads I did get came to nothing, the first day of my search ended in disappointment.

The owner of the Seashore Restaurant in Anjuna, a heavy-set young Maharashtrian named Dashrant, was the last local I spoke to, as the sun began to set. He prepared a hearty meal of cabbage leaves stuffed with potatoes, green beans with ginger, aubergines with sour green chutney, and crisp-fried okra. When the meal was ready, he brought his own plate to my table, and sat with me to eat it. He insisted that we finish the meal with a long glass of the locally brewed coconut feni, and followed that with an equally long glass of cashew feni. Refusing to accept payment for the meal from a gora who spoke his native Marathi, Dashrant locked the restaurant and left with me, as my guide, on the back of my motorcycle. He saw my quest to find Karla as very romantic—very Indian, he said— and he wanted me to stay nearby, as his guest.

'There are a few pretty foreign girls in the area,' he told me. 'One of them, if the Bhagwan wills it, might be your lost love. You sleep first, and search tomorrow—with a clean mind, isn't it?'

Paddling, with our legs outstretched from the bike, along a soft, sandy avenue between tall palms, I followed his directions to a small house. The square structure was made from bamboo, coconut poles, and palm leaves. It stood within sight of his restaurant, and with a wide view of the dark sea. I entered to find a single room, which he lit with candles and lamps. The floor was sand. There was a table and two chairs, a bed with a bare rubber mattress, and a metal rack for hanging clothes. A large matka was filled with clean water. He announced, with pride, that the water had been drawn that day from a local well. There was a bottle of coconut feni on the table, with two glasses. Assuring me that the bike and I would be safe there, because it was known by all in the area to be his house, Dashrant handed me the key to the door's chain and padlock, and told me to stay until I found my girl. Winking a smile at me, he left. I heard him singing as he walked back between the slender palms to his restaurant.

I pulled the bike in against the hut, and tied a length of cord from it to the leg of the bed, covering it with sand. I hoped that if someone tried to steal the bike, the movement would wake me. Exhausted and disappointed, I fell onto the bed and was asleep in seconds. It was a nourishing, dreamless sleep, but I woke after four hours, and I was too alert, too restless, to find sleep again. I pulled my boots on, took a can of water, and visited the toilet at the back of the hut. Like many toilets in Goa, it was nothing more than a smooth, steep slope behind the squatting keyhole. Waste matter rolled down the slope to a narrow lane. Wild, hairy, black

Goan pigs roamed the lanes, eating the waste. As I walked back to the house to wash my hands, I saw a herd of the black swine trotting along the lane. It was an efficient and environmentally benign method of waste disposal, but the sight of those pigs, feasting, was an eloquent argument in favor of vegetarianism.

I walked down to the beach, only fifty paces from Dashrant's hut, and sat on the dunes to smoke a cigarette. It was close to midnight, and the beach was deserted. The moon, almost full, was pinned like a medal to the chest of the sky. *A medal for what?* I thought. *Wounded in action, maybe. A Purple Heart.* Moonlight rushed with every rolling wave to the shore, as if the light itself was pulling the waves, as if the great net of silver light cast by the moon had gathered up the whole of the sea, and was hauling it to the shore, wave by wave.

A woman approached me, carrying a basket on her head. Her hips rolled and swayed in time to the running wavelets that lapped at her feet. She turned from the sea toward me and dropped the basket at my feet, squatting to look into my eyes. She was a watermelon seller, about thirty-five years old, and clearly familiar with tourists and their ways. Chewing forcefully on a mouthful of betel nut, she gestured with an open palm toward the half watermelon that remained in her large basket. It was very late for her to be on the beach. I guessed that she'd been baby-sitting, or nursing a relative, and was returning home. When she saw me sitting alone, she'd hoped for one lucky-last sale for the night.

I told her, in Marathi, that I would be glad to buy a slice of melon. She reacted with happy surprise and, when the routine questions about where and how I'd learned Marathi were resolved, she cut me a generous slice. I ate the delicious sweet *kalinga*, spitting the seeds onto the sand. She watched me eat, and tried to resist when I forced a note rather than a coin into her basket. As she rose, lifting the basket to her head, I began to sing an old, sad, and much-loved song from a Hindi movie.

Ye doonia, ye mehfil
Mere kam, ki nahi ...

All the world, all its people
Mean nothing to me ...

She yelped in appreciation, and danced a few slick moves before walking away slowly along the beach.

'This is why I like you, you know,' Karla said, sitting down beside me in one quick, graceful movement. The sound of her voice and the sight of her face pulled all the air from my lungs, and set my heart thumping. So much had happened since the last time I'd seen her, the first time we'd made love, that a fevered squall of emotion stung my eyes. If I'd been a different man, a better man, I would've cried. And who knows, it might've made the difference.

'I thought you didn't believe in love,' I answered, straining against my feelings, and determined not to let her know the effect that she had on me, the power she had over me.

'What do you mean, *love?*'

'I ... I thought that's what you were talking about.'

'No, I said that's why I *like* you,' she said, laughing and looking up at the moon. 'But I do believe in love. Everyone believes in love.'

'I'm not so sure. I think a lot of people have stopped believing in love.'

'People haven't stopped believing in love. They haven't stopped wanting to be in love. They just don't believe in a happy ending anymore. They still believe in love, and falling in love, but they know now that ... they know that romances almost never end as well as they begin.'

'I thought you hated love. Isn't that what you said, at the Village in the Sky?'

'I do hate love, just like I hate *hate*. But that doesn't mean I don't believe in them.'

'There's no-one in the world like you, Karla,' I said softly, smiling at her profile as she stared at the night and the sea. She didn't reply. 'So ... why do you?'

'Why do I what?'

'Why do you like me—you know, what you said before.'

'Oh, that,' she smiled, facing me, and raising one eyebrow as her eyes met mine. 'Because I knew you'd find me. I knew I didn't have to send you any message, or let you know where I was. I knew you'd find me. I knew you'd come. I don't know how I knew, but I just knew. And then, when I saw you singing to that woman on the beach—you're a very crazy guy, Lin. I love that. I think that's where your goodness comes from —your craziness.'

'My *goodness*?' I asked, genuinely surprised.

'Yes. There's a lot of goodness in you, Lin. It's very ... it's a very hard thing to resist, real goodness, in a tough man. I didn't tell you, did I, when we worked together, in the slum—I was so proud of you. I knew you must've been scared, and very worried, but you only smiled for me, and you were always there, every time I woke up, every time I went to sleep. I admire what you did there, as much as anything I've ever seen in my life. And I don't admire much.'

'What are you doing here in Goa, Karla? Why did you leave?'

'It would make more sense to ask why *you* stay *there*.'

'I've got my reasons.'

'Exactly. And I had my reasons for leaving.'

She turned her head to watch a lone, distant figure on the beach. It seemed to be a wandering holy man, carrying a long staff. I watched her watching the holy man, and I wanted to ask her again, to find out what had driven her from Bombay, but the set of her features was so tense that I decided to wait.

'How much do you know about my stint at Arthur Road?' I asked.

She flinched, or perhaps it was a shiver in response to the breeze from the sea. She was wearing a loose, yellow singlet top, and a green lungi. Her bare feet were buried in the sand, and she hugged her knees.

'What do you mean?'

'I mean, the cops picked me up the night I left your place to meet Ulla. They got me, right after I left you. What did you think happened to me when I didn't come back?'

'I didn't know, that night. I couldn't guess.'

'Did you think I ... did you think I just ditched you?'

She paused, frowning pensively.

'At first, I did think that. Something like that. And I think I hated you. Then I started asking around. When I found out you didn't even come back to the slum clinic, and that nobody saw you, I thought you must've been ... doing something ... important.'

'Important,' I laughed. It wasn't a good laugh. It was bitter, and angry. I tried to push those feelings away. 'I'm sorry, Karla. I couldn't get a message out. I couldn't let you know. I was out of my mind with worry that you ... that ... you'd hate me, for leaving you like that.'

'When I heard about it—that you were in the jail—it kind of broke my heart. It was a very bad time for me. This ... business, I was doing ... it was starting to go wrong. It was so wrong, so bad, Lin, that I think I'll never come back from it. And then, I heard about you. And I was so ... well ... everything changed, just like that. Everything.'

I couldn't understand what she'd said. I was sure it was important, and I wanted to ask her more, but the lone figure was only a few metres away, and he approached us with slow, dignified steps. The moment was lost.

He was indeed a holy man. Tall, lean, and tanned to a dark, earth-brown, he wore a loincloth and was adorned with dozens of necklaces, amulets, and decorative bracelets. His hair was matted in dreadlocks that reached to his waist. Balancing the long staff against his shoulder, he clasped his hands together in a greeting and a blessing. We greeted him in turn, and invited him to sit with us.

'Do you have any charras?' he asked, in Hindi. 'I would like to smoke on this beautiful night.'

I fished a lump of charras from my pocket, and tossed it to him, with a filter cigarette.

'The Bhagwan's blessing be upon your kindness,' he intoned.

'And a blessing of the Bhagwan upon you also,' Karla replied in perfect Hindi. 'We are very happy to see a devotee of the Lord Shiva at this full moon.'

He grinned, showing gaps in his teeth, and set to preparing a chillum. When the clay pipe was ready, he raised his palms to gain our attention.

'Now, before we smoke, I want to give you a gift in return,' he said. 'Do you understand?'

'Yes, we understand,' I said, smiling to match the light in his eyes.

'Good. I give you both a blessing. My blessing will always stay with you. I give you this blessing in this way ...'

He raised his arms above his head, and then bent over on his knees, touching his forehead to the sand, with his arms outstretched. Kneeling upright again and raising his hands, he repeated the gesture several times while mumbling indistinct words.

Eventually, he sat back on his feet, smiled the gap-toothed smile at us, and nodded for me to light the pipe. We smoked in silence. When the pipe was finished, I refused to accept the return of the lump of charras. Acknowledging the gift with a solemn bow of his head, the holy man stood to leave. As we looked up at him, he slowly raised his staff to point it at the almost full moon. At once, we saw and understood what he meant—the pattern on the surface of the moon, that in some cultures is called the *rabbit*, suddenly looked to both of us like a kneeling figure raising his arms in prayer. Chuckling happily, the sadhu walked away along the gentle dunes.

'I love you, Karla,' I said when we were alone again. 'I loved you the first second I saw you. I think I've loved you for as long as there's been love in the world. I love your voice. I love your face. I love your hands. I love everything you do, and I love the way you do everything. It feels like magic when you touch me. I love the way your mind works, and the things you say. And even though it's all true, all that, I don't really understand it, and I can't explain it—to you or to myself. I just love you. I just love you with all my heart. You do what God should do: you give me a reason to live. You give me a reason to love the world.'

She kissed me, and our bodies settled together on the yielding sand. She clasped her hands in mine, and with our arms outstretched above our heads we made love while the praying moon seduced the sea, luring the waves to crash and crumble on the charmed, unfailing shore.

And for a week, then, we played at being tourists in Goa. We visited all the beaches on the coast of the Arabian Sea, from Chapora to Cape Rama. We slept for two nights on the white gold wonder of Colva Beach. We inspected all the churches in the Old Goa settlement. The Festival of St. Francis Xavier, held on the anniversary of the saint's death, every year, bound us in immense crowds of happy, hysterical pilgrims. The streets were thronged with people in their Sunday-best clothes. Merchants and street-stall operators came from all over the territory. Processions of the blind, the lame, and the afflicted, hoping for a miracle, rambled toward the basilica of the saint. Xavier, a Spanish monk, was one of the seven original Jesuits in the order founded by his friend Ignatius Loyola. Xavier died in 1552. He was just forty-six years old, but his spectacular proselytising missions to India, and what was then called the Far East, established his enduring legend. After numerous burials and disinterments, the much-exhumed body of St. Francis was finally installed in the Basilica of Bom Jesus, in Goa, in the early seventeenth century. Still remarkably—some would say miraculously—well preserved, the body was exposed to public view once in every ten years. While seemingly immune to decay, the saint's body had suffered various amputations and subtractions over the centuries. A Portuguese woman had bitten off one of the saint's toes, in the sixteenth century, in the hope of keeping it as a relic. Parts of the right hand had been sent to religious centres, as had chunks of the holy intestines. Karla and I offered outrageously extravagant bribes to the caretakers of the basilica, laughing all the while, but they steadfastly refused to allow us a peek at the venerable corpse.

'Why did you do the robberies?' she asked me on one of those warm nights of satin sky and rolling, mellisonant surf.

'I told you. My marriage broke up, and I lost my daughter. I cracked up, and got into drugs. Then I did the robberies to feed my heroin habit.'

'No, I mean why *robberies*? Why not something else?'

It was a good question, and one that no-one in the justice system — cops, lawyers, judge, psychiatrist, or prison governors — had ever asked me.

'I've thought about it. I've thought about it a lot. It sounds weird, I know, but I think TV had a lot to do with it. Every hero on TV had a gun. And there was something ... *brave* ... about armed robbery. I know there really isn't anything brave about it — it's a gutless thing to do, scaring people with a gun — but it seemed the bravest way to steal money, then. I couldn't bring myself to hit old ladies over the head and steal their handbags, or break into people's private houses. Robbery seemed *fair*, somehow, as if I took a fair chance, every time I did it, of being shot dead — by the people I robbed, or by the cops.'

She watched me in silence, almost matching her breathing to mine.

'And something else — there's this one special hero in Australia ...'

'Go on,' she urged.

'His name was Ned Kelly. He was a young guy who found himself on the wrong side of the local lawmen. He was tough, but he wasn't really a *hard* man. He was young and wild. He was set up, mostly, by cops who had a grudge against him. A drunken cop had a crush on his sister, and tried to molest her. Ned stopped it, and that's when his trouble started. But there was more to it than that. They hated him for a lot of reasons — mostly for what he represented, which was a kind of spirit of rebellion. And I related to him, because I was a revolutionary.'

'They have revolutions, in Australia?' she asked, with a puzzled laugh. 'I never heard this.'

'Not revolutions,' I corrected her, 'just revolutionaries. I was one of them. I was an anarchist. I learned how to shoot, and how to make bombs. We were ready to fight, when the revolution came—which it didn't, of course. And we were trying to stop our government from fighting the Vietnam War.'

'Australia was in the Vietnam War?'

It was my turn to laugh.

'Yeah. Most people outside Australia don't know it, but we were in the war, all the way with the USA. Australian soldiers died beside American soldiers in Vietnam, and Australian boys were drafted to fight. Some of us refused to go, just like the American draft resisters. A lot of guys went to jail because they wouldn't fight. I didn't go to jail. I made bombs, and organised marches, and fought the cops at the barricades, until the government changed and they pulled us out of the war.'

'Are you still one?'

'Still one what?'

'Are you still an anarchist?'

It was a hard question to answer, because it forced me to compare the man I'd once been with the man I'd allowed myself to become.

'Anarchists ...' I began and then faltered. 'No political philosophy I ever heard of loves the human race as much as anarchism. Every other way of looking at the world says that people have to be controlled, and ordered around, and governed. Only the anarchists trust human beings enough to let them work it out for themselves. And I used to be that optimistic once. I used to believe and think like that. But I don't, any more. So, no—I guess I'm not an anarchist now.'

'And that hero—when you did the armed robberies, you identified with him?'

'With Kelly, Ned Kelly, yeah. I think I did. He had a gang of young guys —his younger brother, and his two best friends—and they did these hold-ups, robbing people. The cops sent a hit squad after him, but he beat them, and a couple of cops got killed.'

'What happened to him?'

'They caught him. There was a shoot-out. The government declared war on him. They sent a trainload of cops after him, and they surrounded his gang, at a hotel in the bush.'

'A hotel, in a *bush*?'

'*The* bush—it's what we call the countryside, in Australia. Anyway,

Ned and his guys were surrounded by this army of cops. His best friend was shot in the throat, and killed. His kid brother, and another kid named Steve Hart, shot each other with their last bullets rather than let themselves be captured. They were nineteen years old. Ned had this armour made from steel—a helmet and a chest plate. He came at them, the army of cops, with both guns blazing. He frightened the shit out of them, at first, and they ran away. But their officers drove them back to the fight. They shot Ned's legs out from under him. After a phoney trial, with false statements from witnesses, Ned Kelly was sentenced to death.'

'Did they do it?'

'Yeah. His last words were, *Such is life*. That was the last thing he said. They hanged him, and then cut off his head, and used it as a paperweight. Before he died, he told the judge who'd sentenced him that they'd meet, very soon, in a higher court. The judge died not long after.'

She was watching the story in my face as I told it. I reached out for a handful of sand, and let it run through my fingers. Two large bats passed over our heads. They were close enough for us to hear the dry-leaf rustle of their wings.

'I loved the Ned Kelly story when I was a kid. I wasn't the only one. Artists and writers and musicians and actors have all worked on the story, in one way or another. He put himself inside us, in the Australian psyche. He's the nearest thing we've got to Che Guevara, or Emiliano Zapata. When my brain got scrambled on heroin, I think I started to drown in a fantasy of his life and mine. But it was a messed-up version of the story. He was a thief who became a revolutionary. I was a revolutionary who became a thief. Every time I did a robbery—and I did a lot of them—I was sure the cops would be there, and I'd be killed. I was *hoping* it would happen. I played it out in my mind. I could see them calling me to stop, and I'd reach for a gun, and they'd shoot me dead. I was hoping the cops would shoot me down in the street. I wanted to die that way ...'

She reached out to put an arm around my shoulders. With her free hand, she held my chin, and turned my head to face her smile.

'What are the women like, in Australia?' she asked, running her hand through my short, blonde hair.

I laughed, and she punched me in the ribs.

'I mean it! Tell me what they're like.'

'Well, they're beautiful,' I said, looking at *her* beautiful face. 'There's a lot of beautiful women in Australia. And they like to talk, and they like to party—they're pretty wild. And they're very direct. They hate bullshit. There's nothing like an Australian woman for taking the piss out of you.'

'Taking your *piss*?'

'Taking *the* piss,' I laughed. 'Letting the air out of your chest, you know, ridiculing you, stopping you from getting too many big ideas about yourself. They're great at it. And if they stick a pin in you, to let a bit of hot air out, you can be pretty certain you had it coming.'

She lay back on the sand, with her hands clasped behind her head.

'I think Australians are very crazy,' she said. 'And I would like very much to go there.'

And it should've been as happy, it should've been as easy, it should've been as good for ever as it was in those Goan days and nights of love. We should've built a life from the stars and the sea and the sand. And I should've listened to her—she told me almost nothing, but she did give me clues, and I know now that she put signs in her words and expressions that were as clear as the constellations over our heads. But I didn't listen. It's a fact of being in love that we often pay no attention whatsoever to the substance of what a lover says, while being intoxicated to ecstasy by the way it's said. I was in love with her eyes, but I didn't read them. I loved her voice, but I didn't really hear the fear and the anguish in it.

And when the last night came, and went, and I woke at dawn to prepare for the trip back to Bombay, I found her standing at the doorway, staring at the great shimmering pearl of the sea.

'Don't go back,' she said as I put my hands on her shoulders and kissed her neck.

'What?' I laughed.

'Don't go back to Bombay.'

'Why not?'

'I don't want you to.'

'What's *that* supposed to mean?'

'Just what I said—I don't want you to go.'

I laughed, because I thought it had to be a joke.

'Okay,' I said, smiling and waiting for the punch line. 'So, *why* don't you want me to go?'

'Do I have to have a reason?' she demanded.

'Well … *yeah*.'

'It just so happens, I *do* have reasons. But I'm not going to tell you.'

'You're not?'

'No. I don't think I should have to. If I tell you I've got reasons, it should be enough—if you love me, like you say you do.'

Her manner was so vehement, and the stand she was taking so inflexible and unexpected, that I was too surprised to be angry.

'Okay, okay,' I said reasonably, 'let's try this again. I have to go back to Bombay. So, why don't *you* come *with* me, and then we'll be together, for ever and ever, amen.'

'I won't go back,' she said flatly.

'Why the hell not?'

'I can't ... I just don't *want* to, and I don't want *you* to, either.'

'Well, I don't see the problem. I can do what I have to do in Bombay, and you can wait here. I'll come back when it's all done.'

'I don't want you to go,' she repeated in that same monotone.

'Come on, Karla. I have to go back.'

'No, you don't.'

My smile curled into a frown.

'Yes, I do. I promised Ulla I'd be back in ten days. She's still in trouble. You know that.'

'Ulla can look after herself,' she hissed, still refusing to turn and look at me.

'Are you jealous of Ulla?' I asked, grinning, as I reached out to stroke her hair.

'Oh, don't be stupid!' she snapped. She turned, and there was fury in her eyes. 'I like Ulla, but I'm telling you she can take care of herself.'

'Take it easy. What's the matter? You knew I was going back. We've talked about this. I'm getting into the passport business. You know how important that is for me.'

'I'll *get* you a passport. I'll get you *five* passports!'

My stubbornness began to rouse itself.

'I don't want *you* to get me a passport. I want to learn how to make them and change them myself. I want to learn it all—everything I can. They're going to teach me how to fix passports, and forge them. If I learn that, I'll be free. And I want to be free, Karla. *Free.* That's what I want.'

'Why should *you* be any different?' she demanded.

'What do you mean?'

'Nobody gets what they want,' she said, 'Nobody does. Nobody.'

Her fury dimmed into something worse, something I'd never seen in her: a resigned and defeated sorrow. I knew it was a sin to put such a feeling in such a woman, in any woman. And I knew, watching her little smile fade and die, that sooner or later I would pay for it.

I spoke to her softly, slowly, trying to win her agreement.

'I sent Ulla to my friend Abdullah's. He's looking after her. I can't just leave her there. I have to go back.'

'I won't be here, when you look for me next time,' she said, turning to lean against the doorway once more.

'What's that supposed to mean?'

'Just what I said.'

'Is that some kind of threat? Is that an ultimatum?'

'You can call it what you like,' she answered dully, as if waking from a dream. 'It's just a fact. If you go back to Bombay, I'll give up on you. I won't go with you, and I won't wait for you. Stay with me now, here, or go back alone. The choice is yours. But if you go back, it will finish us.'

I stared at her, bewildered and angry and in love.

'You have to give me more than that,' I said, more softly. 'You've gotta tell me why. You've gotta talk to me, Karla. You can't just give me an ultimatum, without any reason, and expect me to go along with it. There's a difference between a choice and an ultimatum: a choice means that you know what's going on, and why, before you decide. I'm not the kind of man you can give an ultimatum to. If I was, I wouldn't have escaped from jail. You can't *tell* me what to do, Karla. You can't *order* me to do something, without an explanation. I'm not that kind of man. You've gotta tell me what's going on.'

'I can't.'

I sighed, and spoke evenly, but my teeth were clenched.

'I don't think I'm ... doing a very good job ... of explaining this. The fact is, there isn't a lot that I respect about myself. But the little bit that I've still got left—it's *all* I've got. A man has to respect himself, Karla, before he can respect anyone else. If I just give in, and do whatever you want me to do, without any kind of reason, I wouldn't respect myself. And if you tell the truth, *you* wouldn't respect me, either. So, I'm asking you again. What's this all about?'

'I ... can't.'

'You mean, you *won't*.'

'I mean, I can't,' she said softly, and then she looked straight into my eyes. 'And I won't. That's just how it is. You told me, just a little while ago, that you would do anything for me. I want you to stay here. I don't want you to go back to Bombay. If you *do* go back, it's all over between us.'

'What kind of man would I be,' I asked, trying to smile, 'if I went along with that?'

'I guess that's your answer, and you've made your choice,' she sighed, pushing past me to walk out of the hut.

I packed my bag and strapped it to the bike. When all was ready, I went down to the sea. She rose from the waves and walked toward me slowly, dragging her feet through the shifting sand. The singlet and lungi clung to her body. Her black hair gleamed sleek and wet under the soaring sun. The most beautiful woman I'd ever seen.

'I love you,' I said, as she came into my arms and we kissed. I spoke the words against her lips, her face, her eyes. I held her close to me. 'I love you. It'll be okay. You'll see. I'll be back soon.'

'No,' she answered woodenly, her body not stiff, but utterly still, the life and the love drained out of it. 'It won't be all right. It won't be okay. It's over. And I won't be here, after today.'

I looked into her eyes, and felt my own body harden, hollowed out by pride. My hands fell from her shoulders. I turned, and walked back to the bike. Riding to the last little cliff that gave a view of the beach, our beach, I stopped the bike and shielded my eyes to look for her. But she was gone. There was nothing but the waves breaking like the curved spines of playful porpoises, and the traceless, empty, tousled sheets of sand.

CHAPTER TWENTY-FIVE

A SMILING SERVANT opened the door and ushered me into the room, gesturing for me to be silent. He needn't have bothered. The music was so loud in the room that I couldn't have been heard, even if I'd shouted. Cupping his hand as if it were a saucer, and pretending to sip from it, he mimed an offer of chai. I nodded. He closed the door behind him quietly, leaving me alone with Abdul Ghani. The portly figure stood in the broad curve of a high bay window, looking out at a wide view of roof-garden plateaus, balconies ablaze with green and yellow saris hung out to dry, and rust-red herringbone rooftops.

The room was huge. Ornate ceiling rosettes surrounded thick, gold suspension chains for three elaborate chandeliers on the distant ceiling. At the end of the room near the main door, there was a long dining table with twelve high-backed teak chairs. A mahogany armoire ran the length of the table against one wall, and was topped by an immense, rose-glass mirror. Beside the armoire, there was a floor-to-ceiling bookcase running the further length of the wall. On the opposite long wall of the room, four tall windows looked upon the uppermost branches and cool, shading leaves of plane trees lining the street below. The centre of the room, between the wall of books and the tall windows, was set up as an office. A teak-and-leather captain's chair, facing the main door, served a broad, baroque desk. The far end of the room was decorated for entertaining, with leather chesterfields and deep armchairs. Two enormous bay windows in the end wall, behind the couches, dominated the room with arches of brilliant sunlight. French doors set into the two bay windows opened onto a wide balcony, giving the view of Colaba's inner-city rooftop gardens, clotheslines, and neglected gargoyles.

Abdul Ghani stood there, listening to the music and singing that thundered from an expensive sound system built into the wall of books. The voices and the music were familiar, and a few moments of concentration brought them back to me. They were the Blind Singers, the same men I'd heard as Khaderbhai's guest, on the first night that I met him. The song wasn't one I recalled from that concert, but I was struck, at once, by its passion and power. As the thrilling, heart-wrenching chorus of voices finished, we stood in a throbbing silence that seemed to resist the noises of the households within the building and of the street below us.

'Do you know them?' he asked, without turning around.

'Yes. They're the Blind Singers, I think.'

'Indeed, they are,' he said in the mix of Indian lilt and BBC newsreader's tone that I'd come to enjoy. 'I love their music, Lin, more than anything I have ever heard, from any culture. But in the heart of my love for it, I have to say that I am afraid. Every time I hear them—and I play them every day, when I am at home here—I have the feeling that I am hearing the sound of my own requiem.'

He still hadn't turned to face me, and I remained standing near the centre of the long room.

'That ... that must be unsettling.'

'Unsettling ...' he said softly. 'Yes. Yes, it is unsettling. Tell me, Lin, do you think that one great act of genius can allow us to forgive the hundred flaws and failures that bring it into being?'

'It's ... hard to say. I'm not exactly sure what you mean, but I guess it depends on how many people benefit by it, and how many people get hurt.'

He turned to face me, and I saw that he was crying. Tears rolled quickly, easily, and continuously from his large eyes, and spilled across the plump cheeks to the belly of his long silk shirt. His voice, however, was calm and composed.

'Did you know that our Madjid was killed last night?'

'No,' I frowned, shocked by the news. 'Killed?'

'Yes. Murdered. Slaughtered like some beast, in his own house. His body was torn to pieces, and the pieces were found in many different rooms of the house. The name Sapna was daubed on the walls with his own blood. Police are blaming fanatics who follow this Sapna. I'm sorry, Lin. Forgive my tears, please. I'm afraid that this bad business has taken its toll on me.'

'No, not at all. I'll … I'll come back at another time.'

'Of course not. You're here now, and Khader is anxious for you to begin. We'll drink tea, and I will pull myself together, and then we'll examine the passport business, you and I.'

He walked to the hi-fi set, and extracted the cassette tape of the Blind Singers. Sliding it into a gold plastic case, he approached me and pressed it into my hand.

'I want you to have this, as a present from me,' he said, his eyes and cheeks still wet with tears. 'It's time I stopped listening to it, and I feel sure that you will enjoy it.'

'Thank you,' I muttered, almost as confused by the gift as I was by the news of Madjid's death.

'Not at all, Lin. Come, sit with me. You were in Goa, I believe? Do you know our young fighter, Andrew Ferreira? Yes? Then you know he is from Goa. He goes there, often, with Salman and Sanjay, when I have work for them. You must all go there together, some time—they will show you the *special* sights, if you get my meaning. So tell me, how was your trip?'

I answered him, trying to give my whole attention to the conversation, but my mind was thick with thoughts of Madjid; dead Madjid. I couldn't say that I'd liked him, or even that I'd trusted him. Yet his death, his murder, shook me, and filled me with a strange, excited agitation. He'd been killed—*slaughtered*, Abdul had said—in the house at Juhu where we'd studied together, and he'd taught me about gold and golden crimes. I thought of the house. I remembered its view of the sea, its purple-tiled swimming pool, its bare, pale-green prayer room where Madjid had bent his ancient knees, five times every day, and touched his bushy grey eyebrows to the floor. I remembered sitting outside that room, near the pool, waiting for him as he took time out to pray. I remembered staring at the purple water as the murmured syllables of the prayers buzzed past me into the swaying fronds of palms leaning in around the pool.

And once again I had the sense of a trap, of a destiny not shaped by my own deeds and desires. It was as if the constellations themselves were just the outlines of an immense cage that revolved and realigned itself, inscrutably, until the single moment that fate had reserved for me. There was too much that I didn't understand. There was too much that I wouldn't allow myself to ask. And I was excited, in that web of connections and concealments. The scent of danger, the smell of fear, filled my senses. The heart-squeezing, enlivening exhilaration of it was so powerful that it wasn't until an hour later, when we entered Abdul Ghani's passport workshop, that I could give my full attention to the man and the moment that we shared.

'This is Krishna, and this is Villu,' Ghani said, introducing me to two short, slender, dark-skinned men who resembled one another so closely that I thought they might be brothers. 'There are many experts in this business, many men and women with a detective's eye for detail, and a surgeon's confident steadiness of hand. But my experience of ten years in the counterfeiting arts tells me that the Sri Lankans, such as our Krishna and Villu, are the best forgers in the world.'

The men smiled widely, with perfect white teeth, in response to the compliment. They were handsome men, their faces formed from fine, almost delicate features, in a harmony of gentle contours and curves. They returned to their work as we strolled about the large room.

'This is the light-box,' Abdul Ghani explained, waving his plump hand at a long table. It was topped with white opaque glass. Strong lights shone from within its frame. 'Krishna is our best light-box man. He examines the pages of genuine passports, looking for watermarks and concealed patterns. In this way, he can duplicate these effects where we need them.'

I bent over Krishna's shoulder to watch him as he studied the information page of a British passport. A complex pattern of wavy lines descended from the top of the page, across a photograph, and on to the bottom of the page. On another passport beside it, Krishna was matching the pattern of wavy lines on the edge of a substituted photograph, creating the lines with a fine-tipped pen. Using the light-box, he placed one pattern over the other to check for irregularities.

'Villu is our best stamp man,' Abdul Ghani said, guiding me to another long table. On a rack at the back of the table, there were rows of many more rubber stamps.

'Villu can make any stamp, no matter how intricate its design. Visa stamps, exit and entry, special permission stamps—whatever we need. He has three new profile-cutting machines, for reproducing the stamps. The machines cost me dearly—I had to import them, all the way from Germany—and I spent almost as much again, in baksheesh, getting them through customs controls and into our workshop without any unpleasant questions. But our Villu is an artist, and he often prefers to ignore my beautiful machines, and cut the new stamps by hand.'

I watched as Villu created a new stamp on a blank rubber template. He copied a photographic enlargement of the original—a departure stamp from Athens airport—and cut the new stamp with scalpels and jeweller's files. Inkpad tests of the new stamp revealed minor flaws. When those were finally eradicated, Villu used a scrap of wet-and-dry sandpaper to wear away one corner of the stamp. That deliberate imperfection gave the inked image a genuine, natural appearance on the page. The completed stamp joined scores of others in the rack of stamps waiting to be used on newly altered passports.

Abdul Ghani completed his tour of the factory, demonstrating the computers, photocopy equipment, printing presses, profile cutters, and reserves of special parchment papers and inks. When I'd seen all there was to see on a first visit, he offered me a lift back to Colaba. I declined, asking him if I might stay and spend some time with the Sri Lankan forgers. He seemed pleased with my enthusiasm, or perhaps simply amused. When he left me, I heard his heavy sigh as the sadness of bereavement claimed him once more.

Krishna, Villu, and I drank chai and talked for three hours without a pause. Although they weren't brothers, they were both Tamil Sri Lankans who came from the same village on the Jaffna peninsula. Conflict between the Tamil Tigers—the Liberation Tigers for Tamil Eelam—and the Sri Lankan army had obliterated their village. Almost all the members of both families were dead. The two young men escaped, with Villu's sister, a cousin, Krishna's grandparents, and his two young nieces, who were under five years old. A fishing boat brought them to India, on the people-smuggling route between Jaffna and the Coromandel coast. They made their way to Bombay and then lived on a footpath, under a sheet of plastic, as pavement dwellers.

They'd survived that first year by taking ill-paid jobs as day labourers, and by committing a variety of petty crimes. Then, one day, a footpath-neighbour, who'd learned that they could read and write well in English, asked them to change a licence document. Their work was good, and it brought a steadily increasing stream of visitors to their plastic awning on the Bombay footpath. Hearing of their skill, Abdul Ghani had recommended to Khaderbhai that they be given a chance to prove themselves.

Two years later, at the time that I met them, Krishna and Villu shared a large, comfortable apartment with the surviving members of their two families, saved money from their generous salaries, and were arguably the most successful forgers in Bombay, India's counterfeiting capital.

I wanted to learn everything. I wanted the mobility and security that their passport skills offered me. They spoke English well. My enthusiasm fuelled their natural congeniality, and that first conversation flowed with good humour. It was a propitious start to the new friendship.

I visited Krishna and Villu every day for a week after that meeting. The young men worked long hours, and on some days I remained with them for ten hours at a stretch, watching them work, and asking my several hundred questions. The passports that they worked on fell into two main groups—those they obtained as genuine, used passports, and those that were blank and unused. The used passports had been stolen by pickpockets, lost by tourists, or sold by desperate junkies from Europe, Africa, the Americas, and Oceania. The blank passports were rare. They'd been sold by corrupt officials at consulates and embassies and departments of immigration, from France to Turkey to China. Those that found their way into Khaderbhai's area of influence were bought immediately, at any price, and given to Krishna and Villu. They showed me a blank, original, unused passport from Canada, as an example. It was housed in a fireproof safe with others from the United Kingdom, Germany, Portugal and Venezuela.

With sufficient patience, expertise, and resources, the two forgers could change almost anything in a passport to suit a new user's requirements. Photographs were substituted, and the ridge-marks or indentations of a heavy stamp were imitated, using something as humble as a crochet hook. Sometimes the stitching that bound a passport was carefully removed, and whole groups of pages were replaced, using clean pages from a second passport. Dates, details, and stamps were all altered or erased with chemical solvents. New data was inserted in an appropriate shade, selected from a comprehensive catalogue of printer's inks. Some of the changes defied the scrutiny of experts, and none of them was detectable in routine examinations.

During that first week of passport studies, I found a new, safe, comfortable apartment for Ulla in neighbouring Tardeo, not far from the Haji Ali Mosque. Lisa Carter, who'd visited Ulla almost every day at Abdullah's apartment—and visited, far more warmly, with Abdullah himself—agreed to share the new place. We moved them and their belongings in a small fleet of taxis. The two women liked one another, and got on well. They drank vodka, cheated at Scrabble and gin rummy, enjoyed the same kinds of movies on video, and swapped clothes. They'd also discovered, in the weeks they'd spent in Abdullah's surprisingly well-stocked kitchen, that they liked one another's cooking. The new apartment was a new beginning for them and, despite Ulla's lingering fears about Maurizio and his crooked deals, she and Lisa were happy and optimistic.

I continued the weight training and karate with Abdullah, Salman, and Sanjay. We were fit and strong and fast. And as the days of training became weeks, Abdullah and I grew closer, as friends and brothers, just as Salman and Sanjay were with one another. It was the kind of closeness that didn't need conversation to sustain itself: quite often we would meet, travel to the gym, work out on the weights, box a few rounds, spend half an hour sparring at karate, and speak no more than ten words to one another. Sometimes, with no more than a look in my eye or an unusual expression on his face, we would laugh, and keep on laughing so hard that we collapsed to the practice mats. And in that way, without words, I slowly opened my heart to Abdullah, and I began to love him.

I'd spoken to the head man of the slum, Qasim Ali Hussein, and to several others, including Johnny Cigar, when I'd first returned from Goa. I saw Prabaker in his taxi every other day. But there were so many new challenges and rewards in Ghani's passport workshop, and they kept me so busy and excited, that I stopped working, even occasionally, at the slum clinic I'd founded in the little hut that had been my home.

On my first visit to the slum in several weeks, I was surprised to find Prabaker in the wriggling convulsions of a dance while the slum musicians were rehearsing one of their popular songs. The little guide was dressed in his taxi driver's khaki shirt and white trousers. He wore a purple scarf around his neck, and yellow plastic sandals. Approaching him unobserved, I watched him in silence for a while. His dance managed to combine obscenely lewd and suggestive thrusts of his hips with the facial expressions and hand-whirling gestures of a child-like innocence. With clownish charm he held his open palms beside his smiling face one moment, and then pumped his groin back and forth with a determined little grimace the next. When he finally turned and saw me, his face exploded in that huge smile, that uniquely wide and heart-filled smile, and he rushed to greet me.

'Oh, Lin!' he cried, squeezing his head into my chest in an affectionate hug. 'I have a news for you! I have it such a fantastic news! I was looking for you in every place, every hotel with naked ladies, every drinking bar with black-market peoples, every dirty slum, every —'

'I get the picture, Prabu. So, what's your news?'

'I am to be getting married! I am making a marriage on Parvati! Can you believe it?'

'Sure, I can believe it. Congratulations. I take it you were practising, just now, for the wedding party.'

'Oh, yes!' he agreed, lunging at me with his hips a few times. 'I want a very sexy dancing for everybody at the party. It's a pretty good sexy, isn't it?'

'It's ... sexy ... sure. How are things here?'

'Very fine. No problem. Oh, Lin! I forgot! Johnny, he is making a marriage also. He will be married with Sita, the sister of my own beautiful Parvati.'

'Where is he? I want to say hello.'

'He is down at the seashore, you know, at the place where he sits on the rocks, for being lonely — the same place where you also enjoy a good lonely. You'll find him there.'

I walked off, glancing back over my shoulder to see Prabaker encouraging the band with mechanical, piston-like thrusts of his narrow hips. At the edge of the slum, where black boulders tumbled to the sea, I found Johnny Cigar. He was dressed in a white singlet and a chequered green lungi. He braced himself with his arms, leaning back, and staring out to sea. It was almost exactly the same spot where he'd told me about seawater, sweat, and tears on the evening of the cholera outbreak, so many months before.

'Congratulations,' I said, sitting beside him and offering him a beedie cigarette.

'Thanks, Lin,' he smiled, shaking his head. I put the packet away, and for a while we both watched the small petulant waves smack at the rocky shore.

'You know, I was brought into this life — conceived, I mean, not born — just over there, in the Navy Nagar,' he said, nodding his head toward the compound of the Indian Navy. A curve of coastline separated us from the Nagar, but a direct line of sight across the small bay gave us a clear view of the houses, huts, and barracks.

'My mother was from Delhi-side originally. Her family, they were all Christians. They made good money in the service of the British, but they lost their position, and their privileges, after the Independence. They moved to Bombay when my mother was fifteen years old. Her father took employment with the navy, working as a clerk. They lived in a zhopadpatti near here. My mother fell in love with a sailor. He was a tall, young fellow from Amritsar, with the best moustache in the whole Nagar. When she became pregnant with me, her family threw her out. She tried to get some help from the sailor who was my father, but he left the Nagar, and she never saw him or heard about him again.'

He paused, breathing through his nose, with his lips pressed tightly together. His eyes squinted against the glare from the glittering sea, and the fresh, persistent breeze. Behind us we could hear the noises of the slum—hawkers' cries, the slap of clothes on stone in the washing area, children playing, a bickering complaint, and the jangling music for Prabaker's piston-hips.

'She had a tough time of it, Lin. She was heavily pregnant with me when they threw her out. She moved to a pavement-dweller settlement, across in Crawford Market area, and wore the widow's white sari, pretending that she'd had a husband, and pretending that he was dead. She had to do that—she had to become a widow, for life, before she was even married. That's why I never got married. I'm thirty-eight years old. I can read and write very well—my mother made sure I was educated—and I do the bookwork for all the shops and businesses in the slum. I do the taxes for every man who pays them. I make a good living here, and I have respect. I should've been married fifteen or even twenty years ago. But she was a widow, all her life, for me. And I couldn't do it. I just couldn't allow myself to get married. I kept hoping I would see him, the sailor with the best moustache. My mother had one very old, faded photograph of the two of them, looking very serious and stern. That's why I lived in this area. I always hoped I would see him. And I never married. And she died last week, Lin. My mother died last week.'

He turned to me, and the whites of his eyes were blazing with the tears he wouldn't let them shed.

'She died last week. And now, I'm getting married.'

'I'm sorry to hear about your mother, Johnny. But I'm sure she'd want you to get married. I think you'll make a good father. In fact, I *know* you'll make a good father. I'm sure of it.'

He looked at me, his eyes talking to me in a language I could feel but couldn't understand. When I left him, he was staring at the ceaselessness of the sea, irritated to chequered, white rifts by the wind.

I walked back through the slum to the clinic. A conversation with Ayub and Siddhartha, the two young men I'd trained to run the clinic, reassured me that all was well. I gave them some money to keep, as an emergency float, and left money with Prabaker for his wedding preparations. I paid a courtesy visit to Qasim Ali Hussein, allowing him to force the hospitality of chai upon me. Jeetendra and Anand Rao, two of my former neighbours, joined us, with several other men I knew well. Qasim Ali led the conversation, referring to his son Sadiq, who was working in the Gulf. In turn, we spoke of religious and communal conflict in the city, the construction of the twin towers, still at least two years from completion, and the weddings of Prabaker and Johnny Cigar.

It was a genial, sanguine meeting, and I rose to leave with the strength and confidence that those honest, simple, decent men always inspired in me. I'd only walked a few paces, however, when the young Sikh, Anand Rao, caught up, and fell into step beside me.

'Linbaba, there is a problem here,' he said quietly. He was an unusually solemn man at the best of times, but at that moment his expression was unambiguously grim. 'That Rasheed, that fellow I used to be sharing with. Do you remember?'

'Yes. Rasheed. I remember him,' I replied, recalling the thin, bearded face and restless, guilty eyes of the man who'd been my neighbour, with Anand, for more than a year.

'He is making a bad business,' Anand Rao declared bluntly. 'His wife and her sister came from their native place. I went from that hut when they came. He has been living with them alone now, for some time.'

'And ... *what?*' I asked, as we walked out on to the road together. I had no idea what Anand Rao was driving at, and I had no patience for it. It was the kind of vague, insinuated complaint that had come to me almost every day when I'd lived in the slum. Most of the time, such complaints came to nothing. Most of the time, it was in my best interests to have nothing to do with them.

'Well,' Anand Rao hesitated, perhaps sensing my impatience, 'it is ... he is ... something is very bad, and I am ... there must be ...'

He fell silent, staring at his sandaled feet. I reached out to put a hand on his broad, proud, thin shoulder. Gradually his eyes lifted, and met mine in a mute appeal.

'Is it money?' I asked, reaching into my pocket. 'Do you need some money?'

He recoiled as if I'd cursed him. He held the stare, for a moment, before turning and walking back into the slum.

I strode on through familiar streets, and told myself that it was okay. Anand Rao and Rasheed had shared a hut for more than two years. If they were falling out because Rasheed's wife and her sister had moved to the city, and Anand had been forced from the hut, it was probably to be expected. And it was no business of mine. I laughed, shaking my head as I walked, and trying to figure out why Anand Rao had reacted so badly to the offer of money. It wasn't an unreasonable thing for me to assume or to offer. On the thirty-minute walk from the slum to Leopold's, I gave money to five other people, including both of the Zodiac Georges. *He'll get over it, whatever it is,* I told myself. *At any rate, it's got nothing to do with me.* But the lies we tell ourselves are the ghosts that haunt the empty house of midnight. And although I pushed Anand and the slum from my mind, I felt the breath of that ghosted lie on my face as I walked through the long, thronging Causeway on that hot afternoon.

I stepped up into Leopold's, and Didier seized me by the arm before I could speak or sit down, turning me about and leading me to a cab that was waiting outside.

'I have searched for you everywhere,' Didier puffed as the cab pulled out from the kerb. 'I have been to the most unspeakably foul places, looking for you.'

'People keep telling me that.'

'Well, Lin, you really must try to spend more time in places where they serve a decent alcohol. It may not make the finding of you easier, but it will make it far more pleasant.'

'Where are we going, Didier?'

'Vikram's great strategy—my *own* superb strategy, if you please—for the capture of Letitia's cold and stony little English heart unfolds, now, even as we speak.'

'Yeah, well, I wish him all the best,' I frowned, 'but I'm hungry. I was about to make very loud noises in a plate of Leopold's pulao. You can let me off here.'

'But, no! It is not possible!' Didier objected. 'Letitia, she is a very stubborn woman. She would refuse gold and diamonds if someone *insisted* that she should take them. She will not participate in the strategy unless someone convinces her. Someone like you, my friend. And this must be achieved in the next half-hour. At exactly six minutes after three o'clock.'

'What makes you think Lettie will listen to me?'

'You are the only one of us she does not now hate, or has not hated at some time in the past. For Letitia, the statement *I do not hate you* is a poem of passionate love. She will listen to you. I am sure of it. And without you, the plan will fail. And the good Vikram—as if loving such a woman as our Letitia was not sufficient to prove his mental derangement —he has already risked his life, several times, to make the plan possible. You cannot imagine how much preparation we have made, Vikram and I, for just this moment.'

'Well, nobody told *me* anything about it,' I complained, still thinking of the delicious pulao at Leopold's.

'But that is exactly why I have searched for you all over Colaba! You have no choice, Lin. You must help him. I know you. There is in you, as there is in me, a morbid belief in love, and a fascination for the madness that love puts in its victims.'

'I wouldn't put quite that spin on it, Didier.'

'You can spin it how you will,' he replied, laughing for the first time, 'But you have the love disease, Lin, and you know, in your heart, that you must help Vikram, just as *I* must help him.'

'Oh God,' I relented, lighting a beedie to stave off the hunger. 'I'll do what I can to help. What's the plan?'

'Ah, it is quite complicated —'

'Just a minute,' I said, raising my hand to interrupt him quickly. 'Is this scheme of yours dangerous?'

'Well ...'

'And does it involve breaking the law?'

'Well ...'

'I thought so. Then, don't tell me until we get there. I've got enough to worry about.'

'*D'accord.* I knew that we could count on you. *Alors,* speaking of worry, I have a little news that may be of some help to you.'

'Let's have it.'

'The woman who made the complaint about you, the woman who put you in the prison, she is *not* Indian. I have learned it, beyond any doubt. She is a foreigner who lives here, in Bombay.'

'There's nothing else?'

'No. I regret, there is nothing more. Not at this time. But I will not rest until I know all.'

'Thanks, Didier.'

'It's nothing. You are looking well, by the way. Perhaps even better than before you went to the prison.'

'Thanks. I'm a little heavier, and a little fitter.'

'And a little ... crazier ... perhaps?'

I laughed, avoiding his eye, because it was true. The taxi pulled up at Marine Lines Station. Marine Lines was the first railway station after the central city terminus, at Churchgate Depot. We climbed the pedestrian ramp and found Vikram, with several of his friends, waiting for us on the station platform.

'Oh, *fuck*! Thank *God* you're *here*, man!' he said, pumping my hand in a frantic, two-handed shake. 'I thought you weren't coming.'

'Where is Letitia?' Didier asked.

'She's down the platform, *yaar*. She's buying a cold drink. See her there, just past the chai shop?'

'Ah, yes. And she knows nothing of the plan?'

'Not a fuckin' thing, man. I'm so nervous that it's not going to work, *yaar*. And what if she gets killed, Didier? It won't be a good look for us, man, if my proposal kills her!'

'Killing her would definitely be a bad start,' I mused.

'Don't worry. It will be okay,' Didier soothed, although he mopped his brow with a scented handkerchief as his eyes searched the empty tracks for an approaching train. 'It will work. You must have faith.'

'That's what they said at Jonesville, *yaar*.'

'What do you want me to do, Vikram?' I asked, hoping to calm him down.

'Okay,' he replied, puffing as if he'd just run up a flight of steps. 'Okay. First, Lettie has to stand just here, facing you. Just like I'm standing now.'

'U-huh.'

'It has to be right *here*. Exactly *here*. We've checked it out a hundred fuckin' times, man, and it has to be just here. Have you got that?'

'I ... think so. You're saying that she has to stand just —'

'Here!'

'Here?' I teased him.

'Fuck, man, this is serious!'

'Okay! Take it easy. You want me to make Lettie stand here.'

'Yeah. Here. And your job is to get her to put the blindfold on.'

'The ... blindfold?'

'Yeah. She's got to wear a blindfold, Lin. It won't work without it. And she has to leave it on, even when it gets very scary.'

'Scary ...'

'Yeah. That's your job. Just convince her to put the blindfold on, when we give you the signal, and then convince her to keep it on, *yaar*, even if she's screaming a bit.'

'Screaming ...'

'Yeah. We thought about a gag, but we decided, you know, a gag might be a bit counter-fuckin'-productive, *yaar*, because she might freak out a bit, with a gag. And she's going to freak out enough as it is, without using a fuckin' gag on her.'

'A ... gag ...'

'Yeah. Okay, here she comes! Get ready for the signal.'

'Hello, Lin, you fat bastard,' Lettie said, giving me a kiss on the cheek. 'You're really beefing out, aren't you, son?'

'You look good, too,' I replied, smiling at the pleasure of seeing her.

'So, what's this all about then?' she asked. 'It looks like the gang's all here.'

'You don't know?' I shrugged.

'No, of course I don't. Vikram just told me we were meeting you and Didier—hullo, Didier—and here we all are. What's up?'

The train from Churchgate Station came into view, approaching us at a steady pace. Vikram gave me the signal, opening his eyes as widely as the muscles would allow, and shaking his head. I put my hands on Lettie's shoulders, gently turning her until she stood as Vikram had requested, with her back to the tracks.

'Do you trust me, Lettie?' I asked.

She smiled up at me.

'A bit,' she replied.

'Okay,' I nodded. 'Well, I want you to do something. It's gonna sound strange, I know, but if you don't do it, you'll never know how much Vikram loves you—how much we *all* love you. It's a surprise that we figured out for you. It's about love ...'

The train slowed behind her as it entered the station. Her eyes were gleaming. A smile flickered and faded on her open lips. She was intrigued and excited. Vikram and Didier were gesturing wildly, behind her back, for me to hurry. The train stopped with a wheezy creak of metal triumph.

'So, here it is—you have to put a blindfold on, and you have to promise us not to look until we tell you.'

'Is that it?'

'Well, yeah,' I shrugged.

She looked at me. She stared. She smiled into my eyes. She raised her eyebrows, and turned down the corners of her mouth as she considered it. Then she nodded.

'Okay,' she laughed. 'Let's do it.'

Vikram leapt forward with the blindfold and tied it on, asking her if it was too tight. He guided her a step or two backwards, toward the train, and then told her to raise her arms over her head.

'Raise my arms? What, like this? If you tickle me, Vikram, you'll pay!'

Some men appeared at the edge of the roofline on the train carriage. They'd been lying on the roof of the train. They leaned over, and seized Lettie's raised arms, lifting her slight frame effortlessly onto the roof with them. Lettie shrieked, but the piercing sound was lost in the shrill of the train guard's whistle. The train began to move.

'Come on!' Vikram shouted to me, climbing up the outside of the carriage to join her.

I glanced at Didier.

'No, my friend!' he shouted. 'This is not for me. You go! Hurry!'

I jogged along beside the train, and clambered up the outside of the carriage to the roof. There were a dozen men or more on the roof. Some of them were musicians. Sitting together, they cradled tablas, cymbals, flutes, and tambourines in their laps. Further along the dusty roof was a second group. Lettie sat in the middle of them. She still wore the blindfold. Men held her at the shoulders—one on each arm, and two from behind—to keep her safe. Vikram knelt in front of her. I heard his pleading as I crept along the roof toward them at a crouch.

'I promise you, Lettie. It really is a great surprise.'

'Oh, it's a friggin' *surprise* all right,' she shouted. 'And not half as big as the surprise you're gonna get, when we get down from here, Vikram bloody Patel!'

'Hi, Lettie!' I called to her. 'Great view, eh? Oh, sorry. Forgot about the blindfold. Well, it *will* be a great view, when you can see it.'

'This is fuckin' madness, Lin!' she shouted at me. 'Tell these bastards to let go of me!'

'That wouldn't be wise, Lettie,' Vikram answered. 'They're hanging on to you so you don't fall, *yaar*, or stand up, and snag yourself on an overhead wire, or something. It's really only another half a minute, I promise you, and then you'll understand what all is happening.'

'I understand, don't you worry. I understand that you're a dead man, Vikram, when I get down from here. You might as well throw me off the bloody roof now, I'm tellin' ya! If you think I —'

Vikram untied the blindfold, and watched her as she looked around, taking in the perspective from the roof of the fast-moving train. Her mouth fell open, and her face slowly swelled into a wide smile.

'Wow! It's ... Wow! It really *is* a *great* view!'

'Look!' Vikram commanded, turning to point along the roofs of the train carriages. There was something stretched across the tracks, much higher than the roofline of the train. It was strung between the pylon supports for the overhead electric wires. It was a huge banner, puffed like the sail of a ship in the steady breeze. There were words painted on it. As we neared the banner, the writing became clear enough to read. The words were painted in letters as tall as a man. They filled the whole width of the billowing sheet:

LETITIA I LOVE YOU

'I was afraid you would stand up and hurt yourself,' Vikram said. 'That's why those fellows were holding on to your arms.'

Suddenly, the musicians struck up the chiming, thudding strains of a popular love song. Their voices soared over the blood-stirring thump of the tablas and the wail of the flutes. Vikram and Lettie stared at one another, their eyes holding as the train pulled into a station, stopped, and pulled out again. Half way to the next station, we approached another banner. Vikram wrenched his eyes from hers, and looked ahead. She followed his gaze. More words were written across the taut white cloth:

WILL YOU MARRY ME?

We passed beneath the pennant and out into the soft afternoon light. Lettie was crying. They were both crying. Vikram threw himself forward and wrapped her in his arms. They kissed. I watched them for moment and then I turned away to face the musicians. They grinned at me, wagging their heads and laughing as they sang. I did a little victory dance for them as the train rocked and rumbled through the suburbs.

Millions of dreams were born there, around us, every day. Millions of dreams died there, and were born again. The humid air was thick with dreams, everywhere, in my Mumbai. My city was a steaming, sweltering hothouse garden of dreaming. And there, on that red-brown rusting metal roof, a new dream of love was born. And I thought of my family as we rushed through the humid dreaming air. And I thought about Karla. And I danced on that steel serpent as it slithered sinuous beside the scroll and swell of the endless, imperishable sea.

And although Vikram and Lettie disappeared for a week, after she accepted his proposal, a lightness and optimism that was like happiness circulated in the Leopold's crowd. When he finally did return, that positive feeling greeted Vikram with real affection. Abdullah and I had just finished our training and we teased him, mercilessly, for his delirious, exhausted joy. Then, while Vikram blubbered about love, we ate in hungry, purposeful silence. Didier was jubilant, crowing over the triumph of his romantic scheme, and demanding modest tributes, in the form of stiff drinks, from everyone we knew.

I looked up from my plate of food to see a man, one of the street boys who scrounged for the black marketeers, gesturing to me in some anxiety. I left the table, and walked to the footpath to speak with him.

'Lin! Big trouble for you,' he said quickly, looking left and right nervously. 'Three men. Africans. Big men. Very strong. They look for you. They want to kill you.'

'Kill me?'

'Yes. Sure. Better you go. Go fast from Bombay for a while!'

He ran off, and I lost sight of him in the crowd. Puzzled, but not worried, I returned to the table. I'd only eaten two mouthfuls when another man called me out to the street. It was Gemini George.

'I think you're in a spot of bother, old chum,' he said. His tone was cheery, but his face was tense and afraid.

'U-huh.'

'Seems there's three bull-necked African geezers—Nigerians, I think— and they mean to do you a bit of grievous bodily harm, if you know what I mean.'

'Where are they?'

'I dunno, mate. I seen them talkin' with some of the street boys, but then they got in a taxi and took off. They're fuckin' big lads, I tell ya. They filled that taxi, with a bit of flesh to spare. Fairly bulgin' out the windows they were, know what I mean?'

'What's it about?'

'No idea, mate. They didn't say nothin' what they're on about, Lin. They're just lookin' for you, and they got trouble in mind. I'd watch my back, and I'd watch my step, sunshine.'

I reached into my pocket, but he put a hand on my wrist.

'No, mate. On the house. I mean, it's not right, whatever their game is.'

He sauntered off in pursuit of a passing trio of German tourists, and I walked back into the restaurant. With Gemini George's warning to support the first, I *was* worried. It took me longer than usual to finish my meal. Soon after, there was a third visitor. It was Prabaker.

'Lin!' he said, his expression frenzied. 'There is a bad news!'

'I know, Prabu.'

'Three men, African, they are wanting to beat and kill and beat you! They are asking questions everywhere. Such big fellows they are! Like buffalos! You must make a lucky escapes!'

It took me five minutes to calm him down, and even then I had to invent a mission for him—checking for the Africans at the hotels he knew well—in order to prise him from my side. Alone again with Didier, Vikram, and Abdullah, we considered my options, in a lengthening silence. Vikram was the first to speak.

'Okay, so we find the fuckers, and break their heads, *yaar*,' he suggested, looking from face to face for support.

'After we kill them,' Abdullah added.

Vikram wagged his head from side to side in agreement.

'Two things are sure,' Didier said slowly. 'One, you must not be alone, Lin, at any time, until this is resolved.'

Vikram and Abdullah nodded.

'I will call Salman and Sanjay,' Abdullah decided. 'You will not be alone, Lin brother.'

'And two,' Didier continued, 'the others, whoever they are, whatever their reasons, must not remain in Bombay. They must go—one way, or the other way.'

We got up to pay the bill and leave. Didier stopped me when the others walked to the cashier's desk. He pulled me down into a chair beside him. Sliding a napkin from the table, he fumbled under the table's edge for a moment and then slid a bundle across to me. It was a pistol, wrapped in the napkin. No-one knew that Didier carried a gun. I was sure that I was the first to see and handle the weapon. Grasping it tightly in the napkin wrapping, I stood and joined the others as they left the restaurant. I looked back over my shoulder to see him nodding gravely, the curly black hair trembling about his face.

We found them, but it took us all the day and most of the night. In the end it was Hassaan Obikwa, another Nigerian, who gave us the decisive clue. The men were tourists, completely new to the city, and unknown to Obikwa. He had no precise idea of their motive—it was something to do with a drug deal—but his network of contacts had confirmed that they were determined to do me harm.

Hassaan's driver, Raheem, almost fully recovered from the injuries he'd suffered in prison, discovered that they were in one of the Fort area hotels. He offered to *resolve* the matter. He was conscious of the debt he owed me for buying him out of Arthur Road Prison. With an earnest, almost shy expression, he offered to have the men killed, slowly and painfully, as a personal favor to me. He seemed to think that it was the least he could do, under the circumstances. I refused. I had to know what it was all about, and I had to put a stop to it. Clearly disappointed, Raheem accepted the decision, and then led us to the small hotel in the Fort. He waited outside with our two cars while we went inside. Salman and Sanjay remained with him, watching the street. Their brief was to stop the cops, if they arrived, or slow them up long enough for us to leave the hotel.

One of Abdullah's contacts smuggled us, whispering, into a room adjoining that taken by the three Africans. We pressed our ears to the connecting wall, and could hear their voices clearly. They were joking, and talking about trivial, unrelated things. Finally, one of them made a remark that tightened the skin on my skull and face with dread.

'He got that medal,' one of them said. 'Around his neck. That medal is gold. I want that gold medal.'

'I like them shoes, them boots he got,' another voice said. 'I want them shoes.'

They went on to talk about their plan. They argued a little. One of the men was more forceful. The others agreed, at last, with his idea to follow me from Leopold's all the way to the quiet car park beneath my apartment building and then beat me until I was dead, and strip my body.

It was bizarre, standing in the dark and listening to the details of my own murder. My stomach dropped and tightened on a curdling mix of nausea and rage. I hoped to hear some clue, some reference to a motive, but they never mentioned one. Abdullah was listening with his left ear against the thin partition, and I was listening with my right. Our eyes were only a hand's width apart. The signal to move, when I nodded my head, was a gesture so faint and subtle that it was as if our minds had spoken the message.

Vikram, Abdullah, and I stood outside the door to their room, with a passkey poised over the lock. We counted down *three* ... *two* ... *one* ... then I turned the key and tried the door. It wasn't locked from the inside. I stood back, and kicked it open. There was a second, three seconds, of utter stillness, as the surprised and frightened men stared at us, their jaws gaping and their eyes bulging. Nearest to us was a tall, very solid man with a bald head, and deep scars cut into his cheeks in a regular pattern. He wore a singlet and boxer shorts. Standing behind him was a slightly shorter man, who was dressed only in jockey shorts. He was bending over a waist-high dressing table, poised in the act of snorting a line of heroin. The third man was shorter still, but very thick in the chest and arms. He lay on one of the three beds, at the furthest corner of the room, holding a *Playboy* magazine in his hands. There was a strong smell in the room. It was the smell of sweat and fear. Some of it was mine.

Abdullah closed the door of the room behind him, very slowly and gently, and locked it. He was wearing black: he almost always wore a black shirt and pants. Vikram was dressed in his black cowboy rig. By some chance, I too wore a black T-shirt and black trousers. We must've looked like the members of some club, or gang, to the goggle-eyed men in the room.

'What the *fuck* —' the big man bellowed.

I ran at him and rammed a fist into his mouth, but he had time to raise his hands. We grabbed at each other, fists flying, and locked in a hard grapple.

Vikram sprang for the man on the bed. Abdullah closed on the man at the dresser. It was a short fight, and a dirty one. There were six of us — six big men in a small room. There was nowhere to go but into each other.

Abdullah finished his man quickly. I heard a frightened shriek, choked off, as Abdullah snapped a hard, straight, right hand to the man's throat. From the corner of my eye, I was aware that the solid man fell back, grasping and clutching at his throat. The man on the bed jumped to his feet and kicked outward, trying to use the advantage of high ground. Abdullah and Vikram tipped the bed up, sending the man sprawling behind it. They leapt over the upturned bed and fell on him, stomping and kicking him until he stopped moving.

I held the strap of the big man's singlet with my left hand, and pounded at him with my right. Ignoring the blows to his head, he managed to get his hands around my neck, and started to squeeze. My throat locked tight. I knew that the breath I held in me was the last until I finished him. I reached out for his face, desperately, with my right hand. My thumb found his eye. I wanted to push it into his brain, but he moved his head, and the thumb slipped between the eye and the hard ridge of bone at his temple. I drove the thumb in harder and deeper until I gouged his eye from the socket, and it hung there from bloody strands. I tried to reach it, to rip it away or to dig my thumb into the empty socket, but he pulled back to the limit of his reach. The eye hung out on his cheek, and I swung my fist at his head, trying to crush it.

He was a hard man. He didn't give up. His hands squeezed tighter. My neck was strong and the muscles were well developed, but I knew he had the strength to kill me. My hand reached, groping for the pistol in my pocket. I had to shoot him. I had to kill him. That was all right. I didn't care. The air in my lungs was spent, and my brain was exploding in Mandelbrot whirls of colored light, and I was dying, and I *wanted* to kill him.

Vikram crashed a heavy wooden stool into the back of the big man's bald head. It's not as easy to knock a man out as it seems in the movies. It's true that a lucky hit can do it in one shot, but I've been hit with iron bars, lumps of wood, boots, and many hard fists, and I've only ever been knocked out once in my life. Vikram slammed the heavy stool into the back of the man's head five times, with all of his strength, before the big man buckled and fell. He was defeated, and groggy. The back of his head was pulpy. I knew that his skull was fractured in several places. Somehow, he was still conscious.

We worked on them for half an hour, overcoming their initial reluctance to talk. Raheem joined us, speaking in English and their Nigerian dialect. Their passports told us who they were — Nigerian citizens, on tourist visas. Other information in their wallets and luggage told us where they'd stayed in Lagos before they came to Bombay. Little by little, the story emerged. They were muscle: hit men, sent by a gangster in Lagos to punish me for a major heroin and Mandrax tablet deal that had gone wrong. The deal involved some sixty thousand dollars — money that their boss in Lagos had lost in a hustle in Bombay. The hustler, whoever he was, had nominated me as the mastermind of the plan; the man responsible for ripping off the money.

The hired thugs surrendered that much information, but then they balked. They didn't want to give me the man's name. They didn't want to tell me who'd set me up. They didn't want to betray him without the express permission of their Nigerian boss. We insisted, and they were persuaded. The man's name was Maurizio Belcane.

I put the big man's eye back into its socket, but it stared out at a strange angle. From the way that he turned his head to look at me, I guessed that he couldn't see out of it, yet, and I suspected that it would never sit correctly again. We closed the eye with tape, bandaged his head, and tidied the other men up. Then I spoke to them.

'These men will take you to the airport. You're gonna wait in the car park. There's a plane to Lagos tomorrow morning. You're gonna be on it.

We're gonna buy the tickets with your money. And get this straight—I had nothing to do with this. That's not your fault—it's Maurizio's—but that doesn't make me any happier about it. I'm gonna fix Maurizio, for lying about me. That's my business, now. You can go back to your boss, and tell him that Maurizio will get what's coming to him. But if you ever come back here, we'll kill you. Understand? You come back to Bombay, you die.'

'Yeah, you fuckin' under*stand?*' Vikram shouted at them, lashing out with a kick. 'You come here and fuck with *Indians*, you fuckin' *fuck-heads!* India is *finished* for you! You come back here and I will *personally* cut off your fuckin' *balls!* Do you see my hat? You see the mark on my fuckin' hat, you fuckin' *bahinchhud?* You put a mark on my fuckin' *hat!* You don't fuck with an Indian guy's *hat!* You don't fuck with Indian guys for *any* reason, hat or no hat! Not ever! And especially not, if they *do* wear a hat!'

I left them, and took a cab to Ulla's new apartment. She would know where Maurizio was, if anyone knew. My throat was aching, and I could hardly talk. The gun in my pocket was all I could think about. It swelled, in my mind, until it was huge: until the pattern of ridges on the handle was as large as the wale of bark on a cork tree. It was a Walther P38, one of the best semi-automatic pistols ever made. It fired a 9mm round from an eight-shot magazine, and in my mind I saw all eight of them punch their way into Maurizio's body. I mumbled the name, *Maurizio, Maurizio,* and a voice in my head, a voice that I knew very well, said, *Get rid of the gun before you see him ...*

I knocked hard on the door of the apartment, and when Lisa opened it I brushed past her to find Ulla sitting on a couch in the lounge room. She was crying. She looked up when I entered, and I saw that her left eye was swollen, as if she'd been hit.

'*Maurizio!*' I said. 'Where is he?'

'Lin, I can't,' she sobbed. 'Modena ...'

'I'm not interested in Modena. I want Maurizio. Tell me where he is!'

Lisa tapped me on the arm. I turned, and noticed for the first time that she had a large kitchen knife in her hand. She jerked her head toward the nearest bedroom. I looked at Ulla, and then back to Lisa. She nodded at me, slowly.

He was hiding in a wardrobe. When I dragged him out, into the room, he pleaded with me, begging me not to hurt him. I grabbed the belt at the back of his trousers, and marched him to the door of the apartment. He screamed for help, and I hit him in the face with the pistol. He screamed again, and I hit him again, much harder. His lips parted, and he wanted to cry out, once more, but I beat him to it, crunching the gun into the top of his head as he flinched away. He was quiet.

Lisa snarled at him, brandishing the knife.

'You're lucky I didn't put this in your *guts*, you son of a bitch! If you ever hit her again, I'll *kill* you!'

'What did he want here?' I asked her.

'It's all about the money. Modena's got it. Ulla called Maurizio —'

She stopped, shocked by the fury she saw on my face as I glared at Ulla.

'I know, I know, she wasn't supposed to call anyone. But she did, and she told him about this place. She was supposed to meet them both, here, tonight. But Modena didn't show. It's not her fault, Lin. She didn't know Maurizio put you in it. He just told us about it, then, a minute ago. He told us he gave your name to a couple of Nigerian thugs. He put *you* in it, to save himself. He said he had to have the money, to get away, because they'd be after him when they were finished with you. The hero was trying to beat it out of her, where Modena is, when you got here.'

'Where's the money?' I asked Ulla.

'I don't know, Lin,' she cried. '*Fuck* the money! I didn't want it in the first place. Modena was ashamed that I was working. He doesn't understand. I rather would work on the street, and keep him safe, than have this crazy thing happen. He loves me. He loves me. He didn't have anything to do with you and the Nigerians, Lin, I swear it. That was Maurizio's idea. It's been going on for weeks now. That's what I've been so scared about. And then tonight, Modena got hold of the money Maurizio stole—the money he stole from the Africans—and he hid it. He did it for me. He loves me, Lin. Modena loves me.'

She trailed off in stuttering sobs. I turned to Lisa.

'I'm taking him with me.'

'Good!' she snapped.

'Will you be okay?'

'Yeah. We're fine.'

'Have you got any money?'

'Yeah. Don't worry.'

'I'll send Abdullah as soon as I can. Keep the doors locked, and don't let anyone in but us, okay?'

'You got it,' she smiled. 'Thanks, Gilbert. That's the second time you came riding to the rescue.'

'Forget it.'

'No. I won't forget it,' she said, closing and locking the door behind us.

I wish I could say that I didn't hit him. He was big enough and strong enough to defend himself, but he had no heart for fighting, and there wasn't any victory in hitting him. He didn't fight or even struggle. He whimpered and cried and begged. I wish I could say that a stern justice and a righteous revenge for the wrong that he'd done to me had curled my hands into fists, and punched him. But I can't be sure. Even now, long years later, I can't be sure that the violence I did to him didn't come from something darker, deeper, and far less justifiable than angry retribution. The fact was that I'd been jealous of Maurizio for a long time. And in some part, some small but terrible part, I may have struck at his beauty, and not just his treachery.

On the other hand, of course, I should've killed him. When I left him, bloody and broken, near the St. George Hospital, a warning voice told me it wasn't the end of the matter. And I did hesitate, looming over his body with murder in my eyes, but I couldn't take his life. Something he'd said, when he was begging me to stop beating him, stayed my hand. He said that he'd named me, that he'd thrown me to the Nigerian thugs when he had to invent someone else who was responsible for his theft, because he was jealous of me. He was jealous of my confidence, my strength, and my friendships. He was jealous of me. And in his jealousy, he hated me. And in that, we weren't so different, Maurizio and I.

It was still with me, all of it, the next day, when the Nigerians were gone and I went to Leopold's, looking for Didier to return his unused gun. It was still with me, clotting my mind with anger, confused in regret, when I found Johnny Cigar waiting for me outside. It was still there, as I struggled to focus, and understand his words.

'It's a very bad thing,' he said. 'Anand Rao has killed Rasheed this morning. He cut his throat. It's the first time, Lin.'

I knew what he meant. It was the first murder in our slum. It was the first time that one slum-dweller had ever killed another in the Cuffe Parade slum. There were twenty-five thousand people in those little acres, and they fought and argued and bickered all the time, but none, not one of them, had ever killed another. And in the shocked moment, I suddenly remembered Madjid. He, too, had been murdered. I'd managed, somehow, to push the thought of his death away from my waking, working mind, but it had been gnawing through the screen of my composure slowly, steadily, all the while. And it broke through then, with the news of Rasheed's death. And that other murder—the slaughter, Ghani had said —of the old gold smuggler, the mafia don, became confused with the blood that was on Anand's hands. Anand, whose name meant *happy*. Anand, who'd tried to talk to me and tell me about it, who'd come to me that day in the slum for help, and found none.

I pressed my hands to my face, and ran them through my hair. The street around us was as busy and colourful as ever. The crowd at Leopold's were laughing, talking, and drinking, as they usually did. But something had changed in the world that Johnny and I knew. The innocence was lost, and nothing would ever be the same. I heard the words tumbling over and over in my mind. *Nothing is ever gonna be the same ... Nothing is ever gonna be the same ...*

And a vision, the kind of postcard that fate sends you, flashed before my eyes. There was death in that vision. There was madness. There was fear. But it was blurred. I couldn't see it clearly. I couldn't see the detail. I didn't know if the death and madness were happening to me, or happening around me. And in a sense, I didn't care. In too many ways of shame and angry regret, I didn't care. I blinked my eyes, and cleared my swollen throat, and stepped up off the street into the music, the laughter, and the light.

PART FOUR

CHAPTER TWENTY-SIX

'THE INDIANS are the Italians of Asia,' Didier pronounced with a sage and mischievous grin. 'It can be said, certainly, with equal justice, that the Italians are the Indians of Europe, but you do understand me, I think. There is so much Italian in the Indians, and so much Indian in the Italians. They are both people of the Madonna — they demand a goddess, even if the religion does not provide one. Every man in both countries is a singer when he is happy, and every woman is a dancer when she walks to the shop at the corner. For them, food is music inside the body, and music is food inside the heart. The language of India and the language of Italy, they make every man a poet, and make something beautiful from every *banalité*. These are nations where love — *amore, pyaar* — makes a cavalier of a Borsalino on a street corner, and makes a princess of a peasant girl, if only for the second that her eyes meet yours. It is the secret of my love for India, Lin, that my first great love was Italian.'

'Where were you born, Didier?'

'Lin, my body was born in Marseilles, but my heart and my soul were born sixteen years later, in Genova.'

He caught the eye of a waiter, and waved a hand lazily for another drink. He'd hardly taken a sip from the drink on the table in front of him, so I guessed that Didier was settling in for one of his longer discourses. It was two hours past noon on a cloudy Wednesday, three months after the Night of the Assassins. The first rains of the monsoon were still a week away, but there was a sense of expectancy, a tension, that tightened every heartbeat in the city. It was as if a vast army was gathering outside the city for an irresistible assault. I liked the week before monsoon: the tension and excitement I saw in others was like the involuted, emotional disquiet that *I* felt almost all the time.

'My mother was a delicate and beautiful woman, the photographs of her reveal,' Didier continued. 'She was only eighteen years old, when I was born, and not yet twenty when she died. The influenza claimed her. But there were whispers—cruel whispers, and I heard them many times —that my father had neglected her, and was too, how do they say it, *tight* with his money to pay doctors when she fell ill. Whatever the case, she died before I was two years old, and I have no memory of her.

'My father was a teacher of chemistry and mathematics. He was much older than my mother when he married her. By the time I started at school, my father was the headmaster. He was a brilliant man, I was told, for only a brilliant Jew could rise to the position of headmaster in a French school. The *racisme*, the anti-Semitism, in and around Marseilles at that time, so soon after the war, was like a sickness. It was a guilt that pinched at them, I think. My father was a stubborn man—it *is* a kind of stubbornness that permits one to become a mathematician, isn't it? Perhaps mathematics is *itself* a kind of stubbornness, do you think?'

'Maybe,' I replied, smiling. 'I never thought about it that way, but maybe you're right.'

'*Alors*, my father returned to Marseilles, after the war, and returned to the very house that he had been forced to leave when the Jew-haters took control of the town. He had fought with the Resistance, and he was wounded, in hand-to-hand fighting with the Germans. Because of that, no-one dared to challenge him. Not openly. But I am sure that his Jewish face and his Jewish pride and his beautiful young Jewish bride reminded the good citizens of Marseilles of the thousands of French Jews who were betrayed and sent to their deaths. And it was a cold triumph for him, returning to that house he had been forced out of, and to that community that had betrayed him. And that coldness claimed his heart, I believe, when my mother died. Even his touch, when I think of it now, was cold. Even his hand, when he touched me.'

He paused and took a sip from his glass, replacing it slowly and carefully in the precise circle of moisture it had left on the table in front of him.

'Well then, he was a brilliant man,' he continued, raising his eyes to mine with a hastily gathered smile. 'And, with one exception, he was a brilliant teacher. The exception was me. I was his only failure. I had no head for science and mathematics. They were languages I could never decipher or understand. My father responded to my stupidity with a brutal temper. His cold hand, it seemed to me when I was a child, was so large that when he struck me my whole body was shocked and bruised by the giant's hard palm and the whips of his fingers. I was afraid of him, and ashamed of my failures at school, so I played the truant very often, and fell into what the English call a *bad company*. I was many times in the courts, and served two years in the prisons for children before my thirteenth birthday. At sixteen, I left my father's house, my father's city, and my father's country forever.

'By chance I came to Genova. Have you seen it? I tell you, it is the jewel in the tiara of the Ligurian coast. And one day, on the beach at Genova, I met a man who opened my life to every good and beautiful thing that there is in the world. His name was Rinaldo. He was forty-eight years old then, when I was sixteen. His family held some ancient title, a noble line that reached to the time of Columbus. But he lived in his magnificent house on the cliffs without the pretensions of his rank. He was a scholar, the only true Renaissance man I ever met. He taught me the secrets of antiquity, the history of art, the music of poetry, and the poetry of music. He was also a beautiful man. His hair was silver and white, like the full moon, and his very sad eyes were grey. In contrast to the brutish hands of my father, with their chilling touch, Rinaldo's hands were long, slender, warm, expressive, and he made tenderness in everything that he touched. I learned what it is to love, with all of the mind and all of the body, and I was born in his arms.'

He began to cough, and attempted to clear his throat, but the cough became a fit that wracked his body in painful spasms.

'You've got to stop smoking and drinking so much, Didier. And you've gotta do a little exercise now and then.'

'Oh, *please!*' he shuddered, stubbing out a cigarette and fishing another from the pack in front of him as the coughs subsided. 'There is nothing so depressing as good advice, and I will be pleased if you do not inflict it upon me. Frankly, I am shocked at you. You must *know* this, surely? Some years ago I suffered such an offensively gratuitous piece of good advice that I was depressed for six months afterward. It was a very close call—I almost never recovered.'

'Sorry,' I smiled. 'I don't know what came over me.'

'You are forgiven,' he sniffed, downing one glass of whisky as the waiter brought the next.

'You know,' I admonished him, 'Karla says that depression only happens to people who don't know how to be sad.'

'Well she is wrong!' he declared. 'I am an expert in the *tristesse*. It is the perfect, definitive human performance. There are many animals that can express their happiness, but only the human animal has the genius to express a magnificent sadness. And for me it is something special; a daily meditation. Sadness is my one and my only art.'

He pouted for a few moments, too peeved to proceed, but then raised his eyes to meet mine and laughed out loud.

'Have you heard from her?' he asked.

'No.'

'But you know where she is?'

'No.'

'She has left Goa?'

'I asked a guy I know down there, Dashrant—he owns a restaurant on the beach where she was staying—I asked him to keep an eye on her, and make sure she was okay. I called him last week, and he told me she left. He tried to talk her into staying, but she ... well, you know.'

Didier pursed his lips in a reflective frown. We both watched the shuffling, idling, bustling, scurrying street only two metres away, beyond the wide entrance to Leopold's.

'*Et bien*, don't worry yourself about Karla,' Didier said at last. 'At the least, she is well protected.'

I assumed that Didier meant she could take care of herself and, perhaps, that she lived under a good and lucky sign. I was wrong. There was more to the remark than that. I should've asked him what he meant, of course. In the long years since that conversation I've asked myself a thousand times how different my life might've been if only I'd asked him what he meant by that remark. Instead, my head full of assumptions and my heart full of pride, I changed the subject.

'So ... what happened?'

'Happened?' he asked, bewildered.

'What happened to you and Rinaldo in Genova?'

'Ah, yes. He loved me, and I loved him, it was true, but he made an error of the judgment. He gave my love a test. He allowed me to discover the secret place where he kept a large sum of cash. I could not resist the temptation that he offered to me. I took the money and ran away. I loved him, but I took his money, and I ran away. For all his wisdom, he did not know that love cannot be tested. Honesty can be tested, and loyalty. But there is no test for love. Love goes on forever, once it begins, even if we come to hate the one we love. Love goes on forever because love is born in the part of us that does not die.'

'Did you ever see him again?'

'Yes. Yes, I did. Another loop of fortune brought me back to Genova, almost fifteen years later. I walked on the same boulevard of sand where he had taught me to read Rimbaud and Verlaine. And then I saw him. He was sitting with a group of men of his own age—he was more than sixty then—and they were watching two elderly men play chess. He wore a grey cardigan and a black velvet scarf, although the day was not cold. His hair was almost gone. That silver crown of hair, it was ... gone. His face was all hollow spaces, and his skin was a bad mix of bad colours, as if he was recovering from a serious illness. Perhaps he was *succumbing* to it. I do not know. I walked on past him, averting my gaze, so that he should not recognise me. I even pretended a strange, stooping walk to disguise myself. At the last moment I glanced back at him, watching as he coughed violently into a white handkerchief. There was blood, I think, staining that white handkerchief. I walked faster and faster until I ran with the haste of a man in terror.'

Once again we sat in silence and allowed our eyes to rove the passing crowds, following a man in a blue turban in one instant, and a woman in a black mask, veil, and chador the next.

'You know, Lin, I have lived what many—or most—would call a wicked life. I have done things that could put me in prison, and things that, in some nations, could see me executed. There are many things I have done that I can say, I am not proud. But there is only one act in my whole life that I can say, I am truly ashamed of it. I hurried past that great man, and I had money enough and time enough and good health enough to help him. I hurried past him, not because I felt guilty about the theft of his money. And not because I was afraid of his sickness, or the commitment it might cost me. I hurried past that good and brilliant man who loved me, and taught me how to love, simply because he was old—because he was not beautiful any more.'

He drained his glass, examined its emptiness for a moment, and then placed it on the table as gently and attentively as if it was about to explode.

'*Merde!* Let's *drink*, my friend!' he cried at last, but my hand stayed his, preventing him from summoning the waiter.

'I can't, Didier. I have to meet Lisa at the Sea Rock. She asked me to ride out there and meet her. I'll have to leave now, if I'm going to make it.'

He clenched his jaws on something—a request, perhaps, or another confession. My hand still rested on his.

'Look, you can come, if you like. It's not a private meeting, and it's a nice ride out to Juhu.'

He smiled slowly, and slid his hand out from under mine. Still staring into my eyes, he raised his hand, pointing with one finger. A waiter came to the table. Without looking at him, Didier ordered another whisky. When I paid my bill and walked out to the street, he was coughing again, hunched over one hand and clutching his glass with the other.

I'd bought a bike, an Enfield Bullet, a month before. The taste of two-wheeled adrenaline that I'd experienced in Goa had nagged at me until I finally surrendered to it, and went with Abdullah to the mechanic who serviced his bike. The mechanic, a Tamil named Hussein, loved bikes, and loved Abdullah almost as much. The Enfield he sold to me was in perfect condition, and it never once let me down. Vikram was so impressed with it that he bought one from Hussein within a week. Sometimes we rode together, Abdullah, Vikram, and I, our three bikes side by side, and the sun in our laughing mouths.

On that afternoon when I left Didier at Leopold's I rode slowly, and gave myself time and space to think. Karla was gone from the little house on Anjuna beach. I had no idea where she might be. Ulla told me that Karla had stopped writing to her, and I had no reason to think she was lying. So Karla was gone, and there was no way to find her. And every day I woke with a dream or a thought of her. Every night I slept with the knife of regret in my chest.

My thoughts drifted to Khaderbhai as I rode. He seemed well pleased with the niche role that I was playing in his mafia network. I supervised certain movements of smuggled gold through the domestic and international airports, exchanged sums of cash with agents at the five-star hotels and airline offices, and arranged to buy passports from foreigners. They were all jobs that a gora could perform more successfully and less obtrusively than an Indian. My conspicuousness was a strange and ironic form of camouflage. Foreigners were stared at in India. Somewhere in the five or more millennia of its history, the culture had decided to dispense with the casual, nonchalant glance. By the time I came to Bombay, the eye contact ranged from an ogling gaze to a gawping, goggle-eyed glare. There was nothing malicious in it. The staring eyes that found and followed me everywhere I went were innocent, curious, and almost always friendly. And that intense scrutiny had its benefits: for the most part, people stared at what I *was*, not what I *did*. Foreigners were stared into invisibility. So I wandered in and out of travel agencies or grand hotels, airline or business offices, followed in every step by eyes that saw *me*, but not the crimes I committed in the service of the great Khan.

I rode on past the Haji Ali Mosque, accelerating into the wide avenue of afternoon traffic, and as I rode I asked myself why Abdel Khader Khan never referred to the murder of his friend and colleague Madjid. It still nagged at me and I wanted to ask him about it, but the one time that I'd mentioned his name, soon after the murder, Khader had looked so stricken with grief that I'd let the subject lapse. And as the days had passed into weeks, and the weeks had drifted into silent months, I'd found it impossible to drag the subject into our conversations. It was as if *I* was the one who was keeping secrets; and no matter how thick my mind became with thoughts of the murder, I never admitted them to him. Instead, we talked business or we spoke of philosophy. And during the course of our long discussions he finally answered my big question. I remembered the excitement that had refracted in his eyes, and the pride, perhaps, when I'd proved that I understood his teaching. And as I rode from Leopold's to my meeting with Lisa on that day of Didier's confession, I remembered word-by-word and smile-by-smile the great Khan's explanation.

'And so, you understand the principle of the argument to this point?'

'Yes,' I answered him. I'd come to his Dongri mansion that night, a week before, to give him a report on the changes I'd recommended and initiated in the passport factory run by Abdel Ghani. With Ghani's approval and support, we'd expanded the operation to include a full package of identity documents—driver's licences, bank accounts, credit cards, even memberships of sports clubs. Khader was delighted with the progress of those innovations, but he soon changed the subject to talk of his favourite themes: good and evil, and the purpose of life.

'Perhaps you can tell it back to me,' he nodded, looking into the playful fling and splash of the fountain's plumes of water. His elbows rested on the arms of the white cane armchair, and the temple of his fingertips peaked at his lips and the neat, silver-grey moustache.

'Ah ... sure. You were saying that the whole universe is moving toward some ultimate complexity. This has been going on since the universe began, and physicists call it the *tendency toward complexity*. And ... anything that kicks this along and helps it is good, and anything that hinders it is evil.'

'Very good,' Khader said, raising one eyebrow in the smile he offered me. As was so often the case, I wasn't sure if he was expressing approval or mockery or both. It seemed, with Khader, that he never felt or expressed any one emotion without feeling something of its opposite. That might be true for all of us, to some extent. But with him, with lord Abdel Khader Khan, it wasn't possible to know what he really thought or felt about you. The one and only time that I saw the whole of the truth in his eyes—on a snow-covered mountain called Sorrow's Reward—it was already too late, and I never saw it again.

'And this final complexity,' he added, 'it can be called God, or the Universal Spirit, or the Ultimate Complexity, as you please. For myself, there is no problem in calling it God. The whole universe is moving toward God, in a tendency toward the ultimate complexity that God is.'

'That still leaves me with the question I asked you last time. How do you decide how any one thing is good or evil?'

'That is true. I promised you an answer to this very good question then, young Mr. Lin, and you will have it. But, first, you must answer a question for me. Why is killing wrong?'

'Well, I don't think it *is* always wrong.'

'Ah,' he mused, his amber eyes glittering in the same wry smile. 'Well, I must tell you that it *is* always wrong. This will become clear, later in our discussion. For now, concentrate on the type of killing that you *do* think is wrong, and tell me *why* it is wrong.'

'Yeah, well, it's the unlawful taking of a life.'

'By whose law?'

'Society's law. The law of the land,' I offered, sensing that the philosophical ground was slipping away beneath me.

'Who makes this law?' he asked gently.

'Politicians pass laws. Criminal laws are inherited from ... from civilisation. The laws against unlawful killing go all the way back—maybe all the way back to the cave.'

'And why was killing wrong for *them*?'

'You mean ... well, I'd say, because there's only one life. You only get one shot at it, and to take it away is a terrible thing.'

'A lightning storm is a terrible thing. Does that make it wrong, or evil?'

'No, of course not,' I replied more irritably. 'Look, I don't know why we *need* to know what's behind the laws against killing. We have one life, and if you take a life without a good reason you do something wrong.'

'Yes,' he said patiently. 'But *why* is it wrong?'

'It just *is*, that's all.'

'This is the point we all reach,' Khader concluded, more serious in his tone. He put his hand on my wrist as it rested on the arm of my chair beside him, and he tapped out the important points with his fingers. 'If you ask people why killing, or any other crime, is wrong, they will tell you that it is against the law, or that the Bible, or the Upanishads, or the Koran, or the Buddha's eight-fold path, or their parents, or some other authority tells them it is wrong. But they don't know *why* it is wrong. It may be *true*, what they say, but they don't know *why* it is true.

'In order to know about any act or intention or consequence, we must first ask two questions. One, what would happen if *everyone* did this thing? Two, would this *help* or *hinder* the movement toward complexity?'

He paused as a servant entered with Nazeer. The servant brought sweet, black suleimani chai, in long glasses, and a variety of irresistible sweets on a silver tray. Nazeer brought a questioning glance for Khaderbhai and a scowl of unmitigated contempt for me. Khader thanked him and the servant, and they left us alone once more.

'In the case of killing,' Khader continued, after he'd sipped the tea through a cube of white sugar. 'What would happen if *everyone* killed people? Would that *help* or *hinder*? Tell me.'

'Obviously, if everyone killed people, we would wipe each other out. So ... that *wouldn't* help.'

'Yes. We human beings are the most complex arrangement of matter that we know of, but we are not the *last* achievement of the universe. We, too, will develop and change with the rest of the universe. But if we kill indiscriminately, we will not get there. We will wipe out our species, and all the development that led to us across millions of years—billions of years—will be lost. The same can be said for stealing. What would happen if *everyone* stole things? Would that help us, or would it hinder us?'

'Yeah. I get the point. If everyone was stealing off everyone else we'd be so paranoid, and we'd waste so much time and money on it, that it would slow us down, and we'd never get —'

'To the ultimate complexity,' he completed the thought for me. 'This is *why* killing and stealing are wrong—not because a book tells us they are wrong, or a law tells us they are wrong, or a spiritual guide tells us they are wrong, but because if *everyone* did them we would *not* move toward the ultimate complexity that is God, with the rest of the universe. And the opposite of these is also true. Why is love *good*? Well, what would happen if everyone loved everyone else? Would that help us or would it hold us back?'

'It would help,' I agreed, laughing from within the trap he'd set for me.

'Yes. In fact, such universal love would greatly accelerate the movement toward God. Love is good. Friendship is good. Loyalty is good. Freedom is good. Honesty is good. We knew that these things were good before—we have always known this in our hearts, and all the great teachers have always told us this—but now, with this definition of good and evil, we can see *why* they are good. Just as we can see *why* stealing and lying and killing are evil.'

'But sometimes …' I protested, 'you know, what about self-defence? What about killing to defend yourself?'

'Yes, a good point, Lin. I want you to imagine a scene for me. You are standing in a room with a desk in front of you. On the other side of the room is your mother. A vicious man holds a knife to the throat of your mother. The man will kill your mother. On the table in front of you there is a button. If you press it, the man will die. If you do not, he will kill your mother. These are the only possible outcomes. If you do nothing, your mother dies. If you press the button, the man dies and your mother is saved. What would you do?'

'The guy's history,' I answered without hesitation.

'Just so,' he sighed, perhaps wishing that I'd wrestled with the decision a little longer before pressing the button. 'And if you did this, if you saved your mother from this vicious killer, would you be doing the wrong thing or the right thing?'

'The right thing,' I said just as swiftly.

'No, Lin, I'm afraid not,' he frowned. 'We have just seen that in the terms of this new, objective definition of good and evil, killing is always wrong because, if everyone did it, we would not move toward God, the ultimate complexity, with the rest of the universe. So it is wrong to kill. But your reasons were good. So therefore, the truth of this decision is that you did the *wrong* thing, for the *right* reasons ...'

As I rode the wind, a week after Khader's little lecture on ethics, weaving the bike through ancient-modern traffic beneath a darkening, portentous tumble of clouds, those words echoed in my mind. *The wrong thing, for the right reasons.* I rode on and, even when I stopped thinking about Khader's lesson, those words still murmured in the little grey daydream-space where memory meets inspiration. I know now that the words were like a mantra, and that my instinct—fate's whisper in the dark—was trying to warn me of something by repeating them. *The wrong thing ... for the right reasons.*

But on that day, an hour after Didier's confession, I let the murmured warnings fade. Right or wrong, I didn't want to think about the reasons —not my reasons for doing what I did, or Khader's, or anyone's. I enjoyed the discussions of good and evil, but only as a game, as an entertainment. I didn't really want the truth. I was sick of truth, especially my own truth, and I couldn't face it. So the thoughts and premonitions echoed and then whipped past me into the coils of humid wind. And by the time I swept into the last curve of coast near the Sea Rock Hotel, my mind was as clear as the broad horizon clamped upon the limit of a dark and tremulous sea.

The Sea Rock, which was as luxurious and opulently serviced as the other five-star hotels in Bombay, offered the special attraction that it was literally built upon the sea rocks at Juhu. From all its major restaurants, bars, and a hundred other windows, the Sea Rock scanned the endlessly shifting peaks and furrows of the Arabian Sea. The hotel also offered one of the best and most comprehensively eclectic smorgasbord lunches in the city. I was hungry, and glad to see that Lisa was waiting for me in the foyer. She wore a starched, sky-blue shirt with the collar turned up, and sky-blue culottes. Her blonde hair was wound into the praying-fingers of a French braid. She'd been clean, off heroin, for more than a year. She looked tanned and healthy and confident.

'Hi, Lin,' she smiled, greeting me with a kiss on the cheek. 'You're just in time.'

'Great. I'm starving.'

'No, I mean you're just in time to meet Kalpana. Just a minute—here she comes now.'

A young woman with a fashionably western short haircut, hipster jeans, and a tight, red T-shirt approached us. She wore a stopwatch around her neck on a lanyard, and carried a clipboard. She was about twenty-six years old.

'Hello,' I said when Lisa introduced us. 'Is that your rig outside? The broadcast vans, and all the cables? Are you shooting a movie?'

'*Supposed* to be, *yaar*,' she replied in the exaggerated vowels of the Bombay accent that I loved and found myself unconsciously imitating. 'The director has gone off somewhere with one of our dancers. It's meant to be a secret, *yaar*, but the whole damn set is talking about it. We've got a forty-five minute break. Although, mind you, that's about ten times as long as our guy will need, from what all I'm told about his prowess.'

'Okay,' I suggested, smacking my hands together. 'That gives us time for lunch.'

'Fuck lunch, let's get stoned first, *yaar*,' Kalpana demurred. 'Have you got any hash?'

'Yeah,' I shrugged. 'Sure.'

'Did you bring a car?'

'I'm on a Bullet.'

'Okay, let's use my car. It's in the car park.'

We left the hotel, and sat in her new Fiat to smoke. While I prepared the joint, she told me that she was an assistant to the producer of that and several other films. One of her duties was to oversee the casting of minor roles in the films. She'd subcontracted the task to a casting agent, but he was experiencing difficulty in finding foreigners to fill the small, non-speaking, decorative roles.

'Kalpana got talking about this at dinner last week,' Lisa summed up when Kalpana began to smoke. 'She told me that her guys couldn't find foreigners to play the parts in the movies—you know, the people at a disco or a party scene or, like, British people, in the time of the British Raj and like that. So ... I thought of you.'

'U-huh.'

'It would be a great help if you could get the goras for me when we need them,' Kalpana said, offering me what seemed to be a well-practised leer. Practised or not, it was damned effective. 'We provide a cab to bring them to the shoot and take them home again. We give them a full lunch during the break. And we pay about two thousand rupees a day, per person. We pay that to *you*, plus a bonus commission per head. What you pay *them*, well, it's up to you. Most of them are happy to do it for nothing, and are real surprised, you know, when they find out we actually *pay* them to be in the movies.'

'Whaddaya say?' Lisa asked me, her eyes gleaming through the rose filter of her stone.

'I'm interested.'

My mind was trawling through the possible lateral benefits in the arrangement. Some of them were obvious. The moviemakers were a fairly affluent crowd of frequent flyers who might need black-market dollars and documents, from time to time. It was clear to me, as well, that the casting job was important to Lisa. On its own, that was reason enough for me to get involved. I liked her, and I was glad that she wanted to like me.

'Good,' Kalpana concluded, opening the door and stepping out to the car park. We walked back to the hotel foyer, each of us with sunglasses clamped to our eyes. We shook hands at the same spot where we'd met half an hour before.

'Have your lunch,' she said. 'I'll go back to the set. We're in the ballroom. When you're all done, follow the cables and you'll find me. I'll introduce you to the guys, and you can start right away. We need a few foreigners for tomorrow's shoot, here. Two guys and two gals, *yaar*. Blonde, Sweden types, if you can find them. Hey—that was Kashmiri hash, *na*? We'll get along just fine, Lin, you and me. *Ciao! Ciao*, baby.'

In the restaurant, Lisa and I heaped our plates high, and sat facing the sea to eat.

'Kalpana's okay,' she said between mouthfuls. 'She's sarcastic as all hell, sometimes, and she's a real ambitious girl—don't make any mistake about that—but she's a straight talker and a real friend. When she told me about the casting job, I thought about you. I thought you might be able to... make something out of it ...'

'Thanks,' I said, meeting her eye and trying to read her. 'I appreciate the thought. Do you want to be partners in it with me?'

'Yes,' she answered quickly. 'I was hoping ... hoping you'd want to.'

'We could work it out together,' I suggested. 'I don't think I'll have any trouble getting foreigners to work in the movies, but I don't really want to do the rest of it. You could do that part, if you like. You could organise picking them up, looking after them on the set, and making the payments and all that. I'll talk them into it, and you take it from there. I'd be glad to work with you, if you're interested.'

She smiled. It was a good smile; the kind you like to keep.

'I'd love to do it,' she gushed, flushing pink with embarrassment under her tan. 'I really need to do something, Lin, and I think I'm ready. When Kalpana ran this casting thing by me, I wanted to jump at it, but I was too nervous to take it on alone. Thanks.'

'Don't mention it. How's it going with you and Abdullah?'

'Mmmm,' she mumbled, finishing a mouthful of food. 'I'm not *working*, if you know what I mean, so that's something. I'm not working at the Palace, and I'm not using. He gave me money. A lot of money. I don't know where he got it. I don't really care. It's more money than I've ever seen in one bundle before in my whole life. It's in this case, this metal case. He gave it to me, and asked me to look after it for him, and to spend it whenever I need it. It was real spooky, kinda like ... I dunno ... like his last will and testament, or something.'

I raised one eyebrow unconsciously in a quizzical expression. She caught the look, reflected a moment, and then responded.

'I trust you, Lin. You're the only guy in this city I do trust. Funny thing is, Abdullah's the guy gave me the money and all, and I think I love him, in a kind of insane way, but I don't trust him. Is that a horrible thing to say about the guy you live with?'

'No.'

'Do you trust him?'

'With my life.'

'Why?'

I hesitated, and then the words didn't come. We finished our meal and sat back from the table, looking at the sea.

'We've been through some things,' I said after a while. 'But it's not just that. I trusted him before we did any of that. I don't know what it is. A man trusts another man when he sees enough of himself in him, I guess. Or maybe when he sees the things he wishes he had in himself.'

We were silent for a time, each of us troubled, and stubbornly tempting fate in our own ways.

'Are you ready?' I asked her. She nodded in reply. 'Let's go to the movies.'

We followed the black vines of relay cables from the generator vans outside the hotel. They led us through a side entrance and past a procession of bustling assistants to the banquet room, which had been hired as a set. The room was filled with people, powerful lights, dazzling reflector panels, cameras, and equipment. Seconds after we entered, someone shouted *Quiet, please!* And then a riotous musical number began.

Hindi movies aren't to everyone's taste. Some foreigners I'd dealt with had told me that they loathed the kaleidoscopic turmoil of musical numbers, bursting stochastically between weeping mothers, sighing infatuates, and brawling villains. I understood what they meant, but I didn't agree with them. A year before, Johnny Cigar had told me that in former lives I must've been at least six different Indian personalities. I'd taken it as a high compliment, but it wasn't until I saw my first Bollywood movie shoot that I knew at last, and exactly, what he'd meant. I loved the singing, the dancing, and the music with the whole of my heart from the very first instant.

The producers had hired a two-thousand-watt amplifier. The music crashed through the banquet room and rattled into our bones. The colours were from a tropical sea. The million lights were as dazzling as a sun-struck lake. The faces were as beautiful as those carved on temple walls. The dancing was a frenzy of excited, exuberant lasciviousness and ancient classical skills. And the whole, improbably coherent expression of love and life, drama and comedy, was articulated in the delicate, unfurled elegance of a graceful hand, or the wink of a seductive eye.

For an hour we watched as the dance number was rehearsed and refined and finally recorded on film. During a break, after that, Kalpana introduced me to Cliff De Souza and Chandra Mehta, two of the four producers of the film. De Souza was a tall, curly-haired, thirty-year-old Goan with a disarming grin and a loping walk. Chandra Mehta was closer to forty. He was overweight, but comfortable with it: one of those big men who expand to fit a big idea of themselves. I liked both men and, although they were too busy to talk for long, that first meeting was cordial and communicative.

I offered Lisa a lift back to town, but she'd arranged to ride with Kalpana, and she chose to wait. I gave her the phone number at my new apartment, telling her to call if she needed me. On my way out through the foyer, I saw Kavita Singh also leaving the hotel. We'd both been so busy in recent months—she with writing about crimes, and me with committing them—that we hadn't seen one another for many weeks.

'Kavita!' I called out, running forward to catch her. 'Just the woman I wanted to see! The number-one reporter, on Bombay's number-one newspaper. How are you? You... look... *great!*'

She was dressed in a silk pantsuit. It was the colour of bleached bone. She carried a linen handbag in the same colour. The single-breasted jacket descended to a deep décolletage, and it was obvious that she was wearing nothing under the jacket.

'Oh, come off it!' she snapped, grinning and embarrassed. 'This is my dressed-to-kill outfit. I had to interview Vasant Lal. I just came out of there.'

'You're moving in powerful circles,' I said, recalling photos of the populist politician. His incitements to communal violence had resulted in rioting, arson, and murder. Each time I saw him on television or read one of his bigoted speeches in the newspaper, he made me think of the brutal madman who called himself Sapna: a legal, political version of the psychopathic killer.

'It was a snake-pit up there in his suite, I tell you, baba. But I got my interview. He has a weakness for big tits.' She whipped a finger into my face. 'Don't say *anything!*'

'Hey!' I pacified her, raising both hands and wagging my head. 'I'm ... saying nothing at all, *yaar*. Absolutely nothing. I'm *looking*, mind you, and I wish I had three eyes, but I'm saying nothing at all!'

'You bastard!' she hissed, laughing through gritted teeth. 'Ah, shit, what's happening to the world, man, when one of the most important guys in the city won't talk to *you*, but will give a two-hour interview to your *tits*? Men are such sick fuckers, don't you think?'

'You got me there, Kavita,' I sighed.

'Fuckin' pigs, *yaar*.'

'Can't argue with that. When you're right, you're right.'

She eyed me suspiciously.

'What are you being so damn agreeable about, Lin?'

'Listen, where are you going?'

'What?'

'Where are you going? Right now, I mean.'

'I was going to take a cab back to town. I'm living near Flora Fountain now.'

'How about I give you a lift, on my bike? I want to talk to you. I want you to help me with a problem.'

Kavita didn't know me well. Her eyes were the colour of bark on a cinnamon tree, flecked with golden sparks. She looked me up and down with those eyes, and the forensic examination left her somewhere short of inspired reassurance.

'What kind of a problem?' she asked.

'It involves a murder,' I replied. 'And I want you to make it a page-one story. I'll tell you all about it at your place. And on the way you can tell me about Vasant Lal—you'll have to shout on the back of the bike, so that'll help you get it out of your system, na?'

Some forty minutes later, we sat together in her fourth-floor walk-up apartment on the edge of the Fort area, near Flora Fountain. It was a tiny apartment with a foldout bed, a rudimentary kitchen, and a hundred noisy neighbours. It boasted a superb bathroom, however, large enough to hold a washing machine and dryer without crowding. There was also a balcony enclosed in antique wrought iron that looked out on the wide, busy square around the fountain.

'His name is Anand Rao,' I told her, sipping the strong espresso coffee she'd prepared for me. 'He shared a hut, in the slum, with a guy named Rasheed. They were my neighbours when I lived there. Then Rasheed's wife and her sister came to stay, from the village in Rajasthan. Anand moved out of the hut to leave room for Rasheed and the sisters.'

'Hang on,' Kavita interrupted. 'I better get this down.'

She stood up and walked to a wide, cluttered desk, where she gathered up a pad, pen, and cassette recorder. She'd changed out of her pantsuit, and wore loose harem pants and a singlet. Watching her walk, following her quick, purposeful, graceful movements, I realised for the first time just how beautiful she was. When she returned and set up the recorder, tucking her legs beneath her on the armchair as she prepared to write, she caught me staring at her.

'*What?*' she asked.

'Nothing,' I smiled. 'Okay, so Anand Rao got to meet Rasheed's wife and her sister. He got to like them. They were shy, but they were friendly, happy, and kind. I think, now, reading between the lines, that Anand got a little sweet on the sister. Anyway, one day Rasheed tells his wife that the only way they can set themselves up, in the little shop that they want, is if he sells his kidney—one of his kidneys—at this private hospital he knows about. She argues against this, but he finally convinces her that it's their only chance.

'Well, he comes back from the hospital, and he tells her he's got good news and bad news. The good news is that they definitely want a kidney. The bad news is that they don't want a *man's* kidney—they want a *woman's* kidney.'

'Okay,' Kavita sighed, shaking her head.

'Yeah. The guy was a prince. Anyway, his wife balks at this, understandably, but Rasheed convinces her, and she goes off to have the operation.'

'Do you know where this took place?' Kavita asked.

'Yeah. Anand Rao checked into it all, and told Qasim Ali, the head man in the slum. He's got the details. So, anyway, Anand Rao hears about this, when Rasheed's wife returns from the hospital, and he's furious. He knows Rasheed well—they shared the hut together for two years, remember—and he knows that Rasheed is a con man. He has it out with Rasheed, but it comes to nothing. Rasheed gets all indignant. He spills kerosene on himself, and tells Anand Rao to light it, if he doesn't trust him, and if he thinks he's such a bad guy. Anand just warns him to look after the women, and leaves it at that.'

'When did this happen?'

'The operation was six months ago. Well, the next thing is, Rasheed tells his wife that he's been down to the hospital twenty times to sell his own kidney, but they don't want it. He tells her the money they got for her kidney was only half as much as they need to buy their business. He tells her that they still want women's kidneys, and he starts working on her to sell her *sister's* kidney. The wife is against it, but Rasheed works on the young sister, telling her that if she doesn't sell her kidney, then the wife will have sold her kidney for nothing. Finally, the women give in. Rasheed packs the younger sister off to the hospital, and she returns, minus one of her kidneys.'

'This is some guy,' Kavita muttered.

'Yeah. Well, I never liked him. He was one of those guys who smile as a tactic, you know, and not because they actually feel anything worth smiling about. Kind of like the way a chimpanzee smiles.'

'And what happened? He took off with the money, I suppose?'

'Yeah. Rasheed took the money and ran. The two sisters were devastated. Their health deteriorated. They went downhill fast. They ended up in hospital. First one, and then the other—they both fell into a coma. Lying together in their hospital beds, they were pronounced dead within minutes of each other. Anand was there, with a few others from the slum. He stayed long enough to see the sheets pulled over their faces. Then he ran out of the hospital. He went out of his mind with anger and ... guilt, I suppose. He went looking for Rasheed. He knew every one of Rasheed's drinking dives. When he tracked him down, Rasheed was lying in a rubbish pit, sleeping off a binge. He'd paid some kids to keep the rats off his drunken body. Anand chased the kids off and sat down beside Rasheed, and listened to him snore. Then he cut his throat, and waited there until the blood stopped flowing.'

'Pretty messy,' Kavita muttered, not looking up from her pad.

'It was. It is. Anand gave himself up, and made a full confession. He's been charged with murder.'

'And you want me to ...?'

'I want you to make it a front-page story. I want you to build some kind of popular movement around him, so that if they do convict him—which they will, for sure—they'll have to go a little easy on him. I want him to have support while he's in prison, and I want to keep his prison time down to as little as possible.'

'That's a lot of I want.'

'I know.'

'Well,' she frowned, 'it's an interesting story, but I've got to tell you, Lin, we get too many stories like this every day. Wife-burning, dowry murders, child prostitution, slavery, female infanticide—it's a war against women in India, Lin. It's a fight to the death, and mostly it's the women dying. I want to help your guy, but I don't see this as page one, *yaar*. And anyway, I don't have any pull with page one. I'm new there myself, don't forget.'

'There's more,' I pressed her. 'The kicker in the story is that the sisters didn't die. Half an hour after they were pronounced dead, Rasheed's wife stirred beneath the sheet. A few minutes later, her sister moved and groaned. They're alive and well today. Their hut, in the slum, has become a kind of shrine. People come from all over the city to see the miracle sisters who returned from the dead. It's the best thing that's ever happened to the businesses in the slum. They're doing a roaring trade with the pilgrims. And the sisters are richer than they could ever have dreamed. People are throwing money at them, a rupee or two at a time, and it's really adding up. The sisters have set up a charity for abandoned wives. And I think their story—back from the dead, you know—is enough to jump this to page one.'

'*Arrey yaar*, baba!' Kavita yelped. 'Okay, first you have to get me together with the women. They're the key to this. Then I have to interview Anand Rao in prison.'

'I'll take you there.'

'No,' she insisted. 'I have to speak to him alone. I don't want him prompted by you, or responding to you. I have to see how he'll hold up on his own. If we're going to build a campaign around him, he'll have to stand alone, *yaar*. But you can speak to him first and prepare the way before my interview. I'll try to get to see him in the next two or three weeks. We've got a lot to do.'

For two hours we discussed the campaign, and I answered her many questions. I left her in a happy, enthusiastic whirl of pressure and purpose. I rode straight out to Nariman Point, and bought a sizzling meal from one of the fast-food vans parked on the beach. But my appetite wasn't as good as I'd thought, and I ate less than half. I went down to the rocks to rinse my hands in the seawater, within sight of the spot where Abdullah had introduced himself to me three years before.

Khader's words floated on the swift, shallow stream of my thoughts once again: *the wrong thing, for the right reasons* ... I thought of Anand Rao, in Arthur Road Prison, in the big dormitory room with the overseers and the body lice. I shivered the thought off into the breeze. Kavita had asked me why the Anand Rao case was so important to me. I didn't tell her that he'd come to me before he committed the murder, only a week before he cut Rasheed's throat. I didn't tell her that I'd brushed him off, and insulted him, demeaning his dilemma with an offer of money. I smudged an answer to her question, and let her think that I was just trying to help a friend, just trying to do the right thing.

Khaderbhai once said that every virtuous act is inspired by a dark secret. It mightn't be true of everyone, but it was true enough about me. The little good that I've done in the world has always dragged behind it a shadow of dark inspiration. What I do know now, and didn't know then is that, in the long run, motive matters more with good deeds than it does with bad. When all the guilt and shame for the bad we've done have run their course, it's the good we did that can save us. But then, when salvation speaks, the secrets we kept, and the motives we concealed, creep from their shadows. They cling to us, those dark motives for our good deeds. Redemption's climb is steepest if the good we did is soiled with secret shame.

But I didn't know that then. I washed my hands in the cold, uncaring sea, and my conscience was as silent and remote as the mute, unreachable stars.

CHAPTER TWENTY-SEVEN

Used passports, known as books to us, the counterfeiters and smugglers who traded in them, had to be checked before they could be sold or used by black marketeers. It was always possible that the junkies, runaways, or indigent foreigners who'd sold their passports to our agents were wanted for some serious offence in their own or some other country. More than a few smugglers had been caught out in that way. They'd bought passports, changed them to suit, and set out on a mission, only to find themselves arrested at a foreign airport because the original owners were wanted for murder, or robbery, or different smuggling charges. To ensure the satisfaction of our customers and the safety of our couriers, Abdul Ghani subjected every new passport that he bought or stole to two levels of scrutiny.

A customs officer with access to a computer at Bombay's international airport provided the first filter. At a time and place of his choosing, the officer was given a sheet bearing the country of origin, passport number, and original name on each passport to be checked. A day or two later he returned the sheet with a line drawn through those that were flagged in his computer. Some of the passports were flagged because international arrest-warrants had been issued for the original owners. Some passports were flagged because suspicion attached itself to the owner: a hint of involvement in the illegal drugs or arms trade, or some political connection that made security services uneasy. Whatever the reason, flagged passports couldn't be sold on the black market or used by Ghani's couriers.

Flagged books still had their uses. It was possible to cannibalise them by pulling apart the stitching to furnish fresh pages for other, usable books. There were also other uses within India. Although foreigners had to show their passports for C-Form entries when they registered at hotels, every city had its share of places that weren't fastidiously precise about the resemblance, or lack of it, between a passport and its bearer. For those hotels, any passport did the job. Although unable to travel out of India with such a flagged passport, a man or woman could use one to move around *within* the country safely, and satisfy the minimum legal requirements that an obliging hotel manager had to observe.

Unflagged books that did pass the customs check were sent through a second filter at airline offices. All the major airlines kept their own lists of hot or flagged passports. Inclusion of a passport name and number on the list was prompted by anything from a bad credit rating or fraudulent dealings with an airline to any incident involving violent behaviour as a passenger on a plane. Naturally enough, when smugglers were going about the business of their crimes they were eager to avoid any but the most superficial and routine attention from airline staff, customs personnel, or police. A passport that was flagged, for any reason, was useless to them. Abdul Ghani's agents at the offices of most of the major airlines in Bombay checked the numbers and names of the passports we'd acquired, and reported those that were flagged. The clean books that passed through both filters—a little less than half of all those obtained—were sold, or used by Khader's couriers.

The clients who bought Ghani's illegal passports fell into three main categories. The first were economic refugees, people forced from their land by famine or driven to seek a better life in a new country. There were Turks wanting to work in Germany, Albanians wanting to work in Italy, Algerians wanting to work in France, and people from several Asian countries who wanted to work in Canada and the United States. A family, a group of families, and sometimes a whole village community pooled their meagre earnings to purchase one of Abdul's passports and send a favoured son to one of the promised lands. Once there, he worked to repay their loan and eventually buy new passports for other young men and women. The passports sold for anything between five and twenty-five thousand dollars. Khaderbhai's network issued about a hundred of those poverty passports every year, and his annual profit, after all the overheads, was more than a million dollars.

Political refugees made up the second category of clients. The upheavals that sent those people into exile were often violent. They were victims of wars, and of conflicts based on community, religion, or ethnicity. Sometimes the upheaval was legislated: thousands of Hong

Kong residents who weren't recognised as British citizens became potential clients, with the stroke of a pen, when Britain decided in 1984 to return its colonial possession to China in a thirteen-year resolution of sovereignty. Around the world, at any one time, there were twenty million refugees living in camps and safe havens. Abdul Ghani's passport agents were never idle. A new book cost those people anywhere from ten to fifty thousand dollars. The higher price was determined by the greater risks involved in smuggling *into* war zones, and the greater demand to escape *from* them.

The third group of clients for Abdul's illegal books was criminals. Occasionally, those criminals were men like me—thieves, smugglers, contract killers—who needed a new identity to stay one step ahead of the police. For the most part, however, Abdul Ghani's special clients were the kind of men who were more likely to build and fill prisons than to serve time in them. They were dictators, military coup leaders, secret policemen, and bureaucrats from corrupt regimes forced to take flight when their crimes were uncovered or the regime fell. One Ugandan fugitive—a man I dealt with personally—had stolen more than a million dollars, allocated by international monetary agencies for essential service constructions, including a children's hospital. The hospital was never built. Instead, the sick, injured, and dying children were transported to a remote camp and left to fend for themselves. At a meeting that I set up in Kinshasa, Zaïre, the man paid me two hundred thousand dollars for two books—a perfect, unblemished Swiss passport, and a virgin, original Canadian passport—and travelled safely to Venezuela.

Abdul's agents in South America, Asia, and Africa established contact with embezzlers, torturers, mandarins, and martinets who'd supported fallen tyrannies. Dealing with them gave me more angry shame than anything else I ever did in Khaderbhai's service. In the young life I'd known as a free man, I was a dedicated writer of newspaper articles and pamphlets. I'd spent years researching and exposing the crimes and violations perpetrated by such men. I'd put my body on the line, supporting their victims in a hundred violent protest clashes with the police. And I still felt some of the old hatred and a choking sense of outrage when I dealt with them. But that life I'd known was gone. The revolutionary social activist had lost his ideals in heroin and crime. And I, too, was a wanted man. I, too, had a price on my head. I was a gangster, and I lived from one day to the next with only Khader's mafia council standing between me and prison torture.

So, I played my part in Ghani's network, helping mass-murderers to escape from the death sentences they'd passed on so many others and had finally earned from their countrymen in return. But I didn't like it, and I didn't like them, and I let them know it. I drove them to the wall on every deal, taking a little solace from the rage I provoked in them. And they haggled infuriatingly, those human-rights abusers, self-righteously indignant about spending the money they'd gouged from people's mouths. But in the end, they all caved in and agreed to our terms. In the end, they paid well.

No-one else in Khaderbhai's network seemed to share my sense of outrage or my shame. There's probably no single group of citizens who are more cynical about politics and politicians than professional criminals. In their view, all politicians are ruthless and corrupt, and all political systems favour the powerful rich over the defenceless poor. And in time, and in a sense, I began to share their view because I knew the experience in which it was grounded. Prison had given us an intimate acquaintance with human-rights violations, and every day the courts confirmed what we'd learned about the law: the rich in any country, and any system, always got the best justice money could buy.

On the other hand, the criminals in Khader's network displayed a kind of egalitarianism that would've filled communists and Gnostic Christians with admiring envy. They didn't care about the colour, creed, race, or political orientation of clients, and they didn't judge them when asking about their past. Every life, no matter how innocent or evil, reduced to only one question: *How bad do you need the book?* The answer established the going rate, and every customer who had the money to pay it was born again, with no history and no sin, in the moment of the deal. No client was better than any other, and none was worse.

Abdul Ghani, propelled by the purest amoral spirit of market forces, serviced the needs of generals, mercenaries, misappropriators of public funds, and murderous interrogators without a hint of censure or dismay. Their freedom brought in about two million dollars each year in clear profit. But although he wasn't ethically squeamish about the *source* of the income, or receiving it, Abdul Ghani was religiously superstitious about *spending* it. Every dollar earned in saving that poisonous clientele went to a refugee rescue program that Khaderbhai had established for Iranians and Afghans displaced by war. Every passport bought by one of the warlords or their apparatchiks bought fifty more books, identity cards, or travel documents for Iranian and Afghan refugees. Thus, in one of those psychic labyrinths that fate likes to build around greed and fear, the high prices paid by tyrants rescued many of those made wretched by tyranny.

Krishna and Villu taught me everything they knew about the passport business, and in time I began to experiment, creating new identities for myself with American, Canadian, Dutch, German, and British books. My work wasn't as good as theirs, and never would be. Good forgers are artists. Their artistic vision must encompass the deliberate creative smudge that gives each page its counterfeit authenticity, no less than the accuracy of altered or manufactured details. Each page that they create is a miniature painting, a tiny expression of their art. The precise angle of one slightly skewed stamp or the casual blurring of another are as significant to those small canvasses as the shape, position, and colour of a fallen rose might be in a grand master's portrait. The effect, no matter how skilfully achieved, is always born in the artist's intuition. And intuition can't be taught.

My skills, instead, found expression in the stories that had to be invented for every newly created book. There were often gaps of months, or even years, in the record of travel contained within the books that we got from foreigners. Some had overstayed their visas, and that lapse had to be expunged from the book before it could be used. Stamping an exit from Bombay airport *before* the last visa's expiry date, as if the passport holder had left the country within the life of the visa, I then set about establishing a history of movement from one country to another for every book, using the bank of exit and entry stamps that Villu had created. Little by little, I brought each book up to date, and finally supplied it with a new visa for India and an entry stamp at Bombay airport.

The chain of entries and exits that linked that lapsed time was always carefully plotted. Krishna and Villu had a library of logbooks from the major airlines, listing all of the flights in and out of Europe, Asia, Africa, and the Americas with their departure dates and arrival times. If we put a stamp into a British book stating that the holder had arrived in Athens on July the fourth, say, we were sure that a British Airways flight had connected at Athens airport on that day. In that way, every book had a personal history of travel and experience backed up by logs, timetables, and weather details which gave the new bearer a credible personal history.

My first test of the passports I'd forged for myself was on the domestic transfer route, known as the *double-shuffle*. Thousands of Iranian and Afghan refugees in Bombay tried to find asylum in Canada, Australia, the United States, and elsewhere, but the governments of those countries refused to consider them. If they could land there, in those western countries, they could declare themselves to be asylum-seekers and submit to the processes of assessment that determined the merit of their applications. Because they *were* political refugees and genuine asylum-seekers, the applications they launched within the nominated country were often successful. The trick was to get them into Canada, or Sweden, or some other country of choice in the first place.

The *double-shuffle* was the system we used. When Iranians or Afghans in Bombay tried to buy tickets to the asylum countries, they were required to show current visas for those countries. But they couldn't obtain the visas legally, and false visas were impracticable because they were immediately checked against the consular register. So I purchased a ticket to Canada or Sweden with a false visa. As a gora, a well-dressed foreigner of European appearance, I was never subjected to anything but a cursory examination. No-one ever bothered to check if my visa was genuine. The refugee I was helping then purchased a ticket for the domestic leg—from Bombay to Delhi—on the same plane. As we boarded the plane, we received boarding passes: mine was the green international boarding pass, and his was the red domestic pass. Once in the air, we swapped our boarding passes. At Delhi airport, only those with green international boarding passes were permitted to remain on board. Clutching my domestic pass, I got down at Delhi and left the refugee to continue on to Canada, or Sweden, or whatever the destination of the flight we'd chosen. Upon arrival, he would declare himself to be an asylum-seeker, and the process of his recognition would begin. In Delhi, I would spend the night at a five-star and then purchase another ticket to repeat the process—the double-shuffle—with another refugee on the Delhi to Bombay route.

The system worked. In those years we smuggled hundreds of Iranian and Afghan doctors, engineers, architects, academics, and poets into their nominated countries.

I received three thousand dollars for a double-shuffle, and for a while I did two doubles per month. After three months of internal flights from Bombay to Delhi, Calcutta, Madras, and back, Abdul Ghani sent me on my first international courier run. I carried a package of ten passports to Zaïre. Using photographs of the recipients—sent from Kinshasa, the capital—Krishna and Villu had worked the passports into perfect counterfeit books. After sealing them in plastic, I taped them to my body under three layers of clothing, and flew into the steaming, well-armed mayhem of Kinshasa's international airport.

It was a dangerous mission. At that time, Zaïre was a neutral no-man's-land between the bloody proxy wars that raged in Angola, Mozambique, Namibia, Sudan, Uganda, and the Congo. It was the personal fiefdom of the conspicuously insane dictator Mobutu, and a percentage of the profit from every crime in the kingdom slithered into his pocket. Mobutu was a darling of the western powers because he bought every costly killing weapon they offered to sell him. If it mattered to them that Mobutu turned the weapons on trade unionists and other social reformers in his own country, they never expressed the concern publicly. Those governments hosted the dictator in lavish style at royal and presidential receptions while hundreds of men and women were being tortured to death in his prisons. The same governments were hunting me through the international police agency, Interpol, and there was no doubt in my mind that their ally would've taken great pleasure in finishing me off for them—as a bonus, so to speak—if the passport mission had gone wrong and I'd found myself arrested in his capital city.

Still, I liked the wildness of Kinshasa, a city that thrived as an open market-place for the trade in every kind of contraband, from gold and drugs to rocket launchers. The city was full of mercenaries, fugitives, criminals, black-market profiteers, and wild-eyed, bare-knuckled opportunists from all over Africa. I felt at home there, and I would've stayed longer, but within seventy-two hours I'd delivered the books and accepted one hundred and twenty thousand dollars in payment. It was Khaderbhai's money. I was anxious to hand it over. I jumped the first flight back to Bombay, and reported to Abdul Ghani.

What I gained from the mission was ten thousand American dollars, field experience, and an introduction to the African branch of Ghani's network. The network and the experience were worth the risk, it seemed to me then. The money was unimportant. I would've done the job for half the wage or less. I knew that most of the human lives in Bombay came and went much cheaper.

More than that, there was the danger. For some people, danger's a kind of drug or even an aphrodisiac. For me, living as a fugitive, living every day and every night of my life with the fear of being killed or captured, danger was something else. Danger was one of the lances I used to kill the dragon of stress. It helped me to sleep. When I went to dangerous places and I did dangerous things, a rush of new and different fear swept over me. That new fear covered the dread that too often worried me awake. When the job was done, and the new fear subsided and passed away, I drowned in an exhausted peace.

And I wasn't alone in that hunger for dangerous work. In the course of the job I met other agents, smugglers, and mercenaries whose excited eyes and adrenaline-fired reflexes matched my own. Like me, they were all running from something: they were all afraid of something that they couldn't really forget or confront. And only danger money, earned with reckless risk, helped them to escape for a few hours and to sleep.

A second, third, and fourth trip to Africa followed without incident. I used three different passports, departing and arriving from different Indian international airports each time and then taking domestic flights back to Bombay. The double-shuffle flights between Delhi and Bombay continued. The specialist tasks that I performed with Khaled's currency dealers and some of the gold traders kept me busy—busy enough, most of the time, not to think too long and too hard of Karla.

Toward the end of the monsoon I visited the slum, and joined Qasim Ali on his daily tour of inspection. As he checked the drainage channels and ordered the repair of damaged huts, I recalled how much I'd admired and depended upon him when I'd lived there in the slum. Walking beside Qasim Ali in my new boots and black jeans, I watched the strong young men in bare feet and lungis dig and scrape with their hands, as I'd once done. I watched them shore up the retaining walls and clear the clogged drains, ensuring that the slum would remain dry to the end of the rains. And I envied them. I envied the importance of the work and their earnest devotion to it. I'd known it once, so well—that fervent and unquestioning dedication. I'd earned the smiles of pride and gratitude from the slum-dwellers when the dirty work was done. But that life was gone for me. Its virtues and its solaces beyond price were as remote and irrecoverable as the life I'd known and lost in Australia.

Perhaps sensing my sombre mood, Qasim directed us toward the open area where Prabaker and Johnny were making the first preparations for their weddings. Johnny and a dozen or so of his neighbours were erecting the frame for a *shamiana*, or great tent, where the wedding ceremonies would take place. Some distance away, other men were building a small stage where the couples would sit after the ceremonies and receive gifts from family members and friends. Johnny greeted me warmly and explained that Prabaker was working in his rented taxi, and would return after sunset. Together we walked around the framed structure, examining the construction and discussing the relative merits and costs of a plastic or a cotton covering.

Inviting me to drink tea, Johnny led us to the team of stage builders. My former neighbour Jeetendra was the supervisor for the project. He seemed to have recovered from the grief that had enfeebled him for many months after his wife's death in the cholera epidemic. He wasn't so robust —the once-familiar paunch had shrunk to a tight little mound beneath his T-shirt—but his eyes were bright with hope again, and his smile wasn't forced. His son, Satish, had grown in a rapid burst since his mother's death. When I shook hands with him, I passed a hundred-rupee note in the press of hands. He accepted it just as secretively, and slid it into the pocket of his shorts. The smile he gave me was warm, but he was still wounded by his mother's death. There was a hollowness in his eyes: a black hole of shocked grieving that swallowed all the questions and released no answers. When he returned to his work, cutting lengths of coconut-fibre rope for the men to tie around bamboo bracing poles, his young face assumed a numb expression. I knew that expression. I sometimes caught it, by chance, in the mirror: the way we look when the part of happiness that's trusting and innocent is ripped away, and we blame ourselves, rightly or wrongly, for its loss.

'You know where I got my name?' Johnny asked me as we sipped hot, delicious slum chai.

'No,' I answered, smiling to match the laughter in his eyes. 'You never told me.'

'I was born on the footpath, near Crawford Market. My mother had a little place there, a little hut made with plastic and two poles. The plastic was tied to a wall, underneath a sign. The sign was all broken, you know, and only two bits of two different posters were still on the wall. On one side was a little bit of a movie poster with the name *Johnny* written on it. Beside that one, and sticking out a bit, was a poster advertising cigars with—yes, you guessed it—only the word *Cigar* sticking out.'

'And she liked it,' I continued for him, 'and she —'

'Called me Johnny Cigar. Her parents, you know, they had thrown her out. And the man who was my father had dumped her, so she absolutely refused to use either of those family names for me. And all the way through the labour, when she gave birth to me, on that footpath, she stared at those words, Johnny Cigar, and she took it as a *sign*, if you'll forgive the joke. She was a very, very stubborn woman.'

He looked at the little stage, watching as Jeetendra, Satish, and others lifted flat pieces of plywood onto the frame to make the floor.

'It's a good name, Johnny,' I said, after a while. 'I like it. And it brought you good luck.'

He smiled at me, and the smile became a laugh.

'I'm just glad it wasn't an advert for laxatives or some such!' he spluttered, causing me to laugh and spray tea at him in return.

'It's taking you guys quite a while to tie the knot,' I observed when we could talk again. 'What's the delay?'

'Kumar, you know, he wants to play the successful businessman, and put a dowry with each of his daughters. Prabaker and I, we told him we don't believe in all that. We don't want a dowry, you know. It's kind of old fashioned, all that stuff. Mind you, Prabaker's dad is not quite of the same opinion. He sent down a list, from the village—a list of dowry gifts he has in mind. He wants a gold watch—a Seiko automatic—and a new bicycle, among other stuff. The model of bicycle he wants, the one he picked out for himself, we told him it's too big. We told him that his legs are too damn short to reach the pedals, let alone the ground, *yaar*, but he's crazy for that bicycle. Anyway, we're waiting for Kumar to collect all his dowry and such. The weddings are set for the last week in October, before all the Diwali and all that.'

'That'll be quite a week. My friend Vikram gets married that week, too.'

'You're coming to the weddings, Lin?' he asked with a small, tight frown. Johnny was a man who granted favours to others with selfless generosity. As is often the case with such men, he couldn't ask for them, or express his wishes, with anything like the same ease.

'I wouldn't miss it for the world,' I replied, laughing. 'I'll be there with bells on. I mean that literally—when you hear the bells ringing, you'll know I'm on my way.'

When I left him, he was talking to Satish. The boy listened intently and stared into his face, his eyes as expressionless as a gravestone, and I remembered how he'd clutched at my leg on the day that Karla visited me in the slum; how he'd favoured her with a shy, sincere smile. The memory sliced into my dead heart. It's said that you can never go home again, and it's true enough, of course. But the opposite is also true. You must go back, and you always go back, and you can never stop going back, no matter how hard you try.

Needing distraction, I rode my bike out to the R.K. film studios, gunning the engine and swerving too often and too fast between the cars. I'd hired eight foreigners the day before, and had sent them to Lisa. It wasn't difficult for me to find and convince foreigners to fill non-speaking roles in the Bollywood films. The same German, Swiss, Swedish, or American tourists who would've reacted with mistrust and hostility to Indian casting agents responded enthusiastically when I approached them. In the years that I'd lived in the slum and worked as a tour guide, I'd met every kind of foreign tourist. I'd developed a style in dealing with them that won their trust quickly. That style was two parts showman, two parts flatterer, and one part philanderer, combined with a hint of mischief, a sniff of condescension, and a pinch of contempt.

The work as a tour guide had also given me friendships in several key Colaba restaurants. For years I'd steered my tour parties into the Café Mondegar, the Picadilly, Dipty's Juice Bar, Edward the Eighth, Mezban Restaurant, Apsara Café, the Strand Coffee House, the Ideal, and others in the tourist beat, and encouraged them to spend their money. When I needed foreigners to fill bit parts in the Bollywood films, I trawled those cafés and restaurants. The owners, managers, and waiters always greeted me warmly. Whenever I saw a suitable group of young men and women, I approached them with the offer of a chance to work in an Indian movie. With the restaurant staff vouching for me, I usually secured their confidence and agreement within a few minutes. I then phoned Lisa Carter to arrange transport for the following day.

The system worked well. In the few months since we'd started working together, Lisa was drawing casting work from the major studios and producers. Finding the most recent group—the foreigners I'd hired the day before—was our first job for the famous R.K. studio.

I was curious to see the large, prestigious studio complex, and as I rode through the entrance gates my spirits lifted to the tall grey sails of the corrugated gable roofs. For Lisa Carter, and others like her, the dream world of movies inspired an almost reverential awe. I wasn't awed by the movie world, but I wasn't immune to it either. Every time I entered the fantasy-land of a film studio, a little of the magic that makes a movie caught in my heart and lifted me, bright with surprise, from the gloomy sea that, too much and too often, my life had become.

The guards directed me to a sound stage where Lisa and her group of Germans were waiting. I'd arrived during a break in the shooting, and found Lisa serving coffee and tea to the young foreigners. They were seated at two tables—two of several that were arranged around a stage, on a set that was designed to replicate a modern nightclub. I greeted them, exchanging a few pleasantries, and then Lisa took me aside.

'How are they?' I asked her when we were alone.

'They're great,' she answered happily. 'They're patient and relaxed and having a good time, I think. This'll be a good shoot. You've sent some pretty good people in the last couple weeks, Lin. The studios are real pleased. We could ... you know, we could really work this into something, you and me.'

'You like this, don't you?'

'*Sure* I do,' she said, giving me a smile I could feel on the back of my head. Then her expression shifted into something more solemn, something determined—the kind of determination you find in people who do it all the hard way, without hope. She was beautiful: a California beach beauty in the carnal jungle of Bombay; a pom-pom girl who'd pulled herself out of the death-by-leeches of heroin and the sybaritic suffocation of Madame Zhou's Palace. Her skin was clear and tanned. Her sky-blue eyes were radiant with resolve. Her long, curly blonde hair was pulled back from her face, and held in an elegant coiffure that complemented the decorousness of her modest, ivory-coloured pantsuit. *She beat heroin,* I found myself thinking, as I met her stare. *She beat it. She got off the stuff.* I was suddenly aware of how brave she was, and that the courage in her—

when you knew it was there, and you knew how to look for it—was as palpable and riveting as the fierce, impersonal menace in a tiger's eye.

'I like this gig,' she said. 'I like the people, and the work. I like the life. I think *you* should like it, too.'

'I like *you*,' I smiled.

She laughed, and slipped an arm through mine, leading us in a stroll around the set.

'The movie's called *Paanch Paapi*,' she said.

'Five kisses ...'

'No. *paapi*, not *papi*. That's the play on words. *Paapi* means *thief*, and *papi* means *kiss*. So, it's really *Five Thieves*, but there's a joke about it being *Five Kisses*, as well, because it's a romantic comedy. The female lead is Kimi Katkar. I think she's gorgeous. She's not the best dancer in the world, but she's a beautiful girl. The male lead is Chunkey Pandey. He could be good, *real* good, if his head wasn't jammed so far up his own ass.'

'While we're on the subject, have you had any more trouble with Maurizio?'

'Not a thing from him, but I'm worried about Ulla. She's been gone for a whole day and night. She took a call from Modena the night before last, and left in a hurry. It was the first time he surfaced in weeks. I haven't heard from her since, and she promised to call.'

I rubbed the frown from my forehead, up through my untidy hair.

'Ulla knows what she's doing,' I growled. 'She's not your problem, and she's not mine. I helped her because she asked me to. Because I like her. But I'm getting tired of this Ulla-Maurizio-Modena thing, you know what I mean? Did Modena say anything to her about the money?'

'I don't know. Maybe.'

'Well, it's still missing, and so is Modena. The boys on the street have been telling me. Maurizio's going around all over the place looking for Modena. He won't give up until he finds him. And Ulla's no better. Sixty thousand bucks—it's not all that much, but people have been killed for less. If Modena's got it, he better stay clear of Ulla while Maurizio's still after him.'

'I know. I know.'

Her eyes were suddenly glazed and apprehensive.

'I'm not worried about Ulla,' I said more softly. 'I worry about you. If

Modena's back, you should stay close to Abdullah for a while. Or me.'

She looked at me with her lips pressed to white rims around what she *wanted* to say but couldn't or wouldn't.

'Tell me about the scene,' I suggested, trying to shift us from the cold, black whirlpool that Ulla's life was becoming. 'What's going on in this movie?'

'It's a nightclub, or at least it's a movie version of one. The hero steals a jewel from a rich politician, I think—something like that—and he runs in here to hide. He watches the girl, Kimi, doing a big dance number, and he falls for her. When the cops show up, he hides the jewel in her wig. The rest of the movie is about how he tries to get close to her, to get the jewel back.'

She paused, studying my face, and trying to read the expression in my eyes.

'It's ... I guess you think it's kinda stupid.'

'No, I don't,' I laughed. 'I like it. I like all this. In the real world, the guy would just beat her up and take his jewel back. He might even shoot her. I like the Bollywood version better.'

'So do I,' she said, laughing. 'I love it. They put it all together from painted canvas and skinny pieces of wood and it's ... it's like they're making dreams or something. I know that sounds corny, but I mean it. I love this world, Lin, and I don't want to go back to the other one.'

'Hey, Lin!' a voice called out from behind me. It was Chandra Mehta, one of the producers. 'You got a minute?'

I left Lisa with the German tourists and joined Chandra Mehta beneath a metal gantry that supported a complex tree of bright lights. He wore a baseball cap backwards, and the press of the tight band made his plump face seem rounder. Faded blue Levis were buttoned up under his expansive paunch, and a long kurtah shirt almost covered it from above. He was sweating in the mildly humid air of the closed set.

'Hey, man. How is it? I've been wanting to see you, *yaar.*' His voice was breathy with conspiracy. 'Let's go outside and get some air. I'm boiling my fuckin' bonus off in here, *yaar.*'

As we strolled between the metal-domed buildings, actors in costume crossed our path, together with men carrying props and pieces of equipment. At one point, a group of nine pretty dancing girls dressed in exotic, feathered costumes passed us on their way to a sound stage. They turned my head around, forcing my body to follow it until I was walking backwards for a while. Chandra Mehta never gave them so much as a glance.

'Listen, Lin, what I wanted to talk to you about ...' he said, touching my arm at the elbow as we walked. 'I have this friend, you know, and he's a business fellow, with a lot of dealings in the USA. *Achaa*, what to say ... he has a problem of his rupees-to-dollars cash flow, *yaar*. I was kind of hoping that you ... a little bird told me that you are a helpful fellow when the cash is not flowing.'

'I assume this cash should be in U.S. dollars, when it's flowing correctly?'

'Yes,' he smiled. 'I'm very glad that you understand his problem.'

'Just how badly is the flow backed up?'

'Oh, I think that about ten thousand should move things along very nicely.'

I told him Khaled Ansari's current rate for U.S. dollars, and he agreed to the terms. I arranged to meet him on the set the following day. He was to have the rupees—a much larger bundle of notes than the American currency made—in a soft backpack, ready for me to collect on my bike. We shook on the deal. Mindful of the man I represented, lord Abdel Khader Khan, a man whose name would never be mentioned by Mehta or by me, I put a slightly uncomfortable pressure in the handshake. It was a tiny pain I inflicted on him, the merest twinge, but it reinforced the hard eye-contact above my amiable smile.

'Don't start this if you're going to mess it up, Chandra,' I warned, as the handshake pulsed from his pinched hand to his eyes. 'Nobody likes to get jerked around—my friends least of all.'

'Oh, of *course* not, *baba*!' he joked, not quite smothering the blip of alarm that spiked in his eyes. 'No problem. *Koi baht nahi*! *Don't worry*! I'm very grateful that you can help me, my ... what to say, help my *friend*, with his problem, *yaar*.'

We strolled back to the sound stage, and I found Lisa with Mehta's fellow producer, Cliff De Souza.

'Hey, man! You'll do!' Cliff said in greeting, seizing me by the arm and dragging me toward the tables on the nightclub set. I looked at Lisa, but she just raised her hands in a gesture that said *You're on your own, buddy.*

'What's going on, Cliff?'

'We need another guy, *yaar*. We need a guy, a gora, sitting between these two lovely girls.'

'Oh, no you don't.' I resisted him, trying to wrestle myself out of his grip without actually hurting him. We were at the table. The two German girls stood and reached out to drag me into the seat between them. 'I can't do this! I don't act! I'm camera shy! I don't do this!'

'Na, komm' schon! Hör' auf!' one of the girls said. 'You are the one who told us yesterday how easy it is to do this, na?'

They were attractive women. I'd selected their group precisely because they were all healthy and attractive men and women. Their smiles were challenging me to join them. I thought about what it would mean: taking a part in a movie that about three hundred million people in ten or more countries would see while I was on the run as my country's most wanted man. It was foolish. It was dangerous.

'Oh, why the hell not,' I shrugged.

Cliff and the stagehands backed away as the cast members took their places on the set. The star, Chunkey Pandey, was a handsome, athletic, young Bombay guy. I'd seen him in a few of the movies I'd watched with my Indian friends, and I was surprised to discover that he was considerably more handsome and charismatic in person than he was on the screen. A make-up assistant held up a mirror while Chunkey combed and fretted at his hair. The intensity of the gaze that he focused on the mirror was as steadfast as a surgeon's might be in the midst of a complex and critical procedure.

'You missed the best part,' one of the German girls whispered to me. 'It took this guy a big time to learn his dancing moves for this scene. He crapped it up quite a few many times. And every time he crapped it up, this little guy with the Spiegel ... the mirror, he pops out, and we watch him, with the hair combing, all again. If they just used all that stuff of him crapping it up and combing his hair while the little guy holds the mirror, I tell you, this would be a big comedy hit.'

The director of the film stood beside his cinematographer, poised with one eye to the lens of the camera, and then gave his last instructions to the lighting crew. At a signal, the director's assistant called for all-quiet on the set. The cinematographer announced that the film was rolling.

'Cue sound!' the director commanded. 'And ... action!'

Music hammered into the set from large stadium speakers. It was the loudest that I'd ever heard Indian movie music played, and I loved it. The dancers, including the star, Kimi Katkar, pranced onto the artificial stage. Working the set and the crowd of extras, Kimi sashayed across the stage and made her way from table to table, dancing and miming her number all the while. The hero joined in the dance, and then ducked under a table when the actors playing the cops arrived. The whole sequence lasted only five minutes in the film, but it took all the morning to rehearse and most of the afternoon to shoot. My first taste of show business resulted in two brief sweeps of the camera that captured my wide smile as Kimi paused, in her seductive routine, at the back of my chair.

We sent the foreign tourists home in two cabs, and Lisa rode back to town with me on the Bullet. It was a warm evening and she removed her jacket to ride, pulling the clip from her long hair. She wrapped her arms around my waist and pressed her cheek into my back. She was a good passenger: the kind who surrenders her will in unconditional trust, and blends her body to the nuance of the rider. Through my thin white shirt I felt the press of her breasts against my back. The shirt was open in the warm wind, and her hands clung to the tight skin of my waist. I never wore a helmet on the bike. There was a helmet clipped to the back of the seat for a passenger, but she chose not to wear it. Occasionally, when we stopped for the flow of traffic or to make a turn, a gust of wind whipped her long, curly blonde hair over my shoulder and into my mouth. The perfume of verbena flowers lingered on my lips. Her thighs clung to me, gently, and with a promise or a threat of the strength they possessed. I remembered those thighs, the skin as soft as moonlight on the palm of my hand that night at Karla's house. And then, as if she was reading my thoughts or joining them, she spoke when the bike stopped at a traffic signal.

'How's the kid?'

'The kid?'

'That little kid you had with you that night, you remember, at Karla's place.'

'He's fine. I saw him last week, at his uncle's. He's not so little any more. He's growing fast. He's at a private school. He doesn't like it much, but he'll do okay.'

'Do you miss him?'

The signal changed and I kicked the bike into gear, twisting the throttle to send us into the intersection on the staccato throbbing of the engine's growl. I didn't answer her. Of course I missed him. He was a good kid. I missed my daughter. I missed my mother and all of my family. I missed my friends: I missed them all and I was sure, in those desperate years, that I would never see them again. Missing the people I loved was a kind of grieving for me, and it was worse, much worse, for the fact that—so far as I knew—they weren't dead. My heart, sometimes, was a graveyard full of blank stones. And when I was alone in my apartment, night after night, that grieving and missing choked me. There was money in bundles on the dressing table, and there were passports freshly forged that could send me ... anywhere. But there was nowhere to go: nowhere that wasn't emptied of meaning and identity and love by the vacuum of those who were missing and lost forever.

I was the fugitive. I was the vanished one. I was the one who was missing; missing in action. But inside the slipstream of my flight, *they* were the missing ones. Inside my exile, it was the whole world I once knew that was missing. The fugitive kind run, trying against their hearts to annihilate the past, and with it every tell-tale trace of what they were, where they came from, and those who once loved them. And they run into that extinction of themselves, to survive, but they always fail. We can deny the past, but we can't escape its torment because the past is a speaking shadow that keeps pace with the truth of what we are, step for step, until we die.

And from the pink and purple palette of the perished evening, a blue-black night rose up around us as we rode. We plunged with the sea-wind into tunnels of light. The robe of sunset slipped from the shoulders of the city. Lisa's hands moved on my hard skin like the sea; like the surging, swarming caress of the sea. And for a moment, as we rode together, we were one: one desire, one promise dissolving into compromise, one mouth tasting the trickle of danger and delight. And something—it might've been love, or fear—goaded me to the choice, putting whispers in the warming wind: *This is as young, and as free, as you'll ever be.*

'I better go.'

'Don't you want a coffee or something?' she asked, her hand on the key in the door to her apartment.

'I better go.'

'Kavita's really into this story you gave her, about the girls from the slum. The girls who came back from the dead. It's all she talks about. The

Blue Sisters, she calls them. I don't know why she calls them that, but it's a pretty cool name.'

She was making conversation, holding me there. I looked into the sky that was her eyes.

'I better go.'

Two hours later, fully awake, and still feeling the press of her lips in the good-night kiss, I wasn't surprised when the phone rang.

'Can you come over right away?' she said when I answered the call.

I was silent, struggling to find a way to say *no* that sounded like *yes.*

'I've been trying to find Abdullah, but he doesn't answer,' she went on, and then I heard the flattened, frightened, shell-shocked drone in her voice.

'What is it? What's happened?'

'We had some trouble ... there was some trouble ...'

'Was it Maurizio? Are you okay?'

'He's dead,' she mumbled. 'I killed him.'

'Is anyone there?'

'Anyone?' she repeated vaguely.

'Is anyone else there, in the apartment?'

'No. I mean, *yes*—Ulla's here, and him, on the floor. That's ...'

'Listen!' I commanded, 'Lock the door. Don't let anyone in.'

'The door's busted,' she murmured, her voice weakening. 'He smashed the lock off the wall when he busted in here.'

'Okay. Push something up against the door—a chair or something. Keep it closed until I get there.'

'Ulla's a mess. She ... she's pretty upset.'

'It'll be okay. Just block the door. Don't phone anyone else. Don't speak to anyone, and don't let anyone in. Make two cups of coffee, with lots of milk and sugar—four spoons of sugar—and sit down with Ulla to drink them. Give her a stiff drink, as well, if she needs it. I'm on my way. I'll be there in ten minutes. Hang in there, and stay cool.'

Riding the night, cutting into crowded streets, winding the bike into the web of lights, I felt nothing: no fear, no dread, no shiver of excitement. Red-lining a motorcycle means opening the throttle so hard, with every change of gears, that the needle on the rev-counter is twisted all the way round to the red zone of maximum revolutions. And that's what we were doing, all of us, in our different ways, Karla and Didier and

Abdullah and I: we were red-lining our lives. And Lisa. And Maurizio. Twisting the needle to the red zone.

A Dutch mercenary in Kinshasa once told me that the only time he ever stopped hating himself was when the risk he faced became so great that he acted without thinking or feeling anything at all. I wished he hadn't said it to me because I knew exactly what he meant. And I rode that night, I soared that night, and the stillness in my heart was almost like being at peace.

CHAPTER TWENTY-EIGHT

In my first knife fight I learned that there are two kinds of people who enter a deadly conflict: those who kill to live, and those who live to kill. The ones who like killing might come into a fight with most of the fire and fury, but the man or woman who fights just to live, who kills just to survive, will usually come out of it on top. If the killer-type begins to lose the fight, his reason for fighting it fades. If the survivor-type begins to lose, his reason for fighting it flares up fiercer than ever. And killing contests with deadly weapons, unlike common fistfights, are lost and won in the reasons that remain when the blood begins to run. The simple fact is that fighting to save a life is a better and more enduring reason than fighting to end one.

My first knife fight was in prison. Like most prison fights, it started trivially and ended savagely. My adversary was a fit, strong veteran of many fights. He was a stand-over man, which meant that he mugged weaker men for money and tobacco. He inspired fear in most of the men and, not burdened with judiciousness, he confused that fear with respect. I didn't respect him. I detest bullies for their cowardice, and despise them for their cruelty. I never knew a tough man who preyed on the weak. Tough men hate bullies almost as much as bullies hate tough men.

And I was tough enough. I'd grown up in a rough, working-class neighbourhood, and I'd been fighting all my life. No-one in the prison system knew that then because I wasn't a career criminal, and I had no history. I began my prison experience as a first offender. What's more, I was an intellectual, and I sounded and acted like one. Some men respected that and some ridiculed it, but none of them feared it. Nevertheless, the long prison sentence that I was serving—twenty years at hard labour for armed robberies—gave most of them pause. I was a dark horse. No-one knew how I would respond to a real test, and more than a few were curious about it.

The test, when it did come, was flashing steel, and broken teeth, and eyes rolling wide and wild as a frenzied dog. He attacked me in the prison laundry, the one place not observed directly by guards patrolling catwalks between the gun towers. It was the kind of unprovoked surprise attack that's known in prison slang as a *sneak-go*. He was armed with a steel table knife, sharpened with endlessly malignant patience on the stone floor of his cell. Its edge was sharp enough to shave a man or cut his throat. I'd never carried a knife or used one in my life before prison. But in there, where men were attacked and stabbed every other day, I'd followed the advice of the hard men who'd survived long years there. *It's better to have a weapon and not need it,* they'd told me more than once, *than need it and not have it.* My knife was a sharpened spike of metal about as thick as a man's finger and a little longer than a hand. The hilt was formed with packing tape, and fitted into my hand without bunching the fingers. When the fight began he didn't know that I was armed, but we both, in our separate ways, expected that it was a fight to the death. He wanted to kill *me*, and I was sure that I had to kill *him* to survive.

He made two mistakes. The first was to fight on the back foot. In the surprise of his sneak attack he'd first rushed at me and, with two slashes of the knife, he'd cut me across the chest and the forearm. He should've pressed on to finish it, hacking and tearing and stabbing at me, but he stepped back instead and waved the knife in little circles. He might've expected me to submit—most of his foes surrendered quickly, defeated by their fear of him as much as by the sight of their own blood. He might've been so sure he would win that he was simply toying with me and teasing out the thrill of the kill. Whatever the reason, he lost the advantage and he lost the fight in that first backward step. He gave me time to drag my knife from inside my shirt and shape up to box him. I saw the surprise in his eyes, and it was my cue to counter-attack.

His second mistake was that he held the knife as if it was a sword and he was in a fencing match. A man uses an underhand grip when he expects his knife, like a gun, to do the fighting for him. But a knife isn't a gun, of course, and in a knife fight it isn't the weapon that does the fighting: it's the *man*. The knife is just there to help him finish it. The winning grip is a dagger hold, with the blade downward, and the fist that holds it still free to punch. That grip gives a man maximum power in the

585

downward thrust and an extra weapon in his closed fist.

He dodged and weaved in a crouch, slashing the knife in sweeping arcs with his arms out wide. He was right-handed. I adopted a southpaw-boxing stance, the dagger in my right fist. Stepping with the right foot, and dragging the left to keep my balance, I took the fight to him. He ripped the blade at me twice and then lunged forward. I side-stepped, and punched at him with a three-punch combination, right-left-right. One of them was a lucky punch. His nose broke, and his eyes watered and burned, blurring his vision. He lunged again, and tried to bring the knife in from the side. I grabbed at his wrist with my left hand, stepped into the space between his legs, and stabbed him in the chest. I was trying for the heart or a lung. It didn't hit either one, but still I rammed the spike up to the hilt into the meaty flesh beneath his collarbone. It broke the skin of his back just below the shoulder blade.

He was jammed against a section of wall between a washing machine and a clothes-dryer. Using the spike to hold him in place, and with my left hand locked to his knife-wrist, I tried to bite his face and neck, but he whipped his head from side to side so swiftly that I opted for head-butts instead. Our heads cracked together several times until one desperate, wrenching effort of his legs sent us sprawling onto the floor together. He dropped his knife in the fall, but the spike tore free from his chest. He began to drag himself toward the door of the laundry. I couldn't tell if he was trying to escape or seeking a new advantage. I didn't take a chance. My head was level with his legs. Thrashing together on the ground, I reached up and grabbed the belt of his trousers. Using it for leverage, I stabbed him in the thigh twice, and again, and again. I struck bone more than once, feeling the jarring deflection all the way up my arm. Releasing his belt, I stretched my left hand out for his knife, trying to reach it so that I could stab him with that one as well.

He didn't scream. I'll say that much for him. He shouted hard for me to stop, and he shouted that he gave up—*I give up! I give up! I give up!*—but he didn't scream. I did stop, and I let him live. I scrambled to my feet. He tried again to crawl toward the door of the laundry. I stopped him with my foot on his neck, and stomped down on the side of his head. I had to stop him. If he'd made it out of the laundry while I was there, and the prison guards saw him, I would've spent six months or more in the punishment unit.

While he lay there groaning on the floor, I took off my bloody clothes and changed into a clean set. One of the prisoners who cleaned the jail was standing outside the laundry, grinning in at us through the doorway with unspiteful enjoyment. I passed him the bundle of my soiled clothes. He smuggled the bloodied clothes away in his mop-bucket, and threw them into the incinerator behind the kitchen. On my way out of the laundry I handed the weapons to another man, who buried them in the prison garden. When I was safely away from the scene, the man who'd tried to kill me limped into the prison chief's office, and collapsed. He was taken to hospital. I never saw him again, and he never opened his mouth. I'll say that much for him, too. He was a thug and a stand-over man, and he tried to kill me for no good reason, but he wasn't an informer.

Alone in my cell, after the fight, I examined my wounds. The gash on my forearm had made a clean cut through a vein. I couldn't report it to the medical officer because that would've connected me to the fight and the wounded man. I had to hope that it would heal. There was a deep slash from my left shoulder to the centre of my chest. It was also a clean cut, and it was bleeding freely. I burned two packets of cigarette papers all the way down to white ash in a metal bowl, and rubbed the ash into both wounds. It was painful, but it sealed the wounds immediately and stopped the bleeding.

I never spoke of the fight to anyone, but most of the men knew about it soon enough, and they all knew that I'd survived the test. The white scar on my chest, the scar that men saw every day in the prison shower, reminded them of my willingness to fight. It was a warning, like the bright bands of colour on the skin of a sea snake. It's still there, that scar, as long and white after all these years as it ever was. And it's still a kind of warning. I touch it, and I see the killer pleading for his life; I remember, reflected in the fright-filled domes of his eyes, fate's mirror, the sight of the twisted, hating thing that I became in the fight.

My first knife fight wasn't my last, and as I stood over Maurizio Belcane's dead body I felt the cold, sharp memory of my own experiences of stabbing and being stabbed. He was face down in a kneeling posture, with his upper body on a corner of the couch and his legs on the floor. Beside his slackly folded right hand there was a razor-sharp stiletto resting on the carpet. A black-handled carving knife was buried to the crank in his back, a little to the left of his spine and just below the shoulder blade. It was a long, wide, sharp knife. I'd seen that knife before, in Lisa's hand, the last time Maurizio had made the mistake of coming to the apartment uninvited. That was one lesson he should've learned the first time. We don't, of course. *It's okay*, Karla once said, *because if we all learned what we should learn, the first time round, we wouldn't need love at all.* Well, Maurizio had learned that lesson in the end, the hard way—face down in his own blood. He was what Didier called a *fully mature* man. When I'd chided Didier once for being immature, he'd told me that he was proud and delighted to be immature. *The fully mature man or woman*, he said, *has about two seconds left to live.*

Those thoughts rolled over one another in my mind like the steel balls in Captain Queeg's hand. It was the knife that did it, of course: the memory of stabbing and being stabbed. I remembered the vivid seconds every time I'd been stabbed. I remembered the knives cutting me, entering my body. I could still feel the steel blades inside me. It was like burning. It was like hate. It was like the most evil thought in the world. I shook my head and breathed in deeply, and looked at him again.

The knife might've ruptured a lung and penetrated to the heart. Whatever it had done, it had finished him fast. His body had fallen onto the couch and, once there, he'd hardly moved at all. I took a handful of his thick, black hair and lifted his head. His dead eyes were half open, and his lips were pulled back slightly from his teeth in a rictal smile. There was remarkably little blood. The couch had absorbed the big spill. *We've gotta get rid of the couch*, I heard myself thinking. The carpet had suffered no great damage, and could be cleaned. The room was also little disturbed by the violence. A leg was broken on the coffee table, and the locks on the front door hung askew. I turned my attention to the women.

Ulla bore a cut on her face from the cheekbone almost to the chin. I cleaned the wound and pressed it together with tape all along the length of it. The cut wasn't deep, and I expected it to heal quickly, but I was sure it would leave a scar. By chance, the blade had followed the natural curve of her cheek and jaw, adding a flash of emphasis to the shape of her face. Her beauty was injured by the wound but not ravaged by it. Her eyes, however, were abnormally wide and pierced with a terror that refused to fade. There was a lungi on the arm of the couch beside her. I put it around her shoulders, and Lisa gave her a cup of hot, sweet chai. When I covered Maurizio's body with a blanket she shuddered. Her face crumpled into puckers of pain, and she cried for the first time.

Lisa was calm. She was dressed in a pullover and jeans, an outfit that only a Bombay native could wear on such a humid, still, and hot night. There was the mark of a blow around her eye and on her cheek. When Ulla was quiet again we crossed the room to stand near the door, out of her hearing. Lisa took a cigarette, bent her head to light it from my match, and then exhaled, looking directly into my face for the first time since I'd entered the apartment.

'I'm glad you came. I'm glad you're here. I couldn't help it. I had to do it, he —'

'Stop it, Lisa!' I interrupted her. The tone was harsh, but my voice was quiet and warm. 'You didn't stab him. *She* did. I can see it in her eyes. I know the look. She's still stabbing him now, still going over it in her mind. She'll have that look for a while. You're trying to protect her, but you won't help her by lying to me.'

She smiled. Under the circumstances, it was a very good smile. If we hadn't been standing next to a dead man with a knife in his heart, I'd have found it irresistible.

'What happened?'

'I don't want her to get hurt, that's all,' she replied evenly. The smile closed up in the thin, grim line of her pursed lips.

'Neither do I. What happened?'

'He busted in, slashed her up. He was crazy, out of his mind. I think he was on something. He was screaming at her, and she couldn't answer him. She was even crazier than he was. I spent an hour with her before he crashed in here. She told me about Modena. I'm not surprised she was crazy. It's ... fuck, Lin, it's a bad story. She was out of her mind because of it. Anyway, he crashed through the door like a gorilla, and he slashed her. He was covered in blood—Modena's, I think. It was pretty fuckin' scary. I tried to jump him with the knife from the kitchen. He socked me pretty good in the eye and knocked me on my ass. I fell on the couch. He got on top of me, and he was just about to start on me with that switchblade of his when Ulla gave it to him in the back. He was dead in a second. I swear. A second. One second. Just like that. He was looking at me, then he was dead. She saved my life, Lin.'

'I think it's more likely that you saved hers, Lisa. If you weren't here, it would be *her* hugging the couch with a knife in her back.'

She began to tremble and shiver. I took her in my arms and held her for a while, supporting her weight. When she was calm again, I brought her a kitchen chair and she sat down shakily. I phoned around, and found Abdullah. Explaining what had happened in as few words as possible, I told him to contact Hassaan Obikwa in the African ghetto and bring him to the apartment with a car.

Little by little, as we waited for Abdullah and Hassaan, the story emerged. Ulla was suddenly tired, but I couldn't let her sleep. Not yet. After a while she began to speak, adding a detail here and there to Lisa's account, and then gradually telling the whole story herself.

Maurizio Belcane met Sebastian Modena in Bombay, where both of them made money from the work they arranged for foreign prostitutes. Maurizio was the only son of rich Florentine parents who'd died in a plane crash when he was a child. By his own account, repeated to Ulla whenever he was drunk, he was raised with indifferent duteousness by distant relatives who'd tolerated him reluctantly in the loveless shelter of their home. At eighteen he seized the first tranche of his inheritance and fled to Cairo. By the age of twenty-five he'd squandered the fortune left to him by his parents. The remnants of his family cast him out, no less for his penury than for the many scandals that had pursued his profligate progress through the Middle East and Asia. At twenty-seven he found himself in Bombay, brokering sex for European prostitutes.

The point man for Maurizio's operation in Bombay was the diffident, dour Spaniard, Sebastian Modena. The thirty-year-old sought out and approached wealthy Arab and Indian customers. His short, slight frame and timid manner worked to his advantage, putting the customers at ease by allaying their fears and suspicions. He took one-fifth of the cut that Maurizio claimed from the foreign girls. Ulla believed that Modena was happy enough in the unequal relationship, where he did most of the dirty work and Maurizio took most of the dirty money, because he saw himself as a pilot fish and the tall, handsome Italian as a shark.

His background was very different to Maurizio's. One of thirteen children in an Andalusian Gypsy family, Modena had grown up with a notion of himself as the runt of the litter. Schooled more in crime than in scholarship, and barely literate, he'd worked his way from swindle to grift to petty larceny across Turkey, Iran, Pakistan, and India. He preyed on tourists, never taking too much and never remaining too long in any one place. Then he met Maurizio, and for two years he'd pandered for the pimp, procuring clients and putting them together with the girls in Maurizio's stable.

They might've gone on in that way for much longer, but one day Maurizio walked into Leopold's with Ulla. From the first moment that their eyes met, Ulla told us, she knew that Modena was hopelessly in love with her. She encouraged him because his devotion to her was useful. She'd been purchased from Madame Zhou's Palace, and Maurizio was determined to recover his investment costs as quickly as possible. He'd instructed the smitten Modena to find work for her twice a day, every day, until the debt was repaid. Tortured by what he saw as betrayals of his own love, Modena pressed his partner to release Ulla from the obligation. Maurizio refused, ridiculing the Spaniard's affection for a working girl, and insisting that he put her to work day and night.

Ulla paused in her story when a tap at the door announced Abdullah's arrival. The tall Iranian entered silently, dressed in black like a thing made from the night itself. He greeted me with a hug and nodded gently to Lisa. She came forward and kissed him on the cheek. He lifted the blanket to look at Maurizio's body. Nodding and turning down the corners of his mouth in professional approval of the single killing thrust, he let the blanket fall, and muttered a prayer.

'Hassaan is busy. He will be here after about one hour,' he said.

'Did you tell him what I want him to do?'

'He knows,' he replied, raising one eyebrow in a tight smile.

'Is it still quiet outside?'

'I checked, before I came inside. The building is quiet, and the street all around.'

'There's been no reaction from the neighbours, so far. He took the door out with one kick, Lisa says, and there wasn't all that much shouting and screaming. There was loud music playing next door when I got here. It was a party or something. I don't think anyone knows about this.'

'We ... we have to *call* someone!' Ulla shouted suddenly, standing and letting the lungi fall from her shoulders. 'We should ... call a doctor ... call the police ...'

Abdullah sprinted to her, and wrapped her in his arms with surprisingly tender compassion. He sat her down again and rocked her, murmuring reassuringly. I watched them with a little pinch of shame because I knew that I should've comforted her myself, long before that, and in just the same gentle way. But the fact was that Maurizio's death had compromised me, and I was afraid. I'd had reason enough to want him dead, and I'd beaten him with my fists for it. That was, in other words, a motive for murder. People knew that. I was there in the room with Lisa and Ulla, and it seemed that I was helping them, responding to their call for help, but that wasn't all of it. I was also there to help myself. I was there to make sure that no part of the sticky web of his death clung to me. And that's why there was nothing gentle in me, and all the tenderness came from an Iranian killer named Abdullah Taheri.

Ulla began to speak again. Lisa poured her a drink of vodka and lime juice. She gulped at it, and went on with her story. It took quite a while because she was nervous and afraid. She skipped important details from time to time, and she was loose with her chronology, ordering the facts as they occurred to her in the telling rather than as they'd happened. We had to ask questions and prompt her into a more sequential account, but little by little we got it all.

Modena had been the first to meet the Nigerian—the businessman who'd wanted to spend sixty thousand dollars on heroin. He introduced him to Maurizio, and too quickly, too easily, the African had parted with his money. Maurizio stole the money and planned to move on, but Modena had other ideas. He seized his chance to free Ulla and rid himself of Maurizio, the man he resented for enslaving her. He snatched the money from him, and went into hiding, prompting the Nigerian to send his hit-squad to Bombay. To distract the understandably bloodthirsty Africans while he searched for Modena, Maurizio had given them my name and told them I'd stolen their money. Abdullah and I knew the next part of that story well enough.

For all his cringing cowardice with me, and his dread that the Nigerians might return to hunt him down, Maurizio Belcane couldn't cut his losses and leave the city. He couldn't rid his heart of the killing rage he felt for Modena and the righteous lust he felt for the money they'd stolen together. For weeks he watched Ulla and followed her everywhere. He knew that, sooner or later, Modena would contact her. When the Spaniard did make that contact, Ulla went to him. Without realising it, she also led the crazed Italian to the cheap Dadar hotel where his former partner was hiding. Maurizio burst into the room, but he found Modena alone. Ulla was gone. The money was gone. Modena was ill. Some sickness had ruined him. Ulla thought it might've been malaria. Maurizio gagged him, tied him to the sickbed, and went to work on him with the stiletto. Modena, tougher than anyone knew and taciturn to the end, refused to tell him that Ulla was hiding in an adjoining room, only footsteps away, with all the money.

'When Maurizio stopped with the knife ... the cutting ... and left the room, I waited for a long time,' Ulla said, staring at the carpet and shivering beneath the blanket. Lisa was sitting on the floor at her feet. She gently prised the glass from Ulla's fingers, and gave her a cigarette. Ulla accepted it, but she didn't smoke. She looked into Lisa's eyes, and craned her neck around to look into Abdullah's face and then mine.

'I was so afraid,' she pleaded. 'I was too much afraid. After a time I went into the room, and I saw him. He was lying on the bed. There was the rag tied on his mouth. He was tied up to the bed, and he could move only his head. He was cut up all over. On his face. On his body. Everywhere. There was so much blood. So much blood. He kept looking at me, with his black eyes staring, and staring. I left him there ... and I ... I ran away.'

'You just *left* him there?' Lisa gasped.

She nodded.

'You didn't even untie him?'

She nodded again.

'Jesus *Christ!*' Lisa spat out bitterly. She looked up, moving her anguished eyes from Abdullah's face to mine and back again. 'She didn't tell me that part of it.'

'Ulla, listen to me. Do you think he might still be there?' I asked.

She nodded a third time. I looked at Abdullah.

'I have a good friend in Dadar,' he said. 'Where is the hotel? What is the name?'

'I don't know,' she mumbled. 'It's next to a market. At the back, where they throw the rubbish away. The smell is very bad. No wait, I remember, I said the name in the taxi—it is called Kabir's. That's it. That's the name. Oh, God! When I left him, I just thought ... I was sure they would find him ... and ... and make him free. Do you think he might be on that bed until *now*? Do you think?'

Abdullah phoned his friend, and arranged to have someone check the hotel.

'Where's the money?' I demanded.

She hesitated.

'The *money*, Ulla. *Give* it to me.'

She stood up shakily, supported by Lisa, and walked into the bedroom she'd used. Moments later she returned with a travel flight bag. She handed it to me, her expression strangely contradictory—coquette and adversary in equal parts. I opened the bag and took out several bundles of American hundred-dollar bills. I counted out twenty thousand dollars, and pushed the rest back into the bag. I returned the bag to her.

'Ten thousand is for Hassaan,' I declared. 'Five thousand is to get you a new passport and a ticket to Germany. Five thousand is to clean up here, and set Lisa up in a new apartment on the other side of town. The rest is yours. And Modena's, if he makes it.'

She wanted to reply, but a soft tap at the door announced Hassaan's arrival. The stocky, thickly muscled Nigerian entered, and greeted Abdullah and me warmly. Like the rest of us, he was acclimatised to Bombay's heat, and he wore a heavy serge jacket and bottle-green jeans with no trace of discomfort. He pulled the blanket from Maurizio's body and pinched the skin, flexed a dead arm, and sniffed at the corpse.

'I got a good plastic,' he said, dumping a heavy plastic drop-sheet onto the floor and unfolding it. 'We got to take off all them clothes. And any of his rings and chains. Just the man, that's all we want. We'll pull the teeth later.'

He paused, when I didn't reply or react, and looked up to see me staring at the two women. Their faces were stiff with dread.

'How about … you get Ulla in the shower,' I said to Lisa with a grim little smile. 'Have one yourself. I reckon we'll be finished here in a little while.'

Lisa led Ulla into the bathroom, and ran a shower for her. We dumped Maurizio's body onto the plastic sheet and stripped it of its clothes. His skin was pallid, matt, and in some places marbled-grey. In life Maurizio was a tall, well-built man. Dead and naked he looked thinner, feebler somehow. I should've pitied him. Even if we never pity them at any other time, and in any other way, we should pity the dead when we look at them, and touch them. Pity is the one part of love that asks for nothing in return and, because of that, every act of pity is a kind of prayer. And dead men demand prayers. The silent heart, the tumbled nave of the chest unbreathing, and the guttered candles of the eyes—they summon our prayers. Each dead man is a temple in ruins, and when our eyes walk there we should pity, we should pray.

But I didn't pity him. *You got what you deserve,* I thought, as we rolled his body in the plastic sheet. I felt despicable and mean-souled for thinking it, but the words wormed their way through my brain like a murderous whisper working its way through an angry mob. *You got what you deserve.*

Hassaan had brought a laundry-style trolley basket with him. We wheeled it into the room from the corridor. Maurizio's body was beginning to stiffen up, and we were forced to crunch the legs to fit it into the basket. We wheeled and carried it down two flights of stairs unobserved, and out into the quiet street, where Hassaan's delivery van was parked. His men used the van every day to deliver fish, bread, fruit, vegetables, and kerosene to his shops in the African ghetto. We lifted the wheeled basket into the back of the van, and covered the plastic-wrapped body with loaves of bread, baskets of vegetables, and trays of fish.

'Thanks, Hassaan,' I said, shaking his hand and passing him the ten thousand dollars. He stuffed the money into the front of his jacket.

'No,' he rumbled in the *basso* voice that commanded unquestioning respect in his ghetto. 'I am very happy to do this work. Now, Lin, we are even. All even.'

He nodded to Abdullah and left us, walking half a block to his parked car. Raheem leaned out of the van to flash a wide smile at me before turning over the engine with a flick of his wrist. He drove away without looking back. Hassaan's car followed it a few hundred metres behind. We never heard so much as a murmur about Maurizio again. It was rumoured that Hassaan Obikwa kept a pit in the centre of his slum. Some said the pit was full of rats. Some claimed that it was filled with scuttling crabs. Others swore that he kept huge pigs in the pit. Whatever the hungry creatures were, all the whisperers agreed that they were fed from time to time with a dead man, one piece of the corpse at a time.

'Money you did spend well,' Abdullah muttered, with a blank expression, as we watched the van drive away.

We returned to the apartment, and repaired the door locks so the door could be sealed shut when we all left. Abdullah phoned another contact and arranged for two reliable men to visit the apartment on the following day. Their instructions were to bring a saw, cut the couch into pieces, and remove it in rubbish sacks. They were to clean the carpet and leave the apartment in an orderly state, removing every trace of its recent occupants.

He put the phone down, and it rang at once. His contact in Dadar had news. Modena had been discovered by staff in the hotel room, and rushed to hospital. The contact had visited the hospital, and learned that the weak and wounded man had checked himself out of the ward. He was last seen speeding away in a taxi. The doctor who'd attended him doubted that he would survive the night.

'It's weird,' I said when Abdullah had related the news. 'I knew Modena, you know ... I sort of knew him well. I saw him at Leopold's ... I don't know ... a hundred times. But I can't remember his voice. I can't remember what he sounded like. I can't hear his voice in my head, if you know what I mean.'

'I liked him,' Abdullah said.

'I'm surprised to hear you say that.'

'Why?'

'I'm not sure,' I replied. 'He was so ... so *meek*.'

'He would have made a good soldier.'

I raised my eyebrows in greater surprise. Modena wasn't just meek, it seemed to me then, he was a weak man. I couldn't imagine what Abdullah meant. I didn't know then that good soldiers are defined by what they can endure, not by what they can inflict.

And when all the loose ends were cut or tied, when Ulla left the city for Germany, and Lisa moved to a new apartment, and the last questions about Modena and Maurizio and Ulla faltered, faded, and ceased, it was the mysteriously vanished Spaniard who claimed my thoughts most often. I made two double-shuffle flights to Delhi and back in the next two weeks. I followed that by flying a seventy-two hour turnaround to Kinshasa with ten new passports for Abdul Ghani's network. I tried to keep busy, tried to focus on the work, but the screen in my mind was filled too often with an image of him, Modena, tied to the bed and staring at Ulla, watching her leave him there, watching her walk away with the money. And gagged. No way to scream. And what he must've thought when she entered the room ... *I'm saved* ... And what he must've thought when he saw the terror in her face. And was there something else in her eyes: was it revulsion, or was it more terrible than that? Did she look relieved, perhaps? Did she seem glad to be rid of him? And what did he feel when she turned and walked away and left him there, and closed the door behind her?

When I was in prison I fell in love with a woman who was an actress in a popular television program. She came into the prison to teach classes in acting and theatre for our prison drama group. We clicked, as they say. She was a brilliant actress. I was a writer. She was the physical voice and gesture. I saw my words breathe and move in her. We communicated in the shorthand shared by artists everywhere in the world: rhythm, and elation. After a time, she told me that she was in love with me. I believed her, and I still believe that it was true. For months we fed the affair with morsels of time stolen from the acting classes, and long letters that I smuggled to her through the illegal jail mail system known as the stiff-letter run.

Then trouble found me and I was thrown, literally, into the punishment unit. I don't know how the screws found out about our romance, but soon after I arrived in the punishment block they began to interrogate me about it. They were furious. They saw her affair with a prisoner, carried on for months under their noses, as a humiliating affront to their authority and, perhaps, to their manhood. They beat me with boots, fists, and batons, trying to force me to admit that she and I had been lovers. They wanted to use my confession as the basis for laying a charge against her. During one beating they held up a photograph of her. It was a smiling publicity still that they'd found in the prison drama group. They told me that all I had to do to stop the beatings was nod my head at it. *Just nod your head*, they said, holding the picture before my bloody face. *Just nod your head, that's all you have to do, and it'll all be over.*

I never admitted anything. I held her love in the vault of my heart while they tried to reach it through my skin and my bones. Then one day, as I sat in my cell after a beating, trying to stop the blood flowing into my mouth from a chipped bone in my cheek and my broken nose, the trap-door opened in the door of my cell. A letter fluttered in and landed on the floor. The trapdoor shut. I crawled over to the letter, and crawled back to the bed to read it. The letter was from her. It was a Dear John letter. She'd met a man, she said. He was a musician. Her friends had all urged her to break up with me because I was serving a twenty-year sentence in prison, and there was no future in it for either of us. She loved the new man, and she planned to marry him when his concert tour with the symphony orchestra was complete. She hoped I understood. She was sorry, but the letter was goodbye, goodbye forever, and she would never see me again.

Blood dripped onto the page from my broken face. The screws had read the letter, of course, before giving it to me. They laughed outside my door. They laughed. I listened to them as they tried to make a victory of that laughter, and I wondered if her new man, her musician, would stand up under torture for her. Maybe he would. You can never tell what people have inside them until you start taking it away, one hope at a time.

And somehow, in the weeks after Maurizio's death, Modena's face, or my mind's picture of his gagged and bloody and staring face, became confused with my own memories of that love I'd lost in prison. I wasn't sure why: there didn't seem to be any special reason why Modena's fate would twist itself into the strands of my own. But it did, and I felt a darkness growing within me that was too numb for sorrow and too cold for rage.

I tried to fight it. I kept myself as busy as I could. I worked in two more Bollywood films, taking small parts—as an extra at a party and in a street scene. I met with Kavita, urging her once again to visit Anand in prison. Most afternoons, I trained at weights and boxing and karate with Abdullah. I put in a day here and there at the slum clinic. I helped Prabaker and Johnny to prepare for their weddings. I listened to Khaderbhai's lectures, and immersed myself in the books, manuscripts, parchments, and ancient faience carvings in Abdul Ghani's extensive private collection. But no work or weariness could drive the darkness from me. Little by little, the tortured Spaniard's face and silent, screaming eyes became my own remembered moment: blood falling on the page, and no sound escaping my howling mouth. They claim a hidden corner of our hearts, all those moments that stay with us unscreamed. That's where loves, like elephants, drag themselves to die. It's the place where pride allows itself to cry. And in those sleep-lonely nights and think-rambled days, Modena's face was always there, staring at the door.

And while I worked and worried, Leopold's changed forever. The crowd that had coalesced there dispersed and disappeared. Karla was gone. Ulla was gone. Modena was gone, and probably dead. Maurizio was dead. Once, when I was too busy to stop for a drink, I passed the wide entrance arches and I saw no face that I knew. Yet Didier persisted at his favourite table each evening, conducting his business and accepting drinks from old friends. Gradually a new crowd collected around him with a new and different style. Lisa Carter brought Kalpana Iyer with her for drinks one night, and the young assistant producer became a Leopold's regular. Vikram and Lettie were in the last stages of preparation for their wedding, and they stopped for coffee, a snack, or a beer almost every day. Anwar and Dilip, two young journalists who worked with Kavita Singh, accepted her invitation to drop in and look the place over. On their first visit they found Lisa Carter, Kalpana, Kavita, and Lettie, with three German girls who'd worked for Lisa as extras on a film — seven beautiful, intelligent, vivacious young women. Anwar and Dilip were healthy, happy, unattached young men. They came to Leopold's every day and night after that.

The ambience created by the new group was different to that which had flowered around Karla Saaranen. The indelible cleverness and piercing wit that were Karla's gifts had inspired her own group of friends to a more profound discourse and a higher, thinner laughter. The new group took its more erratic tone from Didier, who combined the expressive mordancy of his sarcasm with a proclivity for the vulgar, the obscene, and the scatological. The laughter was louder, and probably more frequent, but there were no phrases that remained with me from the jokes or the jokers.

Then one night, a day after Vikram married Lettie, and a few weeks after Maurizio went into Hassaan Obikwa's pit, as I sat amongst the new group while the cawing, shrieking gulls of good humour settled on them, sending up squawks of laughter and fluttering hands, I saw Prabaker through the open arch. He waved to me, and I left the table to join him in his cab parked nearby.

'Hey, Prabu, what's up? We're celebrating Vikram's wedding! He and Lettie got married yesterday.'

'Yes, Linbaba. Sorry for disturbing the newly-marriages.'

'It's okay. They're not here. They've gone to London, to meet her parents. But what's up?'

'*Up*, Linbaba?'

'Yeah, I mean what are you doing here? Tomorrow's *your* big day. I thought you'd be drinking it up with Johnny and the other guys at the zhopadpatti.'

'After this talk only. Then I will go,' he replied, fidgeting nervously with the steering wheel. Both front doors of the car were open for the breeze. It was a hot night. The streets were crowded with couples, families, and single young men trying to find a cool wind or a curiosity somewhere to distract them from the heat. The crowd who streamed along the road beside the parked cars began to eddy around Prabaker's open door, and he pulled it shut hard.

'Are you okay?'

'Oh, yes, Lin, I am very, very fine,' he said. Then he looked at me. 'No. Not really, baba. In fact of speaking, I am very, very bad.'

'What is it?'

'Well, how to tell you this thing. Linbaba, you know I am getting a marriage to Parvati tomorrow. Do you know, baba, the first time I ever saw her my Parvati, was before six years, when she was sixteen years old only. That first time, when she first came to the zhopadpatti, before her daddy Kumar had his chai shop, she was living in a little hut with her mummy and daddy and sister, the Sita who is a marriage for Johnny Cigar. And that first day, she carried a matka of water back from the company well. She carried it on her head.'

He paused, watching the aquarium of the swirling street through the windscreen of the cab. His fingernail picked at the rubber leopard's skin cover he'd laced onto his steering wheel. I gave him time.

'Anyway,' he continued, 'I was watching her, and she was trying to carry that heavy matka, and walk on the rough track. And that matka, it must have been a very old one, and the clay was weak, because suddenly it just broke up in pieces, and all the water spilled down on her. She cried and cried so much. I looked at her and I felt ...'

He paused, looking up at the strolling street once more.

'Sorry for her?' I offered.

'No, baba. I felt ...'

'Sad? You felt sad for her?'

'No, baba. I felt a erection, in my pants, you know, when the penis is getting all hard, like your thinking.'

'For God's sake, Prabu! I know what an *erection* is!' I grumbled. 'Get on with it. What happened?'

'Nothing happened,' he replied, puzzled by my irritation, and somewhat chastened. 'But from that time only, I never forgot my big, big feeling for her. Now I am making a marriage, and that big, big feeling is getting bigger every day.'

'I'm not sure that I like where this is going, Prabu,' I muttered.

'I am asking you, Lin,' he said, choking on the words. He faced me. Tears bulged and rolled from his eyes into his lap. His voice came in stuttering sobs. 'She is too beautiful. I am a very short and small man. Do you think I can make a good and sexy husband?'

I told Prabaker, sitting in his cab and watching him cry, that love makes men big, and hate makes them small. I told him that my little friend was one of the biggest men I ever met because there wasn't any hate in him. I said that the better I knew him, the bigger he got, and I tried to tell him how rare that was. And I joked with him, and laughed with him until that great smile, as big as a child's biggest wish, returned to his gentle round face. He drove away toward the bachelor party that was waiting for him in the slum, and sounded the horn triumphantly until he was out of sight.

The night that walked me, long after he left, was lonelier than most. I didn't go back to Leopold's. I walked instead along the Causeway, past my apartment, and on to Prabaker's slum at Cuffe Parade. I found the place where Tariq and I fought the vicious pack on the Night of the Wild Dogs. There was still a small pile of scrap timber and stones on the spot. I sat there, smoking the darkness, and watching the slow elegance of the slum-dwellers drifting back along the dusty track to the huddle of huts. I smiled. Thinking of Prabaker's mighty smile always made me smile reflexively, as if I was looking at a happy, healthy baby. Then a vision of Modena's face flowed from the flickering lanterns and vaporous wreaths of smoke, and faded again to nothing before it was fully formed. Music started up inside the slum. A strolling group of young men quickened their pace to jog toward the stirring sound. Prabaker's bachelor party had begun. He'd invited me, but I couldn't bring myself to go. I sat near enough to hear the happiness, but far enough away not to feel it.

For years I'd told myself that love had made me strong when the prison guards tried to force me to betray the actress and our affair. Somehow, Modena had haunted the truth from me. It wasn't love for her that had kept me silent, and it wasn't a brave heart. It was stubbornness that had given me the strength to bite down; stiff-necked, bull-headed stubbornness. There was nothing noble in it. And for all my contempt for the cowardice of bullies, hadn't I become a bully when I was desperate enough? When the dragon-claws of heroin sickness dug into my back I became a small man, a tiny man. I became so small that I had to use a gun. I had to point a gun at people, many of them women, to get money. To get money. How was I different, in that, to Maurizio bullying women to get money? And if they'd shot me during one of those hold-ups, if the cops had gunned me down as I'd wanted and expected at the time, my death would've aroused and deserved as little pity as that of the crazed Italian.

I stood up and stretched, looking around me and thinking of the dogs and the fight and the bravery of the little boy Tariq. When I started back toward the city, I heard a sudden eruption of happy laughter from many voices at Prabaker's party, followed by a cloudburst rattle of applause. And the music dwindled with the distance until it was as faint and diminishable as any moment of truth.

Walking through the night, alone with the city for hours, I loved her with my wandering, just as I'd done when I lived in the slum. Near dawn I bought a newspaper, found a café, and ate a big breakfast, lingering over a second and then a third pot of chai. There was an article on page three of the paper describing the miraculous gifts of the Blue Sisters, as Rasheed's widow and her sister had become known. It was a syndicated article, written by Kavita Singh and published across the country. In it she gave a brief history of their story and then related several first-hand accounts of miraculous cures that had been attributed to the mystical powers the girls exercised. One woman claimed to have been cured of tuberculosis, another insisted that her hearing had been fully restored, and an elderly man declared that his withered lungs were strong and healthy again after he merely touched a hem of their sky-blue garments. Kavita explained that the name Blue Sisters wasn't their own choice: they wore blue, always, because they woke from their comas with a shared dream about floating in the sky, and their devotees had settled on the name. The article concluded with Kavita's own account of a meeting with the girls, and her conviction that they were, beyond any doubt, special—perhaps even supernatural—beings.

I paid the bill, and borrowed a pen from the cashier to circle the article with several lines. As the streets unwound the tangled morning coil of sound, colour, and commotion, I took a cab and jounced through reckless traffic to the Arthur Road Prison. After a wait of three hours, I made my way into the visiting area. It was a single room divided down the centre by two walls of cyclone wire that were separated by an empty space of about two metres. On one side were the visitors, squeezed together and holding their places by clinging to the wire. Across the gap and behind the other wire fence were the prisoners, crushed together and also grasping at the wire to steady themselves. There were about twenty prisoners. Forty of us crowded into an equal space on the visitors' side. Every man, woman, and child in the divided room was shouting. There were so many languages—I recognised six of them, and stopped counting as a door opened on the prisoners' side. Anand entered, pushing his way through to the wire.

'Anand! Anand! Here!' I shouted.

His eyes found me, and he smiled in greeting.

'Linbaba, so good to see you!' he shouted back at me.

'You look good, man!' I called out. He *did* look well. I knew how hard it was to look well in that place. I knew what an effort he'd put into it, cleaning body lice from his clothes every day and washing in the worm-infested water. 'You look real good!'

'*Arrey*, you look very fine, Lin.'

I didn't look fine. I knew that. I looked worried and guilty and tired.

'I'm ... a bit tired. My friend Vikram—you remember him? He got married yesterday. The day before yesterday, actually. I've been walking all night.'

'How is Qasim Ali? Is he well?'

'He's well,' I replied, reddening a little with shame that I didn't see the good and noble head man as often as I used to, when I'd lived in the slum. 'Look! Look at this newspaper. There's an article in it about the sisters. It mentions you. We can use this to help you. We can build up some sympathy for you, before your case comes to court.'

His long, lean, handsome face darkened in a frown that drew his brows together and pressed his lips into a tight, defiant crease.

'You must not do this, Lin!' he shouted back at me. 'That journalist, that Kavita Singh, she was here. I sent her away. If she comes again, I will send her away again. I do not want any help, and I will not allow any help.

I want to have the punishment for what I did to Rasheed.'

'But you don't understand,' I insisted. 'The girls are famous now. People think they're holy. People think they can work miracles. There's thousands of devotees coming to the zhopadpatti every week. When people know you were trying to help them, they'll feel sympathy for you. You'll get *half* the time, or even *less*.'

I was shouting myself hoarse, trying to be heard above or within the clamouring din. It was so hot in the crush of bodies that my shirt was already soaked, and clung to my skin. Had I heard him correctly? It seemed impossible that he would reject any help that might reduce his sentence. Without that help, he was sure to serve a minimum of fifteen years. *Fifteen years in this hell*, I thought, staring through the wire at his frowning face. *How could he refuse our help?*

'Lin! No!' he cried out, louder than before. 'I did that thing to Rasheed. I knew what I was doing. I knew what would happen. I sat with him for a long time, before I did it. I made a choice. I must have the punishment.'

'But I *have* to help you. I have to *try*.'

'No, Lin, please! If you take this punishment away, then there will be no meaning for what I did. There will be no honour. Not for me, not for them. Can't you see it? I have *earned* this punishment. I have become my fate. I am begging you, as a friend. Please do not let them write anything more about me. Write about the ladies. The sisters. Yes! But let me have the peace of my fate. Do you promise me? Linbaba? Do you swear it?'

My fingers clutched at the diamonds of the wire fence. I felt the cold rusty metal bite at the bones within my hands. The noise in that wooden room was like a wild rainstorm on the ragged rooftops of the slum. Beseeching, entreating, adoring, yearning, crying, screaming, and laughing, the hysterical choruses shouted from cage to cage.

'Swear it to me, Lin,' he said, the distress reaching out to me desperately from his pleading eyes.

'Okay, okay,' I answered him, struggling to let the words escape from the little prison of my throat.

'Swear it to me!'

'All right! All right! I swear it. For God's sake, I swear … I won't try to help you.'

His face relaxed, and the smile returned, burning my eyes with the beauty of it.

'Thank you, Linbaba!' he shouted back happily. 'Please don't be thinking I am ungrateful, but I don't want you to come back here again. I don't want you to visit me. You can put some money for me, sometimes, if you think of it. But please don't come back again. This is my life now. This is my life. It will be hard for me, if you come back here. I will *think* about things. I thank you very much, Lin, and I wish a full happiness for you.'

His hands released their hold on the wire fence. He held them together in a praying gesture of blessing, bowing his head slightly, so that I lost contact with his eyes. Without that strong grip on the fence he was at the mercy of the crowd of prisoners, and in seconds he fell back, vanishing into the bubbling wave of faces and hands at the wire. A door at the back of the room opened behind the prisoners, and I watched Anand slip through into the hot yellow light of day with his head high and his thin shoulders bravely squared.

I stepped out onto the street outside the prison. My hair was wet with sweat, and my clothes were soaked. I squinted in the sunlight and stared at the busy street, trying to force myself into its rhythm and rush, trying not to think about Anand in the long room with the overseers, with Big Rahul, with the hunger and the beatings and the filthy, swarming pests. Later that night I would be with Prabaker and Johnny Cigar, Anand's friends, while they celebrated the double wedding. Later that night, Anand would be crammed into a writhing, lice-crawling sleep with two hundred other men on a stone floor. And that would go on, and on, for fifteen years.

I took a cab to my apartment and stood under a hot shower, scorching the slither and itch of memory from my skin. Later, I phoned Chandra Mehta to make the final arrangements for the dancers I'd hired to perform at Prabaker's wedding. Then I phoned Kavita Singh, and told her that Anand wanted us to pull out of the campaign. She was relieved, I think. Her kind heart had fretted for him, and she'd feared from the first that the campaign would fail and then crush him with the weight of fallen hope. She was also glad that he'd given his blessing to her stories about the Blue Sisters. The girls fascinated her, and she'd arranged for a documentary film-maker to visit them in the slum. She wanted to talk about the project, and I heard the sparkling enthusiasm in her voice but I cut her off, promising to call again.

I went out to my little balcony, and let the sound and smell of the city settle on the skin of my bare chest. In a courtyard below, I saw three young men rehearsing the moves and steps of a dance routine they'd copied from a Bollywood film. They laughed helplessly when they messed up the moves of the party piece, and then gave a cheer when they finally danced through one whole routine without error. In another yard some women were squatting together, washing dishes with small anemones of coir rope and a long bar of coral-coloured soap. Their conversation came to me in laughing gasps and shrieks as they scandalised one another with gossip and sardonic commentaries on the peculiar habits of their neighbours' husbands. Then I looked up to see an elderly man sitting in a window opposite me. My eyes met his, and I smiled. He'd been watching me as I'd watched the others below. He wagged his head from side to side, and smiled back at me with a happy grin.

And it was all right. I dressed, and went down to the street. I made the rounds of the black-market currency collection centres, and checked in at Abdul Ghani's passport factory, and inspected the gold-smuggling ring I'd restructured in Khader's name. In three hours I committed thirty crimes or more. And I smiled when people smiled at me. When it was necessary, I gave men enough *bad head*, as gangsters call it, to make them draw back and lower their eyes in fear. I walked the goonda walk, and in three languages I talked the talk. I looked good. I did my job. I made money, and I was still free. But in the black room, deep in my mind, another image added itself to the secret gallery—an image of Anand, holding the palms of his hands together, as his radiant smile became a blessing and a prayer.

Everything you ever sense, in touch or taste or sight or even thought, has an effect on you that's greater than zero. Some things, like the background sound of a bird chirping as it passes your house in the evening, or a flower glimpsed out of the corner of an eye, have such an infinitesimally small effect that you can't detect them. Some things, like triumph and heartbreak, and some images, like the image of yourself reflected in the eyes of a man you've just stabbed, attach themselves to the secret gallery and they change your life forever.

That last image of Anand, the last time I ever saw him, had that effect on me. It wasn't compassion for him that I felt so deeply, although I did pity him as only a chained man could. It wasn't shame, although I was truly ashamed that I hadn't listened when he'd first tried to tell me about Rasheed. It was something else, something so strange that it took me years to fully comprehend. It was envy that nailed the image to my mind. I envied Anand as he turned and walked with his back straight and his head high into the long, suffering years. I envied his peace and his courage and his perfect understanding of himself. Khaderbhai once said that if we envy someone for all the right reasons, we're half way to wisdom. I hope he wasn't right about that. I hope good envy takes you further than that, because a lifetime has passed since that day at the wire, and I still envy Anand's calm communion with fate, and I long for it with all my flawed and striving heart.

CHAPTER TWENTY-NINE

Eyes curved like the sword of Perseus, like the wings of hawks in flight, like the rolled lips of seashells, like eucalyptus leaves in summer—Indian eyes, dancers' eyes, the most beautiful eyes in the world stared with honest, unbeguiling concentration into mirrors held for them by their servants. The dancers I'd hired to perform at the wedding ceremonies for Johnny and Prabaker were already in costume beneath the modest covering of their shawls. In a chai shop near the entrance to the slum, emptied of customers for the purpose, they made the final adjustments to their hair and make-up, professionally swift amid excited chattering. A cotton sheet strung across the doorway was just sheer enough in the golden lamplight to reveal thrillingly indistinct shadows, inflaming fierce desires in many of those who crowded outside, where I stood guard and kept the curious at bay.

At last they were ready, and I threw the cotton screen back. The ten dancers from Film City's chorus lines emerged. They wore traditional tight choli blouses and wrap-around saris. The costumes were lemon yellow, ruby, peacock blue, emerald, sunset pink, gold, royal purple, silver, cream, and tangerine. Their jewels—hair clusters, plait tassels, ear rings, nose rings, necklaces, midriff chains, bangles, and anklets—struck such sparks of light from lanterns and electric bulbs that people blinked and flinched to look at them. Each heavy anklet carried hundreds of tiny bells and, as the dancers began their slow, swaying walk through the hushed and adoring slum, the sizzling clash of those silver bells was the only sound that marked their steps. Then they began to sing:

Aaja Sajan, Aaja
Aaja Sajan, Aaja

Come to me, my lover, come to me
Come to me, my lover, come to me

The crowds that preceded and surrounded them roared their approval. A platoon of small boys scrambled along the rough path ahead of the girls, removing stones or twigs, and sweeping the way clear with palm-leaf brooms. Other young men walked beside the dancers, cooling them with large pear-shaped fans of fine, woven cane. Further ahead along the path, the band of musicians I'd hired with the dancers approached the wedding stage silently in their red and white uniforms. Prabaker and Parvati sat to one side, and Johnny Cigar sat with Sita on the other side. Prabaker's parents, Kishan and Rukhmabai, had travelled from Sunder for the event. They planned to spend a full month in the city, staying in a slum hut beside Prabaker's own. They sat at the front of the stage with Kumar and Nandita Patak. A huge painting of a lotus flower filled the space behind them, and coloured lights formed glowing vines overhead.

When the dancers slowly entered the space, singing love, they stopped as one and stamped their feet. They twirled in place, turning clockwise in perfect unison. Their arms moved with the grace of a swan's neck. Their hands and fingers rolled and swirled like silk scarves sailing the wind. Then suddenly they stamped their feet three times, and the musicians struck up a wild, enravishing rendition of that month's most popular movie song. And with the cheering in every throat around them, the girls danced into a million dreams.

Not a few of those dreams were my own. I'd hired the girls and the musicians, not knowing what kind of show they'd planned to put on for Prabaker's wedding. Chandra Mehta had recommended them to me, and he'd assured me that they always devised their own program. That first black-market money deal Mehta had asked me to transact—the ten thousand American dollars he'd wanted—had borne black fruit. Through him I'd met others in the film world who wanted gold, dollars, and documents. In the previous few months, my visits to the film studios had grown more frequent, and the profit for Khaderbhai accumulated steadily. There was a certain reciprocal cachet in the connection: the *filmi* types, as they were known in Bollywood, found it exhilarating to be associated, at a safe distance, with the notorious mafia don, and the Khan himself wasn't indifferent to the glamour that laminated the movie world. When I approached Chandra Mehta for help in organising the dancers, two weeks before Prabaker's wedding, he'd assumed that the Prabaker in question was an important goonda working for Khaderbhai. He put time and special care into the arrangements, selecting each girl from personal knowledge of her skills, and teaming them with a band of the best studio musicians. The show, when we finally saw it, would've satisfied the manager of the raunchiest nightclub in the city. The band played a long top ten of the season's most popular songs. The girls sang and danced to every one of them, giving seductive and erotic emphasis to the sub-text of each phrase. Some of the thousands of neighbours and guests at the slum wedding were pleasantly scandalised, but most were delighted by the wickedness—Prabaker and Johnny first among them. And I, seeing for the first time how lubricious the uncensored versions of the dances were, gained a new appreciation of the subtler gestures I'd seen so often in the Hindi films.

I gave Johnny Cigar five thousand American dollars as a wedding present. It was enough money for him to buy the little hut that he wanted in the Navy Nagar slum, near the spot where he'd been conceived. The Nagar was a legal slum, and purchasing the hut there meant the end of eviction fears. He would have a secure home from which to continue his work as unofficial accountant and tax consultant to the many hundreds of workers and small businesses in the surrounding slums.

My present to Prabaker was the deed to his taxi. The owner of the small fleet of taxis sold the deed to me in a vicious bout of bare tooth-and-knuckle haggling. I paid too much for the vehicle and its licence, but the money meant nothing to me. It was black money, and black money runs through the fingers faster than legal, hard-earned money. If we can't respect the way we earn it, money has no value. If we can't use it to make life better for our families and loved ones, money has no purpose. Nevertheless, out of respect for the formalities of tradition, I damned the taxi fleet owner, at the conclusion of our deal, with that most polite and hideous of Indian business curses—*May you have ten daughters, and may they all marry well!*—a string of dowry commitments sure to exhaust all but the sturdiest fortunes.

Prabaker was so pleased and excited with the gift that the gravity he'd assumed in the role of the sober groom exploded in a whooping cheer. He leapt to his feet and danced a few pumps of his hip-thrusting sexy dance before the solemnity of the occasion overwhelmed him once more, and he sat down with his bride. I joined the thick, gyrating jungle of men in front of the stage, and danced until my thin shirt clung to me like seaweed in a shallow wave.

Returning to my apartment that night, I smiled to think how different Vikram's wedding had been. Two days before Prabaker and Johnny wed their sister-brides, Vikram was married to Lettie. Against the passionate and occasionally violent opposition of his family, Vikram had opted for a registry office ceremony. He'd responded to the tears and pleading of his loved ones with one formulaic phrase: *This is the modern India, yaar.* Few of his family members could bring themselves to face the agony of that public repudiation of the ancient, gorgeously elaborate Hindu wedding they'd long planned for him. In the end, it was only his sister and his mother who joined the little circle of Lettie's friends, and watched as the bride and groom promised to love and honour one another for the rest of their days. There was no music, no colour, and no dancing. Lettie wore a burnt-gold suit, with a broad, gold straw hat bearing organdie roses. Vikram wore a three-quarter-length black coat, a black-and-white brocade vest, black gaucho pants with silver piping, and his beloved hat. The ceremony was over in minutes and then Vikram and I half-carried his grief-stricken mother to her waiting car.

On the day after their wedding, I drove Vikram and Lettie to the airport. Their plan was to repeat the ceremony in London with Lettie's family. While Lettie phoned her mother to confirm their arrival time, Vikram seized the opportunity for a heart-to-heart with me.

'Thanks for the work you did on my passport, man,' he grinned. 'That fuckin' drug conviction in Denmark—it's only a little thing, but it could've given me a big headache, *yaar*.'

'No problem.'

'And the dollars. That was a fuckin' good rate you got for us. I know you did a special deal on that, *yaar*, and I'll return the favour, somehow, when we get back.'

'It's cool.'

'You know, Lin, you really ought to settle down, man. I don't mean to jinx up your scene or anything. I'm only saying it as a friend, as a friend who loves you like a brother. You're heading for a big fall, man. I got a bad feeling. I ... I think you should settle *down*, like.'

'Settle down ...'

'Yeah, man. That's the whole point of it, *yaar*.'

'The whole point of ... *what*?'

'That's what the whole fuckin' game is all about. You're a man. That's what a man has to do. I don't mean to get into your personal shit, but it's kind of sad that you don't know that already.'

I laughed, but he held the serious frown.

'Lin, a man has to find a good woman, and when he finds her he has to win her love. Then he has to earn her respect. Then he has to cherish her trust. And then he has to, like, go on doing that for as long as they live. Until they both die. That's what it's all about. That's the most important thing in the world. That's what a man is, *yaar*. A man is truly a man when he wins the love of a good woman, earns her respect, and keeps her trust. Until you can do that, you're not a man.'

'Tell that to Didier.'

'No, man, you're not getting it. It's just the same for Didier, but with him it's a good *guy* he has to find and love. It's the same for all of us. What I'm trying to tell you is that you *found* a good woman. You found her *already*. Karla is a good woman, man. And you earned her fuckin' respect. She told me a couple of times, man—about the cholera and all that in the zhopadpatti. You knocked her out with all that Red Cross shit, man. She respects you! But you don't cherish her trust. You don't trust her, Lin, because you don't trust yourself. And I'm afraid for you, man. Without a good woman, a man like you—men like you and me—we're just asking for trouble, *yaar*.'

Lettie approached us. The grim purpose dimmed in his eyes, washed away by the look of love he turned on her.

'They're calling our flight, Lin, me darlin',' she said. Her smile was sadder than I'd expected, and wounding, somehow, because of it. 'We better go. Here, I want you to have this, as a present from both of us.'

She handed me a folded strip of black cloth, about a metre long and a hand-span wide. When I opened it out I found a small card in the centre.

'It's the blindfold,' she said. 'You know, from the train, on the roof, the day Vikram proposed. We want you to have it—as a souvenir, you know. And on the card, that's Karla's address. She wrote to us. She's still in Goa, but in a different part. Just, you know, if you're interested. Goodbye, darlin'. Take care.'

I watched them leave, happy for them, but too busy with Khader's work and the preparations for Prabaker's wedding to give much thought to Vikram's advice. Then the visit to Anand, the last visit, had pushed Vikram's voice even deeper into the choir of competing speeches, warnings, and opinions. But as I sat alone in my apartment on the night of Prabaker's wedding, and took the note and the black strip of the blindfold from my pocket, I remembered every word he'd said to me. I sipped at a drink and smoked cigarettes in a silence so profound that I could hear the susurrus of the blindfold's soft fabric rustle and slip between my fingers. The seductive, bell-bejewelled dancers had been escorted to their bus, and paid a respectful bonus. Prabaker and Johnny had led their brides away to taxis that waited to take them to a simple but comfortable hotel on the outskirts of the city. For two nights they would know the joys of private love before their public loves in the crowded slums resumed. Vikram and Lettie were already in London, preparing to repeat the vows that meant everything to my cowboy-obsessed friend. And I was sitting in the armchair, fully dressed and alone, not trusting *her*, as Vikram said, because I didn't trust myself. Then at last, when I drifted to sleep, the note and the strip of blindfold slipped from my fingers.

And for three weeks, after that night, I tried to lose the loneliness that their three happy marriages had pulled from my heart by taking every job I was offered, and cutting every deal I could devise. I flew one passport run to Kinshasa staying, as instructed, at the Lapierre Hotel. It was a nearly squalid three-storey building in a laneway parallel to Kinshasa's long main street. The mattress was clean, but the floor and the walls seemed to be made from recycled coffin-wood. The grave-like smell was overpowering, and a sweating damp filled my mouth with gloomy, unidentifiable tastes. I chain-smoked Gitanes and gargled Belgian whisky to kill them. Rat-catchers patrolled the corridors, dragging conspicuous hessian sacks that bulged with writhing, fat animals. Cockroach colonies had claimed the drawers of the dresser, so I hung my clothing and toiletries and other personal items from hooks and thick, crooked nails conveniently hammered into every surface that would endure them.

On my first night I was ripped from a light sleep by gunshots in the corridor beyond my door. I heard a crumpling thump, as of a body falling, and then shuffling footsteps pulling something heavy, backwards, along the bare wooden floor of the hallway. I clamped a fist around my knife and opened the door. Men were standing at three other doors in the corridor, drawn as I was by the sounds. They were all Europeans. Two of them held pistols in their hands, and one held a knife similar to my own. We all looked at one another, and then at the trail of blood that smeared its way down the corridor out of sight. As if in response to a secret signal, we all closed our doors again without a word.

When I followed the Kinshasa run with a mission to Mauritius, my hotel on the island-nation provided a welcome and agreeable contrast. It was called the Mandarin, and it was in Curepipe. The original structure was built as a small-scale reproduction of a Scottish castle. The turreted resemblance was clear enough, on the winding approach through a neat English garden. Inside the building, however, the guest entered a kingdom of Chinese baroque designed by the Chinese family who were the new owners of the hotel. I sat beneath huge, fire-breathing dragons and ate Chinese broccoli with snow peas, garlic spinach, fried bean curd, and mushrooms in black bean sauce by the light of paper lanterns, while the windows gave a view of castellated battlements, gothic arches, and rose-studded topiary.

My contacts, two Indians from Bombay who lived in Mauritius, arrived in a yellow BMW, as had been arranged. I got into the back of the car and had barely spoken a greeting when they took off at such tyre-torching speed that I was hurled backwards into a corner of the seat. We screamed along back roads at four times the speed limit for fifteen knuckle-whitening minutes and then they pulled into a silent, deserted grove. The overheated car cooled down with little clinks and clunks of sound. There was a strong smell of rum on both men.

'Okay, let's have the books,' one of the two contacts said, leaning around from the driver's seat.

'I haven't got them,' I snarled at him through clenched teeth.

The contacts looked at one another and then back at me. The driver raised his mercury-lens glasses, revealing eyes that looked as though he kept them in a glass of brown vinegar beside his bed at night.

'You don't got the books?'

'No. I was trying to tell you that on the way here—wherever the fuck we are—but you kept saying, *Keep cool! Keep cool!* And not listening to me. Well, are we *cool* enough now? Huh?'

'I'm not cool, man,' the passenger said.

I saw myself in the lenses of his glasses. I didn't look happy.

'You idiots!' I growled, switching to Hindi. 'You nearly killed us all for nothing! Driving like a speed-freak-arsehole-Bombay-taxi-driver with the cops up his arse! The passports are back at the sister-fucking hotel. I stashed them because I wanted to be sure of you two motherfuckers first. Now the only thing I'm sure of is that you guys haven't got the brains of two fleas on a pariah dog's balls.'

The passenger lifted his glasses, and they both smiled as widely as their hangovers would allow.

'Where the fuck did you learn to speak Hindi like that?' the driver asked. 'It's fuckin' great, *yaar*. You're speaking like a regular Bombay sisterfucker. It's fantastic, *yaar!*'

'Damn impressive, man!' his friend added, wagging his head admiringly.

'Let me see the money,' I snapped.

They laughed.

'The money,' I insisted. 'Let me see it.'

The passenger lifted a bag from between his feet and opened it to reveal many bundles of cash.

'What's *that* shit?'

'It's the money, brother,' the driver replied.

'That's not money,' I said. 'Money is green. Money says, *In God We Trust*. Money has the picture of a dead American on it because money *comes* from America. That's not money.'

'It's Mauritian rupees, brother,' the passenger sniffed, wounded by the insult to his currency.

'You can't spend that shit anywhere but in Mauritius,' I scoffed, recalling what I'd learned about restricted and open currencies while working with Khaled Ansari. 'It's a restricted currency.'

'I know, of course, baba,' the driver smiled. 'We arranged it with Abdul. We don't have the dollars just now, man. All fuckin' tied up in other deals. So we're paying in Mauritian rupees. You can change them back to dollars on your way home, *yaar*.'

I sighed, breathing slowly and forcing calm into the little whirlwind that my mood was making out of my mind. I looked out the window. We were parked in what seemed to be a green forest fire. Tall plants as green as Karla's eyes whirled and shuddered in the wind all around us. There was no-one and nothing else in sight.

'Let's just see what we got here. Ten passports at seven thousand bucks apiece. That's seventy thousand bucks. At the exchange rate of, say, thirty Mauritian roops to the dollar, that gives me no less than two million, one hundred thousand rupees. That's why you got such a big bag. Now, forgive me for seeming obtuse, gentlemen, but just where the fuck am I going to change two million rupees into dollars without a fuckin' *currency certificate!*'

'No problem,' the driver responded quickly. 'We've got a money-changer, *yaar*. A first-class guy. He'll do the deal for you. It's all set up.'

'Okay,' I smiled. 'Let's go and see him.'

'You'll have to go there alone, man,' the passenger said, laughing happily. 'He's in Singapore.'

'*Singa-fuckin'-pore!*' I shouted, as that little whirlwind flared in my mind.

'Don't be all upset, *yaar*,' the driver replied gently. 'It's all arranged. Abdul Ghani is cool about it. He'll call you at the hotel today. Here, take this card. You go to Singapore, on your way home—okay, okay, Singapore is not exactly on the way home to Bombay, but if you fly there first, then it *will* be on the way, isn't it? So when you get down in Singapore, you go and see this guy on the card. He's a licensed money-changer. He's Khader's man. He'll change all the roops into dollars, and you'll be cool. No problem. There's even a bonus in it for you. You'll see.'

'Okay,' I sighed. 'Let's go back to the hotel. If this checks out with Abdul, we'll do the deal.'

'The hotel,' the driver said, sliding his glasses down over the dartboards of his eyes.

'The hotel!' the passenger repeated, and the yellow Exocet hurtled back along the winding roads once more.

The trip through Singapore passed off without a hitch, and the Mauritian currency fiasco provided a few unexpected benefits. I made a valuable, new contact in the Singapore moneychanger—an Indian from Madras named Shekky Ratnam—and I took my first look at the profitable smuggling run of duty free cameras and electrical goods from Singapore to Bombay.

When I rode out to the Oberoi Hotel to meet Lisa Carter, after handing the dollars to Abdul Ghani and collecting my fee, I felt positive and hopeful for the first time in far too long. I began to think that I might've thrown off the dark moods that had settled on me after

Prabaker's wedding night. I'd travelled to Zaïre, Mauritius, and Singapore on forged passports without raising the vaguest suspicion. In the slum, I'd survived from day to day on the small commissions I made from tourists, and I had only my compromised New Zealand passport. Just a year later I lived in a modern apartment, my pockets were bulging with freshly ill-gotten gains, and I had five passports in five different names and nationalities, with my photograph on every one of them. The world of possibility was opening up for me.

The Oberoi Hotel stood at Nariman Point, on the handle of Marine Drive's golden sickle. Churchgate Station and Flora Fountain were a five-minute walk away. Ten minutes more in one direction led to Victoria Terminus and Crawford Market. Ten minutes in the other direction from Flora Fountain led to Colaba and the Gateway Monument. The Oberoi lacked the postcard recognition that the Taj Hotel inspired, but it compensated for that with character and flair. Its piano bar, for example, was a small masterpiece of light and cleverly private spaces, and its brasserie vied determinedly for the title of the best restaurant in Bombay. Walking into the dark, richly textured brasserie from the brilliant day, I paused and blinked until my eyes found Lisa and her group. She and two other young women were sitting with Cliff De Souza and Chandra Mehta.

'Hope I'm not late,' I said, shaking hands all round.

'No, I think *we're* all *early*,' Chandra Mehta joked, his voice booming out across the room.

The girls laughed hysterically. Their names were Reeta and Geeta. They were aspiring actresses on the first rung—a lunch date with key second-tier players—and they gushed it up with a bug-eyed enthusiasm that wasn't far from panic.

I sat down in the vacant chair between Lisa and Geeta. Lisa wore a thin, lava-red pullover beneath a black silk jacket, and a skirt. Geeta's silver spandex top and white jeans were tight enough to be anatomically explicit. She was a pretty girl, maybe twenty years old, with her long hair pulled into a high ponytail. Her hands fretted at the table napkin, folding and unfolding a corner of the cloth. Reeta had a neat short hairstyle that suited her small face and gamine features. She wore a yellow blouse with a deep, confrontation neckline, and blue jeans. Cliff and Chandra both wore suits, and it seemed that they were coming from or going to an appointment of some significance.

'I'm starved,' Lisa said happily. Her voice was light and confident, but she squeezed my hand under the table so hard that her fingernails pinched their way into my skin. It was an important meeting for her. She knew that Mehta planned to offer us a formal partnership in the casting business we'd been running unofficially. Lisa wanted that contractual agreement. She wanted the approval that only a contract could provide. She wanted her future in writing. 'Let's eat!'

'How about—what do you all think—if I make the order for all of us?' Chandra suggested.

'Since you're paying for it, I don't mind,' Cliff said, laughing and winking at the girls.

'Sure,' I agreed. 'Go ahead.'

He summoned the waiter with a glance and waved the menu aside, launching straight into his list of preferences. It began with a white soup entrée made with lamb cooked in blanched-almond milk, worked its way through grilled chicken in a cayenne, cumin, and mango marinade, and ended, after many other side platters, with fruit salad, honey kachori balls, and kulfi ice cream.

Listening to Mehta's lengthy and precise list of dishes, we all knew that it would be a long lunch. I relaxed, and let myself drift in the flow of fine foods and conversation.

'So, you still haven't told me what you think,' Mehta prodded.

'You're giving it more attention than it's worth,' Cliff De Souza declared, fluttering a hand dismissively.

'No, man,' Mehta insisted. 'It happened right outside my damn office, *yaar*. If ten thousand people are shouting about killing you, outside your own damn office window, it's hard not to give it some attention.'

'They weren't shouting about *you personally*, Chandrababu.'

'Not me personally. But it's me, and everyone like me, they want to get. Come on, it's not so bad for you, and you should admit it. Your family is from Goa. You're Konkani speakers. Konkani and Marathi are very close. You speak Marathi as well as you speak English. But I don't speak a damn word of it. Still I'm born here, *yaar*, and my daddy was born here before me. He has his business here in Bombay. We pay taxes here. My kids all go to school here. My whole life is here in Bombay, man. But they're shouting *Maharashtra for the Marathis*, and they want to kick us out of the only home we have.'

'You have to see it from their point of view as well,' Cliff added softly.

'See my *eviction* from *their* point of view,' Mehta retorted, with such vehemence that several heads turned toward him from other tables. He continued more quietly but with just as much passion. 'I should see my *murder* from *their* point of view, is that it?'

'I love you, my friend, like I love my own third brother-in-law,' Cliff replied, grinning widely. Mehta laughed with him and the girls joined in, clearly relieved to have the tension at the table diluted with the little joke. 'I don't want to see anyone hurt, least of all you, Chandrabhai. All I'm saying is, you have to see it from their side if you want to understand why they're feeling all this. They're native Marathi speakers. They're born here in Maharashtra. Their grandfathers, all the way back to ... who knows, three thousand years or more, they were all born here. And then they look around in Bombay, and they see all the best jobs, all the businesses, all the companies owned by people from other places in India. It drives them crazy. And I think they have a point.'

'What about the reserve jobs?' Mehta protested. 'The post office, the police, the schools, the state bank, and lots of others, like the transport authority, they all reserve jobs for Marathi speakers. But that's not enough for these crazy fuckers. They want to kick us all out of Bombay and Maharashtra. But I tell you, if they get their way, if they kick us out, they'll lose most of the money and the talent and the brains that make this place what it is.'

Cliff De Souza shrugged.

'Maybe that's a price they're prepared to pay—not that I agree with them. I just think that people like your grand-dad, who came here from U.P. with nothing, and built a successful business, owe something to the state. The ones who have it all have to share some of it with the ones who have nothing. The people you call fanatics can only get others to listen because there's a grain of truth in what they say. People are angry. The ones who came here from outside and made their fortunes are getting the blame. It's going to get worse, my dear third brother-in-law, and I hate to think where it's going to end.'

'What do you think, Lin?' Chandra Mehta asked me, appealing for support. 'You speak Marathi. You live here. But you're an outsider. What do you think?'

'I learned to speak Marathi in a little village called Sunder,' I said in answer. 'The people there are native Marathi speakers. They don't speak Hindi well, and they don't speak English at all. They're pure, *shudha* Marathi speakers, and Maharashtra has been their home for at least two thousand years. Fifty generations have farmed the land there.'

I paused to give someone else a chance to comment or query what I'd said. They were all eating, and listening intently. I continued.

'When I came back to Bombay with my guide, Prabaker, I went to live in the slum, where he and twenty-five thousand other people live. There were a lot of people like Prabaker there in that slum. They were Maharashtrians, from villages just like Sunder. They lived in the kind of poverty where every meal cost them a crown of thorns in worry, and slaving work. I think it must break their hearts to see people from other parts of India living in fine homes while they wash in the gutters of their own capital city.'

I took a few mouthfuls of food, waiting for a response from Mehta. After a few moments, he obliged.

'But, hey, Lin, come on, that's not all of it,' he said. 'There's a lot more to it than that.'

'No, you're right. That's not all of it,' I agreed. 'They're not just Maharashtrians in that slum. They're Punjabis and Tamils and Karnatakans and Bengalis and Assamese and Kashmiris. And they're not just Hindus. They're Sikhs and Muslims and Christians and Buddhists and Parsis and Jains. The problems here are not just Maharashtrian problems. The poor, like the rich, are from every part of India. But the poor are far too many, and the rich are far too few.'

'*Arrey baap!*' Chandra Mehta puffed. *Holy father!* 'You sound like Cliff. He's a fuckin' communist. That's one of *his* raves, *yaar*.'

'I'm not a communist, or a capitalist,' I said, smiling. 'I'm more of a *leave-me-the-hell-alone-ist*.'

'Don't believe him,' Lisa interjected. 'When you're in trouble, he's the right man to call.'

I looked at her. Our eyes held just long enough to feel good and guilty at the same time.

'Fanaticism is the opposite of love,' I said, recalling one of Khaderbhai's lectures. 'A wise man once told me—he's a Muslim, by the way—that he has more in common with a rational, reasonable-minded Jew than he does with a fanatic from his own religion. He has more in common with a rational, reasonable-minded Christian or Buddhist or Hindu than he does with a fanatic from his own religion. In fact, he has more in common with a rational, reasonable-minded *atheist* than he does with a fanatic from his own religion. I agree with him, and I feel the same way. I also agree with Winston Churchill, who once defined a fanatic as someone who *won't* change his mind and *can't* change the subject.'

'And on that note,' Lisa laughed, 'let's change the subject. Come on, Cliff, I'm relying on you to give me all the gossip about the romance on the set of *Kanoon*. What's really going on there?'

'Yes! Yes!' Reeta cried out excitedly. 'And all about the new girl. There's so much of scandal about her that I can't even say her name out loud, *yaar*. And everything, anything at all about Anil Kapoor! I just love him to pieces!'

'And Sanjay Dutt!' Geeta added, trembling dramatically at the mention of his name. 'Is it true that you actually went to his party in Versova? Oh, my God! How I would *love* to be there! Tell us all about it!'

Encouraged by that febrile curiosity, Cliff De Souza spun out yarns about the Bollywood stars, and Chandra Mehta added titillating ruffles of gossip throughout. It became clear during the lunch that Cliff had an eye for Reeta, and Chandra Mehta directed much of his attention to Geeta. The long lunch was the beginning of a long day and night they'd planned to spend together. Warming to their themes, and with half their minds on the pleasures of the night to come, the movie men gradually shifted their gossip and anecdotes into the area of sex and sexual scandals. They were funny stories, sometimes straying into the bizarre. We were all laughing hard when Kavita Singh entered the restaurant. The laughter was still rippling through us as I introduced Kavita around the table.

'Excuse me,' she said, with the kind of frown that climbs out of deep trouble and refuses to leave. 'I have to speak to you, Lin.'

'You can talk about the case here, Kavita,' I offered, still bright with the laughter of a minute before. 'They'll find it interesting.'

'It's not about the case,' she insisted firmly. 'It's about Abdullah Taheri.'

I stood at once and excused myself, nodding to Lisa that she should stay and wait for me to return. Kavita and I walked to the foyer of the restaurant. When we were alone, she spoke.

'Your friend Taheri is in deep shit.'

'What do you mean?'

'I mean that I heard a whisper from the crime staffer at the *Times*. He said that Abdullah is on a police hit list. *Shoot on sight*, he said.'

'What?'

'The cops' orders are to take him alive, if they can, but to take no chances with him. They're sure he's armed, and they're sure he'll shoot, if they try to arrest him. At the slightest hesitation from him, they're ordered to shoot him down like a dog.'

'Why? What's it all about?'

'They think he's this Sapna guy. They've had a solid tip-off, with solid evidence. They're sure it's him, and they're going to get him. Today. It might have happened already. You can't fuck with the cops in Bombay — not with something this serious. I've been looking for you for two hours.'

'Sapna? It doesn't make sense,' I said. But it did make sense. It made perfect sense, somehow, and I couldn't understand why. There were too many pieces missing; too many questions that I hadn't asked, and should've asked, long before.

'Sensible or not, it's now a reality,' she said, her voice trembling in the shudder of a resigned and pitying shrug. 'I've been looking for you every-where. Didier told me you were here. I know Taheri's a good friend of yours.'

'Yeah. He's a friend,' I said, suddenly remembering that I was talking to a journalist. I stared at the dark carpet, and tried to find sense or direction in the sandstorm of my thoughts. Then I looked up and met her eyes. 'Thanks, Kavita. I really appreciate it. Thanks a lot. I'll have to go.'

'Listen,' she said more softly. 'I filed the story. I phoned it in as soon as I heard it. If it makes the evening news, it might make the cops a little more careful. For the record, I don't think he did it. I can't believe it. I always liked him. I had a little crush on him for a while, right after you brought him to Leopold's the first time. Maybe I've still got a crush on him, *yaar*. Anyway, I don't think he's Sapna, and I don't think he did those ... terrible things.'

She left, smiling for me and crying for him at the same time. At the table, I apologised for breaking up the lunch and offered a vague excuse for leaving. Without asking her if she wanted to come, I pulled back Lisa's chair for her and lifted her handbag from the chair's high back.

'Oh, Lin, do you really have to go?' Chandra complained. 'We haven't even talked about the casting-agency deal.'

'Do you really know Abdullah Taheri?' Cliff asked, the faintest hint of accusation in his curiosity.

I glared at him.

'Yes.'

'And you're taking the lovely Lisa with you,' Chandra pouted. 'That's a double disappointment.'

'I've heard so much about him, *yaar*,' Cliff persisted. 'How did you meet him?'

'He saved my life, Cliff,' I said, a little more harshly than I'd intended. 'The first time I met him, he saved my life, at the hash den run by the Standing Babas.'

I held open the door of the brasserie for Lisa, and looked back at the table. Cliff and Chandra had their heads close together, their whispers excluding the bewildered girls.

On the bike, outside the hotel, I told Lisa everything that I knew. Her healthy tan faded suddenly and her face was pale, but she pulled herself together quickly. She agreed with me that a trip to Leopold's was logical, as a first step. Abdullah might be there, or he might've left a message with someone. She was afraid, and I felt that fear twisting in the muscles of her arms as she clung to my back. We hurtled through the ponderously slow traffic, riding on luck and instinct just as Abdullah might've done. At Leopold's we found Didier drinking himself into the liquid abyss.

'It's over,' he slurred, pouring himself another whisky from a large bottle. 'It's all over. They shot him dead almost an hour ago. Everyone is talking about it. The mosques in Dongri are calling the prayers for the dead.'

'How do you know?' I demanded. 'Who told you?'

'The prayers for the dead,' he mumbled, his head lolling forward. 'What a ridiculous and redundant phrase! There *are* no other kinds of prayers. *Every* prayer is a prayer for the dead.'

I grabbed the front of his shirt and shook him. The waiters, who all liked Didier as much as I did, watched me and calculated how far they would let me go.

'Didier! Listen to me! How do you know? Who told you about it? Where did it happen?'

'The police were here,' he said, suddenly lucid. His pale blue eyes looked into mine as if he was looking for something at the bottom of a pond. 'They were boasting about it to Mehmet, one of the owners. You know Mehmet. He's also Iranian, like Abdullah. Some of the police from the Colaba station, across the road, were in the ambush. They said that he was surrounded in a little street near Crawford Market. They called on him to surrender himself to them. They said he stood perfectly still. They said his long hair was streaming behind him in the wind, and his black clothes. They talked about that for quite some time. It is strange, don't you think, Lin, that they were talking about his clothes ... and his hair? What does it mean? Then they ... they said he took two guns from his jacket, and began to shoot at them. They all returned the fire at once. He was shot so many times that his body was mutilated, they said. It was torn apart by the fusillade.'

Lisa began to cry. She sat down next to Didier, and he wrapped an arm around her in the automatism of grief and shock. He didn't look at her or acknowledge her. He patted at her shoulder and rocked from side to side, but his sorrow-struck expression would've been the same if he were alone and wrapping his arms about himself.

'There was a big crowd,' he continued. 'They were very upset. The police were nervous. They wanted to take his body to the hospital in one of their vans, but the people in the crowd attacked the van, and forced it off the road. The police took the body to the Crawford Market police station. The crowd followed them there, shouting and screaming abuse. They are still there, I think.'

Crawford Market police station. I had to go there. I had to see the body. I had to see him. Maybe he was alive ...

'Wait here,' I told Lisa. 'Wait with Didier, or get a cab home. I'll be back.'

A spear rammed into my side, up beside my heart, and out through the top of my chest. The spear of Abdullah's death, the spear of thinking about his dead, dead body. I rode to Crawford Market, and every breath pushed the rough spear up against my heart.

Near the market police station I was forced to abandon the bike because a milling crowd mobbed the road. Striking out on foot, I soon found myself in a wild, aimlessly rambling frenzy of people. Most of them were Muslims. What I could make out from the many chants and shouted slogans indicated that they weren't simply mourners. Abdullah's death had touched off a prairie fire of discontent and long-nursed grievances in the neglected acres of the poor around the market area. Men were shouting a confusing collection of complaints, and clamouring for their own causes. I could hear prayers ringing out from several places.

Inside the legions of screaming men it was chaos, and every step toward the police station was won with a wrestling, shoving effort of force and will. Men came in waves that swept me sideways and then forward and then back. They pushed and punched and kicked out with their legs. More than once I almost went under those trampling feet, reaching out at the last moment to save myself by grappling my fingers into a shirt or a beard or a shawl. I finally caught sight of the police station and the police. Wearing helmets and carrying shields, they were three or four deep across the whole width of the building.

A man beside me in the crowd seized my shirt and began to punch me about the head and face. I had no idea why he'd attacked me—maybe he didn't understand it himself—but it didn't matter. The blows were struck, and I was in it. I covered myself with my hands and tried to wrench myself free. His hand was locked onto the shirt, and I couldn't shake him off. I stepped in closer, jabbed my fingers into his eyes, and crashed my fist into his head just ahead of the ear. His hand released me and he fell back, but others began to punch at me. The crowd opened out around me and I shaped up, punching out at random and hitting anything within range.

It was a bad situation. I knew that sooner or later I would lose the energy and the surprise that kept the posse of men at bay. Men rushed at me, but only one at a time and with no technique. They took solid hits and drew back. I danced around, hammering anyone who came near me, but I was surrounded and I couldn't win. It was only the crowd's fascination with the fighting that kept them from surging forward in a strangling crush of bodies.

A determined phalanx of eight or ten men broke through the circle, and I was face to face with Khaled Ansari. I was running on instinct, and I almost punched him. He held out both hands, waving for me to stop. His men ploughed their way back into the crowd, and Khaled pushed me in behind them. Someone punched my head from behind, and I turned and ran at the mob again, wanting to fight every man in the city; wanting to fight until they punched me numb; until I couldn't feel that spear, dead Abdullah's spear, in my chest. Khaled and two of his friends wrapped their arms around me and dragged me out of the writhing, lunatic hell that the street had become.

'His body's not there,' Khaled told me when we found my bike. He wiped the blood from my face with a handkerchief. My eye was swelling up quickly, and blood dripped from my nose and a cut on my lower lip. I hadn't felt the blows at all. There was no pain. The pain was all in my chest, right next to my heart, and I breathed it in, and out, and in.

'The crowd stormed the place. Hundreds of them. That was before we got here. When the cops pushed them out again, they went to the cell where they'd put his body, and it was empty. The crowd let all the prisoners out, and they got his body.'

'Ah, Jesus,' I moaned. 'Ah, fuck. Ah, God.'

'We'll get people on it,' Khaled said, quiet and confident. 'We'll find out what happened. We'll find ... it ... him. We'll find his body.'

I rode back to Leopold's, and found Johnny Cigar sitting at Didier's table. Didier and Lisa were gone. I collapsed in a chair beside Johnny, much as Lisa had done beside Didier a few hours before. Leaning my elbows on the table, I rubbed my eyes with the heels of my hands.

'A terrible thing,' Johnny said.

'Yeah.'

'It shouldn't have happened.'

'No.'

'And it didn't need to happen. Not like this.'

'Yeah.'

'He didn't need to take that fare. It was the last one for the night, but he didn't need it. He made plenty yesterday.'

'What?' I asked, looking at him with a frown that was angry in its bewilderment.

'Prabaker's accident,' he said.

'What?'

'The accident,' he repeated.

'What ... *accident?*'

'Oh, my God, Lin, I thought you knew about it,' he said, the blood in his face an ebb tide that receded to his tightening throat. His voice cracked, and his eyes filled with tears. 'I thought you knew. When I saw your face just now, the way you look, I thought you knew about it. I've been waiting for you nearly for one hour. I came to find you as soon as I left the hospital.'

'Hospital ...' I repeated stupidly.

'St. George Hospital. He's in the intensive care. The operation —'

'What operation?'

'He was hurt—very badly hurt, Lin. The operation was ... he's still alive, but ...'

'But what?'

Johnny broke down and wept, bringing himself under control only with deep breaths and a clench-jawed effort of will.

'He took two passengers, very late last night. Actually, it was about three o'clock this morning. A man and his daughter, wanting to go to the airport. There was a handcart on the highway road. You know how these fellows take some short-cuts at night, on the main road. It's forbidden, but still they do it, *yaar*, to save miles of pushing those heavy carts. This cart was full of steel for building. Long steel pieces. They lost the control of that cart on a hill. It slipped from their hands, and it rolled backwards. Prabaker came around the corner in his taxi, and the whole thing went into the front of the car. Some of the steel went through the window. The man and the woman in the back were killed. Their heads came off. Completely off. Prabaker was hit in the face.'

He wept again, and I reached out to comfort him. Tourists and patrons at other tables glanced at us, but quickly looked away. When he recovered, I ordered a whisky for him. He gulped it in one tip of the glass, as Prabaker had done on the first day that I met him.

'How bad is he?'

'The doctor said it's sure he will die, Lin,' Johnny sobbed. 'His jaw is gone. The steel took it away completely. Everything is gone. All his teeth. There is a big hole, just a big hole, where his mouth and his jaw used to be. His neck is open. They haven't even put bandages on his face, because there are so many tubes and pipes going into that hole. To keep him alive. How he survived it, in that car like that, nobody can say. He was trapped in there for two hours. The doctors think that he will die tonight. That's why I tried to find you. He got bad wounds in the chest and stomach and head. He's going to die, Lin. He's going to die. We have to go there.'

We walked into the critical-care ward, and found Kishan and Rukhmabai sitting at the side of his bed and weeping in one another's arms. Parvati, Sita, Jeetendra, and Qasim Ali were all standing in solemn silence at the foot of the bed. Prabaker was unconscious. A bank of machines monitored his vital signs. Tubes and metal pipes were taped to his face — what was left of his face. That great smile, that gorgeous, solar smile, had been ripped from his face. It was simply ... gone.

In a duty room on the ground floor, I found the doctor in charge of his care. I pulled a bundle of American hundred-dollar bills from my belt and offered it to him, asking him to forward any further accounts to me. He wouldn't take it. There was no hope, he said. Prabaker had hours, perhaps only minutes, to live. That was why he'd allowed the family and friends to remain at the bedside. There was nothing to do, he said, but wait with him, and watch him die. I returned to Prabaker's room and gave Parvati the money, together with everything I'd earned on my most recent courier run.

I found a toilet in the hospital and then washed my face and neck. The cuts and wounds on my face filled my aching head with thoughts of Abdullah. I couldn't bear to think those thoughts. I couldn't hold the image of my wild, Iranian friend surrounded by cops and shooting it out until his body was torn and bloodied. I stared into the mirror, feeling the acid burn of tears. I slapped myself hard awake, and returned to Prabaker's floor.

I stood with the others, at the foot of his bed, for three hours. Exhausted, I began to nod off, and I had to admit that I couldn't stay awake. In a relatively quiet corner, I put two chairs against the wall and went to sleep. A dream swallowed me whole, almost at once. It carried me to Sunder. I was floating on the murmuring tide of voices on that first night in the village when Prabaker's father put his hand on my shoulder, and I clenched my teeth against the stars. When I woke from the dream, Kishan *was* sitting there beside me with his hand on my shoulder, and when I met his eyes we both sobbed helplessly.

In the end, when it was sure that Prabaker would die, and we all knew it, and we all accepted the fact that he had to die, we went through four days and nights of watching his brave little body suffer, what was left of him, the almost-Prabaker with the amputated smile. In the end, after days and nights of watching him suffer that pain and bewilderment, I began to hope that he would die, and to wish for it with all my heart. I loved him so much that in the end I found an empty corner in a cleaner's room, where a tap dripped constantly into a concrete trough, and I fell to my knees on a place marked by two wet footprints, and I begged God to let him die. And then he did die.

In the hut he'd once shared with Parvati, Prabaker's mother, Rukhmabai, unfurled her thigh-length hair. She was sitting in the doorway with her back to the world. Her black hair was night's waterfall. She cut across thickly, close to her head, with sharp shears, and the long hair fell like a shadow dying.

At first, when we truly love someone, our greatest fear is that the loved one will stop loving us. What we should fear and dread, of course, is that *we* won't stop loving *them*, even after they're dead and gone. For I still love you with the whole of my heart, Prabaker. I still love you. And sometimes, my friend, the love that I have, and can't give to you, crushes the breath from my chest. Sometimes, even now, my heart is drowning in a sorrow that has no stars without you, and no laughter, and no sleep.

CHAPTER THIRTY

Heroin is a sensory deprivation tank for the soul. Floating on the Dead Sea of the drug stone, there's no sense of pain, no regret or shame, no feelings of guilt or grief, no depression, and no desire. The sleeping universe enters and envelops every atom of existence. Insensible stillness and peace disperse fear and suffering. Thoughts drift like ocean weeds and vanish in the distant, grey somnolency, unperceived and indeterminable. The body succumbs to cryogenic slumber: the listless heart beats faintly, and breathing slowly fades to random whispers. Thick nirvanic numbness clogs the limbs, and downward, deeper, the sleeper slides and glides toward oblivion, the perfect and eternal stone.

That chemical absolution is paid for, like everything else in the universe, with light. The first light that junkies lose is the light in their eyes. A junkie's eyes are as lightless as the eyes of Greek statues, as lightless as hammered lead, as lightless as a bullet hole in a dead man's back. The next light lost is the light of desire. Junkies kill desire with the same weapon they use on hope and dream and honour: the club made from their craving. And when all the other lights of life are gone, the last light lost is the light of love. Sooner or later, when it's down to the last hit, the junkie will give up the woman he loves, rather than go without; sooner or later, every hard junkie becomes a devil in exile.

I levitated. I floated, upraised on the supernatant liquid of the smack in the spoon, and the spoon was as big as a room. The raft of opiate paralysis drifted across the little lake in the spoon, and the rafters intersecting over my head seemed to hold an answer, some kind of answer, in their symmetry. I stared at the rafters, knowing that the answer was there and that it might save me. And then I closed my eyes of hammered lead again, and lost it. And sometimes I woke. Sometimes I was wide-awake enough to want more of the deadening drug. Sometimes I was awake enough to remember it all.

There'd been no funeral for Abdullah because there was no body for them, for us, to bury. His body had disappeared during the brawling riot just as Maurizio's body had disappeared—as completely as a flared, exhausted star. I joined the others to carry Prabaker's body to the ghat, the burning place. I ran with them through the streets. I ran with them beneath the garlanded burden of his little body, chanting names of God, and then I watched his body burn. Grief roamed the lanes of the slum afterward, and I couldn't remain there with the gathering of friends and family who mourned him. They stood near the spot where Prabaker had been married only weeks before. Tattered streamers from the wedding still dangled from the roofs of some of the huts. I spoke to Qasim Ali, Johnny, Jeetendra, and Kishan Mango, but then I left them and rode to Dongri. I had questions for lord Abdel Khader Khan: questions that crawled inside me like the things in Hassaan Obikwa's pit.

The house near the Nabila Mosque was closed, locked up with heavy padlocks and utterly silent. No-one in the forecourt of the mosque or the street of shops could tell me when he'd left, or when he might return. Frustrated and angry, I rode to see Abdul Ghani. His house was open but his servants told me that he was out of the city on a holiday, and wasn't expected home again for weeks. I visited the passport factory, and found Krishna and Villu hard at work. They confirmed that Ghani had left them instructions and sufficient funds for several weeks of work, and had told them that he was taking a holiday. When I rode to Khaled Ansari's apartment, I met a watchman on duty who told me that Khaled was in Pakistan. He had no idea when the dour Palestinian would return.

The other members of Khader's mafia council were just as suddenly and conveniently absent. Farid was in Dubai. General Sobhan Mahmoud was in Kashmir. No-one answered my knock at Keki Dorabjee's house, and every window was darkened with a drawn shade. Rajubhai, who'd never been known to miss a day at his counting house in the Fort, was visiting a sick relative in Delhi. Even the second-level bosses and lieutenants were out of town or simply unavailable.

Those who remained, the gold agents and currency couriers and passport contacts all over the city, were polite and friendly. Work for them seemed to continue at the same pace and with the same routines. My own work was just as secure. I was anticipated at every depot, exchange centre, jewellery store, and other point of contact with Khader's empire. Instructions had been left for me with gold dealers, currency men, and the touts who bought and stole passports. I wasn't sure if it was a compliment to me—that I could be relied upon to function in the absence of the council—or that they saw me as so inconsequential in their scheme of things that I didn't merit an explanation.

Whatever the reason, I felt dishearteningly alone in the city. I'd lost Prabaker and Abdullah, my closest friends, in the same week, and with them I'd lost the mark on the psychic map that says *You Are Here*. Personality and personal identity are in some ways like co-ordinates on the street map drawn by our intersecting relationships. We know who we are and we define what we are by references to the people we love and our reasons for loving them. I *was* that point in space and time where Abdullah's wild violence intersected with Prabaker's happy gentleness. Adrift, then, and somehow un-defined by their deaths, I realised with unease and surprise how much I'd also come to depend upon Khader and his council of bosses. My interactions with most of them had been cursory, it seemed to me, and yet I missed the reassurance of their presence in the city almost as much as I missed the company of my dead friends.

And I was angry. It took me a while to understand that anger, and to realise that Khaderbhai was its instigator and its target. I blamed him for Abdullah's death: for not protecting him and for not saving him. I couldn't bring myself to believe that Abdullah, the friend I'd loved, was the brutal madman Sapna. But I *was* ready to believe that Abdel Khader Khan had some connection to Sapna and to the killings. Moreover, I felt betrayed by his desertion of the city. It was as if he'd abandoned me to face ... everything ... alone. It was a ridiculous notion, of course, and quite self-aggrandising. The truth was that hundreds of Khader's men were still working in Bombay, and I dealt with many of them every day. But still I felt it—betrayed and forsaken. A coldness, formed from doubt and angry fear, began to spread inward toward the core of my feeling for the Khan. I still loved him, and I was still bonded to him as a son to his father, but he was no longer my revered and flawless hero.

A mujaheddin fighter once told me that fate gives all of us three teachers, three friends, three enemies, and three great loves in our lives. But these twelve are always disguised, and we can never know which one is which until we've loved them, left them, or fought them. Khader was one of my twelve, but his disguise was always the best. In those abandoned, angry days, as my grieving heart limped into numbing despair, I began to think of him as my enemy; my beloved enemy.

And deal by deal, crime by crime, day by day my will and purpose and hope staggered toward the pit. Lisa Carter pursued and won her contract with Chandra Mehta and Cliff De Souza. For her sake I sat in at the meeting that clinched the deal, and I signed on as her partner. The producers saw my involvement as important. I was their safe conduit to the black money of the Khader Khan mafia — an untapped and virtually inexhaustible resource. They didn't mention that connection, not then, but it was a key factor in their decision to sign on with Lisa. The contract specified that Lisa and I would supply foreign *junior artists*, as bit players were known, for three major studios. The terms of payment and commissions were set for two years.

After the meeting, Lisa walked me to my bike parked at the sea wall on Marine Drive. We sat together at the precise spot where Abdullah had put his hand on my shoulder, years before, when my mind was filled with the drowning sea. We were lonely, Lisa and I, and at first we talked to one another as lonely people do — in fragments of complaint, and corners clipped from conversations that we'd already had with ourselves, alone.

'He knew it would happen,' she said after a long, silent pause. 'That's why he gave me that money in the case. We talked about it. *He* talked about it. He talked about being killed. You know about the war in Iran? The war with Iraq? He almost got killed there a few times. It got into his head, I'm sure of it. I think he wanted to die, for running away from the war and leaving his friends and family behind. And when it came down to it, if it ever did come down to it, he wanted to go out like that.'

'Maybe,' I answered her, looking at the sublime, indifferent sea. 'Karla once said we all attempt suicide several times in our lives, and sooner or later we all succeed.'

Lisa laughed, because I'd surprised her with the quote, but the laugh ended in a long sigh. She tilted her head to let the wind play with her hair.

'The thing with Ulla,' she said quietly, 'It's been killing me, Lin. I can't get Modena out of my mind. I'm reading all the papers, every day, looking for something about him — about maybe they found him or something. It's weird … the thing with Maurizio, you know, I was sick with it for weeks after. I used to cry all the time, just walking on the street or reading a book or trying to sleep, and I couldn't eat a meal without feeling sick to my stomach. I couldn't stop thinking about his dead body ... and the knife ... what it must've felt like, when Ulla pushed the knife into him ... But now, all that's kind of faded. It's still there, you know, in the bottom of my gut, but it doesn't freak me out any more. And even Abdullah—I don't know if I'm in shock or denial or whatever, but I don't ... let myself think about him. It's like ... like I *accept* it, or something. But Modena—that keeps getting worse. I can't stop thinking about him.'

'I see him, too,' I muttered. 'I see his face, and I wasn't even there in that hotel room. It's not good.'

'I should've hit her.'

'Ulla?'

'*Yes*, Ulla!'

'Why?'

'That ... callous ... *bitch*! She left him there, tied up in that room. She brought you trouble, and me trouble and ... Maurizio ... But when she told us about Modena, I just put my arm around her, and took her to the shower, and looked after her like she'd just told me she hadn't fed her pet goldfish. I should've slapped her or socked her one on the jaw or kicked her ass or something. Now she's gone, and I'm still freaking out about Modena.'

'Some people do that,' I said, smiling at the anger in her because I felt it myself. 'Some people always manage to make us feel sorry for them, no matter how stupid and angry we feel about it after. They're the canaries, kind of, in the coalmines of our hearts. If we stop feeling sorry for them, when they let us down, we're in deep trouble. And anyway, I didn't get involved to help *her*. I did it to help you.'

'Oh, I know, I know,' she sighed. 'It's not Ulla's fault. Not really. The Palace messed her up. It messed with her head completely. Everyone who worked for Madame Zhou got messed up in some way. You should've seen Ulla, back then, when she started work there. She was gorgeous, I gotta tell ya. And kind of ... innocent ... in a way that the rest of us weren't, if you know what I mean. I *went* there *already* crazy when I first started work there. But it fucked me up, too. We all ... we had to ... we did some weird shit there ...'

'You told me about it,' I said gently.

'I told you?'

'Yeah.'

'I told you what?'

'You told me … a lot of it. The night I came around to get my clothes from Karla's. I went there with the kid, Tariq. You were very drunk, and very stoned.'

'And I told you about that?'

'Yeah.'

'*Jesus!* I don't remember that. I was starting to turkey. That was the first night, when I tried to get off the stuff—when I *did* get off the stuff. I remember the kid, though … and I remember you didn't want to have sex with me.'

'Oh, I *wanted* it, alright.'

She turned her head quickly and met my eye. Her expression smiled at the lips, but a tiny frown creased her forehead. She was wearing a red salwar kameez. The long, loose silk shirt clung to her breasts and the outline of her figure in the strong sea breeze. Her blue eyes glittered with courage and other mysteries. She was brave and fragile and tough in the same instant. She'd dragged herself from the life that was drowning her at Madame Zhou's Palace, and she'd beaten heroin. In defence of her friend's life, and her own, she'd helped to kill a man. She'd lost her lover, Abdullah, my friend, his body torn and mutilated by bullets. And it was all there, in her eyes and her thin face, thinner than it should've been. It was all there, if you knew what to look for, and if you knew where to look.

'So, how did you end up at the Palace?' I asked, and she flinched a little as I changed the subject.

'I don't know,' she sighed. 'I ran away from home when I was a kid. I couldn't stand it at home. I got outta there as soon as I could. In a couple years I was a teenage junkie, working the beat in L.A. and getting beat up by that month's pimp. Then a guy came along, a nice, quiet, lonely, gentle guy, named Matt. I fell for him, hard. He was my first real love. He was a musician, and he'd been to India a couple times. He was sure we could make enough money for a new start, if we smuggled some shit from Bombay back home. He said that he'd pay for the tickets, if I agreed to carry the stuff. When we got here, he just took off with everything—all our money, and my passport, and everything. I don't know what happened. I don't know if he got cold feet or found someone else to do the job or just decided to do it himself. I don't know. The end of it was ... that I got stuck in Bombay with a big, raging heroin habit, and no money, and no passport. I started working from a hotel room, turning tricks to keep going. After a couple months of that, a cop came into my room one day and told me I was busted. I was going to an Indian jail—unless I agreed to work for this friend of his.'

'Madame Zhou.'

'Yeah.'

'Tell me, did you ever *see* her? Did you ever talk to her in *person?*'

'Nah. Almost no-one ever talks to her or sees her, except for Rajan and his brother. Karla met her in person. Karla hates her. Karla hates her more than ... I've never seen anything like it in my life. Karla hates her so much that she's a bit crazy with it, if you know what I mean. She thinks about Madame Zhou almost all the time, and she'll get her, sooner or later.'

'The thing with her friend Ahmed, and Christine,' I murmured. 'She thinks Madame Zhou had them killed, and she blames herself for it. She can't let it go.'

'That's right!' she answered wonderingly, her face frowning and smiling in puzzlement. 'Did she tell you about that?'

'Yeah.'

'That's ...' she laughed, 'that's amazing! Karla never talks to anyone about that. I mean, *anyone*. But I guess it's *not* really so amazing. You really got under her skin. You know that time when the cholera was in the slum and all? She talked about that for weeks after. She talked about it like it was some kind of holy experience, some kind of transcendental high. And she talked about you a lot. I've never seen her so ... *inspired*, I guess.'

'When Karla got me to rescue you from the Palace,' I asked, not looking at her, 'was that for you, or was it just a way to score points against Madame Zhou?'

'You mean, were we just pawns in Karla's game, you and me? Is that what you're asking?'

'Something like that.'

'I think I'd have to say yes, we were.' She pulled her long scarf from her neck and drew it across an open palm, staring at it intently. 'Oh, you know, Karla *likes* me and all, I'm sure about that. She's told me things that nobody knows—not even you. And I like her. And she lived in the States, you know. She grew up there, and she felt something about that. I think I was the only American girl who ever worked at the Palace. But the heart of it, deep down, was this war with Madame Zhou. I think we got used up, you and me. But it doesn't matter, you know? She got me out of there —*you* got me out of there, with her, and I'm damn glad. Whatever her reasons were, I don't hold it against her, and I don't think you should either.'

'I don't,' I sighed.

'But?'

'But ... nothing. We didn't work out, Karla and me, but I ...'

'You still love her?'

I turned my head to look at her, but when her blue eyes met mine I changed the subject.

'Have you heard anything from Madame Zhou?'

'Not a thing.'

'Has she been asking questions about you? Anything at all?'

'Nothing, thank God. It's weird—I don't hate Madame Zhou. I don't feel anything for her, one way or the other, except that I never want to go anywhere near her again. But I *do* hate her servant, Rajan. If you worked at the Palace, he's the one you had to deal with and answer to. His brother takes care of the kitchen, but Rajan looks after the girls. And that's one spooky motherfucker, that Rajan. He gets around like a ghost. It's like he's got eyes in the back of his head. He's the scariest thing in the whole world, let me tell ya. Madame Zhou, I never even saw. She talks to you through a metal grille. There's at least one in every room, so she can watch what's going on, and talk to the girls or the customers. It's a fuckin' creepy place, Lin. I'd rather die than go back to that.'

There was another silence. Waves pushed at the shoreline of rocks and pebbles at the base of the wall. Seagulls hovered, prowling the wind for signs of things that slithered and scuttled among the rocks.

'How much money did he leave you?'

'I'm not sure,' she said. 'I never counted it. It's a lot. Seventy, eighty grand—a lot more, you know, than Maurizio carved up Modena for, and got himself killed for. It's crazy, isn't it?'

'You should take it, and get the fuck out of here.'

'That's funny—I thought we just signed a two-year contract with

Mehta and his production company. You know, the *let's-get-on-with our-lives* contract.'

'Fuck the contract.'

'Come on, Lin.'

'Fuck the contract. You've gotta get out of this. We don't know what the fuck's going on. We don't know why Abdullah's dead. We don't know what he did do, or what he didn't do. If he *wasn't* Sapna, then things are bad. If he *was* Sapna, things are much worse. You should take the money and just ... go.'

'And go where?'

'Anywhere.'

'Are you going?'

'No. I've got unfinished business here. And I'm ... I'm finished myself, in a way. But you should go.'

'You don't get it, do you?' she demanded. 'It's not about the money. If I go back now, I'll put the lot of it in my arm. I've gotta have something more than money. I'm trying to *build* something here with this business. And I can do it here. I'm *something* here. I'm somebody. The people look at me, when I just walk down the street, because I'm different.'

'You'd be *something*, wherever you are,' I said, grinning at her.

'Don't make fun of me, Lin.'

'I'm not, Lisa. You're a beautiful girl, and you've got heart—that's why people stare at you.'

'This can work,' she insisted. 'I can feel it in my bones. I don't have any education, Lin, and I'm not smart like you. I'm not trained to do anything. But this ... this could be big. I could, I don't know ... I could start producing movies, maybe, one day. I could ... do something good.'

'You *are* good. You'll do good wherever you go.'

'No. This is my chance. I'm not going back—I'm not going *anywhere* —until I've made it. If I don't do that, if I don't *try*, then the whole thing will be for nothing. Maurizio ... and everything else that's happened will be for nothing. If I leave here, I want to do it with my head on straight, and a pocket full of money that I earned myself.'

I looked into the wind, feeling the day alternately warm and cool and warm again on my face and arms as the breeze turned and returned across the bay. A small fleet of fishing canoes drifted past us on their way back to the fishermen's sandy refuge near the slum. I suddenly remembered the day in the rain, sailing in a canoe across the flooded forecourt of the Taj Mahal Hotel and beneath the booming, resonant dome of the Gateway Monument. I remembered Vinod's love song, and the rain that night as Karla came into my arms.

And staring, then, at the ceaseless, eternal waves, I remembered all that had been lost since that storming night: prison, torture, Karla gone, Ulla gone, Khaderbhai and his council gone, Anand gone, Maurizio dead, Modena probably dead, Rasheed dead, Abdullah dead, and Prabaker—it was impossible—*Prabaker*, also *dead*. And I was one of them: walking and talking and staring at the wilding waves, but as dead in my heart as all the rest.

'And what about you?' she asked. I could feel her eyes on me, and I could hear the emotions in her voice: sympathy, tenderness, maybe even love. 'If I stay—and I'm *definitely* going to stay—what are *you* going to do?'

I looked at her for a while, reading the runes in her sky-blue eyes. Then I stood from the wall, held her in my arms, and kissed her. It was a long kiss. We lived out a life together in that kiss: we lived and loved and grew old together, and we died. Then our lips parted, and that life we might've had retreated, shrinking to a spark of light we would always recognise in one another's eyes.

I could've loved her. Maybe I already did love her a little. But sometimes the worst thing you can do to a woman is to love her. And I still loved Karla. I loved Karla.

'What am *I* going to do?' I said, repeating her question. I held her shoulders in my hands, keeping her at the distance of my arms. I smiled. '*I* am going to get *stoned*.'

I rode away, and never looked back. I paid three months' rent on my apartment, and paid substantial baksheesh to the watchman in the car park and the watchman in the building. I kept one good, forged passport in my pocket, put all my spare passports and a bundle of cash into a satchel, and left it with my Enfield Bullet bike in Didier's care. Then I took a cab to Gupta-ji's opium den near the Street of Ten Thousand Whores, Shoklaji Street. I climbed the worn wooden steps to the third floor and walked into the cage that junkies build for themselves, one shiny, sharp, steel bar at a time.

Gupta-ji provided a large room with twenty sleeping mats and wooden pillows for his opium smokers. For those with special needs he reserved other rooms behind that open den. Through a very small doorway, I entered the discreet corridor that led to those back rooms. It was so low that I had to stoop, almost to crawling. The room I chose had a cot with a kapok mattress, a weathered carpet, a small cabinet with wickerwork doors, a lamp with a silk lampshade, and a large clay matka filled with water. The walls on three sides were made from reed matting stretched upon wooden frames. The last wall, at the head of the bed, looked out over a busy street of Arab and local Muslim traders, but its windows were shuttered so that only a few bright stars of sunlight gleamed in the chinks and gaps. There was no ceiling. Instead, the view overhead was of heavy rafters crossing and joining one another in support of the clay tile roof. I got to know that view very well.

Gupta-ji took money and instructions, and left me alone. The room, so close to the roof, was very hot. I took my shirt off, and switched off the lamp. The dark little room was like a cell; a prison cell at night. I sat on the bed and, almost at once, the tears came. I'd cried before, in Bombay. I'd shed tears after I met Ranjit's lepers, and when the stranger had washed my tortured body in Arthur Road Prison, and with Prabaker's father at the hospital. But that sorrow and suffering had always been stifled: somehow, I'd managed to choke back the worst of it, the flood of it. Then, alone in that little opium cell with my ruined love for those dead friends, Abdullah and Prabaker, I let it go.

The tears, when they come to some men, are worse than beatings. They're wounded worse by sobbing, men like that, than they are by boots and batons. Tears begin in the heart, but some of us deny the heart so often, and for so long, that when it speaks we hear not one but a hundred sorrows in the heartbreak. We know that crying is a good and natural thing. We know that crying isn't a weakness, but a kind of strength. Still, the weeping rips us root by tangled root from the earth, and we crash like fallen trees when we cry.

Gupta-ji gave me time. When at last I heard the sliding, scuffing sound of his chappals as he approached the door I smeared the sorrow from my face, and switched on the lamp. He'd brought what I'd asked for—a steel spoon, distilled water, disposable syringes, heroin, and a carton of cigarettes—and he set the items out on the little dresser. There was a girl with him. He told me that her name was Shilpa, and that he'd assigned her to me as a servant. She was young, years less than twenty, but already scarred with the glum expression of the working professional. Hope, ready to snarl or grovel like a beaten cur, cowered in her eyes. I sent her and Gupta-ji away, and cooked up a taste of heroin.

The dose sat in the syringe for almost an hour. I picked it up and put the needle against a fat, strong, healthy vein in my arm five times, only to put it down again unused. And for the whole of that sweating hour I stared at the liquid in the syringe. That was it. The damnation drug. That was the big one, the drug that had driven me to commit stupid, violent crimes; that had put me in prison; that had cost me my family, and lost my loved ones. The everything-and-nothing drug: it takes everything, and gives you nothing in return. But the *nothing* that it gives you, the unfeeling emptiness it gives you, is sometimes all and everything you want.

I pushed the needle into the vein, pulled back the rose of blood that confirmed the clean puncture of the vein, and pressed the plunger all the way to the stop. Before I could pull the needle from my arm, the drug made my mind Sahara. Warm, dry, shining, and featureless, the dunes of the drug smothered all thought, and buried the forgotten civilisation of my mind. The warmth filled my body as well, killing off the thousand little aches, twinges, and discomforts that we endure and ignore in every sober day. There was no pain. There was nothing.

And then, with the desert still in my mind, I felt my body drowning, and I broke the surface of a suffocating lake. Was it a week after that first taste? Was it a month? I crawled onto the raft and floated there on the lethal lake in the spoon, carrying the Sahara in my blood. And those rafters overhead: there was a kind of message in them, a message about how and why we all intersected, Khader and Karla and Abdullah and I. Our lives, all of us, in the link to Abdullah's death, intersected in some uniquely profound way. It was there, in the rafters, a key to the code.

But I closed my eyes. I remembered Prabaker. I remembered that he was working so hard and so late on the night he died because he owned the taxi, and was working for himself. I'd bought the taxi for him. *He'd be alive if I hadn't bought that taxi for him.* He was the little mouse that I'd trained and fed with crumbs in my prison cell; the mouse that was crucified. And sometimes the breeze of a clear, unstoned hour gave me an image of Abdullah in the minute before he died, alone in the killing circle. Alone. I should've been there. I was with him every day. I should've been with him then. Friends don't let friends die like that—alone with death and fate. And where was his body? And what if he was Sapna? Could my friend, my friend I loved, really have been that ruthless, insane mutilator? What did Ghani say? *Pieces of Madjid's slaughtered body were found all over his house* ... Could I have loved the man who did that? What did it mean, that some small, insistent part of me feared that he *was* Sapna, and loved him anyway?

And I fired the silver bullet into my arm again, and fell back on the floating raft. And I saw the answer in the rafters overhead. And I was sure I would understand it with a little more dope, and a little more, and a little more.

I woke to see a face glaring at me and speaking fiercely in a language I couldn't understand. It was an ugly face, a scowling face, defined by deep lines that descended in curved chines from his eyes and nose and mouth. Then the face had hands, strong hands, and I found myself lifted from the raft of my bed and propped unsteadily on my feet.

'You *come!*' Nazeer growled in English. 'You come, *now!*'

'Fuck ...' I said slowly, pausing for maximum effect, '... off.'

'You *come!*' he repeated. The anger in him was so close to the surface that he trembled with it, and opened his mouth unconsciously to bare his teeth in an underbite.

'No,' I said, turning to the bed once more. 'You ... *go!*'

He pulled me around to face him again. There was enormous power in his arms. He clamped the metal grapples of his hands on my arms.

'*Now!* You *come!*'

I'd been three months in the room at Gupta-ji's. They were three months of heroin every day, and food every other day, and the only exercise a short walk to the toilet and back. I didn't know it then, but I'd lost twelve kilos—the best thirty pounds of muscle on my body. I was thin and weak and still stupid on drugs.

'Okay,' I said, feigning a smile. 'Okay, let me go, will ya. I have to get my stuff.'

He relaxed his grip as I nodded toward the little table where my wallet, watch, and passport rested. Gupta-ji and Shilpa waited in the corridor beyond. I gathered up the possessions and put them into my pockets, pretending to co-operate with Nazeer. When I judged the moment to be right, I swung round at him with an overhand right. It should've hit him. It would've hit him when I was healthy and sober. I missed him completely, and threw myself off balance. Nazeer drove a fist into my solar plexus, just under the heart. I doubled over, winded and helpless, but my knees locked stiffly and my legs wouldn't fold. He raised my head, with his left hand locked into a patch of my hair, pulled his right fist back at shoulder height, hesitated in the precision of his aim, and then rammed his fist into my jaw. The full force of his neck, shoulders, and back were in the blow. I saw Gupta-ji's lips pout and his eyes squint in a wince, and then his face exploded in a shower of sparks that left the world darker than a cave full of sleeping bats.

It was the only time in my life I was ever knocked out cold. It seemed that I was falling forever, and the ground was impossibly far away. After a time I was dimly aware of movement, floating through space, and I thought, *It's okay, this is all a dream, a drug dream, and I'm going to wake up any minute now, and take more drugs.*

Then I came down with a rumpled crash on the raft once more. But the raft-bed that I'd floated on for three long months had changed. It was different, somehow—soft and smooth. And there was a new and wonderful smell, a gorgeous perfume. It was *Coco.* I knew it well. It was Karla. It was the perfume on Karla's skin. Nazeer had carried me over his shoulder all the way down the flights of stairs and out into the street, where he'd dumped me into the back seat of a taxi. Karla was there. My head rested in her lap. And I opened my eyes to look into her lovely face. And her green eyes looked back at me with compassion and concern and something else. I closed my eyes, and in the moving darkness I knew what it was, that something else in her eyes. It was disgust. She was disgusted by my weakness, my heroin habit, my stink of neglect and self-indulgence. Then I felt her hands on my face, and it was like crying, and her fingers moving the caress across my cheek were the tears.

When the taxi finally stopped, Nazeer carried me up two flights of steps as easily as he might've lugged a sack of flour. I came to consciousness again draped over his shoulder, looking down at Karla as she climbed the steps behind us. I tried to smile at her. We entered a big house through a back door that led to a kitchen. Beyond the large, modern kitchen, we came into an enormous, open-plan living room, with one wall of glass that looked out upon a golden beach and the dark sapphire sea. Flipping me over his shoulder, Nazeer lowered me with more gentleness than I'd expected to a pile of cushions near the glass feature wall. The last hit I'd injected, just before he'd kidnapped me from Gupta-ji's, was a big dose. Too big. I was groggy and lapsing. The urge to close my eyes and surrender to the stone swept over me in almost irresistible, immersible waves.

'Don't try to get up,' Karla said, kneeling beside me and washing my face with a wet towel.

I laughed, because standing was the last thing on my mind. In the laugh I felt the soreness, dimly, through the stone, on the point of my chin and the hinge of my jaw.

'What's going on, Karla?' I asked, hearing my voice crack and warble as I spoke. Three months of utter silence and soul-fog had distorted my speech with dysphasic lapses and creaking fumbles. 'What are you doing here? What am *I* doing here?'

'Did you think I would leave you there?'

'How did you know? How did you find me?'

'Your friend Khaderbhai found you. He asked me to bring you here.'

'He asked *you*?'

'Yes,' she said, staring into my eyes with such intensity that it cut through the stone like sunrise piercing the morning's hazy mist.

'Where is he?'

She smiled, and the smile was sad because it was the wrong question. I know that now. I'm not stoned now. That was my chance to know the whole of the truth, or as much of the truth as she knew. If I'd asked her the right question, she would've told me the truth. That was the power behind her intense stare. She was ready to tell me everything. She might've even loved me, or begun to love me. But I hadn't asked the right question. I hadn't asked about her. I'd asked about him.

'I don't know,' she answered, raising herself with her hands to stand beside me. 'He was supposed to be here. I think he'll be here soon. I can't wait, though. I have to go.'

'*What?*' I sat up, and tried to push the stone curtains aside in order to see her, to speak to her, to keep her with me.

'I have to go,' she repeated, walking briskly to the door. Nazeer waited for her there, his thick arms jutting out from the swollen trunk of his body. 'I can't help it. I've got a lot of things to do before I leave.'

'Leave? What do you mean, *leave*?'

'I'm leaving Bombay again. I've got some work. It's important, and I …

well, I have to do it. I'll be back in about six or eight weeks. I'll see you then, maybe.'

'But this is crazy. I don't get it. You should've left me *there*, if you're only going to leave me now.'

'Look,' she said, smiling patiently, 'I just got back yesterday, and I'm trying not to stay. I'm not even going back to Leopold's. I saw Didier this morning—he says hello, by the way—but that's it. I'm not sticking around. I agreed to help get you out of that little suicide pact you had going with yourself at Gupta-ji's. Now you're here, you're safe, and I have to go.'

She turned and spoke to Nazeer. They were speaking Urdu, and I understood only every third or fourth word of their conversation. He laughed, listening to her, and turned to look at me with his customary contempt.

'What did he say?' I asked her when they fell silent.

'You don't want to know.'

'Yes I do.'

'He doesn't think you'll make it,' she replied. 'I told him that you'll do cold turkey here, and be waiting for me when I come back in a couple of months. He doesn't think so. He says you'll run out of here to get a fix the first minute the turkey begins. I made a bet with him that you'd make it.'

'How much did you bet?'

'A thousand bucks.'

'A thousand bucks,' I mused. It was an impressive stake, against the odds.

'Yes. It's all the cash he has—a kind of nest egg. He's betting it all that you'll break down. He says you're a weak man. That's why you take drugs.'

'What do you say?'

She laughed, and it was so rare to see and hear her laugh that I took those bright, round syllables of happiness into me like food, like drink, like the drug. Despite the stone and the sickness, I knew with perfect understanding that the greatest treasure and pleasure I would ever know was in that laugh; to make that woman laugh, and feel the laughter bubbling from her lips against my face, my skin.

'I told him,' she said, 'that a good man is as strong as the right woman needs him to be.'

Then she was gone, and I closed my eyes, and an hour or a day later I opened them to find Khaderbhai sitting beside me.

'*Utna hain*,' I heard Nazeer's voice say. *He's awake.*

I woke unwell. I woke alert and cold and needing heroin. My mouth was filthy and my body ached everywhere at once.

'Hmmm,' Khader murmured. 'You have the pain already.'

I pulled myself up on the pillows and looked around the room. It was the beginning of evening, and night's long shadow was creeping across the sandy beach beyond the window. Nazeer sat on a piece of carpet near the entrance to the kitchen. Khader was dressed in the loose pantaloons, shirt, and tunic-vest of the Pathans. The clothes were green, the favourite colour of the Prophet. He looked older, somehow, after just those few months. He also looked fitter, and more calm and determined than I'd ever seen him.

'Do you need food?' he asked when I stared at him without speaking. 'Do you want to take your bath? There is everything here. You can bath as often as you like. You can eat food—there is plenty. You can put on new clothes. I have them for you.'

'What happened to Abdullah?' I demanded.

'You must get well.'

'What the *fuck* happened to Abdullah?' I shouted, my voice breaking.

Nazeer watched me. He was outwardly calm, but I knew that he was ready to spring.

'What do you want to know?' Khader asked gently, avoiding my eyes, and nodding his head slowly as he stared at the carpet between his crossed knees.

'Was he Sapna?'

'No,' he replied, turning to meet my hard stare. 'I know the people say this, but I give you my word that he was not Sapna.'

I exhaled a full breath in an exhausted sigh of relief. I felt tears stinging my eyes, and I bit the inside of my cheek to kill them.

'Why did they *say* he was Sapna?'

'Abdullah's enemies made the police believe that he was.'

'What enemies? Who are they?'

'Men from Iran. Enemies from his country.'

I remembered the fight; the mysterious fight. Abdullah and I—we'd fought with a group of Iranian men on the street. I tried to remember other details from that day, but I couldn't think past the sharp, guilty twist of regret that I'd never asked Abdullah who the men were or why we'd fought them.

'Where's the *real* Sapna?'

'He is dead. I found the man—the real Sapna. Now he is dead. That much is done, for Abdullah.'

I relaxed against the cushions, and closed my eyes for a moment. My nose was beginning to run, and my throat was clogged and sore. I'd built up a big habit in those three months—three grams of pure Thai-white heroin every day. The turkey was coming on fast, and I knew that it would be two weeks in Hell's punishment unit.

'Why?' I asked him, after a time.

'What do you mean?'

'Why did you find me? Why did you have him—Nazeer—bring me here?'

'You work for me,' he answered, smiling. 'And now, I have a job of work for you to do.'

'Well, I'm afraid I'm not up to it, just at the minute.'

The cramps were creeping into my stomach. I groaned, and looked away.

'Oh, yes,' he agreed. 'You must be well first. But then, in three or four months, you will be the right man to do this job for me.'

'What ... what kind of a job?'

'It is a mission. A kind of holy mission, you might call it. Do you know how to ride a horse?'

'A *horse*? I don't know anything about horses. If I can do the job on a motorcycle—when I get well, *if* I get well—I'm your man.'

'Nazeer will teach you to ride. He is, or he was, the best horseman in a village of men who are the best horsemen in Nangarhar province. There are horses stabled near here, and you can learn to ride on the beach.'

'Learn to ride ...' I muttered, wondering how I was going to survive the next hour, and the hour after that, and the worse that would come.

'Oh, yes, Linbaba,' he said, reaching out with the smile and touching my shoulder with his palm. I flinched at the touch, and shivered, but the warmth of his hand seemed to enter me, and I was still. 'You cannot reach Kandahar in any other way but by horse, at this time, because the roads are all mined and bombed. So you see, when you go with my men to the war in Afghanistan, you must know how to ride a horse.'

'Afghanistan?'

'Yes.'

'What ... what the hell makes you think I'm going to Afghanistan?'

'I don't know if you will do it or not,' he replied with what seemed to be genuine sadness. 'I am going on this mission myself. To Afghanistan— my home, that I have not seen for more than fifty years. And I am inviting you—I am *asking* you—to go with me. The choice, of course, is yours to make. It is a dangerous job. That much is certain. I will not think less about you, if you decide not to go with me.'

'Why me?'

'I need a gora, a foreigner, who is not afraid to break a large number of international laws, and who can pass for an American. Where we will go there are many rival clans, and they have fought with one another for hundreds of years. They have long traditions of raiding one another and taking whatever they can as plunder on their raids. Only two things unite them, just at this time—love for Allah, and hatred for the Russian invaders. At the moment, their chief allies against the Russians are the Americans. They are fighting with American money and American weapons. If I have an American with me, they will leave us alone, and let us pass, without molesting us or stealing more than a reasonable amount from us.'

'Why don't you get an American—a real one, I mean?'

'I tried. I could not find one crazy enough to take the risk. That is why I need you.'

'What are we smuggling on this mission to Afghanistan?'

'The usual things that one smuggles into a war—guns, explosives, passports, money, gold, machine parts, and medicines. It will be an interesting journey. If we pass through the heavily armed clans who would like to take what we have, we will deliver our goods to a unit of mujaheddin fighters who are putting siege to Kandahar city. They have been fighting the Russians in the same place for two years, and they need the supplies.'

Questions writhed in my shivering mind, hundreds of them, but the cold turkey was crippling me. Cold, greasy sweat from the struggle smothered my skin. The words, when they came at last, were rushed and faltering.

'Why are *you* doing this? Why *Kandahar*? Why there?'

'The mujaheddin—the men at the siege of Kandahar—they are my people, from my village. They are from Nazeer's village also. They are fighting a jihad, a holy war, to drive the Russian invaders out of the homeland. We have helped them in many ways, up to this time. Now it is time to help them with guns, and with my blood, if it is necessary.'

He looked at the sickness trembling across my face, and cutting facets from my eyes. He smiled again, pressing his fingers into my shoulder until that pain, that touch, his touch, was all I felt for a moment.

'First you must be well,' he said, releasing the pressure of his fingers and touching his palm to my face. 'Allah be with you, my son. *Allah ya fazak!*'

When he left me, I went to the bathroom. Stomach cramp stabbed me with eagle's claws, and then twisted my insides with talons of agony. Diarrhoea shook me with convulsive spasms. I washed myself, shivering so violently that my teeth clattered together. I looked in the mirror and saw my eyes, the pupils so large that the whole iris was black. When the light comes back, when the heroin stops and the turkey starts and the light returns, it rushes in through the black funnels of the eyes.

Wearing a towel around my waist, I walked back to the big main room. I looked thin. I was stooped, and shivering, and moaning involuntarily. Nazeer looked me up and down, with a sneer curling his thick upper lip. He handed me a pile of clean clothes. They were exact copies of Khader's green Afghan costume. I dressed, shaking and trembling and losing my balance a few times. Nazeer watched me, his knotty fists balled at his hips. The sneer rippled his lip like the opening ridges of a clamshell. His every gesture was so loud and broad that it had the exaggeration of pantomime, but his dark eyes were fierce with menace. I suddenly realised that he reminded me of the Japanese actor Toshiro Mifune. He was an ugly, troll-like caricature of Mifune.

'Do you know Toshiro Mifune?' I asked him through a desperate, pain-smeared laugh. 'You know Mifune? Huh?'

His answer was to walk to the front door of the house and throw it open. He pulled some fifty-rupee notes from his pocket, and hurled them onto the floor.

'*Jaa, bahinchudh!*' he snarled, pointing out the open door. *Go, sister-fucker!*

I staggered to the pile of cushions heaped against the great window and collapsed there. I pulled a blanket over myself, cringing in the flaying wrench and cramp of the craving. Nazeer closed the door of the house and took up his position on the patch of carpet, sitting cross-legged and straight-backed as he watched me.

We all cope with anxiety and stress, to one degree or another, with the help of a cocktail of chemicals produced in the body and released in the brain. Chief among them is the endorphin group. The endorphins are peptide neurotransmitters that have pain-relieving properties. Anxiety and stress and pain bring on the endorphin response as a natural coping mechanism. When we take any of the opiates—morphine or opium or heroin, in particular—the body stops producing endorphins. When we stop taking opiates, there's a lag of between five and fourteen days before the body begins a new endorphin production cycle. In the meanwhile, in that black, tortured crawlspace of one to two weeks without heroin and without endorphins, we learn what anxiety and stress and pain really are.

What's it like, Karla asked me once, *cold turkey off heroin?* I tried to explain it. Think about every time in your life that you've ever been afraid, really afraid. Someone sneaks up behind you when you think you're alone, and shouts to frighten you. The gang of thugs closes in around you. You fall from a great height in a dream, or you stand on the very edge of a steep cliff. Someone holds you under water and you feel the breath gone, and you scramble, fight, and claw your way to the surface. You lose control of the car and see the wall rushing into your soundless shout. Then add them all up, all those chest-tightening terrors, and feel them all at once, all at the same time, hour after hour, and day after day. And think of every pain you've ever known—the burn with hot oil, the sharp sliver of glass, the broken bone, the gravel rash when you fell on the rough road in winter, the headache and the earache and the toothache. Then add them all up, all those groin-squeezing, stomach-tensing shrieks of pain, and feel them all at once, hour after hour, and day after day. Then think of every anguish you've ever known. Remember the death of a loved one. Remember a lover's rejection. Recall your feelings of failure and shame and unspeakably bitter remorse. And add them all up, all the heart-stabbing griefs and miseries, and feel them all at once, hour after hour, and day after day. That's cold turkey. Cold turkey off heroin is life with the skin torn away.

The assault of anxiety on the unprotected mind, the brain without natural endorphins, makes men and women mad. Every junkie going through turkey is mad. The madness is so fierce and cruel that some die of it. And in the temporary insanity of that skinned, excruciated world, we commit crimes. And if we survive, years later, and become well, our healthy recollection of those crimes leaves us wretched, bewildered, and as self-disgusted as men and women who betray their comrades and country under torture.

Two full days and nights into the torment, I knew I wasn't going to make it. Most of the vomiting and the diarrhoea had passed, but the pain and anxieties were worse, much worse, every minute. Beneath the screaming in my blood there was a calm, insistent voice: *You can stop this ... you can fix this ... you can stop this ... take the money ... get a fix ... you can stop this pain ...*

Nazeer's bamboo and coconut-fibre cot was in the far corner of the room. I lurched toward it, watched closely by the burly Afghan, who was still sitting on his mat near the door. Trembling and moaning with pain, I dragged the cot closer to the great window that looked out on the sea. I took up a cotton sheet and began to tear at it with my teeth. It gave way in a few places, and I ripped it along the length, tearing off strips of cloth. Frantic in my movements and close to panic, I hurled two thick, embroidered quilts onto the rope bed for a mattress, and lay down on it. Using two of the strips, I tied my ankles to the bed. With a third strip, I secured my left wrist. Then I lay down, and turned my head to look at Nazeer. I held out the remaining strip, and asked him with my eyes to bind my arm to the bed. It was the first time that we'd ever met one another's eyes in an equally honest stare.

He rose from his square of carpet and walked toward me, holding the stare. He took the strip of cloth from my hand and bound my right wrist to the frame of the bed. A shout of trapped, panic-fear escaped from my open mouth, and another. I bit down on my tongue, biting through the flesh at the sides until blood ran past my lips. Nazeer nodded slowly. He tore another thick strip from the sheet and twirled it into a corkscrew tube. Sliding it between my teeth, he tied the gag behind my head. And I bit down on the devil's tail. And I screamed. And I turned my head to see my own reflection tied to the night in the window. And for a while I was Modena, waiting and watching and screaming with my eyes.

Two days and nights I was tied to the bed. Nazeer nursed me with tenderness and constancy. He was always there. Every time I opened my eyes, I felt his rough hand on my brow, wiping the sweat and the tears into my hair. Every time the lightning strike of cramp twisted a leg or arm or my stomach, he was there, massaging warmth into the knot of pain. Every time I whimpered or screamed into the gag, he held my eyes with his, willing me to endure and succeed. He removed the gag when I choked on a trickle of vomit or my blocked nose let no air pass, but he was a strong man and he knew that I didn't want my screams to be heard. When I nodded my head, he replaced the gag and tied it fast.

And then, when I knew that I was either strong enough to stay or too weak to leave, I nodded to Nazeer, blinking my eyes, and he removed the gag for the last time. One by one he untied the bonds at my wrists and ankles. He brought me a broth made from chicken and barley and tomatoes, unspiced, except for salt. It was the richest and most delicious thing I ever tasted in my life. He fed it to me, spoon by spoon. After an hour, when I finished the little bowl, he smiled at me for the first time, and that smile was like sunlight on sea rocks after summer rain.

Cold turkey goes on for about two weeks, but the first five days are the worst. If you can get through the first five days, if you can crawl and drag yourself into that sixth morning without drugs, you know you're clean, and you know you'll make it. Every hour, for the next eight to ten days, you feel a little better and a little stronger. The cramps fade, the nausea passes, the fever and chills subside. After a while, the worst of it is simply that you can't sleep. You lie on the bed at night, twisting and writhing in discomfort, and sleep never comes. In those last days and very long nights of the turkey, I became a Standing Baba: I never sat or lay down, all day and all night, until exhaustion collapsed my legs at last and I sank into sleep.

And it passes, the turkey passes, and you emerge from the cobra bite of heroin addiction like any survivor from any disaster: dazed, wounded forever, and glad to be alive.

Nazeer took my first sarcastic jokes, twelve days after the turkey began, as the cue for my training to commence. From the sixth day I'd been walking with him as light exercise, and for the fresh air. The first of those walks had been slow and halting, and I'd returned to the house after fifteen minutes. By the twelfth day I was walking the length of the beach with him, hoping to tire myself so much that I could sleep. Finally, he took me to the stable where Khader's horses were kept. The stable was a converted boathouse, one street away from the beach. The horses were trained for beginning riders, and carried tourists up and down the beach in the high season. The white gelding and grey mare were large, docile animals. We took them from Khader's stable-master and led them down to the flat, hard-packed sand of the beach.

There's no animal in the world with a deeper sense of parody than a horse. A cat can make you look clumsy, and a dog can make you look stupid, but only a horse can make you look both at the same time. And then, with nothing more than the flick of a tail or a casual stomp on your foot, it lets you know that it did it on purpose. Some people know from the first contact with the animal that they'll ride well, and bond with the beast. I'm not one of those people. A friend of mine has a strange, antimagnetic effect on machines: watches stop on her wrist, radio receivers crackle, and photocopy machines glitch whenever she's near. My relationship with horses is something like that.

The thickset Afghan cupped his hands to boost me onto the gelding's back, nodding his head for me to climb up, and winking encouragingly. I put my foot into his hands and sprang up onto the white horse, but in the instant that I sat on its back the previously meek, well-trained creature hurled me off with a prodigious, arching kick. I soared over Nazeer's shoulder and landed with a thump on the sand. The gelding galloped away down the beach without me. Nazeer stared after it, gape-mouthed. The animal was only calmed and returned to my presence when he fetched a blinding bag, and placed it over its head.

That was the beginning of Nazeer's slow, reluctant acceptance of the fact that I would never be anything other than the worst horseman he knew. The disappointment should've plunged me deeper into the well of his contempt, but in fact it provoked an opposite reaction. In the weeks that followed he became solicitous and even tender-hearted toward me. For Nazeer, that stumbling ineptitude with horses was a terrible affliction, as pitiable in a man as a painfully debilitating illness. And even at my best, when I managed to remain on the horse for minutes at a time, and work the beast in a circle by flapping my legs at its sides and yanking with both hands at the bridle, my gracelessness moved him close to tears.

Nevertheless, I persevered with the lessons, and I exercised every day. I worked my way up to twenty sets of thirty push-ups, with a minute rest between each set. I followed the push-ups every day with five hundred sit-ups, a five-kilometre run, and a forty-minute swim in the sea. After almost three months of the routine, I was fit and strong.

Nazeer wanted me to gain some experience at riding over rough terrain, so I arranged with Chandra Mehta for us to visit the riding range at the Film City movie studio ranch. Many of the feature films had horse-and-rider sequences. The teams of horses were cared for by squads of men who lived on the vast tracts of hilly land, and were on call for stunt and action scenes. The animals were superbly well trained but, barely two minutes after Nazeer and I had mounted the brown mares assigned to us, my horse threw me into a stack of clay pots. Nazeer took up the reins of my horse and sat in his saddle, shaking his head pityingly.

'Hey, great stunt, *yaar!*' one of the stunt men called out. There were five of them riding with us, and they all laughed. Two men jumped down to help me up.

Two falls later, as I climbed wearily into the saddle, I heard a familiar voice. I looked around to see a group of riders. At their head was a cowboy looking like Emiliano Zapata, with a black hat hanging on his back from a leather thong.

'I fuckin' *knew* it was you!' Vikram shouted. He drew his horse up close to mine and shook my hand warmly. His companions joined Nazeer and our stunt riders, and they trotted away, leaving us alone.

'What are *you* doing here?'

'I *own* the fuckin' place, man!' He spread his arms wide. 'Well, not exactly. Lettie bought a share, as a partner, with Lisa.'

'*My* Lisa?'

He raised one eyebrow quizzically.

'*Your* Lisa?'

'You know what I mean.'

'Sure,' he said, grinning widely. 'Her and Lettie, you know, they're running that casting agency together—the one you guys started up. And they're doin' all right, man. They're good together. I decided to get in on it as well. Your friend, Chandra Mehta, told me there was a share going in the stunt stable. Hey, it's a *natural* for me, wouldn't you say?'

'Oh, no doubt about that, Vikram.'

'So, I put some damn money in it, and now I come out here every week. I'm an extra in a fuckin' movie tomorrow! Come and watch me get shot, brother!'

'It's a tempting offer,' I said, laughing with him. 'But I'm leaving town for a while tomorrow.'

'You're leaving? For how long?'

'I don't know, exactly. A month, maybe longer.'

'Then you'll be back?'

'Sure. Keep a video of the stunt. When I get back, we'll get stoned, and watch you get killed in slow motion.'

'Ha! You got a deal! Come on! Let's ride together, man!'

'No, no!' I shouted. 'I'll never get this horse to ride with you, Vikram. I'm the worst rider you ever saw. I've already fallen off this one three times. If I can get it to *walk* in a straight line I'll be happy.'

'Come on, brother Lin! I tell you what, I'll lend you my hat. It never fails, man. It's a lucky hat. You're having trouble because you got no hat.'

'I ... I don't think the hat's gonna cover it, man.'

'It's a fuckin' magic hat, man, I'm telling you!'

'You haven't seen me ride.'

'And you haven't worn the hat. The hat can fix anything. Plus, you're a gora. No offence to your whiteness, *yaar*, but these are *Indian* horses, man. They just need to get a little Indian *style* from you, that's all. You speak in Hindi to them, and dance a little, then you'll see.'

'I don't think so.'

'*Sure*, man. Come on, get down and dance with me.'

'What?'

'Come on and dance with me.'

'I'm not dancing for the horses, Vikram,' I declared, with as much dignity and sincerity as I could pack into the bizarre string of words.

'Sure you will! You get down with me now, and dance a little Indian magic. The horses have to *see* that cool, Indian motherfucker you got inside your tight, white exterior, man. I swear, the horses will love you, and you'll ride like Clint fuckin' Eastwood!'

'I don't want to ride like Clint fuckin' Eastwood.'

'Yes, you do!' he laughed. 'Everybody does.'

'No, I'm not doing it.'

'Come *on*.'

'No way.'

He climbed down, and began to prise my boots from the stirrups. Exasperated, I climbed down and stood next to him, facing the two horses.

'Like *this*!' Vikram said, shaking his hips and stepping out in a movie dance routine. He began to sing, clapping his hands in time. 'Come on, *yaar*! Put some *India* into it, man. Don't go all fuckin' European on me.'

There are three things that no Indian man can resist: a beautiful face, a beautiful song, and an invitation to dance. I was Indian enough, in my crazy white way, to dance with Vikram, even if it was simply that I couldn't bear to see him dance alone. Shaking my head, and laughing despite myself, I joined in his routine. He guided me through the dance, adding new steps until we had the turns and walks and gestures in perfect time together.

The horses watched us with that peculiarly equine mix of white-eyed timorousness and snorting condescension. Still, we danced and sang to them in that grassy wilderness of rolling hills, under a blue sky as dry as the smoke from a campfire in the desert.

And when the dance was over, Vikram spoke to my horse in Hindi, letting it snuffle at his black hat. He passed the hat to me then, and told me to wear it. I slipped it over my head and we climbed into the saddles.

Damn if it didn't work. The horses cantered off, and gently broke into a gallop. For the first and only time in my life, I almost looked like a horseman. I knew the elation, for a glorious quarter hour, of fearless synergy with the great-hearted animal. Closely following Vikram's lead, I flew at steep inclines and conquered them to plummet over the summit, and hurtle downward into curving loops of wind and scattered shrubs. We stretched out over flatter grasslands in effortless, lunging snatches at the ground, and then Nazeer joined us with his riders at the gallop. For a little while, for a moment, we were as wild-willed and free as the horses could teach us to be.

I was still laughing about it and chattering to Nazeer when we climbed the stairs and entered the house on the beach two hours later. I walked my excited smile through the door and saw Karla standing by the long feature-wall window and staring out at the sea. Nazeer greeted her with gruff fondness. A tiny bright smile rushed from his brow to his chin, trying to hide behind his scowl. He seized a litre bottle of water, a box of matches, and a few sheets of newspaper from the kitchen, and left the house.

'He's leaving us alone,' she said.

'I know. He'll make a fire, down on the beach. He does that sometimes.'

I walked to her, and kissed her. It was a brief kiss, almost shy, but all the love in my heart was in it. When our lips parted, we held one another close, both of us looking at the sea. After a while we saw Nazeer, down at the beach, collecting driftwood and dry scraps for a fire. He wedged the balled up newspaper between the twigs and sticks, lit the fire, and sat down beside it, facing the sea. He wasn't cold. There was a warm breeze leaning in on a hot night. He lit the fire to show us, as night rode the waves across the setting sun, that he was still there, on the beach; that we were still alone.

'I like Nazeer,' she said, her head against my throat and chest. 'He's very kind and good-hearted.'

That was true. I knew that. I'd discovered it, at last, the hard way. But how had *she* come to know it from such a little acquaintance of him? One of the worst of my many failings, in those exile years, was my blindness to the good in people: I never knew how much goodness there was in a man or a woman until I owed them more than I could repay. People like Karla saw goodness with a glance, while I stared, and stared, and too often saw nothing past the scowl or bittering eye.

We looked down at the darkening beach and at Nazeer, sitting straight-backed beside his little fire. One of my small victories over Nazeer, when I was still weak and dependent on his strength, had been with language. I'd learned phrases in his language faster than he'd learned them in mine. My fluency had forced him to communicate with me in Urdu most of the time. When he tried to speak English, the words came out in awkward, truncated couplets, top-heavy with meanings and tottering on small feet of blunt sense. I taunted him often about the crudity of his English, exaggerating my confusion and demanding that he repeat himself, that he stumble from one cryptic phrase to another until he cursed me in Urdu and Pashto, and withdrew into silence.

Yet, in truth, his scissored English was always eloquent, and often a cadenced poetry. It was abbreviated, to be sure, but that was because the superfluous had been hacked from it, and what remained was a pure and precise language of his own—something more than slogans and less than proverbs. Against my will, and unknown to him, I'd begun to repeat some of his phrases. He said to me once, while grooming his grey mare, *All horse good, all man not good.* For years afterward, whenever I encountered cruelty and treachery and other kinds of selfishness, especially my own, I found myself repeating Nazeer's phrase: *All horse good, all man not good.* And on that night, holding Karla's heart against my own as we watched his fire dance on the sand, I remembered another of his English iterations. *No love, is no life,* he used to say. *No love, is no life.*

I held Karla as if holding her could heal me, and we didn't make love until night lit the last star in our wide window of sky. Her hands were kisses on my skin. My lips unrolled the curled leaf of her heart. She breathed in murmurs, guiding me, and I spoke rhythm to her, echoing my needs. Heat joined us, and we enclosed ourselves with touch and taste and perfumed sounds. Reflected on the glass, we were silhouettes, transparent images—mine full of fire from the beach, and hers full of stars. And at last, at the end, those clear reflections of our selves melted, merged, and fused together.

It was good, so good, but she never said she loved me.

'I love you,' I whispered, the words moving from my lips to hers.

'I know you do,' she replied, rewarding me and pitying me. 'I know you do.'

'I don't have to go on this trip, you know.'

'Why *are* you going?'

'I'm not sure. I feel ... a sense of loyalty to him, to Khaderbhai, and I still owe him, in a way. But it's more than that. It's ... have you ever had the feeling—about anything at all—that your whole life is kind of a *prelude*, or something—like everything you've ever done has been leading you up to this one point, and you knew, somehow, that one day you'd get there? I'm not explaining it well, but —'

'I know what you mean,' she interrupted quickly. 'And yes, I *have* felt like that. I did something, once, that was my whole life—even the years I haven't lived yet—in one second.'

'What was it?'

'We were talking about you,' she corrected me, avoiding my eyes. 'About you, not having to go to Afghanistan.'

'Well,' I smiled, 'like I said, I don't have to go.'

'Then don't,' she said flatly, turning her head to look at the night and the sea.

'Do you want me to stay?'

'I want you to be safe. And … I want you to be free.'

'That's not what I meant.'

'I know it's not,' she sighed.

I felt the small stir of restlessness in her body, against mine, that said she wanted to move. I didn't move.

'I'll stay,' I said quietly, fighting my heart, and knowing it was a mistake, 'if you tell me you love me.'

She closed her mouth, and pressed her lips together so tightly that they formed a white scar. Slowly, cell by cell, it seemed, her body drew back into itself all that she'd given to me a few moments before.

'Why are you doing this?' she asked.

I didn't know why. Maybe it was the cold turkey, what I'd been through in the last months, and the new life I felt I'd won. Maybe it was death— Prabaker's death, and Abdullah's, and the death I secretly feared was waiting for me in Afghanistan. Whatever the reason, it was stupid and pointless and even cruel, and I couldn't stop wanting it.

'If you say that you love me,' I said again.

'I don't,' she murmured, at last. I tried to stop her, with my fingertips on her mouth, but she turned her head to face me, and her voice was clearer and strong. 'I don't. I can't. I won't.'

When Nazeer returned from the beach, coughing and clearing his voice loudly to announce his arrival, we were already showered and dressed. He smiled—such a rare thing, that smile—as he looked from me, to her, and back again. But the cold sorrow in our eyes drove the downward curves of his face into willow-wreaths of disappointment, and he looked away.

We watched her leave in a taxi on that long and lonely night before we went to Khader's war, and when Nazeer finally met my eyes he nodded, slowly and solemnly. I held the stare for a few moments, but then it was my turn to look away. I didn't want to face the strange mix of grief and elation I'd seen in his eyes because I knew what it was telling me. Karla was gone, yes, but it was the whole world of love and beauty that we'd lost that night. As soldiers in Khader's cause we had to leave it all behind. And the other world, the once unlimited world of what we might yet be, was shrinking, hour by hour, to a bullet's blood-red full stop.

CHAPTER THIRTY-ONE

Nazeer woke me before dawn, and we left the house as the first yawning rays of light stretched into the fading night. When we climbed from our taxi at the airport we saw Khaderbhai and Khaled Ansari near the entrance to the domestic terminal, but we didn't acknowledge them. Khader had laid out a complex itinerary that would take us, with four major changes of transport, from Bombay to Quetta, in Pakistan, near the Afghan border. His instructions were that we should appear at all times to be individual travellers, and that the travellers shouldn't acknowledge one another in any way. We were setting out with him to commit a score of crimes across three international boundaries, and to interfere in a war between Afghanistan's mujaheddin freedom fighters and the mighty Goliath of the Soviet Union. He was planning to succeed in his mission, but he was also allowing for failure. He was ensuring that if any of us were killed or captured at any stage, the trail of connections back to Bombay would be as cold as a mountain climber's axe.

It was a long journey, and it began as a silent one. Nazeer, scrupulous as ever in his conformity with Khaderbhai's instructions, never uttered a single word on the first leg from Bombay to Karachi. An hour after we'd checked into our separate rooms in the Chandni Hotel, however, I heard a soft tap on the door. Before the door was halfway open he slipped inside and pressed it shut behind him. His eyes were wide with nervous excitement and his manner was agitated, almost frantic. I was unsettled and a little disgusted by the conspicuousness of his fear, and I reached out to put a hand on his shoulder.

'Take it easy, Nazeer. You're freaking me out, brother, with all this cloak-and-dagger shit.'

He saw the condescension behind my smile, even if he didn't understand the full meaning of the words. His jaw locked around some inscrutable resolve, and he frowned at me fiercely. We'd become friends, Nazeer and I. He'd opened his heart to me. But friendship, for him, was measured by what men do and endure for one another, not by what they share and enjoy. It puzzled and even tormented him that I almost always met his earnest gravity with facetiousness and triviality. The irony was that we were, in fact, similarly dour and serious men, but *his* grim severity was so stark that it roused me from my own solemnity, and provoked a childish, prankish desire to mock him.

'Russian ... everywhere,' he said, speaking quietly, but with a hard, breathy intensity. 'Russian ... know everything ... know every man ... pay money for know everything.'

'Russian spies?' I asked. 'In Karachi ...'

'Everywhere Pakistan,' he nodded, turning his head aside to spit on the floor. I wasn't sure if the gesture was in contempt or for luck. 'Too much danger! Not speak anyone! You go ... Faloodah House ... Bohri bazaar ... today ... *saade char baje.*'

'Half past four,' I repeated. 'You want me to meet someone at the Faloodah House, in the Bohri bazaar, at half past four? Is that it? Who do you want me to meet?'

He allowed me a grim little smile and then opened the door. Glancing briefly along the corridor, he slipped out again as swiftly and silently as he'd entered. I looked at my watch. One o'clock. I had three hours to kill. For my passport-smuggling missions, Abdel Ghani had given me a money belt that was his uniquely original design. The belt was made from a tough, waterproof vinyl and was several times wider than the standard money belt. Worn flat against the stomach, the belt could hold up to ten passports and a quantity of cash. On that first day in Karachi it held four of my own books. The first of them was the British book that I'd used to purchase plane and train tickets, and register at the hotel. The second book was the clean American passport that Khaderbhai required me to use for the mission into Afghanistan. The two others, a Swiss book and a Canadian book, were spares for emergency use. There was also a ten thousand dollar contingency fund, paid in advance, as part of my fee for accepting the hazardous mission. I wrapped the thick belt around my waist, beneath my shirt, slipped my switchblade into the scabbard at the back of my trousers, and left the hotel to explore the city.

It was hot, hotter than usual for the mild month of November, and a light, unseasonable rain had left the streets hazy with a thickened, steamy air. Karachi was a tense and dangerous city then. For several years the military junta that had seized power in Pakistan and executed the democratically elected prime minister, Zulfikar Ali Bhutto, had ruled the nation by dividing it. They'd exploited genuine grievances between ethnic and religious communities by inciting violent conflicts. They'd pitted the indigenous ethnic groups—particularly the Sindis, the Pashtuns, and the Punjabis—against the immigrants, known as Mohajirs, who'd streamed into the newly founded nation of Pakistan when it was partitioned from India. The army secretly supported extremists from the rival groups with weapons, money, and the judicious application of favours. When the riots that they'd provoked and fomented finally erupted, the generals ordered their police to open fire. Rage against the police violence was then contained by the deployment of army troops. In that way the army, whose covert operations had *created* the bloody conflicts, were seen to be the only force capable of preserving order and the rule of law.

As massacres and revenge killings tumbled over one another with escalating brutishness, kidnappings and torture became routine events. Fanatics from one group seized supporters from another group, and inflicted sadistic torments on them. Many of those who were abducted died in that fearsome captivity. Some vanished, and their bodies were never found. And when one group or another became powerful enough to threaten the balance of the deadly game, the generals incited violent conflict *within* their group to weaken it. The fanatics then began to feed on themselves, killing and maiming rivals from their own ethnic communities.

Each new cycle of violence and vengeance ensured, of course, that no matter what form of government emerged or dissolved in the nation, only the army would grow stronger, and only the army could exercise real power.

Despite that dramatic tension—and because of it—Karachi was a good place to do business. The generals, who were like a mafia clan without the courage, style, or solidarity of genuine, self-respecting gangsters, had seized the country by force, held the entire nation hostage at the points of many guns, and looted the treasury. They lost no time in assuring the great powers, and the other arms-producing nations, that Pakistan's armed forces were open for their business. The civilised nations responded with enthusiasm, and for years Karachi was host to junketing parties of arms-dealers from America, Britain, China, Sweden, Italy, and other countries. No less industrious in their pursuit of a deal with the camarilla of generals were the illegals—the black marketeers, gunrunners, freebooters, and mercenaries. They crowded into the cafés and hotels: foreigners from fifty countries who had crime in mind and adventure in their hearts.

In a sense, I was one of them, a ravager like the rest of them, profiting from the war in Afghanistan like the rest of them, but I wasn't comfortable in their company. For three hours I drifted from a restaurant to a hotel to a chai shop, sitting near or with groups of foreigners who were searching for a quick buck. Their conversations were dispiritingly calculating. The war in Afghanistan, most of them conjectured cheerily, had a few good years left in it. The generals were, it had to be admitted, under considerable pressure. There were rumours that Benazir, daughter of the executed prime minister, was planning to return to Pakistan from exile in London to lead the democratic alliance opposed to the junta. But with a little luck and skilful connivance, the profiteers hoped, the army might remain in control of the country—and the well-established channels of corruption—for some years yet.

The talk was of *cash crops*, a euphemism for contraband and black-market trade goods, which were in great demand along the entire border between Pakistan and Afghanistan. Cigarettes, particularly American blends, were selling at Khyber Pass for sixteen times their already inflated Karachi price. Medicines of every kind were generating profits that increased in scale from month to month. Winter clothing, suitable for snow habitats, was exceptionally marketable. One enterprising German freebooter had driven a Mercedes truck loaded with surplus German army alpine-issue uniforms, complete with thermal underwear, from Munich to Peshawar. He'd sold the lot, including the truck, for five times its purchase value. The buyer was an Afghan warlord who was favoured by western powers and agencies, including the American CIA. The heavy winter clothing, after a journey of thousands of kilometres through Germany, Austria, Hungary, Romania, Bulgaria, Turkey, Iran, and Pakistan, never reached the fighting men of the mujaheddin in the snow-draped mountains of Afghanistan. Instead, the winter uniforms and underwear were stored in one of the warlord's warehouses in Peshawar, awaiting the end of the war. The renegade and his small army were sitting out the war in the safety of their fortress compounds in Pakistan. His plan was to launch a strike for power with his own troops after the real fighting against the Russians was done, and the war was won.

News of that new market—a warlord, cashed up with CIA money and hungry for supplies at any price—sent thrilling, speculative ripples through the community of foreign opportunists in Karachi. I encountered the story of the venturesome German and his truck full of alpine uniforms in three slightly different incarnations during the course of the afternoon. In a fever, something like gold fever, the foreigners passed the story among themselves as they pursued and closed down deals for shipments of canned foods, bales of brushed fleeces, shipping containers of engine parts, a warehouse full of second-hand spirit stoves, and stocks of every kind of weapon from bayonets to grenade launchers. And everywhere, in every conversation, I heard the dark, desperate incantation: *If the war goes on for another year, we'll have it made …*

Vexed and gloomy with squalling emotions I entered the Faloodah House in the Bohri bazaar, and ordered one of the sweet, technicoloured drinks. The faloodha was an indecently sweet concoction of white noodles, milk, rose flavours, and other melliferous syrups. The Firni House in Bombay's Dongri area, near Khaderbhai's house, was justly famous for its delicious faloodah drinks, but they were insipid when compared to the fabulous confections served at Karachi's Faloodah House. When the tall glass of pink, red, and white sugary milk appeared beside my right hand, I looked up to thank the waiter and saw that it was Khaled Ansari, carrying two drinks.

'You look like you need something stronger than this, man,' he said with a smile—a small, sad smile—as he sat down beside me. 'What's up? Or what's *down*, for that matter?'

'It's nothing,' I sighed, offering him a smile in return.

'Come on,' he insisted. 'Let's have it.'

I looked into his honest, open, scarred face and it occurred to me that Khaled knew me better than I knew him. Would I have noticed and realised how troubled *he* was, I wondered, if our roles were reversed, and *he'd* entered the Faloodah House with such disturbing preoccupations? Probably not. Khaled was so often gloomy that I wouldn't have given it a second thought.

'Well, it's just a bit of soul-searching, I guess. I've been doing some research, digging around in some of the chaikhannas and restaurants you told me about—some of the places where the black-market guys and the mercenaries hang out. It was pretty depressing. There's a lot of people here who want the war to go on forever, and they don't give a shit who's getting killed or who's doing the killing.'

'They're making money,' he shrugged. 'It's not their war. I don't expect them to care. That's just how it is.'

'I know, I know. It's not the *money* thing,' I frowned, searching for the words, rather than the emotion that had prompted them. 'It's just—if you wanted a definition of sick, really *sick*-minded, you could do worse than somebody who *wants* a war—any war—to go on *longer*.'

'And ... you feel ... kind of *tainted* ... kind of like them?' Khaled asked gently, looking down into his glass.

'Maybe I do. I don't know. I wouldn't even think about it—you know, if I heard people talking like that somewhere else. It wouldn't bug me if I wasn't here, and if I wasn't doing exactly the same thing myself.'

'It isn't *exactly* the same.'

'It is. Pretty much. Khader's paying me—so I'm making money out of it, like them—and I'm smuggling new shit into a shit-fight, just like they are.'

'And maybe you're starting to ask yourself what the fuck you're doing here?'

'That, too. Would you believe me if I told you I haven't got a clue? I really, honestly, don't know why the fuck I'm doing it. Khader asked me to be his *American*, and I'm doing it. But I don't know why.'

We were silent for a while, sipping at our drinks and listening to the clatter and buzz surrounding us in the busy Faloodah House. A large portable radio was playing romantic gazals in Urdu. I could hear conversations in three or four languages from customers close to us. I couldn't understand the words, nor could I even identify *which* languages they were: Baluchi, Uzbek, Tajik, Farsi ...

'This is great!' Khaled said, using a long spoon to scoop noodles into his mouth from the glass.

'It's too sweet for my taste,' I answered him, drinking the treat nonetheless.

'Some things *should* be too sweet,' he replied, giving me a wink as he sucked on the straw. 'If faloodahs weren't *too* sweet, we wouldn't drink them.'

We finished our drinks and walked out into the late afternoon sunlight, pausing beyond the doorway to light our cigarettes.

'We'll take off in different directions,' Khaled muttered as he held a match for my cigarette in his cupped hands. 'Just keep walking that way, south, for a few minutes. I'll catch you up. Don't say goodbye.'

He turned on his heel and walked away, stepping out to the edge of the road and into the fast lane of foot traffic between the footpath and the cars.

I turned and walked off in the opposite direction. Some minutes later, at the perimeter of the bazaar, a taxi slid to a stop quickly beside me. The back door opened and I jumped in next to Khaled. Another man was in the front seat beside the driver. He was in his early thirties, with short, dark brown hair receding from a high, wide forehead. His deep-set eyes were of a brown so dark as to seem black until direct sunlight pierced the irises to reveal the auburn earth tones swirling within them. His eyes stared evenly, intelligently, from beneath black brows that all but met in the centre. His nose was straight, descending to a short upper lip, a firm determined mouth, and a blunt, rounded chin. It was obvious that the man had shaved that day, and probably not long ago, but a blue-black shadow darkened the lower half of his face along the neat, sharply defined lines that governed his beard. It was a strong, square, symmetrical face, handsome in its strength and even proportions if not in any one outstanding feature.

'This is Ahmed Zadeh,' Khaled announced as the cab moved off. 'Ahmed, this is Lin.'

We shook hands, sizing one another up with equal candour and affability. His strong face might've seemed severe but for a peculiar expression that screwed his eyes into a gentle squint, and creased the crests of his cheeks with smile lines. Whenever he was concentrating, whenever he wasn't completely relaxed, Ahmed Zadeh wore an expression that made him look as if he was searching for a friend in a crowd of strangers. It was a disarming expression, and it endeared him to me at once.

'I've heard a lot about you,' he said, releasing my hand and resting his arm on the front seat of the taxi. His accent, speaking a hesitant but clear English, was that melodious North African blend of French and Arabic.

'I hope it wasn't all good,' I said, laughing.

'Would you prefer people to say bad things about you?'

'I don't know. My friend Didier says that praising people behind their back is monstrously unfair, because the one thing you can't defend yourself against is the good that people say about you.'

'*D'accord!*' Ahmed laughed. 'Exactly so!'

'Shit, that reminds me,' Khaled interjected, fishing through his pockets until he found a folded envelope. 'I almost forgot. I saw Didier, the night before we left. He was looking for you. I couldn't tell him where you were, so he asked me to give you this letter.'

I took the folded envelope and slipped it into the pocket of my shirt, to read when I was alone.

'Thanks,' I muttered. 'So what's going on? Where are we going?'

'To a mosque,' Khaled replied, with that small, sad smile. 'We're going to pick up a friend first, then we're going to meet Khader and some of the other guys who'll be going with us across the border.'

'How many guys?'

'There'll be thirty or so, I think, once we're all together. Most of them are already in Quetta, or at Chaman, near the border. We leave tomorrow —you, me, Khaderbhai, Nazeer, Ahmed, and one other guy, Mahmoud. He's a friend of mine. I don't think you know him. You'll meet him in a few minutes.'

'We are the small United Nations, *non?*' Ahmed asked rhetorically. 'Abdel Khader Khan from Afghanistan, Khaled from Palestine, Mahmoud from Iran, you from New Zealand—I'm sorry, you are now our *American* —and I am from Algeria.'

'And there's more,' Khaled added. 'We've got one guy from Morocco, one guy from the Gulf, one guy from Tunisia, two from Pakistan, and one from Iraq. The rest are all Afghans, but they're all from different parts of Afghanistan, and different ethnic groups as well.'

'*Jihad,*' Ahmed said, his smile grim and almost fearful. 'Holy war—this is our holy duty, to resist the Russian invaders, and liberate a Muslim land.'

'Don't get him started, Lin,' Khaled winced. 'Ahmed's a communist. He'll be hitting you with Mao and Lenin next.'

'Don't you feel a little … compromised?' I asked, tempting fate. 'Going up against a socialist army?'

'*What* socialists?' he retorted, squinting more furiously. '*What* communists? Please do not misunderstand me—the Russians did some good things in Afghanistan —'

'He's right about that,' Khaled interrupted him. 'They built a lot of bridges, and all the main highways, and a lot of schools and colleges.'

'And also dams, for fresh water, and electric power stations—all good things. And I supported them, when they did those things as a way of helping. But when they invaded Afghanistan, to change the country by force, they threw away all of the principles they are supposed to be believing. They are not true Marxists, not true Leninists. The Russians are imperialists, and I fight them in the name of Marx, Lenin, Mao —'

'And Allah,' Khaled grinned.

'Yes, and Allah,' Ahmed agreed, smiling white teeth at us and slapping the back of the seat with his open palm.

'Why did they do it?' I asked him.

'That is something that Khaled can better explain,' he replied, deferring to the Palestinian veteran of several wars.

'Afghanistan is a prize,' Khaled began. 'There's no major reserves of oil, or gold, or anything else that people might want, but still it's a big prize. The Russians want it because it's right on their border. They tried to control it the diplomatic way, with aid packages and relief programs and all that. Then they worked their own guys into power there, in a government that was really just a puppet outfit. The Americans hated it, because of the cold war and all that brinkmanship crap, so they destabilised the place by supporting the only guys who were really pissed off with the Russian puppets—the religious mullah-types. Those long-beards were out of their minds at the way the Russians were changing the country—letting women work, and go to university, and get around in public without the full burkha covering. When the Americans offered them guns and bombs and money to attack the Russians, they jumped at it. After a while, the Russians decided to cut the pretence, and they invaded the country. Now we've got a war.'

'And Pakistan,' Ahmed Zadeh concluded, 'they want Afghanistan because they are growing very fast, too fast, and they want the land. They want to make a great country by combining the two nations. And Pakistan, because of the military generals, belongs to America. So, America helps them. They are training men now, fighters, in religion schools, madrassahs, all over Pakistan. The fighters are called Talebs, and they will go into Afghanistan when the rest of us win the war. And we will win this war, Lin. But the *next* one, I do not know ...'

I turned my face to the window, and as if that were a signal, the two men began to speak in Arabic. I listened to the smooth, swiftly flowing syllables and I let my thoughts drift on that sibilant music. Beyond the window the streets grew less ordered, and the buildings grew more shabby and unkempt. Many of the mud-brick and sandstone buildings were single-storey dwellings, and although they were obviously inhabited by whole families they seemed unfinished: barely standing before they'd been possessed and used as shelters.

We passed through whole suburbs of such haphazard and impetuously constructed sprawls — dormitory suburbs thrown up to cope with the headlong rush of immigrants from villages to the rapidly expanding city. Side streets and lateral avenues revealed that the duplication of those crude, resemblant structures extended all the way to the horizon of sight, on either side of the main road.

After almost an hour of slow progress through sometimes impassably crowded streets, we stopped momentarily to allow another man to join us in the back seat. Following Khaled's instructions, the cab driver then turned his taxi around and returned along precisely the same congested route.

The new man was Mahmoud Melbaaf, a thirty-year-old Iranian. A first glimpse of his face — the thick, black hair, the high cheek bones, the eyes coloured like a sand dune in a blood-red sunset — reminded me so much of my dead friend Abdullah that I flinched around the pain of it. In a few moments the similarity dissolved: Mahmoud's eyes protruded a little, his lips were less full, and his chin was pointed, as if it was designed to hold a goatee beard. It was, in fact, a very different face.

But in the clear thought of Abdullah Taheri and the piercing pain of missing him, I suddenly understood a part of the reason I was there, with Khaled and the others, on a journey into someone else's war. One part, a vital part of my readiness to face the risks of taking on Khader's mission, was the guilt I still felt that Abdullah had died alone, surrounded by guns. I was putting myself in the nearest equivalent, surrounding myself with enemy guns. And in the instant of thinking that thought, in the moment of daubing the unspoken words on a grey wall of my mind — *death wish* —

I rejected it, with a shudder that shivered across the surface of my skin. And for the first time in all the months since I'd agreed to do the job for Abdel Khader Khan I felt afraid, and I knew that my life, there and then, was no more than a handful of sand squeezed into my clenched fist.

We got out of the car a block away from the Masjid-i-Tuba Mosque. Following one another in single file, with twenty metres between each man, we reached the mosque, and removed our shoes. An ancient hajji attended to the shoes while he muttered his meditational *zikkir*. Khaled pressed a folded bank note into the man's calloused, arthritic hand. As we entered the mosque I looked up and gasped in surprise and joy.

The interior of the mosque was cool and immaculately clean. Marble and stone tiles gleamed from fluted pillars, mosaic arches, and vast stretches of patterned floors. But above and beyond all that, drawing the eye irresistibly, was the enormous white marble dome. The spectacular canopy was a hundred paces across, and bejewelled with tiny, polished mirrors. As I stood there, gaping in wonder at its beauty, the electric lights in the mosque came on and the great curve of marble above us gleamed like sunshine on the million peaks and ripples of a wind-worried lake.

Khaled left us immediately, promising to return as soon as possible. Ahmed, Mahmoud, and I walked to an alcove that gave a view of the dome, and we sat down on the polished tile floor. It was some time since the evening prayer—I'd heard the call of the muezzin while we were driving in the cab—but there were still many men absorbed in private prayer throughout the mosque. When he was sure that I was comfortable, Ahmed announced that he would take the opportunity to pray. He excused himself, and walked to the bathing fount. With his face, hands, and feet washed according to ritual, he returned to a little clear space beneath the dome and commenced his prayer.

I watched him with a tiny germ of envy at the ease with which he opened his communication with God. I felt no urge to join him, but the sincerity of his meditation made me feel much more alone, somehow, in my solitary, unconnected mind.

He completed the prayer and, as he began the walk back to us, Khaled returned. He wore a troubled expression. We sat close together, our heads almost touching.

'We've got trouble,' he whispered. 'The police were at your hotel.'

'The cops?'

'The political police,' Khaled answered. 'The ISI. Inter-Services Intelligence.'

'What did they want?' I asked.

'You. All of us. We've been made. They hit Khader's house, too. You were both lucky. He was out of the house, and they didn't get him. What have you got with you, from your hotel? What did you leave there?'

'I've got my passports, my money, and my knife,' I replied.

Ahmed grinned at me.

'You know, I am going to like you,' he whispered.

'Everything else is still there,' I continued. 'There's not much. Clothes, toiletries, a few books. That's it. But there's the tickets—the plane and the train tickets I bought. I left them in my carry bag. That's the only thing with a name on it, I'm pretty sure.'

'Nazeer got your carry bag, and got out of there just a minute before the cops crashed in,' Khaled said, offering me a reassuring nod. 'But that's all he got time to grab. The manager's one of our guys, and he tipped Nazeer off. The big question is, who told the cops that we're here? It has to be someone from Khader's side. Someone on the inside, very close. I don't like it.'

'I don't get it,' I whispered. 'Why are the cops so interested in us? Pakistan is supporting Afghanistan in the war. They should *want* us to smuggle stuff to the mujaheddin. They should be *helping* us to do it.'

'They *are* helping *some* Afghans, but not *all* of them. The guys we're getting the stuff to, the guys near Kandahar, they're Massoud's men. Pakistan hates them because they won't accept Hekmatyar, or any of the other pro-Pakistan leaders of the resistance. Pakistan and the Americans have picked out Hekmatyar as the next ruler of Afghanistan, after the war. But Massoud's men spit every time they hear his name.'

'It is crazy war,' Mahmoud Melbaaf added in a coarse, throaty whisper. 'Afghans fight each other for so long time, thousands years. The only thing better than fighting each other, is fighting ... how do you say it ... *invasion*. They will beat Russians, sure, but they will keep fighting.'

'The Pakistanis want to be sure that they win the *peace*, after the Afghans win the war,' Ahmed continued for him. 'No matter who wins the war for them, they want to be in control of the peace. If they could do it, they would take all of our weapons and our medicines and our other supplies, and give them to their own ...'

'Proxies,' Khaled murmured, the New York in his accent exploding in the whispered word. 'Hey, you hear that?'

We all listened intently, and heard the sounds of singing and music from somewhere outside the mosque.

'They've started,' Khaled said, rising to his feet with athletic grace. 'It's time to go.'

We stood and followed him out of the mosque to collect our shoes. Walking around the building in the gathering dark, we approached the sound of the singing.

'I've ... I've heard this singing before,' I said to Khaled as we walked.

'You know the Blind Singers?' he asked. 'Oh sure, of *course* you do. You were there in Bombay, with Abdel Khader, when they sang for us. That was the first time I ever saw you.'

'You were there that night?'

'Sure. We were all there. Ahmed, Mahmoud, Siddiqi—you haven't met him yet. A lot of the others who'll be going with us on this trip. They were all there that night. That was the first big meeting for this run to Afghanistan. That's why we got together. That's what the meeting was all about. Didn't you know?'

He laughed as he asked the question, and his tone was as honest and ingenuous as it ever was, but still the words stabbed into my mind. *Didn't you know? Didn't you know?*

Khader was planning the trip all that time ago, I thought, *on the first night that I met him*. I remembered with perfect clarity the large, smoky room where the Blind Singers sang for their private audience. I remembered the food that we ate, the charras we smoked. I remembered the few well-known faces I'd recognised that night. *Were they all involved in the mission?* I remembered the young Afghan who'd greeted Khaderbhai with such respect, bending low enough to reveal the pistol held within a fold of his shawl.

I was still thinking of that first night, still worried by the questions I couldn't answer, when Khaled and I came upon a large group of men, hundreds of them, sitting cross-legged on the tiles of a wide forecourt adjacent to the mosque. The Blind Singers finished a song and the men applauded, shouting *Allah! Allah! Subhaan Allah!* Khaled led us through the crowd of men to a relatively sheltered alcove where Khader sat with Nazeer and several others.

When I caught his eye Khaderbhai raised his hand, signalling for me to join him. As I reached his side he grasped my hand and pulled me down beside him. A number of heads turned in our direction. Conflicting emotions stumbled into one another in my haunted heart: fear, that I was so conspicuously associated with Khader Khan, and a flush of pride that he'd drawn me, over all others, to sit at his side.

'The wheel has moved through one full turn,' he whispered to me, placing his hand on my forearm and speaking close to my ear. 'We met each other, you and I, with the Blind Singers, and now we hear them again, just as we begin this important task.'

He was reading my mind and I was sure, somehow, that it was deliberate: that he was fully aware of the dizzying impact of his words. I was suddenly angry with him, suddenly resentful, even of the touch of his hand on my arm.

'Did you arrange to have the Blind Singers here?' I asked him, staring straight ahead and leaving the razor's edge in my tone. 'You know, just like you arranged everything else the first time we met?'

He remained silent until at last I turned to face him. When my eyes met his I felt the sting of impulsive tears, and I mastered them by grinding my jaws together. It worked, and my burning eyes remained dry, but my mind was in turmoil. The man with the cinnamon-brown skin and the trim, white beard had used and manipulated me and everyone else he knew as if we were his chained slaves. Yet there was such love in his golden eyes that it was, for me, the full measure of something I'd always craved from the innermost coils of my heart. The love in his softly smiling, deeply worried eyes was a father's love: the only father-love I'd ever known.

'From this moment, you stay with us,' he whispered, holding my stare. 'You cannot return to your hotel. The police have a description of you, and they will keep looking. This is my fault, and I must give you my apology. Someone close to us has betrayed us. It is our good luck, and his bad luck, that we were not captured. He will be punished. His mistake has revealed him to us. We know now who he is, and we know what must be done to him. But that will wait until we return from our task. Tomorrow we travel to Quetta. We must remain there for some time. When the time is right, we will make the crossing into Afghanistan. And from that day, for as long as you are in Afghanistan, there will be a price on your head.

The Russians pay well for the capture of foreigners who help the muja-heddin. And we have few friends here in Pakistan. I think we will have to get some local clothes for you. We will dress you like a young man from my village—a Pashtun, like me. Yes, with a cap to cover your white hair, and a pattu, a shawl, to throw over your broad shoulders and chest. We will pass you off, perhaps, as my blue-eyed son. What do you think?'

What did I think? The Blind Singers cleared their throats noisily, and the assembly of musicians began the introduction to a new song with the plaintive wail of the harmonium and the blood-stirring passion of the tablas. I watched the long, slender fingers of the tabla players clap and caress the trembling skins of the drums, and I felt my thoughts drift away from me in the hypnotic flutter and flow of the music. My own govern-ment had put a price on my head, in Australia, as a reward for informa-tion leading to my capture. And there, across the world, I was putting another price on my head. Once more, as the wild grief and rapture of the Blind Singers rippled through a listening crowd, once more, as the eyes of that crowd blazed the ecstasy of their devotions, once more I sur-rendered to the fate-filled moment and felt myself, my whole life, turning with the wheel.

Then I remembered the note in my pocket: the letter from Didier that Khaled had given me in the taxi two hours earlier. Caught up in the superstitious twist of coincidence and history repeating itself, I was sud-denly desperate to know what the letter said. I slipped it from my pocket and held it close to my eyes in the yellow-amber light that reached us from lamps high over our heads.

Dear Lin,

This is to tell you, mon cher ami, that I have discovered who was it—the woman who betrayed you to the police and had you put inside the prison and beaten so badly. Such a terrible thing! Even now I am still desolated by it! Well then, the woman who did this thing is Madame Zhou, the owner of the Palace. Up to this time, I have not learned the reason for what she did, but even without some understanding of her motive for doing this terrible thing to you, I have only the best sources to assure me that it is true.

I hope that I will hear from you soon.

Your dear friend,

Didier.

Madame Zhou. *Why?* Even as I formed the question in my mind, I knew the answer. I suddenly remembered a face staring at me with inexplicable hatred. It was the face of Rajan, Madame Zhou's eunuch servant. I remembered that I'd seen him watching me, on the day of the flood, when we'd rescued Karla from the Taj Mahal Hotel in Vinod's boat. I remembered the malignant hate that had filled his eyes as he'd watched me with Karla, and watched me drive away in Shantu's taxi. Later that night the police had arrested me, and my prison torture had begun. Madame Zhou had punished me for defying her, for daring to challenge her, for impersonating an American consular officer, for taking Lisa Carter away from her and, yes, perhaps for loving Karla.

I tore the letter into pieces and put the fragments back in my pocket. I was calm. The fear was gone. At the end of that long Karachi day, I knew why I was going to Khader's war, and I knew why I would return. I was going because my heart was hungry for Khaderbhai's love, the father-love that streamed from his eyes and filled the father-shaped hole in my life. When so many other loves were lost — my family, my friends, Prabaker, Abdullah, even Karla — that look of love in Khader's eyes was everything and all the world to me.

It seemed stupid, it *was* stupid, to go to war for love. He wasn't a saint and he wasn't a hero: I knew that. He wasn't even my father. But for nothing more than those seconds of his loving gaze, I knew that I would follow him into that war, and any other. And it wasn't any more stupid than surviving just for hate, and returning for revenge. For that's what it came down to: I loved him enough to risk my life, and I hated her enough to survive and to avenge myself. And I would have that revenge, I knew, if I made it through Khader's war: I would find Madame Zhou, and I would kill her.

I closed my mind around that thought as a man might close his hand around the hilt of a knife. The Blind Singers cried the joys and agonies of their love for God. Beside me, surrounding me, hearts soared in response. Khaderbhai turned his head to meet my eyes, and nodded slowly. I smiled into the golden eyes filled with tiny, swaying lamplights, and secrets, and sacred pleasures summoned by the singing. And, God help me, I was content and unafraid and almost happy.

CHAPTER THIRTY-TWO

W E SPENT A MONTH in Quetta — a long month of waiting with the frustration of false starts. The delay was caused by a mujaheddin commander named Asmatullah Achakzai Muslim. He was the leader of the Achakzai people in the region of Kandahar, which was our ultimate destination. The Achakzai were a clan of sheep and goat herders who'd originally been members of the dominant Durrani clan. In 1750, the founder of modern Afghanistan, Ahmed Shah Abdali, divided the Achakzai from the Durrani and established them as a clan in their own right. That was in accordance with Afghan tradition, which allowed a sub-clan to be separated from its parent clan when it reached sufficient size or strength. It was also an admission by the wily warrior and nation-builder Ahmed Shah that the Achakzai were a force to be reckoned with and appeased. Through two centuries the Achakzai increased their status and their power. They earned a well-deserved reputation as fierce fighters, and every man in the clan could be counted on to follow his leader without question. During the early years of the war against the Russians, Asmatullah Achakzai Muslim formed his men into a well-armed, highly disciplined militia. In their region they became the spearhead of the independence struggle: the jihad to drive out the Soviet invaders.

Toward the end of 1985, as we prepared ourselves in Quetta for the crossing into Afghanistan, Asmatullah began to vacillate in his commitment to the war. So much depended on his militia that when he pulled his men back from active service, and began secret peace talks with the Russians and their Afghan puppet government in Kabul, the entire war of resistance in the Kandahar region collapsed. Other mujaheddin units not under Asmatullah's control, such as Khader's men in the mountains north of the city, remained in their positions; but they were isolated, and every supply route to them was perilously vulnerable to Russian attack.

The uncertainty forced us to wait until Asmatullah decided whether to continue the jihad or switch sides and support the Russians. No-one could predict which way he would jump.

Although we were all restive and agitated with the wait — as the days limped into weeks, it seemed interminable — I used the time well. I practised phrases in Farsi, Urdu, and Pashto, and even picked up a few words in some Tajik and Uzbek dialects. I rode horses every day. While I never managed to eliminate my clownish, arm-and-leg-flapping gestures when I made the animals stop or go or turn in a desired direction, I sometimes did succeed in dismounting them by climbing down rather than being hurled to the ground on my back.

I read books every day from a bizarre, eclectic collection supplied to me by Ayub Khan, a Pakistani, and the one member of our group who'd been born in Quetta. Because it was judged too dangerous for me to leave our safe-house compound at a horse ranch on the outskirts of the city, Ayub brought me books from the central library. The library was stocked with obscure and fascinating English-language books that were an inheritance from the days of the British Raj. The name of the city, Quetta, was derived from the Pashto word *kwatta*, meaning *fort*. Its proximity to the Chaman Pass route to Afghanistan, and the Bolan Pass route to India, ensured Quetta's military and economic significance for millennia. The British first occupied the old fort in 1840, but were forced to abandon it after sickness in the troops and ferocious resistance from the Afghans had withered the colonial force. It was reoccupied in 1876, and firmly established as the premier British possession in that region of the North West Frontier of India. The Imperial Staff College for military officers in British India was established there, and a thriving, prosperous market-centre grew up in the spectacular, natural amphitheatre of the surrounding mountains. A cataclysmic earthquake on the last day of May in 1935 destroyed most of the city and killed twenty thousand people, but Quetta was rebuilt, and the clean, wide boulevards and pleasant weather made it one of the most popular holiday resorts in northern Pakistan.

For me, restricted then to the compound, the chief attraction of the city was the random selection of books that Ayub brought to me. Every few days he appeared at my door, grinning hopefully and handing the bundle of books to me as if they were treasures from an archaeological dig.

And so it was that I rode during the day, acclimatising myself to the thinner air above five thousand feet, and at night read the diaries and journals of long-dead explorers, extinct editions of Greek classics, eccentrically annotated volumes of Shakespeare, and a dizzyingly passionate terza rima translation of Dante's *The Divine Comedy*.

'Some of the men think you are a scholar of the holy works,' Abdel Khader Khan said to me from the doorway of my room one night, after we'd been a month in Quetta. I closed the book that I was reading and stood to greet him at once. He took my hand and enclosed it within both of his own, muttering a whispered prayer of blessing. When he accepted the chair that I offered him, I sat down on a stool an arm's reach away. He had a parcel wrapped in cream chamois leather under his arm. He placed it on my bed and settled back comfortably.

'Reading is still something mysterious, in the country of my birth, and the cause of some fear and much superstition,' Khader said wearily, rubbing a hand over his tired, brown face. 'Only four men in ten can read at all, and half that number again for women.'

'Where did you learn ... everything you've learned?' I asked him. 'Where did you learn to speak English so well, for example?'

'I was tutored by a very fine English gentleman,' he laughed softly, brightening with the recollection. 'Just as my little Tariq was tutored by you.'

I took two beedies from a pack, lit them in my hand with the play of a match, and handed one to him.

'My father was the leader of his clan,' Khader continued. 'He was a stern man, but he was also a just man and a wise man. In Afghanistan men become leaders by merit—they are good speakers, wise managers of money, and brave, when fighting is necessary. There is no inherited right to be a leader, and a leader's son who has no wisdom or courage or skill at speaking to the people will be passed over for another man with better skills. My father was very anxious for me to succeed him and to continue his life-work, which was to raise his people from ignorance, and to ensure their future well-being. A wandering Sufi mystic, an old saint who visited our area when I was born, had told my father that I would grow up to become a shining star in the history of my people. My father hoped for this with all his heart but, unfortunately, I showed none of a leader's skills, and no interest in attaining them. I was, in short, a bitter disappointment to him. He sent me to my uncle, here in Quetta. And my uncle, who was a prosperous merchant then, put me in the care of an Englishman, who became my tutor.'

'How old were you?'

'I was ten years old when I left Kandahar, and I spent five years as a student of Mr. Ian Donald Mackenzie Esquire.'

'You must've been a good student,' I suggested.

'Perhaps,' he mused in reply. 'I think, really, that Mackenzie Esquire was a very good teacher. I have heard, in the years since I left him, that the people of Scotland are known for their sour and stern ways. Some people have told me that the people of Scotland are pessimists, who prefer to walk on the dark side of every sunny street. I think that if this is in some way true, it does not also tell us that the people of Scotland find this dark side of things to be very, very funny. My Mackenzie Esquire was a man who laughed in his eyes, even when he was most stern with me. Every time that I think of him, I remember the laughter in his eyes. And he loved it in Quetta. He loved the mountains, and the cold air in winter. His thick, strong legs were built for climbing mountain paths, and he roamed these hills every week, often with me alone for company. He was a happy man who knew how to laugh, and he was a great teacher.'

'What happened when he finished teaching you?' I asked. 'Did you return to Kandahar?'

'I did, but it was not the joyful return that my father hoped for. You see, on the day after my dear Mackenzie Esquire left Quetta, I killed a man, in the bazaar, outside my uncle's warehouse.'

'When you were fifteen?'

'Yes. When I was fifteen years old I killed a man, for the first time.'

He lapsed into silence, and I pondered the weight and measure of that phrase ... *for the first time* ...

'It was a cause that was really no cause, a trick of fate, a fight that grew out of nothing at all. The man was beating a child. It was his own child, and I should not have interfered. But it was a very cruel beating, and I could not bear to watch it. Filled with the importance of being the son of a village leader, and being the nephew of one of Quetta's most prosperous merchants, I commanded the man to stop beating the child. He took offence, of course, and there was an argument. The argument became a fight. And then he was dead, stabbed in the chest with his own dagger — the dagger he had tried to use on me.'

'It was self-defence.'

'Yes. There were many witnesses. It was in the main street of the bazaar. My uncle, who had much influence at that time, spoke for me with all the authorities, and finally arranged for me to return to Kandahar. Unfortunately, the family of the man I had killed refused to accept a blood-money payment from my uncle, and they sent two men to Kandahar after me. I received a warning from my uncle, and I struck first. I killed both men by shooting them with my father's old long rifle.'

He was silent again for a while, staring at a point on the floor between our feet. I could hear music, distant and muffled, coming from the other side of the compound. There were many rooms radiating outward from a central courtyard that was larger but less grand than that in Khader's Bombay home. From some of the nearer rooms I could hear the low, water-bubble murmur of conversation and the tapping drum-roll of an occasional laugh. From the room next door, Khaled Ansari's room, I heard the unmistakable *clikka-k'chuck* of a Kalashnikov AK-74 assault rifle being cocked and cold-fired after cleaning.

'The blood feud that began with those killings—and with their attempt to kill me—destroyed my family and theirs,' Khader said flatly, resuming his story. His expression was sombre, and it seemed as if the spirit was draining invisibly from his downcast eyes as he spoke. 'One on our side, two on theirs. Two on our side, one on theirs. My father tried many times to find a way to end the feud, but it was impossible. It was a demon that moved from man to man, and made each man mad with the love of killing. I tried to leave my home, because I was the cause of the feud, but my father refused to let me leave, and I could not oppose him. The feud went on for years, and the killing went on for years. I lost my two brothers, and both of my uncles, my father's brothers. When my own father was badly wounded in an attack, and unable to stop me, I told my family to spread the rumour that I had been killed. I left my family home. The blood feud ended some time after that, and peace was restored between the two families. But I was dead to my family, because I had sworn an oath to my mother that I would never return.'

The breeze through the metal-framed window that had been cool in the earlier evening was suddenly cold. I stood to close the window, and then poured a glass of water from the clay pitcher on my nightstand. Khader accepted the glass, whispered a prayer, and drank the water. He handed me the glass when he was finished. I poured water into the same glass and sat down on the stool to sip at my drink. I said nothing, afraid that, if I asked the wrong question or made the wrong comment, he would stop talking altogether and leave the room. He was calm, and he seemed to be completely relaxed, but the brilliant, laughing gleam was missing from his eyes. It was also disturbingly out of character for him to be so expansive about his own life. He'd talked to me for long hours about the Koran or the life of the Prophet Mohammed or the scientific, rational basis for his moral philosophy, but I'd never known him to tell me or anyone else so much about himself. In the lengthening silence I looked at the lean, sinewed face and I controlled even the sound of my breathing, lest it disturb him.

We were both dressed in the standard Afghan costume of a long, loose shirt and wide-waisted pants. His clothes were a light, faded green and mine were pale blue-white. We both wore leather sandals as house slippers. Although I was heavier and deeper in the chest than Khaderbhai, we were roughly the same height and build across the shoulders. His short hair and beard were white-silver, and my short hair was white-blonde. My skin was tanned to a shade resembling his natural, almond-shell brown. If it wasn't for the sky in my blue-grey eyes and the alluvial gold in his, we might've been taken for father and son.

'How did you get from Kandahar to the Bombay mafia?' I asked him at last, when I feared that the lengthening silence, more than my questions, might make him leave.

He turned to face me. His smile was radiant: a new, gentle, artless smile that had never moved his face before in any conversation with me.

'When I ran away from my home in Kandahar, I made a journey across Pakistan and India to Bombay. Like a million others, like *millions* of others, I hoped to make my fortune in the city of the Hindi picture heroes. At first, I lived in a slum—like the one that I own now, near the World Trade Centre. I practised the Hindi language every day, and I learned quickly. After a while, I observed that men could make money buying tickets for popular pictures at the cinemas and then selling them for a profit when the cinemas put up the House Full signs. I decided to use the little money I'd saved to buy tickets for the most popular Hindi picture in Bombay. Then I stood outside the cinema, and when the House Full signs went up I sold my tickets for a good profit.'

'Scalping,' I said. 'We call it ticket scalping. It's big business—black-market business—at the most popular football matches in my country.'

'Yes. And I made an excellent profit in the first week of my work. I already began to have dreams of moving to a fine apartment and wearing the best clothes, perhaps even buying a car. Then, one night, I was standing outside the cinema with my tickets when two very big men came to me, showed me their weapons—they had a sword and a meat chopper—and demanded that I go with them.'

'Local goondas,' I laughed.

'Goondas,' he repeated, laughing with me. For those of us who knew him as lord Abdel Khader Khan, the don, the ruler of his kingdom of crime in Bombay, it was hilarious to picture him as a shame-faced eighteen-year-old in the custody of two street thugs.

'They took me to see *Chota Gulab*, the Little Rose. He had that name for the mark on his cheek made by a bullet that had passed through his face, breaking most of his teeth, and leaving a scar that was pinched like a rose. He was the boss of that whole area in those days, and before he had me beaten to death, as an example to others he wanted to take a look at the impudent fellow who had trespassed on his area.

'He was furious. "What are you doing, selling tickets in my area?" he asked me, speaking a mix of Hindi and English. It was a poor English, but he wanted to intimidate me with it, as if he was a judge in a court of law. "Do you know how many men *died*, how many men I had to *kill*, how many good men I *lost*, to take control of the black-market tickets at all the cinemas in this area?"

'I was terrified, I admit it to you, and I thought that my life was but a few minutes' worth. So I threw away my caution, and I spoke boldly. "Now you will have to eliminate one more nuisance, Gulabji," I told him, speaking an English that was far superior to his, "because I have no other way of making money, and I have no family, and I have nothing to lose. Unless, of course, you have some decent job of work that a loyal and resourceful young man can do for you."

'Well, he laughed out loud, and he asked me where I learned to speak English so well, and when I told him, and when I told him my story, he gave me a job right away. Then he showed me his smashed teeth, opening his mouth wide to point out the gold replacements. Looking into Chota Gulab's mouth was a real honour amongst his men, and some of his closest goondas were very jealous that I got such an intimate tour of the famous mouth on my very first meeting with him. Gulab liked me, and he became a kind of father to me in Bombay, but I had enemies around me from the first time that I shook his hand.

'I went to work as a soldier, fighting with my fists and with swords and cleavers and hammers to enforce Chota Gulab's rule in the area. Those were bad days, before the council system, and there was fighting every day and night. After a while, one of his men took a special dislike to me. Resentful of my close relationship with Gulabji, he found a reason to pick a fight with me. So I killed him. And when *his* best friend attacked me, I killed him, too. And then I killed a man for Chota Gulab. And I killed again. And again.'

He fell silent, staring ahead at the floor where it met the mud-brick wall. After a time, he spoke.

'And again,' he said.

He repeated the phrase into a silence that was thickening around us and seeming to press in upon my burning eyes.

'And again.'

I watched him wade through the past, his eyes blazing recollections, and then he shook himself back into the moment.

'It is late. Here, I want to give you a gift.'

He opened the chamois-leather parcel to reveal a pistol in a side holster, several magazines, a box of ammunition, and a metal box. Lifting back the lid of the metal box, he displayed a cleaning kit of oil, graphite powder, tiny files, brushes, and a new, short pull-through cord.

'This is a Stechkin APS pistol,' he said, taking up the weapon and removing its magazine. He checked to ensure that there was no round in the firing chamber, and handed the pistol to me. 'It is Russian. You will find plenty of ammunition on the dead Russians, if you have to fight them. It is a nine-millimetre-calibre weapon, with a magazine of twenty rounds. You can fire it as a single shot, or set it on automatic. It is not the best gun in the world, but it is reliable, and the only light weapon with more bullets in it, where we are going, is a Kalashnikov. I want you to wear it, clearly displayed at all times from now on. You eat with it, you sleep with it, and when you wash yourself, you have it within your reach. I want everyone who is with us, and everyone who sees us, to know that you have it. Do you understand?'

'Yes,' I answered, staring at the gun in my hands.

'I told you that there is a price on the head of every foreigner who helps the mujaheddin. I want it to be so, that someone who might think of this reward, and of claiming it with your head, will also think of the Stechkin at your side. Do you know how to clean an automatic pistol?'

'No.'

'Very well. I will show you how it is done. Then you must try to sleep. We leave for Afghanistan at five, before dawn, tomorrow morning. The waiting is over. The time has come.'

Khaderbhai showed me how to clean the Stechkin. It was more complicated than I'd imagined, and it took the best part of an hour for him to walk me through the instructions for its complete service, repair, and handling protocols. It was a thrilling hour, and men and women of violence will know what I mean when I say that I was drunk with the pleasure of it. I confess with no little shame that I enjoyed that hour with Khader, learning how to use and clean the Stechkin automatic pistol, more than the hundreds of hours that I'd spent with him while learning his philosophy. And I never felt closer to him than I did that night as we hunched over my blanket, stripping and reassembling the killing weapon.

When he left me, I turned out the light and lay back on my cot, but I couldn't sleep. My mind was caffeine-alert in the darkness. At first I thought about the stories Khader had told me. I moved through that different time in the city I'd come to know so well. I imagined the Khan as a young man, fit and dangerous and fighting for Chota Gulab, the gangster boss with a little rose scar on his cheek. I knew other parts of Khader's story—I'd heard them from some of the goondas who worked for him in Bombay. They'd told me how Khaderbhai had seized control of Gulab's little empire when the scarred one was assassinated outside one of his cinemas. They'd described the gang wars that had erupted across the city, and they'd talked of Khader's courage, and his ruthlessness in crushing his enemies. I knew, as well, that Khaderbhai was one of the founders of the council system, which had brought peace to the city by dividing territories and spoils between the surviving gangs.

I wondered, as I lay in a darkness scented with the polished-floor-and-raw-linen odours of the gun and the cleaning oil, why Khaderbhai was going to war. He didn't have to go—there were a hundred more like me, prepared to die for him in his place. I remembered his strangely radiant smile when he'd told me about his first meeting with Chota Gulab. I recalled how quick and youthful his hands had been when he'd shown me how to clean and use the gun. And it occurred to me that he might've been with us, risking his life, simply because he was hungry for the wilder days of his youth. The thought worried me because I was sure that at least some small part of it was true. But that other motive—that he'd judged the time right to end his exile, and to visit his home and family— worried me more. I couldn't forget what he'd told me. The blood feud that had killed so many and driven him from his home had only ended with his promise, to his mother, never to return.

After a while my thoughts drifted, and I found myself reliving, moment for moment, the long night before my escape from prison. That, too, was a night without sleep. That, too, was a night of wheeling fears and exhilaration and dread. And just as I had on that night years before, I rose from bed before the first stir and shuffle of the morning, and pre- pared myself in the dark.

Soon after dawn, we took the train to Chaman Pass. There were twelve from our group on the train, but none of us spoke through the several hours of the journey. Nazeer sat with me, and we were alone for much of the trip, but still he held his stony silence. With my pale eyes concealed behind dark sunglasses, I stared through the window and tried to lose myself in the spectacular view.

The train ride from Quetta to Chaman was one of the glories of the illustrious sub-continental railway system. The tracks wound through deep gorges and crossed riverscapes of astounding beauty. I found myself repeating, as if they were lines of poetry, the very names of the towns through which it passed. From Kuchlaagh to Bostaan, and the small river crossing at Yaaru Kaarez, the train climbed to Shaadizai. At Gulistan there was another climb, with a sweeping curve that followed the ancient dry lake at Qila Abdullah. And the jewel in the twin steel-bands of that crown, of course, was the Khojak Tunnel. Built by the British over several years at the end of the nineteenth century, it smashed its way through four kilometres of solid rock, and was the longest in the sub-continent.

At Khaan Kili the train negotiated a series of sharp curves, and at the last remote regional stop before Chaman we climbed down with a few dusty locals and were met by a covered truck. When the area was deserted we climbed onto the extravagantly decorated truck, and followed the main road toward Chaman. Before we reached the town, however, we took a side road that seemed to end in a deserted track, with a stand of trees and several scrubby pastures, about thirty kilometres north of the main highway and the Chaman Pass.

We climbed down from the truck, and as it drove away we mustered in the shade of the trees with the main group of men, who'd been waiting there for us. It was the first time that we'd assembled in our full number. There were thirty of us, all men, and for a moment I was reminded of the men who gathered in similar groups in prison yards. The fighters seemed tough and determined and, although many of them were lean to the point of being thin, they looked healthy and fit.

I removed my sunglasses. As I scanned the faces, my eyes met those of a man who stared back at me from the heart of darkness. He was in his late forties or early fifties, and perhaps the oldest man in the group after Khaderbhai. His short hair was grey beneath a brown, round-edged Afghan cap, identical to the one I wore myself. His short, straight nose divided a long, pointed face that was so deeply lined beneath the sunken cheeks that it appeared to have been slashed with a machete. Heavy bags hung below his eyes. Theatrically peaked eyebrows like the wings of a black bat spiked above his eyes, but it was the eyes themselves that caught and held me.

As I locked eyes with him, returning his psychotic stare, the man began to stumble toward me. After the first few shambling steps, his body twitched into a more efficient mode, and he began to lope, covering the thirty metres that separated us in long, crouching, feline strides. Forgetting that the gun was strapped to my side, my hand instinctively moved to the hilt of my knife and I took half a pace backward with my right foot. I knew the eyes. I knew the look. The man wanted to fight me, perhaps even to kill me.

Just as he reached me, shouting something in a dialect that I couldn't recognise, Nazeer stepped from nowhere to stand in front of me and bar his way. He shouted something back at the man, but the other ignored him, staring past his head at me and shouting his question, again and again. Nazeer repeated his reply, shouting to match the other. The crazed fighter tried to shove Nazeer out of the way with both hands, but he might as well have tried to push aside a tree. The burly Afghan stood his ground, forcing the madman to shift his gaze from me for the first time.

A crowd had formed around us. Nazeer held the man's lunatic stare, and spoke in softer, pleading tones. I waited, tensed and ready to fight. *We haven't even crossed the border yet*, I thought, *and I'm going to have to stab one of our own men ...*

'He was asking if you are a Russian,' Ahmed Zadeh muttered from beside me, his Algerian accents rolling over the R in Russian. I flicked a glance at him, and he pointed at my hip. 'The gun. And your pale eyes. He thinks you are a Russian.'

Khaderbhai walked between the men, and put his hand on the madman's shoulder. The man turned immediately, and with eyes that seemed ready to weep, searched Khader's face. Khader repeated what Nazeer had been murmuring, in a similarly soothing tone. I couldn't understand all of it, but the sense was clear. *No. He is American. The Americans are here to help us. He is here with us to fight the Russians. He will help us to kill the Russians. He will help us. We will kill many Russians together.*

When the man turned to face me once more, his expression had changed so dramatically that I was moved to pity him, when a moment before I was ready to run my knife into his chest. His eyes were still deranged, hanging unnaturally wide and white beneath the brown irises, but his frenzied expression had collapsed into such wretched, pitiable misery that his face reminded me of the many ruined stone cottages we'd seen beside the roads. He looked once more into Khader's face, and the stutter of a smile flickered across his features as if animated by an electric pulse. He turned and walked away through the crowd. The tough men parted for him warily, compassion vying with fear in their eyes as they watched him pass.

'I am sorry, Lin,' Abdel Khader said softly. 'His name is Habib. Habib Abdur Rahman. He is a schoolteacher—well, he once *was* a schoolteacher, in a village on the other side of these mountains. He taught the little ones, the youngest children. When the Russians invaded, seven years ago, he was a happy man, with a young wife and two strong sons. He joined the resistance, like every other young man in the region. Two years ago he returned from a mission to find that the Russians had attacked his village. They had used gas, some kind of nerve gas.'

'They deny it,' Ahmed Zadeh interjected. 'But while they fight this war they are testing their new weapons. A lot of the weapons used here, land mines and rockets and everything, are new experimental weapons that have never been used in a war before. Like the gas that they used on Habib's village. There is no war like this one.'

'Habib wandered alone through the village,' Khader continued. 'Everyone was dead. All the men and the women and the children. All the generations of his family—his grandparents, from both sides, his parents, his wife's parents, his uncles and aunties, his brothers and sisters, his wife, and his children. All gone, in just one hour of one day. Even the animals, the goats and the sheep and the chickens, were all dead. Even the insects and the birds were dead. Nothing moved. Nothing lived and nothing survived.'

'He make ... a bury ... all men ... all women ... all childrens ...' Nazeer added.

'He buried them all,' Khader nodded. 'All his family, and his friends from childhood, and his neighbours. It took so long to do it, all alone, that it was a very bad business, at the end. Then, when the job was done, he took up his gun and rejoined his mujaheddin unit. But the loss had changed him in a terrible way. This time he was like a different man. This time he did everything in his power to capture a Russian, or an Afghan soldier fighting for the Russians. And when he captured one—and he *did* capture them, many of them, because he was very good at it after that— when he did capture them, he tortured them to death by impaling them on a sharpened steel spike, made from the wooden handle and the blade of the shovel he had used to bury his family. He has it now. You can see it strapped to the top of his pack. He ties the prisoners to the spike by their hands, behind their backs, with the spike touching their backs. At the moment that their strength fails them, and the metal spike begins to tear its way through their bodies, forcing its way out through their stomachs, Habib leans over them, staring into their eyes, and spits into their screaming mouths.'

Khaled Ansari, Nazeer, Ahmed Zadeh, and I stood in a deeply breathing silence, waiting for Khader to speak again.

'There is no man who knows these mountains, and the region between here and Kandahar, better than Habib,' Khader concluded, sighing wearily. 'He is the best guide. He has survived hundreds of missions in this region, and he will get us to our men in Kandahar. And there is no man more loyal or trustworthy, because there is no man in Afghanistan who hates the Russians more than Habib Abdur Rahman. But ...'

'He is completely insane,' Ahmed Zadeh offered into the silence with a Gallic shrug, and I found myself liking him, suddenly, and missing my friend Didier in the same instant. It was just the kind of pragmatic and brutally honest summary that Didier might've made.

'Yes,' Khader agreed. 'He is insane. His grief has destroyed his mind. And for as much as we need him, there is the fact that he must be watched at all times. Every mujaheddin unit from here to Herat has cast him out. We are fighting the Afghan army that serves the Russians, but the fact is that they *are* Afghans. We receive most of our information from soldiers in the Afghan army who want to *help* us to win against their Russian masters. Habib cannot make this fine distinction. He has only one understanding of this war: to kill them all quickly, or to kill them slowly. And he prefers to kill them slowly. There is such a cruel violence in him that it frightens his friends no less than his enemies. So he must be watched, while he is with us.'

'I'll watch over him,' Khaled Ansari declared firmly, and we all turned to look at our Palestinian friend. His face was set in an expression of suffering and anger and determination. The skin was tight across his eyes from brow to brow, and his mouth was drawn into a wide, flat line of tenacious resolve.

'Very well ...' Khader began, and he would've said more, but with those two words of consent Khaled left us and walked toward the slumped, forlorn figure of Habib Abdur Rahman.

Watching him leave, I was struck with a sudden, clutching instinct to cry out and stop him. It was a foolish thing—an irrational stabbing dread that I was losing him, losing another friend. And it was so ridiculous, so petty in its jealousy, that I bit down on it and said nothing. Then I watched him sit down opposite Habib. I watched him reach out to lift the gaping, murderous face of the madman until their eyes met and held, and I knew, without understanding it, that Khaled was lost to us.

I dragged my eyes from the sight of them, as boatmen drag a lake with starry hooks. My mouth was dry. My heart was a prisoner pounding on the walls inside my head. My legs felt leaden, fixed to the earth with roots of shame and dread. And as I looked up at the sheer, impassable mountains, I felt the future shudder through me like thunder trembling through the limbs and wearied vines of a storming willow.

CHAPTER THIRTY-THREE

The main road from Chaman, in those years, crossed a tributary of the Dhari River on the way to Spin Baldak, Dabrai, and Melkaarez on the highway route to Kandahar. The whole journey was less than two hundred kilometres. By car, it took a few hours. We didn't take the highway route, of course, and we didn't have cars. We rode on horseback over a hundred mountain passes, and the same journey took us more than a month.

We spent that first day camped beneath the trees. The baggage—the goods we were smuggling into Afghanistan, and our personal supplies—was scattered in a nearby pasture, covered by sheepskins and goatskins to give the appearance, if seen from the air, of a herd of livestock. There were even a few real goats tethered among the woolly bundles. When dusk finally smothered the sunset, a whisper of excitement went through the camp. We soon heard the muffled tread of hooves as our horses approached. There were twenty riding horses and fifteen pack animals. The horses were a little smaller than those I'd learned to ride on, and my heart lifted with hope that I might find them easier to control. Most of the men moved off at once to hoist and secure the baggage onto the pack animals. I started off to join them, but Nazeer and Ahmed Zadeh intercepted me, leading two horses.

'This one is mine,' Ahmed announced. 'And that one is yours.'

Nazeer handed the reins to me, and checked the straps on the short, thin Afghan saddle. Satisfying himself that all was as it should be, he nodded his approval.

'Horse good,' he said, in his grunting, gravel-throated version of good humour.

'All horse good,' I replied, quoting him. 'All man not good.'

'The horse is superb,' Ahmed concurred, casting an admiring eye over my horse. She was a chestnut mare, with a deep chest and strong, thick, relatively short legs. Her eyes were alert and unafraid. 'Nazeer picked her for you from all that we have. He was the first to reach her, and there are some disappointed men back there. He is a good judge.'

'We've got thirty men, by my count, but there's less than thirty riding horses here, for sure,' I remarked, patting at the neck of my horse, and trying to establish first contact with the beast.

'Yes, some ride and some walk,' Ahmed replied. He put his left foot in his stirrup and swung into the saddle with an effortless spring. 'We take turns. There are goats, ten goats with us, and men will herd them. And we will lose some men on our way, also. The horses are really a gift for Khader's people near Kandahar. We would be better on this trip with camels. Donkeys would be the best, in my opinion, in the narrow passes. But the horses are animals of great status. I think Khader insisted on using horses because it is important how we look when we make contact with the wild clans—the men who will want to kill us, and take our guns and our medicines. The horses will make us important in their eyes. And they will be a gift of much prestige for Khader Khan's people. He plans to give them away on the way back from Kandahar. We will ride some of the way to Kandahar, but we will walk all the way home!'

'Did you say we're going to *lose* some men?' I asked, frowning up at him.

'Yes!' he laughed. 'Some men will leave us on the way, to return to their villages. But yes, also, it might be that some will die on this journey. But *we* will live, you and I, *Inshallah*. We have good horses. It is a good beginning!'

He wheeled the horse expertly and cantered over to a mounted group who'd assembled around Khaderbhai some fifty metres away. I glanced at Nazeer. He nodded for me to mount the horse, offering me an encouraging little grimace and a muttered prayer. We both fully expected that I would be thrown, and his eyes began to close in cringing anticipation. I put my foot in the stirrup and sprang off with my right foot. I hit the saddle with a harder jolt than I'd planned, but the horse responded well to the mount and dipped her head twice, anxious to move off. Nazeer opened one eye to see me sitting comfortably on the new horse. Delighted and flushed with unselfconscious pride, he beamed one of his rare smiles at me. I tugged at the reins to turn the horse's head, and kicked backward. The horse responded calmly, but with a smart, stylish, almost prancing elegance in its movement. Snapping at once into a graceful canter, she took me toward Khaderbhai's group with no further prompting.

Nazeer ran along with us, a little behind and to the left of my horse. I glanced over my shoulder and exchanged equally wide-eyed, bewildered looks with him. The horse was making me look good. *It's gonna be okay*, I whispered to myself, knowing, as the words trotted through the thick fog of vain hope in my mind, that I'd uttered the certain jinx formula. The saying, *pride goeth ... before a fall ...* is condensed from the second collection of the Book of Proverbs, 16:18—*Pride goeth before destruction and a haughty spirit before a fall*. It's attributed to Solomon. If he *did* say it, Solomon was a man who knew horses intimately well; much better than I did as I clicked up to Khader's group and reined the horse in as though I knew—as though I would *ever* know—what I was doing in a saddle.

Khader was speaking in Pashto and Urdu and Farsi, giving the men last-minute instructions. I leaned across to whisper to Ahmed Zadeh.

'Where's the pass? I can't see it in the dark.'

'What pass?' he whispered back.

'The pass through the mountains.'

'You mean *Chaman*?' he asked, mystified by the question. 'It's back there, thirty kilometres behind us.'

'No, I mean how do we get through those mountains into Afghanistan?' I asked, nodding toward the sheer rock walls that began to rise less than a kilometre away from us, and peaked in the black night sky above.

'We don't go *through* the mountains,' Ahmed replied, gesturing a little jab with the reins in his hands. 'We go *over* them.'

'Over ... them ...'

'*Oui.*'

'Tonight.'

'*Oui.*'

'In the dark.'

'*Oui,*' he repeated seriously. 'But no problem. Habib, the *fou*, the crazy one, he knows the way. He will lead us.'

'I'm glad you told me that. I was worried, I admit, but I feel a lot better about it now.'

His white teeth flashed a laugh at me and then, with a signal from Khaled, we moved off, churning slowly into a single column that stretched to almost a hundred metres. There were ten men walking, twenty men riding, fifteen packhorses, and a herd of ten goats. I noticed with deep chagrin that Nazeer was one of the men walking. It was absurd and unnatural, somehow, that such a fine horseman was walking while I rode. I watched him, ahead of me in the darkness, watched the rhythmic roll of his thick, slightly bowed legs, and I swore to myself that I would convince him, at the first rest break, to take turns with me in riding my horse. I did eventually succeed in that resolve, but Nazeer was so reluctantly persuaded that he glowered miserably at me from the saddle, and only ever brightened when our positions reversed and he looked up at me from the rocky path.

You don't *ride* a horse over a mountain, of course. You push and drag and sometimes help to *carry* a horse over a mountain. As we neared the base of the sheer cliffs that form the Chaman range, dividing the southwestern part of Afghanistan from Pakistan, it became clear that there were in fact gaps and pathways and trails leading into and over them. What had seemed to be smooth walls of bare, mountainous rock proved on closer inspection to be formed in undulating waves of ravines and tiered crevices. Ledges of stone and lime-encrusted barren earth wound through those rocky slopes. In places the ledges were so wide and well flattened as to seem like a man-made road. In places they were so jagged and narrow that every footstep of horse or man was brooded over with careful, trembling consideration before it was made. And the whole of it, the whole stumbling, slipping, dragging, shoving breach of the mountain barrier, was done in the dark.

Ours was a small caravan when compared to the once mighty tribal processions that had plied the silk route between Turkey and China and India, but in that time of war our numbers were remarkable. The fear of being seen from the air was a constant worry. Khaderbhai imposed a strict blackout: no cigarettes, torches, or lamps on the march. There was a quarter moon that first night, but occasionally the slippery paths led us through narrow defiles where smooth rock rose up sharply, drowning us in shadows. In those black-walled corridors it was impossible to see my own hand held in front of my face. The whole column inched its way along the blind clefts in the rock wall, men and horses and goats pressed hard against the stone, and shuffling into one another.

In the centre of just such a black ravine, I heard a low whining sound that rose quickly in pitch. I was walking, or sliding my feet, between two horses. I had the reins of my horse in my right hand, and the tail of the horse in front wrapped around my left hand. My face was sliding against the granite wall, and the path beneath my feet was no wider than the length of my arm. As the sound rose in its pitch and intensity, the two horses reared in the same instinct, and stamped their hooves in staccato fear. Then the whining sound suddenly erupted in a roar that rattled the whole mountain, and ripped into an explosive, shrieking scream of satanic noise directly over our heads.

The horse to my left bucked and reared in front of me, pulling its tail from my hand. Trying to retrieve it, I lost my footing in the dark and slid to my knees, my face scraping against the rock wall. My own horse was terrified, as frightened as I was myself, and it struggled forward on the narrow path, following an impulse to run. I still held the reins, and I used them to pull myself to my feet, but the horse rammed into me again with its head, and I felt myself slide backward from the path. Fear stabbed into my chest and crushed my heart as I stumbled, slid, and fell off the path into the lightless void. I fell the full length of my body, and stopped with a wrenching snap as the reins in my hand held fast.

I was dangling in free space over a black abyss. Millimetre by millimetre I felt the downward creep, the easing, slipping creak of leather as I slid further from the edge of the narrow ledge. I could hear the shouts of men, all along the ledge above me. They were trying to calm the animals, and they were calling out names to account for their friends. I could hear the horses screaming their fear and snorting in protest. The air in the ravine was thick with the smells of piss and horseshit and frightened man-sweat. And I could hear the scrabbling, scraping clatter of hooves as my own horse struggled to maintain its footing. I suddenly realised that as strong as the horse undoubtedly was, its foothold on the crumbling, jagged path was so precarious that my weight might've been enough to drag it over the ledge with me.

Flailing with my left hand in the impenetrable dark, I grasped the reins and began to drag myself back up to the ledge. I put one set of fingertips on the edge of the stony path and then choked a scream as I slipped backwards into the dark crevasse. The reins held again, and I dangled over the gap, but my situation was desperate. The horse, fearing that it would be dragged over the edge, was shaking and dipping its head violently. An intelligent animal, she was trying to rid herself of the bridle, bit, and harness. At any moment, I knew, she would succeed. I gave a snarl of rage through clenched teeth and dragged myself to the ledge once more.

Scrambling up to my knees, I gasped in sweating exhaustion and then, working to an intuition that starts in fear and spikes on a jet of adrenaline, I jumped up and to my right as my neighbour's horse kicked out in the black, blind night. If I hadn't moved, it would've struck me on the side of the head, and my war would've ended there and then. Instead, the life-saving reflex to jump meant that the blow struck my hip and thigh, driving me into the wall and against my own horse's head. I threw my arms around the animal's neck, as much to comfort myself with its touch as to support my numb leg and aching hip. I was still cradling her head in my arms when I heard shuffling steps and felt someone's hands slide from the wall onto my back.

'Lin! Is that you?' Khaled Ansari asked into the darkness.

'Khaled! Yeah! Are you okay?'

'Sure. Jet fighters! Fuck me! Two of them. Not far overhead. A hundred feet, man, no more than that. *Fuck*! They were really smashing up the sound barrier! What a noise!'

'Were they Russians?'

'No, I don't think so. Not this close to the border. More likely they were Pakistani fighters, American planes with Pak pilots, crossing a little into Afghan space to keep the Russians on their toes. They won't go too far. The Russian MiG pilots are too good. But the Paks like to remind them they're here, just the same. Are you sure you're all right?'

'Sure, sure,' I lied. 'I'll be a lot better when we get out of this fuckin' dark. Call me a weak motherfucker, but I like to see where I'm going when I'm trying to lead a horse along a ledge outside a ten-storey building.'

'Me, too,' Khaled laughed. It was the small, sad laugh, but I drenched myself in the reassurance of it. 'Who was behind you?'

'Ahmed,' I replied. 'Ahmed Zadeh. I heard him swearing in French back there. I think he's okay. Nazeer was behind him. And I know Mahmoud, the Iranian, was near him somewhere. There were about ten behind me, I think, counting the two guys herding the goats.'

'I'll go check,' Khaled said, giving me a comforting slap on the shoulder. 'You keep going. Just slide along the wall for another hundred yards or so. It's not far. There's still some moonlight when you get out there, outside this ravine. Good luck.'

And for a few moments, when I reached that pale oasis of moonlight, I felt safe and sure of myself. Then we pushed on, hugging the cold, grey stone of the canyon-silo, and in minutes we were in blackness again, with nothing but faith and fear and the will to survive.

We travelled so often at night that we sometimes seemed to be *feeling* our way to Kandahar like blind men, with our fingertips. And, like blind men, we trusted Habib, without question, as our guide. None of the Afghans in our group lived in the border region, and they were as dependent on his knowledge of those secret passes and fortuitous ledge-pathways as I was.

When he wasn't leading the column, however, Habib inspired far less confidence. I came upon him once as I scrambled over some rocks to find a place to take a piss during a rest stop. He was kneeling in front of a roughly square slab of stone, and beating his forehead against it. I leapt down to stop him, and discovered that he was weeping, sobbing. The blood from his torn forehead ran down his face to mix with the tears in his beard. I poured a little water from my canteen onto a corner of my scarf, and wiped the blood from his head to examine the wounds. They were rough and jagged, but largely superficial. He allowed me to lead him, unprotesting, back to the camp. Khaled rushed up at once and helped me to apply ointment and a clean bandage to his forehead.

'I left him alone,' Khaled muttered when the job was done. 'I thought he was praying. He told me he wanted to pray. But I had a feeling ...'

'I think he *was* praying,' I answered.

'I'm worried,' Khaled confessed, looking into my eyes with a febrile mix of heartbreak and fear. 'He keeps setting mantraps all over the place. He's got twenty grenades on him under that cloak. I've tried to explain to him that a mantrap has no conscience—it might just as easily kill a local nomad shepherd, or one of *us*, as a Russian or an Afghan soldier. He doesn't get it. He just grins at me, and does it a little bit more secret. He rigged some of the horses with explosives yesterday. He said it was to make sure the Russians didn't get their hands on them. I said to him, what about us? What if the Russians get their hands on us? Should *we* be rigged with explosives, too? He said it was a problem he worried about all the time — how to make sure we were dead before the Russians got their hands on us, and how to kill more Russians *after* we were dead.'

'Does Khader know?'

'No. I'm trying to keep Habib in line. I know where he's coming from, Lin. I've been there. The first couple years after my family was killed, I was as crazy as he is. I know what's going on inside him. He's filled up with so many dead friends and enemies that he's kind of locked on one course — killing Russians — and until he snaps out of it, I just gotta stay with him as much as I can, and watch his ass.'

'I think you should tell Khader,' I sighed, shaking my head.

'I will,' he sighed in return. 'I will. Soon. I'll talk to him soon. He'll get better. Habib will get better. He's getting better in some ways. I can talk to him real well now. He'll make it.'

But as the weeks of the journey passed, we all watched Habib more closely, more fearfully, and little by little we all realised why so many other mujaheddin units had cast him out.

With our senses alert for menace from without and within, we travelled by night, and sometimes by day, north along the mountainous border towards Pathaan Khel. Near the *khel*, or village, we swung north-north-west into deserted mountainous terrain that was veined with cold, fresh, sweet-water streams. Habib laid out a route that was roughly equidistant between towns and larger villages, always avoiding the main arteries that local people used. We trudged between Pathaan Khel and Khairo Thaana; between Humai Khaarez and Haji Aagha Muhammad. We forded rivers between Loe Kaarez and Yaaru. We zigzagged between Mullah Mustafa and the little village of Abdul Hamid.

Local pirates, demanding tribute, stopped us three times on the way. Each time, they revealed themselves at first in high vantage points, with guns trained on us, before their ground forces swept from hiding to lock the way forward and cut off our retreat. Each time, Khader raised his green-and-white mujaheddin flag emblazoned with the Koranic phrase:

Inalillahey wa ina illai hi rajiaon
We come from God, and unto God do we return

Although the local clans didn't recognise Khader's standard, they respected its language and intent. Their fierce, belligerent postures remained, however, until Khader, Nazeer, and our Afghan fighters explained to them that the group was travelling with, and under the protection of, an American. When the local pirates had examined my passport and stared hard into my blue-grey eyes, they welcomed us as comrades-in-arms, and invited us to drink tea and feast with them. The invitation was a euphemism for the honour of paying them a tribute. Although none of the pirates we encountered wanted to upset the critically important American aid that helped to sustain them in the long years of the war by attacking an American-sponsored caravan, it was unthinkable that we might pass through their territory without providing some plunder. Khader had brought a supply of baksheesh goods for that very purpose. There were silks in peacock blue and green, with rich interweavings of gold thread. There were hatchets and thick-bladed knives and sewing kits. There were Zeiss binoculars—Khader had given me a pair, and I used them every day—and magnifying spectacles for reading the Koran, and solid, Indian-made automatic watches. And for the clan leaders there was a small hoard of gold tablets, each weighing one tola, or about ten grams, and embossed with the Afghan laurel.

Khader hadn't merely anticipated those pirate attacks; he'd counted on them. Once the formal courtesies and tribute negotiations were concluded, Khader arranged with each local clan leader to re-supply our caravan. The re-supply provided us with rations while we were on the move, and also guaranteed us food and animal feed at fraternal villages that were under the control or protection of the clan leader.

The re-supply was essential. The munitions, machine parts, and medicines that we carried were priorities, and left us little room for surplus cargo. Thus we carried a little food for the horses—two days' ration at most—but we carried no food at all for ourselves. Each man had a canteen of water, but it was understood that it was an emergency ration, to be used sparingly for ourselves and the horses. Many were the days we passed with no more than one glass of water to drink, and one small piece of naan bread to eat. I was a vegetarian, without being a fanatic about it, when I started on that journey. For years I'd usually preferred to eat my fruit and vegetable diet when it was available. Three weeks into the trek, after dragging horses across mountains and freezing rivers, and trembling from hunger, I fell on the lamb and goat meat that the pirates offered us, and ripped the flesh half-cooked from the bones with my teeth.

The steep mountain slopes of the country were barren, burned of life by biting wintry winds, but every flat plain, no matter how small, was a vivid, living green. There were wild flowers with red, starry faces, and others with sky-blue pom-pom heads. There were short, scrubby bushes with tiny yellow leaves that the goats enjoyed, and many varieties of wild grasses topped with feathery bowers of dried seed for the horses. There were lime-green mosses on many of the rocks, and paler lichens on others. The impact of those tender, viridescent carpets between the endlessly undulating crocodile's back of naked stone mountains was far greater than it might've been in a more fertile and equable landscape. We responded to each new sight of a softly carpeted incline or tufted, leafy moor with similar pleasure—a deep, subliminal response to the vitality in the colour green. More than a few of the tough, hardened fighters, trudging between the walking horses, stooped to gather a little clutch of flowers so that they might simply feel the beauty of them in their dry and calloused hands.

My status as Khader's American helped us to negotiate the badlands of the local pirates, but it also cost us a week when we were stopped for the third and last time. In an effort to avoid the little village of Abdul Hamid, our guide Habib led us into a small canyon that was just wide enough for three or four horses to ride side-by-side. Steep rock walls rose up on either side of the canyon trail for almost a kilometre before the funnel opened out into a much longer, wider valley. It was the perfect place for an ambush and, in anticipation, Khader rode at the head of our column with his green-and-white banner unfurled.

The challenge came before we were a hundred metres into the gorge. There was a chilling ululation from high above—men's voices raised in an imitation of the high-pitched, warbling wail of tribal women—and a sudden tumble of small boulders as a little avalanche spilled into the canyon before us. Like others, I turned in my saddle to see that a platoon of local tribesmen had taken up positions behind us with a variety of weapons trained on our backs. We halted immediately, at the first sound. Khader slowly rode on alone for some two hundred metres. He stopped there, with his back straight in the saddle, and his standard fluttering in the strong, chill breeze.

The seconds of a long minute ticked away with the guns behind us, and the rocks poised above. Then a lone figure appeared, riding toward Khader on a tall camel. Although the two-humped Bactrian camel is native to Afghanistan, the rider's was a single-humped Arabian camel; the type bred by long distance cameleers of the northern Tajik region for use in extremes of cold. It had a mop of hair on its head, thick and shaggy neck-fur, and long, powerful legs. The man riding that impressive beast was tall and lean, and appeared to be at least ten years older than Khader's fit sixty-plus. He wore a long, white shirt over white Afghan pants, and a knee-length, sleeveless, black serge vest. A snowy-white turban of sumptuous length was piled majestically on his head. His grey-white beard was trimmed away from the upper lip and the mouth, descending from his chin to nudge his thin chest.

Some of my friends in Bombay had called that kind of beard a Wahabi, after the sternly orthodox Saudi Arabian Muslims who trimmed their beards in that way to imitate the style preferred by the Prophet. It was a sign to us, in the canyon, that the stranger possessed at least as much moral authority as temporal power. The latter was emphasised with spectacular effect by the antique, long-barrelled jezail that he held upright, balanced on his hip. The muzzle-loaded rifle was decorated along all of its wooden surfaces with gleaming discs, scrolls, and diamond shapes fashioned from brass and silver coins and polished to a dazzling brilliance.

The man drew up beside Khaderbhai, facing us and within a hand's reach of our Khan. His bearing was commanding, and it was clear that he was accustomed to a comprehensive respect. He was, in fact, one of the very few men I ever came to know who equalled Abdel Khader Khan in the esteem—perhaps even the veneration—that he commanded from others with nothing more, or less, than his bearing and the sheer force of his fully realised life.

After a lengthy discussion, Khaderbhai wheeled his horse gently to face us.

'Mister John!' he called to me, using the first name in my false American passport, and speaking in English. 'Come here to me, please!'

I kicked backward, uttering what I hoped was an encouraging sound. All eyes on the ground and above us were on me, I knew, and in the swollen, silent seconds I had a vision of the horse throwing me to the ground at Khader's feet. But the mare responded with a smart, prancing canter, and found her own way through the column to stop at Khader's side.

'This is Hajji Mohammed,' Khader announced. He swept around us with a broad movement of his open palm. 'He is the Khan, the leader of all the people, in all the clans, and all the families here.'

'*Asalaam aleikum*,' I said in greeting, holding my hand over my heart as a gesture of respect.

Believing me to be an infidel, the leader didn't respond to my greeting. The Prophet Mohammed adjured his followers to return the peaceful greeting of a believer with an even more polite greeting. Thus the greeting *Asalaam aleikum, Peace be with you*, should've been answered, at the very least, with *Wa aleikum salaam wa rahmatullah, And with you be peace and the compassion of Allah*. Instead, the old man stared down from his perch on the camel and greeted me with a hard question.

'When will you give us Stingers to fight with?'

It was the same question every Afghan had asked me, the American, since we'd entered the country. And although Khaderbhai translated it for me again, I understood the words and I'd rehearsed the answer.

'It will be soon, if Allah wills it, and the sky will be as free as the mountains.'

It was a good answer and Hajji Mohammed was pleased with it, but it was a much better question, and it deserved a better response than my hopeful lie. The Afghans, from Mazar-i-Sharif to Kandahar, knew that if the Americans had given them Stinger missiles at the outbreak of the war, the mujaheddin would've beaten the invaders back within months. Stingers meant that the hated and mortally effective Russian helicopters could be smashed from the skies. Even the formidable MiG fighters were vulnerable to a hand-launched Stinger missile. Without the insuperable advantage of the air, the Russians and their Afghan army proxies would be forced to fight a ground war against the mujaheddin resistance—a ground war they could never win.

Cynics among the Afghans believed that the Americans refused to supply Stingers, for the first seven years of the conflict, because they wanted Russia to win just enough of the Afghan War to over-reach and over-commit themselves. If and when the Stingers finally arrived, the Russians would suffer a defeat that cost them so much in men and resources that their entire Soviet Empire would collapse.

And whether the cynics were right or wrong, the deadly game did play itself out in exactly that way. The Stinger missiles did turn the tide of the conflict, when they were finally introduced, a few months after Khader led us into Afghanistan. The Russians were so weakened by the war of resistance fought by those very Afghan villagers, and millions like them, that their monstrous, Caligulan empire crumbled around them. It worked, it played out that way, and what it cost was a million Afghan lives. What it cost was one-third of the population forced from their homeland. What it cost was one of the largest forced migrations in human history—three-and-a-half million refugees moving through the Khyber Pass to Peshawar, and a million more exiled in Iran, India, and the Muslim republics of the Soviet Union. What it cost was fifty thousand men, women, and children with one or more limbs amputated through land-mine explosions. What it cost was the Afghan heart and soul.

And I, a wanted criminal, working for a mafia crime lord, impersonated an American and looked those people in the eye, and lied to them about the weapons I couldn't give them.

Hajji Mohammed liked my answer so much that he invited our group to attend the wedding celebrations of his youngest son. Concerned that a refusal might offend the elderly leader, and genuinely touched by the generous invitation, Khader accepted. When all the tributes were exacted —Hajji Mohammed drove a hard bargain, demanding and receiving Khader's own horse as an additional, personal gift—Khaderbhai, Nazeer, and I agreed to accompany the leader to his khel.

The rest of our column made camp in a pastured valley with plentiful fresh water. The break in our forced march allowed the men to groom and rest the horses. The pack animals were in constant need of attention and, with the cargo concealed in a protected cave, the unburdened beasts were free to gambol and roam. Our men prepared to feast on four roasting sheep, aromatic Indian rice, and fresh green-leaf tea provided by Hajji's village as their contribution to our part in the jihad. With the practical business of tributes negotiated and received, the senior men of Hajji Mohammed's village—like all the Afghan clan leaders we'd encountered on the journey—acknowledged us as fighters in the same cause, and offered every help they could provide. As Khader, Nazeer, and I rode away from the temporary camp toward the khel, the sounds of singing and laughter followed us, echo chasing playful echo. It was the first time we'd heard that lightness of heart from our men in the twenty-three days of the journey.

Hajji Mohammed's village was in celebration when we arrived. His profitable, bloodless encounter with our column of armed men had added to the gathering thrill of anticipation for the wedding. Khader explained how the elaborate rituals of Afghan matrimony had been unfolding for months before we'd arrived. There'd been ceremonial visits between the family of the groom, and the family of the bride. In every case, small gifts such as handkerchiefs or scented sweets had been exchanged, and precise courtesies were observed. The bride's dowry of extravagantly embroidered cloths, imported silks, perfumes, and jewellery had been publicly displayed for all to admire, and was then held in trust for her by the groom's family. The groom had even visited his bride-to-be in secret, and he'd presented her with personal gifts as he spoke to her. According to custom, it was strictly forbidden for him to be seen by the men in her family during that secret visit, but custom also required him to be helped by the girl's mother. The dutiful mother, Khader assured me, had remained with the couple while they spoke to one another for the first time, and had acted as their chaperone. With all that achieved, the couple was ready for the culmination of the marriage ceremony itself, to be held in three days' time.

Khader took me through the finest details of the rituals, and it seemed to me that there was a kind of urgency in his normally gentle, teacher's manner. At first I guessed—rightly, I think—that he was reacquainting himself with the customs of his people, after his five long decades in exile. He was reliving the scenes and celebrations of his youth, and he was proving to himself that he was still Afghan, in all that his heart knew and felt. But as the lessons continued through the following days, and the intensity of his attention to them never failed, I finally realised that the long explanations and histories were for my benefit more than his. He was giving me a crash course in the culture of the nation where I might be killed and where my body might be laid to rest. He was making sense of it—my life with him, and my possible death—in the only way that he knew. And understanding that, without ever speaking of it to him, I listened dutifully and learned everything I could.

Kinsmen, friends, and other invitees streamed into Hajji's village during those days. The four main houses of Hajji Mohammed's fortress-like men's *kal'a*, or compound, were tall, square, mud-brick buildings. High walls surrounded the kal'a, and one large dwelling stood in each of the four corners. The women's kal'a was a separate set of buildings behind even higher walls. In the men's compound we slept on the floor and cooked all our own meals. It was already crowded in the house that Khader, Nazeer, and I joined but, as new men arrived from distant villages, we all simply squashed in further. Sleeping in our clothes, we top-and-tailed across the whole floor, each man sleeping with his head beside the feet of the next. There's a theory that snoring at night in sleep is a sub-conscious defence reflex—a warning sound that frightened potential predators away from the mouth of the cave when our lower-Palaeolithic ancestors huddled in vulnerable sleep. That group of Afghan nomads, cameleers, sheep and goat herders, farmers, and guerrilla fighters lent credibility to the idea, for they snored so thunderously and with such persistent ferocity through the long, cold night that they would've frightened a pride of ravenous lions into scattering like startled mice.

During the day, the same men prepared complex food dishes for the Friday wedding. Those dishes included flavoured yoghurts, piquant goat's or sheep's milk cheeses, oven-baked cakes made with corn flour, dates, nuts, and wild honey, biscuits baked with richly churned goat's milk butter and, of course, a variety of halal meats and vegetable pulao. While the foods were being prepared, I watched as men dragged a foot-operated grinding wheel into an open space, and the groom devoted a tense hour to putting a razor's edge to a large, ornate dagger. The bride's father watched that effort with a critical eye. After satisfying himself that the weapon was suitably lethal, he gravely accepted it as a gift from the younger man.

'The groom has just sharpened the knife that the bride's father will use on him, if he ever mistreats the girl,' Khader explained to me as we watched.

'That's a pretty good custom,' I mused.

'It is not a custom,' Khader corrected me, with a laugh. 'It is his idea— the bride's father. I have never heard of it before this. But if it works, it might *become* a custom.'

Each day the men also rehearsed ritual group-dances with the musicians and singers who'd been hired to complement the formal, public celebration. The dancing gave me the chance to see a new and completely unexpected side of Nazeer. He hurled himself into the whirling chorus line of men with grace and passion. Moreover, my short, bow-legged

friend, whose bulky arms seemed to jut outward from the tree-trunk of his thick neck and chest, was by far the best dancer in the entire assembly, and quickly earned their admiration. The whole secret and invisible inner life of the man, his full creative and spiritual endowment, was expressed in the dance. And that face—I'd said, once, that I'd never seen another human face in which the smile was so utterly defeated—that scowl-creased face was transfigured in the dance until his honest, selfless beauty was so radiant that it filled my eyes with tears.

'Tell me once more,' Abdel Khader Khan commanded, with a roguish smile in his eye, as we watched the dancers from a vantage point beneath a shaded wall.

I laughed. When I turned to look at him, he laughed as well.

'Go on,' he urged. 'Do it to please me.'

'But you've heard this twenty times from me already. How about you answer me a question instead?'

'You tell me once more, and then I will answer your question.'

'Okay. Here goes. The universe began about fifteen billion years ago, in almost absolute simplicity, and it's been getting more and more complex ever since. This movement from the simple to the complex is built into the web and weave of the universe, and it's called the tendency toward complexity. We're the products of this complexification, and so are the birds, and the bees, and the trees, and the stars, and even the *galaxies* of stars. And if we were to get wiped out in a cosmic explosion, like an aster-oid impact or something, some other expression of our level of complex-ity would emerge, because that's what the universe *does*. And this is likely to be going on all over the universe. How am I doing so far?'

I waited, but he didn't reply, so I continued with my summary.

'Okay, the final or ultimate complexity—the place where all this com-plexity is going—is what, or *who*, we might call God. And anything that promotes, enhances, or accelerates this movement toward God is good. Anything that inhibits, impedes, or prevents it is evil. And if we want to know if something is good or evil—something like war and killing and smuggling guns to mujaheddin guerrillas, for example—then we ask the questions: *What if everyone did this thing? Would that help us, in this bit of the universe, to get there, or would it hold us back?* And then we have a pretty good idea whether it's good or evil. What's more important, we know *why* it's good or evil. There, how was that?'

'Very good,' he said without looking at me. While I'd run through the summary of his cosmological model, he'd closed his eyes and nodded his head, pursing his lips in a half smile. When I concluded it, he turned to look at me, and the smile widened as the pleasure and the mischief sparked in his eyes. 'You know, if you wanted to do it, you could express this idea every bit as well and as accurately as I do. And I've been working on it and thinking about it for almost all of my life. I cannot tell you how happy it makes me feel to hear you tell it to me in your own words.'

'I think the words are yours, Khaderji. You've coached me often enough. But I do have a couple of problems. Do I get my question now?'

'Yes.'

'Okay. We've got things like rocks in the world that *aren't* alive, and living things like trees and fish and people. Your cosmology doesn't tell me where life and consciousness come from. If rocks are made out of the same stuff that people are made out of, how come rocks aren't alive, but people are? I mean, where does life come from?'

'I know you well enough to be sure that you want me to give you a short, direct answer to this question.'

'I think I'd like a short, direct answer to *every* question,' I replied, laughing.

He raised an eyebrow at the foolishness of my flippant response and then shook his head slowly.

'Do you know the English philosopher Bertrand Russell? Have you read any of his books?'

'Yeah. I read some of his stuff—at university, and in prison.'

'He was a favourite of my dear Mr. Mackenzie Esquire,' Khader smiled. 'I do not often agree with Bertrand Russell's conclusions, but I do like the way he arrives at them. Anyway, he once said, *Anything that can be put in a nutshell should remain there.* And I do agree with him about that. But now, the answer to your question is this: life is a feature of all things. We could call it a characteristic, which is one of my favourite English words. If you do not speak English as your first language, the word "characteristic" has an amazing sound—like rapping on a drum, or breaking kindling wood for a fire. To continue, every atom in the universe has the characteristic of life. The more complex way that atoms get put together, the more complex is the expression of the characteristic of life. A rock is a very simple arrangement of atoms, so the life in a rock is so simple that we cannot see it. A cat is a very complex arrangement of atoms, so the life in a cat is very obvious. But life is there, in everything, even in a rock, and even when we cannot see it.'

'Where did you get this idea? Is it in the Koran?'

'Actually, it is a concept that appears in one way or another in most of the great religions. I have changed it slightly to suit what we have learned about the world in the last few hundred years. But the Holy Koran gives me my inspiration for this kind of study, because the Koran commands me to study everything, and learn everything, in order to serve Allah.'

'But where does this *life characteristic* come from?' I insisted, sure that I had him trapped in a reductionist dead-end at last.

'Life, and all the other characteristics of all the things in the universe, such as consciousness, and free will, and the tendency toward complexity, and even love, was given to the universe by light, at the beginning of time as we know it.'

'At the Big Bang? Is that what you're talking about?'

'Yes. The Big Bang expansion happened from a point called a singularity—another of my favourite five-syllable English words—that is almost infinitely dense, and almost infinitely hot, and yet it occupies no space and no time, as we know those things. The point is a boiling cauldron of light energy. Something caused it to expand—we don't know yet what caused it—and from light, all the particles and all the atoms came to exist, along with space and time and all the forces that we know. So, light gave every little particle at the beginning of the universe a set of characteristics, and as those particles combine in more complex ways, the characteristics show themselves in more and more complex ways.'

He paused, watching my face as I struggled with the concepts and questions and emotions that looped in my mind. *He got away from me again*, I thought, suddenly furious with him for having an answer to my question, and yet struck with admiring respect for the same reason. There was always something eerily incongruous in the wise lectures— sometimes they were like sermons—of the mafia don Abdel Khader Khan. Sitting there against a stone wall in an all-but-Stone Age village in Afghanistan, with a cargo of smuggled guns and antibiotics nearby, the dissonance created by his calm, profound discourse about good and evil, and light and life and consciousness, was enough to fill me with exasperated irritation.

'What I have just told you is the relationship between consciousness and matter,' Khader proclaimed, pausing again until he had my eye. 'This is a kind of test, and now you know it. This is a test that you should apply to every man who tells you that he knows the meaning of life. Every guru you meet and every teacher, every prophet and every philosopher, should answer these two questions for you: *What is an objective, universally acceptable definition of good and evil?* And, *What is the relationship between consciousness and matter?* If he cannot answer these two questions, as I have done, you know that he has not passed the test.'

'How do you *know* all this physics?' I demanded. 'All this about particles and singularities and Big Bangs?'

He stared at me, reading the full measure of the unconscious insult: *How is it that an Afghan gangster like you knows so much about science and higher knowledge?* I looked back at him, remembering a day at the slum with Johnny Cigar when I'd made the cruel mistake of assuming him to be ignorant simply because he was poor.

'There is a saying—*When the student is ready, the teacher appears*—do you know it?' he asked, laughing. It seemed that he was laughing at me, rather than with me.

'Yes,' I whistled patiently, through clenched teeth.

'Well, just at the point in my studies of philosophy and religion when I came to need the special knowledge of a scientist, one appeared for me. I knew that there were many answers for me in the science of life and stars and chemistry. But, unfortunately, these were not the things that my dear Mackenzie Esquire taught to me, except in the most elementary fashion. Then I met a physicist, a man who was working at the Bhabha Atomic Research Centre in Bombay. He was a very good man, but he had a weakness for gambling at that time. He found himself in big trouble. He lost a lot of money that was not his to lose. He was gambling at one of the clubs owned by a man I knew well—a man who worked for me, if I needed it. And there was more trouble. The scientist was involved with a woman—he fell in love with her, and he did stupid things for the sake of this love, and so there were many dangers. When he came to me, I solved the problems of this scientist, and kept all the matters strictly between us. No-one else ever knew the details of his indiscretions, or of my involvement in solving them. And, in exchange for this, the man has been teaching me ever since that day. His name is Wolfgang Persis, and I have arranged it that you will meet him, if you wish, soon after we return.'

'How long has he been teaching you?'

'We have been studying together once every week for the past seven years.'

'*Jesus!*' I gasped, thinking, with a little curl of mean delight, that wise and mighty Khader hacked out his pound of flesh when it suited him. In another heartbeat I was ashamed of the thought: I loved Khader Khan enough to follow him into a war. Wasn't it possible that the scientist loved him just as well? And in thinking that, I knew I was jealous of the man, the scientist I didn't know and probably would never meet. Jealousy, like the flawed love that bears it, has no respect for time or space or wisely reasoned argument. Jealousy can raise the dead with a single, spiteful taunt, or hate a perfect stranger for nothing more than the sound of his name.

'You are asking about life,' Khader said gently, changing tack, 'because you are thinking about death. And you are thinking about the taking of a life, if it happens that you must shoot a man. Am I right in this?'

'Yeah,' I muttered. He was right, but the killing that preoccupied me wasn't in Afghanistan. The life I wanted to take was perched on a throne, in a secret room in a grotesque brothel called The Palace, in Bombay. Madame Zhou.

'Remember,' Khader said insistently, resting his hand on my forearm to emphasise his words. 'Sometimes it is necessary to do the wrong thing for the right reasons. The important thing is to be sure that our reasons are right, and that we admit the wrong—that we do not lie to ourselves, and convince ourselves that what we do is right.'

And later, as the wedding whirled and clamoured to the last wail of its rejoicing, and as we rejoined our men and scrambled, clattered, and strained our way across new mountains, I tried to unwind the wreath of thorns that Khader had coiled around my heart with his words. *The wrong thing for the right reasons* ... Once before he'd tormented me with that phrase. I chewed at it, in my mind, as a bear will chew at a leather strap that binds it by the leg. In my life, the wrong things were almost always done for the wrong reasons. Even the *right* things that I did were too often goaded by the wrong reasons.

A gloomy mood enwrapped me. It was a sullen, doubting temper that I couldn't shake off, and as we rode into the winter I thought often of

Anand Rao, my neighbour from the slum. I remembered Anand's face smiling at me through the metal grille of the visitor's room at Arthur Road Prison: that gentle, handsome face, so serene, and softened with the peace that had suffused his heart. He'd done the wrong thing for the right reasons, as he saw it. He'd calmly accepted the punishment that he'd *earned*, as he said to me, as if it was a privilege or a right. And at last, after too many thinking days and nights, I cursed Anand. I cursed him to drive him from my mind because a voice kept telling me—my own voice, or maybe it was my father's—that I would never know that peace. I would never come to that Eden in the soul, where acceptance of punishment and acknowledgement of wrong and right roll away the troubles that lodge like stones in the barren field of an exiled heart.

Moving north again at night, we climbed and crossed the narrow Kussa Pass in the Hada Mountains. The journey of thirty crow-kilometres was closer to one hundred and fifty climbing-and-descending-kilometres for us. Then, exposed to the wide sky, we travelled over flatter land for almost fifty kilometres to cross the Arghastan River and its tributaries three times before we reached the foothills of the Shahbad Pass. And there, with my mind still choked on its rights and wrongs, we were fired on for the first time.

Khader's command that we commence the climb of the Shahbad Pass without a rest saved many lives, including my own, that cold evening. We were exhausted after the headlong, trotting march across the open plain. Every man among us hoped for rest at the foothills of the pass, but Khader urged us on, riding the length of the column and shouting for us to keep on, keep on, and keep up the pace. Thus we were moving fast when the first shots were fired. I heard the sound: a hollow metal tapping, as if someone was rapping on the side of an empty gasoline can with a piece of copper pipe. Stupidly, I didn't associate it with gunfire at first, and I kept trudging forward, leading my horse by the reins. Then the bullets found their range, and they smashed into the ground, our column, and the rock walls around us. The men scrambled for cover. I fell to the ground, grinding my face into the dust of the stony path and telling myself that it wasn't really happening, that I hadn't seen the man in front of me ripped open across his back as he stumbled forward. Our men began firing from all around me. And rapid-breathing the dust into my mouth, stiff with fear, I was in the war.

I might've stayed there, with my face in the dirt and my heart thumping seismic terror into the earth, if it wasn't for my horse. I'd lost the reins, and the horse was rearing in fright. Fearing that it might trample me, I scrambled to my feet and scrabbled at the flailing reins to regain control of her. The horse that had been so impressively obedient to that point was suddenly the worst of the entire column. She reared and then bucked. She stamped her hooves and tried to drag me backward. She thrashed and drove us in tight circles, trying to find an angle where she could kick backward at me. She even bit me, snapping at my forearm and causing intense pain through three layers of clothes.

I glanced along the line, left and right. Those nearest to the pass were making a run for it, leading their animals toward the rocky shelves for shelter. Those immediately in front of me and behind me had managed to bring their horses down, and they crouched beside or behind them. Only my horse was still rearing and widely visible. Without a horseman's skill, it's a damn hard thing to convince a horse to lie down in a battle zone. Other horses were screaming in fear, and each whinny of terror put more panic into mine. I wanted to save her, to bring her down and make less of a target of her, but I was afraid for myself as well. The enemy fire slammed into the rocks above and beside me, and with every shattering sound I flinched like a deer nudging a thorn-hedge.

It's a bizarre feeling, waiting for a bullet to strike: the nearest experience I can recall that's anything like it is falling through space, and waiting for the safety chute to open. There's a special taste; a unique taste. There's a different smell on your skin. And there's a hardness in the eyes, as if they're suddenly made of cold metal. Just when I decided to give up and let the animal fend for herself, she buckled easily and followed my dragging arms down and onto her side. I hurled myself down with her, using her swollen middle as a shield. In an attempt to calm her, I reached over to pat at her shoulder. My hand squelched in a bloody wound. Raising my head, I saw that the horse had been struck twice, once high on the shoulder and once in the belly. The wounds were streaming blood with every heaving breath, and the horse was crying—I have no other word for it. The sound was a breathy, stuttering, whining sob. I put my head against hers, and wrapped my arm around her neck.

The men in my group concentrated their fire on a ridge about one hundred and fifty metres away. With my body pressed hard against the ground, I peeked over the mane of my horse to see dusty plumes rise and spill over the distant ridge as bullet after bullet rammed into the earth.

And then it was over. I heard Khader shouting in three languages for the men to stop shooting. We waited for long minutes, in a stillness that groaned and moaned and sobbed. I heard footsteps crunching the stones nearby, and looked up to see Khaled Ansari running toward me at a crouch.

'Are you okay, Lin?'

'Yeah,' I answered, wondering then for the first time if I, too, had been shot. I ran my hands over my legs and arms. 'Yeah, I'm all here. I think I'm still in one piece. But they shot my horse. She's —'

'I'm doing a count!' he interrupted me, holding up the palms of both hands to calm me and stop me speaking. 'Khader sent me to see if you're okay and do a head count. I'll be back soon. Stay here and don't move.'

'But she's —'

'She's *finished*!' he hissed and then softened his tone. 'The horse is gone, Lin. She's done for. She's not the only one. Habib's gonna finish them off. Just stay here and keep your head down. I'll be back.'

He ran off at a crouch, stopping here and there along the column behind me. My horse was breathing hard, whimpering with every third or fourth chugging breath. The flow of blood was slow but steady. The wound in her belly was oozing a dark fluid that was darker than blood. I tried to soothe her, stroking her neck, and then I realised that I hadn't given her a name. It seemed grievously cruel, somehow, for her to die without a name. I searched my mind, and when I pulled the net of thought up from the blue-black deep there was a name, glittering and true.

'I'm going to call you Claire,' I whispered into the mare's ear. 'She was a beautiful girl. She always made me look good, wherever we went. When I was with her I always looked like I knew what I was doing. And I didn't start to love her, really, until she walked away from me for the last time. She said I was *interested in everything and committed to nothing*. She said that to me once. And she was right. She was right.'

I was babbling, raving, in shock. I know the symptoms now. I've seen other men under fire for the first time. A rare few know exactly what to do: their weapons are returning fire before their bodies have finished an instinctive crouch and roll. Others laugh, and can't stop laughing. Some cry, and call for their mama, or their wife, or their God. Some get so quiet, shrinking down inside themselves, that even their friends get spooked by it. And some talk, just like I talked to my dying horse.

Habib scrambled up to me in a slithering, zigzag run, and saw me talking into the mare's ear. He checked her over thoroughly, running his hands over the wounds and probing under the thickly veined hide to feel for the bullets. He pulled his knife out of its scabbard. It was a long knife, with a dog's tooth point. He positioned it over the horse's throat and then paused. His mad eyes met mine. There was a sunburst of gold around the pupils of his eyes that seemed to pulse and whirl. They were big eyes, but the madness in them was bigger, straining and bulging at them as if it wanted to burst outward from his very brain. And yet he was sane enough to sense my helpless grief, and to offer me the knife.

It may be that I should've taken the knife and killed the horse, my horse, myself. Maybe that's what a good man, a committed man, would've done. I couldn't. I looked at the knife and the trembling throat of the horse, and I couldn't do it. I shook my head. Habib pushed the knife into the horse's neck and gave it a subtle, almost elegant twist of his wrist. The mare shuddered, but allowed herself to be calmed. When the knife left her throat, the blood gushed in heart-thrusted bursts onto her chest and the sodden ground. Slowly, the straining jaw relaxed, and the eyes glazed over, and then the great heart was still.

I looked from the gentle, dead, unfearing eyes of the horse into the sickness that careered in Habib's eyes, and the moment that we shared was so charged with emotion, so surreally alien to the worlds I knew, that my hand slid involuntarily along my body to the gun in my holster. Habib grinned at me, a toothy baboon grin that was impossible to read, and scrambled away along the line to the next wounded horse.

'Are you okay?'

'Are you okay?'

'Are you okay?'

'What?'

'I said, are you okay?' Khaled asked, shaking a handful of clothing at my chest until I looked him in the eye.

'Yeah. Sure.' I focused on his face, wondering how long I'd been staring at my dead horse, with my hand resting on her punctured throat. I looked around me at the sky. The night was close, only minutes away.

'How bad ... how bad was it?'

'We lost one man. Madjid. A local guy.'

'I saw it. He was right in front of me. The bullets cut him open like a can opener. Fuck, man, it was so quick. He was alive, and then his back opened up, and he dropped over like a cut puppet. I'm sure he was dead before his knees hit the ground. It was *that* fast!'

'Are you sure you're okay?' Khaled asked when I paused for breath.

'Of course I'm *fuckun* okay!' I snapped, a purely Australian accent punching into the expletive. The gleam in his eyes goaded me for another heartbeat of vexation and I almost shouted at him, but then I saw the warmth in his expression, and the concern. I laughed instead. Relieved, he laughed with me. 'Of course I'm okay. And I'd be a lot better if you'd stop asking me. I'm just a bit ... talkative ... that's all. Gimme some slack. *Jesus!* A man just got killed on one side of me, and my horse got killed on the other side. I don't know whether I'm lucky or jinxed.'

'You're lucky,' Khaled answered quickly. His tone was more serious than his laughing eyes. 'It's a mess, but it could've been worse.'

'Worse?'

'They didn't use anything heavy—no mortars, no heavy machine guns. They would've used them if they had them, and it would've been a lot worse. That means it was a small patrol, probably Afghans, not Russians, just testing us out or trying their luck. As it is, we've got three wounded, and we lost four horses.'

'Where are the wounded guys?'

'Up ahead, in the pass. You wanna take a look at them with me?'

'Sure. Sure. Gimme a hand with my gear.'

We wrenched the saddle and bridle from my dead horse, and trotted up the line of men and horses to the mouth of the narrow pass. The wounded men were lying within the cover of a shoulder of rock. Khader stood nearby, frowning watchfully at the plain behind me. Ahmed Zadeh was gently but hurriedly removing the clothing from one of the wounded men. I glanced at the darkening sky.

One man had a broken arm. His horse had fallen on him when it was shot. The break was a bad one, a compound fracture of the forearm, near the wrist. One bone protruded at a sickeningly unnatural angle, but it remained within the envelope of flesh, and nowhere pierced the skin. It had to be set. When Ahmed Zadeh removed the second man's shirt, we saw that he'd been shot twice. Both bullets were still in his body, and they were too deep to reach without major surgery. One, in the upper chest, had shattered the collarbone, and the other had lodged in his stomach, tearing a wide and undoubtedly fatal wound from hip to hip. The third man, a farmer named Siddiqi, had a bad head-wound. His horse had thrown him against the rocks, and he'd struck a boulder with the top of his head, near the crown. It was bleeding, and there was a clear fracture of the cranium. My fingers slid along the ridge of broken bone, greasy-wet with his blood. The broken scalp had split into three chunks. One of them was so loose that I knew it would come away in my hand if I tugged at it. His matted hair was all that held his skull together. There was also a thick swelling at the base of the skull, where his head met his neck. He was unconscious, and I doubted that he would ever open his eyes again.

I glanced at the sky once more. There was so little daylight left, so little time. I had to make a decision, a choice, and help one man to live, maybe, while I let other men die. I wasn't a doctor, and I had no experience under fire. The work had fallen to me, it seemed, because I knew a little more than the next man, and I was willing to do it. It was cold. I was cold. I was kneeling in a sticky smear of blood, and I could feel it soaking through the knees of my pants. When I looked up at Khader he nodded, as if he was reading my thoughts. Feeling sick with guilt and fear, I pulled a blanket over Siddiqi, to keep him warm, and then I abandoned him to work on the man with the broken arm.

Khaled pulled open the comprehensive first-aid kit beside me. I threw a plastic bottle of antibiotic powder, antiseptic wash, bandages, and scissors on the ground at Ahmed Zadeh's feet, beside the man who'd been shot. I snapped out brief instructions for cleaning and dressing the wounds, and as Ahmed went to work, covering the bullet wounds, I turned my attention to the broken arm. The man spoke to me urgently. I knew his face well. He had a special talent for herding the unruly goats, and I'd often seen the temperamental creatures following him, unbidden, as he wandered around our camp.

'What did he say? I didn't get it.'

'He asked you if it's going to hurt,' Khaled muttered, trying to keep his voice and his expression reassuringly neutral.

'I had this happen to me once,' I said in reply. 'Something just like this.

I know exactly how much it hurts. It hurts so much, brother, that I think you should take his gun away.'

'Right,' Khaled replied. 'Fuck.'

He smiled broadly, and brushed at the ground beside the wounded man, gradually easing the Kalashnikov out of the man's hand and out of reach. Then, as darkness closed over us, and five of the man's friends held him down, I wrenched and twisted his shattered arm until it resembled the straight, healthy limb that it once had been and never would be again.

'*Ee-Allah! Ee-Allah!*' he shouted, over and over through clenched teeth.

When the break was wrapped and set with hard plastic splints, and we'd patched over the wounds on the man who'd been shot, I hastily wrapped a dressing around unconscious Siddiqi's head. At once we set off into the narrow pass. The cargo was distributed among all the remaining horses. The man with the bullet wounds rode a horse, supported on both sides by his friends. Siddiqi was strapped across one of the packhorses, as was the body of Madjid, the Afghan who'd been killed in the attack. The rest of us walked.

The climb was steep but short. Puffing hard in the thin air and shivering in a cold that penetrated to my bones, I pushed and dragged the reluctant horses with the rest of the men. The Afghan fighters never once complained or grumbled. When the pitch of one climb was steeper than anything I'd known on the whole trip, I paused at last, panting heavily to regain my strength. Two men turned to see that I'd halted, and they slid down the path to me, giving up the precious metres they'd just gained. With huge smiles and encouraging claps on the shoulder, they helped me to drag a horse up the slope and then bounded off to help those ahead.

'These Afghans may not be the best men in the world to live with,' Ahmed Zadeh puffed as he struggled up the scrambling trail behind me. 'But they are certainly the best men in the world to *die* with!'

After five hours of the climb we reached our destination, a camp in the Shar-i-Safa Mountains. The camp was sheltered from the air by a prodigious ledge of rock. The ground beneath had been excavated to form a vast cave leading to a network of other caves. Several smaller, camouflaged bunkers surrounded the cave in a ring that reached to the fringe of the flat, rugged mountain plateau.

Khader called us to a halt in the light of the rising full moon. His scout Habib had alerted the camp to our arrival, and the mujaheddin were waiting for us—and the supplies we brought—with great excitement. A message was sent back to me, in the centre of the column, that Khader wanted me. I jogged forward to join him.

'We will ride into the camp along this path. Khaled, Ahmed, Nazeer, Mahmoud, and some others. We do not know exactly who is in the camp. The attack on us at Shahbad Pass tells me that Asmatullah Achakzai has changed sides again, and joined the Russians. The Pass has been his for three years, and we should have been safe there. Habib tells me that the camp is friendly, and that these are our own men, waiting for us. But they are still behind cover, and they will not come out to greet us. I think it will be better for us if our American is riding with us, near the front, behind me. I cannot tell you to do this. I can only ask it. Will you ride with us?'

'Yes,' I replied, hoping that the word sounded firmer in his ears than it did in my own.

'Good. Nazeer and the others have prepared the horses. We will leave at once.'

Nazeer led several horses forward, and we climbed wearily into the saddles. Khader must've been far more tired than I was, and his body must've wrestled with many more pains and complaints, but he was straight-backed in the saddle and he held the green-and-white standard at his hip with a rigid arm. Imitating him, I sat up straight and kicked back smartly to start the horse forward. Our small column moved off slowly into a silvered moonlight so strong that it cast looming shadows on the grey rock walls.

The approach to the camp from that southern climb was along a narrow stone path that swept in a graceful, even curve from right to left. Beside the path on our left was a steep drop of some thirty metres to a rubble of broken boulders. On our right was the smooth rock face of a sheer wall. When we were perhaps half way along the path, watched attentively by our own men and the mujaheddin in the camp, I developed an irritating cramp in my right hip. The cramp quickly became a piercing knot of pain; and the more that I tried to ignore it, the more agonising it felt. Attempting to relieve the stress on my hip, I took my right foot out of the stirrup and tried to stretch my leg. With all the weight on my left leg, I stood a little in the saddle. Without warning, my left foot gave way beneath me as my boot slipped from the stirrup, and I felt myself falling sideways out of the saddle toward the deep, hard drop to the stones.

Self-preservation instincts set my limbs flailing, and I clutched at the horse's neck with my arms and my free right leg as I swung down and around. In the time it takes to clench your teeth, I'd fallen from the saddle and coiled myself upside-down around the neck of the horse. I called on it to stop, but it ignored me, plodding onward along the narrow track. I couldn't let go. The path was so narrow, and the drop so steep, that I was sure I would fall if I released my grip. And the horse wouldn't stop. So I hung on, with my arms and my legs wrapped around its neck, upside-down, while its head gently bobbed and dipped next to mine.

I heard my own men laughing first. It was that helpless, stuttering, choking laughter that makes men suffer for days with the ache of it in their ribs. It was the kind of laughter that you're sure will kill you if you can't get that next gasping breath. And then I heard the mujaheddin fighters laughing from the camp. And I arched my head backward to see Khader, facing around in his saddle and laughing as hard as the rest. And then *I* started to laugh, and when the laughter weakened my arms, as I clutched at the horse, I laughed again. And as I choked out an anguished, croaky *Whoa! Stop! Band karo!* the men laughed harder than ever.

And so I entered the camp of the mujaheddin fighters. Men crouched around me at once, helping me from the horse's neck and steadying me on my feet. My own column of men followed us across the narrow path, and reached out to pat me on the back and slap at my shoulders. Seeing that familiarity, the mujaheddin joined in the slapping chorus, and it was fully fifteen minutes before the last man left my side and I could sit down to rest my jelly legs.

'Getting you to ride with him wasn't Khader's best-ever idea,' Khaled Ansari said, sliding down a boulder face to sit beside me with his back to the stone. 'But *fuck*, man, you are *real* popular after that trick. That's easily the funniest thing those guys have ever seen in their lives.'

'For Christ's sake!' I sighed, with a last reflexive giggle of laughter. 'I rode over a hundred mountains and crossed ten rivers, most of it in the dark, for a whole month, and everything was okay. I roll into the camp, and I'm hangin' on my horse's neck like a fuckin' monkey.'

'Don't get me started again!' Khaled spluttered, laughing and clutching at his side.

I laughed with him, and although I was exhausted and resigned to the ridicule, I didn't want to laugh any more, so I glanced around to my right to avoid his eye. A canvas shamiana in camouflage colours provided shelter for our wounded men. In the shadows beside it, men were pulling cargo from the horses and ferrying it into the cavern. I saw Habib dragging something long and heavy away from behind the working line, and deeper into the darkness beyond.

'What's ...' I began, still chuckling. 'What's Habib doing over there?'

Khaled was instantly alert, and jumped to his feet. His urgency quickened me, and I leapt up after him. We ran to the line of rocks that formed one edge of the flattened mountain plateau, and as we rounded them we saw him kneeling, legs astride the body of a man. It was Siddiqi. While all the attention was on the fascinating bundles of the cargo, Habib had dragged the unconscious man from beneath the canvas awning. Just as we reached him, Habib drove his long knife into the man's neck and gave it that delicate twist. Siddiqi's legs twitched a tiny, trembling shake and then were still. Habib pulled the knife away and turned to see us staring back at him. The horror and rage in our faces seemed only to fuel the burning madness in his eyes. He grinned at us.

'Khader!' Khaled shouted, his face as pale as the moon-washed stone around us. 'Khaderbhai! *Iddar ao!' Come here!*

I heard an answering shout from behind us somewhere, but I didn't move. My eyes were on Habib. He turned to face me, swinging his leg over the murdered man and crouching on his haunches as if he was about to spring at me. The manic grin locked on his features, but his eyes grew darker—more afraid, perhaps, or more cunning. He turned his head quickly and tilted it at an eccentric angle, as if listening with feral intensity to a faint sound in the distant night. I heard nothing but the noises of the camp behind me and the soft wail of the wind as it coursed through the canyons and ravines and secret pathways. In that instant, the land, the mountains, the very country of Afghanistan seemed to me so desolate, so bleached of loveliness and tenderness that it was like the landscape of Habib's insanity. I felt that I was trapped inside the stony maze of his hallucinated brain.

While he listened, tense in his animal crouch, with his face turned away from me, I slipped the stud-clip off my holster. I eased the gun out, and into my hands. Breathing hard, I followed Khader's instructions automatically, not realising until it was done that I'd flicked off the safety, chambered a round by pulling back the sliding return, and cocked the hammer. The sounds brought Habib round to face me. He looked at the gun in my hand. It was aimed at his chest. He looked back to my eyes, moving his gaze slowly, almost languorously. The long knife was still in his hand. I don't know what expression lit my face in the moonlight. It can't have been good. My mind was made up: if he moved a millimetre toward me, I would pull the trigger as many times as it took to finish him.

His grin widened into a laugh—at least, it looked like a laugh. His mouth moved, and his head shook, but there was no sound. And his eyes, ignoring Khaled completely, stared a message into mine. And then I could hear him, hear his voice in my head. *You see?* his eyes said to me. *I'm right not to trust any of you ... You want to kill me ... All of you ... You want me dead ... But it's all right ... I don't mind ... I give you my permission ... I want you to do it ...*

We heard a sound, a footstep, behind us. Khaled and I jumped and whirled in fright to see Khader, Nazeer, and Ahmed Zadeh rushing to join us. When we looked back, Habib was gone.

'What is wrong?' Khader asked.

'It's Habib,' Khaled answered, searching the darkness for a sign of the madman. 'He went crazy ... he *is* crazy ... he killed Siddiqi ... dragged his body here, and stabbed him in the throat.'

'Where he is?' Nazeer demanded angrily.

'I don't know,' Khaled replied, shaking his head. 'Did you see him go, Lin?'

'No. I turned with you, to see Khader, and when I looked back he was ... just ... gone. I think he must've jumped down into the ravine.'

'He *can't* have jumped,' Khaled frowned. 'It's gotta be fifty yards down there. He *can't* have jumped.'

Abdel Khader was kneeling beside the dead man, whispering prayers with his hands held palms upwards.

'We can look for him tomorrow,' Ahmed said, putting a comforting hand on Khaled's shoulder. He looked up at the night sky. 'There is not much of this moonlight left for us to work. We still have a lot to do. Don't worry. If he's still around here, we will find him tomorrow. And if we do not—if he is gone—perhaps it is not the worst for us, *non?*'

'I want the guard to watch for him tonight,' Khaled ordered. 'Our own guys—the men who know Habib well—not the guys from here.'

'*Oui,*' Zadeh agreed.

'I don't want them to shoot him, if they can help it,' Khaled continued, 'but I don't want them to take any chances, either. Make a check of all his stuff—check his horse, and his pack. See what weapons or explosives he might've had on him. I didn't get too good a look, before, but I think he had some stuff under his jacket. *Fuck*, this is a mess!'

'Don't worry,' Zadeh muttered, putting a hand on Khaled's shoulder once more.

'I can't help it,' the Palestinian insisted, looking around him into the darkness. 'It's a fuckin' bad start. I think he's out there, staring at us, right now.'

When Khader completed his prayers, we carried Siddiqi's body back to the canvas shamiana, and wrapped it in cloth until the rituals of burial could be performed on the following day. We worked for a few hours more and then lay down in the cavern, side by side for sleep. The snoring was loud, and the exhausted men were restless in their slumber, but I lay awake for other reasons. My eyes kept drifting back to the place, moonless and thickly shadowed, where Habib had disappeared. Khaled was right. It had started badly, Khader's war, and the words echoed in my wakeful mind. *A bad start ...*

I tried to fix my eyes on the clear and perfect stars of that fated night's black heaven, but again and again my concentration lapsed, and I found myself staring at the dark edge of the plateau. And I knew, in the way we know without a word that love is lost, or in the sudden, sure way we know that a friend is false and doesn't really like us at all, that Khader's war would end much worse, for all of us, than it had begun.

CHAPTER THIRTY-FOUR

For two months of cold and ever colder days we lived with the guerrilla fighters in their cave complex on the Shar-i-Safa range. They were hard months in many ways, but our mountain stronghold never came under direct fire, and we were relatively safe. The camp was only fifty crow-kilometres from Kandahar. It was about twenty kilometres from the main Kabul highway and about fifty kilometres south-east of the Arghandab Dam. The Russians occupied Kandahar, but their hold on the southern capital was tenuous and the city was subject to recurring sieges. Rockets had been fired into the city centre, and guerrilla fighting on the outskirts claimed a steady toll of lives. The main highway was in the hands of several well-armed mujaheddin units. Russian tank and truck convoys from Kabul were forced to blast their way through blockades to resupply Kandahar, and that they did, from month to month. Afghan regular army units loyal to the Kabul puppet government protected the strategically important Arghandab Dam, but frequent attacks on the dam threatened their hold on the precious resource. Thus we were roughly in the centre of a triad of violent conflict zones, each of which constantly demanded new men and guns. The Shar-i-Safa range offered no strategic advantage to our enemies, so the fighting didn't find us in our well-disguised mountain caverns.

The weather shifted during those weeks to the cold heart of a severe winter. Snow fell in fitful gusts and squalls that left us sodden in our many-layered patchwork uniforms. A freezing mist drifted so slowly through the mountains that it sometimes hung suspended for hours at a time: still and white and as impenetrable to the gaze as frosted glass. The ground was always muddy or frozen, and even the stone walls of the caves we lived in seemed to ring and tremble with the icy chill of the season.

Part of Khader's cargo had consisted of hand tools and machine components. We'd set up two workshops in the first days after our arrival, and they were busy throughout the creeping weeks of the winter. There was a small capstan lathe, which we'd bolted to a homemade table. The lathe ran on a diesel engine. The fighters felt certain that there were no enemy forces within earshot, but still we dampened its noise with a little igloo of burlap sacks that covered the engine, leaving gaps for the air inlet and exhaust gas outlet. The same engine powered a grinding wheel and a speed drill.

With that assembly, the fighters repaired their weapons and sometimes adapted them to suit new and different purposes. First among those weapons were the mortars. After aircraft and tanks, the most effective battle weapon in Afghanistan was the Russian 82-millimetre mortar. The guerrillas bought the mortars, stole them, or captured them in hand-to-hand fighting, often at the cost of human lives. The weapons were then turned on the Russians, who'd brought them into the country in order to conquer it. Our workshops stripped the mortars down, refitted them, and packed them in waxed bags for use in combat zones as far away as Zaranj in the west, and Kunduz in the north.

Apart from the cartridge pliers and crimping tools, the ammunition and the explosives, Khader's cargo also included new parts for the Kalashnikovs that he'd purchased in the arms bazaars in Peshawar. The Russian AK—*Avtomat Kalashnikova*—was designed by Mikhail Kalashnikov in the 1940s, in response to German armament innovations. Toward the end of the Second World War, German army generals disobeyed the explicit orders of Adolph Hitler and produced an automatic assault rifle. The armaments engineer Hugo Schmeisser, using the germ of an earlier Russian concept, developed a weapon that was short, light, and fired its magazine of thirty bullets at a practical rate of more than a hundred rounds per minute. Hitler was so impressed with the weapon he'd previously forbidden that he named it the *Sturmgewehr*, or *Storm Weapon*, and immediately ordered its intensive production. It was too little, too late for the Nazi war effort, but Schmeisser's Storm Weapon set the trend for all assault rifles for the rest of the century.

Kalashnikov's AK-47, the most influential and widely manufactured of the new assault rifles, operated by diverting some of the propellant gases produced by a fired bullet into a cylinder above the barrel. The gas drove a piston that forced the bolt back against its spring, and cocked the hammer for the next round. The rifle weighed about five kilos, carried thirty rounds in its curved metal magazine, and fired the 7.62-millimetre rounds at around 2,300 feet per second, over an effective range greater than 300 metres. It fired more than a hundred rounds per minute on auto, and about forty rounds every minute on the semi-automatic, single-shot function.

The rifle had its limitations, and the mujaheddin fighters were quick to explain them to me. The low muzzle-velocity of the heavy 7.62-millimetre round defined a looping trajectory that called for tricky adjustments to hit a target at three hundred metres or more. Muzzle flash on firing the AK was so bright, particularly with the new 74 series, that it blinded the firer at night, and often betrayed his position. The barrel overheated rapidly, becoming too hot to hold. Sometimes a round grew so hot in the chamber that it exploded in the user's face. That fact explained why so many guerrilla fighters held the gun away from their bodies, or over their heads, in battle operations.

Nevertheless, the rifle worked perfectly after total immersion in water, mud, or snow, and it remained one of the most efficient and reliable killing machines ever devised. In the first four decades after its development, fifty million of them were produced—more than any other firearm in history—and the Kalashnikov, in all its forms, was carried as a preferred strike weapon by revolutionaries, regular soldiers, mercenaries, and gangsters all over the fighting world.

The original AK-47 was made of forged and milled steel. The AK-74, produced in the 1970s, was made from stamped metal parts. Some of the older Afghan fighters rejected the newer weapon, with its smaller 5.45-millimetre round and its orange plastic magazine, preferring the solidity of the heavier AK-47. Some younger fighters chose the 74 model, dismissing the heavier gun as an antique. The models they used were produced in Egypt, Syria, Russia, and China. Although they were essentially identical, the fighters often preferred one to another, and the trade in the weapons, even within the same unit, was energetic and intense.

Khader's workshops repaired and refitted the AKs of every series, and modified them as required. The workshops were popular places. The Afghan men were insatiable in their desire to know about weapons and learn new skills with them. It wasn't a frenzied or brutal curiosity. It was simply necessary to know how to handle guns in a land that had been invaded by Alexander the Great, the Huns, the Sakas, the Scythians, the Mongols, the Moghuls, the Safavids, the British, and the Russians, among many others. Even when they weren't studying at the workshops or helping out with the work, the men gathered there to drink tea made on spirit stoves, smoke cigarettes, and talk about their loved ones.

And for two months I worked with them every day. I melted lead and other metals in the little forge. I helped to gather scraps of firewood, and carried water from a spring at the foot of a nearby ravine. Trudging through the light snow I dug out new latrines, and carefully covered them over and concealed them again when they were full. I turned new parts on the turret lathe, and melted the helical metal shavings to make more parts. In the mornings I tended to the horses, which were billeted in another cave further down the mountain. When it was my turn to milk the goats, I churned the milk into butter and helped to cook naan bread. If any man needed attention for a cut or graze or sprained ankle, I set up the first-aid kit and did my best to heal him.

I learned the answering choruses of a few songs, and in the evenings when the fires were smothered and we huddled together for warmth, I sang with the men as softly as they did. I listened to the stories that they whispered into the dark, and that Khaled, Mahmoud, and Nazeer translated for me. Each day when the men prayed, I knelt with them in silence. And at night, enclosed within the breathing, snoring swathe of their soldier-scented sleep—smells of wood-smoke, gun oil, cheap sandalwood soap, piss, shit, sweat soaking into wet-serge, unwashed human and horse hair, liniment and saddle-softener, cumin and coriander, peppermint tooth powder, chai, tobacco, and a hundred others—I dreamed with them of homes and hearts we longed to see again.

Then, when the second month ended, and the last weapons were repaired and modified, and the supplies we'd brought with us were all but exhausted, Khaderbhai ordered us to prepare for the long walk home. He planned to make a detour west, toward Kandahar and away from the border with Pakistan, to deliver some horses to his family. After that, with marching packs and light weapons, we would march by night until we reached the safety of the Pakistan border.

'The horses are nearly loaded,' I reported to Khader when I'd packed my own gear. 'Khaled and Nazeer will be back up here when it's all done. They told me to let you know.'

We were on the flattened top of a tor that gave a commanding view of the valleys and then the desert plain that stretched from the foot of the mountains all the way to Kandahar at the horizon. For once, the cloudy mists and snow had cleared enough for us to take in the whole, panoramic sweep of the view. There were dark, thick clouds massed to the east of us, and the cold air was damp with the rain and snow they would bring, but for the moment we could see all the way to the end of the world, and our wintry eyes were drowning in the beauty of it.

'In November of 1878, the same month that we started this mission, the British forced their way through the Khyber Pass, and the second Afghan war with them began,' Khader said, ignoring my report, or perhaps responding to it in his own way. He stared toward the ripple of haze on the horizon caused by the smoke and fire of distant Kandahar. I knew that some of the horizon's shimmer and drizzle might've been exploding rockets, fired into the city by men who'd lived there once as teachers and merchants. In the war against the Russian invaders, they'd become devils in exile, raining fire upon their own homes and shops and schools.

'Through Khyber Pass, there came one of the most feared, brave, and brutal soldiers in the whole British Raj. His name was Roberts, Lord Frederick Roberts. He captured Kabul, and began a ruthless martial law there. On one day, eighty-seven Afghan soldiers were killed by hanging in the public square. Buildings and markets were destroyed, villages were burned, and hundreds of Afghan people were killed. In June, an Afghan Prince named Ayub Khan announced a jihad to drive out the British. He left Herat with ten thousand men. He was an ancestor of mine, a man of my family, and many of my kinsmen were in the army that he raised.'

He stopped talking and flicked a glance at me, his golden eyes gleaming beneath the silver-grey brows. His eyes were smiling, but his jaw was set and his lips were compressed so tightly that they showed white at the rims. Reassured, perhaps, that I was listening to him, he looked back to the smouldering horizon, and spoke again.

'The British officer in charge of Kandahar city at that time, a man named Burrows, was sixty-three years old, the same age that I am today. He marched out of Kandahar with one thousand five hundred men— British and Indian soldiers—and he met Prince Ayub at a place called Maiwand. You can see the place from here, where we sit, when the weather is good enough. In the battle, both armies fired canons, killing hundreds of men in the most terrible ways that can be imagined. When they met each other, as one man to another man, they fired their guns at such close range that the bullets went through one body to strike the next. The British lost half their number. The Afghans lost two thousand five hundred men. But they won the battle, and the British were forced to retreat to Kandahar. Prince Ayub immediately surrounded the city, and the siege of Kandahar began.'

It was cold, bitterly cold on the windy tor, despite the unusually bright, clear sunlight. I felt my legs and arms growing numb, and I longed to stand up and stamp my feet, but I didn't want to disturb him. Instead, I lit two beedies, and passed one to him. He accepted it, raising his eyebrow in thanks, and took two long puffs before continuing.

'Lord Roberts—do you know something, Lin, my first teacher, my dear Mackenzie Esquire, always said this thing, *Bobs your uncle*, all the time, and it became a thing that I also said, to imitate him. Then, one day, he told me that the saying came from him, from Lord Frederick Roberts, because, you see, the man who killed my people in hundreds was so kind to his own soldiers that they called him *Uncle Bobs*. And they said that if *he* was in charge, everything would be well—*Bobs your uncle*. I never said that again, not ever, after he told me that. And something that is very strange—my dear Mackenzie Esquire was the grandson of a man who fought in the army of Lord Roberts. His grandfather and my kinsmen fought each other in the second British war against Afghanistan. That is why Mackenzie Esquire had such fascination for the history of my country and such knowledge about the wars. And, thanks be to Allah, I did have him as my friend, and my teacher, while men were still alive who bore the scars of fighting the war that killed his grandfather, and killed mine.'

He paused again, and we listened to the wind, feeling the first sting of the new snow that it was bringing to us: the shivering wind that began in distant Bamiyan, and dragged the snow and ice and frosty air from every mountain all the way to Kandahar.

'And so Lord Roberts went from Kabul, with a force of ten thousand men, to relieve the siege of Kandahar. Two-thirds of his men were Indian soldiers—and they were good fighting men, those Indian Sepoys. Roberts marched them from Kabul to Kandahar, a distance of three hundred miles, in twenty-two days. Much more than the distance we covered, you and I, from Chaman, on our journey—and you know that took us a month, with good horses, and help from villages along the way. And they marched, from freezing snow mountains to burning desert, and then, after twenty days of this unbelievable march through hell, they fought a great battle with the army of Prince Ayub Khan, and they defeated him. Roberts saved the British in the city, and from that day, even after he became the field marshal of all the soldiers in the British Empire, he was always known as Roberts of Kandahar.'

'Was Prince Ayub killed?'

'No. He escaped. Then the British put his close kinsman Abdul Rahman Khan on the throne of Afghanistan. Abdul Rahman Khan, also an ancestor of mine, ruled the country with such a special wisdom that the British had no real power in Afghanistan. The situation was exactly the same as it was before—before the great soldier and great killer, *Bobs your uncle*, forced his way through the Khyber Pass to fight the war. But the point of this story, now that we sit here and look at the fires of my burning city, is that Kandahar is the key to Afghanistan. Kabul is the heart, but Kandahar is the soul of this nation, and who rules Kandahar also rules Afghanistan. When the Russians are forced to leave my city, they will lose this war. Not until then.'

'I hate it all,' I sighed, sure in my own mind that the new war would change nothing: that wars can't really change things. *It's peace that makes the deepest cuts*, I thought. And I remember thinking it—I remember thinking that it was a clever phrase, and hoping for a chance to work it into our conversation. I remember everything about that day. I remember every word, and all those foolish, vain, unwary thoughts, as if fate had just now slapped my face with them. 'I hate it all, and I'm glad we're going home today.'

'Who are your friends here?' he asked me. The question surprised me, and I couldn't guess at his intention. Reading my baffled expression, and clearly amused, he asked me again. 'Of those you have come to know here, on this mountain, who are your friends?'

'Well, Khaled, obviously, and Nazeer —'

'So, Nazeer is your friend now?'

'Yeah,' I laughed. 'He's a friend. And I like Ahmed Zadeh. And Mahmoud Melbaaf, the Iranian. And Suleiman is okay, and Jalalaad—he's a wild kid—and Zaher Rasul, the farmer.'

Khader nodded as I ran through the list, but when he made no comment I felt moved to speak again.

'They're *all* good men, I think. Everyone here. But those ... those are the men I get on with the best. Is that what you mean?'

'What is your favourite task here?' he asked, changing the subject as quickly and unexpectedly as his portly friend Abdul Ghani might've done.

'My favourite ... it's crazy, and I never thought I'd ever say this, but I think tending the horses is my favourite job.'

He smiled, and the smile bubbled into a laugh. I was sure, somehow, that he was thinking about the night I'd ridden into the camp hanging from the neck of my horse.

'Okay,' I grinned, 'I'm not the best horseman in the world.'

He laughed the harder.

'But I really started to miss them when we got here and you told us to stable the horses down the mountain. It's funny—I sort of got used to them being around, and it's always made me feel good, somehow, going down to see them and brush them and feed them.'

'I understand,' he murmured, reading my eyes. 'Tell me, when the others are praying and you join them—I've seen you sometimes, kneeling behind them and not very close—what words are you saying? Are they prayers?'

'I'm ... not really saying anything at all,' I replied, frowning. I lit two more beedies, not for the need of them, but for the distraction they provided, and their little warmth.

'What are you thinking, then, if you're not speaking?' he asked, accepting the second cigarette as he tossed away the butt of the first.

'I couldn't call them prayers. I don't think so. I think about people, mostly. I think about my mother ... and my daughter. I think about Abdullah ... and Prabaker—I've told you about him, my friend who died. I remember friends, and people I love.'

'You think about your mother. What about your father?'

'No.'

I said it quickly—too quickly, perhaps—and I felt him watching me closely as the seconds passed.

'Is you father living, Lin?'

'I think so. But I ... I can't be sure. And I don't care, one way or the other.'

'You must care about your father,' he declared, looking away again. It seemed such a condescending admonition to me then: he knew nothing about my father or my relationship to him. I was so caught up in resentments, new and old, that I didn't hear the anguish in his voice. I didn't realise, as I do now, that he, too, was an exiled son talking about his own father.

'You're more of a father to me than he is,' I said, and although I felt it to be true, and I was opening my heart to him, the words came out sounding sulky and almost spiteful.

'Don't say that!' he snapped, glaring at me. It was the closest he ever came to showing anger in my presence, and I flinched involuntarily at the sudden vehemence. His expression softened at once, and he reached out to put a hand on my shoulder. 'What about your dreams? What are you dreaming about here?'

'Dreams?'

'Yes. Tell me about your dreams.'

'I'm not having many,' I replied, trying hard to recall. 'It's weird, you know, but I've had nightmares for a long time—pretty much since the escape from jail. Nightmares about being caught, or fighting to stop them catching me. But since we've been up here, I don't know if it's the thin air, or being so damn tired and cold when I get to sleep, or maybe just worry about the war, but I'm not having those nightmares. Not here. I've had a couple of good dreams, in fact.'

'Go on.'

I didn't want to go on: the dreams had been about Karla.

'Just ... happy dreams, about being in love.'

'Good,' he murmured, nodding several times, and taking his hand from my shoulder. He seemed satisfied with my reply, but his expression was downcast and almost grim. 'I, too, have had dreams here. I dreamed about the Prophet. We Muslims, you know, we are not supposed to tell anyone, if we dream about the Prophet. It is a very good thing, a very wonderful thing, and quite common among the faithful, but we are forbidden to tell what we have dreamed.'

'Why?' I asked, shivering in the cold.

'It is because we are strictly forbidden to describe the features of the Prophet, or to talk about him as someone who is *seen*. This was the Prophet's own wish, so that no man or woman would adore him, or take any of their devotions away from God. That is why there are no images of the Prophet—no drawings, or paintings, or statues. But I *did* dream of him. And I am not a very good Muslim, am I? Because I am telling you about my dream. He was on foot, walking somewhere. I rode up behind him on my horse—it was a perfect, beautiful white horse—and although I didn't see his face, I knew it was him. So I got down from my horse, and gave it to him. And my face was lowered, out of respect, all the time. But at last, I lifted my eyes to see him riding away into the light of the setting sun. That was my dream.'

He was calm, but I knew him well enough to see the dejection that hooded his eyes. And there was something else, something so new and strange that it took me a few moments to realise what it was: fear. Abdel Khader Khan was afraid, and I felt my own skin creep and tighten in response. It was unimaginable. Until that moment I'd truly believed that Khaderbhai was afraid of nothing. Unnerved and worried, I moved to change the subject.

'Khaderji, I know I'm changing the subject, but can you answer this question for me? I've been thinking about something you said a while ago. You said that life and consciousness and all that other stuff comes from light, at the Big Bang. Are you saying that light is God?'

'No,' he answered, and that sudden, fearful depression lifted from his features, driven off by a look that I could only read as a loving smile. 'I do not think that light is God. I think it is possible, and it is reasonable to say, that light is the *language* of God. Light may be the way that God speaks to the universe, and to us.'

I congratulated myself on the successful change of theme and mood by standing up. I stamped my feet and slapped at my sides to get the blood moving. Khader joined me and we began the short walk back to the camp, blowing warmth into our frozen hands.

'*This* is a strange light, speaking about light,' I puffed. 'The sun shines, but it's a cold sun. There's no warmth in it, and you feel stranded between the cold sun and the even colder shadows.'

'*Beached there in tangles of flicker ...*' Khader quoted, and I snapped my head around so quickly that I felt a twinge of pain in my neck.

'What did you say?'

'It was a quote,' Khader replied slowly, sensing how important it was to me. 'It is a line from a poem.'

I pulled my wallet from my pocket, reached into it, and took out a folded paper. The page was so creased and rubbed by wear that when I opened it the fold-lines showed gaps and tears. It was Karla's poem: the one I'd copied from her journal, two years before, when I went to her apartment with Tariq on the Night of the Wild Dogs. I'd carried it with me ever since. In Arthur Road Prison the officers had taken the page from me and torn it into pieces. When Vikram bribed my way out of the prison I wrote it out again from memory, and I carried it with me every day, everywhere I went. Karla's poem.

'This poem,' I said excitedly, holding the tattered, fluttering sheet out for him to see. 'It was written by a woman. A woman named Karla Saaranen. The woman you sent to Guptaji's place with Nazeer to ... to get me out of there. I'm amazed that you know it. It's incredible.'

'No, Lin,' he answered evenly. 'The poem was written by a Sufi poet named Sadiq Khan. I know his poems by heart, many of them. He is my favourite poet. And he is Karla's favourite poet also.'

The words were ice around my heart.

'Karla's favourite poet?'

'I do believe so.'

'Just how well ... how well do you know Karla?'

'I know her very well.'

'I thought ... I thought you met her when you got me out of Gupta's. She said ... I mean, I *thought* she said *that* was when she met you.'

'No, Lin, that is not correct. I have known Karla for years. She works for me. Or at least, she works for Abdul Ghani, and Ghani works for me. But she *must* have told you about it, didn't she? Didn't you know this? I am very surprised. I was *sure* that Karla would have talked to you about me. Certainly, I have talked to her about *you*, many times.'

My mind was like the screaming jets that had screeched over us in the dark ravine: all noise and black fears. What had Karla said as we lay together, struggling against sleep, after fighting the cholera epidemic? *I was on a plane, and I met a businessman, an Indian businessman, and my life changed forever* ... Was that Abdul Ghani? Is that what she meant? Why hadn't I asked her more about her work? Why didn't she tell me about it? And what did she do for Abdul Ghani?

'What does she do for you—for Abdul?'

'Many things. She has many skills.'

'I know about her skills,' I growled at him angrily. 'What does she do for you?'

'Among other things,' Khader answered, slowly and precisely, 'she finds useful and talented foreigners, such as you are. She finds people who can work for us, when we need them.'

'What?' I asked, gasping out the word that wasn't really a question, and feeling as if pieces of myself—frozen pieces of my face and my heart—were falling splintered around me.

He began to speak again, but I cut him off quickly.

'Are you saying that Karla recruited me—for *you*?'

'Yes. She did. And I am very glad that she did.'

The cold was suddenly inside me, running through my veins, and my eyes were made of snow. Khader kept walking, but when he noticed that I'd stopped, he halted. He was still smiling when he turned to face me. Khaled Ansari approached us at that instant, and clapped his hands together loudly.

'Khader! Lin!' he greeted us with the sad, small smile that I'd come to love. 'I've made up my mind. I gave it some thought, Khaderji, just like you said, but I've decided to stay. At least for a while. Habib was here last night. The sentries saw him. He's been doing so much crazy stuff—the things he's done to Russian prisoners, and even some of the Afghan prisoners near here on the Kandahar road in the last couple weeks are ... well, it's grisly shit—and I'm hard to impress in that way. It's so weird, the men are going to do something about it. They're so spooked, they're gonna shoot him on sight. They're talking about hunting him down like a wild animal. I have to ... I have to try to help him, somehow. I'm gonna stay, and try to find him, and try to talk him into coming back to Pakistan with me. So ... you go on without me tonight, and I'll ... I'll come through in a couple of weeks, on the next trip out. That's ... that's it, I guess. That's ... what I came to say.'

There was a cold silence after the little speech. I stared at Khader, waiting for him to speak. I was angry, and I was afraid. It was a special fear—the kind of arctic dread that only love can inspire. Khader stared back at my face, reading me. Khaled looked from one to the other of us, confused and concerned.

'What about the night I met you and Abdullah?' I asked, speaking through teeth clenched against the cold and the even colder fear that ripped through me like spasms of cramp.

'You forget,' Khader Khan replied a little more sternly. His face was as dark and determined as my own. It never occurred to me then that he, too, was feeling deceived and betrayed. I'd forgotten about Karachi and the police raids. I'd forgotten that there was a traitor in his own circle, someone close to him, who'd tried to have him and me and the rest of us captured or killed. I never saw his grim detachment as anything but a cruel disregard for what I felt. 'You met Abdullah a long time before the night that we met. You met him at the temple of the Standing Babas, isn't it true? He was there to look after Karla on that night. She did not know you well. She was not sure of you, not sure that she could trust you, in a place that she did not know. She wanted someone there who could help her, if you had no good intention with her.'

'He was her bodyguard ...' I muttered, thinking *she didn't trust me ...*

'Yes, Lin, he was, and a good one. I understand it that there was some violence, on that night. Abdullah did do something to save her—and perhaps to save you. Isn't that true? This was Abdullah's job, to protect the people for me. That is why I sent him to follow you when my nephew Tariq went to stay with you in the zhopadpatti. And on the very first night, he did help you to fight some wild dogs, isn't it true? And for the whole time that Tariq was with you, Abdullah was close to you, and to Tariq, just as I told him to be.'

I wasn't listening. My mind was all angry arrows, whistling backward to a much earlier time and place. I was searching for Karla—for the Karla I knew and loved—but every moment with her began to give up its secret and its lie. I remembered the first time I'd met her, the first second, how she'd reached out to stop me from walking in front of the bus. It was on Arthur Bunder Road, on the corner near the Causeway, not far from the India Guest House. It was the heart of the tourist beat. Was she waiting there, hunting for foreigners like me, looking for useful recruits who could work for Khader when he needed them? Of course she was. I'd done it myself, in a way, when I'd lived in the slum. I'd loitered there, in the same place, looking for foreigners just off the plane who wanted to change money or buy some charras.

Nazeer walked up to join us. Ahmed Zadeh was a few paces behind him. They stood together with Khaderbhai and Khaled, facing me. Nazeer screwed his face into a scowl, and scanned the sky from south to north, calculating the minutes before the snowstorm hit us. The packing for the return journey was complete and double-checked, and he was anxious to leave.

'And the help you gave me with the clinic?' I asked, feeling sick, and knowing that if I unlocked my knees and let my legs relax, they would crumple and fold beneath me. When Khader didn't speak, I repeated the question. 'What about the clinic? Why did you help me with the clinic? Was that part of your plan? Of *this* plan?'

A freezing wind blew into the broad plateau, and we all shuddered, unsteadied, as the force of it whipped at our clothes and faces. The sky darkened swiftly as a dirty, grey tide of cloud crossed the mountains and tumbled on toward the distant plain and the shimmering, dying city.

'You did good work there,' he replied.

'That's not what I asked you.'

'I don't think this is the right time to talk of such things, Lin.'

'Yes, it is,' I insisted.

'There are things you will not understand,' he stated, as if he'd thought it through many times.

'Just tell me.'

'Very well. All of the medicine that we brought here to this camp, all of the antibiotics and penicillin for the war, was supplied to us by Ranjit's lepers. I had to know if it was safe to use here.'

'Ah, Jesus ...' I moaned.

'So I used the opportunity, the strange fact that you, a foreigner, with no connection to a family or an embassy, set up a clinic in my own slum —I took that chance to test the supplies on the people in the zhopadpatti. I had to be sure, you understand, before I brought the medicines into the war.'

'For God's sake, Khader!' I snarled.

'I had to be —'

'Only a fuckin' *maniac* would do that!'

'Take it easy, Lin!' Khaled snapped back at me. The other men tensed on either side of Khader, as if they feared that I might attack him. 'You're way outta line, man!'

'*I'm* out of line!' I spluttered, feeling my teeth chatter, and struggling to make my numb limbs obey my mind. '*I'm* out of fuckin' line! He uses the people in the slum as guinea pigs or lab rats or whatever the fuck, to test his antibiotics—using *me* to trick them into doing it, because they believed in me—and *I'm* the one who's out of line!'

'No-one got hurt,' Khaled shouted back at me. 'The medicines were all good, and the work you did there was good. People got well.'

'We should get out of the cold, now, and talk about it,' Ahmed Zadeh put in quickly, hoping to conciliate. 'Khader, you'll have to wait for this snow to clear before you leave. Let's get inside.'

'You must understand,' Khader said firmly, ignoring him. 'It was a decision of war—twenty lives risked against the saving of a thousand, and a thousand risked to save a million. And you must believe me, we knew that the medicines were good. The chance of Ranjit's lepers supplying impure medicines was very low. We were almost completely sure that the medicine was safe when we gave it to you.'

'Tell me about Sapna.' There it was, out in the open, my deepest secret fear about him, and about my closeness to him. 'Was that your work, too?'

'I was not Sapna. But the responsibility for his killings does come back to me. Sapna killed for me—for this cause. And if you want me to tell you the whole of the truth, I did make a great benefit from Sapna's bloody work. Because of Sapna, because he existed, and because of their fear of him, and because I made a commitment to find him and stop him, the politicians and the police allowed me to bring guns and other weapons through Bombay to Karachi and Quetta, and to this war. The blood Sapna spilled—it did oil the wheels for us. And I would do this again. I would use Sapna's killings, and I would do more killings, with my own hands, if it would help our cause. We have a *cause*, Lin, all of us here. And we fight and we live and perhaps we will also die for that cause. If we win this fight, we will change the whole of history, forever, from this time, and in this place, and with these battles. That is our cause—to change the whole world. What is *your* cause? What is *your* cause, Lin?'

I was so cold, as the first flakes whirled about us, that I shivered and shook and couldn't stop my jaw from shuddering.

'What about ... what about Madame Zhou ... when Karla got me to pretend I was an American. Was that *your* idea? Was that *your* plan?'

'No. Karla has her own war with Zhou, and she had her own reasons. But I approved of her plan to use you, to get her friend out of the Palace. I wanted to see if you could do it. I had the thought, even then, that you would one day be my American in Afghanistan. And you did well, Lin.

Not many people do so well against Zhou in her own Palace.'

'One last thing, Khader,' I stammered. 'When I was in jail … did you have anything to do with that?'

There was a hard silence, the kind of deadly, breathing silence that insinuates itself into the memory more deeply than the sharpest sound.

'No,' he replied at last. 'But the truth is that I could have taken you out of there, even after the first week, if I chose to do it. I knew about it almost at once. And I had the power to help you, but I did not. Not when I could have done it.'

I looked at Nazeer and Ahmed Zadeh. They stared back evenly. My eyes shifted to Khaled Ansari. He returned my stare with an anguished and angrily defiant grimace that pulled his whole face into the jagged lash of the scar that divided his features.

They all knew. They all knew that Khader had left me in there. But it was okay. Khader didn't owe me anything. He wasn't the one who put me there. He didn't have to get me out. And he did, in the end: he did get me out of jail in the end, and he did save my life. It was just that I'd taken so many beatings, and other men had taken beatings for me, trying to get a message out to him … and even if we'd succeeded, even if we'd managed to get a message to him, Khader would've ignored it, and left me there, until he was ready to act. It was just that all the hope had been so empty, so meaningless. And if you prove to a man how vain his hope is, how vain his hoping was, you kill the bright, believing part of him that wants to be loved.

'You wanted to be sure that … that I'd be … so grateful to you. So you … you left me there. Was that it?'

'No, Lin. It was just unfortunate, just your *kismet* at that time. I had an arrangement with Madame Zhou. She was helping us to meet with the politicians, and get favours from one of the generals from Pakistan. He was a … contact … of hers. He was, in truth, Karla's special client. She was the one who first brought him, that Pakistani general, to Madame Zhou. And it was a critical connection. He was critically important to my plans. And she was so very angry with you, Madame Zhou, that nothing less than prison would satisfy her. She wanted to have you killed in there. As soon as my work was done, at the earliest day, I sent your friend Vikram for you. You must believe me when I tell you that I never wanted to hurt you. I like you. I —'

He stopped suddenly because I put my hand on the holster at my hip. Khaled, Ahmed, and Nazeer tensed at once and raised their hands, but they were too far away to reach me in a single springing leap, and they knew it.

'If you don't turn around and walk away now, Khader, I swear to God, I swear to God, I'll do something that'll finish us both. I don't care what happens to me, just so long as I don't have to look at you, or speak to you, or listen to you, ever again.'

Nazeer took a slow, almost casual step, and stood in front of Khader, shielding him with his body.

'I swear to God, Khader. Right now, I don't care much if I live or die.'

'But, we're leaving now, for Chaman, when the snow clears,' Khader replied, and it was the only time I ever heard his voice waver and falter.

'I mean it. I'm not going with you. I'm staying here. I'll go on my own. Or I'll stay here. It doesn't matter. Just ... get ... the fuck ... out of my sight. It's making me sick to my stomach to *look* at you!'

He stood his ground a moment more, and I could feel the urge to take the gun out and shoot him: an urge that was drowning me in cold, shivering waves of revulsion and rage.

'You must know this,' he said at last, 'whatever wrong I have done, I did for the right reasons. I never did more to you than I thought you could bear. And you should know, you must know, that I always felt for you as if you were my friend, and my beloved son.'

'And you should know this,' I answered him, the snow thickening on my hair and shoulders. 'I hate you with the whole of my heart, Khader. All your wisdom, that's just what it comes down to, isn't it? Putting hate in people. You asked me what my cause is. The only cause I've got is my own freedom. And right now that means being free of you, forever.'

His face was stiff with cold. Snow had settled on his moustache and beard, and it was impossible to read his expression. But his golden eyes gleamed through the grey-white mist, and the old love was in them still. Then he turned, and he was gone. The others turned with him, and I was alone in the storm with my hand frozen and trembling on the holster. I snapped the safety clip off, pulled the Stechkin out, and cocked it quickly and expertly, just as he'd taught me. I held it at my side, pointed at the ground.

The minutes passed—the killing minutes, when I might've gone after him and killed him, and myself. And I tried to drop the gun then, but it wouldn't fall from my numbed and icy fingers. I tried to prise the gun free with my left hand, but all my fingers were so cramped that I gave it up. And in the whirling white snow-dome that my world had become I lifted my arms to the white rain, as I once had done beneath the warm rain in Prabaker's village. And I was alone.

When I'd climbed the wall of the prison all those years before, it was as if I'd climbed a wall on the rim of the world. When I slid down to freedom I lost the whole world that I knew, and all the love it held. In Bombay I'd tried, without realising it, to make a new world of loving that could resemble the lost one, and even replace it. Khader was my father. Prabaker and Abdullah were my brothers. Karla was my lover. And then, one by one, they were all lost. Another whole world was lost.

A clear thought came to me, unbidden, and surging in my mind like the spoken words of a poem. I knew why Khaled Ansari was so determined to help Habib. I suddenly knew with perfect understanding what Khaled was really trying to do. *He's trying to save himself,* I said, more than once, feeling my numb lips tremble with the words, but hearing them in my head. And I knew, as I said the words and thought them, that I didn't hate Khader or Karla: that I couldn't hate them.

I don't know why my heart changed so suddenly and so completely. It might've been the gun in my hand—the power it gave me to take life, or let it be—and the instincts, from my deepest nature, that had prevented me from using it. It might've been the fact of losing Khaderbhai. For, as he walked away from me, I knew in my blood—the blood I could smell in the thick, white air, the blood I could taste in my mouth—that it was over. Whatever the reason, the change moved through me like monsoon rain in the steel bazaar, and left no trace of the swirling, murderous hate I'd felt only moments before.

I was still angry that I'd put so much of a son's love into Khader, and that my soul, against the wishes of my conscious mind, had begged for his love. I was angry that he'd considered me expendable, to be used as a means to achieve his ends. And I was enraged that he'd taken away the one thing in my whole life—my work as the slum doctor—that might've redeemed me, in my own mind if nowhere else, and might've gone some way to balance all the wrong I'd done. Even that little good had been polluted and defiled. The anger in me was as hard and heavy as a basalt hearthstone, and I knew it would take years to wear down, but I couldn't hate them.

They'd lied to me and betrayed me, leaving jagged edges where all my trust had been, and I didn't like or respect or admire them any more, but still I loved them. I had no choice. I understood that, perfectly, standing in the white wilderness of snow. You can't kill love. You can't even kill it with hate. You can kill *in*-love, and loving, and even loveliness. You can kill them all, or numb them into dense, leaden regret, but you can't kill love itself. Love is the passionate search for a truth other than your own; and once you feel it, honestly and completely, love is forever. Every act of love, every moment of the heart reaching out, is a part of the universal good: it's a part of God, or what we call God, and it can never die.

Afterwards, when the snow cleared, I stood a little apart from Khaled to watch Khaderbhai and Nazeer and their men leave the camp with the horses. The great Khan, the mafia don, my father, sat straight-backed in his saddle. He held his standard, furled about the lance in his hand. And he never once looked back.

My decision to separate myself from Khaderbhai and to stay with Khaled and the others in the camp had increased the danger for me. I was far more vulnerable without the Khan than I was in his company. It was reasonable to assume, watching him leave, that I wouldn't make it back to Pakistan. I even said those words to myself: *I'm not gonna make it ... I'm not gonna make it ...*

But it wasn't fear that I felt as lord Abdel Khader Khan rode into the light-consuming snow. I accepted my fate, and even welcomed it. *At last,* I thought, *I'm gonna get what I deserve.* Somehow, that thought left me clean and clear. What I felt, instead of fear, was hope that he would live. It was over, and finished, and I never wanted to see him again; but as I watched him ride into that valley of white shadows I hoped he would live. I prayed he would be safe. I prayed my heartbreak into him, and I loved him. I loved him.

CHAPTER THIRTY-FIVE

Men wage wars for profit and principle, but they fight them for land and women. Sooner or later, the other causes and compelling reasons drown in blood and lose their meaning. Sooner or later, death and survival clog the senses. Sooner or later, surviving is the only logic, and dying is the only voice and vision. Then, when best friends die screaming, and good men maddened with pain and fury lose their minds in the bloody pit, when all the fairness and justice and beauty in the world is blown away with arms and legs and heads of brothers and sons and fathers, then, what makes men fight on, and die, and keep on dying, year after year, is the will to protect the land and the women.

You know that's true when you listen to them, in the hours before they go into battle. They talk about home, and they talk about the women they love. And you know it's true when you watch them die. If he's near the earth or on the earth in the last moments, a dying man reaches out for it, to squeeze a grasp of soil in his hand. If he can, he'll raise his head to look at the mountain, the valley, or the plain. If he's a long way from home, he'll think about it, and he'll talk about it. He'll talk about his village, or his home town, or the city where he grew up. The land matters, at the end. And at the very last, he won't scream of causes. At the very last, he'll murmur or he'll cry out the name of a sister or a daughter or a lover or a mother, even as he speaks the name of his God. The end mirrors the beginning. In the end, it's a woman, and a city.

Three days after Khaderbhai left the camp, three days after I watched him ride away from us through the soft new snow, sentries at the southern lookout on the Kandahar side of the camp shouted that men were approaching. We rushed to the southern edge to see a lumpy confusion of shapes, perhaps two or three human figures, struggling up the steep slope. Several of us reached for binoculars in the same instant and trained them on the spot. I made out one man crawling, inching his way up the slope on his knees, and dragging two prone figures. After a few moments of study I recognised the powerful shoulders, the bowed legs, and the distinctive grey-blue fatigues. I handed the binoculars to Khaled Ansari and bounded over the edge in a sliding run.

'It's Nazeer!' I shouted. 'I think it's Nazeer!'

I was one of the first to reach him. He was face down in the snow, and he was breathing hard. His legs were pushing against the snow, seeking purchase, and his hands were locked in wraps of clothing at the throats of two men. He'd dragged them to that spot on their backs, one in each hand. It was impossible to guess how far he'd come, but it looked to be a long way, most of it uphill. The man in Nazeer's left hand, nearest to me, was Ahmed Zadeh. He was alive, but seemed to be badly wounded. The other man was Abdel Khader Khan. He was dead.

It took three of us to wrench Nazeer's fingers from the clothes. He was so exhausted and so cold that he couldn't speak. His mouth opened and closed, but the voice was a long, unsteady croak. Two men seized the shoulders of his clothes and dragged him back up to the camp. I pulled open Khader's clothes at the chest, hoping to revive him, but when I put my hand on his body the skin was ice-cold and stiffened and woody. He'd been dead for many hours, perhaps more than a day. The body was rigid. The arms and legs were bent a little at the elbows and knees, and the hands were curled into claws. His face, however, was serene and unblemished beneath its thin shroud of snow. His eyes and his mouth were closed as if in a peaceful sleep, and he was so gently dead that my heart refused to believe him gone.

When Khaled Ansari shook my shoulder, I came to the moment as if from a dream, although I knew that I'd been awake for the whole of the time since the sentries had first given us the alarm. I was kneeling in the snow, against Khader's body, and cradling the handsome head in my arms, against my chest, but I had no recollection of doing it. Ahmed Zadeh was gone. Men had dragged him back to the camp. Khaled, Mahmoud, and I dragged and half-carried Khader's body back with us and into the big cave.

I joined a group of three men who were working on Ahmed Zadeh. The Algerian's clothes were stiff with frozen blood around the middle, below the chest. Piece by piece we cut them away, and just as we reached the torn, minced, bloody wounds on his raw skin, he opened his eyes to look at us.

'I'm wounded ...' he said in French, then Arabic, then English.

'Yes, mate,' I answered him, meeting his eyes. I tried a little smile, but it felt numb and awkward, and I'm sure he drew little comfort from it.

There were at least three wounds, but it was difficult to be sure. His abdomen had been ripped open with a vicious, gouging tear that might've been caused by shrapnel from a mortar shell. For all that I could tell, the piece of metal could've been inside him, nudging up against his spine. There were other gaping wounds in his thigh and groin. He'd lost so much blood that his flesh was curled and grey around the wounds. I couldn't begin to guess what damage had been done to his stomach and other internal organs. There was a strong smell of urine and other wastes and fluids. That he'd survived so long was a miracle. It seemed that the cold alone had kept him alive. But the clock was ticking on him: he had hours or only minutes to live, and there was nothing I could do for him.

'It is very bad?'

'Yes, mate,' I answered him, and I couldn't help it—my voice broke as I said it. 'There's nothing I can do.'

I wish now that I didn't say it. Of the hundred things that I wish I'd never said or done in my wicked life, that little quirk of honesty is right up there, near the top of the list. I hadn't realised how much the hope of being rescued had held him up. And then, with those words of mine, I watched him fall backward into the black lake. The colour left his skin, and the small tension of will that had kept his skin taut collapsed, with little twitches of quivering surrender, from his jaw to his knees. I wanted to prepare an injection of morphine for him, but I knew that I was watching him die, and I couldn't bring myself to take my hand from his.

His eyes cleared, and he looked around him at the cave walls as if seeing them for the first time. Mahmoud and Khaled were on one side of him. I knelt on the other. He looked into our faces. His eyes were starting from their sockets with fear. It was the desolate terror of a man who knows that fate has abandoned him, and death's already inside, stretching and swelling and filling up the life-space that used to be his. It was a look I came to know too well in the weeks that followed, and in the years beyond. But there, on that day, it was new to me, and I felt my scalp tighten with a fear that mimed his.

'It should have been donkeys,' he rasped.

'What?'

'Khader should have used donkeys. I told him that from the beginning. You heard me. You all heard me.'

'Yes, mate.'

'Donkeys ... on this kind of job. I grew up in the mountains. I know the mountains.'

'Yes, mate.'

'It should have been donkeys.'

'Yes,' I said again, not knowing how to respond.

'But he was too proud, Khader Khan. He wanted to feel ... the moment ... the returning hero ... for his people. He wanted to bring horses to them ... so many fine horses.'

He stopped talking, choked by a little series of grunting gasps that began in his wounded stomach, and thumped upwards into his stuttering chest. A trickle of dark fluid, blood and bile, dribbled from his nose and the corner of his mouth. He seemed not to notice.

'For that, only, we went back to Pakistan in the wrong direction. For that, to deliver those horses to his people, we went to die.'

He closed his eyes, moaning in pain, but then just as quickly opened them again.

'If not for those horses ... we would have gone east, toward the border, direct toward the border. It was ... it was his *pride*, do you see?'

I looked up, exchanging a glance with Khaled and Mahmoud. Khaled met my eye, but then shifted his gaze quickly to concentrate on his dying friend. Mahmoud held my stare until we both nodded. It was a gesture so subtle that it would've been imperceptible to an observer, but we both knew what we'd acknowledged and what we'd agreed upon with that little nod. It was true. It was pride that had brought the great man to his end. And strange as it may seem to someone else, it was only then, understanding the pride in his fall, that I began to truly accept that Khaderbhai was gone, and to feel the gaping, hollow sense of his death.

Ahmed talked for a while longer. He told us the name of his village, and he gave us directions for how to find it in relation to the nearest big city. He told us about his father and mother, about his sisters and brothers. He wanted us to let them know that he'd died thinking of them. And he did, that brave, laughing Algerian, who'd always looked as though he was searching for a friend in a crowd of strangers: he did die with his mother's love on his lips. And the name of God escaped with his last breath.

We were freezing, chilled to the bones by the stillness we'd assumed while Ahmed lay dying. Other men took over the task of cleaning his body according to the rituals of Muslim burial. Khaled, Mahmoud, and I checked on Nazeer. He wasn't wounded, but he was so utterly and crushingly exhausted that his sleep resembled that of a man in a coma. His mouth was open, and his eyes were slitted to show the whites within. He was warm, and he seemed to be recovering from his ordeal. We left him, and examined the body of our dead Khan.

A single bullet had entered Khader's side, below the ribs, and seemed to have travelled directly to his heart. There was no exit wound, but there was extensive blood coagulation and bruising on the left side of his chest. The bullet fired by Russian AK-74s in those years had a hollow tip. The steel core of the bullet was weighted towards the rear, causing it to tumble. It crashed and ripped its way into a body, rather than simply piercing it. Such ammunition was banned under international law, but almost every one of the Afghans who was killed in battle bore the terrible wounds of those brutal bullets. So it was with our Khan. The bullet had smashed its way through his body. The gaping, jagged wound in his side had left a streak of bruising across his chest that ended in a blue-black lotus over his heart.

Knowing that Nazeer would want to prepare Khaderbhai's body for burial himself, we wrapped the Khan in blankets and left him in a shallow, scooped-out trench of snow near the entrance to the caves. We'd just finished the task when a warbling, fluttering, whistle of sound drew us to our feet. We looked at one another in fearful confusion. Then a violent explosion shook the ground beneath us with a flash of orange and dirty grey smoke. The mortar shell had struck the ground more than a hundred metres away, at the far edge of the compound, but the air near us was already filthy with its smell and smoke. Then a second shell burst, and a third, and we ran for the cave-mouth and flung ourselves into the squirming octopus of men who were there ahead of us. Arms, legs, and heads crushed in on one another as we hunkered down in terror while the mortars tore up the rocky ground outside as if it was papier-mâché.

It was bad, and it got worse every day after that. When the attack was over, we searched among the blackened stipple and crater of the compound. Two men were dead. One of them was Kareem, the man whose broken forearm I'd set on the night before we'd reached the camp. Two others were so badly wounded that we were sure they would die. Many of the supplies were destroyed. First among them were the drums of fuel we'd used for the generator and the stoves. The stoves and lamps were critically important for heating and cooking. Most of the fuel was gone, and all of our water reserves. We set to cleaning up the debris— my medical kit was blackened and scorched by the fire—and consolidating the remaining supplies in the great cave. The men were quiet. They were worried and afraid. They had reason enough.

While others busied themselves with those tasks, I tended to the wounded men. One man had lost a foot and a part of his leg below the knee. There were fragments of shrapnel in his neck and upper arm. He was eighteen years old. He'd joined the unit with his elder brother six months before we arrived. His brother had been killed during an attack on a Russian outpost near Kandahar. The boy was dying. I pulled the metal pieces from his body with long stainless steel tweezers and a pair of long-nosed pliers I pilfered from the mechanic's kit.

There was nothing substantial that I could do for the savaged leg. I cleaned the wound, and tried to remove as much of the shattered bone as I could wrench free with the pliers. His screams settled on my skin in an oily sweat, and I shivered with every gust of frosty wind. I put sutures into the ragged flesh where clean, hard skin would support them, but there was no way to close the gap over completely. One thick chunk of bone protruded from the lumpy meat. It occurred to me that I should take a saw, and hack the long bone off to make a neat wound of the stump, but I wasn't sure if that was the right procedure. I wasn't sure that it wouldn't make the wound worse than it was. I wasn't sure ... And there's only so much screaming you can bring yourself to cause when you're not sure what you're doing. In the end, I smothered the wound in antibiotic powder and wrapped it in non-adhesive gauze.

The second wounded man had taken a blast in the face and throat. His eyes were destroyed, and most of the nose and mouth were gone. In some ways, he resembled Ranjit's lepers, but his wounds were so raw and bloody, and the teeth were so smashed, that Ranjit's disfigurements seemed benign in comparison. I took the metal pieces from his eyes and his scalp and his throat. The wounds at his throat were bad, and although he was breathing fairly evenly, my guess was that his condition would worsen. After dressing his wounds, I gave both men a shot of penicillin and an ampoule of morphine.

My biggest problem was blood, and the need to replace what the wounded men had lost. Not one of the mujaheddin fighters I'd asked during the last weeks had known his own or anyone else's blood type. Thus it was impossible for me to blood-match the men, or to build up a bank of donors. Because my own blood type was O, which is known as the universal donor type, my body was the only source of blood for transfusions, and I was the walking blood bank for the whole combat unit.

Typically, a donor provides about half a litre of blood in a session. The body holds about six litres, so the blood lost in donation amounts to less than one-tenth of the body's supply. I put a little more than half a litre into each of the wounded men, rigging up the intravenous drips that Khader had brought with him as part of his smuggled cargo. I wondered whether the equipment had come from Ranjit and his lepers as I tapped my veins and those of the wounded fighters with needles that were stored in loose containers rather than sealed packets. The transfusions took nearly 20 per cent of my blood. It was too much. I felt dizzy and faintly nauseous, unsure if they were real symptoms or simply the slithering tricks of my fear. I knew that I wouldn't be able to give more blood for some time, and the hopelessness of the situation—mine and theirs—crushed my chest with a flush and spasm of anguish.

It was dirty, frightening work, and I wasn't trained for it. The first-aid course that I'd completed as a young man had been comprehensive, but it hadn't covered combat injuries. And the work I'd done at my clinic in the slum was little help in those mountains. Beyond that, I was running on instinct—the same instinct to help and heal that had compelled me to save overdosed heroin addicts in my own city, a lifetime before. It was, of course, in great part a secret wish—like Khaled, with the vicious madman Habib—to be helped and saved and healed myself. And though it wasn't much, and it wasn't enough, it was all I had. So I did my best, trying not to vomit or cry or show my fear, and then I washed my hands in the snow.

When Nazeer was sufficiently recovered, he insisted on burying Abdel Khader Khan with the strictest adherence to ritual. He did that before he ate a meal or even drank a glass of water. I watched as Khaled, Mahmoud, and Nazeer cleaned themselves, prayed together, and then prepared Khaderbhai's body for burial. His green-and-white standard was lost, but one of the mujaheddin provided his own flag as a shroud. On a simple white background, it carried the phrase:

La illa ha ill'Allah
There is no god but God

Mahmoud Melbaaf, the Iranian who'd been with us since the Karachi taxi ride, was so tender and devoted and loving in his ministrations that my eyes went again and again to his calm, strong face as he worked and prayed. If he'd been burying his own child, he couldn't have been more gentle or clement, and it was from those moments during the burial that I began to cherish him as a friend.

I caught Nazeer's eye at the end of the ceremony, and at once I dropped my face to stare at the frozen ground beside my boots. He was in a wilderness of grieving and sorrowing shame. He'd lived to protect and serve Khader Khan. But the Khan was dead, and he was alive. Worse than that, he wasn't even wounded. His own life, the mere fact of his existence in the world, seemed like a betrayal. Every heartbeat was a new act of treachery. And that grief, and his exhaustion, took such a toll on him that he was quite seriously ill. He looked as much as ten kilos lighter. His cheeks were hollow, and there were black troughs beneath his eyes. His lips were cracked and peeling. His hands and feet worried me. I'd examined them, and I knew that the colour and warmth hadn't fully returned to them. I thought he might've suffered frostbite in his crawl through the snow.

There was, in fact, a task that did give his life purpose at that time, if not meaning, but I didn't know that then. Khaderbhai had given a last instruction, a last duty to perform, in the event of his death during the mission. He'd named a man, and ordered Nazeer to kill him. Nazeer was following that instruction even then, simply by staying alive long enough to carry out the murder. It was what sustained him, and his whole life had shrunk to that forlorn obsession. Knowing nothing of that then, as the cold days after Khader's burial became colder weeks, I worried constantly for the tough, loyal Afghan's sanity.

Khaled Ansari was changed by Khader's death in ways that were less obvious but equally profound. Where many of us were shocked into a dull, dense attention to routines, Khaled became sharper and more energetic. Where I often found myself adrift in stunned, heart-broken, bitter-sweet meditations on the man we'd loved and lost, Khaled took on new jobs almost every day, and never lost his focus. As a veteran of several wars, he assumed Khaderbhai's role of adviser to the mujaheddin commander Suleiman Shahbadi. In all his deliberations, the Palestinian was intense and tireless and judicious, to the point of being solemn. They weren't new qualities for Khaled—he was ever a dour, fervent man—but there was in him, after Khader's death, a hopefulness and a will to win that I'd never seen before. And he prayed. From the day we buried the Khan, Khaled was the first to call the men to prayer, and the last to lift his knees from the frozen stone.

Suleiman Shahbadi, the most senior Afghan left in our group—there were twenty of us, including the wounded—was a former community leader, or *Kandeedar*, from a clutch of villages near Ghazni, two-thirds of the way to Kabul. He was fifty-two years old, and a five-year veteran of the war. He was experienced in all forms of combat, from siege to guerrilla skirmish to pitched battle. Ahmed Shah Massoud, the unofficial leader of the nation-wide war to expel the Russians, had personally appointed Suleiman to set up the southern commands near Kandahar. All the men in our ethnically eclectic unit felt such awe-struck admiration for Massoud that it wasn't too strong to call it a kind of love. And because Suleiman's commission had come directly from Massoud, the Lion of the Panjsher, the men gave him an equally reverential respect.

When Nazeer was well enough to give a full report, just three days after we'd found him in the snow, Suleiman Shahbadi called a meeting. He was a short man with big hands and feet, and a sorrowful expression. Seven lines and ridges like planter's furrows creased his broad, high brow. A thickly coiled white turban covered his bald head. The dark, grey beard was trimmed around the mouth, and cut short beneath the jaw. His ears were slightly pointed—an effect that was exaggerated against the white turban—and that puckish touch combined with his wide mouth to hint at the cheeky humour that once might've been his. But then, on the mountain, his face was dominated by the expression in his eyes. They were the eyes of an unutterable sadness; a sadness withered and emptied of tears. It was an expression that engaged our sympathy yet prevented us from befriending him. For all that he was a wise, brave, and kindly man, that sadness was so deep in him that no man risked its touch.

With four sentries at their posts around the camp, and two men wounded, there were fourteen of us gathered in the cave to hear Suleiman speak. It was extremely cold—at or below zero—and we sat together to share our warmth.

I wished that I'd been more assiduous in my study of Dari and Pashto during the long wait in Quetta. Men spoke in both languages at that meeting, and every one after it. Mahmoud Melbaaf translated the Dari into Arabic for Khaled, who transformed the Arabic into English, leaning first to his left to listen to Mahmoud, and then leaning right as he whispered to me. It was a long, slow process, and I was amazed and humbled that the men waited patiently for every exchange to be translated for me. The popular European and American caricature of Afghans as wild, bloodthirsty men—a description that delighted Afghans themselves endlessly when they heard it—was contradicted by every direct contact I had with them. Face to face, Afghan men were generous, friendly, honest, and scrupulously courteous to me. I didn't say anything at that first meeting, or at any of those that followed, but still the men included me in every word they shared.

Nazeer's report on the attack that had killed our Khan was alarming. Khader had left the camp with twenty-six men, and all the riding and pack horses, on what should've been a safe-passage route to the village of his birth. On the second day of the march, still a full day and night from Khaderbhai's village, they were forced to stop for what they thought was a routine tribute exchange with a local clan leader.

There were hard questions asked about Habib Abdur Rahman at the meeting. In the two months since he'd left us, after killing poor, unconscious Siddiqi, Habib had instituted a one-man war of terror in what was for him a new area of operations—the Shar-i-Safa mountain range. He'd tortured a Russian officer to death. He'd dealt similar justice, as he saw it, to Afghan army men, and even mujaheddin fighters whom he judged to be less than fully committed to the cause. The horrors of those tortures had succeeded in nailing terror to everyone in the region. It was said that he was a ghost, or the *Shaitaan*, the Great Satan himself, come to rend men's bodies and peel the masks of their human faces back from their very skulls. What had been a relatively quiet corridor between the war zones was suddenly a turmoil of angry, terrified soldiers and other fighters, all pledged to find and kill the demon Habib.

Realising that he was in a trap designed to capture Habib, and that the men surrounding him were hostile to his cause, Khaderbhai tried to leave peacefully. He surrendered four horses as a tribute, and gathered his men. They were almost free of the enemy high ground when the first shots rattled into the little canyon. The battle raged for half an hour. When it was over, Nazeer counted eighteen bodies from Khader's column. Some of them had been killed as they lay wounded. Their throats had been cut. Nazeer and Ahmed Zadeh had only survived because they were crushed in a tangle of bodies, of horses and men, and appeared to be dead.

One horse had survived the encounter with a serious wound. Nazeer roused the animal, and strapped Khader's dead body and Ahmed's dying one to its back. The horse trudged through the snow for a day and half a night before it crumpled, collapsed, and died almost three kilometres from our camp. Nazeer then dragged both bodies through the snow until we found him. He had no idea what had happened to the five men who were not accounted for from Khader's column. They might've escaped, he thought, or they might've been captured. One thing was certain: among the enemy dead, Nazeer had seen Afghan army uniforms and some new Russian equipment.

Suleiman and Khaled Ansari assumed that the mortar attack on our position was linked to the battle that had claimed Abdel Khader's life. They guessed that the Afghan army unit had regrouped and, perhaps following Nazeer's trail, or acting on information gouged from prisoners, they'd launched the mortar attack. Suleiman assumed that there would be more attacks, but he doubted that they would launch a full frontal assault on the position. Such an attack would cost many lives, and might-n't succeed. If Russian soldiers supported the Afghan army units, how-ever, there might be helicopter attacks as soon as the sky was clear enough. Either way, we would lose men. Eventually, we might lose the high ground altogether.

After much discussion of the limited options open to us, Suleiman decided to launch two counter attacks with mortar units of our own. To that end, we needed reliable information about the enemy positions and their relative strength. He began to brief a fit, young Hazarbuz nomad named Jalalaad for the scouting mission, but then he froze, staring at the mouth of the cave. We all turned and gaped in surprise at the wild, ragged silhouette of a man in the oval frame of light at the opening of the cave. It was Habib. He'd slipped into the camp unseen by the sentries —an enigmatically difficult task—and he stood with us, two short steps away. I'm glad to say I wasn't the only one who reached for a weapon.

Khaled rushed forward with such a wide and heartfelt smile that I resented it, and resented Habib more for inspiring it. He brought the madman into the cave and sat him down beside the startled Suleiman. And then, with perfect calm and clarity, Habib began to speak.

He'd seen the enemy positions, he said, and he knew their strength. He'd watched the mortar attack on our camp, and then he'd crept down to their camps, so close that he'd heard them decide what to eat for lunch. He could guide us to new vantage points where we could fire mortars into their camps, and kill them. Those who didn't die outright, he wanted it understood, belonged to him. That was his price.

The men debated Habib's proposal, speaking openly in front of him. It worried some that we were putting ourselves in the hands of the very lunatic whose monstrous tortures had brought the war to our cave. It was bad luck to link ourselves to his evil, those men said; bad morals and bad luck. It worried others that we would kill so many Afghan army regulars.

One of the seemingly bizarre contradictions of the war was that Afghan met Afghan with real reluctance, and sincerely regretted every death. There was such a long history of division and conflict between the clans and ethnic divisions in Afghanistan that no man, with the exception of Habib, truly hated the Afghans who fought on the side of the Russians. Real hatred, where it existed at all, was reserved for the Afghan version of the KGB, known as the KHAD. The Afghan traitor Najibullah, who eventually seized power and appointed himself ruler of the country, headed that infamous police force for years, and was responsible for many of its unspeakable tortures. There wasn't a resistance fighter in the country who didn't dream of dragging on a rope and hoisting him into the air by his neck. The soldiers and even the officers of the Afghan army, however, were a different matter: they were kinsmen, many of them conscripts, doing what they had to do in order to survive. And for their part, the Afghan regulars often sent vital information concerning Russian troop movements or bombardments to mujaheddin fighters. In fact, the war could never be won without their secret help. And a surprise mortar attack on the two Afghan army positions, identified by Habib, would cost many Afghan lives.

The long discussion ended with a decision to fight. Our situation was judged to be so perilous that we had no choice but to counter-attack and drive the enemy from the mountain.

The plan was good, and it should've worked, but like so much else in that war it brought only chaos and death. Four sentries remained to guard the camp, and I stayed behind as well to care for the wounded. The fourteen men of the strike force were divided into two teams. Khaled and Habib led the first team; Suleiman led the second. Following Habib's directions, they set up their mortars about a kilometre away from the enemy camps—a distance that was well inside the maximum effective range. The bombardment commenced just after dawn, and continued for half an hour. The strike teams found eight Afghan soldiers when they entered the ruined camps. Not all of them were dead. Habib went to work on the survivors. Sickened by what they'd agreed to let him do, our men returned to the camp, hoping never to see the madman again.

Less than one hour after their return, a counter-bombardment rained on our compound with whining, whistling, thumping explosions. As the deadly attack subsided, we crawled from our hiding places to hear a strange, vibrating hum. Khaled was a few metres away from me. I saw the fear rasp across his scarred face. He began to run toward the small cover provided by clefts in the rock walls opposite the caves. He was shouting and waving for me to join him. I took a step towards him and then froze as a Russian helicopter rose like some huge, monstrous insect over the rim of the compound. It's impossible to describe how immense and predatory those machines seem when you're under fire from them. The monster fills the eye and the mind, and for a second or two there seems to be nothing else in the world but the metal and the noise and the terror.

In the instant that it appeared, it fired on us and wheeled away like a falcon falling to the kill. Two rockets scorched the air as they streaked toward the caves. They travelled with incredible speed, much faster than my eyes could follow. I swung round to see one rocket smash into the stone cliff above the entrance to the cave complex and explode with a shower of smoke, flame, rock, and metal fragments. Immediately after it, the second rocket entered the cave-mouth and exploded.

The shock wave that hit me was a physical thing, like standing on the edge of a swimming pool and having someone push me in with the flat of his hands. I slammed onto my back and gasped, choking for air, with the wind knocked out of me. I could see the entrance to the caves. The wounded men were in there. Other men were hiding in there. Bursting through the black smoke and flames, men began running or crawling out of the cave. One of the men was a Pashtun trader named Alef. He'd been a favourite of Khaderbhai's for his jokes and irreverent satires of pompous mullahs and local political figures. His back was blown out from the head to the thighs. His clothes were on fire. They burned and smouldered around the bare, erupted meat of his back. Bones — a hipbone and a shoulder blade — were clearly visible, and moving in the open wound as he crawled.

He was screaming out for help. I gritted my teeth to make the run to him, but the helicopter appeared again. It roared past us at great speed, twice turning in tight circles to attack us from new angles in passing rushes. Then it hovered with arrogant, fearless nonchalance near the edge of the plateau that had been our haven. Just as I started to move forward it fired two more rockets at the caves and then another two. The salvo lit up the whole interior of the cavern for an instant, and melted the snow with a rolling fireball of flames and white-hot metal pieces. One fragment landed only an arm's reach away from me. It crashed into the snow and sizzled with a blistering hiss for several seconds. I crawled away after Khaled, and squeezed my body into the narrow cleft in the rocks.

The gunship opened up with machine guns, raking the open ground and chopping up the bodies of the wounded men who were exposed there. Then I heard another gun with a different tone, and I realised that one of our men was firing back at the helicopter. It was the sound of a PK, one of our Russian machine guns, returning fire. It was quickly followed by a second, long *chun-chun-chun-chun* burst from another PK. Two of our men were firing at the helicopter. My only instinct had been to hide myself from the ruthlessly efficient killing machine, but they not only exposed themselves to the beast, they actually challenged it and drew its fire.

There was a shout from somewhere behind me and then a rocket fizzed past my hideaway cleft in the stone toward the chopper. It was a rocket, fired from an AK-74 by one of our men. It missed the helicopter, and so did the next two rockets, but the return fire from our men was finding its target, and convinced the pilot to cut his losses and leave.

A great shout went up from our men: *Allah hu Akbar! Allah hu Akbar! Allah hu Akbar!* Khaled and I eased our way out of the wedge of stone to find four men rushing forward and firing at the aircraft. A thin stream of rusty black smoke dribbled from a point about two-thirds of the way along the length of the machine as it plunged away from us, to the metal screech of a wildly racing engine.

The young man who'd opened up the counter attack was Jalalaad, the Hazarbuz nomad. He handed the heavy PK off to a friend, snatched up an AK-74 with a taped double magazine, and bounded away in search of enemy soldiers who might've crept close under cover of the chopper. Two other young men ran after him, slipping and jumping down the snow-covered slope.

We searched the compound for survivors. We were twenty men at the start of the attack, including our two wounded. After it, we were eleven: Jalalaad and the two young men, Juma and Hanif, who'd left with him to find any Afghan regulars or Russians within our defensive perimeter; Khaled; Nazeer; a very young fighter named Ala-ud-Din; three wounded men; Suleiman; and myself. We'd lost nine men—one more than the eight Afghan army men we'd killed in our mortar attack on them.

Our wounded were in a bad way. One man was so badly burned that his fingers had fused together like a crab's claws, and his face wasn't recognisably human. He was breathing through a hole in the red skin of his face. It might've been his mouth, that trembling hole in his face, but there was no way to be sure. The breaths were laboured, scraping sounds that faded and weakened as I listened to them. I gave him morphine, and moved on to the next man. He was a farmer from Ghazni named Zaher Rasul. He'd taken to bringing me green tea whenever I read a book or made notes in my journal. He was a kindly, self-effacing forty-two year old—a senior man in a country where the average life span for men was forty-five. His arm was missing below the shoulder. The same projectile, whatever it was, that had severed his arm, had torn him open along his body, from the chest to the hip, on the right-hand side. There was no way of knowing what pieces of metal or stone might be lodged inside his wounds. He was praying a repetitive *zikkir*:

God is great
God forgive me
God is merciful
God forgive me

Mahmoud Melbaaf was holding a tourniquet on the ragged stump of shoulder that remained. When he released it, the blood spattered us in strong warm spurts. Mahmoud pulled the tourniquet tight once more. I looked into his eyes.

'Artery,' I said, crushed by the task that confronted me.

'Yes. Under his arm. Did you see?'

'Yeah. It'sgotta be stitched up or clamped or something. We've gotta stop the blood. He's lost too much already.'

The blackened, ash-covered remains of the medical kit were grouped on a piece of canvas in front of my knees. I found a suture needle, a rusty mechanic's pliers, and some silk thread. Freezing cold on the snowy ground, and with my bare hands cramped, I ran stitches into the artery, and the flesh, and the whole area, desperate to lock off the gush of hot, red blood. The thread snagged several times. My stiffened fingers trembled. The man was awake and aware, and in terrible pain. He screamed and howled intermittently, but returned always to his prayer.

My eyes were full of sweat, despite the shivering cold, when I nodded to Mahmoud to release the tourniquet. Blood oozed through the stitches. It was a much slower flow, but I knew the trickle would still kill him in the long run. I began to pack wads of bandage into the wound and then to wind on a pressure dressing, but Mahmoud's bloody hands seized my wrists in a powerful grip. I looked up to see that Zaher Rasul had stopped praying and stopped bleeding. He was dead.

I was breathing hard. It was the kind of breathing that does more harm than good. I suddenly realised that I hadn't eaten for too many hours, and I was very hungry. With that thought—hunger, food—I felt sick for the first time. I felt the sweaty wave of nausea surge over me, and I shook my head free of it.

When we returned our attention to the burned man we found that he, too, had succumbed. I covered the still body with a canvas camouflage drop-sheet. My last glimpse of his scorched, featureless, melted face became a prayer of thanks. One of the agonising truths for a battle medic is that you pray as hard and almost as often for men to die as you pray for them to live. The third wounded man was Mahmoud Melbaaf himself. There were tiny grey-black fragments of metal and what seemed to be melted plastic in his back, his neck, and the back of his head. Fortunately, the spray of that hot material had only penetrated the upper layers of his skin, much like splinters. Nevertheless, it was the work of an hour to rid him of them. I washed the wounds and applied antibiotic powder, dressing them wherever it was possible.

We checked our supplies and reserves. We'd had two goats at the start of the attack. One of them had run off, and we never sighted it again. The other was found cowering in a blind alcove formed between high, rocky escarpments. That goat was our only food. The flour had burned to soot with the rice and ghee and sugar. The fuel reserves were completely exhausted. The stainless steel medical instruments had suffered a direct hit, and most of them had deformed into useless lumps of metal. I scraped through the wreckage to retrieve some antibiotics, disinfectants, ointments, bandages, suture needles, thread, syringes, and morphine ampoules. We had ammunition, and some medicines, and we could melt the snow to make water, but the lack of food was a very serious concern.

We were nine men. Suleiman and Khaled decided that we had to leave the camp. There was a cave on another mountain, about twelve hours' march away to the east, which they hoped might give us adequate protection from attack. The Russians were sure to have another helicopter in the air within a few hours at most. Ground forces wouldn't be far behind.

'Every man fill two canteens with snow, and keep them inside his clothes, next to his body, on the march,' Khaled said to me, translating Suleiman's orders. 'We carry weapons, ammunition, medicines, blankets, some fuel, some wood, and the goat. Nothing else. Let's go!'

We left on the march with empty stomachs, and that state defined us for the next four weeks as we hunkered down in the new mountain cave. One of Jalalaad's young friends, Hanif, had been a halal butcher in his home village. He slaughtered, skinned, gutted, and quartered the goat when we arrived. We prepared a fire with wood that we'd carried from the ruined camp, and a sprinkle of spirit from one of the lamps. The meat was cooked—every last morsel, except for the parts, such as the legs of the animal below the knee joint, which were regarded as *haram*, or forbidden for Muslims to eat. The carefully cooked meat was then rationed into small daily shares. We stored the bulk of the cooked flesh in an improvised refrigerator scooped out of the ice and snow. And then, for four weeks, we nibbled at the dry meat and cringed inwardly as hunger twisted us around the craving for more.

It was an expression of our discipline and good-natured support for one another that the meat from one goat kept nine men alive for four weeks. We tried many times to slip away from the camp and reach one of the neighbouring khels to secure some extra food. But all the local villages were occupied by enemy troops, and the entire mountain range was surrounded by patrols of Afghan army units led by Russians. Habib's tortures had combined with the damage we'd done to the helicopter to rouse a furious determination in the Russians and Afghan regulars. On one foraging mission, our scouts heard an announcement echoing through the nearest valley. The Russians had attached a loudspeaker to a military jeep. An Afghan, speaking in Pashto, described us as bandits and criminals, and said that a special task force had been set up to capture us. They'd put a reward on our heads. Our scouts wanted to shoot at the vehicle, but they thought it might be a trap designed to draw us out of hiding. They let it pass, and the words of the hunters echoed in the sheer, stone canyons like the howl of prowling wolves.

Apparently acting on false information—or perhaps following the trail of Habib's bloody executions—the Russians, working from all the surrounding villages, concentrated their searches on another mountain range to the north of us. For so long as we remained in our remote cave, we seemed to be safe. So we waited, trapped and hungering and afraid, through the four coldest weeks of the year. We hid, creeping through shadows in the daylight hours, and huddled together without light or heat in the darkness every night. And slowly, one ice-edged hour at a time, the knife of war whittled the wishing and hoping away until all that was left to us, within the hard, disconsolate wrap of our own arms around our own shivering bodies, was the lonely will to survive.

CHAPTER THIRTY-SIX

I COULDN'T FACE the loss of Khaderbhai, my father-dream. I'd helped to bury him, for God's sake, with my own hands. But I didn't grieve, and I didn't mourn him. There wasn't enough truth in me for that kind of sorrowing because my heart wouldn't believe him dead. I'd loved him too much, it seemed to me in that winter of war, for him to simply be gone, to be dead. If so much love could vanish into the earth and speak no more, smile no more, then love was nothing. And I wouldn't believe that. I was sure there had to be a pay-off, somehow, and I kept waiting for it. I didn't know then, as I do now, that love's a one-way street. Love, like respect, isn't something you get; it's something you give. But not knowing that in those bitter weeks, not thinking that, I turned from the hole in my life where so much loving hope had been, and I refused to feel the longing or the loss. I cringed within the bleak, concealing camouflage of snow and shadowed stone. I chewed the leathered fragments of goat's meat left to us. And each minute crammed with heartbeats and hunger dragged me further from the grieving and the truth.

Eventually, of course, we exhausted the supply of meat, and a meeting was called to discuss our options. Jalalaad and the younger Afghans wanted to make a run for it: to fight our way through enemy lines, and strike out for the desert region of Zabul province, close to the Pakistan border. Suleiman and Khaled reluctantly agreed that there was no other option, but they wanted clear intelligence of the enemy disposition before choosing where to launch a breakout attack. To that end, Suleiman sent young Hanif on a scouting mission that would take him on a sweeping curve from the south-west to the north and south-east of our position. He ordered the young man to return within twenty-four hours, and to travel only at night.

It was a long, cold, hungry wait for Hanif to return. We were drinking water, but that only staved off the torment for a few minutes, and left us even hungrier. Twenty-four hours stretched to two days, and then into a third, with no sign of him. On the morning of the third day, we accepted that Hanif was dead or captured. Juma, a cameleer from the tiny Tajik enclave in the south-west of Afghanistan near Iran, volunteered to search for him. He was a dark, thin-faced man with a hawk-like nose and a thickly emotive mouth. He was close to Hanif and Jalalaad—the closeness that men in wars and prisons find, against their every expectation, and rarely express in words or gestures.

Juma's Tajik clans of cameleers were traditional rivals of the Mohmand Hazarbuz people of Hanif and Jalalaad in the nomadic transport of trade goods. The competition between the groups had become intense as Afghanistan rapidly modernised. In 1920, fully one in every three Afghans was a nomad. Just two generations later, by 1970, only 2 per cent of the people were nomads. Rivals though they were, the three young men had been thrown into close co-operation with one another by the war, and they'd become inseparable friends. Their friendship had developed in the insidiously dull months that troughed between the peaks of fighting, and was tested many times in combat. In their most successful battle, they'd used land mines and grenades to destroy a Russian tank. Each of them wore, on a leather thong around his neck, a small piece of metal taken from the tank as a souvenir.

When Juma declared that he would search for Hanif, we all knew that we couldn't prevent him from doing it. With a weary sigh, Suleiman agreed to let him go. Refusing to wait until nightfall, Juma shouldered his weapon and crept from the camp at once. He'd gone without food for three days, just as we had, but the smile that he sent back to Jalalaad, as he looked over his shoulder for the last time, was bright with strength and courage. We watched him leave, watched his thin, retreating shadow sweep the sundial of the snowy slopes beneath us.

Hunger exaggerated the cold. It was a long, hard winter, with snow falling on the mountains around us every other day. The temperature fluttered above zero during the daylight hours, but sank into icy, teeth-chattering sub-zero levels from dusk until well after dawn. My hands and feet were constantly cold; achingly cold. The skin on my face was wooden, and as riven with cracks as the feet of the farmers in Prabaker's village. We pissed on our hands, to fight off the aching sting of the cold, and it helped to bring feeling back to them momentarily. But we were so cold that taking a piss was a serious issue. First there was the dread inspired by having to open our clothes at all, and then there was the chill that followed the release of a bladder of warm fluid. Losing that warmth caused the body temperature to drop quickly, and we always put it off until the last moment.

Juma failed to return that night. At midnight, with hunger and fear prodding us awake, we all jumped at a little crickle of sound in the darkness. Seven guns aimed at the spot. Then we gasped as a face loomed from the shadows, much closer than we'd expected. It was Habib.

'What are you doing, my brother?' Khaled asked him gently, in Urdu. 'You gave us a big fright.'

'They are here,' he answered in a rational, calm voice that seemed to rise from another mind or another place, as if he was a medium speaking in a trance. His face was filthy. We were all unwashed and bearded, but Habib's filth was something so repulsive and thickly smeared that it was shocking. Like poison pouring from an infected wound, the foulness seemed to squeeze outward through the pores of his skin from some feculence deep within. 'They are everywhere, all around you. And they are coming up to here to get you, to kill you all, when more men come, tomorrow, or the day after that. Soon. They know where you are. They will kill you all. There is only one way out of here now.'

'How did you find us here, brother?' Khaled asked, his voice as calm and remote as Habib's.

'I came with you. I have always been near you. Did you not see me?'

'My friends,' Jalalaad asked, 'Juma and Hanif—did you see them anywhere?'

Habib didn't reply. Jalalaad asked the question again, more forcefully.

'Did you see them? Were they in the Russian camp? Were they captured?'

We listened in a silence thick with our fear and the poisonous smells of decayed flesh that clung to Habib. He seemed to be meditating, or perhaps listening to something no-one else could hear.

'Tell me, *bach-e-kaka*,' Suleiman asked gently, using the familiar term for *nephew*, 'what did you mean, there is only *one* way out of here now?'

'They are everywhere,' Habib answered, his face deformed by its wide-mouthed, psychotic stare. Mahmoud Melbaaf was translating for me, whispering close to my ear. 'They don't have enough men. They have mined all the easiest ways out of the mountains. The north, the east, the west, all mined. Only the south-east is clear, because they think you will not try to escape that way. They left that way clear, so they can come up here to get you.'

'We can't go out that way,' Mahmoud whispered to me when Habib stopped suddenly. 'The Russians, they hold the valley south-east of here. It is their way to Kandahar. When they come for us, they will come from that direction. If we go that way, we will all die, and they know it.'

'Now, they are in the south-east. But for tomorrow, for one day, they are all on the far side of the mountain, in the north-west,' Habib said. His voice was still calm and composed, but his face was a gargoyle's leer, and the contrast unnerved us all. 'Only a few of them stay here tomorrow. Only a few will stay, while the rest of them put the last mines on the north-west slopes, just after dawn. If you run at them, attack them, fight them tomorrow, in the south-east, there will only be a few of them. You can break through and escape. But only tomorrow.'

'How many are they altogether?' Jalalaad asked.

'Sixty-eight men. They have mortars, rockets, and six heavy machine guns. There are too many of them for you to sneak past them at night.'

'But *you* sneaked past them,' Jalalaad insisted defiantly.

'They cannot see me,' Habib replied serenely. 'I am invisible to them. They cannot see me until I am pushing my knife into their throats.'

'That's ridiculous!' Jalalaad hissed at him. 'They are soldiers. You are a soldier. If you can get past them, we can do it.'

'Did your men return to you?' Habib asked him, turning his maniac stare on the young fighter for the first time. Jalalaad opened his mouth to speak, but the words sank into the small heaving sea of his heart. He cast his eyes down, and shook his head. 'Could you enter this camp without being seen or heard, as I did? If you try to get past them, you will die, like your friends. You cannot get past them. I can do it, but you cannot.'

'But you think we can fight our way out of here?' Khaled put the question to him gently, quietly, but we all heard the urgency in it.

'You can. It is the only way. I have been everywhere on this mountain, and I have been so close to them that I can hear them scratch their skin. That is the reason why I am here. I came to tell you how to save yourselves. But there is a price for my help. All the ones you do not kill tomorrow, the ones who survive, they will be mine. You will give them to me.'

'Yes, yes,' Suleiman agreed soothingly. 'Come, *bach-e-kaka*, tell us what you know. We want to share your knowledge. Sit with us, and tell us what you know. We have no food, so we cannot offer you a meal. I'm sorry.'

'There is food,' Habib interrupted, pointing beyond us to the shadows at the edge of our camp. 'I smell food there.'

True enough, the rotting pieces of the dead goat—the haram cuts from the animal—lay in a little heap in the slushy snow. Cold as it was, and even in the snow, the bits of raw meat had long begun to decay. We couldn't smell them from that distance, but it seemed that Habib could.

The madman's comment provoked a long discussion of the religious rights and wrongs of eating haram food. The men weren't rigid in the observation of their faith. They prayed every day, but not in strict adherence to the timetable of three sessions, ordained by Shia Islam, or the five sessions of the Sunni Muslims. They were good men of faith, rather than overtly religious men. Nevertheless, in a time of war, and with the great dangers we faced, the last power they wanted ranged against them was God's. They were holy warriors, mujaheddin: men who believed that they would become martyrs at the instant that they died in battle, and that they were assured a place in the heavens, where beautiful maidens would attend them. They didn't want to pollute themselves with forbidden foods when they were so close to the martyr's rush for paradise. It was a tribute to their faith, in fact, that the mere discussion of the haram meat hadn't occurred until we'd hungered for a month and then starved for five days.

For my part, I confessed to Mahmoud Melbaaf that I'd been thinking about the discarded meat almost constantly for the last few days. I wasn't a Muslim, and the meat wasn't forbidden to me. But I'd lived so closely with the fighters, and for so many painful weeks, that I'd linked my fate to theirs. I would never have eaten anything while they hungered. I wanted to eat the meat, but only if they agreed and ate it with me.

Suleiman delivered the decisive opinion on the matter. He reminded the men that while it was indeed evil for a Muslim to eat haram food, it was an even greater evil for a Muslim to starve himself to death when haram food was available to be eaten. The men decided that we would cook the rotting meat in a soup, before the first light. Then, fortified by that meal, we would use Habib's information on the enemy positions to fight our way out of the mountains.

During the long weeks of hiding and waiting without heat or hot food, we'd entertained and supported one another with the stories we'd told. On that last night, after several others had spoken, it was my turn once more. For my first story, weeks before, I'd told them about my escape from prison. Although they'd been scandalised by my admissions about being a *gunaa*, or sinner, and being imprisoned as a criminal, they'd been thrilled by the account, and asked many questions afterwards. My second story had been about the Night of the Assassins: how Abdullah, Vikram, and I had tracked the Nigerian killers down; how we'd fought with them, defeated them, and then expelled them from the country; how I'd hunted Maurizio, the man who'd caused it all, and beat him with my fists; and how I'd wanted to kill him, but had spared his life, only to regret that pity when he'd attacked Lisa Carter and forced Ulla to kill him.

That story, too, had been very well received, and as Mahmoud Melbaaf took his place beside me to translate my third story, I wondered what might capture their enthusiasm anew. My mind scanned its list of heroes. There were many, so many men and women, beginning with my own mother, whose courage and sacrifice inspired the memory of them. But when I began to speak, I found myself telling Prabaker's story. The words, like some kind of desperate prayer, came unbidden from my heart.

I told them how Prabaker had left his village-Eden for the city when he was still a child; how he'd returned as a teenager, with the wild street boy Raju and other friends to confront the menace of the dacoits; how Rukhmabai, Prabaker's mother, had put courage into the men of the village; how young Raju had fired his revolver as he walked toward the boastful leader of the dacoits until the man fell dead; how Prabaker had loved feasting and dancing and music; how he'd saved the woman he loved from the cholera epidemic, and married her; and how he'd died, in a hospital bed, surrounded by our sorrowing love.

After Mahmoud finished translating the last of my words there was a lengthy silence while they considered the tale. I was just convincing myself that they were as moved by the life of my little friend as I was myself when the first questions began.

'So, how many *goats* did they have in that village?' Suleiman asked gravely.

'He wants to know how many goats —' Mahmoud began translating.

'I got it, I got it,' I smiled. 'Well, near as I can tell, about eighty, maybe as many as a hundred. Each household had about two or three goats, but some had as many as six or eight.'

That information inspired a little gesticulating buzz of discussion that was more animated and partisan than any of the political or religious debates that had occasionally stirred among the men.

'What ... *colour* ... were these goats?' Jalalaad asked.

'The colours,' Mahmoud explained solemnly. 'He wants to know the colors of those goats.'

'Well, gee, they were brown, I guess, and white, and a few black ones.'

'Were they big goats, like the ones in Iran?' Mahmoud translated for Suleiman. 'Or were they skinny, like the ones in Pakistan?'

'Well, about *so* big ...' I suggested, gesturing with my hands.

'How much milk,' Nazeer asked, caught up in the discussion in spite of himself, 'did they get from those goats, every day?'

'I'm ... not really an expert on goats ...'

'Try,' Nazeer insisted. 'Try to remember.'

'Oh, shit. I ... it's just a wild stab in the dark, mind you, but I'd say, maybe, a couple of litres a day ...' I offered, raising the palms of my hands helplessly.

'This friend of yours, how much did he earn as a taxi driver?' Suleiman asked.

'Did this friend go out with a woman, alone, before his marriage?' Jalalaad wanted to know, causing all the men to laugh and some of them to throw small stones at him.

In that way the session moved through all the themes that concerned them, until at last I excused myself and found a relatively sheltered spot where I could stare at the misty nothing of the frozen, shrouded sky. I was trying to fight down the fear that prowled in my empty belly, and leapt up with sharp claws at my heart in its cage of ribs.

Tomorrow. We were going to fight our way out. No-one had said it, but I knew that all the others were thinking we would die. They were too cheerful, too relaxed. All the tension and dread of the last weeks had drained from them once we'd made the decision to fight. It wasn't the joyful relief of men who know they're saved. It was something else — something I'd seen in the mirror, in my cell, on the night before my desperate escape from prison, and something I'd seen in the eyes of the man who'd escaped with me. It was the exhilaration of men who were risking everything, risking life and death, on one throw of the dice. Some time on the next day we would be free, or we would be dead. The same resolution that had sent me over the front wall of a prison was sending us over the ridge, and into the enemy guns: it's better to die fighting than to die like a rat in a trap. I'd escaped from prison, and crossed the world, and crossed the years, to find myself in the company of men who felt exactly as I did about freedom and death.

And still I was afraid: afraid of being wounded, afraid of being shot in the spine and paralysed, afraid of being captured alive and tortured in another prison by yet another prison guard. It occurred to me that Karla and Khaderbhai would've had something clever to say to me about fear. And in thinking that, I realised how remote they were from the moment, and the mountain, and me. I realised that I didn't need their brilliance any more: it couldn't help me. All the cleverness in all the world couldn't stop my stomach from knotting around its prowling fear. When you know you're going to die, there's no comfort in cleverness. Genius is vain, and cleverness is hollow, at the end. The comfort that does come, if it comes at all, is that strangely marbled mix of time and place and feeling that we usually call wisdom. For me, on that last night before the battle, it was the sound of my mother's voice, and it was the life and death of my friend Prabaker ... *God give you rest, Prabaker. I still love you, and the grieving, when I think of you, is pinned to my heart and my eyes with bright and burning stars ...* My comfort, on that freezing ridge, was the memory of Prabaker's smiling face, and the sound of my mother's voice: *Whatever you do in life, do it with courage, and you won't go far wrong ...*

'Here, take one,' Khaled said, sliding down beside me to squat on his heels, and offering me one of two half-cigarettes that he held in his bare hand.

'Jesus!' I gawked. 'Where'd you get those? I thought we all ran out last week.'

'We did,' he said, lighting the cigarettes with a small gas lighter. 'Except for these. I kept them for a special occasion. I think this is it. I got a bad feeling, Lin. A real bad feeling. It's inside me, and I can't shake it tonight.'

It was the first time that we'd spoken more than the essential word or two since the night that Khader had left. We'd worked and slept side by side, every day and night, but I almost never met his eye, and I'd avoided conversation with him so coldly that he, too, had been silent with me.

'Look … Khaled … about Khader, and Karla … don't feel… I mean, I'm not —'

'No,' he interrupted. 'You had plenty of reason to be mad. I can see it from your side. I always could. You got a raw deal, and I told Khader that, too, on the night he left. He should've trusted you. It's a funny thing— the guy he trusted most, the only guy in the whole world he really trusted all the way, turned out to be a crazy killer, and the one who sold us all out.'

The New York accent, with its Arabic swell, rolled over me like a warm, frothy wave, and I almost reached out to hug him. I'd missed the assurances I'd always found in the sound of that voice, and the honest suffering I saw in the scarred face. I was so glad to have his friendship again that I confused what he'd said about Khaderbhai. I thought, without really thinking at all, that he was talking about Abdullah. He wasn't, and that, too, like a hundred other chances to know all the truth in the one conversation, was lost.

'How well did you know Abdullah?' I asked him.

'Pretty well,' he answered, his little smile becoming an asking frown: *Where is this going?*

'Did you like him?'

'Not really.'

'Why not?'

'Abdullah didn't believe in anything. He was a rebel without a cause, in a world that doesn't have enough rebels for the real causes. I don't like— and I don't really trust—people who don't believe in anything.'

'Does that include me?'

'No,' he laughed. 'You believe in a lot of things. That's why I like you. That's why Khader loved you. He did love you, you know. He told me so, a couple different times.'

'What do I believe in?' I scoffed.

'You believe in people,' he replied quickly. 'That stuff with the slum clinic and all. The story you told the guys tonight, that about the village. You'd forget that shit if you didn't believe in people. That work in the slum, when the cholera went through the place—Khader loved that, what you did then, and so did I. Shit, for a while there, I think you even had

Karla believing, too. You gotta understand, Lin. If Khader had a choice, if there was a better way to do what he had to do, he would've taken it. It all played out the way it had to. Nobody wanted to fuck you over.'

'Not even Karla?' I smiled, savouring the last puff of the cigarette and then stubbing it out on the ground.

'Well, maybe Karla,' he conceded, laughing the small, sad laugh. 'But that's Karla. I think the only guy she never fucked over was Abdullah.'

'Were they together?' I asked, so surprised that I couldn't help the pinch of jealousy that pulled my brows together in a hard, little frown.

'Well, you couldn't say *together*,' he answered evenly, staring into my eyes. 'But *I* was, once. I used to live with her.'

'You *what*?'

'I lived with her—for six months.'

'What happened?' I asked, gritting my teeth and feeling stupid for it. I had no right to be angry or jealous. I'd never asked Karla about her lovers, and she'd never asked me about mine.

'You don't know, do you?'

'I wouldn't ask, if I knew.'

'She dumped me,' he said slowly, 'just about the time you came along.'

'Ah, fuck, man ...'

'It's okay,' he smiled.

We were silent for a moment, both of us reeling back through the years. I remembered Abdullah, at the sea wall near the Haji Ali Mosque, on the night that I met him with Khaderbhai. I remembered him saying that a woman had taught him the clever phrase he'd used in English. It must've been Karla. Of course it was Karla. And I remembered the stiffness that was in Khaled's manner when I first met him, and I realised, suddenly, that he must've been hurting then, and maybe blaming me for it. I saw clearly what it must've taken for him to be as friendly and kind to me as he was at the beginning.

'You know,' he added after a while, 'you really got to go careful with Karla, Lin. She's ... *angry* ... you know? And she's hurt. She's hurt bad, in all the places that count. They really fucked her up when she was a kid. She's a bit crazy. She did something, in the States, before she came to India. And that fucked her up, too.'

'What did she do?'

'I don't know. Something pretty serious. She never told me what it was.

We talked *around* it, if you get my meaning. I think Khaderbhai knew about it because, you know, he was the first one to meet her.'

'No, I didn't know that,' I answered him, frowning with the thought of how little I knew about the woman I'd loved for so long. 'Why ... why do you think she never told me about Khaderbhai? I knew her a long time — when we were both working for him — and she didn't say a word. *I* talked about him, but she never said a word. She didn't mention his name once.'

'I think she's just loyal to him, you know? I don't think there's anything against you, Lin. She's just incredibly loyal — well, she *was* incredibly loyal to him. She thought of him like a father, I think. Her own father died when she was a kid. And her stepfather died when she was still pretty young. Khader came along just in time to save her, so he got to be her father.'

'You said he was the first one who met her?'

'Yeah, on a plane. It's kind of a weird story, the way she told me. She didn't remember getting on the plane. She was running from something — something she did — and she was in trouble. She ended up going on a few different planes from different airports — for a few days, I think. And then she was on this plane that was going to Singapore from ... I don't know ... somewhere. And she must've had, like, a nervous breakdown or something, because she cracked up, and the next thing she knew, she was in this cave, in India, with Khaderbhai. And then he left her with Ahmed, who looked after her.'

'She told me about him.'

'Did she? She doesn't talk about it much. She liked that guy. He nursed her for near about six months until she got herself together again. He brought her back — into the light, like. They were pretty close. I think he was the closest thing to a brother she ever knew.'

'Were you with her — I mean, did you *know* her then, when he was killed?'

'I don't know that he *was* killed, Lin,' Khaled stated, frowning hard as the knot of recollections turned in his memory. 'I know Karla believes it — that Madame Zhou killed him, and the girl ...'

'Christine.'

'Yeah, Christine. But I knew Ahmed pretty well. He was a very gentle guy — a very simple, soft kind of a guy. He was just the type to take poison with his girlfriend, like in a romantic movie, if he thought he couldn't ever be free with her. Khader looked into it, real close, because Ahmed was one of his guys, and he was sure Zhou had nothing to do with it. He cleared her.'

'But Karla wouldn't accept it?'

'No, she didn't buy it. And coming on top of everything else, it really fucked her up. Did she ever tell you she loves you?'

I hesitated, partly from reluctance to surrender the little advantage I might've had over him if he believed that she did say it, and partly from loyalty to Karla—because it was her business, after all. In the end, I answered him: I had to know why he'd asked me the question.

'No.'

'That's too bad,' he said flatly. 'I thought you might be the one.'

'The one?'

'The one to help her—to break through, I guess. Something really bad happened to that girl. A lot of bad things happened to her. Khader made it worse, I think.'

'How?'

'He put her to work for him. He saved her, when he met her, and he protected her from what she was scared of, back in the States. But then she met this guy, a politician, and he fell for her pretty hard. Khader needed the guy, so he got her to work for him, and I don't think she was cut out for it.'

'What kind of work?'

'You know how beautiful she is—those green eyes, and that white, white skin.'

'Ah, fuck,' I sighed, remembering a lecture Khader had given me once, about the amount of crime in the sin, and the sin in the crime.

'I don't know what was in Khader's head,' Khaled concluded, shaking his own head in doubt and wonder. 'It was ... out of character, to say the least. I honestly don't think he saw it as ... *damaging* her. But she, kind of, froze up, inside. It was like her own father ... was getting her to do that shit. And I don't think she forgave him for it. But she was incredibly loyal to him, all the same. I never understood it. But that's how I got together with her—I saw all that happening, and I felt kind of sorry for her, if you know what I mean. After a while, one thing led to another. But I never really got through to her. And you didn't, neither. I don't think anyone will. Ever.'

'Ever is a long time.'

'Okay, you got a point. But I'm just trying to warn you. I don't want you to get hurt any more, brother. We've been through too much, *na*? And I don't want *her* to get hurt.'

He fell silent again. We stared at the rocks and the frosty ground, avoiding one another's eyes. A few shivering minutes passed. At last he took a deep breath and stood up, slapping at the chill in his arms and legs. I stood as well, trembling with cold and stamping my numb feet. At the last possible moment, and with an impulsive rush as if he was breaking through a tangle of vines, Khaled flung his arms around me and hugged me. The strength in his arms was fierce, but his head slowly came to rest against mine as tenderly as the lolling head of a sleeping child.

When he pulled away from me, his face was averted and I couldn't see his eyes. He walked off, and I followed more slowly, hugging my hands under my arms to fight off the cold. It was only when I was alone that I recalled what he'd said to me: *I got a bad feeling, Lin. A real bad feeling* ...

I resolved to talk to him about it, but just at that moment Habib stepped out of a shadow beside me, and I jumped in fright.

'For *fuck's* sake!' I hissed. 'You scared the fuckin' *shit* outta me! Don't *do* that shit, Habib!'

'It's okay, it's okay,' Mahmoud Melbaaf said, stepping up beside the madman.

Habib garbled something at me, speaking so quickly that I couldn't make out a single clear syllable. His eyes were starting from his head. The effect was exaggerated by the dark, heavy pouches beneath his eyes, which dragged the lower lids with them and showed too much white below the fractured, scattered wheel of the iris.

'What?'

'It's okay,' Mahmoud repeated. 'He wants to talk with everybody. He talks to every man, tonight. He comes to me. He asks me to make it English for you, what he says. You are the last, before Khaled. He wants to speak to Khaled last.'

'What did he say?'

Mahmoud asked him to repeat what he'd said to me. Habib did speak again, in exactly the same too-rapid, hyper-energetic manner, staring into my eyes as if he expected an enemy or a monstrous beast to emerge from them. I was just as steadfast in returning the stare: I'd been locked up with violent, crazy men, and I knew better than to take my eyes off him.

'He says that strong men make the luck to happen,' Mahmoud translated for us.

'What?'

'Strong men, they make it for itself, the luck.'

'Strong men make their own luck? Is that what he means?'

'Yes, exactly so,' Mahmoud agreed. 'A strong man can make his own luck.'

'What does he mean?'

'I do not know,' Mahmoud replied, smiling patiently. 'He just says it.'

'He's just going around, telling everybody this?' I asked. 'That a strong man makes his own luck?'

'No. For me, he said that the Prophet, peace be upon Him, was a great soldier before he was a great teacher. For Jalalaad, he said that the stars shine because they are full with secrets. It is different for every man. And he was in too much a hurry for telling us these things. It is very important for him. I do not understand, Lin. I think it is because we fight tomorrow morning.'

'Was there anything else?' I asked, mystified by the exchange.

Mahmoud asked Habib if there was anything else that he wanted to say. Holding the stare into my eyes, Habib rattled away in Pashto and Farsi.

'He says only that there is no such a thing as luck. He wants you to believe him. He says again that a strong man —'

'Makes his own luck,' I completed the translation for him. 'Well, tell him I appreciate the message.'

Mahmoud spoke, and for a few moments Habib stared harder, searching in my eyes for a recognition or response that I couldn't give him. He turned and loped away with the stooped, crouching run that I found more chilling and alarming, somehow, than the more obvious, bulging madness in his eyes.

'*Now* what's he up to?' I asked Mahmoud, relieved that he was gone.

'He will find Khaled, I think,' Mahmoud replied.

'Damn, it's cold!' I spluttered.

'Yes. I am too cold, like you. I am all day dreaming that this cold will be gone.'

'Mahmoud, you were in Bombay when we went to hear the Blind

Singers, with Khaderbhai, weren't you?'

'Yes. It was the first meeting, for all of us, at the same time together. I saw you there the first time.'

'I'm sorry. I didn't meet you that night, and I didn't notice you there. What I wanted to ask you is how you got together with Khaderbhai in the first place.'

Mahmoud laughed. It was so rare to see him laugh out loud that I felt myself smiling in response. He'd lost weight on the mission—we'd all lost weight. His face was drawn tight to the high cheekbones and the pointed chin, covered with a thick, dark beard. His eyes, even in the cold moonlight, were the polished bronze of a temple vase.

'I am standing on the street, in Bombay, and I am doing some passport business with my friend. There is a hand on my shoulder. It is Abdullah. He tells me that Khader Khan wants to see me. I go to Khader, in his car. We drive together, we talk, and after, I am his man.'

'Why did he pick you? What made him pick you, and what made you agree to join him?'

Mahmoud frowned, and it seemed that he might be considering the question for the first time.

'I was against Pahlavi Shah,' he began. 'The secret police of the Shah, the Savak, they killed many people, and they put many people in the jail for beating. My father killed in the jail. My mother killed in the jail. For fighting against Shah. I was a small boy that time. When I grow up, I fight Shah. Two times in the jail. Two times beating, and electricity on my body, and too much pain. I fight for revolution in Iran. Ayatollah Khomeini makes the revolution in Iran, and he is the new power, when Shah runs away to America. But Savak secret police still the same. Now they work for Khomeini. Again I go in the jail. Again the beating and the electric pain. The same people from the Shah—the exactly same people in the jail—now they work for Khomeini. All my friends die in the jail, and in the war against Iraq. I escape, and come to Bombay. I make business, black-market business, with other Iran people. Then, Abdel Khader Khan makes me his man. In my life, I meet only one great man. That is Khader. Now, he is dead ...'

He choked off the words, and rubbed a tear from each eye with the sleeve of his rough jacket.

It was a long speech, and we were freezing cold, yet still I would've asked him more. I wanted to know it all—everything that filled the gaps between what Khaderbhai had told me and the secrets Khaled had shared. But at that moment we heard a piercingly piteous scream of terror. It died suddenly, as if the thread of sound had been cut with a pair of shears. We looked at one another, and reached for weapons in the same instinct.

'This way!' Mahmoud shouted, running over the slippery snow and slush with short, careful steps.

We reached the origin of the sound at the same time as the other men. Nazeer and Suleiman rushed through our group to see what we were staring at. They froze, silent and still, at the sight of Khaled Ansari kneeling over the body of Habib Abdur Rahman. The madman was on his back. He was dead. There was a knife in his throat where the words about luck had been only minutes before. The knife had been pushed into his neck and twisted, just as Habib himself had done to our horses and to Siddiqi. But it wasn't Habib's knife that we stared at, jutting out of the muddy, sinewed throat like a branch from a riverbed. We all knew the knife well. We'd all seen its distinctive, carved, horn handle a hundred times. It was Khaled's knife.

Nazeer and Suleiman put their hands under Khaled's arms, and lifted him gently from the corpse. He accepted the help momentarily, but then he shrugged them off and knelt beside the body. Habib's pattu shawl was rucked up around his chest. Khaled pulled something from the front of the dead man's flak jacket. It was metal, two pieces of metal, hanging from Habib's neck on leather thongs. Jalalaad rushed forward and snatched them. They were the souvenir fragments of the tank that he and Hanif and Juma had destroyed; the pieces that his friends had worn around their necks.

Khaled stood and turned and walked slowly away from the killing. I put my hand on his shoulder as he passed me, and walked with him. Behind me there was a howl of rage as Jalalaad attacked Habib's corpse with the butt of his Kalashnikov. I looked over my shoulder to see the mad eyes of the lunatic crushed beneath the rise and smashing fall of the weapon. And in one of those perversities of the pitying heart, I found myself feeling sorry for Habib. I'd wanted to kill him myself, more than once, and I knew that I was glad he was dead, but my heart was so sorry for him in that moment that I grieved as if he was a friend. *He was a teacher*, I heard myself thinking. The most violent and dangerous man I'd ever known had been a kindergarten teacher. I couldn't shake that thought—as if it was the only truth, in that moment, that really mattered.

And when the men finally dragged Jalalaad away, there was nothing left: nothing but blood and snow and hair and shattered bone where the life and the tortured mind had been.

Khaled returned to our cave. He was muttering something in Arabic. His eyes were radiant, filled with a vision that illuminated him, and put an almost frightening resolve in the set of his scarred features.

At the cave, he removed the belt around his waist that held his canteen. He let it slip to the ground. He lifted the cartridge belt over his head from his shoulder and let that too fall. Next he rummaged through his pockets, emptying them of their contents one by one until there was nothing on him but the clothes he wore. At his feet were his false passports, his money, his letters, his wallet, his weapons, his jewellery, and even the bruised, wrinkle-eared photos of his long-dead family.

'What's he saying?' I asked Mahmoud desperately. I'd spent the last four weeks avoiding Khaled's eye and coldly rejecting his friendship. Suddenly, I was unbearably afraid that I was going to lose him; that I'd already lost him.

'It is the Koran,' Mahmoud replied in a whisper. 'He is telling Suras from the Koran.'

Khaled left the cave and walked to the edge of the compound. I ran to stop him, and pushed him back with both hands. He allowed the shove, and then came on toward me again. I threw my arms around him and dragged him back a few paces. He didn't resist me. He stared directly ahead at that infuriating vision only he could see while he chanted the hypnotically poetic verses of the Koran. And when I let him go, he continued his walk out of the camp.

'Help me!' I shouted. 'Can't you see? He's going! He's going out there!'

Mahmoud, Nazeer, and Suleiman came forward but, instead of helping me to restrain Khaled, they grasped my arms and gently prised them away from him. Khaled immediately began to walk forward. I wrestled myself free, and rushed to stop him again. I shouted at him and slapped at his face to waken him to the danger. He didn't resist and he didn't react. I felt the tears hot on my cold face, stinging in the cracks that split my frozen lips. I felt the sobbing in my chest like a river rappling and rolling against worn and rounded rocks, on and on and on. I held him tight, with one arm around his neck and the other around his waist, my hands locked together at his back.

Nazeer, even as thin and weakened as he'd become in those weeks, was too strong for me. His steel hands grabbed at my wrists and peeled them away from Khaled. Mahmoud and Suleiman helped him to hold me back as I struggled and reached out to grab Khaled's jacket. And then we watched him walk from the camp into the winter that one way or another had ruined or killed us all.

'Didn't you see it?' Mahmoud asked me when he was gone. 'Didn't you see his face?'

'Yes, I saw it, I saw it,' I sobbed, staggering back to the cave to fall into the crumpled cell of my misery.

I lay there for hours unsleeping, filthy, starving, angry, and broken-hearted. And I might've died there—some pain, sometimes, leaves you without legs or arms—but the smell of food brought me round. The men had decided that they couldn't wait to cook the last of the rotting meat. They'd boiled it in a pot during those hours, fanning the smoke away continuously and concealing the flame with blankets.

The soup was ready long before dawn, and every man took a bowl, glass, or mug of it. The stink of the rotting meat was more than our empty stomachs could bear, at first. We all vomited the foul, retching sips we took. But hunger has a will of its own, a will that's much older than the other will we praise and flatter in the palace of the mind. We were too hungry to refuse the food, and by the third try, or the fifth for some of us, we kept the repulsive, stinking brew down. Then the pain caused by the hot soup in our empty stomachs was as sharp as a belly full of fish-hooks; yet that too passed, and every man forced himself to drink three helpings, and to chew the rubbery, rotting chunks of meat.

For two hours after that we took turns to dash into the rocks as the food worked through intestines and bowels that had seized in our starving bodies, and suddenly erupted.

At last, when we recovered, and when all the prayers were said, and when each man was ready, we gathered near the south-eastern edge of the compound at the place Habib had recommended for our attack. He'd assured us that the steep slope was our one chance to fight our way to freedom; and since he'd planned to fight in the attack with us, we had no reason to distrust the advice.

We were six men. The five others were Suleiman, Mahmoud Melbaaf, Nazeer, Jalalaad, and young Ala-ud-Din. He was a shy man of twenty with a boy's grin beneath an old man's faded green eyes. He caught my eye, and nodded encouragingly. I returned the nod with a smile, and his face broke into a wider grin while his head nodded more vigorously. I looked away, ashamed that I'd spent so much time with him, months of hard time, without once trying to engage him in a conversation. We were going to die together, and I knew nothing about him. Nothing.

Dawn put fire in the sky. Wind-driven clouds streaming across the far plain were aflame, crimsoned with the first burning kisses of the morning sun. We shook hands, embraced, hugged one another, checked our weapons again and again, and stared down the steep slopes toward forever.

The end, when it comes, is always too soon. My skin was tight on my face, drawn back by the muscles of my neck and jaw, those muscles in turn pulled taut by the shoulders and arms and frostbitten hands, clutching the final agony of the gun.

Suleiman gave the order. My stomach dropped and locked, and froze as hard as the cold unfeeling earth beneath my boots. I stood up, and crossed the lip of the ridge. We started down the slope. It was a magnificent day, the best clear day for months. I remembered thinking, weeks before, that Afghanistan, like prison, had no dawns and no sunsets in the stone cages of its mountains. Yet the dawn that morning was more lovely than any I'd ever known. When the steeper slopes eased into a more gradual decline, we picked up the pace, jogging over the last of the rose-pink snow and into the grey-green rough ground beyond.

The first explosions we heard were too far away from us to frighten me. *Okay. Here it comes. This is it* ... The words chattered through my mind as if someone else spoke them: as if someone, like a coach, was preparing me for the end. Then the explosions were closer, as the enemy mortars found their range.

I looked along our line, and saw that the others were running harder than I was. Only Nazeer was still beside me. I tried to run faster. My legs seemed wooden and numb: I saw them moving, running, step after step, but I couldn't feel them. It took a gigantic effort of will to send the message to my legs, and command them to greater speed. At last I stumbled into a faster run.

Two mortars exploded quite close to me. I kept running, waiting for the pain, and waiting for the killing joke. My heart was churning in my chest, and my breathing came in gasping, grunting little puffs of cold air. I couldn't see the enemy positions. The mortar's range was well over a kilometre, but I knew they had to be closer than that. And then the first shots spattered, the *tun-tun-tun-tun* of the AK-74s—theirs and ours. I knew they were close. They were close enough to kill us, and close enough for us to kill them.

My eyes raced ahead on the rough ground, looking for holes or boulders, trying to find the safest path. A man went down, left of me, along the line. It was Jalalaad. He was running beside Nazeer, and less than a hundred metres from me. A mortar shell exploded directly in front of him and ripped his young body into pieces. Looking down again, I jumped over rocks and boulders, and I stumbled but didn't fall. I saw Suleiman, fifty metres in front of me, clutch at his throat and then fall forward, running a few more paces doubled-up as if he was searching for something on the ground in front of him. His body crumpled and collapsed over his face, tumbling to the side. His face and throat were bloodied and broken and torn open. I tried to run around him, but the ground was rough and strewn with rocks, and I had to jump over his body as I ran.

I saw the first flashes of fire from the enemy Kalashnikovs. They were far away, at least two hundred metres, much further than I'd guessed. A tracer bullet fizzed past me, only one step to my left. We wouldn't make it. We couldn't make it. There weren't many of them—there weren't many guns firing—but they had so much time to get a sight on us and shoot us down. They were going to kill us all. Then a wild flurry of explosions crunched into the enemy lines. *The idiots! They blew up their own mortar shells,* I thought, and gunfire like fireworks rattled the world from everywhere at once. And Nazeer raised his assault rifle, and fired as he ran, and I saw Mahmoud Melbaaf firing ahead of me, on my right, where Suleiman had been, and I raised my weapon, and pulled the trigger.

There was a horrible, blood-freezing scream somewhere very close. I suddenly recognised it as my own, but I couldn't stop it. And I looked at the men, the brave and beautiful men beside me, running into the guns, and God help me for thinking it, and God forgive me for saying it, but it was glorious, it was glorious, if glory is a magnificent and raptured exaltation. It was what love would be like, if love was a sin. It was what music would be, if music could kill you. And I climbed a prison wall with every running step.

And then, in a world suddenly soundless as the deepest sea, my legs stopped still, and hot, gritty, filthy, exploding earth clogged my eyes and my mouth. Something had hit my legs. Something hard and hot and viciously sharp had hit my legs. I fell forward as if I'd been running in the dark and I'd smashed into a fallen tree trunk. A mortar round. The metal fragments. The shock-deafened silence. The burning skin. The blinding earth. The choking struggle for breath. There was a smell that filled my head. It was the smell of my own death—it smells of blood, and seawater, and damp earth, and the ash of burned wood when you smell your own death before you die—and then I hit the ground so hard that I plunged through it into a deep, undreaming darkness. And the fall was forever. And there was no light, no light.

PART FIVE

CHAPTER THIRTY-SEVEN

IF YOU STARE into its cold dead eye, the camera always mocks you with the truth. The black-and-white photograph showed almost all the men of Khader's mujaheddin unit assembled for the kind of formal portrait that makes the people of Afghanistan, Pakistan, and India seem more stiff and gloweringly self-conscious than they really are. It was impossible to tell from that photo how much those men had loved to laugh, and how readily they'd smiled. But none of them were looking directly into the lens of the camera. All the eyes but mine were a little above or below, a little to the left or the right. Only my own eyes stared back at me as I held the picture in my bandaged hands, and remembered the names of the men leaning together in the ragged lines.

Mazdur Gul, the stonemason, whose name means *labourer*, and whose hands were permanently grey-white from decades of work with granite ... Daoud, who liked to be called by the English version of his name, David, and whose dream it was to visit the great city of New York and eat a meal in a fine restaurant ... Zamaanat, whose name means *trust*, and whose brave smile concealed the agony of shame he'd felt that his whole family lived in hungry squalor at Jalozai, a huge refugee camp near Peshawar ... Hajji Akbar, who'd been appointed as the doctor in the unit for no other reason than that he'd once spent two months as a patient in a Kabul hospital, and who'd greeted my acceptance of the doctor's job, when I arrived at the mountain camp, with prayers and a little Dervish dance of joy ... Alef, the mischievously satirical Pashtun trader, who died crawling in the snow with his back torn open and his clothes on fire ... Juma and Hanif, the two wild boys who were killed by the madman Habib ... Jalalaad, their fearless young friend, who died in the last charge ... Ala-ud-Din, whose name in English is shortened to Aladdin, and who escaped unscathed ... Suleiman Shahbadi, of the furrowed brow and sorrowing eyes, who died leading us into the guns.

And in the centre of the assembly there was a smaller, tighter group around Abdel Khader Khan: Ahmed Zadeh, the Algerian, who died with one hand clenched in the frozen earth and the other knotted into mine ... Khaled Ansari, who murdered the madman Habib and then walked into the lost world of the smothering snow ... Mahmoud Melbaaf, who survived the last charge like Ala-ud-Din, unwounded and unmarked ... Nazeer, who ignored his own wounds to drag my unconscious body to safety ... and me. Standing behind and a little to the left of Khaderbhai, my expression in the photograph was confident, resolute, and self-possessed. And the camera, they say, doesn't lie.

It was Nazeer who'd saved me. The mortar shell that had exploded so close to us, as we ran into the guns, ripped and ruptured the air. The shock wave burst my left eardrum. In the same deafened moment, pieces of the exploded shell passed us in a hot metal blizzard. None of the larger chunks of metal hit me, but eight small pieces of the shrapnel smashed into my legs below the knees—five in one leg, and three in the other. Two smaller pieces hit my body—one in the stomach, and one in the chest. They tore through the heavy layers of my clothing, and even pierced my thick money belt and the solid leather straps of my medic's bag, burning their way into my skin. Another chunk hit my forehead, high above the left eye.

They were tiny fragments, the largest of them about the size of Abe Lincoln's face on an American penny coin. Still, they were travelling at such a speed that they took my legs out from under me. Earth, thrown up by the explosion, peppered my face, blinding and choking me. I hit the ground hard, just managing to turn my face aside before the impact. Unfortunately, I turned the burst eardrum to the ground, and the violence of the blow rived the wound even further. I blacked out.

Nazeer, who was wounded in the legs and the arm, pulled my unconscious body into the shelter of a shallow, trench-like depression. He collapsed himself, then, covering my body with his own until the bombardment stopped. Lying there with his arms around my neck, he took a hit in the back of his right shoulder. It was a piece of metal that would've hit me, and might've killed me, had Khader's man not protected me with his love. When all was quiet, he dragged me to safety.

'It was Sayeed, yes?' Mahmoud Melbaaf asked.

'Sorry?'

'It was Sayeed who took the picture, was it not?'

'Yes. Yes. It was Sayeed. They called him *Kishmishi* ...'

The word swept us into remembrances of the shy, young Pashtun fighter. He'd seen Khaderbhai as the embodiment of all his warrior heroes, and he'd followed him everywhere, adoringly, with eyes he quickly cast down when the Khan looked his way. He'd survived smallpox as a child, and his face was severely pockmarked with dozens of small, brown, dish-like spots. His nickname, *Kishmishi*, used with great affection by the older fighters, meant *Raisins*. He'd been too shy to pose with us in the photograph, so he'd volunteered to operate the camera.

'He was with Khader,' I muttered.

'Yes, at the end. Nazeer saw his body, at the side of Khader, very close to him. I think he would ask to be with Abdel Khader even if he knew, *before* the attack, that they would get an attack, and get killed. I think he would ask to die like that. And he was not the only one.'

'Where did you get this?'

'Khaled had the roll of film. Remember? He had the only camera that Khader give his permission. The film was with other things he let fall down to the ground from his pockets when he went from us. I take it with me. I put it in the photo studio last week. They return the photos this morning. I thought you would like it to see them, before we leave.'

'Leave? Where are we going?'

'We have to get out of here. How are you feeling?'

'I'm fine,' I lied. 'I'm okay.'

I sat up on the cot bed and swung my legs over the side. When my feet hit the floor there was a pain so excruciating in my shins that I moaned aloud. Another fierce pain throbbed at my forehead. I probed with my blunt, bandaged fingers at a wad of dressing beneath a bandage that wound round my head like a turban. A third pain in my left ear nagged for my attention. My hands were aching, and my feet, swaddled in three or more layers of socks, felt as if they were burning. There was a painful ache in my left hip, where the horse had kicked me when the jets had torn up the sky above us, months before. The wound had never properly healed, and I suspected that a bone was chipped beneath the tender flesh. My forearm felt numb near the elbow, where my own horse had bitten me in its panic. That wound was also months old, and it too had never really healed.

Doubled over, resting on my thighs, I could feel the tightness of my stomach and the leaner flesh of my legs. I was thin, after starving on the mountain. Too thin. All in all, it was a mess. I was in a bad way. Then my mind came back to the bandages on my hands, and a sensation close to panic rose like a spear in my spine.

'What are you doing?'

'I've gotta get these bandages off,' I snapped, tearing at them with my teeth.

'Wait! Wait!' Mahmoud cried. 'I will do it for you.'

He unwound the bulky bandages slowly, and I felt the sweat run from my eyebrows onto my cheeks. When both lots of bindings were removed, I stared at the disfigured claws that my hands had become, and I moved them, flexing the fingers. Frostbite had split my hands open at all the knuckle joints, and the bruise-black wounds were hideous, but all the fingers and all the fingertips were there.

'You can thank Nazeer,' Mahmoud muttered softly as he examined my cracked and peeling hands. 'They were thinking to cut off your fingers, but he would not let them. And he would not let them leave you until they treated all your injuries. He did force them to help the frostbite injuries on your face, also. He had the Kalashnikov and your automatic pistol. Here—he asked me to give it to you, when you wake up.'

He produced the Stechkin, wrapped in a coil of cheesecloth. I tried to take it, but my hands couldn't hold the bundle.

'I will keep it for you,' Mahmoud offered with a stiff little smile.

'Where is he?' I asked, still dazed and drilled by the pain, but feeling better and stronger by the minute.

'Over there,' Mahmoud indicated, nodding his head. I turned to see Nazeer, sleeping on his side on a cot similar to my own. 'He is resting, but he is ready to move. We must leave here soon. Our friends will come for us at any time now, and we must be ready to move.'

I looked around me. We were in a large, sand-coloured tent with pallet floors and about fifteen folding cot-beds. Several men wearing Afghan clothing—loose pants, tunic shirts, and long, sleeveless vests in the same shades of pale green—moved among the beds. They were fanning the wounded men with straw fans, washing them with buckets of soapy water, or carrying away wastes through a narrow slit in the canvas door. Some of the wounded were moaning or speaking out their pain in languages I couldn't understand. The air in that Pakistani plain, after months in the snowy peaks of Afghanistan, was thick and hot and heavy. There were so many strong smells, one upon another, that my senses rejected them and concentrated on one particularly pungent aroma: the unmistakable smell of perfumed Indian basmati rice, cooking somewhere close to the tent.

'I'm fuckin' hungry, man, I gotta tell ya.'

'We will eat good food soon,' Mahmoud assured me, allowing himself a laugh.

'Are we ...? This is Pakistan?'

'Yes,' he laughed again. 'What can you remember?'

'Not much. Running. They were shooting at us ... from a long way off. Mortars everywhere. I remember ... I was hit ...'

I felt along the padded bandages that swathed my shins, from knees to ankles.

'And I hit the ground. Then ... I remember ... was it a jeep? Or a truck? Did that happen?'

'Yes. They took us. Massoud's men.'

'Massoud?'

'Ahmed Shah. The Lion himself. His men made the attack on the dam and the two main roads—to Kabul and to Quetta. They put a siege on Kandahar. They are still there, outside the city, and they will not leave, I think so, until the war is over. We ran into the middle of it, my friend.'

'They rescued us ...'

'It was, how to say, the less they do for us.'

'The *least* they could do for us?'

'Yes. Because it was them who killed us.'

'What?'

'Yes. When we made our escaping out of the mountain, running down, the Afghan army shoot at us. Massoud's men see us, and think we are some of the enemy. They are a long way from us. They start to shoot at us with mortars.'

'Our own people shot at us?'

'Everybody was shooting—I mean, everyone shooting in the same time. Afghan army, they were shooting at us also, but the mortars that did hit us, I think they were our own side. And that made Afghan army and Russian soldiers run away. I killed two of them myself when they run away. The men of Ahmed Shah Massoud, they had Stingers. The Americans give them the Stingers, in April, and since that time, the Russians having no helicopters. Now the mujaheddin fight back in every place. Now the war is over, in two years, or maybe three, *Inshallah.*'

'April … what month is this?'

'Now is May.'

'How long have I been here?'

'Four days, Lin,' he answered softly.

'Four days …' I'd thought it was one night, one long sleep. I looked over my shoulder again at the sleeping form of Nazeer. 'Are you sure he's okay?'

'He is injured—here … and here—but he is strong, and he can move himself. He will be well, *Inshallah.* He is like a *shotor!*' he laughed, using the Farsi word for camel. 'He makes his mind, and nobody can change him.'

I laughed with him for the first time since I'd woken. The laugh sent my hands to my head in an effort to contain the throbbing pain it caused.

'I wouldn't like to be the one who tried to change Nazeer's mind about anything, once it was made up.'

'Me too not.' Mahmoud agreed. 'The soldiers of Massoud, they carried you and Nazeer, with me, to a car, a good Russian car. After the car, we moved you and Nazeer to a truck, for the road to Chaman. At Chaman, the Pakistanis, border guards, they want to take Nazeer's guns. He give them money—some of your money, from your money belt—and he keep his guns. We hide you in the blankets, with two dead men. We put them on top of you, and we show them to border guards, and tell that we want to give good Muslim burial for these men. Then we come into Quetta, to this hospital, and again they want to take Nazeer's guns. Again he give them money. They want to cut your fingers, because of the smell …'

I put my hands to my nose, and sniffed at them. There was a rotten, death-foetid smell to them still. It was faint, but clear enough to remind me of the rotting goat's feet we'd eaten as our last supper on the mountain. My stomach churned, arching like a fighting cat. Mahmoud quickly reached for a metal dish and thrust it under my face. I vomited, spitting black-green bile into the bowl, and fell forward helplessly onto my knees.

When the nausea attack passed, I sat back on the cot and snatched gratefully at the cigarette Mahmoud lit for me.

'Go on.' I stuttered.

'What?'

'You were saying … about Nazeer …'

'Oh yes, yes, he pull his Kalashnikov out from under his pattu and point it at them. He tell them he will kill them all, if they cut you. They want to call the guards, the camp police, but Nazeer, he is in the door of the tent, with his gun. They cannot go past him. And I am on his other side, looking for his back. So they fix you.'

'That's a hell of a health plan—an Afghan with a Kalashnikov pointed at your doctor.'

'Yes,' he agreed without irony. 'And after, they fix Nazeer. And then, after two days with no sleep, and many wounds, Nazeer sleep.'

'They didn't call the guards, when he went to sleep?'

'No. They are all Afghans here. Doctors, wounded men, guards, everybody is Afghan. But not the camp police. They are Pakistani. The Afghans, they don't like the Pakistan police. They have big trouble with Pakistan police. Everybody has trouble with Pakistan police. So they give a permission to me, and I take Nazeer's guns when he sleep. And I look after him. And I look after you. Wait—I think our friends are here!'

The long flaps of the tent's doorway opened all the way back, stunning us with the yellow light of a warm day. Four men entered. They were Afghans, veteran fighters; hard men, with eyes that stared at me as if they were looking along the decorated barrel of a jezail rifle. Mahmoud rose to greet them, and whispered a few words. Two of the men woke Nazeer. He'd been in a deep sleep, and spun round at the first touch, grasping at the men and ready to fight. Reassured by their gentle expressions, he then turned his head to check on me. Seeing me awake and sitting up, he grinned so broadly that it was a little alarming in a face so seldom struck with a smile.

The two men helped him to his feet. There was a wad of bandage strapped to his right thigh. Supporting himself on their shoulders, he limped out into the sunlight. The other men helped me to my feet. I tried to walk, but my wounded shins refused to obey me, and the best I could manage was a tottering shuffle. After a few seconds of that embarrassingly feeble scuffling, the men formed a chair with their arms and swept me up effortlessly between them.

For the next six weeks, that was the pattern of our recovery: a few days, perhaps as long as a week, in one location before an abrupt shift to a new tent or slum hut or hidden room. The Pakistan secret service, the ISI, had a malign interest in every foreigner who entered Afghanistan without their sanction during the war. The problem for Mahmoud Melbaaf, who was our guardian in those vulnerable weeks, was the fascination our story held for the refugees and exiles who harboured us. I'd darkened my blonde hair, and I wore sunglasses almost all the time. But, no matter how careful and secretive we were in the slums and camps where we stayed, there was always someone who knew who I was. The temptation to talk about the American gunrunner who was wounded in battle, fighting with the mujaheddin, was irresistible. Talk like that would've been enough to pique the curiosity of any intelligence agent from any agency. And had the secret police found me, they would've discovered that the American was in fact an escaped convict from Australia. That would've meant promotions for some, and a special thrill for the torturers who would get to work on me before they handed me over to the Australian authorities. So we moved often and we moved quickly, and we spoke to none but the few we trusted with our wounded lives.

Little by little, the details emerged: the more complete story of the battle we'd run into, and our rescue after it. The Russian and Afghan soldiers who'd surrounded our mountain comprised the best part of a company and, as such, were probably led by a captain. Their sole purpose in operating among the Shar-i-Safa Mountains was to catch and kill Habib Abdur Rahman. A huge reward had been posted for his arrest, but the terror and the horror that his atrocities had forced into their minds made the hunt for him a much more personal operation for the searchers. So mesmerised were they by his savage hatred, and so obsessed were they with his capture, that they failed to detect the stealthy advance of Ahmed Shah Massoud's forces. When we made our break for freedom, acting on Habib's information that most of the Russians and the Afghans were busy laying mines and other traps on the far side of the mountain, the startled sentries in the deserted enemy camp had opened fire. They'd thought, perhaps, that Habib himself was coming for them, because their fire was wild and undisciplined. That action had precipitated the attack that was being planned by Massoud's mujaheddin, who must've seen the firing as a pre-emptive strike by the Russians. The explosions I'd seen and heard as I ran toward the enemy—*they blew up their own mortar shells, the idiots*—

were actually direct hits on the Russian positions by Massoud's mortars. The wider mortar strikes that tore into our line were mere accidents: friendly fire, as they say.

And that was the elated moment I'd called *glorious*, in my mind, as I ran into the guns: that stupid waste of lives, that friendly fire. There wasn't any glory in it. There never is. There's only courage and fear and love. And war kills them all, one by one. Glory belongs to God, of course; that's what the word really means. And you can't serve God with a gun.

When we fell, Massoud's men pursued the fleeing enemy all the way around the mountain and into the returning company of minelayers. The battle that followed was a massacre. Not one man of the force sent to catch and kill Habib Abdur Rahman survived. He would've liked that, the madman, had he been alive to hear it. I know exactly how he would've grinned, with his wide mouth gaping soundless and his grief-crazed eyes bulging on swollen hatreds.

All that cold day, and into the sudden evening, Nazeer and I had remained on the battleground. As we shivered in the swiftly falling shadows of sunset, the mujaheddin and the survivors from our own unit returned from the fighting to find us. Mahmoud and Ala-ud-Din brought the dead—Suleiman and Jalalaad—from the barren mountain.

Massoud's men had combined with independent Achakzai fighters to claim the Chaman highway from the Pass all the way to the Russian defensive perimeter of besieged Kandahar, less than fifty kilometres from the city. The evacuation to Chaman, and through the Pass to Pakistan, was rapid and without incident. We rode in a truck, carrying our dead friends with us, and reached the checkpoint in hours—the journey that had taken us a month of mountains on Khader's horses.

Nazeer healed rapidly and began to regain weight. The wounds in his arm and the back of his shoulder closed over well, and gave him little trouble. But the larger and deeper wound to his right thigh seemed to have damaged the ligamentary relationship between muscle, bone, and tendons, from his hip to his knee. The upper leg was stiff, and he still walked with a limp as he swung his right step around the hip, instead of through it.

His spirits were relatively high, however, and he was anxious to return to Bombay—so anxious, in fact, that his fretting attention to my slower recovery became irritating. I snapped at him a couple of times when his solicitous urging—*You better? You come now? We go now?*—became unendurably annoying. I didn't know then that he had a mission, Khader's last mission, waiting for him in Bombay. The mission was all that held his grief and his shame at surviving Abdel Khader in check. And every day, as our health improved, the obligations of Khader's last command to him grew more suffocating; and his dereliction, as he saw it, more profane.

I had preoccupations of my own. The wounds on my legs were healing readily enough, and the skin on my forehead closed safely over a small, lumpy ridge of bone, but my ruptured eardrum became infected, and it was the source of a constant and almost unbearable pain. Every mouthful of food, every sip of water, every word I spoke, and every loud noise that I heard sent piercing little scorpion stings along the nerves of my face and throat, and deep into my fevered brain. Every movement of my body, or turn of the head, stabbed into that sweating excruciation. Every inward breath, and sneeze or cough, magnified the torment. Shifting accidentally in my sleep and bumping the damaged ear sent me starting up from the cot with a shout that woke every man for fifty metres around.

And then, after three weeks of that maddening, torturous pain and massive, self-medicated doses of penicillin and hot antibiotic washes, the wound healed and the pain receded from me just as memories do, like landmarks on a distant, foggy shore.

My hands healed around the deadened tissue on the knuckle joints. Truly frozen tissue never really heals, of course, and the injury was one of many that settled in my flesh in those exile years. I took the suffering from Khader's mountain into my hands, and every cold day sends me back there with my hands aching, just as they did when I clutched at the gun before the battle. Nevertheless, in the warmer air of Pakistan my fingers flexed and moved and obeyed me. My hands were ready for the work I had waiting; the little matter of revenge in Bombay. Although my body was thinner after the ordeal, it was harder and tougher than it had been all those plump months before, when we'd first set out for Khader's war.

Nazeer and Mahmoud organised our return trip by a series of connecting trains. They'd acquired a small arsenal of weapons in Pakistan, and were intent on smuggling them into Bombay. They concealed the guns in bales of fabric, and shipped them in the care of three Afghans who were fluent in Hindi. We rode in different carriages, and never acknowledged the men, but the illicit cargo was always on our minds. The irony of it—we'd set off to smuggle guns into Afghanistan, and we were returning to smuggle guns into Bombay—made me laugh, when it occurred to me, as I sat in my first-class carriage. But the laughter was bitter, and the expression it left on my face turned the eyes of my fellow passengers away.

It took us a little over two days to get back to Bombay. I was travelling on my false British book, the one I'd used to enter Pakistan. According to the entries in the book, I'd overstayed on my visa. Using the little smiling charm I could muster and the last of the money Khader had paid me, the last American dollars, I bribed the officials on both the Pakistani and Indian sides of the border without raising so much as the flicker of an eye. And an hour after dawn, eight months after we left her, we walked into the deep heat and frantic, toiling fervency of my beloved Bombay.

From a discreet distance, Nazeer and Mahmoud Melbaaf supervised the unloading and transport of their military cargo. Promising Nazeer that I would meet up with him that night at Leopold's, I left them at the station.

I took a cab. I felt drunk on the sound and colour and gorgeous flowing kinesis of the island city. But I had to concentrate. I was almost out of money. I directed the driver to the black-market currency-collection centre in the Fort area. With the taxi waiting below, I ran up the three narrow wooden flights to the counting room. A memory of Khaled wrung out my heart—*I used to run up these stairs with Khaled, with Khaled, with Khaled*—and I clenched my jaw against it, just as I bit down on the pain in my wounded shins. The two big men, loitering with intent on the landing outside the room, recognised me. We shook hands, all of us smiling widely.

'What's the news of Khaderbhai?' one of the men asked.

I looked into his tough young face. His name was Amir. I knew him to be brave and reliable and devoted to the Khan. For the blink of an eye it seemed, incredibly, that he was making a joke about Khader's death, and I felt a quick, angry impulse to stiffen him. Then I realised that he simply didn't know. *How is that possible? Why don't they know?* Instinct told me not to answer his question. I held my eyes and my mouth in a hard, impassive little smile, and brushed past him to knock at the door.

A short, fat, balding man in a white singlet and dhoti opened the door and thrust out his hands at once in a double handshake. It was Rajubhai, controller of the currency collections for Abdel Khader Khan's mafia council. He pulled me into the room, and closed the door. The counting room was the core of his personal and business universe, and he spent twenty out of every twenty-four hours there. The thin, faded, pink-white cord across his shoulder, under his singlet, declared that he was a devout Hindu, one of many who worked within Abdel Khader's largely Muslim empire.

'Linbaba! So good to see you!' he said with a happy grin. '*Khaderbhai kahan hain?*' *Where is Khaderbhai?*

I struggled to keep the surprise from my face. Rajubhai was a senior man. He held a seat at the council meetings. If *he* didn't know that Khader was dead, then nobody in the city would know. And if Khader's death was still a secret, then Mahmoud and Nazeer must've insisted on the suppression of the news. They hadn't said anything to me about it. I couldn't understand it. Whatever their reasons, I decided to support them and to keep my silence on the matter.

'*Hum akela hain,*' I replied, returning his smile. *I'm alone.*

It wasn't an answer to his question, and his eyes narrowed on the word.

'*Akela ...*' he repeated. *Alone ...*

'Yes, Rajubhai, and I need some money, fast. I've got a taxi waiting.'

'You need dollars, Lin?'

'Dollars *nahin. Sirf rupia.*' *Not dollars. Only rupees.*

'How much you need?'

'*Do-do-teen hazaar,*' I answered, using the slang phrase two-two-three thousand, which always means three.

'*Teen hazaar!*' he huffed, more from habit than any real concern. Three thousand rupees was a considerable sum to the street runners, or in the slums, but it was a trifling amount in the context of the black-market currency trade. Rajubhai's office collected a hundred times that much and more every day, and he'd often paid me sixty thousand rupees at a time as my wage and my share of commissions.

'*Abi, bhai-ya, abi!*' *Now, brother, now!*

Rajubhai turned his head and gestured, with a twitch of his eyebrows, to one of his clerks. The man handed over three thousand rupees in used but clean hundred-rupee notes. Riffling the small bundle first, from habit, as a double check, Rajubhai handed the notes across. I peeled off two notes to put in my shirt pocket, and pushed the rest inside a deeper pocket in my long vest.

'*Shukria, chacha,*' I smiled. '*Main jata hu.*' Thanks, uncle. I'm going.

'Lin!' he cried, stopping me by grasping at my sleeve. '*Hamara beta Khaled, kaisa hain?*' *How is our son, Khaled?*

'Khaled is not with us,' I said, struggling to keep my voice and my expression neutral. 'He went on a journey, a *yatra*, and I don't know when we'll see him.'

I took the steps two at a time on the way down to the cab, feeling the shock of each jump shudder into my shins. The driver swung out into the traffic at once, and I directed him to a clothing shop that I knew on the Colaba Causeway. One of the sybaritic splendours of Bombay is the limitless variety of relatively inexpensive, well-made clothes constantly changing to reflect the newest Indian and foreign trends. In the refugee camp, Mahmoud Melbaaf had given me a long, blue-serge vest, a white shirt, and coarse brown trousers. The clothes had served for the trip from Quetta, but in Bombay they were too hot and too strange: they drew curious attention to me when I needed the camouflage of current fashion. I chose a pair of black jeans with strong, deep pockets, a new pair of joggers to replace my ruined boots, and a loose, white silk shirt to wear over the jeans. I changed in the dressing room, sliding my knife in its scabbard under the belt of my jeans and concealing it with the shirt.

While waiting at the cashier's desk, I caught sight of myself unexpectedly in an angled mirror that showed my face in three-quarter profile. It was a face so hard and unfamiliar that it startled me to recognise it as my own. I remembered the photograph taken by shy Kishmishi, and looked again into the mirror. There was a cold impassiveness in my face—and a determination, perhaps—which hadn't even begun to gleam in the eyes that had stared so confidently into the lens of Khaled's camera. I snatched up my sunglasses and put them on. *Have I changed so much?* I hoped that a hot shower, and shaving off my thick beard, would soften some of the hard edges. But the real hardness was inside me, and I wasn't sure if it was simply tough and tenacious or if it was something much more cruel.

The cab driver followed my instructions and pulled up near the entrance to Leopold's. I paid him, and stood on the busy Causeway for a minute, staring at the wide doorway of the restaurant where my fated connection to Karla and Khaderbhai had really begun. Every door is a portal leading through time as well as space. The same doorway that leads us into and out of a room also leads us into the past of the room and its ceaselessly unfolding future. People knew that once, deep within the ur-mind, the ur-imagination. You can still find those who decorate doorways, and reverently salute them, in every culture, from Ireland to Japan. I stepped up one, two steps, and reached out with my right hand to touch the doorjamb and then touch my chest, over the heart, in a salaam to fate and a homage to the dead friends and enemies who entered with me.

Didier Levy was sitting in his usual chair, commanding a view of the patrons and of the busy street beyond. He was talking to Kavita Singh. Her eyes were averted, but he looked up and saw me as I approached the table. Our eyes met and held for a second, each of us reading the other's shifting expressions like diviners finding meanings in the magic of scattered bones.

'Lin!' he shouted, hurling himself forward, flinging his arms around me, and kissing me on both cheeks.

'It's good to see you, Didier.'

'Bah!' he spat, wiping his lips with the back of his hand. 'If this beard is the fashion for holy warriors, I thank whatever powers protect me that I am an atheist, and a coward!'

There was a little more grey, I thought, in the mop of dark curls that brushed the collar of his jacket. The pale blue eyes were a little more tired, a little more bloodshot. Yet the wicked, leering mischief still arched his eyebrow, and the playful sneer I knew so well, and loved, was still there, curling his upper lip. He was the same man, in the same city, and it was good to be home.

'Hello, Lin,' Kavita greeted me, pushing Didier aside to give me a hug.

She was beautiful. Her thick, dark brown hair was tousled and awry. Her back was straight. Her eyes were clear. And, as she held me, the casual, friendly touch of her fingers on my neck seemed like such a tender ravishment—after the blood and snow of Afghanistan—that I can still feel it, through all the years since.

'Sit down, sit down!' Didier shouted, waving to the waiters for more drinks. '*Merde*, I heard that you were dead, but I didn't believe it! It is so *good* to see you! We shall be famously drunk tonight, *non?*'

'No,' I replied, resisting the pressure he placed on my shoulder. The disappointment in his eyes moderated my tone, if not my mood. 'It's a little early in the day, and I have to get going. I've got ... something to do.'

'Very well,' he yielded with a sigh. 'But you *must* have *one* drink with me. It would be too uncivilised for you to leave my company without allowing me at least this little corruption of your holy warring self. After all, what is the point of a man returning from the dead, if it is not to drink strong spirits with his friends?'

'Okay,' I relented, smiling at him but still standing. 'One drink. I'll have a whisky. Make it a double. Is that corrupt enough for you?'

'Ah, Lin,' he grinned, 'Is there anyone, in this sickly sweet world of ours, who is corrupt enough for me?'

'Where there's a weak will, there's a way, Didier. We live in hope.'

'But of course,' he said, and we both laughed.

'I'll leave you to it,' Kavita announced, leaning over to kiss my cheek. 'I've got to get back to the office. Let's get together, Lin. You look ... you look pretty wild. You look like a story, *yaar*, if ever I saw one.'

'Sure,' I smiled. 'There's a story or two. Off the record, of course. Probably keep us going over dinner.'

'I look forward to it,' she said, holding my eye long enough to make sure I felt it in several places at once. She broke the contact to flash a smile at Didier. 'Be nasty to someone for me, Didier. I don't want to hear that you've got all sentimental, *yaar*, just because Lin is back.'

She walked out with my eyes on her, and when the drinks arrived Didier insisted that I sit down with him at last.

'My dear friend, you can stand to eat a meal—if you must—and you can stand to make love—if you are able—but it is impossible to stand and drink whisky. It is the act of a barbarian. A man who stands up to drink a noble alcohol like whisky, in all but a toast to some noble thing or purpose, is a beast—a man who will stop at nothing.'

So we sat, and he raised his glass immediately to toast with mine.

'To the living!' he offered.

'And the dead?' I asked, my glass still on the table.

'And the dead!' he replied, his smile wide and warm.

I raised my glass in turn, clinked it against his, and threw back the double.

'Now,' he said firmly, the smile discarded as swiftly as it had risen to his eyes. 'What is the trouble?'

'Where do you want me to start?' I scoffed.

'No, my friend. I am not talking just about the war. There is something else, something very determined in your face, and I want to know the heart of it.'

I stared back at him in silence, secretly delighted to be back in the company of someone who knew me well enough to read between the frown lines.

'Come on, Lin. There is too much trouble in your eyes. What is the problem? If you want, if it is easier, you can begin by telling me what happened in Afghanistan.'

'Khader's dead,' I said flatly, staring at the empty glass in my hand.

'No!' he gasped, fearful and resentful, somehow, in the same quick response.

'Yes.'

'No, no, no. I would hear something ... The whole city would know it.'

'I saw his body. I helped to drag it up the mountain to our camp. I helped them bury him. He's dead. They're all dead. We're the only ones left from here—Nazeer, Mahmoud, and me.'

'Abdel Khader ... It can't be ...'

Didier was ashen-faced, and the grey seemed to move even into his eyes. Stricken by the news—he looked as though someone had struck him hard on the face—he slumped in his chair and his jaw fell open. He began to slip sideways in the chair, and I was afraid that he would fall to the floor or even suffer a stroke.

'Take it easy,' I said softly. 'Don't go to fuckin' pieces on me, Didier. You look like shit, man. Snap out of it!'

His weary eyes drifted up to meet mine.

'There are some things, Lin, that simply cannot be. I am twelve, thirteen years in Bombay, and always there is Abdel Khader Khan ...'

He dropped his gaze again, and lapsed into a reverie so rich in thought and feeling that his head twitched and his lower lip trembled in the turbulence of it. I was worried. I'd seen men go under before. In prison, I'd watched men succumb, fragmented by fear and shame, and then slaughtered by solitude. But that was a process: it took weeks, months, or years. Didier's collapse was the work of seconds, and I was watching him crumple and fade from one heartbeat to the next.

I moved around the table and sat beside him, pulling him close to me with an arm around his shoulder.

'Didier!' I hissed in a harsh whisper. 'I've got to go. Do you hear me? I came in to find out about my stuff—the stuff I left with you while I was at Nazeer's, getting off the dope. Remember? I left my bike, my Enfield, with you. I left my passports and my money and some other stuff. Do you remember? It's very important. I need that stuff, Didier. Do you remember?'

'Yes, but of course,' he replied, coming to himself with a grumpy little shake of his jaw. 'Your things are all safe. Have no fear of that. I have all your things.'

'Do you still have the apartment in Merriweather Road?'

'Yes.'

'Is that where my things are? Do you have my things there?'

'What?'

'For God's sake, Didier! Snap out of it! Come on. We're going to get up together and walk to your apartment. I need to shave and shower and get organised. I've got something … something important to do. I *need* you, man. Don't fuck up on me now!'

He blinked, and turned his head to look at me, his upper lip curling in the familiar sneer.

'What is the meaning of such a remark?' he demanded indignantly. 'Didier Levy does not fuck up on *anyone*! Unless, of course, it is very, very early in the morning. You know, Lin, how I hate *morning people*, almost as much as I hate the police. *Alors*, let's go!'

At Didier's apartment I shaved, showered, and changed into the new clothes. Didier insisted that I eat something. He cooked an omelette while I went through the two boxes of my belongings to find my stash of money—about nine thousand American dollars—the keys to my bike, and my best false passport. It was a Canadian book, with my photo and details inserted in it. The false tourist visa had expired. I had to renew it quickly. If anything went wrong in what I planned to do, I would need plenty of money and a good, clean book.

'Where are you going now?' Didier asked as I pushed the last forkful of food into my mouth, and stood to rinse the dishes in the sink.

'First, I have to fix up my passport,' I answered him, still chewing. 'Then I'm going to see Madame Zhou.'

'You *what*?'

'I'm going to deal with Madame Zhou. I'm going to clear the slate. Khaled gave ...' I broke off, the words failing, and the thought of Khaled Ansari momentarily bleaching my mind with the mention of his name. It was a white blizzard of emotion storming from the last memory, the last image of him, walking away into the night and the snow. I pushed past it with an effort of will. 'Khaled gave me your note in Pakistan. Thanks for letting me know, by the way. I still don't really get it. I still don't know how she got so mad that she had to put me in jail. There was never anything personal in it, from my side. But it's personal now. Four months in Arthur Road made it personal. That's why I need the bike. I don't want to use cabs. And that's why I've got to get my passport tidied up. If the cops get in on it, I'll need a clean book to hand over.'

'But you don't *know*? Madame Zhou was attacked last week—no, ten days ago. The mob, a mob of Sena people, they attacked her Palace and destroyed it. There was a great fire. They ran inside the building and they destroyed everything, then they put the place on fire. The building still stands. The staircases and the upstairs rooms still exist. But the place is ruined, and it will never again open. They will pull it down at some time soon. The building is finished, Lin, and so is she, *La Madame*.'

'Is she dead?' I asked through clenched teeth.

'No. She is alive. And she is still there, so they say. But her power is destroyed. She has nothing. She *is* nothing. She is a beggar. Her servants are searching the streets for scraps of food to bring to her while she waits for the building to come down. She is finished, Lin.'

'Not quite. Not yet.'

I moved to the door of his apartment, and he ran to join me. It was the fastest I'd ever seen him move, and I smiled at the strangeness of it.

'Please, Lin, will you not reconsider this action? We can sit here, together, and drink a bottle or two, *non*? You will calm down.'

'I'm calm enough *now*,' I replied, smiling at his concern for me. 'I don't know ... what I'm going to do. But I have to close the door on this, Didier. I can't just ... let it go. I wish I could. But there's too much that's—I don't know—tied up in it, I guess.'

I couldn't explain it to him. It was more than just revenge—I knew that—but the web of connections between Zhou, Khaderbhai, Karla, and me was so sticky with shame and secrets and betrayals that I couldn't bring myself to face it clearly or talk about it to my friend.

'*Bien*,' he sighed, reading the determination in my face. 'If you must go to her, then I will come with you.'

'No way —' I began, but he cut me off with a furious gesture of his hand.

'Lin! I am the one who told you of this ... this *horrible* thing she did to you. Now I must go with you, or I will be responsible for all that happens. And you know, my friend, that I hate responsibility almost as much as I hate the police.'

CHAPTER THIRTY-EIGHT

D IDIER L EVY was the worst pillion passenger I've ever known. He held on to me so tightly, and with such rigid tensity, that it was difficult to steer the bike. He howled as we approached cars, and shrieked when we sped up to pass them. On critical, sweeping turns he wriggled in terror, trying to straighten the bike from its necessary lean into the curve. Every time I stopped the bike at a traffic signal, he put both feet down to the ground to stretch his legs and moan about the cramps in his hips. Every time I accelerated away, he dragged his feet on the road and fidgeted for several seconds until he found the footrests. And when taxis or other cars ventured too close to us, he kicked out at them or waved his fist in frantic outrage. By the time we reached our destination, I calculated that the danger faced during a thirty-minute ride in fast traffic with Didier was roughly equivalent to a month under fire in Afghanistan.

I pulled up outside the factory run by my Sri Lankan friends Villu and Krishna. Something was wrong. The signs outside had changed, and the double front doors were wide open. I went up the steps and leaned inside to see that the passport workshop was gone, replaced by an assembly line producing garlands of flowers.

'There is something wrong?' Didier asked as I climbed back on the bike and kicked the starter.

'Yeah. We have to make another stop. They've moved it. I'll have to see Abdul to find out where the new workshop is.'

'Alors,' he whined, squeezing me as tightly as if we were sharing a parachute. 'The nightmare, it goes on!'

Minutes later I left him with the bike near the entrance to Abdul Ghani's mansion. The watchman at the street door recognised me, and snapped his hand up in a theatrical salute. I put a twenty-rupee note in his other hand as he opened the door, and I stepped into the cool, shadowed foyer to be greeted by two servants. They knew me well, and led me upstairs with wide, friendly smiles and a little mime-show of comments on the length of my hair and the weight I'd lost. One of the men knocked on the door of Abdul Ghani's large study, and waited with his ear to the door.

'*Ao!*' Ghani called from within. *Come!*

The servant entered, closing the door behind him, and returned a few moments later. He wagged his head at me and opened the door wide. I walked inside, and the door closed. Brilliant sunshine blazed at the high, arched windows. Shadows reached in spikes and claws across the polished floor. Abdul was sitting in a wing chair that faced the window, and only his plump hands were visible, steepled together like sausages in a butcher's window.

'So it's true.'

'What's true?' I asked, walking around the chair to look at him. I was shocked to see how the months, the nine months since I'd seen him, had aged Khader's old friend. The thick hair was grey to white, and his eyebrows were frosted with silver. The fine nose was pinched by deep lines that swept past the curve of his mouth to a sagging jaw. His lips, once the most sumptuously sensual I'd seen in Bombay, were as split and cracked as Nazeer's had been in the snow mountains. The pouches beneath his eyes drooped past the peak of his cheekbones and reminded me, with a shiver, of those that had dragged down the eyes of the madman Habib. And the eyes—the laughing, golden, amber eyes—were dull, and drained of the soaring joys and vain deceits that once had shone in his passionate life.

'You are here,' he replied in the familiar Oxford accent, without looking at me. 'And *that* is the truth. Where is Khader?'

'Abdul, I'm sorry—he's dead.' I answered at once. 'He ... he was killed by the Russians. He was trying to reach his village, on the way back to Chaman, to deliver some horses.'

Abdul clutched at his chest and sobbed like a child, mewling and moaning incoherently as the tears rolled fat and freely from his large eyes. After a few moments he recovered, and looked up at me.

'Who survived with you?' he asked, his mouth agape.

'Nazeer ... and Mahmoud. And a boy named Ala-ud-Din. Only four of us.'

'Not Khaled? Where is Khaled?'

'He … he went out into the snow on the last night, and he never came back. The men said they heard shooting, later, from a long way off. I don't know if it was Khaled they were shooting at. I … I don't know what happened to him.'

'Then it will be Nazeer …' he muttered.

The sobbing spilled over again, and he plunged his face into his fleshy hands. I watched him uncomfortably, not knowing what to do or say. Since the moment that I'd cradled Khader's body in my arms on the snowy slope of the mountain, I'd refused to face the fact of his death. And I was still angry with Khader Khan. So long as I held that anger before me like a shield, loving Khader and grieving for him were deep and distant wonders of my heart. So long as I was angry, I could fight off the tears and miserable longing that made Ghani so wretched. So long as I was angry, I could concentrate on the job at hand—information about Krishna, Villu, and the passport workshop. I was on the point of asking him about them when he spoke again.

'Do you know what it cost us—apart from his … his unique life— Khader's hero curse? Millions. It cost us millions to fight his war. We've been supporting it, in one way and another, for years. You might think we could afford it. The sum is not so great, after all. But you're wrong. There is no organisation that can support such an insane hero curse as Khader's. And I couldn't change his mind. I couldn't save him. The money didn't mean anything to him, don't you see? You can't reason with a man who has no sense of money and its … its value. It's the one thing all civilised men have in common, don't you agree? If money doesn't mean anything, there is no civilisation. There is nothing.'

He trailed off into indecipherable mumbles. Tears rolled into the little rivers they found on his cheeks, and dropped through the yellow light into his lap.

'Abdulbhai,' I said, after a time.

'What? When? Is it *now*?' he asked, terror suddenly bright in his eyes. His lower lip stiffened in a cruel curve of malice I'd never seen or even imagined in him before that moment.

'Abdulbhai, I want to know where you moved the workshop. Where are Krishna and Villu? I went to the old workshop, but there's no-one there. I need some work on my book. I need to know where you moved to.'

The fear shrank to a pinpoint in his eyes, and they glittered with it. His mouth swelled in something like the old voluptuary smile, and he looked into my eyes with avid, hungering concentration.

'Of *course* you want to know,' he grinned, using the palms of his hands to wipe at the tears. 'It's right here, Lin, in this house. We rebuilt the cellar, and fitted it out. There is a trapdoor in the kitchen floor. Iqbal will show you the way. The boys are working there now.'

'Thanks,' I said, hesitating a moment. 'I've got a job to do, but ... I'll be back later tonight, or tomorrow, at the latest. I'll see you then.'

'Inshallah,' he said softly, turning his face to the windows once more. 'Inshallah.'

I went down through the house to the kitchen and lifted the heavy trapdoor. A dozen steps led into the floodlit cellar. Krishna and Villu greeted me happily, and went to work on my passport immediately. Few things excited them more than a counterfeiting challenge, and they chattered in a spirited little argument before agreeing on the best approach.

While they worked, I examined Ghani's new workshop. It was a large space—much larger than the basement of Abdul Ghani's mansion alone. I walked some thirty to fifty metres past light-tables, printing machines, photocopiers, and storage cupboards. I guessed that the basement extended beneath the next large house in the street beside Ghani's. It seemed likely that they'd bought the house next door, and connected the two cellars. If that were so, I assumed, there would be another exit, leading into the neighbouring house. I was searching for it when Krishna called to tell me that my rush-jobs visa was ready. Intrigued by the new set-up beneath the houses, I promised myself that as soon as possible I would return and inspect the workshop thoroughly.

'Sorry to keep you,' I muttered to Didier as I climbed back onto the bike. 'It took longer than I expected. But the passport's done. We can go straight to Madame Zhou's now.'

'Don't hurry, Lin,' Didier sighed, clutching at me with all his strength as we moved out into the traffic. 'The best revenge, like the best sex, is performed slowly and with the eyes open.'

'Karla?' I shouted over my shoulder, as the bike accelerated into the metal stream.

'*Non*, I think it's mine! But ... but I can't be sure!' he shouted back, and we both laughed for love of her.

I parked the bike in the driveway of an apartment building a block away from the Palace. We walked on the other side of the road until we passed the building by half a block, studying it for signs of activity within. The façade of the Palace seemed intact and undamaged, although metal and wooden sheets on the windows, and planks nailed across the main door, hinted at the destruction the mob had wrought inside. We turned and walked back, passing the building again and searching for an entrance.

'If she's in there, and if her servants are bringing her food, they're not coming and going through *that* door.'

'Yes, exactly my own thought,' he agreed. 'There must be another way inside.'

We found a narrow lane that gave access to the rear of the buildings in the street. In contrast to the proud, clean, main street, the access lane was filthy. We stepped carefully between rank, scum-covered pools of black liquid, and skirted piles of oily, unidentifiable debris. I glanced at Didier, knowing from his wretched grimace that he was calculating how many drinks it would take to rid himself of the stench that filled his nostrils. The walls and fences on either side of the lane were made of stone, brick, and cement, patched together over many decades, and swarming with a wormy writhe of plants, mosses, and creepers.

Counting back from the corner, building by building, we found the rear of the Palace and pressed on a short wooden gate, set into a high stone wall. The gate opened at the touch, and we stepped into a spacious rear courtyard that must've been a luxurious and beautiful retreat before the mob had attacked it. Heavy clay pots had been toppled and shattered, their burdens of earth and flowers spilled in muddy confusion. Garden furniture had been smashed to kindling. Even the paving tiles were cracked in many places, as if they'd been struck with hammers.

We found a blackened door that led into the house. It was unlocked, and swung inward with a rusty creak of complaint.

'You wait here.' My tone allowed no possibility of protest. 'Keep watch for me. If someone comes in through that gate, slow them up, or give me a signal.'

'As you say,' he sighed. 'Don't be too long. I don't like it here. *Bonne chance.*'

I stepped inside. The door swung shut behind me, and I wished that I'd thought to bring a torch. It was dark, and the floor was treacherously cluttered with broken dishes, pots, pans, and other vessels strewn amid the black lumps of furniture and fallen beams. I picked my way slowly through the ground-floor kitchen and on into a long corridor that led toward the front of the big house. I passed several rooms that were burned. In one of them, the fire had been so fierce that the floor was missing, and the charred bearers showed through the gaps like the ribs of some great animal's remains.

Near the front of the house I found the stairway that I'd taken, years before, when I'd come there with Karla to save Lisa Carter. The Compton wallpaper, once so rich in colour and texture, was scorched and peeling from the blistered walls. The stairway itself was carbonised, its carpet scorched to stringy clumps of ash. I climbed up slowly, testing each step before pressing down with my full weight. One step collapsed beneath me when I was halfway to the top, and I scrambled upward more quickly to the landing on the first floor.

On the upper level I had to pause while my eyes adjusted to the darkness. After a few moments I could make out the gaps in the floor, and I began to inch my way around them. The fire had incinerated some parts of the house, leaving holes and blackened stumps, while sparing other parts of the house altogether. Those pristine sections were so clean, and so precisely as I remembered them, that they heightened the eerie strangeness of the place. I felt as if I was moving between the past, before the fire, and the ruined present: as if my own memories were creating those grandiose, unconsumed zones in the house.

Some way along that wide passage on the upper level my foot plunged through a papery section of floor, and in my hard reaction I drove backward into the wall behind me. The wall itself collapsed and I found myself falling, in a clumsy stumble, flaying out with my hands to find something solid to cling to amid the crumbling rubble. I landed with a thump, much more quickly than I expected, and realised at once that I was inside one of Madame Zhou's secret corridors. The wall I'd fallen through appeared to be as solid as all the others, but it was merely a plywood screen papered over with her ubiquitous Compton pattern.

I stood up and brushed myself off in a very narrow, low corridor that snaked ahead, following the shapes and corners of the rooms it circumscribed. Metal grates were set into the walls of the rooms that the secret corridor passed. Some of them were low, near the floor, and others were higher. Beneath the higher metal grates were boxed steps. From the lowest of those steps I looked into a room through the heart-shaped gaps in the metal grille. I could see the whole room beyond: the cracked mirror on the wall, the burned and collapsed bed, and the rusted metal nightstand beside it. There were several steps above the one on which I stood, and I imagined her, Madame Zhou, crouched there on the topmost step and breathing silently while she watched, and watched.

The corridor wound through several turns, and I lost my bearings, unsure in the enshrouding darkness if I faced the front of the house or the rear. At one point the secret corridor inclined sharply. I climbed upward until the higher metal grilles disappeared, and I stumbled in the dark upon a flight of steps. Feeling my way upward, I encountered a door. It was a small, paneled wooden door—so small and perfectly proportioned that it might've been furnished for a child's playhouse. I tried the doorknob. It turned easily in my hand. I pushed it open, and shrank back immediately at the inward rush of light from beyond.

I stepped into an attic room lit by a row of four stained-glass dormer windows that peaked like little chapels and reached out over the external roof of the house. The fire had reached the room, but it had failed to destroy it. The walls were darkened, splashed with streaky burn-shadows, and the floor was holed in places to reveal a deep sandwich layer between it and the ceiling of the room below. Parts of the long room, however, were quite solid and untouched by the flames. In those islands of exotically carpeted floor and unblemished wall-space, furniture still stood intact and unmarked. And in the stiff, enwrapping arms of a throne-like chair, her face twisted in a manic stare, was Madame Zhou.

As I approached her I realised that the malevolent stare wasn't directed at me. She was staring with hatred and spite at some point in the past, some place or person or event that held her mind as firmly as a chain holds a dancing bear. Her face was made up with a thick smear and powdering of cosmetics. It was a mask—more tragic, for all its deluded exaggerations, than grotesque. The painted mouth was bigger than her own lips. The scrawled eyebrows were larger than the real ones. The daubed cheeks were higher than the bones beneath them. When I stood near enough, I saw that there was a trickle of drool dripping, dripping, from the corner of her mouth into her lap. The smell of alcohol, undiluted gin, wreathed her and coiled into other smells, more foul and sickening. Her hair was almost concealed by a wig. The thick coils of the black, pompadour wig hung slightly askew, revealing the short, sparse grey hair beneath. She was dressed in a green silk cheongsam. The neck of the dress covered her throat almost to her chin. Her legs were folded, with her feet resting on the seat of the chair beside her. They were tiny feet—the size of a small child's feet—enclosed in soft, silk slippers. Her hands, as limp and expressionless as her slack mouth, lay in her lap like things washed up on a deserted shore.

It was impossible for me to tell her age or her nationality. She might've been Spanish. She might've been Russian. She might've been Indian, in part, or Chinese, or even Greek. And Karla was right—she *had* been beautiful once. It was the kind of beauty that grows from the sum of its parts rather than from any one outstanding feature: a beauty that strikes the eye rather than the heart, and a beauty that sours if it isn't nourished by some goodness from within. And she wasn't beautiful then, in that moment. She was ugly. And Didier was right, too: she was beaten and broken and finished. She was floating on the black lake, and soon the dark water would drag her under. There was a deep silence where her mind used to be, and a blank, uncraving emptiness where once her cruel and scheming life had ruled.

Standing there, invisible to her, I was astonished and bewildered to realise that I felt not angry or vengeful, but ashamed. I felt ashamed that I'd filled my heart with revenge. The part of me that had wanted to— *What? Had I really wanted to kill her?*—was the very part that was like her. I looked at her, and I knew that I was looking at myself, my own future, my destiny, if I couldn't rid my heart of its vindictiveness.

And I knew, as well, that the revenge I'd fed myself with and planned through the weeks of my recuperation in Pakistan was not merely hers, not only hers. I was striking out at myself, and at a guilt I could only face in that moment of shame as I looked at her. It was the guilt I felt for Khader's death. I was his American—his guarantee against the warlords and pirates. If I'd been with him, as I was supposed to be, when he'd tried to take the horses to his village, the enemy might not have fired on him.

It was foolish and, like most guilt, it only told one half of the story. There were Russian uniforms and weapons on some of the dead around Khader's body: Nazeer had told me that. My being there probably wouldn't have changed a thing. They would've captured me or killed me, and the result for Khader would've been the same. But reason didn't play a big part in the guilt I'd felt, deep in my heart, since the moment I'd seen his dead face beneath its shroud of snow. Once I'd faced it, I couldn't shake the shame. And somehow, the blame and repining sorrow changed me. I felt the vengeful stone fall from the hating hand that had wanted to throw it. I felt light, as if light itself filled me and lifted me up. And I felt free — free enough to pity Madame Zhou, and even to forgive her. And then I heard the scream.

A heart-piercing shriek, as shrill as a wild pig's, pulled me round just in time to see Rajan, Madame Zhou's eunuch servant, running at me at full speed. Caught off balance by the charge, I stumbled backward with his arms wrapped around my chest, and we crashed into and then through one of the attic windows. I was leaning out backwards, looking up under blue sky at the crazed servant and the eaves of the house behind his head. I felt the unmistakable cold trickle of blood on the top and the back of my head where the broken glass had made deep cuts. More glass fell in jagged shards as we wrestled in the smashed window, and I shook my head from side to side to save my eyes. Rajan clung to me and drove forward with his feet in a weird, running shuffle that gained him no space at all. It took me a moment to understand that he was trying to push me out through the window — to push us both out, into the big fall. And it was working. I felt my feet beginning to lift off the floor under the pressure of his effort, and I slipped further out through the little steeple of the dormer window.

Growling with fury and desperation, I clutched at the window frame and dragged us back into the attic with all my strength. Rajan fell backward, and scrambled to his feet with astonishing speed to run shrieking at me again. There was no way to step around his quick charge, so we closed again in a murderous grapple. His hands locked on my throat. My left hand clawed at his face, looking for the eye. His long, curved fingernails were sharp, and they pierced the skin of my neck. Shouting from the pain, I found his ear with the fingers of my left hand, and used it to pull his head close enough to punch with my right. I hammered my fist into his face, six, seven, eight times until he wrenched free from me, tearing the ear half away from his head.

He fell back a step and stood there, panting heavily and glaring at me with a hatred that was beyond reason or fear. His face was bloody. His lips were split into a broken tooth, and the skin over one eye, where the eyebrow had been shaved off, had opened up in an ugly cut. His bald head was cut and bleeding where he'd crashed through the glass. The blood was in one eye, and I guessed that his nose was broken. He should've quit. He had to quit. He didn't.

Shrieking, shrill and weird, he ran at me. I sidestepped and slammed a hard, short right hand into the side of his head, but he reached out with his clawed hand as he fell, and clutched at my trousers. His momentum pulled us both down and then he scrambled, crab-like, to cover me, reaching out for my neck. Once more the claws bit into my shoulder and my throat.

He was lean, but he was strong and tall. I'd lost so much weight in Khader's war that we were evenly matched for strength. I rolled once, twice, but couldn't shake him. His head was tucked in close to mine, and I couldn't punch at him. I felt his mouth and his teeth against my neck. He was straining forward, butting heads with me and biting. His long, sharp claws punctured my throat to the stubs of his fingers.

I reached down and found my knife. I pulled it out and around, and rammed it into his body. The blade went into his thigh, high up near the hip. He raised his head in a howl of pain, and I stabbed him in the neck, close to the shoulder. The knife went in through the front and deep into the shoulder, crunching an edge of bone and gristle on the way. He scrabbled at his throat, and rolled away from me until his body met the wall. He was beaten. There was no fight left in him. It was over. And then I heard the scream.

I jerked my head around to see Rajan creeping out of the gap between the broken floor and the ceiling of the room below. It was the same man, or so it seemed, but whole and unharmed: the same bald head, shaved eyebrows, decorated eyes, and clawed fingernails painted as green as a grass snake. I swung round quickly to see that Rajan was still there, curled in a moaning heap against the wall. *It's a twin*, I thought stupidly. *There's two of them. Why didn't anyone tell me?* And I turned again, just as the screeching twin rushed at me. The second one had a knife in his hand.

He held the thin, curved blade like a sword, sweeping it in a vicious arc as he ran. I allowed his frenzied sweep to pass and then stepped in close, jabbing downward with my own knife. It cut his arm and shoulder, but he was still free to move. His knife slashed backward toward me. He was fast —fast enough to cut my forearm. Blood ran quickly from the wound, and rage pulled me into him with my right fist punching and jabbing with the knife. Then a sudden black, blood-tasting pain crashed into the back of my head, and I knew I'd been hit from behind. I scrambled past the twin, and twisted round to see wounded Rajan, his shirt painted on his skin with his own blood. There was a lump of wood in his hand. My head was ringing with the force of the blow he'd struck. Blood was running from wounds on my head, my neck, my shoulder, and the soft inside of my forearm. The twins began wailing again, and I knew they were about to make a new charge. A tiny seed of doubt ripened and burst open in my mind for the first time since the bizarre contest had begun: *I might not win this …*

I grinned at them, shaping up for their charge with my fists high and my left foot forward. *Okay*, I thought. *Let's go. Let's finish it.* They ran at me, keening that high-pitched scream again. The one with the lump of wood, Rajan, swung it at me. I raised my left arm to block the blow. It came down hard on my shoulder, but I rammed my right fist into his face and he fell backward, his knees folding before he hit the floor. His brother slashed at my face with the knife. I ducked and weaved, but the knife cut my head at the back, above the neck. I came up under his guard and jammed my knife into his shoulder, all the way to the crank. I'd aimed for his chest, but it was still a useful wound because his arm below the knife went as limp as seaweed, and he screeched away from me in panic.

Years of anger broke through: all the prison-anger I'd buried in the shallow grave of my resentful self-control. The blood running down my face from the cuts and gashes on my head was liquid anger, thick and red and spilling from my mind. A furious strength ripped the muscles of my arms, shoulders, and back. I looked from Rajan and his twin to the imbecile in the chair. *Kill them all*, I thought, dragging the air in through clenched teeth, and growling it out again. *I'll kill them all.*

I heard someone calling me, calling me, calling me back from the edge of the abyss into which Habib, and all those like him, had plunged.

'Lin! Where are you, Lin?'

'In here, Didier!' I shouted back. 'In the attic! You're very close! Can you hear me?'

'I hear you!' he shouted. 'I'm coming at once.'

'Be careful!' I called back, panting. 'There's two guys up here, and they're ... fuck, man ... they're none too friendly!'

I heard the sound of his footsteps, and I heard him curse as he stumbled in the dark. He pushed open the little door and stooped to enter the room. There was a gun in his hand, and I was glad to see him. I watched his face as he quickly took in the scene—the blood on my face and arms, the blood on the bodies of the twins, the drooling figure in the chair. I saw his shocked surprise harden and settle into the grim, angry line of his mouth. Then he heard the scream.

Rajan's brother, the one with the knife, let out that blood-numbing waul and ran at Didier, who swung his pistol round without hesitation and shot the man in the groin, near the hip. He crumpled and flung himself sideways, yowling sobs of pain as he rolled on the floor, doubled over his bleeding wound. Rajan limped to the throne-like chair and draped his body in front of Madame Zhou, shielding her with his bare chest. He stared his hatred into Didier's eyes, and we knew that he was willing to take a bullet to protect her. Didier took a step towards him, and levelled the pistol at Rajan's heart. The Frenchman's face was set in a severe frown, but his pale eyes were calm, and gleaming with his cool and absolute dominion. That was the real man, the steel blade within the shabby, rusting scabbard. Didier Levy: one of the most capable and dangerous men in Bombay.

'Do you want to do it?' he asked me, his face harder than anything else in the room.

'No.'

'No?' he breathed, his eyes never leaving Rajan. 'Take a look at yourself. Look at what they did, Lin. You should shoot them.'

'No.'

'You should wound them, at the very least.'

'No.'

'It is dangerous to let them live. Your history with these people is ... not good.'

'It's okay,' I muttered.

'You should shoot at least *one* of them, *non*?'

'No.'

'Very well. Then I will shoot them for you.'

'No,' I insisted. I was grateful that he'd stopped them from killing me, but far more thankful that he'd arrived in time to prevent me from killing them. Surging waves of nausea and relief crashed into my blood-red mind, draining the rage from me. I shivered as the last smile of shame trembled in my eyes. 'I don't want to shoot them ... and I don't want *you* to shoot them, either. I didn't want to fight them in the first place. I wouldn't have, if they hadn't attacked me first. They're only doing what I'd do, if I loved her. They're only trying to protect her. They're not against me. It's not about me. It's about her. Leave them alone.'

'And *what* about her?'

'You were right,' I said quietly. 'She's finished. She's already dead. I'm sorry I didn't listen to you. I guess ... I had to see it for myself.'

I reached out to cover the gun in Didier's hand. Rajan flinched and flexed. His twin, crying out in pain, began to drag himself away from us along the edge of the wall. Then I slowly pushed Didier's hand downward until the gun was at his side. Rajan met my eyes. I saw the surprise and fear in his black eyes soften into relief. He held the stare a moment longer and then limped to his brother's side.

With Didier close behind me, I made my way along the secret corridor and back to the blackened stairs.

'I owe you one, Didier,' I admitted, grinning into the dark.

'Certainly you do,' he replied, and then the stairs crumbled beneath us and we fell, tumbling in and through the burned and broken wood until we hit the hard floor below.

Spluttering and coughing in the cloud of charcoal dust and floating fibres, I wriggled against my fallen friend to sit upright. My neck was stiff and sore, and I'd landed on my wrist and shoulder, spraining them both, but I seemed to be intact and otherwise unbroken. Didier had landed on me, and I heard him moaning grumpily.

'Are you okay, man? Jesus, what a fall! Are you all right?'

'That's it,' Didier snarled. 'I'm going back up there to *shoot* that woman!'

We laughed as we hobbled out of the ruined Palace together, and the laughter stayed with us in the hours that followed while we bathed our wounds and dressed them. Didier gave me a clean shirt and trousers to wear. His wardrobe was surprisingly stylish and colourful for a man who dressed in such a drab uniform at Leopold's. He explained that most of those bright new clothes had been left with him by lovers who'd never returned for them, and I thought of Karla, giving me clothes that had once belonged to her lovers. And the laughter bubbled up anew as we ate a meal together at Leopold's while Didier talked of his most recent romantic disasters. We were laughing still when Vikram Patel ran up the steps with his arms wide in an excited greeting.

'Lin!'

'Vikram!'

I stood just in time to receive his flying hug. Holding my shoulders with his arms straight, he looked me over, frowning at the cuts on my head and face.

'Fuck, man, what happened to you?' he asked. His clothes were still black, and still inspired by the cowboy dream, but they were much more subdued and subtle. That was Lettie's influence, I guessed. Although the new, inexcessive look suited him, I was relieved and comforted to see that his beloved hat still hung on his back from the cord at his throat.

'You should see the other guys,' I answered, flicking a glance at Didier.

'So why didn't you tell me you're back, man?'

'I only got back today, and I've been kind of busy. How's Lettie?'

'She's great, *yaar*,' he responded cheerily, taking a seat. 'She's going into this business thing, this multi-fuckin-media thing, with Karla and her new boyfriend. It's going to be damn good.'

I turned my head to look at Didier, who shrugged non-committally and then glared at Vikram with his teeth bared in fury.

'Shit, man!' Vikram apologised, clearly stricken. 'I thought you knew. I thought Didier would've told you, *yaar*.'

'Karla is back in Bombay,' Didier explained, silencing Vikram with another stern frown. 'She has a new man—a boyfriend, she calls him. His name is Ranjit, but he likes everyone to call him Jeet.'

'He's not a bad guy,' Vikram added, smiling hopefully. 'I think you'll like him, Lin.'

'Oh, really, Vikram!' Didier hissed, wincing for me.

'It's okay,' I said, smiling at each of them in turn.

I caught the eye of our waiter and nodded to him, gesturing for a new round of drinks. We were silent until they arrived and the drinks were poured, and then, with the glasses in the air, I proposed a toast.

'To Karla!' I proposed. 'May she have ten daughters, and may they all marry well!'

'To Karla!' the others echoed, clashing glasses and throwing back the drinks.

We were sharing our third toast—to someone's pet dog, I think—when Mahmoud Melbaaf walked into the happy, noisy, chattering restaurant and looked at me with eyes that were still up there, on the frozen mountains of the war.

'What happened to you?' he asked quickly, looking at the cuts on my face and head when I rose to greet him.

'Nothing,' I smiled.

'Who did this?' he asked more urgently.

'I had a run-in with Madame Zhou's guys,' I answered, and he relaxed a little. 'Why? What's up?'

'Nazeer told me you would be here,' he whispered through a tight, anguished little frown. 'I am happy to find you. Nazeer says to you, don't go anywhere. Don't do anything, for some days. There is a war now—a war of the gangs. They fight for Khader's power. It is not safe. Stay away from the dundah places.'

The word *dundah*, or business, was the slang term we used for all of Khader's black-market operations in Bombay. They'd become targets, somehow.

'What happened? What's it all about?'

'The traitor, Ghani, is dead,' he replied. His voice was calm, but his eyes were hard and determined. 'The men with him, his men in Khader's gang, will also die.'

'Ghani?'

'Yes. Do you have money, Lin?'

'Sure,' I muttered, thinking about Abdul Ghani. *He was from Pakistan. That had to be it. The connections to the secret police, the Pakistan ISI, must've been his. Of course it was him. Of course he was the traitor. Of course he was the one who'd tried to have us arrested and killed in Karachi. That's who Khaled had been talking about on the night before the battle: not Abdullah, but Ghani. Abdul Ghani ...*

'Do you have a place? A safe place?'

'What? Yes.'

'Good,' he said, shaking my hand warmly. 'Then I will see you here, in three days' time, in the day, at one o'clock, *Inshallah*.'

'*Inshallah*,' I responded, and he walked out. His handsome head was high, in his brave, righteous step, and his back was straight.

I sat down again, avoiding the eyes of my friends until I could disguise the dread that I knew they would read in them.

'What is it?' Didier asked.

'Nothing,' I lied, shaking my head and faking a smile. I reached for my glass and lifted it to clink against theirs. 'Where were we?'

'We were just going to toast Ranjit's dog,' Vikram recalled, grinning widely, 'but I'd like to include his horse in that toast, if it's not too late.'

'You do not know if he *has* a horse!' Didier objected.

'We don't know if he's got a dog, either,' Vikram pointed out, 'but that's not stopping us. To Ranjit's dog!'

'Ranjit's dog!' we all replied.

'And his horse!' Vikram added. 'And his neighbour's horse!'

'Ranjit's horse!'

'And ... horses ... in general!'

'And to lovers, everywhere!' Didier proposed.

'And to lovers ... everywhere ...' I answered.

But somehow, in some way, for some reason, the love had died in me, and I suddenly realised it, and was suddenly sure. It wasn't completely over, my feeling for Karla. It never is completely over. But there was nothing of the jealousy I once would've felt for the stranger Ranjit. There was no rage against him, and no feeling of hurt inspired by her. I felt numbed and empty sitting there, as if the war, and the loss of Khaderbhai and Khaled, and the face-off with Madame Zhou and her twins had poured anaesthetic into my heart.

And there was, instead of pain, a sense of wonder—I could think of no other way to describe what I was feeling—at Abdul Ghani's treachery. And behind that almost spiritual awe there was a dull, throbbing, fatalistic dread. For even then the bloody future his betrayal had forced on us was unfolding and spilling into our lives, like the sudden blossom of a drought-forced rose in a red, falling rush to dry, unyielding earth.

CHAPTER THIRTY-NINE

ONE HOUR after I'd left Abdul Ghani's mansion to confront Madame Zhou, Nazeer and three of his most trusted men forced the door of the house next to Ghani's and made their way through the long basement workshop that connected the two houses. At about the time that I picked my way through the rubble of Madame Zhou's ruined Palace, Nazeer and his men, wearing black knitted masks, pushed up the trapdoor in Ghani's kitchen and entered the house. They seized the cook, the yard-man, Abdul's two servants, and the Sri Lankan counterfeiters, Villu and Krishna, and locked them in a small room in the basement. As I climbed the blackened stairs of the Palace to the attic and found Madame Zhou, Nazeer crept upstairs to Abdul's grand study and found him sitting in the wing chair, weeping and still. Then, at about the time that I uncurled the knotted fist of my revenge to pity my broken enemy, the drooling Madame, Nazeer avenged himself and Khader Khan by killing the traitor who'd betrayed us all in Pakistan.

Two men held Abdul's arms against the chair. A third man forced his head back and his eyes open. Nazeer removed his mask. Staring into Abdul's eyes, Nazeer stabbed him in the heart. Abdul must've known he had to die. He was sitting there, alone, waiting for his killers. But his scream, they say, came all the way from hell to claim him.

They rolled his body off the chair and onto the polished floor. Then, as I struggled with Rajan and his twin in the attic across the city, Nazeer and his men used heavy cleavers to hack off Abdul's hands, his feet, and his head. They scattered the pieces of his corpse around the great house, just as Abdul Ghani had ordered the Sapna killers to do with the butchered pieces of loyal old Madjid's body. And as I left the ruined Palace, my heart free and almost at peace for the first time in too many vengeful months, Nazeer and his men released Krishna, Villu, and the servants—all deemed to have had no part in Ghani's treachery—and then left the mansion to hunt down the members of Ghani's faction, and kill them all.

'Ghani was freakin' out for a long time, *yaar*.' Sanjay Kumar said, translating freely from Nazeer's Urdu into English. 'He thought Khader had gone crazy. He thought he was, like, *obsessed*, you know? He got the idea that Khader was going to lose all the business and the money and the power of the council. He thought Khader was spending too much time on Afghanistan, the war, and all that. And he knew Khader had all these other missions planned—stuff in Sri Lanka and Nigeria and such like. So when he couldn't talk Khader out of it, and he couldn't get him to change, he decided to use all this Sapna business. The Sapna thing was Ghani's operation, right from the start.'

'All of it?' I asked.

'Sure,' Sanjay answered. 'Khader and Ghani, both. But Ghani was in charge. They were using the Sapna thing, you know, to get what they wanted from the cops and the government.'

'How?'

'Ghani's idea was to freak everybody out—the cops and the politicians and the other councils—with a common enemy. That was Sapna. When the Sapna guys started chopping people up all over the place, and talking about a revolution, and Sapna being the king of thieves and all that, everybody got worried. Nobody knew who was behind it. That got them to work *with* us, to catch the fucker, in exchange for our help. But Ghani, he was hoping to get a shot at Khader himself.'

'I'm not sure he wanted that from the start,' Salman Mustaan interrupted, shaking his head at his close friend to emphasise his point. 'I think he started out just like always, backing Khader all the way. But that Sapna thing—that was some weird shit, man, and I think, you know, it bent his mind.'

'Whatever,' Sanjay continued, shrugging off the fine point. 'The result's the same. Ghani has this gang—the Sapna guys—his own gang, that only answer to him. And he's killing fuckers all over the place. Most of them were people he wanted to get rid of anyway, for business reasons, which I got no problem with. So everything's going fine, *yaar*. The whole fuckin' city is going crazy looking for this Sapna fucker, and all Khader's traditional enemies, they're falling all over themselves to help him smuggle guns and explosives and other heavy shit through Bombay because they want *him* to help *them* find out who this Sapna is, and take him out. It's a fuckin' crazy plan, but it's working, *yaar*. Then, one day, a cop comes to see him. It was that Patil—you know the guy, Lin—that sub-inspector Suresh Patil. He used to work out of Colaba. And he's such a cunt, *yaar*.'

'But a smart one,' Salman muttered respectfully.

'Oh, yeah, he's smart. He's a very smart cunt. And he tells Ghani that the Sapna killers have left a clue at the scene of their latest murder, and it leads back to the Khader Khan council. Ghani freaks out. He can see all that shit he's been doing coming right home to his doorstep. So he decides that he's got to have a sacrifice. Someone from the Khader Khan council itself, you know, right in the fuckin' heart of it all, that the Sapna guys can chop up to throw the cops off. They figured, if the cops saw one of our own guys get all chopped up, they'd have to think that Sapna was our enemy.'

'And he picked Madjid,' Salman concluded for him. 'And it worked. Patil was the cop in charge of the case, and he was there when they were putting the pieces of Madjid's body into carry bags. He knew how close Madjid was to Khaderbhai. Patil's dad—now *there's* a tough cop, *yaar*—had some history with Khaderbhai. He put him in jail once.'

'Khaderbhai did time?' I asked, disappointed that I'd never asked the Khan myself: we'd talked about prison often enough.

'Sure,' Salman laughed. 'He even escaped, you know, from Arthur Road.'

'You're fuckin' kidding!'

'You didn't know that, Lin?'

'No.'

'It's a damn fine story, *yaar*,' Salman stated, wagging his head enthusiastically. 'You should get Nazeer to tell it some time. He was the outside man for Khader Khan during the escape. They were fuckin' wild guys, Nazeer and Khaderbhai, in those days, *yaar*.'

Sanjay, in agreement, clapped Nazeer on the back with a hard, good-natured slap. It was almost exactly the place where Nazeer had been wounded, and I knew the slap must've hurt, but he showed no sign of pain. Instead, he studied my face. It was my first formal debriefing after Abdul Ghani's death and the end of the two-week gangster war that had cost six lives and put the power of the mafia council back in the hands of

Nazeer and the Khader faction. I met his gaze, and nodded slowly. His stern, unsmiling face softened for an instant and then quickly set in its customary severity.

'Poor old Madjid,' Sanjay said, sighing heavily. 'He was just a—what the fuck do you call those red things? Those fish?'

'A red herring,' I said.

'Yeah, one of those herring fuckers. The cops—that Patil cunt and his guys—they decided that there wasn't any connection between Sapna and Khader's council. They knew how much Khader loved Madjid, and they started looking in other places. Ghani was off the hook, and after a while his guys started chopping fuckers up again. Business as usual.'

'How did Khader feel about it?'

'About what?' Sanjay asked.

'He means about Madjid being killed,' Salman cut in. 'Don't you, Lin?'

'Yeah.'

There was a small hesitation as all three men looked at me. Their features were set in grim and almost resentful stillness, as if I'd asked them an impolite or embarrassing question. But their eyes, lit with secrets and lies, seemed regretful and saddened.

'Khader was cool with it,' Salman answered. I felt my heart stutter, murmuring its pain.

We were in the Mocambo, a restaurant and coffee bar in the Fort Area. It was clean, well serviced, and fashionably bohemian. Rich businessmen from the Fort mixed with gangsters, lawyers, and celebrities from the movies and the rapidly developing television industries. I liked the place, and I'd been glad that Sanjay had chosen it for our meeting. We'd worked our way through a big but healthy lunch and kulfi dessert, and had moved on to our second coffee. Nazeer sat at my left, with his back in a corner space, and facing the main street door. Next to him was Sanjay Kumar, the tough, young Hindu gangster from the suburb of Bandra who'd once been my training partner. He'd worked his way into a permanent position on what remained of Khader's mafia council. He was thirty years old, fit and heavy-set, with thick, dark-brown hair that he blow-dried to match the bouffant of the movie heroes. His face was handsome. Wide-apart brown eyes, set deep into the shelter of a high brow, looked out with humour and confidence over a wide nose, a smiler's mouth, and a softly rounded chin. He laughed easily, and it was always a good, warm laugh, no matter how often he provoked himself to it. And he was generous: it was almost impossible to pay a bill in his company—not, as some thought, because he aggrandised himself with the gesture, but rather because it was his instinct to give and to share. He was also brave, and as dependable in a violent crisis as he was from day to mundane day. He was an easy man to like, and I *did* like him, and I had to remind myself with a little nudge of will, now and then, that he was one of the men who'd hacked off Abdul Ghani's hands and feet and head with a butcher's cleaver.

The fourth man at our table, sitting next to Sanjay, as always, was Salman, his best friend. Salman Mustaan was born in the same year as Sanjay, and had grown up with him in the bustling, crowded suburb of Bandra. He'd been a precocious child, I'd been told, who'd surprised his impoverished parents by topping every subject in every class at his junior school. His success was the more remarkable for the fact that, from the day of his fifth birthday, the boy had worked twenty hours a week with his father, plucking chickens and sweeping out at the local poultry yard.

I knew his history well, piecing it together from stories and confidences he'd shared when we'd worked out together at Abdullah's gym. When Salman had announced that he had to leave school to work longer hours in support of his family, a teacher who knew Abdel Khader Khan asked the don to intercede on his behalf. Salman became one of Khaderbhai's scholarship children—like my adviser, in the slum clinic, Doctor Hamid—and it was decided that he should be groomed toward a career as a lawyer. Khader enrolled Salman in a Catholic college run by Jesuit priests, and every day the boy from the slum dressed in a clean, white uniform and took his place among the sons of the rich elite. It was a good education—Salman's spoken English was eloquent, and his general knowledge roved through history and geography to literature, science, and art. But there was a wildness in the boy and a restless hunger for excitement that even the strong arms and the hard canes of the Jesuits couldn't tame.

While Salman struggled with the Jesuits, Sanjay had found a job in Khaderbhai's gang. He worked as a runner, carrying messages and contraband between mafia offices throughout the city. In the first weeks of that service, Sanjay was stabbed during a fight with men from a rival gang who'd tried to rob him. The boy fought back and evaded his attackers, delivering his contraband parcel to Khader's collection centre, but his wound was serious and he took two months to recover from it. Salman, his lifelong friend, blamed himself for not being with Sanjay, and he left school immediately. He begged the Khan for permission to join his friend and work with him as a runner. Khader agreed, and from that day the boys worked together at every crime in the council's catalogue.

They were just sixteen then, at the beginning. They both turned thirty in the weeks before our meeting in the Mocambo. The wild boys had become hard men who lavished gifts on their families, and lived with a certain gaudy, aggressive cool. Although they'd supported their sisters into prestigious marriages, both men were unmarried, in a country where that was unpatriotic at the least, and sacrilegious at worst. They'd refused to marry, Salman told me, because of a shared belief or presentiment that they would die violently and they would die young. The prospect didn't frighten or worry them. They saw it as a reasonable trade-off: excitement and power and wealth enough to provide for their families, balanced against short lives that rushed into the dead-end of a knife or a gun. And when Nazeer's group won the gangster war against Ghani's group, the two friends found themselves on the new council; young mafia dons in their own right.

'I think Ghani did *try* to warn Khaderbhai what was in his heart,' Salman said thoughtfully, his voice clear and his English rounded to the nearest decibel point. 'He talked about that hero curse thing for a good year or so before he decided to create Sapna.'

'Fuck him, *yaar*,' Sanjay snarled. 'Who the fuck was he to be giving Khaderbhai warnings? Who the fuck was he to get us all in the shit with Patil, so he had to have his guys cut up old Madjid? And then, after everything, he went and sold everybody out to the fuckin' Pakistani cops, *yaar*. Fuck him. If I could dig the madachudh up and kill him again, I'd do it today. I'd do it *every* day. It would be my fuckin' hobby, like.'

'Who was the real Sapna?' I asked. 'Who actually did the killings for Abdul? I remember Khader told me once, after Abdullah was killed, that he found the real Sapna. He said he killed him. Who was he? And why did he kill him, if he was working for him in the first place?'

The two younger men turned to face Nazeer. Sanjay asked him a few questions in Urdu. It was an act of respect toward the older man: they knew the facts as well as Nazeer did, but they deferred to his recollection of them and included him in the discussion. I understood most of Nazeer's reply, but I waited for Sanjay to translate.

'His name was Jeetendra. Jeetudada, they called him. He was a gun and machete guy from Delhi-side. Ghani brought him down here, with four other guys. He actually kept them in five-star hotels, like, the whole fuckin' time—two *years*, man! *Bahinchudh*! Complaining about Khader spending money on the mujaheddin and the war and all, and meanwhile he was keeping these psycho fuckers in five-star hotels for two fuckin years!'

'Jeetudada got drunk when Abdullah was killed,' Salman added. 'It really got to him, you know, that everyone was saying Sapna was dead. He'd been doing the Sapna thing for nearly two years, and it had started to twist his brain. He started to believe his own—or Ghani's—bullshit.'

'Stupid fuckin' name, *yaar*,' Sanjay cut in. 'It's a *girl's* name, Sapna. It's a fuckin' *girl's* name. It's like me calling myself fuckin' Lucy, or some such. What kind of a bad fucker calls himself a girl's name, *yaar*?'

'The kind who kills eleven people,' Salman answered, 'and almost gets away with it. Anyway, he got completely drunk the night Abdullah was killed and everybody was saying that Sapna was dead. And he started shooting his mouth off, telling anyone who would listen that *he* was the real Sapna. They were in a bar in the President Hotel. Then he starts shouting that he was ready to tell it all—who was behind the Sapna killings, you know, and who planned it all and paid for it all.'

'Fuckin' *gandu*,' Sanjay growled, using the slang word for arsehole. 'I never met one of these psycho types who wasn't a fuckin' squealer, *yaar*.'

'Lucky for us, there were mostly foreigners in the place that night, so they didn't know what he was talking about. One of our guys was there, in the bar, and he told Jeetu to shut the fuck up. Jeetudada said he wasn't afraid of Abdel Khader Khan because he had plans for Khader, as well. He said Khader was going to end up in pieces, just like Madjid. Then he starts waving a gun around. Our guy called Khader right away. And the Khan, he went and did that one himself. He went with Nazeer and Khaled, and Farid, and Ahmed Zadeh, and young Andrew Ferreira, and some others.'

'I missed that one, fuck it!' Sanjay cursed. 'I wanted to fix that maakachudh from the first day, and especially after Madjid. But I was on a job, in Goa. Anyway, Khader fixed them up.'

'They found them near the car park of the President Hotel. Jeetudada and his guys put up a fight. There was a big shoot-out. Two of our guys got hit. One of them was Hussein—you know, he runs the numbers in Ballard Pier now. That's how he lost his arm—he took a shotgun blast, both barrels of a crowd-pleaser, a sawn-off, and it tore his arm right off his body. If Ahmed Zadeh hadn't wrapped him up and dragged him out of there, and off to hospital, he would've bled to death, right there in the car park. All four of them who were there—Jeetudada and his three guys —got wasted. Khaderbhai put the last bullets into their heads himself. But one of those Sapna guys wasn't in the car park, and he got away. We never tracked him down. He went back to Delhi, and he disappeared from there. We haven't heard anything since.'

'I liked that Ahmed Zadeh,' Sanjay said quietly, dispensing what was, for him, extravagantly high praise with a little sigh of sorrowing recollection.

'Yeah,' I agreed, remembering the man who'd always looked as though he was searching for a friend in a crowd; the man who'd died with his hand clenched in mine. 'He was a good guy.'

Nazeer spoke again, grunting the words at us in his wrathful style as if they were threats.

'When the Pakistani cops were tipped off about Khaderbhai,' Sanjay translated, 'it was obvious that it had to be Abdul Ghani behind it.'

I nodded my agreement. It *was* obvious. Abdul Ghani was from Pakistan. His connections there went deep, and high. He'd told me about it more than once when I'd worked for him. I wondered why I hadn't seen it at the time, when the cops raided our hotel in Pakistan. My first thought was that I'd simply liked him too much to suspect him, and that was true. More to the point, perhaps, was how flattered I'd been by his attention: Ghani had been my patron on the council, after Khader himself, and he'd invested time, energy, and affection in our friendship. And there was something else that might have distracted me in Karachi: my mind had been filled with shame and revenge—I remembered that much from the visit to the mosque when I'd sat beside Khaderbhai and Khaled to hear the Blind Singers. I remembered reading Didier's letter and deciding, in that shifting, yellow lamplight, that I would kill Madame Zhou. I remembered thinking that and then turning my head to see the love in Khader's golden eyes. Could that love and that anger have smothered something so important, something so obvious, as Ghani's treachery? And if I'd missed that, what else had I missed?

'Khader wasn't supposed to make it out of Pakistan,' Salman added. 'Khaderbhai, Nazeer, Khaled—even you. Abdul Ghani thought it was his chance to take out the whole council in one shot—all the guys on the council who weren't with him. But Khaderbhai had his own friends in Pakistan, and they warned him, and you made it out of the trap. I think Abdul must've known he was finished from that day on. But he held his peace, and he didn't make any moves here. He was hoping, I guess, that Khader, and the whole lot of you, might be killed in the war —'

Nazeer interrupted him, impatient with the English that he despised. I thought I understood what he'd said, and I translated his words, looking to Sanjay for confirmation that my guess was correct.

'Khader told Nazeer to keep the truth about Abdul Ghani a secret. He said that if anything happened to him in the war, Nazeer was to return to Bombay and avenge him. Was that it?'

'Yeah,' Sanjay wagged his head. 'You got it. And after we did that, we had to fix the rest of the guys who were on Ghani's side. There's none of them left now. They're all dead, or they got the fuck out of Bombay.'

'Which brings us to the point,' Salman smiled. It was a rare smile, but a good one: a tired man's smile; an unhappy man's smile; a tough man's smile. His long face was a little lopsided with one eye lower than the other by the thickness of a finger, a break in his nose that had settled crookedly, and a mouth that hitched in one corner where a fist had split the lip and a suture had pulled the skin too tightly. His short hair formed a perfectly round hairline on his brow like a dark halo that pressed down hard on his slightly jugged ears. 'We want you to run the passports for a while. Krishna and Villu are very insistent. They're a little ...'

'They're freaked out of their fuckin' brains,' Sanjay cut in. 'They're scared stupid because guys were getting chopped all over Bombay— starting with Ghani while they were right there in the fuckin' cellar. Now the war's over, and we won, but they're still scared. We can't afford to lose them, Lin. We want you to work with them, and settle them down, like. They're asking about you all the time, and they want you to work with them. They like you, man.'

I looked at each of them in turn, and settled my eyes on Nazeer. If my understanding was correct, it was a tempting offer. The victorious Khader faction had reformed the local mafia council under old Sobhan Mahmoud. Nazeer had become a full member of the council, as had

Mahmoud Melbaaf. The others included Sanjay and Salman, Farid, and three other Bombay-born dons. All of the last six spoke Marathi every bit as well as they spoke Hindi or English. That gave me a unique and very significant point of contact with them because I was the only gora any of them knew who could speak Marathi. I was the only gora any of them knew who'd been leg-ironed at Arthur Road Prison. And I was one of the very few men, brown or white, who'd survived Khader's war. They liked me. They trusted me. They saw me as a valuable asset. The gangster war was over. In the new *Pax Mafia* that ruled their part of the city, fortunes could be made. And I needed the money. I'd been living on my savings, and I was almost broke.

'What exactly did you have in mind?' I asked Nazeer, knowing that Sanjay would reply.

'You run the books, the stamps, all the passport stuff, and the licences, permits, and credit cards,' he answered quickly. 'You get complete control. Just the way it was with Ghani. No fuckin' problem. Whatever you need, you get it. You take a piece of that action—I'm thinkin' about 5 per cent, but we can talk about that if you don't think it's enough, *yaar.*'

'And you can visit the council whenever you want,' Salman added. 'Sort of an observer status, if you get my meaning. What do you say?'

'You'd have to move the operation from Ghani's basement,' I said quietly. 'I'd never feel happy about working there, and I'm not surprised the place has got Villu and Krishna spooked.'

'No problem,' Sanjay laughed, slapping the table. 'We're going to sell the place anyway. You know, Lin-brother, that fat fuck Ghani put the two big houses—his own one and the place next door—in his brother-in-law's name. Nothin' wrong with that—fuck, man, we *all* do that. But they're worth fuckin' *crores,* Lin. They're fuckin' mansions, baba. And then, after we sliced and diced the fat fuck, his brother-in-law decides he doesn't want to sign the places over to us. Then he gets tough, and starts talking lawyers and police. So we had to tie him up over a big dubba of acid, *yaar.* Then he's not tough any more. Then he can't wait to sign the places over to us. We sent Farid to do the job. He took care of it. But he got so fucked up, *yaar,* with the disrespect Ghani's brother-in-law showed us, and he was real angry with the madachudh for making him set up the acid barrel and all. He likes to keep things simple, our brother Farid. The whole hanging-the-cunt-up-over-the-acid-thing, it was all a bit—what did you call it, Salman? What was the word?'

'Tawdry,' Salman suggested.

'Yeah. Taw-fuckin-dry, the whole thing. Farid, he likes to get respect, or cut to the chase and gun the motherfucker down, like. So, angry as he is, he takes the brother-in-law's own house as well—makes him sign over his *own* house, just for being such a big madachudh about Ghani's houses. So now he's got nothing, that guy, and we got *three* houses on the market instead of one.'

'It's a vicious and bloodthirsty racket, that property business,' Salman concluded with a wry smile. 'I'm moving us into it as soon as I can. We're taking over one of the big agencies. I've got Farid working on it. Okay, Lin, if you don't want to work at Ghani's place, where would you like us to set it up for you?'

'I like Tardeo,' I suggested. 'Somewhere near Haji Ali.'

'Why Tardeo?' Sanjay asked.

'I like Tardeo. It's clean … and it's quiet. And it's near Haji Ali. I like Haji Ali. I've got kind of a sentimental connection to the place.'

'*Thik hain*, Lin,' Salman agreed. 'Tardeo it is. We'll tell Farid to start looking right away. Anything else?'

'I'll need a couple of runners—guys I can trust. I'd like to pick my own men.'

'Who've you got in mind?' Sanjay asked.

'You don't know them. They're outside guys. But they're both good men. Johnny Cigar and Kishore. I trust them, and I know I can rely on them.'

Sanjay and Salman exchanged a glance and looked to Nazeer. He nodded.

'No problem,' Salman said. 'Is that it?'

'One more thing,' I added, turning to Nazeer. 'I want Nazeer as my contact on the council. If there's any problem, for any reason, I want to deal with Nazeer first.'

Nazeer nodded again, favouring me with a little smile deep in his eyes.

I shook hands with each man in turn to seal the deal. The exchange was a little more formal and solemn than I'd expected it to be, and I had to clench my jaw to stifle a laugh. And those attitudes, their gravitas and my recusant impulse to laugh, registered the difference between us. For all that I liked Salman, Sanjay, and the others—and the truth was that I loved Nazeer, and owed him my life — the mafia was, for me, a means to an end and not an end in itself. For them, the mafia was a family, an infrangible bond that held them from minute to minute and all the way to the dying breath. Their solemnity expressed that kin-sacred obligation from eye to eye and hand to hand, but I knew they never believed it was like that for me. They took me in and worked with me — the white guy, the wild gora who went to the war with Abdel Khader Khan — but they expected me to leave them, sooner or later, and return to the other world of my memory and my blood.

I didn't think that, and I didn't expect it, because I'd burned all the bridges that might've led me home. And although I had to stop myself from laughing at the earnestness of the little ceremony, the handshake had, in fact, formally inducted me into the ranks of professional criminals. Until that moment, the crimes I'd committed had been in the service of Khader Khan. As difficult as it is for anyone outside that world to understand, there was a sense in which I'd been able to say, with sincerity, that I'd committed them for love of him: for my own safety, certainly; but, beyond every other reason, for the father's love I'd craved from him. With Khader gone, I could've made the break completely. I could've gone ... almost anywhere. I could've done ... something else. But I didn't. I joined my fate to theirs and became a gangster for nothing more than the money, and the power, and the protection that their brotherhood promised.

And it kept me busy, breaking laws for a living: so busy that I managed to hide most of what I felt from the heart that was feeling it. Everything moved quickly after that meeting at the Mocambo. Farid found new premises within a week. The two-story building, only a short walk from the floating mosque, Haji Ali, had been a records office for a branch of the Bombay Municipal Corporation. When the BMC had moved to larger, more modern offices, they'd left most of the old benches, desks, storage cupboards, and shelves behind as stock fittings. They were well suited to our needs, and I spent a week supervising a team of cleaners and labourers, who dusted and polished every surface while moving the furniture around to make way for the machinery and light-tables from Ghani's basement.

Our men loaded that specialist equipment onto a large, covered truck and delivered it to the new premises late at night. The street was unusually quiet as the heavy truck backed up to the double folding doors of our new factory. But alarm bells and the heavier clang of fire-engine bells jangled in the distance. Standing beside our truck, I looked along the deserted street in the direction of the frantic sound.

'It must be a big fire,' I muttered to Sanjay, and he laughed out loud.

'Farid started a fire,' Salman said, answering for his friend. 'We told him we didn't want anyone watching us move this stuff into the new place, so he started the fire as a diversion. That's why the street is so empty. Everybody who is awake has gone to the fire.'

'He burned down a rival company,' Sanjay laughed. 'Now we are officially in the real estate business because our biggest rivals have just closed down, due to fire damage. We start our new real estate office not far from here tomorrow. And tonight, no curious fuckers are here to see us move our stuff into your new workshop. Farid killed two birds with one match, *na*?'

So, while fire and smoke singed the midnight sky, and bells and sirens railed about a kilometre away, we directed our men as they moved the heavy equipment into the new factory. And Krishna and Villu went to work almost at once.

In the months that I'd been away, Ghani had followed my suggestion to push the focus of the operation laterally into the production of permits, certificates, diplomas, licences, letters of credit, security passes, and other documents. It was a booming trade in the booming economy of Bombay, and we often worked through the dawn to satisfy the demand. And the business was generational: as licensing authorities and other bodies modified their documents in response to our forgeries, we dutifully copied and then counterfeited them again, at additional cost.

'It's a kind of Red Queen contest,' I said to Salman Mustaan when the new passport factory had been running for six diligent months.

'*Lal ka Rani*?' he asked. *A Red Queen?*

'Yeah. It's a biology thing. It's about hosts, like human bodies, and parasites, like viruses and such. I studied it when I was running my clinic in the zhopadpatti. The hosts—our bodies—and the viruses—any bug that makes us sick—are locked in a competition with each other. When the parasite attacks, the host develops a defence. Then the virus changes to beat that defence, so the host gets a new defence. And that keeps on going. They call it a Red Queen contest. It's from the story, you know, Alice in Wonderland.'

'I know it,' Salman answered. 'We did it at school. But I never understood it.'

'That's okay—nobody does. Anyway, the little girl, Alice, she meets this Red Queen, who runs incredibly fast but never seems to get anywhere. She tells Alice that, in her country, it takes all the running you can do, to keep in the same place. And that's like us with the passport authorities, and the licensing boards, and the banks all over the world. They keep changing the passports and other documents to make it harder for us. And we keep finding new ways to fake them. And they keep changing the way they make them, and we keep finding new ways to fake them and forge them and adapt them for ourselves. It's a Red Queen contest, and we all have to run real fast just to stand still.'

'I think you're doing better than standing still,' he asserted. His tone was quiet but adamant. 'You've done a damn fine job, Lin. The ID stuff is deadly—it's a real big market. They can't get enough. And it's good work. So far, all our guys who've used your books have gone through without any problems, *yaar*. As a matter of fact, that's why I've called you to have lunch with us today. I've got a surprise for you—kind of a present, like, and I'm sure you're going to like it. It's a way of saying thanks, *yaar*, for the great job you've been doing.'

I didn't look at him. We were walking quickly, side by side, along Mahatma Gandhi Road toward the Regal Circle roundabout on a hot, cloudless afternoon. Where the footpath was clogged with shoppers halting at the tabletop street stalls, we walked on the road with a slow, unceasing stream of traffic behind and beside us. I didn't look at Salman because I'd come to know him well enough during those six months to be sure he was embarrassed by the praise he'd felt moved to lavish on me. Salman was a natural leader but, like many men who have the gift of command and the instinct to rule, he was deeply troubled by every expression of the leadership art. He was, at heart, a humble man, and that humility made him an honourable man.

Lettie had once said that she found it strange and incongruous to hear me describe criminals, killers, and mafiosi as men of honour. The confusion, I think, was hers, not mine. She'd confused honour with virtue. Virtue is concerned with what we do, and honour is concerned with how we do it. You can fight a war in an honourable way—the Geneva Convention exists for that very reason—and you can enforce the peace without any honour at all. In its essence, honour is the art of being humble. And gangsters, just like cops, politicians, soldiers, and holy men, are only ever good at what they do if they stay humble.

'You know,' he remarked, as we moved to the wider footpath opposite the cloisters of the university buildings, 'I'm glad it didn't work out with your friends—the ones you wanted to help you with the passports, right at the start.'

I frowned, and remained silent, keeping pace with his rapid step. Johnny Cigar and Kishore had refused to join me in the passport factory, and it had shocked and disappointed me. I'd assumed that they would jump at the chance to make money—to make more money with me than either of them had ever dreamed of making alone. I'd never anticipated the saddened and offended expressions that closed their smiles when they understood, at last, that I was offering them nothing more than the golden opportunity to commit crimes with me. It had never occurred to me that they wouldn't want to do it. It had never occurred to me that they would refuse to work with criminals, and for criminals.

I remembered turning away from their stony, closed, embarrassed smiles that day. I remembered the question that had knotted into a fist in my mind, right behind the eyes: *Was I so far out of touch with the thoughts and feelings of decent men?* The question still rankled six months later. The answer still stared back at me from the mirrored windows of the shops we passed as we walked.

'If those guys of yours had worked out,' Salman continued, 'I wouldn't have put Farid with you. And I'm damn glad that I *did* put him with you. He's a much happier guy now. He's a much more relaxed kind of guy. He likes you, Lin.'

'I like him, too,' I replied quickly, smiling through my frown. And it was true. I did like Farid, and I was glad that we'd become close friends.

Farid, the shy but capable youngster I'd met on my first visit to Khader's mafia council more than three years before, had toughened up to a hard, fearless, angry man whose sense of loyalty assumed the full measure of his young life. When Johnny Cigar and Kishore rejected my offers of work, Salman had put Farid and the Goan, Andrew Ferreira, to work with me. Andrew had been genial and talkative, but he'd moved only reluctantly from the company of his young gangster friends, and we hadn't become close. Farid, however, had spent most days and many nights with me, and we liked and understood one another.

'He was right on the edge, I think, when Khader died and we had to clean out Ghani's guys' Salman confided. 'It got pretty rough—you remember—we all did some ... *unusual* things. But Farid was wild. He was starting to worry me. You have to get heavy sometimes in our business. That's just how it is. But you got a problem on your hands when you start to *enjoy* it, *na?* I had to talk to him. "Farid", I said to him, "cutting people up should not be the first option. It should be a long way down the list. It shouldn't even be on the same page as the first option." But he went right on doing it. Then I put him with you. And now, after six months, he's a much calmer guy. It worked out well, *yaar*. I think I'll just have to put all the really bad and mad motherfuckers with you, Lin, to straighten them out.'

'He blamed himself for not being there when Khader died,' I said as we rounded the curve of the domed Jehangir Art Gallery. Seeing a small gap in the traffic, we jogged across the roundabout at Regal Circle junction, dodging and weaving between the cars.

'We *all* did,' Salman muttered softly when we took up a position outside the Regal Cinema.

It was a tiny phrase, three small words, and it said nothing new, nothing more than I already knew to be true. Yet that little phrase thundered in my heart, and an avalanche of grieving began to tremble, shift, and slide. For almost a year, and until that very moment, my anger at Khaderbhai had shielded me from the pain of grieving for him. Others had crumbled and withered and raged in their shock and sorrow at his death. I'd been so angry with him that my share of grief was still up there, beneath the smothering snow, in those mountains where he'd died. I'd felt a sense of loss. I'd suffered almost from the start. And I didn't hate the Khan—I'd loved him, always, and still loved him in that instant as we stood outside the cinema, waiting for our friends. But I hadn't really grieved for him—not in the way that I'd grieved for Prabaker or even Abdullah. Somehow, Salman's casual remark that we all blamed ourselves for not being with Khader when he died had shaken my frozen sorrowing free, and the slow, inexorable snowslip of its heartache began, right there and then.

'We must be a bit early,' Salman observed cheerily, and I flinched as I forced myself into the moment with him.

'Yeah.'

'They're coming by car, we're walking, and *still* we beat them here.'

'It's a good walk. At night it's even better. I do that walk a lot: the Causeway to V.T. and back. It's one of my favourite walks in the whole city.'

Salman looked at me, a smile on his lips and a frown exaggerating the slightly crooked tilt of his almond-brown eyes.

'You really love this place, don't you?' he asked.

'Sure I do,' I replied, a little defensively. 'That doesn't mean I *like* everything about it. There's a lot that I *don't* like. But I do love the place. I love Bombay, and I think I always will.'

He grinned and looked away down the street. I struggled to hold the set of my features, to keep my expression calm and even. But it was too late. The heartgrief had already begun.

I know now what was happening to me, what was overwhelming me, what was about to consume and almost destroy me. Didier had even given me a name for it—assassin grief, he'd once called it: the kind of grief that lies in wait and attacks from ambush, with no warning and no mercy. I know now that assassin grief can hide for years and then strike suddenly, on the happiest day, without discernible reason or exegesis. But on that day, six months after my work in the passport factory had begun, and almost a year after Khader's death, I couldn't understand the dark and trembling mood that was moving in me, swelling to the sorrow I'd too long denied. I couldn't understand it, so I tried to fight it as a man fights pain or despair. But you can't bite down on assassin grief, and will it away. The enemy stalks you, step for step, and knows your every move before you make it. The enemy is your own grieving heart and, when it strikes, it can't miss.

Salman turned to me once more, his amber eyes gleaming in the cast of his thoughts.

'That time, when we had the war to get rid of Ghani's guys, Farid was trying to be a new Abdullah. He loved him, you know. He loved him like a brother. And I think he was trying to *be* Abdullah. I think he got the idea that we needed a new Abdullah to win the war for us. But it doesn't work, does it? I tried to tell him that. I tell that to all the young guys— especially the ones who try to be like *me*. You can only ever be yourself. The more you try to be like someone else, the more you find yourself standing in the way. Hey, here's the guys!'

A white Ambassador stopped in front of us. Farid, Sanjay, Andrew Ferreira, and a tough, forty-year-old Bombay Muslim named Amir got out of the car and joined us. We shook hands as the car drove off.

'Let's wait a minute, guys, while Faisal parks the car,' Sanjay suggested.

It was true that Faisal, who ran the protection racket with Amir, was parking the car. It was also true, and more to the point, that Sanjay was enjoying himself, standing in our conspicuous group on a warm afternoon and sparking furtive but fervent looks from most of the girls passing us on the busy street. We were goondas, gangsters, and almost everyone knew it. Our clothes were new and expensive and cut to the edge of fashion. We were all fit. We were all confident. We were all armed and dangerous.

Faisal loped around the corner and wagged his head to signal that the car was safely parked. We joined him, and walked the three blocks to the Taj Mahal Hotel in a single, wide line. The route from Regal Circle to the Taj Hotel crossed spacious, open, crowded squares. We held our line easily as the crowds parted for us. Heads turned as we passed, and whispers whirled in our wake.

We climbed the white marble steps at the Taj, and walked through to the Shamiana Restaurant on the ground floor. Two waiters settled our group at a long, reserved table near a tall window with a courtyard view. I sat at one end of the table, nearest to the exit. The strange and overpoweringly dark mood that had stirred in me with Salman's little phrase grew stronger by the minute. I wanted to be free to leave at any moment, without upsetting the balance of the group. The waiters greeted me with broad smiles, calling me *gao-alay*, or countryman, the Indian equivalent of the Italian *paisano*. They knew me well—the gora who spoke Marathi— and we chatted for a while in the village dialect I'd learned in Sunder more than four years before.

Food arrived, and the men ate with good appetite. I, too, was hungry, but I couldn't eat, and I just pushed at the food to make a polite show. I drank two cups of black coffee and tried to bring my troubled, storming mind into the run of conversations. Amir was describing the movie he'd seen the night before—a Hindi gangster picture, in which the gangsters were vicious thugs and the hero conquered them all, unarmed and alone. He described every fight sequence in detail, and the men hooted with laughter. Amir was a scarred, blunt-headed man with thick, tangled eye-brows and a moustache that rode the cresting wave of his full upper lip like the wide prow of a Kashmiri houseboat. He loved to laugh and tell stories, and his self-assured, sonorous voice compelled attention.

Amir's constant companion, Faisal, had been a champion boxer in the youth league. On his nineteenth birthday, after a year of tough profes-sional bouts, he'd discovered that his manager had embezzled and squan-dered all the money he'd been entrusted to save from his boxers' fights. Faisal had tracked the manager down. When he'd found him, he hit him and then kept on hitting him until the man was dead. He'd served eight years in prison for the crime, and was banned from boxing for life. In prison, the naïve, hot-tempered teenager had become a calculating, cold-tempered young man. One of Khaderbhai's talent scouts had recruited him in the prison, and he'd served his apprenticeship to the mafia through the last three years of his sentence. During the four years since his release, Faisal had worked as Amir's principal strong-arm man in the burgeoning protection racket. He was quick, ruthless, and driven to suc-ceed at whatever task was set for him. His flattened, broken nose, and a neat scar that dissected his left eyebrow gave him a fearsome appearance, and toughened what might otherwise have been a too-regular and too-handsome face.

They were the new blood, the new mafia dons, the new lords of the city: Sanjay, the efficient killer with the movie-star looks; Andrew, the genial Goan who dreamed of taking his seat on the mafia council; Amir, the grizzled veteran with the story-teller's gift; Faisal, the cold-hearted enforcer who only asked one question—*Finger, arm, leg, or neck?*—when he was given an assignment; Farid, known as the Fixer, who solved prob-lems with fire and fear, and who'd raised six much younger brothers and sisters, alone, when his parents died in a cholera-infested slum; and Salman, the quiet one, the humble one, the natural leader, who con-trolled the lives of hundreds in the little empire that he'd inherited and held by force.

And they were my friends. More than friends, they were my brothers in their brotherhood of crime. We were bonded to one another in blood —not all of it other people's—and boundless obligation. If I needed them, no matter what I'd done, no matter what I wanted them to do, they would come. If they needed me, I was there, without cavil or regret.

They knew they could count on me. They knew that when Khader had asked me to join him in his war I'd gone with him, and I'd put my life on the line. I knew I could count on them. When I'd needed him, Abdullah had been there to help me deal with Maurizio's body. It's a significant test, asking someone to help you dispose of a murdered man's body. Not many pass it. Every man at the table had passed that test; some of them more than once. They were a solid crew, to use the Australian prison slang. They were the perfect crew for me, an outlaw with a price on my head. I'd never felt so safe—not even with Khaderbhai's protection—and I never should've felt alone.

But I *was* alone, and for two reasons. The mafia was theirs, not mine. For them, the organisation always came first. But I was loyal to the men, not the mafia; to the brothers, not the brotherhood. I worked for the mafia, but I didn't join it. I'm not a joiner. I never found a club or clan or idea that was more important to me than the men and women who believed in it.

And there was another difference between the men in that group and me—a difference so profound that friendship, on its own, couldn't surmount it. I was the only man at that table who hadn't killed a human being, in hot blood or cold. Even Andrew, amiable and garrulous young Andrew, had fired his Beretta at a cornered enemy—one of the Sapna killers—and emptied all seven rounds of the magazine into the man's chest until he was, as Sanjay would've said, two or three times dead.

Just at that moment the differences suddenly seemed immense and unconquerable to me—far greater and more significant than the hundred talents, desires, and tendencies that we had in common. I was slipping away from them, right there and then, at the long table in the Taj. While Amir told his stories and I tried to nod and smile and laugh with the others, grief came to claim me. The day that had started well, and should've been like any other, had spun askew with Salman's little words. The room was warm, but I was cold. My belly hungered, but I couldn't eat. I was surrounded by friends, in a vast, crowded restaurant, but I was lonelier than a mujaheddin sentry on the night before battle.

And then I looked up to see Lisa Carter walk into the restaurant. Her long, blonde hair had been cut. The new short style suited her open, honest, pretty face. She was dressed in pale blue—her favourite colour—a loose shirt and pants, with matching blue sunglasses propped in her thick hair. She looked like a creature of light, a creature made out of sky and clean, white light.

Without considering what I was doing, I stood and excused myself, and left my friends. She saw me as I approached her. A smile as big as a gambler's promise unveiled her face as she opened her arms to hug me. And then she knew. One hand reached up to touch my face, her fingertips reading the braille of scars, while the other hand took my arm to lead me out of the restaurant and into the foyer.

'I haven't seen you for weeks,' she said as we sat together in a quiet corner. 'What's wrong?'

'Nothing,' I lied. 'Were you going in to have some lunch?'

'No. Just coffee. I've got a room here, in the old part, looking out over the Gateway. It's a million-dollar view, and a great room. I've got it for three days while Lettie sews up a deal with a big producer. This is one of the fringe benefits she managed to squeeze out of him. The movie business—what can I say?'

'How's it going?'

'Great,' she smiled. 'Lettie loves every minute of it. She deals with all the studios and the booking agents now. She's better at it than me. She drives a better deal for us every time. And I do the tourists. I like that part better. I like meeting them and working with them.'

'And you like it that sooner or later, no matter how nice they are, they always go away?'

'Yeah. That, too.'

'How's Vikram? I haven't seen him since—since the last time I saw you and Lettie.'

'He's cool. You know Vikram. He's got a lot more time on his hands now. He misses the stunt thing. He was really big on that, and he was great at it. But it drove Lettie crazy. He was always jumping off moving trucks and crashing through windows and stuff. And she worried a lot. So she made him give it up.'

'What's he doing now?'

'He's kind of the boss, you know? Like the executive vice-president of the company—the one Lettie started, with Kavita and Karla and Jeet. And me.' She paused, on the verge of saying something, and then plunged on. 'She was asking after you.'

I stared back at her, saying nothing.

'Karla,' she explained. 'She wants to see you, I think.'

I held the silence. I was enjoying it, a little, that so many emotions were chasing one another across the soft, unblemished landscape of her face.

'Have you seen any of his stunts?' she asked.

'Vikram's?'

'Yeah. He did a whole lot before Lettie made him stop.'

'I've been busy. But I really want to catch up with Vikram.'

'Why don't you?'

'I will. I heard he's hanging out at the Colaba Market every day, and I've been wanting to see him. I'm working a lot of nights, so I haven't been to Leopold's lately. It's just ... I've been ... busy.'

'I know,' she said softly. 'Maybe *too* busy, Lin. You don't look too good.'

'Gimme a break,' I sighed, trying to laugh. 'I work out every day. I do boxing or karate every other day. I can't get any fitter than this.'

'You know what I mean,' she insisted.

'Yeah, I know what you mean. Listen, I should let you go ...'

'No. You shouldn't.'

'I shouldn't?' I asked, faking a smile.

'No. You should come with me, now, to my room. We can have coffee sent up. Come on. Let's go.'

And she was right: it was a spectacular view. Tourist ferries bound for the caves on Elephanta Island, or returning to shore, rose up the wavelets and rolled over them in proud, practised glissades. Hundreds of smaller craft dipped and nodded like preening birds in the shallow water while huge cargo vessels, anchored to the horizon, lay motionless on that cusp of calm where the ocean became the bay. On the street below us, parading tourists wove coloured garlands with their movements through and around the tall, stony gallery of the Gateway Monument.

She kicked off her shoes and sat cross-legged on the bed. I sat near her on the edge of the bed. I stared at the floor near the door. We were quiet for a while, listening to the noises that pushed their way into the room with a breeze that caused the curtains to riffle, swell, and fall.

'I think,' she began, taking a deep breath, 'you should come and live with me.'

'Well, that's —'

'Hear me out,' she cut in, raising both palms to silence me. 'Please.'

'I just don't think —'

'Please.'

'Okay,' I smiled, sitting further along the bed to rest my back against the bed-head.

'I found a new place. It's in Tardeo. I know you like Tardeo. So do I. And I *know* you'll like the apartment, because it's exactly the kind of place we both like. And I think that's what I'm trying to get at, or trying to say — we like the same things, Lin. And we got a lot in common. We both beat the dope. That's a fuckin' hard thing to do, and you know it. And not many people do it. But we did — we both did — and I think that's because we're alike, you and me. We'd be good, Lin. We'd be ... we'd be real good.'

'I can't say ... for sure ... that I beat the dope, Lisa.'

'You did, Lin.'

'No. I can't say I won't ever touch it again, so I can't say I beat it.'

'But that's even more reason to get together, don't you see?' she insisted, her eyes pleading and close to tears. 'I'll keep you straight. I *can* say I won't ever touch it again, because I *hate* the stuff. If we're together, we can work the movie business, and have fun, and watch out for each other.'

'There's too much ...'

'Listen, if you're worried about Australia, and jail, we could go somewhere else — somewhere they'll never find us.'

'Who told you about that?' I asked, keeping my face straight.

'Karla did,' she answered evenly. 'It was in the same little conversation we had once, where she told me to look after you.'

'Karla said that?'

'Yeah.'

'When?'

'A long time ago. I asked her about you — about what her feelings were, and what she wanted to do.'

'Why?'

'Whaddaya mean, *why*?'

'I mean,' I replied slowly, reaching out to cover her hand with mine, 'why did you ask Karla about her feelings?'

'Because I had a crush on you, stupid!' she explained, holding my eye for a second and then looking away again. 'That's why I went with

Abdullah—to make you jealous, or interested, and just to be close to you, through him, because he was your friend.'

'Jesus,' I sighed. 'I'm sorry.'

'Is it still Karla?' she asked, her eyes following the rise and breathless fall of the curtains at the window. 'Are you still in love with her?'

'No.'

'But you still *love* her.'

'Yes.'

'And ... how about me?' she asked.

I didn't answer because I didn't want her to know the truth. I didn't want to know the truth myself. And the silence thickened and swelled until I could feel the tingling pressure of it on my skin.

'I've got this friend,' she said at last. 'He's an artist. A sculptor. His name's Jason. Have you ever met him?'

'No, I don't think so.'

'He's an English guy, and he's got a real English way of looking at things. It's different than our way, our American way, I mean. He's got a big studio out near Juhu Beach. I go there sometimes.'

She was silent again. We sat there, feeling the breeze alternately warm and cool as the air from the street and the bay swirled into the room. I could feel her eyes on me like a blush of shame. I stared at our two hands joined and resting on the bed.

'The last time I went there, he was working on this new idea. He was filling empty packaging with plaster, using the bubble packs that used to have toys in them, you know, and the foam boxes you get packed around a new T.V. set. He calls them negative spaces. He uses them like a mould, and he makes a sculpture out of them. He had a hundred things there— shapes made out of egg cartons, and the blister-pack that a new tooth-brush came in, and the empty package that had a set of headphones in it.'

I turned to look at her. The sky in her eyes held tiny storms. Her lips, embossed with secret thoughts, were swollen to the truth she was trying to tell me.

'I walked around there, in his studio, you know, looking at all these white sculptures, and I thought, that's what *I* am. That's what I've always been. All my life. Negative space. Always waiting for someone, or some-thing, or some kind of real feeling to fill me up and give me a reason ...'

When I kissed her, the storm from her blue eyes came into our mouths, and the tears that slid across her lemon-scented skin were sweeter than honey from the sacred bees in Mombadevi's Jasmine Temple garden. I let her cry for us. I let her live and die for us in the long, slow stories our bodies told. Then, when the tears stopped, she surrounded us with poised and fluent beauty—a beauty that was hers alone: born in her brave heart, and substantialised in the truth of her love and her flesh. And it almost worked.

We kissed again as I prepared to leave her room—good friends, lovers, gathered into one another then and forever by the clash and caress of our bodies, but not quite healed by it, not quite cured by it. Not yet.

'She's still there, isn't she?' Lisa said, wrapping a towel around her body to stand in the breeze at the window.

'I've got the blues today, Lisa. I don't know why. It's been a long day. But that's nothing to do with us. You and me ... that was good—for me, anyway.'

'For me, too. But I think she's still there, Lin.'

'No, I wasn't lying before. I'm not in love with her any more. Something happened, when I came back from Afghanistan. Or maybe it happened *in* Afghanistan. It just ... stopped.'

'I'm going to tell you something,' she murmured and then turned to face me, speaking in a stronger, clearer voice. 'It's about her. I believe you, what you said, but I think you have to know this before you can really say it's over with her.'

'I don't need —'

'Please, Lin! It's a girl thing. I *have* to tell you because you can't really say it's over with her unless you know the truth about her—unless you know what makes her tick. If I tell you, and it doesn't change anything or make you feel different than how you feel now, then I'll know you're free.'

'And if it *does* make a difference?'

'Well, maybe she deserves a second chance. I don't know. I can only tell you I never understood Karla at all until she told me. She made sense, after that. So ... I guess you have to know. Anyway, if there's anything gonna happen for us, I want it to be clear—the past, I mean.'

'Okay,' I relented, sitting in a chair near the door. 'Go ahead.'

She sat on the bed once more, drawing her knees up under her chin in the tight wrap of the towel. There were changes in her, and I couldn't help noticing them—a kind of honesty, maybe, in the way her body moved, and a new, almost languorous release that softened her eyes. They were love-changes, and beautiful for that, and I wondered if she saw any of them in me, sitting still and quiet near the door.

'Did Karla tell you why she left the States?' she asked, knowing the answer.

'No,' I replied, choosing not to repeat the little that Khaled had told me on the night that he walked into the snow.

'I didn't think so. She told me she wasn't going to tell you about it. I said she was crazy. I said she had to level with you. But she wouldn't. It's funny how it goes, isn't it? I wanted her to tell you, then, because I thought it might put you off her. Now, *I'm* telling you, so that you can give her one more chance—if you want to. Anyway, here it is. Karla left the States because she had to. She was running away ... because she killed a guy.'

I laughed. It was a small chuckle, at first, but it rolled and rumbled helplessly into a belly laugh. I doubled over, leaning on my thighs for support.

'It's really not that funny, Lin.' Lisa frowned.

'No,' I laughed, struggling to regain control. 'It's not ... that. It's just ... *Shit*! If you knew how many times I worried about bringing *my* crazy, fucked up life to *her*! I kept telling myself I had no right to love her because *I* was on the run. You gotta admit, it's pretty funny.'

She stared at me, rocking slightly as she hugged her knees. She wasn't laughing.

'Okay,' I exhaled, pulling myself together. 'Okay. Go on.'

'There was this guy,' she continued, in a tone that made it clear how serious she considered the subject. 'He was the father of one of the kids she used to baby-sit for, when she was a kid herself.'

'She told me about it.'

'She did? Okay, then you know. And nobody did anything about it. And it messed her up pretty bad. And then, one day, she got herself a gun, and she went to his house when he was alone, and she shot him. Six times. Two in the chest, she said, and four in the crotch.'

'Did they know it was her?'

'She's not sure. She knows she didn't leave any prints there, at the house. And nobody saw her leave. She got rid of the gun. And she scrammed out of there, right out of the country, real fast. She's never been back, so she doesn't know if there's a sheet on her or not.'

I sat back in the chair and let out a long, slow breath. Lisa watched me closely, her blue eyes narrowing slightly and reminding me of the way she'd looked at me on that night, years before, in Karla's apartment.

'Is there any more?'

'No,' she answered, shaking her head slowly, but holding my eyes in the stare. 'That's it.'

'Okay,' I sighed, running a hand over my face, and standing to leave. I went to her, and knelt on the bed beside her, with my face close to hers. 'I'm glad you told me, Lisa. It makes a lot of things ... clearer ... I guess. But it doesn't change anything in how I feel. I'd like to help her, if I could, but I can't forget ... what happened ... and I can't forgive it, either. I wish I could. It'd make things a lot easier. It's bad, loving someone you can't forgive.'

'It's not as bad as loving someone you can't have,' she countered, and I kissed her.

I rode the elevator down to the foyer alone with the crowd of my mirror selves: beside and behind me, still and silent, not one of them was able to meet my eye. Once through the glass doors, I walked down the marble steps and across the wide forecourt of the Gateway Monument to the sea. Beneath the arched shadow I leaned on the sea wall and looked out at the boats carrying tourists back to the marina. *How many of those lives*, I wondered, watching the travellers pose for one another's cameras, *are happy and carefree and ... simply free? How many of them are sorrowing? How many are ...*

And then the full darkness of that long-resisted grieving closed around me. I realised that for some time I'd been gritting my teeth and that my jaw was cramped and stiff, but I couldn't unlock the muscles. I turned my head to see one of the street boys, someone I knew well, doing business with a young tourist. The boy, Mukul, sent his eyes left and right, lizard quick, and passed a small, white packet to the tourist. The man was about twenty years old: tall and fit and handsome. I guessed him to be a German student, and I had a good eye. He hadn't been in the city long. I knew the signs. He was new blood, with money to burn and the whole world of experience open to him. And there was a spring in his step as he walked away to join his friends. But there was poison in the packet in his hand. If it didn't kill him outright, in a hotel room somewhere, it would deepen in his life, maybe, as it did once in mine, until it poisoned every breathing second.

I didn't care — not about him or me or anyone. I wanted it. I wanted the drug, just then, more than anything in the world. My skin remembered the satin-flush of ecstasy and the lichen-stippled creep of fever and fear. The smell-taste was so strong that I felt myself retching it. The hunger for oblivion, painless, guiltless, and unsorrowing, swirled in me, shivering from my spine to the thick, healthy veins in my arms. And I wanted it: the golden minute in heroin's long leaden night.

Mukul caught my eye and smiled from habit, but the smile twitched and crumbled into uncertainty. And then he knew. He had a good eye, too. He lived on the street, and he knew the look. So the smile returned, but it was different. There was seduction in it — *It's right here ... I've got it right here ... It's good stuff ... Come and get it* — and the dealer's tiny, vicious, little sneer of triumph. *You're no better than me ... You're not much at all ... And sooner or later, you'll beg me for it ...*

The day was dying. Each jewelled shimmer, dazzling from the waves in the bay, turned from glittering white to pink, and weak, blood red. Sweat ran into my eyes as I stared back at Mukul. My jaws ached, and my lips quivered with the strain of it: the strain of not responding, not speaking, not nodding my head. I heard a voice or remembered it: *All you have to do is nod your head, that's all you have to do, and it'll all be over ...* And grieving tears boiled up in me, relentless as the gathering tide that slapped against the sea wall. But I couldn't cry them, those tears, and I felt that I was drowning in a sorrow that was bigger than the heart that tried to hold it. I pressed my hands down on the little mountain range of the faceted bluestones on the top of the sea wall, as if I could drive my fingers into the city and save myself by clinging to her.

But Mukul ... Mukul smiled, promising peace. And I knew there were so many ways to find that peace — I could smoke it in a cigarette, or chase it on a piece of foil, or snort it, or puff it in a chillum, or spike it into my vein, or just eat it, just swallow it and wait for the creeping numbness to smother every pain on the planet. And Mukul, reading the sweating agony like a dirty page in a dirty book, inched his way closer to me, sliding along the wet stone wall. And he knew it. He knew everything.

A hand touched my shoulder. Mukul flinched as if he'd been kicked, and backed away from me, his dead eyes dwindling to nothing in the burning splendour of the setting sun. And I turned my head to stare into the face of a ghost. It was Abdullah, my Abdullah, my dead friend, killed in a police ambush too many suffering months before. His long hair was cut short and thick like a movie star's. His black clothes were gone. He wore a white shirt and grey trousers with a fashionable cut. And they seemed strange, those different clothes—almost as strange as seeing him standing there. But it was Abdullah Taheri, his ghost, as handsome as Omar Sharif on his thirtieth birthday, as lethal as a big cat prowling, a black panther, and with those eyes the colour of sand in the palm of your hand a half-hour before sunset. Abdullah.

'It is so good to see you, Lin brother. Shall we go inside and drink some chai?'

That was it. Just that.

'Well, I ... I can't do that.'

'Why not?' the ghost asked, frowning.

'Well, for starters,' I mumbled, shielding my eyes from the late-afternoon sun with my hand as I stared up at him, 'because you're dead.'

'I am not dead, Lin brother.'

'Yes ...'

'No. Did you speak to Salman?'

'Salman?'

'Yes. He arranged it, for me to meet with you, in the restaurant. It was a surprise.'

'Salman ... told me ... there was a surprise.'

'And *I* am the surprise, Lin brother,' the ghost smiled. 'You were coming to meet *me*. He was supposed to be making it a surprise for you. But you left the restaurant. And the others, they have been waiting for you. But you didn't come back, so I went to find you. Now the surprise is really a shocks.'

'Don't say that!' I snapped, remembering something Prabaker had once said to me, and still reeling, still confused.

'Why not?'

'It doesn't matter! Fuck, Abdullah ... this is ... this is a fuckin' weird dream, man.'

'I am back,' he said calmly, a little frown of worry creasing his brow. 'I am here, again. I was shot. The police. You know about it.'

The tone of the conversation was matter-of-fact. The fading sky behind his head, and the passers-by on the street, were unremarkable. Nothing matched the blur and streak of a dream. Yet it had to be a dream. Then the ghost lifted his white shirt to reveal his many wounds, healed and healing into dark-skinned rings, whirls, and thumb-thick gashes.

'Look, Lin brother,' the dead man said. 'I was shot, yes, many times, but I did live. They took my body from the Crawford Market police station. They took me to Thana for the first two months. Then they took me to Delhi. I was in hospital for one year. It was a private hospital, not far from Delhi. It was a year of many operations. Not a good year, Lin brother. Then it was almost another year to become well, *Nushkur'allah*.'

'Abdullah,' I said, reaching out to hug him. The body was strong. Warm. Alive. I held him tightly, clamping my hand to my wrist behind his back. I felt the press of his ear against my face, and smelt the soap on his skin. I heard his voice passing from his chest to mine like ocean sonancies, sounding and resounding, wave on wave through shores of tight-wet sand at night. Eyes closed, and clinging to him, I floated on the dark water of the sorrowing I'd done for him, for both of us. Heart-crippled with fear that I was mad, that it really was a dream, a nightmare, I held him until I felt the strong hands push me gently to the length of his extended arms.

'It is okay, Lin,' he smiled. The smile was complex, shifting from affection to solace, and a little shocked, perhaps, at the emotion in my eyes. 'It is okay.'

'It's *not* okay!' I growled, breaking away from him. 'What the fuck happened? Where the fuck have you been? And why the fuck didn't you *tell* me?'

'No. I could not tell you.'

'Bullshit! Of course you could! Don't be so stupid!'

'No,' he insisted, running a hand through his hair and squinting his eyes to fix me with a determined stare. 'Do you remember, one time, we were riding the motorcycles, and we saw some men? They were from Iran. I told you to wait at the motorcycles, but you did not. You followed me, and we fought those men together. Do you remember?'

'Yes.'

'They were enemies of mine. And they were Khader Khan's enemies, also. They had a connect to the Iran secret police, the new Savak.'

'Can we—wait a minute,' I interrupted, reaching backwards to support myself against the sea wall. 'I need a cigarette.'

I flipped open the box to offer him one.

'Did you forget?' he asked, grinning happily. 'I do not smoke the cigarettes. And you should not also, Lin brother. I only smoke the hashish. I have some, if you would like?'

'Fuck that,' I laughed, lighting up. 'I'm not getting stoned with a ghost.'

'Those men—the men we fought—they did some business here. Mostly drugs business, but sometimes guns business and sometimes passports. And they were spies against us, reporting about any of us from Iran who ran away from the Iraq war. I was one man who ran away from the Iraq war. Many thousands ran away to here, India, and many thousands who hate Ayatollah Khomeini. The spies from Iran, they made reports about us to the new Savak in Iran. And they hate Khader because he want to help the mujaheddin in Afghanistan and because he did help so many of us from Iran. You understand this business, Lin brother?'

I understood it. The Iranian expatriate community in Bombay was huge, and I had many friends who'd lost their homeland and their families, and were struggling to survive. Some of them worked in existing mafia gangs like Khader's council. Others had formed their own gangs, hiring themselves out to do the wet work, in a business that got a little bloodier every working day. I knew that the Iranian secret police had spies circulating among the exiles, reporting on them and sometimes getting their own hands a little damp.

'Go on,' I said, taking a gulp of smoky air from my cigarette.

'When those men, those spies, made their reports, our families in Iran had very bad suffering. Some mothers, brothers, fathers, they put them into the secret police prison. They torture people in that place. Some of the people, they died. My own sister—they torture and rape her because of the reports about me. My own uncle, he is killed when my family cannot pay to the secret police quick enough. When I find out about that, I told to Abdel Khader Khan that I want to leave him, so I can fight them, those men who are spies from Iran. He told me not to leave. He said to me that we will fight them together. He told me that we will find them, one by one, and he promise me that he will help me to kill them all.'

'Khaderbhai ...' I said, breathing smoke.

'And we found them, some of them, Farid and me, with Khader's help. There was nine men, at the start. We found six men. Those men, we finished. The other three of them did live. Three men. And they knew something about us—they knew that there is a spy in the council, very close to Khader Khan.'

'Abdul Ghani.'

'Yes,' he said, turning his head to spit at the mention of the traitor's name. 'Ghani, he came from Pakistan. He had many friends in the Pakistan secret police. The ISI. They work in secret with the Iran secret police, the new Savak, and with CIA, and with Mossad.'

I nodded, listening to him, and thinking about something Abdul Ghani had said to me once: *All the secret police of the world work together, Lin, and that is their biggest secret.*

'So, the Pakistan ISI told the Iranian secret police about their contact on the Khader council.'

'Abdul Ghani. Yes,' he replied. 'In Iran they were very worried. Six good traitors gone. Nobody ever can find the bodies of those traitors. Only three were left. The three men from Iran, so then they work with Abdul Ghani. He told them how to make a trap for me. At that time, do you remember, we did not know it, that Sapna, he was working for Ghani and planning to move against us. Khader did not know. I did not know. If I knew that, I would put the pieces of those Sapna men into Hassaan Obikwa's hole in the ground myself. But I did not know. When I came into the trap, near to Crawford Market, the men from Iran fire the first time from a place near me. The police, they think that I am firing my gun. They fire at me. I am dying, I know, so I take my guns and I shoot at the police. The rest, you know.'

'Not all of it,' I grunted. 'Not enough. I was there that night, the night you got shot. I was in the crowd at Crawford Market police station. It was wild. Everyone said you were shot so many times that your face was unrecognisable.'

'There was so much blood. But Khader's men, they *did* know me. They make a riot and then they fight step and step into the police station, and they take my body out of there and away to the hospital. Khader had a truck near there, and he had a doctor—you know him, Doctor Hamid, do you remember him?—and they saved me.'

'Khaled was there that night. Was he the one who rescued you?'

'No. Khaled was one of the men who make the riot. It was Farid who took my body.'

'Farid the Fixer got you out of there?' I gasped, stunned that he'd said nothing about it in all the close months we'd worked together. 'And he's known about it all this time?'

'Yes. If you have a secret, Lin, put it in the heart of Farid. He is the best of them, my brother, now that Abdel Khader is gone. After Nazeer, Farid is the best of them. Never forget that.'

'What about the three guys? The three Iranian guys? What happened to them after you got shot? Did Khader get them?'

'No. When Abdel Khader killed Sapna and his men, they ran away to Delhi.'

'One of the Sapna guys got away. You know that?'

'Yes, he went to Delhi also. When I was strong again—not completely fix up yet, but strong enough to fight—just two months ago, I went to look for the four men and their friends. I found one of them. One from Iran. I finish him. Now there are only three left from that time—two spies from Iran, and one Sapna killer from Ghani.'

'Do you know where they are?'

'Here. In the city.'

'You're sure?'

'I am sure. That is why I have come back to Bombay. But now, Lin brother, we must return to the hotel. Salman and the others, they are waiting for us, upstairs. They want to make a party. They will be happy I can find you—they did see you leaving, hours before, with a beautiful girl, and they told me I will not find you.'

'It was Lisa,' I said, glancing unconsciously over my shoulder at the bedroom window on the first floor of the Taj. 'Do you ... want to see her?'

'No,' he smiled. 'I did meet someone—Farid's cousin, Ameena. She has been looking after me for more than a year. She is a good girl. We want to be married.'

'Get the fuck outta here!' I spluttered, more shocked by his intention to marry than I was by his survival of the killing fusillade.

'Yes,' he grinned, reaching out to give me an impulsive hug. 'But come on, the others are waiting. *Challo*.'

'You go ahead,' I answered him, smiling to match his happy grin. 'I'll be with you soon.'

'No, come, Lin,' he urged. 'Come now.'

'I need a minute,' I insisted. 'I'll be there ... in a minute.'

He hesitated a moment more but then smiled, nodded his head, and walked back through the domed arch toward the Taj Hotel.

Evening dimmed the afternoon's bright halo. A haze of dusty smoke and vapour misted the horizon, sizzling soundlessly, as if the sky at the distant wall of the world was dissolving into the waters of the bay. Most of the boats and ferries were safely tied to their mooring posts at the dock beneath me. Others rose and fell and rose again, swaying on the secure tethers of their sea anchors. High tide pushed the swollen waves against the long stone wall where I stood. Here and there along the boulevard, frothy plumes, like gasps of effort, slapped up, over, and onto the white footpaths. Strollers walked around the intermittent fountains, or ran laughing through the sudden boom and spray. In the little seas of my eyes, those tiny blue-grey oceans, waves of tears pushed hard against the wall of my will.

Did you send him? I whispered to the dead Khan, my father. Assassin grief had pushed me to that wall where the street boys sold heroin. And then, when it was almost too late, Abdullah had appeared. *Did you send him to save me?*

The setting sun, that funeral fire in the sky, seared my eyes, and I looked away to follow the last flares of cerise and magenta streaming out and fading in the ocean-mirrored sapphire of the evening. And staring out across the rile and ruffle of the bay, I tried to fit my feelings within a frame of thought and fact. Strangely, weirdly, I'd re-found Abdullah and re-lost Khaderbhai on the same day, in the same hour. And the experience of it, the fact of it, the inescapably fated imperative of it, helped me to understand. The sorrowing I'd shunned had taken so long to find me because I couldn't let him go. In my heart, I still held him as tightly as I'd hugged Abdullah only minutes before. In my heart, I was still there on the mountain, kneeling in the snow and cradling the handsome head in my arms.

As the stars slowly reappeared in the silent endlessness of sky, I cut the last mooring rope of grief, and surrendered to the all-sustaining tide of destiny. I let him go. I said the words, the sacred words: *I forgive you ...*

And it was good. And it was right. I let the tears fall. I let my heart break on my father's love, like the tall waves beside me that hurled their chests against the wall, and bled onto the wide, white path.

CHAPTER FORTY

THE WORD MAFIA comes from the Sicilian word for bragging. And if you ask any serious man who commits serious crimes for a living, he'll tell you it's just that—the boasting, the pride—that gets most of us in the end. But we never learn. Maybe it's not possible to break laws without boasting about it to someone. Maybe it's not possible to be an outlaw without being proud in some way. Certainly, in those last months of the old mafia, the brotherhood that Khaderbhai had designed, steered, and ruled, there was plenty of boasting and no less pride. But it was the last time that any of us in that corner of Bombay's underworlds of crime could've said, with complete honesty, that we were proud to be gangsters.

Khader Khan had been dead for almost two years, but his precepts and principles still dominated the day-to-day operations of the mafia council he'd founded. Khader had hated heroin, and he'd refused to deal in the drug or permit anyone else but desperately addicted street junkies to trade in it within the areas he'd controlled. Prostitution had also appalled him. He'd seen it as a business that injured women, degraded men, and blighted the community where it occurred. The hemisphere of his influence had extended to all the streets, parks, and buildings across several square kilometres. Within that little kingdom, any man or woman who hadn't kept their involvement with prostitution and pornography to very low, very discreet, levels of activity had risked his condign punishment. And that situation prevailed under the new council headed by Salman Mustaan.

Old Sobhan Mahmoud, still the nominal head of the council, was gravely ill. In the years since Khader died, he'd suffered two strokes that had left his speech and much of his movement severely impaired. The council moved him into Khader's beach house in Versova—the same house where I'd gone through cold turkey with Nazeer. They ensured that the aged don had access to the best medical treatments, and arranged for his family and his servants to attend him.

Nazeer slowly groomed Khader's nephew, young Tariq, for what most on the council assumed would be a leading role. Despite the boy's pedigree, his maturity, and his unusually solemn demeanour—there was no-one, man or boy, whose dour, fervent intensity reminded me so much of Khaled—Tariq was deemed to be too young to claim a council position or even to attend the council meetings. Instead, Nazeer gave him duties and responsibilities that more gradually acquainted him with the world he might one day command. In all practical senses, Salman Mustaan was the don, the new Khan, the leader of the council and the ruler of Khaderbhai's mafia. And Salman, as everyone who knew him testified, was Khaderbhai's man, body and soul. He governed the actions of the clan as if the grey-haired lord was still there, still alive, advising and cautioning him in private sessions every night.

Most of the men supported Salman unquestioningly. They understood the principles involved, and agreed that they were worth upholding. In our area of the city, the words goonda and gangster weren't an insult. Local people knew that our branch of the mafia did a better job than the police at keeping heroin and salacious crimes from their streets. The police, after all, were susceptible to bribes. Indeed, Salman's mafia clan found itself in the unique position of bribing the police—the same cops who'd just been paid off by pimps and pushers—to look away whenever they had to run a recalcitrant heroin dealer into a brick wall, or take a mash hammer to a pornographer's hands.

Old men in the district nodded to one another, and compared the relative calm on their streets with the chaos that tumbled and trawled through the streets of other districts. Children looked up to the young gangsters, sometimes adopting one as a local hero. Restaurants, bars, and other businesses welcomed Salman's men as preservers of peace and comparatively high moral standards. And the informing rate in the areas of his control, the amount of unsolicited information supplied to the police—a sure indicator of public popularity or displeasure—was lower than in any other area across the whole seething sprawl of Bombay. We had pride, and we had principle, and we were almost the men of honour that we believed ourselves to be.

Still, there *were* a few grumbles of complaint within the clan, and some council meetings hosted fierce, unresolved arguments about the future of the group. The heroin trade was making other mafia councils rich. New smack millionaires flaunted their imported cars, designer clothes, and state-of-the-art electronic gadgets at the most exclusive and expensive venues in the city. More significantly, they used their inexhaustible, opiate-based income streams to hire new men: mercenaries who were paid well to fight dirty and to fight hard. Little by little, those gangs expanded their territories in turf wars that left a few of the toughest men dead, many more wounded, and cops all over the city lighting incense sticks to give thanks for their luck.

With similarly high profits derived from the new and insatiable market for imported, hard-core pornographic videos, some of the rival councils had accumulated enough money to acquire that ultimate status symbol for any criminal gang: a hoard of guns. Envious of the wealth amassed by such gangs, infuriated by their territorial gains, and wary of their growing power, some of Salman Mustaan's men urged him to change his policy. First among those critical voices was that of Sanjay, Salman's oldest and closest friend.

'You should meet with Chuha,' Sanjay said earnestly as he, Farid, Salman, and I drank chai at a little shop on Maulana Azad Road near the brilliant, green mirages of the Mahalaxmi Racecourse. He was talking about Ashok Chandrashekar, an influential strong-arm man in the Walidlalla gang. He'd used Ashok's nickname, *Chuha*, meaning *the Rat*.

'I've met with the fucker, *yaar*,' Salman sighed. 'I meet him all the time. Every time one of his guys tries to squeeze out a corner of our territory, I meet with Chuha to set it straight. Every time our guys get in a fight with his guys, and give them a solid pasting, I meet with Chuha. Every time he makes an offer to join our council to his, I meet with him. I know the fucker *too* well. That's the problem.'

The Walidlalla council held a contiguous border with our own. Relations between the gangs were generally respectful but not cordial. Walid, the leader of the rival council, had been a close friend of Khaderbhai and, with him, was one of the original founders of the council system. Although Walid had led his council into the heroin and pornography trade that he, like Khaderbhai, had once despised, he'd also insisted that no conflict with Salman's council should occur. Chuha, his second in command, had ambitions that strained at the leash of Walid's control. Those ambitions led to disputes and even battles between the gangs, and all too often forced Salman to meet with the Rat at stiffly formal dinners held on neutral ground in a suite at a five-star hotel.

'No, but you haven't really *talked* to him, one on one like, about the *money* we can make. If you did, Salman brother, I know you'd find out he talks a lot of sense. He's making crores out of the fuckin' garad, man. The junkies can't get enough of the shit. He has to bring it in by fuckin' *train*. And the blue movies thing, man—it's going crazy. I swear! It's a fuckin' deadly business, *yaar*. He's making five hundred copies of every movie, and selling them for five hundred each. That's two-and-a-half lakhs, Salman, for every fuckin' blue movie! If you could make money like that by killing people, India's population problem would be solved in a month! You should just talk to him, Salman brother.'

'I don't like him,' Salman declared. 'And I don't trust him, either. One of these days, I think I'll have to finish the madachudh once and for all. That's not a very promising way to start up a business, *na*?'

'If it comes to that, I'll kill the gandu for you, brother, and it will be my pleasure. But up to then, like, before we actually have to *kill* him, we can still make a lot of money with him.'

'I don't think so.'

Sanjay looked around the table for support, and finally appealed to me.

'Come on, Lin. What do you think?'

'It's council business, Sanju,' I replied, smiling at his earnestness. 'It's got nothing to do with me.'

'But that's why I'm asking you, Linbaba. You can give us an independent point of view, like. You know Chuha. And you know how much money there is in the heroin. He's got some good money ideas, don't you think so?'

'*Arrey*, don't ask him!' Farid cut in. 'Not unless you want the truth.'

'No, go on,' Sanjay persisted, the gleam in his eyes brightening. He liked me, and he knew that I liked him. 'Tell me the truth. What do you think of him?'

I glanced around at Salman and he nodded, just as Khader might've done.

'I think Chuha's the kind of guy who gives violent crime a bad name,' I said.

Salman and Farid spluttered their tea, laughing, and then mopped at themselves with their handkerchiefs.

'Okay,' Sanjay frowned, his eyes still gleaming. 'So, what … *exactly* … don't you like about him?'

I glanced again at Salman. He grinned back at me, raising his eyebrows and the palms of his hands in a *Don't look at me* gesture.

'Chuha's a stand-over man,' I replied. 'And I don't like stand-over men.'

'He's a what?'

'A stand-over man, Sanjay. He beats up on men he knows can't fight back, and takes whatever he wants from them. In my country, we call those guys stand-over men because they really do stand *over* little guys and steal from them.'

Sanjay looked at Farid and Salman with a blank expression of confused innocence.

'I don't see the problem,' he said.

'No, I know *you* don't have a problem with it. And that's okay. I don't expect everyone to think like me. Fact is, most people don't. And I understand that. I get it. I know that's how a lot of guys make their way. But just because I understand it, that doesn't mean I like it. I met some of them in jail. A couple of them tried to stand over me. I stabbed them. None of the others ever tried it again. The word got around. Try to stand over this guy, and he'll put a hole in you. So they left me alone. And that's just the thing. I would've had more respect for them if they'd kept on trying to stand over me. I wouldn't have stopped fighting them—I still would've cut them up, you know, but I would've respected them more while I did it. Ask the waiter here, Santosh, what he thinks of Chuha. They came in here last week, Chuha and his guys, and slapped him around for fifty bucks.'

The word bucks was Bombay slang for rupees. Fifty rupees was the same amount, I knew, that Sanjay customarily tipped waiters and better-than-average cab drivers.

'The guy's a fuckin' millionaire, if you believe his bullshit,' I said, 'and he stands over a decent working guy like Santosh for fifty bucks. I don't respect that. And in your heart of hearts, Sanjay, I don't think you do, either. I'm not going to do anything about it. That's not my job. Chuha makes his graft by slapping people. I understand that. But if he ever tries to stand over *me*, I'll cut him. And I tell you, man, I'll enjoy doing it.'

There was a little silence while Sanjay pursed his lips, twirled his hand palm upward, and looked from Salman to Farid. Then all three of them burst out laughing.

'You asked him!' Farid giggled.

'Okay, okay,' Sanjay conceded. 'I asked the wrong guy. Lin is a wild guy, *yaar*. He gets wild notions. He went to Afghanistan with Khader, man! Why did I ask a guy who's crazy enough to do that? You ran that clinic in the zhopadpatti, and you never made a fuckin' paise out of it. Remind me of that, Lin brother, if I ever ask you for your business opinion again, *na*?'

'And another thing,' I added, keeping a straight face.

'Eh, *Baghwan*!' Sanjay cried. 'He's got another thing, yet!'

'If you think about the slogans, you'll understand where I'm coming from on this.'

'The *slogans*?' Sanjay protested, provoking his friends to bigger laughter. 'What fuckin' slogans, *yaar*?'

'You know what I mean. The slogan, or the motto, of the Walidlalla gang is *Pahiley Shahad, Tab Julm*. I think I'm right in translating it as *First Honey, Then Outrage*, or even *Atrocity*. Isn't that right? And isn't that what they say to each other as their slogan?'

'Yeah, yeah, that's their thing, man.'

'And what's our slogan? Khader's slogan?'

They looked at one another, and smiled.

'*Saatch aur Himmat*.' I spoke it aloud for them. '*Truth and Courage*. I know a lot of guys who'd like Chuha's slogan. They'd think it was clever and funny. And it sounds ruthless, so they'd think it was tough. But I don't like it. I like Khader's.'

At the sound of an Enfield engine, I looked up to see Abdullah park his bike outside the chai shop and wave to me. It was time for me to go.

I'd spoken the truth, as I saw it, and I meant every word, but in my *own* heart of hearts I knew that Sanjay's argument, although not better, would turn out to be stronger than mine. The Walidlalla gang under Chuha was the future of all the mafia councils, in a sense, and we all knew it. Walid was still the head of the council that bore his name, but he was old and he was ill. He'd ceded so much power to Chuha that it was the younger don who ruled. Chuha was aggressive and successful, and he gained new ground by conquest or coercion every few months. Sooner or later, if Salman didn't agree to merge with Chuha, that expansion would come to open conflict, and there would be a war.

I hoped, of course, that Khader's council, under Salman, would win. But I knew that, if we did win, it would be impossible to claim Chuha's territory without also absorbing his trade in heroin, women, and porn. It was the future, and it was inevitable. There was simply too much money in it. And money, if the pile gets high enough, is something like a big political party: it does as much harm as it does good, it puts too much power in too few hands, and the closer you come to it the dirtier you get. In the long run, Salman could walk away from the fight with Chuha, or he could defeat him and become him. *Fate always gives you two choices,* Scorpio George once said: *the one you should take, and the one you do.*

'But hey,' I said, standing to leave, 'it's got nothing to do with me. And frankly, I don't really give a damn one way or the other. My ride is here. I'll see you guys later.'

I walked out, with Sanjay's protests and his friends' laughter rattling above the clatter of cups and glasses.

'*Bahinchudh! Gandu!*' Sanjay shouted. 'You can't fuck up my rave like that and then walk out, *yaar!* Come back here!'

As I approached him, Abdullah kick-started the bike and straightened it from the side stand, ready to ride.

'You're in a hurry for your workout,' I said, settling myself onto the saddle of the bike behind him. 'Relax. No matter how fast we get there, I'm still going to beat you, brother.'

For nine months, we'd trained together at a small, dark, sweaty, and very serious gym near the Elephant Gate section of Ballard Pier. It was a goonda's gym set up by Hussein, the one-armed survivor of Khader's battle with the Sapna assassins. There were weights and benches, a judo mat, and a boxing ring. The smell of man-sweat, both fresh and fouled into the stitching of leather gloves and belts and turnbuckles, was so eye-wateringly rancid that the gym was the only building in the city block that rats and cockroaches spurned. There were bloodstains on the walls and the wooden floor, and the young gangsters who trained there accumulated more wounds and injuries in a workout week than the emergency ward of a city hospital on a hot Saturday night.

'Not today,' Abdullah laughed over his shoulder, pulling the bike into a faster lane of traffic. 'No fighting today, Lin. I am taking you for a surprise. A good surprise!'

'Now I'm worried,' I called back. 'What kind of surprise?'

'You remember when I took you to see Doctor Hamid? You remember that surprise?'

'Yeah, I remember.'

'Well, it is better than that. Much better.'

'U-huh. Well, I'm still not very relaxed about it. Gimme another hint.'

'You remember when I sent you the bear, for hugging?'

'Kano, sure, I remember.'

'Well, it is *much* better than that!'

'A doctor and a bear,' I called out above the growl of the engine. 'There's a lot of space between them, brother. One more hint.'

'Ha!' he laughed, coming to a stop at a set of traffic lights. 'I will say to you this—the surprise is so good that you will forgive me for all that you suffered when you thought I was dead.'

'I do forgive you, Abdullah.'

'No, Lin brother. I know you do not forgive me. I have too many bruises, and I am too much sore from our boxing and karate.'

It wasn't true: I never hit him as hard as he hit me. Although he was healing well, and he was very fit, he'd never fully recovered the uncanny strength and charismatic vitality he'd known before the police shooting. And when he removed his shirt to box with me, the sight of his scarred body—it was as if he'd been savaged by the claws of wild animals and burned with hot iron brands—always made me pull my punches. Still, I never admitted that to *him*.

'Okay,' I laughed. 'If that's the way you're gonna play it, I don't forgive you!'

'But when you see this surprise,' he called out, laughing with me, 'you will forgive me completely, with a full heart. Now, come on! Stop asking me about it, and tell me, what did Salman say to Sanjay about that pig— that Chuha?'

'How did you know that's what we were talking about?'

'I can see the look in Salman's face,' he shouted back. 'And Sanjay, he told me, this morning, that he wants to ask Salman—again—to make business with Chuha. So, what did Salman say?'

'You know the answer to that one,' I replied a little more quietly as we stopped in traffic.

'Good! *Nushkur'Allah.*' *Thanks be to God.*

'You really hate Chuha, don't you?'

'I don't hate him,' he clarified, moving off with the flow of cars. 'I just want to kill him.'

We were silent for a while, breathing the warm wind and watching the black business unfold on the streets we'd both roamed so often. There were a hundred large and small scams and deals going down around us every minute, and we knew them all.

When we found ourselves twisted into a knot of traffic behind a stalled bus, I looked along the footpath and noticed Taj Raj, a pickpocket who usually worked the Gateway area near the Taj Mahal Hotel. He'd survived a machete attack years before that had all but severed his neck. The wound caused him to speak in a rattling whisper, and his head was set at such an ill-balanced angle that when he wagged it to agree with someone he almost fell over. He was working the stumble-fall-pilfer game with his friend Indra serving as the stumbler. Indra, known as the Poet, spoke almost all of his sentences in rhyming couplets. They were deeply moving in their beauty, for the first few stanzas, but always found their way into sexual descriptions and allusions so perverse and abhorrent that strong, wicked men winced to hear them. Legend had it that Indra had once recited his poetry through a microphone during a street festival, and had cleared the entire Colaba Market of shoppers and traders alike. Even the police, it was said, had shrunk back in horror until exhaustion overcame the Poet, and then they'd rushed him as he paused for breath. I knew both men, and liked them, though I never let them get closer than an arm's stretch from my pockets. And sure enough, as the bus finally grumbled to life and the traffic began to ease forward, I watched Indra pretending to be blind—not his best performance, but good enough—and stumbling into a foreigner. And Taj Raj, the helpful passer-by, assisted both of them to their feet, and relieved the foreigner of his burdensome wallet.

'Why?' I asked, when we were moving through free space again.

'Why what?'

'Why do you want to kill Chuha?'

'I know he had a meeting ... with the men from Iran,' Abdullah shouted over his shoulder. 'People say it was just business—Sanjay, he says it was just business. But I think more than business. I think he work with them, against Khader Khan. Against us. For that reason, Lin.'

'Okay,' I called back, pleased to have my own instincts about Chuha confirmed, but worried for my wild, Iranian friend. 'But don't do anything without me, okay?'

He laughed, and turned his head to show me the white teeth of his smile.

'I'm serious, Abdullah. Promise me!'

'*Thik hain*, Lin brother!' he shouted in reply. 'I will call you, when the time is right!'

He coasted the bike to a stop and parked it outside the Strand Coffee House, one of my favourite breakfast dives, near the Colaba Market.

'What the hell's going on?' I demanded as we walked toward the market. 'Some surprise—I come here nearly every day.'

'I know,' he answered, grinning enigmatically. 'And I am not the only one who knows it.'

'What's *that* supposed to mean?'

'You will find out, Lin brother. Here are your friends.'

We came upon Vikram Patel and the Zodiac Georges, Scorpio and Gemini, sitting comfortably on bulging sacks of lentils beside a pulses stall, and drinking chai from glasses.

'Hey, man!' Vikram greeted me. 'Pull up a sack and make yourself at home.'

Abdullah and I shook hands all round and, as we sat down on the row of sacks, Scorpio George signalled a chai-runner to bring two more glasses. The passport work was often keeping me busy at night because Krishna and Villu—both of them with young children in their growing families—had taken to staggering their shifts, giving themselves valuable hours at home during the day. That work with the books, and other commitments to the Salman council, prevented me from going to Leopold's as often as I once had. Whenever I could, I'd met with Vikram and the Georges near Vikram's apartment on the edge of the Colaba Market. Vikram was there most days, after his lunch with Lettie. He kept me up to date with the news from Leopold's—Didier had fallen in love, again, and Ranjit, Karla's new boyfriend, was becoming popular—and the Georges filled me in on what was going down on the streets.

'We thought you weren't coming today, man,' Vikram said as the chai arrived.

'Abdullah gave me a lift,' I replied, frowning at my friend's mysterious smile, 'and we got stuck in traffic. It was worth it, though. I had a front row seat for Taj Raj and Indra doing their stumble routine on MG Road. It was quite a show.'

'He's not what he used to be, our Taj Raj,' Gemini commented, hurling South London at us in the vowels of the last two words. 'Not as nimble, like. Since the accident, y'know, his timing's a bit off. I mean, it's only reasonable, innit? His whole bleedin' head was damn near off, an' all, so it's no wonder his timing's got a kink in it.'

'At this point,' Scorpio George interrupted, lowering his head and assuming the solemn piety we all knew well and dreaded more, 'I think we should all bow our heads in prayer.'

We glanced at one another, our eyes widening with alarm. There was no escape. We were too comfortable to move, and Scorpio knew it. We were trapped.

'Oh, Lord,' Scorpio began.

'Oh, Gawd,' Gemini grumbled.

'And Lady,' Scorpio continued, 'infinite yin-yang spirit in the sky, we humbly ask you to hear the prayers, today, of five souls that you put into the world, and left in the temporary care of Scorpio, Gemini, Abdullah, Vikram, and Lin.'

'What does he mean, *temporary*?' Vikram whispered to me, and I shrugged in reply.

'Please help us, Lord,' Scorpio intoned, his eyes shut and his face raised to heaven, which seemed, roughly, to be in the middle of the balcony on the third floor of the Veejay Premnaath Academy of Hair Colouring and Ear Boring. 'Please guide us to know what's right, and to do the right thing. And you can start, God, if you're of a mind, by helping out with the little business deal we're doing with the Belgian couple tonight. I don't have to tell you, Lord and Lady, how tricky it is to supply customers with good-quality cocaine in Bombay. But, thanks to your providence, we managed to find ten grams of A-grade snow—and, given the real bad drought on the streets, that was a mighty slick piece of work on your part, God, if you'll accept my professional admiration. Anyway, Gemini and me, we sure could use the commission on that deal, and it would be kinda nice not to get ripped off, or beaten up, or maimed, or killed— unless, of course, that's in your plan. So, please light the way, and fill our hearts with love. Signing off now, but keeping the line open, as always, I'll say Amen.'

'Amen!' Gemini responded, clearly relieved that the prayer was far shorter than Scorpio's more usual efforts.

'Amen,' Vikram sobbed, nudging a tear from his eye with the knuckles of a balled fist.

'*Astagfirullah*,' Abdullah muttered. *Forgive me, Allah.*

'So how about a bite to eat then?' Gemini suggested cheerily. 'There's nothing like a bit of religion to put you in the frame of mind to make a pig of yourself, is there?'

At that moment Abdullah leaned forward to whisper into my left ear.

'Look slowly—no, slowly! Look over there, behind the peanuts shop, near the corner. Do you see him? Your surprise, brother Lin. Do you see him?'

And then, still smiling, my eyes were drawn to a stooped figure watching us from the shadows beneath an awning.

'He is here every day,' Abdullah whispered. 'And not only here—in some other places that you go, also. He watches you. He waits, and he watches you.'

'Vikram!' I mumbled, wanting some other testament to what I was seeing. 'Look! There, on the corner!'

'Look at *what*, man?'

With my attention upon him, the figure drew back into the shadows and then turned and loped away, limping, as if the whole left side of his body was damaged.

'Didn't you see him?'

'No, man. See who?' Vikram complained, standing with me to squint in the direction of my frantic stare.

'It's Modena!' I shouted, running after the limping Spaniard. I didn't look back at Vikram, Abdullah, and the Zodiacs. I didn't answer Vikram's call. I didn't think about what I was doing or why I was pursuing him. My mind was only one thought, one image, and one word. *Modena* ...

He was fast, and he knew the streets well. It occurred to me, as he ducked into hidden doorways and all but invisible gaps between buildings, that I was probably the only foreigner in the city who knew those streets as well as he did. For that matter, there were few Indians—only touts and thieves and junkies—who could've kept up with him. He scrambled into a hole that someone had knocked through a high stone wall to create an access hatch from one street to another. He stepped around a partition that seemed as solid as brick, but was made from stretched and painted canvas. He took short cuts through improvised shops in sheltering archways, and weaved his way along the labyrinth lines of washed, brightly coloured saris hung out to dry.

And then he made a mistake. He ran into a narrow lane that had been commandeered by homeless pavement dwellers and extended families that were crowded out of local apartments. I knew it well. About a hundred men, women, and children were living in the converted lane. They slept in shifts, in a loft space they'd built above the cobbled lane and between the walls of adjacent buildings. They did everything else in the long, dark, narrow room that the lane had become. Modena dodged between the seated and standing groups; between cooking stoves and bathing stalls and a blanket of card players. Then, at the end of the lane-room, he turned left instead of right. It was a cul-de-sac surrounded by high sheer walls. It was completely dark, and it ended in a little dogleg where the space curved around the blind corner of another building. We'd used it, sometimes, to make buys with drug dealers we didn't completely trust, because there was only one way in or out. I rounded the corner, only a few steps behind him, and stood there, panting and straining my eyes to pierce the darkness. I couldn't see him, but I knew he had to be in there.

'Modena,' I said softly into the black echoes. 'It's Lin. I just want to talk to you. I'm not trying to … I know you're in here. I'll just put my bag down, and light us up a beedie, okay? One for you. One for me.'

I put the bag down slowly, expecting him to make a rush past me. I took a bundle of beedies from my shirt pocket, and extracted two from the pack. Holding them between my third and fourth fingers, thick ends inwards, as every poor man in the city did, I worked open a box of matches and struck one. With the flame playing over the ends of the cigarettes, I allowed myself a glimpse upward and I saw him, cringing away from the little arc of light thrown by the match. Just as the match died, I extended my arm to offer him one of the glowing beedie cigarettes. In the new dark, after the match failed, I waited for a second, two seconds, three seconds, and then I felt his fingers, softer and more delicate in their grasp than I would've believed, close around my own and accept the cigarette.

When he puffed at the beedie I saw his face clearly for the first time. It was grotesque. Maurizio had sliced and slashed so much suffering into the soft skin that it was almost frightening simply to look at it. In the faint orange light, I saw the sneering smile that gleamed in Modena's eyes as he recognised the horror in my own. How many times, I wondered, had he seen that horror in the eyes of others—that wide, white dread as they imagined his scars on their own faces and his torment in their souls? How many times had he seen others flinch, as I'd flinched, and shrink away from his wounds as if from the open sores of a disease? How many times had he seen men ask themselves: *What did he do? What did he do to deserve this?*

Maurizio's knife had opened both cheeks beneath the dark brown eyes. The cuts had healed into long Y-shaped scars that dragged down the lower lids of his eyes and ran like the trails of hideous, mocking tears. The lower lids, permanently red and raw, gaped open in little trenches of agony that revealed the whole globe of each eye. The wings and septum of his nose had been cut through to the bone. The skin, when it closed together, had fused in jagged whorls at the sides but not at all in the centre, where the laceration was too deep. The wide hole where his nostrils had been resembled the snout of a pig, and flared with every inward breath. There were many more cuts beside the eyes, around the jaw, and along the full width of his brow below the hairline.

It looked as though Maurizio had tried to peel off the whole layer of Modena's face, and the hundred scars that encircled his features were puckered, here and there, into little mounds of flesh that might've matched the outstretched fingers of a man's hands. I knew that there had to be other scars and injuries beneath his clothes: the movements of his arm and leg on the left side of his body were awkward, as if the hinges at elbow, shoulder, and knee had stiffened around wounds that had never really healed.

It was a monstrous mutilation; a disfigurement so calculated in its cruelty that I felt numbed by it and unable to respond. I noticed that there were no marks on or near his mouth. I wondered at the fortune that had left his sensuous and finely sculpted lips so perfect, so flawlessly unscarred. Then I remembered that Maurizio had gagged him when he'd tied him to the bed, only lifting the twisted cloth from time to time as he'd commanded him to speak. And it seemed to me, as I watched Modena puff at the cigarette, that his smooth, unblemished mouth was the worst and most terrible wound of them all.

We smoked the beedies down to stubs in silence, and my eyes adjusted to the darkness. I became aware, gradually, of how small he was; how much smaller he'd become with the shrivelling effect of the wounds on his left side. I felt that I was towering over him. I stepped back a pace into the light, picked up my bag, and wagged my head encouragingly.

'*Garam chai pio?*' I asked. *Shall we drink hot tea?*

'*Thik hain,*' he replied. *Okay.*

I led the way back through the converted lane and into a chai shop where workers from a local flourmill and bakery were resting between shifts. The men, several of them, shuffled along the wooden bench to make room for us. They were powdered with white flour in their hair and over the whole of their bodies. They looked like phantoms or so many stone statues come to life. Their eyes, no doubt irritated by the dusty flour, were as red as coals from the fiery pit beneath their ovens. Their wet lips, where they sipped the tea, were black leeches against the ghostly white of their skin. They stared at us with the usual frank, Indian curiosity, but looked away quickly when Modena raised his gaping eyes to them.

'I'm sorry for running away,' he said quietly, his eyes fixed on his hands as they fidgeted in his lap.

I waited for him to say something more, but he locked his mouth in a tight little grimace and breathed loudly, evenly, through his wide, flaring nose.

'Are you … are you okay?' I asked, when the tea arrived.

'*Jarur,*' he answered, with a little smile. *Certainly.* 'Are *you* okay?'

I thought he was being facetious, and I didn't hide the irritation in my frown.

'I do not mean to offend you,' he said, smiling again. It was a strange smile, so perfect in the curve of the mouth, and so deformed in the stiffened cheeks that dragged the lower lids of his eyes down into little wells of misery. 'I am only offering my help, if you need it. I have money. I always carry ten thousand rupees with me.'

'What?'

'I always carry —'

'Yes, yes, I heard you.' He was speaking softly, but still I glanced up at the bakery men to see if they'd heard him as well. 'Why were you watching me today in the market?'

'I watch you very often. Almost every day. I watch you and Karla and Lisa and Vikram.'

'Why?'

'I *must* watch you. It is one of the ways I will know how to find her.'

'To find who?'

'Ulla. When she returns. She won't know where I am. I don't go … I don't go to Leopold's any more or any of the other places we used to be together. When she looks for me, she will come to you or to one of the others. And I will see her. And we will be together.'

He made the little speech so calmly, and then sipped at his tea with such contented abstraction, that it exaggerated the weirdness of his delusion. How could he think that Ulla, who'd left him on the bloody bed to die, would return from Germany to be with him? And even if she *were* to return, how could she react to his face, deformed into that mourner's mask, with anything but horror?

'Ulla … went to Germany, Modena.'

'I know,' he smiled. 'I am glad for her.'

'She won't be coming back.'

'Oh, yes,' he said flatly. 'She'll come back. She loves me. She'll come back for me.'

'Why —' I began, and then abandoned the thought. 'How do you live?'

'I have a job. A good job. It pays good money. I work with a friend, Ramesh. I met him when … after I was hurt. He looked after me. At the houses of the rich, when a son is born, we go there, and I put on my special clothes. I put on my costume.'

The dire emphasis he'd put on the last word, and the fractured little smile that accompanied it, sent a creeping unease along the skin of my arms. Some of that disquiet croaked into my voice as I repeated the word.

'Costume?'

'Yes. It has a long tail and sharp ears, and a chain of little skulls around the neck. I make it that I am a demon, an evil spirit. And Ramesh, he makes that he is a holy sadhu, looking like a holy man, and he beats me away from the house. And I come back, and I make it that I am trying to steal the baby. And the women scream when I come near the baby. And Ramesh, he beats me away again. Again I come back, and again he beats me until, at the very last, he beats me so badly that I make like I am dying, and I run away. The people pay us good money for the show.'

'I never heard of it before.'

'No. It is our own idea, Ramesh and me. But after the first rich family paid us, all the others wanted to be sure to beat the evil spirit away from their new baby son. And they pay us good money, all of them. I have an apartment. I don't own it, of course, but I have paid more than a year of rent in advance already. It is small, but it is comfortable. It will be a good place for Ulla and me to live together. You can see the waves of the sea from the main window. My Ulla, she loves the sea. She always wanted a house near to the sea ...'

I stared at him, fascinated no less by the fact of his speech than its meaning. Modena had been one of the most taciturn men I'd ever known. When we'd both been regulars at Leopold's he'd gone for weeks at a time, and sometimes as long as a month, without uttering a word in my presence. But the new Modena, the scarred survivor, was a talker. I'd been forced to run him down in a blind alley to get him to talk at all, it was true; but once he started, he became disconcertingly chatty. As I listened to him, as I reoriented myself to the disfigured, voluble version of the man, I became aware of the melodies that his Spanish accent made as it moved fluently between Hindi and English, mixing the two seamlessly, and incorporating words from each into a hybrid language that was his own. Adrift on the softness in his voice, I asked myself if that was the key to the mysterious bond that had existed between them, Ulla and Modena: if they'd talked to one another, for hours, when they were alone, and if that tender euphony, that voice music, had held them together.

And then, with a suddenness that caught me off-guard, the meeting with Modena was over. He stood to pay the bill and walked out into the lane, waiting for me just beyond the doorway.

'I must go,' he said, looking nervously to his left and right before raising his wounded eyes to mine. 'Ramesh is there by now, outside the President Hotel. When she comes back, Ulla will be there, she will stay there. She loves that hotel. It is her favourite. She loves the Back Bay area. And there was a plane this morning from Germany. A Lufthansa plane. She might be there.'

'You check ... after every flight?'

'Yes. I do not go in,' he murmured, lifting his hand as if to touch his face, but running it through his short, greying hair instead. 'Ramesh goes in the hotel for me. He checks her name—Ulla Volkenberg—to see if she is there. One day she will be there. She will be there.'

He began to walk away from me, but I stopped him with a hand on his shoulder.

'Listen, Modena, don't run away from me next time, okay? If you need anything, if there's anything I can do, just ask me. Is it a deal?'

'I will not run away again,' he said solemnly. 'It is just my habit to run. And it was just my habit that was running away from you. It was not me running, just my habit. I am not afraid of you. You are my friend.'

He turned to leave, but I stopped him again, drawing him closer to me so that I could whisper into his ear.

'Modena, don't tell anyone else that you keep so much money on you. Promise me.'

'Nobody else knows that, Lin,' he assured me, smiling that deep-eyed grimace at me. 'Only you. I would not say that to anyone. Not even Ramesh knows that I have money with me. He does not know that I save my money. He does not even know about my apartment. He thinks that I spend my share of the money that we earn together on drugs. And I do not take any drugs, Lin. You know that. I never did any drugs. I just let him think that I do. But you are different, Lin. You are my friend. I can tell you the truth. I can trust you. Why should I not trust the man who killed the devil himself?'

'What do you mean?'

'I'm talking about Maurizio, the enemy of my blood.'

'I didn't kill Maurizio,' I said, frowning down into the red-walled caves of his eyes.

His perfect mouth widened into an accomplice's leer. The expression dragged harder on the Y-shaped scars that once were the lower lids of his eyes. The gape of those eyes was so unnerving in the flame-lit lane that I had to steel myself not to flinch or draw back when he reached out to put his palm on my chest.

'Do not worry, Lin. The secret is safe with me. I am *glad* that you killed him. Not just for me. I knew him. I was his best friend—his *only* friend. If he lived, after he did this to me, there was no limit to his evil. That is how a man destroys his own soul—he loses the last limit to his evil. And I watched him, when he cut me with his knife, and when he walked away the last time, and I knew that he lost his soul. It cost him his soul, what he did … the things he did to me.'

'You don't have to talk about it.'

'No, it is okay, now, to talk about him. Maurizio was afraid. He was always afraid. He lived all his life in fear of … everything. And he was cruel. That is what gave him his power. I have known a lot of powerful men in my life, and this much I know—all the powerful men I knew were afraid, and cruel. That is the … *mix* … that gave them power over other men. I was not afraid. I was not cruel. I had no power. I was … you know, it was like the feeling for my Ulla—I was *in love* with Maurizio's power. And then, after he left me there, on the bed, and Ulla came into the room, I saw the fear in her eyes. He put his fear into her. He made her so afraid, when she saw what he did to me, that she ran away and left me there. And when I watched her leave, and shut the door …'

He hesitated, swallowing hard, the full, unmarked lips trembling on the words. I wanted to stop him, to spare him the memory of it and maybe save myself from it as well. But as I began to speak he put a little more pressure in the palm that he held against my chest, silencing me, and looking up into my eyes once more.

'I hated Maurizio for the first time, then. My people, the people of my blood, we do not want to hate, because when we do hate, it is with the whole of the soul, and it can never forgive the hated one. But I hated Maurizio, and I wished him dead, and I cursed him with that wish. Not for what he did to *me*, but for what he did to my Ulla, and for what he would do in the future as a man without a soul. So, do not worry, Lin. I do not speak of it to anyone, what you did. And I am glad, I am truly grateful that you killed him.'

A clear voice within me said that I should tell him what had really happened. He had a right to know the truth. And I *wanted* to tell him. An emotion that I couldn't fully understand—the last vestige of anger at Ulla, perhaps, or a jealous contempt for his faith in her—made me want to shake him, and shout the truth at him, and hurt him with it. But I couldn't speak. I couldn't move. And as his eyes reddened and simmered into tears that ran, exactly, in the channelling scars that pierced his cheeks I held the stare, and nodded my head, and said nothing at all. He nodded his head, slowly, in reply. He misread me, I think, or I misread him. I'll never know.

Silences can wound as surely as the twisting lash, the poet Sadiq Khan once wrote. But sometimes, being silent is the only way to tell the truth. I watched Modena turn and limp away, and I knew that the wordless minute we'd shared, with his hand on my chest and his breached and weeping eyes close to mine, would always be more precious and even more honest for both of us, no matter how errable or misunderstood, than the cold, unloving truth of his world alone, or of mine.

And maybe he's right, I thought. Maybe his way of remembering Maurizio and Ulla was right. Certainly, he'd dealt with the pain they'd caused him a lot better than I'd dealt with that kind of pain when it had happened to me. When my marriage fell apart in betrayal and bitterness, I became a junkie. I couldn't bear it that love was broken, and that happiness had cindered so suddenly into sorrow. So I ruined my life, and hurt a lot of people on the long way down. Modena, instead, had worked and saved and waited for love to return. And thinking about that—how he'd lived with what had been done to him—and wondering at it on the long walk back to Abdullah and the others, I discovered something that I should've known, as Modena did, right from the start. It was something simple: so simple that it took a pain as great as Modena's to shake me into seeing it. He'd been able to deal with that pain because he'd accepted his own part in causing it. I'd never accepted my share of responsibility— right up to that moment—for the way my marriage had failed or for the heartache that had followed it. That was why I'd never dealt with it.

And then, as I entered the bright, bartering bustle of the market, I did: I did accept that blame, and I felt my heart expand and unfold as it released its burdens of fear, resentment, and self-doubt. I walked back between the busy stalls and, by the time I joined Abdullah, Vikram, and the Georges, I was smiling. I answered their questions about Modena, and I thanked Abdullah for his surprise. He was right—I did forgive him everything, after that. And although I couldn't find the words to tell him of the change that had happened to me, he sensed, I think, that the difference in the smile I shared with him came from a new peace that was born in me that day, and slowly began to grow.

The cloak of the past is cut from patches of feeling, and sewn with rebus threads. Most of the time, the best we can do is wrap it around ourselves for comfort or drag it behind us as we struggle to go on. But everything has its cause and its meaning. Every life, every love, every action and feeling and thought has its reason and significance: its beginning, and the part it plays in the end. Sometimes, we do see.

Sometimes, we see the past so clearly, and read the legend of its parts with such acuity, that every stitch of time reveals its purpose, and a kind of message is enfolded in it. Nothing in any life, no matter how well or poorly lived, is wiser than failure or clearer than sorrow. And in the tiny, precious wisdom that they give to us, even those dread and hated enemies, suffering and failure, have their reason and their right to be.

CHAPTER FORTY-ONE

MONEY STINKS. A stack of new money smells of ink and acid and bleach like the fingerprinting room in a city police station. Old money, vexed with hope and coveting, smells stale like dead flowers kept too long between the pages of a cheap novel. When you put a lot of money, new and old, into one room—millions of rupees counted twice and snapped into bundles with rubber bands—it stinks. *I love money,* Didier once said to me, *but I hate the smell of it. The more happiness I get from it, the more thoroughly I have to wash my hands afterwards.* I knew exactly what he meant. In the counting-room for the mafia money-change racket, an airless cavern in the Fort area where the hot lights were bright enough to search through the best counterfeit, and the overhead fans never turned fast enough to lift a stray note from the counting tables, the smell of money was like the sweat and the dirt on a gravedigger's boots.

Some weeks after the meeting with Modena, I pushed my way out through the door of Rajubhai's counting room, shoving the goondas aside with the kind of childish rough play we all enjoyed, and gasped at the fresher air in the stairway. A voice called my name, and I stopped on the third step, my hand on the wooden rail. I looked up to see Rajubhai leaning out of the doorway. The short, fat, bald currency-controller for Khader's—no, *Salman's*—mafia council was dressed, as always, in a dhoti and a white singlet. He leaned out of the doorway, I knew, because he never actually left the room until he sealed it, at close to midnight, every night. When he needed to relieve himself, he used a private facility that was fitted with a one-way mirror so that he could watch the room. He was a dedicated accountant—the mafia's best—but it wasn't just the duty of his profession that held Rajubhai to the activity on his counting tables. Away from the busy room he was a grumpy, suspicious, and strangely wizened man. In the counting room he was plumper, somehow, and expansively self-assured. It was as if the physical attachment linked him to a psychic force: so long as a part of his body was still in the room, he was still connected to the energy, the power, the money.

'Linbaba!' he shouted down at me, with the lower part of his body hidden by the door frame. 'Don't forget the wedding! You are coming, isn't it?'

'Sure,' I smiled back at him. 'I'll be there!'

I did the quick walk-fall down three flights of the stairway, teasing and shoving the goondas on duty at every level, and bumped past the men at the street door. At the end of the street I acknowledged the smiles of two more men watching the door. There were some exceptions, but for the most part the young mafia gangsters liked me. I wasn't the only foreigner working with the Bombay mafia—there was an Irish gangster in the Bandra council, an American freelancer making a name in major drug deals, a Dutchman working with a gang in Khar, and there were other men across the city—but I was the only gora in the Salman council. I was *their* foreigner. And those years, as Indian pride was rising like new green, white, and orange vines from the scorched post-colonial earth, were the last years when being foreign, being British, or looking and sounding British was enough to win hearts and intrigue minds.

Rajubhai's invitation to his daughter's wedding was significant: it meant that I was accepted as one of them. For months I'd worked side by side with Salman, Sanjay, Farid, Rajubhai, and others on the council. My work in the passport section was bringing in almost as much money as the entire currency operation. My own contacts on the streets threw large sums into the gold, goods, and money-change pots. I worked out in the boxing gym with Salman Mustaan and Abdullah Taheri every other day. Using my friendship with Hassaan Obikwa, I'd forged a new alliance with his men in the black ghetto. It was a useful connection which had brought us new men, money, and markets. At Nazeer's request, I'd joined the delegation that had struck an arms agreement with Afghan exiles in the city—a deal that had ensured a steady supply of weapons to the Salman council from the semi-autonomous tribal regions on the Pakistan-Afghanistan border. I had friendship and respect and more money than I cared to spend, but it wasn't until Rajubhai invited me to his daughter's wedding that I knew I was truly accepted. He was a senior man on the Salman council. His invitation was the endorsement that welcomed me into the inner circle of trust and affection. You can work with the mafia, and for the mafia, and do the kind of job that earns high esteem, but you're not really one of them until they invite you home to kiss the babies.

I walked out through the invisible boundaries of the Fort area and approached Flora Fountain. A roving taxi slowed beside me, the driver gesturing aggressively for my fare. I waved him away. Not realising that I could speak Hindi, he drove up beside me at a crawling pace and leaned from the window to talk.

'Hey, white sisterfucker, can't you see the taxi's empty? What are you doing? Walking in the hot afternoon like somebody's lost white goat?'

'*Kai paijey tum?*' I asked in rude Marathi. *Whaddaya want?*

'*Kai paijey?*' he repeated, stunned to hear the Marathi phrase.

'What's your problem?' I asked, speaking in the rough Marathi dialect of Bombay's back streets. 'You don't understand Marathi? This is our Bombay, and Bombay is ours. If you can't speak Marathi, what are you doing in Bombay? Have you got a goat's brain inside your sisterfucking head?'

'*Arrey!*' he grinned, switching to English. 'You speak Marathi, *baba?*'

'*Gora chierra, kala maan,*' I said in answer, making circling gestures over my face and my heart. *White face, black heart.* I moved into Hindi, using the most polite form of the word *you* to put him at ease. 'I'm white on the outside, brother, but full Hindustani on the inside. I'm just taking a walk, passing time. Why don't you look for some real tourists, and leave poor Indian fuckers like me alone, *na?*'

He laughed aloud and passed his hand across the window of his cab to shake mine gently, and then sped away.

I walked on, avoiding the crowded footpaths to join the swifter lines on the road beside the passing cars. Deep breaths of the city finally drove the smell of the currency-room from my nostrils. I was heading back toward Colaba, to Leopold's, to meet Didier. I wanted to walk because I was glad to be back in the part of the city I loved most. Work for Salman's mafia council took me to every distant suburb of the great city, and there were many favoured places: from Mahalaxmi to Malad; from Cotton Green to Thana; from Santa Cruz and Andheri to the Lakes District on the Film City Road. But the real seat of his council's power was in the long peninsula that began in the sweeping curve of Marine Drive and followed the scimitar shore all the way to the World Trade Centre. And it was there in those thriving streets, never more than a few bus stops from the sea, that I'd lost my heart to the city and learned to love her.

It was hot on the street, hot enough to burn all but the deepest thoughts from troubled minds. Like every other Bombayite, every other *Mumbaiker*, I'd made that walk from Flora Fountain to the Causeway a thousand times, and like them I knew where to find the cool breezes and refreshing shades on the way. My scalp, my face, and my shirt were wet with sweat in any few seconds of bare sunlight—the baptism in every daylight walk—and then cooled all the way to dry again in a minute of shaded wind.

My thoughts, as I moved between the traffic and the browsing shoppers, were on the future. Paradoxically, even perversely, just as I was being accepted into the secret heart of Bombay, I also felt the strongest urge to leave. I understood the two forces, contradictory as they seemed. So much of what I'd loved about Bombay had been in the hearts and minds and words of human beings—Karla, Prabaker, Khaderbhai, and Khaled Ansari. They were all gone, in one way or another, yet there was a constant, melancholy sense of them in every street, shrine, and strip of seacoast that I loved in the city. Still, there were new sources of love and inspiration—new beginnings rising from the fallow fields of loss and disillusion. My position with Salman's mafia council was secure. Business opportunities were opening up in the Bollywood film industry and the newer fields of television and multi-media: I received offers of work every other week. I had a good apartment, with a view of the Haji Ali Mosque, and plenty of money. And night by night I grew a little closer in loving affection for Lisa Carter.

A sadness that lingered in all my favourite places was pressing me to leave the city, just as new love and acceptance pulled me closer to her heart. And I couldn't decide, as I walked that long, baptismal stretch from Flora to the Causeway, which way to jump. No matter how often or deeply I thought about the struggled past or the sorrow and promise of the present, I couldn't make that leap of confidence or trust or faith into the future. There was something missing: some calculation, some piece of evidence or parallax view of my life that would make it all clear to me, I was sure, but I didn't know what it was. So I moved between the frantic flow of cars, bikes, buses, trucks, and push-carts, and the meandering progress of tourists and shoppers, and let my thoughts drift into the heat and the street.

'Lin!' Didier shouted as I stepped through the wide arch and up to his long raft of joined tables. 'Direct from your training, *non?*'

'No, I've been walking. Thinking. More of a workout for the mind— and maybe the soul.'

'Do not fear!' he commanded, signalling for the waiter. 'I cure this sickness every day of every week. Or every night, at the least. Make a place for him, Arturo. Move down a little, and let him sit next to me.'

Arturo, a young Italian hiding in Bombay from an undisclosed problem with the police in Naples, was Didier's new infatuation. He was a short, slight man with a doll-like face that many a girl might've envied. He spoke very little English and reacted to every approach, no matter how friendly, with the same petulantly surly shudder of irritation. Consequently, Didier's many friends ignored him and set the alarms in their mental clocks to give the relationship from a few months, at most, to a few weeks, before it collapsed.

'You just missed Karla,' Didier told me more quietly when I shook his hand. 'She will be upset. She wanted to —'

'I know,' I smiled. 'She wanted to see me.'

The drinks arrived, and Didier clattered his glass against mine. I took a sip from it and put it down on the table next to him.

Several people from the movie crowd that worked with Lisa Carter were at the long table, joining in a party with some of Kavita Singh's press group. Sitting next to Didier were Vikram and Lettie. They were both happier and healthier than I'd ever known them to be. They'd bought the new apartment in the heart of Colaba near the market only months before. While the commitment had exhausted their savings and forced them to borrow from Vikram's parents, it was proof of their faith in one another and the future of their burgeoning movie business, and they were still excited with the change.

Vikram greeted me warmly, rising from his chair to give me a hug. His gunslinger's clothes had disappeared, item by item, under Lettie's persuasion and his own maturing taste. All that remained of the Clint Eastwood costume were the silver belt and the black cowboy boots. His beloved hat, surrendered with no little reluctance when he'd found himself more frequently in the boardrooms of major companies than in the stuntmen's corral, was hanging from a hook in my apartment. It was one of my most treasured possessions.

When I leaned over to kiss Lettie, she seized the shoulder of my shirt and pulled me closer to whisper in my ear.

'Keep your cool, lad,' she murmured inscrutably. 'Keep your cool.'

Sitting next to Lettie were the movie producers Cliff De Souza and Chandra Mehta. As sometimes happens with close friends, Cliff and Chandra seemed to exchange the substance of their bodies between them over time, so that Cliff had become slightly thinner and more angular, while Chandra had gained weight in almost perfect proportion. The more they differed physically, however, the more they resembled one another in other ways. In fact, the close colleagues, who often worked and played together for forty hours at a stretch, used so many of the same gestures, facial expressions, and phrases that they were known on the sets of the movies they produced as Fat Uncle and Skinny Uncle.

They raised their arms in identically enthusiastic greeting when I approached them, although each was pleased to see me for his own reasons. Cliff De Souza had developed a passionate affection for Kavita Singh since I'd introduced them, and he'd hoped I might influence her in his favour. Having a far longer acquaintance with her, I knew that no power could influence Kavita toward anything not fully consonant with her will and her wish. Still, she seemed to like him well enough, and they had much in common. They were both almost thirty and unmarried—a status so unusual in the Indian upper middle class, in those years, that their families anguished over it at every feast and festival in the crowded calendar. They were both media professionals who prided themselves on their independence and artistic flair. They were also driven by the same instinctive tolerance to seek out, and fairly examine, each point of view in any apparent conflict of interests. And they were attractive people. Kavita's shapely figure and perilously seductive eye seemed the perfect complement to Cliff's rangy angularity and the boyishness of his artless, lopsided grin.

For my part, liking them both, I saw no reason to resist the matchmaker's urge to meddle. In public I made it clear that I liked Cliff De Souza, and in private I praised him discreetly to her whenever the natural opportunity arose. They had a chance—a good chance, it seemed to me —and my heart put a wishing star in my eyes for them.

Chandra Mehta, on the other hand, was pleased to see me because I was his closest link to the black money in Salman's mafia council, and the only link he could describe as amicable. Like Khader before him, Salman Mustaan saw great advantage in the access to Bombay's film world that Chandra Mehta provided. New regulations at federal and state levels had tightened restrictions on the flow of capital, making it ever more difficult to launder black money. For many reasons—not least because of the irresistible glamour attached to the industry—politicians had exempted the movie business from many of those monetary and investment controls. They were boom economy years, and Bollywood films were going through a renaissance in style and confidence. The films got bigger and better, and had begun to reach out to a wider world market. As the budgets for successful films soared, however, producers exhausted the traditional sources of revenue. That convergence of interests drove more than a few producers and production houses into strange syzygies with gangsters: films about mafia goondas were financed by the mafia, and the profits from hit movies about hit men went into new crimes and real hits on real people, which in turn became the subjects for screenplays and new films financed by more mafia money.

And I played my part, so to speak, by working as the connection between Chandra Mehta and Salman Mustaan. The relationship was a lucrative one. The Salman council had put *crores*, each *crore* being ten million rupees, through Mehta-De Souza Productions, and drew clean, untraceable profits from the bottom line. That first contact with Chandra Mehta, when he'd asked me to find a few thousand American dollars on the black market, had fattened into a nexus that the portly producer couldn't resist or refuse. He was rich, and getting richer. But the men who poured their wealth into his company frightened him, and every contact with them was menaced with the scent of their distrust. So Chandra Mehta smiled at me, and was glad to see me, and tried to pull me tighter into the tremulous clutch of his friendship whenever our paths crossed.

I didn't mind. I liked Chandra Mehta, and I liked Bollywood movies. I allowed him to drag me into the worried, wealthy world of his friendship.

Next to him at the table was Lisa Carter. Her thick, blonde hair had grown long enough, after the short cut, to fall beside the oval cameo of her face. Her blue eyes were clear and glittering with passionate intent.

She was tanned and very healthy. She'd even gained a little extra weight — something she decried, but that I and every other man within her sight-horizon was bound to admire. And there was something new and very different in her manner: a warm, unhurried softness in her smile; a willing laugh that won the laughter of others; and a lightness of spirit that looked for and often found the best in those she met. For weeks, months, I'd watched those changes shift and settle in her, and at first I'd thought they'd grown from my affection. Although no formal relationship had been declared — she continued to live in her apartment, and I lived in mine — we were lovers, and we were far more than friends. After a time, I realised that the changes were not mine, but hers alone. After a time, I began to see how deep the well of her loving was, and how much her happiness and confidence depended on drawing that love into the light, and sharing it. And love was beautiful in her. It was a clear sky she gave us with those eyes, and a summer morning with her smile.

She kissed my cheek when I greeted her. I returned the kiss, wondering, as I stepped back, why a small concerned frown rippled from her brow to her cornflower-blue eyes.

Sitting next around the long table were the print journalists Dilip and Anwar. They were young, only a few years out of college, and still learning their trade in the anonymous vaults of *The Noonday*, a Bombay daily. At night, with Didier and his little court, they discussed the big breaking stories of the day as if they'd played key parts in the scoops or had followed their own instincts to the investigation's end. Their excitement, enthusiasm, ambition, and limitless hope for the future so delighted everyone in the Leopold's crowd that Kavita and Didier felt obliged to respond, occasionally, with sardonic sniping. Dilip and Anwar reacted well, laughing and often giving as good as they got until the whole group was shouting and pounding the table in delight.

Dilip was a tall, fair, almond-eyed Punjabi. Anwar, a third-generation native of Bombay, was shorter, darker, and the more serious of the two. *New blood*, Lettie had said to me with a smile, a few days before that afternoon. It was a phrase she'd once used about me, soon after I'd arrived in Bombay. And as I made my way around the table and looked at the two young men talking with such passion and purpose, it occurred to me that once, before heroin and crime, my life had been like theirs. Once I'd been just as happy and healthy and hopeful as they were. And I was glad to know them, and to know they were a part of the pleasure and promise of the Leopold's crowd. It was right that they were there, just as it was right that Maurizio was gone, and Ulla and Modena were gone, and that I, too, would one day be gone.

Returning their warm handshakes, I moved past the young men to Kavita Singh sitting beside them. Kavita stood to give me a hug. It was the tender, close hug that a woman gives a man when she knows she can trust him, or when she's sure his heart belongs to someone else. It was a rare enough embrace between foreigners. Coming from an Indian woman, it was uniquely intimate in my experience. And it was important. I'd been in the city for years; I could make myself understood in Marathi, Hindi, and Urdu; I could sit with gangsters, slum-dwellers, or Bollywood actors, claiming their goodwill and sometimes their respect; but few things made me feel as accepted, in all the Indian worlds of Bombay, as Kavita Singh's fond embrace.

I never told her that—what her affectionate and unconditional acceptance meant to me. So much, too much, of the good that I felt in those years of exile was locked in the prison cell of my heart: those tall walls of fear; that small, barred window of hope; that hard bed of shame. I do speak out now. I know now that when the loving, honest moment comes it should be seized, and spoken, because it may never come again. And unvoiced, unmoving, unlived in the things we declare from heart to heart, those true and real feelings wither and crumble in the remembering hand that tries too late to reach for them.

On that day, as the grey-pink veil of evening slowly enclosed the afternoon, I said nothing to Kavita. I let my smile, like a thing made of broken stones, fall and slide from the peak of her affection to the ground beneath her feet. She took my arm and steered me into an introduction to the man who sat beside her.

'Lin, I don't think you've met Ranjit,' she said as he stood and we shook hands. 'Ranjit is ... Karla's friend. Ranjit Choudry, meet Lin.'

I suddenly knew what Lettie had meant with her cryptic comment, *Keep your cool, lad*, and why Lisa couldn't shift the frown that creased her brow.

'Call me Jeet,' he offered. His smile was wide, natural, and confident.

'O-*kay*,' I answered evenly, not really smiling. 'Pleased to meet you, *Jeet*.'

'And it's a pleasure to meet you,' he countered, with the well-rounded and musical inflection of Bombay's best private schools and universities: my favourite accent in all the beautiful ways to speak the English language. 'I've heard so much about you.'

'*Achaa*?' I responded without thinking, exactly as an Indian of my age might've done. The word, in its literal translation, means *good*. In that context and with that inflection it meant *Oh, yeah*?

'Yes,' he laughed, releasing my hand. 'Karla talks about you often. You're quite the hero to her, I'm sure you know.'

'That's funny,' I answered, not sure if he was as ingenuous as he seemed to be. 'She once told me that heroes only come in three kinds: dead, damaged, or dubious.'

He tipped his head back and roared with laughter, his mouth open wide enough to reveal a perfect set of perfect Indian teeth. Still laughing, he met my eye and wagged his head in wonder.

So that's part of it, I thought. *He gets her jokes. He likes her play with words. He understands her love of them and her cleverness. That's one of the reasons why she likes him. Okay.*

The rest of it was more obvious. He had a lithe build, and was average tall, my height, with an open, handsome face. More than just the sum of good features—high cheekbones, a high, wide forehead, expressive topaz-coloured eyes, a strong nose, smiling mouth, and firm chin—it was the kind of face that once would've been called dashing: the lone yachtsman, the mountaineer, the jungle adventurer. He wore his hair short. The hairline was receding, but even that seemed to suit him, as if it was the preferred option for healthy, athletic men. And the clothes—I knew them well from the shopping expeditions that Sanjay, Andrew, Faisal, and the other mafiosi made to the most expensive stores in the city. There wasn't a self-respecting gangster in Bombay who wouldn't have pursed his lips and wagged his head in approval of Ranjit's clothes.

'Well,' I said, shuffling my feet to move around him and greet Kalpana, the last friend sitting in the loop of the table. She was working as a first-assistant director for Mehta-De Souza productions, and in training to become a director in her own right. She looked up at me and winked.

'Wait,' Ranjit requested, softly but quickly. 'I wanted to tell you … about your stories … your short stories …'

I turned to flinch a frown at Kavita Singh, who hunched her shoulders and raised the palms of her hands as she looked away.

'Kavita let me read them, and I wanted to tell you how good they are. I mean, how good *I* think they are.'

'Well, thanks,' I muttered, trying once again to move past him.

'Really. I read them all, and I think they're really great.'

There are few things more discomfiting than a spontaneous outburst of genuine decency from someone you're determined to dislike for no good reason. I felt a little blush of shame beginning to spread across my cheeks.

'Thanks,' I said, putting truth into my eyes and my voice for the first time. 'It's damn nice to hear, even if Kavita wasn't supposed to show them to anyone.'

'I know she wasn't,' he said quickly. 'But I think you *should*—show them to someone, I mean. They're not right for my paper. It's not the right forum. But *The Noonday*, well, it would be the perfect forum for them. And I know they'd buy them for a very fair price. The editor of *The Noonday*, Anil, is a friend of mine. I know what he likes, and I know he'll like your stories. I didn't show him your work, of course. Not without your permission. But I did tell him that I read them, and that I think they're good. He wants to meet you. If you take your stories to him, I'm sure you'll get on well with him. Anyway, I'll leave it at that. He's hoping to see you. But it's up to you. Whatever you decide, I wish you all the best.'

He sat down, and I moved past him to greet Kalpana and then take my place beside Didier. I was so distracted by the exchange with Ranjit—*Jeet*—Choudry that I only half-listened to Didier's announcement of his planned trip to Italy with Arturo. *Three months*, I heard him say, and I remember thinking that three months in Italy could become three years, and that I might lose him. The thought was so strange that I wouldn't let myself consider it. Bombay without Didier was like … Bombay without Leopold's, or the Haji Ali Mosque, or the Gateway Monument. It was unthinkable.

Pushing the thought away, I looked around the laughing, drinking, talking table of friends, and filled the empty glass within me, pouring their successes and their hopes into my eyes. Then I returned my attention to Ranjit, Karla's boyfriend. I'd done my homework on him in recent months. I knew that he was the second eldest—some said the favourite—of four sons born to Ramprakash Choudry, a truck driver who'd made his fortune resupplying coastal towns in Bangladesh that had been hit by cyclones. The first government tenders had grown into major contracts, requiring fleets of trucks and, eventually, chartered aircraft and ships. Along the way, Choudry had acquired a small-circulation Bombay newspaper as part of a merger with a more diversified transport and communications firm. He'd handed the paper to his son Ranjit, who'd just graduated with a business degree and was the first, on both sides of his family, to complete high school and to attend any kind of further-education college. Ranjit had been running the paper, re-badged as *The Daily Post*, for eight years. His success with *The Post*, as it was known, had allowed Ranjit to segue into the incipient field of independent television production.

He was wealthy, influential, popular, and possessed of an entrepreneurial élan in print, movies, and television: a media baron in the making. There were rumours of resentments stirring in the heart of Ranjit's older brother Rahul, who'd joined his father in the transport business in his early teenage years, and had never enjoyed the private-school education lavished upon Ranjit and the younger siblings. There was gossip, also, about the two younger brothers, the wild parties they sometimes threw, and the large bribes required to keep them out of trouble. There was no criticism of Ranjit, however, in any connection; and apart from those few simmering concerns, his life seemed almost charmed.

He was, as Lettie had once said, quite a fat and shiny catch. And as I watched him with friends—listening more than he talked, smiling more than he frowned, self-deprecating and considerate, tactful and attentive—I had to admit to myself that he was a very likeable man. And, strangely, I felt sorry for him. A few years or even months before, I would've been jealous that he was such a likeable man—*such a very nice guy*, as more than a few people said to me when I'd asked them about him. I would've hated him. But I felt nothing like that for Ranjit Choudry. Instead, as I watched him, remembering too much of what I'd felt for Karla, and thinking about her clearly for the first time in … a long time, I felt sorry for the rich, handsome media baron, and I wished him luck.

For half an hour I talked across the table with Lisa and the others and then I looked up to see Johnny Cigar, standing in the wide doorway and gesturing to catch my eye. Delighted to have an excuse to leave, I turned to Didier and drew him around to face me.

'Listen, if you're really serious about going to Italy for three months—'

'Certainly, I am —' he began, but I cut him off quickly.

'And if you're really serious about needing someone to look after your place for you while you're away, I think I've got just the guys for the job.'

'Oh, yes? And who are they?'

'The Georges,' I replied. 'The Zodiac Georges. Gemini and Scorpio.'

Didier was appalled.

'But these ... these *George* people ... they are, how can I say it?'

'Reliable?' I suggested. 'Honest. Clean. Loyal. Brave. And, above all, the most important qualification for situations like this, they're absolutely *not* interested in staying in your apartment for a minute longer than you want them to. In fact, I'll have a damn hard job talking them into it in the first place. They *like* the street. They won't want to do it. But if I let them know they're doing me a favour, they might agree. They'll do a good job of looking after your place for you, and they'll get three months of safe living in a decent place.'

'*Decent*?' Didier scoffed. 'What do you mean, *decent*? My apartment is without parallel in Bombay, Lin. You know that. *Excellent*, I can understand. *Superb*, I can accept. But *decent—non*! It is like saying that I live in the fish market and, er, what do you say, *whoosh* it out every day with a water hose!'

'So what do you think? I've gotta go.'

'*Decent!*' he sniffed.

'Come on, man, will you forget about that!'

'Well, yes, perhaps you are right. I have nothing against them. The George from Canada, the Scorpio, he does speak some French. That is true. Yes. Yes. Tell them I think it is a good idea. Tell them to see me, and I will speak to them—with very careful instructions.'

Laughing as I said goodbye, I joined Johnny Cigar at the doorway of the restaurant. He pulled me close to him.

'Can you come with me? Now?' he asked.

'Sure. Walking or taxi?'

'I think taxi, Lin.'

We pushed our way through the breaking waves of walkers to the road and found a taxi. I was smiling as we waved the taxi down and climbed inside. For months, I'd been trying to find a way to help Gemini and Scorpio George that was more meaningful than the money I gave them from time to time. Didier's holiday with Arturo provided the perfect opportunity. I knew that three months in Didier's apartment would add years to their lives: three months without the stress of street living and with the secure good health that only a home and home cooking can provide. And I also knew that, with the Zodiac Georges in his apartment while he was gone, Didier would worry just enough to make his return to Bombay a little more likely, and a little sooner.

'Where to?' I asked Johnny.

'World Trade Centre,' he told the driver, smiling at me but clearly concerned about something.

'What's up?'

'There is a problem at the zhopadpatti,' he answered me.

'Okay,' I said, knowing that he wouldn't say anything else about the problem until he thought the moment was right. 'How's the baby?'

'Fine, very fine,' he laughed. 'He has such a strong grab on my fingers. He will be big and strong—bigger than his father, sure. And Prabaker's baby, from the sister of my Sita, Parvati, that baby is also very beautiful. He is very much like Prabaker ... in his face and his smiling.'

I didn't want to think about my dead, beloved friend.

'And how's Sita? And the girls?' I asked.

'They are fine, Lin, all fine.'

'You'll have to watch out, Johnny,' I warned him. 'Three kids in less than three years—before you know it, you'll be a fat, old guy with nine kids climbing all around you.'

'It is a fine dream,' he sighed happily.

'How's work? How are you ... how you doing for money?'

'Also fine, very fine, Lin. Everybody pays taxes, and nobody likes it. My business is good. Sita and me, we decided to buy the house next to ours, and make a bigger house for the family.'

'That's fantastic! I can't wait to see it.'

There was a little silence and then Johnny turned to me with an expression of worry, almost of torment.

'Lin, that time when you asked me to work for you, to work with you, and I refused —'

'It's okay, Johnny.'

'No, it is not okay. I want to tell you, I should have said yes, and I should have worked beside you.'

'Are you in trouble?' I asked, not understanding him. 'Is business not as good as you said it was? Do you need money?'

'No, no, everything is fine with me. But if I was with you that time, watching you, maybe you would not still be working for all these months at the black business, with those goondas.'

'No, Johnny.'

'I blame myself every day, Lin,' he said, his lips pulled wide in an anguished grimace. 'I think that you asked me to work with you, to be your friend, because you did need a friend at that time. I was a bad friend, Lin, and I blame myself. Every day I feel bad about it. I am so sorry that I refused you.'

I put my hand on his shoulder, but he wouldn't meet my eye.

'Look, Johnny, you've got to understand. What I do, I don't feel good about it, but I don't feel bad about it, either. You do feel bad about it. And I respect that. I admire it. And you're a good friend.'

'No,' he murmured, his eyes still downcast.

'Yes,' I insisted. 'I love you, man.'

'Lin!' he said, grabbing my arm with sudden, urgent concern. 'Please, please, be careful with these goondas. Please!'

I smiled, trying to put him at ease.

'Man,' I protested, 'are you ever gonna tell me what this damn trip is about?'

'Bears!' he said.

'Bears?'

'Well, actually, you know, only *one* bear is our problem. You know Kano? Kano the bear?'

'Sure I know him,' I muttered. 'Bahinchudh bear—what's happened? Has he got himself put in jail again?'

'No, no, Lin. He is not in the jail.'

'Good. At least he's not a recidivist.'

'Actually, you know, he *escaped* from the jail.'

'Shit …'

'And now he is a fugitive bear, with a reward price on his head, or his paws, or any part of him they can catch.'

'Kano's on the run?'

'Yes. They even have a wanted poster.'

'A *what*?'

'A wanted poster,' he explained patiently. 'They took a photo of him, that Kano, with his two blue bear-wallahs, when they arrested them again. Now, they are using that photo for the wanted poster.'

'Who's *they*?'

'The state government, the Maharashtra police, the Border Security Force, and the Wildlife Protection Authority.'

'Christ, what did Kano do? Who did he kill?'

'Not killed anyone, Lin. The story, what happened, the Wildlife Authority has a new policy, to stop cruelty to the dancing bears. They don't know that Kano's bear-wallahs, they love him so much, like a big brother, and he loves them also, and they would never hurt him. But the policy is the policy. So, the Wildlife-wallahs, they captured Kano, and they took him to the animal jail. And he was crying and crying for his blue bear-wallahs. And the bear-wallahs, they were outside the animal jail, and they were also crying and crying. And two of those Wildlife-wallahs, two watchmen on duty, they got very upset about all the crying, so they went outside, and they started beating Kano's blue men with lathis. They gave them a solid pasting. And Kano, he saw his two blue men getting that beating, and he just lost his control. He broke down that cage and made an escape. The two bear-wallahs got a big feeling of courage, and they beat up the Wildlife fellows and ran away with Kano. Now they are hiding in our zhopadpatti, in the same hut that you used to have as your house. And we have to try to get them out of the city without getting captured. Our problem is how to get that Kano from the zhopadpatti to Nariman Point. There is a truck waiting there, and the driver has agreed to take Kano away with his bear-wallahs.'

'Not easy,' I murmured. 'And with a goddamn *wanted* poster for the blue guys and the bear. *Jesus!*'

'Will you help us, Lin? We feel very sorry for that bear. Love is a special thing in the world. When two men have so much love in their hearts, even so it is for a bear, it must be protected, isn't it?'

'Well …'

'Isn't it?'

'Sure it is,' I smiled. 'Sure it is. I'll be glad to help, if I can. And you can do me a favour as well.'

'Anything.'

'Try to get me one of those wanted posters with the picture of the bear and the blue guys. I gotta have one of those posters.'

'The poster?'

'Yeah. It's a long story. Don't worry about it. Just, if you see one, grab it for me. Have you got a plan?'

The taxi pulled up outside the slum as the evening, emptied of its sunset and pale enough to unveil the first few stars, drew squealing, playing faronades of children back to their huts, where plumes of smoke from cooking fires fluttered into the cooling air.

'The plan,' Johnny announced as we walked quickly through the familiar lanes, nodding and smiling to friends along the way, 'is to dress up the bear in a disguise.'

'I dunno,' I said doubtfully. 'He's real tall, as I remember, and kinda big.'

'At first, we put a hat and a coat on him, and even an umbrella hanging from his coat, like an office-working fellow.'

'How did he look?'

'Not so good,' Johnny replied without a trace of irony or sarcasm. 'He still looked quite a lot like a bear, but a bear with clothes.'

'You don't say.'

'Yes. So, now the plan is to get a big Muslim dress, you know the one? From Afghanistan? Covering all the whole body, with only a few holes to see out of it.'

'A burkha.'

'Exactly. The boys went to Mohammed Ali Road to buy the biggest one they could find. They should be — ah! Look! They are here already, and we can try it, to see how does it look.'

We came upon a group of a dozen men and a similar number of women and children gathered near the hut where I'd lived and worked for almost two years. And although I'd left the zhopadpatti, convinced that I could never live there again, it always gave me a thrill of pleasure to see the humble little hut, and stand near it. The few foreigners I'd taken to the slum — and even the Indians, such as Kavita Singh and Vikram, who'd visited me there — had been horrified by the place and aghast to think that I'd chosen to stay there so long. They couldn't understand that every time I entered the slum I felt the urge to let go and surrender to a simpler, poorer life that was yet richer in respect, and love, and a vicinal connectedness to the surrounding sea of human hearts. They couldn't understand what I meant when I talked about the purity of the slum: they'd been there, and seen the wretchedness and filth for themselves. They saw no purity. But they hadn't *lived* in those miraculous acres, and they hadn't learned that to survive in such a writhe of hope and sorrow the people had to be scrupulously and heartbreakingly honest. That was the source of their purity: above all things, they were true to themselves.

So, with my dishonest heart thrilling at the nearness of my once and favourite home, I joined the group and then gasped as a huge, shrouded figure emerged from beside the hut and stood among us.

'Holy shit!' I said, gawking at the towering, immense form. The blue-grey burkha covered the standing bear from its head to the ground. I found myself wondering at the size of the woman that garment had been intended to cover, because the standing bear was a full head taller than the tallest man in our group. 'Holy shit!'

As we watched, the shapeless form took a few lumbering steps, knocking over a stool and water pot as it swayed and lurched forward.

'Maybe,' Jeetendra suggested helpfully, 'she is a very tall, fat ... *clumsy* kind of a woman.'

The bear suddenly stooped and then fell forward onto its four paws. We followed it with our eyes. The blue-grey, burkha-clad figure trundled forward, all the while emitting a low, grumbling moan.

'Maybe,' Jeetendra amended, 'she is a small, fat ... *growling* woman.'

'A *growling* woman?' Johnny Cigar protested. 'What the hell is a *growling* woman?'

'I don't know,' Jeetendra whined. 'I am only trying to be helping.'

'You're going to help this bear all the way back to jail,' I muttered, 'if you let it go out of here like that.'

'We could try the hat and coat again,' Joseph offered. 'Maybe a bigger hat ... and ... and a more fashionable coat.'

'I don't think fashion's your problem,' I sighed. 'From what Johnny tells me, you have to get Kano from here to Nariman Point without the cops spotting you, is that right?'

'Yes, Linbaba,' Joseph answered. In the absence of Qasim Ali Hussein, who was enjoying a six-month holiday in his home village with most of his family, Joseph was the head man of the slum. The man who'd been beaten and disciplined by his neighbours for the brutal, drunken attack on his wife had become a leader. In the years since that day of the beating, Joseph had given up drinking, regained his wife's love, and earned the respect of his neighbours. He'd joined every important council or committee, and worked harder than any other in the group. Such was the extent of his reform and his sober dedication to the well-being of his family and his community that, when Qasim Ali nominated Joseph as his temporary replacement, no other name was tendered for consideration. 'There is a truck parked near to the Nariman Point. The driver says that he will take the Kano and carry him out of the municipality, out of the state, also. He will put him and the bear-wallahs back in their native place, back in U.P., all the way back to Gorakhpur side, near to the Nepal. But that truck driver, he is afraid to come near this place to collect the Kano. He wants that we take that bear to *him* only. But how to do it, Linbaba? How to get such a big bears to that place? Sure thing a police patrol will see Kano and make an arrest of him. And they will be arresting us, also, for the help of escaping bears. And then? What then? How to do it, Linbaba? That is the problem. That is why we were thinking about the disguises.'

'*Kano-walleh kahan hey?*' I asked. *Where are Kano's handlers?*

'Here, baba!' Jeetendra replied, pushing the two bear-handlers forward.

They'd washed themselves clean of the brilliant blue dye that usually covered their bodies, and they'd stripped away all of their silver ornaments. Their long dreadlocks and decorated plaits were concealed beneath turbans, and they wore plain white shirts and trousers. Unadorned and decolourised, the blue men seemed spiritless, and much smaller and slighter than the fantastic beings I'd first encountered in the slum.

'Tell me, will Kano sit on a platform?'

'Yes, baba!' they said with pride.

'For how long will he sit still?'

'For an hour, if we are with him, near him, talking to him. Maybe more than one hour, baba—unless he needs to make a wee. And if so, he is always telling first.'

'Okay. Will he sit on a small, moving platform—one on wheels—if we push it?' I asked them.

There was some discussion while I tried to explain what kind of platform or table I had in mind: one mounted on wheels for carrying fruit, vegetables, and other goods around the slum and displaying them for sale. When it was clear, and such a hawker's cart was found and wheeled into the clearing, the bear-handlers waggled their heads excitedly that yes, yes, yes, Kano would sit on such a moving table. They added that it was possible to steady him on the table by using ropes, and that he wouldn't find that secure fastening objectionable if they first explained its necessity to him. But what, they wanted to know, did I have in mind?

'On my way in with Johnny just now, I passed old Rakeshbaba's workshop,' I explained quickly. 'The lamps were lit, and I saw a lot of pieces from his Ganesh sculptures. Some of them are pretty big. They're made from papier-mâché, so they're not very heavy, and they're all hollow inside. They're big enough, I think, to fit right over the top of Kano's head, and to cover his body if he's sitting down. With a bit of silk for trimming, and a few garlands of flowers for decoration ...'

'So ... you think ...' Jeetendra stammered.

'We should disguise Kano as Ganesh,' Johnny Cigar concluded, 'and push him on the trolley, like a Ganpatti devotion, all the way to Nariman Point, right down the middle of the street. It's a great idea, Lin!'

'But Ganesh Chaturthi finished last week,' Joseph said, referring to the annual festival where hundreds of Ganesh figures—some small enough to hold in the hand, and others towering ten metres tall—were pushed through the city to Chowpatty Beach and then hurled into the sea amid a crowd of close to a million people. 'I myself was in the *mela* at Chowpatty. The time for it has finished, Linbaba.'

'I know. I was there, too. That's what gave me the idea. I don't think it'll matter that the festival is over. I wouldn't think twice if I saw a Ganpatti at *any* time of the year. Would any of you ask questions if you saw a Ganesha, on a trolley, being wheeled down the street?'

Ganesh, the elephant-headed God, was arguably the most popular in all the Hindu pantheon, and I was sure no-one would think to stop and search a little procession featuring a large sculpture of his form on a moving trolley.

'I think he is right,' Jeetendra agreed. 'Nobody will say anything about a Ganesha. After all, Lord Ganesha is the Lord of Obstacles, *na?*'

The elephant-headed god was known as the Lord of Obstacles and the Great Solver of Problems. People in trouble appealed to him with prayers in much the same way that some Christians appealed to their patron saints. He was also the divine ministrant of writers.

'It will be not a problem to push a Ganesha to Nariman Point,' Joseph's wife, Maria, pointed out. 'But how to put that Kano bear into the disguise —that is a problem. Just putting him in the dress was a very difficult job.'

'He did not like the dress,' one of the bear-handlers declared reasonably. 'He is a man bear, you know, and sensitive about such things.'

'But he will not mind the Ganesha disguise,' his friend added. 'I know he will think it is very good fun. He is very greedy for attention, I have to say. That is one of his two bad habits: that, and flirtations with girls.'

We were speaking in Hindi, and the last exchange was too swift for me to follow.

'What did he say?' I asked Johnny. 'What was Kano's bad habit?'

'Flirtations,' Johnny replied. 'With girls.'

'Flirtations? What the hell do they mean?'

'Well, I'm not exactly sure, but I think —'

'No, don't!' I interrupted him, disowning the question. 'Please ... don't tell me what it means.'

I looked around me at the press of expectant faces. For a moment I felt a thrill of wonder and envy that the little community of neighbours and friends worried so much about the problems of two itinerant bear-handlers —and the bear, of course. That unequivocal involvement, one with another, and its unquestioning support—stronger and more urgent than even the co-operation I'd seen in Prabaker's village—was something I'd lost when I'd left the slum to live in the comfortable, richer world. I'd never really found it anywhere else, except within the high-sierra of my mother's love. And because I knew it with them, once, in the sublime and wretched acres of those ragged huts, I never stopped wanting it and searching for it.

'Well, I really can't think of another way,' I sighed again. 'If we just cover him with rags or fruit or something and try to push him there, he'll move and make a noise. And if they see us, we'll get stopped. But if we make him look like Ganesh, we can chant and sing and crowd around him and make our own noise—as much noise as we want. And I don't think the cops would ever stop us. What do *you* think, Johnny?'

'I *like* it,' Johnny said, grinning happily in appreciation of the plan. 'I think it's a fine plan, and I say we give it a try.'

'Yes, also *I* like it,' Jeetendra said, his eyes wide with excitement. 'But, you know, we must better hurry—the truck will only wait for one or two hours more, I think so.'

They all nodded or wagged their heads in agreement: Satish, Jeetendra's son; Maria; Faroukh and Raghuram, the two friends who'd fought and been tied at the ankle by Qasim Ali as a punishment; and Ayub and Siddhartha, the two young men who'd run the free clinic since I'd left the slum. Finally, Joseph smiled and gave his assent. With Kano trundling along on all fours beside us, we made our way through the darkening lanes to the large double-hut that was old Rakeshbaba's workshop.

The elderly sculptor raised his grizzled brows when we entered his hut, but affected to ignore us and continued with the work of sanding and polishing a newly moulded section of a fibreglass religious frieze almost two metres in length. He worked at a long table made from thick builder's planks, lashed together and resting on two carpenter's trestles. Wood and fibreglass shavings covered the table and lay in chips and whorls, along with rinds of papier-mâché, at his bare feet. Sections of the sculpted and moulded forms—heads and limbs and bodies with gorgeously rounded bellies—rested on the floor of the hut amid a venerable profusion of plaques, reliefs, statues, and other pieces.

He took some convincing. The artist was notoriously cantankerous and he assumed, at first, that we were trying to mock the gods, and him, with a prank or a hoax. In the end, three elements persuaded him to help us. First was the bear-handlers' impassioned appeal to the problem-solving genius of Ganesha, the Lord of Obstacles. The elephant-headed one was, as it turned out, old Rakeshbaba's personal favourite from the abundant plane of the divine. Second, Johnny's subtle suggestion that perhaps the task was beyond the creative skill of the old sculptor proved a telling blow. Rakeshbaba shouted that he could disguise the Taj Mahal itself in a Ganesha sculpture, if he so desired, and the camouflage of a bear was a mere trifle to such a gifted artist, as the whole world knew and proclaimed him to be. Third, and perhaps most influential, was Kano himself. Apparently growing impatient in the lane outside, the burly creature forced its way into the hut and then lay down on its back beside Rakeshbaba, with all four paws in the air. The grouchy sculptor was transformed immediately into a giggling, cackling child as he bent to scratch the creature's belly and play with its gently whirling paws.

He stood at last to shove all of us but the bear-handlers and the bear from his workshop. The wooden cart was wheeled inside, and the wiry, grey-haired artist drew his reed curtains across the entrance.

Worried but excited, we waited outside, swapping stories and popping bubbles of news. The slum had survived the last monsoon with little real damage, Siddhartha told me, and no serious outbreaks of illness. Qasim Ali Hussein, celebrating the birth of his fourth grandson, had taken his extended family to his birth village in Karnataka State. He was well, and in good spirits, all of the voices confirmed. Jeetendra seemed to have recovered, inasmuch as such a thing is possible, from the death of his wife in the cholera epidemic. Although he'd vowed never to remarry, he worked and prayed and laughed enough to keep the soul bright within his eyes. His son Satish, who'd been sullen and quarrelsome for a time after his mother's death, had at last overcome the aloofness of grieving, and was engaged to a girl he'd known since his earliest memory in the slum. The promised pair was still too young to marry, but their betrothal gave them both joy, and was a commitment to the future that gladdened Jeetendra's heart. And one by one, each in his own way, everyone in the group that night praised Joseph, the redeemed one, the new leader who lowered his gaze shyly and only raised his eyes to share his embarrassed smile with Maria, standing at his side.

At last, Rakeshbaba pulled aside the reed curtains and beckoned us to enter his workshop. We crowded together and stepped into the golden lamplight. A gasp, some of us breathing in and some puffing out, rustled through our group as we looked at the completed sculpture. Kano was not simply disguised—he was transfigured into the form of the elephant-headed god. A huge head had been fitted over the bear's head, and rested on a pink, round-bellied body, with arms attached. Swathes of light blue silk surrounded the base of the figure where it rested on the trolley. Garlands of flowers were heaped on the flat table and around the neck of the god, concealing the join for the head.

'Is it really in there, that Kano-bear?' Jeetendra asked.

At the sound of his voice, the bear turned his head. What we saw was the living god, Ganesha, turn his elephant head to stare at us from his painted eyes. It was the movement of an animal, of course, and utterly unlike a human gesture. The whole group, myself included, flinched in surprise and fright. The children with us squealed, and pushed themselves backwards into the protective vines of adult legs and arms.

'*Bhagwaaaaan,*' Jeetendra breathed.

'Wow,' Johnny Cigar agreed. 'What do you think, Lin?'

'I'm … glad I'm not stoned,' I muttered, staring as the god tilted his head and uttered a low, moaning sound. I forced myself to act. 'Come on, let's do it!'

We rolled out of the slum with a knot of supporters. Once past the World Trade Centre and into the residential boulevard leading to the Back Bay area, we began a tentative chant. Those nearest to the cart put their hands on it and helped to push or pull it along. Those like Johnny and me, on the fringe, clung to the others and added our voices to the chant. As we gathered speed to a fast walk, the chanting grew more vigorous. In a while, many of the helpers seemed to forget that we were bear-smugglers, and hurled their voices into devoutly passionate chants and responses, no less inspired, I was sure, than they'd been a week before on the real pilgrimage.

As we walked, it occurred to me that the slum had been strangely devoid of pariah dogs. I noticed that there were none visible anywhere on the streets. Remembering how violently the dogs had reacted to Kano's first visit to the slum, I felt moved to mention it to Johnny.

'Arrey, kutta nahin,' I said. *Gee, there's no dogs here.*

Johnny, Narayan, Ali, and the few other men who'd heard the comment turned their faces to me quickly and stared, wide-eyed with amazement and worry. Sure enough, seconds later a shrill, whining howl broke out from the footpath to our left. A dog rushed out from its cover and launched itself at us, barking furiously. It was a small, wizened, mangy cur of a thing, not much bigger than a fair-sized Bombay rat, yet the barking was loud enough to pierce the screen of sound in our chanting.

It took only seconds, of course, for more pariah dogs to join in the howling affray. They came from left and right, single animals and groups of them, yelping and yowling and growling hideously. In an attempt to drown them out, we raised our chants to greater volume, all the while keeping our wary eyes on the snapping jaws of the dogs.

As we approached the Back Bay area we passed an open *maidan*, or field, where a party of wedding musicians dressed in bright red-and-yellow uniforms, complete with tall, plumed hats, was rehearsing its songs. Seeing our little procession as an opportunity to practise their music on the march, they swung in behind us and struck up a rousing, if not particularly canorous, version of a popular devotional song. Incited by the spectacle that our smuggling mission had become, happy children and pious adults left the footpaths and streamed toward us, joining in the thunderous chants and swelling our numbers to more than a hundred souls.

Agitated, no doubt, by the wild throng and frenzied barking, Kano the bear swayed from side to side on the cart, turning his head to follow the peaks of sound. At one point we passed a group of strolling policemen, and I risked a glance to see them standing completely still, their mouths open and their heads turning as one, like a row of mouth-clown dummies at a carnival sideshow, as we passed.

After too many long minutes of that brawling and roistering, we were near enough to Nariman Point to see the tower of the Oberoi Hotel. Worried that we'd never rid ourselves of the wedding band, I ran back to press a bundle of notes into the hand of their bandmaster, with instructions that he should turn right, away from us, and march along Marine Drive. As we neared the sea, he led his men right when we moved left. Emboldened, perhaps, by their successful tour with our little parade, the musicians launched into a medley of dance hits as they marched away toward the brighter lights of the ocean drive. Most of the crowd jigged and danced away with them. Even the dogs, lured too far beyond their prowling domain, turned away from us and crept back into the mean shadows that had spawned them.

We pushed the cart further along the sea road toward the deserted spot where the truck was parked. Just then I heard a car horn sounding, close by. My heart sinking at the thought that it was the police, I slowly turned to look. Instead, I saw Abdullah, Salman, Sanjay, and Farid standing beside Salman's car. They'd stopped in a wide parking bay, surfaced with gravel stones, that was empty but for them.

'Are you all right, Johnny?' I asked. 'Can you take it from here?'

'Sure, Lin,' he replied. 'The truck is just there, ahead of us, you see? We can do it.'

'Okay, I'll peel off here, man. Let me know how it all goes. I'll see you tomorrow. And, hey, see if you can find me one of those wanted posters, brother!'

'No problem,' he laughed, as I walked away.

I crossed the road to join Salman, Abdullah, and the others. They'd been eating take-away food bought at one of the Nariman caravans parked near the sea wall. As I greeted them, Farid swept the rubble of containers and paper towels from the roof of the car onto the gravel park space. I felt the wince of guilt that litter-conscious westerners invariably experience, and reminded myself that the mess on the road would be collected by rag-pickers who depended on the litter for their livelihood.

'What the fuck were you doing in that show?' Sanjay asked me when the greetings were made and received.

'It's a long story,' I grinned.

'That's a damn scary Ganpatti you got there,' he said. 'I never saw anything like it. It looked so real. It was like it was moving. I got quite a religious feeling. I tell you, man, I'm going to pay a bahinchudh to light some incense when I get home.'

'Come on, Lin,' Salman prodded. 'What's it all about, *yaar*?'

'Well,' I groaned, knowing that no explanation would seem sensible. 'We had to smuggle a bear out of the slum, and get him up to this spot, right here, because the cops had a warrant out on him and wanted to arrest him.'

'Smuggle a what?' Farid asked politely.

'A bear.'

'What ... kind of a bear?'

'A dancing bear, of course,' I said stiffly.

'You know, Lin,' Sanjay pronounced, grimacing happily as he picked his teeth clean with a match, 'you do some very weird shit.'

'Are you talking about *my* bear?' Abdullah asked, suddenly interested.

'Yes, fuck you. It's really all your fault, if you want to go back far enough.'

'Why do you say it was your bear?' Salman wanted to know.

'Because I arranged that bear,' Abdullah replied. 'I sent him to Lin brother, a long time ago.'

'Why?'

'Well, it was all about the hugging,' Abdullah began, laughing.

'Don't start,' I said through pressed lips, warning him off the subject with my eyes.

'What *is* all this with fuckin' *bears*?' Sanjay asked. 'Are we still talking about bears?'

'Oh, shit!' Salman cut in, looking over Sanjay's shoulder. 'Faisal is in a big hurry. And he's got Nazeer with him. This looks like trouble.'

Another Ambassador gravelled to a stop near us. A second car followed, only two seconds behind it. Faisal and Amir leapt from the first car. Nazeer and Andrew rushed forward from the second. I saw that another man got out of Faisal's car and waited there, watching the approach road. I recognised the fine features of my friend Mahmoud Melbaaf. One more man, a heavy-set gangster named Raj, waited with the boy Tariq in the second car.

'They're here!' Faisal announced breathlessly when he joined us. 'They're supposed to come tomorrow, I know, but they're already here. They just joined up with Chuha and his guys.'

'Already? How many?' Salman asked.

'Just them,' Faisal replied. 'If we move now, we get all of them. The rest of the gang is at a wedding in Thana. It's like a sign from heaven or something. It's the best chance we'll ever have. But we've got to be damn quick!'

'I can't believe it,' Salman muttered, as if to himself.

My stomach dropped and then set hard. I knew exactly what they were talking about, and what it meant for us. There'd been reports and rumours for days that Chuha and his gang within the Walidlalla council had made contact with the Sapna survivor and two of his family members, a brother and a brother-in-law. They were planning a strike against our group. The border war for new gang territory had flared, pitting Chuha's mafia council against ours, and Chuha was hungry.

The Sapna-Iran connection, all survivors from Abdul Ghani's treacherous attempted coup, had learned of the hostility between the councils, and had appeared at just the right moment to capitalise on Chuha's greed and ambition. They'd promised to bring weapons—new guns—and lucrative contacts in the Pakistani heroin trade. They were renegades: the Sapna killers were working without Abdul Ghani, and the Iranians had no official support from the Savak. It was hatred that had brought them together. They wanted revenge for the deaths of their friends, and their hate had combined with Chuha's to put murder in their minds.

The situation had been so tense, for so long, that Salman had infiltrated the Chuha gang with his own man, Little Tony, a gangster from Goa who was unknown in Bombay. He'd provided information from the inside. They were his reports that had alerted Salman to the Sapna-Iran connection and the imminent attack. With Faisal's confirmation of their arrival at Chuha's house, we all knew there was only one option Salman would consider. Fight. Make war. Put an end to the Sapna killers and the Iranian spies, once and for all. Finish Chuha. Absorb his territory. Seize his operations.

'Fuck, man! How lucky can we get?' Sanjay whooped, his eyes glittering in the grey-white streetlight.

'Are you sure?' Salman asked, fixing his friend Amir, an older man, with his sternest frown.

'I'm sure, Salman,' Amir drawled, running his hand over the short, grey hair on his blunt head. He twirled the ends of his thick moustache with the same hand as he spoke. 'I saw them myself. Abdullah's guys, from Iran, they came half an hour ago. The Sapna fucks, you know, they've been there all day. They came in the morning. Little Tony, he told us as soon as he could. We've been watching them for two hours at Chuha's place. The last time he talked to me, Little Tony said they were all getting together—Chuha and his closest guys, the Sapnas, and the guys from Iran. They were waiting for the Iran guys to get here and then they want to hit us. Soon. Maybe tomorrow night. The day after tomorrow, at the latest. Chuha sent word for a lot more guys. They're coming from Delhi and Calcutta. They're working out some kind of a plan where they hit us at about ten places at once, like, to stop us from coming back at them. I told Tony to go back and to let us know when the Iran guys got there. We were watching the place, like usual. Then we saw them walk in, a day early like, but we were pretty sure. Not long after, Little Tony came out and lit a cigarette. That was the signal. They're the ones—the ones who are after Abdullah. Now they're all in there together, and we're only two minutes away. I know it's early, but we have to go. We have to do it now, Salman, in the next five minutes.'

'How many, all together?' Salman demanded.

'Chuha and his buddies,' Amir answered in his lazy drawl. I think the slow, softly slurring style of the man gave everyone there new heart: he wasn't, or didn't seem to be, anywhere near as nervous as the rest of us. 'That makes six. One of them, Manu, is a good man. You know him. He put the Harshan brothers down, all three of them, on his own. His cousin Bichchu is also a good fighter—they don't call him the Scorpion for nothing. The rest of them, including Chuha, that madachudh, are not much. Then there's the Sapnas. That makes three more. And from Iran, two more. That's eleven. Maybe one or two more, at the most. Hussein is watching the place. He'll tell us if any more arrived.'

'Eleven,' Salman murmured, avoiding the eyes of the men while he considered the situation. 'And we are … eleven—twelve, counting Little Tony. But we have to lose two, on the street outside Chuha's house—one on each side, to slow up the cops if they come screaming on us while we're inside. I'll make a call before we go in, to keep the cops away, but we need to be sure. Chuha might have more guys coming, as well, so we need at least two on the outside. I don't mind fighting my way in there, but I don't want to fight my way out again if I don't have to. Hussein is already there. Faisal, you're the number two on the street outside, okay? Nobody goes in, or out, but us.'

'No problem,' the young fighter agreed.

'Check the guns, now, with Raj. Get them ready.'

'I'm on it,' he said, collecting guns from a few of the men and then jogging over to the cars, where Raj and Mahmoud waited.

'And two will have to go back to Khader's house with Tariq,' Salman continued.

'It was Nazeer's idea to bring him with us,' Andrew put in. 'He didn't want to leave him behind there when Faisal and Amir came to give us the news. I told him not to bring the kid, but you know how Nazeer is when he gets an idea in his head.'

'Nazeer can take the boy to Sobhan Mahmoud's house in Versova, and watch over him,' Salman declared. 'And you'll go with him.'

'Oh, come on, man!' Andrew complained. 'Why do I have to do that? Why do I have to miss all the action?'

'I need two men to watch over old Sobhan and the boy. Especially the boy—Nazeer was right not to leave him. Tariq is a target. As long as he's alive, the council is still Khader's council. If they kill him, Chuha will take a lot of power from it. The same goes for old Sobhan. Take the boy out of the city, and keep him and Sobhan Mahmoud safe.'

'But why do I have to miss the action, man? Why does it have to be me? Send someone else, Salman. Let me go with you to Chuha's.'

'Are you going to argue with me?' Salman said, his lip curling with anger.

'No, man,' Andrew snarled petulantly. 'I'll do it. I'll take the kid.'

'That leaves eight of us,' Salman concluded. 'Sanjay and me, Abdullah and Amir, Raj and little Tony, Farid and Mahmoud —'

'Nine,' I cut in. 'There's nine of us.'

'You should take off, Lin,' Salman said quietly, raising his eyes to meet mine. 'I was just now going to ask you to take a cab and pass the word to Rajubhai, and the boys at your passport shop.'

'I'm not leaving Abdullah,' I said flatly.

'Maybe you can go back with Nazeer,' Amir, who was Andrew's close friend, suggested.

'I left Abdullah once,' I declared. 'I'm not doing it again. It's like fate or something. I've got a feeling, Salman. I've got a feeling not to leave Abdullah. I'm in it. I'm not leaving Mahmoud Melbaaf, either. I'm with them. I'm with you.'

Salman held the stare, frowning pensively. It occurred to me, stupidly, that his slightly crooked face—one eye a little lower than the other, his nose bent from a bad break, his mouth scarred in the corner—found a handsome symmetry only then, when the burden of his thoughts creased his features into a determined frown.

'Okay,' he agreed, at last.

'What the *fuck*!' Andrew exploded. '*He* gets to go, but I do the *baby-sitting* job?'

'Settle down, Andrew,' Farid said soothingly.

'No, fuck him! I'm sick of this fuckin' gora, man. So Khader liked him, so he went to Afghanistan, so fuckin' what? Khader's dead, *yaar*. Khader's day is gone.'

'Relax, man,' Amir put in.

'*What* relax? Fuck Khader, and fuck his gora, too!'

'You should watch your mouth,' I muttered through clenched teeth.

'I should?' he asked, thrusting his face forward pugnaciously. 'Well, fuck your sister! How's my mouth now? You like that?'

'I don't have a sister,' I said evenly in Hindi. A few men laughed.

'Well, maybe I'll go fuck your mother,' he snarled, 'and make you a new sister!'

'That's good enough,' I growled, shaping up to fight him. 'Get 'em up! Get your fuckin' hands up! Let's go!'

It would've been messy. I wasn't a good fighter, but I knew the moves. I could hit hard. And if I got into real trouble in those years, I wasn't afraid to put the wet end of a knife into another man's body. Andrew was capable. With a gun in his hand, he was deadly. As Amir moved around to support him, directly behind his right shoulder, Abdullah took up a similar position beside me. A fight would become a brawl. We all knew it. But the young Goan didn't raise his hands, and as one second became five, and ten, and fifteen, it seemed that he wasn't as willing with his fists as he was with his mouth.

Nazeer broke the stand-off. Pushing between us, he seized Andrew by the wrist and a scruff of shirtsleeve. I knew that grip well. I knew that Andrew had to kill the burly Afghan if he wanted to break it. Nazeer paused only long enough to give me a bewilderingly cryptic look, part censure and part pride, part anger and part red-eyed affection, before he shoved the young Goan backwards through the circle of men. At the car, he pushed Andrew into the driver's seat and then climbed into the back with Tariq. Andrew started the car and sped away, spitting gravel and dust as he wheeled around and headed back toward Marine Drive. As the car swept past me I saw Tariq's face at the window. It was pale, with only the eyes, like wild paw prints in snow, betraying any hint of the mind or the mood within.

'Mai jata hu,' I repeated when the car had passed. *I'm going.* Everyone laughed. I wasn't sure if it was at the vehemence of my tone or the blunt simplicity of the Hindi phrase.

'I think we got that, Lin,' Salman said. 'I think that's very clear, *na?* Okay, I'll put you with Abdullah, out the back. There's a lane behind Chuha's house—Abdullah, you know it. It has two feeds from other lanes, one into the main street, and one around the corner to other houses in the block. At the back of Chuha's house there's a yard. I've seen it. There are two windows, both with heavy bars, and only one door to the house. It's down two steps. You two hold that place. Nobody goes in when we start. If we do right, some of them will try to make a run for it out there. Don't let them get past you. Stop them right there, in the yard. The rest of us will go in through the front. What about the guns, Faisal?'

'Seven,' he answered. 'Two short shotgun, two automatic, three revolver.'

'Give me one of the automatics,' Salman ordered. 'Abdullah, you take the other one. You'll have to share it, Lin. The shotguns are no good inside—it's gonna get very close in there, and we want to be real sure what we're shooting at. I want them on the street outside, for maximum coverage if we need it. Faisal, you take the shotguns, and give one to Hussein. When we're finished, we'll go out the back way, past Abdullah and Lin. We won't go out the front, so put holes in anything that tries to go in or out once we're in there. The three other guns are for Farid, Amir, and Mahmoud. Raj, you'll have to share with us. Okay?'

The men nodded, and wagged their heads in agreement.

'Listen, if we wait, we can get thirty more men and thirty guns to go in with us. You know that. But we might miss them. As it is, we've already talked for ten minutes too long. If we hit them now, quick and hard, before they know it, we can take them out, and none of them will get away. I want to finish them, and finish this business, right now, tonight. But I want to leave it up to you. I don't want to make you go in if you don't feel ready. Do you want to wait for more men, or go now?'

One by one the men spoke, quickly, most of them using the one word, *Abi*, meaning now. Salman nodded, then closed his eyes and muttered a prayer in Arabic. When he looked up again, he was committed, fully committed for the first time. His eyes were blazing with hatred and the fearsome killing rage he'd kept at bay.

'Saatch ... *aur himmat*,' he said, looking each man in the eye. *Truth ... and courage.*

'Saatch aur himmat,' they replied.

Without another word, the men claimed their guns, climbed into the two cars, and drove the few short minutes to Chuha's home on fashionable Sardar Patel Road. Before I could order my thoughts and even consider, clearly, what I was doing, I found myself creeping along a narrow lane with Abdullah in a darkness deep enough for me to feel the widening of my straining eyes. Then we climbed over a sheer wooden fence and dropped down into the backyard of the enemy's house.

We stood together in the dark for a few moments, checking the luminous dials on our watches, and listening hard as we let our eyes adjust. Abdullah whispered beside me, and I almost jumped at the sound.

'Nothing,' he breathed, his voice like the rustle of a woollen blanket. 'There's no-one here, no-one near.'

'Looks okay,' I answered, aware that my whispering voice was raspy with hard-breathing fear. There were no lights at the windows or behind the blue door at the rear of the house.

'Well, I kept my promise,' Abdullah whispered mysteriously.

'What?'

'You made me promise to take you with me, when I kill Chuha. Remember?'

'Yeah,' I answered, my heart beating faster than a healthy heart should. 'You gotta be careful, I guess.'

'I will be careful, Lin brother.'

'No—I mean, you gotta be careful what you wish for in life, *na*?'

'I will try to open that door,' Abdullah breathed, close to my ear. 'If it will open, I will go inside.'

'*What?*'

'You wait here, and stay near the door.'

'*What?*'

'You wait here, and —'

'We're *both* supposed to stay here!' I hissed.

'I know,' he replied, creeping with leopard stealth toward the door.

In my clumsier way, looking more like a cat waking stiffly from a long sleep, I crept after him. As I reached the two wide steps leading down to the blue door, I saw him open it and slip inside the house like a shadow thrown by a swooping bird. He pushed the door shut soundlessly behind him.

Alone, in the dark, I took my knife from the sheath in the small of my back, and enclosed the hilt in my right fist, dagger-point down. Staring out into the darkness, I put all of my focus on the beating of my heart, trying by force of will to slow its too-rapid pace. It worked, after a time. I felt the count reducing, calming me further in turn as the meditative loop closed around a single, still thought. That thought was of Khaderbhai, and the formula he'd made me repeat so often: *The wrong thing, for the right reasons.* And I knew, as I repeated the words in the fearing dark, that the fight with Chuha, the war, the struggle for power, was always the same, everywhere, and it was always wrong.

Salman and the others, no less than Chuha and the Sapna killers and all the rest of them, were pretending that their little kingdoms made them kings; that their power struggles made them powerful. And they didn't. They couldn't. I saw that then so clearly that it was like understanding a mathematical theorem for the first time. The only kingdom that makes any man a king is the kingdom of his own soul. The only power that has any real meaning is the power to better the world. And only men like

Qasim Ali Hussein and Johnny Cigar were such kings and had such power.

Unnerved and afraid, I pressed my ear to the door and strained to hear anything of Abdullah or the others within. The fear that twisted in me wasn't the fear of death. I wasn't afraid to die. I was afraid of being so injured or wounded that I couldn't walk, or couldn't see or, for some other reason, couldn't run from capture. Above all things I was afraid of that—of being captured and caged again. As I pressed my ear to the door, I prayed that no wound would weaken me. *Let it happen here*, I prayed. *Let me get through this, or let me die here ...*

I don't know where they came from. I felt the hands on me before I heard a single sound. Two men slammed me round and hard up against the door. Instinctively, I struck out with my right hand.

'*Chaku! Chaku!*' one of the men shouted. *Knife! Knife!*

I couldn't swing the knife up quickly enough to stop them. One man pinned me to the door by the throat. He was a big man, and very strong. The other man used two hands, trying to force me to drop the knife. He wasn't quite so strong, and he couldn't make me drop the weapon. Then a third man hopped down the steps from the darkness, and with those extra hands they twisted my grip and forced me to drop the knife.

'*Gora kaun hai?*' the new man asked. *Who's the white guy?*

'*Bahinchudh! Malum nahi,*' the strong man replied. *The sisterfucker! I don't know.*

He stared at me, obviously bewildered to have stumbled on a foreigner who was listening at the door and armed with a knife.

'*Kaun hai tum?*' he asked in an almost friendly tone. *Who are you?*

I didn't reply. All I could think was that I had to warn Abdullah somehow. I couldn't understand how they'd reached that spot without making a sound. The back gate must've swung silently on its hinges. Their shoes or chappals must've been soled with soft rubber. Whatever. I'd let them sneak up on me, and I had to warn Abdullah.

I suddenly struggled as if I was trying to break free. The feint had its effect. The men all shouted at me, and three pairs of hands slammed me against the blue door. One of the smaller men scrambled to my left side, pinning my left arm to the door. The other short man held my right arm. In the wrestle, I managed to kick my boots hard against the door three times. *Abdullah must've heard it*, I thought. *It's okay ... I've warned him ...*

He must know something's wrong ...

'Kaun hai tum?' the big man asked again. He took one hand from my throat, and bunched it into a fist poised menacingly close to my head, just below the line of sight of my eyes. *Who are you?*

Again I refused to answer, staring at him. Their hands, as hard as shackles, held me to the door.

He slammed his fist into my face. I managed to move my head, just slightly, but I felt the blow on my jaw and cheek. He had rings on his fingers, or he was using a knuckleduster. I couldn't see it, but I could feel the hard metal chipping bone.

'What you are doing here?' he asked in English. 'Who you are?'

I kept silent, and he struck me again, the fist ramming into my face three times. *I know this ...* I thought. *I know this ...* I was back in prison, in Australia, in the punishment unit—the fists and boots and batons.. *I know this ...*

He paused, waiting for me to speak. The two smaller men grinned at him, then at me. *Aur,* one of them said. *More. Hit him again.* The big man drew back and punched at my body. They were slow, deliberate, professional punches. I felt the wind empty from my body, and it was as if my life itself was draining from me. He moved up the body to my chest and throat and face. I felt myself wading into that black water where beaten boxers stagger and fall. I was done. I was finished.

I wasn't angry with them. I'd fucked up. I'd let them sneak up on me— *walk* up on me, probably. I'd gone there to fight, and I should've been on guard. It was my fault. Somehow, I'd missed them, and messed up, and it was my own fault. All I wanted to do was warn Abdullah. I kicked back feebly at the door, hoping he would hear it and get away, get away, get away ...

I fell through perfect darkness, and the weight of all the world fell with me. When I hit the floor I heard shouts, and I realised that Abdullah had wrenched open the door, letting us fall into him. In the dark, bloody-eyed and swollen, I heard a gun firing twice, and saw the flashes. Then light filled the world, and I blinked into the glare as another door opened somewhere, and I saw men rushing in on us. The gun fired again twice, three times, and I rolled out from under the big man to see my knife, close to my eyes, shining on the ground near the open blue door.

I grabbed for the knife just as one of the smaller men tried to crawl over me and out the door. Without thinking, I swept it backwards and into his hip. He screamed, and I scrambled up to him, slashing the knife across his face near the eyes.

It's amazing how a little of the other guy's blood, or a lot of it, if you can manage it, puts power in your arms and pain-killing adrenaline in your aching wounds. Wild with rage, I swung round to see Abdullah locked in a struggle with two men. There were bodies on the floor of the room. I couldn't tell how many. Gunshots cracked and drummed from all around and above us in the other rooms of the building. They seemed to come from several places in the house at the same time. There were shouts and screams. I could smell shit and piss and blood in the room. Someone had a gut wound. I hoped that it wasn't me. My left hand slapped at my belly and searched, frisking myself for wounds.

Abdullah was punching it out with the two men. They were wrestling, gouging, biting. I began to crawl toward them, but I felt a hand on my leg pulling me backward. It was a strong hand. A very strong hand. It was the big guy.

He'd been shot, I was sure, but I couldn't see any blood on his shirt or his pants. He dragged me in as if I was a turtle caught in a net. When I reached him, I raised the knife to stab him, but he beat me to it. He slammed his fist into the right side of my groin. He'd missed the killing blow, a direct hit, but it was still enough to make me curl and roll over in agonising pain. I felt him lurch past me, actually using my body for leverage as he pushed himself to his feet. I rolled back, retching bile, to see him stand and take a step toward Abdullah.

I couldn't let it happen. Too many times, my heart had withered on the thought of Abdullah's death: alone, in a circle of guns. I thrashed against the pain, and in a scrabble of bloody, slipping movements I sprang up and plunged my knife into the big guy's back. It was high, just under the scapula. I felt the bone shiver under the blade, diverting the point sideways toward the shoulder. He was strong. He took two more steps, dragging my body with him on the hook of the knife, before he crumpled and fell. I fell on top of him, looking up to see Abdullah. He had his fingers in a man's eyes. The man's head was bent backwards against Abdullah's knee. The man's jaw gave way, and his neck cracked like a piece of kindling.

Hands pulled at me, dragging me toward the back door. I struck out, but strong, gentle hands twisted the knife from my fingers. Then I heard the voice, Mahmoud Melbaaf's voice, and I knew we were safe.

'Come on, Lin,' the Iranian said, quickly and too quietly, it seemed, for the bloody violence that had just roared around us.

'I need a gun,' I mumbled.

'No, Lin. It is over.'

'Abdullah?' I asked, as Mahmoud dragged me into the yard.

'He's working,' he replied. I heard the screams inside the house ending, one by one, like birds falling silent as night moves across the stillness of a lake. 'Can you stand? Can you walk? We must leave now!'

'Fuck, yes! I can make it.'

As we reached the back gate, a column of our men rushed past us. Faisal and Hussein carried one man between them. Farid and Little Tony carried another. Sanjay had a man's body on his right shoulder. He was sobbing as he clutched the body to his chest and shoulder.

'We lost Salman,' Mahmoud announced, following my gaze as we let the men rush past us. 'And Raj, also. Amir is bad—alive, but hurt bad.'

Salman. The last voice of reason in the Khader council. The last Khader man. I hurried down the lane to the waiting cars and I felt the life draining from me, just as it had when the big man was hitting me at the blue door. It was over. The old mafia council was gone with Salman. Everything had changed. I looked at the others in my car: Mahmoud, Farid, and the wounded Amir. They'd won their war. The Sapna killers were gone at last. A chapter, a book of life and death that had opened with Sapna's name, was closed forever. Khader was avenged. Abdul Ghani's mutinous betrayal was finally defeated. And the Iranians, Abdullah's enemies, were no more: as silent as that bloody, unscreaming house where Abdullah was ... working. And Chuha's gang was crushed. The border war was over. It was over. The wheel had turned through one full revolution, and nothing would ever be the same. They'd won, but they were all crying. All of them. Crying.

I let my head fall back on the seat of the car. Night, that tunnel of lights joining promise to prayer, flew with us at the windows. Slowly, des-olately, the fist of what we'd done unclenched the clawed palm of what we'd become. Anger softened into sorrow, as it always does, as it always must. And no part of what we'd wanted, just an hour's life before, was as rich in hope or meaning as a single teardrop's fall.

'What?' Mahmoud asked, his face close to mine. 'What did you say?'

'I hope that bear got away,' I mumbled through broken, bleeding lips as the stricken spirit began to rise from my wounded body, and sleep, like fog in morning forests, moved through my sorrowing mind. 'I hope that bear got away.'

CHAPTER FORTY-TWO

Sunlight shattered on the water, shedding streaks in crystal-brilliant slivers across waves rolling swollen on the broad meniscus of the bay. Birds of fire in the approaching sunset wheeled and turned as one in their flocks, like banners of waving silk. From a low-walled courtyard on the white marble island of Haji Ali Mosque, I watched pilgrims and pious local residents wend and weave, leaving the shrine for the shore along the flat stone path. The incoming tide would submerge the path, they knew, and then only boats could bring them home. Those who'd sorrowed or repented, like others on previous days, had cast garlands of flowers upon the shallower, receding sea. Riding the returning tide, those orange-red and faded grey-white flowers floated back, garlanding the path itself with the love, loss, and longing that was prayed upon the water by a thousand broken hearts each wave-determined day.

And we, that band of brothers, had come to the shrine to pay our last respects, as they say, and pray for the soul of our friend Salman Mustaan. It was the first time since the night he'd been killed that we'd gathered as a group. For weeks after the battle with Chuha and his gang we'd separated, to hide and to heal our wounds. There'd been an outcry in the press, of course. The words *carnage* and *massacre* were spread across the pages of the Bombay dailies like butter on a prison guard's sugared bun. Calls had rung out for justice, undefined, and punishment, unremitting. And there was no doubt that the Bombay police could've made arrests. They certainly knew which gang was responsible for the little heaps of bodies they'd found in Chuha's house. But there were four good reasons not to act: reasons that were more compelling, for the city's cops, than the unrighteous indignation of the press.

First, there was no-one from inside the house, on the streets outside, or anywhere else in Bombay who was willing to testify against us, even off the record. Second, the battle had put an end to the Sapna killers, which was something the cops would've been very glad to take care of personally. Third, the Walidlalla gang under Chuha's leadership had killed a policeman, months before, when he'd stumbled into one of their major drug deals near Flora Fountain. The case had remained unsolved, officially, because the cops had nothing they could take into court. But they'd known, almost from the day it had happened, that Chuha's men had spilled the blood. The bloodshed in Chuha's house was very close to what the cops themselves had wanted to do to the Rat and his men—and would've accomplished, sooner or later, if Salman hadn't beaten them to it. And fourth, the payment of a crore of rupees, appropriated from Chuha's operations and applied in liberal smears to a small multitude of forensic palms, had put a helpless shrug in all the right constabulary shoulders.

Privately, the cops told Sanjay, who was the new leader of the Khader Khan council, that the clock was ticking on him, and he'd used up all his chances on that one throw of the dice. They wanted peace—and continued prosperity, of course—and, if he didn't pull his men into line, they would do it for him. *And by the way*, they told him after accepting his ten-million-rupee bribe, and just before they threw him back onto the street, *that guy Abdullah, in your outfit, we don't want to see him again. Ever. He was dead once, in Bombay. He'll be dead again, for good this time, if we see him ...*

One by one, after weeks of lying low, we'd made our way back into the city and back to the jobs we'd done in the Sanjay gang, as it had become known. I returned from hiding in Goa and took up my position in the passport operation with Villu and Krishna. When the call finally went out for us to gather at Haji Ali, I rode to the shrine on my Enfield bike, and walked with Abdullah and Mahmoud Melbaaf across the rippling wavelets of the bay.

Mahmoud led the prayers, kneeling at the front of our group. The little balcony, one of many surrounding the island mosque, was ours alone. Facing toward Mecca, and with the breeze filling and then falling from his white shirt, Mahmoud spoke for all the men who knelt or stood behind him:

> Praise be to God, Lord of the Universe,
> The Compassionate, the Merciful,
> Sovereign of the Day of Judgement!

You alone we worship, and to You alone we turn for help.
Guide us to the straight path ...

Farid, Abdullah, Amir, Faisal, and Nazeer—the Muslim core of the council—knelt behind Mahmoud. Sanjay was a Hindu. Andrew was a Christian. They knelt beside me and behind the praying group. I stood with my head bowed and my hands clasped in front of me. I knew the words of the prayers and I knew the simple standing, kneeling, and bowing observations. I could've joined in. I knew that Mahmoud and the others would've been delighted if I had. But I couldn't bring myself to kneel with them. The separation that they found so easy and instinctual—this is my criminal life, over here, and that's my religious life, over there—was impossible for me. I did speak to Salman, whispering my hope that he'd found peace, wherever he was. Yet I was too self-consciously aware of the darkness in my heart to offer more than that tiny prayer. So I stood in silence, feeling like an impostor, a spy on that island of devotions, as the amethyst evening blessed the balcony of praying men with gold-and-lilac light. And the words of Mahmoud's prayer seemed a perfect fit for my withered honour and my thinning pride: *those who have incurred your wrath ... those who have gone astray ...*

At the end of prayers we hugged one another, according to custom, and made our way back along the path toward the shore. Mahmoud was leading the way. We'd all prayed, in our own ways, and we'd all cried for Salman, but we didn't look the part of devout visitors to the holy shrine. We all wore sunglasses. We all wore new clothes. Everyone, except me, carried a year or more of smuggler's wages in gold chains, first-tier watches, rings, and bracelets. And we swaggered. We walked the walk: the little dance-step that fighting-fit gangsters do when they're armed and dangerous. It was a bizarre procession, and one so menacing that we had to work hard to make the professional beggars on the island pathway take the sheaves of rupee notes we'd brought as alms.

The men had three cars parked near the sea wall. It was almost exactly where I'd stood with Abdullah on the night I met Khaderbhai. My bike was parked beyond them, and at the cars I paused to say goodbye.

'Come and have a meal with us, Lin,' Sanjay offered, putting real affection in the invitation.

I knew the meal would be fun, after the melancholy observations at the shrine, and that it would include a choice of drugs and a choice of happy, silly, pretty girls. I was grateful for the offer, but I refused.

'Thanks, man, but I'm meeting someone.'

'*Arrey*, bring her along, *yaar*,' Sanjay suggested. 'It's a girl, isn't it?'

'Yeah. It's a girl. But … we have to talk. I'll see you guys later.'

Abdullah and Nazeer wanted to walk me to my bike. We'd only taken a few steps when Andrew ran up behind us and called me to stop.

'Lin,' he said quickly, nervously, 'what happened with us in the car park and all. I … I just want to say … I'm sorry, *yaar*. I've been wanting to make—well—an apology, you know?'

'It's okay.'

'No—it's not okay.'

He pulled at my arm, near the elbow, leading me away from Nazeer and just out of his hearing. Leaning in close to me, he spoke softly and quickly.

'I'm not sorry for what I said about Khaderbhai. I know he was the boss and all, and I know you … you kind of loved him …'

'Yeah. I kinda did.'

'But still, I'm not sorry for what I said about him. You know, all his holy preaching, it didn't stop him from handing old Madjid over to Ghani and his Sapna guys when he needed someone to take the fuckin' fall, and keep the cops off his back. Madjid was supposed to be his friend, *yaar*. But he let them cut him up, just to throw the cops off the case.'

'Well …'

'And all those rules, about this and that and what-all, you know, they came to nothing—Sanjay has put me in charge of Chuha's girls, and the videos. And Faisal and Amir, they're running the garad. We're gonna make fuckin' crores out of it. I'm getting my place on the council, and so are they. So, Khaderbhai's day is over, just like I said it was.'

I looked back into Andrew's camel-brown eyes, and let out a deep breath. Dislike had been simmering since the night in the car park. I hadn't forgotten what he'd said, and how close we'd come to fighting it out. His little speech had made me angrier still. If we hadn't just been to a funeral service for a friend we'd both liked, I probably would've hit him already.

'You know, Andrew,' I muttered, not smiling, 'I gotta tell ya, I'm not gettin' much comfort from this little apology of yours.'

'That's not the apology, Lin,' he explained, frowning in puzzlement. 'The apology is for your mother, and for what I said about her. I'm sorry, man. I'm really, really, sorry for what I said. It was a very shitty thing to say—about *your* mother, or *anybody's* mother. Nobody should say shitty things like that about a guy's mother. You would've been well within your rights, *yaar*, to take a fuckin' shot at me. And … I'm damn glad you didn't. Mothers are sacred, *yaar*, and I'm sure your mother is a very fine lady. So, please, I'm asking you, like—please accept my apology.'

'It's okay,' I said, putting out my hand. He seized the hand in both of his, and shook it vigorously.

Abdullah, Nazeer, and I turned away and walked to the bike. Abdullah was unusually quiet. The silence he carried with him was ominous and unsettling.

'Are you going back to Delhi tonight?' I asked.

'Yes,' he answered. 'At midnight.'

'You want me to go to the airport with you?'

'No. Thank you. It is better not. There should be no police looking at me. If you are there, they will look at us. But maybe I will see you in Delhi. There is a job in Sri Lanka—you should do it with me.'

'I don't know, man,' I demurred, grinning in surprise at his earnestness. 'There's a war on in Sri Lanka.'

'There is no man, and no place, without war,' he replied, and it struck me that it was the most profound thing he'd ever said to me. 'The only thing we can do is choose a side, and fight. That is the only choice we get —who we fight for, who we fight against. That is life.'

'I … I hope there's more to it than that, brother. But, shit, maybe you're right.'

'I think you can do this with me,' he pressed, clearly troubled by what he was asking me to do. 'This is the last work for Khaderbhai.'

'What do you mean?'

'Khader Khan, he asked me to do this job for him, when the … what is it—the *sign*, I think, or the message—when it comes from Sri Lanka. Now, the message, it has come.'

'I'm sorry, brother, I don't know what you're talking about,' I stated softly, not wanting to make it harder for him. 'Just take it easy, and explain it to me. What message?'

He spoke to Nazeer quickly, in Urdu. The older man nodded several times and then said something about names, or not mentioning names. Nazeer turned his head to face me, and favoured me with a wide, warm smile.

'In the Sri Lanka war,' Abdullah explained, 'there is fighting—Tamil Tigers against Sri Lanka army. Tigers are Hindus. Sinhalese, they are Buddhist. But in the middle of them, there are the others—Tamil Muslims—with no guns and no army. Everybody kill them, and nobody fight for them. They need passports and money—gold money. We go to help them.'

'Khaderbhai,' Nazeer added, 'he make this plan. Only three men. Abdullah, and me, and one gora—you. Three men. We go.'

I owed him. Nazeer would never mention that fact, I knew, and he wouldn't hold it against me if I didn't go with him. We'd been through too much together. But I *did* owe him my life. It would be very hard to refuse him. And there was something else—something wise, perhaps, and fervently generous—in that rare, wide smile he'd given me. It seemed that he was offering me more than just the chance to work with him, and work off my debt. He blamed himself for Khader's death, but he knew that I still felt guilty and ashamed that I hadn't been there with him, pretending to be his American, when Khader had died. *He's giving me a chance*, I thought, as I let my eyes move from his to Abdullah's and back again. *He's giving me a way to close the book on it.*

'So, when would you be going on this trip? Roughly speaking?'

'Soon,' Abdullah laughed. 'A few months, no more than that. I am going to Delhi. I will send someone to bring you, when the time is coming. Two, three months, Lin brother.'

I heard a voice in my head—or not a voice, really, but just words in whispered echoes like stones hissing across the still surface of a lake— *Killer ... He's a killer ... Don't do it ... Get away ... Get away now ...* And the voice was right, of course. Dead right. And I wish I could say that it took me more than those few heartbeats to make up my mind to join him.

'Two, three months,' I replied, offering my hand. He shook it, putting both of his hands over mine. I looked at Nazeer and smiled as I spoke into his eyes. 'We'll do Khader's job. We'll finish it.'

Nazeer's jaw locked tight, bunching the muscles of his cheeks and exaggerating the downward curve of his mouth. He frowned at his sandaled feet as if they were disobedient puppies. Then he suddenly hurled himself at me, and locked his hands behind me in a punishing hug. It was the violent, wrestler's hug of a man whose body had never learned to speak the language of his heart—except when he was dancing—and it ended as abruptly and furiously as it had begun. He whipped his thick arms away and shoved me backward with his chest, shaking his head and shuddering as if a shark had passed him in shallow water. He looked up quickly, and the warmth that reddened his eyes vied with a grim warning clamped in the bad-luck horseshoe of his mouth. I knew that if I ever raised that moment of affection with him, or referred to it in any way, I would lose his friendship forever.

I kicked the bike to life and straddled it, pushing away from the kerb with my legs and pointing it in the direction of Nana Chowk and Colaba.

'*Saatch aur himmat,*' Abdullah called out as I rode past him.

I waved, and nodded, but I couldn't give the answering call to the slogan. I didn't know how much truth or courage was in my decision to join them on their mission to Sri Lanka. Not much, it seemed to me, as I rode away from them, from all of them, and surrendered to the warm night, and the press and pause of traffic.

A blood-red moon was rising from the sea as I reached the Back Bay road leading to Nariman Point. I parked the bike beside a cold-drink stall, locked it, and threw the keys to the manager, who was a friend from the slum. With the moon behind me, I set out along the footpath beside a long curve of sandy beach where fishermen often repaired their nets and battered boats. There was a festival on that night in the Sassoon Dock area. The celebrations had drawn most of the local people from the huts and shelters on the beach. The road where I walked was almost deserted.

And then I saw her. She was sitting on the edge of an old fishing boat that was half-buried on the beach. Only the prow and a few metres of the long boat's gunnels protruded from the surrounding waves of sand. She was wearing a long, salwar top over loose pants. Her knees were drawn up, and she was resting her chin on her arms as she stared out at the dark water.

'This is why I like you, you know,' I said, sitting down beside her on the rail of the beached fishing boat.

'Hello, Lin,' she replied, smiling, her green eyes as dark as the water. 'I'm glad to see you. I thought you weren't coming.'

'Your message sounded kind of ... urgent. I nearly didn't get it. It was just lucky that I ran into Didier on his way to the airport, and he told me.'

'Luck is what happens to you when fate gets tired of waiting,' she murmured.

'Fuck you, Karla,' I replied, laughing.

'Old habits,' she grinned, 'die hard—and lie harder.'

Her eyes moved across my features for a moment, as if she was searching a map for a familiar reference point. Her smile slowly faded.

'I'm going to miss Didier.'

'Me, too,' I muttered, thinking that he was probably in the air already, and on his way to Italy. 'But I think he'll be back before too long.'

'Why?'

'I put the Zodiac Georges in his apartment, to look after it.'

'Ooooh!' she winced, making a perfect kiss of her perfect mouth.

'Yeah. If that doesn't bring him back quick, nothing will. You know how he loves that apartment.'

She didn't answer, but her stare tightened in the intensity of her concentration.

'Khaled's here, in India,' she remarked flatly, watching my eyes.

'Where?'

'In Delhi—well, *near* Delhi, actually.'

'When?'

'The report came in two days ago. I had it checked. I think it's him.'

'What report?'

She looked away, towards the sea, and breathed a long, slow sigh.

'Jeet has access to all the wire services. One of them sent a report about a new spiritual leader named Khaled Ansari, who walked all the way from Afghanistan, and was pulling in big crowds of followers wherever he went. When I saw it, I asked Jeet to check it out for me. His people sent a description, and it fits.'

'Wow ... thank God ... thank God.'

'Yeah, maybe,' she murmured. Something of the old mischief and mystery flared in her eyes.

'And you're sure it's him?'

'Sure enough to go there myself,' she answered, looking at me once more.

'Do you know where he is—now, I mean?'

'Not exactly, but I think I know where he's going.'

'Where?'

'Varanasi. Khaderbhai's teacher, Idriss, lives there. He's very old now, but he still teaches there.'

'Khaderbhai's *teacher?*' I asked, stunned to think that in all the hundreds of hours I'd spent with Khader, listening to his philosophy lectures, he'd never mentioned the name.

'Yes. I met him once, right at the start, when I first came to India, with Khader. I was ... I don't know ... I guess you'd call it a nervous breakdown. There was this plane, going to Singapore. I don't even know how I got on it. And I broke down—just, kind of, cracked up. And Khader, he was on the same plane. And he put his arm around me. I told him everything ... absolutely ... everything. And next thing, I'm in this cave with a giant Buddha statue and this teacher named Idriss—Khader's teacher.'

There was a pause while she let those memories pull her into the past, but then she shook herself free, and back into the moment.

'I think that's where Khaled is going—to see Idriss. The old guru fascinated him. He was obsessed about meeting him. I don't know why he never got around to it then, but I think that's where he's headed now. Or maybe he's already there. He used to ask me about him all the time. Idriss taught Khader everything he knew about Resolution theory, and —'

'About what?'

'Resolution theory. That's what Khader called it, but he said it was Idriss who gave it that name. It was his philosophy of life, Khader's philosophy, about how the universe is always moving toward —'

'Complexity,' I interrupted. 'I know. I talked about it a lot with him. But he never called it Resolution theory. And he never talked about Idriss.'

'That's funny, because I think he loved Idriss, you know, like a father. Once, he called him the teacher of all teachers. And I know he wanted to retire up there, not far from Varanasi, with Idriss. Anyway, that's where I'm going to start looking for Khaled.'

'When?'

'Tomorrow.'

'O-*kay*,' I responded, avoiding her eyes. 'Is this ... is this anything to do with ... well, you and Khaled, from before?'

'You can be such a *fuck* sometimes, Lin, you know that?'

I looked up sharply, but I didn't respond.

'Did you know Ulla's in town?' she asked after a while.

'No. When did she get in? Have you seen her?'

'That's just it. I got a message from her. She was at the President, and she wanted to see me right away.'

'Did you go?'

'I didn't want to,' she mused. 'If *you* got the message, would *you* have gone?'

'I guess,' I answered, staring out at the bay where moonlight crested on the serpent curves of a gently rolling sea. 'But not for *her*. For Modena. I saw him a while ago. He's still nuts about her.'

'I saw him tonight,' she said quietly.

'Tonight?'

'Yes. Just before. With her. It freaked me out. I went to the hotel and up to her room. There was another guy there, a guy named Ramesh —'

'Modena told me about him. They're friends.'

'So, he opens the door, and I walk in, and I see Ulla, sitting on the bed, resting her back against the wall. And Modena, he's lying across her legs, with his head back near her shoulder. That face ...'

'I know. It's a hell of a mess.'

'It was weird. It was freaking me out, the whole scene. I'm not sure why. And Ulla, she tells me she inherited a lot of money from her father —they're very rich, you know, Ulla's family. They practically own the town in Germany where she was born, but they cut her off cold when she was heavy into drugs. She never got a thing from them for years— not until her father died. So when she inherited the money, she got this idea to come back and look for Modena. She felt guilty, she said, and she couldn't live with herself. And she found him. He was waiting for her. And they were together, when I went to see her, like some ... some kind of a love story.'

'Damn, if he wasn't right about her,' I said softly. 'He told me—he *knew* she'd come back for him, and she really did. I never believed it for a second. I thought he was just crazy.'

'The way they were sitting together, with him across her legs. You know the Pieta? Michelangelo? It looked exactly like that. It was so strange. It really shook me up. Some things are so weird they make you angry, you know?'

'What did she want?'

'What do you mean?'

'Why did she call you to the hotel?'

'Oh, I get it,' she said, with a little smile. 'Ulla always wants *something*.'

I raised an eyebrow, returning her stare, but said nothing.

'She wanted me to arrange a passport for Modena. He's been here for years. He's an overstayer. And he's got a few problems with the Spanish police, under his own name. He needs a new passport to get back into Europe. He could pass for Italian. Or maybe Portuguese.'

'Leave it to me,' I said calmly, thinking that I knew the reason, at last, why she'd asked me to meet with her. 'I'll get on it tomorrow. I know how to get in touch with him, for photos and whatever—although there'd be no mistaking *his* face at a customs check. I'll fix it.'

'Thanks,' she said, meeting my eyes with such fervent intensity that my heart began to beat hard against my chest. *It is always a fool's mistake,* Didier once said to me, *to be alone with someone you shouldn't have loved.* 'What are you doing, Lin?'

'Sitting here with you,' I replied, smiling.

'No, I mean, what are you going to do? Are you going to stay in Bombay?'

'Why?'

'I was going to ask you … if you want to come with me, to find Khaled.'

I laughed, but she didn't laugh with me.

'That's the second-best offer I've had today.'

'The *second* best?' she drawled. 'What was the first?'

'Someone invited me to go to the war, in Sri Lanka.'

She clamped her lips tightly around an angry response, but I held my hands up in surrender, and spoke quickly.

'I'm just kidding, Karla, just kidding. Take it easy. I mean, it's *true* about the invitation to go to Sri Lanka, but I'm just … you know.'

She relaxed, smiling again.

'I'm out of practice. It's been a long time, Lin.'

'So … why the invitation now?'

'Why not?'

'That's not good enough, Karla, and you know it.'

'Okay,' she sighed, glancing at me and then looking away to follow the breeze weaving wave-patterns on the sand. 'I guess I was hoping to find something like … like what we had in Goa.'

'What about … *Jeet*?' I asked, ignoring the opening she'd given me. 'How does he feel about you going off to find Khaled?'

'We lead separate lives. We do what we want. We go where we want.'

'Sounds … *breezy*,' I offered, struggling to find a word that wasn't a lie, but wouldn't offend. 'Didier made it sound more serious than that—told me the guy asked you to marry him.'

'He did,' she said flatly.

'And?'

'And what?'

'And will you—marry him, I mean?'

'Yes. I think I will.'

'Why?'

'Why not?'

'Don't start that again.'

'Sorry,' she said, sighing through a tired smile. 'I've been running with a different crowd. Why marry Jeet? He's a nice guy, he's healthy, and he's loaded. And, hey, I think I'll do a better job of spending his money than he does.'

'So what you're telling me is that you're ready to die for this love.'

She laughed and then turned to me, suddenly serious again. Her eyes, pale with moonlight; her eyes, the green of water lilies after the rain; her long hair, black as forest river stones; her hair that was like holding the night itself in the wrap of my fingers; her lips, starred with incandescent light; lips of camellia-petal softness warmed with secret whispers. Beautiful. And I loved her. I loved her still so much, so hard, but with no heat or heart at all. That falling love, that helpless, dreaming, soaring love, was gone. And I suddenly knew in those seconds of … cold adoration, I suppose … that the power she'd once held over me was also gone. Or, more than that, her power had moved into me, and had become mine. I held all the cards. And then I wanted to know. It wasn't good enough to just accept what had happened between us. I wanted to know everything.

'Why didn't you tell me, Karla?'

She gave an anguished little sigh, and stretched her legs out to bury her bare feet in the sand. Watching the small cascades of soft sand spill over her moving feet, she spoke in a dull, flat tone, as if she was composing a letter—or recalling a letter, perhaps, that she'd written once and never sent to me.

'I knew you were going to ask me, and I think that's why I've waited so long to get in touch with you. I let people know that I was around, and I asked after you, but I didn't do anything, until today, because … I knew you'd ask me.'

'If it makes it any easier,' I interrupted, sounding harder than I'd intended, 'I know you burned down Madame Zhou's place —'

'Did Ghani tell you that?'

'Ghani? No. I figured that one out myself.'

'Ghani did it for me—he arranged it. That was the last time I spoke to him.'

'The last time I spoke to him was about an hour before he died.'

'Did he tell you anything about her?' she asked, perhaps hoping that there were some parts of it she wouldn't have to tell me.

'About Madame Zhou? No. He didn't say a word.'

'He told me … a lot,' she sighed. 'He filled in a few gaps. I think it was Ghani who tipped me over the edge with her. He told me she had Rajan following you, and she only pulled her strings with the cops to get you arrested when Rajan told her you made love to me. I always hated her, but that did it. I just … it was one thing too many. She couldn't let me have it, that time with you. She wouldn't let me have it. So I called in some dues with Ghani, and he arranged it. The riot. It was a great fire. I lit some of it myself.'

She broke off, staring at her feet in the sand, and clamped her jaw shut. Reflected lights gleamed in her eyes. For a moment I let myself imagine how those green eyes must've blazed with firelight as she'd watched the Palace burn.

'I know about the States, too,' I said after a while. 'I know what happened there.'

She looked at me quickly, reading my eyes.

'Lisa,' she said. I didn't answer. Then, knowing instantly, as women do, what she couldn't possibly know, she smiled. 'That's good—Lisa and you. You and Lisa. That's … very good.'

My expression didn't change, and her smile faded as she looked down at the sand once more.

'Did you kill anyone, Lin?'

'When?' I asked, not sure if she was talking about Afghanistan or the much-smaller war against Chuha and his gang.

'Ever.'

'No.'

'I'm glad,' she breathed, sighing again. 'I wish ...'

She was silent again for a while. From somewhere beyond the deserted beach we heard the sounds of the festival: happy, roaring laughter rising over the blare of a brass band. Much closer, ocean music gushed onto the soft assenting shore, and the palms above us trembled in the cooling breeze.

'When I went there ... when I walked into his house, into the room where he was standing, he smiled at me. He was ... actually ... happy to see me. And for a split second, I changed my mind, and I thought it was ... over. Then, I saw something else, right there in the middle of his smile ... something dirty, and ... he said ... *I knew you'd be back for more, one of these days* ... or something like that. And he ... he kind of, he started looking around like he was making sure nobody was gonna bust in on us ...'

'It's okay, Karla.'

'When he saw the gun, it was worse, because he started ... not begging ... but *apologising* ... and it was real clear, real clear, that he knew what he did to me ... he knew ... every part of it, and how bad it was. And that was much worse. And then he was dead. There wasn't a lot of blood. I thought there would be. Maybe there was later. And I don't remember the rest, until I was in the plane with Khader's arm around me.'

She was quiet. I leaned over to pick up a conical shell descending in spirals to a sharp, eroded point. I pressed it into my palm until it pierced the skin, and then threw it away across the rippled sand. When I looked at her again, I found that she was staring at me and frowning hard.

'What do you want?' she asked bluntly.

'I want to know why you never told me about Khaderbhai.'

'Do you want it straight?'

'Of course I do.'

'I couldn't trust you,' she declared, looking away again. 'That's not exactly right—I mean, I didn't *know* if I could trust you. I think ... now—I *know*—I could've trusted you all along.'

'Okay.' My teeth were touching, and my lips didn't move.

'I tried to tell you. I tried to get you to stay with me in Goa. You know that.'

'It would've made a difference,' I snapped, but then sighed just as she had, and relaxed my tone. 'It *might've* made a difference if you'd told me that you worked for him—that you recruited me for him.'

'When I ran away ... when I went to Goa, I was in a bad way. The Sapna thing—that was my idea. Did you know that?'

'No. *Jesus*, Karla.'

Her eyes narrowed as she read the angry disappointment in my face.

'Not the killing part,' she explained, and her expression was shocked, I think, to realise that I'd misunderstood what she'd said, and that I believed her capable of devising the Sapna killings. 'That was all Ghani's idea—his spin on it. They needed to get stuff in and out, through Bombay, and they needed help from people who didn't want to give it. My idea was to create a common enemy—Sapna—and to get everybody working with us to defeat him. It was supposed to be done with posters, and graffiti, and some harmless bomb hoaxes—to make it seem like there was a dangerous, charismatic leader out there. But Ghani didn't think it was scary enough. That's why he started the killings ...'

'And you left ... for Goa.'

'Yeah. You know the very first place I heard about the killings—what Ghani was doing with my idea? It was at that Village in the Sky ... that lunch you took me to. Your friends were talking about it. And it really shook me up that day. I stuck it out for a while, trying to stop it, somehow. But it was hopeless. And then Khader told me you were in jail—but you had to stay there until Madame Zhou did what he wanted her to do. And then he ... he got me to work on the Pakistani, the young general. He was a contact of mine, and he liked me. So I ... I did it. I worked him, while you were in there, until Khader got what he wanted. And then I just ... quit. I'd had enough.'

'But you went back to him.'

'I tried to get you to stay with me.'

'Why?'

'What do you mean?'

She was frowning, and seemed irritated by the question.

'Why did you want me to stay with you?'

'Isn't that obvious?'

'No. I'm sorry. It's not. Did you love me, Karla? I'm not asking if you loved me like I loved you. I mean ... did you love me at all? Did you love me at all, Karla?'

'I liked you ...'

'Yeah ...'

'No, it's true. I liked you, more than anyone else I knew. That's a lot for me, Lin.'

My jaw was locked tight, and I turned my head away from her. She waited for a few moments and then spoke again.

'I couldn't tell you about Khader. I couldn't. It would've felt like I was betraying him.'

'Betraying me was different, I guess ...'

'Fuck, Lin, it wasn't like that. If you'd stayed with me, we *both* would've been out of that world, but even then I couldn't have told you. Anyway, it doesn't matter. You wouldn't stay with me, so I never thought I'd see you again. Then I got a message from Khader saying you were in Gupta's place, killing yourself with smack, and he needed me to help him get you out of there. That's how I got back into it. That's how I went back to him.'

'I just don't get it, Karla.'

'*What* don't you get?'

'You worked for him, and Ghani, for how long—before the Sapna thing?'

'About four years.'

'So, you must've seen a lot of other stuff go down—you must've *heard* about it, at the very least. You're working for the Bombay mafia, for fuck's sake, or a goddamn branch of it. You're working for one of Bombay's biggest gangsters, like I was. You *knew* they killed people, *before* Ghani went psycho with his Sapna gang. Why ... after all that, did you suddenly get freaked out with the Sapna thing? I don't get it.'

She'd been watching me closely. I knew she was clever enough to see that I was striking back at her with the questions, but her eyes told me that she saw more than that. Although I'd tried to hide it, I knew she'd picked up the scepticism barbed with righteous censure in my tone. When I finished she took a breath, and seemed about to speak, but then she paused as if reconsidering her reply.

'You think I left them,' she began at last, with a little frown of surprise, 'and went to Goa because I wanted to be ... what ... *forgiven*, for what I'd done? Or for what I'd been part of? Is that it?'

'Did you?'

'No. I wanted to be forgiven, and I still do, but not for that. I left them because I didn't feel anything at all about the Sapna killings. I was stunned … and … sort of, freaked out, at first, that Ghani had turned the idea around so much. And I didn't like it. I thought it was stupid. I thought it was unnecessary and it would get us all into trouble we didn't need. And I tried to talk Khaderbhai out of it. I tried to get them to stop. But I didn't *feel* anything about it, even when they killed Madjid. And I … I used to like him, you know? I liked old Madjid. He was the best of them, in a way. But I didn't feel anything when he died. And I didn't feel it, not even a bit, when Khader told me he had to leave you in jail and let you get beaten up. I liked you—more than I liked anyone else—but I didn't feel bad or sorry. I kind of understood it—that it had to happen, and it was just bad luck that it was happening to *you*. I felt nothing. And that's when it hit me —that's when I knew I had to get away.'

'What about Goa? You can't tell me that was nothing.'

'No. When you came to Goa and you found me, like I knew you would, it was … pretty good. I started to think, *this is what it's like … this is what they're talking about* … But then you wouldn't stay. You had to go back—back to *him*—and I knew he wanted you, maybe even needed you. And I couldn't tell you what I knew about him, because I owed him, and I didn't know if I could trust you. So I let you go. And when you left, I didn't feel anything at all. Not a thing. I didn't want to be forgiven because of what I did. I wanted to be forgiven—and I still want it, and that's why I'm going to Khaled and Idriss—because I don't feel *sorry* for any of it, and I don't regret a thing. I'm cold inside, Lin. I like people, and I like things, but I don't love any of them—not even myself—and I don't really care about them. And, you know, the strange thing is, I don't really wish that I *did* care.'

And there it was. I had it all—all the truth and detail that I'd needed to know since that day on the mountain, in the withering snow, when Khader had told me about her. I think I'd expected to feel … nourished, perhaps, and vindicated, by forcing her to tell me what she'd done and why she'd done it. I think I'd hoped to be released by it, and solaced, just by hearing her tell me. But it wasn't like that. I felt empty: the kind of emptiness that's sad but not distressed, pitying but not broken-hearted, and damaged, somehow, but clearer and cleaner for it. And then I knew what it was, that emptiness: there's a name for it, a word we use often, without realising the universe of peace that's enfolded in it. The word is *free*.

'For what it's worth,' I said, reaching out to put my hand against her cheek, 'I forgive you, Karla. I forgive you, and I love you, and I always will.'

Our lips met like waves that crest and merge the whirl of storming seas. I felt that I was falling: free and falling at last from the love that had opened, lotus-layered, within me. And together we did fall the length of her black hair to the still-warm sand in the hollow of the sunken boat.

When our lips parted, stars rushed through that kiss into her sea-green eyes. An age of longing passed from those eyes into mine. An age of passion passed from my grey eyes into hers. All the hunger, all the fleshed and hope-starved craving, streamed from eye to eye: the moment we met; the laughing wit of Leopold's; the Standing Babas; the Village in the Sky; the cholera; the swarm of rats; the secrets that she'd whispered near exhausted sleep; the singing boat on the flood beneath the Gateway; the storm when we made love the first time; the joy and loneliness in Goa; and our love reflecting shadows into glass, on the last night before the war.

And there were no more words. There was no more cleverness as I walked her to a taxi parked nearby. I kissed her again. A long kiss, good-bye. She smiled at me. It was a good smile, a beautiful smile, and almost her best. I watched the red lights of the taxi fuzz and blur and then vanish in the furtherness of night.

Alone on the strangely quiet street, I began to walk back to Prabaker's slum—I always thought of it as Prabaker's slum, and I still do—to retrieve my bike. My shadows twirled with every street light, dragging loath behind me and then rushing on ahead. Ocean songs receded. The road moved beyond the span of coast and into the wide, tree-lined streets of the new peninsula reclaimed from the sea, stone on mortared stone, by the ever-expanding island city.

Sounds of celebration streamed into the road from streets around me. The festival had ended, and the people were beginning to return. Daring boys on bicycles flashed between the walkers much too fast, but never touching so much as a flap of sleeve. Impossibly beautiful girls in bright new saris glided between the glances of young men who'd scented their shirts, as well as their skin, with sandalwood soap. Children slept on shoulders, their unwilled arms and legs hanging limp as wet washing on a line. Someone sang a love song, and a dozen voices joined the choruses for each verse. Every man and woman, walking home to slum hut or fine apartment, smiled, listening to the romantic, foolish words.

Three young men singing near me saw my smile, and raised the palms of their hands in question. I lifted my arms and sang the chorus, joining my voice to theirs, and shocking and delighting them with what I knew. They threw their strangers' arms around me and swept our song-connected souls toward the unvanquishable ruin of the slum. *Everyone in the whole world,* Karla once said, *was Indian in at least one past life.* And I laughed to think of her.

I didn't know what I would do. The first part of it was clear enough—there was the debt to the burly Afghan, Nazeer. He'd said to me once, when I'd talked to him of the guilt I continued to feel for Khader's death: *Good gun, good horse, good friend, good battle—you know better way that Great Khan, he can die?* And a tiny fragment of that thought or feeling applied to me, too. It was right, somehow—although I couldn't have explained it, even to myself—and fitting for me to risk my life in the company of good friends, and in the course of an important mission.

And there was so much more that I had to learn, so much that Khaderbhai had wanted to teach me. I knew that his physics teacher, the man he'd told me about in Afghanistan, was in Bombay. And the other teacher, Idriss, was in Varanasi. If I made it back to Bombay from Nazeer's mission to Sri Lanka, there was a world of learning to discover and enjoy.

In the meanwhile, in the city, my place with Sanjay's council was assured. There was work there, and money, and a little power. For a while there was safety, in the brotherhood, from the long reach of Australian law. There were friends on the council, and at Leopold's, and in the slum. And, yes, maybe there was even a chance for love.

When I reached the bike I kept walking on into the slum. I wasn't sure why. I was following an instinct, and drawn, perhaps, by the swollen moon. The narrow lanes, those writhing alleys of struggle and dream, were so familiar to me and so comfortingly safe that I marvelled at the fear I'd once felt there. I wandered without purpose or plan, and moved from smile to smile as men and women and children who'd been my patients and neighbours looked up to see me pass. I moved in mists of cooking scent and shower soap, of animal stalls and kerosene lamps, of frankincense and sandalwood streaming upward from a thousand tiny temples in a thousand tiny homes.

At a corner of one lane I bumped into a man, and as our faces rose to their apologies we recognised one another in the same instant. It was Mukesh, the young thief who'd helped me in the Colaba lock-up and the Arthur Road jail: the man whose freedom I'd demanded when Vikram had paid me out of prison.

'Linbaba!' he cried, seizing my upper arms in his hands. 'So good to see you! *Arrey!* What's happening?'

'I'm just visiting,' I answered, laughing with him. 'What are *you* doing here? You look great! How the hell *are* you?'

'No problem, baba! *Bilkul fit, hain!' I'm absolutely fit!*

'Have you eaten? Will you take chai?'

'Thank you, baba, no. I am late for a meeting.'

'*Achcha?*' I muttered. *Oh, yes?*

He leaned in close to whisper.

'It is a secret, but I know I can trust you, Linbaba. We are meeting with some of those fellows who are with Sapna, the king of thieves.'

'What?'

'Yes,' he whispered. 'These fellows, they actually *know* that Sapna. They speak to him almost of every day.'

'That's not possible,' I said.

'Oh yes, Linbaba. They are his friends. And we are making the army—the army of poor fellows. We will teach those Muslims who is the real boss here in Maharashtra! That Sapna, he killed the mafia boss, Abdul Ghani, in his own mansion, and put the pieces of his body all around his house! And the Muslims, after that they are learning how to fear us. I must go now. We will see us, before too much time, isn't it? Goodbye, Linbaba!'

He ran off through the lanes. I turned away, to walk unsmiling into a sudden mood that was anxious and angry and forlorn. And then, as it always did, the city, Bombay, my Mumbai, held me up on the broad back of a nourishing constancy. I found myself at the edge of a devoted crowd gathered before the new, large hut belonging to the Blue Sisters. Men and women stood at the rear of the crowd, while others sat or knelt in a semi-circle of soft light at the threshold of the hut. And there in the doorway, framed by haloes of lamplight and wreathed about with streamers of blue incense smoke, were the Blue Sisters themselves. Radiant. Serene. Beings of such lambent compassion, such sublime equanimity, that in my broken, exiled heart I pledged to love them, as every man and woman who saw them did.

At that moment I felt a tug at my shirtsleeve and I turned my head to see what seemed to be the ghost of a gigantic smile with a very small man attached to it. The ghost shook me, grinning happily, and I reached out to enclose it in a hug and then bent forward quickly to touch its feet, in the traditional greeting to a father or mother. It was Kishan, Prabaker's father. He explained that he was in the city for a holiday with Rukhmabai, Prabaker's mother, and Parvati, his widow.

'Shantaram!' he admonished me when I started speaking to him in Hindi. 'Have you forgotten all your lovely Marathi?'

'Sorry, father!' I laughed, switching to Marathi. 'I'm just so happy to see you. Where is Rukhmabai?'

'Come!' he answered, taking my hand as if I was a child, and leading me through the slum.

We arrived at the little group of huts, including my own, that clustered around Kumar's chai shop near the crescent of the sea. Johnny Cigar was there, with Jeetendra, Qasim Ali Hussein, and Joseph's wife, Maria.

'We were just talking about you!' Johnny cried as I shook hands and nodded my greetings. 'We were just saying that your hut is empty again— and we were remembering the fire, on that first day. It was a big one, *na*?'

'It was,' I muttered, thinking of Raju and the others who'd died in that fire.

'So, Shantaram,' a voice scolded in Marathi from behind me, 'now you are too big a fellow to speak to your simple village mother?'

I swung round to see Rukhmabai standing close to us. I bent to touch her feet, but she restrained me, and joined her hands together in a greeting. She looked sadder and older within the soft endearments of her smile, and grieving had put a swipe of grey in the black pelt of her hair. But the hair was growing back. The long hair I'd seen falling like a shadow dying was growing back, and there was living hope in the thick, upward sweep of it.

Then she directed my gaze to the woman in widow's white standing beside her. It was Parvati, and a child, a son, was standing with her. He was clinging to her sari skirt for support. I greeted Parvati, and when I gave my attention to the boy and looked into his face I was so shocked that my jaw dropped open. I turned to the adults and they all smiled, waggling their heads in the same wonder, for the child was the image of Prabaker. More than merely resembling him, the boy was the exact duplicate of the man we'd all loved more than any other we knew. And when he smiled at me it was his smile, Prabaker's vast, world-encompassing smile, that I saw in that small, perfectly round face.

'*Baby dijiye?*' I asked. *Can I hold him?*

Parvati nodded. I held my arms out to him, and he came to me without protest.

'What's his name?' I asked, jigging the boy on my hip and watching him smile.

'Prabu,' Parvati answered. 'We called him Prabaker.'

'Oh Prabu,' Rukhmabai commanded, 'give Shantaram-uncle a kiss.'

The boy kissed me on the cheek, quickly, and then wrapped his tiny arms around my neck with impetuous strength, and squeezed me. I hugged him in return, and held him to my heart.

'You know, Shantu,' Kishan suggested, patting at his round belly, and smiling to fill the world, 'your house is empty. We are all here. You could stay with us tonight. You could sleep here.'

'Think hard, Lin,' Johnny Cigar warned, grinning at me. The full moon was in his eyes, and pearling his strong white teeth. 'If you stay, word will get out. First, there'll be a party tonight, and then, when you wake up, there'll be a damn long line of patients, *yaar*, waiting to see you.'

I gave the boy back into Parvati's arms, and wiped a hand across my face and into my hair. Looking at the people, listening to the breathing, heaving, laughing, struggling music of the slum, all around me, I remembered one of Khaderbhai's favourite phrases. *Every human heartbeat*, he'd said many times, *is a universe of possibilities*. And it seemed to me that I finally understood exactly what he'd meant. He'd been trying to tell me that every human will has the power to transform its fate. I'd always thought that fate was something unchangeable: fixed for every one of us at birth, and as constant as the circuit of the stars. But I suddenly realised that life is stranger and more beautiful than that. The truth is that, no matter what kind of game you find yourself in, no matter how good or bad the luck, you can change your life completely with a single thought or a single act of love.

'Well, I'm out of practice sleeping on the ground,' I said, smiling at Rukhmabai.

'You can have *my* bed,' Kishan offered.

'Oh no you don't!' I protested.

'Oh yes I do!' he insisted, dragging his cot from outside his hut to mine while Johnny, Jeetendra, and the others hugged and mock-wrestled me into submission, and our cries and laughter rolled away toward the time-dissolving everness of the sea.

For this is what we do. Put one foot forward and then the other. Lift our eyes to the snarl and smile of the world once more. Think. Act. Feel. Add our little consequence to the tides of good and evil that flood and drain the world. Drag our shadowed crosses into the hope of another night. Push our brave hearts into the promise of a new day. With love: the passionate search for a truth other than our own. With longing: the pure, ineffable yearning to be saved. For so long as fate keeps waiting, we live on. God help us. God forgive us. We live on.

ACKNOWLEDGEMENTS

It took me thirteen long and troubled years to write *Shantaram*. The first two drafts of the book—six years' work and six hundred pages—were destroyed in prison. My hands, damaged by the residual effects of frost-bite, suffered so badly during the winters in the punishment unit of the prison that many pages of the manuscript journal, which survived and which I still have with me, are stained and streaked with my blood. When I was released, the hardships were severe and unrelenting. I almost, but not quite ever, despaired of finishing the book. The fact that I did complete it, this novel written in blood and tears and exultation that you've just read, is a testament to the help and involvement of a great many people. In making this grateful acknowledgement to them I'm sure that, unintentionally, some names will be omitted from my personal honour roll. I ask those friends and colleagues to forgive me.

I want to thank my manager, Tammy Michaels, for whom the true beauty of art is its passionate exaltations; my editor, Margot Rosenbloom; the agent for the project, Joe Regal; the first commissioning editor in the USA, Tim Bent; and George Witte, at St. Martin's Press, whose erudition, urbanity, and love for the world of the word are an artist's inspiration.

I thank Jessica and Nick, for their being and their forgiveness and their love; Nick, Mary, Paris, and Blaise, for the wondrous gift of their faith in me; my best friend, Shula, who was always the first to read the words, and to speak love for them; and my mother and my stepfather, whose unflagging moral, spiritual, and financial support—beyond what I've ever deserved or could repay—has sustained me, and uplifted this work.

Reaching back from this moment through those thirteen years, I also want to thank the following colleagues and loved ones: Alan and Maria Almeida, Trish Anderson, Mike and Jenny Arnold, Don Arnold, Chloris and Chris Bath, Christine Boyle, Kerry Boxall, Buckley Bullock, Nick and Helen Burrows, Roger Bushell, Grant Carey, William Carey, Sarah

Carroll, Tracy Carroll, Alfredo Cerda, Paul Chamberlain, Narayan Chandrashekar, Julia Chennels, Glen and Bindi Choyce, Sue Coley, Celia Conor, Tom Cooper, Graeme Corcoran, Laurie Cosgrove, Peter Craven, Daniella Cripa, Malcolm Crook, Li Cunxin, Alison Davidson, Mark Davis, Danny Ders, James Dorabjee, Paul Dornbusch, Cameron Drake, Suzannah Espie, Peter Ferne, Lindsay Forbes, Lisa Freedman, Kate Galloway, Con Gantinas, Richard Gelemanovic, Claudia Glenewinkel, Linnet Good, Nicholas Goodwin, Sherridan Green, David Greenman, Ingrid Grobel, Lutz Grossman, Anna Hampson, Justine Hampson, Meredith Harsh, Jason and Victoria Hartcup, Wendy Hatfield, Robbie Heazlewood, Mark Holden, Chris, Lee, and Ian Hunter, Pietro The Colonel Iodice, Izumi, Bashka Jacobs, Sue Jamison, Sandy Jarrett, Jenny and Stewart, Kate Jones, Julie Jordanou, Katsuya and Michelle, Yusuf Mohammed Khan, Daniel Keays, Judi Kenneally, Val Keogh, Ranyana Kothari, Glen King, Andy Kirkland, Dr. Sue Knight, Clay Lafferty, Dr. John Lattanzio, Marc Lawrence, Kevin Leighton, Myriam Leo, Paul Linacre, Graham Lodge, Ian Lovell, Günter Lück, Dr. Mohammed al Mahdi, Amad Malkoun, Elie Malkoun, Big Mick Mantzaris, Pat Martin, Nick and Christine Matheou, Maximillian, Elaine May, John McAuslan, Jim McManus, Joan McQueen, Martin and Claudia Meurer, Marjorie Michael, Mark Mitchell, Wendy Joy Morrissey, Myriam, Jenny Nagle, Kim Albert Ng, Blaise Oarsman, Donna Palma, Kylie Parish, Lindon Parker, Vikram Patel, Jan Paull, Sally Paxton, Joyce Petrie, Susan Rokich, Max Rosenbloom, Andrew Rule, Aysha Rowe, Fabian Salamon, Kristina Schelldorfer, Michael Starkman, Sven Schmidt, David and Michelle Shipworth, Kathy Simota, Jo Skipwith, Dave Stevens, Barry and Steven Stockley, Anand Subramaniam, Sue and Phyl, Gregory and Mary Szczepaniak, Rosie Tovie, Lizette Twistleton, Gillian Upton, Rosalie Vaccari, Chandrakant Vishwanath, Void, Werner and Linda Weber, Cheryl Weinstein, Shelley and Barbara Weisberg, Chris Wilson, Cameron Woodhead, John Wooller, and Lee Xiaoshin.